Two
Wings
to
Veil
My
Face

BOOKS BY LEON FORREST

There Is a Tree More Ancient Than Eden
The Bloodworth Orphans

Two Wings to Veil My Face

LEON FORREST

RANDOM HOUSE/NEW YORK

For Aunt Maude Richardson
And in Memory of Aunt Maude White

Library of Congress Cataloging in Publication Data
Forrest, Leon.
   Two wings to veil my face.
   I. Title.
PS3556.0738T85   1983   813'.54   83-42777
ISBN 0-394-52965-0

Manufactured in the United States of America

9 8 7 6 5 4 3 2

"MOTHER OF MINE, WHY DO YOU OBJECT TO
OUR TRUSTY SINGER
GIVING DELIGHT IN WHATEVER WAY HIS
MIND INSPIRES HIM?
THE POETS ARE NOT RESPONSIBLE FOR THEIR
SUBJECT MATTER BUT ZEUS RATHER
WHO GIVES TO EACH MAN WHAT HE WILL.
SO ATTACH NO BLAME TO THIS MAN FOR
SINGING OF THE GREEKS' SORRY FATE.
FOR MEN MUCH MORE PRAISE WHICHEVER
SONG
COMES NEWEST TO THEIR EARS."

—*THE ODYSSEY,* HOMER

–I INTEND TO MAKE A COLLECTION OF YOUR
SAYINGS IF YOU WILL LET ME.
SPEAKING TO ME. THEY WASH AND TUB AND
SCRUB. AGENBITE OF INWIT. CONSCIENCE.
YET HERE'S A SPOT.
–THAT ONE ABOUT THE CRACKED LOOKING-
GLASS OF A SERVANT BEING THE SYMBOL
OF IRISH ART IS DEUCED GOOD.
BUCK MULLIGAN KICKED STEPHEN'S FOOT
UNDER THE TABLE AND SAID WITH
WARMTH OF TONE:
–WAIT TILL YOU HEAR HIM ON HAMLET,
HAINES.

—*ULYSSES,* JAMES JOYCE

"BLACK WILL MAKE YOU . . ."
"BLACK . . ."
". . . OR BLACK WILL UN-MAKE YOU."
"AIN'T IT THE TRUTH, LAWD?"
AND AT THAT POINT A VOICE OF TROMBONE
TIMBRE SCREAMED AT ME, "GIT OUT OF
THERE, YOU FOOL! IS YOU READY TO COM-
MIT TREASON?"
AND I TORE MYSELF AWAY, HEARING THE
OLD SINGER OF SPIRITUALS MOANING, "GO
CURSE YOUR GOD, BOY, AND DIE."

—*INVISIBLE MAN,* RALPH ELLISON

Two
Wings
to
Veil
My
Face

1

Of
Kith
and
Kin

I n the young man's earliest memories, whenever they visited Great-Momma Sweetie Reed—as Nathaniel and his father Arthur Witherspoon did that morning on June 5, 1944, after Grandfather Witherspoon's death—the boy Nathaniel sat there in the ancient rocking chair and opened himself up to the aroma of steaming-hot rolls, biscuits, lightbread, cornbread or muffins that his grandmother always kept bound up snugly in a series of interwoven Santa Fe bar towels, fashioned into sleeves that Great-Momma Sweetie Reed called warming sleeves; but they in turn were bound about by ancient, faded rainbow-colored, Mississippi-spun bathing towels that she brought with her from the Reed plantation, and which she pronounced as warm-up jackets.

The steam was always great for delivering the boy into the kingdom of daydreaming, even as the moist breathing of the breads opened him up to Great-Momma Sweetie Reed's storytelling powers and recollecting of leftovers to be remade once again by the boy when Great-Momma Sweetie unveiled the last of the sleeves and his imagination produced a vision of preserved mummies sliding forth (perhaps because of the thinning, see-through condition of the warm-up jackets) as if to play a joke on himself, but instead (as always) a bevy of life-giving celebrants of bread emerged almost bursting with life, not crumbling.

But today, as he sat in that same creaking rocking chair, any dreams he had then of Grandfather Witherspoon's last, babelike days only led him to the aged figure of Great-Momma Sweetie Reed lying there now upon the bed, coming and going in and out of memories and reveries. As a child in the early times of memory, imagination always flung the boy to his grandmother's sleeve for direction in the steam-filled room; but now fourteen years later she was dependent upon him; the room was stripped down to its bare essentials for living and the only steam in the room would eventually issue from the teapot he had on the burner, so that soon he would arise, rouse her from the knit of sleep and fix his grandmother a cup of powerful sassafras tea with two shots of brandy and place the cup at her elbow and this stirred-up combination seemed always to illuminate her memory, when she wanted to deliver talk about family history, or some business in need of handling.

Nathaniel Witherspoon's audience with his grandmother this day came not only as one of his regular visits to the ninety-one-year-old woman's side to give her aid and comfort, but from a pledge made some fourteen years earlier by the four-foot, eight-inch Sweetie Reed when she was feeding and serving down-and-out neighbors, that she would explain her erratic behavior; her reason for planning not to attend Grandfather Jericho Witherspoon's funeral. And then the statement made that morning after his death, that she would explain it all to the boy Nathaniel when he reached his majority.

And he wondered then, as he wondered now, how Great-Momma Sweetie had in fact dared to believe that she would live another fourteen years. But if you lived to be seventy-seven you might feel that you could make another fourteen years, or even embrace the mountaintop marking a century of living; that indeed she more than likely felt touched with the gift of immortality. Or, if you lived to see a husband (or more properly, a former husband) live to be a hundred and seventeen years old, then you came to believe in every human possibility, particularly when you considered the dangers they both had passed, Nathaniel noted as he thought of the boiling water pouring over the sassafras leaves: a powerful incandescent odor arising, as a genie let from a bottle, then two dashes of brandy stirred together that would open Great-Momma Sweetie Reed up to memory and this history she wanted to pass on to him. But what memories did he need to sharpen at twenty-one?

On that morning after Grandfather Witherspoon's death they could barely see Great-Momma Sweetie Reed; rather they seemed to see something of her form, beneath an expanding, encircling halo that made her appear to be a spirit dancing at her work. The boy Nathaniel laughed to think how she had the watchful eyes of warning memory itself (behind the earlobe; where she wore the hearing aid; beneath a strawberry-colored bonnet). But he also thought of the other side of Great-Momma Sweetie's word as two veiled wings to hide from; especially when he got into hot water with her and she said she was *going to pay him back for old and new;* this was also a part of her *backwater time;* and those hands that made such wonderful bread, or dabbed away the boy's tears, or even had wiped his behind, could be used to bring down wrath; even as she winged to God by nightfall, with lifted hands, the words for his salvation. And the boy Nathaniel was back into his grandmother's arms again; as she begged God forgiveness for her temper and her pride, he begged her forgiveness for his disobedience, upsetting this awesome, harsh and generous-spirited goddess.

But now the young man Nathaniel Witherspoon (a college dropout) wondered if all the storytelling, the loving, the harsh disciplining, the praying and the direction had been but a preparation for the day, *this* day, when he would have to take over her memories, and business, and even participate in the state of her soul's progress. So that he would have to be many kinds of men brought together as one, in one flesh, and soul, and mind. Each man must re-create himself, Nathaniel Witherspoon thought, out of all that's given to him and placed upon his shoulders; Great-Momma Sweetie Reed had contributed to that shaping of the young man. You could not escape from the yoke of history, ancestors, lovers, and the demons and gifts of living, only

5

transcend and remake yourself through all of it as a man, he thought, as wincing he now loosened the red, gold and green necktie given to him by Candy Cummings in happier days.

But on that fateful day in 1944 the warning wisdom pitched forth, with plenty of steam of its own, lodged behind those foreknowing, deeply set, haunting eyes of Great-Momma Sweetie Reed, where she saw things other people could not see, dared not dream of seeing. She was nearly deaf, but she heard what she wanted to hear, his father once said. She also heard other voices in other rooms and confided in them, too, argued with them, such as the voice of her long-dead and loathed father, the manservant I. V. Reed, whose body had been touched to *the wishbone of his master; a tongue flapped backwards and pressed to the sole of a footless shoe,* she said.

Now he laughed at the way the boy Nathaniel stubbornly held to this idea that Sweetie Reed did indeed speak to others in a chamber of a world not open to the average soul. And the boy wondered if Almighty God gave her, allowed her, a special gift of entering another world of hearing and seeing since He had taken her hearing. But Nathaniel Witherspoon, boy and man, wondered just how Great-Momma Sweetie Reed had come to lose her hearing.

The boy Nathaniel hoped that Great-Momma Sweetie would not fade away as the steam in the room started to evaporate, but remain in the very breath of life, visible in his mind and heart with those words of hers spun from the wet-wash accents of the Southland and the beginning time of all memory. With the exception of what was said in church, or at Mass, few if any practiced service to man in God as did this former preacher woman; even Grandfather Witherspoon himself, but his service had been purely to man, not God. The boy was also sure Great-Momma Sweetie would always be with the family in spirit, power and voice, and return to them with her words about the poor that touched the hearing of God; he felt the same about Grandpa Witherspoon, yet different, for he was so ancient and awesome and godless. Grandfather Witherspoon was only newly dead, so that his spirit had not had the time to drift very far from the garment of his body.

In his heart the boy wanted them to be as one when they met in death, just as they had been once upon a time, and to put their old habits aside.

The young man Nathaniel Witherspoon merely scoffed at this memory, for now he could never dream that these warring spirits would speak with one voice, or be as one even though they were bride and bridegroom, and of one flesh, sixty years before. But he did believe Sweetie Reed when she said that Jesus Christ was the bridegroom of her soul: *Jesus promised never to leave me alone. No never. Never alone.* This marriage with Christ—not made of hands and without flesh— forged the pearl ring of memory in his imagination, from the earliest storytelling when Great-Momma Sweetie first spoke of the small but moving figure of an early conversion; he who came to her in the depths of night, something like High-John the Conqueror, but with the troubling good news; the Negro preacher Stigwood, who had been a slave on the Bloodworth plantation. He seemed to haunt her dreams, or nightmares, along with her father, I. V. Reed, Grandfather Rollins Reed, the slaver, and somebody named Reece Shank Haywood, and in back of them all in the beginning times, her mother, Angelina, and the distant, awesome figure of Auntie Foisty.

And Nathaniel had often thought that those figures too would emerge from the steam in the room out of the power of Great-Momma Sweetie's storytelling. Yet to this very hour they remained shadows from Sweetie Reed's past, spoken of in gems of memory . . . So that when she told him to come to her this day, and she would try to bring all of the recollections together, the young man had suggested that he bring along a tape recorder, and his grandmother had said simply: *No. Just bring along a pen and pad, not a pencil, either, because too much has been erased in time. Nor an indelible pencil. Write it all down in longhand, with blue-black ink on the pad, in your notebook, and then it all will be recorded on the tablet of your memory and in your heart, as it's transformed from your longhand to your short memory. It's time we moved from listening and half hearing to listening and recording in longhand,* she said.

You are always waiting on the appearance of the deliverance from women, the young man now laughed to himself as he listened to the sleeping woman's breathing (perhaps she's warming up memory even now, he mused,) and waited to hear the steam whistle in the teapot, as an alarm-clock signal to rouse Great-Momma Sweetie Reed from her slumber.

On that other morning when father and son had waited for Great-Momma Sweetie Reed to finish kitchen preparations, she had commenced to sing, *He arose. He arose from the Dead, and the Lord shall make my spirit whole,* which always revealed that she was nearing the completion of her tasks. Arthur Witherspoon had brought along to

7

discuss with Great-Momma Sweetie Reed, if she was in the proper mood, documents that he would take later to the undertaker, Memphis Raven-Snow. The boy noted the angry crow's-feet at the edges of his father's bloodshot eyes, slanted towards the kitchen like those red rubber bands in the slingshots drawn back in the hands of bad boys down near the foggy lagoon and fired at quick-witted rabbits; the boy thought his father's mind seemed stretched back to an earlier time, where some other heated arguments between his father and Great-Momma Sweetie Reed lived suspended beyond the pull of his brain and memory.

But as he glimpsed the print on those documents and deeds going back even to the slave past, with words beyond his schooling and vocabulary (in his father's reddish yellow hand), the boy remembered how Grandfather Witherspoon had taught Great-Momma Sweetie to read and write over sixty years before and how she had coupled this with the fine speaking and pronunciation of her mother, Angelina Reed, until her mother was killed before her very eyes at the age of seven, the boy's own age.

Great-Momma Sweetie was born two years after the Surrender and married to Jericho Witherspoon when she was fifteen and he was fifty-five, all of which made the boy's eyes buck out of his head when he overheard it through the family grapevine; and not only that, but how all of it suggested that on this side of the family tree, too, there was the strange hidden history, like the family trees out of Eden that Great-Momma Sweetie, or Aunt Harriet or Aunt Breedlove had read out loud to him from the book of Genesis, in the Good Book, and had started him to reading when he was three; but none of the family history was put down in books, in the way it was for the families of the Hebrew children, Great-Momma Sweetie Reed said. And he wondered if even those documents and deeds now trembling in his father's hand carried an important chapter in their story; and were there missing pages inside of these papers?

In the boy's imagination all of this was tied up with the beginning time on both sides of his family, like two wings of a strange angel struggling to rise . . . Just as it was difficult, in another way, for Nathaniel to conjure up clearly the idea that Great-Momma Sweetie Reed was a decade older than Aunt Hattie Breedlove, more like a big sister to Breedie, and that it was the slave-born mother of Hattie Breedlove Wordlaw, Lovelady Breedlove, with whom she and Jericho Witherspoon had lived. He wondered why it was easier to imagine

8

Great-Momma Sweetie's eyes in the back of her head seeing other worlds of long-forgotten and dead life that he could not see, than it was to see clearly how the life of the beginning time was so close to the present.

For the boy Nathaniel, the sweep of all this was something akin to trying to gulp down too many of her leftovers and the belching, chamber-echoing, day-old wonders—particularly Great-Momma Sweetie's cabbages—like her recollections, coming from an angry, hungry stomach, growling through the boy's being for the truth-tongue of her stirring, warming foods so loaded, rich and lined out with gospel possessions, and slave passages, inside of remade recipes never forgotten, always remade out of remembering and reshaped like the words to a kind of gospel (that nobody ever wrote down on paper) which Great-Momma Sweetie said was also the first boy cousin to a blues. The lips and mouth of the boy, and then his galloping tongue, found those leftovers, those rolled-up gospel scrolls for the gut and the soul, as Great-Momma Sweetie Reed also proclaimed them, so bedeviling to his taste buds that the mystery of overpowering taste was like *the mystery of history,* as Uncle Hampton commanded.

The boy tasted it and felt it, but it was beyond his powers of understanding. He had a deep appetite for history, since he had heard so much of it along with the leftovers, from the wee-winking, beginning time, amid all of the history that appeared to be left out of the storytelling time . . . And the boy also thought of what they said at Mass about the mystery of the water and the wine, and the bread and the wine that mysteriously took the place of Jesus Christ's body and blood. And the beautiful prayer the priest prayed, at the Epistle side of the altar as he poured wine into the chalice, and Aunt DuDora pouring the English translation into the boy's ears:

> *O God, who hast established the nature of*
> *man in wondrous dignity and even more*
> *wondrously hast renewed it, grant that*
> *through the mystery of this water and wine,*
> *we may be made partakers of his divinity,*
> *who has deigned to become partaker of our*
> *humanity, Jesus Christ, your Son, our Lord,*
> *who lives and reigns with you in the unity of*
> *the Holy Spirit, God forever and ever. Amen.*

9

And Aunt DuDora explaining how the water mixed with wine showed the human and the divine in our Lord and our redemption by blood (and water) from the side of the crucified but resurrected Savior; as she prepared herself for Holy Communion. And the boy wondered could you taste Christ's body when the priest placed the wondrous bread upon your tongue? Would his body feel new and wondrous when the bread of life hit his gut, when he experienced First Holy Communion? Was the host made from day-old bread, and therefore improved? Uncle Hampton said that Colored Catholic mysteries of the Mass only add to the mystery of our History. *The boy will come out more mucked up than the mystery of Mars and those Creoles. I prefer the mystery of Frederick Douglass as my tie to the wonders of man.*

But the young man in the rocker now thought yes, give me Frederick Douglass in whose shadow the great President was worthy to walk, but only his shadow, and the mighty Bard in whose shadow Hamlet was worthy to talk, but only his shadow, and whispering in the ears of the world, what a piece of work is a man . . . Yes, and all mucked up, too.

These leftovers of Great-Momma Sweetie Reed's were day-old dishes rolled into warming sleeves of delight, in the breadbasket, because the ingredients had time to suffer and instruct together; yes, and as Great-Momma Sweetie Reed also said to Nathaniel, *deepening as they stir and rise* and extra precious when she served her cabbages or soups, or stews and breads during cold weather, along with something to stick to your ribs like ham hocks, licked to the soul of black-eyed peas, or red beans and rice or butter beans and collards. And if Nathaniel was really a good boy he might sit there in this same rocking chair and chew and absorb these leftovers until he felt them in his gut along with what she said about the strange, nourishing beginning times. So that sometimes the boy found himself letting out a long-low belch from leftover food and story. Was this what Uncle Hampton meant when he spoke of his gut reaction to a series of stirring-up events?

But from those leftover cabbages left out too long in this steamy room a decaying smell would emerge that could chase you out of this world. And this made the boy think of all of the parts of her stories that Great-Momma Sweetie Reed always left out, even as she added to her stories inside of stories; but the stories were also wonders and mysteries, the boy thought, because of all of the things she left out.

Just as with the food, it was only when they had time to suffer together that the parts of the recipe came together; you didn't taste them at first because they were newly cooked. But sometimes the adults could taste everything in recipes, even the finest detail of spice. Like the family history, your auntie did this and it led to that kind of taste, as when he learned the ABC's; but it was different, too. Because in the ABC's you went from A to B to C. But in these stories of the family, the boy felt he often went from A to C to E and then maybe later on learned of B. But often, maybe not. Learning to play piano as he was now doing, the boy thought of how you skipped over notes to Every Good Boy Does Fine. *E G B D F.* And it took perhaps forever to learn what those notes could do, when brought together in different combinations. One day he would learn the meaning of chords, his teacher had said. But there, too, certain notes were left out to make other notes when played together seem stronger, or softer, but not necessarily weakening the piece, adding even more mysterious wonders. Uncle Hampton played out blue notes and created chords on the organ and discord in life, his mother said. He often made *Clair de Lune* into a blues. Uncle V. I. DuPont could hear notes inside of notes, as whispering echoes warming up, inside the sleeves of ghosts, as he stripped the intestine from the shrimps for gumbo and imitated the sound of Armstrong's horn, playing "Potato-Head Blues."

And just as the boy Nathaniel became overstuffed in Great-Momma Sweetie Reed's rocking chair (as loaded down with history as a lumpy cotton sack, bearing harvest after harvest), he also had to be careful where he sat in that chair lest a loose spring pop up and stick him amid all the cushiony comfort of her grandfather's rocker. But then suddenly Great-Momma Sweetie Reed would bounce him onto his feet and off he would go running a slew of errands for the poorer neighbors she served.

Many of these neighbors had been owned and operated upon by gutless white landowners down in the old country and were unable to handle the new-found jobless slavery without skill, opportunity, a crop or seed, a pot or a window, the boy's father had said. It seemed as if bringing them bread and meat formed the very bread sacrament, not sacrifice, of her life—and the boy thought how much he enjoyed being her messenger, doing the route work of this missioned woman, much more than he ever longed to study the roles, motions, and then drape the vestments of an altarboy over his street clothes.

The boy often brought her wondrous dishes to the shut-ins and the drifters, the wind-blasted winos and the lost-found; the good families in bad strait-jackets as well as those Negroes who flew to the city in flapping sleeves of desperation. And the boy nicknamed himself Nattie-Joe Turner, along with Great-Momma Sweetie calling him her Splendid Spoons (which also started when he licked the silver-edged cake bowl clean), but in the mirrors of Great-Momma Sweetie's oval-shaped, piercing eyes there were indeed no respective persons; nor restricted covenants, nor appointed, nor anointed folks; for the eyes of Jesus glowed when He was at work amongst the least of the despised, and the troubled, she declared, with that hand arched upon her frail hipbone. Not that she had any money: Grandfather Witherspoon had purchased this old frame house for her forty years ago; she lived on the rents of two families, but much of that money was rolled back to her mission work; and occasionally she still gave a sermon, or spoke before a well-known Colored Women's Club.

Now as Great-Momma Sweetie Reed emerged from the steam of her tasks, Arthur Witherspoon asked her if she wanted to accompany them to the Memphis Raven-Snow Funeral Home and help cover the arrangements and the selection of clothing for Jericho Witherspoon's body and to discuss his business affairs; as he slipped the documents back into his briefcase. It was cool even for early June, this day after Arthur Witherspoon's birthday and the first morning after Grandfather Witherspoon's death. But even in death Aunt Bella-Lenore Boltwood, the seamstress, had told Nathaniel to look for the silver lining, that the old man had left a treasury of human contributions behind. Well, that was all right, the boy thought, but when it was your very own grandfather, not somebody you read about in the newspapers, then it was different and her advice hard to swallow.

The boy wondered if Great-Momma Sweetie Reed had her hearing aid turned up enough to catch his father's words. They could still not totally see the tiny, cedar-colored, cotton-headed woman with the strawberry bonnet on her head, for the last breath of steam in the room; they could see her angular outline loosely fitting the air, as she swooped about the four huge-bellied pots on the stove for a last-minute check, cooking stew meat and collard greens, cabbages, soups, and now she stood next to her dresser, where she was unwinding the last of the warming sleeves, extracting seven biscuits with her right hand, as she placed her long left hand onto her hip; a warning high-water mark, that she was either about to read you out of this world, or just plain read you, or take those present on a long-forgotten journey road of contention, or down a peg or two and back down into the unrecorded backbone of history and what really stirred at the bottom—never to rise unless she touched down upon it—or what Great-Momma Sweetie Reed decreed as *backwater time.* As she came out of the steam, her face carried its faint screen as a veil, but the boy thought of what happened when you blew your breath upon a mirror, and how it screened the picture of your face in the looking-glass. Great-Momma Sweetie Reed had heard Arthur Witherspoon, all right.

—What clothing? Arthur Witherspoon, they'll have to defreeze Jerry's body first to raise his right arm; all that man ever desired to be buried up in, as yoking thread, was that subzero high judge's majesty robe; all of that unfolding meant more to him than his wedding vows and his warming bed; even as I warned him way back *when,* that he had to get right on the inside before he could ever hope to get right on the outside; though everybody—including me, I confess it— praised him dawn-up to sundown. I never weaved no spite-work up in my head for Jericho Witherspoon, but that praise was the bad part of his long suit—even as it meant him catching his arm up in the sleeve of his jacket and thinking it went through as silk velvet . . . but maybe we were as those folks I hear tell about who had convinced themselves and their naked master that he was parading before them wearing new clothes, over his old body.—

—Mother Sweetie, my father never asked anyone to prop him up in this world.—

—But now, Arthur, as for his business affairs: it ain't hardly my disposition to invest my time in nobody's will, that willed themselves away from me; I'm about too busy with the Lord's warning will and urgent business, circulating and working up the backbone of my soul; He's the one what clothed my soul and fed me when I was hungry, even famished and dying out in the world of sorrows, and put water to my lips when I was thirsty and troubled and thought I needed only water. And He's keeping a strict account on my time journal, right down to this minute; it's to Him I'm bound over; obligated, invested and obliged; not to Jerry Witherspoon, though he spotted ingratitude in my eyes, forty-odd years ago, when mine eyes were only a-begging and a-pleading for him to turn with me to the beam of Almighty God and to turn away from himself in the mirror which was his world within his word; his long suit and his straight jacket . . . For if you got God (oh, how many times did I say it to you, Jerry), if you got

Him invested in the inner lining of your soul, no harm can come to you . . . Like the moonlight showing the proper path to take and not to take. Because despite all the good Jerry did in His world, he was about to drown looking at his own self in the pool of his good deeds; and the public's back-patting was filled with back-biting to bring him down, as they lifted him up off of his feet, before the world.—

—I never heard him—once in my life—accuse you of ingratitude, Mother Sweetie.—

—. . . Oh yes, he gave me my first lady's dress, sixty-two years ago, I freely admit to it; and I also admit that it ain't covered this body frame since; though I still got it hanging there in that closet—drooping.—

Now she was handing the boy three of the beloved biscuits upon a plate, draped down in butter and dressed in honey; giving biscuits now also as a way, he thought, of closing his gaping mouth, as the boy's head bobbed back and forth between the two adults. His father was jabbing his arm into the sleeve of his topcoat with great anger, but he kept getting his arm caught up in a slit in the sleeve. His face appeared to reveal that he had made a mistake in coming here in the first place and that he never cared to cross the door of Sweetie Reed's again.

Not only had Grandfather Witherspoon bought her first dress, her off-white wedding dress with the rose-colored fringes; he had helped her to read and print and write before he sent her to night school.

And Sweetie Reed still had the promissory note of her mother's purchase out of slavery amongst her papers in the chest of drawers like a file cabinet right in front of her huge four-poster bed, with the cardboard printed sign affixed to the drawer, hanging from a string, marked *Personal Instrument Papers*—documents that Grandpa Witherspoon had used to teach her to read by, along with the Declaration of Independence and the Emancipation Proclamation, starting off her education with the alphabet and then using some of the fundamental lawbooks as instructional models; so that Great-Momma Sweetie Reed had to think as she learned, she confided, but that was the other way around from the way he was taught in school, for the most part, Nathaniel thought.

Now in another voice, personal and warm as if unleashed from a curving tributary, Great-Momma Sweetie Reed was saying:

—. . . And so you have to take it all onto the high road, Arthur, from there I reckon God'll be my judge and my jury—as He'll guide your steps to the Light; and sometimes the Light of His deliverance is so strong that you just kind of forced to stumble onto it like old man Rollins Reed was stumbled upon through a satanic man's greed for gold, through guilt and guilt through diamonds—yet because of all of that I was momentarily saved for the world, so that I could be saved later for His calling, through man. Though it was not me he was after saving in the beginning time.—

But then Great-Momma Sweetie started to drift off; her right hand, no longer arched high upon her left hipbone, wandered.

—I tried to pass it all on to Jerry, he who had given me so much, I admit that freely: Take a search warrant, Jerry, and see where God brought you up from out of the wilderness to hear and to accept your calling; but *now* to know your deeper nature—He provided me with a lighthouse in the stormy waters by sending me to you; and it took a long time to get the deeper understanding of that, too. But now he's sending you back to me. Let it come between us, Jerry, and stir and rise and deep'n us, as troubling counsel . . . Jerry needed to save himself and search himself out clean to the bone, as he was trying to save folks from jail and rising in his own law career—when he became a prisoner of another injustice. Another jail. *Self-cell.* Don't match up with the man down in the old country going around taking names, Jerry. I think Jerry must have thought he had built a platform in the middle of the air . . . He looked long and troubled into my face, when I said these things. Hovering up there as some suspended kind of God of Judgment.—

Arthur Witherspoon's sweat-drenched brow was knitted; his face brooding and troubled. He started mumbling something to himself about:

—Hot air.— And then:

—Oh, the pole vault of ambition plagued the garland of his ascent, as maggots dwell within the wrathful grapes of his memory. But who's to acclaim his greatest—

And the boy thought this was always his father's way of saying something you could barely hear but understand, followed by something you could hear plainly and not understand, though the words made an impression of great weight and fear in his soul about his father, who was always troubling over everything, and now putting the documents back into the briefcase and preparing to leave.

Now Great-Momma Sweetie Reed was suggesting that she would be willing to supply the food for the wake. And the boy saw in his father's face a look of *There now, that's my real and true Mother Sweetie's spirit.* But he also knew for a fact that Great-Momma Sweetie Reed and Grandfather Witherspoon had not lived together since June of 1905; she had started back to using her maiden name shortly after that. Why this separation but not divorce had occurred was as unclear to the boy as the mysteries of the Mass that he believed, because he was told it from the beginning time; but did not understand why. He remembered how his father had said:

—What a blow to the old man for Mother Sweetie to turn her name back to the slaver's name, Reed, and against Witherspoon—a slaver's name, too, but the old man has turned it around to the name of honor.— The boy felt badly at the moment that she was apparently not going to pay respect to his grandfather, even though he loved her almost more than anybody in the whole wide world. How could someone who loved as much as Great-Momma Sweetie also dislike so strongly? What had Grandfather Witherspoon done to Great-Momma Sweetie Reed to make her feel this way? The announcement to what she was also about to announce—and why hadn't his father seen this, the young man now wondered.

—But, Arthur, I know you don't expect me to be there at that wake; and if you do—how could you? And be fair now—to me—Artie?—

—Charity begins at home.—

—From *you!*—

—Mother Sweetie, I thought you would understand on this occasion; would relent in this situation, Arthur Witherspoon started in a shrill, emotional manner that Nathaniel rarely heard, so that he now looked up to where his father's lower lip was trembling; and after a deep, breath-sucking action that seemed to draw all of the tears and coloring back into his lean face and down into his body, not only did his lower lip quake but his body seemed to shake as a meal sack of skeleton bones. The boy thought this a signal of his father's diabetes performing and he knew enough to know that his unsettled feelings could mark the moment of trouble in mind and body for Arthur Witherspoon. These were old emotions; the doctor had explained that Arthur Witherspoon "could not trace down even on a graph, even though your inner body carries a recorder like the journal you carry in your inner jacket pocket, noting the fitful flight of your diabetes for the week—food intake, urinalysis, domestic strife, exercise program; your life on the gram scale, your sleeping patterns; your diet-wrecking alcoholic intake, which your body records long before you record it in blue-black ink on paper."

—Not to see him ever again? Not to pay him the last respect? Mother Sweetie—how could your large heart be so icy pale?

And the boy saw his father make a fist of his left hand, squeeze the fingers of the palm in a back-and-forth motion, as he often did in order to show his son the pulsating, blood-pumping action—the throb of the heart, he called it; usually he placed a cellophane wrapper over a deflated football in his palm before commencing the illustration: *Nathaniel, the heart is enclosed within a delicate two-chambered membrane,* and then he would enclose a double fold of see-through, heart-shaped, plastic membrane about the football.

—Respect? Arthur, how could I—oh, not in front of the boy, now —let's not wake up the dead with old-time revivals and new-time troubles of mind—too smoldering to touch down on and too hot not to grab without the aid of a cloth handle, she said as she stirred at her stew.

And that was when the boy first started to understand a little bit more about himself and how hard it was to take to the heart the way women looked down at a man's eyes, when you looked up to that same man with more respect than you could hold for any priest or minister. And as he looked again he tried to place himself into his father's shoes and thought back onto the arguments of his parents and how his mother's winging words always scaled down the flight of his father's vision; as if he were a snowman down in the playground near James· town's lagoon site, easily melted by the heated assault of the glaring sun, not unlike the one that spun out of the cradle of the skies and kept Great-Momma Sweetie's breads warmed and alive—summer or winter. Just then the boy felt his father's icy cold fingers pinch at the elbow sleeve of his jacket where there was a slightly worn spot, at the crazy bone. His father had once said that life places you into a straight jacket and there you must twist and dangle; yet in the next breath his father would tell how much he wanted his son to become an accomplished surgeon, to mend the sick and not be overcome by a sin-sick world.

Now sitting in the rocking chair and listening to Great-Momma Sweetie's heavy breathing and the stirring-up warmth in the teapot, the young man found himself rustling about, still unsettled over those arguments between his parents, still at war with his own confronta-

tions with his parents in life—though his mother resided in date-filled
night, his father a skeleton of the man he was in a hospital. And his
own failures. Not a doctor, lawyer, nor Indian chief, despite the Hopi
blood. Why not a baker? At least he could have learned that from
Great-Mother Sweetie's hand and her wisdom could have dispensed
that knowledge. To be a healer. Not a doctor of men. But Great-
Momma Sweetie Reed had sought out healing all of her life and what
had it rendered her privately? The world of her riddled soul and a
dropout for a grandson.

Privately, then and now, she was still at war with her father, I. V.
Reed, and her estranged husband, Jericho Witherspoon . . . You could
save the world, at least a piece of it; but you could also lose your way
and your soul in the inner circle of the family. Perhaps that was what
the dear woman now wanted to expostulate. He had decided to stay
in school the rest of his life; a life of learning, not as an escape from
the world but as a way of allowing the beacon light of wisdom from
knowledge to give illumination to the ruptured world of his family
and his reality. Yet here he was *not* reading before the grand altar of
books but rather trying to read out history through the final words
of an old woman nearing death, even as his father had gone to see
Jericho Witherspoon in the final months of his life in order to gain
the space of history, in order to fill in the gaps left there in time.

The boy found himself trying to replace Grandfather Witherspoon's parts and recollections, the image he held of him, which was
lofty and grand despite Great-Momma Sweetie's words. He didn't
fully understand what was behind them; they placed unscaled weight
upon him and forced him to wrestle with what he knew his father had
known about his own father as well as what he knew and felt for his
grandfather and back to the knowledge of what his mother said she
knew of the boy's father in the private world of marriage, if women
could do this—have this power over what you thought you knew
about men like Grandfather and Father—then what hope was there
for me, he wondered, in their arms?

And the young man thought now how powerless he was in the
hands of women; how they made you as you made them, out of the
clay of emptiness and loneliness that was so delicate that you shaped
a relationship as with the two hands of a magician, playing with
love-words, as so many silks in a rainbow of beauty and agony until
your body and soul were as one, as you spent long hours trying to tear
away the silken linen that went into fashioning the beautiful fabric of

oneness, in order to reassert your selfhood, your manhood, perhaps fearful of the feminizing power of her womanhood over you, what it drew out of you to make the relationship work. But how was this love-binding and love-destroying assertion any different from what went between parents and children? Yes, and surely it was more than a fractious moment with the grand old lady that turned Candy Cummings' once groovy heart to a frost-bitten apple, he now thought, pounding his fist beneath his heart at the memory of the lost body and soul of Candy Cummings. How divine it would be just now to rock and roll with her on that water bed.

The young man thought that what had started everything off on the wrong foot, that day long ago, started when Great-Momma Sweetie had said Grandfather *needed to get right on the inside before he could ever hope to get right on the outside,* in a way that suggested a judgment against him all of his days that didn't account for his many assets.

In the boy's eyes, his own father appeared to see Grandfather Witherspoon as an archangel and everything of perfection and high-mindedness, even though he had debated the old judge on many issues of the day. And as the boy turned towards his father now, as Witherspoon backed out of the door, he saw his father's forehead as a wrinkled network of creases in the sleeves of a starchless shirt hanging down over a straight-back chair. The father said:

—Give him credit enough to merely appear at his funeral, you don't have to say anything or even do anything.—

But as they backed out of the room (as if leave-taking before the throne of a queen) the boy felt himself torn once again between wanting to leave with his father immediately or rush back to Great-Momma Sweetie and hug her, as he had always embraced her; finally he came to her and she hugged his body with such fierce energy, need and strength that he thought he would snap in two like a string bean. And the boy looked past Great-Momma Sweetie to the huge feather bed—so ample and springy and loose-fitting yet snug and ever so soft —in which she and Grandfather Witherspoon had once upon a time slept, a bed so old and powerful and huge and gaunt, and the wooden tower of posts standing like a man's biceps; and the legs beneath like those of a football player's or the powerful wooden legs that the bathtub stood upon.

And the bed always warm where she appeared at the brink of wakefulness and this recalling the lingering memory of her body pouring down deep as she settled back down after her workday, and the boy sleeping in the curve her body made in the bed, as her body shifted from left to right alone, so that there were at least three body-cradling places in that bed for the frame to find its way back into. (Whenever he slept over, he donned one of his father's shirts—the front tails hung to his kneecaps—but it was at home that he sometimes wore Grandpa Witherspoon's slave tunic; and he wondered had his own father as a babe slept in this same bed.) Now the young man looked past her to the huge bed where she kept an electric pad down upon her soft mattress, and the bed was always radiant like smoldering logs and his memory of her body pouring down as she settled down; especially when he had a temperature, and reclining in that bed as his body sank down, the temperature seemed to abate from his warmth when combined with the goose grease to his chest, an iron-hot flannel cloth atop the grease; a prayer cloth to his temple, and then Great-Momma Sweetie gave him a hot toddy of bourbon, sassafras tea, lemon and sugar (and he often laughed, though sadly, to think of Aunt Genevieve's way of taking Antoine's temperature—a thermometer used in the way a soap-stick is inserted up the rectum). As Great-Momma Sweetie shook out the sheets, aired the bed the next day, the presence of their personalities remained in the rising, swooping, popping sheets as a clay mask retains the cast of the features when removed from the face (and since Grandfather Witherspoon had slept in this very same bed once upon a time, he wondered if his mighty form wasn't still in the shape of the huge, sloping downfall softness of the mattress).

But now the young man mused how Great-Momma Sweetie Reed had never been able to rid herself of the bed where she and Jericho Witherspoon had slept ever so long ago as one, even as she had never been able to rid herself of the warring memory of the man she loved once upon a time.

Great-Momma Sweetie's hands were red and callused, work-soured and overhauled with a hard crust to them, that was mean to the touch and brittle and sometimes cracking at the edges of her palms. Those old hands had touched the news of so many temperatures, climes, stoves, heats, icicles, deaths and births; she often measured up cups for lengthy distances and how many feet tall you were by how many hands you were: so as to measure up your rise in the world, she laughingly declared; so that as he reclined there Great-Momma Sweetie often used that hand, those dear and callused hands to fan his overheated forehead; except for that lost top of her thumb, missing from her right hand—lost back on the plantation many years before, when a wooden steel-edged bucket, filled with green-mint ice cream she was making for old man Rollins Reed, came tumbling down on her thumb as she was rushing between making his green-mint ice cream and trying to nurse her father, I. V. Reed, *whose heart was never in the right place.* I. V. Reed, himself sick on his skin-slick palate, rolled out from underneath the former master's bed. *And I got careless,* she said; *and that's why you see me taking my own sweet time with everything now.*

In her bed, and at her touch, the boy felt insulated against the whole world of hurts; still and all, he felt the sudden sharp need to go to his father, who seemed abandoned, and he broke himself free from her clutching and clinging and ran down the steps to his father to drift off to the funeral home. But as he broke and spun out of her reach, he felt her tapping upon his shoulders, in the long-reaching measure of those arms attached to her short body:

—Son, you don't understand it all now, but when you reach your majority, you come on back to Great-Momma Sweetie Reed and she'll unfold it all to you, without leaving out a jot of the picture so you can look into the mirror for yourself and know the full of my hurts, my wrongs, my history, our history, and what went wrong, from the beginning time.

2

"Angel Got Two Wings to Hide My Face"

Early the next morning they were back at Memphis Raven-Snow's funeral home. The offices were in the basement, three rooms from where the attendants brought in the bodies. Raven-Snow always kept the trapdoor leading to the basement tilted so that he might see upstairs in case anybody (or any "unanointed bodies," Uncle Hampton said, or any "body snatchers") arrived without warning. Nathaniel thought the funeral director had locked the front door when he let the boy and his father in; Raven-Snow certainly had slammed the door hard enough to wake up the dead, as the saying goes. The last of the business concerning Grandfather Witherspoon's funeral was soon settled and signed regarding a second mortgage on the dead man's summer cottage.

The boy and his father stood in front of the casket for half an hour, looking down upon Grandfather Witherspoon in the front of Raven-Snow's largest parlor room before descending the trapdoor ladder. His father was "satisfied" with the work of Raven-Snow and his helpers in "restoring a quality of life beyond life" to the ancient man's face. Grandfather Witherspoon's body wore the dark blue suit (one of three in his possession at the time of his death), and inside the suit, the invisible, tightly wrapped tissue paper and then the overriding robes of ebony justice. A red tie lightened the somber study. Nathaniel's father took a small comb-and-brush set from his inner overcoat pocket and applied them—rather heatedly, the boy thought—to Grandfather Witherspoon's unruly clusters of nappy red hair (which stood on the dead man's head as frozen puffs of cotton candy about angular-shaped wires) at the sides of his temple and rear of the huge, bald dome of the judge's head.

The boy felt one with his grandfather's head on the green cushiony pillow; even as he had felt one with Grandfather Witherspoon when the great man had lifted him in his caring arms a thousand times, or more it seemed, into the tree house, or to touch out to the very texture of the leaves; or to see the red-and-blue-faced clowns, shot from a cannon, at the circus, and the floats in the annual Negro parade in August. Cradled in the long sleeves of the grandfather's caring dreams: "My long suit into eternity," Jericho Witherspoon had often sweetly wept as they went along the streets in the dark, arm in arm.

Jericho Witherspoon's upper lip was slightly curled upwards in life, mockingly so, and it appeared all the more in death. And the boy recalled how his grandfather had often laughed at things that few others saw right away as funny. His father said that humor was "a many-sided personal instrument for survival; the deeper life cuts you, the deeper runs the lacing waves of your humor," as if to convince himself, the boy thought. The many wild, whitish red wiry hairs in the grandfather's nose and yellowish red earlobes made the boy feel a strange kind of humor, but also think of the wisps of cobwebs upon the screen of the enclosed porch at the small summer cottage; and it hurt the boy to think that the cottage might no longer be in the family.

The image of the enclosed porch recalled the boy's earliest memory (below the threshold all seemed garbled, passionate sounds, fuzzy and soupy with scenes as before a film starts pouring forth upon the extended screen with pictures of famous film stars and the kids screech and scream for the make-believe to begin), Grandfather Witherspoon lifting him up in his wrinkled, ropy arms on that porch . . . And the lyrical lullaby of the grandfather's voice reciting the ballad about the robin that covered dead bodies with leaves, the ancient "Babe in the Woods":

No burial this pretty pair
From any man receives
Till Robin Redbreast piously
Did cover them with leaves.

Jericho Witherspoon had kept no insurance; he had not believed in the institution as it was practiced against Negroes; the fragile little cottage had to be mortgaged a second time now, in order to bury the judge. Except for the old three-story frame house, where Great-Momma Sweetie Reed lived, Grandfather Witherspoon had lost nearly all of his estate in bad investments and the Depression; he had never made much money as a lawyer anyway, giving over half his time to taking on cases for the beleaguered Negro poor, who could not afford legal fees; and since in the beginning he was the only Negro lawyer in the state, he felt honor-bound to take these cases without financial reward.

Jericho Witherspoon had pushed his age back some fifteen years, but even then he was over seventy when he became a judge. His library was worth more than gold, and diamonds, the boy's father said. Three white universities had written for his private papers; yet none had offered money. Nathaniel's mother and Uncle Hampton said that these universities might give a tidy sum, and the boy could use the money for college. Arthur Witherspoon seemed embittered though not shocked that no Negro college had offered to house Jericho Witherspoon's private papers in its library.

Grandfather Witherspoon's six-foot, six-and-a-half-inch form had carried 250 pounds before the boy's knowledge of the grand old gentleman's weighty presence in the world, before words existed for the boy; but this was passed down through retelling. Awesome words spoke of the many dimensions of the outer man, as the conversation drifted into the stature of the inner man; but in the last months, his head bowed and back stooped, in the autumn, and then taken to the University Hospital in October, his speech slurred and the weight scalded down to less than one hundred pounds—ninety-nine, ninety-eight, ninety-seven . . . the way a snow melts away, the boy wept.

He threw away the magazine advertisement that boasted of making a man of you, if you weighed only ninety-seven pounds. That was for the foolish older guys, he thought. *I don't need to become Mr. Atlas; he was my Atlas; when I sat upon his shoulders, I was upon an axis* . . . Besides, hadn't he heard from his own father's lips the words of the Bard: "Golden lads and girls all must as chimney sweepers, come to dust." The brain itself, he had heard, weighed less than the body of most infants no more than three pounds. But there were brains and then there were brains. *Most people don't use 75 percent of the light of the body, which is the brain and the golden radiance of the soul,* his father said. This made the boy think: the brains of most people are dusty, long before their death; and that's what being dimwitted must mean. But did you go on living after the wheels in your brain stopped clicking? Or when your heart stopped beating? Grandfather Witherspoon's brain had gone to sleep, like so many furious bees, and brilliant butterflies, suddenly gassed in a net; yet his heart went on beating for a long time, after that sleeping away of the brain.

Grandfather Witherspoon's mouth was opened ever so slightly. His irregular teeth, half his own, half dentures and caps, were like withered kernels of corn; his cupped-up lower lip seemed to be asking a curt question—suggesting that even his one hundred seventeen years upon this earth had not provided any of the answers to certain questions asked in the beginning to the end of his justice-seeking days. The boy became snugly knit with his grandfather's invisible soul, feeling the beginning of quest for life and answers to the riddle of death in life. Yet he was constantly saying, "Yes, I understand" to the adult world's problems, as they were explained. Or the questions others' actions placed before his own brain; but seeing only opened up all kinds of new questions. Nor did the seeing make you understand, the boy thought as he looked upon Jericho Witherspoon, who had seen so much of life yet claimed towards the end of his days how little he understood of this world . . . *Now and at the hour of our death, amen,* he had said, just before going into the hospital that autumn.

Most adults didn't like for you to ask a lot of questions; even though they were always encouraging you to be curious, and to seek knowledge, they would also say, "Curiosity killed the cat." But Grandfather Witherspoon had encouraged questions of the boy. In his quiet way the boy seemed to be saying yes and to believe in little or nothing; only

25

question. In that way, he thought out loud as he looked down upon Grandpa Witherspoon's mocking lip, he was definitely his father's child and particularly Grandpa Witherspoon's; he was the light of his father's beam but particularly Grandpa Witherspoon's Short-Ribs; but he was also a child of his own day and light and darkness; Great-Momma Sweetie Reed said that he was *solely God's child, when all was said and done.* More like his grandfather than his father about the questioning lip; he saw none of Great-Momma Sweetie Reed in his father's face, nor in his own; nor, for that matter, did he particularly favor his own mother. His playmate, Maxwell "Blackball" Saltport, said he had a face only a mother could love.

Now the boy looked at Grandfather Witherspoon's curling lip that seemed to be answering the lower cupped questioning one, not with an answer but rather with a sour, mocking response; not an evasion, but as a charge that hinted a constant battle as the commanding, all-consuming troubled and bittered counter-call to the upper lip's demand. And as the boy looked again he seemed to see ever so fine liquid trickle over the curling upper lip. He thought maybe Grandfather Witherspoon still held some of the juices from his favorite chewing tobacco in the rear of his wisdom teeth, that had trickled forth, as if neither death nor the arts of the body-draining mortician were able to clear off nor defeat the juices inside of the man.

Seated there in Great-Momma Sweetie's bedroom, the remembering young man, at this point, speculated that the old man had held on to his juices—not tobacco juices, but those of life—and had just enough electrical strength in him after dying to send forth a bitter, mocking laugh over the answers life had provided; the non-answers; still rebuking and scorning and spitting back at life, at the very brink of death, that he would mock life better after death.

Now the boy wondered just how many of the scores of mourners who visited the lying-in-state ceremony for his grandfather would notice this film of juice upon the upper lip of the famous dead man's face. He shivered as he thought of the scalelike film over the brand JW upon Grandfather Witherspoon's back, placed there by the slave's very own father and that the old man would take into eternity . . . "Here, Riley, here"—he shuddered as he thought of how the young escaped slave's very own uncle had set the bloodhounds upon Jericho Witherspoon's trails over a century ago . . . *Angel,* he thought, *got two wings to hide my face . . . two wings to fly me away,* but those were Great-Momma Sweetie's words.

Nathaniel's mother had provided Grandfather Witherspoon's face with some slight pancake makeup, but that only gave the gaunt face a flush; highlighting the red clay of his yellowish red coloring, and the mixed gray with the bubbly, nappy red-hair puff balls at the sides of his head.

. . . *Making Big Red (as his fellow slaves had called him) appear rather like an actor in a movie made from a novel concerning an actor's life, the remembering young man Nathaniel now reflected. He thought of the many outfits and disguises that Jericho Witherspoon had donned along the way to his freedom . . . Refining the refinements into sheaths and sleeves of liberation . . . Gifted in the art of freehand drawing, as well as calligraphy, Jericho Witherspoon had drawn pictures of the many garbs, wigs and disguises he had used along the way of his journey from the South, on the last pages of his journal.*

One hundred and seventeen years seemed beyond time to the boy. It had taken him his first three years to learn to count to one hundred, although he had learned to sight-read quickly; he didn't start walking until he was sixteen months old; Grandfather Witherspoon had started walking when he was six months old, and according to Great-Momma Sweetie Reed his father had started walking when he was nine months old.

Grandfather Witherspoon didn't have any socks on—the boy knew this because one of his tasks was to select the linen for the ancient man's body. His feet were all calluses, like his hands—now that was different from the baby picture that the boy also had to carry in his own mind forever and ever, which would never fade from his mind, the way the sprinkle of Holy Water faded upon the fingertips.

He was to be the boy's baby-king. Nathaniel suddenly started weeping as he thought back over his grandfather's last months. Sleeping like a baby in its cradle. Cousin Viola, "Aunt" Harriet's wild and churchgoing daughter—had said "when a baby dies, its clothes should never be put on another baby, and that next baby can't be placed in the dead baby's cradle—because that will place it into the arms of Death." Maybe, the boy thought, this also meant that he should never put on the old man's slave tunic again, when going off to bed and sleep, because the old man had seemed cradled in the suckling sleep of a babe without a care—despite the mocking, questioning lips—there at the University Hospital.

Or would the old man's memory haunt him if he returned to wearing that ancient garment that he loved so well? Though he had learned to hate what the tunic stood for, he loved the story of the grandfather's escape; and when he put on the tunic (that Jericho Witherspoon had worn when he was five), always in secret, he felt as one with his grandfather's memory; and he always felt this way when the meaning of the word "Covenant" was explained to him. For now, even if he was a little frightened of stealing into the dead man's childhood garment, the boy knew that he would always be haunted by the memory and presence of Jericho Witherspoon . . . blood of my blood, the words ran through his body like deep waters renewing the spirit of the troubled river.

His other task was to read from a newspaper account at the funeral the next day. The newspaper story told of the first important promotion Jericho Witherspoon had won, on his way up the ladder of success. The boy had read the account over and over again, so that he could learn it by heart, as he had learned the Apostles' Creed. But each time he read the account aloud, he felt more and more that he would never be able to fill the dead man's shoes.

Now the boy's father turned around to look down into his sad, dark eyes; the troubled beam of light in Arthur Witherspoon's right eye was filled with salty tears—like tiny bubbles in an eyedropper—about to pop and trickle off into the long eyelash. The eyelash of the left eye was beating like the furious wings of a bird—flapping to keep the strong sunlight away from the eyes of the infant sparrow . . . Great-Momma Sweetie Reed often quoted Luke: "The Light of the body is of the eye."

But just now a bell pealed three times and then the side doors (which were normally locked) shot open, revealing a towering flock of flowers and three men, dressed in white uniforms, bearing tall stands of floral arrangements. The flowers spreading outwards from their bodies, so that other than their white-gloved hands, ballooning sleeves, legs and shoe tops, their bodies remained momentarily invisible; instantly they installed the flowers sharply adjacent to the casket, left and right; then swiftly the men abandoned the room to the watch of the father and the son. With the flowers jammed tightly to either side of the golden casket (which stood upon a platform, briefly elevated), the oblong box appeared to the boy's eyes suspended in space upon the wings of the angelic breathing of the flowers.

The rainbow of colors and the powerful odor, sweet and swimming with radiant heartbreak, as at Easter sunrise, made the chapel throb to the brink of life with the strange presence of the grand man come

28

alive, as in a daydream. It was too much for the boy. He thought of holy water in the font at church that would never go away; even as it dried so quickly in the heat of the sun, like Great-Momma Sweetie Reed's fingertips when touched to the iron, in order to test the flatiron's heat.

But who had sent the white-uniformed men with the flowers? The family had requested that the money for flowers should be sent to the University Hospital for heart research, in Jericho Witherspoon's name. Now the presence of the freshly cut flowers made the boy feel a presence of his grandfather's breathing in the casket, even as the ancient man had gone on breathing in his hospital bed after he no longer recognized any family members, and his eyes were also closed . . .

He was my baby-king, the boy thought. In the last months it had been necessary for Grandfather Witherspoon to wear diapers; they put him in the hospital, starting in late October.

By March he had descended into a deep sleep. And thinking of this now made the boy suddenly angry with Great-Momma Sweetie for abandoning his grandfather, some thirty-nine years earlier, although in truth he had abandoned her, or had he? And why was it that in death, and especially now, he found himself putting the blame on Great-Momma Sweetie Reed? She at least could give him the respect of appearing at the funeral, the boy thought; in this at least his father was right. He felt a deep set of confusions, as with two wings no longer willing to go in one direction—each hurling him in opposite directions.

In Great-Momma Sweetie's arms the boy felt that he was in the possession of a great and everlasting queen, and in Grandfather Witherspoon's arms he knew that he had been in the presence of a great and goodly king, even though the boy said to himself how peaceful he seemed to sleep, as a babe at the hospital . . . The white silk hose of the boy's choosing seemed more like silk stockings, fit for a king, but also like booties, when he beheld them upon his own outstretched palms. The seams in the white socks made the boy think of the pathway of Grandfather Witherspoon's labors to freedom, stitched to the threads of memory forever and ever, that the runaway slave had worn on the patch beneath his sleeve. Aunt Genevieve had said, "If you carry the right eye of a wolf sewn inside the right sleeve, you remain free from all injuries." "No injury was worst than injustice," Grandpa Witherspoon had said.

Grandfather Witherspoon's body was like lightbread, ready to crumble in the heat of the long sleeve of slumber; even though Memphis Raven-Snow and his helpers had placed ballooning tissue paper that formed an inner lining between his robes and the dark blue suit to add body to the appearance of the famous jurist's life-stripped form. And as his father now touched Nathaniel's sleeve, indicating that it was time to go, he took a last look at his grandfather's face, noting this time how those three little knitted veins at either side of the temple, once upon a time so prominent (as if ready to flood over), were now exhausted, dried-up where Nathaniel projected his grandfather had kept, stored up: his wisdom . . . Taking yet another last look upon his grandfather's body, the boy placed his hand upon the withered, ancient dead man's hand—thinking of him, saying out loud, as he so often did: "This is the Roof, this is the Steeple, but Lord, open it up, and Short-Ribs, *here's the problem—the People.*" Spinning in and out of each other's arms: children lost and afraid of the dark.

And so the boy and his father descended the white ladder to the basement, where Arthur Witherspoon signed the second mortgage on the cottage in order to bury his father: a grove for the judge in the earth. The boy felt a grievous knot in his stomach; finally he sat down upon a high chair in the corner and tried to look through the annual mortuary magazine taken by Memphis Raven-Snow. But before his eyes the words from the magazine (concerning burial insurance) only seemed to unleash bulletins from the past, clusters of ideas and phrases he had heard . . . Slavery . . . Up north, many thousands gone to jail on trumped-up charges and Jericho Witherspoon getting them out on writs of habeas corpus, Negroes arrested at the very train station as they descended the platform, because the authorities were looking for runaways, in order to pin injustices upon them. "Negroes up here, too, wanted Dead or Alive," Grandfather Witherspoon said.

And Great-Momma Sweetie's voice: "Jericho Witherspoon extended my vision into the meaning of words by candlelight; starting off with the very papers of my freedom to his hand in marriage and then my mother's freedom paper by old man Rollins Reed's hand, that receipt my father received from the patroller, on which Angelina Reed's name was crossed out and my own name put in exchange for my mother's place, and the *purchase* deed for me, signed by old man Rollins Reed's shaky hand; he who had sent the paper north in the darkness of his vision to Lovelady Breedlove, born 1833 and died 1907. She who had once been his slave; he'd nodded upon the marriage of his granddaughter for a price and a pledge in a letter he could no longer clearly read, nor could I read it, so that we had to turn to I. V. Reed, who was slumbering beneath his old master's bed because he was needed to be up all night with the old man, who was suffering indigestion and hardening of the arteries. And I. V. Reed was trying to catch up on his long sleep. He was the only one who could read around the whole of the plantation . . . But one day I shall tell you his full hand in it all.

"And so it was I. V. Reed who struck the deal in the final deed, helped the old man sign the agreement, the covenant: I. V. Reed's dark walnut-colored hand atop the pinkish blueberry shaking hand and quivering fingers of Rollins Reed's—guiding it into a signature, piggyback-like, and with the sweet harmonious voice of a choir director's to knee-shaking, shrill-voiced members of the children's choir, soothingly directing it along; that I would be married to this man of fifty-five—the age of my own father; the marriage set for June 5, at high noon, 1882 . . . And Rollins Reed twisting me back around I. V. Reed to get at him in a covenant with Jericho Witherspoon, weaved as a veil through it all . . . But one day, my Splendid Spoons, I will reveal it all to you." And I. V. Reed, himself, making certain that the agreement was fair and honest to all parties concerned as he aided the old slaver to give his granddaughter's hand away in marriage, "pointing to the five hundred dollars on the bottom line, as if his own blood wasn't knotted to the deed, in double trust . . . like the thread of a needle darning up the sole of a sock."

But just then the front door suddenly slammed and the three looked up the shaking ladder in wonder—only to see the cedar-colored face of Great-Momma Sweetie Reed, who was wearing that strawberry bonnet of her mother's. Great-Momma Sweetie didn't know they were immediately watching her from the ladder leading up the steps and they stood witnessing her through the basement trapdoor, so that Arthur Witherspoon and Memphis Raven-Snow climbed up the steps on tiptoe like little boys and Nathaniel followed close behind them, wondering breathlessly what she was about to do and at the same time hearing her commence to a-moaning and a-humming, as if in preparation for a sermon, as she breathed heavily three feet in front of Grandfather Witherspoon's casket, where the boy and his father had stood only moments earlier. Had she been hovering, perched somewhere within the presence of the funeral home, all along, watching over them as a witness and waiting until they descended to make her appearance? And why had she decided to come?

Great-Momma Sweetie Reed had a sprig of lilies of the valley in her white-gloved left hand as she now approached the final three steps leading up to the brief platform, just before the golden casket bearing Grandfather Witherspoon's body . . . "God, I thought I had slammed that door completely shut," Memphis Raven-Snow whispered heavily in an awed voice; but just at that moment they heard her move from humming and whispering.

". . . And so, Jerry, you didn't think I was going to come to see you —pay you any portion of last respects. But you see the chamber of my soul is not sealed away in a cold bloodstream."

The boy heard his father scream out in the voice of one announcing bloody murder; a wordless shrill that could awaken the dead. Memphis Raven-Snow shot withering looks between the woman and Arthur Witherspoon.

Did Great-Momma Sweetie think Grandfather Witherspoon's spirit still hovered above his body, as she had thought of her mother's spirit hovering, like a halo? Or was she simply continuing a conversation started *before we knew Grandfather,* the boy wondered.

". . . Because your children are not your children—they are the sons and daughters of their own breath and being and brightness and darkness. Jerry, we can never be saved from Death, but we can be saved in the midst of Death—and for that occasion, as a wheel cast within a bright-faced wheel, I've been praying for sixty years—even as the very wings of the spirit are preparing for flight at the moment of the Lightning that shatters Life, you can be reborn by such a bolting power as the fitful discharging of one wheel from its moorings, flinging outwards like a wing, within the larger wheel, cradled upon the platform; moving counterclockwise, yet another, greater circulation spirit can be there, troubling and rising in the very falling off of the primary body wing; as love's careless sleeves stirring up old still waters, rising out of them in the pitch of night, in a greater ecstasy than the mind can conceive . . . Put a shell-shape to your eardrum, there by the rolling waters, Jerry; and you can hear all kinds of sounds from the heart-shape inside the anointed roaring waters of Almighty God's message drifting upon the waters, as that old inner wheel rolling upon a platform like a chariot-carriage.

". . . We got to get back to the beginning time; for I hope and I believe that was the case in your dying and the commencing of your

32

spirit off of this old world, that a deepening was rising up in you in the last gasp of bubbling breath, upon the waters and towards your final will and testimony—or Lawd, why else would you appear to me before the dawn's early light?"

Memphis Raven-Snow and the boy Nathaniel had to hold Arthur Witherspoon back from ascending the ladder of the trapdoor; he was weeping and screaming frantically for Great-Momma Sweetie to shut up, as far as the boy could understand his words. The son on one side and the mortician on the other, holding on to the outstretched spread of the father's flying, flaying arms; and the boy recalled learning to swim, at two, with his father at one end, holding up his head and the arms, and the teacher at the other end holding the feet (all three knee-deep) as his body touched down upon the icy waters; the ladder to the diving board within a stone's throw; and they took him up and down and down and up to get his body used to the chilling waters; in the very same waters where many were baptized in the summer months. His father seemed as shocked by the chilling presence of Great-Momma Sweetie Reed as he himself had been by the cold waters of the pool to his body.

Arthur Witherspoon was shuddering, saliva streaming down from the sides of his mouth; what on earth was she talking about, the boy himself wondered, and he grew fearful that his father's diabetes was about to flare up. Now Sweetie Reed was praying:

". . . How horrible it would be to live for any more years than Jerry Witherspoon consumed this earth; dominated it; to struggle and crawl with the breathless, troubling heartbeat that reduced to a trickle throb; man can't take it; to struggle with the bleeding heart in the dreadful prisoner's clutches of mind and body—if we couldn't die, what a deeper curse than death itself it would all be, if, in fact, we couldn't fly away upon the wings of the morning; ripened in Death. Out of the sorrow of our suckling shadow. For life is never completely consummated, only destroyed, until it is embraced by Death. Reborn out of the flying chamber of dispatching life, undefeated; discharged from the wheel within a wheel, out of the troubling waters of Time —to know the two wings of Mankind's riddled redemption.

". . . Bones too brittle; legs too fra-gile; arms can't be propelling wings in the morning time. When the light of winter's day comes tumbling down (as avalanching rocks from high, mighty mountains crashing into the sea), creating sleeves of rippling renewal within the waters about to burst into life-giving, though agony-ridden for the groomed swimmer—Lawd, which is also where we are in the beginning time of Jericho Witherspoon's days.

". . . Lawd, even as decomposition bereaves us on our way from the time we are infants until our two-score, if we breathe that long; just as life is said to be beginning and coming back down to the baby napkin and non-talk but babble like the deep river; and we etch our first, stumbling ways towards crawling in the great gathering-up morning of our brief day; as a child learning to dress its body in shrouding grief and we go from stuttering to word-shaping talk after coming out of the chilly sleeves of the river's eternity."

Amid his father's howling for Great-Momma Sweetie to cease, the boy remembered now Grandfather Witherspoon lifting him up out of the hot bathing waters of the huge tin tub on the floor, as a baby, and toweling his feet, legs, backside, neck and arms in the ballooning gray robelike towel, so that his very body seemed to spin in the coarse gray material.

And the remembering young man Nathaniel reflected: Yes, spinning as a wheel within a wheel, and as the delicate streams of the river are embodied in wing-fluttering, encircling motions, to insulate the robes of the river's being, even as the circular motion stirs the river's depths —was this what Great-Momma Sweetie was talking about, he wondered, as a picture of early-morning fishing with Uncle Ulysses came before his vision; the pool of circles declaring the presence of a catch before the hooked fish emerged only to somersault above the riverbed.

Now Arthur Witherspoon fairly spun out of the care and keeping of Memphis Raven-Snow and Nathaniel. He was screeching and howling and leaping up the ladder steps, as one caught up in a holy-jump dance of madness, and Memphis Raven-Snow captured one leg and bounded up to catch the other; the obese sweating mortician pulling the furious man back, even as he tried to surge forward . . . Crying out aloud: "Douse cold water on that wicked woman; I'll douse some ice water on her. She's vexed as a dragon lady."

But Nathaniel heard Great-Momma Sweetie's continuing voice:

". . . That don't mean we don't get unsettled on the Pilgrim's Highway, Jerry, that don't mean we stop asking up the robe of Heaven's long light as you did in your way all of your days for Justice, as Job did, in his grief—for a deep-river revelation to carry you on through—all right, Jerry, I understand that—I hear you, but you forgot the God part, the arms of your perfect soul appealed out of your sleeves as a beseeching chorus scoring for Justice: an Eagle's wings clawing and scaling the mountain for Truth."

And the boy cried out: *Then why can't she hear my father's voice?* —but realizing just as suddenly that Sweetie Reed couldn't hear him because her hearing aid was not on, on purpose, the boy imagined, yet usually some peals of sound peeked through, just enough from the outer world for her to avoid an answer if she so desired.

But the remembering young man Nathaniel thought: *Even if her hearing aid was on, she would not have heard his father's muttering and screeching words to know his voice, nor to know the voice of his heartbreak in his words. Why should Great-Momma Sweetie Reed hear his father—if he understood what she was getting at, in her many-sided way—through Grandfather Witherspoon, her only husband, if not the sole bridegroom of her soul.*

But this was also the moment when the boy Nathaniel started to see that Great-Momma Sweetie was stumbling towards what she was trying to show. Why couldn't his father, who loved words so much, see it all now? But the boy could understand this stumbling way towards the path of the right answers. He often felt this way when his father—who was a great but impatient and intimidating teacher— attempted to show him how to do his homework, or to instruct him in ideas just above a boy's head; and then getting vexed with the son's slower flowing learning passages. Then he always felt as a child stealing in and out of the garments of grownups in one way; and in another, as a child lost in the dark, trying to escape but only going into the chamber door that folded in on itself into a new chamber door, like those set up in "Prank-City Paradise" at the circus sideshows—and the guiding hand of Grandpa Witherspoon lost, seemingly, forever and ever.

And the reflecting Nathaniel Witherspoon said to himself: *Yes, we are all as God's children wandering about in His garden, trying to spell the names of His creatures and using the wrong alphabet; because we've suffered too many blows to the brain, living in this paradise lost.*

Now Arthur Witherspoon floundered in the arms and hands of Raven-Snow as if his very soul was beset by a mixture of madness and a yearning for mercy. And Nathaniel suddenly thought, then why did he want her to come to see the body that had brought on such pain in life, and then expect Great-Momma Sweetie not to be herself, or to act as one who has simply covered herself body and soul, in lamb's wool. Hadn't he invited her saying, 'You don't have to say anything or do anything.' Now she cried out in a shrill voice:

". . . Oh now, Jerry, I used to tell you that all those security locks and jail cells you stole through to free up falsely accused folk wouldn't pick nothing clean, or bolt up nothing in the final go-around, if they and you didn't have the spirit stuck to your ribs . . . And all the locks and bolted-up folks here in freeway North used to keep doors locked away from wife-stealing; and thieves that come in before the Dawn; where there's no springtime of the soul and folks got to go around with their hard-clothes on to melt the mean ice in their souls; and nobody leaves food out on the stove all day long for nourishment; and the old service pan might have pitchforks tucked away, as if to get back at poison-sprinkling slaves . . . Because after you free all of *that* up—there is no bolt to the heart, even though you may think you've locked up the chambers to feeling and *an enslaving Jesus;* and secured yourself against Death's enterprise and sent him to the padlocked back door, with the malignant jailer . . . No, Jerry, hold still, listen to what I'm saying, hear me out for once in your—"

"What the hell is that crazy woman talking about?" Nathaniel heard his father yell, but not wanting to look into his face; the words shocked the boy into a desire to cry out in defense of Great-Momma Sweetie Reed, but he knew that his father would only read his words as mannish back talk.

Now the boy realized his father was having an insulin reaction, as Arthur Witherspoon's body rolled backwards into the arms of Memphis Raven-Snow; meantime the son held on to his father's flopping legs, and they descended the steps in order to place the sick man on a couch . . . And it appeared to the boy as if his father were being carried down the ladder like a dying man carried upon the shoulders by friends and kin; the very ones who might be called upon to be the pallbearers later. Even though he knew his father was having an insulin reaction and that with a candy bar, or sugar water, or orange juice he might be restored to his normal self again; he felt that this is the way he will also be when he, my only father, is dying and I am called on to hold my father in my arms and he breathes his last breath. And sprinkling drops of water, like beads from a font of holy water, filled the son's eyes.

As the body of Arthur Witherspoon began to contort and the mouth twisted and he slobbered like a babe, the limbs stiffened and seemed to leap forward as spiritually estranged contraband in the holding arms of two sentinels, unprepared for the spiraling motions of the man's frame. The honey-colored temple of the heavy-huffing undertaker was pouring sweat, as he tried to hold the moaning Arthur Witherspoon down; meantime they could hear Great-Momma humming and singing before the body of Jericho Witherspoon, her voice filled with vapors of music that sounded like a commingling of steamy blues and divine radiating.

The boy stripped a Baby Ruth candy bar of its wrapper and placed it to his father's quaking lips while the other hand was wanting to slap him into respect and to surprise him out of his shock—though the boy knew this was not the way—even as that hand was trying to keep the father's body afloat on the couch; just as another part of the son was feeling a peculiar sense of fear of and keen interest in Great-Momma Sweetie's humming and chanting and what her hovering words meant.

Raven-Snow—with those tiny, fat but nimble fingers of his—somehow was able to get Arthur Witherspoon out of his jacket; but Nathaniel's father seemed like a man in a straitjacket, trying to wrestle his way free of his very flesh; even as he munched savagely upon the candy bar. The son wondered what vision his father saw while under the insulin shock. Did he see visions of his own death? He seemed to fight so hard to come from beneath the shock, where his very personality had vanished; as a small child fighting to say in words the pictures his imagination presents to his mind in the unknitting garments of a dream . . . This made the boy think back to the whispered words of Dr. Brudderstone, at the hospital months before, as Grandfather Witherspoon hovered, breathlessly, or so it seemed, at the very edge of death—that the family reconsider ending the ancient man's embarrassing agony, with an injection of insulin . . . And Arthur Witherspoon's violent reaction against the cold, blond physician's gently stated, icy whisper in the ear of the dying man's son . . . When suddenly now, as the boy looked down upon his father, the words of old came tumbling down to the son, as if in a kind of deliverance, and as a waterfall from the mountain's side: *Your arms too short to box with God.* But then as Arthur Witherspoon munched greedily upon the Baby Ruth candy bar and seemed to emerge ever so slowly from the first stages of the insulin shock, the boy recalled Great-Momma Sweetie's words: *"For a man who doesn't believe in God, Arthur sure fights to get from out under those reactions, as one laboring to bring life back into His world."*

37

Now as Arthur Witherspoon finished the last of the candy bar, he tossed the wrapper aside and freed himself from the reach of the mortician and Nathaniel. He was still rather groggy and glassy-eyed as he climbed up to the top of the ladder, with Raven-Snow and the boy at his heels. He stood there in a state of amazement, listening to her words; from time to time reaching his hands out as if to cut off her breathing. Just now Sweetie Reed was saying:

". . . Because you can have some tribulation of the heart and it can suddenly miss a faint beat, like a tributary caught up in a lightning cord to a bighearted river at baptizing time, as a throbbing breast come alive to suckle, and then you feel a sudden bolt and that can tear down the walls protecting and saving the heart; the body cannot evade; and there's no covenant can overturn *that* bolting time. But, Jerry, there is a covenant to the heart, that comes down to us from Day One of the blood transfusion of How we got over from down under in the storm, without a life raft, to just swimming and then climbing that mountain, like you, Jerry.

". . . And I believe I heard it this morning, Jerry, because my two mothers told me long before you arrived. Heard my Lovelady crying out to me, 'Yes, though we enslaved and in a long-haul prison, I'm so glad I got my religion in time.' And then I thought I heard Mother Angelina saying, 'I'm so glad trouble don't last always,' and then, Jerry, I thought I heard her saying, as she did on the night they killed her, as she lay dying, 'I'm so glad Death can't do me no wrong.'

". . . Because in the very midst of the Lightning of Death—ah, the wings a-stirring like a baby chick's, in the nest at its mother's breast-bone—I heard my long-dead mother call down to me, from the mountaintop:

Hurry, Angel, hurry! Down to the pool
Lord, I want you to trouble the waters
This morning to bathe my weary soul.
Angel got two wings to hide my face,
Two wings to fly me away.

And the boy Nathaniel saw Great-Momma Sweetie Reed move to the tiny platform so that her face was almost one with his Grandfather Witherspoon's face. The boy's father cried out in a loud voice. But Great-Momma Sweetie's cry outdistanced Arthur Witherspoon's, as if she had heard him and picked it up, not as a source of defiance that she must shut off but rather as a tune of vexing inspiration that drove her on.

"... Cataracts cut from your eyes but they were simply to leave only reflecting pools of light in your soul—which was always bent on doing right and bringing justice up from the waters, as the smeared beacon of a lighthouse in the storm vaulting upwards the lost vessels. Oh, that you would have placed an eternal flame in that smeared beacon lamp—but still what a lamp to light the slate upon which I learned how my name looked, spelled out by your very hand upon my hand, Jerry; and I learned to recognize the words on the papers that said my mother, Angelina Reed, would be free, when her father died who did not die out in time—to get his religion—words that signified not deeds but the meaning of words beyond deeds; and how to read with an understanding; and it was *that* helped me to learn to read and recognize, understand and even wrestle for the wisdom with the angel of that old Bible my slaver grandpappy sent me.

"... Oh yes, I learned from you that we got to go up the rugged side of the mountain. And if it's rugged, then it's meant for us; and if the swimming is rough through choppy waters, then you know for sure you in the sleeves and robes of the ancestors—and then you know the mountain'll be rugged and thereby fair and unfair, fouled as the waters and slated for our testing—hand- and body-shaping and mind-making out of fury and set to unleash new confusion in the citadel of the mind.

"... But, Jerry, if you got God's word sewed to the inner lining of your soul as a prayer cloth, you got the map; no harm can come to sound you away—in the moonlight ... 'Cause I'm so glad trouble don't last always. Yes, showing the path as it reveals you face to face with the pale posse of Death, storming its way to the innocents. Jerry, you taught me a portion of this, as a suckling remnant of the unbridled Truth, when you presented the babe of innocence upon the bed of woe as my portion.

"... Rugged is the word, so you can keep on climbing and learning how to fall and rise and hook into the edges and slabs and crevices and niches and keep on climbing in the slipping breach, yea though it's steeplejack steep and tricky and loaded down with disasters as life's calamitous land mines, at every glance of the eye and turn (as you moving with the feet of a toddler in your constant newness) so that the mountain's very personality becomes scrawled out and fleshed in you as tongue-lashing meanness, backbone courage, arm-winging generosity, and waxed to your body parts, as another skin to the anklebone to your backbone and implanted in your skullbone, as survival knowledge. When you emerge out of the waters, you just getting ready for the real climb up the jagged mountain, babe in your manhood, and mannish in your innocence; blissful in your daring and full of the savvy of a snake in your caring. Ready for your climb and nervous as a virgin bride—up, *Up,* UP the jagged mountain; your new baptism after the baptism by waterfall. Baptism by brimstone—because by the time you finished, your baby fat's burned away and you back down to the way you come into this world but this time a rugged skeleton, a replica of the mountain; you're as a savage, sacred spent from the swim and worn as blood-smeared parchment from the climb; can't talk because you've seen too much. Can't walk because the burdens of life have backed you down to a crippling crawl.

". . . Yes, and if you climb it you'll never forget one solitary lesson when you out there by yourself, by your lonesome, hanging by a thread of your humanity, and His Divinity; in your body-bleeding lessons, carved rock to rock and crevice to hand and ankles bleeding and head bloody and yes, bowed, as a lynched man's physique . . . And only the foul winds of circumstance there to let you know and not to know of the valley below and the waters from whence you have come up to climb. Bellowing and howling below up at you, in mockery, you think, with your puny brainpower: the voices of weeping babes and screaming old folks, and beneath that the curses of all who prayed that you would slip and fall back down. But you, Jerry, came to doubt sometimes if that old watchful mountain God lives . . ." Then Arthur Witherspoon fell back into their arms. Thunderstruck by her words. What had he heard in those words? The boy wondered about why Great-Momma Sweetie Reed's words had shook his father so.

Nathaniel saw Great-Momma Sweetie Reed extract from her large purse a small bag—where she kept the lock of her mother's hair—and then place the clip of the deceased Angelina Reed's chestnut-colored tresses just beneath Grandfather Witherspoon's left sleeve; sternly rearrange her bonnet, as if before a long, oval-shaped, floor-length mirror. Then she placed the sprig of lilies of the valley on the cushioned step, leading up to the casket, as if to block the way for those that might kneel there, the boy thought; and now just as suddenly as she had appeared, spun out of a dream, Great-Momma Sweetie Reed vanished . . .

Vanished indeed, because her sudden departure occurred as Memphis Raven-Snow and the boy carted Arthur Witherspoon back to an old battered rocking chair—near the embalming room. Nathaniel placed a footstool underneath his father's feet, as the heaving Raven-Snow straightened Arthur Witherspoon's body out. Arthur Witherspoon seemed to suckle upon the last portion of the Baby Ruth candy bar as bitter grapes; his eyes were still glassy, but now ablaze with tears, as one taken to the top of a mountain suddenly, and left there to die. Spittle ran down upon his white shirt. His long nails had torn into the flesh of his throat. Raven-Snow had vanished, too. The boy was left with his trembling father, terrified over what he saw and not understanding what his father heard and saw in the words of Great-Momma Sweetie; coming from beneath the last stages of the insulin shock, only to be struck low by her words.

Now the returned Raven-Snow applied steaming-hot and then cold compresses to Arthur Witherspoon's temple, all of which, the boy explained as delicately and respectfully as he could, wouldn't help put his father back together again, though he appreciated Mr. Raven-Snow's act of concern; but please get him another bar of candy. The boy felt that Memphis Raven-Snow should have known better with his medical school training and that he should not have suffered what his own father often called "an immediate brainstorm" of applying compresses, one hot the other cold to the temple of Arthur Witherspoon. To the boy's understanding, adults seemed to love humility in children, much more than they respected the truth. Though they always wanted you to tell the truth and shame the devil. But the truth could get you into troubled waters, if it was seen as back talk about an adult subject.

He heard the front door of the funeral parlor slam . . . Was he hearing things, too? Just then the obese Memphis Raven-Snow extracted a Brach Way candy bar from his upper desk drawer. The son applied it to the teeth of his father in a grinding manner; then the father opened his mouth as his son broke off a piece of candy bar and placed it upon the tongue. Arthur Witherspoon chewed violently amid his tears, crying out for Great-Momma Sweetie Reed in the voice of a screeching babe. But now, to his surprise, in a voice that was almost pleading; even as his father bit down upon the candy bar (as an infant learning to masticate his food) the son heard his beloved and brilliant father cry out amid his slobbering: "Mother Sweetie, sugar water, sugar water, Momma Sweetie . . . Sugar. Water. Sugar-tit."

After they left the funeral home, the father thought he had under-gone a nightmare in the wilderness, in which Great-Momma Sweetie had only appeared during the insulin-induced shock, the deep choco-late and white mint from the candy smeared upon his tie like slob-bered dessert upon a baby's bib.

*   *   *

But now the remembering young man Nathaniel Turner Wither-spoon discovered to his strange surprise that the teapot had not just begun to whistle, but apparently had been whistling for some time. And the rising steam was a steam-piping train engine to his shattered and uncomfortable reverie, enough to awaken the dead. Now the stroke from the grandfather clock rendered up three muffled peals. He arose. Snapped off the heat beneath the boiling pot of water. Glanced over at the still sleeping Great-Momma Sweetie, who was wrestling with life in sleep, as she had always done, all of his remembering life (and giving no quarter), while wide awake.

The sweat of steam poured off the bronzed teapot. He took down a tall cup from the glass-faced cupboard. Now he poured out the boiling water upon the autumn-colored leaves of the sassafras tea; a wickedly alluring odor leapt from the cup; he ran a slit with a razor blade about the yoke of the fifth of Rémy Martin brandy, uncapped the cork of the bottle at the sideboard.

For comfort's sake he kicked off his black and white Oxfords and observed that the sole of each shoe was in dire need of mending. Oh, why hadn't he gone along and accepted one of the two university offers in exchange for his grandfather's private papers, a tuition-free status as student-at-large? The easy way out. I'll not ride those be-loved shoulders to a sheepskin. The shoulders I rode so richly well as a boy to the top of the tree house. I'll work my own way up, hand over hand, to the top of the mountain. But to the top of which mountain? A bleeding heart for massive causes, Candy Cummings gave no quarter to the individual, fragile lost souls of God's intellec-tual wandering kingdom. Candy Cummings thought I had something up my sleeve by not accepting one of the offers. No wonder Candy Cummings (surely richer than all of my tribe) called me "a fool—an eternal student-at-large with a hole in your head to match the one in your scuffed-up Oxfords. Working for some nickel-and-dime newspa-per; writing a column and selling ads. A shiftless wonder. Part-time and half-ass." A dropout, deserted by his Delta deserted Queen of hearts; abandoned finally via the backwater wrath of Sweetie Reed's saucy words.

Now he took a long, last look at Great-Momma Sweetie Reed, wondered if in fact he was doing the right thing in taking her orders; then doused a jigger of the soul-flaming brandy into the tall cup, poured off a full measure of sugar. Stirred the brew vigorously with the small paddle she often used to stir cream. The odor filled the room with the insatiable authority of fire upon beechwood, bathed in gasoline, in the wilderness, so it seemed to Nathaniel.

Then ever so lightly he touched his fingers to Great-Momma Sweetie's temple; it was cold and rather clammy. He touched his fingers to the balled-up fists she held up high in her sleep, boxing her way out of the last sleeves of sleep; *backwater time* indeed, he mused.

Soon now Great-Momma Sweetie was roused almost completely.

Now she was still groggy but definitely awake. Nathaniel propped her up with the aid of three pillows. He handed her the cup of steaming tea. From his briefcase he took out seven legal pads, pens and a bottle of blue-black ink and sat these essentials down upon the dresser, adorned by a red, black and green padding, next to her bed; then he selected one of his favorite pens, took one of the yellow legal pads in hand and sat rocking for a moment in the chair of Rollins Reed; then he moved it closer to the bed of Great-Momma Sweetie Reed. He started rocking again, pen in hand. Sweetie Reed blew upon the steamy brew, sipped at the brothy substance and sighed and (like an actress taking a last potion before making her legendary entrance) Sweetie Reed then cleared her throat. Now the lyrical soprano voice, seemingly untouched by her advanced years, took stage center.

3

The
Deaths
of
Rapture

Nathaniel, you see all eleven years after the bought-off patroller man with the long silver beard returned me to the plantation of my grandfather Rollins Reed, I tried to seek out my very own father, I. V. Reed, but he'd be gone off to the quarters playing on that mouth harp of his songs for Angelina.

Or he'd be under Master Rollins' bed or cursing his fate, our fate, as he was polishing up Rollins Reed's shoes—so they shone like two dancing diamonds—and shining up his own, grunting, whispering and babbling something about Shank Haywood to himself like he's uncovering old soles inside a pair of new shoes and the old soles are backed with torn greenbacks below and he don't want to give away his new foundlings, and don't know what to do with the greenbacks.

When I. V. Reed was on his deathbed, I went back down to the Rollins Reed plantation to say goodbye; fifty-two years ago to this very day; after all, this was the father, I said to myself. I had not seen him since I left that plantation, twenty-four years before. Maybe I wanted to hear him say just simply *I tried to love you, Sweetie;* discover those old tongues of feeling, as a water-pump rod to the well water, covered and gutted by tons of leaves and old shoes, soles and tongues and lapsed life insurance policies, and free papers, discarded there as a refuse dump in the well of time and memory. But I thought those old tongues would fly up in his face as a plague of stinging bees if he ever opened himself up that much, I said in my spitefulness.

Yet I knew his word would be a foundling lie, so maybe not even that; but to give me a portion of recognition as his child, that never sprang from his tongue while I was there. In turn I had pledged myself to give out a show of the daughter's gift of feeling, even though I knew it only came from a hurt and father-cut-off heart. Over my pride I wore a garment of tenderness; but I wondered as I stood there before I. V. Reed, the master liar, whether my true feelings—like a drooping garment hem—didn't show out as a brightly marked shroud over my shoe tops.

This time I. V. Reed was on top of Rollins Reed's bed. Nathaniel, his body put me in the mind of those balloon men I used to see the circus clowns blowing up, puffed-up bodies, but weightless, for the next day's performance, as we came out exhausted but revived and glorified in Jesus' name, out of the campground meetings . . . Over there where they shot up another one of those projects as a mound to Heaven, last year.

Nathaniel recalled that for a long time Great-Momma Sweetie Reed had been a most fiery minister at camp meetings and revivals; but by her own admittal *too much of the cash had become the very capital of the minister's soul-seeking sermons and they were all the time tithing and questing and not putting anything back into the flock— think they buying mansions in my father's house; and letting rooms like kitchenettes for rent and sale; even trying to rent out daybeds in Heaven; trying to buy up this ground; we ain't in real estate . . . Christ fed the children with the loaves they scraped up together . . . But if a campground flock was unprofitable they moved on. The covenant my Father set up with me when I came under Lovelady's hand sprung from*

the covenant my Angelina commenced for me with with Almighty God
—that's my inheritance and it's a good stock and a powerful cross and
you give back to the poor because with us, too, we know there is always
the many in the one and the one in the many with less than a scrap of
fish, or a fishbone—and you simply have to depend on Him and your
own mother wit and wisdom and what the old folks passed on and
re-create a miracle . . . But these here preachers would make profit out
of fish in the backwaters.

And so Great-Momma Sweetie Reed left preaching stints and
finally churchgoing, and devoted herself exclusively to the profitless
fulfillment of her mission started by Miss Lovelady Breedlove, in 1852
. . . But this didn't stop her from speaking out in a preaching voice
—she who had heard and often spoken of Harriet Tubman's preaching style to Nathaniel—when on occasion she in fact would enter an
assemblage, or even a church. *(You can't get away from it, and it's my*
own hardheadedness and God's goading that made me leave off for a
calling back down to Lovelady's mission, but that don't mean that you
all should ever follow that pathway—the church needs you; and God
knows you need the church and to remake it in His face and form out
of His radiance.) Sometimes going to a church, but never to beg for
her mission *(I made my bed and cast my lot);* rather to plead for the
widows and orphans and the lost-found of the storm-blown in the
northward winds; in the storm so long, with less than a crust of bread.
Nathaniel had gone with her on several occasions, and her eloquence
and power were astonishing and terrible, wonderfully fashioned and
forged with racial memory, history, personal witness and largeness of
Biblical memory, as tributaries flowing into a mighty river.

—Nathaniel, I. V. Reed was shoeless and there was a hole in his
left sock; and when I looked again I saw how the thick wool socks
were mismated ever so slightly, the left one purple and the right one
dark blue; he always talked about having cold feet. His crumpled but
expensive pants were dark brown, and he wore a coffee-and-wine-
stained white dinner jacket; the sleeves seemed a mite too short for
the measure of his arm's length; and underneath a heavy logger's
long-sleeved baby blue sweater ran the measure of his arms and wrist
and then some, just nipping over to the commencing of his long but
brittle-looking fingernails (making the sweater appear at that point
like a child's cut-away mittens); just at the border of each nostril seven
dead straight hairs, like the prongs of a pitchfork.

On the top of his head and overlapping his forehead: a sheeny foreskin, you might say, pressed down on top of skin. It was a lady's scarlet silk stocking (the kind they wear sometimes to masquerade balls) tied to his head in a fitful knot, like a stocking cap, and screened so tightly to his skull and temple that it had left a permanent high-water mark, you might say; then in the very center of I. V. Reed's forehead was a round, tiny backwater hole in the stocking about the very size where you put a dime in—like those machines nowadays for a cup of black coffee, or with cream and sugar in it. The stocking cap covered much of the length of his goatlike ears. And I. V. Reed had the tiniest green diamond earbob in his left earlobe: a picture of a whispering green toad of evil, stuck on a blood-red apple in a green garden, slid across my mind's eye.

I. V. Reed needed a shave, but I didn't have a razor about me. And he was kind of coo-gasping and suddenly the thought come over me, why, he ain't nothing but bleating breath and baggy britches; as I once again looked down into his mahogany face, the features and the high cheekbones a little like those Seminole Indians I used to hear him whispering to himself about. And now I realized how much I had loathed his presence below that bed all of those years, even as I was also here to find out what he might tell me to know myself better— if he would just give me that gift of recognizing me in a slightly feeling way, as daughter on his dying bed (since he had spent most of his life pretending, and lying, why not use these last breaths to make his own feel kinship).

Nathaniel, I. V. Reed was dying in a strange way; a body so consumed in itself, so self-sufficient unto death's sting, his own manservant. But I also thought, well, maybe in his pride he's made, or is making right this moment, in his silence, some last-ditch covenant with the Master over his sins, and regrets, and misdeeds, that he's finally stopped casting out as simply accursed misfortunes. But I also thought, yes, but why doesn't he come clean with me, too, in this last hour, if he has been meditating upon the Son of Man? Then another thought crossed my vision: maybe he knows my presence before his bed, figures if he lies there perfectly still, like a man pretending he's dead, I'll steal away back up north and leave him to His Maker—or is it his Master? He should live so long. For I been standing there for about an hour now, calling his name kind of soft and low but firm.

Now as I. V. Reed's body stirred a bit, I also thought if I could hold his memories to me (to quiet not his soul but my heaving heart) and take part of his words in along with his barefaced lies and hold on for dear life no matter how many directions he threw the truth and me into abuse and scorn and misuse—if only I could get and keep my arms and hands about his stories and shape it all up for myself, as when my very own mother took scraps of lace cloth from a curtain and made a wedding gown, even though she wanted the real thing with all of her heart and soul, in order to marry this man: then I could learn the deeper parts of my unknown, untold story, even though I would have to work from the bottom up to reshape it all out. But standing there now in the shadow of his body slightly stirring towards wakefulness, I could not help but remember how when as a little girl I'd come into the room to seek out my father and he'd be propped up on a pillow, making out he was asleep like a child.

And all of those years, Nathaniel, I. V. Reed pretending he was the captain of his soul and the master of his fate; yet he had been a great storyteller and maybe he believed his own grand lies. Even thinking of his great storytelling ways racked my heart with memory now, because you see he told it all lying down on that mattress below Rollins Reed's bed, that's how come his voice seemed clothed barely above a whisper speaking to Rollins Reed, sitting there in that very rocking chair where you are now sitting. I had to steal away to hear it, in the raven-hearted darkness of the cellar, to get at his weaving words, breathing like echoes through a sleeve; only the threads of sound could be picked up, but I got enough of that yarn, you might say, to start a quilt pattern forever, though it took so many directions. What I heard made me hungry-hearted for more. But more was to be nevermore for my especial ears, if it was left to I. V. Reed. Only the remnant sounds of words aimed at the ears of Rollins Reed, on top of the bed or sitting in that rocker, and spun in that singer's voice of I. V. Reed's.

For I. V. Reed most likely knew the ground and history of this land, as the lines in the palms of his hand slanting out as rivers and limbs of wild pointing branches upon a trembling tree; besides the lakes, rivers and streams; as well as every clue and inch of water for the best fishing and the worst, and the bottoms where rumors of drowned ancestors remained and stories of monsters festered and foamed in the whites of the master's eyes. I. V. Reed's seeing eyes pierced depths and had lived with the sea horses and come to take on their tricky swimming ways and saw what would come up from the troubled bottom of the riverbed with blinding vision; as if he had also lived in the belly of the whale but was unredeemed by the journey. Now in his billing-

and-cooing sleep, I. V. Reed started to lick his lips; he always liked
to set up his thin lips with his tongue before he spoke—so as to water
down the truth, I thought.

He slept under his master's bed even after Surrender, and down to
the time when I left the plantation (in 1882) to marry Jericho Witherspoon, your grandfather. The certain trusted body attendant, the role
I. V. Reed had commenced in slavery: to be on call in case Master
Rollins Reed wanted a blanket, a log on the fire, a cooling towel, a
bedpan, wiping paper; or a drink of cool cedar water during the night
dipped from the bucket near the spring in the garden . . . Or rising
at midnight to prepare a bath water for the master's whispered whims,
placing his elbow into the water to make certain of its sweet-back
warmth of temperature to his crazy bone. And, Nathaniel, in my
mind, I blamed I. V. Reed for being tied to that mattress so that it
left us wide open in the barn for those patrollers to steal my mother
and me away, when we should've been under the safety of the roof
of the Big House. But finally, when all was said and done, I said to
myself: if you Master Jesus will just allow for a portion of taint-
hearted feeling, then surely I will know something of comfort and
please let him die out peacefully, in the pose of his repose, and I'll steal
away quietly as a hand slipped from the pallbearers' white glove.

But all of a sudden his lips opened, like a preacher who's been
waiting in the wings for his call at the campground meeting, but
decides to wait so as to make the congregation thirst for his presence
a few moments, so that his arrival on the stage is even more dramatic
. . . and the choir has to make up by heart a new chorus of humming
or chanting to keep the souls at a fever pitch on high. Finally we are
talking easy at first without touching on too much. But when I. V.
Reed asked me how I'm getting along, looking out towards my face
but not into my eyes, I told him, *I've seen some better days, but I'm
hanging these here out to dry this early morning and see what kind of
sunup today brings;* but as I said this I realized how much I wanted
to raise pure hell with that man for staying down so long as a serpent
inside of a shell and seeming to adore it so and mainly denying our
blood tie: my husbandless heart, a tattered girl's sleeve, was needful
of mending now. But just then I. V. Reed says to me up out of the
slit his eyes knit in his wakefulness:

—Now, Angelina, I thought you spoilt Mistress Sylvia. She taught
me a learning—what could I do with it, but come to think of myself
as so special no nigger was good enough to hold society in the mirror

of my high presence, for no longer than Saturday night (when I had the only pure fun, even joy I ever possessed, without stealing it, when they'd steal a hog, go barbecue him; I'd steal away; come amongst my own, and they be dressing it down, barbecuing, hidden in the shadows, the trees made of the gulley); and they'd call on me to play my mouth harp. I was always to stay at a separating-line distance of about seventy-five paces; then afterwards a gal would bring a tin of barbecue up to me, like she was bringing it down to me, her eyes cutting to the ground, as a coffin slicing down to the bubbling hole . . .

—For you see I was the only one who knew all the old-time whooping cries, as they birth to be praise tunes, some born out of warbling, warning curses; I had perfect pitch, you see; I didn't understand how much it all meant to me then, I guess. Sometimes I'd climb up into the highest branch of the tree; the soles of my feet would strike a balance; I could see those dancers better, the tops of their flinging heads as they were dancing after the barbecuing; then sometimes I'd balance myself on a real good sturdy limb while I tried to play on my mouth harp (like a juggler man in the circus flipping weights in the middle of the air). I pitched out verses through the trees at them; they made new music with their limbs, with those whooping, wooing chants. I could see them real good then: niggers, dancing wild, free-hearted, wonderful, sassy, impish, saucy, bold-butt, brazen, reckless, but keen in time out of time. Those hips moving like when you slice apples in halves; dips them into a bucket of water, shoots the rapid pump water to them; flipping their backsides up, down into all kinds of shaking shapes . . .

—Now, I don't mean I worshiped being old man Rollins Reed's personal body servant—though my mind stayed glued on his wants like white on balls of cotton—but I did love being a special-regarded nigger in men's eyes, all right, I freely admit it, no two ways about it; despite the price I had to pay for my actions—*also* Auntie Foisty, the African's left-handed command. But you must see, as I tried to explain to you over again, why run off to be free—so-called free? Then I'd lose all my special, polished-up yoke, my own pearl brand, just be another, maybe surly nigger . . . Don't you see, child?—

—I can see you blind to your own child's presence, from that mattress . . . You want me to praise you for staying below his bed for the duration and at his beck and call into eternity—even after you were set free by the bluecoats, and Mr. Lincoln, when you can't acknowledge my face . . . You, I. V. Reed, playing both ends against the middle and trying to make ends meet, as the old folks used to warn.—

—I'm on top of his bed now, don't you see? Been up here ten-odd years. I'm top dog around here, don't you see? I done warmed down this bed so long it's come to wear the shape of my body; just as a old sleeve wrinkled by the arm's stretching. His no longer! I declare it! Angelina—oh, can't you see it! Been up here for years. Why, niggers up north, in Hell, can't harness up no bloodhounds.—

—Yeah, looks of the years, plenty souls love to bootlick heel to toe to be your kinda free soul. Those who know too much sleep below the bed, in a long-suit, until they snore, their eyes slit wide open with a mouthful of give me to Jesus.—

—Free woman. Free to be; to tell you a mind-shape you never knew *was* and still *is*.—

—Free what? How? Where even? Sucking Reed's spit in his beard, like dangling grapes, because you supped near his supper table—and laid the length of his bed, like you sleeping in the vineyard. You nigh unto high quality, all right.—

—Rather be a free manservant than a freeman slave.—

—. . . Felled in the light of your days, son of the morning; yes, I know you were his brightest invention . . . Patented you, and you leapt from his head.—

—Your oily split tongue comes to my bed as the wings of Death, flapping torment after me; but your poison breath gonna roll off my backbone like water off a duck's back, and I'll keep floating on upstream, not downstream.— I. V. Reed was shivering.

—I. V. Reed, that's because your body's oiled down. Greased. I. V. Reed, your sole delight is to make all ill who come to know your words, jawbone to heelbone.—

—Fool woman, *I* supported him.—

—Your back's no turtle's shell.—

Nathaniel, now I turned about to look once again on the mildewed decay and the cobwebs that made a whirlwind of the once grand Big House—the confusion of cobwebs whirling about like wine-drunk dancing ghosts, who wore a lace of tattered white curtain and flinging about as bride and bridegroom; but seen only by the tormented living who entered these doors, chambers of images blown out of looking-glass mirrors; but that made me think how could I. V. Reed be cold in all those double sleeves of body caring—lest he be kin to one of these bloodless, ghostly, whirling cobwebs. And if that be true then what of me, oh Lord, standing knee-deep in the need of prayer? And as my head fell to this unsteady refuge, I also wondered how much the old mulatto woman whom I saw earlier did look out and care for I. V. Reed. And who was she, anyhow?

Nathaniel, the sheriff had to awaken his deputy up by ringing his doorbell three times to take me out there and it was hard breathing and coming through to get anywhere near the old plantation house, so much was around and about it; obsessed by woods and foliage. The old Reed Big House seemed like a cottage you come upon in a trance, when your unrested soul is sucked away through the reflecting glass of a nightmare; you wonder if you'll ever be delivered. My body seemed more to reel when I came up to stand once more in the clearing—with the Big house in view, but over a thousand yards away —and thinking of how it had changed in the going and coming; even though I had played as a young girl (once returned to the Reed plantation) in these very woods, many's the time gathering rocks and stones to toss at the birds of the woods and the fields, or to collect wood chips for the fireplace.

Nathaniel, I could see the fear in the sheriff's deputy's eyes as he turned me over at this point to the waiting local Negro preacher, who turned out to be Stigwood Bloodworth's grandson, whose grandfather had given me my first conversion by water. It was young Stigwood who had sent me the telegram, too:

> COME QUICK IF YOU EVER HOPE TO SEE YOUR
> PAP'S BREATH IN LIFE/BREATHING BEING
> SUCKED FROM HIS WINDPIPE FAST AS RAIN-
> WATER DOWN A DRAINPIPE/HIS BACKBONE
> IS RACKED AND RENT/SINKING ON HIS
> DEATHBED, LOW/DOWN, DOWN, DOWN.
>
> WOE UNTO THE WORLD,
> REV. STIGWOOD BLOODWORTH

Nathaniel, now Stigwood was to get me through part of the rest of the way of sunken trees, bushes and foliage that I had not seen until I was in closer range of the house—that presented another world that so surrounded the plantation's Big House, like a care-tossed but magical shroud that keeps spreading itself out before your very eyes, in a deep-down nightmare of death; and you think you must've been blind to have missed it in the second place. But then this old mulatto woman appears out of nowhere from the tumbled-down Bloodworth plantation; the preacher called her Cuz Angel-Crust; she led me to the Big House and up to the very porch of my beginning time; Stigwood turned me over to her hand and ran like he'd seen a spreading fire through the treetops. Immediately backwater leapt to my mind: *What you setting me up for, Preacher man!* I howled; he was long gone . . . On that porch it come down on me full force as a blow to the brain from an unseen rock, hung in time and waiting for you to remake the wrong move this time, when I was returned to the old Reed plantation by the bought-off patroller, way back in the beginning time; when I saw that porch; and I. V. Reed's face at that screen door.

Nathaniel, that woman showed me the way, the rest of the five hundred yards; and how to get down on both of my knees and crawl in a peculiar way—but her mouth didn't let out any words, in her offering up of help . . . She showed through gestures and motions; also she pointed out how she served I. V. Reed a meal of leavings on a silver platter, from where she warmed them up in a broken-down praise shack; pointing out now a portion of the cracking wooden steps of old Rollins Reed's Big House, as a unsteady portion of the Praise Shack. She was using sign language, and making up new signs to describe things unseen by sign-making folks.

Now the full force of the blow to the remembering portion of my brain came shocking-clear as I stood on those cracking porch steps, with the two smashed alabaster statues of angels kneeling on either side—a male on the left side, female on the right, with harps in their hands. Master Rollins Reed himself had placed them there before my time; the wings set for flight. I had to shake my head, even as I was shaking the weeds from my clothing, covering me head to toe, from where we had been crawling, because it was hard not to believe I was in a dream that I thought I had come out of long ago in the beginning time. And I remembered the Good Book saying: *He that loseth his life shall find it.* I sure hoped so, because in my soul I felt like a widow woman.

Nathaniel, as I stood before that shattered screen door (a-flapping like a tongue and baying me come in or go away, I knew not which), my mind flew back to the time when that patroller sat me down on Rollins Reed's knees and I. V. Reed stood there behind that screen door scratching upon it and saying nothing: only a rattling warning to how much he would break my heart with his silence or with his tongue unleashed in spitework as a spider's web in hot air taking on the shape of his breath.

For somewhere in the heart of my little seven-year-old life, I had felt sure that day, that I. V. Reed's grief for me being stolen and lost would be at least like a bird's whooping for its hawk-stolen young; stolen out the nest and then suddenly found, while the hawk's on the wing. But the way he acted, scratching and clawing at that screen door, started me as a small child to feel (rightly or wrongly) that men do not have this feeling from their heart to the soles of their feet for grief and love-memory to give out—because standing there that day, I had also hoped that he would see me as the gift of return and as a portion of Angelina returned to him from the drowning waters of the new slavery I had by misfortune (and the grace of God) survived.

Well, I might as well have climbed the back of one of those angel statues and expected it to fly me off, as expect I. V. Reed to come to life. It was almost like he seemed to despise me for surviving my own mother . . . But this day I fell to my knees on that porch between those two angels and I wondered of my fate to be returned here by the message of enslaving Bloodworth's black offspring, or to be returned here by the turncoat patroller . . . Nathaniel, I was the age you were when your grandfather died, when they stole me back to Rollins Reed's plantation; his covenant, he called it, with the patroller, who turned his coat inside out (where I could see the blood-knives up his sleeves) when he drove off with me around midnight, and donned his long silver beard, in case some of the other patrollers spotted him with this little cedar-colored bounty.

Nathaniel, now as we talked, or I. V. Reed talked and I listened, he kept on confusing me at points with my mother, Angelina, though we didn't favor. Finally I took her strawberry bonnet off, and put it aside on the little nightstand next to the bed by the water pitcher. Then after a while I gave up on trying . . . but for now I did say:

—I. V. Fath—I'm Sweetie, not Angelina, she was my mother; your woman, I mean your wife.—

—We jumped the broom in 1855. Remember? Master Reed gave up a wonder wedding and Rev. Stigwood Bloodworth rung us up together. Remember? Grand wedding. You even had a dram. Remember?—

—The wife you treated like a child. And the child you refused to see.—

—Shut your defiling tongue—the very stream of life-blood in me has been drying up since Sweet Angelina was snatched up by those body snatchers—.

—Oh, you *do* remember, when you want to see through the spiteweave in time. I'm Sweetie, not Angelina. Sweetie Reed. Not Angelina Reed. And I was snatched away, too; from my mother's arms, not your arms. Your arms were like your backbone.—

—When Sweet finally comes along—didn't die out like the others . . . Marked my end, though . . . Miz Angel Sweet, you didn't have to eat the heel of the bread. You remember! Sweet Angel then . . . Don't you know when freedom come, I passes Mistress Sylvia's coffin —one of Golightly Braidwood's making—I looks down on her with tears in my eyes. Then I saw her heel print in Hell. I was crying, but wasn't sorry. I seen everything, was consoled because now I knew Master Rollins Reed come more to depending on me to keep everything underfoot, in hand, in harness, in stock, up to snuff.—

—You still trying to answer Angelina through me, and me through her, like trying to swoop a hive of bees up the sleeves of a wedding gown, but only working yourself into a ghost's lace, Mister I. V. Reed, sir.—

—. . . But I weren't tickled to death as some slaves, who rolled on the ground, muddy in merriment. Master Rollins thinking they draping sorrow on their arms; their sleeves at their eyes. But whooping spirits plowed up in their faces. By now his sight ebbing on him. With her dead, freedom come; Master Rollins Reed forced to playing possum in a tar bush for a time. I went out there to slip him supper whilst bluecoats were here: plundering, thieving, looting, like pilgrims what done heard a bell to riot. We come back in, found Mistress Sylvia dead in the basement . . . She got her propers, all right; no two ways about it.

—Master Rollins Reed had me play on my mouth harp, Mistress Sylvia's favorite—*Clair de Lune.* Had me sing it—ohohoh, I remember long patches of her song so well; it's as real to me as scripture, like my very fingers touched to the sleeves of fine silk made with care . . . *Honest, honest Ivy,* she used to say, in her playful way in the good old dark times . . . *Don't abuse De-Bussey,* her laugh as light as a lark.

Nathaniel, I. V. Reed commenced to singing in an unbelievable voice, like a man in soaring delight of conjuring yet another voice in flight, as he sang by heart:

—*Only God's strong arms could guide his children well. I gaze in*

wonder and know that no harm could come to a heart . . . Shining,
bright moonlight . . . When the Sun sets you give us light, you shone
so clearly, the road that's dreary . . . I know that only God could this
vision express.—

Nathaniel, I staggered backwards from the bed, shocked at his
voice, as he continued to sing; why he was a perfect imitation of the
Irish tenors I had heard at the Opera House, when I first come north
to marry your grandfather, Jericho Witherspoon. But where had I. V.
Reed picked up the sound? That voice? And what voice did he use
when he sang at her funeral, I wondered. And what voice did he use
to pray to his God, if he possessed one? He had so many voices. And
now I remembered as a child how he was known to have a thousand
voices by the old slaves, in the old days! From old Master Rollins
Reed—to birdcalls. Had he picked up the imitation from some soul-
bidding voice in the long ago, when on a trip with Rollins Reed to
pick up new slaves in the marketplace and they stopped to hear a
traveling troupe of singers come over from Europe; for Mistress Sylvia
just loved the peasant singing of many European lands, Angelina told
me; and had he stood outside the great hall and heard the singing?
Or had he picked it up from the levee in their travels down the river?
But how had he come to refine these Irish voices so that they sounded
almost English with the Irish soul sewed away within the spirit of the
song? But now he was saying in his regular speaking voice:

—Then the number she loved to hear me play and sing at masquerade balls, "Turkey in the Straw." I brought new words back up from
those barbecues, along with new dance steps stirred up in the black
bottom down in the gulley; like them big women sopping hog slabs
twisting on firebed pits. Bringing the hog back into life, too, with
sweet-souring, suckling sauces, spices, herbs. Niggers had a *mean*
sauce down there going they never did allow to trickle up to the Big
House; though some gave up a watery portion, covered over by a
soupy veil; set every palate of the Big House in a pure riot—watering
on down for more.

—Yet I, honest Ivy, as Mistress Sylvia useda call me, shunned frolic
the better part of my days; I was dyed-in-the wool true-blue indigo;
ate of Master's red table though not *at* his table. Tar-brushed a bright
grin on my face as a screwed-on vise of correction—but had to be
careful not to pitch it too tight, lest Master Rollins Reed cripple
completely back into his old-time self, rationing, running dog ways
before Auntie Foisty's anointing time; I be on third-grade shorts, sure

as you think you standing there before me, Miz Smarty-Sweet . . . Fact of the business is you *had* to get back. Stay on low down so as you could stay long off short-grade rations; I tried to tell you, Sweet Angelina, many's the time. Then there was memories of meanness. How Mistress Sylvia ordered the water cure for Reece Shank Haywood—thinking the clay-washed-down skin of Master Rollins' body had touched his mind by Auntie Foisty's magical pitchfork—when Reece Haywood was dragged back. But that was a hanging order from Rollins Reed himself, the master, for all caught runaways . . . Mistress Sylvia got her proper fitting for her part in it all, as a vise.

4

"A Motherless Child"

Nathaniel, you asked me once in your uneasy innocence why my mother didn't leave when she was free, and I couldn't tell you then all of it, though some folks say if a child is old enough to ask a question, then he's old enough to get a proper answer regardless to his age. But there are questions that deserve a long-haul answer; questions that go beyond the mind of a child's knowing time to understand, in his leap of curiosity; so that's part of why I'm waiting for you to hear it all now. So let me now unfold to you what I. V. Reed told me, but just you remember from whose lips the *truth* smiled.

Nathaniel, some of it had to do with the Yankees. And what Angelina had seen and experienced at their hands. Yet and still as I looked down into I. V. Reed's face I wondered about the same question—at first I thought I wouldn't ask him, because he would lie about that, too. But that was Mother. And I knew why she didn't leave—couldn't leave—or I thought I did. Yet I put it to him anyway; I thought in his lying condition he'd touch some truth and I would have to peel the rest of it out, by hand, like you have to cull out the bottom meat of a nut and then see what you set to your own lips for the eating.

Nathaniel, my mother was so peculiar, God bless her soul, I must say so—probably feeling guilty about leaving her husband, I. V. Reed, who was tied to his master's bed, as a shoelace to the boot. (Though plenty of men leave their womenfolks with less weight to carry and I'm here to tell you about that, which is part of why I'm telling you about this.) But she was also tied in some peculiar ways to old lady Sylvia Reed, who had commenced now sometimes to speak as if she could see her heart throbbing and gasping on my mother's sleeve and sought out a softer spot for herself beneath there, though surely not by her words, my mother said, in a constant way. And mother was right close to the field slaves and for a long time felt that they depended on her to hear out their complaints and many of them wasn't leaving. And too, Nathaniel, don't forget old man Rollins Reed was not only the slave master, he was her father, and now he seemed to be near death's door; and the question was: going off to what?—the Yankees didn't offer up any answer. Still, after I settled his wrestling spirit down, and got him to speak in a civil tongue, partially anyhow, I did ask I. V. Reed the question you asked of me, that time when your grandfather went into the hospital and we was having one of our little talks and he was coming and going. But then I. V. Reed said to me:

—Sweet Angelina was going to, all right. Useda threaten me leastways with leaving. Yankees was coming through; yes, word had trickled down slaves set free by Mr. Lincoln's almighty hand in blue-black ink . . . One evening we heard they about a day's hard ride away, though I heard about the freeing up from under the porch of the Big House weeks before. Well, now Mistress Sylvia Reed calls Angelina away from her own mending basket. Told her of those bluecoats' closeness to our skin; she was giving Angelina run of her household, until *those Devils* moved through; I was down low in the basement, squatting; I made darkness shelter me in my secret hiding place; I heard every word, deep as owls' eyes in tree branches of moonlight;

I could see the shapes of Angelina and Mistress Sylvia in the faces of those oval mirrors. Mistress standing there rubbing the angles of her diamond rings on her hands with a velvet cloth so to make them like stars, as she spoke to her slave girl, body and soul.

—Sweet Angel, Mistress Sylvia was pure-featured with hyacinth hair; she spoke now with a voice sounding lowdown-hearted; the powder on her cheeks made her face look like a biscuit about to crumble. Angelina seemed taller. Mistress Sylvia said she was about to lock herself up in the wine cellar; *though who knows if I'll be safe from myself away from my mirrors and my sacred diamonds,* she said. But she tricked us because she took her knitting basket from Angelina's sewing table 'neath the picture frame—the one she gave Angelina . . . a netlike strawberry handkerchief she was going to work on in the basement by candlelight, with a golden key on a chain around the white tower of her neck look like a swan's throat rung in wrinkles of baby snakes slowly winding about her throat, with each turn of her face, now to catch up a last look at herself in the mirrors at every angle.

—But now after Mistress Sylvia had come three steps down the basement ladder, she turned about to face Angelina (I hid in the corner, over there with the dog, Caledonia, where I could spot them better from the crack of light shot through the opened door). Then Mistress Sylvia took from the starched white apron Angelina had washed out for her, two fists of diamonds, sparkling so I had to duck my head down lower, lest they catch up my reflection below; Lord, them was sure some brilliant jagged-edged stones—almost looked too keen to touch without bringing blood to the fingertips; seemed of a mystery power. Handed them up to Angelina (who stood above her at the top of the steps now); the mistress' hand upon hers like she was smuggling a secret love letter to a messenger for private keeping to her secret lover, on the other side of a combat line, at midnight, I felt a heaviness in my chest for the scene before my very eyes, you see. Not looking into Angelina's face, but into the seven oval-shaped mirrors in her front room, where she could see the back of Angelina's glory-crown of rich chestnut hair, like the slopes of her mind. But what broke my heart, made tears come to my eyelids, was when she took off those rings from her hand, shining in the dark like the sun before a storm; but now in the mirror it's like she's not handing them to her body servant but acting like she's a defeated warrior handing over those last, best diamonds to the victor, who hasn't so much as raised a hand to win the prize, but whose soldiers have taken over the kingdom, the occupied country, body and soul; the diamonds themselves seemed now as cut-glass teardrops in my eyes; Sweet Angelina had turned ever so smartly about, after receiving those diamonds in the cup of her hands, as the soldier who doesn't want to face the embarrassment of the defeated warrior's face in his own eyes; but then she was forced to turn again, as Mistress Sylvia now said:

Take my diamonds and hide them upon your person, the lowdown Yankees aren't about to touch their sacred darkies . . . For you are no longer our darkies to have and to hold, though our breeding is meshed into the marrow of your bones, fathoms deep, sole to pearly crown, just as you are no longer proper Africans, when we took them over, and they bartered you to us, and we sold you to each other—your souls enriched by each lap of the auctioneer's unbloodied tongue . . .

Mr. Reed purchased these gems and the necklace for me at great expense, many and many a year ago; and no one will ever sever my soul from the soul within the castle of their beauty. I'll reclaim them when the blackhearted Yankees leave if it be unto Almighty God's will that I should live out my claim to you and your people's freeing up for a worsening enslavement . . . I place them in your care and keeping, with an anointing touch of duty, as mistress to her lady, Angelina—but then, where would you take them, where would you flee without that good and faithful body servant, honest, honest Ivy? (What she always called me, above a drylongso.) Then Mistress Sylvia said: Why not place them inside that high-pile of thick chestnut hair you braided-up so grandly . . . a five-fathom plot, as if you were a pure white lady preparing for a masquerade! None would think to seek out booty there.

—But Sweet Angelina turned on Mistress Sylvia like a snake flipping its rattles in the dying sun for new skin, as she juggled those diamonds in the cup she made of her hands, gripping the fingers together so the hands seemed as red as blood out of the lantern's face in the mirrors . . . Lord have mercy if the poor Mistress Sylvia wasn't already struck down dead to life, you might say, from the cook Wayland Woods, the black scoundrel's poison letters early in January. Fool done ran off to the Yankee soldiers; sending crazy nigger letters to Mistress Sylvia. Stirring up slop for them Yankees' pots in the hospital while he's coming back from being shot down. Left for dead. Them was some terrible words to behold in his letters, but I ain't never heard the like of Angelina's words, leastways from her lips, no two ways about it . . . Said unto Mistress Sylvia:

Look, white bitch, you benefiting by these diamonds and that neck-
lace that hung by your throat, as a water-cured body from a stock, with
his eyes going from shocked to glowering, out of money come out of the
bodies of my grandmother, auntie and uncle—auctioned by your Devil
husband's life-choking hands.

—Mistress Sylvia was so shocked and fell at first to stammering in
tongues; she caught the railing for balance, comfort; I'm glad for the
railing 'cause I think I might have to catch her, prop her up, but I
been into master's wine there in the cellar, in my bitterness over
everything bringing down; I am high as a Georgia pine . . . Mistress
Sylvia is now losing her grip on the polished railing Angelina had
worked up to a glow earlier in the day. The very shape of her heart
slid down to the silver buckles she gave Angelina to put on her
slippers; but Angelina was crying herself in her heaving bosoms, too.
I can see it all in the looking-glass of crazy shapes, drooping diamonds
in Angelina's bloody-looking cupped hand; she keeps juggling them;
as if to give her strength to say what she's saying . . .

—Because after all she had learned to read the Bible, to write, to
sew . . . How to set a table, how to cook certain dishes of self-refining
from her mistress. How to express herself proper; she practiced imitating Mistress Sylvia at being a pure lady; reading out Shakespeare.
Reciting those poems of praise aloud of Miss Phillis Wheatley, the
nigger lady poet, who dreamed of sleeping in President Washington's
bed all of the time . . . *All* of this by the commandment of Mistress
Sylvia's tolerance and generosity . . . But then Angelina got to doing
it all better than Mistress Sylvia. More in the shape of her own style,
till after a time Mistress Sylvia couldn't see her own reflection, nor
hardly her hand-shaping in Angelina's step, grace and fashioning. Yet
she called Angelina her doll baby . . . Angelina only remembering her
own grandmother, auntie, *then* Auntie Foisty's words—not writ on
tablets, but swimming, clinging at the edges of her mind, like the old
clothes of a drowned man tossed out to find his whereabouts, seeking
out their master's body parts in the tide . . .

—Now Mistress Sylvia's shoulders was trembling. I thought she
needed her robe about her shuddering body; but I was too high to help
her. So it was then Mistress Sylvia cried out:

No, you heifer . . . You would call your Sire a lowdown hellish name
—and in dirt, after all I've done to clean your fortunes up to the level
of civility out of the wilderness, I call you out—you slave scullion; and
just because the black-hearted, classless Yankees are going to come and

take away the only home you've ever known to claim, upon this earth,
so that you can be so-called free to have nothing but the wilderness as
the cottage to surround your naked arms . . . Since you are without
arms.

—It was the first time anybody had ever heard Mistress Sylvia
admit Rollins Reed was Angelina's pappy. She staggered like she was
drunk at one of her masquerade charity balls, right on down to the
last steps of the wine cellar, where the dog commenced barking from
where it was tied on a chain harness, tossed aside by some runaway,
chased down by bloodhounds. Caledonia chained up in the corner,
opposite of me (the gold key flaring from a green chain around Mistress Sylvia's throat) . . . Very cellar where we had stowed some
escaping slaves once long before, in another part of the basement, had
dug out and sealed a portion off, like a folding closet in the wall, so
smooth as tide-washed stones, you couldn't see no remnant, or difference from it and the natural white wall.

—And Angelina (who used to plait and dress up Mistress' hair;
black plaits circled her head, loops making a dark crown, as a hyacinth halo) now calling her with words gulping out of her like vomit
after our banquet feast before our masquerade ball:

Father? You didn't speak to me for three months after you found out
who sired me; spat me from your arms (as if you didn't know in your
buried, unburdened heart what the slaves had been knowing and whis-
pering for years); because that meant I could no longer be your doll
baby doll to recite Phillis' words, next to your knitting-reading; you
fruitless She-Devil; you didn't know the price you had to pay for being
spoilt and ruint by Papa Sire!

—Rollins Reed had started wanting her to call him, not master, but
Papa Reed, even Papa, when they were alone; but it was the first time
I ever heard Papa—even as spittle—drip down her lips, now as water
out of the mouth of a rain-drenched, bloody drainpipe. But just then
I heard the shadow of Mistress Sylvia's voice as a flapping shade
backlashing in a windstorm, out at my Angelina, up the ladder at the
tops of the slave girl's polished shoe buckles.

Wench, I named you Angelina, re-created you; everything that you
possess is fired from my being, culled from the rapture of my history.
Refined you as silver. If you think you are solely a nigger slave, then
you don't know how deeply I placed my brand within your very soul,
unto the end of time and the judgment.

—And then Angelina cried out:

63

You! All you've done . . . so that I might serve your body and your soul, your eyes, your wicked tongue. When I wished that the diamonds you handed me down would have become fingers clawed about your wretched lily wrinkled throat and choked and strangled the very neck upon which they clung—till you could barely gasp for breath—in the flaming cottage of your satanic lover's arms, forever and ever.

—Why, Sweet Angelina had more spewing back-sass than any slave I'd ever heard since many long years before when Old Master Rollins Reed, the minister, was alive—the one who converted Auntie Foisty —and they tell me he was out trying to straighten out Percy Inchmore on his proper duties to Master Jesus; as the slave was knee-deep at his hay-binding work. This was long before Percy got saved and became Rev. Inchmore. Old Master was serving Percy with papers of all shapes of torment in Hell; in particular about how Satan would buy up his soul if he continued to seek the unnatural knowledge of this world against his natural nature and how Satan would turn him into changing stalks of hay into flames by way of a pitchfork, and then Satan would fire off bolts of lightning, twenty-four hours a day down on Inchmore's back. Then he, Percy Inchmore, would have to pitch some of the hay-turned-to-flames onto the other slaves' backs in Hell, hotter than any branding irons, Rev. Reed said; and strapping a slave boy attendant with him across the back to show out how Satan would drive Inchmore against the slaves down there . . . With twenty-four hours on, catching hell, and twenty-four off giving Hell's flames to the slaves of Hell. And no time off for good behavior.

—And Percy says, up from his hay-binding work, *Mass'r, you sure Mass'r Satan ain't got no helpers crawling on their bellies down the river? Well, then he bes a hard-working old Mass'r sure as you born, work like a nigger twenty-four a day. I hopeful Mass'r Satan won't be so powerful cruel and tear out his taxation past his nature on Percy's natural backbone . . .* Old Master Rollins Reed says to Percy: *Inchmore, you shouldn't call Satan master.* Percy says up to him; *I didn't mean to call him out of his name, but see, Mass'r Reed, no telling but your foe might catch me up, and seeing as how he's as powerful as you says, and then pray he bes remembering how as I spoke right reverently of him just the same as he be in the body of a white man.* And Old Master Rollins Reed says: *He that believeth on me, as the scripture hath said, out his belly shall flow rivers of living waters.* And with this, Inchworm falls to both of his knees, holding to his ribs for dear life,

muffling his laughing so hard it sounds out like crying: Old Master
Reed can only hear his crying and he thinks the nigger Inchmore is on
his way to conversion; and he's making himself a man.—

And now Nathaniel Witherspoon found himself remembering that
time Aunt Genevieve—high on her wine—made a high-powered
blowgun and fired it the length of the street, ringing the church bell
in the mock church tower at Sacred Heart, and picking off the pigeons
lodged or tipping about the steeple. Aunt Genevieve saying this was
her contribution to pure air and to clean out all of the bullshit impurities off the wall of the Cathedral and she hoped the hint of her rifled
"BULL" would descend into the church proper and also ring up to
the ears of the princes of the church. And her anger at the church's
do-nothing clan going back first of all to the time that the whites had
burned down the original church rather than see it be turned over to
the coloreds; starting the fire with the cloth that lined the Communion
rail; and seven children perished at the railing; so that the church
fathers made a church of the old school building that stood across the
street; and secondly when Mussolini fired off soldiers into Ethiopia
and the Pope blessed their actions, anointed their heads, as a fire-
worshiping idolator, she said.

Aunt Genevieve at the window of her upper room squeezing the
trigger of her homemade rifle on each of two Sundays before Easter
and then on the Holy Day of the Resurrection. The rifle projecting
baseballs at 150 m.p.h., gonging against the church bell in the mock
steeple, where a tiny Nativity scene stood and the wee Redeemer lay
in a bed of straw. And the rifle-blasted baseballs alarming the church-
goers into fantastic yells of personal revelations—particularly those in
Confession, thinking the church was on fire, again—and driving many
true believers out of the church. On three occasions firemen proceeded
to run ladders up to the top of the mock steeple and ascend their
ladders to find nothing but a cracked church bell, seven dead doves
and a ripped-up Nativity scene.

. . . Talking about I'll huff and I'll puff and I'll blow your house
in, Nathaniel laughed, finally the pigeons lost their faith, too, in the
safety if not the sanctity of Holy Mother of Church . . . But Great-
Momma Sweetie Reed was remembering I. V. Reed's words:

—Now in the seven oval mirrors I saw Angelina's eyes meeting, like
she's gone cross-eyed in her fury, as two darning needles threaded by
fire. Then as I slid deeper into the darkness of the wine cellar, I heard

Mistress Sylvia cry out as her heels clicked furious on the wine-cellar floor—her voice like a wounded but dangerous coyote when its foot is caught in a trap:

I am possessed by niggers . . . not slaves, solely by niggers my soul is owned . . .

—Now coming to the tops of the bronze-edged steps, I can see the silver buckles on Angelina's dainty feet; she screams down:

And what do you think my grandmother felt, the one you helped sell into a deeper slavery down the river? She who suckled you at her very breast? And why don't you tell me if you dare dream of Reece Haywood? Where's his body moldering? Now? Who's possessed by him?

—The sheep dog, Caledonia, was baying, panting, slobbering. Looking like seven dogs turned to monsters' heads, leaping from the chain in the corner; Mistress Sylvia off with her knitting basket of crepe lace handkerchiefs. Nevermore to hear a word croaked from her lips in this life, except: *I'll see you dead in Hell with Reece Shank Haywood,* over and over again; and then all is silence.—

Nathaniel, at this mention of the name *Reece Shank Haywood,* I. V. Reed started to choke and weep and I went over to the nightstand to pour him out a cup of water; and sitting down on the bed, I handed him the cup; and waited for the other shoe to drop, as they say. Finally, he puts his face together.

—Well now, I thought Angelina felt herself pretty proud with Mistress Sylvia, her rival in the household, turned out to the cellar, told off. Angelina running the house; Mistress Sylvia getting consolation only from her dog, Caledonia. Knitting, not speaking words. Well, I slipped past the notice of her vision. But instead of Angelina finding comfort in her unburdening words, I found her now seated before one of them seven oval mirrors in the front room weeping, her spirit grieved. Undelivered, no two ways about it. Because you see of a sudden now, Angelina's words let out how she felt about Mistress Sylvia, but with those diamonds inside the tower of her hair (like demons inside of a castle) she now commenced to see the money piled up from the sale of slaves turned into those diamonds, hot inside of her hair; like teardrops of blood parading before her; it all coming down on her, pouring out of her like gems long buried in the mud of the earth below.

—Angelina said she felt horrible as the bodies of her kin came drooping before her eyes in two golden scales hanging from chains, down on a auction block. Sold off to Arlington Bloodworth's plantation, now come spawning in her head. Leaping out the diamonds and swooping into haystacks of money to be used for freedom in the North but with the bodies *of my kin to follow and haunt down my days and nights.* Then I found myself weeping for her, even as I am pitying Mistress Sylvia who loved her, had learn to love her, as a way of becoming a Christian over against the loathing she felt for her husband for siring this child into the world. Making her, Angelina, her sacrifice to Christ Jesus, maybe as a way of getting back at Auntie Foisty, Rollins Reed, even poor Shank Haywood, too. I'm so drunk with wine, heartbreak and torment, I think my body is going to split into not two faces but a thousand parts, like a broken shell in the moonlight. Almighty God's going to command I get down on both knees; collect all the parts of my nerve-racked being. Then Angelina said to me in the voice of a wounded lamb how she had longed to hold those very diamonds in her hair (I thought they were going to fall out) for all to see—just as she had helped prepare Mistress Sylvia's body. Dress her and place those plaits and those diamonds in her plaited hair for masquerade balls and charity dances, years before. A time out of a time we thought once to be forever what was never to be again; and now down inside of Angelina's hair and me thinking during those times how Mistress Sylvia wore the flower of such a gentle face, and even as I thought of it all, I couldn't help but see how terrible and beautiful Angelina looked, more glorified than Mistress Sylvia even was in the long ago.

—Yet hadn't she set the necklace at the base of Mistress' skull? Countless times I saw how she was trying with all of her mind and heart to wash her out of her memory, how those gems came to be put in the jewelry case each night in the first place deep down in the bosom of Mistress Sylvia's love chest as she plaited diamonds in her mistress' hair; the necklace upon her neck; then watching from the keyhole the whole night through the dancing, the prancing, the promenading, the jigs, the flings, she would turn back into the steps she learned in turn from the field slaves . . . Somewhere in the recollecting of it all, the mainspring in Angelina broke; I blamed the Yankees' near coming for the breakdown of Angelina with her new-found truth . . . So though I'm proud this beautiful-looking woman was my own, I feared her most strange, violent nature, so unnatural to her nature now.

—But now slavery was at an end, Sweet Angelina seem to wonder if she weren't haunted by the diamonds so much they would show through her heavy chestnut hair, and I said to her, *You mean as flares*

*in a lantern come to be jabbering tongues in the whispering branches
of trees in the deep woods from where they dangling in their time-
talking as jack-o'-lanterns!* She sobs in wonder at me. No two ways
about it, she felt guilt streaking up through her with every strand of
her upswept hair. Fear, too, in every turn she made in those mirrors
surrounding and enfolding her body like she was being redressed in
those mirrors, body upon body. Put me in the mind of somebody
trying to run out of a chamber of mirrors—don't know what to do
with the faces they've seen. Said how she kept hearing them old slaves'
voices full of trouble: coming after her. Then I said:

*Gal, you better get out of facing them looking-glasses, 'specially in
your weeping-eyed, body-whipped condition, you gonna see too much.*

—But this 'zactly the minute I started backing out of the room,
projecting a warning at screaming Angelina: *Even to look into the
mirrors, fool child, is to guarantee blindness; the darkness shall dress
your shuddering body down in beads of ice . . . choking on the tongue
into non-talk . . . with no name in the street . . . with no lamps for the
feet to fly by . . . those seven mirrors done commence to enfold your very
soul already.* But from Angelina's voice I heard the long song of a
sorrow wail:

*That's the curse I bear to carry these diamonds in my hair and run
the risk of my own death, 'cause my soul is auctioned in Hell since I
went along with the life of this lying evil—Lord, Lawd, delighting with
this she-wolf wench and her bloodhound master in their evil designs and
deadly delights; and now I, even as I cry out in the song of old for two
wings to hide my face, two wings to carry me away, where may I go and
what must I do? The darkness will blind my body, even the darkness
will be as a fierce light about my body and my soul. Oh, Ivy, in my
torment, my soul is woefully famished and fearfully made; for now even
as I turn and turn again, the darkness and the light are both a haunting, sucking shield over my soul. But why didn't I cry out for right in
the morning of my tribulations? Oh, the proud must be brought low in
these final days. Oh, why didn't I die there in my mother's womb so
that I might not see the light of my days in this dark terrible time?* And,
Sweet Angelina, you fell to your knees and crawled to the main
window. But the rock in the soul of your words knocked loose a knot
tucked away in my guts and I said:

*You afraid them niggers going to kill you like the blacks did the
mulattoes over across the sea, I hear tell of . . .* Sweet Angelina says
to me in a voice as properfied as Mistress Sylvia's with her hands

arched on her hips: *You don't have to worry none, honest, honest Ivy,*
they know where to find your proud, hiding soul below the surface of
the earth.

Nathaniel, that's when I fell once again upon my knees and wept
out at the foot of this hellion's bed.

—Why didn't you take her into your arms and bring comfort and
assurance to her then, as a man, I sobbed, and end her tormenting,
oh, you sheath of a man.—He said nothing for a long time.

—Fool child, what's choking up from the pit in my stomach I'm
trying to offer up as a cup shaped in Hell . . . Softening words are
what's done corrupted us both into careless slumber . . . Naw, it
weren't my words so much not saying enough, but something deepening as it arose in her made her run off to warn the field slaves, for she
also believed these here were not only the last days of slavery but the
last days of God's earth. So full of a lightning-struck-down spirit now;
long loathing being the Reeds' soul-sweetening cream. But she wanted
to believe in the Yankees, she let me know—and the bottom rail was
coming on top now, as the best of the cream rises, you might say; but
fearful of what the death of this old skin might mean in the way it
would bring down a hellish new world, or tie up with the hell of the
last flames of the old world tumbling down. Made an even greater
destruction, as the hooves of them Yankees was swift upon us all. We
don't know if they the ones Mistress Sylvia read about out loud in the
Revelations as the Four Horsemen, or the Pale Rider old folks spoke
of.

—But, Sweet Angelina, you also loathed the field slaves, no two
ways about it, you see; yet said they would need to hear the news of
the closeness of the horses carrying the Yankee soldiers' runaway
bodies. You poor soul, you looked like you don't know if you should
sweep into all seven of the collapsing mirrors that oval like the heart-
shape around your body, as Mistress Sylvia sometimes does in stark
nakedness to redress herself for them masquerade balls, and hide
there, or pray you'll disappear in them, let them looking-glasses serve
your body, or fly to the slaves. Warn and flee from them lest they
capture your body and soul. But you see it was I, honest, honest Ivy,
who first warned them all week before of what I had heard in the very
wine cellar of Master Rollins Reed's unraveling words to Mistress
Sylvia about Mr. Lincoln signing them freeing-up papers: the coming-
down death notice of them Yankees.

—But I know what Sweet Angelina don't know from firsthand

experience, how them field slaves got more sides to them than a turtle got different meats, so when Angelina went out to the quarters, some told her hurry sundown and see what tomorrow brings, others said tomorrow may be the coachman's day for plowing; some said all who wore blue coats didn't have to be bonified Yankees' flesh to the tailbone. Those what did believe them to be coming Yankees said they might still be died-in-the-wool buckras to their skullbone. Not to think of any of them as being no soldiers of the cross, climbing ladders for her freeing up. Still some others crying, Well, I'm glad I got my 'ligion in time . . . She might warn them on a point from household news, as I had done, but they would end up giving it deep meaning stirred with old wisdom. I seen it happen time and again. But it don't always mean they right neither 'cause their lanterns is trimmed low; only flares they trust are those they learn to blow on with their own breath, you always had to keep this in the back of your second mind in dealing with them bottom-rail niggers. They ain't gonna trust no wind blast, yea even if it be lightning-struck, if they can't feel with their own hands, breathing, pulse and heart. Some want to see how the blood done signed Mister Lincoln's name—wondering if there is a Mister Lincoln to begin with; some saying if there is, then he's some runaway God done struck down dead, turned to radiance for a second coming . . . How the buckras'll crucify him, too, soon enough, or baptize him with the water cure.

—Now I see her going out there later in the moonlight as I'm feeding Master Rollins his supper on this very silver dinner tin on the nightstand there. She had blood streaked through her eyes, like the quartered moon's brought her nature down on her. I says to myself, woman, you hypocriting yourself to make yourself feel good about yourself. I wondering if some of them all-seeing slaves who knows everything in their stubbornness can see them gems sewed away in her hair. I'm saying to myself, hellfire, nigger slaves what's half free is plum half crazy in the moonlight and half past a colored woman.

—Well now, come next morning at dawn delivering Yankees raid plantations for all their looting souls can suck up, forty days and forty nights they in the area, like they got a bat's wing on one side, a dove's wing on the other. Stealing some; giving some. But now first up three of them come in the yard out of nowhere; Angelina was not sure if these weren't Confederate soldiers—acting as patrollers out black-birding—dressed in Yankee true blue. Puffing up accents like a set of magicians doing stunts at a masquerade ball; ending up by aping them

Abolitionists . . . Because you see Sweet Angelina was still knee-deep in Mistress Sylvia's warning words (like the sunlight on mirrors in the morning, what won't go out of her heart, or them first words Angelina heard of Miss Wheatley's refining poems) that said Yankees were still at least a hard day's ride away, in one side of her body servant's heart. The other side doting on them field slaves' warning peculiar words, what's also streaked up from many tongues; signifying everything is counterfeit.

—But soon the private soldiers' true-blue cloth turned inside out to show, 'cause a Yankee can ape a peckerwood and be lined out in the flesh of their flesh . . . Now these three soldiers bent on raping Angelina toppled her to the ground. Starts in on her but out falls diamonds inside the tower of her hair to the mud in front of the house; they looked on them gems, she told me, like the old masters useda gaze on the bodies of a set of naked beautiful-shaped slave women undressed for a body-bidding auction.

—Come long or short those diamonds saved Angelina, no two ways about it. Bluecoats so amazed like they seen radiance. Glory in those diamonds greater than the grace of seven naked bodies. Soon they down on both knees cupping up the gems out of the muddy earth. Stop tearing her dress off, the one Mistress Sylvia give her years before— this give Sweet Angelina just the speck of time to run away off into the woods . . . Flee the Yankees' arms to freedom. She could hear bluecoats wrestling with each other over diamonds; one was killed. But soon the other two was after her as bloodhounds . . . Shouting out: *Hold on there, you pretty little bright-skinned black gal; you Miz Sly, ain't you? Come back here, we got something real good for your deliverance; you free now—come unto us. Got a parcel to deliver, something real good for you; you free now—come unto us.* She went on streaking deeper into the woods. But the little dove sure did find rest for the sole of her feet, as they say; she tumbled right into my protection. For you see she stumbled over in the darkness, where me and Master Rollins was buried in a deep hole covered over with a plaitwork of limbs, leaves and mud. In crushing down on our hiding spot she hurt the sole of her foot some but she was thankfully saved. Stayed out there; the three of us down in the hole till the Yankee soldiers was put under commandment by their high, big-voiced officers.

—Now when we returned after the Yankees had gone back to their camps—except for their big officers—I found the dead soldier in the front yard with his throat slit, from earlobe to earlobe like the fitting design of a blood-red necklace . . . Clay Birthwright, the Reeds' overseer, was more powerful than the straight jacket Rollins Reed tailored for him to wear and we seen this now, because he run off with some of the Yankees to a contraband camp like he's outfitted with wings on his back; but he had the only full set of keys on the premises to all the locks (and taking with him a flock of the hardest-working hands—like they suddenly been delivered up by miracle-giving angels). I can see him just as plain flying off with Old Master Rollins Reed's patched-up trousers on, the ones he useda do his special preaching in when I was a small boy; a Yankee blue shortcoat, flapping in the wind, with a carpetbag hooked about his torn sleeve. Even had laced on a pair of my shoes to his feet. After the Surrender, Clay Birthwright reappears wearing Old Master Rollins' best suit of clothes; we didn't see him take this—musta had them stuck away in the carpetbag. But soon as he spotted Birthwright's cut of cloth he took him back in like the claim the father made to the prodigal son, Master Rollins Reed said. Come back while my Angelina was taken away from my bed.

We ain't got no keys so we got to tear down the door.

—Well now, you see, we found old lady Sylvia Reed dead on the cellar floor. Caledonia broke off of her harness chain. I started to slide down a bowl of poison milk for her lapping, yelping tongue's pacifying. But I thought it more merciful to her and Mistress Sylvia's memory if I killed her quick and dead, so I turned to Old Master Rollins Reed's revolver, hidden 'neath his Bible, to snatch her out of her misery with mercy, as fast as I could so we could get to Mistress Sylvia's body, so crazy was the animal with grieving; snapping at us, guarding her dead mistress' body.

—Then it was we uncovered how Mistress Sylvia had swallowed up the gold key; but it weren't gold but only goldish-looking; it was hardened like rock candy to run through many locks; it was what they call a master key. But it was shot through with poison of a bluing nature—like turpentine shot through with tar. Maybe zipping through her body as a turkey shooting through the straw.

—Now the three of us put Mistress Sylvia's body on a bench; I could see the gold turn blue-dark blue on the lap of her tongue, peculiar to her lips, teeth and gums. But it was my Sweet Angelina, to tell the honest truth, who told us how Mistress Sylvia must've bit down on the goldish key for the deliverance of the poison; it turned blue in her mouth, as the poisoning shot through her system, like when you shoots out a life raft to a drowning man by way of a bighearted bow, and the tide of the waves sweeps it downstream. Because to tell the truth and shame the Devil, all Master Rollins Reed and I needed was one look; we shot back upstairs with jugs of wine after spotting the blue-gummed Mistress Sylvia—'specially Master Rollins Reed, who said: It's Foisty's hand at the reins of the Pale Horse; he had taken to slipping everything, good yet powerful bad, over Foisty's dead-head as a sack over a bail of cotton. Upstairs now I settled myself down (out of the light of them mirrors) to see through my thinking; it come down to how Mistress Sylvia had been preparing herself for this day in many ways, not solely with this key business, but also Mistress Sylvia reciting scripture in Isaiah about them Yankees, where it reads something about: *Why should you be stricken anymore? The whole head is sick and the heart is faint from the sole of the feet, even unto the heel there is no soundness in it . . . but wounds and bruises and putrifying sores: they have not been closed, neither nullified with ointment.*

—But now as I am doting on this upstairs I commences to cover all seven of Mistress Sylvia's oval mirrors in the drawing room—with some of her old masquerade dresses; but I move about those mirrors in their shadows and in back of them, like I seen one time in some of those books where them bullfighters slips outside the reach of them deadly bulls over the waters in Spain. Plenty good room to spare in those closets now; I did this lest Mistress Sylvia's soul be stolen by Satan. I didn't look into those mirrors 'case the self-reflection of her corpse be locked away in those looking-glass faces, but the masquerade gowns captured her old body there; kept her true soul's nature from Satan's snatching up because after all her soul's newly dead. Let Satan gnaw away on them gowns till his heart's content, I says to myself, turn into the magic of a butterfly, I laugh.

—Sweet Angelina meantime gone to Mistress Sylvia's other closet in the bedroom; got the wedding gown from out of the huge trunk where she kept some of her boss bosom-diamonds, what's costume. But when Angelina opens the trunk what comes leaping out was some powerful peculiar odors . . . almost knocks the soul out of her body. For weeks after she's sick with new pains, colds, aching like she's been caught up in the arms of a sudden storm. Naked, sore-boned with chills. Some of them odor-spats of fever never seem to leave her alone —like they was eternal leftovers gone to lockjaw rot.

73

—Hopeless, she comes back whooping and coughing with Mistress Sylvia's wedding gown across her arms like she's carrying a patched-up cotton sack to fit over a scarecrow. Sweet Angelina fixed Mistress Sylvia's dead straight hair back up into plaits as a twirled crown; but then I told her how she better let it hang loose lest Satan send down his blackbirds and loosen those plaits, even unto the wooden coffin where they would find their way like specks of floating grain inside of a seashell, but the way them chills and coughing spells, fevers swept across my hopeless Angelina—like she's got death rattles also as a price for yanking up her mistress' trunk too fast, without at least stepping to the side or opening it with respect.

—We got one of the coffins from the barn Braidwood had made and left for one of the slaves' burying. I feared those blackbirds would work in her coffin by night plucking away; loosen the plaits in Mistress Sylvia's hair, as birds picking for worms where fishermen already dug up for bait, even though Master Rollins Reed kept insisting up how Angelina *must* replait Mistress Sylvia's hair in the way she wore it for their wedding day. The only shoes we can find—he commands how Mistress Sylvia preaches to be buried in shoes—were those finest ones she wore to the last masquerade balls, special from Paris; they are silver with fake rhinestones in them; but the heel is made of glass, it look like a spike. You can take the heel off the shoes: the shoe turns into a ballet slipper, sweet to the soles of tired, dancing feet.

—But now Sweet Angelina was undressing Mistress Sylvia for the burying. Cleaning and scrubbing her with tears falling upon her mistress' body. She had to wash the body down and clean her even though who's to inspect the body (Mistress Sylvia is embraced in Death, by Death all around her) when suddenly Mistress Sylvia's pure waste *productions* fell to the cellar floor as Angelina took off the last of the undergarments; but among the waste productions was seven green diamonds, more precious than any of the ones she gave Angelina to hold inside the cast of her person, even if she didn't mean for her to hold them outright . . . Come down to Angelina's mind how Mistress Sylvia had taped these pure diamonds up inside of her rectum with the gummy blue cloth she used to fix the masks over her earlobes for the masquerade balls to look like large, wound-about earbobs. But this is 'zactly when Angelina, in her high false pride, says bury them alive with her. I says shoot down a fury of pump water on them: if they dulls out to tar, green or yellow, we know they no-account all along; if not, we can slip into town with Braidwood, sell them to the highest bidder. Main thing, though, is not to let on to Master Rollins Reed, whether those diamonds are alive, dead, stillborn or ever exists. Finally I hides them in a old pair of shoes socked away with some paper filler.

—So as we shoveling the last grounds on Mistress Sylvia's coffin we hear Yankee officers' shuffling steps on the rickety clapboard porch out there. After burying, Master Rollins Reed collects us all together, in a fanned-out circle, in front of the porch, with the head of the Yankee troops, Colonel T. J. Delano Bloodcoate, at his side holding a long white scroll, with the blue-black ink bearing through like tar on the seat of a rabbit's bottom; but in the high-noon sun we can see the slanting shadow of the hand writing on our side in a blur of lines and shapes.

—Rollins Reed was sure as silk can't come from a pig's ear it was Wayland Woods who done tip his hat to the Yanks 'bout our plantation. But now he tolls out the words (like the slow drumbeat of a dying man's heart in the first frost) come down from Mr. Lincoln's handwriting in black and blue; but most us desires to hear Rollins Reed himself, as he stands alongside of the Yankee, also speak in his own words, unrolled from his own tongue. See him, hear him, feel him, set his mouth, fix his lips round his own wording of those words, after those write-down words, drop off the mask of those longhand words *and* say out bareface, even if it be in a cold morning tongue, we'd understand, the hot words *Niggers, you free.* Knowing he could never say, Niggers, you free as any white man, but you free like me, in this kind of personality way; and maybe not even what his words might mean in living-flesh actions; but what it meant in his heart's turning.

—Slaves standing round with mussel shells they useda take up their food with, in their hands; most slaves didn't understand, with purity, Mr. Lincoln's words though they knew what was meant and not meant in some ways, too; like white folks knows right from wrong, but puts words on white paper in blue-black ink, changing things back to a worse condition than the previous condition, black as the skillet calling the kettle black, as the white folks say. I seen some free papers, but then I could read. What did it mean to you, free papers, if you couldn't read them; they may say free but . . . or free only here or free only there. Part of why I never went nowhere, just because of how the Yankees would read; make up their own mind about what those freeing-up papers might mean. Be and not be. Fact of the business is, Rollins Reed had offered me some free papers three different times.

—Most slaves loved the idea of Mr. Lincoln or somebody freeing us up, what did it mean past words on paper is lies. Past this, too: we wanted one of our own white folks to put their lips to those words so we could see 'zactly what kind of old lie it sounded like in the fullness of his heart, *and* our own recollection . . . Some want to see Mr. Lincoln's name dipped in blood on the scroll before they'll commence believing those words got any blood, muscle, teeth in them. They don't want be like the poor fool off in a Free State with his master: goes for free, high court tells him; fool, you still property to your master. See what I'm getting at? Then too with Colonel Bloodcoate reading them words we couldn't be sure if they weren't changing them words, a word here or a word there (like a cook slipping a drop of poison here and pinch of poison there into the master's supper, to kill him off slow), as he reads out those words. Changing them, turning the shape of them against us, changing them words, as our names been changed over and over again; maybe now changing those words as he come to them on these holy freeing-up papers . . . Remaking those words like Mistress Sylvia and some of the others remakes our dance steps, what we give away as a rich man gives away loose change . . . John says in the beginning was the Word; but I come to find out how the white man made the word into his own flesh and likeness. But then you married up to a lawyer man and you know how folks can practice trick-nology—play acting with words over their hearts, as pictures on face cards.

—Like them Hebrew children of old, *by the waters of Babylon we were sat down—*but we didn't have no comforting Zion to think about; not with our repeating words of Foisty dying away on our lips. Sweet Angel, I swear this was the onlyest time I felt one with the lowest field nigger in the confusion of our condition . . . But from the looks of your eyes I see you don't believe me like you don't believe so much of what I've said . . . But like the old song says out—on the last day you shall have no hiding place. I looked down at my wonderful shoes from the master; I wondered what kind of slave would I be in the next unfolding. Seeing now how some would want to get back at me, now had the freedom to do it; I thought of my words to Angelina.

—But the words they wanted to hear never poured or trickled from Master Rollins Reed's lips, not purely. Maybe some wants to hear the blood sign in his words to mock his condition. His voice was weeping; but it was cracking. Weeping because we were no longer his, or 'cause of the death of his wife by her election, the burying off of her earlier?

Or 'cause she had taken her own life rather than live to see us free
—or her body enslaved in the new Cross of freedom. Looking down
upon us full of loathing, knowing, wanting, needing us like a man full
of nakedness who wants to be dressed, but knows the ones who may
dress him may be outfitting him for his funeral—standing there next
to the colonel, Master Rollins Reed put me in the mind of a slave on
the auction block whose body and soul is for sale. Him not knowing
what he could do with us, or without us, or what we could do without
him; because a slave and a master is one in the same persons, don't
you know? We, the cause of his Hell and the source of his fool's
paradise of a creation on this earth he had not made but enjoyed to
the fullest, like a dinner sat before you night after night you ain't
prepared but enjoy, ain't sure one fine morning you gonna have it
much longer. In this way, too, Master Rollins Reed reminds me of a
dying man, wondering how many hours is left. I looked around to see
my Angelina's eyes. But Rollins Reed's eyes are now full on her. She
who was all he had out of the Hell of all of this. For after all was said
and done, Mistress Sylvia had not given him the fulfillment a slave
woman had given him—who he had *raped,* way back when *Reece
Shank Haywood* brought him down.—

Nathaniel, now I started into screaming and crying but I. V. Reed
was moaning and shaking like a dying man who begs to be released
from the living and wants to hold on to see what the end will reveal—since he's never had the backbone to face it in the heat of
the sun . . . just upon that word raped; and then Reece Shank
Haywood . . .

Or maybe I. V. was weeping because of some lacking between their
marriage bed beyond having a child—or maybe guilty now, I see, after
what he was to say later because Reece Shank Haywood was such a
haunting man hanging over his very perfect soul. But suddenly now
some of the slaves on that plantation were singing before my eyes, in
shrieking voices, that pealed as a bell broken that's been sealed over
at the crack—*He arose, He arose, He arose from the dead, and the
Lord shall make my spirit whole;* and I saw with my own eyes, Mother
Angelina move past I. V. Reed's eyes, towards those field slaves in the
back; and then Lord, I could see those horrible men lifting her up
again and again. Stripping her naked body and falling down upon her
body and lifting her up again in a savage ritual of violation and
sacrifice . . .

And now Great-Momma Sweetie Reed's voice faded off into mumbling and chanting and weeping, forgetfulness and snatches of phrases, that the recording young man could not understand.

Now the young man Nathaniel took the teacup from Great-Momma Sweetie Reed's encircling hands and placed it upon the dresser top. He went to the sink and let cold water onto his weary writing hand for about three minutes and then letting some of the icy water pour down upon and across the wrist of his right hand. Oh, would that I was ambidextrous, he mused. He dried his writing hand on an old Santa Fe bar towel. From the bed he heard Sweetie Reed's voice now drifting off into fitful sleep; her lips making a popping sound, as the garments of a wet wash go *pop* as they dry out in the wind and in the heat of the sun. Occasionally he would hear words as voices from sleeping, pouting lips; the ninety-one-year-old lady going up and down several layers of sleep, the threshold of wakefulness. Oh, would that I had the intelligence of Dante, he scoffed. Lord, she's troubling the waters even in sleep, he thought to himself as he began to feel the nerve of sleep at his brain tissue. The grandfather clock directly across from her bed now struck five.

He looked over at the thick layers of writing paper, the legal pad he had used; the heavy blue-black ink of his dreadful scrawl. Snatches of her recall of I. V. Reed's words coming back to him now, and Nathaniel Witherspoon thought, she's cleaning up his language here and there, through the process of re-creation, memory transformed. Editing whereever possible, as a preacher who renders up her version of a sermon she heard from her father; making it her own. How will it all look when I transform it, at the Underwood, he wondered. Or should I say, transpose it. Lest my longhand turn to shorthand and short-circuit my memory of what I've set down upon the long yellow legal pad. Who aided this Wayland Woods, hand to hand as soul to soul? Or was he mainly self-educated in the hospital? Did his hot letters to Sylvia come totally from his own outlawed longhand? Suppose Sylvia had taught him the alphabet. Wayland Woods: you clever, courageous soul. Would that I could claim you as kinsman, rather than this I. V. Reed.

But he also thought: I. V. Reed, you devious man, are you sure you're not a Creole at heart and soul? Or some reincarnated, deviant, peasant Venetian . . . If the backbone of my heritage is lined to the labyrinth of your vertebrae, then the matrix of my mix must look like a furious mesh of crossroads; ports pouring into ports. Crisscrossed to zigzagging. Threads of psychic madness, richness and troubling horror; shadows of shadows to come and not to be understood. Oh, poor Othello bound to the straps of unbonneted Iago's Janus-headed soul forever. And Jesus thinks he had a burden to unburden us all. Go melt down Hamlet's flesh and make me a canon and a pallet on your floor.

And then he heard Great-Momma Sweetie Reed humming in her fitful sleep the spiritual "Live A-Humble."

5

To Get Right on the Inside

And Nathaniel remembered how as a boy of seven he first learned what rape meant, not from the lips of the men who spoke of the horror in the Southland, but from Great-Momma Sweetie Reed's lips. Asking her what the newspaper account meant that he overheard the men talking about: the report from down south that a black woman had been gang-raped by the same men who lynched the woman's husband and while he watched, too. First they stripped the man of his clothing naked to the loins, then they lifted him up to a platform; yoked his neck to the branch, roped and bound his body at the stomach to the trunk of the poplar tree; then as some started to rape the wife, others, who were also to participate in the act, stripped the man of his loin cloth; he almost tore the tree up from its roots in the earth, the report said, in his rage, as the men fell upon his wife, each taking turns back down upon her. But as the husband attempted to tear his body from the tree and vault from the tree he ran the risk of hanging himself. After the dreadful men finished, they proceeded to kick the platform from beneath the man's naked, wildly kicking feet, so that he appeared to come out of the tree, off the tree where they had lain his body and bound his body in hoops of steel like chains. Even as a boy of seven he had heard of lynchings back to the very nightmare slits of beginning memory and Grandfather Wither-spoon had spoken of them before sleep and wakefulness.

But when the boy asked what rape meant he didn't understand. He knew it was so fierce it seemed beyond murder in what it did to the mind and spirit of a woman (and a man, too, if he loved her); he also knew it was something men alone did to women; and he also knew enough not to ask the men in childish shame about what he didn't understand, he had felt a deeper shame in the peculiar horror in the welling-up recall of their voices, at Williemain's barbershop amid the clippers, razors and scissors.

At seven the boy Nathaniel had asked Great-Momma Sweetie Reed about it all, not even sure with her, because even she had not used the word in telling of what had happened to her mother, but rather *violated,* or *assaulted.* When Sweetie Reed explained what the word "rape" meant to the boy in connection with what happened to her mother (and to the woman and husband in the newspaper story), the boy felt sick deep in his stomach, and shame crept up about his loins; where already in recent days the boy had commenced to feel some stirrings in the presence of female power and glory in the form of his third cousin Lily-Beth Michaelson and in the cupcake presence of little Beatrice Treadwell.

Great-Momma Sweetie went by the premise if you were old enough to ask a question, then you were old enough to get an answer. Yet even here she told you what she wanted you to know, just as they said she heard what she wanted to hear. The young man Nathaniel Turner Witherspoon felt more than shame, but horror and wanton evil when the word "rape" came up. Now at twenty-one he felt the rapist at every turn and corner of his life along with the lyrical lushness of female loins. For even in the most perfectly normal moments of seduction and passion (not the vulgar fool who hides in the shadows and leaps upon some woman on her way home) but the male aggressor in lovemaking. What was the line between aggressor and rapist? He felt that those men who had treated Angelina as so much meat upon a slab, or the men who had raped the black woman before her husband's eyes, should be castrated. But the close, perverse connection between rape and sexual aggression tormented him body and soul. His love of women was worshipful, even as his body was afire, as leaping flame in a dark cathedral. He felt not only fury over this urge for sex but confusion about it, commingled as it was with lovemaking and worship and behind this guilt and fear and this desperate attempt to put everything on a higher altar plane of thought, deed and spirit with a girl. The life of her mind and the life in his body; the life in her body and the life in his mind.

But down in the dark of lovers' lane, with row upon row of cars swarming with lovemaking or attempts at getting a girl's sweater and panties off, stripping the body to the bone, if lucky—hadn't some of the frat guys who loved electronics wired up Uncle Hampton's Dodge, the very car he was tooling, for sound; and put out the badmouth on his action, or inaction.—

—Man, Spoons be in there working out, doing some down heavy third finger work and all of a sudden when he's supposed to be copping his plea and popping the loaded question, his mind goes acrobat, his soul goes berserk, and his hard-on goes iceberg slim on him . . . Man, a stream of twelve cars picked up on his sounds they vio-lated the very nut of man's nature; I can hear him now telling the mollie: Girl, your mind's too lightweight to receive the philosophical ramifications of my erection and the plight and state of human existence on the same plane . . . You have no concept of how brilliance is related to the sheer madness of a dancing star—your virginal mind is untouched by Freud, Marx and Shakespeare . . . So get out of this coupet Miss Uncopped, Uncouth.—

This had never occurred, Nathaniel swore. But the guys had something garbled on tape and played it at some of their smokers and dubbed in the lines they swore were a part of the original conversation. But Nathaniel had to carry the image for the last three years; and his badly tarnished image had kept him off the scene. Meanwhile his inability to ask for it, in simple language, had made him suddenly attractive to certain girls, who now attempted to see how far they could make him go before he let go and asked them in plain English . . . The priest had said would you take a beautiful, dazzling jewel and throw it upon the black mud and smash it and stamp upon it? Then how could you abuse one of God's creatures—more alluring and beautiful in the Master's eyes than the lilies of the field in all of their glory? Well, a lot of those lilies were twisted up with weeds and some of the weeds were as attractive as lilies. Some enjoyed wrestling in the dirt as much as he did. And although by now he had spat out the priest's words, collar and all upon the ground, he could hear those words and the word of his mother whenever he got down to the point of stripping the panties off the loins, and heard the eternal no no no stopped as the voice of some victimized woman; or whenever he fumbled with the infernally complicated and elusive bra strap hook. The cries of no no no were often sobs of yes yes yes and therefore many times he plunged ahead; but not always. For he believed with the other men that he knew his sexuality was his jewel and his source of manhood and his was not to be put off; still a mindless girl never brought him back for more; still he despised the frank term of the guys, a hard dick has no conscience.

His father, in his pride over literature and learning, always was saying in the abstract how Dostoevsky taught us all that we are potential murderers and rapists. But Arthur Witherspoon could not bring himself to speak of sex to the boy, nor to the young man, as son in the light of reality and the inner workings of daily confrontation with female flesh, and the citadel of the woman, mind, spirit and soul inside the slopes of overpowering succulent flesh. How much his father allowed for the female mind was questionable, for one thing. But the deeper implications of his father's lack of advice, and Uncle Hampton's wanton jokes, which said nothing about the complex nature of male/female relations, also stemmed from the fact that they both believed that you got your knowledge through your own experience; that you paid for it. As bookish as his father was, Nathaniel knew this also to be the case with him, too.

Then there was the fear that the girl would get pregnant. Or the fear that the rubber sheath would break. Or that the girl-woman would shun the rubber as so much blubber over natural reality. He heard that one enough times, as well. Obsessed with the fury of ideas, and the fury of the loins, and the need to have something spiritual going with a girl, he howled at his body—in the naked mirror of stripped-away reality—how fearfully and wonderfully made, yet where could he hide from the spirit of the fire—he seemed to possess no reins over the leap for sex. Yet the mind demanded discipline at every turn, particularly of the body. Nor did he particularly want reins. Yet the sexual act itself implied reins over one's powers: lest he waste his powers in lascivious pleasure; or lest the girl take the reins; or lest he come too quickly. Did not the passion for sexual embrace mean that he would make his bed in Hell? Yet to abstain seemed freaky and surely not manly. For it seemed as if he was always to be suspended between the bedroom of the flesh and the altar of candlelights, bedded down with ideas and a pillow awash with books and history and literature, all of which offered up no scapegoat but the mind and body, only alive to sex and ideas but one igniting the other. If my mind takes the wings of the morning, then it seems my wings are as vultures for the stripping down of every garment sleeve of care and the triumph of the ripping loins. Lord, the darkness is my gospel of wealth and the genesis of my secret days. But the intellectual girls did not care for sex in body, only in the spiritual lip service. Wanted dead or alive: books, they said.

Nathaniel felt enormous guilt when visiting a whorehouse and yet he could not stay his hand from knocking upon the door, like he was going to knock it down, with the pounding bell clapper. He thought of the great artists who had spent their lives suspended between the rock and the hard-place of whorehouse beds and bedded down in the creative act of the soul and mind. But hadn't they sold their souls to Lucifer for the stiff proposition of too much perverse knowledge? Yet wasn't perverse knowledge and experience the key to the deeper impulses of the creative mind? Ah, the literature of deviance! How often, as he knocked upon those doors, had he thought of Aunt Genevieve's fabulous whorehouse and found himself laughing wildly over the lusty stories spun from her lips, over the fables and tall tales of life at Madam Genevieve's Mansion back in New Orleans . . . Lord, must my mind carry me upon the wings of the morning, eternally, as some fallen angel's spirit back down to that branch of the family's beginnings? Yet women used you, too, and they were to be used; and as he thought of this he thought of the earliest memory of the embittered Uncle Hampton, who had such a shaping shadow power upon his mind, as a child. Coming into his room—upon the young boy's birthday—and rendering up the souring news of his own heartbreak, even as he sat before the record player in the boy's room playing over and over again "The Tennessee Waltz" and crying in his beer: *Marry the woman who loves you and the one you care for* . . . But I did care enough for Candy Cummings to accept her returned engagement ring

84

and not press the issue. And she loved herself, enough, not to get over her head into a careless love. Had Great-Momma Sweetie seen all of this and acted out, accordingly, from this knowledge? Met Candy Cummings at a Herskovits lecture. She had just returned in mid-March, the year before, from Ghana's independence celebration, as an Inquiring Reporter for some Negro newspaper chain; she had paid her way.

But just now Great-Momma Sweetie Reed was coming back from her tossing and her rest-broken state.

—Sweet Angel, as I wondered and pondered what this new-found freedom might mean in my second mind, all of a sudden, right there in the yard, old Bluestone takes out a mouth harp he stole from me. He commence to play a jigging tune of freedom; started off like a mourning wail for deliverance; broke off again. Some, like Angelina, wanted to know what freedom meant—if it signified we was to live among Yankees, maybe we would become like them, too, act like them; they be as us? But the way those three bluecoats came at my Sweet Angelina signified enough of Yankees for her; she decided to stay on. Yankees was to occupy us; so some wondered would the Yankees be some new kind of slave masters whipping us to the tune of Yankee Doodle Dandy, sunup till can't see at night, eight to the bar? Even as they stood there for our protection (like a groom supposed to be protecting his bridely beloved), they laughed at our ways worse than Old Master; they understood even less of Bluestone's wailing-jig turned to a spritely hot tune than Master Rollins, who thought Bluestone's freedom-wail turned to a jig was answering up my quailing sound of *Clair de Lune* for Mistress Sylvia's soul, as some kind of birdcalling runaway signal . . . With Mistress Sylvia dead, come out *where* she hid the super of her *last* diamonds. She was scandalized in memory, but her reputation got some yoking propers, all right, about Reece Haywood, too.—

Nathaniel, at the mention of Reece Haywood's name, I. V. Reed starts to coughing and slobbering like he's lost control of his natural self. And I recalled how the old folks had always whispered the name of Reece Shank Haywood as a handkerchief covering a fitful, cracked jawbone, whenever I came around, I do remember that . . . *Whose propers?* I started to say . . . Why, I see a nigger who suffered from mattress fever all of my remembering days on this broken-down plantation and now wears that purple patch of heartbreak, as a tattered coat-of-arms on his wrinkled sleeve. But I held my peace—at body length. I held on as Lovelady had instructed me out to do—when faced with wise man or fool. And maybe this father was both. And I wondered at Honest Ivy's role in all of this . . . And then it come to me why I. V. Reed kept a-calling me Sweet Angelina too (or so I thought), because maybe he wanted to get right with her through me, in death, or get at her through me, and maybe both; and thinking yes, life is lined out in softness but as the pink silk in a Northern casket.

—Look here, I. V. Reed, you face me face to face. I'm Sweetie Reed, your only child. And as the Lord's my witness, you going to speak to me directly. Not my mother. Though I worshiped the ground she walked on. But I'm not going to let you salve the scabs of your soul by talking to her through me. Say Sweetie or speak no more words to me, evil man. You might even allow yourself to call me daughter.—

—Yes, all right, Sweet, I'll try to remember, he said in a voice humble enough to startle; maybe the talk of Reece Shank Haywood had unleashed this voice.

—Reece Shank Haywood, you see I go back to before Angelina's beginning, as I'm trying to get you to see. I'm thirteen years her senior. My remembrance is back to when Master Reed was an unleashed bloodhound to his niggers. I recollect when he'd whip them soon up in the morning till nightfall can't stand moonlight's shadow; he'd shake down hot red peppers into their wound lashes; other times drop hot wax from candles into their bleeding sores and scabs, left there from the master's earlier lashes . . . Love to go cutting after slave women till one night under the moonlight when I tiptoes to a witness from a high branch; somehow some of his body-bile was choked off . . . and later swimming in the rescuing arms of Auntie Foisty.

—From the soles of his feet to the temple of his crown Rollins Reed was baptized in pure meanness and cruelty; even his gifts to me were designed to blind my eyes, I now know, as they soothed me into comfort, like when a man put his soles into hot water filled with salts, to rid them of calluses, after while you ain't got no calluses but you keep on dipping them soles into the salty hot water. The soles of your feet goes dainty on you, they ain't fitting enough to do a sudden patch of hard day's work when called on . . . As a small boy I useda tote water-boy buckets to field slaves at their cotton-picking, where I first saw Reece Shank Haywood the driver; sometimes I'd collect up wood chips in those long woods for Master Reed's fireplace; or blacken and shine up his handsome shoes, strop down his striding boots to tiptop shape till I'd give a natural birth to brightness in them, so as he could see his natural, white walnut of a face delivered up in those black toe-top-tips as the face on a coin washed up from the bottom of the sea, and a half-blind man would see his reflection in the sunlight in them. And I'd come to know Master Rollins Reed's wrath *and* his lash if he couldn't see the pure outline of his face in those shoes and boots; my face would flash in the dark-buffed shine of his fancy boots; Rollins Reed got 'em from off those boats over in New Orleans from France; sometimes I could see halves of both our faces as quarter-cuts of the moon in those shoe-top faces.

—But still I wanted to butcher him down low so bad, no two ways about it; come down on me one of old Auntie Foisty's omens and got me a dried-out blue shell and ladled up a portion from a high ground his left track made in the earth, into the shell; full-body shape, heel to toe of his sole-shape. Then I sealed off the shell's lips with the master's left-sole print inside with cotton and hot wax and licked the edges up from trickling drops off the mouth of Master's private whiskey bottle. Oh, I was going to fix him up proper for a watery grave, all right . . . Him so proud strutting around like he was God's gift to life's brightness.

—I scurries to the trembling river—deepening in its rising—and buries the shell at the edges of the water so it would wiggle and crawl-like as it floats downstream, a shivering, soulless body. But it didn't work; though so many of Auntie Foisty's misery remedies and omens did will out. Fact of the business is, one day I come on what was left of the blue shell broken in a hundred tiny pieces glaring in the sun, like blue chips of bright-faced stars, on the other side of the river; shell seemed like it had been caught up, crushed in a whirlwind against a powerful rock. I was fastened to the brightness of them shattered pieces. I bent to touch one, and when I did I got the deepest kind of cut on my fingers; bled for three days and three nights; couldn't stop the blood; except by using one of Auntie Foisty's remedies she used to call up for curing of snakebite poison.

—But no ill fortune for Master Rollins Reed—*then;* for he made more sole prints over us slaves' backs as branding irons; the way they did over at on the Bloodworth plantation. 'Peared like he was more powerful. Had shed his old skin for a even tougher crust—I almost wished for the old one I had wished away in the smashed shell—until one moonlight midnight started his downfalling in front of Jubell's shack . . . Lawd, but my prime-pumping mistake was not bringing

Auntie Foisty in on enough of the truth about whose good fortunes I'd plotted against to lay his body down low—and then later on not showing her how Reece Shank Haywood's hand was touched to the firing clay of it all.

—Sweet, faced with Master Rollins Reed, I thought of myself like a teapot dare not whistle too high . . . Just kinda like it ain't hardly got but a little trickling of water and soup in it, much for boiling sake. Teapot whistling high-pitched at the top is dangerous. Just brew enough so foamy white-head bubbles come to the top. Not even to show on the outside, as the steam moistens the black pot's face— couldn't show your face in your sweaty news; or your news in your face. Don't reveal time your sweet-sweat, in your boiling-up anger. Best keep it all below parboil temperature. You better watch out how sweaty you get, down to the kind of sweat lathered up in your sweating, 'cause it all might show out . . . Will out if you give up a wine-sapped odor, from where in your bitter-grapes you had to drink too much of the master's wrathful wine the night before. Sometimes they could smell what you've done like a bloodhound scent. *Now tell me my white folks ain't keen to ass-hole knowing, if it's grapes to garlic,* sly, old Bluestone useda say . . . So of a sudden you'd look as if you aping up one of them white minstrel made-up faces; like second-face polish over the foundation, but a skin beneath a pearly pair of off-white slippers you've buffed to a glowing grin. Then they'd stroke your hair, give up some silver coins. Why you'd be like them; then they'd love you so . . . Master Rollins would, Mistress Sylvia would.

—Come long or short you was expected to work like a nigger, though, sweat like a slave; no brow-knitting about it. Just so as your face kept a white folks shine of brightness to it. Watch out how potlicker weaved a wonder-smelling mask across your face, for the pure envy it caused in their faces. Never mind about keeping cool. Forget all about it . . . But don't get icy . . . 'cause you suposed to be as the dew, not first frost. Don't get steamed over like hot ice. I useda dream the foul, liquor-stinking lining of Master Rollins Reed's underwear was visited by a plague of bees, so devoured his backbone to his skullbone he had to crawl to move, then only backwards with the speed of a terrapin, but not with its wisdom.

—I had deep spite in a shroud up in the wind (but praying for the master's death, like a boll weevil of wickedness in the cotton) for Rollins Reed to go down dead, all right. Though I learned myself to sweat like a nigger, I wore a maiden's starched white apron about the centerpiece of my actions—so none would know the crepe paleness of my hidden thoughts. Oh, the slaves might fling to flying in their dancing or shouting; though on their second mind's command it might mean to be free or to go for broke or to go to Heaven or later on Jubilee—but we had to wear a shield over our hearts so no blood-throb would shine through; or show out through trembling jug-gu-lar vein; 'cept in a hipbone action, or a dancing passion. But you can't pluck out your talking, mocking eye-spirit, so we, I had to be careful the way I glimpses him but things come up and will out. I kept my eyes glued to the ground like I had wax in a candle gutter; tried to size up my days like the old limp-head rabbit useda say: fleeing tracks cost too much when you buys them grieving memories out of a rattrap.

—But Master Rollins Reed loved to go cutting after slave women —blackbirding—and I didn't like it deep down in the quartered chambers of my heart; then, too, he had sold my mother off, just after I was born. He would slip off from Mistress Sylvia's bed like a thief suited up in the dark, and off he'd go. I knew his routes, his routines by heart—but in this, I was determined not to be his body servant; I stay at a pace; till one time he went after Angelina's mother, the full-circle African. Well, he had his way with her: 'zactly how your mammy came springing out to be.—

Nathaniel, I. V. Reed was sly as a fox, never cared about how my eyes saw into the quartering paleness of his words; but all of this was his way of being just *honest Ivy;* as long as his words were stinging somebody else; and I remembered as a child how he had to whip me to flesh out his affection and feelings. And that was when I realized one of the reasons why I hated this man so, because he could say things that uprooted the deepest wounds, tearing away scab and healing, as if this alone might be excused because he was known as honest, honest Ivy. Every glance of his body revealed to me the vexations of my troubled and terrible being, as when you look into a crooked, cloudy mirror, and it makes you think you got your hat on lopsided, too. It made me think of coals to sores in a peculiar way: he allowed for his disregard to trouble the waters of my caring to a point of heartbreak; he talked like he didn't know to whose lips his words cut—especially to me, his sole daughter. He had blanched affection and marked disregard to a point of madness in the scarred temple of my childhood memory. Almost as if he needed to make me feel loved and despised, so that I would know complete madness all of my days. Anything, anything was up for grabs, in the mock of an honest presentation of the truth . . . Bring the way of my mother's birth low, so you can rise on the wings of your foulness, I. V. Reed. And you see how all of this spite-work from his lips was so veiled I can't tell the victim from the rapist. Looking down upon his body, I wondered was my father *soulless*—and cried aloud, and how many heads does Lucifer have in Hell? And in giving up her body to you, I. V. Reed, Angelina cast pearls before swine.

Nathaniel, then I said to myself: go on, careless I. V. Reed, break my heart with the way you shape out the past (like the swift cut of a man's sleeve) as long as I can't see your hand choking out the sleep-broken past, as a fierce arm twisting in a straight jacket; I who watched my mother defiled—must I take this, too? Yet I didn't want him to sugarcoat the past—or did I? He had hungered for a shroud over old man Rollins Reed's naked form—but I looked down on him as a lapsed life-insurance policy that could not be revived. Yet there I was, standing there before his dying bed now . . . And maybe in the need of prayer myself . . . Why? He knew that it was my grandmother and mother he was talking about—even if he had removed his seed from my very being in his vulgar mind. Not even being able to allow himself to call me Sweet for the longest, much less daughter. He needed to get right on the inside before he could ever hope to get right on the outside; history couldn't save him, no matter how many slabs of it he unearthed, like so much befouled yet usable treasure.

For even in the unearthing wasn't he using it all as a ground-covering monument to shadow his naked memory? As far as I. V. Reed was concerned, that was his long suit of appearing to be righteous, with his wrongside outsideness. His face to face the truth as honest, honest Ivy. Hadn't I heard the chorus at church singing of *those who shall have no hiding place that day,* sung out by the biggest hypocrites in the church, on that dawn of Easter Sunday, sunrise Resurrection? But thinking in this way suddenly subjected my mind to a strange release of the heart and it come down to my second mind also—why I was here, too, because of what it all might make me, force me, to see in the darkness of time . . . so that even as his words were spun to hurt, to quarter my heart, but to look as if they were drawn up from a seventh part of his blood made unlucky by the glaze of my presence; yet the truth of my being was to admit the way my grandmother was in fact ravaged as part of the family genesis; maybe being up north and winning so many audiences and then being known as the former wife of Jericho Witherspoon had made me not so much forget, but decline to remember the horror of that part of the past in my heart.

Lord, I had spoken of so many of these things in public, but perhaps this was part of some strange, peculiar performance, in which I had forced others to see what I dared not look back on, other than in a deep melancholy. But to hear the satanic one's voice allowed to bear witness to history was something I had to get used to because amongst other things I had so grown used to being called upon as the counsel for the wretched, I'd forgotten how it is always a fool, or a wise fool, who gives us a quarter of the truth, because it is he who has lived so many sides of the truth, turned inside out. So that out of the voice of the serpent came coiled memory but what spat from off of his tongue in its mockery was the base truth and a side of my truthful history. But then life shows us how sometimes out of violence and evil springs some good, if you can live through it; and how in good times, times that look like peace, more evil and corruption is going on than you can shake a stick at . . . I wanted to shake a stick at I. V. Reed's heart, I can tell you that.

6

Big
House
Praise
Shack

S weet, come midnight . . . Well, one of the tough young bucks
got wind of it; one who had his hat cocked for Angelina's
mother, Jubell—this was Reece Shank Haywood, the driver.
Now, I'm the guilt-party what opened up Reece Shank Haywood's
eyes, bright as pennies, bending over as if looking deep down through
a keyhole—pinched round out of a wishbone . . . *Master Rollins down
at Jubell's shack—now let's see how passion-boned and stirred-up-
natured you can be about his sleeping laces lashed cross your careless
face,* I says, laying my left-hand fingertips to the throbbing jug-gu-lar
vein in his purple-black throat, ever so lightly as I spoke. I told 'cause

I loathed Reece Shank Haywood out; he stole my gal, even though I was big at the Big House. I could steal things for her with my light-fingers in my sweethearted manner, but I was thirteen and she was fourteen; even though the flame in my heart waxed on Minnie-Bea. I shoulda known I couldn't keep her; hold up to her. I lied—hoping to snap them apart, as the chicken's wishbone I had split, then cracked in my hands, saying, *Minnie-Bea: Reece Haywood is a blue-gummed man* to steal her heart back away, my greasy hands reaching out for her arms.

—Sweet, it just tempted her all the more; apple-faced Minnie-Bea's bold all right, I thought, 'cause you see I was still young, ain't yet learn to fly. Falling, before I'm rising; but Minnie-Bea's falling in her flying, too. She's a fool if she thinks she can shoot down rubbery Shank for long. I didn't think to realize if she was being some parts of Shank's gal, behind my back; she sure knew about his tongue, and his gums. First time I spied them was down twisting round behind this poplar tree; woke me up then to make a voice—tell the truth, I couldn't tell who was tempting up who . . .

—Anyway, Minnie-Bea's chicken-greasy mouth spat my words into the woods, like brittle bones or birdshot through the treetops. Then showed me out her tongue and with her hand on her hip gave up the one-butt shuffle in my face to boot; I wanted to shoot an arrow through Minnie-Bea's apple face. I raced after her seeing the strawberry sunbonnet my grandmother made; the one I gave up to her, flopping over Minnie-Bea's ears. My heart quivering like skin over a sparrow's eyeballs. I took my homemade bow and arrow, shot a sparrow on the wing in my spite.

—Minnie-Bea was fourteen. Already shaped up from the ground and fine. I was a little old scrawny kid and Reece Shank Haywood—why, he's a big, muscle-flexing nigger could own any number of gals to call his own, how come he got to own the sleepy-eyed, apple-faced one I was sweet on, eyeing up and suckling after; but I'm too young to take to heart how crow and corn can't stalk the same field. It was during this whole Minnie-Bea time I commences to develop—'cause of her—bowel spasms, cause by a nervous stomach caused by gas. All caused by my heart-burn over her.

—Well now, Minnie-Bea didn't even seem to hear the music I made with my mouth harp what comes winding up from my ribcage; even went and put wax in her eyes to cut me off; though she sure sopped the grease off my chicken. She left me holding the wings, the wishbone, backbone in the bleeding heart of the high-noonday sun, with my bow and arrow and my lunch basket . . . I reckon I'm not going to let my heart be as wax in your hands, I said as I looked down on my greasy hands and the chickens' barebones; as I watched her flip off into the woods, I wished if only I had wings to swoop down on her with bow and arrow in the talons . . . Wishing as Minnie-Bea flung away into the woods a blood-tongued snake would rise up: sting her in the sole. I was so heartsick I felt a lump in my throat; a crack in the pit of my stomach; a hollow below my ribs.

—But now I asked Reece Shank Haywood if he wanted a cup of Master Rollins Reed's wine to take him flying off to the shack—for I knew where Master kept his pleasures stored, as fingers flexing in rich but holely leather gloves. Shank swiftly rebukes my offer with an elbow in my ribs; it bends me over, and of a sudden I spies Minnie-Bea's strawberry bonnet strapped to his belt on the left-hip side, drooping as a gun holster. There it was, all right, sewed to Shank's trousers at the thigh part like moonlight consoling on the lap of night. I was rebuked in sadness: my grandmother's bonnet; the one I gave up to Minnie-Bea. I hated Reece Haywood with Hell's breath as I saw him loping off towards Jubell's shack. Now hearing his last words ring out at me, kinda of tossed over his shoulder like a mouth full of bitter grapes; the shoe leather of his almighty brogans swishing—as whipping lashes—through the green grass; as easy riders—making tracks sweet to his sole.

—I hoped he'd act crazy, as he all the time could. Go down there, speak out of turn. Get his forty lashes while his black ass was stropped across a mule; *'cause pride goeth before destruction and a haughty spirit before a fall,* Good Book lines us out to this. But funny how my second mind come to remembering about the tale Auntie Foisty heard back up from her mother: when a new king comes in, they kill a brave battle prisoner, the king eats his heart for courage. Still, honest to my heart's command, I didn't think Master Rollins Reed would do much more then whip Reece Shank Haywood—at six foot, six inches; arms of steel down to his knees, hams and legs, so powerful and hard, we called him horse-shanks; a pair of canoes for feet. A valuable driver to boot, who many niggers feared more than they ever did Jesus Christ coming in a chariot driven by a windstorm, to carry them home in His arms. As for boldness, both Master and Shank were more bodacious than a pair of unchained eagles . . .

—Now Shank Haywood had shot spittle over his shoulder, as he loped off so tall and proud, with just these words, winging back at me, in my face: *Lit-tle Nig', ya say Rolley's makin' time wid who?* I nodded to his backbone in a arching bend a bow makes. But off he trots and lopes just as cool and mean, licking up his lips as his head is going from side to side, like he's got apple pie toothed away from last night and he don't want to get rid of it—on his mind or in his back teeth. His tongue is at the roof of his mouth enjoying it down to his natural aching gums, come hell or ice water.

—I follows Reece at a tiptoe safe pace . . . Shank Haywood waits outside, don't go knocking on the cabin door, or busting it down, like he's giving Master Rollins Reed the benefit of his last wish as they allow some prisoners who's clocked to burn, or hang, or are choked to death, with a hood over their heads, their last request for favorite venison meat; don't disturb them their last hour at their plate before they face death at the stroke of midnight.—

Nathaniel, I had to hang back from spitting upon I. V. Reed's body crown to his sole. But I held on to my peace a pace and my tongue, knowing my turn would surely come, though that didn't predict no consolation.

—Now you see, Sweet, I stands behind this tree of a distance, say hundred paces from the shack. Climbs up into the highest limbs to watch at a special angle the action to come, my bow and arrow slung over my shoulder—laughing, but kind of nervous now to myself over Shank's cockiness, his gumption; but to tell the honest-to-heart truth it was coming down on me now, no telling what Shank might do in this shivering moonlight; I got some smooth stones in my pockets. I starts to rock them at Jubell's shack door to hurry the action, with my slingshot made from strips off of Mistress Sylvia's throwed-away rubber corset and her bursted water bag . . . 'Cause the longer Master Rollins Reed's in there, the shorter Shank's temper going to get, I 'specks, from where I'm hanging on tiptoe in the branches like them ballet dancers Mistress Sylvia useda have in for entertainment at them masquerade balls . . . So I don't fire my slingshot yet, for fear of losing my proper balance, should I hit the shack, or dare I hit Haywood— if I miss, I pray the Master my soul to keep. I can now see how Shank's temper is doing a flapping spread-eagle, deepening, rising and throbbing in his temple. His chest is heaving, like the brooding, churning coldness of this night what's got a storm brooding below its cloudy tar shroud, with only the white moon clear, beautiful, showing out.

—It's January cold hanging in those tree limbs, as a soul chilling in a ice-house cage—and the sleeves of my jacket ain't proper warm enough 'cause they full of holes and unraveling patches, like they could be used for a scarecrow man in the corn patch. Wind's commencing to howl in the trees; I can barely balance for falling—hoping the soles of these old shoes don't slip me for a loss. I'm thinking wouldn't it be lovely to be playing the *Nutcracker* for them ballet dancers' straining legs—which is the role Mistress Sylvia allows for me—'stead of hanging out here with a freezing ass up a tree.

—Well now, pretty soon Master Rollins Reed comes out yawning on tiptoe like a proud man walking on stilts. Still clothing up and buttoning on down. He's as pink in the face as a bowl of milk choked up with strawberries in January; 'pearing like all he needs is his pipe for pure contentment; maybe he's just stepped out for a breath of fresh air, 'cause it's so breathless inside; his rich man's shoes ain't laced up proper, but slunk on his feet as slippers. His crotch is wide open; one suspender's up on his shoulder, one's drooping down to this thigh.

—Well, now you see Reece Haywood takes three paces up behind Master Rollins Reed, smooth as a rabbit tipping over dead-heads, brings Master Rollins to his knees with a swift-hearted, powerful, chop to the backbone (like you cracks off the dead limb of a tree with an ax, not to destroy the tree but to cut off its harming, from hurting other branches, but on the other hand a middling blow like this one from Reece, who's as strong as Jack Johnson nowadays and don't know his own strength, is enough to sew snoring across a one-eyed giant's eye). Then Shank commences into choking Master, like vengeance getting good to him; but I'm thinking now: oh *naw,* flying almighty fortresses of shivering sheep's shit in a windstorm, what is he doing? Mainly what have I done *now?* . . . what have I created . . . ?

—Trying to think of what to do to undo crazy Reece Shank Haywood's flame-knitted soul; I knew he was topping Jubell (and my lips was sealed as candle wax) but I didn't see, maybe too young to understand what it all might do to a grown man, whose power—in his deeper nature, rising in him; sap just starting to rise in me about Minnie-Bea—didn't know how he was so long-haul fitful sweet on Jubell's body, like he's got pearls of honeysuckle stropped up in both his nostrils and he's a easy rider to the backbone about her round-eye . . . I'd heard tell he was a sweetback man, but this was new news about lover's sweat for me; even though it's January he's on fire, as foul with liquor to his lips on the Fourth of July at high noon. Reece

Shank Haywood is choking and strangling his master for all he's worth. Master Rollins' face is turn from rosy red to plum strawberry now in the pearly moonlight to purple like them dancing and clowning white minstrels. His eyes is glowering as greedy green diamonds; they going to turn backwards in his natural head as green dice, drop down to these shining black shoe tops I polished over. Then them plowing green dice like eyes is rolling about in his head.

—Reece Shank Haywood will kill Master Rollins Reed sure as you born on the Sabbath and your name ain't Kwasi; his cup done run over with revenge, I announces to myself out loud (as the midwife Auntie Foisty, declaring a newborn's sex nature, but then seeing the babe's got a caul over both eyes, and her voice goes from shouting to praise-shout-screeching) but to awake my shivering soul from the shock, as if my hands was crime-free of any bloodspot, even though I want him to chastise Master Rollins Reed—want to read it off his lips—'cause he's whipped my complete ass down to a spasm's shiver enough times for me to feel my bones shivering, hot to cold. He sold my mother before I came to know her. Tried to keep Mistress Sylvia from learning me to read and write. Thinking of Mistress Sylvia as I watch them struggling there in the moonlight, I thought of how when your body fed up with misery beyond knowing or even understanding, how she would give you a dose of pure salts, you vomit till you was plum dizzy in the head to clean everything out you of your system, like the bloodlettings of olden times (particularly your evil, remembering-natureed side, she say) . . . Well, Shank was sure giving his master a shit-splitting fit down there; if he was doing a bloodletting on him, he sure was letting the master's breath slip out of his body —with both hands about the white man's throat.

—But come long or short, no two ways about it, I had not prayed for all of this, I thought out loud to *the* master. I didn't know rightly or wrongly what I expected to happen, more than the chastising of them both. But Lawd no, naw, not all of this! And in the naked moonlight, too, that seemed to strip them down to masquerade dancers doing a dance of war, but whose masks been dropped from their faces in the struggle. Then it come to my mind, Shank figgers he better make his bad boldness good, 'cause long or short he's in tribulation's pure clutches, even as he's now got his powerful hands to Master Rollins Reed's throat, like two twisting lynch ropes—but for me Reece's hands become as two forks pitched to Master Rollins Reed's windpipe. And I'm wondering if my master got any breath in his soul for goodness or badness; but his feet is pitching out for all he's got left so some pure devilment is in him yet.

—Quick as a jack rabbit it come to me to draw Reece Haywood's attention away from Master Reed's throat; if I uses the bow and arrow, arrow might go astray, kill one of 'em—so I picks out a smooth stone from the five I had in my left-hand pocket; my fingers too chilly at each tip to aim it pure straight and crown Haywood; I lets the slingshot fly—hits Shank smack-dab in the temple, as my eyes got refocused in tears, I guess, too, but it lands at the side of his long head: left ear, I almost loses my balance in the tree limbs; all I can see at first is trembling branches from the weight of my throwing body and growing force of gathering wind—juggling limbs up and down like they possessed by the flowering ghost of my throbbing heart. The fierce moonlight throws a furious spotlight on the men in front of the shack.

—Now Shank drops Master from his hands as a sack of meal; his right hand leaps to his ear; as he drops to his knees, then he reclaims some of his strength; staggers backwards against Jubell's rickety shack, swaying with wind force; I see blood trickling down Shank's ear to the tip of his lobe, like the penciling on a map marking off a deep river at the part you can drown easiest; fitted there: a dripping blood-red earbob of a pearl, blooming, finding its way to the surface of the earth below . . . Dripping and making me think of them cut-glass pieces in Mistress Sylvia's chandelier, when she covers them over with strips of crimson paper for her masquerade and charity balls . . .

—Shank shakes himself, wipes away the blood, but it comes right back all the faster, as off a slit-tongue drainpipe; then Shank Haywood's looking wild all about to camp out the direction where the stone flung from what's done felled him—all of a sudden Shank falls to his knees again, searching trees, skies, bright moonlight of the heavens for a sign from where the horror of the stone came, like he's been hit by the wing-tip portion of a falling star and he ain't for sure if it ain't a wonder or a sign. But I'm fearing all the time, the shaking branches gonna unveil the heart of my whereabouts and display my face as mourning news in the mask of moonlight cast in the face of shivering nightfall upon them branches; I'm praying the mask of the night is enough to cover me; I'm praying Shank can't see in deep as I can see him out pure long, in the spreading light of the moon's false-hearted apple-face. But I guess every tree looks the same, as bent to breaking, to Reece in the howling wind's winter light, though he peers out as a royal man brought low by some unknown, unpredicted sign, but just let from his prison pen. Hungry to slit the throat of his hiding jailer who's set him up in the moonlight, for a deeper catch, if he can find the jailer in a hurry, lest he be repossessed and set off to a deeper prison pit, 'cause to be free he's sure got to get moving in a scurry; ain't got time for the evil part of his mind to hatch no eggs of light in the night.

—Then Reece Shank Haywood commences to straighten himself out, starts running off into the woods behind the shack—blood flinging in the soles of his tracks making to his front and his back—like a searchlight lantern swinging back and forth—encircling his every step. But, Angel Sweet, Shank was natural flying—make me commence to thinking of those slaves plotting up escapes, useda whisper inside the long sleeves of humming songs, behind the praise shack: *When I leaves this temptation, I'll be running dodging trees... You'll see the soles of my feet so many times you'll swear I'm flying on my knees...* Go on, fool, I sings out; wings you don't have on your back —them you got to possess in your natural soles, as greased lightning; but watch out for them unnatural traps; I also thought of him as a prisoner running from the naked truth, 'cause my rebuked heart was pierced as his ear.

—Now you see, Sweet, I leap from the tree and hit the ground; it seems like another world all about me, like I been up in the tree past time; it takes me a while to get my bearings, then I rushes over to Rollins Reed's side, I can't see no parts of breathing stirring up in him; so I put my head down to his chest to where his heart is susposed to be, then of a sudden I can hear but a faint beating throb, like the motion sound of an old man flexing his hand into a fist over and over; but it don't seem hardly to be pumping no life into his breathing, like a weak-crocking water pump ain't gasping up nothing but ruint red-yellowish trickles and nothing the body can go by. You better go on and be thirsty than drink of this pumped-up water. Right now I'd rather drink muddy water, sleep in a hollow log than be Master Rollins Reed. Seems like Master Rollins Reed's choked his breathing to the gasp of a trickle. Then some foolish command come down to me to get down on both knees and try to breathe my breathing into Master Rollins' mouth 'cause facts of the business is—he 'pears like a man been captured up from out of a drowning water; even his mouth making little quick gasping, half-moon motions like he's part man and part fish . . . So I lies my body down atop of his and breathes my breath into his last for all I'm worth, like I seen old Rev. Inchmore do down at the baptizing when some fool got holy, happy and hellified-crazy and damn near drowned for Jesus' sake, when I was a small boy no more then commencing my wood-chip collecting . . .

—Why, it's all as foolish as me trying to get him to vomit a chicken bone when he's swallowed his tongue by beating him on the back plum to death, as a drum tap, warning his soul to get right . . . I'm thinking if only I had a cup of the wine I'd offered Reece Haywood, I'd take the master up into my arms and try to get a trickle to his lips, might unleash his tongue, even his breath of life . . . Well, you see I'm pure frantic of what to do and not to do through my shivering being in the moonlight; we must look like lost souls one standing over the one, shot down by the foolish hunters; or the blind leading the blind. In the night I can feel the gathering brew of the windstorm, and feel as a soul what been plucked up out its natural habitat and sat down by a river beneath—'cause even as I'm moving and dragging Master Reed, I don't feel as if I'm moving forward none, in my second mind. So I starts to run back to tell Mistress Sylvia, leave him there for the second, I ain't but a thousand yards from the big house. Confess everything, tell all; she'll give him more hell than she would me. By the time he gets well, all will be well. Well, no, I better . . . just the thought of Master well makes me think I better leave well enough alone on this peculiar score and keep on pulling my load. No, give Reece Shank Haywood time to make more tracks, a voice says aloud; besides, if I go to Mistress Sylvia, I got to think of some new trails in my story, more powerful than a lie; and this right here ain't no more a pure lie than a fly in the buttermilk.

—So now I starts to dragging Master Rollins' body past the tree where I been witnessing it all, into the long-faced woods; hoping to get out of the bright-eyed moonlight, casting a life breathing remark over my motions. Me thinking out loud: *So now what you going to do with his body, mister smart-assed I. V. Reed? Your brains up a mosquito's ass make him fly backwards, in the moonlight.* It was a powerful ticklish situation—no heads or tails about it. Then it all come down to me about the old Praise House, old shack, really, you heard tell of the one, Sweet Angel, where the slaves useda steal away long before you thought of to pray; to hold their own kind of service off from the master's words *and* the sounding of his hearing. But nobody hardly used it anymore; it's so tumbled down, broken, twisted, rain-

gathered and vine-bound; on land all worn out with too much cropping, turned back finally. It was old Auntie Foisty who suggest Master
grow up some trees near it; them trees now seem bent on climbing to
the Heavens.

—But now Master Rollins Reed is getting heavier. I'm getting more
afraid, but bold in my fearing as chill in the wind is gathering sharper,
making my hands numb and my fingers icy biting as they are clutching about Master Rollins' collar, pulling him deeper into the long
arms of the woods, where I sometimes useda still go to get wood chips
for the fireplace. Now with all of this I starts praying for Master
Rollins to be alive, because without him, what I, we going to do? Then
of a sudden I wishes for those leather-kid gloves, though patched up,
his hairy hand passed on down to me last wintertime.

—Now in the darkness with only the light of the moon on my
shoulders I thinks how this light does seem to have a spirit shining
in the darkness, but it can't see the darkness out of which its own light
came back from; like a masquerade them minstrels wears greased over
their natural face . . . Then it come down to me like the windstorming
element, *Fool, you going to choke the master to death by the collar;* so
I comes to drag him at the shoulders. But now as we halfway to the
Praise House, I commences to spot blood marks inside of Reece
Haywood's sole print in the moonlight—everywhere, as a body being
flung in all kinds of directions, the size of grapes, as Death trying to
hang on to Shank's shoulders. The bleeding man's body making more
motions to toss old man Death from his shoulders than a buzzard's
wings flapping over a field of dying, huddled-together, half-buried
bodies; commence to come to my hearing Reece's very bloodspots
sweeping bitter from his earlobe, from the earth where the dripping
flung about as wild seed in a farmer's field, and I thinks, *Well, fool,
it's the wind and nothing more—hurling these visions up before your
very eyes,* but then another voice comes down on me with the element,
*Fool, what you gonna do when you get the master to the Praise House,
pray over him, you of all people;* I takes it up, says right smart, How
can God hear my prayers in this howling night? But I half expect to
see witches mixing up the storming brew in the moonlight.

—I thinks my natural mind's done turn to nut-cracking up; wasn't
Reece going off in one direction, *flying,* at first? Was Shank as lost as
I was now before he straighten himself out? Or did he ever get hisself
straighten out down a crooked path? So now I got to zigzag Master
Rollins' body to 'void dragging the master's body into the tongues of

Reece's bloodspots I see before my eyes, what seem unleash from fathoms deep in my memory. They seem to be gathering my very soul in as a fisherman's net gathering in seashells. It's hard 'voiding them bloodspots before my eyes. My sight goes pealing off as bells to warn me where bloodspot tongues don't live. Only patches of moonlight as giveaway guides. Seems like Reece's blood marks are everywhere, in time with Master Rollins Reed's half-moon mouth gasps, like he's choking up flexing fists of blood for his own breathing sake.

—I wonder how Shank could ever think he could outrun death and be saved. Then it come down to me, how do you know it's Reece's blood babbling in the tongues of red scattered markings? Because I can hear them mouths babbling in wailing, moaning talk. They different from Master's gasping, flexing sounds, I cries down to my shoe tops with the weight of dragging master, numbing my strength. Hoping my core-soul will hear out my heart's plea. But suppose all I'm hearing is the voices of the coming windstorm. Or suppose all I'm hearing proper are witches' voices mixing up this brewing night with *hail, Hell?* Even the step of my dragging sole makes a loud noise unto the night; I'm thinking if somebody don't see me, they sure as Satan will hear my step, and tapped to master's clumping-along body. But now even the winds seem to be double-talking in tongues of judgment, as pig Latin . . . I tries to console myself God will hear my innocence in all of this mixed-up brew; trying as I was to warn Shank away and now trying to save my master, with the scripture words of one of Mistress Sylvia's favorites: *In the fullness of the heart the mouth speaketh. . . .*

Nathaniel, that was when it come across my mind not to scorn I. V. Reed for his giving praise, horror and delight to all things that came newest to his ears and his eyes and filled his mouth. For God gives each soul different portions of what He wants all men to know, and even portions of the mystery of life that He only wants them to know in part. But it was I. V. Reed's own actions in his words, or his avoiding action, that made me wonder of the condition of his back-bone, even as I clasped my ears and my hearing fast to his words, as the child I never was in his arms, and wrapping my arms about myself in the huddling dark to catch a glimpse of his words in the darkness of the cellar many and many a year ago. Still, that old business about *in the fullness of the heart the mouth speaketh* had to be tussled with for all of his tormented revelation and release, as Almighty God was my witness.

—Now, the Praise Shack is about fifteen hundred yards from the tree where my sighting of it all commenced, so first one minute and then the next I'm dragging, resting and putting my head to Master Rollins' heart-spot. I'm huffing and puffing. He's gasping though his face has gone from purple to darker. I can't help but laugh, despite the shape I'm in: *My God, I'm going to live to see Master Rollins' blood turn his face from purplish blue to black! Then maybe I'll be seeing his soul print rising in his face, like a flood deepening as it rises.*

—But now a peculiar cloud overcomes my second mind: if the master circles back round too soon, he's bound over to think I'm somehow tied up with his downfall, though he sure would know I ain't the one cracked him in the spine and tried to choke him to death; but he's gonna need him a nigger sure as you born to die, to fall back on and play the straight part, nut-role. So as I'm pleased to see him stirring a bit, I'm fearful of what'll untie. Then spiteful of him for not dying, even though I'm afraid as hell of what it'll mean if the light bursts out in him. Then there's the role of my softer feelings, like the leavings from a supper what's been for the most part bad: you are famished and thirsty, the wine they send up is full of vinegar but it's all you got to depend on for tomorrow's belly-plate and tongue, as it was middling today, but the onlyest supper you got, in the last word when all is said and done.

—'Cause as I'm dragging Master Rollins Reed along, he don't seem so suffering loathsome, as he does standing above us, stropping niggers to death, like he's beating time solely to some different evil-hearted tune played out by a mad, drunk-plucked fiddler-man in his temple—now he ain't no heavier than his blacksnake whip, which is heavy enough on my back, now as I'm getting used to toting him by dragging him. Seem like I'm getting stronger inside myself as I'm pulling his limp load of empty meal sack; not half the bad man as when he's ruling fierce wrath down upon us slaves' backs, for pleasure —for all he's worth and striding about like he's stonewalling Jackson; or maybe it's I'm getting useda dragging and toting helpless weight, from Genesis to Revelations; but all the time I'm finding out I'm praying up he don't die out for my sake and also to my surprise for Shank Haywood's life. Then saying to myself: *Nig', you in a whole gully of trouble and ain't a bottom wind stirring in your behalf to set your sure-to-be-barbecued ass free from becoming ashy.*

—But now as I dotes on Reece Shank Haywood running for all he's worth and straightening out, too, I think about those other slaves run off in these very same woods, on the slim errand of deliverance, fleeing the Bloodworth boys, with the bloodhounds hotter than the breathing flames lapping up from Hell, after them, and it all makes my pure blood turn; now I'm dragging this white man in these selfsame chilly, storm-gasping naked woods, what's like a dying man's breathing or the icy huffing of a escaping prisoner; it makes me think too how a contented heart must be the host chamber of a soul: a shelter from the storm.

—Even the same old trees I know as I do the crackling lines in the palms of these here hands seems like men on slanting stilts spooked out with hands, arms, wild limbs hurled in every direction, in flaying sleeves of rags and sticks flinging down peculiar on me. Pointing to the blood-spouting mouths Shank's blood making, as seed, in the churned-up floor of the woods at every other yard's sole-pace condition. These very selfsame woods where old man Rollins Reed's nephew, the brutish Calhoun, was buried. Slaves got him out there on a pretense of gold found below a tree, touched up his skullbone with the shovel blade, 'zact spot where they dug a six-by-six-foot hole for a played-out gold spot, while they digging his pure grave. He thought they had tapped down on a chest of gold treasure and wanted to get right on the inside with their master. As old cruel Calhoun commence bending over looking for the chest of gold, they cracked his skull with the spade; then wrapped his body in a cloth, bathed in tar and leaves, and buried him. Onlyest time I seen bloodhounds set to the trail of a white master's scent; never found where he was buried.

—Well now, Sweet Angel, finally we reaches the old tumbled down Praise Shack—I 'most never go there—it's pitch-blackness. Come down to me how the pure Night and Day must live right here. I kicks open the door and it crackles out like a cracked eggshell. But it seems even darker, more inky black in there than night ever appeared before my eyes before. I find I can't make a fire as quick as I can light a candle; for I know 'zactly where the old slaves useda keep them seven candles in a silver stand on a worn and battered table-top slab, shaped in a circle; Master Rollins used it for the dinner meats. Mistress Sylvia throw'd it away with some pig's feet; slaves used the cutting table for a altar-block. Inchmore used it for a preaching stand, where he would pound down his huge, sour fists on the Deliverance; and light up the blackness of our deep darkness. Now the little ruint room of the Praise Shack was given the same shape as those oval looking-glasses in Mistress Sylvia's front room. There are more cobwebs and spider's webs out there making nets of curtains than you can shake a robe at, I see now in the new flare-up of light, and in my mad craziness I fear the candles gonna catch those webs inside of spider's webs, start a fire I won't be able to put out . . . All I need, I says to myself as I pound my chest in weeping over my new-found woe of Master's body, the curtains of knotted-up webs . . . What's to be done, and undone.

—Now I light the candles. I take two smooth stones and put them underneath my master's head so as to prop him up; take off his shoes —and notice how he's got a hole in the sole of his left sock—like moths had 'em a supper there with toe-jam for dessert, all the same I feel embarrassed for him. I loosens the collar of his shirt for the deliverance of air, and breath. I think maybe the rocks are not smooth and soothing enough so I finds an old worn-out Bible, loose and leaf-stained. With one hand I raise the master's head, with the other I places the Bible on the stones, then rests his head down on the Good Book for a soothing prop, but as I bring my right hand away I spots blood markings on my hand from the back of the base of the master's skull, or his shirt—come from Reece Shank Haywood's bleeding earlobe, as the throb of talking tongues, collected up from the drag-ging of Master Rollins' body through the woods to the Praise Shack. I look at my hands. What appears before my eyes leads me to howling, as I recollect what the old folks say: the wounds of a murdered man will bleed in the presence of his murderer. I ain't gone crazy enough to think my stone upsides Shank's head shattered his life, but I do feel chills about how my stone shed his blood as a dead giveaway and will cost his life, for it's worth half a cent to kill a nigger and half a cent to bury him in the best of times nowadays.

—But as I look down on Master Rollins Reed again now, I see the darkening spots under his left eye, I think of the pirates' black eye he sometime wears at the masquerade charity balls; when he would dress up in his sea merchant's get-up, the pirates' patch over his left eye. I tremble to keep myself from dashing one of the seven candles to pieces in his left eye but hoping the light from the candles would burn forever and ever more, as guides to his way to burning Hell; for as the Good Book teaches, *If thine left eye offend thee, pluck it out,* as I dotes for a moment on how he's had sport of pouring hot wax into strips of wounds on my back three times. Yes, let the candlelight burn him to Hell and back; but what of those bloodspots, like grapes what made an imprint on my hand? Let the master be a one-eyed jack shooting craps on the floor of Hell with Satan for his naked soul; or his freedom. Then let the light from this candle lead his way to the land of dusty eternal burning, never to return, nor be able to turn around to see his pappy but only dote on the vision of his burning mother, for eternity; he's so ruled and ruint my life at every turn.

—I had to catch holt my estranged mind from disturbing my natural peaceful nature; another side of me saying aloud: *If thine left eye offend thee, pluck it out and hurl it into the darkness;* yea but he was my left eye, is my left eye. I am his left eye, and his right eye, as God can spot a sparrow. Still his left eye, if he's to be saved from death. But then, who's to save me, if he lives or dies, from Death? I shiver as I make the Bible on the smooth stones comfortable, as mercy to a widow woman. And I says, go on now, Rolley, dream sweet princely dreams as you tiptoe down the ladder to Hell and Death's Row, with my dreams of this candle in your eye for light.

—But now I'm wondering will those slaves what bathes his body down and scrubs his clothing ever be able to clean away at their wet wash these pure bloodspots, before my natural eyes, for I'll have none of it. Yet as I make him comfortable—as I had so often—I think how his hair needs a barbering; I'd like to give him a nice trim, all right. But then it come down all about my head as a drooping shroud lifted up in a windstorm—what's going to be next, fool? What to do? What's to be done? I put my fingertips underneath his shirt to touch his heart with them, these same fingertips what touches so light as a feather to make music for him I know not how many times . . . Heart beating out as a natural man's beat, but slow as the roll of muffled drums.

—Well, it come down all 'bout my mind to call upon old Auntie Foisty, who's Jubell's great-grandauntie . . . She who knows a mite of everything 'bout anything in the way of bringing people back from the dead and how to help the living to keep on holding on. She can save 'em.

—Auntie Foisty can yet revive them breathless slaves down by the riverside—souls steaming over as a wet wash with the word made flesh at daybreak, by her powerful commandment! Now I blow out the candlelights lest the Praise Shack catch on fire. Then I laugh as I think now in this very room on Inchworm's sermon about *Set this house on fire,* as he tried to charge up the spirit of the slaves, who've formed themselves in a circle, when I was a little child, come up just past her knee, holding tight to her hand. I'm wondering now what it would feel like for Master Rollins Reed to wake from his downfall in this room in the pitch-blackness of this Praise Shack, what seems about to fall on top of us all. Would he feel those bloodspots since he couldn't see them at the base of his skull on his clothing? 'Cause he may be the master but sure as hell ain't got eyes in the back of his head, like they say Auntie Foisty has . . . Still, Auntie Foisty ain't always right about everything, as I recollects: her telling some runaways to bathe down the soles of their feet with red peppers or sleek down their soles with turpentine—don't always throw the bloodhounds' scent of sole trail off then, fleeting, foxy niggers. Then, too, her word on the shell curse didn't work, either, against Master Rollins Reed. Still, Auntie Foisty is powerful wise and folks breathe her name as High John the Conqueror's older blood-sister.

—Then I worry some more as I nears Auntie Foisty's shack, 'cause her younger sister, Chastity, might be home guarding the door to keep folks out, pouring up spells over the living. Old folks had it out how Chastity skinned old man Reed's brother into young manhood before he converted over in the Wakening . . . Chastity dreamt into being a chariot—with a tub of boiling spirits, brewing in the cab—what shot through the sky like a falling star, drawn by nine snakes as horsemen, their tongues of fire flaring the way in the night. When the chariot touched ground, Chastity got down on both knees, slit brother Reed's neck with a carving knife, the blood gush out of his throat; and with a water-pump dipper, she poured the hot juices of the spirits' brew— lapping over onto the cab floor—into his mouth, and into the slit-open part cross his throat; sealed his neck back into place with candle wax, burned down by the snakes' tongues. Fed them snakes his Adam's apple laying there on the ground next to the chariot . . . Presently revived Brother Reed was back to form of a man he hadn't known since the springtime of his days, more devilish than ever. His voice come out as shrill as a girl's. Well now, sure 'nough there Chastity was breathing like she's made for sleep; I slips past her on tiptoe, her unbonneted head sweeping in circles as if she's brewing up something even in her dozing. I can't help but muse a bit as some nonbelievers had it out how the tub in the cab of the chariot was filled with moonshine, as I glimpse her head going in circles. As I scurried to the back door, I thought and who will guard the guards themselves.

—Tied as Auntie Foisty is to my salvation and my way out of this condition, I find Auntie Foisty for all of her terribleness is a sight for sore eyes. Now Auntie Foisty is even more of an African than her sister, or her great-grandniece, she could remember coming off the slave ship; but she was delivered up to a Christian all mixed up together like dough and water, tar and turpentine, or water and wine; with all her omens and conjurings and mixings and worship ways. Then, too, come to me how she's something special to Rollins Reed, since it was she what nursed his dead pappy as a baby at her breast. How she was midwife to Master Rollins and half the slaves on the Reed plantation, including me in the circle, so if the master wakes to her soul-toting arms, I must be safe from harm's way, for the time being. But as Mistress Sylvia says, anytime you get a portion of what you want it only unknits new cares, so I'm also wondering what Auntie Foisty's going to think—yea though she brought him into the world—about me bringing the first white man ever set foot in the Praise Shack, to our Praise House, even though Master Rollins owns the very timber with saved gold piled up from sales from our bodies, and they, not me, cut down the timber, Shank Haywood had a marked hand in it all.

—Now bright moonlight seems proper cooing light for lovers' arms and bodies (and this all makes me think back to apple-faced Minnie-Bea and evil-tongued Reece Shank Haywood all the more) but a pure giveaway for a fugitive from justice, thereby making me pity old Haywood again.

—The face of this bright moonlight is grieving to burst open with the power of the brewing windstorm. Auntie Foisty's shack is about a mile and half away from the Praise Shack; I'm sailing as a messenger of Almighty God who ain't for sure what's to become of him once he's delivered up the message, or what spirit's going to overcome him once he tries to give up the word; so many commands at my earlobe. My heart's so filled up.

—But before Auntie Foisty's face where I dare not look, but better aim towards looking, I'm praying I don't develop the lockjaw. My flinging elbows at the sleeve in the wind seems as wings to me in my flying and streaking towards her shack; but pretty soon I starts to see them marked spots before my eyes, as a vision again, sure as you born. Bloodspots as talking tongues grieving upon the ground, I'm zigzagging and leap-frogging to keep my sole from coming down in them —lest they devour my substance, and suck me into the earth with them. And as I'm running and streaking as a messenger with an errand of mercy, I'm thinking to the pound of my brogans of Shank, too, wondering what direction the wind is carrying him into . . . what arms awaits his dreadful body. Thinking of him makes the bloodspots as mouths speak out to me one second and turn to twisting tongues the next—and they plain everywhere as seed, but the size of grape, for a new crop, in an old, overplowed-up field, when you decided to rotate crops . . . And thinking of Shank but 'specially Auntie Foisty, I weeps to myself over it all: *Got two wings to hide my face* . . . Those seven unforgettable words of song wisdom and deathly, pearly woe.

—Well now, Sweet Angel, don't ask me how old Auntie Foisty was —'cause all I know is when I dare look into her face it 'pears like she seen the first dark stirring-up waters of creation rising in the flood waters of Mother Time herself. Now I had to drag and prop Master Rollins Reed up in the Praise House and now I had to support and deliver Auntie Foisty (who had the longest arms I ever seen hung out on a woman) to the Praise Shack with the aid of a cane whittled into being by Golightly Braidwood. My shoulder underneath her other arm and she constant 'bout bringing along *all* in her picnic basket, covered over with a handkerchief she used to clothe about her temple when she's conjuring.

Now it's the covering under where she's got a hand of bat wings, grasshoppers, snake heads all dried out and a hank of hair dried up, and crackled fingernails, a Bible, a wooden crucifix, and a huge, blood-and-wine-stained blue berry-patterned handkerchief, not so much sewed into life as stirred into being of seven lace veils, and snake oil in a small, delicate-shaped bottle once used for one of Mistress Sylvia's precious scents from Paris; some herbs and roots and a jar of blessed water she anoints three times a week with her foamy spittle to keep it pure for healing and cursing. I hear tell how she drinks her urination for purifying those waters, how she keeps it in a black-bodied kettle. She sleeps on a bed made of rocks, her pillow is made of stones with a big rock in the center—all to keep her humble and in tune with her ancestors, who she says she dreams of each and every night, and her coming over on the slave ship, but the ancestors won't come to her in the dreams without her head upon the dreaming rock. There is a glowing stone in the center of the rock; she calls it her diamond-head stone.

—Auntie Foisty's tall as man shot up from the very earth, as a naked arrow from a bed of pine needles, almost tall it seems as Reece Shank Haywood (maybe taller since ain't none seen her stand to full height since she was taken into slavery), she's so spare of flesh to judgment like she done carved all fat from her living body by the blade of wisdom's cutting edge; some say if you want to make a scarecrow, go take one look at Auntie Foisty, then you can make one what would scare Lucifer and all crows back to Hell on a tiger's back. As we cripples along I note the breathing wind-whipped moonlight with each show of her body angles, how she's like the tree branches and limbs we passing, naked of leaves (but under the cover of night rattling branches looks spooky as bats' wings, too) as they crisscross one another and seems like they pointing us out to invisible bloodhounds in a moonlight what wears a mask over night and might be sweet to the lips of unknowing lovers but pure pearl of a giveaway to runaways, and thinking of this I now thinks of myself as a kind of runaway, more than Haywood, whose either a dead man by now or found some secrets to freedom but maybe not to deliverance; maybe from something he's learn from Auntie Foisty's magical hand, who had herself helped many a slave escape.

—Auntie Foisty's as black as a barrel of pitched tar uncovered in the mourning light of hovering moonlight; nearly as black as the Praise House inside where we are now heading, like soldiers on a death march, our pace is about the same it seems. Some folks claim this elderess of evil and good news is as bald as the naked soles of her feet, but few if any ever seen her clean head without those seven different-colored handkerchiefs she saved, sewed and stirred up into one shocking witness of a vow, as a turban—sits on her head like the church steeple, caught up in a lightning rod so as to 'pear to change colors as you look on, and pointed straight and out to the North Star and making Auntie Foisty 'pear even taller, sharper and more almighty—a terrible swift sword of a turban (but as a rainbow of colors so furious) which she holds *all* together inside, sewed from body of a dried-out snake, like catguts. Some of the old folks says if you touch the rainbow-changing turban you'll die on the spot; others hold to the idea of it possessing the spirit of seven different African judgment gods, and if she suffers you to touch it, you'll sleep in death with your ancestors.

—Now in the moonlight Auntie Foisty's face is so horrible, wondrous, powerful and maybe even beautiful—who knows? 'Specially wondrous for me tonight. I can't look up directly into its ebony glow with a knotted looping rainbow tower upon her head (without fearing my limbs could be turned to a plowshare what can't move). I don't want to look at her pure face, lest those grape-size bloodspots return, I think. But cut off my legs and declare me shorty—throw my body to a school of sharks, my soul on the mercy of the pale-hearted high court of the land, for from the nerve streaking through my skullbone to my backbone to my quaking kneebone to my quivering anklebone I can't get free of her tar-blackness, in this moonlight, as if my second nature is glued to it. Also, I've lied to get her out here. Auntie Foisty knows some speck of everything from a eye spasm in a baby's eye to a streak of lightning over a church steeple to a moth's wings bathed over Hell's flames 'bout everything visible and peculiarly invisible upon God's unearthly kingdom, even unto the changing meaning of the faint stars pitched in the face of this night, as teary-eyed bloodspots.

—This heavy basket Auntie Foisty's got under her other arm seems to make her body droop down all the more, with them long-reaching arms, to judgment, so we are measured closer. The old white cane, which was Master Rollins' blind father's, is in her other shaking hand; her fingernails are about three inches long from the quick, on her hands, what's known to palm up watermelons (without dropping one of them) at their belly center. And I say to myself I sure hope those nails don't claw out my sight for seeing the truth.

—Auntie Foisty's so ancient, lame, tall and crippled up, she can barely make tracks plain in the earth with those old patched-up, half-soled black brogan shoes, what looks as canoes, slit at seven different window-points for "breathing rumors," she says. Auntie Foisty never seems to be picking 'em up and laying down—just seems to be laying down, laying down; so it scurries through my mind how I've got to hurry her through the night. Might as well try to lead a witch down the paths of righteousness; force January cold to shiver through a plate of molasses, or split the drawers of night into egg-cracking day. She senses me hurrying her ever so slightly, at the edges of my extra heavy puffing, and says:

Take ya time, boy. All Gawd's chillen got shoes. When I get to heben, gonna put on my shoes . . . Gonna walk all over Gawd's heben.

—Well, not a shadow of a doubt 'bout it, she's something like a mountain what knows inside of an echo sound before its release to the world's hearing ear; always talking to another question, before it reaches her second mind. She may not have wings in her soles, but she plum has 'em in her mind; they can fly her backwards when you think she's winging forwards . . . Mistress Sylvia always useda repeat what some man said 'bout *east is east and west is west.* How they'll never meet, but he ain't never seen the mind of Auntie Foisty.

—Then, too, Auntie Foisty's mind seems to get sharper, more supple, deeper with each fork-turning in the long woods of her days;

so much so, Master Rollins himself bends to her for recollecting 'bout the rightness of Old Master's records on the crop books unto the peculiar weather bend of each stripped-down branch and blade of grass of the seasons, what his pappy, Old Man Rollins Reed, kept fifty-odd years before, in the beginning time. Those books partly burned in a fire, so who do they turn on, Auntie Foisty, who can't read or write; even asking her what each slave was sold for, hour, day and year of the auction. Most of the time she ain't for sure about the money part of it; but knows where each and every one of 'em was sold off to. So here she is called on to correct them books, where the fire burnt off the face of the blue-black ink to curling ash, or give the justice to the pages and the ledger where the sheets burned out. But seasons, crops and slaves she remembers whole; when each slave was sold out this plantation; when they come into this world and how they went out: backwards or forwards.

—Now, even though I'm supporting Auntie Foisty it comes down how she's depending on me. Guilt feelings commences in my soul— as she's now humming with pure evil and lightning wisdom and streaks of sour spite and fomenting trickery and belching and troubling and musing over Jesus. She got this black smock on like someone hovering towards a funeral; I'm thinking Auntie Foisty's gonna trip over the hem of her garment, pitch us both to the earth (with her pageant of peekaboo petticoats drooping on down to the tip of her brogan tops and seems precious up to a queen's throne; each one a different shade of blue, as if bathed in different lights of blue moonlight shavings, back to her beginning time when she first stepped onto those shores). Each blue petticoat thread, marking years of slaving time, stitched to her troubling memory right along with her cooing and humming and moaning and grunting sounds, like she don't trust the birth of words, either, but is warming up and preparing the way for a conjuring and a prayerful moan-whooping, what matches seven different birdcalling voices, from an eagle to a dove.

—Auntie Foisty's breathing is smoky with chewing tobacco, the herbs she swoops up into her cooking. Even though she's gone past all time clocks in the steeple and shooting stars, 'clipses and rainmakers in duration of living, grieving memory, her teeth are white as the pearly, glowing teeth in Minnie-Bea's head, whose mouth ain't never knowed a cut of chewing tobacco (less it be cracked out of blue-gum Shank's jawbone), and the pipe in Auntie Foisty's mouth is rocking back and forth like her second mind is stirring and chewing over my story to see if it's a blue-blood tale, toothed by a blue-gum; ain't sure if she going to cast out the pearly baby with the hot water and the chilly afterbirth.

—But she's gonna go along 'cause she's got to slip her hand to the backbone and skullbone of every living thing to keep knowing some of every breath in nature, no matter how foul or glorified; Almighty God or Mister Lucifer himself ain't gonna stop her tracks in time, without her getting first wind of it; yea though it be as wild, crazy and driven as this storm-brewing night; what *now* 'pears to be so mad, I half expects it to turn into day, in the twinkling of an eye. Auntie Foisty's life is one long, learning season; she can recollect the peculiar way the sun rose and set on nearly every day of the year for high nigh a century or more . . . Just you call out the day, say April 4, 18———, and she'll tell you something about it. But I can't help but think, at the pace we setting, by the time we get to Master Rollins Reed he'll be so dead his soul'll be as a moth's wings hovering over Hell; if his soul ain't already winged the coop of his body; sure as you born, it's going to take a miracle of her long-reaching memory to pull breath back to a body whose soul is flipping flames.

—Now you see, Sweet Angel, as we come to the place where Shank's blood marks first showed out, I don't seem to spot 'em, I wonder as how if I can't spot 'em soon, they never was in the first place. Maybe my mind gone turncoat, as the cartwheeling windstorm through this witch-brewing night. But no contentment for the weariness brewing up my fortune, 'cause soon I starts to see the blood before my eyes, I know full well she's already seen blood-tongues, heard *them* talking. Her seeing's so razor-keen, stropped to her swift-reaching hearing, I know she can see, let alone hear them blood-tongues stowed away in them blood-seeds (what's shaped up from the ground as grapes). Turned again to the shape of Shank's ear in her imagination. Then I starts to humming, to outhum her humming, or to distract the track-pace of her present mind, fool as I am; then I starts to hear them weeping voices again crying through the trees as mumbling, woofing, dying voices in a watery grave, in a deep river: a man's arms twisting in his sleeves . . . Making his body as many bodies, come out of one body. I'm feeling like Mister Nobody, without a granddaddy, or a McDaddy. Come to my mind, too, how this Auntie Foisty is stone coldhearted; but I sure hope Master Rollins Reed ain't coldblooded by now. The only pure sound I gets is from their last gasp breathing and weeping. In my mind now I see how I'm getting the shape of Reece and Rollins all confused as one man's sorry lot. The words *Woe is me, Woe is me* seems slicked to my lips as a seal on a coffin. Tongues give up a whining sound from an old woman's voice moaning woe to the sounds of a baby's crushed throat behind me. At first I think Auntie Foisty's throwing her voice upon the backwards motion of her winging, beating brain; then I think it's the wind them witches is brewing up, in their huffing and puffing voices. I think if I turn to hear them or see them I'll be turned to stone, sure as you born. But if I do get turned to stone leastways I'll be out of the shape I'm in, which is 'bout as good as the measure between a rock and a hard-place.

—Lawd, can Auntie Foisty hear this, too? I catch myself looking up at her throat to see if she's preparing mocking-room and tongue-shape for them sounds hurled over her shoulders on the wings of her mind, in the bloodspots before my eyes. Can Auntie Foisty's eyes inside of her soul see the heavy sorrows on my eyelids, size of red apples, grown out the pool of blood, now seed on the land? . . . Going back to the gasping, heaving waves in the beginning time, when she came over out of the breath of waters? Can Auntie Foisty see the same spirit of souls—like a steaming wet wash—now in the clear-eyed moonlight flying in the air, color of blood spat down upon the earth? The ground has drunk of Haywood's blood, as a split tongue of a bloody crop, to the core. Now I know I'm going crazy for sure. For why is it, as I'm going to take her, or be led by her to the Praise Shack to save Rollins Reed, whose dying would mean a lot more to the saving of my life, I can't think, see and hear nothing but what don't go back to the delivering-up memory of Reece Shank Haywood's blood?

—Just now I hear a dog's howling carry long and loud, then shrill and terrible, swept up by the wind through these trees and a pure sign of Death going around taking names—but I muses to myself, *It don't thunder every time a pig squeals;* well, it's cold enough to slaughter up a hog tonight so to chill its meat but not too cold to freeze a body —Lawd, could it be they were already hot to Haywood's swift-footed trail with frothy-mouthed hounds lapping at his heels from the spirit rising from them bloodspots down these woods? A score of other folks could've been about watching and waiting when Shank fell my master and left him for dead; and Shank's blood smeared across the pearly white of the moonlight kept stretching and stretching inside the stormy veil of the night, like the moonlight's wearing a gray shroud.

—And I'm thinking as we trampling towards the old Praise House in these slave-fleeing woods (which some say is still haunted by Wilks Jackson's body-hung ghost, what rises up sometimes at the hour of the wolf to walk and babble with the carving knife of his loins), Auntie Foisty's shack ain't much different from where we bound for right this moment; and wondering how if Master Rollins body give over to death, what's mastering up his soul, it come down to me how the shadow for Master's death don't deliver up no different moon shadow —the Big House roof—than it do on the Praise Shack top; but this thinking solely makes me tremble to my knees: a hollow man as a shealth made man.

—Now in the clear moonlight I think of the first time I ever laid eyes, almost, on Auntie Foisty's eyes; I was going out in the fishing boat with Rollins Reed, I fell asleep. Her eyes are as beams in them lighthouses miles and miles away, as when I failed to wake up in time and the last thing I thought I saw, or remember, but the first thing I thought I saw and lost were them eyes, steadfast to judgment. Then the peculiar notion comes over my eyes: Auntie Foisty was the midwife what brought you into the world, fool; the first person, even before your very own mammy, to lay her eyes on you, before you opened your eyes.

—Her eyes come to make me think of two split-off blackhearted diamonds, too, set in mud slits, each haunted over by two drooping, cupped caves, where them runaway slaves done gone; but them eye lights—as the lighthouse lights in the night—slunk so far back in her head (like she pitched the light back there to dare you to look and not to look) as they connected to her skullbone where she hears the troubling word of the Lord fly from one eye and the word of Satan wing in the other eye. They are out tonight, plain as a shack to the moonlight, to save you in trouble and damn you if you running from the truth . . . I remembered how it was the lighthouse eyes what saved us. I woke first before Master, roused him from where he'd fell to sleep over his rod and reel. First thing I thought I saw was not them lighthouse lights but the lights in Auntie Foisty's deep purple to black, flaring-up eyes; I was a little old bitty boy. I howled for three nights and three days over how she touched this light to my eyes what saved our lives.

—They say Auntie Foisty was born with a caul over both eyes, I believe it. But to get to those eyes, if you dare or if I dare, you had to look over past them jutting mountain slabs of quick sloping-out ebony cheekbones—making her jaws seem like she's toothless, they so sharp. If you do rise on tiptoe to look, some old folks say, you might turn to stone . . . But what also shock my judgment when Auntie Foisty opens her mouth, past talking to breathing, are a full set of those pure pearly perfect white teeth.

—Then you got to go around about the mountain, you might say, of her huge nose, so proud, ugly, handsome and dangerfied. Winging wild with scent charging, then knowing, and scent scorning. Stewing with thought, twitching with tribulation, evil and wisdom. Lawd, she's delighting in all-time rememberance. Sweet Angel, she's got backwater stayed on her second mind, no two ways 'bout it. Makes me think of what old Rev. Inchmore says 'bout trying to pull a fast one pass Auntie Foisty—how it's like trying to slip the dawn past the eye of a rooster, just because its back is turned.

—Now Auntie Foisty stops her humming and chanting and says unto me: *Ivy, BOY, I spy flies in you honey tale—plain as the North Star in this moonlight.* And I ain't daring up enough to say nothing, much less do nothing, but *Yes'm* . . . All the time looking down at her scarred-up shoes. Then the pageant of blue-tinted petticoats. Now my heart's beating as if it is going to break down under her weight. My lungs full of Reece's bloodspots and my lying; quaking to my very soles in this moonlight. I start to praying way back deep down, some long-forgotten, stone-diamond prayers, even though service to Master Jesus seems false to my tongue, and breathing as a gentleman's sleeve sewed to the patches of a magician's shoulder. My mind's leaping 'bout what to do once I get her there from groping, moping like they say a blind pig finds an acorn up a bitch's ass in his stumbling for food. And I'm thinking I best be fending and proving soon; but I also think the die is cast, and my dice-shot shaking up, only a cast of snake eyes, as I tries now to spy what's pitching in the distant light of Auntie Foisty's long light eyes. Just then she says plain as anything: *Roddy dead: Don't ya see?* I don't see. I don't say anything to her—'cause if I disagree, I'm nigh unto dead; 'cause she's liable to curse me. In my case, leaving me in these woods would leave me with my curse. Lord knows I sure need Auntie Foisty a hay-heap higher than she needs me, ain't no two ways to judgment 'bout it. But suppose she spots the living proof of those marks caked on the back of the master's skull? Maybe she's too farsighted to see it, in her vision-suckled imagination.

—Well now, Sweet Angel, Auntie Foisty cripples on up to the door of the Praise Shack (with this little child, who's me) as I slides from underneath her arm. Soon as she steps inside the pitch-black room, I commences to light the seven candles. They shimmer and quake, before her awful presence. Now Auntie Foisty commences to a-huffing and a-chanting some of them broken-down African words over Master Rollins and then calling on Jesus Christ, the Master. Massaging, conjuring and preparing his body for blessed waters. Then telling me to hurry off and make swift tracks to the Big House. Call sleeping Mistress Sylvia out of herself; I see arrows of trouble slanting in the light of Auntie Foisty's eyes, as I say, Yes'm, with more humbleness than I ever conjures up to Mistress Sylvia's ears. Distrusting Auntie Foisty no doubt reads my words as No'm, but she's bee-busy 'bout her calling. She can't stop for a fool infidel, in the body of a slave, what can't get his head out of his shell-house long enough tell his hind legs what to do and not to do. Finally I streaks out the Praise Shack like I been hit by lightning in my backbone, fairly knocking down the Praise Shack door.

—Then it comes down to my second mind's command: I better not go to Mistress Sylvia just yet. I don't tell Auntie Foisty. I want to ask her is there any faith in hoping Master Rollins will live; but I draw back, do 'bout-face. I balances for a breath on tiptoe as a squirrel on a branch of a tree, when he of a sudden spots a cloven hoof at the edges of the woods; in fact I spin round backwards . . . I'll wait till morning's breathing light; give dirty dog Shank chance to break free and drift off to wherever he can send his body. Hoping Auntie Foisty's spirit'll keep breathing over Master Rollins like when I blow on a dying ember to keep it panting light, in front of the master's fireplace (just as I seen her breathing over my master, as wind to stir dying coals), when I cracked open the Praise Shack door; my head turned back for a gasping last look at them both; then I flew off into the moonlight, like a runaway loose to the howling wind.

—I'm determine I won't let sleep settle on my eyes, or slumber settle shade on my eyelids, till I look into Mistress Sylvia's face with the news. But when I get inside of the Big House, I discover how I'm all played out; I ain't lying. I fall upon the mattress dead for the arms of sleep; I don't wake up till 'bout seven o'clock and Mistress Sylvia, who sleeps until ready, usually 'bout eleven, is dead in the embrace of sleep, naturally; for I know each of her seven kinds of snoring. I peep into her room, the master bedroom, and tiptoes to her bed and she's got one of her old masks over her eyes—dead to the world—

plainly I decide to let her sleep on and remember she's been up preparing for the masquerade charity ball clocked for the stroke of midnight, Saturday. Now the window's open and there's a wild, swift-breeze stropping the lace curtains, with just the slightest faint-breathing beads of rain.

Mistress Sylvia's resting those large blue-green eyes of hers in sleep —dreaming, I suspects, about the masked ball, and doting on some of those steps she ask me to teach her, gathered up from down in the slave quarters. With my head lowered I showed her some old ones, remade. She said, *Ivy, you certainly do have long eyelashes.* I think of it now as it come to me how Mistress Sylvia's eyelashes dusting her tear ducts 'neath her mask, like dusting powders for all over the body she uses. Now I look down on the uncovered parts of her naked face, not touched by the black mask. The shape of her cheeks, the coloring, as two, smooth pink stones bleached to beauty by the caressing foam of the seas' changing whirlwind of waves. She is cooing; like she's shooing a goose. I'm thinking: *When trouble sleeps, let it sew up a sleeve over the arms of woe, without caring.*

—Now from the closet I can see Mistress Sylvia's Marie Antoinette gown; her jet-black diamond-studded mask hanging from the open-faced door; each eye-shape of the mask like a carved-out rabbit's pouch with a false eye inside to make you think her real eyes are cocked at you: only you. Alongside of Mistress Sylvia's dress hangs master's magician's dark blue cape and the black high-top hat, where he pulls out white doves and sometimes butterflies at masquerade balls. He learned this from Merlin Spottswood, the black magician. Then I see Master's beard and his mustache piece; his magic ring dangling from his watch pocket.

—When Master Rollins shakes the cloak-cape out hard enough, it unfurls into the shape of a lady's long gown. If he presses up a button at his cuff, a rod is set free in the chambers of each sleeve, from the wired shoulder pad knitted there. Then two veiled wings flip and fling out, starched like they been stayed by wax. They are sprinkled with green rhinestones; but as I look at them rhinestones they turn to glaring bloodshot eyes. They remind the light of my eye of the blood-spots on the back of Master Rollins' skull, from Reece Shank Haywood's drops of blood . . . Is Auntie Foisty looking now down upon those very bloodspots? But I think of the mask Master Rollins wears, the one with two and a half faces draped over a wire-shaped skull; he slips the skull over his head—one side of the mask is the profile of an angel's face turned upside down; the other side is a face: half monster, half man . . . So as he spins 'bout at the dance, turning and turning, after they been drinking the wine, and trying to do some of the turns I give up to him, he's like somebody gone possessed at one of them revivals for Jesus; always turning another face; going so fast-face you can't hardly tell one face from the other; as he spins another face at you. 'Specially when he gets stone drunk on his wine 'bout three in the morning. But now I tremble with fear once again; for all of a sudden as I am quivering over what's to be done and maybe how I've done enough already to bring down a whole plantation, if this brewing storm outside don't bring it down first. I finds myself laughing as I look at their costumes row on row, lined up for the masquerade charity balls. I sure hope Auntie Foisty has some charity for me, in her *hand*.

—I'm laughing so I'll have to leave the room, lest I disturb Mistress Sylvia's repose with my own teary-hearted dark laughter, as I recollect again where Master Rollins Reed got all of this heart for mask-hearted faces, up his sleeve, the sapphire magic ring in his traveling up north, wild young days, even wilder than he is now; but I don't mean *right now*.

—Because you see, Sweet Angels, it all springs up like a wire trap in the shoulders of a magic box from when he run up on Merlin Spottswood, *the Masters' Magician,* as this nigger outfitted himself to be; up there in them cold states. My master learned from Spottswood the black arts: pulling pigeons, sparrows, butterflies from his cloak; juggling, card trickery, masking and unmasking into masks hidden below, as shadows inside of shades plotting their way to become shadows, all mixed together as a streak of lean and a streak of fat, or wine and water. He taught my master to ape the sounds of doves and lambs, and certain voice-throwing accents of geese and especially hogs.

—But I don't care how smart Master was at learning them tricks, which was Spottswood's main-man trick—and sword swallowing; he kept the mind-reading trick hid and offered to learn Master Rollins Reed sword swallowing instead. Which puts me all in the mind of the story Master Rollins give out this time of how old Spottswood showed off sword swallowing himself, it was the first time Master ever met the magician. Seems like Spottswood was finishing up his face card shuffling act at a high Yankee masquerade charity ball, they hand-clapped, but when it come time for dinner the host banished him off to the kitchen to eat like any other nigger body servant or white-trash help, and out with his white kitchen-nigger help, who so delighted in Spottswood they had marked up they faces with cork, in appreciation, mock and imitation, Master Rollins Reed said.

—Now Merlin Spottswood's real high and proud, and don't believe in no separating line, Master Rollins warns as he explains to Mistress Sylvia why niggers and white folks got to stay separate even when niggers are free in certain cold snowy spots as any white man, 'specially when they misrepresents themselves as free men of color; I hear 'em talking from the cellar basement, getting ready for a masquerade ball. But now pretty soon head supper host master, Mister Waterfill, the local minister, sets his elbows out as spread-eagle wings, points and perches for the knife carving up of the roasted pig laid out before him, on a silver platter, with an apple prop plum in its mouth; but Lawd, Sweet Angels, just before he centers the searing side of the blade down, a yelping-bleeding-bloodchilling shower of squeals stuns the whole high, royal, costumed gathering—some dressed like overseas, royalty white folks. Now head host Master Waterfill's false teeth commences to rattling to the back of his jawbone, his face turns pink like he done seen a two-headed ghost, first head eating the other munching cheese from out of a rabbit trap. Anything but admit where the pig squeal done come from, leads Waterfill to direct one of his manservants and Master Rollins Reed to go and shut the shutters to the windows, where they think some woodpeckers done pecked they way in and now can't peck they way out of there, as they in cages. But it's a decoy 'cause they know full well it ain't woodpeckers what gone wrong.

—Finally all is silent again and host Waterfill recollects himself from his petrified previous condition and starts up again, looking even more properfied than ever before. Master Rollins howls as he tells Mistress Sylvia, as another sampling of how Yankees don't understand niggers, 'specially those they color up as freemen. But just as the carving knife 'bout to fall, a pig's squeal-yelp like his nuts been slit slaughters up a blue-black thunder through the great gathering room of people; teeth of one grand mistress—who looks like a lizard and is dressed like a frog—plops out into her water gobbler; another royalty-dressed lady has her heart attacked; several people starts to screaming bloody murder, with their forks set for pitching; them high white folks is pitch putrified. At Waterfill's direction Master Rollins Reed goes out to the kitchen, personal, and tells the nigger magic-man

Spottswood to come forth and have a seat in the middle of the banquet where he can keep an eye on him, and where high host Waterfill can keep him under lock-and-key eye watch.

—Master Rollins leads Spottswood back and Mister Waterfill tells him to keep his natural mouth shut till he's through cutting the hog. Mister Waterfill is a minister of the Word of God, and he says real serious to this Spottswood person, *God hath given you one face and you make yourself another.* Just then he says to Waterfill, *I's gonna guarantee ya to keep my lips seal up as a stewing lamb,* talking like a nigger himself, though Master Rollins says *that darky kin spout English better than me, like a pure-d white man, got nerve to spout like it's his sole, native tongue; but then he can ape anything in nature,* he tells Mistress Sylvia as they finish dressing now for one of their masquerade charity balls.

—Well now, Sweet Angels, head high host Waterfill nods, not knowing why the black magic man is so certain but happy he's happy, quiet and obeying; Spottswood's nodding and seated. Now host Waterfill raises on high his carving knife for serious work again. But just as he rises on his tiptoes to start, fork in one hand, knife in the other, he takes a last look to see if Spottswood's stayed put in his new place. But Merlin Spottswood's in the shadow of Waterfill's eye-spot vision like a blur.

—He rises in the shadow of Waterfill's motion; just a few drops of a second behind the host. Spottswood slowly brings out a sword of his own, slipped from underneath his black magician's cloak. With his head tossed backwards, he starts to swallowing the sword down his throat, easy.

—High, proud company in costumes roars and yells. Some scream as they nearly choke on their salads—between terror over this outrageous nigger and fearful laughing at his butt-bold antics. Meantime head host Waterfill, known around in them parts to be a master carver of all kinds of meat, done split the hog damn near in two, as he falls apart in the act of hog cutting with a beam in the corner of his right eye caught between hog splitting and Spottswood watching. Spottswood crying: *Well, you told me to keep my mouth shut*—and then Spottswood commences to bleating like a wounded lamb. And the listening Mistress Sylvia taking in all of the master's words, says: *Well, the Bard teaches false face must hide what false heart doth know;* which is also bent to mean, and why did you take up with the nigger? But she can't hardly say the Bard part full-faced 'cause part of the delight she has at them masquerade balls leaps from wonders Master Rollins does at those parties, spring all out of what he picked up and ape from Merlin Spottswood; but the steps she sprung up from us, and those we got from what he brought back from Europe as he tailed Spottswood about and we now mocks, she never would have a face to see, face to face, no, not in a pig's eye.

One of Spottswood's favorites and the one his audiences seemed to like most was when they bound him up into a stock, tied his feet backwards by a rope and handcuffed his wrists, then placed him, the stock and all, into a huge steel-box coffin; then they placed a gag in his mouth, locked up the steel coffin with an iron bolt and pitched him into the middle of the Mississippi River . . . They'd be in one of the big steamboats going down the river, ladies waving their lily-white handkerchiefs and the men laughing with their grand cigars puffing like the steam from the boat and howling, *He'll never get out this one* . . . But just as the boat arrives in New Orleans, the gambling men all drunk and the ladies sick of the cigars and the liquor, what do they see at the dock but the stevedores helping this Spottswood lift up the discarded steel coffin out the river and he's done bent the iron-bolt lock around his neck like a necklace.

—Sweet Angels, just now I think I see stepping from out the front mirror the shape of Reece Shank Haywood, and I scurries out the room and races back down to the Praise Shack, where I see the commencing of some weird sights and sounds. But the elements gone from fierce shuddering to a rebuking downpour, and I flies back to the Big House drenched to my natural skin, as rainy storms tore its face from the Heavens. Power of Heaven and Hell seem near to uprooting trees and as sleep-broken as I am I would rise to start to the window standing back a pace—and wondering over the light of my days and terribleness of my nights, in this house, and fearful the storm would break this glass and shatter it backwards as brimstone into my face, stripped down in terror and to the skeleton in my jawbone, even unto the nerve of my backbone, swaying as limbs on the trees, outside about to break.

—I thought of Shank Haywood driven mad and far and near. I saw bloodspots in the wind at every turn of his heels, where maybe there weren't none; and then it was I fell, Sweet Angel, down on my knees and wept in a pool of Reece Shank Haywood's blood what changed from a grape-shape to a heart there from the ceiling to the floor of my room; I was amazed. And, Sweet Angel, I swear to you this day, I tried to pray out loud so my soul could hear the voice inside of me, for Reece Shank Haywood's skin, bending low, coming down to both of my knees, as I had bent low to help pick up the terrible master, who I loved, too, on the earth before Jubell's shack, and hearing some old-time words not from the old slaves either but from something Master Rollins Reed had picked up from Merlin Spottswood, who picked 'em up from God know where, *Watch closely the eye of him who bows the lowest,* I fell to banging both fists on the mattress . . . Just then I thought of Master Rollins Reed saying one time how we darkies would go to heaven if we were in the state of a perfect soul; but how we would be in a different part or room, sealed off in heaven from them, close but ever so far, near enough to hear commands and callings for serving them up there; there'd be a kind of tarred-off part, sealed away, but where we could slip trays through of melons, and honey and pitchers of milk. God would allow us to see through, too, face to face. They wouldn't see us, but we'd be able to see them; be tiny holes in the screened-off part, as in a veil. We could see Mistress Sylvia, as she floated by, from her face to the hem of her garment so as we could continue to try to match up our actions and ways to her motions and gestures; cut off but closed in . . . And now I wondered would she be wearing one of those masquerade ball gowns up there.

—Well now, Auntie Foisty did nurse Master Rollins (but I remember her saying three times when she first looked down on him: *Massa Rod, he thirst*); seems as how the crack to his backbone fractured his constitution and pinched his nerve, near quick and dead. He barely can walk out of the Praise Shack; but as Auntie Foisty was breathing life to him, in him, she was praying over him. Schooling him in a scolding voice, then in a dreadful voice. Learning him how to pray, what to say, what not to be and to be . . . I'm afraid to tell the world, even now, of what I saw out there in the Praise Shack, in those six days of his confining . . . But 'cause of it all, too, his moving towards the Big House was on unstable legs—put me in the mind of them vets, shocked out their eye-teeth, thinking every cord of lightning is a house on fire.

—Mistress Sylvia dreads to go out there; she's scared of Auntie Foisty with all of her herbs, chants, age, blackness, wicked witherings; her blue gums, Jesus, snake oil, blessed waters, *hand* and rainbow veils stirred into a turban; her urination and conjuring and peculiarness of prophesying out of the limp nothingness of her being but what seems no more than a rag, a hank of bone, *a rod and wires spun out of chains,* Mistress Sylvia told me once upon a time.

—But Mistress Sylvia also scared of crossing Auntie Foisty out, 'cause rumor held it to the heart how she wanted Auntie Foisty's magic wrinkle cream recipe, held in a small gold jar on a little four-legged platform; kept the cheeks, temple and neck soft and smooth as a baby's butt, but it strong-scented and made up from the mud; open the jar up and out leaps seven different odors and stenches more powerful than a sermon on the destruction of the world and the opening up of all them graves; stench could knock your face off, like God done struck you down dead, if you opened it pure. You had to open it with your face turned away nigh backwards—let the potions there breathe air a bit and poison the element long as you kept your face turned and bowed. But, Sweet Angels, what Auntie Foisty put on Master Rollins was out of the books. When he come crawling out the grieving Praise House; she been in there mourning with him, but Lawd, when we all looked on the skin of his body parts; they all went up in a riot. Let me shed some light on what happened inside the lightning change.

—See, Auntie Foisty stayed out there with Master Rollins Reed for six days and every time I'd go out there and peep in I could see her lifting him up out of a deep hole in the earth by the will of those whipping long arms spread inside of her black tunic, powerful as two angels' flapping wings; up and down, up and down and Up and Down —like she's exercising his body muscles to strengthen up his soul tissues and tendencies . . . As the flapping cloaklike wings made the sound of a thunderclap I heard her saying over and over again, with each motion and movement she's using to shape up his body, words of the song: *Angel got two wings to veil my face, Angel got two wings to fly me away.*

—Now, when I got to the crack for a window in the wall of the Praise House, I stood on a rock, tiptoed upwards; then it was I also heard Auntie Foisty saying each time as she scooped Master Rollins out of the earth and up into her long arms: *Why plague us wid mo woe, Massa Roddy?* This hole was just deep enough to serve up a natural man. Her face was hid from my viewing powers, Sweet Angels. I flew away in terror as the looking-glass view of her flying arms kept reminding me of swimming and rowing and Rev. Inchmore trying to baptize Shank Haywood many years before. Then I remember one of the stories 'bout Auntie Foisty, up from the white folks, how she was so powerful cunning and touched. She cut a trapdoor in the hole of the slave ship on the way over with her long nails, sealed it back up with her lips so as no one could tell and then outswam the sharks, the slavers and Satan—but thought she was on her way back to Africa —when low and behold if she ain't delivered up in a storm to the arms of a missionary off the coast of Virginia, who saw her terrible vision in the face of a huge, smooth-faced rock, while out fishing; thought she was a bastard angel, whose wings got shattered by a streak of lightning—its light brought low as one of them lost, shooting stars, from worlds, eyeballs beyond this one.

—Well now, Sweet Angels, when they come out of the Praise Shack, Master Rollins Reed II is a changed man, very near, but at first he can barely walk; crawling like a turtle what's slow in deciding if he's gonna bring his head out and mainly if he's still in contact with his hind legs. Still unstable to judgment. He's as a man come out an awaking storm in the arms of Jesus Christ, but wearing somebody's garments. Not even sure unto his own sole prints. Wondering if he ain't into somebody else's limbs, eyes, face, skin, wrinkles. He's trying to re-collect his old strength inside these new members and body garments, without the old-time religion of his natural evil self; 'fraid he might find his old face steamed inside his new glowing skin.

—But what's got near all the slaves down on both knees—excepting me—ain't the jawbone of the Word made flesh, but how Auntie Foisty's delivered up Rollins Reed's body and bathed Master down to a radiant clay, holy fit: done set the Word alive by the flesh. It's worse off than her taming his hide to a sun tanning; 'cause he's bronzed from his anklebone to his temple, 'cept for the soles of his feet. And it made me think of the joke some tell of how Negroes were the last to be dipped into the waters of Creation . . . Or how they put a house frame over the place where they keeps the meats, wines and ice below the ground, as to protect it over at the Bloodworth plantation.

—All this clay glowing and radiating ain't a revealing element to me, no indeed—facts of the business is, the last time I went out there, Sweet Angels, I saw what she was doing, almost knocked me off my knees to a-humble.

—Auntie Foisty had Master Rollins down in a grave-hole for a whole day; stripped his body clean to his pure underlinens and I saw her washing his body down with a *mud* she made up from her own spat-water, bubbly urination, holy water and the earth from the very floor of the Praise Shack (touching it to her fingertips and then her lips like it was sacred venison offering), adding little special pinches of clay tucked away in a earbob box, stuck in the back pocket of her black smock. But what was so howling crazy was how serious her face was: sweet, confident, prideful as all get-out, and caring like she was anointing the body of a sacred newborn baby—her hands so long she could reach large portions of Master's quarters with one swoop, and Lawd, those fingernails in her man-making motion. It was the first time I ever looked directly to the profile of her face; from where I was tiptoeing on the huge rock.

—But then on this last day I saw Auntie Foisty wash Master's naked body down complete, rub him all over with a special ointment of her own so strongly scented it made my nostrils burn and quiver though I'm outside peeking in through the crack of a window. Then I saw her wrap Master's body; the clay itself 'peared as a glorious net cloth; a veil over the body, like a magician? Auntie Foisty pulled out a cord of beads from her rainbow turban, without so much as disturbing the sewed-together handkerchief veils. I saw her dip the cord of grape-shaped beads in the cup of spittle, urination, blessed waters and mud. I saw her touch the cord of beads, with a flick of her wrist, whip-popping motion to the master's heelbone, his backbone, his skullbone, his jawbone; holding the cord below his jawbone for a long count . . . Like his jaw was cracked (not his backbone). Auntie Foisty trying to set it, or reset it, by the face of this cord. I didn't know rightly from wrongly what it all meant . . . Then there was the part about the crackling leaves.

—All I know for sure is when Master come out of the wilderness, clay over his body, 'peared as a glorious cloth in a net, but the leaves commence to fall away. Come down to me as I peeked in on her the last day—Auntie Foisty's making herself a man. Auntie Foisty weeping and wailing over and over again, as she touched up his heelbone, backbone, skullbone and jawbone:

Sur-ren-der to me, Sur-ren-der to Him . . . He is you Rock! I am you Rock! Sur-ren-der to the Rock, the Cross, the Lad-der. He you Rock, Roddy. I you Sur-ren-der . . . Give it Up! Sur-ren-der . . . Angel got two wings to fly you a-way . . . See the chariot, feel the fire, know the suffering . . . Sur-ren-der to the Rock, Roddy. I flew away as if a kennel of bloodhounds—unleashed from 'neath my mistress' masquerade gown—was hot to my trail; spitting Hell's flaming breath; chasing me the length of the sky, across the hem and outreaching arms of Heaven, demanding me to name by claim, but not to change my very name.

—Now, Sweet Angels, when Master Rollins come out with all the mud-made clay sole to crown, Mistress Sylvia was furious as if Auntie Foisty had burn down one of the pictures of her grandfather in the front room. I think now it was the main reason why she decided to give the order for Reece Shank Haywood to get the water cure, as a prime way of getting back at Auntie Foisty. She didn't have to act on Master Rollins Reed's commandment of old: all captured runaways to be given the water cure. But the first thing she did was this: Mistress Sylvia sent by me a silver cup of *touched* white wine out to Auntie Foisty, what's known to make you forget everything, amongst the white folks (and telling me to tell Auntie Foisty *the wine is for remembrance of her saving Master Rollins' life*), but Auntie Foisty read it by viewing the foamy seven beads on top and splashed the contents to the hog trough, then washed the silver cup spit-shine clean; went back of her shack and to the well; I did see her put a bucket down into the well; came around the side so as I didn't see her; and past her dozing, head-swoop-whooping sister Chastity; and sent Mistress Sylvia back, by me, the silver cup of clear water; but as I neared the Big House I saw seven little bubbles of aqua foam spew up to the surface of the cup, as I handed it back to Mistress Sylvia; I kept my eyes glued to my gem-bright shoes.

—Master Rollins Reed's the color of cedar wood and looks like a wild man with those blue-green eyes blazing in his head; diamonds flung to a watery grave; the mud made over into clay, made out of her mud-making, I thinks to myself. With the pale red of Master Rollins' natural skin underneath, he's got something of a crazy glow to the persons of his natural body. His eyes is pure fiendish like them made-over eyes in masks at masquerade balls.

But now he starts to dancing and leaping and weeping and speaking out in many tongues about how he seen two angels in a pool of light and was wrestling with one of them and how one was choking him down and he was hairy, and another choking the water out of his condition and beating him on the back and he was smooth, as the other lifts the hand away from his throat and then the other one lifts his body and told the master to change his ways and stop trying to choke the niggers down so, and stop lashing them (and he felt his backbone crackle) and if he promised to do this and pledge to give his soul up to Jesus then he could see God Almighty coming out of a vessel like a cradle, in the cab of a chariot in a windstorm; and to stop drinking and fornicating he could know eternal life in a cradle made from a chariot; but to get down on both knees and beg for the breath of life; to surrender to the waters of Jordan; to sleep with his wife at night and read the Bible and let old Stigwood Bloodworth (the one who had a hitch and a who-who-who-WHOA tremble in the deep breathing part of his chanted sermons) come round and preach out loud to us darkies, by firelight (and he felt his jawbone tremble and freeze).

And Master claiming as how he heard *through a giant rock, music and gunpowder throughout, like the Heavens had opened their ears and let the pearly angels hear the music out of the rainbow, floating across the waters, stirring as it also rises from five fathoms below in time; not out of the Heavens but from the clear-water wells, from a chord of notes out of new-made earth, clay, wind and fire of Creation; and it wasn't shouting-for-joy music but shouting, all right, a little like our darkies' transplanting the ferns of our Christian words and preacher-chant, trying to say them like they was long-song voices; these very old-time song words made flesh chanted in a voice I heard akin, yet like none I had ever heard before; chanting over me as oily lapping waters, up from my heelbone to my skullbone as the life-breathing clay engulfing my being: Hurry, Angel! Hurry . . . Hurry down to the pool/I want you to trouble the waters this morning/to bathe my weary soul/Angel got two wings to veil my face/Two wings to fly me away; and then how the angel flew up a ladder as bats' wings made to fly in the night, made of clay, and icy chain-snake-heads, seven lace veils and wings and I felt it down to my very feet set on fire so as to leap me to Heaven out of my heelbone to my very soles. And I turned every whichaway to look for Ivy, but he had abandoned me. I was naked before my very eyes with every one of the pouring shapes of my sins etched and branded on the serpent skin of my blindfold to the world before the Word, and without my transgressions paid for but paraded on a platform kept flapping more as an eagle's wings than an angel's wings. Seems I lost my skin in the wind as a sheet.—*

And now the exhausted Great-Momma Sweetie Reed fell backwards into fitful tossing and finally to drowsiness and sleep; as if in the unraveling of I. V. Reed's part of her story, she was now spent yet still frustrated because the deliverance of her story was far from completed. Nathaniel felt his imagination carry him back to the Rev.

Pompey c. j. Browne's church where many and many a year ago he had gone with his grandmother on Easter Sunday to hear the wild, six-foot-seven minister deliver the sermon.

". . . He *ain't* here, Church, gone home soon this one last morning to get ready to reassemble the living and the dead and yet He is the same man today He was on Friday, but *different*. But one morning He'll return to shepherd you upon an elect chariot-carriage, with a rainbow around His shoulder; with woolly, nappy hair, just like ours was in the *muggified* genesis—and then you'll be straight—if I can ever straighten you out without the help of Madame Walker and tear the bandages, blindfolds and the shades away from your eyes, so as you can come face to face with yourself—and before that undertaker, Mr. Memphis Raven-Snow, gets to your body and if I can ever pluck you from the steering wheel of those priceless, but perishable chrome-dripping Cadillacs spilling over with sardine oil, which is all you can afford to eat as you circle around, transforming your soul into small change in one of those bloodsucking creme-de-coo-coo shorts. We constantly losing ground in this land—ploughing up old tracks and thinking we driving in a new way to the North Star, as we simply reinvent the wheel; meantime you think you navigating at breakneck speed (which is about right, too); Church, you ain't even marking time; believing you can cruise, float or crawl to Jesus in your own tooling time; and He'll be waiting there with open arms to wheel you on in, and you'll throw the fishtail into overdrive on time; but, Church, I *ain't* never heard of a turtle with a convertible shell that can propel into wings; with piston power in its hind legs. Church, time you ought to be driving a buggy if I know anything about your financial position; your soul situation; your previous condition and your sardine salaries and all that chrome you thump down in the collection plate, a buggy 'stead of those rattling, stomach-growling fishtail chariots of rambling dis-enfranchisement and ru-i-nation, that you seem to cherish more than you do the Savior's liberal gait . . .

"Why, I hear tell some of you trying to pour off that sardine oil into the carburator towards the end of the month. You're out there celebrating that chrome like you anointing, buffing and accelerating the Word into chrome—making it whiter and lighter than snow, with your steaming wet-wash rags as prayer cloths worshiping up your lily-white mule machines, which are as stubborn as you are . . . Church, you've strapped down the radiance of your ancestral memory like those despair-filled slaves who delivered up the word on the runaways' route to the slave catchers in the days of our previous condition. But my master and our Jesus spun into Jerusalem sweet, cool and low in the saddle upon a jackass; that was his surrey and his chariot. What do you think the old folks meant when they sang, *Ride on, King Jesus, no man can hinder me.* You, Church, are looking for a miracle to medicate the malice within our maladies; but I say upon this Easter Sunday morning, Arise, turn about and come on out of the wilderness and turn a new face to God's Radiance . . . Those sheens don't wheel in a balm in Gilead." And then Rev. Browne vanished, seemingly, in midair from God's Golden Leaves.

But now the door was suddenly opened; the crack of thunder was heard; Nathaniel's mouth popped open like Charlie McCarthy's; he was surprised to the quick of his backbone, thinking he had awakened to a new dream; the church was indeed amazed that morning ("Pressed dead to the quicksand Sunday silk come sleek, glorious and gorgeous," as Great-Momma Sweetie Reed had said), but by now the preacher himself—like a ducking cowboy—came through the side-door entrance normally bolted (and opened only on Emergency for a fire hazard or when the spiritual fire got too hot in the church and sealed off in the form of a no-entry painting of a rock) . . . Rev. Pompey c. j. Browne filled with the spirit of the good news and dressed to kill in fine though crumpled (from furious preaching) linen robes; now a woolly headpiece atop his process and flanked by three imperially dressed church deacons on each side, in high church collars and blue jackets, with golden leaf buttons the size of silver dollars, in their lapels, marching on each side of "Preacher" and then lifting the six-seven, two hundred fifty pounds (as if in sacrifice), carrying and then elevating him upon their grand shoulders as powerful wings; Rev. Browne revivified, yet still moldering, back to the pulpit now and Rev. Browne standing before the altar slab, hewed out of a rock from the Holy Land, which stood next to a table of wine in a golden cup that glowed like a trombone, and the Saltine crackers, for Communion, lay upon a bronze, canoe-shaped platter; and a glowing candelabra of seven candles to the left of the crackers.

And the moldering soul of Rev. Browne coming through the wilderness of grumbling now grunting, moaning now chanting rage-eloquence and glory-majesty and humility and shocking elegance *sang* through a series of humming voices, spun out of tongues . . . words beyond words into The Word, his trembling flesh alive, and leaping within the huge frame. The material of his robes winging like the old clothes of a scarecrow, caught up in a windstorm; even the lights in the candelabra flaring and quickening.

And then the Tenderness Sisters (whom Rev. Browne dressed in long white gowns, with golden leaf clusters clinging to the breast over the heart) appeared as beautiful bronzed bouquets accompanied by the high-stepping teenaged usherettes. Their bodies moving as if in preparation for a sacred dance in black patten-leather flats (with golden bows, fashioned as leaves) and silk-sheer blue stockings; baby-blue skirts (hemmed at the calf); and upon their backs, lily-white wings; white gloves that glowed in the dark of twilight processions; and golden ribbons in their precisely pressed, oiled down, super-curly hair.

And as Rev. Browne hit the moment of ecstasy in his chanting, he suddenly fell to his knees, sobbing and weeping, his head sweeping about in circles, then falling into a state of collapse; the congregation shrieks in pain and wonder, trembling in harmony with his withering form downed, as a mighty eagle, in the well before the altar. Immediately the high-brown lead usherette leaps forth on the glad tidings of a ballet dancer's legs, produces a lily-white cape from her small purse, unfolds its many layers and drapes the garment over the spirit-felled preacher's body, completely encompassing the huge man's form, except for his sweeping head; the tears streaking down his cheeks. The shivering, limp man appears as one suffering from a nervous breakdown. The hand of the medium-sized narrow-hipped usherette leads the preacher, who is still on his knees, his torso falling, heaving, rising, towards the exit door, off to the left of the altar. The choir has gone from singing to humming "Hear the Lambs A-Crying." Now dependent on the aid of the usherette at his right-hand side, the struck-down, crawling Rev. Browne's head is wobbling and rolling about on the back of his neck, as if it is about to roll off . . . But as they reach the exit door and the usherette's fingertips touch the panel ever so lightly to open the door, Rev. Browne hurls the lily-white cape to the floor and comes up from the knee-crawling position, babbling in tongues of fire, and doing holy leaps, and somersaults in his Jesus' name, with the adroitness of an acrobat half his size and age; the organist now sweeps into "Didn't It Rain." Rev. Browne places the lily-white cape upon the usherette's slim shoulders; he lifts the startled girl upon his shoulders, elevating her to new heights; they reenter and down to the well of the church. The recharged congregation is awe-struck. Rev. Browne is still quaking; his yellowish brown face is lathered in sweat; his eyes other-worldly . . . Now chanting a life-giving call to the organist rendition of "Didn't It Rain."

Now the usherettes taking off Rev. Browne's old robes, befouled with glory and God and preacher sweat, and crumpled (fairly stripping and tearing the outer garments off the inner man's body, as he snapped his fingers to hurry them at their task, amid his trembling and quivering); now passing his garment back onto the matronly, majestic group of God's Golden Leaves' twelve Tenderness Sisters; as they then placed over Pompey c. j. Browne's head (somehow not disturbing the delicately balanced wig) a new long lily-white winging tunic that drooped to his shiny black shoe tops; and then a tiny bejeweled crown of both thorns and diamonds, spires of gold and spear-shapened beacons of lights made in the form of tiny lanterns, with wee flickering lights inside, but rocking like diamonds upon the pointed, mushy hill that his matty headpiece made atop his process, like a three-layered, quaking cake at a Tom Thumb wedding, Nathaniel thought at the time; and Great-Momma Sweetie Reed looked shocked—this was not her church—nor Nathaniel's and he wondered did he have one made of weighing hands, *even back then*—but she was mad at Rev. Foxworth, at River Rock of Eden. And then Great-Momma Sweetie Reed saying: *My Lawd arose in a windstorm.* Nathaniel had a rosary in his pocket and a High-John the Conqueror leaf there and a prayer cloth Sister Rachel Flowers had given him . . .

And now the young man Nathaniel felt in his pocket for the prayer cloth, that the blind singing-choir directress and prophetess Sister Rachel had given him; still carrying it, starched now, in his pocket and thinking suddenly how a simple prayer cloth could be turned into a snot rag (ah, mighty Joyce); or to drive the Moor mad; or to cover the hand in the basket of Auntie Foisty; or dipped in the Lamb's Blood, or used to wipe the face of the bedraggled, falling and rising Redeemer's face of glory to the world, forever and ever; or to wipe the tears and then the blood from his feet . . . His feet. Now he thought of the holes in his own eternally college-boy shoes. Madly for Adlai. And like Abu Kasem—or Adlai—he would not throw away these least of these shoes—lest some shipwrecked brother see them and take heart. The bedraggled shoes of the perpetual, idea-fishing student. Wandering Afro-American/Jew; who looked like an Arab on location and dislocation (and mistaken time and again for a Latino,) and thought to be a Sephardic Jew; not a Hebrew; nor Bloom's butler-*cum*-body servant. And you ain't never had a molly till you've been rocked by a high-rolling high-brown. Perhaps the wings of his soul had holes in them, too, he thought, and the new rosary beads shaped as bellybuttons, back then like the small beady holes in the starched prayer cloth.

Now seated in Rollins Reed's rocker, with his hand touched to Great-Momma Sweetie Reed's knuckles he thought of those rosary beads and the Indian Birth Control plot . . . Presented by the militant *happenings* feminist-beatnik to Jacob V. I. Sivasankara, the gambler and stock exchange speculator and perpetual student; Indian-Oxford (Afro-American brown with inky-black dead-straight hair, like Antoine's); intellectual, bittersweet, crafty beyond savvy; mockery his touchstone to reality; disdaining all skins darker than his own; despising all whites, even those making up his lonely, soured coterie, now encircling his presence and Jacob living part-time with a lily-white-skinned lamb, Milk-Maiden Molly . . . and loving his prime rib and his Guccis . . . Loathing more than anything else ignorance and arrogance amid his furious audacity and superiority of total knowledge, as he and he alone, all five feet, six inches of him, as a Pan-world-Indian individualist-*cum*-perfecto held in his head as gestalt-happening now and forever and never again the answer to the world's soul . . . Prime-pumping atheist who knew that the world was slated for its own destruction any day now . . . And the young feminist beat stabbing away at the pot-filled air of the room at International House and claiming that the Indian women would wear the chain with beads spun upon it (the beads portioned out as rosary bead points or non-happening, happening stations of the Cross), each section a different color to mark the days of the cycle, like a parody on a rosary; but then the crude joke offered up in totally serious mockery of it all by Jacob: *"But, you see, my idealistic Frau-frump-colleague, they won't see your beads; the beads don't glow in the dark."* He who would never ever return home again in the dark; seated there upon his high pile of dusky medical books as a rocking chair.

Now Nathaniel once again let the cold water bathe his weary writing hand, and his wrist. Recalled Great-Momma Sweetie's voice recalling Spottswood's antic disposition and then Auntie Foisty's bathing of Master Rollins Reed's body, as he sipped upon a Rémy Martin over ice, and all of this suddenly unleashed the voice of Aunt Genevieve within him, in the long ago, talking to Uncle Hampton about her mansion back down in New Orleans, the year before they closed it down, in 1917.

". . . But, Hamp, that was when Big Smidley Shockley came bare-butt into *my* house of worship, with a huge flowered bird cage atop his head and Professor Tenderloin, my parrot mascot, going up and down in his cage like he was bobbing for a dangling string of now-you-see-them, now-you-don't bananas, and crying *Get that Turkey-Strutter out of here*—he looked like the Leaning Tower of Pisa, that damn Shockley did—unpainted—he was as naked as a jaybird stripped of his flesh, down to the bone, by an admiring kitty . . . That god damn pissoir of a bird cage on his head just a-jangling and a-shaking, Baa-bay, like a bowl of jelly-belly kinda oozing on his sleeked-down head, like he was fixing to do a rumba step and then lindy hop and him acting dicty, too, about his bird-turd cage, Baa-bay, like he got a secret hard-on and all the girls wants to do is ball his jack, or jack his balls, or jerk his jack, take your cake, or a cone of titty for an appetizer, or an all-day sucker and I'll be an estranged blueberry pie Muth-Planter.

"But that's when Ma-Dam, for Mutha Genevieve, appears as a miracle upon the arching staircase, rising towards the Heavens like a marvelous climax, the rosary beads about my throat, from my admiring bishop . . . And that's when himself, Mister Mother Merriment, places the bird cage down atop Professor Tenderloin's bird cage and then *gets down* (like he's gonna sit in it) on both of his knees and kisses the floor and by this time Professor Tenderloin is hopping-jack mad; thinking this fool Shockley is bringing another bird into his paradise and a lady parrot at that (don't look funny-money, Hamp, because everybody knows Professor Tenderloin is a virgin and ain't giving up none of that prime heat of his funky-butt, not even a lash from his bitter tongue) . . . I can see his eyes through both cages now, eyeing down *Mutha* coming down the stairs with my midget carrying my drooping silk-spun gown, and a beloved Oc-*toe*-genarian Bishop holding on to my monocle.

"Shockley starts crying like some cantor as he kisses the floor, like it was the missing part of Venus de Milo's arm, and claiming how he is dedicating these preserves to Holy Mother of Church, and then he takes the veil off his bird cage and what should emit from the steeple-like peak but twelve cocaine-snorted-down pheasants who ain't going nowhere for going everywhere and he starts to dangling an incenser of powerful herbs and spices mixed with the cocaine, consecrating my Mansion; my Oc-*toe*-genarian Bishop is furious, like he's caught Satan's hand in the poor box on Good Friday. Meantime the pheasants going around in circles, like they *also* hooked on some private wire, invisible to the naked eye of redemption. Hamp, Baa-bay, I tell you Professor Tenderloin almost having a shit hemorrhage—the Mansion went up like the Holy Father had decreed that all the priests in New Orleans could have a free day on the Sabbath . . . My girls all looking up at me to find out what's to be done now; I'm shaking so, the rosary beads tumble off my neck and go tripping down the golden staircase. And my Oc-*toe*-genarian Bishop—who thinks that I am Mary Magdalene reincarnated—now raises my monocle to his one good eye and screams down there for all he's worth to Smidley Shockley: "Fool, Get thee to a nunnery." Because he also thinks Shockley is a faggot, now in drag. The monocle's made Shockley's pecker seem twice its size; and ain't nobody natural hung like that . . .

"Why, the nerve of that sonofabitch Shockley, consecrating my Mansion—when the old bishop at my right hand (who owns half the Palace) has consecrated it beyond that poor ass-bugger's powers to add or detract . . . Everybody with an informed body knew that. And every living with a swinging understood!

". . . Finally one of the ladies-in-waiting took a fly net and captured the spinning pheasants, as they nodded on freeze; on high, in the middle of the air, floating in their flying and not moving more than nine inches per hour; we had pheasant under glass that evening, Baa-bay. But the only way we could quiet old Professor Tenderloin down was to slip some of that prime pheasant meat into his cage; he stayed high for a week."

*   *   *

But now Nathaniel was looking over at the bottle of blue-black ink and wondering if there was enough left in the inkwell for him to finish recording Great-Momma Sweetie's story. About one-third of the ink left . . . If my hand doesn't drop off first, he laughed, flexing its iciness. Outside he heard a siren-wail, announcing an ambulance speeding past the frame house.

If he left the sleeping woman now to return tomorrow, would she want to finish? Would she be able to pick up where she had left off? He longed for some of Great-Momma Sweetie's old-time cooking. He opened the small refrigerator and fixed a ham-on-rye sandwich; for the insides of the refrigerator no longer contained the many foods it had in the old days of her mission. Tumbling and heaving in her sleep now upon the bed, Great-Momma Sweetie called out his name. *Here*

I am, Grandmother, he said. Now as he hurried to her side, pen and pad in hand, he thought back to Grandfather Witherspoon's early occupation as typewriter and stenographer. But had the great man ever been in such a position of writing down the words of any boss as long-winded as the fabulous Great-Momma Sweetie Reed? He doubted it.

Just then Nathaniel put down his pen and yellow legal pad.

—Wait a moment, Great-Momma Sweetie Reed! This lost soul of a father of yours is a horror; a nightmare. More of magician gone daft than Spottswood, hiding as he was behind the magician's cape or sleight of hand with his sleight of searing tongue. He's guilty as hell in all of this. Why, he set Shank up. Envied him over the unworthy Minnie-Bea's bonnet, simply as an excuse. *Pride goeth before the fall indeed.* He should've let Master Rollins Reed die out, I tell you! Ah, and think of the lot of poor Shank Haywood, as loathsome as that of Emmett Till. Why do you have to claim kin with him? Why not hold Foisty and Shank fast as your our blood kin? Kissing cousins. They are the ones who are the true blood of our vision; not that spineless rascal, that Iago-like rat, I. V. Reed. You are right, though, you need to scorn him. Put him on the rack. But you are too philosophical, Great-Momma Sweetie, about the meaning of the *fullness of the heart the mouth speaketh* business. Your interpretation, I mean, does not reflect the true loathing in your heart for him.

—Foisty is even harder to deal with. Some cousin to convert to cousin, bag and baggage. She should have plucked out the light of Rollins Reed's life . . . Not stooped to save him . . . And yet didn't this sinister but gifted storyteller, this narrow-spirited liar, I. V. Reed, ever get called down? Didn't Auntie Foisty find out something, if she was so prophetic? And what of your role in all of this, Great-Momma Sweetie, couldn't you take him on?—

—I'm about to tell you what I did. But let me tell you what else he did. And how all of this led to his promotion and his demotion, you might say, too. Oh, he was proud as he spoke, but I could detect some of his change of spirit, as he confessed to me.—

7

"The
Ravelled
Sleeve
of Care"

Well now, Sweet Angels, out of all of this is how I come to be Master Rollins' body servant. Auntie Foisty found a place for me to be remembered by Master Rollins, too, when he came up to know himself; I had been there a while asleep below his bed—living up in the Big House—wasn't sure of my station. But didn't do no good in the long haul, 'cause in a few days they returned Reece Shank Haywood to the plantation with bloodhounds baying on both sides of him; Mistress Sylvia had them give him the water cure. Master Rollins was still in a state of babbling 'bout his lost-found Jesus, two angels and Auntie Foisty. Scared to skin the mud-clay off

his face and body lest he reveal his old body self to hisself; Mistress
Sylvia saying Auntie Foisty gave him the mud cure of her wrinkle
creams so as he would stay young, get young gals in his arms . . . Leave
her as spite-work upon her very own bed.—
   Nathaniel, that was when I said to I. V. Reed:
   —You lied to Auntie Foisty, didn't you, to get her out there to the
Praise House? Didn't you?—And I. V. Reed, this father, wept and
didn't create up a mumbling word for about five minutes.
   Then:
   —Sweet Angel, I told her he had a bad fall from a tree while out
hunting and he swallowed up his tongue because see he was munching
on something at the time of his fall and had hurt his backbone (I kept
my lips sealed about Reece Haywood, 'cause I knew how a rattling
jawbone will jimmy up a jinx) . . . How Master Rollins Reed's windpipe was choking him to death and whatever he had been munching
on had stuck up in his windpipe, twisted about. I knew this was
enough to get Auntie Foisty going; this and the fact she had delivered
his father into this world, nursed him. I admit I knew my tale
wouldn't set too well on her stomach for long, like a tin of cold sweet
potatoes. But Auntie Foisty uncovers it all, too, when they return
Reece Haywood three days later and give him the water cure at
Mistress Sylvia's direction. This was after she discovers Master Rollins Reed suddenly sitting there one fine morning at her breakfast
table, bathed down in clay . . . Babbling and learning how he had been
out there cutting swift after your grandmother 'cause you see Auntie
Foisty had told him to confess everything to his woman. Him sitting
there naked and babbling at the mistress' front table . . . Calling into
super-rule the commandment he himself had about what was to happen to all runaways . . . and no respective persons.
   —Now, when all of this come out, Reece died; his mother, a cousin
of Auntie Foisty's, hanged herself on hearing of Shank's death by
tying the ropes and the chains they used to hogtie Shank and drag him
through the woods to a tree near Jubell's shack. In the morning they
found her yoked upon the tree. Auntie Foisty calls me down to her
shack house, where she's pulling out a shroud of remembering for
Shank, with those long arms circling it all 'bout the walls, from what
'pears as bathing towels of dark clouds. I find she starts from nothing
more than a wrapper, made from cloth she used for her long black
tunic . . . Telling me I'd never walk upright as a man again. As I look
—dare look up—into her face I saw how she wore the most horrible

scowl; ain't seen since time long ago when she was telling the little ones 'bout her knee of how them slaves suffer in the hole of the ship coming over; what they had to do to get over and come on through, past master, sharks, blindness, and slime of sins, horror of soulless men.

—Yes, and Auntie Foisty saying as long as she lives out I must stay up there in the Big House (she points out, pass layers of shroud seem to cling, twist and climb the walls; what's holding them up God knows, maybe a snake's body) and never come down to her quarters again. I was *lower den the weebil in the cotton . . .* And then Auntie Foisty said:

Cor-rupting chile, you baby breathing in the crib slay the hogs in the smokehouse wid poison, I 'members now, what it was I ask my Mass'r . . . when I saw it in here . . . And He says, Naw, Foisty, babe mussa live so we might know the deeps, as my hands as was set to the breathing . . . Hollowness super-rule in you nat-chile skullbone unto the tiniest nerve up you anklebone and the bleeding peppers of you sleek-heart-sole.

—Auntie Foisty told me before she passed, slaves would see me as a bloodhound all my days yet they would never tell on me—but would whisper my name in their heart of hearts and never trust me. The sole way I could ever hope for salvation was to tell the whole story out loud before I died out to each of my children and each of their children's children unto my last breathing gasp . . . Me personal, not through any hired third hand, but by my very own lapping tongue.—

Nathaniel, tears flowed about the chiseled features of I. V. Reed's face, as rainwater over a great stoneface in a mountain slab; but that don't seem to leap from the tear ducts now as fountain water from the wells of the spring; and I thought of the gas on his stomach all the days under Rollins Reed's bed and his epileptic fits visited on him, my mother said, before she could remember, in the beginning time.

—Sweet Angelina, I mean Sweet Reed, it ain't stop there 'cause she told Master Rollins Reed to keep me sleeping under his bed; knit to it the rest of my days, not only as body servant but even if we slaves were ever to be set free. Master Rollins just knew it was all a part of his new covenant with her; his salvation opportunity to be free, to redeem himself; something special about me, too, his curse; his father's curse all mixed up in it; I was the tar and the turpentine of his new blest condition . . . Dragging him off into the *wilderness as a shell of a man and back to her hands, the breathing one, who brought me forth as babe, now as new man.* But then Auntie Foisty told Master Rollins Reed, for a year I was to wear his old, discarded shoes and those holely and full of patches, too.

—Sweet Angel, old Auntie Foisty died out on the day Jubell told her she was with a child. This was all of how your mother come to be. As she come up to know herself, my second mind told me by marrying Angelina I'd get spite-salt out of my eyes after old Auntie Foisty, who saw my hand in Shank's slaughter so his body burst unto his kidneys, by water, but I was heart-tricked when Angelina come up to be so beautiful to look on, from the soles of her feet to the glory of her crown weren't a blemish in her; the breath of angels winging in her eyelashes set my heart to throbbing; her breath as a cup of ambrosia; cured just right by Mistress Sylvia's hand—my heart was bubbling over with gladness to take her up into my arms as wife when she was fifteen. She became my heart's only business . . . But, Angelina, you kept miscarrying and losing up babes. I thought old Auntie Foisty's hand is damning you up, Angelina, for Reece Shank Haywood's lot, as spite-work against me, just as I had commenced to suffering fits 'bout the same time Angelina was born . . . Then Sweet come along . . .

—But marrying didn't bring no consolation inside the previous condition of my burning heart 'cause Reece Shank Haywood's ghost haunted my nights under Master Rollins' bed—as a voice inside of a coffin (even though some of the slaves then took and stole away and shrouded it in the woods and buried Reece in a worn-out patch east of the plantation, after Auntie Foisty had buried him in an old praise shack, high on a hill; later on, after Stigwood Bloodworth got the parched-out patch into a parcel of land set aside as the Negroes' pure graveyard; but the Negroes made Reece's plot as the centerpiece of the cemetery) coming down through the ceiling at first, then through his bed as if up there dodging, ducking, and sliding round through the bedsprings and right down to me. Those hands, bleeding earlobe and Reece Haywood babbling: a ghost trying to speak out to me with water soaked through. The bell ringing in my head getting louder as his swollen body getting more like it's gonna burst open. Near each time it would happen for years I dazzled over how Master Rollins Reed (on the top bed) slipped Reece's clutches as the hands and body like the streams and streak of a fountain bed come over me, in a spring shower turned to a thunderclap in the garden.

—Well now, Master Rollins Reed's religion last long enough and hard enough for him never to peel back into the serpent skin of his old black-snake days—yet some of his Pale Rider ways seep into service through his high-riding temper, after the clay-mud fell away as a clown's grease mask. But he never left off praising Auntie Foisty and what she stamped down upon his natural mind as commandment. Giving her titles of tribute such as: *The Breathing One; Furious Auntie Foisty;* and *Unforgettable Foisty.* But he couldn't escape Reece Haywood's icy fingers and memory. Sometimes he'd don Mistress Sylvia's mask to blind Reece away from his seeing—the one with the rhinestones cast in it to blind Reece—which he commence to loose up.

—Sweet, I still young enough when Auntie Foisty cursed me and died to go right on living 'spite Reece Haywood's visits almost nightly. No brass-toe brogans for me like those field niggers; Master Rollins Reed hand me down those old shoes like Auntie Foisty command him out to do. I thought; why, her curse is laced up with a buried treasure; anyway she can't be so great, after all, she died out when she got wind of the news 'bout your grandmother pregnant; she couldn't stop it or me from going on living—curse and all. But I thought, too, watch out, I. V. Reed, you getting too many slabs of satisfaction (though no consolation from old hovering Haywood); and fatting hogs ain't bawn and bred for no patch of grazing luck.

—Master Rollins' sole was a little keener than mine, and by his own measuring three-fifths inch longer, so I'd add a pinch of scroll to fill it out, let the shoes sit in a lengthing wooden stock cast so as all of his hand-me-down black shoes, hipboots or lower-quarters, with gold buckles sewed in them, fitted out my soles as pairs, heel to sole; looked better on my feet than they did on his in the long run. Plunk my feet right side of his; hellfire to a icy tree limb, a muskmelon vine ain't shame to grow 'side of the morning glory—if his shoes outglowed mine; his face didn't shine up no different, in his sweat. Then Braidwood, the coachman, knew something of leathers, and when he drove Master Rollins Reed to Memphis where he, Golightly Braidwood, was learning to be a carpenter (ambition was his long suit, but he useda say: *Tomorrow morning may be the coachman's day for ploughing*) he'd take a pair to one of them free Negroes who not only fixed shoes but made them. I full remember well, *if the soles wears you out, you going to be poor all your livelong days; and if your heels wear out, you going to steal all your moonlight wasting-away nights.*

—Now this freed slave even come up with some new inventions for

sole and heelbone connections; he was a part-time preacher, too.
Good shoes, child. I could rock well, heel to the balls of my soles—
slope well, resting upon my feet with a pinch of scroll or cotton at the
toe part, as my feet still growing. I come to know I don't need no
cotton in the toe part; I'm a full-footed man now, sure as you born.
Could flex them shoes on my feet, instep to back heel as a young man
with a muscle to show off. I'd strut 'bout in those fine shoes all over
the Reed's plantation in the green grass; my soles sweet in those shoes
as peas bawn to a pod, but I guess boll-weevil sweet on cotton; no two
ways 'bout it. Old folks say I stepping around in them shoes—like a
soul waiting for dead man's shoes, meaning his buried treasure.

—But then one day after the War between the States, I try to peddle
off a pair of old shoes to one of those nigger preachers, and he spats
in the very tracks my sole makes and gives me up the one-butt shuffle
to boot; but says I ain't fit to wear the master's shoes; seems kinda
fishy to me . . . I never could understand how come . . . Try out others
but all rebuke the shoes and me in them . . . Soles mended up. Still
walking and humming good to the nerve center of the heelbone. Why,
even my backbone felt good in them steady walkers, on up to my
skullbone . . . Like the shoes those ballet dancers useda wear at one
of Mistress Sylvia's charity balls; slippers fit so fine they seem to be
the *understandings* what help them dancers go from leaping to flying,
up in the middle of the air, near to move the chandeliers to shaking
. . . Never could understand why them niggers wouldn't take to them.
'Cept Auntie Foisty's word-plague kept they association 'way from
any knot-tying backbone of feeling; 'cause of how part of me was tied
to Reece Haywood. Just like I don't understand why she told Master
Rollins Reed to hand them old shoes down for one year only. But he
stopped 'zactly to the one year of her commandment wishes.—

With those words I. V. Reed's body flipping on that mattress now
into all sorts of shapes. And, Nathaniel, that's when I said:

—Because you plagued out, fool, she knew those were the shoes of
a dead man.—

—Dead man? You the one with a unraveling veil, as a raving bat's
wing.—

—Did you think your master wouldn't have to taste Death, before
he perished, without *her* arms; just because he was famished to rule
forever? Or because *you* were supping in the shadow you sewed in the
shade of his rule, as a linen cloth for the feast table of duration?—

—Weren't no caul over *your* eyes when you was bawn to light, Miz

Sweet, I lay claim and witness. I was there, I brought you into this world smooth as a tailor's handiwork out your mammy's womb.—

—You what! Why, your soul's a stocking sewed by Satan, wrong side out.—

—Yes! I was hovering over your mammy's face. Good Book says: *of the fullness of the heart the mouth speaketh.*—

—. . . And did you think, I. V. Reed, that lily-livered white man would never have to flap up the ghost?—

—Sweet, your religion makes you forget elements prime learned from a proper-stitched heart such as respect for elders and the truth-spirit, face to face.—

—I. V. Reed, truth never had a pumping bloodline to your heart.—

—Ain't dead to my heart, but coupled with spirit and truth there, as the tongues of true lovers, Miz Sweetie.—

—Dead man! Auntie Foisty knew your master had died, *inside.* Then wrapped in the sleeves of her long, mourning-out, caring arms; and was cradled there; reborn there but as yet an infant in the spring. But his soul condition was as the shoes of a fisherman sunk in fathoms of mud by the fishing waters. She pulled him out about sixty percent of the sopping, sucking-down mud . . . But, fool, why do you think those poor, freed niggers didn't wear your shoes; want his shoes; couldn't give his bootlaces away at a flea circus, I bet; did you think to remember—you remember everything else with your long-head, like a tattered sleeve, flexing with gossip of a wind-gathering, rotting corpse—the curse about wearing the shoes of a dead man?—

—. . . *You* can't ease-drop on Death, daughter. Anyway, who you? Where you pump your prime wisdom? Not the well, or the getting place.—

—Don't I know a curse when I stare one down through the soul's veil, *Master* I. V. Reed, *sir?* Do I have to see the face in the mirror to know the soul? Or the hoof print of Satan to know the flaming breath of Hell.—

—. . . I'm trying to deliver the word out to you in the *fullness of my heart.* Listen as I delivers the rod down to you, colored woman, from on high; see if you can take your spirit out of your heart, up to the mountaintop. Let me show you the sides of the truth. What you think I been trying to do for you.—

—You listen up to me, for once in your lifetime, and learn how to re-collect them bones, old man, who's lost the shape of his days, turning and twisting into a hundred masks on his very afflicted bed.—

—Woman, who *you* to spew out a parable from the seed of my story on how you come to be straddling where you standing; when you oughta be kneeling to receive the father's final blessing . . . Instead you reminding me of yet another curse: my pumped-out bloodline.—

—I. V. Reed, what you know, other than how long it takes spittle of bread to drip down old man Rollins Reed's beard, where you stepped in and fetched it before it hit the floor. You could concentrate on that duty longer than you could the face of your returned baby-child.—

—Woman, didn't I walk with him, talk with him? Look into his green eyes, eyeball to eyeball? Face to face? Make him think I was his own? I ain't never lied to myself. Don't I in peculiar know what Mr. Lincoln said about *you can fool all the people some of the time; you can even fool some of the people all the time; but you can't fool all the people all of the time.*—

—. . . Mr. Lincoln sure was a good one to know all about fooling people, all right . . . Did you have to scoop up the blue-green diamonds of Rollins Reed's eyes turned backwards in his temple not to know the pale death in his face?—

—Woman, I'm telling you how I served him body and soul. Dressed the master underlinen, suit, shirts, socks to cap to his boots; undressed and stripped him down to his very loin-cloth . . . Still you of all peoples tell me, schooling me, I didn't know the man's soul condition as my own cut of cloth, when facts of the business is, I knew my master years before, during and after Auntie Foisty sowed a spell, a trance over Master's clay-tan temple. Him like a small child at first whose head's in a sack of butterflies; gone crazy over the shape and colors of their wings; *but* Master still ruling. Not dead, no two heads about it.—

—What does it mean, I. V. Reed, when you couldn't see inside out for serving your master's body and soul, wrong side out in your straight jacket?—

—Sweet Witherspoon, you trying me out to ride me, as a galloping ghost, on how I knew not my master inside out, wrong side up . . . Watching over him to the very second the clay-tanning commence to peel out of his face, as paint shavings on the front porch; the blood seem now to creep out of his face . . . He was stropped to me as much

as I bound over to him; I drew his water, but he drank from my cup, though it was thinly cracked; slit to my doing.—
—I. V. Reed, you more of a fiend than a fool.—
—Bootstrap to long johns, crown of the man's head to sole of his feet on the green grass of the mountain's side and back again to the pure wisdom teeth, as worn pearls in his mouth. Who *you* schooling, Sweet? What year you graduate by Ole Miss? Master was tight with me as soul fit to the body. Tell me he didn't still rule, super-rule, 'spite . . . Shit, Sweet, I'm the one who's just now delivered down the words on how my master come out the Praise Shack, his condition, his 'pearance, his pure words; unstitched from a long night's deep sleep. I ain't jawboning, I'm facking. Can't you read my words on my lips and see the breath of the truth blowing hard behind them? You ain't so old, blackhearted woman! Smart, either. Why, I even come to be as Master's seeing-eye dog till his death in eighteen and ninety-six. But by then he starting to call me Uncle Ivy, though he's the oldest; as we sat by the fireplace I'd be telling him stories, as songs of old. Why, he got in such a failing state, he'd put on mismatch shoes. A dark blue shoe and then a black one. I'd say, *Master, you got mismated shoes on.* He'd say, *Which one, left or right?*—
—I'll wager hell in a feather bed you warmed up the soles of your feet to dream of being close to a fireplace in January—with a bowl of berries and milk—and watching the flames go turning the logs upside down . . . But facts of the business is, you sucking out the spittle crumbs in Reed's beard as supper; or under the bed when the house was cold to the heart and you don't have long knitted sleeves to welcome in sleep, by the fireplace.—
—Yeah, all I had to worry 'bout was hanting, flying Reece Shank Haywood's hovering spirit. Trouble enough to carry me away. Now you come here with new-found shit to spread, Sweet, *your* lips foul as sow's-belly breath. Listen up here, woman, to the word I'm trying to flesh out to you, deliver you up by. Haywood's steamy spirit commence to prey on my mind—suspended from a stock on a platform in the middle of this very room, come branching out of the ceiling; hovering over me in a wingspread damn near every night: outfitted in bloodspots.—
—Oh, so you did get some troubling parts of your fit propers. Heaven's ear isn't stone deaf to righteous music if the mourning's in tune.—

—Damn you, Sweet, to the skeleton breastbone of Auntie Foisty in the boneyard, 'cause you sure ain't no angel of mine . . . She didn't tell how Haywood would follow me out, hover over me as a buzzard near each night for a dead body with his choking fingers as claws at my throat so I never knowed a night's peace till Master Rollins Reed died out in ninety-six. But I'm commencing to see a mite of how you lacing your sass; though you feeling 'bout as fast as molasses in January; but NAW shit, Foisty can't sew no shadow curse from the grave so long it outrun the shade of Time and up through the sole of a man's heel to his anklebone to his hipbone to his backbone slab. Lawd, oh *naw,* up, up, UP! Her arms weren't so long, to play God, her fingers not so skillful they anointed into Death-kneeling time. Hell, even a patch of moonlight give way to a crack of bleeding dawn, Praise Shack to the Big House.—

—Auntie Foisty knew, all right. Her curse didn't slip out from an unknit tongue of a orge's flapping lip.—

—Her arms can't cast, too short, can't box.—

—Don't you know you had to taste some parts of death for the poison Ivy crop you grew, fallen son of the morning.—

—Foisty's arms weren't so long and just and powerful to cast a fishnet over time past the graveyard . . . Hell, Foisty weren't ninety-nine and a half percent when alive. Didn't I hear tell how she kill every nigger twin bawn for a time—thinking in them old-time African ways how twins was a curse . . . Folks say she seven different women borrowed together as seven meats in a turtle; I say she loathed the natural nature of men to the soles of her feet.—

—Yeah, and you turn into more shapes than earth, wind and fire . . . She knew what she wanted you to know, I. V. Reed, and not to know. Be and not be; because she knew the nature of the kind of man you are; now, grieve on that! Like a seeing-eyed dog with his master's favorite slipper at its nose. Maybe Auntie Foisty's lips were sealed and her tongue tight to her gums because she had her covenant to keep, before she slept away in Death's deep, dark, reviving arms . . . Keeping her own counsel, as they say; like the laces of a pair of brogans waxed and tied to the style of her own gait in her own time, rhythm and step . . . Why, even you, I. V. Reed, allowed as how backwater time stayed on her second mind's command. Who are you to say Auntie Foisty's wings were full of patches?—

—You a prophetess? How you know so much, Sweet Mistress

Reed? You weren't even thought of—still a corner beam sunk in the whites of my waxing eyes . . . Then: you was darting round there as a sparrow's wings. Knee-high to a 'squito and lacing spittle with sass since they bought you, not my Angelina, back home in a sack; I done heard tell of hindsight but you a sight to see with your watching, batting eyeballs in the back of your nappy head before you had a head-to-be . . . Like you born knowing; who gave you a halo? You ain't got no blood tie to Foisty; though you got enough gumption to give a rabbit backbone to try a bear . . . Then you flew off to the North soon as you come to smelling your nature . . . Flying off like a bird lost from its flock, going off on the wrong way backwards towards the dying sun, up in the cold Northern states. 'Zactly how come you can't 'proach your father's dying bed a-humble? Love? Lawd, love's another pair of silk slippers I don't believe you possess in your nature to slip on.—

—You tied the knot so as I could be married away from this plantation . . . I. V. Reed, let me address something to your second mind's command: how long you wear those shoes? His shoes? How long did you say that white man's soles measured out the gait of your days?—

—Sweetie *Reed*, don't say just simple *white* man; 'cause he was and is your grandpappy and don't you ever forget it, Miz Smarty Sweet . . . Even though he tried to forget it. I had the last of those pairs half-soled, year before Master Rollins give up the ghost—then the tongue come unstitched in the left one. The heel broke off the right one; had them sewed up and repaired. Young Rev. Stigwood Bloodworth delivers them up from Braidwood. There they be over in the corner; one pair full-soled in the back room. I could never bring myself to stepping them off to the grave.—

—They've might near outran you—as this strawberry bonnet of my mother's, your wife Angelina's bonnet.—

—Don't bring up no Angelina's bonnet . . . You two-faced vixen, Minnie-Bea.—

—Two-faced? You were the rattlesnake my mother should've turned on or crushed, after she cursed Mistress Sylvia to her natural accursed face.—

—Vixen woman, live away from my bed; lies might blossom out into a shroud from your shit-spreading tongue. You think I'm coming apart, but every goodbye ain't gone.—

—Your soul going off in seven different directions, and only the bat wings of Satan's going to collect your parts on his back and fly you on home to your pale, eternal reward—.

—Why don't you put the bonnet back on at a distance, so I can see you better; colored womens need something to brighten they face so you can make them out plain in the darkening light. So we can stand to look at you face to face. Sunbonnet, ain't I give it down to her? It was my own mother's; she had three; gave one to Minnie-Bea, the whore.—

—And now it's all unraveling, I. V. Reed, I'll leave it off for sure. It's been on too long, with all my cares and her woes; but not knowing, seeing too much; but if you . . . If you don't want me to wear it, it must surely be something wrong in my needing to wear it.—

—. . . Master Rollins died at seventy-nine and here you come spite-eyed to bury me off on my dying bed at seventy-nine. Thinking I got ten thousand dollars stowed away in the soles of my shoes, I wager . . . You mean to tell? Naw, you trying to outfox the shadow of Foisty, in the hanting and the cursing.—

—Fiend . . . Your soul is mended out in woe by Satan's patch-work.—

—You stop calling me a fiend. I'm your needing pap in Almighty God's sight. Those plaits crisscrossing each other on your head solely hiding the scabs and sores of your spiteful brain.—

—I. V. Fath—I'm trying to tell you that you were wearing the shoes from the body of a dead man! She, Auntie Foisty, had only healed up enough of Rollins Reed so as his soul would not come unraveling out of his crawling condition. But he was dead in his previous condition.—

—When pigs fly north to Hell . . . Master didn't need no nursery.—

—But then, after coming out of her arms, recollecting up enough of his drying-out spirit power so he could walk without crawling the rest of his creeping days; though he came out crawling at first as parched bones, first crackling together to live. You yourself said that, and he wasn't nothing but a pod of a man when you pulled him into that Praise Shack to deliver him up from death's door, you hoped, and all carried away with yourself like a hog gliding on see-through ice; then spying on Auntie Foisty's reviving Reed's soul.

—I. V. Reed, Auntie Foisty wound the sleeve of her long-arm curse over you, as a shroud to not only walk the earth harnessed to your master's shadow in stride, like a flock of poisoned buzzards shadowing a wounded horse, with his dead rider drooped in the saddle; but your spirit was marked, your very soul was to crawl the gates of hell the balance of your days to the bottom of his bed—like a bedbug saddled to the cot as a prisoner of a dying master's mattress, without the will of a bedbug to bite your master's pale hand, or back.—

—Get your buzzard's breath out of my scenting.—

—Yes, and Rollins Reed didn't want to wear those shoes, too, no wonder he gave them up with such a free spirit . . . They were paired to your soles and to take them would mean going down dead in the soles of a dead man twice, that's what those freed slaves knew within their bones.—

—. . . You half-white bitch, get, I. V. Reed said, his arms flapping about as wings to cover his face, though they appeared as a skeleton's flouncing sleeves in a windstorm.

—So now you call me out of my name, you half-blind man. I thought at least you could see clear out of one of those eyes, as you were his seeing-eyed pup. His lap dog . . . Who you think you looking at? Maybe Death delivered up your proper eyesight and left your body as a sack of leavings to moan out the past. But you haven't got the insight to grieve out your unmourning, woeful soul; you like to dip your mind in the waters of remembering for its forgetting powers and the forgiving waters they can spat up on you, as foam beads. Because you are after all righteous, honest, honest Ivy to the bone of your body, like the feathers in a whore's bed.—

—Commandment says out plain as salt through a widow woman, honor thy father and thy mother; and you suppose to be a Christian, 'bout as much one as old persecuting Saul. If only I had a rod, I would reel your spoilt body in till spilt blood racked your hide as drops of rainsalt cross a bee-bit back; sure would be sweetmeat to my good eyes to learn you some humility. Woman, I was hoping the spirit of Auntie Foisty's long-arm sleeve would flap after Shank Haywood, as whipping winds lengthening breath to a torchlight, as his pure guide.—

—What in the moonlight! And what if the breath you breathing on those coals in Hell wakes Satan to wrap you in his flaming arms, in a whirlwind seven times, sevenfold? And you all of a sudden see a pair of arms; reach out to be taken up and it's Reece Shank Haywood's being, but just at that second he hides his face from you in the hover of his wings.—

—Where's my flaming strop for this hounding vixen? A torch would be as a e-ternal flame of his memory for all to see.—

—Oh, so it would glow for all and be a deadbeat giveaway in the moonlight . . . But the light touches not your soul.—

—I'll set lacing fire to your hide before I die, Sweet Angels.—

—Your body's wrapped in flaming chains on that burning River to Hell.—

—I'm still breathing and I ain't 'bout to go out less I take your hide to Hell with me, if it be God's Almighty's will.—

—I. V. Reed, I see every form of Evil seething in each new drop of breath you draw; and *that's* but the web of your terribleness.—

—Woman, you got up there north and let your lawyer man learn your nature, your meat was sweet. But you ain't nothing but a rack of fatback on a grill to me. You remember your very being come from the cracked slumber of my shank.—

—I. V. Reed, you fiendish bat out of Hell; you remember everything, but you can't allow yourself to recollect and understand what you fat-mouthing, like something inside of you was cut off in the beginning time, disconnected bones, deep inside of you sputtering in the dark creeping to the edge of the river; try as you might sometimes your breath can give truth nothing but a brief light—as a stuttering candle, and even that you have to blow out; but that's how you got an eternal light in Hell, mister honest, honest Ivy.—

—I wasted all my breath and the fullness of my heart, as I did the fire of my loins, in bringing honest life to you, simple-minded harlot of this morning's two-faced light.—

—Honest Ivy, my foot . . . Why do you . . . What do you think in the name of heaven that old woman, Auntie Foisty, the one who brought you into this world, meant that time when she kept on saying: *Massa Roddy dead, don't you see?* Super-ruled over what? Misrule? With you his footman! And his foot up your.—

—You don't understand nothing of them bloodspots; or the duty you have to me, the creator of your being; your breath.—

—. . . The more the wonder of His works—that He could create you out of nothing in His terribleness; the whirlwind of His wonders.—

—. . . 'Cause you was not there in the beginning time, when Auntie Foisty gathered Reece Shank Haywood up into her arms; when they left him for dead after the water cure and carried him away stock and all to her shack but she fell with Shank in her arms several times along the way; her tears falling on the ground—and the ground seemed to cry aloud. To be receiving them old bloodspots with each fall of him' in her arms, drinking the blood from the murdered Shank's body, as his body burst by the water cure and the ground itself seemed to be mourning as tongues and seen out of my other eyes the bloodspots, again as tongues of receiving and mourning out ... I'm trying to learn you, blackhearted woman of the curse, the curse what's on you, too.—

Nathaniel, it was then that I. V. Reed commenced to huffing and puffing and spitting about the ingratitude of a child, but soon he is choking and like he got something down his windpipe and I think he's having one those epileptic fits. Rubbing the tiny green diamond ear-bob in his earlobe in a pinching fit: if he rubbed it in the proper way, I thought, he would disappear. I rushed in on I. V. Reed to help him, in his ailing; full of loathing on my second mind's command, deep to my heart's core. I saw he was famished for sleep but feared what the twin seamstress of sleep might sew across his windpipe.

—Water, water, water, I. V. Reed cries out as a whistling wind in a teapot. His dark face breathing and pouring sweat. His right eye-brow arching like a tom cat's back awakened to his scorching fur before a fireplace, where he's been dozing in comfort his long days and nights away. That wee green earbob in his left earlobe like a clown's joke below the big top at the circus. A luster to his cheeks touched there by the rosy fingertips of rouge; the jowls bloated as roasted apples. His body commencing to flip in every direction, even in death he can't let the Angel of Death hold him to a shape, and a definition of anything that doesn't shoot into twelve different directions of wind circles; nor give him peace. Maybe I think Satan sewed the stocking of his soul so fast that even the Angel of Death can't unbind him to bind him up for the journey.

Nathaniel, I hurry to the nightstand to get I. V. Reed a drink of cool water and I trip over the shoes he's been talking about and I spill half the water in the jug; finally, I get some water trickling into a white cup with the shape of a swooning swan's neck turned about backwards and I try to sprinkle some drops from the cup down on I. V. Reed's scaly-chapped lips with my fingertips; then of a sudden his lips are parting but are weak as a babe and slobbering like one, too, but then I think yes, and you better watch out lest *it* bite you; like a python dozes on death.

Nathaniel, I'm lifting I. V. Reed partial into my arms; before I know quite what I am doing; I am trembling with him in my arms with new-found tears streaming down my cheeks, locked in this awful embrace with the father's arms about me for the first time; but it was too late to let him go away back down on his bed of roses, I think aloud; he's light as a bird shorn of its feathers; then I'm raising him full way up in the bed into my arms to something of a sitting-down position and finding out how heavy he is to lift up, though his body seems so fragile it is weightless. Then I'm beating him on the back for all he's worth—like he's got a crust of bread or a fishbone trapped in his windpipe—and then I'm wondering of what Auntie Foisty must have felt when she lifted Reece Shank Haywood up. I see how he's near choking to death and I put the cup down and hear a lowdown condition stirring within my naked soul, past loathing and grief and from way back when; my very heart seems to tumble down to my dull boot tops, and my fingertips shaking. And that's exactly when I cried out in another voice to I. V. Reed:

—And when that patroller man plunked me down on Rollins Reed's knee and you stood there looking down at me from behind that screen door and scratched on it when I lifted my arms out to you, up to you; and I wondered what does my daddy have to say to me with my arms lifted out to you. You kept on scratching on that screen door with your long fingernails as if to scratch out my eyes for an apology, reappearing in your life as the vision of your wife's life taken from you. Blaming me because you dared not blame them. And I wondered what was wrong with me that you would not want to take me up into your arms; you who had not seen me since I was four and they had taken me and your wife off to another slavery. And without your wife to hold on to the mask of your greasy face; that screen door, as but a veil. Nathaniel, I had him in my arms. Oh, what ailed me, I. V. Reed, that you shunned your own baby doll so? Nathaniel, his sole answer was to keep on choking. In his choking there was a babbling; he seem to have lost his tongue as a going-down slow swimmer in his stroke.

Nathaniel, I found myself shaking I. V. Reed up and down and down and up and begging and cursing him, and tearing at his powder blue sweater to know. As I shook and tore at him, and he choked, I commenced to thinking of that big old angel doll, with wings of porcelain, that I found in the closet the week they returned me, that had been Mistress Sylvia's as a child. If you shook the doll hard enough, a sobbing bell sound would come out like a hollow dry cough.

Once I got so mad with I. V. Reed for shunning me that I tore the big angel doll apart with a butcher knife to find the sobbing bell on the inside and smashed it, I guess forever and ever, and only found nothing but stuffings inside of torn-up British paper money, then inside of that packets of cotton balls, till finally at the very center of the angel doll's makings I discovered a chain linked about two twisted crossed sticks glued to the cotton balls and wound and bound through the doll's body to its crimson dress; Mistress Sylvia must've called her angel doll Dogwood, because on the back of the doll, below its neck, in a child's scrawling print was the name: *Dogwood*. Nathaniel, I cried out as I heard I. V. Reed choking:

—Did you hate me for surviving your wife, who was my beloved mother, after all? Even when he left off looking at me with the spite scratching out the feeling part of his eyes so that he was blinded to life and love, I must have kept my arms lifted out to him because finally it was old man Rollins Reed who forced my arms down one at a time as you close down the coffin. That's when Angelina's song come back to me, that time on the porch and now: *Angel got two wings to hide my face, two wings to carry me away.* I cried out, *Dadda,* three times. You, I. V. Reed, denied your blood being there.

Oh, how could I know then that Rollins Reed's closing down of my arms was a signal to me that my little arms were only remnants from Angelina in his sight and should not start the seeking out of his clasp because . . .

I. V. Reed arms were never there to have and to hold but to mock and ridicule. Nathaniel, I guess that's when I could see the evil of spite-work upon not only I. V. Reed's soul, but how it had come to transform my soul whenever I was away from my church and my God. I thought upon I. V. Reed's presence in my life or faced the shadow of his life, upon my very life, across it, me his only blood, marking he had ever existenced.

Nathaniel, then it was that I. V. Reed starts to yelling, screaming and pointing towards the ceiling, his arms flinging out like the winging branches of a tree in a storm knocked back away from his quivering mattress; me thinking aloud, why, this very bed is a pagan altar; his thorny bed of roses forever and ever. Just then, Nathaniel, he cries out:

—It's Reece Shank Haywood, Angel-Sweet Angelina. It's Shank. I sees the dawn of his bloated fingers drowning me down; him who took my apple-faced gal. Lawd, his body 'bout to explode with water.

In my mind he cast me away with a rock-shattering blow to the mirror in the moonlight; as my body seem to crash into the mirrors. Shank 'buked and scorned at every doorway, even unto me what's bent on helping him, in the long run. Earlobe bleeding. No one listening. Listening to his words. Reece trying to fly to freedom to a freedom past men's arms, and eyes. Them bloodhounds baying to where he cries out, *Souls can be reborn,* like his mind has flipped out of the wings of his spirit and ain't no place to hide in the windstorm.—

Nathaniel, I. V. Reed collapses on that mattress; I try to beat more water out of him, as I'm trying to beat breath back into him again. Or am I beating him to beat him to death? Lawd, today! He's holding on to the flap of my sleeves for dear life; as if to tear me into caring. In our non-talk now, I wonder fitfully why am I trying so hard to save his life, even as earlier I had tried to hard to slit his throat with the razor my tongue made, down to his very backbone. And thinking of this I dared not put my mouth near his breathing; he's about to tear the sleeves of my shirt with new-found strength now, in those arms, just as I'm commencing to pity him with less loathing and my power over him. And I think, well now, the strength of a dying man is something to contend with, all right; for the light of his living seems to be fading fast and he's still swimming strong; hateful in death.

Nathaniel, now I put my head to his chest where his heart's suppose to be yet pumping blood, because of a sudden he fades on me, almost completely. All light of his limbs comes to a sack of dry weeds in my arms. I can't hear no heart throbbing. But he was always complaining of a previous condition of the heart before the beginning time of my return. He has cold feet. I am excited. Not to hear that he no longer has a heart for life? I wonder. For if he is no longer alive that don't make him my father no longer? Does that make me free of his will? Though father he never was of a will to be. Now that comes down to me pure and simple, as the first gentle raindrops upon the green tender leaves of blessed summer and why was I, why had I been trying to force him to be something that I. V. Reed had never honestly felt, nor tried to feel within the circulation of his heart?

Nathaniel, I also realize that I. V. Reed is not given of the gift to feel fatherly; yet that don't lead him out of the path of duty to me of trying to feel. But that's the moment when something says to me: But, Sweetie you haven't spoke very daughterly to him, either. Now that he is purely dying you feeling some parts of guilt, which is proper, you trying to beat that fear part out of yourself by beating him to death on the back—even as you trying to beat feeling into him—as you beating to help stop what's choking and ailing him. But this feeling, this thought don't reveal no new skin off the hideaway of my heart. I had been trying to not only beat *father* into him, that never was his natural spirit's nature; but was trying to beat him to death to boot.

Facing all of this in me now, Nathaniel, I fell back for a time and gasped. Then I found a small mirror in my purse and held it before his face with my right hand, while I cradled him with my left arm, and then to his nose to see if I could see any faint-breathing shadow frost on the mirror's face. Not the faintest gasping seem to make a picture of breathing on the mirror's facing. I think maybe I. V. Reed's dead for sure, by my hand or choked to death by his notion or vision of what Shank Haywood's ghost did to him in death, as if Justice could speak from the grave, much less in life. I catch myself now gasping harder than ever, as if I'm trying to gasp for the both of us. But as I now ease him back down and rest his head upon the pillow, something rolls off the edge of his bed; I. V. Reed gasps aloud again, like a small child that's been holding his breath to make his parents fearful as a way of punishing them; or maybe he's spotted what's rolled to the edge of his bed, what's been below his twisting, worm-wretched body, and caught up in the sheet, and rolled now onto the floor, suddenly possessed of legs. I pick it up and discover a small pinch-folded waxed article out of his gray snuff pouch; a black wing-shaped masquerade mask creased and frazzled and frayed pale at the edges with some scratched letters at the sides.

Nathaniel, now as I undo the mask from its tiny pinched binding, it keeps getting larger and larger. I see how it's the shape of two black wings. I rush to the bureau drawers in Sylvia's old room to get a mirror, that I might see the markings better. Don't find even a look-ing-glass. But what I do discover is one of Wayland Woods' letters written to Sylvia and Rollins Reed. I take it with me and now I look at that masquerade mask closer in one of Mistress Sylvia's huge floor-length, oval-faced mirrors in the front of the Big House, with the aid of a little mirror I find glued to the big mirror's backing. Makes things twice the shape of their natural size and now I see Mistress Sylvia's initials are thinly outfitted, as a dressmaker's design (and recalling to my mind those window curtains Mistress Sylvia helped my Angelina sew into the wedding gown for Mother's marrying up to this mattress-bedded-down I. V. Reed). For a time, Nathaniel, I can't help but think out loud that maybe I. V. Reed wore Mistress

Sylvia's mask to frighten off the ghost of Reece Shank Haywood, the same one that Rollins Reed donned to escape Haywood's sight. I can hear I. V. Reed heaving in the bedroom.

Nathaniel, then I come to myself and move swift out of the mirror's presence—recollecting how the old folks used to warn that mirrors fleece spirits, steal and suck away souls like a voodoo man sucking away on a black cat bone—then I'm suddenly howling at myself; why did I take the mirror out to catch up I. V. Reed's breath, if he had any? Now I commenced to read Wayland Wood's letter through and through. Especially where he wrote of his tender feelings for his daughters and his fierce intentions to redeem them from bondage. Tears ran down my cheeks without mercy but as impatient raindrops. I hurry back to the shuddering I. V. Reed, twisting and vaulting now into new shapes upon his master's bed, like a sparrow on a limb of a tree hanging upsides down and spinning about, flung broadcast in a windstorm, but Lawd most alive! as if because of the watching eye, Death had suddenly focused his eyes upon my heart, and the last gasps of his soul, once he realized that Death had focused his wild, pale beam on him. For maybe the will to live isn't any greater than the will to die, until that last fraction of a split second when you realize the pale rider ain't playing and his eye is cocked for you, lasso in hand.

Nathaniel, me thinking: I. V. Reed, no wonder Death marked you down in a corpse's suit. For now that I. V. Reed had summoned up as his last fit of strength to tackle Death and me too, I found myself laughing as a dry coughing coming up from a pump before white water spittles forth, thinking of his spirit as his garb, as half fire, half smoke, a touch of thunder, what they all call the eighth-day wonder . . . For when I thought about it I. V. Reed was the only one who had survived this place, from the old days, the beginning time, though the plantation itself seemed about to collapse upon him. Maybe it had something to do with a combination as mysterious as a conjurer's mix of *his* stubbornness and *his* willfulness on the one hand (he still refused to call me by my rightful name without mixing it up with mother's) and his terribleness of bending to anything, as a branch in a windstorm; all made manifest by his reverence for the master's will and his silver supper tin, while licking the platter—to suck it down as an odd way of conquering, and conjuring. As I thought of this I said to myself: *You be careful, Sweet, yourself, if you fool enough to cradle your horrible father in your arms again as he seems to collapse, that he don't drag you along with him into death, choke off your breathing, as he appears like he's going go down dead.* But just then I. V. Reed is calling out:

—Reece . . . Reece . . . Reece.—

—If it would please Gawd I pray you'd hanged yourself by the straps you made into a slingshot from Mistress Sylvia's masquerade gown.—

—I did *not* kill Shank.—

—Then he's yet alive; you're a well man hanging at a balance on a limb, bird watching, and aping tricks Spottswood taught your master. And my name is Angelina.—

—I'm hanted but ain't no guilt riding on my shoulders; his hands at my windpipe, turn night into day, as breathing coals of accursed light.—

—Stocked breath of your betraying smokes in Shank's blood.—

—What was Shank to you other than what you hear you know and what you hear not you know more of?—

—More man than memory; and more memory than you can ever run away from in your knowing.—

—You name Shank a man. Gal, why can't you call me father, who named you.—

—Named me but can't call me by my name. My mother *named* you as my father; that doesn't mean you are a man; nor a father.—

—Then I'll start the game and show you my hand and my sleeve when I oughta show you the back of my hand, daughter; you hurl poison words at the father like dice all coming up snake eyes. And you feel like Miz Lady Luck eyeing me tossed: a knotted sheet on this mattress as a loser.—

—You played dice with Satan all your days, so you could be free to play the role of slave, that's all you've had rolled up your sleeve was a sleeve about your soul washed in blood, inside out, shaken before my eyes to see, that I might not see, like the steam before a wet wash; you want me to believe your naked soul is more than a knot inside of a rolled-away knot, as a rock and yet like a rock; smooth as a heart of stone.—

—My Redeemer lives: I await his judgment call. Who you to roll my soul to Hell? Coming here with your face half made up; and looking cross-eyed.—

But then suddenly he said:

—Reece . . . Reece, don't harm me no more . . . Reece, it ain't me who's the witness. I ain't no more to blame than the land, the river flooding. Knotted and froze-up ground seem to take to his bloodspots as seed to a new season of a sudden come in winter, and me, I look to the sky to see if one them earth-face-changing 'clipses weren't pregnant in the witch-brewing storm.—

—Old dying nigger—you to blame, all right, for his giveaway and his downfall. Just like you to blame for the selling of me and the yeaing of it.—

Saying this now, Nathaniel, as I looked down now on that mask in my shaking hands that I've rolled up. Reminds me now somehow a little of those oxygen masks they use, the way they wing out, today in the hospitals.

—Reece, you can't hear me but I can see you plain as a riding ghost without a saddle. Shank, I was praying out for your pure escape though I gave you time to gallop and fly away. Why plague me out with more woe? Why woe-plague me? How could I know you couldn't hear me to know.—

—There you go lying out again, I doubt if you prayed for him or anybody; or if you did, Almighty God was so shocked by your voice he probably thought your echo-breathing came from off the veil of Lucifer's flapping wings—trying to spite his way back to the Kingdom using reverse english in flight . . . Thought it was the spittle off the wings of your cooing sleep, or the spittle from bread crumbs in Rollins Reed's beard . . . Your memory's but a wheel greased with leaves that you can't hardly turn away. Why the master couldn't hear you so, how could Shank? Talking about couldn't hear nobody praying—way down here. Auntie Foisty wanted you buried under Reed's bed; he, who was *your* perfect master; and allowing as how he believed without you below he would not believe he was saved above, without finding you below, as he would look down in the morning to find his bedroom slippers, and not finding them, look for you to find them . . . a prisoner to your devilish delights and his delights.—

—. . . 'Cause you see, Sweet Angel, in the lullaby of naked time, ahahah; it was my rock what slammed upsides Reece's head at his eardrum; yes, leaving more than a pearl mark of blood dripping into the sole-step his prints made and falling, in back of him, as the talking tongues of his shadowing grave. A bloodhood, hanting, 'bout his earlobe, as a voice from a face coming out from a mountain slab in the wilderness . . . speaking to him 'cause he can't hear . . . a double ear of remembering in the mirror.—

—Come clean, I. V. Reed, ain't no rock shelter in your dungeon; though you cleaving to my sleeves, as the straps on the gown of truth; your mistress' masquerade may have dropped from the master's mattress to the floor but you ain't dropped your masquerade yet.—

—. . . AhAHAH . . . Knocking off his hearing senses forever and ever.—

Nathaniel, I had heard him without listening, spoken too fast, without my mind taking on the shape of what his words were unveiling. Then it struck me.

I seemed to see cobwebs whirling about like wine-drunken dancing ghosts; their dance without form, substance, shape of color and then the words *of the fullness of the heart the mouth speaketh* came down on me, not so much as he had been saying that, and trying to use that as a hiding place for his tongue, but what that Bible verse had forced out of his mouth—if you use the Good Book to hide behind, you got to live with what it forces you to live by . . . Then I heard myself crying out:

—. . . Oh NAW . . . Lawd! How many heads have the demons of Hell?—

—Yes, a curse I tell you, woman, a pure curse . . . When Shank ran along the roadside and picked his way to cellars or praise shacks known to plantation slaves . . . Secret passageways in church towers, and barns; they tried to give him out directions but he couldn't make out their words. I guess he couldn't make out their sign language, talk, none too much . . . What he could only led to his confusion of steps . . . Maybe he couldn't settle on being without ear-hearing.—

—Settle? Without his hearing? Did I hear you right, honest, honest Ivy? Without his . . . Lawd, today! Why hast Thou forsaken me by giving me too much knowledge before I could stand and gird myself to know the weight of this accused cross, spat forth from the mouth of this water-and-blood-spouting creature of the morning?—

—. . . Haywood's blood outflinging his shadow.—

—Reece Shank Haywood had to exist on the directions of what? Motions? And gestures? Back to all of that? Your rock? The blow from your rock that drove him to his freedom took his hearing and left him open as a church door to chains, bloodhounds, death and the whirlwind of chance as a shell sailing upon the waters . . . I. V. Reed, you still *ain't* got the commencing of your propers.—

—Even through it all, Reece Haywood was able to get away for a time. But he couldn't hear them when they got close to his trail. Some slaves 'fraid to help 'cause they thought some patrollers hit him upsides the head with a rifle and he had 'scaped them for the second, with new-fell blood flying everywhere and bloodhounds hot from Hell would be scenting closer to his trail; there by their trail.—

—Fiend. Didn't you know his blood meant that you were cursed from the soles up, where his blood dropped at every pace of his flinging footfall; each time you slipped so easily and swiftly into the shoes of your master's shoes; Reed's body still foul; laced with after-birth forever and ever of his previous condition, no matter how much Auntie Foisty had tried to tame, deliver and order him.—

—. . . Lawd as talking seed: drums of the throbbing heart.—

—No more foul than a hooked fish's last gasping breath.—

—Earth was sucking up Reece's blood, as mouths. Fast as the rainwater fell from his earlobe . . . Self-righteous bitch's breath; I'm the one what told you of grieving and the falling of his blood. Don't remake my woe no deeper than the watery grave of his water cure.—

Nathaniel, Reece had to exist on what? Motions? Gestures? Then my mind was flung back to the time the converted patroller man came after me to carry me home; I sat upon Rollins Reed's lap and saw I. V. Reed scratching away at the screen door.

—I. V. Reed, you had to re-create yourself out of that white man's shoes to know your soul and veil your face behind the screen of cares and masks.—

—Your education turns my words out their flesh; scratch the lights out my eyes, so you can find your way home straight in the clear moonlight.—

—You got more faces than the man in the moon.—

—Sweet, you like the waste productions we found of Mistress Sylvia's body. You see yourself as the gems we found; but your tongue turned green, as corrupt as your body's wasteful tongue.—

—I. V. Reed, in your straight jacket you still had span enough to scratch me out of your life; I sat there as little seven-year-old child, lost and found . . . Now lost again, too.—

—Sick woman, you sick from the soles of your feet to the balls of your heels; you without a lick of soundness in you. How I going to heal you from my dying bed, if you ain't willing to submit to the truth?—

—Love, old man . . . No wonder you loathed Wayland Woods. He knew how to love his daughters past the letter of love to the spirit of sacrifice, as the *cause* of his soul. Love: I screamed for it, scratched out for it, as a new-found daughter of seven. Reached my arms out to you. You scratched my heart out with your nails: that screen door was a coffin you were closing in a clawing off of my soul . . . Then you scratched me out of your life to be rid of me and sent me to marry when I was still a child.—

—Child brides weren't curiosity in the land, woman; your bonnet was set and cocked.—

—You and Rollins Reed and Jericho Witherspoon struck a deal over my body and soul; but masked it as a covenant that's been anointed.—

—You stood in the oval mirrors smelling yourself for me to know you was in the time of your beginning, mooning period . . . to know the shape of a man's feel.—

—That's when a child becomes a woman to you, when she starts her.—

—Yeah, and when she stops is when she ceases being.—

—Never mind if I was ready or not to take a groom to bed as a husband.—

—How you get shaped up by a different rib? You made in the figure and form of woman to be made over into a lady by a man's cutting figure.—

—I was a girl in a woman's body.—

—'Zactly what I'm talking 'bout, I wasn't 'bout to see my own flesh and blood go counterfeit and become a perfume woman like Minnie-Bea. Besides, Jericho Witherspoon seemed like a pretty good catch to slice you into womanhood. Tried to save your mammy; yea though it be to take her from my arms.—

—Saved what? Saved whom?—

—'Cause, woman, it was Jericho Witherspoon who sent money to save Angelina . . . Because—

—Because. What 'cause?—

—'Cause, woman, when he came through here in his runaway to the North, he saw Angelina. And never forgot what he looked upon.—

—Not to say . . . You don't mean to say he thought I was she or she was me? He never told me that. Wait a minute, liar. Don't mount another lie 'cause you got to tell a tale to make me feel low and abandoned as a jackass, from your high horse. What are you conjuring up now?—

—You weren't even in the picture. Drew out her face on his slave's sleeve. We hid him. I hid him. I hid your man-to-be, *woman,* in the sealed-off part of the basement down there, what folds in and unfolds like a closet door, in a chamber.—

—As God's my witness to this nightmare, my dreams have ever held such a story of Jericho Witherspoon always holding something back from me, even as he held the truth from me last year, when all of a sudden he appear at the door with—

—Drew her face on his sleeve, inside. Scratched her visage, he said, in a letter to Rollins Reed, upon his heart for ever and ever.—

—How did he get here, murderer of truth; 'cause lies and truth drip from your tongue as showers and spittle. You don't know where one starts and the other begins.—

—Oh, you can't take it when a revelation goes against your grain, black woman, can you? But it was Angelina. My Angelina, the one you call mother, he wanted. Not you, woman, not at first.—

—Now you want to break my heart again by using my mother as the sword of your foulness to lance my heart.—

—Woman, learn one thing if you can't learn anything in the time what's left to you on this earth . . . Sift and screen out the old hard ways and truth. Then let the best new light ones come a-borning as the dirt-clodded mustard seed to the sun.—

—As *you* sift and screen out the substance of the seed from the grain.—

—This all come into being before you. I'm trying to make you *see,* fool woman . . . Jericho was on the run from the old Witherspoon plantation. We hid him in the folding-away part of the basement. He saw Angelina and never forgot her. When them patrollers stole Angelina off (and you with her), Master Rollins was of a fit to get her back. He saw I was heartbroken. He loved her, too. He's broken down. Ain't got enough money left over from slavery, he says, to purchase her back. Sent word to your lawyer man, this was before he became your lawyer man, 'cause Jericho don't know you exist. I figures now part of Rollins Reed wants her back, safe and sound, the father part in him. But he also wants to get back at me, or to keep me in my place; so he up and writes Jericho Witherspoon who he knows wants my woman, for money to purchase his daughter and my woman out of slavery. Telling Witherspoon in the letter if he sends the money, he can have the woman, in time; he'll send her along. Witherspoon sent along the money like he's purchasing himself a bride. Master Rollins claims Auntie Foisty came to him in a dream and told him this the way to handle the matter, but it was her sister Chastity's voice what spoke to him through Foisty's body—.

—You went along as always.—

—Fool, what could I do to undo what was done . . . Once Angelina returned, I planned out how to keep her even if I had to put poison in Rollins Reed's ear, in his sleep.—

—Jericho Witherspoon's money paid for my return. No! How did Rollins Reed know about him in the first place?—

—I made the mistake—mistake in a way, I guess—of reading something about Jericho Witherspoon what was in the newspapers out loud for Master Rollins Reed's dimming vision. Then I half laughing told him how I had helped Jericho to freedom. So this was part of it, too, Master Rollins' way of getting back at me for helping Witherspoon escape.—

—You could joke with him about things like this?—

—Why, sure, I was his body servant, fool . . . But it was for Angelina's return; you was tossed into the bargain. When the patroller man sat you down on Reed's knee, and you all the time talking about me scratching on the screen. I was hating you out; not you, child-woman . . . But loathing the child what survived the woman of my body and soul. Didn't have nothing to do with Mother and Child, or father and daughter. Like the husband what loathes the babe whose life-bearing kills the woman of his bed . . . My Angelina. Not your Angelina. Your mother? Okay. Angelina had kept losing babies; so when you was born, I was happy for her.—

—For her!—

—Yes, for her, 'cause every time I'd touch her she'd get knocked up, then keep me on the outskirts of her bed for all them pregnant months, every time I'd rap at her door to harmonize with her.—

—Yea and you'd be content to sleep beneath your master's bed.—

—Then she'd up and *lose the babes* or it'd died out in infant-time sickness to the grave . . . as God's my witness.—

—God never knew you as a watchman or wit.—

Upon the words *lose the babes,* the young man now heard Sweetie Reed start babbling these words again, *June 5, 1905,* over and over again. And now he looked down once again to the Bible before him. Nathaniel thought how much Great-Momma Sweet Reed had worshiped his father, because he was the child of her midlife as he was the child of Grandpa Witherspoon's ancient years—their one remaining common bond, since they had separated on that fateful day in June, 1905. Although as a boy he had known almost from the beginning time of their separation; he knew, or was told little else and certainly not the date. Yet the boy Nathaniel had come upon the edge of the history of this bitterness quite by accident, and when he was not looking for it; nor old enough to know what he was looking at, even as he read the Bible aloud for Great-Momma Sweetie, to her, starting when he was three, but remembered seeing the *markings* when he was seven, next to his father's name in the lengthy, childish scrawl print, half written in longhand, in a kind of etching, and just below the three names of the children born and soon dead in their stillborn, or short-lived condition . . . Lost souls?

> January 1, Jerry Jr., 1883, June 5, 1884;
> Angelina-Kay, April 14, 1887, stillborn;
> Minor-Ray, May 29, 1891, stillborn;
> Lovelady-Sue, January 15–April 4, 1900,
>   *Rheumatic Heart*

The deceased children of their loins along with tiny crosses, etched by each name. The boy of seven had read aloud from Genesis to her and she had fallen asleep. Reading from the Bible that old man Rollins Reed had given to her, his family Bible, that his forebears had brought over from England two hundred years earlier . . . But then noticing just after the words *Rheumatic Heart,* those quotation marks and . . .

> *"Arthur R. Witherspoon, June 5, 1905."*

But the boy of seven didn't understand; after all, his father's birthday was celebrated on April 4 (1905) . . . Nor *why* the quotation marks which appeared on the fourteenth page of the provided leafs for family dates and after old Rollins Reed's family-line, which was listed on the first thirteen pages—and written in a pinched, tiny, yet precise and even commanding handwriting—that went back to the very signing of the Magna Carta on page one, as a beginning fingerprint in the back of beginning time.

Shaking his weary writing hand pressed into the service of recording Great-Momma Sweetie Reed's saga, as he stood before the icebox, Nathaniel found his whole body shaking now as the last leaf upon an all but barren tree, with this latest connection, June 5, 1905. He looked about for Sweetie Reed's green ice bucket, found it in the closet and filled it with chunks of ice slabs from the refrigerator. If I place my burning hand into this ice bucket, he thought, perhaps I'll be revived. He placed the green ice bucket at the foot of the rocker.

But now the exhausted young man was suddenly at Great-Momma Sweetie Reed's elbow, nudging her ever so lightly in order to arouse her from sleep and ask her about this last, stinging point. (The ninety-one-year-old woman was not to ascend from sleep for a long time, though her voice babbled and bathed in snatches of song.)

Nathaniel Witherspoon backed off from her bed, stumbled backwards into the rocker and collapsed upon the cushion seat—thinking he knew now the meaning of the quotes. He drifted off into sleep in a kind of fitful discordant rhythm with Great-Momma Sweetie Reed's sleeping motion. Her singing voice scaling, swooping and descending down into various stages of sleep, as one going up and down the rungs of a blood-dripping ladder, hand over hand. And he heard her singing voice:

> *Plenty Good Room/Plenty good room,*
> *Good room in my Father's Kingdom . . .*
> *Just choose your seat and sit down . . .*
> *Hosanna to the Prince of Peace who*
> *Clothed Himself with clay and Entered*
> *The iron gates of Death and*
> *Took its sting away.*

8

Prayers
for a
Patriarch

nd now the young man Nathaniel thought back to Grandpa
Witherspoon turning the pages of his lifelong journal at midnight; the pages rattling in his shaking, crackling, withered
hands, as if the very feel of history was ingrained in the texture of the
paper; he could no longer read closely. His memory was so profound
and trouble-remembering that the boy had only to turn to the numbered page of Grandpa Witherspoon's life, and the life of the Race,
and the Country, for the ancient memory and mind to be rekindled.
Just you call it out, Short-Ribs, he'd say. The numbered pages
matched out his ancient life, as arm in sleeve, and going back to 1831

—when he was four, the year before his shoulder was branded by his own father; until he had stopped reciting aloud, in 1943, the year before, and shortly after his eyesight fled and he learned of the death of his friend George Washington Carver.

And Grandfather Witherspoon asked the boy to go into his study and bring down the huge journal that was so heavy the grandson could barely cradle the monumental tablet-journal in his hands and arms (and sometimes he thought of the mighty journal-log as the body of a living human being inside a coffin in his arms) or his own arms were as wings, too short. But cradling the journal aloft as he climbed down the stepladder and carrying it in his arms by balling up two fists smacked together—side by side—and the elbows winging out at forty-five-degree angles, his arms extended; and now the young man Nathaniel thought: and that's why "tote" is such a perfect word for tasks of carting, yea though it be a Southern term and therefore improper to the tongue, he scoffed . . . Grandfather Witherspoon's acolyte, too.

And Grandfather Witherspoon—who was all but blind by now—would ask his only grandson to turn to certain select pages in the journal, and he would, and *Read it aloud, Nattie . . . Just you call it out, Short-Ribs*—the first paragraph to jog his memory and then the mighty architecture of Grandfather Witherspoon's mind (after three fingers of bourbon) was soon seen flinging forth towards the heavens of recall; and them reading together for hours on end, in a kind of winging call-and-response manner to jog his memory, and to develop and fill in the grandson's mind, waxing imagination and memory. Yet never once were the grandfather's days with Great-Momma Sweetie called forth for recital; never calling out those numbered pages . . . One thousand pages, too. Always telling the grandson never to take the middle course, but to go for the stars in flight.

They were on their way to the funeral home that morning in the limousine provided for the family by Memphis Raven-Snow; the boy sat on the jump seat, looking down upon that same newspaper account his eye now beheld, concerning one of Jericho Witherspoon's earliest "first" appointments, blurred now as well, in his tear-filled eyes . . .

There were at least three hundred people in the Memphis Raven-Snow Funeral Home that late morning. Yet none knew Grandfather Witherspoon during the days of his power and influence, so that he was to them and indeed to the community a kind of legendary hero, who had helped many of their grandparents and oldest of kin in memory when they first came north fleeing trouble into new trials; and others in the beginning time, who were escaped slaves. And despite all of the family requests, the parlor was filled with flowers from some of the leaders in the city, as well as average folk; the NAACP had sent flowers; Walter White had sent a personal message and a representative from the oldest civil rights organization.

Nathaniel's parents thought that Great-Momma Sweetie Reed would not show up and he hoped that she wouldn't but prayed that she would; but be silent though not without showing a wounded heart; Great-Momma Sweetie was in fact shook to the depths of her soul by Grandfather Witherspoon's death, the boy Nathaniel saw that, as he thought about what had happened the day before, when without warning she had appeared before the grandfather's casket and spoken over his body in such moving words. Maybe she was stirred at first by his death, because Grandfather Witherspoon was so old and their broken marriage had bent as the branch of a tree so long ago; but sometime between the time of the visit to her house and her arrival at the funeral home, during the night, the meaning of their life together had come back to Great-Momma Sweetie as in a dream, and he thought, the old folks said that when you are dying you see your whole life go before your very eyes, and this thought made the boy wonder if you didn't see the lives of those you loved and your closeness to them, when they died; after all, hadn't he thought about his closeness to Grandfather Witherspoon more than ever, since the old man's death?

Great-Momma Sweetie Reed was in communion with his grandfather's spirit, at least in her own mind; the boy believed this, too, because she was so often in communication with her own mother and other long-dead spirits, arguing with her father's spirit, I. V. Reed, and talking about Reece Shank Haywood. Jericho Witherspoon had appeared before her; the boy believed this, no matter what his father said against it. And the fact that Great-Momma Sweetie Reed had placed a clip of her mother's hair beneath Grandpa Witherspoon's sleeve had left a deep print on the boy's imagination. Still, he wondered at what else this act meant. Did this mean Great-Momma Sweetie had forgiven Grandpa Witherspoon and wanted to leave this gift next to her dead husband's body, as a way of bringing the life that was between them back again, even though it be through the lock of hair from a dead woman's body? This is too deep for me, the boy said, echoing the words he had heard from the adults, when a matter of history went beyond their own recalling understanding.

. . . Observing the sleeping Sweetie Reed, the young man Nathaniel thought, yes, her greatest gift in death to him, to carry as a keepsake-beacon into eternity—a lock of her mother's unbraided hair—where it would become a part of the particles of dust, devoured by the worms, indivisible from the bent of Jericho Witherspoon's body, skeleton, then dust in the mouth of the worms' dust one day; and where none could tell the beginning of things, lest it be unto John's prophetic words.

Perhaps it was Great-Momma Sweetie Reed's way of saying, Yes, Jerry, I forgive you your love for Angelina . . . But also because, Jerry, your death can't do me no wrong and trouble don't last always? Or was there some other hidden meaning lurking there, in the lodging there in the ear of time? He remembered that his father had plainly not seen Great-Momma Sweetie Reed leave the clip of Angelina Reed's chest-nut-colored hair, beneath Grandfather Witherspoon's dark blue left jacket sleeve. And now that he knew how Angelina's hair had once upon a time contained those diamonds from the hand of the withering away Mistress Sylvia (if you could trust the winsome trickster's words of I. V. Reed), he mused to think of how you never knew what the outside of the face, or balloon of sleeve, or upsweep of hair contained. In the popular song they sang of the day, there was this woman who had blond hair, and black roots—oh, Harry, would that it were that simple. And gentle King Duncan saying of the newly murdered former Thane of Cawdor: "There's no art to find the mind's construction in the face: He was a gentleman on whom I built an absolute trust." Oh that he would have heeded those words over the form of the newly anointed Macbeth; but if that be the case he would not have elevated Macbeth, and we would not have a tragedy to instruct our mirroring tragedies of unfold-ing life.

But in the long ago the boy Nathaniel thought: surely Great-Momma Sweetie would not appear at the funeral because of her vast pride, with all of the mourners in the funeral parlor. After all, she had only stolen to the side of the casket, when she thought the parlor was empty. Great-Momma Sweetie thought that she was continuing a long, previously disconnected conversation, like what had happened the day Grandfather Witherspoon died, and the boy's mother was having a telephone conversation with a beloved friend of the judge's and both were speaking in grieving voices, when suddenly, without warning, a storm broke forth, downing the power line on the south side of the city. Nathaniel's mother, Madeline, had to wait until the next morning to continue the conversation. The boy had wondered how could you pick up what you were saying when what you were talking about was dead. With the death of the grandfather, the boy thought that his world was coming to an end.

The family left a vacant seat in the front row for Great-Momma Sweetie out of respect, at the very end of the row of seven chairs, his parents said. The boy became even more certain that Great-Momma Sweetie would not appear again, when he observed the flowers sent yesterday afternoon (as he and his father stood before the casket) and the lengthy tag attached to the red roses and fashioned in an oval-hearted bouquet. The inscription upon the dangling white card read:

THE SOUL IS NEVER FORFEITED, ONLY
IMPRISONED; THE SOUL IS EVER
TROUBLED, BUT NEVER POSSESSED;
FATHERS DIE, BUT FATHERHOOD'S BIGGER
THAN YOUR BODY PARTS—IT'S LIKE A
RIVER; MUSICIANS DIE BUT MUSIC NEVER
DEPARTS FROM ITS TUNEFUL CRY TO THE
HEAVENS' SOULFUL, WINGING NEED,
TROUBLES AND JOYS . . . BROTHERS DIE
BUT BROTHERHOOD IS EVER AS THE CORN
IS GREEN . . . HUSBANDS DIE, BUT
MARRIAGE NEVER FADES AWAY, AS THE
HEART BLEEDS AWAY . . . SWEETIE TO
JERRY . . .

Then too the boy thought of the everlasting summing-up words Great-Momma Sweetie Reed had rendered down upon Jericho Witherspoon's body the day before—the first time since she had looked into her ancient, former husband's face, since that fateful day of June 5, 1905.

The boy's father prepared a eulogy leaflet from the page in the old *Herald City Free-Courier's Journal* upon Jericho Witherspoon's death, under the headline: "Former Jurist, former slave, succumbs at age 117"; and as a preface to his obituary, the Wanted Dead or Alive advertisement the grandfather's uncle, Corley Witherspoon, a former clerk in the State Supreme Court, had placed in the *Southern Worldly Word,* on April 4, 1855. And the ushers handed it out to each mourner. The family had decided that the boy Nathaniel should read that clipping from a newspaper of one of Jericho Witherspoon's first appointments, as a sign of the accomplishments the great man had achieved, and as an inspiration to the younger people present at the funeral. His father felt having the boy read the clipping would also suggest a continuity of family, community, past, present and the future. The boy's mother had helped him with some of the more difficult words. He had been reading since he was three, but now as the seven-year-old Nathaniel Witherspoon Turner arose to read from the clipping he felt his stomach churn over several times. Lifting his voice so that he might be heard in the back row, the boy read the newspaper account from a local Negro newspaper of the day:

JERICHO WITHERSPOON

*Sketch of the life of one
of our Most Promising
Young Men.*

*His appointment as Stenographer and
Typewriter, in the Office of Hon. S. K.
O'Casey, Clerk of the Probate Court,
at a salary of $100 per Month*

The appointment of Mr. Jericho Witherspoon to the position of Stenographer and Typewriter in the Office of the Hon. S. K. O'Casey, Clerk of the Probate Court, at a salary of $100 per month for four years, was one of the highest political honors which has ever been bestowed upon the Colored race in the State history, and coming from the Democrats, the event is all the more important.

Mr. Witherspoon is well known in the city, having resided in the area for the past decade. He has held down several important and trustworthy positions and the action of the Hon. K. C. O'Casey in appointing Mr. Witherspoon to this high post, requiring much executive intelligence, as well as a balanced head, will undoubtedly make many converts among the Colored people of this state.

When he first came to the City, he entered the employ of Swift-Waterhouse, as an office boy, but later resigned to pursue the common school studies at the Summitt School. During this period he roomed with the noble Lovelady Breedlove; he sold papers, blacked boots and did any number of chores which fortune might bestow upon him, after school hours, in order to continue his matriculation.

While at school he was regarded as an exceptionally bright scholar and was the recognized leader of his class. Later on he secured the position of strand boy for the Birmingham Clothing Co., working after school hours, all day Saturday and on Sunday mornings. By means of this position, he was able to continue his school studies, which he maintained until he took a position of office clerk and wrapped for the Ludlow-Young Manufacturers, which demanded his full time. He was thus forced to discontinue his school studies, much to his sorrow, but being resolved to make something out of himself he took up the study of shorthand at the West Side Evening High School, each alternate evening, while thus engaged with the Ludlow-Young Manufacturers. After a period of three months, he had mastered the fundamental principles of shorthand and was soon called to the law office of the well-known firm of Peacock's and Moore as a Stenographer and Clerk, which position he held for five years, winning many friends among the legal fraternity and business community; and at the same time improving his general education, and reading for the law by candlelight in the late of the evening at the boardinghouse of that noble gentlewoman, Lovelady Breedlove.

But the following year, as the result of laborious mental labors his health commenced to fail, so he opened a grocery, on the first floor, just beneath the house, where the venerable Lovelady Breedlove resides. He ran the store for six months, when circumstances rendered liquidating his assets advisable. He then returned to his selected profession—stenography and typewriting—and opened a Shorthand and Typewriting Bureau at the Lincoln Hotel, in which

he has been highly successful. At the same time he
continued to read for the Law.

During the last Presidential election, Mr. Witherspoon made his maiden political speech, and has
taken an active interest in politics ever since. He is
a champion of the Colored man's rights, and argues
upon the broad theory that a division of votes of the
Negro people between the Republican and Democratic parties would result in an effort being made to
secure their votes by both parties and thus ensure a
"Free Ballot and Fair Count." This paper, which is
personally acquainted with Mr. Witherspoon,
wishes him success in his new field of employment,
and submits his past career to other young men for
emulation. Immediately prior to his appointment
Mr. Witherspoon underwent a competitive examination for the position, the examination resulting in
his favor. His appointment is accredited to the Hon.
Michael C. McDonald, J. Q. Reid, J. G. Jones, H.
C. Carter, and Judge Kettelle.

As the boy took his place at his father's side, the Rev. Pompey C.
J. Browne arose to give the eulogy. The boy's eyes were still filled with
tears from the personal memories of his grandfather that the public
reading of the Judge's early career had engendered. So that at first he
only allowed the words of the minister to bounce off of his hearing,
but the seven-year-old Nathaniel solely listened to his own heart's
eulogy in the secret chambers of his being . . .

Now in the young man's remembering eyes, cast back in time,
fourteen years earlier . . . Fingertips touched out towards wakefulness
as his tiny fingers touched upon JW. Alphabet learning his left from
his right, before tying shoestrings in the upright to lift up to Grandfather Witherspoon's knees, leaning forth in the crawling, beginning
time—in the *lift up as you pull up beginning way,* Great-Momma
Sweetie said at every turn of thought—like the induction letters upon
the school slate on the scroll (A to Z), so high you can't get over it,
and above the pulled-down blackboard, where only a man upon stilts
needed apply. The young man plunged back down into the nursery
waters of his beholding, troubled, awakening eyes. The mark upon the
grandfather's back, JW, a lens of his eyes upon the world affixed in

his trouble-lighted soul. As weighty scales. His grandfather's body stripped clean to the waist. The rib cage of a wasted away swimmer. His flesh a long, red clay gathered out of the icy tide of times and wrapped about his skeleton. He was *a long drink of ice water or a rusty old halo, skinny red cloud, with secondhand wings full of patches,* Great-Momma Sweetie Reed had observed . . . Too much to carry; carried off into troubled history . . . To be given the water cure, if the mortgaged body be captured by his own uncle Corley Witherspoon's mandate, *personally.* The JW marks were an ancient lens, as liquid-dripping scales, and behind them the young man now saw: *Wanted more Dead than Alive.* And then the cataracts as in the awakening scenes in the beginning time of tides . . . *The scales of history are weighed down to admit no light and make us all appear as sleepwalkers,* the young man's father had said weightily from behind the heat of his fogged-up spectacles . . . *By the waters of Babylon, we were sat down,* Great-Momma Sweetie's voice rang out in a thunderclap.

. . . Or coming out of the bath tub water into his toweling, robing, troubled arms, pulled up by his uplifting, in the soon morning light upon the dew, or towards the ladder ascending world of his schooling, shouldering, warning, pool of ringlet-casting echoes: his stirring word. Beginnings. Choral stories and time. His body swollen as a river now. Cradled in the sleeves of the grandfather's caring history in the long robe of dust, forever and ever . . . Shouldered in his grandfather's commandment, his feet harnessed in the old man's sleeves, climbing to his shoulders to lift off into life, or ascend into the highest tree of God's invention. Granddaddy. Daddy's daddy. Father's father remembered in prayer after the close of *Our Father and Hail Mary and Hail Holy Queen, Mother of Mercy, our life our sweetness and our hope, to thee we cry poor banished children of Eve* (oh, blessed Martin de Porres); and before Whom It May Concern especially bless. Beginnings: Wanted *Alive* not Dead—to die twice in his uncle's avenging arms, who spat poison in the ears of history/was not to be . . . Grandfather Jericho named me. *Nathaniel? Here I am, Grandfather. I would lay down my life, in sacrifice for that boy,* he said. He loved goat's meat. A recipe Nathaniel's mother had learned from a Jamaican woman in New Orleans. I served goat's meat to him upon a silver platter. He gave me his blessing. His reembodiment. The offertory.

Touched out upon JW and still deeply implanted into his back towards the left shoulder blade. The hot throat a cord of his backbone (like his wreath-combed, protruding Adam's apple), lashed and salt-ed-down memory wounds on fire. Memory. *The descent of memory stitches the sheath of slumber,* his father said. The birthmark that God gave me near the apex of the armpit but a faint echo of the one God gave him; not Daddy. And maybe that started him to tie the other mark in mind with that one branded by the hand of his father . . . *Here riley, here. The bloodhounds of paradise lost,* his mocking upper lip unfurled. *Tell 'em I was flying boys; tell them I was swimming, Short-Ribs . . .* Remembering as how *they* butchered up the "disloyal ones" as you might cut away the parts of a chicken, because the old-time Africans believed if they were only killed out, and not cut away, they could re-collect those bones and return to the old soil . . . *Death is an uninvited nightraider who awakes at the babe's first tolling tears,* Great-Momma Sweetie Reed said.

That old I. V. Reed kept gas on his stomach below old man Rollins Reed's bed, and used to laugh like he was going into convulsions, the tears streaming down his walnut-colored Seminole cheeks, all down his days and his epileptic fits, Great-Momma Sweetie Reed was saying and then *Angel got two wings to hide my face, two wings to fly me away.* Watching Grandfather Witherspoon as he dressed and the black robes of justice pressed down upon his shoulders. Starched robes. Your Honor hiding beneath the naked story. His truth, branded. (But a wig too, and a beard, once upon a time.) *The quality of the man may be masqueraded by the apparel he shapes upon the slipshod form Nature created for him,* he once said. Feeding me his favorite by his hand: ambrosia; upon his knee—endlessly rocking. Giving me a miniature lighthouse that shone in the dark and beckoned; and his tunic. *Christmas gift. Give.* The beard, then Santa Claus. I pulled down upon his beard. There were tears in the eyelashes back to the threshold of remembering. Saying that I was a *a rainbow about his shoulders.*

My blinking eyes first alive in his wakefulness to the light in the darkness of the scale smoothed out JW upon his shoulder blade, as a shock of red sunlight upon the grieving sleeve of the waters: we were on the enclosed porch. The brand yet vivid as a visitation—Great-Momma Sweetie's Jesus still glowing in the darkness—I watched over it in all of my shuddering as Mother laid out his underclothes, shirt, socks, red necktie and the black robe pressed neatly. The dark blue suit hanging too on the wall upon a nail high up the ladder-like high chair. (Aunt Bella-Lenore placed her fallen hair in the braided, plaited bag upon the nail on a panel next to her doorway—it looked as the body of rabbit hanging there). He gave me a rabbit's foot made in the fashion of a bracelet, that a friendly magician-slave had given him upon his escape.

I climbed as if to enter into the doors of a mysterious chamber-garden, face to face; but I climbed upwards, outwards, upon tiptoes, as upon the limbs of a powerful tree, in my bare feet, my arms extended in the tunic, as an outsized, nightgown shirt—it had clung to his back as kidskin gloves, skin of my skin, flesh of my flesh—upon his shoulders to the tree house with the tiny lighthouse in it—he had been given to wear as a young slave (then later, the tributary network to freedom down on the inside of the left sleeve) but giving it not to his father, his only son, alive, but to me, because he/we could keep it alive in his (father's) time but maybe not in my lost time, anymore, the way things got away in flight and faded, as upon the silent screen. Lost and never found in the wilderness of North America. *After the major surgery of Tragedy, Farce appears in white coat and blackface and droops the masquerade of birth pangs and arrogant agony—like me and my shadow,* Father said. *Away.* Grandfather's flight to light-house light. My arms were a membrane of wings in the tunic. Lost. Fix me, Jesus. Fix me. Remember what Heraclitus said, *No man bathes twice in the same stream,* Grandfather Witherspoon reflected, his eyes as scales upon the waters. 1070.

. . . And when I reached out—his arms extending as if presenting the host and branching forth from an angular tree—with my soft hand fingertips onto the parchment letters (*letters of introduction,* he often called them) appearing sometimes to me as a yellowed, reddish salty membrane (resembling his cold palms, where they were not fiercely callused, but smoothly worn, as a reddish brown elastic sheath, that could be used as a slingshot, but that bound an ancient parchment together), I felt suspended between a millstone and a sheaf of miracles. The blister-like italicized brand JW transformed as reflected tributaries of rivers: the stamp of the personality of rivers: the stamp of the personality of his escape; it had been with him so long, as a body servant, defiant with a razor beneath the membrane of all actions, thoughts and deeds, as the machinery of the mind beneath the outer throbbing temple. Beginnings of it all buried in the branded blood, a mere child when it all and all had happened in the beginning time.

. . . Fingertips of the wakefulness at the JW script as it appeared as a birthmark, or a cross, or a forged chain, a rabbit's-foot bracelet; a shadow casting as the gourd before the cup—remember. Anchored in his blood memory, in the shape of a heart, most sacred. At the left shoulder blade—three and three-fourths inches above the birthmark God gave him—a back like an infant's and an ancient warrior's shoulder—the slaves had called him Big Red—now as a slate in time, riddled in the whirlwind waters of circumstance, the backwaters, all right. Of memories of Calvary retold how it came to be when he was five, my beginning age in school. Though schooling begins in the nursery of branding, leaf-bloody memories before paradise bliss was auctioned. *Blood at the leaf and blood at the root* . . . *Lawd,* when his father stood him upon a mountainside, before his kneeling redheaded blood; the father's hand touched to his slave son's shoulder blade, as if preparation before a tunic fitting, and placed the firebrand in place, for the sacrificed son to know his place in this world, forever and ever . . . And *this sickness is not unto death?* And him stirring and rising like the river memory of the body banks it drinks and drains and keeps forever and ever in its essence and personality and memory bank, in the red-clay country . . . What did the father think when he placed the robe about the boy's shoulders and they ascended the mountain for the glory of his god, and he told the boy Jericho Witherspoon to kneel? What did the boy think, when the redheaded father (with the same color head of hair) told Jericho Witherspoon, his only son, to kneel upon the mountain slab?

. . . And me in his arms, too short to shadowbox with almighty Grandfather, who art; and out upon his shoulders, ascending as if in flight; waxed in his shaping. His arms still spread out in an imitation of a river in flight driving the sea out to open up—not too short to box with God. An angular man once upon a time; *I shall not see his construction of figure and form, nor his soul's embodiment this side of paradise, no matter what she make of him,* Father said in the garden to the tree house . . . *The wrinkled sleeve of living cannot be washed and starched anew without the aged lines reflecting the creases of soilage and the "society" of the cloth even as it suggests the silent but not sleeping muscle fiber, tissue and tone of the covered limb,* Grandfather Witherspoon said as I took down his journal's history . . . The pattern of his intelligence route stitched on a patch beneath the armpit of his tunic.

. . . In from planting in his garden . . . Helping him make the scarecrow in the garden . . . *To thee we send up our sighs, mournings, weepings into the valley of tears; turn then, most gracious advocate, thine eyes of mercy towards us, and then show unto us the blessed fruit of thy womb,* His outstretched hands trembled as the leaves upon the

Tree to Heaven. He was wearing a pitcher's warm-up jacket. And then causing me to dream of a white basket, beneath the arm, delivering the head; the body dangling from the poplar tree and the birds devouring . . . *strange fruit; blood on the leaves and blood at the root.* And *for the crows to pluck, for the wind to gather, for the rain to suck; here is a strange and bitter crop.* The water cure of The Blood . . . And this from both sides of the family: that the old clothes of a drowned man can ensnarl his body if thrown in the river, in the approximate area where he went down dead . . .

Mother was showing our cousin, the Goddess Lily-Beth, in . . . *And show unto us the blessed fruit of thy womb, Jesus.* Walking and waking the garden in the cool of the evening upon his shoulders to touch the ladder where he went up in the tree like a man on stilts, in order to build me a tree house amid the apex of the apples—God's creation, in that summer home we would have to sell to bury him—that stirred as Lily-Beth's dangling red earrings. The crimson waters at low tide, even as his breath. And then I looked down upon him as he prepared the glue for my kite to wax in boldness—in parable, as were all his words and visions—beyond the flight of my father's waxing of words, beyond the melting brand upon my heart. Beyond action. *Oh, heir of my heir,* Jericho Witherspoon hailed, as he carted me upwards as if in a chair. The garland of his crown, he wept. And then my fingertips placed to the fire of memory—as chapter and verse in the journal-Bible—of memory and wakened as in the casting off of knitted sleep; bathing, scalding water upon my winter-cold body parts. Crying: Remember down to the bone, and to the backbone to the shoulder-bone: *honor.* And a high chair as a ladder. Sleep dropped away from eyelids, with the yawning motion of a fountain swaying its head back and forth in harness—out of all harness to be free . . . Grandfather wanted me charged with energy as a shaken furious foil. Wearing his robes though he had not ascended the bench—other than the swinging one, as scales, on the enclosed porch of his lectures—for decades—but they were laid out for him; without them he was unsheathed. He slept a great deal but blissful, evil, brittle to tears and wise by turns as wheels inside of wheels: his crown; finally only sleeping; then to the University Hospital . . . Lily-Beth placed the white gardenia from her long, beautiful, heavy, wavy black hair in the alabaster vase next to his deathbed. Remember?

. . . I could smell out the three fingers of bourbon, like Daddy and his words, as a harp at the cooking stove, but then me up into his arms enfolded—swooped upwards—in a gentle, powerful way: glided off by chariot. His Short-Ribs, his Cornbread, his LightBread. His Long-Gone Division, his Birthmark, his Mustard Seed, his Stirring Waters, his Birthright. (He used to tickle me beneath the rib cage.) With my right hand linked into his skeleton bone left hand he/we learned to love to play the Roof, the Steeple, and the People; the bones of quaking arthritic fingers as his hand and mine evolved the game . . . palm to palm and the interlocking fingers and the everlasting arms . . . Christ mixed clay and water and anointed the man's eyes and told the blind man to go to the pool and bathe . . . He was re-created, Aunt Harriet said at his bedside, deathbed, and then she hummed "The Blind Man Stood at the Road and Cried."

Weeping in his arms. He must be circumsised too, he said. Sacrificial skin. His hairy arms coming towards me. And the spittle upon his red stubble from his favorite tobacco juice and his gray-bluish washed-out eyes of his branding sire and his murder-mouthing uncle. Hundred and seventeen, now and at the hour of. And me trembling upwards into his arms. And the next breath trying to explain it all and understandingly and mockingly. And Hattie Breedlove Wordlaw talking about *a judgment and a tax and a wisdom and a reckoning and a rendering and a healing and a blinding, not scaled by hands, beyond all else.* And Great-Momma Sweetie Reed saying that *each man dies alone and* her mother used to sing, *And I couldn't hear nobody praying . . . Oh, way down yonder by myself, I couldn't hear nobody praying. Nobody.*

Looking at the sacrificial skin marks as if he had eyes in the back of his head, like Great-Momma Sweetie—and the marks were branded before him, dripped with blood, daggers of his father's fingers . . . *A driven vagabond for years, though schooled in books and in the Inferno,* Father said. And a neck of red clay and baked bricks painted over in red and blood and the paint was cracking and peeling with lived-in long-song weariness and wilderness and accomplishments and now at the hour of our strange death. *Oh clement, oh loving, oh Sweet Virgin Mary.*

But now as the Rev. Browne started to bring his eulogy to a conclusion, the boy Nathaniel heard him declaring:

". . . But Jericho Witherspoon's coat of many colors was lined out with the preferred stock of introductory letters, written in a fiery calligraphy of the anguished, heart soaring to be free; yes, and a sheaf of royal opinion concerning his blue-chipped service to our yoked-down people, who have been in the storm too long; this was hidden stock and his treasured notes of authority. And many of you sitting in this chapel parlor today are beneficiaries, because of what he invested in us, forever and ever.

"... The very odyssey of this grand, audacious man traces the outline of our story with such vivid visage that the longevity of his preservation seems a tapestry stitched in the agony riddles and wonders and tribulations of our Great Awakening from slavery to freedom to quasi-slavery. Our history-frozen chains dangling upon the magnolia tree. Maybe that's why Almighty God decided in His eagle-screaming, invisible wisdom not to take His hand to Jericho Witherspoon, and because He knows how short the memory glows in us.

"Jericho Witherspoon had only to touch his back, place his ancient shaking fingers across his own shoulders—look into the mirror—and touch back down with his fingertips to remember the wounds of his genesis, and to remind himself of his history and our sorrowful mouths of history; from the time he was five until Mother Nature commenced to place the garments of eternal slumber about his body and clothe his mind in the final winter shroud of unsettling sleep and into the caring Kingdom of His Father's Almighty Arms. But, mourners, don't you think that was meant to be a soothing solitude because the mind goes on, as a flood-babbling, thunder-filled river in which everything is thrown up and the floating citadels of suppressed memories outrage the normal banks of contentment, discipline and control even unto the brink of death *and* anything that took Jericho Witherspoon back to the days of his earliest memories, snapped open his nightmarish crib and the imprisoned crawling infancy . . . No wonder the slaves of old used to sing, as my Grandmother Browne taught me, at her knees, 'I wish I had died in Egypt's land.'

"... Now, there is a leader among us who threatened a March on Washington recently, if the President didn't sign a scroll giving us employment. We who have never known peace in this Kingdom absolutely fare better during stormy weather and wartime condition. Don't forget it took a military action to free our people; and we been under the gun ever since. Yea tho' our very bodies are often the final estate turned fodder of these wars.

"But Mr. A. Philip knew that, just as Jericho Witherspoon was forged in that wartime intelligence of knowing how to use what leverage we have in the battle with the white man. And they both knew that the Big White Man only understands threats that are based on the imminent possibilities of follow-through when caught up in a power situation. That's his sanctuary and the very nature of his bedtime hiding place.

"My beloved Grandmother Browne, a former slave, used to tell how after the Civil War old Massa was most humble in begging her to come back to the plantation and cook for the family and take care of things—sported the so-called 'darky act' for a spell, she said; even was willing to participate in a mock of what we would call *collective bargaining* today, with Mammy Browne, whom his father had placed upon the auction block once upon a time; yes, because the Big House was about to crumble and Ole Miss couldn't boil water without endangering the chicken coop.

". . . The Big White Man is worst than those Asians about losing face, but that's linked to power in his reality, and his heavy thinkers go around picturing us as faceless in the crowd so he don't have to deal with our humanity and his inhumanity; for this rickety Republic to be embarrassed to have its public face of Democracy blown off by divisions of marching slaves in striking distance of the White House lawn was too much for our ole friend Massa FDR to countenance—that don't mean he understood a damn thing about our troubles, even though he understands the Four Freedoms; but he did understand what a Fifth Column might mean . . . And he knew that scores of Negroes fought in the Abraham Lincoln Brigade, and that nearly two hundred thousand of us fought in this Civil War . . . But don't get fooled, he stills thinks in stereotypes about us—didn't he ask the eloquent A. Phillip, 'Asa, what year did you graduate from Harvard?' Because our leader knows how to pronounce the language with precision, resonance and in the proper manner. *To say nothing of a Hyde Park accent.*

". . . Just like old Cassius Browne—whom my family is named for —understood his plantation couldn't move without Grandmama, or Grandmammy Browne, bringing some order to the chaos—but he also knew that if he and others did not hurry up and get those darkies back to work he was going to have to face some kind of guerilla warfare—that would have made the Indian wars seem pale-faced; and my grandmother knew where he kept everything from the silverware that sparkled like diamonds to rifles that glowed like gold. But now when my grandmother tried to bargain a schoolhouse for those just freed slaves and especially for their children and a portion of the crop —that was as frightening to old man Browne as these modern-day

Negroes who have been clamoring to fly airplanes and bombers during this World War, as freedom fighters against Master Hitler (who resembles that Devil my grandmother used to tell me about all the time, who had to take off all of his clothing before he could nourish his bloodhounds on the odors and fumes of burning bodies—in the name of a Supreme white-cloud God) . . . Because they know if we fly bombers over there, we might send bombs down *there* when we come back home to face 'a worser man than Satan,' as my grandmother used to say . . .

"Because all Mr. Asa had to do would be to bring Jericho Witherspoon to the White House and take off his shirt and let the President of this Divided House see what a white father did to his own mulatto blood and then he'd stop asking why the Negro wants to be free to be, to work for equal pay, and yes, Lawd, to *Fly*—and then know how our story is absorbed in, yet goes beyond those Four Freedoms—and how we will stop at nothing to get it; for didn't my grandmother Browne often sing: 'Sometimes I feel like/A Eagle in the sky/spread my wings and fly, *fly*, FLY.' Yes, and to *fly* away from the warfare of welfare, too. Now, Josh White may sing of 'The Man with a Long Chain On' for old Miss Eleanor and some of her best friends, but there is something to the story in the gospels of man's need to place his hands in the wounds and the sides before he believes, Jericho Witherspoon told me once.

". . . You see, my beloved brothers and sisters, both Mr. Asa and Mr. Jericho Witherspoon knew you never show the Big White Man your hole card—you trace our story with our children first, let them place their hands in the wounds, that's what my grandmother knew, in her basement hideaway of blood-remembering instruction. For Massa Browne was willing to give my grandmother a fraction of the crop, but not willing to set the school up with the help of the Yankee missionaries unless *he* could control the welfare, and act as the HNIC schoolmaster; so she went along with a portion of that—but then in the evening hours when Massa Browne was gone off from the quarters cockfighting, and blackbirding, she reinvented her own school, in the basement, sunken earth of a place that was an outhouse once upon a time. Putting a new rock of old wisdom underneath the young ones' heads, inducting and conducting them into the maze of rock-foundation lessons old Massa Browne had left out and crisscrossing over his falsehoods—like the very route to escape a train to freedom makes within the soul, for the glory of the mind and salvation and survival; knowing and seeing how Massa Browne had only set up the school to keep the darkies locked in snake-eyed ignorance by the dozens, so to speak . . . Content with his schooling them, or reschooling them, in the new slavery of peonage, to believe his word, as he did in the beginning time and not calling it Education, but *The Word* . . . She went about her work in a kind of daring solitude the way Jericho Witherspoon kept that route to freedom stitched upon a patch in the sleeve of his slave tunic, as a secret calligraphy.

". . . All three of these souls—and particularly Jericho Witherspoon —knew that you don't show the white man all of the story; you let him see only the outside, like a poker player only lets his enemy see the outside of his cards and the outside of his face, which like the Brown Bomber's reflects nothing but steadfastness. He let the pistons of his brain—with the help of that old master teacher, Mr. Chappie Blackburn, and the fierce precision of his fists—tell our deeper story, as he decked out yet another opponent on the canvas, in red, white and blue. The Big White Man would be intimidated by too much show —if you notice the Brown Bomber never *performs* in the ring, in a showboating manner, nor does he depend on some white man's judgment, if he can help it—and let our tragic story turn to farce in the judge's eyes and decision-manipulating hands; just like old Massa Browne tried to do to my grandmother's plans by flooding the minds of the innocent lambs in pale reverence for his kingdom. And that's why, too, when she started off her lesson plan each day, she commenced with a song:

> *The Lamb, the Lamb, the Lamb,*
> *I hear thy voice a-calling.*
> *The Lamb, the Lamb, the Lamb,*
> *I feel thy grace a-falling.*

But then, my beloved mourners, she'd go on to lead them in singing another verse:

> *The Lamb, the Lamb, the Lamb,*
> *Tell me again your story.*
> *The Lamb, the Lamb, the Lamb,*
> *Flood my soul with your glory.*

And that's when she would flood their minds with the glory of their story; yea the horror and the honor of it. Let them not be cut off from Heavenly Light, as she revealed the maze of their condition, by nightfall, down in that old reinvented basement of an outhouse; and let not their sight be knitted away in blindness, as Massa Browne tried to take the lambs to slaughter, with one hand, as he attempted to stitch their souls to the thread of his wanton wicked words, in the eye of a needle, with the other, in the fierce light of day; as he poured his poison into their ears.

". . . Because she knew that old Massa didn't mind the darkies singing . . . Thought those old slave songs were safe, soothing balms. Didn't realize that we never asked with Jeremiah, *Is there no balm in Gilead?* But turned that around, too, and declared: *There is a balm in Gilead!* Because, you see, although Grandmother got old Massa Browne to use the old Praise House shack for the new school day, she held her own classes a mile away in the woods, at the hush-harbor they used in slavery times for deep praying and bellowing long-songs. Encircled the area off, as she had before the surrender with wet rugs and old sheets, upon a close-line, believing it all would keep the sounds of the word and their call-and-response learning voices from being blown in the wind and flying and disturbing the peace and sleep of old man Browne . . . But then she had to move her schoolhouse to the outhouse, 'cause the wind might whip the truth away to his ears in sleep . . . And praying within her soul: *Fix me, Jesus. Fix me.* Now I want you to tell each other that story—and let that riverbed of flooding power and felt, lived-out history inform your protest, that's what I had to relearn from my Grandmother Browne, Mr. Randolph and Jericho Witherspoon, so as I could constantly reinvent life out whatever material of chaos that came my way.

". . . The weight of Mr. Asa's threat was so powerful in possible numbers, because the numbers game was based in memories like those of Jericho Witherspoon's history; and FDR knew Mr. Randolph meant business. And the power we possess is a meaningful leverage in the world—and if you don't believe it, have faith in it, why do you suppose FDR himself got on that telephone to encourage the Brown Bomber to let loose some of those heavyweight bombs on Max Schmeling's dark jaw—and ole Joe was probably humming through his mouthpiece all the while, the words to 'Go Down, Moses.'

". . . Jericho Witherspoon had to teach me, and us all, when and when not to be, or not to go *public;* and he knew when to take that

Big White Man to the ropes, and when to knit his mind to sleep through craft and wiles. Using the face as a mask, that reveals nothing of the soul or the mind's intention. Like the ole poker-faced Brown Bomber still does—turning the cold steel of his fury on and off, not in a showboating performance, but rather into an immemorial art form like those bullfighters in Spain. And like the art form Jericho Witherspoon made of that stitched map to freedom he wore on the inside of his sleeve and the way he turned that savage branding JW upon his back into a testimonial to suffering and sacrifice.

"... Now, don't you also know FDR is aware of how many Negroes get lynched each year? Don't you know that rich white man—who's regarded as a traitor to his own class—can read the reports of the FBI, many of whose numbers are informed at night by sheets when they oughta be asleep beneath those lily-white sheets, with *the* Miss Ann they claim they worship so much. And Lawd today, that docket ain't a tenth of the tithing, tolling truth—don't you think FDR can read beneath the Mason-Dixon line? And don't you know he heard about those race riots in these army camps, and the riots in Harlem last year, hot off the wires like bulletins from the war zones? Hell, FDR don't need a brain trust, or the First Lady, to tell him the one thing he respects and fears most about the potential power in a man that's been crippled down most of his entrapped days in this land. That old white man—whom many of you love more than some of our ancestors loved a beneficent slave master, or so I'm told—wouldn't be in the impure White House today if he didn't know about the numbers game, and didn't possess the killer instinct—but don't you tell me the Brown Bomber was simply his runner, when it was a white man's jaw Louis was encouraged to break and when that Alabama boy's been going around taking names for more than a decade now!

"... Jericho Witherspoon taught me how to get smart, even as he stayed my mind on freedom, through the long suit of his story. Jericho Witherspoon carried the weight of his history and our history on his left shoulder blade (like a soldier carries his rifle at all times in a combat zone), without having a chip on his shoulder.

"... And so I believe this late morning that we ought to grieve for this great man's passage with a new dedication to the lighthouse spirit he forged for us, at the edge of every wide river we must cross . . . And so I believe this coming high noon that the blue-chipped stock of his spirit was a legacy to our poor, the least of these our brothers . . . And so I want to celebrate and to affirm the values Jericho

Witherspoon stood for, and not the counterfeit values so sweeping our land, and our people; and the false prophets, who try to make you daydream over their precious personalities, like day-star rocks for worship; and so I want you to shun the way some of our people don't question and challenge their faith with inquiry; and decline to wrestle with the Angel for the deeper answer and forget how Job struggled with God's meaning as with the afflictions false-faced Satan laid upon him. Don't be like those old slaves who listen to masters like Massa Browne, who taught and preached continually on Paul's advice of slaves be obedient to masters . . . And so I believe that too many of us have shunned Jericho Witherspoon's advice about the vitality of the mind as an instrument for survival and in that you remind me of a story he once told me concerning a people who existed in ancient times who worshiped after smooth stones and slept upon them for inspiration and connection with their Gods for intervention and praying and daydreaming, and that they would oil down another set of stones and place yams (one of our old mother-lode crops) on the face of these smooth-faced stones; daydreaming a faith that suggested the very spirit of their gods was possessed and reflected in the shining faces of those old smooth stones; before they went out to hunt in the late evening, daydreaming that the sacrificed yams would sweeten and smooth out the disposition of their gods' spirits locked away in those old vanity-mirror stones, so as to guarantee good hunting.

". . . And Jericho Witherspoon told me that even folks coming through those woods with baskets hooked about their arms would lay down morsels for those gods, just as some of us lay up treasures of Vanity-Sheen upon our heavenly Caddies and our divine Lincolns, as showboating daydreamers all day long on Gospel Sunday. Now, Mr. Witherspoon revealed how these folks of yesteryear believed that those possessed stones were some kind of manifest of their gods' personality enshrined; just like some of you think those shorts are charged chariots to Paradise Valley . . . But the only smooth path in life is paved to Hell and old David didn't just sing and compose psalms, he knew what to do with those old five smooth stones!

". . . But Jericho Witherspoon then said: when the local rats and dogs (and here I don't mean those kinds of dogs like Miss Ann has minked about her throat, and I sure ain't talking about no little ole Pekingese, nor those little old French poodles that walk like an obscene harlot, either; I'm talking about bloodhound dogs—like those they set upon our escaping forebearers' trails and the kind Jericho

Witherspoon's very own uncle set upon his nephew's path and those bloodhounds they are using to bring order to lynching parties right this very high noon down in the old country. My beloved mourners, Jericho Witherspoon was not talking about those foot-long rats that beset our slums—nor their cousins, the ones caged up for experimentation that get better treatment from the government than your children and mine—nor am I talking about those third-degree, cardinal-sized original rodents, that earned their rep by outdistancing and chasing primitive man back into those caves)—when these animals ate the yams by night and the people returned the next morning and found the sacrificed food missing in action, they convinced themselves that their Gods had become momentarily embodied in these animals, in order to consume their food. So right there they became stone animal worshipers: *dead in the market.* When they should have found some gunpowder and a silver bullet and blasted those rodents, as werewolves to the gates of Hell, instead they embodied those primitive animals with a naked soul and a Godlike spirit.

". . . Now, Jericho Witherspoon's point in the story was how stone crazy these folks were and that's the kind of thinking we are doomed to right here and now—thinking that the spirit of God is manifested in every seed of commercial folly flung broadcast, as the very trajectory of our seedy spiritual wasteland-wilderness: in the silver bullet upon the silver screen; in a Lincoln, in a Caddy, talking about a wheel inside of a wheel; in an Electrolux; in a Maytag; in a talking-box Philco, the very wireless to our soul; in a sleek set of diamond stones, thinking they can outglow the Star of Bethlehem; in a fifth of Cutty, in a fifth of Creme-de-Coo-Coo, as voo-doo; flaked away in a foxed-out fur piece.

"My beloved mourners, when that happens to us, Jericho Witherspoon taught me, then we have become stone cold dead in the marketplace. Learn not to nourish your souls, nor incorporate your spirits in symbols of quicksand, as the very visage of God's manifest to mankind, reflected in a stone polluted and corrupted soul; as those ancients who thought they worshiped God's house when they worshiped the sun in reverence . . . But, mourners, you are backing right up into an auction block; feeling up the chains that bind and declaring, in the chambers of our blindness: Lock me up, with or without a gravestone for dead to the heart in the chamber door of idolatry. But rather *do* something about human existence, within the society of man's convict ways; strip the foreskin of your heart, look deeply into the mirroring images there, as you accuse your neighbor of desiring the worldly goods inside of your chamber door. Do something about human existence, Jericho Witherspoon preached; don't mirror God to God just because He made you in His image; He wants more out of you than simply a carbon copy. And so, in this context, I believe that Jericho Witherspoon's spirit must be rekindled in the darkness."

And now as Pompey c. j. Browne came towards the last words of his sermon, the fiery violinist, Jenkins "Lodestar" James, played background for the minister's last words by portraying Jericho Witherspoon's favorite spiritual: *Oh, Mary, don't you weep, don't you mourn* . . . Rev. Browne's nodding head signaling Lodestar as a downbeat, into harmony with the minister's last words; so that sermon and song became as one; voice to voice, as soul to soul.

But suddenly, from the rear of the parlor-chapel, they all heard the door open and shut with a strange kind of bell-ringing yet questioning finality; and then slowly down the aisle, with the aid of a cane, came the tiny, cedar-colored Sweetie Reed; and dressed in that wedding gown of her mother's; and the strawberry bonnet of Angelina Reed's atop her proud head. She wore the high-top laced-up boots of a lady of the late nineteenth century and a plain, dark blue cloth coat. The hem of the wedding gown (made from the material of window curtains) peeked out, ever so delicately, to touch with the grace of a lady's handkerchief, and covered the shining shoe tops.

9

To
Trouble
the
Waters

Great-Momma Sweetie Reed came forward now in front of the casket; Nathaniel's parents started to wrench and stir in their seats, with fear, trembling and embarrassment; but the boy refrained from joining them. A startled murmur issued from some of the mourners. Others looked upon her sudden appearance with whimsy. A few seemed to have real delight in their faces, somewhere between the desire for gossip and the pleasure of an instructive, charged proverb, that takes on a surprisingly hidden twist when examined, that resembles, finally, the trajectory of an oracle.

Arthur Witherspoon stepped forward as Great-Momma Sweetie

commenced to open her mouth, with his hands cupped outwards; as a Muslim at prayer, it appeared, but his was not the motion of a supplicant, or an acolyte, suddenly faced with a prophetess, who dares come inside the chambers of the temple; but rather a prefiguring of what his voice was about to utter—

"Why?"

But Great-Momma Sweetie Reed was in a trance of concentration—having a muted spell-stirring in the middle of the air—and the boy thought of her hearing aid, invisible now because it was covered over by the strap of her mother's strawberry bonnet and how she was often given to hearing voices as if she could hold her own séance (or her own revival). Great-Momma Sweetie was still talking to Grandfather Witherspoon—in a deep conversation that seemed to rise as a river from the basin depths of its being to the middle of the air in the Heavens, as she stood there humming and nodding and whispering then chanting, in a communion with her dead husband's spirit. Her non-words of music and Jericho Witherspoon's invisible ones appeared to exist in spirits assigned to a distant drumbeat in a chariot, beyond the reaches and hearing of the mourners (weaving in and out of each other's arms), within the secret sleeves of marriage. The boy thought that this invisible conversation commenced the day before. Just then the nonbelieving Arthur Witherspoon declared:

"*Why!* He was a great river who never forgot his place; the sources of his energy and his power . . . Mother Sweetie, please—*please,* let him be, in death; and proudly respected."

The pallbearers moved forward towards actively settling the seventy-seven-year-old lady down into the vacant seat provided for her by the family and next to the boy Nathaniel. Nathaniel now saw how he knew her better than they did. And so did Rev. Browne, for he nodded them away as she was coming out of her humming and chanting and saying:

". . . All of it coming to me out of the constant nightmare of the patrollers taking Mother and me off and then being taken up and off again. Then the two Angels of Death descended down for me but they found my soul wasn't knitted tightly enough—despite all of my good works and my prayers (and there was some unsettlement concerning just what was to become of my spirit in the sheath of my body) but Jerry was with them and behind him, my Sweet Jesus!—though it was my Savior I saw at first. And I thought: Yes, *Honor, honor unto the dying Lamb.*" Then Arthur Witherspoon said in a calm, measured voice:

"Oh, Mother Sweetie, *naw,* don't do this to us; us all . . . Don't bathe us in more woe than we can bear. We are the children of his light—all of us, this boy, me, you—yes, even you—of not solely his fame alone, but his particular blessedness, his security, his conceits. No man crawls to death unburdened, I realize that, Mother Sweetie. But he died out a poor man. More ancient than life itself ever warrants, or guarantees. Stripped down to a baby's way of uselessness; *he,* Jericho Witherspoon, not simply *just* your former husband, who served humanity in the most manful of ways; *he* now needs the final resting place. Let your hot arguments go down in an untroubling way, as well." The boy struggled uneasily in his chair, as he thought that his father was trying on this way of talking, as a way of cooling her down. Though some of the words he used were not so hot, but had heat pitched inside of them; as a flexing muscle inside of a sleeve.

"I know, I visited Jerry, your pappy, in a hospital once to have it all out with him—none of you knew that. It was at the beginning of October. But he was asleep in the care and keeping of his Maker; without a wrinkle upon the knitted brow of slumber . . . Knowing, then not knowing me through snatches of words and whispers, then only nodding, then nothing, at the last of my visit: the nurses in lily white coming in and out of the room. I could see the fishing pond and the rods from the top-floor window. Left a vase of glads."

"Oh, I don't believe you went there!"

"I know. But that's your trouble, Arthur, you don't believe in anything that you can't see and think into being—that's not bloody with the claws of your ever questioning mind concerning what you want to feel."

"You aren't talking about *your* Biblical Nicodemus—you are talking about my very own father."

Just then several mourners vacated their seats in a kind of respectful embarrassment, but others had come down front in interest, speculation and probably love for the sensational, as spectators at a movie of a boxing match, who can't see for looking. The boy found himself lost yet captured between Great-Momma Sweetie Reed and his father. Agreeing with Great-Momma Sweetie Reed at one point and then with his father the next moment; even as he placed his hand upon his mother's icy hands in order to calm her naked anger, with Arthur

Witherspoon and Sweetie Reed. The Rev. Browne himself was caught as in a photo flash between gesturing towards them in a cooling-down manner and bending his own knees, in order to be seated.

Now the boy believed Great-Momma Sweetie had been there and gone, for hadn't the gladiolas, standing in the dark blue vase upon the hospital nightstand next to Grandfather Witherspoon's body in the bed, lasted so long that several of the nurses remarked in wonderment at their existence, and endurance? The boy knew Great-Momma Sweetie's formula of babying the glads: two teaspoons of sugar and a shot glass of cedar water. Yet because he had not recognized the vase, and believed that Sweetie Reed was in fact through with Jericho Witherspoon, forever and ever, he had failed to believe his own eyes and secret heart, as he looked at the long sword-shaped leaves: with the colors of a rainbow, within a touching distance of his grandfather's bed.

Arthur Witherspoon remained standing but now Great-Momma Sweetie wheeled on him . . .

"You misread us, Arthur. I too realized Jerry was a wizard, a worker and a warrior . . . he was also my former husband. All right."

Nathaniel knew his father had a few bourbons to bolster him before the family left home and that bothered the son, too, because he knew of the meanness of tongue that liquor sometimes soured within his father's spirit; though at first he maintained his calm and cool. He could become as hot ice. What of his diabetes? (The boy had a Baby Ruth candy bar at the ready—but that would look foolish at a funeral.) Nathaniel's mother pulled at his father's sleeve in an attempt to draw him back down.

Several local Negro photographers and newsmen moved forward now, setting up for the impending action, as before a boxing match, when suddenly a fight breaks out in the crowd at ringside and their attention is drawn away from the announced main event. Their cameras and pens drawn to the ready as gloves pulled across the hands of prizefighters; then laced up. All ready for the match. "Mother Sweetie, there was a grand side to him enfolded tightly in a stormy privacy—where no man, and no woman, dared enter; you never saw the hurricane, a-flood in his heart; that he somehow or other was able to gather within his encircling, powerful arms . . . But *why*—this *appearance?*"

"*Why?* Because even still waters don't run deep enough, needs new stirring up to trouble the appearance of calm; yes, and for enriching sake, even fulfillment. Needs some of that old-time religion-bank to mingle with its grieving bones, in the waters. Needs to get unharnessed soon up one of these old mornings, so as it can get unleashed, before the gathering-up storm.

"*Why?* Because Jerry appeared to me yesterday at dawn, in a windstorm. But at first down at the very pool where I was baptized; and where I sought out a bathing balm for the troubled spirit of my weary soul, where old Packwood submerged my body; renamed my soul, in a windstorm; but soon we were back down near those waters of my Angelina's death and went back and forth against each other and no one dared enter, vocally or physically, for long, as a slack soul fearful of flying into the eye of the storm.

". . . No, Arthur, you set down because more ears than yours and especially ours need to hear all of this—all the way out. Clean to the bone; yea though it *all* may ache the plucked liver and wrench the chamber to the shuddering heart, in sackcloth. For even in death Jerry gave me yet another learning task, as when he taught me to read and write and how to type, in the long ago—though it was Jesus Christ made this first assignment, hand in hand. Raised the beam of my hearing aid so *high* I couldn't get over it, around it, nor under it and made me think a miracle had happened to me; as shocking as when I fell and lost my hearing thirty-eight years ago. Now I heard too much—in my stubbornness trying to get around it.

". . . But the odd thing about it all is that I thought it was Jesus, alone, taking me over on the other side, too—with Him, and His two angels—and to see Angelina first, because we were near the waters of her burying-up place; then discovering my presence was causing a stirring up and a confusion down; and maybe that I wasn't ready to go; had to come in through the chamber door; and that's when I saw out at Jerry plainly, and recognized that I was being brought over to be with Jerry, or to confront him, which also made me think for a spell that I was sure 'nough dead to life. Lord God, I thought You had struck me down dead with life.

"I thought: This is the cause, the cause of my Soul, the very center of why my preoccupied soul was shocked down dead to life and down to my very soles. I went baby-to-matron and back to a baby who's had the breast of its mother suddenly torn from its lips. Then I understood that I was to confront not the Master but Jericho Witherspoon. I saw myself as that girl he met at the train station in early June, 1882. He was high in the saddle of his horse, Charger. And *me* more lost than a babe separated from Mother and screened out by Father, and *me* more sassy than a matron . . . And Jericho Witherspoon, whose soul's center was stuffed with causes for Justice, as kindling.

". . . For suddenly I saw the Master's very hand bringing me to Jerry's hand, where I found myself; His hand upon mine, leaving a furious imprint of *Himself!* My soul's bridegroom and the master spirit of my three stages of being; His almighty hand upon mine, leaving an imprint of Himself, I tell you, as a wheel within a wheel; like those revealing x-ray pictures in the hospital, wherein from the portrait of the hand you see each and every little detail bone, down to the tiniest, witnessing nerve, sprung as rhythm from the throbbing heart.

"Then I looked again and I found Master Jesus had placed Jericho Witherspoon and I hand in hand, yet when I saw this I thought of hand-to-hand combat and wrestling for truth and power with a stubborn angel. I uncovered myself this morning, Church, as a bride's body is stripped down to the flesh and bone upon her wedding night . . . Jerry, you know that, because it all started yesterday at dawn and I was brought low and naked to my body and soul . . ."

The boy saw his father go blushing in shame and fury. The beam in his light brown eyes as hopeless as the sun upon the faces of flipped pennies that fall and roll over for dead, far short of the line, lit in the face of the pavement. (And he thought of his father once telling how in the times of great Rome, that the early gladiators were actually outlaws given the choice between death and freedom when they fought in the ring. And how they first appeared at funerals.) But knowing the open-endedness to so many things of Great-Momma Sweetie's words—when she bore witness—made him feel less shocked than troubled over what she was about to get at next. And, in his innocence of seven years, the idea of nakedness did not unleash the sexual images that older children might have found intriguing in her words.

The congregation of mourners sat on the edges of their benches— their knees bending a bit—as if to become even more intimate with this tiny woman's words; not so much with what they meant, but what might be unveiled as naked gossip, body and soul, at the very next turn of her unmended speech. Her unraveling witness appeared to them spun without care, aroused from the slumber of thoughtless sleep.

". . . We were down at my mother's grave at the beginning, near the waters and me thinking we were coming out of a flood, because

all of our clothing was clinging to our bodies; Jesus, Jerry and me
. . . and those two angels . . . I had fallen off to sleep thinking about
what I was going to fix for the wake, so you could pick up the trays
of food in time, Arthur, you and my Splendid Spoons over there;
because I was plainly not going to be standing where I am standing
now.

". . . For, Arthur, as you know, I had no plans to be here. I came
yesterday afternoon—spoke with Jerry's spirit, where I had left off
from that time when I visited him, still alive in the hospital, in early
October—and left soon to continue where Jerry and I had started to
talking by early light, when he appeared to me coming out of the dark
background in the form of a cloud from a windstorm, with his judge's
robe on. All the time I was hoping Master Jesus—whom I saw first
—would block his way and take me with Him, up the ladder, that I
saw drooping down before me, but instead He insisted on *us* talking.

"And now I'm reaching around myself to find Angelina to help me
out of all of this, finding that I felt some anger towards her, my
beloved mother, even as I was wearing her old bonnet and expecting
to find her *there,* as when I used to find myself back on old man
Rollins Reed's plantation and that nightmare. Feeling out for her not
only in the turmoil of the nightmare but still upon wakefulness even
though she had been dead for years . . . a part of me never accepting
the fact that I was a motherless child, apparently, and a long ways
from the home of her arms (or any arms). No, never. Never to leave
me alone.

". . . So I prayed that Master Jesus would block Jerry's way and
Mother Angelina would counsel me, just like I know you all hoped
some of them elders, and deacons' board members, and pallbearers
were going to block my way from coming up to the head of this
chapel, when I came in this minute—you had a mind to do it, leastways . . . Yes, all right, Jerry, I sent some flowers and a message over
and I intended after I visited yesterday for that to be that—but No!
For I found the imprint Jesus had *possessed* upon my soul, now after
His restoring *Jerry & Sweetie* hand in hand. And of a sudden this
imprint is as sweet to my dreaming lips as the polished golden brim
of a spilling-over wine cup of fleeing lovers in the moonlight.

"And I wanted to spit in my own reflection at the body's emotion
and I desired to embrace emotion, as a virgin bride, thirsty for love
in the dawn the morning's light cast across her fiery bed and sheets,
twisted there, as a wild, flexing hand in a glove. When all of a sudden

one of those angels cried out, *Yes, and He's got the whole wide world in His hands . . . yes, even the little-bitty babes innocence in His hands.* And in my dumbness, Lawd, I heard too much: *Oh, see the little children when they truly baptized in their nakedness . . . Oh, Honor, Honor, unto the dying Lamb's sacred blood.*

Just then Pompey c. j. Browne leaned over to Arthur Witherspoon and whispered in an unsettling, subdued voice:

"Arthur, let her have it on out, *this way*—apparently *it* will out; she's been to the valley, and if you are ever to have any kind of communication with her upon this earth, and peace within yourself besides, let Miz Reed have her say. She's trying to free herself from the shadow of this great man (even as her very soul's been anchored in the deep rivers of the Lord's tossed and driven word) as much as you were, are, still are, Arthur; trying to free yourself to understand his power over you. We all are trying to deal with his almighty presence over our lives. And how to live out our days without his presence, in an intimate way, to find some parts of commandment over our existence without the shadow of his presence."

The two men stood there staring at each other. Meantime Great-Momma Sweetie was humming, sweet and low: *Nobody knows the trouble I've seen.* Or was she also humming to say, Well, when you two have finished whispering about me (for she almost always thought somebody was whispering about her; taking advantage of her lack of hearing), I'll continue to unburden my mind and my spirit.

Only once before had the boy noted Rev. Browne's unsettled condition along with the coolness of his words. It was at Easter time, when he had gone with Great-Momma Sweetie Reed to the minister's church of God's Golden Leaves (the original one, on 37th and State next to the tailor shop), where Rev. Browne pastored the tiny flock who sat and sang upon the thirty silver benches, directly in back of the window where the site of the dying lamb was also scrawled out in the corner of the freshly washed-down windowpane below the tip of the milk-white beard . . . And the stomping shoes, soles and heels of the brothers, exposing white socks and trembling jugular veins; and the sisters, glorious in their cloth-ripened hats, that appeared to celebrate the arisen Redeemer as layered orchard crowns to Paradise. Fanning, shouting, jangling their tambourines as new money to the old witnessing-church organ, as they cried out: "Ride on, King Jesus, no man can hinder me."

The boy knew that Rev. Browne's words to Arthur Witherspoon

were to act as a shield of protection for Sweetie Reed. For not only had Sweetie Reed spoken out at his church on the great issues of the day; she had once upon a time typed out the sermons of Rev. Browne, on long white pages of typing paper that looked like scrolls—handed along by kings to their messengers, concerning fierce matters of state —in the movies the boy saw at the Joe Louis Theatre.

Rev. Browne sold these gospel scrolls containing the words of his best sermons at his church's national convention each year. But Great-Momma Sweetie Reed didn't receive any money for her typing service; instead the understanding bargain they struck (based upon a mere handshake) revolved around Rev. Browne teaching several neighborhood boys, designated out by Sweetie Reed, carpentry: the art that supported the Rev. Browne, in the early days, in order that he might live to preach and guide his flock through the week. But the boy's father said: "Fine idea but who's going to crack the unions open to get those young men a license and a job?"

Now Nathaniel saw his own father bring his balled-up fist down and pound it against his heart three times in a flash of anguish, terror and discovery—as a man uncovering a secret ambush in the dark—across his wounded, truth-slapped face. But he only said, as a man who suddenly sees his embattled spirit in the steam of a wet wash over the ditch at daybreak:

"I won't have it; I won't hear of it. No one can call this man down, to heel; who carried our hopes and outrages upon his shoulders, as the natural garment of his burdens, for over a century; not to speak of the seal of history upon his branded back—just to satisfy the whims of an unhinged woman," in a voice of both rage and heartache; his body doubled up at the fierce point of his fist banging three times, at the heart.

The boy Nathaniel was brought up short himself, now. Standing and trying to settle his father down, as his own spirit seemed unable to sit down . . . Inside the child's heart there was the cry: But who is Father really talking to, inside the chamber of his own heart? He felt one with his father, babe and man, as he wondered what he would feel like if his own father was taken from him and someone brought forth words, stirring and unsettling memories before the public view about Arthur Witherspoon. Even if the person was the woman sitting next to them, his very own mother . . . But now Great-Momma Sweetie Reed was remembering . . .

". . . Because, Jerry, when you climbed out of that water and up that mountain, what was left? The vision you saw headed out before you, the territory beyond; the wilderness of man's existence—its shocking loneliness, insecure in Justice, even, without the embrace of God . . . The desert of death, not to know His presence. You did not recognize this, did you? Then Jerry, as always, answered my question with a statement. But this time it was different. For he said to me:

" 'Sweet, I want you to trouble the waters, this morning, with the agitation in the distress, the discord, the discomfort, the anxieties, the frustrations, the provoking, the exasperations; the lying at the building, and in the temples of wisdom; the torment of the defiled dreamers and the soul-suckling horrors of this life; as you bathe my body with the baptizing and the healing, bathing balms, down at the well near the river (which looks like a shallow pool to me), with *your* baptizing waters and your singing, trying to redeem' . . . But that's when I cried out, 'No, I'll be weeping, Jerry:

> *Don't come early in the morning*
> *Neither in the heat of the day*
> *But come in the sweet cool of the*
> *Evening and wash my sins away . . .'*

Then Jerry said to me:

" 'Because, my beloved Sweetie Witherspoon, I want you to show the blood in the water and the grieving water in the blood, the affliction and the bruised-blood contour, the meaning of the condition service cup, the service pan; the floundering and especially the forgetting amid the forging (preserved in your remembering heart, as an echo-throbbing tributary) but now unlocking it all and letting it flow, as the flood-time of the River prepares itself . . . But you've got to charge those guests of yours with the sense of the constant terror of life . . . You give them too much pity. (Something you never gave me.) They are getting too comfortable in their poverty; too soft in your care and keeping. Oh, they're trying; but they are looking upon themselves as not only condemned but cursed to the bottom of humanity . . . They aren't lifting up enough as you trying to pull them up to a higher ground; mainly because they know they have you to fall back on. But they've got to learn to do without you . . . And not just make do, either.'

"And I said, 'Yes, Jerry, as Noah collecting two of every kind, even you and even unto me.'

"But I'm looking down at my hand upon Jerry's hand, with the very presence of Jesus' hand, as the soul of God, over both of our hands, that still somehow remained unclasped. And I start to sing out: *I'm gonna live the life I sing about in my song . . . Folks may watch me, say I'm foolish, I don't care . . . Not for gold, nor for fame, but for the love of Jesus' name.* But almost as a way of not dealing with Jerry's presence and his accusation; surely not to face the Master's hand that keeps shifting and changing its shape (like an escaping slave shifting the meager bundles of his escape and drifting and changing the rerouting of his flight). The three of us are tossed and driven about in the fast-paced leap and vault of the river, as before a storm and sea change of the river. There we are like new world pilgrims and a long ways from home.

"I'm Joshua and Nicodemus; Job and Lucifer; Mary and Magdalene; but new Mary inside of old Mary; pilgrim and nigger-woman slave, spinning in my head like Joseph's coat of many colors, now as Jesus' hand turns to me like the pointing finger on the short hand of time of that clock old Miss Sylvia left behind and Rollins Reed sent along with the Bible and the rocker, in 1895 after hearing Mr. Washington and six months before he, my grandfather, died . . . Lawd, must I go back to that, too; when you, and solely you, whose eye is spun to the trembling, quivering eyelid of the sparrow's throb, remembers what reflected in my brow, face to face. And then it comes down to me what the old folks went through in order to sing out so boldly amid the trembling tribulations: *So grateful, Lawd, woke up this morning clothed in my right mind.* Unlocking all, face to face to the inner face. Letting it flow out—Heaven inside of Hell—as babes unable to flow in the robes of the river, choked off from life yet still being born, soon up in the sundown Sabbath." Sweetie Reed's face smeared with tears and awful with weeping words. Her spirit seemed swept up as that of a whirling dervish.

"Jerry is solely asking me to rub his back down, as he always did in the prime days of our marriage; every time I did, I was faced with the meaning of time and that branded scar as an undying tributary of the river: JW. And this bathing down, oiling was and is to face the nature of human cruelty. To face the meaning of suffering but on Jericho Witherspoon's terms. And to face something of that covenant that brought us together. The transactions that brought me here to the North, the nakedness of that act, and the desirous nakedness that brought me to Jericho Witherspoon's arms and the embracing of him, my husband before God and man.

"Well, now I'm shocked down to the soles of my feet to hear Jerry's soul condition wrapped up in the garment of those words: *Sweetie, I want you to trouble the waters this morning,* as I ever was over those last seven words of the Redeemer's upon the Cross at Golgotha. Especially too, since those words came from a song that my beloved Angelina loved to sing. But she was a Christian, through and through. Jerry ain't hardly ever had any use for the word of the Lord.

"Now Jerry's getting me mad (because once again Jericho Wither-spoon is assigning me a task); even though his words sound like a new man, the wife part in me is thinking he sounds familiarly like the old-time embossing husband. I'm looking over at Jesus, for some help and comfort . . . A way out of no-way. As I try to look at Jesus Christ, for Him, I find myself thinking of what the preacher Packwood said when I was converted, that second time, that *when Jesus came out of that tomb, he was the same man, but different.* But Jerry's words got me caught up like the stays in a kite to a point that I ain't realizing what direction he's going, not just the direction he's heading out towards—as when I was a gal and we first married up. He was explaining my lessons and using that old blue-backed speller. I was so awed by his words and his terrible beauty that I plain sometimes didn't hear a *continental* thing he was saying much less understand it! And at the same time I shouted back, 'Jerry, I know these waters as the lines in my palms; you think I need directions' as I now oiled down his burdensome back; 'You better let me bathe your body, so as the Master can take your soul.' I looked again for Jesus but He was gone, as if to say this is a domestic quarrel, I can lead them to waters but I can't make them take part in the redemption of their marriage; leaving only the handprint flooding over my bathing hand, *and* across my soul; the other *side* of the Master saying: *Whatsoever I have meshed together; let no fool think he can turn wine back to water without turning to vinegar.*

"I was brought over by Jesus and the angels to see Angelina and be reunited with Jerry in this dream, while slumbering as a babe tied to a bough upon a tree. Suddenly the windstorm; and then Jerry and I were in hand-to-hand combat, as quarrelsome lovers—but I was also baptizing him with balmy waters, with my right hand, which was what I had desired to do all of our days together. Jerry would hear none of it—I come to know anything he's *baptizing* me back to remember the other side of a witness is spun out of troubling calamity; 'That's man's touchstone back to reality, troubles,' he said; now here

I'm spending my days and evenings helping folks who's hungry for food and trying to overcome the troubles of this old Herod and Nicodemus suited-up world—like this hearing aid helps me to know life—but I ain't troubling waters, *enough.* Maybe *that's* in his mind. Jerry thinks I'm actually *comforting the tribulation within the waters of time.* The wife in me collapses back into mocking merriment, as how you just can't satisfy these men; but this thing has gone far beyond a domestic quarrel; it's now exploded as a brook of bubbles out of a holy bay into an all-out war. You know, mourners, a husband can create a crisis in a household by coveting his wife's egg money, but this *ex-* husband of mine is trampling upon the grapes and the lilies of what I perceive as perhaps my only gift to God and man. This man is coveting power over my soul condition, even in death.

"I wanted to stir Jerry up, to know there was still time to embrace the Redeemer, in the sleeve of his long sleep there in the hospital, and now he's stirring something up in me and stripping me down, out of school, to the very bone of my *contentiousness,* and my consciousness. I said these poor souls are troubled enough; and he's trying to show me in his way that I'm making them *soft,* even as I'm trying to be helpful and tender with them and soothe out the wrinkles in their bellies and counsel their heads clear as water, so they'll be tender to each other and not get drowned by the icestorms of the North; but once in the storm not get drowned by the flood's storm of rocks and choked to death by the seaweeds that hang about the throat as tarnished necklaces, and the smell of blood in the waters for each downcast man's throat in this dog-eat-dog driving current of breakneck speed. Jerry's trying to tell me that the flood never stops for a respite but deepens trouble as it rises. So like all children of God, when they caught in a heartbreaking question they turn to look for Mother. I look. All I can see is the beating wings of angels; so fast they could veil the quickness of a sparrow's eye. I try to pick up what they were covering over. Angelina's behind them, I tell myself. I'm shocked as I once was in the long ago to discover that Jerry was looking for her face; though his words were slated for me, in the long, oval-faced mirror, in the wake of the angels' wings, just before my face.

". . . Then I try to look for Jesus' face again for an answer, but His face is too powerful and radiant to look upon; shattering the glass of the mirror. I can see the tips of His beautiful naked feet at the edges of the horizon, I think.

"That's when I see and hear old Braidwood, the coachman turned carpenter, moving like a terrapin. His voice warning me, like he did that time when I was a child back down on old man Rollins Reed's plantation. Telling me not to look into the face of the sun, 'directly.' I'm standing there on that rocking chair swaying porch. Rising on the balls of my naked feet; the planks shaking and trembling. The Negroes who are still there have to place shoulder props underneath, as pillars for the house to stand against the winds of circumstance. (Wings on the shoulders of each plaster angel are cracked.) Now I believe I see a life beyond the horizon, as I'm on my tiptoes, though I'm thinking the terrible light's going to scratch out my eyes. But I'm young and I ain't hardly afraid of anything. Braidwood's saying, 'Don't try to stare it down, Thursday's child, ain't no win . . . melt the light out your eyeballs, like poison rot shot through the body of an apple to its seed.' And I think to say but don't say: *The light of the body is of the eye.* But I said to him: 'You sought the sun of your horizon. You went away, learned to be a carpenter.' And he said, 'Yes, because I'm a man, and I got little-bitty children to support, and a wife who is my prop.'

"And I felt like I had stumped my toe in the dark, as I was stomping a jubilee dance, and suddenly somebody blew out all the slit-eyed candles; their flares pitched out of their heads and back to the darkness. But then I said, in her voice (mother's), 'Mother declared that I had a kingdom beyond the heat of the sun, and even unto the breath when the last light explodes out of the Heavens . . . and the glow of that good dew will mark our dwelling place as buds of new-found light.' And behind our voices I heard old I. V. Reed saying, 'Gal, this here plantation *is* your kingdom come. Now that black Yankee slave giving you a chance to rise out the backwaters; throwing you a black-snake rope of deliverance. Let it dangle and you'll surely go down dead in the tide.' Now I don't know whether to rise out of the waters on tiptoe. Go seek the wings of morning or drown myself in the tide, or look to this Jerry for yet another turn in the wheel of survival, as I had when I arrived at the train station, in June of 1882. And he had a wedding present in his hand.

". . . So now Jerry is trying to make me see that I haven't stirred up nothing in my guests; haven't troubled the waters; they are coming to me as to a wealthy lady, whose rich clothes can hide their raggedy, patched-up and mended-over set of wings, without them doing any natural sewing. Like *victory* was *ours.* Most of those clothes I give them aren't hand-me-downs from my back, but the discarded apparel of charity-giving rich white ladies. They need firing up more than ever, Jerry is telling me—and they leave my apartment too cooled down, veiled with the steam of sweets, potlikker, vegetables, slumber-breads and stomach-stirring meats; instead of being increased in sourness, as a soul seasoned in sorrow and swiftly acquainted with the perils of each taste of light at daybreak upon the eyelids and the spade-smack of an earth clod upon the lips, as lyrical bitter licorice of our condition.

". . . This is what he's trying to get at me through them, and them through me, and just as mean as that, too, as his final will and testament, inside the sleeve of death. I'm offering them a hot meal, and hard-clothes advice, as the long suit of our survival, but it's coming up as a sugar-tit: a scolding rap upon their knuckles once they get away, that's how I then start to interpret his words, for I also know all what he's saying ain't necessarily so. Jerry's tongue was always smooth but never golden and his mouth was too narrow to be a Bible; I never was known to spoil any children in my rodding care and keeping. And that's when I said up to Jerry, whose face is all too plain, 'But that would be like shaking salt down into their wounds.' And he says: 'They need *remembering* and *troubling* and *rekindling.*' And I says, 'But, Jerry,' trying to avoid his face after what I've just said (and the JW brand upon his back that I've continued to rub, oil and stroke) despite his words, 'They have got to eat to live; can't nothing much happen till that meal and meat commences its pure percolating, even as I'm trying to spell out the bread of life . . . For just as I'm rubbing down your back I'm not kneading it to bread. Besides, Jerry, I'm not fattening them for the slaughter, I'm feeding them the bread of survival.' Yes, but I'm also thinking at the same time, maybe a worldly-wise man can light the way out of the chamber needle of one's own imagery by resorting to the wisdom robes of a natural fool, if I learn from the mock in his masquerade; and don't allow myself to get all heated up and steamy-eyed; as a widow woman wearing a veil."

And now the boy Nathaniel looked over at his Grandfather Witherspoon's face there in the casket and knew those idea-words were true, *remembering,* and *troubling* and *rekindling;* how often had he heard them from Grandfather Witherspoon's lips, during, before and after his own reading out loud with the patriarch. Sometimes shuffling the words around into new light, and direction, as in *troubling remembering* and *rekindling troubling* in the *slumber sleeve of perilous sleep.* And the boy thought of his Grandfather Witherspoon's slave tunic that often adorned his own naked form; and he looked again upon those mocking lips and the invisible yet highly visible film of juice, that screen of spittle he took even into eternity, where he no doubt would spat upon the wings of the angel's easy flight. Grandfather Witherspoon's personal instrument words of life: remembering, troubling, and rekindling.

Now the soaring Sweetie Reed cried out:

"I realized that all of this could only take place inside the wrinkled, flexing sleeve of a dream, because you can't find your way out until you're delivered from sleep, by a force not made of hands, even as those dreams in the suggestive fulsomeness of their strutting, mocking garment sometimes strip you—as they unravel your daydreams, too —naked as a virgin on her wedding night of her finest silk cloth— resembling beauty, though the form and face may not be as beauteous as a maiden delivered of the covenant of her virginity, without a knife at her throat. It occurs to me how Jerry's changing the subject to get me to change my mind; when in fact everything's on my mind. But that's when I start in on him; yet still rubbing his back with oil in a sweethearting manner and stirring him up at the same time . . . Deed, and now word, though unveiled, commenced last October, when he first started unraveling.

". . . But now no man can deliver you from your time of death; you may find deliverance and a new baptism in death, I now thought out loud (which it seemed to me was my task down there in the troubling waters, now dripping with the oils slipped down from his backbone) . . . Even Almighty God, Himself, can only postpone death; he cannot stop death's cycle (just like He couldn't stop those October leaves from trembling, turning and falling off the tree outside your hospital window, Jericho Witherspoon), lest He stop the flow of His creation, His process; and He can't do that because it is all within the genesis cycle of His imagination and beyond His Being and His stirring Rest and His uneasy Wakefulness to the knowledge of man and nature . . . When He blew breath in man in Eden, He blew His own first breath out of His own being so much He cracked His own rib cage!

"That's when Jerry starts to howling: 'Sweet, you more radical in your taste buds for treason than I am.' For I tell you the bridegroom may not deliver the virgin if her time is upon her and extended over her wedding night as a bloody veil of nonsurrender, even as he will also search the sheets for her blood to know and not to know if she was a virgin bride, if she can't, with a razor gleaming in his hand,

when the morning sun comes screaming through the night shade
. . . But, mourners, that's about exactly the time I now discovered that
I was standing naked in the tide; the sun gleaming upon my naked,
fallen breasts. I'm too old to desire up a man, but what in the world
is the Master doing exposing my nakedness for all the world to see
by the light of day? And oiling down my former husband's back,
who's newly dead?"

And the remembering young man Nathaniel Witherspoon—seated
in Rollins Reed's rocker—reflected how that upon those last words
of Sweetie Reed's the mourners started to stirring up and shuddering
and trembling . . . Some laughing and some weeping and the unsettlement seemed fullsome, wild and fearful. As when some new, lost-
found spirit bares her soul on the threshing floor, at a midnight
campground meeting; so that the congregation of mourners from
every link and corner of the community with deep ties in the church
comes alive to a new set of warnings and tidal anxieties, behind the
veil of propriety.

They were a people who had gathered as so many strands to celebrate their oneness with the honorable dead man. They had come to
listen to the sermon of Rev. Browne, and pay tribute to one of their
patriarchs, prepare themselves to see him buried and go home, but not
this . . . Yet they had also gathered that day to see how the great old
man was put away—if he was celebrated in the grand manner. They
were mightily interested in recording which family members demonstrated their love for Jericho Witherspoon most . . . which ones would
reveal their heartbreak by displaying uncontrollable anguish. Which
family member would yield up to a stream of flowing, unstoppable
tears, behind the veil of grief.

But nothing in their ceremonial history, nor memory, had prepared
them for this outrage and Sweetie Reed's revelations of her dream
within a dream of intimacy . . . She had moved that day from a
spiritual oracle to a secular remembrance Rock of her own, personal
ritual of redemption, the young man now reflected. But all was based
in part, he speculated, upon the way in which the dead man, this
Jericho Witherspoon, had spoken to her in her depths, knee-deep in
the backwaters of time and space, out of a most fierce secular rage,
that for the church had no place in the funeral service; but belonged
on the threshing floor of revelation, on a witness-bearing occasion
. . . Many were attracted to her naked honesty—even as they were
shocked to find how much they loved the gossip aspect of what she

unveiled—while they disdained her wrenching of this occasion, set aside solely for glorifying the deceased . . . But rage, rage indeed, the young man scoffed and celebrated as he wept, amid *the dying of the light,* recalled now of the long ago time, only fourteen years before this day. Oh, Thomas' tapping upon the light of man's chains to death, in death, about his own father. And he heard Sweetie Reed turn and weep upon the bed of shuddering sleep . . . Oh, blood of my blood, Grandfather Witherspoon.

But the small boy in Raven-Snow's funeral home that noonday had his arms around his slumped father's shoulder; Arthur Witherspoon's body stretched out; Sweetie Reed's words had struck him down to a deadly fit. As she now cried out in the delivering of the lost tongues within her being:

". . . In the heat of the day you can stare up into the face of the sun, but no answer comes back to you from the other side, only you are knocked down and blinded by the light, as old Braidwood was trying to tell me, by too much exposure—not knowledge . . . We need dreams for deliverance and revelation, all right, but though eyes can scream as eagle's wings for a new blinding light beyond the sun's eye, we may be scarred forever trying to stare down the radiance of God's meaning, as the virgin who's seen an early death in the well waters and now is blinded by studying the sun on a rooftop and tries to fly off that roof to capture it in her arms, when she suddenly dreams of herself with child; and anyway our arms are far too short to box with the Almighty Father, I wanted to scream out to Jerry, because that's where all of this *troubling* business of his is leading and streaking up my body and flowing back down to the soul trouble of our old-time marriage situation: not blended with that old-time religion. What Braidwood and Jerry didn't understand was that *the Light of the Body is of the Eye,* as Luke tells us and as Angelina had told me. I was too young to understand but could only repeat it. Now I see in that oval glass of reflection what that statement was meant to mean.

"Yet my second mind is also saying, Yes, but if all of these things be so, then why has Almighty God set him down here to *set you out* . . . to set my house on fire, down here? Finally I said out to him, 'Jerry, I do believe you still got some spite-work for Almighty God, like He was your father. He's the Father who delivered you as far as He could; you never went the rest of the journey. Spirit got lost in those waters (like a bridegroom gets his arm caught up in his sleeve, hurrying to dress and fly swift to the side of his veiled, beloved bride's arms) even though your body climbed and became the shape of a mountain's grievous and hardy shoulder slabs. Then you got lost in the wilderness.'

"I'm also thinking Almighty God's postponed Jerry's leave-taking upon the wings of Death so as to school me of something by His Son's hand, His only begotten Son, Jesus—whose feet and hem are visible to me now on the horizon—even as His light is blinding; and Jerry, who is now kind of a sacred infidel, has a piercing voice and the hand print of the Master's still bright upon my own oiling hand as the raised lighthouse is a watchman to the night.

"This is the exact moment when Jerry says to me, 'Sweet, your God has struck you down dead; you thought that it was I who was soley troubled but you are struck *down* dead!' I was shocked to the soles of my feet, thinking that I was hooked in the heart come alive on the pole as a bait of the fisherman; pitched to the quaking, thirsty life of the sea, to save it; and in so doing, as a sacrifice, I sacrificed my life for them, my blood, but mainly to Him, for Him. Jericho Witherspoon's centering down on the barrenness of my efforts, *naturally.*

"I saw the mountain's very personality etched and slated out as tongue-lashing meanness, backbone courage, arm-winging justice, waxed in his body parts as a mirror reflecting his lightless soul condition, as another skin to the anklebone to the nerve center and housed in the skullbone, as survival knowledge; so that when Jerry initially emerged out of the waters he was ready for the real climb up the jagged mountain. Then faced with the wilderness of wasteland; to go through that and then back down to the waters of time where we were now, knee-deep in death.

"But I also saw my own personality as an active agency for Jesus, and Jerry Witherspoon's terrible face trying to show me up as a simple-minded mouthpiece of the Maker, my Master Jesus Christ; without will power, argument and contention with the Christ. It came down to me why Jerry's jealous of my special relationship with Jesus Christ, the lover of my soul. Here I'm stroking down Jerry's back— husband and wife in the waters of time and butt-naked, as newborn babes—in order to smooth out the pain of his burdensome days; but he thinks I'm rubbing his back for his pleasure. The man part in him needs this good turn of soothing oils, that might be used to light the lanterns of the poor. But I'm preparing his body with these oils in my own mind for his redemption. Jerry doesn't realize this. I just agreed to start with the back because that was what he thought he wanted and the brand touched us all back to the beginning time. But I'm rubbing Jerry down with the preparing oils . . . Using the very hand where Jesus' visage is imprinted, now . . . Because I had to break free of our hand-to-hand sealed over by the Redeemer, Himself, in order to oil down Jerry's nakedness."

"Mother Sweetie, sit down," Nathaniel's father cried aloud. "We've heard about enough from you this morning to last a lifetime. Pompey gave us the eulogy. Woman, whatever trouble there was between you and my father is half a century old; he didn't appear to you in the upper room nor in any other room, nor in the troubled waters of your imagination. Even if your fancy tells you his ghost spoke to you at dawn. Your normal courtesy would tell you not to live out the figments of a dream, for the world to hear and see, as an appeal for sympathy. Even an imagined ghost would not appeal to you to come here and preach out the length and breadth of the dead man's days, like a galloping, headless rider on a pale horse and on the day of this great man's funeral—that's your trouble; settle it all, as an old account, in silence."

"Arthur, Jerry never accepted Jesus as his Savior, in the heat of the sun, and that's your trouble—but perhaps not his, in the long haul . . . Because he came to me in the windstorm of the flood's arms. He didn't know it *perhaps,* but he was acting as an agent of Jesus. I'm trying to retell you as well, lest you inherit the whirlwind; find yourself one fine day gasping in death for eternal life upon the shores, with nothing in the bank to go up under you when the Master calls you in for a reckoning and an accounting, there ain't gotta be any *collective bargaining* up there."

"*Master?* Seems as if your eulogy is an old confession, Mother Sweetie—*Reed.*"

"Hold your spiteful, salty tongue there, Arthur *Witherspoon,* lest the Almighty turn it dumb as my right ear without a hearing aid . . . I will be heard out!" Pompey c. j. Browne moved in at his side, in order to usher the son of Jericho Witherspoon down onto his bench.

"If I say to you sit down, woman . . . Don't you know I'm telling you what you know is right in your heart—come back out of the wilderness of your imagination and—"

"Arthur, don't put anything out there in life unless you willing to be embraced by it before you go home to face your Maker."

"I'm prepared to take my family and leave this chapel, Mother Sweetie," Nathaniel's father said, "if you don't sit down and let us finish the last of this funeral in peace, which plainly isn't your funeral, although you are trying to take it over like you take everything else over."

Great-Momma Sweetie Reed just stood there for a few minutes with her hand arched upon her backbone, as if to say, Isn't this signal enough for you to calm down and let me finish? Two minutes went by, then she continued:

". . . For if Jesus let Jerry appear to me with something He wanted me to know, then why should I not appear to you this morning to *trouble* you into recognition, even as the Master has something for you to know through me? To guarantee that we all ain't having a nightmare, even as He's become the bridegroom of my soul, since that day in June of 1905—and I guess like a good chaperon, too, He's staying in the background, because He ain't chaperoning young courting folks, He's interceding husband and wife. The man part of Him knows that's dangerous, as the God part knows that He don't have to hide His face to show His hand; He can stand before us without coming between us, even as He en-joins us through argument; *that* caused our coming asunder, and will cause our healing."

The boy realized that his father was getting caught up in the argument part of what Great-Momma Sweetie Reed was trying to reveal. He loved argument; but he apparently also saw this as the one way to settle Great-Momma Sweetie Reed down, which Nathaniel guessed his father felt was the mistake he had made the day before, when he had allowed her presence to so intimidate him that it drove him to the insulin reaction and probably, too, Nathaniel imagined, he's never taken Great-Momma Sweetie on about Grandfather Witherspoon, just as he had failed to take her on two days before at her apartment, when he invited her to take part in the funeral arrangements.

The boy also wondered how sincere his father had been about wanting her to be a part of the arrangements. Had he wanted her to only be a silent partner, as they said in the movies? Had that been a part of the reason why she and his grandfather had also split up? Sweetie Reed as a silent partner? Never, the boy thought to himself now, looking at the four-foot-eight, ninety-eight-pound lady, as she hummed before the casket, refreshing herself before she started in on Arthur Witherspoon again. Who would dare take on this cedar-colored, tiny, impish, saintly woman of so much earthly power and heavenly delight, and particularly when she put that hand upon her hip, and arched it over her backbone, as she did again for an especial reading and rendering and yes, showdown. Nathaniel's mother looked about to go into a state of shock, herself. And the boy wondered, what did Great-Momma Sweetie Reed have up her sleeve *now?*

Once again they were holding on to Arthur Witherspoon. Holding him down. Nathaniel also tried to hold on to his own spirit and contain his own questions. As his mother was comforting his father, Nathaniel observed how his father became more quarrelsome with her than he was with Raven-Snow and Rev. Browne, who was a pretty strong presence to struggle with, at six-seven. One side of his father seemed to be listening to Great-Momma Sweetie Reed for new light and another side seemed to desperately cry out to shut her up. Was it that he feared what she might say in that light? She had already said enough to shake the mourners and the family up. Nathaniel believed that his father was now more quarrelsome with Madeline, his mother, than any of the rest of them, who were trying to settle him down because he couldn't take any of his fury and anger out on Great-Momma Sweetie Reed, directly.

Now Memphis Raven-Snow, as if to show that he had some control in his business establishment, started to usher the mourners out of the chapel, leaving only the first two rows of benches for the ten or twelve family members.

". . . So, Arthur, kindly let me speak out, because what I'm trying to get at this noonday is a confession, mixed up with a transformation. God revealing something new to me through Jerry of all the people —although Jerry had revealed so much to me of book knowledge as a girl bride—when it was I who thought *she,* Angelina, was God's agency all these years to teach me what Jerry had spurned to know all of his days . . . 'You go on baptize me,' Jerry Witherspoon said, 'even as you are oiling down my back; if you must; but my soul can't be rested until it's bathed in the pool of trouble-faced waters, cracking the calm—that you got to stir up, Sweet . . . Does your Jesus exist there in those tributaries of tribulation?'

"But now I was saying to him: 'This very moment of the bathing of sorrow and baptism must be sewed to the drowning and the dunking of the body so as you come up against it again; that your body is being washed away in the waters as the old self, that old skin, if flung broadcast, away into the tide,' and Jerry saying, 'That can't happen, lest I drown the best parts of me and you and your Jesus are going to have to accept that . . . How can I be renewed without the unadulterated flesh of my very existence that was formed and pounded to my skeleton, boy to man, and kept me alive, branded in me; not simply in earthly form but in the form of my memory etched days—wrestled together as wheat is bound together, but the chaff gets through. How can that be cast away in the tide of times, or wrapped up in faith?' And that's when I said, 'No, Jerry, because the skin of our old ways must be discarded, as the foreskin of flesh in the circumcision . . . That's what death does, discards the body, so as we can concentrate and recollect the soul.' And as I rubbed the oil upon his back and his shoulders, his chest, his loins, his legs, I took the form of the servant, to know the likeness of men . . . obedient to death, even the death of the cross, and I sang that song of old:

> *Prepare me one body, I'll go down. I'll go down.*
> *Prepare me one body like a man.*
> *The man of sorrows, sinner, see—*
> *I'll go down, I'll go down—*
> *He died for you and He died for me—*
> *I'll go down and die.*
> *Prepare me, Lord, one body,*
> *Prepare me one body like a man.*
> *I'll go down and die, I'll go down,*
> *I'll go down, I'll go down and die . . .*

Nathaniel's father cried forth like that wounded Lamb the boy had seen giving birth when he had gone with Uncle Ulysses on the hunting party for deer meat: "Mother Sweet—no, NAW!"

But Nathaniel was also thinking, as Great-Momma Sweetie spoke those last words of the time he brought his grandfather's favorite goat's meat dinner on a platter and he would recite the poem of Blake's in such a tender and yet powerful voice . . . "The Lamb." Yet that was a religious poem, it seemed. It was also a song, when Paul Robeson sang it.

Grandfather Witherspoon was plainly not religious. But if this was true, how could he make you feel that poem, when he recited it aloud? A simple poem, too, yet what did it mean behind those words? He could hear his grandfather's voice even now, especially with those last lines of the poem. God did live there in that voice for a moment, no matter if Great-Momma had called him part infidel or not.

Little lamb, who made thee?
Does thou know who made thee?

Little Lamb, I'll tell thee,
Little Lamb, I'll tell thee:

He is called by thy name,
For He calls Himself a Lamb.
He is meek and He is mild:
He became a little child.
I a child and thou a lamb,
We are called by His name.

Little Lamb, God bless thee.
Little Lamb, God bless thee.

What Great-Momma Sweetie Reed had been saying recalled to Nathaniel's mind an argument between his parents that he had overheard. His father had said: "Madeline, your face is too perfect and it has nothing in it yet—it's too calm with innocence and purity; until it shows the imprint of grief and trouble you can't know joy. It's without a stamp and a personality—it's calm as a virgin spring." He had some nerve, all right, Nathaniel thought. But his mother, who was given to dramatic moments of violence, simply took a lovely hand mirror his father had given her for a birthday present and cracked into the very middle of the looking glass with a small hammer, saying, "And is that what you would like to see looking down upon your memorable face every time you cry out for relief in the bed?"

Great-Momma Sweetie now moved even closer to the casket, as she said:

". . . But that's when Jerry cried forth to me, 'I'm dead, fool woman, how are you going to negotiate eternal life for a man that's dead . . . Other than by stormy waters. Ha!' and I said: 'Stormy waters brought me to you and you to me, *this morning, too soon.*' And he said: 'You think these waters are eternal—why, you'll never baptize again in the same stream, Sweet, that you think of as a holy spring river; foolish old woman, we still are in that swamp flood, like the one down near where they buried your mother, the beautiful Angelina.'

"Then when I looked down upon the waters, through the rippling and the roaring and the thundering I saw a shocking face of Jerry's there just as plain. Reminding me of that time I saw a visage of the hoped-for man I might marry, when I was a gal, back down on old man Rollins Reed's plantation, deep into that well: the outlined face of my daydream man; but I looked until my eyes got sore trying to make him out, and I started to let the ladder down partway; crawl down upon it to get a closer look at the reflection upon the well water caused by the face of the sun, when suddenly I recalled the words of that old slave, Minnie-Bea Bowers—'Gal, anytime you wishes to see your future husband, just pull off all your clothes at night and turn them wrongside out, then hang them on the foot of your bed. Now kneel and say your prayers, but say them backwards and get into bed backwards, pure naked. You will see your future husband at the crack of dawn, sure as the rooster crows.' " Upon those words of Minnie-Bea Bowers several mourners fled from the chapel. But others scurried to the front, knocking over benches. Arthur Witherspoon fell back in dread.

". . . Just then Jerry collapsed for dead, again, on the face of the tide; everything froze, as before the world was said to be and not to be . . . But now as I looked again I saw this Jerry-face turn into a young man who resembled a young Jerry. The young Jerry-man is naked, only a goatskin about his loins. And even though the tide and current are rushing swiftly his body is full-length still, like it is right there in that casket. That's when my first mind had the old memory lost in the long tide of time but it now surfaced: if you want the body of a drowned man to emerge, just throw some of his old clothes in the general direction of the tide where he fell and the clothes will find the soul of his old body and cling to his form. I looked longer and deeper on the sides of him and beneath him; I saw in the swirling waters some gold coins, homemade ladder of braided ropes, chains, chicken-coop wire, stone tablets, several pairs of diamond-eyed dice, smooth stones, some knocking-bones and a huge jagged slab from a rugged-face mountain cliff.

"Come to me to turn the body of the dead, or not breathing young man's body over, who resembled a young Jerry so, in the tide—to see if . . . When I thought I heard him say: 'Sweetie, your heart is as cold as a river of ice; I got the light juices of a younger man's body in me yet.' How could a dead man float as lightbread upon the water without descending? I wondered. And talk to me in a spite-filled voice. Yet when I put my ear to his heart, I found his heart was not beating and something wild in my heart leapt, like the heart of a young gal. Tears upon my cheeks and I followed my impulse and bent to kiss his lips before I turned him over to see if . . . Then the tide started to flow again, with blood.

"And as my lips touched his, which had not touched a man's in forty years, I realized that he was still slightly breathing—even though his heart condition was unheard of. Lord, I thought, maybe I can't hear out of both ears. I could smell his body; and it gave off the odor of the oils I had used to bathe down and prepare Jericho Witherspoon's body. I almost fell back in the tide with shock. Now I righted myself and with all of my might I finally turned him over to see if—when I looked upon his left shoulder blade—and sure enough, Lord, Lawd God Almighty, there was the branded scar JW —as vivid as the feet of the Lord, upon the horizon, placed there upon Jericho Witherspoon's back by his father over one hundred years before; I fell to my knees in the tide. Clinging to the young man's body I must have drifted for hours; all of my life seemed to swirl up before me; I thought I was sure gone.

"Just as I am hugging and holding, he starts to calling me what Jerry used to call me when we first married up, Precious Pone; but just hearing old Jerry's voice—I thought the tide would carry us away in the whirlwind's voice as we were cradled in each others arms. Lord, I don't rightly know, but the world went still for a peculiar moment in my imagination; behind us I could hear Jerry's voice now more powerful and commanding than even in real life, rippling and roaring through the current of our certain motion: an ever increasing echo bouncing louder and still louder off the mountain slab and through the wilderness . . .

" 'Sweet, I want you to trouble the covered-over conscience in the depths of these waters; I want you to stir them with the trouble we've seen so that dunking in the waters can mean something else, not only to the inner lining of the being you and your Jesus would throw away, but to the tribe's so-called soul-caressing wings . . . Preach, if you must, but teach and lacerate you will, into our sheer enchantment with aggravation—making us bewitched by the sheer monotony of trouble, as a rhythm, but not as yet another source of gossip, or reflex action and slippery scandal, or even an endurance cup, but as life's ordering condition, purifying as water is supposed to be; so that trouble loses the garment of its personality inside the inner lining of our hearts and spirits; we cull no joy from the state of life's weariness but are revitalized in defeat to come to know that we cannot be defeated, but also that we can be destroyed; as you, Sweet, reset the troubled, tottering, swollen, water-logged jubilee table that emerges trembling, splintering, and unleashed forth from the spewing flood.'

" 'But, Jerry, Mother Angelina taught, and Sister Lovelady preached—that trouble don't last always.'

" 'Forget it,' he cried, 'even unto the rising sun and the dewy campgrounds: the unfolded truth in the flood . . . the mission of madness in the very texture of man's days upon this earth.'

"But in the nightmare of the flooding I could not hear his voice but only perceive his sobbing . . . I'm hugging on to this young man, this boy-child-man Jerry, like a schoolgirl for all I'm worth—trying to listen out for his old voice for new word pictures to puzzles beyond answers to patterns I'd thought about myself, that went past the cry of old, 'By the Waters of Babylon, we were sat down'; and now only hearing his weeping as sobs of a brokenhearted child. That's when it came to me why this young Jerry (the one I had never seen, nor held in my arms before) meant so much to me and how much I needed love that only a dream of my life in sleep in the darkness of the nightmare could unfold, not during my awakening time in the heat of the stark sun's stare; because there was I. V. Reed's strong-sounding voice, sterling clear as when they tap upon a bell and it peals away—behind Jerry's commanding harp-drum sounding, an organ in the storm. And that's when old I. V. Reed, *my father,* even those words, *my father* —I had hardly ever spoken out loud in the heat of the sun, though he was sometimes in my bedtimes prayers too (years after I came back down there to his deathbed to bury him, when he died out at seventy-nine, in the spring of 1906) asked for forgiveness and redemption and salvation. I. V. Reed coming back to my mind now as backwater in a flood, lodged away in the loathing, and pitying, grieving, troubling, and remembering secret places in my heart, so as I was spinning off with the new Jerry in my arms. My old father came to my mind and I was a little gal again, being lifted up on to the steps of that old rickety white porch back down on old man Rollins Reed's plantation, my grandfather-slaver—some seventy years and more ago—by that pa-troller man; *now* whilst one foot remained sucked down in the muddy flood and I was crying and weeping and one leg up on old man Rollins Reed's lap. I. V. Reed just now coming forth towards the porch. Just barely able to make out his face in the screen, and Lawd, I cried out: 'Daddy!' Lord, Lawd, must I go back to that time, too—when only my Jesus was left for me to call on though I was seven, and memories of what my mother had told me start to weave about my mind: an encircling robe all about my body. But he didn't seem to know, hear nor care about my voice, nor see my arms reaching to him, up to him, and past old man Rollins Reed's beard.

"And that's when old man Rollins Reed said out to I. V. Reed, tears in his eyes, 'Angelina, the one who loved you, is gone, Ivy—they killed her and here's the child.'

"And I can still hear the hooves of the patroller's horse-drawn wagon racing off and that screen door to the porch swatting closed, like a folded scroll slapping down upon a mosquito."

But now the ushers, led by Arthur Witherspoon, Rev. Browne and Memphis Raven-Snow, moved in on the seventy-seven-year-old Sweetie Reed and led her away as she went off into weeping and singing in an enraged voice.

10

Troubling,
Remembering,
Revealing

He had fallen asleep an hour before, but now the young man Nathaniel Witherspoon found that his hot writing hand was still burning and weary to the bone of numbness; yet sharpened by his sudden stage of wakefulness. He dipped it into the green wooden bucket of crushed ice, where he wished a bottle of Mums stood, alongside the watchtower of ice for relief; with a warmed-up Candy Cummings at his side. Most of the ice in the bucket had melted away. His tongue felt thick and dry; his palate thirsty, as if he, not Great-Momma Sweetie Reed, had been talking for so long. He had been remembering her confession and memoir at the chapel for what seemed an hour now.

Nathaniel flexed the fingers of his writing hand in the motion of trying on a new pair of gloves; wiggled the fingers as fluttering wings. Thank God I took piano lessons for six years, he mused. Hypersensitive to the marrow of the bone. If only I had learned to master *The Flight of the Bumblebee* . . . Why not quit? Ah, that early American dropout Bartleby had the right idea: "I prefer not to." But he didn't have a Sweetie Reed to contend with.

Now with his left hand Nathaniel flecked icy droplets from the bucket about his eyes, his jowls and his neck to get fully aroused from the last clutches of steamy sleep. Some of the ice water tricklets got caught up in his eyelids, causing his long, dark lashes to beat like a sparrow's wings in the wind. As he bathed his face he thought of an actor bathing off the layers of greasepaint after a performance. Sweetie Reed was still asleep, though emerging towards wakefulness.

The young man looked over at the labyrinth of memories (as layers of leaves of every suit, color and shape, piled high upon the legal pad) thick with the intricacies of his longhand pitched to the flight of Sweetie Reed's far-flung saga; he thought: the steam may have gone out of my writing hand, but not out of my appetite and spirit for her story. The elaborate inner-ear weave of her oracle appeared all but indecipherable on the yellow legal pad now, as the faintly smeared ink grew cold. The writing lay still in longish, strangely official-looking, curling threads of blue-black penmanship of proclamations, puns and perils, he smiled. The penmanship itself culled from a thousand influences, going back to the beginning time.

Now the scrawled-out longhand appeared as shorthand about to leap from the boundaries of the legal pad, as he finished off a jigger of Rémy Martin and ice—more than a labyrinth of calligraphy but as an etching in relief spun and sculpted out upon the straw-colored legal scroll, and as whirled cobwebs spun back to dancing ghosts in time.

But what of her hand and the meaning behind it that recorded "Arthur R. Witherspoon, June 5, 1905," when Daddy always celebrated his birthday on April 4? Was this some more slippage of dates, in the memory bank of time—but surely not two months? Ah, let me not think of it. *Frailty, thy name is.* . . . But no. This was all to signal the date when Jericho Witherspoon had left her. What a putdown.

As Nathaniel Witherspoon dried off his iced hand on a thin, ropy old Santa Fe bar towel, he thought: but the garment of memory certainly was Sweetie Reed's long suit. Grandpa's even more so. Film of juice spat in the face of the pale horse, pale rider. Laughed up his sleeve at Mr. Death. Carve my grandfather's name in stone, though eternity should be embraced by his light forever and ever. World without the word in the end. JW.

But I. V. Reed—who pitched his voice to fit all occasions—if I'm knotted to your line then I'm a labyrinth of lies more jagged than the neckbone connected by cartilage to the backbone, with a milk-white liver and a cracked-up wishbone for sure. Shit on a shingle mixed with grits. And lambs' wool and sheeps' skin beyond degrees of storytelling. You fabulous fishmonger with a little green-eyed diamond whirled away inside of a twisting wheel of a tale. Hermes' kin, the signifying monkey.

. . . Perhaps it's best, he thought, to come prepared not only with Shakespeare, Freud, the Bible and Marx, but with Auntie Foisty's *hand* touched to the vertebrate of it all. A rainbow as her glory crown, but no pot of gold for I. V. Reed at the end. Callously consecrated into Sweetie's song. Flying him away, while revealing aspects of his revelling, corked-up faces and blood-curdling voices, pealed off in the shimmer cast by the moonlight. And oh, upon that bed he was in nigger heaven, a magical handkerchief gagged to the rhythm of his fitful breathing, body and soul. Olé solar eclipse and the soft shoe. Tambo and bones as one. He who dressed himself in humility, plucked from a scarecrow's garb of deceits. Iago cracked out of Othello's essence, Cereno cracked from the rib cage of Babo . . . But my grand kin, too. Lord. Lawd.

Nathaniel looked down on the blank yellow page awaiting Sweetie Reed's continuance: the fourth legal pad upon his rocking knee now. Plenty good room. And the transformed word shall be my bond, and out of the bond Great-Momma Sweetie Reed's word.

He heard a distant church bell peal off the hour at six o'clock. Outside—through the strawberry lace curtains—he could see it was getting dark. The street lights flickered as just before the start of a new act at the theater; the lights were dimmed; and the last light was enunciated. It suddenly occurred to Nathaniel: I'll capture her dear conscious right away, while still suspended in flight, as soon as her flowing memory comes to the threshold of wakefulness, and she emerges from the strange twilight—with the date and the question. Now he heard the wail of a small boy paddled homewards amid the wrathful screams of a woman in the streets below. Blood-curdling:

"And now you just wait till I get your pitch-black ass . . . home."

As Nathaniel Witherspoon sat there waiting for the other shoe to drop; he observed how Great-Momma Sweetie was coming out of the sleeve of sleep (as one emerging from the last steamy stages of a deeply troubling, wrestling, unraveling nightmare, but trying to shake herself into a wrinkled housecoat in order to answer the doorbell ringing). What steaming genie would escape from the oval, haunted caves of those eyes in the mocking merriment of time, he wondered. But she's guaranteed that I'm persona non grata in Candy's water bed, so I can't go there, even if she read my thoughts. He looked at her cedar-colored face; her head upon the silver pillow slip; the nearly invisible gray lace nightcap over her snow-white flutter of puffed-out hair, stiffened and light upon her crown; as layers of fiercely stirred-up egg whites.

Now the words of memory experienced were spun gifts of golden garments (and rainbows of faded veils) clothing her nakedness of soul and giving refinement to her being, form to her mind. *And* amid her total, angular recall, he saw the shuddering, as fleeing figures upon shades in the moonlight leaped from her passionate words (a sinewy collective clay-fashioning calligraphy) so that even the lace curtains seemed to curl. Ah, the young man thought, memory stirs you with autumn leaves many times before it covers you through the spade-smack and the turning over the surface of the earth and the rolling away of the rock towards revelation. Ah, the characters within her cedar-colored clay, the richest kind and kin of calligraphy in its broadness, he thought. For hadn't she often said, as she stood before the sideboard in the old days when the kitchen—indeed the apartment —was filled with the steam of the good news of the good old leftovers: "Splendid Spoons, it's a mighty poor bee who doesn't make more honey than he wants." But look what she did to my Candy Cummings.

. . . Ah, but the problem of breaking into the flow of an adult's memory bank of storytelling, rebirth. Children shall be seen and not heard (nor heard of and off to bed without a hearing; only a fierce hugging) still haunted Nathaniel into his majority. You may vote but you may not elect to speak. Even though she was an early feminist —of sorts, and active. Poor little Candy Cummings had sorely mis-read her parts, when called to the altar of Sweetie Reed's bed. And surely don't ask any sudden new questions—lest they be those that had suffered together, in the repetition of enunciated thought, in troubling time. Ah, the split in the generations, yet wasn't all of this part of the reason why she had gone home, not only to question I. V. Reed, in the long ago, but also to interrogate history? Just then the words of Jericho Witherspoon came to him: *The mind's rage to know the meaning of existence can never outdo the heart's galloping courage for life, and justice.*

And then he found himself face-to-face arousing the gradually awakening eyes of Great-Momma Sweetie Reed and declaring: *Grandfather's point was that the soul was so enmeshed in the body's riddled-through experience of remembering, troubling and rekindling, that he couldn't relinquish one for the other, nor the one for the many . . . so that when the body withered away the other did, too . . . Maybe that's why he held to the name Witherspoon (so fit-fully remade). Ha!* But now her eyes seemed to be coming back from way back when, as she emerged from some deeply perilous waters, as one indeed wondering how they got out and over . . . Nathaniel thought, to find a drowned man's body—you know this, Great-Momma Sweetie—you don't pray him into existence, you pitch a set of his old clothes in the general direction of where he floated off or where he went down dead and the clothing will turn its way to the cut of the man's body, as a tailor's measure. The rest is silence. No Yorick's skull to weep over, in the time-tanned trade of talk. To be not in time is to be conscious of time. Oh, how can the body coexist with the soul? And the river filled with cities of souls emerging out of the tide in the vaulting flood of Grandfather's eyes . . . the pearls and diamonds that were I. V. Reed's eyes in the back of his head: chains of oyster beds and men's icy eyes . . . the sudden smell of decayed flesh. Lawd, Sweetie's cabbage left out too long in the long ago. Oh, the sudden body of Reece Shank Haywood, water-cured and buried. *It* was buried in a watery grave. Oh, pastoral Pietà of the gallant soul. I. V. soul stuck to the bloody instrument of Haywood's horror and his downfall . . . Oh, let me own up to the wisdom of Grandfather and the flares of his folly . . . The cargoes of Bloods in the silenced Western belly of the Whale . . . Our demonic and hidden American repression down under the sea, clothed in our madness . . . Remembering, troubling and revealing: cargoes of discarded Negroes in the new, immeasurable middle passage down the length and breadth of the Mississippi River. By the waters of Babylon we were sat . . . indeed.

Now Great-Momma Sweetie Reed picked up her story where she left off when captured by the nightmare angel of memory. She had wrestled with that angular shape not so much to free herself but to subdue and pin it; despite the fiery angel's life-flipping, smoky forms; to hold it in flight until after she knit in her unraveling cares by sleep. Revived, too, by the very troubling shapes revealed in the wrestling anguish of voices. Her story coming now as churned butter, bits and pieces sticking together until a clear amount, solely butter and no longer cream, clung to the whipping paddle . . . Ah, but the cream, he thought now (with the pen in hand) was the date and question you, Great-Momma Sweetie, left behind. Yet how shall I ever wrestle that information, that intelligence, from your storytelling powers now? Wings you haven't got on your back you better get into your skull-bone, he cracked. But his rambling could not longer override the ascending chariot of Great-Momma Sweetie Reed's recollecting, and he heard her saying . . .

Nathaniel, I was shocked backwards as I moved away from I. V. Reed's presence, this father, a lost arrow quivering there upon old man Rollins Reed's warring bed. Now I let slip my tongue a slew of curses, as I backed away from *his* bed, staggering toward the front of Big House. But this I do remember as the day they stole my mother and me off to a new slavery (*and the diamonds of Mistress Sylvia haunted Angelina when she was stolen by the nightraiders and she came to believe that this was her payment for being sown to slavery body and soul; cursed from the beginning time for being cracked from the slavers' loins, too; all right; yes, I'll admit this freely, Nathaniel*) the day Rollins Reed and I. V. Reed *contracted* me to Jericho Witherspoon, who thought in marrying me up he was making me the bride of glory. On the day when I was returned to the porch and I saw I. V. Reed scratching out against me at the screen door—my rage and fury to look deeper down upon the instep of my sole to see what foundation I stood upon: I guess upon evil gone to a crushing curse in a madhouse (that I was not suited up for anything they tell you in a steamy sermon). Or that day, June 5, 1905, Jerry came home with . . . to take flight from . . .

Seemed to me if I did try to help I. V. Reed struggle with himself to live I would find much more of his accursedness and thinking he ought to die out and take his evil spell back to Satan with him. And behind this something bubbling as foam of a deepening water to surface in a blood-drenched river, but a nonrecognizable voice echoing: *Yes, all right, now you know part of why Almighty God has allowed him to low-lip life, you even admitted some of it yourself, that he wasn't in a way duty-bound to what came to his crusty lips; but that it was*

Almighty God who solely gives the accursed-blessing of tongues, yea though they be river-foul, that we might know those basin-hearted meats and humors of the soul, that others so lofty cannot say, nor know how to say; forgotten in fear and wonder and snobbery. The idea of I. V. Reed being blessed with tongues in itself was beyond my understanding and only visible to my witness as the tip of an iceberg to the whole. For all of it coming from the harping lips of the Prince of Snobs; the light of the body was his mouth harp. Lawd, today. But wasn't there a rank honesty, too, as those words were indeed new to his lips suddenly unknit (unrehearsed?), in the steaming memory from way back when in the beginning time. But maybe not unrehearsed? Maybe he retold himself his stories over and over again at night as some folks say their prayers all through the night.

I. V. Reed is your poppa, gal, this *fathering one* (as you like to say, Splendid Spoons) more siring than fathering. But I. V. Reed, your own damning spite-work ain't your propers to hardly give up, anoint down, like the lady with scales for Justice on those courthouse buildings where I used to go with Jericho Witherspoon. But then, all the evenhanded justice in the world ain't hardly sealed away inside those walnut wall facings, with pictures framing the faces of stern-faced judges, spread about the court in a horseshoe shape.

Must you plunge your hands in the sides of the blood, you, Miss Sweetie Reed, in all of your pride, before you believe how many manifestations are above and beyond your ability to see into the scales of time and to know and not to be—the layers of blood passed down . . . in a bundle of grief, patched out of tattered sleeves of caring? I said backwards over my shoulders—and where did I. V. Reed's snake-tongue become unknit in the basket of Mistress Sylvia's? Talk about troubling the waters? But what are you going to do with the smoke in the getting place, I. V. Reed, of your dungeon of rattling chains? Another voice echoing out of bloodspots before my eyes now, as a kind of imitation of I. V.'s voice (not one of his thousand and one put-on voices): *self-righteous?* Well, yes, he was right there, all right. You, too. And another starts to chanting and humming of sounds leapt from the winds of word gestures, something of the spirit sound of Jerry himself. I said aloud to that voice: *You mean you going to make me relearn believing through the voice and by the deeds of Satan, that's to lead me back to a revelation of Jesus. Troubling, remembering, revealing.* Through these nonbelievers.

Nathaniel, I kept staggering backwards and then fell straight back when I tripped over the rusty bolts propped up in the trapdoor leading down to the cellar, where the carpet was worn thin as a frayed rope; veil-masked threads of a spider's web. The back of my skullbone came down sharp on the iron frame bottom of one of Mistress Sylvia's oval mirrors still on the wall; the force of my head from the weight of my falling body, hitting the bottom, knocked the light clean out of me and caused the whole mirror to come down—the mirror-frame backing nailed and bound to those walls in the beginning time.

Nathaniel, all I can remember is that it seemed my body and soul fell into a great white well of fierce lights and I'd come in and out of the pale shadows of wakefulness surrounded by I. V. Reed; and that night rider man, who returned me to the plantation in 1874, and old man Rollins Reed; all three knee-deep in troubling waters and gambling in the muddy past; tossing diamond-bright green dice against the sides of the paint-peeling Big House porch and then tossing them up against the sides of that alabaster angel's peeling form (as curdling blood) for my naked soul. Your grandfather, Jericho Witherspoon, astride of it all (but all I can see are his polished black boots upon the porch, next to the alabaster angel, and his golden belt buckle), standing before us all so powerful. Then I see his elbows, winged outwards in a cradling angle. He can stoop to save me, or leave my soul (and perhaps my body) to them, it occurs to me now. I'm wondering amid my tears can he not see my soul in the whirlwind of my circumstance and know the cause of its shattered light. Just then I see a babe in Jerry's arms and I fall backwards seeing only its arms reaching out . . . and then Angelina's voice: *Angel got two wings to veil my face* (down here), *two wings to fly me away.* Then I commence to go in and out of dreadful dreams of that time they stole me and my mother away . . . yet alive by some exact, invisible force stowed away within the private power of her being which released new energies from within, as in our time of high-powered batteries of harnessed energy worn in a secret lining of a power plant to be unleashed when all other systems of the body-plant wane, and based on the ebb, flow and gush of currents within riverbeds harnessed to replenish and flush out the body of a town . . . Lawd, vaulting, cradling death can't do me no wrong, I'll take on his sting in the morning.

Nathaniel, there I was to discover myself the next morning completely unhidden and awake in a strange world, the bright bursting sunshine on the cracked mirror bits and pieces, glinting as oily stars on fire, seemed to hail in the morning's light and became a part of it, surrounding me on every side. The empty iron frame: a rectangle stock upon my shoulder. I managed to get it off, place it down and avoid cutting my hands on the sides of the gems of glass, as slippery as a serpent's body, and so bright-faced they seemed ember-eyes of flames. I felt some cuts on my neck and hands, however, from the splatter of the mirror, but the blood had stopped quick and lay dead upon my hands and my neck. I felt thirsty.

Nathaniel, I lifted the frame, not by pure strength so much but by leverage, using my hands, backpiece and feet against the wall in a rowing-up motion to gather leverage. I wept to myself—*Fix me, Jesus, fix me.* Finally I had it done, lifted from my body; I heard myself cry: *So grateful, Lawd, woke up this morning clothed in my right mind.* But now the light from the window and particularly the gems of glass were so blinding; I had to keep my eyes closed to think back on what to do and I wondered if my right mind hadn't gone counterfeit and confederate—playing cross-eyed dice with me.

Nathaniel, long before the frame held reflecting glass, once in Mistress Sylvia's youth, her very own father's stalking eyes dominating the face that stood there in the oval portion, old Inchmore told I. V. Reed. He had been a slaver and in the deeps of his eyes—the eyelids as wings—you could see the rendezvous of cruelty spat out the eyeteeth of love and the mercy mocking of one who's gone down dead to life, forgot everything of what connected the bones of life to living slabs of substance, so that he keeps on practicing what his second mind wants him to practice even though he's saved with a new body; as the salvation of his empire depended on piles of bodies.

Nathaniel, they moved his picture into Mistress Sylvia's old room where she used to sew her gowns for the masquerade balls with my mother's help and upon the closet door, up high, a foot length from the top. As a child I had looked there as you might look into a well and wonder how deep it goes and see only a beam of light within the darkness and think there must be something to the life below and pitch a body-blasted rabbit down and mark how long it is before you hear a sound or anything as a note to how deep the well goes and never get an echo sound back. You wonder whatever happened to your long-lost rabbit; when all of a sudden on the other side of the river you see a hobbling rabbit limping off into the woods, blood smeared across its shanks.

Nathaniel, a painting in oils kept alive by the quivering light of a hot wax candle—in the beginning time—a hanging vigil of light stuck in a deeply rooted prong until some slave—later I. V. Reed himself would wipe sleep from his bitter-brewing eyes and blow the flame into a flare and then low with his awakening, hot spittle breath until he cut off its breathing light, with a long-winded wad of spittle. Because Rollins Reed himself told his body servant, I. V. Reed, that he must rise soon in the morning and put out the light of the candle flame because it might lick the window curtain lace, near the body of the painting, and set this house on fire. Ceremony still going on—even where the picture hung upon her closet door—when they returned my body in 1874 . . . So that even unto today, whenever I enter a certain kind of church in the darkness, I can see those rabbit-running, supreme and mercy-mocking lights in the eyes of Reed, especially alive in the pitch-blackness of the altar lights upon the altar-like stage; but at high noon when the church is in its swim of light, as the sun gives birth to brightness.

Nathaniel, I was so startled up and blinded down by light *then* only in a nonreflecting way; and *now* noticing of a numbness in my brain. I didn't realize what had happened to me in the silence. I tried clapping my hands but nothing came of it. Now as I was crying and gasping and praying that I was only struck dead in the temple for the moment—and could be put together again soon—it was then I came to make out something in front of me . . . Someone I thought at first (the bits and pieces of wrinkled and wrenched, tore-up fistfuls of cotton balls spun out of gems, as nuggets of new money, in the sun) out there projected in the middle of the air before me.

Nathaniel, you see I couldn't hear the words in the shells of my ears, made out by this figure in front of me that was neither black nor white but a spasm of both the darkness of the light and the fierce light within the darkness behind the impaling sunshine—I don't believe you see what I'm talking about this late afternoon into evening, son, my Splendid Spoons . . . *Oh, light and dark wrinkled into madness.* And thinking as I tried to rise above my shattered circumstance, how much of a curse had befallen me—driving me from my father's bed, by the *implications of it all,* as Jerry used to say about so many things, legal and illegal; or *direction by indirection.* And my heart beating as an eagle's wing to the chant of *light and life to all He brings, risen with healing in His fiery wings.*

Nathaniel, I thought I was still in a dream world twilight time before you awake to light or that I was losing the light of my vision, too; that I would exist forever in a state of romantic moonlight and not knowing, as your grandfather once said of me. But as my eyes got adjusted a little more to the new-time light of my condition, I saw now before me that barefoot mulatto woman, atop a ladder pitched high to the ceiling. Her hair was piled high upon her head as my mother used to wear her hair. This woman appeared wigged out in goodness; sniveling in rigid face sorrow. She looked stage-struck to me, there atop the ladder.

Nathaniel, the ladder pitched not only zenith-high, but the legs spread as wide as the skirts of a dancer's about to do the splits on the stage before your naked eyes; the legs suddenly suspended on *freeze*. This woman's hands arched upon her hips (and I'm thinking, *London Bridge is falling down, falling down, my fair lady;* but I ain't hardly got time for playacting) and like she's growing disgusted with waiting for me, in my non-answering-back confusion of lifting myself up and out of the heavy frame. Nathaniel, I could not make out the meaning of her gestures, nor her attempts at mouthing words. Her frantic signs were spun out by her special garments of sign language, made over. But as I shuddered at her non-talk, I couldn't help but laugh to think of those folks who used pig Latin to throw you off the scenting trail of their conversation valuables—till you caught up with the drift of their meaning, long before you caught on to their code, even as they spoke in front of your face, like they were talking behind your back. Nathaniel, I. V. Reed's dinner plate tin was face down upon the ladder platform top (the one she served his meals in?) and the one he had used to serve Rollins Reed. In the morning's light of crashed brightness, the service plate appeared as a silver crown turned upside down, or perhaps a high-top hat.

Nathaniel, the Adam's apple gesturing in that woman's throat and the movement of her lips were as blind sparrow's caught up at the bottom of a sewed-up sleeve cuff, making throbbing motions against the shape of the cloth, and I thought there's some boldface trick going on behind my back; and her lips trembled as a sparrow's wings when hooded and bagged by an evil-eyed poacher. Nathaniel, then I slapped my face with a ringing whelp in order to shake loose my hearing. What hearing? Lawd, I cried out, had I been truly struck down stone deaf? How much of a non-hearing cross would I too have to settle on for the rest of my days when I escaped the presence of this house? What directions would my brain give to my gestures?

But then I cried out, Almighty Gawd—through the image of my beloved Angel-Angelina—what ailed me, I. V. Reed, when you beheld me in your scratching-out eyes, as I was lifted out of the patroller man's arms and down onto Rollins Reed's knee? You expected me to apologize for it being me who was returned. Yes, you bastard, father who delivered me from my mother's loins, who seeded me there out of the fire of your own loins. How can a child apologize for its being the survivor? Humble itself, before a denying father. Just then I. V. Reed's words came up from the core of my being: *Drew out a picture of Angelina's face upon his sleeve,* and then for the first time I recognized, though failed to understand, my condition. For in the fullness of *what* heart made my mouth to speak?

. . . Nathaniel, in my sudden moment of new non-hearing I cried out, Oh, Shank Haywood, why didn't Almighty God send down two angels with wings to hide you away and cover your steps and capture the rock when it winged towards your earlobe—wording out? But was Haywood's spirit a halo of anguish or ghastly crown to be worshiped as a touchstone relic hovering? To be believed; but also feared as a sacred warning and curse. Why didn't the angels stay those patrollers who stole Mother Angelina and her baby when those men placed their hands over our faces, dressed in their dove-white sheets, sole to crown, and winging us out into the midnight of their madness, as the sheets beat in the wind: the garment of their being from another country, another world. Why not a miracle for that nighttime? When suddenly I realized how much I was sounding in my non-hearing like that Nicodemus, Jericho Witherspoon, my husband from 1882 to 1905, when he divorced my soul . . . separated from my body. Sounding like what he accused me of being—matron on the one hand, little girl on the other.

Nathaniel, that old mulatto woman would not come more than twenty paces to my body, even after she climbed down from that ladder and to the edge of the broken mirror-glass. Now as she stood upon that off-white-colored ladder; her face tilted to the bright chandelier from the sunlight, and the sunlight upon the broken glass so as not to blind her vision, she cocked her head back off to the side. Listening to other voices in other rooms and chambers of her silent, yet gesturing, mysterious being.

I had to cup and hood my hands about my eyes to see out at her; she acted in a dream. I thought of my mother Angelina's dream the week before the patrollers carried us off. Mother had seen a precious statue shattered in its winging (at a stage just before her awakening), but wasn't for certain if she did not have her hand in the shattering, not sure if she ought to help out by lending a hand—whatever that might mean—but she thought, too, the closer she gets, the more the spirit world in its savage parts might get caught up with the sleeve of her spirit breathing and suck out her soul. Just then the broken limbs came together again in space and time; but possessed now, suddenly, of flesh, and bones. Then sprouting tongues of blood. My mother thinking the dead mistress' spirit will return to life; her very body not clothed before Mother's eyes, but plucked and naked crown to sole down to a bony skeleton; but her hands thick with blood. Shaking as my cupped hands were *now* extended out in questioning, as I prayed and wondered about the extent of my lost hearing.

Nathaniel, this speechless mulatto woman—who had led me back, the final leg, to this place—now got a huge rope out, that I recognized right away. They had used this rope in the beginning time to drag in slave boats and fish vessels—so old Inchmore told I. V. Reed, it was that old. Braided in seven waxen strands together; she climbed back up the ladder, threw the rugged old rope out towards me; its edges as brittle ends of a broken-off toenail. She had re-collected the other end of the rope and yoked it about the bedpost in the back room— to the bed where I. V. Reed's body lay upon his all-time master's bed. Then as I'm gathering in the huge rope, this mulatto rice-colored woman pitches me a note, that flew through the air and landed at my feet; gesturing out that she dared not come any closer to my body: —*far suckin up fyears.*

Nathaniel, before I read anymore of the note I laughed and I wept to think that at first I simply imagined she was only scared to come closer because she might cut the soles of her naked feet.

But using briefed-out words and half-crosses and X'd-out markings to mean I don't know what to this very day, she tries to signify many meanings. Her scrawling takes the shape of a child's who keeps putting on the left shoe on the right foot in the dark and then ties the laces of both shoes together. But as always you got to go with what you got left over, so I try to read out her meaning amid her scrawling. It all seems to suggest I'd have to lift myself up by the power of my own body and the power of the strong rope.

Nathaniel, as I'm reading out the *transcription* of her meaning from the paper (like those folks who learn to read out the scrolls of meaning almost washed out from the bottom of a missionary ship that went down hundreds of years earlier and is discovered by whaling boats) she tries to help me out by using new kinds of gestures and movements out of old-time motions of hipbone, hands, eyes, elbows, as to add body substance to her scrawled-out, shorthand-looking jottings. Her hand printing is worse than a three-year-old child learning to print the alphabet backwards, though she knows more, but unclear as to whether the characters' meaning would carry the meaning even if she knew how to properly print like the person who tried to teach her penmanship. She, too, doesn't trust anything written down, even when she herself scrawls it from the early markings of memory of how you can hurry things along if you scratch them down, as you scratch upon a brick to stone and another stone to stone to make a fire to warm the blood, but afraid of the trouble the fire can lead to the next time you strike the stones together. Well, I learned long before that to make do out of dust and as the old folks used to say, better to have gravy than no grease at all.

Finally it comes clear she wants me to tie the big rope to the huge prong in the wall as an anchor; wind the rope about the prong (that once was used to prop up one of those small square platforms where Rollins Reed's granddaddy I hear tell sat a model of a slave ship). I extended myself upon the rope and balanced my way out of the cutting-glass gems like those folks on a high wire I guess you and I, Splendid Spoons, saw at the Barnum & Bailey Brothers Circus. I am wondering if the walls of this old house can take it; so worn out and fragile to tumbling down as they appear to be. But now she goes on to say on the other side of the scrap of paper, that I. V. Reed's body lay dead upon the bed of Master Rollins and this:

Did ya sa a sturbin woe word at mye pappap
years his natchile beathin & cuss hymn ta a
lung hart deapness. angelina clea.

Nathaniel—I. V. Reed, my father, giving this woman Angelina's name. My mother. Her father. And pappap, too. Men! Nathaniel, I can't tell you what I said out loud in plain-spoken English for that writing pad of yours and hold on to the lady part of my dignity. Was Clea cut short from *clean,* which she surely was not? My head shook and my feet almost arched out of the soles of my own shoes as a cat's back arching. Where did I. V. Reed shoot his seed in the darkness to get this puffy daughter of brightness? And so fair? Though her origins be streaked as curdled milk. Perhaps this Angelina leapt from I. V. Reed's other heated head fully clothed; though her garment be that of rags and tatters. Oh, I was evil, all right—and to my surprise, jealous as that green little pearl in his foul earlobe, that looked like the weird beads on a toad's back. I suppose I'd have to call her Sister Clea (or little sister of Death—she would be Martha and I Mary, oh never ever). And then too: hadn't I had to adjust to this—all of this —all before? Lord, must I go back to that too? . . . *And within the last year. Men!*

Nathaniel, now as I followed out the written word of this Clea, my second mind was still pitched back in anger at your grandfather, Jericho Witherspoon, but as I started to climb out I also thought of Jerry talking about his crossing from one mountain to the next bent on his escape and journeying over by rigged-up rope set up by one of those underground agents, but as he's crossing over with the icy-glass valley below—hand over hand—down to where his eye dare not look down for sanity's sake. It came over his deeper mind, as a warning, hovering shroud, that agent might be one of their patrollers in a dark blue suit, in that cloth he was susposed to be suited up in at a certain set-up checkpoint, as friend, not your foe, our foe.

And Jerry recounting in his grand voice: *This might be one of the rumored ones who turned his coat, that he might enfold his sharp purposes as the mask of an eclipse.* And the rope seemed thinner at each section in his sweating hands. He could see the heavy rope tied to the tree and the tree seemed to sway ever so gentle and slight as the sway of lovers dancing in one embrace, and he couldn't tell if the tree swayed because of the cool, swift breeze, or from the force of his body upon the rope. He got over all right but he said he aged a decade. Maybe he told you about that experience and him thinking too that by this very rope that saved him, he would have to hang the man who stood awaiting for him, if that man turned out to be not friend but foe. Well, I didn't know if this mulatto woman was friend or foe, either. And thinking about your grandfather in this light helped some, too, but then it drove my recollecting to what I. V. Reed said of poor Reece Shank Haywood. The full meaning of the curse, even beyond I. V. Reed's words, came down upon me as I thought not only will I never hear his words again—would I ever hear *any* words again! This curse across my hearing couldn't last any longer than the ringing in my head, which had to clear up soon; despite Clea's wrinkled and wretched presence.

Nathaniel, thinking of your grandfather and the times we had together, and what he had done to me, but then again our love; then

I. V. Reed, and the way he scorned my presence, through complete ignoring of me; how Jericho escaped and how Reece Shank Haywood didn't escape, it come to my mind the story Angelina told me of that freedom-loving slave from Arlington Bloodworth's plantation who risked his life for love. How he rode the last one hundred miles to a Free State, bound and strapped up to the underbelly of a stout stallion; his legs pitted backwards and clinging to the very stripped-down straps under the belly of the horse, like they were *his rearranged* commandments; harnessed to his deepest nature. Straps that his master had turned into whips to strop his body down and no longer used because they didn't seem sturdy enough for lashing out sake. Straps now as useful to the slave as those straps, stripped into eights, that were laced tight and rigged up to the stallion's saddle. And atop that saddle was the trusted coachman, Golightly Braidwood.

Nathaniel, this story was most sweet to me, all the days of my growing up till I went north to marry your grandfather. For my mother said that the slave was bound on going north to catch up with the gal he loved, whose parents had escaped with his beloved earlier that year. Mother said the slave had stripped himself down to be as light (and unseen) as a joint in a backbone for the journey and Master Bloodworth thought that this weight lost was bound over to some wild religious cavorting he had undergone at the very hands of Stigwood Bloodworth and his assistant old Inchmore down by the pool —trying to fast out his evilness, his impurities out of his system and that he was also punishing himself up from some original sin against Master; as good a sign, Master believed, as fish in the window to a lost traveler, she overheard Bloodworth telling Rollins Reed.

Nathaniel, as long as the slave's constitution didn't wither away, Master Arlington Bloodworth had said he went along because the fasting out had seemed to make the slave meek as a lamb. He went after his labors in the master's yard as a man who knew the voice of the master and was obsessed to do his bidding and didn't fret; thinking the slave was working and starving also, for his religion as a frame for his pining but not grieving heart, after (not the runaway girl's heart) but her beautiful-to-look-upon body parts; and suffering out what he had done against the master's words, in thought or deed. So stripped down did the slave become that Bloodworth thought of making him into a jockey, if he stripped down five more pounds from his body. Bloodworth stood the slave naked on the auction platform scales each morning, in order to keep him humble and nervous about his future each day, at high noon. The breakfast meal was accounted for in the weighing in; and calling the slave Shorty-George. Now in my womanhood, with everything coming down upon me, I realized why she had kept telling me that story over and over again, for if she did not, had not, I would never believe a man could love a woman, risk everything, his life for her. This was before I read Wayland Woods' letter to Mistress Sylvia and Rollins Reed, revealing his love for his daughters . . . Nathaniel, so much of our history never gets told —buried as it is in the troubled waters of time—or it doesn't get to us in time.

Nathaniel, finally I went into the bedroom where I. V. Reed's body lay—yet twisting; Good Lord, couldn't this Clea of his see? Was she as blind to seeing as I was to hearing? Or as she was to speaking? Cursed, too? Or had he made yet another comeback, while we were both away overnight? I. V. Reed twisting as if yoked in chains; his body fitful as if he existed upon a deep, burning river; and making sounds like he's got a gag in his windpipe.

Nathaniel, I had to catch myself up before I started staggering backwards again upon shakey legs, as stammering tongues, in the beginning time. The plaited web of I. V. Reed's days even surfaced unto the folds of sheets (as a hant's underwear visible solely to my eyes, with its trapdoor flapping) upon his master's broken-in, re-shapen mattress. A wrack of ruin and wrestling; snatches of I. V. Reed's clawed-away, bloody skin upon the linen. Now that I could no longer hear, would my eyes scratch out too much light of seeing and knowing so that I would have to apologize for my very being—his blood? Scratch into existence a forgiveness, as a blind beggar's scratching out, filthy nails for money on the palm? Scratched out into being the fierce facts that perhaps my very fighting words had hastened the foul man's hovering death.

Nathaniel, the unkind cut of I. V. Reed's mouth: two slivers of glass slit into a puppet's face on the muddy wall—as the springs underneath the mattress seemed to dance with his very body in leaping waves; I. V. Reed was dead, all right, but his body leapt like burning wood chips mounted atop a bed of coals in the fire consuming and the mattress-bed floating downstream to the land of the dead; but hearing a private trumpet, screaming to the angel of the morning I also seemed to hear an angel with two wings aflutter, singing:

Behold the terrible trumpet sounds,
The restless dead to raise,
And calls the blood underground:
Oh, how the souls will praise;
Behold the Savior how He comes
Decending from His throne
To burst asunder all our tombs
And bid his grieving children home.

. . . Oh yes, I. V. Reed, oh yes, your propers indeed; yes, and if you make yourself a grinning ass before not only the world, but yourself, the Pale Rider will ride you backwards to the river of forgetfulness, where you'll surely drink of the cup, and even your remembering won't be recollection enough, I cried in my bitterness . . . This cup as sweet as ambrosia to me for a moment, before the face of this father who had denied me all the days of my living upon that plantation, and now to take the curse of non-hearing, as a last spat in the face through him, no matter how indirectly his hand was in it all as the curse from Auntie Foisty over him that came from the haunting spirit of Reece Shank Haywood's *yet* hovering spirit. As I now looked once again at that sliver of a mouth, the very slit and cut of my own lips, unto my dying day.

Nathaniel, I. V. Reed's mattress: from a foundry of coffins. I thought, Yes indeed, the old head rabbit's grieving tracks cost too much, when he has to purchase them out from a rat's trap. But, Nathaniel, that was exactly when it came down full measure to me, Sweetie Reed, how righteous is your bloated righteousness; your so-called righteousness. Could I face the fact that perhaps my words had hastened his death? Was I in league with the Pale Rider—Just like I. V. Reed's rock had brought on the daring, foolish Reece Shank Haywood's unlucky, accursed death? Made Reece escape into a soundless, thereby sound-filled impossibility; sound-filled to the horsemen and hounds, streaking for the very form, for the very scent of Shank's gait, conjured and shaken pace, as the hounded, clever driver scratched his way. And, Nathaniel, I thought of those dead, stripped-down rabbits in the marketplace strung upside down; their bodies bloated.

Nathaniel, all men sought the mending ways in the sleeve sleep sewed with Death, as a rehearsal and a bargain, but for Reece, Death would not heal the salty wounds of memory before his bulging eyes, his twisted sore-ridden lips; and one side of me wondered, with I. V.

Reed gone, would Reece Shank Haywood now come haunting after me, for already I was struck down deaf to hearing words, maybe even to I. V. Reed's lamentations, as he, Shank, had stalked I. V. Reed down the rest of his life; hovering just above his head as a dark angel, suspended in the middle of the air. Just then, the other side of me heard an angel's voice:

> *You'll hear the trumpet sound*
> *Wake bleeding tribes underground,*
> *Looking to my God's right hand,*
> *Touch falling stars upon this land.*

But then I wondered whether I. V. Reed would find sleep in death, either, as spite or dread; and the crying bloodspots as grieving tongues speaking out to me forever and ever, restless world without end, as tribulations' falling stars blasting through my very new non-hearing in the real world sacked of understanding amid my new reborn understanding of the *ways* of Light; a light shattered, as the broken mirrors in the front room, even as a voice wept in song:

> *The trumpet shall sound, the dead shall rise*
> *Rocks and mountains don't fall on me;*
> *And go to the mansions in-a the skies;*
> *Fly home to my Lawd and be free?*

Nathaniel, I. V. Reed's daughter couldn't hear, and Lawd, his other daughter, whom he had dared to name for my mother, was left *to be* speechless at his graveside, but full of signs and wonders of signals, and noddings. Was this her payment for her blessing and my inheritance and my new knowledge for the rock to Reece's head, as he then took Rollins Reed into the circle of his arms in order . . . And past this, didn't Reece know his act meant, signified his certain death . . . without any angels' wings to hide his face, to carry him home to freedom. I wept, loathing him, and pitying him not because he had tried to kill Grandfather, Rollins Reed, because he deserved something, just this side of killing, as he this grandfather was in that shack assaulting my grandmother but Lord that's how Mother came to be as that foul-mouth father of mine had said; and must I erase this Rollins Reed's raping act, if I could, then how would I come to know the mother I knew, who was gentle as a dove at dawn?

Yet, Nathaniel, how did I know he had raped my grandmother? Perhaps at the moment of assault she had not accepted his loins, surely not his act, nor his foul body, but his presence as master over her body, not her will, as women so often had done—had to do, short of being killed in the resistance . . . Or had she in her despair resisted him at all? Lord, must I go back to that beginning time, too, though now it came down to me that Rollins Reed had seemed to play father more than I. V. Reed had seemed willing to act out the role, at best . . . Maybe the world of humankind sprung from a long series of rapes and Almighty God had turned his back believing that after this calamitous beginning woman would refine man into a higher condition. If God was of a male nature, then perhaps he cared less about the genesis of the human family than we knew . . . I have to tell you this, Nathaniel, that this too crossed my mind, like the crossed sticks of war. If this was true, then women alone could only protect themselves against men . . . Maybe that was why that old story of the slave who stripped his body down to virtually nothing stayed with me, and I came north; there were some men in the world, perhaps only a fraction of the breed, who could love . . . And I believed this until June 5, 1905.

 . . . Nathaniel, loathing I. V. Reed, and pitying him, as Clea and I dug into the earth, and thinking of all of this abuse, I could not stand for long on hating Clea, who was my sister in blood. We were using one of old man Rollins Reed's tarnished green gardening spades; the very mattress-bed I. V. Reed slept on, for a bloated casket-bed. Clea and I could barely see each other plain for the steam and fog. Dawn's delivering early-light fall, as broken stars in the Negro graveyard three hours later; as that day when they returned me to the Reed plantation, and I. V. Reed had stood there in the mirror of the screen door and I saw him through a veil; he scratched on that screen as if to scratch out my eyes and the light of my existence. I sat upon Rollins Reed's knee. Not simply my grandfather, either, Nathaniel, because my return, too, based on Rollins Reed's dream of getting Angelina, his only blood daughter, back in the beginning place, even I knew that as a child of seven when that patroller man placed me on Reed's knee; and Rollins Reed's eyes, too, scratched me out of primary blood existence, but held on to me because I was all there was to hold to of his being without his hands touching me: and Lord, standing in the graveyard now as we dug the grave for I. V. Reed and thinking back to the porch with the two winging angels on either side placed there after Auntie

Foisty had taken Rollins Reed into her arms for his *deliverance.*
Nathaniel, as Clea and I took turns digging I. V. Reed's grave, I
came to see in the solitude that it was Auntie Foisty who had delivered
him, Rollins Reed, to whatever mercy and half-love—no, not love but
confused blood-love-loathing he had for that part of me that was his
own to claim though he could never claim it was a deed. That the
more I was removed from his primary seed and consumed by the seed
of slaves, the less I was his own. Scratched from his existence, as they
placed an X across a set of slave records marking out their existence
in death . . . and their existence from the mind; records consumed by
the fire, until it was she, the Unforgettable One, who remembered the
ledger and tablet, the crop and the sword and the weather and the
beginning time. And Auntie Foisty's curse and Shank Haywood's
memory charged over I. V. Reed's existence forever and ever. I still
brooded upon his face that day the patroller man sat me down upon
Rollins Reed's knee. But if that was true, then how much more had
I needed I. V. Reed's love? So as I dug the grave for I. V. Reed, the
father, that morning with Angelina-Clea, part of my mind was back
in the coffin where I helped some captured slaves bury my mother,
in that old swamp plantation in the long ago.

Nathaniel, apparently a river load of that love was needed—as a
well, that can't be called a well until it knows water to its depths; and
too, since nobody commanded that I return to this plantation and
combat I. V. Reed across his bed (not for love but recognition, I see
that plainly now) where he and my mother had known fitful love and
argument, when the Reeds were out of the house . . . Yes, and to battle
the father to recognize me in his need for love, only to see that he,
honest, honest Ivy, didn't possess this need. But the instrument of my
surgery to the heart: the very knife of my flaming tongue. Yes, and
hadn't I loved those winging parts of his story, too (the magician,
Spottswood) as he talked, told, spun his wild and wonderful *lies*—in
a dread-filled way.

And hadn't they, both of them, I. V. Reed and Rollins Reed, sold
me off to marriage with Jericho Witherspoon, your grandfather, in a
spite-riddled deal to be rid of me forever and ever; my presence as a
reminder of Angelina, my mother, and to a man obsessed with her
memory, the picture of her face, so that he drew it in upon his sleeve.
And, Nathaniel, it was at that moment, piled high upon what had
happened to me, the year before, June 5, 1905, as I dug up the earth
for burying, that I commenced to hear again I. V. Reed's voice saying:

Ain't got enough money left over from slavery, he says to purchase her back. Sent word to your lawyer man, this was before he became your lawyer man, 'cause Jericho don't know you exist . . . (Foolish man, you didn't know that I existed) . . . *I figures now part of Rollins Reed wants her back, safe and sound, the father part in him* . . . (What father part, where was that buried then in his clay—give Foisty credit for that human remnant if it existed at all) . . . *But he also wants to get back at me, or to keep me in my place; so he up and writes Jericho Wither-spoon, who he knows wants my woman, for money to purchase his daughter and my woman out of slavery* . . . (Purchased into a new slavery, you mean, with me to be thrown into the bargain, as a proxy) . . . *Telling Witherspoon in the letter if he sends the money, he can have the woman, in time; he'll send her along. Witherspoon sent along the money like he's purchasing himself a bride* . . . (Nathaniel, is it little wonder that given Jerry's personality, too, he would think of me solely as his property, body and soul; and making it even harder for me because he was so liberal by the husband's ways of the day) . . . *Master Rollins claims Auntie Foisty came to him in a dream and told him this was the way to handle the matter, but it was her sister Chastity's voice what spoke to him through Foisty's body* . . . (How clever of him, the magician). And, Nathaniel, it was upon that moment that I decided to do something about Woman's Condition, well, at least *this* woman's condition . . .

But him, I. V. Reed, unable to get rid of the picture of her in his mind, too; naming his other daughter after Angelina and Rollins Reed, trying to be like Miz Sylvia on the one hand and like Auntie Foisty on the other and the slaves loving Angelina's memory, even more in their troubling recall of her, but in death, of course; recalling her grace and her magic, her cleverness and dancing, her bright skin, her rowdy gracefulness in dancing, her singing; *and* yes, all right, and despising her closeness to them in power and warning her and advising her and *reschooling* her information. Even as they loathed her for bright-facedness, and the fabulous chestnut hair, her dainty dumbness, and her refinements, that were not only the refinements of the Big House, but also those of the Praise Shack, *and* those spun as dark gold up from the quarters, that they had put there themselves, thereby making her into a new kind of person—a new clay image—that they themselves hardly recognized, *and* it was of, by and from them.

Despising her, for the way she was used by Mistress Sylvia (and probably not seeing how much Mistress Sylvia, no doubt, was dependent on her) and one of them telling me, in more of a pitying voice as if to mask the mocking of *their* loathing: how Mistress Sylvia suffered from the yaller jaundice and Angelina used to set her down in the tub; then glide away and scoop up spring water in a bucket, sweeping back and forth like a jack rabbit doing a figure eight and Angelina drifting over Mistress Sylvia's body waves of chilly spring waters again and again until it seemed Angelina's numbed arms would fall off, in the relief, bringing to Mistress Sylvia's body of swabs of painful *yaller skin.* Mistress leapt in the tub (as ice to fire) in the fullness of a fit before the mirrors all the night through until dawn cracked light upon her long body-length looking-glass mirrors, where she stood in all of her nakedness to see everything, charred in ecstasy as one caught up in the clutches of death while feverishly dancing in the light of flames.

Must I go back to that, too, and her telling me all of what she dared to say and not say that night before the new slavers killed her, and still talking about love, too, and that story of the slave that stripped himself down to nothing to flee the plantation under the belly of a stallion, in order to escape to his beloved's arms; the night before the new slavers killed her, some of whose hands were in the return of Reece Haywood (and maybe my return, too) I'll believe unto my dying day. Nathaniel, must I go back to day one of our shattered deliverance? And back to why I could not go to the burying of Rollins Reed when I'd have to sit in the nigger train, and the nigger coach, next to the steam heat to pay last respects to this loathsome grandfather, who had kept unloading me with the freight of his existence for the last five years: by getting rid of all of his belongings, though he was not so much piling the cargo of his consciousness and history on me but binding me to the history of his conscience (even unto that very rocker where you are now sitting, Nathaniel, and recording in longhand this story) as when they unite a baggage car to the cattle car, with yoking chains in the yards and bound for cities, new and old through the opening-up country. Adding new touchstones to old calamities, you might say, Nathaniel, each and every time you rock in that creaking, wheezing rocker, as a train rocking on the rail, and guaranteeing that it'll never get derailed in time from his memory; or if it does get derailed in time, how I'm the one that's got to pick up the baggage, and if not me, then you, and that's part of why I'm telling you all of this . . .

Nathaniel, to a graveyard I could not enter less the town's white

239

fathers make an especial case, plea and covenant or I. V. Reed, himself, go down dead on both knees and unburden himself with a begging plea for my entry, me who was Rollins Reed's only living flesh and blood. Not only because *I'm black but comely,* as the saying goes, but because I had escaped in their thoughts, at least, and gone wrong like a derailed train, by going north. And me loathing but determined to go down there at first because I'm still evil to clever and vengeful to nonforgiving and long-headed in my remembering to see this once mighty house and its master in ruins, though he's sent me a remnant of those ruins right along with a portion of all that was precious to him as well, some of which was tied and bound to our own refinement of our enslavement . . . Ruins, yes, but didn't I enjoy showing them off, keeping them out, I didn't try to get rid of them, like that rocker, for example, prima facie evidence, as Jerry used to say . . . Not admitting that I not only wanted to see Rollins Reed dead but also to see him; that I could not strip my soul from his bond, that he was part of the little that marked my existence, though it be shrouded in rape and wretchedness. Yes, I wanted to look upon my grandfather's face again. All right, yes—grandfather, once and for all. That I wanted to see I. V. Reed, even to do something for him, thereby wanting to undo some of the past estrangement; me with my losing of babies. Oh Lord, that too. My body seemingly not as substantial to hold life for long in it as that old rocker that can still hold up the weight of your young body, even Arthur's when he was here among us . . . Lord, must I go back to that too; and June 5, 1905.

Nathaniel, now as I'm thinking and reflecting over all of this and digging I. V. Reed's grave in my non-hearing, therefore I'm dwelling within myself (like those blues women who come clean with their spirit when they sing about sleeping by themselves after their men have gone off) more than ever and remembering and partially too, I guess, because this Sister Clea can't hold a decent conversation without sign language and I can't do that and dig at the same time, nor can she. I'm trying to forget exactly what I'm doing; to hold back the tears falling as rain upon the spading-up earth, revealing the turned-over ground that shall hold my father's body, as a season-bruised leaf, when of a sudden it occurs to me what I. V. Reed had said earlier about the diamonds of Mistress Sylvia's and how in the long ago *I hides them diamonds in a old pair of shoes socked away with some paper filler.* So one side of me is saying hurry and finish off honest I. V. Reed's grave and another is saying those diamonds have now fallen into your hands though they are not in your hands but in some old shoes, and nobody knows where they are buried less it's this Clea-*cum*-Angelina! Ha! Yes, *but* now I can't get away from the previous condition . . . Train system can't run now without the third rail; yet touch it and be electrocuted.

Nathaniel, I tried to drive these diamond-thoughts from my mind; they hurled me back in time to my mother's torment; I fiercely dug into the ground and the bitter, knotted earth fell back by the force of my spade and my tears fell upon the clods of dirt like rain from a choked-up and now released mist from the heavens. And I recalled another telegram to me from Stigwood Bloodworth, that when all was said and done it was left to the Negroes to bury Rollins Reed, since the whites would not go out to the Reed plantation, most them, anyway, because he was forever and ever praising his great awakening at the hands of Auntie Foisty, the transformed African, as if she was some kind of saint. They were yet unsettled about which Negroes could go and wanted all numbered who went out there, and that he, he alone, was slated to check those who would be allowed to stand at the edges of the white cemetery with their approval solely; though they were in disagreement as to the actual number that should be in attendance and would watch over it all from a distance, with long-eyed spyglasses.

Nathaniel, it was left to the former slaves of the Reed plantation to bury him since all of their children were now gone north. And the former slaves resurging from out of nowhere to bury Rollins Reed in neither the Negro grave in their hard-won pride nor go by midnight and risk their lives and bury him in the white graveyard; so that finally I was made to understand (when I telegramed back saying I would not come down there to help, either, and risk my life) that it was I. V. Reed and two others (perhaps this very Clea) who made a new grave for Rollins Reed, along the side of the road, between the two graveyards, the separating line of the two burying sites.

Yes, and part of the reason I didn't go back, too, was that I didn't want to face that train—though I often traveled segregated trains to go to rallies for our struggle against discrimination, but, Splendid Spoons, never to go back down, because I had become a transformed soul in the North; yes, and because I couldn't deal with the Deep South and, son, when I say South, I also especially mean the Negroes there as well. And I could not take what those of the old Bloodworth, Witherspoon and Reed plantations, those left behind, would think of me—leaving them behind, because they despised my leaving as if I had stole out by not staying down there and going down with whatever happened to them, and the South. They were, you see, some strange kind of patriots. And the religious ones thought I had sold my soul to the Devil by going north to the freedom of that evil wilderness of snow and new marketplaces of flesh for profit. And then, too, in a personal way, they knew I was married to your grandfather, and though they knew he was working for Negro freedom in a general way, they thought of it all as some sort of a deal he was working with the Yankees that could not be trusted, like the Emancipation that had never worked out for them, though they respected what Lincoln had done, and honored Frederick Douglass as a distant kind of saint . . .

Nathaniel, this Angelina-Clea wore a veil and after we spent ourselves dragging the rope-bound mattress of a casket out with I. V. Reed's body bound upon it, we stood there trying to look each other in the face, through the steamy mist. Splendid Spoons, we took that huge sailing-vessel-pulling rope she had tossed to me earlier and bound it about the body of I. V. Reed to the mattress; we dragged the body of the mattress-bound father-man out to the edge of the deep hole we had dug to receive his clay-colored body. Then this almighty Clea, called Angelina, dragged forth a huge cotton sack. And as we struggled to bring down his body bound to the mattress without falling over the grave edge ourselves, I thought of that line from that song of old . . . *Prepared me one body, like man, I'll go down and die* . . .

Nathaniel, then I did see Angelina-Clea put down on either side of I. V. Reed on the mattress, the following: a slingshot, a pair of old shoes and a masquerade mask. Then she gestured to me and I followed and we went to the shed in back of the Big House and found an old coffin (left there by Golightly Braidwood, the coffin was full of termites); with the mattress as a filler, we were made to feel more comfortable about putting I. V. Reed's body in the hole-ridden wooden coffin. We rolled the wooden coffin out to the gravesite as if we were rolling a ship to shore; placed the mattress-bound body of I. V. down inside of it and then with all of our strength lowered the coffin into the ground. We each said some prayers privately. Angelina-Clea offered up a praise worship in sign language. We shoveled the earth back down upon the coffin. The fog made another veil across her face.

Now this Clea called Angelina commenced to place other items from the cotton sack about the grave of I. V. Reed. I saw her put down a series of empty shells that looked like a spider's web left upon the earth after a flood.

As we turned to go, I saw where I. V. Reed had marked off Reece Shank Haywood's grave in that delicate tiny scrawl of his, as delicate as a twig or a young girl's ankle, in a circle almost perfect, as a waiter's circling arm then hand setting the dishes in front of the invisible guest and host, and then words upon the glass-stained tombstone:

LIES HERE MISTER REECE SHANK HAYWOOD,
18—— TO 18——

Great-Momma Sweetie Reed commenced to drift off to sleep; and with his hand upon her hand, Nathaniel Witherspoon himself started to drift off to sleep; but as he slipped away within the sleeve of care-riddled sleep he heard the only grandmother he had ever known, since he had not seen his mother's mother, saying in sobs of sleep:

Why, that woman, that Angelina-Clea, was gesturing in sign language as I was left to shovel the earth over the buried man's coffin back in place:

Plenty Good Room Plenty good room,
Good room in my Father's Kingdom . . .
Just choose your seat and sit down . . .
Hosanna to the Prince of Peace who
Clothed Himself with clay and Entered
The iron gates of Death and
Took its sting away.

11

Angel
Two Wings
to Veil
My Face

ow Nathaniel wondered if Great-Momma Sweetie's saga was
to reach a higher stage of consecration, what was to be his
specific role in the storytelling, beyond that of mere recorder
of deeds. For this was not simply the swelling stage of someone with
an incandescent saga to sing, whom a talented, offbeat, student dropout happened upon while visiting a relative at a home for the city's
ancient citizens. This was his grand-kin, the illuminating Sweetie
Reed Witherspoon, a woman vitally linked to everything in his world
of remembrances, and the knowing connection to the gaps in his
history. Ah, but that dreadful interval, April 4–June 5, 1905.

Not only was there the question of how to be good as his word but true to her word, he thought aloud. Her Baruch, her Boswell. . . . How to become illuminated through the torchlight of her saga to a higher stage of his own evolvement to know the light of the North Star? He must speak out, though he might be brought low to the well for his payment. He must prod her not so much for more story—the legal pads upon the bureau flowed with the copyright of her eloquence and were now unto the fifth generation, he smiled to himself. But also to spin the story, transform it into an eternal gold beyond the radiance of the here and the now of men's eyes.

Without my own imprint recorded somewhere within the soul of the saga—past the blue-black ink on the yellow legal pad, or the hot type in cold print on the sleek white bond—I will remain but an idle ludlow; a designated executor, he thought, full of steam heat; sound and fury, signifying everything; not remaking that estate my own, but simply an actor, as instrument. Yet my property, but not via my process in the possession. And how to make her eloquence more eloquent, so that it possessed the miraculous stamp of permanence. If I can be a part of that transformation, magician-like, I'll be happy to be quiet, if not still, serving as acolyte at her High Mass. For who could sit still without rocking from her rendered-up incantation of eloquence? The rest should indeed be silence, where one might study the significance in solitude—unless there is a golden mean to June 5, yet to be offered up. A dénouement wrought without expostulation?

Great-Momma Sweetie Reed's troubling, revealing story deserved at least the dimension of believable, immemorial preservation he offered. Now he wondered after those men, the priests and other writers, who in their solitude had rewritten the words of the orally delivered, handed-down public utterances of the prophets, in the beginning time of his memory, when Sweetie Reed read aloud from the Old Testament to him, and then his reading to her. The prophets' original oracles enriched, heightened and embellished.

But the priests and writers could bring a certain impassioned detachment, primal and golden, to the peculiar testifying, amid their own religious fervor, years after the initial word was flung forth by those soapbox drifters who stood outside the temple, bewailing the values going against the native spiritual grain, on the inside and outside, within the body politic. Scribes who could rewrite through a fanatical figure and go virtually undetected until scholars centuries later found their particular "contribution," their "strand," as yet another layer in the labyrinth of luminosity, polished into a sacredness beyond the original word of the prophet, if he in fact of flesh ever existed, as more than a collection of brilliant, streaklike, tributary-swirling voices of protestation; outlawish dervish, in the first holy-jumping, word-weaving place. Ah, the relationship of the mustard seed to the sun. The flesh made word, incarnate. But my informant, my most unruly prophetess, as it were, is very much alive and kicking. At the moment, however, looking over at the bed, he thought, Great-Momma Sweetie Reed is dozing exquisitely.

And shall I record, too, he wondered now, in order to recharge her memory, keep her light going (when to the summons of sweet silent thought I jotted upon yellow legal pad, then transformed to bond, things of remembrance past) how I fed my beloved grand-kin a jigger of Rémy Martin dashed over a bed of boiling sassafras tea leaves to sweeten and kindle the unwritten oracles of her sundered past, articles of her constitution, beyond the scripture of her emancipation procla-mation: those long, personal tracts of eloquence lodged away within the fabulous memory bank of Sweetie Reed, and distilled out of the fierce, fiery tongue of that demigod, I. V. Reed. Great-Momma Sweetie, who could make caviar out of short rations. "Of the fullness of the heart the mouth speaketh" indeed.

For in her retelling had she not reshaped the voices of her yellow-streaked, storytelling I. V. Reed, that shape-changing, now-you-see-him, now-you-don't, laminated onion of soul; beyond all peeling, but flavorful in the soup of any stewing story; and the others as well—pruning and culling, superimposing (editing?) even as the word was given to her, *charged* and *changed*. Yes, and as an actress, too, who reshapes the role night after night from the multilayered collectivity of words spun out of time about the play to the director's hypersensi-tive ear of experience—and the word of the sacred text—upon two boards and a passion, even unto the holy, irredeemable Bard himself. Enriched again by the actress' personal roles in life upon many pas-sionate stages, out of many stages, without the sound of applause or wages. But that was reshaping the word within the world of the role made flesh through spirit, memory, intellect, agony, enunciation and accents. Dare he change the word, rearrange the Bardlike Sweetie's words . . . Ah, but a "woman colored ill" or not, I suspect, Nathaniel chuckled, that the Bard in all of his glory, never came upon such a peculiar institution as Great-Momma Sweetie Reed, made flesh.

Oh, how many times in the deep well of night unto the pitch of daybreak had Sweetie Reed rehearsed her story and her lines, for this afternoon's curtain call of sessions with the lives of her soul, he wondered. And particularly so because of the estranging membrane to hearing. Surely in the secret sleeve of solitude and sleep she had re-created her story upon the two boards and a passion that was her bed. And there found no peace, nor peaceful sleep—ah, there indeed was the rub. Yes, and there found no peace, nor acceptable person, despite her getting into the bed, but not to fall asleep, either, but rather to start reading from any one of a half-dozen Bibles, linked binding to binding upon her nightstand:

"Until my mind drops my body off to sleep; and troubled dreaming, Nattie . . . Because my mind, ah, that heartache to the brain! But you see, Splendid Spoons, I want my soul to be ready in case I get called off in the night, or by dawn's light," she said time and again.

"And if the Lord decides now, let's descend by the light of the North Star and pick up Sister Sweetie Reed, I want this extra layer of praying and reading wrapped tight about my body and soul, warning off any icy evil I might have conjured up during the day, as I comforted His wayward children, and covered up my own wayward mind . . . and warming up my soul. But not in the way some of those feverish churchwomen *promenade* two hundred body pounds all about the one hundred and forty pounds of flesh God supplied them with—on loan—as a tottling mountain cast over a molehill, in order to attract attention, since I suspect ain't nobody watching them very much (so they think) without that extra flopping baggage of slabs and crevices and jutting jaws (but they gonna have to learn to travel light if they gonna ever see God's radiance); and thinking that weight makes them much woman, or that might means right; well now, Nattie, I want to be very much woman on the inside, they can have the shaky outside, and think it's sleek silk. They think all that baby fat around their hearts and hips going to keep them warm, give them *airs* of innocence; make menfolk, particularly the preacher, believe they got good natural softness and warmth on the inside—but I'm here to tell you, Nathaniel, they lining themselves out for a heart attack. And to God's eye, these shapeless souls in a spiritual sack dress ain't nothing but a stocking cap sewed by Satan wrong side out.

"Or now, you take the way some women wear minks and sables and fox wraps and even bears out on their man-hunting parties; skinning and stripping those animals in order to trap body warmth inside to their souls; hugging that fur to their bodies to trap a man in a bear trap, with a bear hug. But all they are doing, son, is turning their temperature up and their inner warmth down, that's why you see them swearing all the time inside those beavers' bodies, like an ice-storm across the face of the sky. Meantime they think they are really radiating. But the palpitations of even a natural man are tricky; for a rabbit knows a fox trap same as a hound knows Hell. Those women are like some city men who send up a whistling rhapsody of steam heat to the female ear, when their boiling hearts ain't nothing but hot ice. Yes, and those women going off to church like they are going off to a masquerade ball, dressed to kill. Why, they desire to be worshiped by God through man as a golden sunset—meantime their souls suited up to top a golden calf.

"But Sweetie Reed desires only to have that band of powerful reading and text touched to the context of her living deeds and inner soul . . . and in the last breathing, thinking and doting hours fixed upon Him—that's the radiance I want about me, within me. That's my hope for a halo . . . so He'll know that in the terrors of the night's storm the radiant lighthouse pool from this window—coming forth from my voice reading those verses from this little old upper room— is out there shining, this little light of mine, and as a beacon pitched to the North Star, for Him and His band of angels to take me on home, where I can meet my mother, and Lovelady. Now, Nattie, don't get me wrong, I ain't courting up Death for a ring.

"But then if He doesn't send down His band of angels, these pray-ers, text readings, verses and living deeds will and do guide me to fight off those demons that come from under the sea after me in my sleep. Though I never beat them back all the way. The verses and deeds knit a life jacket of protection about my soul—every night as demons chase me, hover about, like hounding patrollers chased my mother and me to another world . . . So that I can float upon the waters and be as lightbread and not get unsettled nor drowned; a life jacket; and as long as that air stays in the sleeves of my soul and don't go to my head to a point of getting me dizzy with devilment, nor drunk over my inner heat and warmth—then I'll be in the ripe condition; and not filled up and puffed out like those fur-bound women, draped out as water bags with spite-work." Yet when Nathaniel knelt down beside Great-Momma Sweetie Reed, in the long ago, he could hear her mumbling and humming and praying aloud over and over again, in a fervor:

Hurry, Angel, hurry! Hurry down to the pool.
I want you to trouble the waters this morning.
To bathe my weary soul.
Angel got two wings to hide me away
Two wings to fly me away.
I would not be a hypocrite
I tell you the reason why
'Cause death might overtake me
And I wouldn't be ready to die.
Angel got two wings to veil my face.
Angel got two wings to fly me away.

Then she was saying, "Yes, but when you have reached your majority, my Splendid Spoons, I will try to unload, yield up this burden to you, not in a madness but in a sharing." Nathaniel observing even then in the long ago that her mind was not satisfied though her spirit seemed to have found a way of centering down for the evening's long-haul solitude of agony . . . Ah, but, Great-Momma Sweetie, the trauma of another calamitous kingdom alive in the afterlife makes this native son quake in the embrace of the here and the now forever and ever, rather than fly to the ills I've never seen in my wildest nightmares. Yet to deliver her saga might signal a call to readiness and announce the commencement of a golden age. Not of pleasure nor prosperity, but enlightenment of spirit as transformed by the mind soaring to new heights, albeit in the eye of the storm.

Nathaniel wondered what could be more disenchanting in life than passionate attachment without engagement? How could I be a part of it all and manifest myself without becoming a showoff, a Merlin-Spoofing Spottswood (but oh, to have his parts and his indivisible shrewdness of genius); and even the skullbone, if not the backbone of I. V. Reed, who was not exactly your garden-variety Yorick. Should I write a preface and bow out? Or play the role of Prologue announcing the warring kingdoms upon the stage of Sweetie Reed's embattled country? Backwater time, indeed. I have no intention of being rendered speechless like Angelina-Clea, he announced . . . If it were my cue to speak, I'd need no prompter, nor censor, either; ah, the majestic Moor, he mused.

But now as Nathaniel heard Great-Momma Sweetie clearing her throat, he swiftly turned to face her with the deeper question, *his* very own 1877, he projected wildly. His hands extended, cupped with a perfectly shaped urn of boiling sassafras leaves doused with Rémy Martin: an offering up for her continued revelation of the soul. But Sweetie Reed was saying:

—No, Nathaniel, not another hot toddy, lest I become a pure tall-tale-telling tattletale. Besides, your right hand must be ready to drop off to sleep. I can even see your sleeve trembling as a wet-washed garment caught up in a breeze, with its shaking; nerves in your biceps quivering with the chores of my writing assignment in longhand, like a nerve opened to the quick.—

Nathaniel heard his soul commanding him if not to take charge then to charge forth with his question.

—Great-Momma Sweetie, I know that June 5 is not your juneteenth, but since you've spelled out everything to me in order that I might get some order over my disorder.—

—In order, son, that I might get some peace of mind, and that's very different from peace of soul, church folks haven't understood that part of the good news yet. They still can't deal with Nicodemus, who was about as close to us as anything in the New Testament I can think of in our modern-day finery . . . Yet they allow for his presence at the tomb.—

—I feel that I'm somewhere between Nicodemus and Hamlet, Fred Douglass and Lincoln, a rock and a hard-place and Joe Williams singing "Every Day I Have the Blues," all the time, Great-Momma Sweetie.—

—That day, June 5, Nathaniel, is a burden still fierce for me to center down upon.—

—Great-Momma Sweetie, it's not for the story alone that I need to fill out that date and what it meant to get the story right. But to get right what is missing from you and me. Between us, too. For myself and my own troubled mind within. I came upon those dates in your Bible long ago. And now I want to know what is hidden from me and what you have hidden maybe from yourself, as unspeakable in the long ago . . . especially when you confessed everything else.—

—Told, not confessed. I'm not Catholic, like those DuPonts, they confess everything without revealing anything. Still the Bible, where you found the date, is about genesis and then some, so hold on, as my Lovelady used to say, when I came north to marry your grandfather and work for her and went to her for advice and counsel, two years before she died . . . Must I go back to that, too, when only Jericho Witherspoon knows the truth and he's the beloved culprit who's long gone? And you, Splendid Spoons, stand as his remnant to the new day. Mine, too, I don't mean that you aren't. No, not for a moment. You're all I'll ever have, Nathaniel. And as the old folks used to say, a one-eyed mule can't be handled on the blind side, without you misleading your second mind; I see you are smiling and that's good. I sure wasn't smiling on June 5, 1905, that midnight when your grandfather appeared, after being away for two months, out of a windstorm, and out at elbow.

—But, Nathaniel, as the old folks also used to say, proudness of a man don't count when his head is cold, which Jerry used when he defended poor folks in court. Lovelady interpreted it to also mean, in her wisdom, that a *cold head* was one that was unsatisfied by the lukewarm answers people gave about hot questions, raised up by hotheads so that the temple grows ice-cold with anger for the answers.—

—Momma Sweetie, I'm not a hothead and you know it. But June 5 will not go away from you, nor me, and you know it . . . Set off, too, as it was next to my father's name in quotation marks, in your main Bible, and just beneath the listing of the babies you . . . of the genealogy . . .—

—Nathaniel, go on and say it, *lost*. Babies I had lost and then the name of Arthur Witherspoon and the date in quotation marks. All right, all right, Nathaniel Witherspoon. And I realize you are not a hothead. Still, you have a hot question burning in your head, I also know that. Lovelady wasn't knocking hotheads and there were plenty of them back then, but she was trying to shape hotheads into fiery-tempered instruments, cold and calculating for freedom, that's what I was getting at through her. But no, son, this goes way back, this June 5 business.

—Nathaniel, when the word got back to Rollins Reed that his daughter Angelina was dead, but her child was still alive, the patroller-turncoat stole me back from my heathen captors, who lived near the swamps on one side of a river; two-hundred-fifty-acre parcel of land with twenty captured Negroes, whose fortunes had been turned back to slavery.

—I was snatched up by those huge gloved hands out of the hay where I was hiding from both the new masters and the patroller, whom I'd seen sleepy-eyed coming after me in the barn around midnight and thought that he was somebody else. I was in a fitful state of not trusting anybody.

—Because you see, Nathaniel, my mother's life had been taken three days earlier, before my very eyes. She told me many times how this place we were standing on was not our home; our other home was in another part of this country; a cruel place; it was nothing as horrible as this country; but we had a true home where we might see each other one day. She was always trying to prepare me for her death and what to do at every turn and stage, in case I lived.

—. . . Nathaniel, that tall man doused out the torchlight and picked me up by the ear and neck from out of the hay where I lay hiding. He looked something like one of the three men who had raped and murdered my mother; and like one of the seven who snatched us up from Reed's barn. I was holding on to that strawberry bonnet my mother had worn on her head when they left her for dead.

—I was just coming out of another nightmare of my mother's rape and then murder and shaking off sleep in the hay when he entered the barn, in a masquerade and throwing up a silver-sounding voice of sweetness. When he picked out my whereabouts with his torch, his voice changed to a roaring sea. I was certain it was my turn now, my time had come to join her.

—When he discovered my whereabouts, I thought he was going to set the barn afire as the others had done to Reed's barn. He circled the torch about his head three times, little sparks flying from it and him spitting through his yellowed and clawish teeth. His gray-green snapping eyes. The chicken pock marks, as hickeys on a gater's flesh, bounded about his scrawny red neck and bit to the skin of his hollow jaws. In the flare of the torchlight he looked albino. He was dressed in layers of clothing: a mud-splattered white uniform with a work-man's apron pulled over his overalls. He wore a battered, hole-ridden hat he must've stolen off the head of a scarecrow. Then he slipped on tar-covered gloves out of his back pocket before he went in after me in the hiding place I had swept into being with my hands and made a cave in the hay, next to the chicken coop and eggs.

—At first I thought he was going to burn the barn down if I didn't come out to the bid of his roaring: "Nigger gal, I'm going to burn up your little black ass if you don't come unto me." Even the chickens' cackling seemed slit to the screech of a pregnant woman caught up in a fire. But I was a little too smart to believe he was going to set the barn on fire, because I was sure he didn't know about the ins and outs of the barn the way I did; not like that other time, when they burned the barn alive with Mother and me. I thought if he tried to burn it to the ground he might be killed in the fire, or he might be caught up by the masters of this plantation.

—I knew where a secret slit in the side of the barn could easily be opened, directly behind me now, and if I could scamper back to it I could rush out of this barn and from the presence of his awful face that was imprinted in my mind through the torchlight and the way the others had looked like him as a chain of brothers and cousins. But rush out to what? My hideous master for protection? Why not rush these masters to fists and then throw them against each other so that they would kill each other in a fight, while I hid behind trees, as they fought over their property, and I fled from this property. But suppose the slit in the side of the barn door was bolted on the outside before he entered. I convinced myself that he was one of the seven who captured us, or one of three who raped and killed my mother. I held a butcher knife inside of the tiny girl's apron my mother had sewed for me at the Reed plantation and it was too small for me now, though I still wore it for her memory sake. I would come up to his arms sweetly, then slip the butcher knife at the place where his heart was suppose to be with all of my heart.

—But spotting me now, he stomped the torchlight out and commenced to put on those tar-splattered gloves, as his gray-green snapping eyes fastened upon the gentle shake of hay from the chest heaving of my heartthrob, buried beneath in the hay revealed me. As if whatever he was about to do was too foul to touch with his naked hands, he rubbed the gloves together in a hand-washing motion. Dashed the last of the torchlight sparks out two feet from the edge of the hay where I spied out at his huge boots up to his snappy eyes; then clawed me up with one hand by the throat, as a chicken's head to be wrenched off. Other hand cuffed me up by my right ear. I thought he was set to murder me now for sure.

—Nathaniel, I was too little and unfit to do any really hard labor, not worth the money for feed. Mother had said that they were planning something horrible for me and she hoped to steal us away soon. But at seven my period had not come down yet and they (men) didn't want you, Mother said, until the time your blood starts to flow.

—Nathaniel, as that man lifted me to the door, I heard the sound of my stolen butcher knife hit the barnyard floor as a tin whistle. I had no idea that he was there to save me (which he wasn't, but to save the last money strand of the bargain he had struck as a flare in the darkness with Reed, that had gone astray). I barely could catch my breath and I prayed God aloud that He would waste this man's body away, like that white-heat torch cone he had dashed to pieces on the barn floor.

—Then I thought he was going to take me off to yet another plantation—as he strode swiftly with me as a meal sack towards an awaiting horse-drawn wagon—worse than this one, for mother had often wept of a place called Hell, where fire burned alive eternally. He was sent from that place by Satan to carry me there where I would find a burning home forever and ever and sunken in a raging sea but the water was swept up in a wave of flames, so that you dared not try to swim out of it, though your earthly mind made you always think of water and escape and swimming and you had to free yourself from that kind of thinking when pitched down there, she said. He, this man, I thought, was sent from that place by Satan to carry me there where I would find a burning home forever and ever more.

—Then I thought the flaring up of his torchlight and the dashing out of it was just to show me a little of what it must be like where his fire-thirsty soul lived and nursed as the mouth to the breast cone of those flames, and what a mighty force he was down there; a driver in Hell, I guessed. He was capable of anything and everything, like the driver on this plantation they were building up, and I suddenly thought this man's gonna drive me to market where they will set me on an auction block naked, as I had heard my mother speak of in her nightmares out of her girlhood memories; and he was mixed up in my first mind with those seven who took us away and the three that raped and murdered my Angel. Angelina. My mother. Now as he buried me beneath the hay in the wagon, I found myself binding bits of hay together in a wild sort of plan suggested by her once upon a time . . .

—Nathaniel, the way Angelina had described the man taking us off from Reed's barn, well, that all came down on me now, in a fixed, bloody memory. Touched as a torchlight to what I saw in my wakefulness because at first I was asleep and awoke trembling from a dream in slumber to a nightmare; my head tucked to her breast; suddenly her arms were beating them off and kicking, as their hands flew into our flesh and pawed and tore away at her body. Later in the wagon mother hugging me close into her, cupping me to her breast, and me crying and asking for *water;* trying to hush me into a sobbing silence the length of the long ride, from my screaming out loud for *water, water, water.* And, Nathaniel, I heard her praying to God for our deliverance and please . . . *God, just don't let them hear Sweetie and give my baby girl up to the water cure.*

—She knew them also to be full of savage games firsthand; they forced us to run to their arms, by tossing us into the corner; torching the barn and fleeing to where they stood as soldiers on either side of the barn door; as some owners did at weddings, down the aisle at the Big House; the hay going up in flames; watching for us, waiting for us as we flew out. They had bolted the front door. Standing there as if to congratulate us for escaping to the freedom of their blissful, awaiting hands and arms. Our saviors.

—Now at the bottom of the hay I could feel the wheels smashing and crushing the pebbles and rocks beneath in my teeth, stomach and backbone. Where he was taking me must be that Hell she had talked about. Down a river *alive* in waves of flames, chained to an auction block, erected upon a frozen slab, that could not melt, two feet above the naked slaves' feet, where the body was forced to twist and dance and leap to avoid the flames, which it could not do, to the howls of laughter from the bidders. With the auctioneer's voice alive in savage preacher rhythms and Christian-minted words of all accents: blood and rebirth, diamonds, and seed, cotton and gold good as a mustard seed, Christ, and anklebones and backbones, good white teeth, and blood ties, heavy-hipped, and duty, honor, country, and nigger toes and salt-bathed lashes and ships called *Sweet Jesus,* weighing scales and many a thousands up the river heathens to flaming salvation. Then, Nathaniel, she'd fall weeping about *stuffed away diamonds in my soul, my soul, my soul.*

—Then I thought if I leaped from this wagon, as fast it was going, and fall out he'd be punished when he returns to Hell without me, because I thought he was given the task of bringing little girls down to the River to Hell with him regularly and if he didn't return with one, me this time, he would be mightily punished and I laughed in pitiful glee, Nathaniel. I set myself to leap, but just then he swirled the wagon about and took yet another direction (and my mind sped back to Mother's old plans, one of three hundred, I can still count out ways to either escape or deal with terror; some foolish, some clever, some cunning, all spun out of what she had heard and based in another time and another world). Wagon seemed to reroute itself and so I said to myself, let it be, I'll try to kill them right back, and then weeping too over my own babyishness as I thought I heard the sound of the butcher knife falling not upon the barnyard floor but upon the water and hearing it popping in flames. Yet if I leapt from the wagon, all right too, because surely I would break my neck and die, and all right too, because in that way I hoped I might see Mother, in another form that I had not known, more beautiful than in life, because she would be mine where we might remain untouched by human hands, which were always inhuman. And her new form would be in the holy glory of an angel's spirit, with wings to hide me away from the troubles of this world.

—Nathaniel, my mother saying that last night we might not ever see each other again; but if I lived it would be through His mercy; the river would always be a mind-troubled passage the length of my days, with the body on land barely kept alive at best and kept alive solely for the dreams of another kingdom that no traveler had ever seen other than by the miracle of His redeeming grace . . . But it was in the middle of the air, and then the Heavens, that I should project my soul, even as my mind, my feet must remain clever to the evil tracks that lay out before me at every turn. No man could be trusted, and no embrace sacred but that of Jesus' hold on me. Hold to that. Which was what Lovelady said in another way after your grandfather left me and came home with that living gift for me, on June 5, 1905, out of a windstorm.

—Nathaniel, now as my body was flung in every direction in that wagon I thought of mother's sunup to nightfall advice of three hundred plans about everything; hope on the one hand and constant terrorized warning, born out of despair of hopelessness and ruggedness, on the other . . . Her saying to me now from an old echoing-up voice within my soul, as the wagon juggled my buried body along . . . *If trapped one day on a journey against your will (which will many a thousand times be the case), throw off bits of whatever you possess along the roadside; if carted off from one place to another, so that you can find your way back.* If I needed to or wanted to—or find my way partial back and then take yet another route . . . *Hide in a church sometimes,* she offered, *in the tower,* she suggested in her despair over answers to the riddle of our condition. *Though church folks can be our greatest enemies amongst our almighty enemies* . . . Then hopeful: *Anything you can turn your hands to, rocks, clumps of hay tied together, pebbles—then pray they don't get seen—the pattern, I mean— nor blown in the wind of hopelessness, try to stick them to the sides of the road* . . .

Then she would throw up her hands in despair over that plan and go on to another and yet another. Teaching me the alphabet A to Z through plans for escape, living and honor. *A* for *Alert* and then how to be Alert to everything that moved on earth and in the Heavens . . . *B* for *Bravery* . . . *C* for *Cunning* and sometimes *C* for *Courage* . . . and sometimes *C* for *Campground,* and in that way teaching me spirituals, too. So that before I could read—and Jericho Witherspoon never quite knew this—I could shape words into action before I knew their shape on a slate . . . An alphabet letter and a word for all kinds of impossible situations, until my head almost dropped from my shoulders with weariness; she was filled with a troubled despair; her head rolling in her hands and her head heavy upon the ground and her carriage jerking her backbone into the motion of a dance to offset the horror of words . . . and then down to *L* for *Love,* because that was when she would tell me once again about that slave who loved so much he risked his life to flee to the arms of his beloved . . . That was a wondrous presence in my mind's eye over the state of Love but prepared me not for a love life, made of hands and power and leverage which is the living condition of love . . . between man and woman.

—And so, Nathaniel, I squeezed and rubbed that chunk of hay and binding it together, in that wagon, as the strands in the braid she used to weave my hair in, as one braid, and then I rubbed the hay for all it was worth, as if the strands were my very own mother's bony fingers brought back to me now with my fingers to make a onesome woman's clasp of daughter and mother, mother and daughter, bound together in one binding lock. Recalling to my mind, too, how as Mother plaited my hair, she also had said that its nappy, cottony strands were as every soldier on his own station, but maybe it was a better grade for all of it, as I now touched upon the lock her dark chestnut, heavy, wavy hair that I had clipped from her head with the garden shears before I/we reburied her—and that I kept in a little wee bag beneath my meal-sack gown, sewed in a sleeve next to my heartbeat, so that it was kept secret beneath my breast, in case I was stripped down of every stitch I would still cling to that inner locket . . .—

—*Reburied,* Momma Sweetie?—

—Yes, child, *reburied.* Because you see after they shot her and took her out there near the swamp and tossed her into a makeshift grave, that was only three feet deep, she was not dead, not for a long spell, and I slipped out there by nightfall to see after her, and she was moaning and weeping and one of the other taken "slaves" was out there with me and we stayed out there with her the night trying to make her comfortable, and old Bluestone trying to make her grave-going easy with old-time slave ointments and new ones he had stolen from the master's household. But Mother died by morning's first light near the river where we washed clothes, on Mondays. Her voice lingering on and echoing that soon she would be done with the troubles of this world, going off to see her mother; crying out for her mother, she who had never spoken much of her mother before; calling out for her now ... Then placing my hand into the hands of Bluestone and his wife; the left hand in Bluestone's and the right hand in his wife's right hand and then she heaved a sigh of horror and fell away. But my body clung to her form. I would not move. I was fixed there, despite my hands being clasped to theirs. Then I wrestled my hands free from their old hands so work-racked. I held her up in my arms, embraced her—hoping that I might fly off with her spirit. And the old Negro Bluestone trying to pull and part me from my mother, I felt in my heart. Calling his woman to help him, and they pulled and strained to take me away. It took all of their strength.

—Then all we had were those shears that I used to cut off a locket of her hair for my very own, as I saw her dying off earlier; and we used those shears and our hands, all three of us, to dig my mother's grave out of the hardened earth of knots. Yes, Nathaniel, *reburied* her now. I fell out as Bluestone put Mother down into the grave we had dug; and he and his wife-woman took me into their hut. A thin, tall woman who moved with a great silence, her body had become numb with its solitaireness, claiming silence eternal as her commandment and portion, even as it had possessed her; and my mother had often used this woman as a source to point out how the death of life was upon this woman and how her spirit had descended into the earth—her spirit no longer brooded over life, as the spirit of death hovered over her body and consumed her body actions and spoke to her spirit; though Martha was very devoted to Bluestone, she was as one who lived her life upon the very edge of a cliff, five thousand feet above a valley, awake even in sleep to the fact that the wrong turn would spell her doom.

—Nathaniel, in the digging for her reburying I had cut off part of myself from the labor and been cut off from myself by the task, the meaning of why we were digging the grave in the first place, amid my tears upon my digging hands and the cutting edge of the shears. I was gone, I know that now; though I was only seven; but when I saw the hole I suddenly expected to see water—and a deep river to carry her

258

body off to the other side. The psalm said: "If I take the wings of the morning, *and* dwell in the uttermost parts of the sea; even there shall thy hand lead me, and thy right hand shall hold me." I would see the angel descend that she so often sang about . . . *Angel got two wings to hide my face, two wings to fly me away.*

—But, Nathaniel, when those shears hit a huge rock and a spark lit off from its face, I saw the faces of those patrollers sparkle as flaming diamonds in a sea of troubles, even as my digging-away hands were awaiting the angel to descend down and take up my mother's soul upon *her wings*—as she lifted my mother's body from the waters to sea . . . But no, that spasm turned to flames in their faces, their red necks and those tearing-away hands and fingers digging away about her body. I fell over; Bluestone swept up my body; I tore myself from his clasp, feeling his grasp was lit to the torch of their touch . . . Lord Gawd, must I go back to that, too? . . . And me reaching out for the angel's touch to touch my fingers to know that she, the angel, was there to claim my mother's body, so that she, my mother, might be possessed by the wings of the morning.—

—*Her* wings?—

—Yes, Nathaniel, because no man-angel could take wings after I saw what I had seen at the hands of foul-faced man. It *was* a man who did the most part of the gravedigging to set my mother's body free at last. But it was also men who slaughtered her down to an early grave so low. No man appeared to me of any account, except Jesus Christ, and that runaway slave my mother always praised for his escape to be with his beloved. But both Jesus and this slave were more —what shall I say?—mythical, I guess, than real in my soul, thereby greater, too, but more distant; at the center of my vision but obscure, larger than the life of the body in the middle of the air.

—. . . Now, Nathaniel, later, after we buried I. V. Reed, and I returned home with Wayland Woods' letter in my purse, I used to read his brave words over and over again for inspiration and instruction about how the heart of a man could have the shape and charge of courage carried along by a merciful current of caring. I still keep Wayland Woods' letter in that top drawer. Lawd, son, that was 1906, and I was nearly forty years old by then, when I discovered it. But read it. Read Wayland Woods' letter for yourself and see the pure soul of black folks. I didn't know enough of the courage as I grew up of Woods and his kind. None to tell me his story, everything happened so fast. So now, Nathaniel, go to the bureau drawer and find it and read it aloud not so much to me but for yourself. And you learn it by heart . . . You can do two things at once. Search and write at the same time.—

Nathaniel commenced to search through her top drawer for the letter.

—Men indeed, the patroller man standing there on that crumbling white porch with angels to either side and old man Rollins Reed seated in his rocking chair. I saw the patroller man open his mouth and bare his yellowish teeth: "Well, since I couldn't bring back your dead gal's body to prove that she was killed, I brought back the wench's stool. And because you gave me that five hundred dollars up front in good faith" (I could see Rollins Reed's face grow disgusted, his jaws drop like soured grapes on a vine) "and I always keeps my word, as it is my bond . . . Come here, little nigger gal," he called out without looking to see me, "Come on over and greet up with your grandpappy's knee," and then he put his gloves back on and lifted me up like I was an empty meal sack and onto Rollins Reed's knee, atop that Bible which was rocking upon his knee, there in the same rocking chair where you are now sitting, Nathaniel.

—And then the patroller man drifted off underneath the gray cloth that was folded up as another layer of the hood that covered his hay wagon. And I sat there atop Rollins Reed's Bible, in that meal sack dress and bonnet my mother had worn on her head when they left her for dead, flopping down unto my ears; and I cried. I wanted to spit into those whiskers of this grandpappy as he looked down upon me with a hateful, loathing look. All the blood ran clean out of his heart, making him grow pale. Locket of Angelina's hair sewn to my heart-beat inside the sack dress and her strawberry bonnet were all I had to touch me back to her form; but as I'm rubbing the locket of hair for faith, whom do I see scratching out upon the screen door other than my father, I. V. Reed.

—At first I wanted to believe he was commencing to wave at me, but it wasn't to be that kind of greeting. Scratching upon that screen door as if he was trying to scratch my eyes out even if I *did* apologize for returning to his sight. If I apologized for being born, that would not be enough for him. Nathaniel, I felt I had been left for dead to melt away upon my grandfather's knee; my pappy's scratching was in tune with my gradual melting away into nothing, until I completely vanished from his sight. And I heard Rollins Reed weeping amid his laughter; someone sure played a joke on me, he seemed to be saying, and then repeating the name *Auntie Foisty* over and over again, as if dumbfounded in the caught-up sleeves of a curse. That was my greeting by these two sentinels of fatherhood, Nathaniel . . . You find that letter yet?

—So that when I came north, Nathaniel, I arrived at the depot as part of a bargain and married Jericho Witherspoon, for himself, and not for me. I can remember his face from the beginning time when he greeted me at the train station; he seemed to search my face for an image, an impression he was dreaming to discover, and not finding it there, turned from me and pondered for a few minutes, readjusted himself and his face; turned to face me.

—Jericho Witherspoon was like a man who strikes a bargain and loses in the main, but gets something out of the transaction; then tries to see how what he got stacks up with what he had dreamed of getting and bargained for and how the compromise will appear in the marketplace. Just now he seemed as if one side of him wanted to do an about-face, but the other said, *No, I struck a bargain and I must submit to the results, though the terms were changed and hidden from my eyes and appear now to be unfair; still I must keep to my word and besides she's young and in youth there is hope.* But I was only speculating then and filling it out now with the second mind of experience, because in fact I didn't know how he fitted into the buying of my freedom.

—I wasn't to a mind of marrying up yet, as they say; it wasn't in my body needs, you know what I mean, Nathaniel; you're grown now. Marriage bed wasn't in my thoughts other than that runaway slave who risked his life for love. But that was the romantic part. *This here,* as the old folks used to start off a statement with, was a full-blown natural man; six feet, six inches tall and higher up than Mr. Lincoln, and huge in flesh, with a high-top hat on. In Jericho's right hand he held a long silver cane given to him by the father of the Governor. In his left hand he offered a bunch of gladiolas, as a greeting gift. Jerry was fifty-five years old but he looked young enough to pass for forty. He had a powerful, rugged face; his coloring a peculiar mixture of glowing pinkish red-brown. What I had on my back was all I had in the world to show a man. He looked like the royal emperor of some kingdom, or the grand general who guarded the palace, and I was to be picked up at the train station and delivered as the new chambermaid for the household by him because it was his right by design to see and know every emplóyee that came to work in the royal household.

—Nathaniel, as he drove us off to Lovelady's house, where we were to stay, I thought if he touches my clothing perhaps I'll be shed of my rags and be as beautiful before him as that escaped slave girl must have been in the mind's eye of her lover. And then maybe I'll be as beautiful as that picture he was looking for when he looked into my face and turned away. But since it was not a hateful look but only one of disappointment, I thought, well, this can be a new start for me.

—Now he took off his gloves and placed his huge reddish brown hand over both of my little ones, as if to say you are safe now, girl, and gave a rapid-fire call of the address to the driver. Not a love embrace, though surely I didn't know what that meant altogether, but a comforting hand. My hands were icy cold. I felt my knees go weak and soon I was on my knees, and before I knew anything about it, I was kissing his hands in appreciation and my tears falling upon his hands, as the gentle rain upon powerful, bare branches. Not because he had purchased me from down there for marriage, for I plainly wasn't ready for marrying (nor did I know how I fitted into the business affair, as a substitute, in the wheel of fortune). This was the first time in my life someone other than my mother had touched me with kindness and sweetness, if not love. And a man, too. I was starved and thirsty for love. Now he lifted me back up from my knees, and in my husband-to-be I found comfort. I could not help but wonder how could this runaway slave be so secure within himself. The warm power of his hands suggested an anchor for me and I felt transformed in a new and different way from what I had envisioned earlier.

—We stayed with Lovelady Breedlove, where he had been rooming. I helped her in the kitchen she had set up for runaways during slavery and now it was more active than ever because more Negroes were coming north with nothing to make a living with. This was 1882 and I was fifteen. I won't go into our private ways between man and woman, Nathaniel, about your grandfather, but let it be enough for me to say that I kept losing babies and your grandfather was middle-aged by then. So I could not tell if it was because his seed was weak that the babies came here weak and opened to all the diseases of the day, or was it because I was not a good enough woman, for that was the way it was looked upon; and not to keep them alive cast even more frowns upon me from Jerry's friends. I appeared as a cursed woman. Cursed in his eyes as well, after a time.

—And though he was very good to me, I was as a child in his eyes, partially because I was a woman and partially because I was in fact a child bride, though that was nothing unusual, I had never had a proper growing up. So he educated me. I became the child we seemed not to be able to keep alive. But I was dissatisfied, I wanted to do something with the mind I was developing and he wanted me to have his child and see it grow up, though he drew pleasure transforming me into a brilliant student of his teachings. I was as the mustard seed before his mighty sun.

—But the absence of a child went between us and filtered through nearly every word of the give-and-take that makes up the daily routine of marriage. And by Jerry being so grand in the world and successful for a Negro—or anyone, for that manner of the day—a shadow seemed cast over all of his intercourse with the outside world, that in turn tied us to a social situation, for everything in our society seemed to reflect back to the shortcomings of our marriage bed. He was quite vulnerable to what people would say about his true stature; and in this people had a field day. Jericho Witherspoon, where's your heir? they'd imply. You are so great, but where's your seed that grows up to a crop? Who's going to take your place when you are dead and gone? Meantime I felt was this a curse, too, because my mother had also lost many babies before my coming.

—Nathaniel, night after night he hounded me, and became less than the grand man I had held so dear. I was still young enough and romantic to think of that slave runaway who risked his life to be with his beloved, why couldn't Jerry be satisfied with what we had and that was a lot. We were making a contribution in the grand old way of *lift up as you pull up*. Jerry with the law and me with that important work in Lovelady's kitchen; and I was going to school in the evenings. We were a couple that the good folks—not generally the society colored people—respected; although all respected him, they dared not; except for that one mark upon us. With Jerry so grand and a giant of a man and me so tiny, certain so-called society ladies delighted in seeing us so that they might make sex jokes of this *imbalance* in size, too, as if it also was tied to my not being able to mother an infant into its childhood and beyond. Naturally in all social occasions I was the darkest woman and the high yellows and the high browns made sharp barbs at *Jerry's cedar-colored slave girl.* Or *his wee woman who can't hold her water.* Many were jealous that he had selected me over them.

—Nathaniel, by now we were coming toward the end of the century, I was nearing thirty-three and already some women were talking to me about the change of life, in a mocking tone. You know what the change is, son . . . Well, of course you do, they talk about everything in school nowadays. And they should, I guess. But women in society can be so cruel, too. Now another matter cropped up in our marriage. Jerry started off with my education from scratch, not knowing what I might develop into, just as he had taken me for a bride sight unseen. I was not satisfied with the role he had slated for me and I knew women—colored women, too—who were doing things, women's issues, racial issues, of course. That role he could not take, so much. He didn't deny me a role to play—in fact, he enjoyed showing off my activities, but they had to be in cooperation with his schedule, his daily log of routines, business and social engagements. At the same time Lovelady was growing old and I was taking over more of the duties operating her kitchen.

—So that by 1905 I was what, thirty-eight, and we had stopped dreaming that I would get pregnant. Jerry was seventy-eight. We were at a party one night and I overheard one of the evil mistresses of fashion make a crack about not only the imbalance in size but the imbalance in age. I had been dancing with one young man in particular that evening. Jerry didn't like to dance even in the early days when I first came to the city. I won't repeat what she said but it was cutting to Jerry's manhood, and I didn't think he heard, but sure enough he did and he stormed out of the dance hall in a huff. This was in late March of 1905. I didn't see Jerry's face for a little over two months and then he appeared at our door, out of a windstorm, with a bundle in his arms.

12

Lost Souls:
The Light,
the Body,
the Eye

L ooking up from where he continued searching for Wayland
Woods' letter in the top bureau drawer, Nathaniel now declared:
—Wait a minute, Momma Sweetie Reed, hold on. Maybe I, as a lost
soul, don't want to hear what you are about to tell me. Grandpa was
always saying a woman is as old as she appears at midnight, just before
she disappears behind her vanishing creams, at the stroke of the hour,
but that the midnight of manhood appears long before it *dawns* on the
rider he's been sailing into a vanished sunset; and other such jokes
which were in part kept from my ears, if not my hearing.—

—. . .At midnight when Jerry came thumping on my door—sounding like a bloody cat's paw—I was sitting in that rocker, between nodding and sewing. I was altering a dress he bought for me that was too wide at the hips. But I didn't want Jerry to exchange it; I had cleaned a bloodstain away from the hem with a sprinkle of cold water.

—Now as I was trying to thread the needle for the last stitch—and drowsy for sleep—Jerry appeared out of the windstorm with this bundle in his arms. The screaming of this red-ruddy baby when rolled out of my husband's blue robe made my shocked voice seem more shrill than quarrelsome and alarmed. The baby's surging cry was loud enough for me to think God had damned all my hearing out of this windstorm. I was surely awake now.

—Jerry points to the baby on the unfolded blue robe and says: *"See, that's what's been absent . . . What we are talking about. What's been missing between us."* I rushed to the bed to serve the screaming, reddish baby but wanting to beat the man who held it a moment ago over the head with a rolling pin and toss a rock at Jerry's head in case he tried to flee from my sight. But before I knew anything I was down on my knees gathering this infant up into my arms. Still screaming like blue-bloody murder; it was enough to wake up the dead.—

—Hold on. Hold it right there, *please,* Momma Sweetie. Because . . .—

—Nathaniel, I got disengaged from my Hell-raising intention, in the howl of this baby. Caught off balance on the blind side of my womanhood. I thought a pin had popped on its napkin—or worse, that a deadly chill had hit the infant's nervous system, coming through that storm and all, so long. That's when I discovered the baby needed its napkin changed. After I changed the babe, I wrapped it in seven towels folded and looped in ties so that it was bound in warm towels head to toe.—

—Hold it right there, Momma Sweetie. Because I'm trying to hold on for dear life, like you were holding on to the dear life in your arms. What babe? Not my . . . I never. Now I know why I was always so afraid to get after you, lest you get unsettled and set before me the truth and nothing but the truth amid the Justice, so help you . . . God . . . No wonder I didn't break our compact of waiting until I was twenty-one to engage you about the meaning of June 5.—

—Wouldn't have told you *if* as you asked, a pageant of all the Sabbaths of Sundays, since 1905, suddenly paraded before my eyes.—

Now Nathaniel touched his lips to the cup of Rémy Martin, doused over the sassafras tea leaves; it was bitter to his palate, but his throat was dry as a hollow cough, and so he drank; saying aloud:

—Oh reddish baby tuckoo through a glass darkly—

—So, Nathaniel Witherspoon, I speak to you in plain English of June 5, 1905. The baby rolled up in the bundle of Jerry's blue robe was your father—

—My father who art . . . I feel like the wishbone that told two lovers don't pull my legs . . . apart—

—. . . Baby just as cute. But so red you can't tell what color it is and I'm trying to attend it, because it needs a fresh napkin.

—About two months old, I calculate. And raising enough storm of its own to challenge the roaring storm outside. Jerry standing there shamefaced—after he spat out that remark about what was absent between us—but proud like that tower over in Italy and dripping rain from head to toe; all wet. Must've kept the baby under his overcoat. Men! "Fool," I called him. "You could've killed this baby with the pure pneumonia bringing it through that storm, from wherever you . . . Ain't *enough* babies died . . .?" Then I catch myself up with that last remark. "Take off your dripping clothes, Jerry Witherspoon; judge or not, men are plain fools beyond judgment when it comes to common sense about babies . . . though not about how to get 'em."

—Nathaniel, imagine a tiny baby all rolled up in that six-foot-six man's blue robe. Then suddenly unfurled and unfolded, as a blue-red flag upon my bed. I'd rather have the wisdom of a fool, Nathaniel . . . though I feared I was being played the fool. Men always overdo in their undertaking of the role common sense plays. You know what Paul said: "If any man among you seemeth to be wise in this world, let him become a fool, that he may be wise. For wisdom of this world is foolishness with God."—

Nathaniel started to say, It's a wise fool who knows his father. Ah, the Bard. But he simply said:

—Paul also said it was better than burning . . . Marriage, I mean.—

—Now Jerry sits down in that rocker where you are sitting and starts to strip off his shoes and socks, slowly and bitterly, like his mind's engaged elsewhere . . . gazing upon that baby and beyond. One shoe overturns and I can see it has a hole in it . . . *Don't give your man too much rope,* Lovelady used to counsel—

—. . . Momma Sweetie, are you trying to tell me that this love that flows between us is not based upon, tied to a bloodline? Not that it matters, though it signifies everything . . . the love that flows between us *is* as blood, I mean—

—Nathaniel, just let your first mind unfold to what your second mind recognized long ago, but didn't want you to understand. Now the baby starts up crying again and I'm redirected from wifely charge after Jerry to get this infant-orphan a bottle of milk. I tossed the wet napkin, made up of three separate rags, into the wastebasket. Does it have a formula? Well, only one person could answer that and it most probably won't be Jerry Witherspoon. Though he sure would know whom to ask, in his profound wisdom. So off I scurry down those creaky steps to get some of the milk we give to our guests and I'm hoping that Lovelady won't hear me and I hope the baby's screaming hasn't roused her from her sleep; if the storm hasn't stirred her up already.

—Realizing too that I'll have to go to her for aid, and understanding of how to handle this uprising, this occurrence, this eclipse over my life, our life. Jerry appeared to be no longer clothed in his right mind. Some men at his age turn to young girls, gambling, or return to their second childhood. Appeared to me Jerry's soul had been turned over by all three, as a vessel in a storm.—

—But, Momma Sweetie, he didn't come to you as a torn-up fisherman-beggar. He threw, or should I say he gently laid down the gauntlet—out of the fallen raindrops of his overcoat—and in the form of an infant tumbled out of a blue bath robe, my father. There, I've said it. I have to keep that presence before me. My father, upon your bed, or the bed that you shared with Grandfather, as husband and wife; that you are now sleeping in . . . Yet not of your flesh—

—Yes, no doubt his boldness was audacious. Jerry had plenty of nerve, or he would never have survived . . . But the woman part in the engagement tore open that old healed-over chamber of my heart. Opened up self-doubt: that vulnerable, inadequate sense. Compromised again. Or I ought to say our bed had been compromised. I returned with the bottle of milk in one hand and a thirst for vengeance in the other. Jerry's back was to the door when I came in . . . Him rocking your father in his arms. I could see the JW brand upon the shoulder in the mirror of my runaway slave husband. Didn't change an iota of spirit-thunder stirring up in my hard heart. Then I looked in the mirror at myself. I didn't exactly look like Aunt Hagar, nor a withered chamber maid-hag with pail and soap and rag, and a dust cloth; and a rainbow-colored handkerchief about my head. I didn't need a masquerade to go dancing. But a steady trickle of pity was dropping merciful rain down upon a knotted-up heart: hard as clods with rocks at its core. Meantime, Jerry is humming a lullaby to the babe in his arms . . . Nathaniel, you must've suspected something—

Nathaniel wanted to say, *You should have suspected something, Sweetie Reed.* But he said:

—Well, I suspected something all right. I haven't been a babe in the woods covered over with green leaves for a long time. But Grandfather Witherspoon was such a miracle of a man that with him all things appeared possible. And at seventy-eight men have been known to father a child. Well, all right, not many men, but a few. Then when I was taking this psychology class last winter, they forced us to remember, in one class project, what we'd forgotten, how in the primal memory we all at one time or other, in childhood; yes, and during moments of anger with our parents, feel so rejected that we come to doubt if our real parents are really in fact our natural parents. In our spite we dream of being offspring of royalty, stolen from our origins, or something like that . . . Anyway, Grandfather Witherspoon always treated me like I was his royal offspring. He was no Methuselah, but he was surely a long-distance runner. I'd better be quiet. I'm going too far; because I'll ask where did my father come from. And Lord, I must be going through my second childhood before I get out of the garments of my first. Next I'll be asking where do babies come from. Well, where did this . . . You're getting teary-eyed, *and* do you want to change the subject, Momma Sweetie, we—

—Appears like it's getting to you far more than it got to me, well, almost. Besides, who said Jerry couldn't father a child?—

—. . . I didn't bargain for all of this, I guess.—

—*You* didn't bargain? What in the Halifax do you think I felt like? Dew on the petals of a June rose at dawn?—

—But then what did you do when you returned to him? The baby, I mean—

Momma Sweetie replied laughingly:

—I'm glad you didn't ask me what I started to do when Jerry returned to me with him. My second mind saved my first mind from sending my body to jail for performing an act of mayhem upon the body of a judge.—

—Momma Sweetie, you apparently were able to approach this gross embarrassment with an admirable amount of restraint, even a healthy kind of mocking humor.—

—What did you expect me to do, bleed all over the place? Men expect hysteria from women as they expect us to pull a fit once a month.—

—That's pretty hot!—

—*Now* is cooled down. Not *then;* but not cracking up and going to pieces, either. Men create a bellyful of chaos, then we have to straighten it out . . . But *then* is always *now* in my heart.

—I'll take you up on that mocking business because soon it comes to mind about Jerry always using that term, prima facie evidence, in court. And as the baby now seems secure with the suck of the milk-bottle nipple at his lips, I quickly turn on Jerry, lest he get at my sympathy again: "You, Jerry, you got exactly until that rain stops falling to explain yourself or get out of this house with your bundle of joy and in that blue robe of grief, that I purchased for you. You always talking about prima facie evidence, well, there it is on *our* bed. Now you, Mr. Lawyer, Mr. Judge, explain and expostulate your way out of *that* one." I'm trembling with rage, not misdirected by that sweet little baby on the bed cooing away now.—

—Look, Momma Sweetie, you can be open with me about your reaction. I know—*firsthand*—the wrath of your sour temper too well to believe for very long that you were so contained within the tempestuous teapot that is your spirit, not to let off more than this steam. Even now, look at that temple of yours, wrinkling up with backwater time, remember Clea? The lash of your tongue about that Clea's origins allowed me, if I had any doubts to see, how the loathing of your tongue can unleash fierce wages.—

—I'm an old woman, son, so naturally my temple's wrinkled.—

—But you seem so . . . unruffled is not quite the word I want.—

—Oh, I didn't know any of the Witherspoons had difficulty finding words. And are you calling me a liar to the heart? You see, now I can bring all of those feelings into play, and description. Not then. Then my mind and heart were going in a hundred different directions as tributaries to a bighearted river, that ain't hardly as bounteous as it appears . . . Now run and tell that—

—But didn't Grandpa have any comeback? As you've said, a Witherspoon always has a word at the ready, even if it isn't the last word; as if all were in readiness before the word is given.—

—No. He won't answer me. Just staring at the babe. Your father. So I come at him proper now, like I guess you are angling to hear, so you can avoid yourself in *this.* Write that down! "Jerry," I said, "let's have some fun since you're a great one for playing jokes at others' expense, as long as somebody else is the butt . . . You gave a young virgin chambermaid a bit of advice in your private chambers about how to handle the advances of her master, I mean her boss, and then she let you slip into her private quarters, after-hours in exchange. But, Jerry, I didn't know you were the kind of judge who'd take a bribe over a bride; then make a bribe into a bride, without first getting a divorce. Why, that makes you something of a bigamist. To say nothing of an adulterous husband, to boot."—

—You told him what? Sweetie Reed, Great-Momma . . . I never said you were a liar. But you do have a fabulous imagination, as those piles of yellow sheets of saga on that bureau will testify. But hold on. Nobody mocked the Judge that way. Not even Bert Williams, in jest. Why, this is prima facie evidence of backwater time, in living black and blue. And you are not going to remain reclined in that bed and tell me that Grandfather Witherspoon remained silent? You were keenly honest to report what back talk I. V. Reed gave you, now what did my grandfather Jericho Witherspoon say? Momma Sweetie, had you no pity for the old man and what this child, this babe in his arms, meant to him, as an heir, a link to tomorrow.—

—Jerry still thought of me as a child, grown up. Wasn't all his fault, either. People everywhere bowed to his desires; and laughed behind his back. I came to him in swaddling clothes, you might say. That's what I'm getting at, trying to, leastways, so I had to come at him as a woman, full bloom and full of bitchery, too, and not afraid to let that icy side drip out as drops of acid rain. But now Jerry commences to blame my work with the "Woman's Question," didn't call it a movement or organization.—

—Wait a minute. Grandfather Witherspoon stood full square for Women's Rights. A matter of public record, in black-and-blue print, on the vote and so on, the whole smear and without alteration or expostulation. Give him his day in court, Momma Sweetie Reed Witherspoon.—

—Oh, in public, yes. Absolutely. But privately was a roan of a different color. I felt hemmed in . . . to a narrow gait. *I* had to constantly fight for elbow room in his imagination.—

—He was not two-faced.—

—Oh? You're fighting mad now, aren't you! I haven't used *Witherspoon* in fifty-three years. You ain't too big for me to get a switch.—

—Pity, woman. Great-Momma Sweetie, I mean, who's talking

about switches? Nor switching? We are talking about the truth and pity, compassion; the words you trained me to believe in. I thought we were speaking as adults, man and woman.—

—I thought it was still grandson and grandmother. Has something I've said changed that? *Pity, woman* indeed, Nathaniel. You getting my backwater time confused with your back talk . . . You letting your university education soften your respect. Maybe it's best you've dropped out for a spell. So you can learn the wisdom of a fool. You can't get right on the outside before you get right on the inside.—

—Momma Sweetie, maybe your gnawing away at I. V. Reed's soul influenced me to duel with you. Didn't you stop to think of how sitting here listening to you for hours would loosen me up to speak out to you?—

—I never trained you not to stand your ground when you knew what you were talking about.—

—Momma Sweetie, you bent your knees in respect and kissed his hands in sweetness for his kindness. A kindness he was to sustain, and you know it. You have this house because of Grandfather Witherspoon.—

—Yes, and that was my first mistake; bending a knee; because a husband can't hardly be *no* daddy; if you know what I mean . . . Closing ranks against me now, aren't you, son?—

—He gave you everything. Saved your life, in ways, *that* I've heard you imply (plainly not today). But I've heard you suggest it, in more blissful times.—

—Yes, and today you heard me tell you—certain that you were not only writing in longhand, but listening—Jerry first struck a bargain over my mother Angelina's face, outlined on his sleeve . . . I was the substitute.—

—He married you, not your mother Angelina . . . Besides, you didn't know about that bargain, the full meaning of it, at midnight on June 5, 1905.—

—Married me by mistaken identity, maybe . . . *You* know it? How come I can't reflect on that information? When I gave it to you to reflect on. Maybe he was marrying her by marrying me as a proxy. I don't know, men are so peculiar. I. V. Reed giving that Clea woman Angelina's name. Men!—

—All right. All right. But now you've got him (and me, too). He didn't come to you as a beggar. But he would have to be beholding to you for your support and breeding, rearing and raising of the baby. So you had him.—

—. . . Had his babies, too. Wasn't my fault no more than yours, Jerry, they took the wings of morning . . . Oh, fool, how did I have him? Possession isn't nine-tenths of the law in the cycle of man versus woman. I've seen women who were doormats to the world dominate their husbands in ninety-nine ways out of a hundred encounters, and the foolish men didn't have any sense of how powerless they were at home. Son, look, how did I have him when this baby, your red-clay father, lay cooing on *our* bed . . . Conceived in another woman's bed.—

—I'm going to fix myself a drink, Momma Sweetie.—

—Yes and deedy, you sorely need refreshing . . . You found that letter yet?—

Nathaniel put down the dreary cup of Rémy Martin and sassafras leaves and stirred up a new, leafless drink with the once hot writing hand, as he continued to search for Wayland Woods' letter with the other. But his writing hand now seemed to him as limp as the leaves in the old urn of tears and brandy . . . Ah, brandy is dandy but Candy ain't handy even though Candy Cummings sure stays on my mind. But look what Great-Momma Sweetie did when I brought my now former sweetheart around for a preview of the part of the family I dared to show off, without expostulation, in the light of day. Those few you could expose to the darkness . . . Still stuck on stacked and stuck-up Candy, though. God, that dark brown tenderloin with gams as succulent gospel-fire would turn Aunt DuPont to . . . red flames.

Candy: "You and your fucked-up family . . . Here we are on the brink of a Revolution—and I don't mean Dulles' brinksmanship—and *them* still in the dark with their lightness." And Nathaniel declaring: "Baby, you ain't seen 'em yet, you just heard tell of 'em." Telling her one of the family horrors: the DuPonts sold White Lightning Bleaching Creme and slaves. My blood, my blood—ah, honesty is the worst impaling policy of the heart. And Candy Cummings: "Color-struck is one thing, but those niggers scare the Klan to turn in their sheets and join the NAACP by dawn's early light . . . I thought the Deltas were bad enough . . ." Our lips came together: a rendezvous by candlelight. We met in evening school: Psychology 369: *Catharsis* . . .

Candy Cummings taking an immediate liking to Great-Momma Sweetie, the myth of her as well. Wanting to meet a progressive

woman of Sweetie's day as a connection, gauge and guide. To touch
her hand as a way of feeling her own way back into the darkness of
history and time; back to Lovelady, Slavery, the Women's Movement,
the Underground Railroad, through Sweetie Reed and as a way to
gather up strength for the new opportunities now finally upon the
horizon. A Smith girl come home to roost, as it were. Candy Cummings, too dark and intellectual for the local sororities. And talk
about the preoccupations of the souls of the new talented tenth, too
much of a snob on the one hand and a tag-wearing, sign-carrying
radical on the other to use whatever social leverage that might deflect
to her, as Dwight Cummings, her uncle and newly elected to Congress, went off to Washington.

But at leave-taking time, Momma Sweetie said: "You all sweethearting? Come here, young lady, Miss Candy Cummings, I want you
to promise me one thing." Candy, who played the guitar and sang folk
songs, at the Cellar Boheme on weekends, now placed the instrument
down upon the floor, and went to the edge of the cedar-colored
woman's bed. Earlier she had played and sang some Negro spirituals
and her favorite folk song, "Joe Hill," for the grand old lady. Candy
was a good guitar player, with a lousy singing voice for spirituals,
Nathaniel observed. Sweetie Reed appeared to enjoy the spirit in
which the offerings were rendered up. Candy Cummings always carried the guitar with her like a weapon and a security blanket, practically everywhere she went. But precious Candy walked over to Great-
Momma Sweetie's bed; one hundred pounds of shapely clay.
Nathaniel thought that Candy Cummings—standing there at the edge
of the bed, with such reverence in her eyes for Mrs. Reed—was now
about to kneel down in respect, for an anointing, woman to woman.
But Sweetie said in a simple voice: "I want you to promise me just
one thing, young lady. You'll stop inviting my grandson over to your
chambers and he'll stop inviting you over to his quarters." Nathaniel
almost fell to his knees in a faint. Candy Cummings backed out of the
apartment (and out of his life), dropping the guitar several times; the
strings offered up a wrenched, creaking sound, as the covered heart
of the instrument was accidentally bumped upon the steps marking
Candy's hurried escape and descent. Candy's bottom lip drooped in
horror, as she backed out of his world.

Candy Cummings had planned to be a June bride. Knit her own
gown. Wear a lily-white veil . . . In June I'll be laced in bourbon,
Nathaniel thought now.

Candy Cummings changed her number; now it was unlisted. Nathaniel turned in his key, dropped it in her empty mailbox. She returned his engagement ring via messenger-boy express service, in a small urn, usually reserved for ashes. Nathaniel left her Josh White record albums with the handsome Negro doorman, who looked like the suave Billy Eckstine, at the exclusive building where she lived. Reflecting now upon the occupation of his soul by Candy Cummings' memory, Nathaniel was suddenly now brought up short by the haunting advice of Uncle Ulysses Hampton . . . As the slit of a diamond across the skin of the back of the hand: marry the woman who loves you and the one you care for . . . Marriage and burning.

Just how did the ninety-one-year-old woman surmise so much? Was she related to this legendary Auntie Foisty? Well, I wasn't ready for marriage, the young man now told himself (too soon, no doubt, meeting her on the rebound, after an affair with a belly dancer, an ex-nun, who kept a model of the Nativity scene upon her nightstand by the window), when suddenly his hand touched upon the delicate pages of Wayland Woods' letter. But now Great-Momma Sweetie Reed was saying:

—Nathaniel, look, I could take the baby. I was taking to the baby and didn't know it. Part of me reacting against my attraction for it. Soon I was telling Jerry he could stay till the storm stopped. And I probably said that so the baby would not leave my sight. For tonight. The mothering part in me. But I didn't know how I would react in the morning. No, it was the *engagement* that brought it here, that I had no . . . Couldn't hold up to that.—

—*Engagement?* Oh, I see what you are talking around.—

—I'm not talking around anything.—

—When did you find out about this other person? The woman involved.—

—The Virgin. That breastless wonder of a girl.—

—Virgin? Girl? You are trying to make an evil man out of Grandfather. A Svidrigailov.—

—A Svid . . . What? We speak English around here, Nathaniel, plain and otherwise.—

—What was her name? This grand . . . I can't say it.—

—Her name? Uncertain. But she was named Lucasta Jones. Miss Lucasta Jones.—

—Oh, I see.—

—Oh, and what do you see?—

—You, Great-Momma Sweetie, you.—

—What of the mint your DuPonts, your mother's people made off of slaves and bleach.—

He looked down at her snow-white flutter of puffed-out hair; light upon her crown as layers of fiercely stirred-up egg whites that now appeared to collapse away . . . How could you? How could you dare bring that up now? She said:

—Nathaniel, what do *you* see when you are seeing it all through my eyes, when you see solely what I want to let you see and not see. Don't know too much about what you haven't seen. Get the order of learning your grandfather was always talking about, *troubling, remembering* and then *revealing.*—

Nathaniel's long, dark eyelashes beat as a sparrow's wings in defiance at her deep gaze up at him and beyond.

—All right, Momma Sweetie. All right. More butter and less cream. More substance and less art, all right? Perhaps if I don't say anything. Refuse the gift of speech in my brain as it signals my tongue; in other words, keep my jaws tight. Then you'll only say, Nathaniel's a good boy. But his jaws are always tight. Why did you tell me to come to you when I reached my majority and then you would truly speak? You wanted me to write a saga of some of your experiences down on paper. I can't match wits with you, and if I appear to then I'm a bigger fool than even you think I am; but, Great-Momma Sweetie, you seem to have no appreciation of what this is doing to me. If we can't talk adult to adult, then why should I speak when all the wisdom is locked up in the chambers of your imagery . . . He wasn't asking for alms of wisdom and you should not be asking for total agreement at every pitch and turn.—

—Her name was Lucasta Jones. Do you want to see her picture, in black and white?—

—Who was she?—

—Why not ask *what* was she?—

—A lost soul?—

—A soul lost? Yes.—

Nathaniel mumbled aloud:

—The Bard knew that crabbed age and youth cannot live together, in one chamber, turn to Lear for lyrical light.—

—Boy, you better put down that Rémy Martin.—

The young man of twenty-one now felt he *had* overstepped his position with the only grandmother he had ever known. And the aged woman of ninety-one felt that she was limiting his way; she needed him. Needed him to possess the ability to act in an adult way now and surely in the immediate future. In a few years, or a few months, he would have to be her eyes. He was all she could trust. If he didn't ask questions, stand up and cut his own path, then how could he defend her from the outside world that was surely closing in on her, with each passing midnight? Yet just recently when he had brought a lovely girl to meet her, hadn't she said something that was beyond her business at the end of the evening's engagement when Nathaniel arose to take the girl home? Wasn't it not to take the young woman home to his apartment? She remembered asking: "Young lady, I'll caution you not to spend the night at my grandson's apartment." But I was trying to protect her, the ancient women wept aloud. Her from him and certainly him from her, in their youth. Now looking at Nathaniel seated in the rocker, she could see how he was trembling. Just like me, Sweetie surmised, he doesn't want to deal with nor see another woman in the picture. Poor little Lucasta, poor Jerry, poor all of God's creatures great and small and particularly great who don't see how small we all are.

Nathaniel thought: Lost souls. This Lucasta Jones too was a lost soul. Now he thought of Aunt Genevieve's description of the girls at her Palace of Pleasure in New Orleans. Lost souls, too. Bones laid to rest, but where? Lodged now in death's date-filled night. No mansion in the Father's kingdom for them. What valley of dry bones was there for them? To arise from?

My true grandmother in blood, this Lucasta Jones. Surely she was no longer of this world. But my true grand-kin lies there upon that bed. The Rémy Martin poured over ice in a clean cup seemed to enflame his spirit. Her picture? Was Sweetie pulling my leg? To embrace the picture of this woman sight unseen was to be one with Sweetie Reed who saw Lucasta Jones, sight unseen, through this baby, he speculated. A motherless child herself, perhaps, and a long way from. He thought to ask Great-Momma Sweetie of April 4 . . . Ah, the days of the warming sleeves and warm-up jacket have turned to one difficult straight jacket. Ah, for the days when this room was filled with the steam from those divine dinners; not clear as the peal of an ice cube, stirring. He tried without success to focus his tearful eyes upon Woods' letter.

—Momma Sweetie. April 4? April 4.—

—. . . Now I realized Jerry's fallen asleep. He's an old man in his

277

pride. Naked to the waist, and I think, well, maybe I've got two babies. Then I looked over to where Jerry is *looking* in his frozen-eyed sleep state at the baby. The little angel is rolling back and forth between the two pillows Jerry laid across the bed, while I was out of the room, to keep the infant from rolling off. The bottle has rolled out its lips. Is it ever hot in that room now and the storm's ceased.

—I scooped up the baby in my arms, its presence there now seeming to unleash deep memories and feelings. For when I started to play with this infant's tiny toes, fingers and its wee fingernails, I could see before me I. V. Reed's scratching nails huge and ugly upon the screen door. The worst man in the world since Filthy McNasty, who dropped dead from scratching his flea-bitten self down to skeleton, cut off all of his flesh, in search for his soul beneath his haunted skin that tormented him so. When they got to him, at a safe distance, he was all smoky powder of clawed-away bones; odor's so foul they couldn't come close. I shuddered at this memory; suddenly the little lamb's presence recalled the little lost souls of my loins and in particular my last, Lovelady-Sue, who lived less than three months, died on April 4, 1900 . . . Memories as sleepwalking ghosts . . . Unrelieved pitter-patter of time powdered by fruitless Death . . . Tiny togs and toys brim as flowing bloody bubbles sucked up by a windstorm.

—Now I find myself humming, "What Month Was Jesus Born In/Last Month in the Year." But I'm thinking: cradling this life in my arms, Jerry's sting can't do me no wrong; besides, he's dozing like a man dipped in snuff before a fireplace; yet his fixed gaze is frozen upon the infant. (Jerry's like a baby fighting sleep.) Then I'm singing the words to the song I was humming, not a lullaby when I break into: "Meeting at the building will soon be over."

—When I take hold of the babe at the wrists to keep time with its sweet, plump hand, in playfulness to my singing and humming, I see a red band about the infant's right arm—slipped down from the wrists to its elbow—and the marked label on the red band reads: "*April 4, 1905.* Lucasta Jones, Mother" . . . For so locked up in melancholy am I that I still can't get free to know more than me and discovering things by sheer accident. Those lost souls that come by the kitchen for food, clues to shelter, job messages and counsel, ain't freed me up yet because I got giving all confused with possessing. Me and Jerry are one, ain't we, son? Lost souls, as our kitchen kin. Spun north in the windstorm to a wilderness—. Her voice seemed to fade away; her eyelids drooped into dozing. Her hair a staunch swirl of egg-white batter, as a lily-white crown upon her ancient head.

—Yes and no, Momma Sweetie . . . It wasn't exactly a marriage hatched in Heaven. More of a mingling of tiger and lamb. Lamb and tiger.

—. . . Because you see I could touch the tops of the trees in his arms and then we would work on our tree house in my tree to Heaven and then he would say, *Keep climbing, rib of my rib* . . . My foot upon his shoulder to climb upwards and outwards and even the profile of stars he reshaped out my heart-shaping figures upon kites could not/ were not to hold me back as they had held my father.—

Lost souls. And Nathaniel thought back in the talk to the sundered breech of how Great-Momma Sweetie would turn in their (the "guests") wake with only their bags of food visible, now, as she turned away to allow them a pinch of dignity. Not facing them so they could escape (particularly the men) with a sliver of respect and then she would do an about-face to find any one of a world of "gifts" . . . a tin of snuff, a pair of shoelaces, a pint box of salt, a pencil, a ten-page, yellow-colored writing tablet, a red-faced razor, a bottle of blue-black ink, half empty; an original picture of Teddy Roosevelt with Booker T. Washington at the White House (stolen, Sweetie Reed later discovered, from a Klansman's cache); a bottle of wintergreen oil, a bottle of Father John's cough syrup, a bottle of Peacock's cough syrup; an original recording of Bessie Smith's "Somebody's Little Angel Child"; a gold-lined placard turned green which read: "Whatsoever God Has Put Together, Let No Man Drive Asunder"; a set of cracked dice, cast out of ivory; a bowl of pecans from the old country, shelled; a copy of *Uncle Remus: His Songs and His Sayings;* a white and bronzed sign proclaiming "Trade Like Blood Should Flow Freely"; a picture of Phillis Wheatley; a pair of spats; a forty-second splice of motion picture film depicting Marcus Garvey at a rally and parade in Harlem; a death notice concerning Oscar Charleston; a photo album of the life of Jean Harlow . . . Scores of plants . . . A cracked-faced tambourine with a sketch of Martin Delaney superimposed in pencil over a portrait of Haile Selasssie . . . A recipe for gumbo scrawled out in an arched handwriting: an adult's imitation of calligraphy . . . an autograph of Josephine Baker on the outside of a Christmas card; a picture of a famous Negro poet at the front line of the Abraham Lincoln Brigade; a picture in the *Chicago-Defender* of the young lawyer Jericho Witherspoon emerging from the courthouse with his arm around a young black man, with the overline: "Free on a writ of Habeas

Corpus" . . . a slingshot; a pair of old brown shoes slit on the sides; a Halloween mask. A series of tintypes picturing the Negroes who lost their jobs as a result of President Wilson's decree barring Negroes from Civil Service jobs . . . Several sets of baby shoes . . . A jar of White Lightning Bleaching Creme, and a bloodstained slave chain. All of these gifts now placed in a huge trunk in the basement.

She called their offerings "gifts" though not to the faces of the "guests." Lovelady called them "guests" because in that way the bargain was consummated without embarrassment, though embarrassment was implicit in the transaction, but "this was not the South, nor a previous condition," Sweetie Reed said. Her "foster mother," Lovelady Breedlove, had fed the slaves their first free meal at the last station of the Underground Railroad. Always with that obligation to help another escaped slave (in the original kitchen at that little AME Church founded by a freeborn Philadelphia Negro). Lovelady had been a mother to Sweetie Reed; and Aunt Hattie Breedlove (born in 1877) was to become Sweetie's "little sister." Lovelady and Sweetie's mother, Angelina, had been fast friends and worked in the kitchen on old man Rollins Reed's plantation, many years before she escaped to the North, via the Underground Railroad. Then they moved the kitchen from the church to Lovelady's rooming house in 1888.

And so these lost souls would ascend to Great-Momma Sweetie Reed's upper room (remade after Lovelady's death in 1907) to know her breads and greens and cabbages and chops and ham hocks and lamb and cracked crockery filled with homemade ice cream and a variety of salads. Dishes slid inside of old worn paper brown bags, or encircled and bound up with one of the hundreds of sheets of newspapers which stood in the corner of her room, stacked to the height of Jericho Witherspoon himself; which also constituted a fire hazard, Nathaniel's father often warned—although so forceful was her obsession for her "guests" and duty that Arthur Witherspoon himself often brought her newspapers and supplied her with Santa Fe bar towels that he used as a bartender. Proudly stating about his mother (the only mother he ever knew, Nathaniel now thought to himself): ". . . knows not that she is a Communist and still believes and votes the straight Republican ticket, even as she runs the kitchen with more efficiency than any budding mom-and-pop capitalist; FDR could benefit from her advice . . . but then they are a couple of felled aristocrats, too proud to speak to each other unless that other aristocrat, A. Philip Randolph, introduced them)."

Lost souls, he thought, yet when the moment for the vexing question (so unappetizing to her deeper nature) forged its way into the embarrassed covenant between giver and receiver, hostess and guest, she would say: "Just leave whatever portion you can; and if you cannot, then just leave and make a mark of it when you get home on your own books—'cause this ain't no service-pan operation. And I sure hope you are keeping some kind of books about everything you do with your days; let your days be warm-warnings, even radiant beams of new light so that your nights can be worthy of cool memories." Often nothing at all was left; but Sweetie Reed's remarks where intended to assist the dignity and the challenge to try and not accept charity. It occurred to him now that the charity of the kitchen and the insistence upon a gift from the guests was to set up a counterweight relationship, so that eventually the kitchen would no longer exist but the idea of charity at both ends would remain within the scope and vision of living no matter where you found them, and no matter who you might be . . . And then one day Great-Momma Sweetie Reed doing an about-face and saying to him:

"Splendid Spoons, maybe that's the hardest part in all the sums, that's hidden behind the faces we put on to the world and then remake over again. Because it seems like it's such a hard thing for one person to give to the brethren without feeling sorry for that soul to a point of despising him or her for their poverty of bread, meat of knowledge, and particularly thinking that somewhere down deep in the castaway (runaway Jerry made me aware of this) that there is something lacking in that lost soul, fundamentally. So that soon your attitude for the poorest is that of the despot you are both trying to escape. Yes, and soon feeling supreme over them and never willing to forgive them for their power over you, for without their poverty you are nothing; yet it is their constant poverty that you are told is the reason that you cannot rise, even as you know you cannot rise without their being pulled up." But now as his eyes focused upon the first sentence of Wayland Woods' letter, he heard her voice again, revived, vaulting and angrier than before:

—I was awake now, Nathaniel, to the babe's screaming and I'm screaming, too. Lost souls because you see . . . In the light it was the woman not the baby who was the cause . . . Not only to love Justice but to seek out mercy and learn the horror mysteries of this breastless girl's inner face that had allured Jericho so . . . Oh, never let me put out that light lest I snuff out the breath of the light in my soul

. . . And Lord, this little light of mine I'm gonna let it shine, because of and despite Sweetie Reed.—

—And so you were willing to keep the baby and allow Grandfather Witherspoon to stay on.—

—Not much of a choice for them when you think about it, since apparently nobody wanted them or they wouldn't be there now. So the next morning I told Jerry he might stay here and I'd keep the babe alive. Not that he was welcomed but that he could stay until he made other arrangements. Stay in the back room and I'd keep the baby until either *she* or he found a way to keep it. But I was rattled to the bone when Jerry said, "No. You keep the baby here until I can find another way. I'll pay for its keep and yours. But I'll not stay in the house where a wife sets limits." I shook my head in wonderment and that's when he said: "Sweetie, if I stayed, that would simply be a call to your spite-work. I would never know an hour of peace and solitude. I'll not allow you to bargain over my freedom."

—I opened the door and pointed to the wind. But Jerry was gone out of the back door when I looked around, with a hundred-dollar bill left on the pillow of the bed next to the baby . . . Take this bill to your breastless, kept gal, I screamed.—

—This is completely different from the story I've always heard, Momma Sweetie. Is nothing as it seems but the visions we have in nightmares that demand that we question the easy sleeve of sleep? But it must have taken all of your pride to just admit this to me, your only grand, grandson.—

—No, not pride, Splendid Spoons, but the dividing away of pride from my soul, which I haven't commenced to clean up, though I'm trying.—

—Then what got you through after his double insult?—

—I stooped to scoop up the baby. Cradling life in my arms, even though it wasn't hardly mine, I knew Jerry's sting can't do me no wrong, even as his rejection has made me know my fragility and my pride and how I'm going to have to get over him to go on living. But that's the selfish part; I'm so angry I don't see that part quite clear. So I go downstairs to Lovelady, whom I've told about my condition that morning. And, Nathaniel, it was she who carried me over, as a newborn babe through the redeeming and the baptizing; but not by waters. And her telling me:

"Hold on, Sweetie, and back up before you leap forward and thereby cross over before you've redirected your legs and trip over your own high-stepping shoelaces in your darkness, so filled up with *your* light. But definitely leap forward in faith, as you hold on. Hold on means everything. A call to action. Means reshape, don't despair. Means lift up as you pull up. Means cling to strength without wrenching and becoming a wretch for any man. Means hold on, but not hold to. Means hold on even as you give it up. Hold on means don't let your freedom get away as you hold on. Hold on for you means cling to the babe, too, Sweetie."

"But the babe, too—hold on to it, too, that's not of my loins? And cast upon me by a man who thinks he's Noah, or worse, or better thereby worse?"

"I thought they said hold on for better or worse."

"But, Miz Love, this is just too much."

"Ain't nothing too much . . . You suppose to hold on and ask for more, more burden. You holding on to the kitchen, helping out in a wonderful way, but that's for them what drop ins."

"But isn't that enough?"

"Not if more is your portion; then that kitchen ain't but a molehill to a mountain."

"I shouldn't burden you, Miz Love."

"Gal, you can't escape from me holding on to you, now."

"Precious Lord, why am I so miserable?"

" 'Cause you can't 'cept the facts that Jerry can live without you. Baby ain't got nothing to do with this at all. And you can't say a woman's in the thing. Have yet to call out a woman's name in the seed . . . Gal, you ain't learned yet how all our opportunities planted in horror. You want me to go back to your momma and how she came to be an angel!"

"Opportunity? I'm blind, Miz Lovelady, to the light you see in all of this."

"Yes, Sweetie, *opportunity.* 'Cause part of your problem is you worried that you are already taking a liking to the babe 'cause it's part Jerry's, and that makes it part yours though you untouched in the matter and the making. And you scared too that you might lose another and therefore look upon . . ."

"No, Miz Lovelady, no. I don't want to see that. How come I as a woman have to always bend? Take the losses. Take low. Take seconds."

"Ain't that funny, and here you make seconds into dishes queens would rise at dawn to eat. Lawd, girl, what am I to do with this opportunity, with you, if you don't see this thing proper . . . Who took you in? Somebody had to smooth out the rock in private into a foundation stone and then into a platform out an auction block for you to stand up on in public and be so proud . . ."

"But to look upon this orphan as an opportunity?"

"And why not?"

"What of the scandal?"

"What scandal? You *can* bring this one through, Sweetie. 'Sides, who's to judge? Colored society? Where they come from, other than a scandal? And their talk delights in scandal. White folks? Where they come running and slave-running from? Their society sowed in scandal. The Savior had a opportunity for that adulterous woman He met at the well. If her, why not you? You just cannot hold on to the form the opportunity is taking. Who you, Sweetie, to dictate what form life of redemption suspose to shape . . . Don't try to be wise before wisdom, Sweet, and become a smart fool, Sweetie."

"Wait a minute, Miz Lovelady . . . Redemption?"

"Yes, the baby cast down here as an opportunity for you to let go of your pride so your pride could be redeemed by giving it up."

"Suspose the baby's mother doesn't want to give *it* up?"

"Lucasta Jones? She's a lost soul; needs a way out of this thicket. She ain't gonna make no blood claim on her kid. Or make no claims on you. How you think Jericho got the babe? Force? No. She's a free-soul woman. There's a bargain if not a covenant here and Lucasta's a free-soul woman. He's trying to cap up his honor, too. He knows she can't hold up; can't hold on; and he can't hold up for her; can't hold up himself, without you holding up and holding on."

"How did you know her name?"

"You spelled it out this morning. Wouldn't say her name."

"Fix me, Jesus, fix me, lest I go mad. Churchfolks surely will be talking behind our backs."

"What, to give birth to the light of truth? Why, they tried to scandalize His name. Oh, they'll corrupt their opportunity to help His wayward children in their righteousness. They always do . . . That's part of the reason why we still got to keep this kitchen going."

"Then the next minute they'll be singing 'Sweet Little Jesus Boy, We Didn't Know Who You Were,' ain't it so, Miz Lovelady?"

"Sweetie, I been meaning to bring this up for a long time. We partners in the kitchen now. Been that way for a long time. Why don't you start to calling me just Lovelady? Or Love. Not Miz Lovelady . . . We equals, daughter. And *now* I know we are more than equals.—

Then Nathaniel leaped forward, shaking the urn of Rémy Martin in one hand and the five legal pads of yellow papers in the other, in a state of fitful ecstasy:

—Grandmother Sweetie, that's more beautiful than anything contained in these legal pads . . . What you just recalled between you and Lovelady. Miz Lovelady.—

—What do you know? How do you know it? She was beautiful and wonderful and helped bring me through. But that was for then. I'm a constant backslider. You ain't *hardly* read over those legal pads of paper to see what is and isn't in there, lodged away. You got a memory longer than Auntie Foisty's? Nathaniel, I'm so evil I need a conversion almost daily and then some.—

—But look how all of this holding-on business helped to save you from abandoning my father.—

—Yes, even as I was abandoned.—

—Miz Lovelady's words strengthened your resolve.—

—. . . But I was not five minutes back up here without seeing those three figures before me . . . shooting dice for my naked soul. Lovelady could be good because wasn't nothing in her that knew evil as a living wage to do battle with. She knew evil fiercely, as an eternal condition in the world of others. Thought I was of value because she saw the battle being waged daily, nightly within my soul and knew that the baby was being forced upon me, not by your grandfather but by your grandfather as an agent. I accepted that answer for the moment, still accept a remnant of it.—

—I can't think of anything as wonderful as—

—Be quiet a moment. Stop getting up and waving those yellow papers at a face you don't know. And stop waving that liquor cup in the face you can see. Can't you hold on to your liquor? No wonder *your* Candy gal can't use you no more.—

—I must be heard though my heart shuns to hear how you still need to harpoon.—

Nathaniel took off the necktie given to him by Candy Cummings and placed it upon the mantle.

—But, Great-Momma Sweetie, didn't Father know . . . recognize? Lucasta . . . That Miss Jones was . . . And that you were not—

—That I was not! Was not what?—

—You are right. I cannot say what would be meaningless to name. Since you were all and all more than his mother . . . Seedy wombs have borne fruitful sons.—

—Yes, he knew! Found out. But, Nathaniel, see how you smoke-screen what you do not want to hear . . . to bear . . . Scratch sight from the light of your body when you want to, so that the eyes are fixed in a decoy of patience.—

—Momma Sweetie, the soul of my grandfather blooms within me . . . But I'm no less bound to you than I would be if Father were the very spirit and the flesh of *all* those babes that came tumbling from your womb; but this time reached past birth to know fruition and maturity, in the form of Arthur Witherspoon . . . All revealed in my father's shape, substance and being.—

—. . . No more words, words, words, Nathaniel . . . We kept it from your hearing. See the trick up our sleeves? Stopped up your ears with other stories. See? See how you were kept from the light and now give that deception a name.—

The room now seemed steamy with the heat of the voices, bodies and ghostly spirits of those lost souls and the dead brought to life. The room seemed almost funky. He started to open up the window but dared not. He slipped his Oxfords back on.

—Did you ever find Wayland Woods' letter? 'Cause it was what helped reaffirm me, boy, when I used to find my resolve wasting away on me . . . And I started to give up on everything and call Jericho Witherspoon and tell him to come get your—

—Yes, I have it in my hands.—

—Well then, read it aloud.—

Nathaniel now stood upon shaking legs as he looked down upon the yellowish paper; the script apparently scrawled out in the longhand of more than one person. And he thought of that time he had stood up at the Raven-Snow Funeral Home and read the brief life history of Jericho Witherspoon's early days, when he himself was but a lad of seven. And then Nathaniel read aloud:

NEWTON BARRACKS   JANUARY 1, 1864

THE DEAREST MISTRESS SYLVIA,
AND HER DEAREST MASTER ROLLINS:

GOD NEVER SO MISHUSE NATCHILE BLOOD THAT A
MAN WERE PIT TO STEAL AWAY SO AS TO STEAL

BACK HIS NATCHILE FLESH AND BLOOD . . . TO HIS
SIDES OUT FROM UNDER THE BONDAGE PITS OF
HELL THAT WE WAS BRED-UP TO SEE AS THE
HOLY GHOST HOUSE NOT MADE OF HANDS TO
EVERLASTING IN THE HEAVENS.

I REMEMBERS RITE WELL MISTRESS SYLVIA YOUR
BREATHING LIPS AS POUTING HOT COALS SPATTING
HEAT UP FROM HELL AS LICKING TONGUES AND
BACKING IT ALL OFF WITH A SOUL SWEET AS A
DOVE-COOING VOICE AT THE REDEEMING FOUNT.
MASTER SATAN IS YOUR SOULMATE AND YOU IS
MASTER SATAN'S SOUL PROPERTY UNTO THE
SHADOW OF WINGING DOWN DEATH. SO AS YOU
MISTROUBLES MY BLOOD LET YOUR CONCHOSENCE
KEEP ON BEING YOUR MASTER, MISTRESS. YOU
MAY HUM THEM HYMNS OF OVER THE SEA IN A
WARM QUAIL, BUT SPITE IS THE LEAD VOICE IN
THE SABBATH SONG OF YOUR COLD-BLOODED,
JACK 'O LANTERN FACE FOR A SOUL . . .

SYLVY REED YOU CLOSE INTO SATAN'S FLAMING
CLUTCHES AS FALL-TIME LEAVES IN WITHERING
WINTER TREES FIRE FOR THE COMFORTING.
BLOOD BELIEVING AS YOU IS TO THE ROOT OF
YOUR OWN AS THE RITE-EYED HOLY GHOST, THAT
IN YOUR HEAVEN THERE ART SLAVES TO BOOT, SO
SISTER AND BROTHER BEHOLD YOUR SOUL AS
GEMS TO THE DEAD. BUT BE OF ONE TRUE FAITH,
SCARECROW WOMAN, BOUT YOUR FAITHFULNESS
SERVANT WAYLAND WOODS, IF IT COST ME THE
BREATH OF MY SOUL, I'LL PURCHASE MY DAUGH-
TERS OUT THE BONDAGE-PIT OF SLAVERY'S BLOOD
—NOT WITH SILVER OR GOLD—BUT WITH A
SWOOP AND A GRASP WITH THE LAST LEAP OF MY
BLOOD AND RAISING UP OF THE SWORD AND
BREATH AS WINGS TO THE MORNING. HERE MY
HAND BE LIFT TO THIS ALMIGHTY GOD GIVEN TO
ME BY YOUR WORDS AND HIM TO STRIKE DOWN BY
YOUR WORDS AND HAND, EYES, AND FEET, HIP-
BONE AND TONGUES, AND BACKBONE, SPECIALLY,
AS SWORD TO DOVE'S TENDER-BRIDE'S NECK.

BUT MAINLY I'M AIMING THE BLACK INK OF THIS
BLUE-BLACK PEN AT ROLLEY WHO NATCHILE
WAYS I KNOWS UNTO JUDDMENT TYME, YOU WOE-
FUL MAN. GOING OFF STRUTTING YOURSELF AS
THE HOLY GHOST . . . TAKING NAMES AND KICK-
ING ASS—WHO YOU BES, BOY? YOU TALK ABOUT

TROUBLE! BUT ROLLEY YOU PURE DON'T KNOW WHAT TROUBLE IS. CAUSE ONLY TROUBLE YOU GOT IS THE TROUBLE YOU DONE CAUSE ME AND MINES TO SWING BY DOWN THE THICKETS AND TREES OF TYME.

ROLLEY AND SYLVY IF YOU THINK I LOVE YANKEES THEN YOU CAN BELIEVE I LOVE SLAVERY MORE YEARS THAN I LOVE MY GOD AND FREEDOM. FOR FROM THE LAWD'S COCKED HAND SET YOU DOWN NO TYME TO SET AGAINST MY TENDER DAUGHTERS TYME LEST I CONVICT YOU TO DREAD. TOUCH NOT THE CHEEKS OF MY DAUGHTERS WITH THE SCORN AND SPITTLE OF YOUR TERRIBLE TEAR DROPS OF YOURS AS SMEARED GRIEF A JACK O' LANTERNS FACE. AND FROM THE LAWD'S HAND SET FOR THE JUSTICE I'LL TAKE MY WORD OUT HIS DIVINE-TYME HANDS AND DO GOD'S SURE-FOOT BUSINESS AND REEK DOWN WAYLAND'S VENGANCE IN A WINDSTORM OF RAMBLING RUSHING STALLION UPON YOUR HOUSE MADE FROM THE MUD UP BY MY HOT HANDS . . . CAST NOT YOUR EYES UPON MY DAUGHTERS' FRESH FLESHING LOINS ROLLEY, LEST YOU TURN YOURSELF TO THE STONE THAT IS YOUR HARD HART CONDITION. CAUSE YOU THE DEFILING OF HIS VESTMENT PLATE OF NATCHILENESS UNTO THE SLEEVE OF MAN'S SOUL.

FOR BE IT KNOWN THIS HIGH NOON I'M GONNA HAVE MY WOMAN PEAK MY DAUGHTERS LOINS TO SEE AND IF THEY AIN'T YET VIRGINS DOWN TO A NATCHILE BLOODY CLOTH—THEN KNOW ITS THE WRONG TYME OF MONTH FOR YOU BY THE MOONLIGHT'S SET TO MASKING UP A JACK MUH LANTERNS SMILE OVER YOUR NATCHILE GRAVE, IF THEM GALS AIN'T STILL VIRGINS BY LANTERNS. IF YOUR HANDS TREMBLING WITH THESE WORDS SET DOWN BY ME AND YANKEES AND MY WORDS TO THEM SO THEY KNOW HOW TO WRITE IN A PROPER-TONGUE WAY, THEN THINK HOW MANY MESSAGES I'VE SIT DOWN TO MY DAUGHTERS IN BLUE-BLACK INK AND IF THEY AIN'T RECEIVE THEM ALL DON'T MEAN A SECOND I AIN'T RITE EVEN MORE IN MY HART OF HARTS. THESE DAUGHTERS THEY BE MY BOND AND MY BALM.

ROLLEY YOU AND I EVER BE NATCHILE ENMAYS, SKIN-TO-SKIN UNTO CALVARY AND YOKE OF OUR

BONDAGE BE LIFT IN THE LAST GO ROUND. ROL-
LEY YOU OUGHT TROUBLE YOUR EVER DAY SHAK-
ING WHEN YOU DOTES ON HAYWOOD SHANK AS
YOU WRAP FOISTY'S SAVING SHROUD BOUT YOUR
SOUL AS WARMING SLEEVES IN JANJEWARY;
CAUSE IT AIN'T THIS OLD DARKY BUT THE MASTER
I REPRESENTS TO TAKE YOU HOME, WHAT YOU
NEEDS TO DREAD; I'M SIMPLE HIS VESSEL OF VEN-
GEANCE. BECAUSE YOU SEE I KNEW YOUR FATHER
IN THE BEGINNING TIME.

HOW CAN YOU CALL YOURSELF A CHILE OF THE
LIVING WORD, SON OF MAN. MASTER AND MIS-
TRESS YOU AND YOUR BRIDE HOW CAN YOU CALL
UP YOURSELF TO BE CHILE OF HIS CLAY WHEN YOU
YOKE UP HIS LAMBS IN A WAY DREAD OF MERCY,
IN YOUR HALLELUJAH. PIT BOND CONDITION.
LASHES AWAY OUT TO CRAWL BACK DEEP DOWN
TO PAST ALL KNOWING TYME OF.

OH BUT ROLLEY AND SYLVY IT GIVES MY SOUL
CHEER TO SET THESE LAST WORDS TO PEN, AS
CHIPS TO THE FIREPLACE NO LONGER YOUR OBEDI-
ENT COOKING SERVANT OR SLAVE OR BODY SER-
VANT, FOREVER AND A DAY TIME, I REMAINS NO
LONGER YOURS FOR THE OFFERING BUT MINE OWN
SERVANT TO GOD FOR THE GIVING UP, WITNESS
AND HIM BE MY MASTER. SINCERELY BELIEVE OF
IT.

(MISTER-MAN) WAYLAND WOODS

P.S. WHEN I RIDES IN THE DISTRICT WITH THEM
BLACK AND WHITE SOLDERS IN ARMS (EVEN AS
HAND IN HAND ME AND THIS PURE WHITE BLUE
COAT RITE THESE WORDS UNTO YOU IN UNISON) I
PLANS TO SWOOP BACK DOWN AND UP-SWEEP MY
TWO TENDER DAUGHTERS IN A WINDSTORM OF
HIS WRATH AND KEEP ON RIDING. BUT YOU, MIS-
TRESS SLY AND MASTERABLE ROLLEY WILL NOT
HAVE A WHISPER OF A HANT'S HOOT OWL WISH,
THE HOUR NEITHER THE LIGHT OR DARK OF THE
TIME OF THE DOOM YOU SO SPECIAL BEEN KNOW-
ING BOUT IN YOUR LONG FACE JACK 'O LANTER'S
LIGHT, IN THE DEEPS OF THESE HERE WOODS. FOR
GOD SO LOVED UP THE WORLD. BUT YOU MAY
KNOW THE HOUR OR DAY AND THEN KNOW IT
NOT. LOOK NOT TO THE NORTH OR THE SEAS BUT
WOE-EYED TO DREAD AND WILD-EYED TO THE

DREAD AT EVERY TURN OF YOUR TAIL, AS YOU TURNS IN YOUR COATS.

P.S.S. FOR MY FAITH AIN'T IN THE EVER(Y) LASTING WITH THESE YANKS WITHOUT LIGHT IN THE BLUE COAT BRIGHTNESS. CAUSE MY DAUGHTERS SAFETY PREYS ON MY MIND TO A CURLING FONDNESS OF THEIR KEEN PLIGHT DOWN THERE IN THAT DREAD. JOY FOR FREEDOM LIFTING ME UP WHEN I'M DOWN PAST EVERYTHING ELSE TO SEE MY BRIGHT-EYED LITTLE ANGELS ONCE MORE. OH MASTERS DON'T YOU SEE MY LIGHT IN YOUR BRIGHT-FACE DARKNESS, EVERY LIGHT. FOREVER. BECAUSE YOU SEE ROLLEY, I KNEW YOUR FATHER MAN.

OH THEY MAY BURY ME IN THE EAST. YOU, ROLLEY MAY BURY ME IN THE WEST. BUT I HEARS THE TRUMPET'S LONG SONG AS A LOG IN THE LONG WOODS DROPPING OFF INTO THE SPRING WATER, NEAR THE PRAISE HOUSE, AS THE SPRING TO EVERY DAY'S WITNESS SABBATH LIGHTNING SOUL TREMBLING IN ITS TERRIBLE SWIFT TIME . . . I'M OUT IN THIS WORLD SOMEWHERE, COMING AFTER YOU ALL . . . SOMEWHERE.

WOODS, WAYLAND, PRIVATE.

Nathaniel said, after a long fitful pause . . .
—. . . Lawd today . . . Speaking of Black and Unknown bards . . . Why wasn't I made aware of this letter before . . . in my education here and especially here?—Throbbing upon his chest.
—Nathaniel, now you see why I. V. Reed never showed it to me, in his strange worship for the Mistress Sylvia . . . And how this letter, shaped by more than one hand, could give me some revealing power to stay me in my lostness . . . even as it was also scrawled out by one who no doubt laughed in the misspellings even as he was swept up, no doubt, in the courageous outrage of this riddle of a freedom-driven man before him, who wrote part of the letter because of the learning he as slave had received from the mistress who damned him . . . —
—I see this letter for the first time. But why was I cut off from its history? This folio to help enlighten the way. Let alone its power, until now?—

For five minutes Nathaniel Witherspoon sat in the chair rocking back and forth, trying to shake off the impact that the letter from Wayland Woods had upon him. But Sweetie Reed declined to reveal herself with an answer. Finally she said:

—Spoons, how you going to embrace sweetness in me without seeing the I. V. Reed in your former grandmother?—

—. . . Ah, He spat upon the ground and made clay of the spittle and earth, the Old Bible says.—

—I had to bear out the brunt of that scandal of raising a son that wasn't my own. Love him? Yes. But Lovelady could give advice, sacred though it was, because she didn't have to live by it. Where were her children . . . Oh, you don't like me saying that, do you? And you didn't like me telling your sweetheart the truth. Demanding a license on love be clamped upon your wrists. That gal had some Lucasta in her bones. In a beam of her eye. Men? What do they know. She was harlot and angel and you weren't ready for either . . . Just as you aren't ready to look upon your blood-kin grandmammy's face. Are you, boy?—

—I'm looking at her now.—

—Who do you think you are? One of Lucasta Jones' wayward children? It's my hand in your raising, Artie!—

—Oh, Great-Momma Sweetie, it's me you are talking to. Don't destroy everything!—

—Destruction is part of the redemption. You little fool.—

—If I'm wayward and a dropout, you made me.—

—Now you talking, Nattie, blame me for everything . . . He was reborn in a windstorm. I don't want you starry-eyed anymore, why do you think I've spent all that time rendering up the shape of two or three years of my life to you, so that you could shape out your days in the profile of Lucasta Jones? How could Lovelady ever see how I saw Lucasta Jones as a curse. Broke up my home . . . Yes, and even your beloved father, that drying-out alcoholic as a manifestation of that curse. Now go deep into those yellow papers and that blue-black ink on them and find that light. Yes, and now reread Wayland Woods' letter for light as prayers in your darkness.—

Nathaniel quietly knelt down on one knee:

—Oh God . . . Oh God whom I never call upon . . . Please now find a final resting place for the bones of all who beseech my grandmother's mind. And settle the wretched sourness in Sweetie's soul.—

—Jesus wept would be shorter. Nathaniel, life is evil. Listen to your prayers. Look how that evil woman stabbed that brilliant young preacher in a bookstore. What's his name? Martin Luther?—

—King.—

—He had better be careful.—

—Momma Sweetie, when I think of all that history on those yellow sheets. And your goodness in raising my father. That wonderful kitchen you and Miz Lovelady kept open for the down and out . . . Or when I think of those little skinny-legged girls breaking barriers down there in Little Rock; and Candy Cummings' uncle going off to Congress . . . Why, despite everything I believe we are entering a new age.—

—What new age in my old age are you instructing me about? Nathaniel, stand up on those skinny legs of yours and go into that closet and look down upon that floor. In the breadbox you'll find out about this golden age. Breadbox is locked to a combination. On the inside there is a tintype hidden in one shoe and something else that you need to see and know in the other.—

Standing up now away from the rocker, his knees shaking, Nathaniel said:

—No! I've seen enough. Heard enough. Can't I believe without seeing? Plunging my hand into space and time.—

—I. V. Reed's shoes in there. You want to accept me as your saving grandmother, then go get I. V. Reed's shoes; he's part of your bloodline, too, forever and ever . . . Her tintype, too. Lucasta Jones. She's you. She's yours, take her. I've had enough. Jericho wills that I *wither* it to you! In a windstorm of truth. Now run and tell that to the wind! I command you, sir.—

With his long, dark eyelashes beating furiously as a sparrow's wings when trapped as a bird of prey, Nathaniel headed for the closet. His mind shocked by what he saw as the unraveling of Great-Momma Sweetie.

—I won't look. Grandmother. Old lady. Great-Momma Sweetie Reed Witherspoon, I won't . . . I won't look. As a lost soul, I don't want to look upon the fate that you want to show me, but not yourself.—

But now kneeling down at the foot of the opened closet door, he pulled out the breadbox. He could hear Sweetie's voice screaming aloud over and over again the combination: 4–11–44. He turned the dials, the door leapt open. As he stuck his hand past the chamber door, he felt as one entering a forbidden, closed-off city.

—Now, Nathaniel, tell me you don't love me. Claim me not as your own. That's right, look down upon your inheritance and tell me you do love me? Shriek out loud to the moon upon this night.—

Now in the deep dark blue shoe he saw socked away amid paper filler, down the length of the sole, a fist of diamonds so bright they sparkled in his eyes to blazing lights. Gems flaring up in time and space as lights upon an altar in a church at midnight, he winced . . . oh no. Sylvia's diamonds . . . oh no . . . Even Wayland Woods didn't know of this . . .

—Yes, boy, that's your inheritance. Part of it. Now Candy'll find you mighty handy, I'll bet. Add that to your Creole inheritance of money from White Lightning Bleaching Creme and slaves. Now look inside that other shoe.—

There he saw a tintype of a girl of fifteen or so; poised upon a love seat, with the inscription "To Jerry, Lucasta—with the love from my heart, free flowing."

—Now you know why I loathe Lucasta so, Great-Momma Sweetie said as she heard Nathaniel read the inscription aloud three times.

But for Nathaniel the picture looked exactly like the pictures Jericho Witherspoon must have drawn out upon the sleeve of his memory, and fitting those descriptions of Angelina that Great-Momma Sweetie had given.

She screamed:

—It's Lucasta, all right, that your eyes are seeing.—

—No, but it's Angelina, too, he wept aloud.

But Nathaniel Witherspoon wasn't thinking of either woman now, he was thinking of his deceased mother. She's just like Madeline, she looks just like . . .

He fell backwards upon the floor, clutching the diamonds and the tintype.

—It's Lucasta, boy. Not Angelina. I tell you it's not her your eyes are seeing, not Angelina your eyes are revealing.—

—I know what I've come to see in what I am looking at.—

—Now do you see the diamonds of your soul, Nathaniel? Nathaniel, do you see the diamonds of your soul? Now can you say you love me? Can you stand the diamond-heads of your existence as your inheritance, forever and ever, world without end?—

293

Nathaniel wept to himself those Biblical words: "Woe unto the world because of offences! for it must needs be that offences come; but woe to that man by whom the offence cometh!" *Oh mighty, broken-hearted and soul-divided Redeemer,* he sobbed. And oh darkened North Star angel, oh darkened angel "so superb in love and logic" in whose shadow the Redeemer stood in the baptizing beginning.

—I tell you it's not Angelina and you keep saying . . . calling her out.—

—Mother Sweetie. Great-Mother Sweetie, I do love you. But do you love Clea?—

—Clea: that babbling brook that made sounds as bubbles popping!—

—. . . Oh, too much is in readiness for my loaded-down soul to be saved.—

—. . . Despite your loathing of me for the truth. Can you say it and be sorry and say it, how much you love and face the prima facie evidence of your existence and *then* kneel at the foot of my bed to me with love in your heart?—

—I do love the truth of Justice, no matter where the beacon's taper light falls, Mother Sweetie Witherspoon Reed . . . But can you recognize Lucasta from Angelina? Oh, you never lied, most sacred liar-prophetess. I do. I do love within my/our loathsome inheritance . . . But do I only love the enlightened cause of Justice? Oh no way out but to burn out the alabaster blight of this blindness; oh, light of the body is luminously of the eye . . . No two wings to hide the riddled features upon my fated American face . . . By dawn's early light He spat upon the ground and swiped up clay from, of and by and out of the spat-upon darkened earth's surface and the red clay, and up spirals man, soon a prisoner within the chambers of his imagery. Oh, Great-Momma Sweetie, look at what we moderns do in the dark. Oh, the center holds too much. Oh, I can see it, this form, this phantom of light, luminous with savagery and brighter than any accursed gems. Amid the radiance forged out of the light of affliction: quaking altar-light eyes. A bloody head fixed upon a stony stick in the thunder-breaking seven seasons after the beginning of dawning light . . .

—Oh, Great-Momma Sweetie: troubling, remembering, believing, indeed: and I can see the radiant halo about the fixed head upon the cross-stick, amid the cistern of toads within (five fathoms deep?) still coming, slouching, Great-Momma Sweetie, more horrid and awesome than ever, forever since thunderous lightning down through four rivers and shocked up through clay, spittle and mud, a driven spiritual fountain: the miracle coursing through man's bloody blood. But coming in waves of wonders in a windstorm (sharper than a shark's scent for the blood of a slave ship) to strike out the blazing North Star light within the halo and the ever so dim and quaking, too, little light of mine; oh so fitful in its glowing; a folio of illuminating light licks up from this folio-sheaf of yellow sheets for tomorrow. I see the eyes within the head upon the stick glow in hope and horror. But the stick man's soul light radiant beyond the cistern of toads, turds and trouble, beyond butchers and belief . . . Oh, fix me, Jesus, fix me . . .

—Troubling, remembering and believing: oh, you black and unknown bards of Calvary, Auntie Foisty, Shank Haywood, Wayland Woods, Angelina, Grandfather Witherspoon, the lyrical Lovelady, yes and even I. V. Reed. But, Great-Momma Sweetie, who can escape his fate and know I. V. Reed within us all? What's to be done indeed, when old repressed deeds come to light?

—Oh, you may bury me in the east, bury me in the west, but I heard the trumpet radiant as the resonant bells of the morning; oh Kyrie eleison, oh Christe eleison . . . And the glowing soul within JW: marked man forever marked, his soul branded upon memory forever and ever as a halo of horror and history. And, Great-Momma Sweetie, you, forever engaged at the soul of his fated features . . . Oh dear God, grant that through the mystery and the miracle of water and the bitter grapes of Golgotha's wrath and the broken bread of His flesh (all suffering together), we may know the meaning of our furnace-refined chalice cup of suffering and affliction, forever, Great-Momma Sweetie, and ever, world without end . . . Oh, to live in luminous light ever rekindled is to live forever in doubt, as pure as faith is . . . Tomorrow and tomorrow's tomorrow weep in a blind cell and each man in the chamber of his own self-seeking metaphor: our American curse.—

But as Nathaniel unleashed his soul, at her bedside altar, Great-Momma Sweetie Reed nodded in agreement upon certain utterances and then shook her head violently in stalking disagreement, upon the very next phrase, as one wrangling over a bruised-blood covenant. Her body vaulting, rising and falling with the light of her body, heat, argument, spittle (spitting on occasion upon the tea leaves in his bitter cup) . . . Commanding him to silence, cursing, praying, denouncing, rendering up counter-memoirs, phrases from scriptures, spirituals, then only gestures; the gestures of sign language, and homemade ones spun up from the grievousness of her soul's captivity in a windstorm; in flight as two wings unveiling her soul . . . an unfolding and a parting away . . . Only grief-stricken gestures, as her soul chased and chastened his words, long and deep into the night and unto the dawning light of the new day.

Forest County, Illinois, 1958

ABOUT THE AUTHOR

LEON FORREST was born in Chicago and was educated
at Wilson Junior College, Roosevelt University and the
University of Chicago. He edited Chicago community
weeklies from 1965 to 1969, and he was managing
editor of *Muhammad Speaks* in 1972–1973. Ralph
Ellison wrote the introduction to his first novel, *There
Is a Tree More Ancient Than Eden* (1973); his second
novel, *The Bloodworth Orphans,* was published in 1977.
The opera with his libretto, *Soldier Boy, Soldier,* was
premiered at the University of Indiana in 1982.

Mr. Forrest delivered the first annual Allison Davis
lecture, on Benito Cereno, in 1981. He served as
president of the Society of Midland Authors in
1981–1982. He has lectured on Ellison, Faulkner and
Dostoevsky at Yale, Rochester and Brown. Currently
he is an associate professor in the Afro-American
Studies Department, Northwestern University.

100 Years of AMERICAN NEWSPAPER COMICS

100 Years of AMERICAN NEWSPAPER COMICS

AN ILLUSTRATED ENCYCLOPEDIA

Edited by
Maurice Horn

GRAMERCY BOOKS
New York • Avenel

Project Editor: Gregory Suriano

Text Design: Barbara Marks

Layout: Helene Berinsky

Jacket Design: Bill Akunevicz, Jr.

Electronic Publishing Advisor: Frank Finamore

Production Supervisor: Ellen Reed

Copyright © 1996 by Maurice Horn

Published by Random House Value Publishing, Inc. All rights reserved under International and Pan-American Copyright Conventions.
No part of this book may be reproduced or trans-mitted in any form or by any means electronic or mechanical including photocopying, recording, or by any information storage and retrieval system, without permission in writing from the publisher.

This edition is published by Gramercy Books, a division of Random House Value Publishing, Inc., 40 Engelhard Avenue, Avenel, New Jersey 07001.

Random House
New York • Toronto • London • Sydney • Auckland
http://www.randomhouse.com/

Printed and bound in the United States of America

Library of Congress Cataloging-in-Publication Data
Horn, Maurice.
    100 years of American newspaper comics / Maurice Horn.
    p. cm.
      ISBN 0-517-12447-5 (HC)
      1. Comic books, strips, etc.—United States—History and criticism.
    I. Title
PN6725.H59 1996
741.5´0973—dc20   95-45979
                       CIP

10   9   8   7   6   5   4   3

ACKNOWLEDGMENTS

*T*he authors of *100 Years of American Newspaper Comics* wish to thank the following persons for their assistance: Alain Beyrand, Bill Blackbeard, Chance and Chris Browne, Alfredo Castelli, Javier Coma, Leon Friedman, Jan Guszynski of Tribune Media Services, Johnny and Bobby Hart, Corinta Kotula of the Newspaper Features Council, Mell Lazarus, Michel Mandry of Disney-Europe, Fred Schwab, Janice Silverman, Joe Szabo, Mort Walker, and Dean Young. Special appreciation is extended to the staff at Random House Value Publishing: to Gregory Suriano, for his editorial guidance, organization, and copyediting; to Bill Akunevicz, Jr., Barbara Marks, and Helene Berinsky, for their design creativity; to Frank Finamore, for his electronic-publishing expertise; and to Ellen Reed, Don Bender, and other members of the Random House production and art departments for their knowledge and support.

THE CONTRIBUTORS

MaryBeth Calhoun (M.B.C.)
Bill Crouch, Jr. (B.C., Jr.)
Maurice Horn (M.H.)
Pierre Horn (P.H.)
Bill Janocha (B.J.)
John A. Lent (J.A.L.)
Fred Patten (F.P.)
Dennis Wepman (D.W.)
Tom Whissen (T.W.)

For complete information on the contributors see page 407

Contents

PREFACE

*T*his is the first encyclopedic study of the comic strips that have adorned, and sometimes even graced, the pages of American newspapers for the past hundred years, in all their breadth and variety. It covers the field from all angles, alphabetically from *A. Piker Clerk* and *Abbie an' Slats* to *Ziggy* and *Zippy the Pinhead*, chronologically from *The Yellow Kid* of 1894 to *Terry and the Pirates* of 1995, and thematically from the broad farce of *The Katzenjammer Kids* to the delicate fantasy of *Little Nemo*, from the futuristic thrills of *Buck Rogers* to the political commentary of *Doonesbury*.

There are 420 entries, arranged alphabetically, each of them devoted to a single title: they constitute the heart and center of the book. All major and most second-rank features are included, along with some not-so-major strips and a few oddities. The strips have been selected on the basis of their historical importance, the excellence of their drawing and/or writing, or simply because they reflect some facet of their times or have had an interesting history. The entries have been written by a team of contributors headed by the editor. All the important aspects of each strip are discussed in detail, giving flavor and background to the particulars, essentially bringing the strips and their creators to life. The black-and-white illustrations, profusely interspersed with the text, supply additional information as well as visual enjoyment; while the color section presents an appropriately pictorial overview of a century of Sunday comics.

A further note on the strips covered in this volume: We have included a number (perhaps a dozen) of foreign-originated features that have received wide circulation in American newspapers. It would seem ridiculous to exclude such a popular comic strip as *Andy Capp,* for instance, on the flimsy pretext that the author is British. In the case of comics of foreign origin, the dates indicated in parentheses are the dates of syndication in the United States. Similarly, with comics derived from other media (e.g., *Mickey Mouse* or *Batman*) the dates given are those of their first appearances in newspapers.

This book is more—much more, we hope—than a compendium of entries listed in alphabetical order. The introduction surveying a hundred years of newspaper comics, gives an appropriate context to and a general understanding of the field covered in greater detail in the entries; while the chronology provides a succint perspective and a valuable timeline to the facts and dates. Summary biographies of the hundred most important creators of the last century complement the information on individual comic titles. Finally, there is an extensive bibliography for those interested in further reading on the subject.

Above all, the texts have been written in entertaining as well as informative prose. It is our hope that this romp through the colorful world of comics will be as fun to read as the medium it thoroughly and lovingly surveys.

The Editors

100 Years of Comics: An Introduction

Of all the questions facing any study of the comics, fixing the exact birthdate and birthplace of the art form has been one of the most perplexing for the specialists. The common notion that the comics as we know them were born in the United States at the tail end of the nineteenth century is still not universally accepted (with France and England as the chief demurrers). In order to disentangle this thorny thicket it is therefore necessary to step back into history.

Some apologists of the form, as well as a few detractors, have claimed for the comics a more ancient and noble lineage, going all the way back to the cave paintings of Altamira and Lascaux, the Egyptian bas-reliefs, the Pompeii murals, Trajan's column in Rome, or the Queen Mathilde tapestry in Bayeux. These examples may be amusing, but they are hardly conducive to an enlightened discussion of the subject at hand: a few pictures may be worth a thousand words but they do not an art form make. Closer to our own century, however, there are no fewer than four prior claims worthy of investigation.

One strong contender for the title of "father of the comics" is Rodolphe Töpffer, the Swiss artist and author who in the 1830s and 1840s penned an entertaining series of stories in pictures (which he called *"histoires en estampes"*), and whose case has most eloquently been advocated in America by Ellen Wiese in *Enter the Comics* and in France by Alain Beyrand in his many writings on the subject. Their claim that Töpffer

R. F. Outcault, *The Yellow Kid*, 1896. The first example of Outcault's use of sequential narrative and speech-balloons in his Sunday page.

THE KATZENJAMMER KIDS CHANGE GRANDPA'S GLASSES.

Everything seems bigger through these spectacles until Grandpa discovers the joke.

THEN THINGS BEGIN TO LOOK LIVELY FOR THE KIDS.

Rudolph Dirks, *The Katzenjammer Kids,* **1898**

had invented a new art form seems overreaching, however; Töpffer's work, inspired as it undoubtedly is, is still too overloaded with extraneous literary preoccupations, and it signaled not the birth of a new art form but the brilliant end of an already outmoded artistic concept.

Another claimant in the comics sweepstakes has been Wilhelm Busch, who started turning out picture-stories in Germany as early as 1864, and whose most famous creation, *Max und Moritz,* appeared some years later. *"Max und Moritz,"* Wolfgang Fuchs stated, "fills most if not all of the classic requirements that define a comic strip." It did not, however, make use of the speech-balloon; more importantly, influential though it was, it did not mark any significant advance in graphic storytelling. It is best remembered today as the inspiration for *The Katzenjammer Kids:* an important antecedent, yes; the starting point of a new art form, definitely no.

Much has also been made in France of Christophe's *La famille Fenouillard,* which first appeared in 1889, but this claim can be dismissed on the same grounds that were used for *Max und Moritz.* For all his qualities (and they were many), Christophe blazed no trail and inspired no following. The modern french *bande dessinée* does not issue from his works; at best he can be regarded as a somewhat eccentric grand uncle.

Not so easily disposed of is the claim advanced by some British historians (led by the noted comics scholar Denis Gifford) that the form was invented in their sceptered isle. The *Ally Sloper* stories, for which the honor is most commonly claimed, were not that different in form and content from *Max und Moritz* and other such continental picture-stories; they did, however, spawn progeny, and therein lies the difference. Yet these progeny, like their dubious begetter, are by and large rather undesirable: *Comic Cuts* and other weeklies in the same vein were pointedly aimed at children, and over the years they never quite broke out of their self-imposed ghetto—no wonder that they too eventually came to a dead end. Their influence on the world's comics has been negligible; and it is largely because of the stigma still attached to them that Britain today is the only major country where the comics are still not acknowledged as a legitimate art form.

In view of the foregoing it is therefore no surprise that the Eurocentric, elitist view is most stubbornly held by the British-born academic David Kunzle, who in two ponderous tomes, respectively titled *The Early Comic Strip* and *The History of the Comic Strip,* has tried to deny to America the distinction of inventing the comic strip with a zeal comparable to those who strive to deny to Christopher Columbus the honor of discovering America. While the good professor claims that the form was created in Europe as early as the fifteenth century, it is interesting to point out that he uses a term *(comic strip)* coined in America in the twentieth century, which brings up the old existential conundrum: If a tree falls unobserved in the forest, is there a tree falling? Or in terms more germane to the discussion at hand, if someone discovers a new continent or a new art form and there is no contemporary historian to record it for posterity, is there a discovery? Most objective analysts would say not.

Clearly the answer must come from another direction, and from another continent, and it is indeed paradoxical that this continent should turn out to be America. Toward the end of the nineteenth century nothing pointed to an American breakthrough in a field that had been pioneered and explored almost exclusively by European artists. True, American newspapers and magazines displayed a robust vitality to which editorial cartoonists and pictorial reporters contributed their legitimate share. Of particular significance was the popularity of the humor magazines: *Puck, Judge, Life,* and others, in whose pages it was already possible to discern the artists who

Gus Dirks, *The Latest News from Bugville,* **1901. Gus Dirks, Rudolph's younger brother, was also a cartoonist of talent whose life was unfortunately cut short.**

Winsor McCay, *Little Sammy Sneeze*, 1904

R. F. Outcault, *Buster Brown*, 1907. Buster receives a visit from the Yellow Kid.

George McManus, *Bringing Up Father*, 1919. An early discussion of manners between the immortal Jiggs and Maggie.

would later become famous for their comics. At the same time the American daily newspapers, competing for readership among themselves, brought forth the Sunday supplement, which made increasingly generous use of illustration and color. Now, almost at the end of the century, all conditions seemed ripe for the bursting forth of a new form of communication, neither merely literature nor merely graphic art, but borrowing freely from both.

To answer the growing demand for illustrators and cartoonists, new and sometimes untried talent was brought to the fore, producing the artistic ferment necessary for all radical departures from the accepted norm. The importation of new and more advanced presses from Europe allowed newspapers to print more copies better and faster, thus reaching an ever-increasing public. The enormous influx of new immigrants from eastern and southern Europe, with little or no knowledge of the English language, gave the medium of visual communication a steady and safe audience, free from the shibboleths of established literary and artistic forms. Finally, the circulation wars among newspapers also worked to the advantage of the artist who, unlike his writing colleague, had a style that was recognizable at first glance.

It was Joseph Pulitzer who first seized upon the Sunday supplement as a showcase for his newspaper, the *New York World*. To attract a new readership to his publication, Pulitzer made increasing use of illustrations and color, combining both in his car-

Bud Fisher: Mutt and Jeff toast some other famous comic characters of the period, 1913.

toons. The conjunction of all these innovations led directly to Richard Felton Outcault's celebrated feature, *The Doings in Hogan's Alley*. This was not yet a genuine comic strip, as it is defined today, but its creation was pivotal, foreshadowing as it did the birth of the comics as a distinct medium.

The often-told struggle of Joseph Pulitzer and his upstart rival, William Randolph Hearst, for hegemony over the New York newspaper market in the waning years of the nineteenth century provided the ultimate catalyst in the synthesis of the disparate elements of narrative and illustration into a single whole. In a frantic scramble Hearst and Pulitzer placed greater and greater reliance on their Sunday supplements and lured employees away from each other (culminating in Outcault's defection to Hearst's *Journal* in 1896).

In a matter of months a new cultural form was born, characterized by a narrative told in a sequence of pictures, a continuing cast of characters, the inclusion of dialogue and/or text within the picture frame, as well as by a dynamic method of story-

Tad Dorgan, *Judge Rummy (Silk Hat Harry's Divorce Suit),* **1920**

telling that would compel the eye to travel forward from one panel to the next. This last distinction is very important, in that it separates the comics proper from most of the pictorial narratives of centuries past in which compositions were static and mainly served as illustrations to the text or the captions. The comics are more than just a sequence of pictures in the same way that the movies are more than just a succession of photographs.

This kinetic dimension the American cartoonists imparted to their drawings struck contemporary observers as such a startling departure that for the first time they groped for a name to give to what they rightly perceived as a new way of telling stories in words and pictures. However inappropriate the term *comics* appears to describe this complex form, it has now passed into universal usage, and the innovation it encapsulates has now become the universally accepted norm. In a recent (November 1995) lecture at New York University, the noted Italian writer and editor Alfredo Castelli had this to say on the subject: "America has inevitably exercised a great influence on the industry of Italian (and world) comics, if only because the first internationally known representatives of the medium are of American origin. As the homeland of comics, America was—and still is—idealized by cartoonists as a somewhat ultimate goal."

While the comics' place of birth no longer seems in doubt in the minds of the overwhelming majority of observers, their exact birthdate has caused much debate among scholars; but the consensus of opinion squarely places it in 1896, when Outcault's creation acquired its definitive characteristics along with the appellation *Yellow Kid,* and the year in which the Pulitzer-Hearst rivalry reached a fever pitch, resulting in the creation of the explosive new medium that came to be called "the comics." The year 1896 has been upheld by every historian from Coulton Waugh on, and it has been officially reaffirmed by an international panel of scholars meeting in Lucca, Italy, in 1989.

A few years ago a small coterie of self-proclaimed experts (with not one of the recognized historians of the medium among them) came out in favor of 1895 as a birth year on the dubious basis that the year marked the first appearance of Outcault's Kid; in actuality, the character first appeared in 1894, a well-documented fact. The erroneous 1895 claim met with some initial success, but in the anniversary year of 1996 good sense and good scholarship again prevailed.

Milton Caniff, *Terry and the Pirates*, © 1943 Chicago Tribune–New York News Syndicate. The famous page reprinted in the *Congressional Record*.

In the course of their hundred-year existence the comics have encompassed virtually every aspect of American life and American endeavor, from the down-to-earth (as in *Gasoline Alley*) to the esoteric (as in *Krazy Kat*), and the illustrated anthology that accompanies this text will give the reader a small sample of the medium's diversity. In the last few decades, unfortunately, this diversity has increasingly given way to gag-a-day uniformity, with greeting-card cuteness predominating. The continuity strips, and particularly the action strips, have been the chief victims of the general reduction of newspaper strips to postage-stamp size: the resulting loss of space for detail and spectacle has predictably caused a sharp drop in readership. The continuity strips are caught in the vortex of a vicious circle: the less popular they have become with the readers the more neglected they are; the more neglected they are (by authors, syndicates, and newspapers) the fewer readers they attract; and so on. There is no doubt that a comic page bereft of adventure, continuity, and suspense—as most comic pages of newspapers have become—looks woefully inadequate.

This mournful situation seems to illustrate Nietzsche's theory of eternal return: we are headed back to the early years of the medium, when the "funnies" were just what that name implies, with only a handful of continuity strips spattered over the landscape. In very recent years there have been hopeful signs of a modest return to narrative structure: *Peanuts* and *Calvin and Hobbes* have played with the notion of day-to-day continuity, Garry Trudeau in *Doonesbury* has developed longer and longer story lines, while the revival of *Terry and the Pirates* gives hope to all aficionados of the

Will Eisner, *The Spirit,* © **1948 Will Eisner. A superb example of Eisner's cinematic storytelling.**

Mort Walker, *Beetle Bailey*, © 1995 King Features Syndicate. A salute to the hundredth anniversary of the comics. The old-time comic characters were drawn with the assistance of Bill Janocha.

adventure strip. Cartoonists, as well as syndicate and newspaper comic editors, seem to have belatedly realized how much continuity is the glue that binds newspaper readers to the daily strip.

What of the future? In 1995 the Newspaper Features Council conducted a survey of its members on the theme "Where Do We Go from Here?" The responses, as could be expected, were varied and contradictory, ranging from Joseph D'Angelo, president of King Features Syndicate, asserting, "All this talk about comics and newspapers heading for oblivion seems to me to be just that—talk" to Lee Salem, vice-president of the clear-sighted Universal Press Syndicate, declaring, "Whatever cyberspace becomes may well afford cartoonists other creative outlets, and it's easy to envision thousands—even millions—of people subscribing to a cartoonist's work for a penny a day. (Even better, the cartoonist won't need a syndicate to edit, sell, and distribute the work.)" These advances in technology, coupled with the "intellectual rights" provisions of the GATT Treaty of 1994, to which the U.S. is a signatory, may indeed restore primacy to the creators over the sales-obsessed types who have for too long dominated the medium; and that would be a most welcome development.

Cynics, pointing to the low state of newspaper comics today, as compared to earlier, happier days, when the syndicates were coming out with more trail-blazing strips in one year than they now seem able to do in a decade, might snidely argue that the comics, born in the nineteenth century, will indeed not make it into the twenty-first. I prefer to remain cautiously optimistic: a medium that has weathered all the vicissitudes of the twentieth century is not likely to disappear overnight. Try as they may, syndicate editors won't be able to kill the comics any more than film producers have been able to kill the movies. So, no cause for celebration perhaps, but a subdued hurrah, and on to the next century.

Maurice Horn

100 Years of Comics: A Chronology

The direct forerunners of the comics were the nineteenth-century picture-stories that combined text and image to tell extended narratives. The Swiss Rodolphe Töpffer, the German Wilhelm Busch, and the French Georges Colomb ("Christophe") were masters of the form. At the same time anecdotes told in cartoon sequences were a fixture of the humor magazines; in the course of the years progressively more complex sequences of drawings led to the creation, toward the end of the century, of an independent and distinct art form that later came to be called *the comics*.

1894 "Feudal Pride in Hogan's Alley," a large cartoon by R. F. Outcault featuring a bald-headed, night-shirted kid, appears in the humor magazine *Truth*.

1895 Outcault's *Hogan's Alley* starts appearing in Joseph Pulitzer's *New York World;* James Swinnerton's *Little Bears* debuts in the *San Francisco Examiner*.

1896 The Yellow Kid in his definitive form appears in *Hogan's Alley;* Outcault is hired away by W. R. Hearst's rival *New York Journal*, taking the Yellow Kid with him. All these developments mark for most historians the birthdate of the comics.

R. F. Outcault, *The Yellow Kid,* 1897

James Swinnerton, *Little Jimmy*, 1905

Winsor McCay, *Dream of the Rarebit Fiend*, 1905

C. W. Kahles, *Hairbreadth Harry*, 1906. The very first episode of the strip.

1897 Rudolph Dirks's *The Katzenjammer Kids,* the oldest comic strip in existence, is first published.

1898 Swinnerton moves to New York, where he creates *The Journal Tigers* for Hearst.

1900 The first year of the twentieth century marks the appearance of F. B. Opper's *Happy Hooligan* and of Charles Schultze's *Foxy Grandpa.*

1902 Outcault's *Buster Brown* and Swinnerton's *Mr. Jack* first appear.

1903 Winsor McCay's *Tales of the Jungle Imps* comes out; H. H. Knerr originates *Die Fineheimer Twins,* first successful imitation of the Katzenjammers; Gustave Verbeck publishes *The Upside Downs.* First attempt at a daily newspaper strip, Clare Briggs's *A. Piker Clerk,* proves short-lived.

1904 The vitality of the new form asserts itself in an outpouring of original creations: Swinnerton's *Little Jimmy,* McCay's *Dream of the Rarebit Fiend,* Opper's *And Her Name Was Maud!,* George McManus's *The Newlyweds* all first appear. C. V. Dwiggins ("Dwig") embarks on his long cycle of *School Days* and Gus Mager draws the first of his "Monks."

1905 McCay's masterpiece, *Little Nemo in Slumberland,* premieres in the pages of the *New York Herald.*

1906 From Germany Lyonel Feininger makes two short-lived but vitally important contributions to the art of the comics: *The Kin-der-Kids* and *Wee Willie Winkie's World.* C. W. Kahles creates *Hairbreadth Harry.*

1907 The first successful daily newspaper strip appears in the pages of the *San Francisco Examiner:* Bud Fisher's *A. Mutt* (later *Mutt and Jeff*).

1909 George Herriman starts *Baron Mooch,* in whose panels appears a Krazy Kat prototype.

Winsor McCay, *Little Nemo in Slumberland*, 1909

George Herriman, *Baron Mooch*, 1909. We can already recognize a prefiguration of Krazy Kat in the third panel.

1910   *Desperate Desmond,* created by Harry Hershfield, and *Slim Jim* by George Frink first appear. George Herriman starts *The Dingbat Family.*

1911   Sidney Smith's *Old Doc Yak* debuts.

1912   *Polly and Her Pals* is first published (as *Positive Polly*). Lawsuit opposing Dirks and Hearst over ownership of *The Katzenjammer Kids* started.

1913   McManus creates *Bringing Up Father, Hawkshaw the Detective* originated by Mager, *Krazy Kat* established as an independent strip (it had hitherto appeared at the bottom of *The Dingbat Family*).

1914   Formation of King Features Syndicate. The Dirks-Hearst suit settled by the Federal Court of Appeals, setting precedent: Dirks draws his version of the characters as *Hans and Fritz* (later *The Captain and the Kids*), while Knerr takes over *The Original Katzenjammer Kids. Abie the Agent* started by Hershfield.

1915   The year sees the birth of *Boob McNutt, Freckles and His Friends,* and *Toonerville Folks.*

1916   McManus's *Rosie's Beau* premieres.

1917   *The Gumps* and *Reg'lar Fellers* started.

1918   Frank King creates *Gasoline Alley.*

1919   Another great year for the comics: *Barney Google, Harold Teen, Mr. and Mrs.,* and *Thimble Theatre* all debut.

1920   Chicago Tribune–New York News Syndicate (today Tribune Media Services) established. *Winnie Winkle* premieres.

1921   The year sees the creation of *Minute Movies, Our Boarding House, Out Our Way,* and *Tillie the Toiler.*

1922   *Fritzi Ritz* and *Smitty* first published.

H. H. Knerr, *The Katzenjammer Kids,* © 1924 King Features Syndicate

Phil Nowlan and Dick Calkins, *Buck Rogers*, © 1929 John F. Dille Co.

1923 *Just Kids, Moon Mullins,* and *The Nebbs* created. Felix the Cat is the first animated cartoon character to successfully make it to the newspaper page.

1924 Roy Crane creates *Wash Tubbs.* Harold Gray comes up with *Little Orphan Annie. Boots and Her Buddies* makes its debut.

1925 *Ella Cinders* first published. Percy Crosby's *Skippy* premieres.

1927 Frank Godwin's *Connie* first syndicated.

1928 *Tailspin Tommy* and *Tim Tyler's Luck* start aviation-strip craze.

1929 *Buck Rogers* and *Tarzan* first appear, on the same day (January 7). The year also gives birth to such diverse strips as *Count Screwloose, Skyroads,* and *Show Girl* (later retitled *Dixie Dugan*). Popeye the Sailor makes his debut in *Thimble Theatre.*

1930 United Feature Syndicate established. Comic strips continue to sprout in all directions, with *Blondie, Mickey Mouse, Scorchy Smith,* and *Joe Palooka* coming out that year.

1931 Chester Gould creates *Dick Tracy,* the first detective strip.

Cliff Sterrett, *Polly and Her Pals*, © 1936 King Features Syndicate

Harold Foster, *Prince Valiant*, © 1941 King Features Syndicate

Crockett Johnson, *Barnaby*, © 1942 Crockett Johnson

1932 *Apple Mary, Pete the Tramp,* and *Napoleon and Uncle Elby* are some of the year's premiere offerings.

1933 And they still keep coming, *Alley Oop, Brick Bradford, Dickie Dare, Smilin' Jack,* and *White Boy* among them.

1934 A signal year for the adventure strip: Alex Raymond brings out *Flash Gordon, Jungle Jim,* and (with Dashiell Hammett) *Secret Agent X-9;* Lee Falk and Phil Davis originate *Mandrake the Magician;* Milton Caniff creates *Terry and the Pirates; Don Winslow* and *Red Barry* also first published. On another front, Al Capp comes up with *Li'l Abner.*

1935 *Don Dixon, King of the Royal Mounted, Oaky Doaks,* and *Smokey Stover* testify to the continuing vitality and diversity of the comics.

1936 *The Phantom* premieres. *Donald Duck* newspaper strip permanently established.

1937 Hal Foster creates *Prince Valiant,* leaving *Tarzan* in the able hands of his successor, Burne Hogarth.

Fred Harman, *Red Ryder* promotion piece, © 1945 NEA Service

Burne Hogarth, *Drago,* © 1946 New York Post Corp.

1938   *Red Ryder* and *The Lone Ranger* revitalize the western strip. *Charlie Chan* adapted to the comics page. *Fritzi Ritz* becomes *Fritzi Ritz and Nancy* (and later simply *Nancy*).

1939   *Superman* finally makes it to the newspaper page.

1940   Newspapers experiment with the so-called comic-book supplement: Will Eisner's *The Spirit* and Dale Messick's *Brenda Starr* are born there.

1942   Military-service strips flourish, including *G.I. Joe, The Sad Sack,* and Caniff's army version of *Terry*. Crockett Johnson creates *Barnaby*.

1943   For copyright reasons Caniff replaces his service version of *Terry* with *Male Call*. Crane creates *Buz Sawyer,* and Al Andriola comes up with *Kerry Drake*

1944   Frank Robbins's *Johnny Hazard* starts.

1945   Hogarth's *Drago* and Ray Bailey's *Bruce Gentry* first appear.

1946   The National Cartoonists Society founded. Raymond creates *Rip Kirby*.

1947   Caniff creates *Steve Canyon*. Coulton Waugh's *The Comics* published: Waugh propounds 1896 as the birth year of the comics.

1948   *Rex Morgan, M.D.,* and *Rusty Riley* both appear. Walt Kelly's *Pogo* first published as a newspaper strip.

1949   Warren Tufts starts *Casey Ruggles*.

1950   Charles Schulz's *Peanuts* and Mort Walker's *Beetle Bailey* start publication.

1951   *The Cisco Kid* and *Dennis the Menace* debut.

1952   First publication of *Judge Parker*.

1953   *The Heart of Juliet Jones* first appears.

1954   *Hi and Lois* created by Mort Walker and Dik Browne.

1955   First appearance of *Dondi*.

1956   Jules Feiffer starts his series of polemical strips in the *Village Voice*.

1957   *Miss Peach* and *On Stage* come out.

1958   *B.C., Short Ribs,* and *The Strange World of Mr. Mum* signal a renewal of the humor strip. Stan Lynde's *Rick O'Shay* first published.

1959   Stephen Becker publishes *Comic Art in America:* 1896 is reaffirmed as the year of birth of the comics.

1960   Bil Keane creates *The Family Circus*.

1964   *The Wizard of Id* by Johnny Hart and Brant Parker begins.

1965   *The Born Loser, Tumbleweed*s, and *Wee Pals* all premiere.

1967   The first international exhibition devoted to the comics by a major museum, "Bande Dessinée et Figuration Narrative," opens at the Musée des Arts Décoratifs, the Louvre, in Paris.

1970   Universal Press Syndicate organized: among its first offerings is Garry Trudeau's *Doonesbury. Broom-Hilda, Friday Foster,* and *Momma* also premiere this year.

1971   The diamond jubilee of the comics is celebrated throughout the year, culminating in the "75 Years of the Comics" exhibition at the New York Cultural Center.

1972   Bob Thaves's *Frank and Ernest* begins.

1973   Dik Browne creates *Hagar the Horrible*.

1976   Publication of *The World Encyclopedia of Comics:* again 1896 is upheld as the year of the comics' birth.

1977   Jeff McNelly originates *Shoe*.

1978   Jim Davis's *Garfield* sees the light of print.

1979   Lynn Johnston creates *For Better or For Worse*. The success of the musical *Annie* prompts a revival of *Little Orphan Annie* (as *Annie*).

Johnny Hart, *B.C.*, © 1987 Creators Syndicate

1980   Berke Breathed starts *Bloom County.*

1985   Bill Watterson creates *Calvin and Hobbes,* one of the very few contemporary strips to deserve ranking alongside the classics of the comics.

1989   A panel of internationally recognized scholars and authorities on the comics, meeting in Lucca, Italy, proclaims 1896 as the birthdate of the comics.

1995   *Terry and the Pirates* given a second lease on life. In October the U.S. Postal Service issues a set of twenty stamps commemorating "Comic Strip Classics"—a rare instance of early delivery by the Post Office.

1996   The International Museum of Cartoon Art opens its doors for the hundredth anniversary of the comics. Other commemorative events take place throughout the world.

WHAT THEY DID TO THE DOG-CATCHER IN HOGAN'S ALLEY.

R. F. Outcault, *The Yellow Kid,* **1896. A typical Outcault page, teeming with life. The parade of motley characters is firmly led by the Yellow Kid, in the very first year of the comics.**

ENTRIES: A TO Z

A. PIKER CLERK
1903–1904

Clare Briggs's *A. Piker Clerk* was not the first daily newspaper strip (for one thing it didn't appear every day), but it was an early, perhaps the earliest, step in that direction. The whole concept was reportedly hatched by Moses Koenigsberg, then the editor of the Hearst-owned *Chicago American* (and later the first president of King Features Syndicate) as a ploy to get the readers to buy the newspaper every day. Koenigsberg and cartoonist Briggs then devised the idea of a weekday strip running in the sports section of the *American*, and so *A. Piker Clerk* made its appearance early in 1903.

A. Piker Clerk (that was his name) was a scrawny, bug-eyed, big-nosed, chinless man with a passion for horses. He would go to any length to ferret out a hot tip from jockeys, trainers, racetrack touts, even the proverbial horse's mouth. A generous man, he was willing to share his knowledge with everyone, all in a noble cause (to try and save an impoverished widow and her five small children from eviction, for example, or to help the financially strapped city of Chicago out of its fiscal mess). Clerk gave out tips on real horses in actual races, and the suspense for the reader consisted in finding out in the next day's paper (there was no radio then) whether the selected horse had won its race. Obviously the gimmick could only work during the racing season, and there were huge gaps between Clerk's appearances in the sports pages of the *American*. In order to remedy the situation Briggs tried to have his gambling hero give tips on other sports, and even featured him in nonsports activities, such as trying to crash high society, but to no avail. The strip was awkwardly drawn (Briggs hadn't found his style yet) and poorly scripted (necessitating a typeset explanatory text below the pictures), and it died an early death in June 1904.

Some commentators have based their assessment of *A. Piker Clerk* on Koenigsberg's highly selective memoir *King News* (1941): written almost forty years after the event, riddled with factual errors, and peppered with self-serving statements, as a source of reference it is almost useless.

M.H.

ABBIE AN' SLATS
1937–1971

Flushed with the growing success of *Li'l Abner*, Al Capp hit upon the idea of a straight story strip that would blend action, humor, and sentiment, all rolled into one neat package. Having written several weeks of continuity at top speed, he then turned to the established magazine illustrator Raeburn Van Buren with the offer to draw the projected feature. Van Buren eventually assented, and the fruit of their collaboration, called *Abbie an' Slats*, made its debut as a daily strip on July 7, 1937. Capp's theme of a tough kid from New York's slums transplanted to the sticks had already been the subject of countless Hollywood movies, but it was given a high gloss by Van Buren's accomplished pen-and-ink illustrations. It all came together somehow in the finished product, and after a brief breaking-in period, the new feature whirred confidently ahead.

The teenaged Aubrey Eustace Scrapple ("my pals on th' east side Noo York all calls me Slats") was soon reformed by the tough love of his spinster aunt Abbie, and the tender care of her sister Sally. He soon aged by a few years and rose to become "flyweight champeen" of the world and the pride of Crabtree Corners, the provincial town where the Scrapple clan resided. Slats also acquired a permanent love interest in the person of Becky Groggins, a dark-haired, sprightly beauty, as well as a mortal enemy in the form of Jasper Hagstone, a representative of that familiar stock-figure of the 1930s, the bloated capitalist shark.

Abbie an' Slats (Capp and Van Buren), © 1941 United Feature Syndicate

While the dailies had overtones of soap opera, humor and slapstick, along with a touch of the grotesque, became the hallmarks of the Sunday pages, which had been launched on January 15, 1939. These were the special province of John Pierpont (better known as Bathless) Groggins, Becky's reprobate father. His adventures often took place in exotic lands, in remembrance of his rowdy past as an old salt. When he was not roaming the seven seas, or consorting with a variety of cheats and swindlers, he could be found disturbing the quiet of Crabtree Corners with his crackpot inventions.

In 1946 Capp relinquished the writing of the strip to his younger brother, Elliot Caplin. A competent craftsman, Caplin did not possess his sibling's effortless virtuosity at situation-building, but he acquitted himself creditably, piloting the feature for another quarter-century. In later years the romance between Becky's no less gorgeous sister Sue and Slats's friend Charlie Dobbs frequently took center stage. In the best soap-opera tradition it was a stormy relationship, traversed by countless adversities, many of them caused by the schemes of the despicable Hagstone, who was hell-bent on marrying off his daughter Judy to the socially connected Charlie.

In the 1960s *Abbie an' Slats*'s popularity steadily declined, and as he was approaching his eightieth birthday, Van Buren decided to call it quits. The daily strips ended on January 30, 1971, while the Sunday page lingered a while longer, until July of the same year.

M.H.

ABIE THE AGENT
1914–1932, 1935–1940

Harry Hershfield's droll little dumpling of a character, Abie the Agent, seems an unlikely figure to lead a revolution in the comics, but in at least two ways he heralded a new age in the medium. First of all, the strip was addressed to a grown-up audience, enough of a novelty in 1914 to give it the claim, made by *New York Journal* editor Arthur Brisbane, of being "the first of the adult comics in America." No less remarkable in a period in which racial minorities were subjected to unrestrained ridicule in the public press, Hershfield broke new ground in presenting a Jewish stereotype sympathetically in a nationally syndicated comic strip. Debuting on February 2, 1914, as a daily strip in the *Journal* and soon to include a Sunday feature as well, *Abie the Agent* was to outlast many of its contemporaries.

According to legend, the character grew out of an inside joke in Hershfield's successful earlier strip *Desperate Desmond*. A cannibal in that pioneering melodrama-spoof, needing an unintelligible native tongue, was given a few words of Yiddish to speak, and the idea so tickled a friend of Brisbane's that he suggested a strip centered on a Yiddish-dialect character. And so was born the rotund Jewish businessman Abe Mendel Kabibble, complete with thick mustache, bulbous nose, and a speech-style owing something to *The Katzenjammer Kids,* something to a stock vaudeville type, and perhaps most to such characters in popular magazine fiction as Montague Glass's Potash and Perlmutter. Abie is no hero, but he is no anti-Semitic cari-

Abie the Agent (H. Hershfield), © 1930 International Feature Services

cature, either. Abie's Yiddish accent is amusingly, but not maliciously, presented. If its sometimes tortured grammar reveals ignorance, it does not (as Jewish and African-American dialect in the mass media so often did) suggest pretension.

The strip is relatively sympathetic to its hero and is without the acid edge of satire, but it has none of the social realism of serious Yiddish literature. Abe is gently mocked, but he does not suffer the hardships and discrimination of the Jewish immigrant in urban America. In fact, he is a rather skillful businessman (a car salesman, or "agent" as the current job title was). He works hard, and apparently prospers.

Hershfield recognized the offensiveness of ethnic caricature; in 1916 he identified his hero as "a clean-cut, well-dressed specimen of Jewish humor," and he succeeded in making him entertaining to Jew and gentile alike. More remarkable for the comics of the time, the character is a believable human being. As husband, father, and man of business, he reveals a wide range of personal emotions, positive and negative. A loving and generous family man, he is warmly supported by his patient and devoted girlfriend and later wife Reba Mine Gold Pearlman. Abe Kabibble is an aggressive and diligent entrepreneur who battles fiercely and shrewdly in a competitive professional arena.

On the other hand, much of the humor in the strip grew out of less likable elements in Abie's personality, traits that in later years would probably have been seen as offensive to a Jewish audience. As African Americans came in time to resent the good-natured kidding of their race in Amos and Andy, Jews would surely have found in Abie's greed, parsimony, cunning, and social climbing some of the Jewish stereotypes in anti-Semitic humor. Most of the cynicism of the strip was directed at the world of business itself, rather than at its Jewish exemplars, but many of the daily gags in *Abie the Agent* depended on the uniquely skewed logic of Jewish jokes: Abie considers himself lucky because he wins $10 by proving he has lost more money than a rival; a character stays in a business that is ruining him because he has to make a living. Abie is the ultimate pragmatist, and a compulsive attention to fiscal detail underlies his every decision: generous and openhanded to his wife, he will fight to the death over a disputed ten-cent charge in a restaurant, explaining to the waiter that "it's not the principle, either, it's the ten cents." He intervenes to save Nate Nixnook's marriage in 1929, not from concern for his colleague's domestic welfare but because "if he has to pay alimony, what chance have I got with the $200 he owes me!!!?"

Though making and keeping money is Abie's central preoccupation, he has the social aspirations of most self-made figures in the comics. In a 1922 strip he seeks to impress a colleague with his love for good books by buying classics and writing early dates to suggest he's been reading for years; in a 1938 Sunday story he varies the gag by buying an elegant library and then reading books from the library to protect his own fine editions from wear. As naive a parvenu as Jiggs's wife Maggie, he is proud to be a member of the Eppes Club (an *eppes* is a "somebody" in Yiddish), and is never seen without a black dress-tie and striped "pents." While most of his colleagues smoke cigars, Abie is seldom without the more fashionable cigarette in his mouth.

Hershfield was a staunch defender of his profession, and *Abie* was such a hit that he had a powerful bargaining position with it. When Brisbane ordered that cartoonists' signatures be omitted from their drawings (in order, as comics historian Jerry Robinson explains, "to reduce their personal following and thereby their salary demands"), Hershfield protested personally to publisher William Randolph Hearst and won not only the right of cartoonists to sign their work but the publication of a byline as well. However, in 1931 he lost a contractual fight with Hearst and King Features Syndicate, then distributing *Abie*. When he tried to take his strip to the *Chicago Daily News*, the courts decided that the title belonged to his original employer, which could continue it with another artist. The *News* wouldn't take the strip without the name, and the *Journal* was unable to find anyone else who could do it in Hershfield's style, so Abie disappeared for four years while Hershfield drew another strip for the *New York Herald-Tribune*. In 1935, Hershfield and Hearst settled their differences, the contract was renewed, and Abie returned to the *Journal*.

The strip continued for another five years, but by the end of the 1930s its characters and gags, as well as its primitive draftsmanship and extensive crosshatching, had begun to seem a little dated. One of the longest-running staples in the comics, Abie the Agent had remained virtually unchanged for over a quarter of a century when he retired with dignity in 1940.

D.W.

ACE DRUMMOND
1935–1940

Drawn by one World War I air ace, Clayton Knight, and allegedly written by another, Eddie Rickenbacker, at the height of the airplane-strip craze, *Ace Drummond* must have looked like a sure bet to the editors at King Features, with the sky the limit, but unfortunately the strip never really took wing.

Launched amid much fanfare touting the credentials of the two creators involved, in February 1935, *Ace Drummond* featured the predictable team of youthful aviator-hero Ace Drummond and old-timer Jerry, his grizzled, cynical mechanic. The action took place in all corners of the world from China to South America. The antagonists consisted of an unsavory lot of air pirates, gang lords, and other shadowy figures, among whom the international outlaw known as the Viper was the most persistent. Later on Ace was joined in his adventures by copilot Dinny Doyle, as well as by a boy sidekick intended to appeal to a juvenile audience, freckle-faced, tousled-haired Bill.

The continuities (written by an anonymous scribe and only lightly glanced over by Rickenbacker) were not terribly inventive, involving the heroes in a series of disjointed adventures. The soaring depiction of flight scenes and of limitless skies were Knight's forte, and he excelled at atmospheric compositions that showed a lone biplane emerging from a cloud-bank or a squadron of fighter planes flying over rugged mountain peaks. His drawing of human faces, however, was not up to the same standards, and all his characters looked bland. In 1937 he relinquished the artwork to Royal King Cole who proved not much of an airplane artist; *Ace Drummond,* after a few more lame exercises, was finally grounded in 1940.

Ace's companion feature on the Sunday page, *The Hall of Fame of the Air,* proved somewhat longer-lasting, surviving well into the late 1940s. In it Knight, who drew the feature throughout its existence, extolled the lives and times of flyers from all parts of the world. After the start of World War II it restricted itself, however, to the exploits of Allied pilots.

M.H.

ACE McCOY
See JOHNNY COMET

THE ADVENTURES OF PATSY
See PATSY

AGATHA CRUMM
1977–present

Started in the last week of October 1977, *Agatha Crumm* was Bill Hoest's second comic creation for King Features Syndicate. Appearing both daily and Sunday, the strip soon approached the cartoonist's earlier *The Lockhorns* in popularity.

The head of a business empire spanning the continent, Agatha Crumm is to greed and avarice what Wimpy is to gluttony and Snuffy Smith to sloth. Always dressed completely in black, the elderly widow makes that notorious miser of history and legend, Hettie Green, look like a spendthrift. Not only does she save paper clips, thumbtacks, and rubber bands, she has been known to unglue unobliterated stamps from envelopes and swipe waiters' tips from restaurant tables; and when she has a bone to pick with the president she calls the White House collect. As tyrannical as she is stingy, she strikes terror in the hearts of the employees of her far-flung enterprises, reserving her choicest barbs for her private secretary, Winsome. Her middle-aged son, Junior, also cringes in fear before his mother, who on occasion is not averse to hitting him with a ruler. She owns only a black-and-white TV set, and never goes to the theater or

The Airship Man (C. W. Kahles), 1902

to the movies, her favorite pastime being "rolling the competition and gouging the public." The only person able to stand up to her is her physician, Dr. Bernhang, who succeeds in quieting down the old biddy by reminding her of her mortality ("And this too shall pass, Agatha...").

Hoest died in 1988, and his work is now being carried on by his widow, Bunny, while the drawings are done by John Reiner, Hoest's former assistant. *Agatha Crumm* looks exactly as it did almost twenty years ago, rendered in the same cartoony, angular style (in keeping with the cartoony, slightly angular spirit of its feisty protagonist).

M.H.

THE AIRSHIP MAN
1902–1903

In the course of a career that extended only a little more than thirty years, from 1898 to the time of his death in 1931, C. W. (Charles William) Kahles managed to create no fewer than twenty-five comic series. These ranged over a wide spectrum, but Kahles found his métier in the mixture of humor and derring-do that became his hallmark. *The Airship Man,* which debuted in the *Philadelphia North American* on May 5, 1902, represents his earliest effort in this vein.

Sandy Highflier, the hero of the piece, was characteristically in the line of the plucky young lads that had populated Victorian boys' fiction (Queen Victoria died the year before *The Airship Man* came out), fiction represented by such titles as *Frank Merriwell* and *Frank Reade, Jr.* Kahles combined these strands with the no less contemporary strain of science fiction exemplified by H. G. Wells, notably in *When*

the Sleeper Wakes (1899), to design the curious airship that transported Sandy to his adventures. Consisting of a motorboat suspended from a blimp, it was capable of high speed and fast acceleration, qualities that came in handy at those not infrequent times when Sandy had to outdistance packs of hunger-crazed wolves or tribes of spear-throwing savages. When it did not bump into church steeples or get tangled in telephone wires, the ship was also used to carry precious cargo, which inevitably brought on air pirates in hot (and fruitless) pursuit of Sandy's craft.

The Airship Man was finally grounded for good in October 1903, shortly before the Wright Brothers' historic flight, anticipating the time when the dirigible would be replaced in boys' imaginations by the newfangled aeroplane.

M.H.

ALLEY OOP
1933–present

One of the greatest adventure strips and one steeped in world history, Vincent T. Hamlin's *Alley Oop* debuted on August 7, 1933, in daily format and September 9, 1934, as a Sunday page. At age 24 Hamlin discovered dinosaur fossils in a Texas oil field, giving him his first impetus to create work based on prehistory.

Anatomically akin to comic-strip contemporary Popeye, Oop is a caveman from the Mesozoic period and of the Kingdom of Moo. In an era sometime between the time of dinosaurs and the Ice Age, the Valley of Moo is the last refuge of these ancient reptiles. Named after the expression used by French tumblers, Alley Oop is a sturdy, simianlike warrior whose loyalty and warm heart match his fearless, athletic prowess and determination. He is first assistant to King Guzzle, who rules over Moo with his daughter Wootietoot and the tenacious Queen Umpateedle.

Prominent citizens include Guz's scheming wizard the Grand Wizer, Oop's beautiful and equally stalwart girlfriend Oola, and their companion Foozy, a philosopher who always speaks in verse. A powerful and affectionate stegosaurus named Dinny is Oop's loyal mount, who has saved him from many a predicament.

Hamlin's handling of narrative and character development and his striking artistry matured quickly. On Sundays, incredible tales of men interacting with reptilian beasts were balanced with a factual panel on subjects of archeology, paleontology, science, and history. Various titles for these educational spots include *Dinny's Family Album, Fragments, Scientists Say,* and *Odds'n'Ends.* During the early 1940s, Hamlin used this extra space not for facts but for espousing personal and nationalistic principles, via *Foozy's Foolosophies.*

By 1938 Hamlin felt it necessary to expand beyond the limitations of primitive exploits. On April 7, 1939, the feature literally entered a new dimension, as contemporary physicist Dr. Elbert Wonmug (after Albert Einstein: "one mug") bridged the gap of time with his introduction of the Time Machine. Oop and Oola were transported instantly into the modern era, and the fourth dimension was conquered. Along with historian Dr. Amos Bronson and, later, rogue rocket engineer G. Oscar Boom, the characters undertook fantastic adventures among the most prominent figures of history and legend, first embarking to the ancient city of Troy during the Trojan War. From this point Hamlin's imagination was unbridled, as he transformed Oop and the others into true soldiers of fortune, propelled into courageous and horrific adventures arguably unequaled elsewhere in the comics. In 1940 Oop encountered Ulysses, Hercules, and Cleopatra, followed in later years by Blackbeard, King John, Genghis Khan, Robin

Alley Oop (V. T. Hamlin), © 1934 NEA Service

Hood, Napoleon, Pocahontas, Aladdin, Nero, and countless others. The time travelers were transported to noted points of world history, and even into the realm of fantasy, confronting an evil giant from Fairyland, Santa Claus, and alien beings during intergalactic excursions to the moon, Venus, and the planet Zoron. Imparting an ability to its subjects to communicate in the foreign languages they encountered and able to follow their actions by viewscreen, Wonmug's Time Machine provided Hamlin the perfect vehicle to indulge his interests in science fiction and historical conjecture. When the United States entered World War II, Oop, King Guz, and Foozy were denied induction into the military service when they were deemed "aliens." Undaunted, they single-handedly fought the Japanese in the Pacific, Oscar Boom perfected rocket explosives for use against the Nazis, and, upon returning to Moo, Oop saved citizens enslaved in a "concentration cave" from Eeny the Dictator.

Hamlin kept the pacing quick, rarely allowing a week to pass between adventures. Equally quick were the tempers of his cast, for there was constant bickering and outbursts of violence; an interesting juxtaposition of human foible and scientific perfection. This current of tension helped create an atmosphere ripe with conflict, the perfect chemistry for explosive developments.

In 1947, Dave Graue began assisting in the drawing of *Alley Oop;* he was hired permanently in 1950. As the decade progressed, the subject of time travel was limited only to the daily sequences, as the Sunday version devoted itself solely to life in Moo. Graue's drawing style slowly dominated the look of the feature, and by 1966 he was allowed to cosign it. Although Graue's art lacked some of the magical nuances and atmospheric range that dominated Hamlin's artistry at its peak, he was the perfect choice to continue the work, providing a smooth transition of writing and art. When Hamlin retired in 1973, Graue continued the strip with much the same intent, and in late 1991 he handed the artistic chores to the very capable Jack Bender, while continuing to script the feature.

At its peak, *Alley Oop* was syndicated in some eight hundred newspapers. There were two *Alley Oop* Big Little Books, as well as fourteen comic-book titles. In 1960 a hit song based on the strip topped the pop charts. Thirty-five years later, a U.S. postage stamp honoring Oop was issued, as part of a "Comic Strip Classics" series, which hopefully reminded the public of the important folk hero V. T. Hamlin had created.

B.J.

ALPHONSE AND GASTON
1902–1920s

Not content to rest on the laurels *Happy Hooligan* had earned for him, the indefatigable Frederick Opper created another comic feature about two ludicrously polite Frenchmen whose names have by now entered the language. *Alphonse and Gaston* made its bow in the Hearst papers sometime in 1902.

Attired in nineteenth-century dandy clothes, they never once lost their good manners, even in the face of every con-

Alphonse and Gaston (F. B. Opper), ca. 1905

ceivable catastrophe. Their constant scraping and bowing and their repeated exchanges of courtesy constituted most of the strip's appeal. "After you, my dear Alphonse," "No, after *you*, my dear Gaston," phrases that recurred like a leitmotif, have now come to ironically symbolize the pitfalls of unbridled decorum.

Opper introduced week-to-week continuity in his new feature (which ran under descriptive titles, changing with each episode, before acquiring its definitive name) ahead of his use of the same device in *Happy Hooligan*. Thus the two dapper Frenchmen, often in the company of their equally daffy but less fastidious Parisian friend Leon, found themselves in the throes of some awful predicament — such as being captured by Indians, or falling down a raging torrent (usually caused by their stubborn sticking to etiquette; but somehow they always succeeded in extricating themselves from peril in the following week's installment.

Alphonse and Gaston enjoyed tremendous success in the first decade of this century and might have continued indefinitely had not Opper tired of its basic situation. The characters appeared more and more rarely after 1910, only turning up in other Opper strips after losing their own title, and they virtually faded from view in the 1920s. Their names, however, endure to this day.

M.H.

THE AMAZING ADVENTURES OF JOHNNY-ROUND-THE-WORLD
See JOHNNY-ROUND-THE-WORLD

THE AMAZING SPIDER-MAN
1977–present

In 1963 comic-book writer and editor Stan Lee teamed up with artist Steve Ditko to create *The Amazing Spider-Man*, a series about a troubled teenager who suddenly and unexpectedly acquired superhuman powers. The outlandish premise (unabashedly exploiting male adolescent power fantasies), coupled with Ditko's snazzy style and Lee's fulsome phraseology, caught on like wildfire among pimpled youths all over the land, on and off campus. This led to Spi-

der-Man toys, tee-shirts, posters, paperbacks—and in 1977 to a newspaper daily and Sunday feature also called *The Amazing Spider-Man* and initially distributed by the Register and Tribune Syndicate.

As in the comic-book version, the shy, insecure high school student Peter Parker got his abilities to climb walls, his superstrength, and his superagility from the bite of a radioactive spider (how the arachnid and its victim survived radioactive poisoning was never made clear). Thus turned into Spider-Man (also known as Spidey and the Webslinger), the superpowered youth donned a skintight costume and went out battling an endless array of supervillains with names like the Green Goblin and Kraven the Hunter. The story lines alternate between superheroics and soap-opera melodramatics, and are narrated by Lee in his characteristically arch and cliché-ridden prose.

The hokum that attaches to any superhero fantasy was in the case of Spider-Man redeemed in great part by the talent of the first artist to work on the newspaper strip, John Romita, whose breathless depictions of action scenes and eye-catching layouts (especially in the Sunday color pages) glossed over the pompous first-person narration and the verbose dialogue. Unfortunately Romita was succeeded in the early 1980s by Lee's brother Larry Lieber, whose tenure has resulted in the strips going into a marked artistic decline. Spider-Man's juvenile adventures, still scripted by the septuagenarian Lee in an increasingly creaky mode, are now being distributed by King Features Syndicate.

M.H.

AND HER NAME WAS MAUD!
1904–1932

One Sunday in July a Vermont farmer named Si Slocum bought a mule: her name was Maud and she proved to be the most stubborn, vindictive, and ornery creature this side of the galaxy. This could have been the opening sen-

And Her Name Was Maud! (F. B. Opper), ca. 1910

tence of a morality tale, but it was in fact the starting episode of Frederick Opper's latest comic series, which made its debut in W. R. Hearst's newspaper pages on July 24, 1904.

Kicking her way to fame, Maud first displayed her prowess by catapulting the hapless Si clear across the field, under the eyes of his wife Mirandy. This turned into a weekly ritual, and the feature became firmly established as *And Her Name Was Maud!,* with the mule demonstrating her propulsive skills on farmhands, debt collectors, visiting relatives, and undesirable vagabonds alike. The strip, Stephen Becker wrote in *Comic Art in America,* "was an endless variation on an ancient and explosive theme...and the plot varied only in nonessentials." All through the years the bewhiskered (and bewildered) Si tried to get rid of the intractable mule, only to be rewarded with a cataclysmic kick. Maud often dropped in on Opper's other creations, *Happy Hooligan* and *Alphonse and Gaston,* seemingly just to practice her skills on characters other than the rustics populating her own strip.

Maud has been viewed in later years as the embodiment of indomitable nature rebelling against the forces of civilization trying to tame her. It doesn't seem, however, that Opper intended his creation to be much more than a boisterous entertainment, and if he was still alive, he would probably express his amused puzzlement at this conceit.

Maud herself was temporarily dropped from Opper's gallery of characters in the mid-1910s, but the feature was revived in 1926 and ran as the companion strip to *Happy Hooligan,* until they both came to an end after Opper's retirement in 1932.

M.H.

ANDY CAPP
1963–present

robably the most famous naturalized American of the comic pages, Andy Capp was born a British subject on August 5, 1957, in the northern edition of the *Daily Mirror.* His origins may have been English, but his appeal was universal and he soon conquered the world, starting with the United States, where he made his first appearance on September 16, 1963, in a daily strip distributed by Publishers Syndicate; a Sunday version soon followed.

Under either nationality Andy is undoubtedly the king of the layabouts and the ne'er-do-wells (his crown is a cap too big for his head). When not busy dodging creditors, he can usually be found at the corner saloon in the company of his equally disreputable pal Chalky. There, cigarette dangling from his lips, he holds forth on any subject under the sun, particularly after the imbibing of countless pints of beer. His favorite companions are barflies, racetrack touts, smalltime crooks, and other low types of the same ilk. His wife Flo is much put-upon, abused, and exploited, but she shows no sign of leaving Andy or even standing up to him. The strip would seem to go against the grain of modern sensibilities, yet *Andy Capp* enjoys tremendous success with the highbrows and the progressive crowd.

The fact is that the main character displays a certain flair in his nonactivities. Work is sacred to him (he never touches it), and when Flo calls him good at nothing, he replies:

Apartment 3-G (**Dallis and Kotzky**), © 1968 Publishers Newspaper Syndicate

"I'm not good at it, I'm *very* good." Again told by his wife that a pal of his had tried to kiss her, Andy remarks without rising from the sofa on which he had been taking his afternoon nap: "I'll belt him tonight when 'e's sober." In this age of gender equality Andy stands as a figure of wish-fulfillment for husbands everywhere, as he goes blissfully his own way, guzzling down his beer and pinching the bar waitresses, in total oblivion of the obligations of work and home.

M.H.

ANNIE
See LITTLE ORPHAN ANNIE

APARTMENT 3-G
1961–present

r. Nicholas Dallis, a psychiatrist turned comic-strip writer, had in the early 1960s two successful soap-opera strips to his credit, *Rex Morgan, M.D.,* and *Judge Parker,* both starring male protagonists. To correct this glaring gender imbalance the good doctor decided on not one but three female leads for his new feature. Called *Apartment 3-G,* it came out daily and Sunday in May 1961, with illustrations done by Alex Kotzky and distribution assured by Publishers Syndicate.

The three women sharing apartment 3-G in a New York City building all wear their natural hair color and run true to stereotype. Margo Magee, an executive secretary, is a brainy brunette; the redheaded Tommy Thompson, big-hearted and short-tempered, started as a nurse; and the blonde LuAnn was initially a school teacher with a tendency to ebullience and flirtiness. The familiar plots revolve around the trio of heroines trying to get ahead in the world and to cope with the myriad problems, big and small, faced by young women in the big city. Romantic interludes abound, and the three attractive leads have each known a number of sentimental attachments (always short of consummation). So far only the bubbly LuAnn got married, but her husband, an Air Force pilot, was shot down over

Vietnam a few years later; declared missing in action he was eventually listed as killed in combat. LuAnn, now a wealthy widow, puts her money in the service of worthy causes, such as the environment and help for troubled youths in disadvantaged neighborhoods.

The only permanent male presence in the strip is Professor Papagoras, a very Hemingway-like character who happens to live in the same building. Through him Dr. Dallis was able to dispense psychological advice to his characters, and through them to the readers. For a brief period in the 1970s the strip's name was changed to *The Girls in Apartment 3-G,* but protest from women readers prompted the syndicate to revert to the original title.

If the plot lines are predictable, special praise should be given to Alex Kotzky, whose sophisticated style reflects a very appealing exuberance, freshness, and joie de vivre. Since Dallis's death in 1991, Kotzky has also taken over the scripting of the feature.

M.H.

APPLE MARY
See MARY WORTH

ARCHIE
1947–present

A newspaper comic strip generated by a comic-book series, *Archie* had already attracted a large following by the time the daily and Sunday newspaper feature debuted. It originated in *Pep Comics* #22 and *Jackpot Comics* #4, both published by MLJ Magazines, Inc., in December 1941, as a six-page supporting feature. Despite its inauspicious birth, it was a hit from the start, and Archie went on to become the leading nonsuperhero in the comics.

Created by MLJ partner John Goldwater (whose first-name initial provided the final letter in the publisher's corporate name), Archie is a wholesome middle-class youngster epitomizing the emerging teenage subculture. Based in

part on such then popular characters as Andy Hardy in the movies and Henry Aldrich on the radio, he gets into comical scrapes by innocently overreaching himself, never as a result of malice, greed, or cruelty. So popular were this nice young fellow and his one-dimensional associates that the comic-book feature soon displaced all the rest of MLJ's series, and the company ultimately changed its name to Archie Comic Publications, Inc. The character eventually gave rise to a giant industry, spawning no fewer than thirty-five comic-book titles, ten digest series, and many foreign-language versions, along with radio and television shows, a rock-and-roll group named the Archies, and numberless licensed products. By 1969, the *Archie* comic books were the industry leaders, selling over a million issues a month. Among their most enduring progeny was a newspaper strip, written and drawn by Bob Montana, the first artist Goldwater assigned to the project, and initially distributed by King Features Syndicate in 1947.

The newspaper strip starred a somewhat older and more worldly hero than Montana's original figure, but it surrounded him with the same cast of characters. By 1947, Archie Andrews's buck teeth had been straightened out and he had matured from a barefoot boy with cheek of tan to a sanitized version of the "typical teenager," a freckle-faced redhead living in the idealized suburban community of Riverdale. Fred and Mary Andrews, his patient and somewhat bewildered parents, are a model middle-aged and middle-class couple, eternally bemused by the younger generation but exercising little influence on it. Archie may try their understanding, but there is no hint of domestic conflict.

Similarly there is little real conflict in Archie's idyllic social life. His best pal, an esurient beanpole called Jughead (Forsythe P. Jones III), represents neither intellectual nor romantic competition, since the primary focus of his life is food. Archie's chaste love life centers on the twin temptations of a wholesome girl-next-door type, the blonde Betty Cooper, and the slinky subdeb Veronica Lodge. His efforts at juggling the affections of both involve him in the sort of merry mix-ups appropriate to such a dilemma. To add some

Archie, TM & © 1988 Archie Comic Pub., Inc.

TM & ©1988 ARCHIE COMIC PUB., INC.

tension to this innocent triangle, the sleek lounge-lizard Reggie Mantle keeps Archie on his toes by competing for the attentions of both girls.

A vast array of stock characters play supporting roles in the saga. Veronica's rich parents, a caricature of the haughty upper class, are perpetually shocked at the plebeian behavior of their daughter's friends. Archie's athletic ineptitude is the despair of Riverdale High School's gym teacher, Coach Kleats, and his inevitable mistakes in the school lab and chemical experiments terrify the science teacher, Mr. Flutesnoot, as well as Mr. Svenson, the Swedish janitor. The skinny spinster Miss Grundy hounds Archie for his homework, and the irascible principal Mr. Weatherbee is forever falling into helpless rages, his cheap toupée flying off his head in classic cartoon style. For comfort and support, and as an antidote to Miss Beazly's repulsive school cafeteria food, the student body of Riverdale High turns to the hamburgers and milkshakes at Pop's Choklit Shoppe and to its proprietor, the ever genial Pop Tate.

Archie's schoolmates include such standard types as Moose, a hulking simpleton on the Riverdale High football team, and the bespectacled brain Dilton Doily, who depends on his slide rule for answers to all of life's problems. The minor characters have their own little romantic involvements: Moose is devoted to his girlfriend Midge and threatens anyone who looks too closely at her, and the wallflower Big Ethel haplessly pursues the misogynist Jughead.

Sustained by Bob Montana until his death in 1975, the newspaper strip was taken over by Dan DeCarlo, one of the Archie Publications staff artists, who wrote and drew it until 1993. Since then it has been produced by Henry Scarpelli, joined by Craig Boldman in March 1994. Respectful of the positive tone and the animated drawing of what had become an American institution, Montana's successors have remained true to the strip's cheerful, upbeat style. It has remained contemporary in its props and its references —Archie has replaced his antique jalopy with an up-to-date car and the characters all use electronic gadgets—but it has never deviated from the positive outlook that won the hearts of teenagers and their parents in the 1940s. *Archie* is now distributed by Creators Syndicate.

D.W.

B.C.
`1958–present`

This humorous farce of prehistoric man by former magazine cartoonist Johnny Hart debuted daily on February 17, 1958; the Sunday version followed on October 19. Distributed by the New York Herald-Tribune Syndicate, it is set during the dawn of recorded time and is the quintessential gag strip, ribbing the foibles and follies of contemporary life from its anachronistic milieu. A groundbreaking mixture of concept and structure from the outset, it was a sophisticated model that mixed significance with slapstick.

B.C., the unassuming title character, is a naive, humble Everyman, surrounded by more colorful neophytes like Thor, ladies' man and inventor of the wheel and other practical or obtuse inventions, and the sarcastic punster Curls. Two women simply called Fat Broad and Cute Chick provide the heavy and romantic interests respectively, while offering an attempted female perspective. Philosopher, huckster, and egotist, Peter is the resident shrink whose periodic correspondence with a nameless "pen" pal across the ocean proves the existence of other, equally sardonic civilizations. Sight gags abound—from the hirsute, subhuman Grog, a surreal clown discovered frozen in a glacier, to the aptly named Clumsy Carp, a near-sighted ichthyologist most adroit when submerged, who can actually make waterballs. His counterpart is peg-legged Wiley, a superstitious poet who abhors water in any form. Like a comic Casey Stengel, he coaches hapless sports teams, despite the lack of opponents.

Wiley's introspective and whimsical poetry display the cartoonist's love of limerick and wordplay, and of late these verbal puzzles, anagrams, and daffynitions have comprised much of the strip via *The Book of Phrases, Show Me,* and *Wiley's Dictionary.* Writing assistants Dick Boland, Jack Caprio, and former *Winthrop* cartoonist Dick Cavalli help Hart create these grammatical games. Literal manifestations of slang expressions playfully reflect our language, such as "dip (idiot) in road" and "paying three (shellfish) clams". Another unique convention is the playful correlation of invented sound to action; "Zot" for the strike of lightning or the anteater's tongue, "Gronk" for a dinosaur's scream, and "Zak" for the striking of an object are onomatopoeic trademarks for this visceral strip.

An eclectic menagerie of talking flora and fauna share the spotlight, adding a unique and loony dimension. Originally B.C.'s pet, an anteater, wanders the plain, nabbing prey with its adroit tongue, a droll scavenger whose occasional consort is an armadillo. The ant colony represents a separate fractured modality: a diminutive subculture disassociated from the general purlieus. This entomological burlesque provides the strip's best vehicle for its wry slant on social ills. Ol' John the turtle and his companion and passenger the Dookey bird are zoological parodies of Bob and Ray, a comedic team perfectly suited for *B.C.*'s one-liners and usual slapstick, delivered in Hart's most endearing fashion. The struggle against intolerance is personified by the inexorable Fat Broad's pursuit of the pitiful snake, a despised creature who is pummeled by this invidious woman and the seemingly malevolent whims of fate. A dinosaur, walking clams, a neurotic turkey, and a verbose kiwi are additional players, providing the artist with a diverse cast and unlimited framework for gag potential.

Since the mid-1980s, Hart's increased religious commitment has found its way into *B.C.* Spiritually inspired stories mix with the usual fare, creating a shared entity of humor and message, providing theological answers to the existential questions raised throughout the run of the strip. Sitting atop a mountain, a Great Guru answers the inquiries of the bewildered cavemen with amusing insight. This, along with regular features like Free Advice, Miss Know-It-All, and the Truth Pedestal, convey the characters' yearning for answers within a framework of incongruous absurdity.

Hart has always reduced his visual presentation to its simplest form, creating a masterful blend of concision and controlled spontaneity. Visual ideas are often derived by manipulating environmental elements, instilling further the creative edge that separates this feature from its peers.

B.C. (J. Hart), © 1972 Field Enterprises

Syndicated currently in some twelve hundred newspapers, *B.C.* has been reprinted in over thirty-five collections and animated for several television commercials and specials. Recipient of the 1968 Reuben Award for Outstanding Cartoonist of the Year by the National Cartoonists Society, Hart's greatest achievement is the pleasure he has brought to millions of readers daily for decades, and the legions of younger cartoonists who marvel and derive influence from his mastery.

B.J.

BANANA OIL
1921–1930

Banana Oil was started by the irrepressible Milt Gross in December 1921 as a daily strip for the *New York World.* In 1926 it evolved into the top strip of the author's new Sunday color feature, *Nize Baby,* distributed by the *World*'s Press Publishing Company.

Banana Oil has been termed by some "not a strip," but this is a mischaracterization. The feature was certainly a strip in the formal sense since it appeared in a row of panels laid across the newspaper page; while it did not have a recurrent cast of characters, it did have a recurrent theme succinctly summarized by its title.

In his strip Gross endeavored to deflate the small hypocrisies without which life would be unbearable and communication between people almost impossible. In one example a portly, middle-aged father declared to a pretty schoolteacher that he had come only because of his "being naturally interested in the lad's education," while from the corner where he was standing, dunce cap on his head, his grinning offspring gleefully exclaimed, "Banana oil!" At another time a male actor was dutifully declaiming to his female partner in the play, "Marry me, and later love will come!," when a married spectator cried out from his orchestra seat, "Banana oil!" On yet another occasion a penurious suitor in a posh restaurant declared to the steward that no wine on the list was good enough for his taste, with his date grumbling *sotto voce,* "Banana oil!" The expression was adopted throughout the 1920s as a catchphrase signifying amused disbelief at a really egregious piece of cant, much as the later and still-used "baloney" that replaced it.

Banana Oil (M. Gross), © 1924 Press Publishing Co.

Gross spun out his little vignettes debunking human foibles and pretensions with almost unflagging imagination and infinite wit. *Banana Oil* ceased publication, along with *Nize Baby,* when the *World* came to an end in 1930.

M.H.

THE BANTAM PRINCE
See BODYGUARD

BARNABY
1942–1952, 1963

One of the most highly praised comic strips in the history of the medium, Crockett Johnson's literate satire-fantasy *Barnaby* was perhaps always caviar to the general public. Its syndicate never claimed a larger circulation than fifty-two newspapers in the United States and twelve overseas, yet the strip was described by the *Philadelphia Record* as "in every sense a major creation" and received the enthusiastic acclaim of *Life, Time,* and *Newsweek* and from such artists and writers as Rockwell Kent, Louis Untermeyer, and Robert Nathan. Dorothy Parker wrote, in a review of the first published collection of the strip, that "Barnaby and his friends are the most important additions to American arts and letters in Lord knows how many years."

Crockett Johnson, born David Johnson Leisk, had been a magazine art director and a freelance advertising artist and gag cartoonist before creating *Barnaby.* Subtly ironic, allusive, and visually innovative, the strip took Johnson two years to sell, but it was finally accepted by the liberal New York newspaper *P.M.,* where it debuted on April 20, 1942. The next year it was picked up by the Chicago Sun-Times Syndicate (it was later transferred to the Bell Syndicate), and within a year of its inception the daily strip had developed a small but enthusiastic following among intellectuals. Hardcover book collections published in 1942 and 1943, a quarterly magazine, an animated film, a stage play, a radio series, a TV special, and a popular song attested to its popularity, and even after its demise in 1952 it continued to appear in translation and as a weekly radio show in Japan.

Surprisingly for so cerebral a strip, it was much loved by children. Johnson himself found the fact puzzling; "I never aimed at the kids," he has been quoted as saying. The animated version he did for television, however, was not successful and was discontinued after a single trial episode. *Barnaby* also had a Sunday page in color in 1950, but it lasted only a few months.

The strip centered on a bright, clear-headed little boy, Barnaby Baxter, and his orotund fairy godfather Jackeen J. O'Malley, who combined the rhetorical style of a medicine-show huckster with that of Dickens's Mr. Micawber. In its first three days, the tone and the theme of the strip's entire run was established with the five-year-old wishing he had a fairy godmother and Mr. O'Malley flying through his window and smashing the cigar he used as a magic wand as he crash-landed on the floor. The diminutive elf, about the size of Barnaby, then introduced himself grandly, taking off on his pink wings, and falling into the rosebushes.

The failure of Mr. O'Malley's showy magic ever to come off quite as planned was one of the recurring motifs of the strip. Another was Barnaby's futile efforts at convincing his parents, or any other adult, of O'Malley's existence; in fact, at one point O'Malley himself was bewildered by their lack of contact and observes, "If, and sometimes I doubt it, your parents actually do exist, I cannot but conclude they're avoiding me!" Circumstantial evidence abounded, and O'Malley and the Baxters *almost* met repeatedly, but somehow Barnaby's relentlessly realistic parents remained convinced that the child's companion was imaginary. Only Barnaby's contemporaries, and the strip's fortunate readers, knew the real truth.

The issue of imagination versus reality that provided the underlying theme of *Barnaby* was complicated and enriched by a supporting cast of players on each side: the Baxters' friends, relatives, and colleagues, who continued to smile at the child's fantasy, and O'Malley's strange circle of companions, who remained just outside the scope of adult perception. Between the two planes of existence were Barnaby and his equally perceptive little friend Jane, along with Barnaby's pooch Gorgon, who discovered one day in 1943 that he could talk, although grown-ups never seemed to hear him. O'Malley's pals and adversaries included Gus, the timid, bespectacled ghost, who fainted at seeing mortals and found haunting houses frightening; Atlas, the minuscule giant (actually a mental giant who answered the most obvious questions, usually incorrectly, by means of a slide rule); Lancelot McSnoyd, a wise-cracking invisible leprechaun with a Brooklyn accent whose greatest pleasure was trying to deflate the grandiloquent O'Malley; and various ogres, witches, and assorted members of his club, the Elves, Leprechauns, Gnomes, and Little Men's Chowder and Marching Society.

The somewhat casually plotted stories in *Barnaby*, which neatly dovetailed into each other through the years, were always subordinated to the strip's characters and sophisticated wordplay, and often depended for such coherence as they had on O'Malley's personality. Almost invariably Barnaby and the forces of good triumphed through O'Malley's unique combination of magical powers and personal ineptitude. He blundered, for example, into defeating Nazi spies, war profiteers, and other villains appropriate to the early 1940s, and in defiance of all logic pulled down a corrupt politician and got himself elected to Congress by not showing up for the campaign; and as a Hollywood screenwriter, he almost got away with selling *The Decline and Fall of the Roman Empire*. Whatever happened, the unflappable little pixie emerged unscathed and undismayed.

Drawn with an austere elegance that lent great visual distinction to the strip, *Barnaby* included backgrounds re-

Barnaby (C. Johnson), © 1946 The Newspaper P.M.

duced to almost Asian simplicity and included no superfluous detail or shading. The figures, animate and inanimate, were rendered entirely in outlines and solid patches of black, and the facial expressions were expressively conveyed with the most minimal lines. An unprecedented feature of the strip was its use of typeset dialogue. Johnson admitted to being less than expert at the laborious job of lettering, and so, having studied typography at Cooper Union, he set the text of his speeches in a clear, legible typeface and had them printed before sending the strip in for publication. According to the artist's estimate, the device enabled him to increase the word count by 60 percent.

Johnson reported that he had undertaken the strip as a way to assure himself a steady living, but within four or five years he began to find the demand of a daily strip oppressive and turned to assistants for help. His signature stopped appearing on the strip on December 28, 1945, and during the fall of the next year it was signed by Ted Ferro, who had taken over the writing, and Jack Morley, who was drawing it. Johnson retained artistic control and reportedly sat in on story conferences with his successors, which assured continuity of style in both the art and the story line. Nevertheless, some critics have written that although Morley's art was indistinguishable from Johnson's and the transition was virtually unnoticeable in the scripting, the strip had begun to slip. After a year Johnson resumed the authorship of the strip, and it appeared signed "Jack Morley & C.J.," but it had already begun to lose papers. In 1952, when Johnson decided to bring *Barnaby* to an end, he took over the full job to deliver the *coup de grace*. Ten years later, he undertook to bring the strip back to life for the Hall Syndicate, rewriting and modernizing some of the stories from the first year, but the spirit was gone, and the venture was abandoned after a short run.

But *Barnaby* has never lost its loyal, if small, following. Although the strip was rich in topical references in its first years, the two collections of early strips have not become dated, and they have been reprinted frequently.

D.W.

BARNEY BAXTER
1935–1950

*I*nitially called *Barney Baxter in the Air*, this aviation strip was created at the end of 1935 by cartoonist and illustrator Frank Miller as a special feature for the junior page of the Denver-based *Rocky Mountain News*, on whose staff the artist was employed at the time. Later transferred to Hearst's *New York Mirror* it soon gained wider recognition, and on December 7, 1936, it received national distribution as a daily strip by King Features Syndicate, which added a Sunday page on February 21, 1937.

Barney Baxter (F. Miller), © 1942 King Features Syndicate

In his Colorado personification Barney had been a freckle-faced, ebullient lad of about 12 who loved airplanes and flying, and through his strip he had been instructing his juvenile audience in the finer points of the science of aeronautics. The mountain air must have stunted his growth, for no sooner did he get a New York outlet than he grew into young adulthood overnight; he was to remain in his twenties for the rest of his career.

The first continuities had Barney spreading his wings in the company of his contemporary, Hap Walters, and under the tutelage of an older, bemustached pilot called Cyclone Smith who introduced the fledgling to the subtler maneuvers in the art of flying, such as making an Immelman turn from a takeoff.

Late in 1937 Barney went adventuring solo, and in the course of his aerial wanderings he met a South Seas beauty named Maura who became his on-again, off-again love interest for the remainder of the feature. In another episode, forced to make a crash landing in Alaska, he was rescued by a grizzled gold prospector, Gopher Gus, who later turned into his constant companion and comic sidekick. Gopher Gus was drawn with a cartoony, caricatural line that detracted from the straight tone of the story lines.

Miller was an ardent supporter of the Allied cause in World War II, and in September 1941, months before the attack on Pearl Harbor, he had his protagonist enlist in the Royal Air Force to take part "in the crusade against the destroyers of civilization." By maintaining the Sunday continuities separate from the dailies, the author could keep his hero fighting the Nazis and the Japanese simultaneously. Thus on weekdays Barney snatched young King Jan of Slavania out of the clutches of the invading German armies in the nick of time, while in the Sundays he bombed Tokyo in a sequence drawn weeks ahead of the Doolittle raid, one of the many instances of art anticipating life.

Late in 1942 Miller suffered a heart attack, and as a replacement the syndicate called on Bob Naylor, who involved Barney and Gus in some of the most bloodcur-

dling encounters with the Japanese ever depicted in the comics. In 1946 Miller, having recovered and back from a stint in the Coast Guard, came to reclaim *Barney Baxter*. His hero, now much more sedate and adult, stopped collecting girlfriends and eventually married the long-suffering Maura. For his part Gopher Gus got himself elected Grand Lama in Tibet after flying a much needed cargo of penicillin there.

Miller died of another heart attack in December 1949, and his strip died with him. The last daily appeared on January 7, 1950, while the Sunday came to an end on January 22. While it lasted, *Barney Baxter* was an entertaining, accurately drawn aviation feature that at its best more than held its own against the competition in a crowded field.

M.H.

BARNEY GOOGLE AND SNUFFY SMITH
1919–present

*T*he history of *Barney Google and Snuffy Smith* is that of two strips, loosely tied together by occasional appearances of the first lead character and by the line of authorship from the strip's creator to his protégé.

The strip created by Billy DeBeck in 1919 featured the antics of a saucer-eyed runt of a loser named Barney Google, usually bedecked in a silk hat, tie, and black coat and ever on the prowl for gorgeous chorus girls, enough money to enter his horse in a derby, or a scheme that allowed him to accumulate some prestige. As Stephen Becker wrote in *Comic Art in America*, his adventures were those of "the fool, the dupe, the pawn of society." The settings and language of *Barney Google* were those of city life— the racetrack, the nightclub, the sporting arena, and the street. Movie stars, famous athletes, and beautiful women, whom DeBeck learned to draw in his youth when he copied the drawings of Charles Dana Gibson and sold them as originals, made cameo appearances in early stories.

The strip fashioned by DeBeck after 1934, and inherited upon his death in 1942 by his assistant, Fred Lasswell, was a world removed. The setting was the remotest back hills of Appalachia, where the main character was attired in patched trousers, a checkered or polka-dotted shirt, and a floppy, oversized black hat; where the language was spiced with backwoodsy dialect that required its own lexicon; and where the main preoccupation was evading and occasionally shooting it out with the revenooers.

Running through the more than seventy-five years of work were the creative geniuses of DeBeck and Lasswell, responsible for the total run of the strip, except for a few months in 1942–43, when Joe Musial drew it. DeBeck had a career before *Barney*, having been employed by newspapers in Youngstown, Ohio, Pittsburgh, and Chicago to draw editorial cartoons and create strips, among which were *Finn an' Haddie*, *Married Life*, and *Ollie Moses and O'Mara, Inc.* He started as a staff artist on the *Chicago Daily News* in 1908 at age 18, and ten years later he found himself working for Hearst when the tycoon bought the

Chicago Herald, where DeBeck was comic artist, and merged it with the *Examiner.* Traces of Barney were already visible, notably in *Married Life,* which showcased a taller version of Barney named Aleck.

Take Barney Google, F'rinstance first appeared in the *Chicago Herald and Examiner* on June 17, 1919, signed "DeBeck Toledo Ohio." DeBeck was in Toledo as a sports cartoonist covering the Dempsey/Willard championship fight. The cartoon, which ran across the length of the *Herald and Examiner* sports page, showed Barney scheming to sneak away from his wife and daughter at an outing so that he could hang around prizefighters at Willard's camp. After the fight, the strip became a regular feature, concentrating on Barney's attempts at being a song promoter, booking agent, and office worker before he went off to the World Series in October. In the space of that quarter year, *Take Barney Google F'rinstance* became nationally syndicated through King Features. During the next few months, Barney was established as a character, the type of guy who loses his money playing poker or chasing Ziegfeld showgirls and suffers the wrath of his much larger wife, "Sweet Woman." As henpecked as Aleck, Barney actually shrinks in size by the 1920s, probably to more accurately represent the power relationship with his wife.

DeBeck's fame and salary skyrocketed to near the top in the 1920s, as *Barney* became the subject of the 1923 hit tune, "Barney Google with the Goo-Goo Googly Eyes," written by Billy Rose, and a slew of all types of merchandise. The strip left its imprint, adding to the language such words and phrases as "goo-goo eyes," "horsefeathers," "hotsy totsy," "yardbird," "heebie jeebies," and after Snuffy's advent, "time's a-wastin," "jughaid," "shifless skonk," "balls o' fire," and "tetched in the haid."

Much of the strip's success was owed to the introduction in 1922 of Spark Plug, a very expressive horse draped to its ankles in a checked blanket that buttoned. Barney inherited Spark Plug in an unusual way; he was given the pick of a bunch of two-year-olds as a reward for breaking the fall of the rotund stable owner when he was unceremoniously

tossed out of a tavern window. Spark Plug changed the strip and Barney's life. Soon after receiving him, Barney entered Spark Plug in the Abadaba Handicap, which he miraculously won, making his new owner $50,000 richer. The money was squandered quickly as Barney continued his pursuit of "sweet mammas" (very pleasantly different from the "Sweet Woman"), winning horses, and poker hands. Throughout the rest of the Spark Plug saga, Barney was constantly conniving to scrape together enough money to enter his horse in the derbies; at the same time he was trying to keep his black jockey Sunshine in check. In most races, Spark Plug "also ran," but occasionally he did win, thus avoiding a kick in the rear and sustaining the love-hate relationship he had with Barney.

After four years of this routine, DeBeck was ready for changes, which he sought from 1927 until 1934, a period when he was "all over the map," according to Brian Walker in his book *Barney Google and Snuffy Smith.* He experimented with themes that involved Barney as a flagpole sitter, candidate for U.S. president (both in 1928 and 1932), friend of Horseface Klotz, wealthy manager of world wrestling champion Sully, and leader of a secret society. DeBeck had fun with the latter, at times satirizing these fraternal orders; the Mysterious and Secret Order of the Brotherhood of Billy Goats lasted more than nine months, in 1927–28, as the strip's plot.

During more than seven years spent searching for a blockbuster formula, DeBeck studiously read on mountain lore, learning the peculiar dialect, supernatural beliefs, and history of family feuds of the mountaineers. On June 14, 1934, he radically reoriented the feature, taking it to the hills. In that strip, Barney was in a lawyer's office where he learned he had just inherited a relative's estate in North Carolina. The frenetic Barney was not very welcome in laid-back Hootin' Holler, even less so when Snuffy Smith and his wife Lowizie (later changed to Loweezey) showed up as a teaser in the November 17 strip.

Lasswell started as a letterer for DeBeck in 1934 when he was 17. His only time away from the strip was when he served in Africa as a Pan-American radio operator in 1942. After DeBeck's death that year, Lasswell returned to take over the strip and drew it even after he joined the Marines. Snuffy and Barney had already gone into the military earlier; Snuffy, partly because he was "countin' on that thutty dulers a month." During the war years, Snuffy turned up everywhere—in Bermuda, somewhere in Africa, at the Taj Mahal, and in Tokyo itself, where he had become the "Tokyo Terror." After the war, Barney and Snuffy were involved with schemes aplenty, such as their All American Bug Race, and an assortment of characters, including the sexy nightclub dancer Tiger L'il, Sadie the Bearded Lady, the sculptor Plaster from Paris, and Tieless Ty Tyler, the Tie Tycoon.

Gradually, Lasswell eased Barney out, so that by 1954 he no longer was a regular character. In his place, Lasswell put the hound dog Ol Bullet, Little Tater, Elviney, Lukey, and many more mountain folk; he also simplified the hillbilly dialect, at the same time adding words and phrases of his own coinage.

Both DeBeck and Lasswell varied panel sizes. *Barney* strips often contained one long panel without dividing

Barney Google (B. DeBeck), ca. 1925, © King Features Syndicate

Baron Bean (G. Herriman), 1918

lines that incorporated as many as six action or dialogue situations, while Snuffy could be seen during the Lasswell years, all alone in one panel, enjoying a panoramic view of his world.

DeBeck's widow Mary established the Billy DeBeck Award for best cartoonist in 1947, which was won in 1963 by Lasswell for *Barney Google and Snuffy Smith;* by that time, the award was called the Reuben.

J.A.L.

BARON BEAN
1916–1919

Probably George Herriman's most famous creation outside of *Krazy Kat, Baron Bean* started appearing daily on January 5, 1916, under syndication by Hearst's International News Service.

Baron Bean was a nobleman whose title was supposedly British and possibly not altogether genuine. Aided and abetted by his faithful retainer Grimes, he tried vainly to crash high society and to find his own fortune in the land of opportunity in the elusive person of that legendary creature known as the American heiress. His efforts were thwarted every time by his total and abject penuriousness: once on the verge of wedding a Pittsburgh heiress, he couldn't scrounge up the ten dollars for a marriage license. So, in order to survive, the baron had to resort to any low expedient to get a free meal, even when it involved getting thrown out of free-lunch bars, beaten up by hot tamale vendors, or cozying up to the neighbor's elephantine cook. No matter how low he had fallen, a full meal would always bring back his aristocratic cockiness. "With such a diet, I can acquire the noble bravery of the caveman, and still retain the customs of civilization," he once declared to the admiring Grimes. (Herriman had earlier dealt with the theme of the aristocratic moocher in his short-lived 1909 strip, *Baron Mooch.*)

As it eventually turned out, the baron was already married, and so was Grimes, and their wives jointly caught up with them. In a bit of typical irony, Herriman had Grimes's wife cowering in front of her shrimpish husband, while the baroness ("baronette," as she liked to be called) was pretty much in charge in her noble household. The wife was named Lucinda, and together with her husband they formed a perfect couple of harebrained dreamers ("barren bean" and "loose in the bean"). Many of the happenings now revolved around the baron's more or less sustained attempts to get away from his spouse, and his wife's stubborn efforts to get back her footloose husband, generally through her cooking.

Baron Bean's gallery of human characters was quite small. In addition to the baron, Grimes, and their wives, the only other people to appear with any regularity were Barney, the owner of the tavern where the baron repaired in search of a free meal or a soft touch, and Tomas Dorgano, the Mexican purveyor of tamales. (The name was in playful reference to Herriman's cartooning friend Thomas Dorgan.) On the other hand, animals were plentiful. "Animals are of great importance to a cartoonist," Herriman once wrote, "no matter what kind of strip he is drawing." In this particular strip there appeared hordes of dogs, legions of cats, a sea-horse, an ostrich, and even a zoo-escaped gnu (which the baron mistook for a cow, thus losing out on the $500 reward for bringing it back).

In its last months *Baron Bean* turned into another domestic-life strip, and Herriman grew increasingly disenchanted with it. He had various characters from his *Krazy Kat* page make cameo appearances for a change of pace, but ultimately he decided to terminate the feature. The last strip appeared on January 22, 1919.

M.H.

BARRY NOBLE
See HAP HOPPER

BATMAN
1943–1946, 1966–1974, 1989–1991

By the time Batman was launched in a newspaper strip in 1943, he was already one of the most popular comic-book costumed heroes in America. The Batman first appeared in National Periodical Publications' DC Comics title, *Detective Comics* #27 (May 1939), created to add to DC's stable of fantastic costumed heroes like Superman. Unlike most such comic-book heroes, however, the Batman (or just plain Batman) had no incredible powers. His creator, DC artist Bob Kane (with the collaboration of writer Bill Finger) modeled him after such mortal mysterious avengers as the Scarlet Pimpernel, El Zorro, and the Shadow.

The Batman was originally a grim vigilante who fought criminals in Gotham City, a stereotypical modern metropolis. He was really Bruce Wayne, a wealthy young socialite whose parents had been murdered before his eyes by a robber when he was a boy. Pledging his life to fighting crime, Wayne trained himself to the peak of athletic perfection and used his fortune to secretly develop such superscientific aids as a crime-analysis lab, the Batmobile, the Batplane, the Batarang (a boomerang to knock out criminals), and many others. In *Detective* #38 (April 1940), Batman met the boy who would become his lifelong companion: Dick Grayson, an almost-adolescent acrobat who was orphaned when his parents, the Flying Graysons, were killed by racketeers trying to shake down their circus. Bruce Wayne adopted Dick as his ward, and Batman acquired a partner in Robin, the Boy Wonder.

Such larger-than-life heroes needed appropriate adversaries against whom to pit themselves. A cast of flamboyantly grotesque supervillains slowly grew, dominated by the Joker, the "Clown Prince of Crime"—a homicidal maniac whose calling card was a venom that made his victims laugh themselves to death. Others included the Penguin, Two-Face, and Catwoman. In the 1940s DC Comics came under social pressure to tone down Batman's more legally questionable activities, such as personally killing criminals. The Dynamic Duo evolved from vigilantes into unofficial auxiliaries of Gotham City's Police Department, who could be summoned by Commissioner Gordon with a rooftop Bat-Signal searchlight for special cases.

Batman and Robin quickly grew beyond the lead feature in *Detective Comics*. They won their own title, *Batman*, in Spring 1940, and then expanded into *World's Finest Comics* (Spring 1941), where they regularly teamed up with Superman. But it was the appearance of the duo in *The Batman*, a 1943 Columbia movie serial, that led to their own newspaper strip. The McClure Syndicate expressed interest in a *Batman and Robin* newspaper strip while the Columbia serial was in production, and arrangements were made with the DC management for the regular *Batman* comic-book production team to supply it.

The head of the crew was the comic book's editor, Jack Schiff, who edited the comic strip during its three-year run. The only credit on the strip was to Bob Kane, the creator of *Batman*. Kane did personally draw the first few dailies, but soon cut back to penciling the strip only. Later stories were penciled by Jack Burnley. Charles Paris became the regular inker. Writers were Bill Finger, Don Cameron, and Alvin Schwartz. There were occasional exceptions: one daily story was written by Schiff himself, penciled by Dick Sprang, and inked by Stan Kaye, and a couple of Sunday stories were inked by Winslow Mortimer. Some of these stories were reworked comic-book adventures.

Batman and Robin began as a daily strip on October 25, 1943, with a separate Sunday strip starting on November 7. The strip was never as popular as the comic book, but the McClure Syndicate distributed it for three years. The Sunday strip ended on October 27, 1946, and the daily concluded on November 2. This strip was much more sedate than the comic-book adventures. The Dynamic Duo's exaggerated villains appeared occasionally—mostly in the Sunday pages—but most of the tales were detective puzzlers that did not require masked vigilantes. In fact, they were little different from the situations that Kerry Drake or the newspaper-strip incarnation of Perry Mason found themselves in.

The 1943–46 *Batman and Robin* was forgotten by the time of the second great wave of Batman popularity in the late 1960s. This was created by the camped-up *Biff! Pow! Zowie!* Batman TV program created for ABC-TV by producer William Dozier and writer Lorenzo Semple, Jr., starring Adam West and Burt Ward. It ran for 120 episodes, from January 12, 1966, through March 14, 1968.

DC Comics was again asked to produce a newspaper strip to take advantage of the show's popularity, this time for the Ledger Syndicate. This incarnation started out emulating the new TV persona of the Batman as a squeaky-clean do-gooder to the point of naiveté, but it gradually evolved closer to the regular comic-book dramatics. It ran from May 29, 1966 (Sundays) and May 30 (dailies) until July 1969 (Sundays) and February 26, 1972 (dailies). Bob Kane's name again appeared on it, but it was actually written by Whitney Ellsworth from its beginning until July 1970, and then by E. Nelson Bridwell until the beginning of 1972. Sheldon Moldoff drew both dailies and Sundays for the first three months, followed by Joe Giella from August 1966 until mid-March 1968 (with the exception that Carmine Infantino penciled the Sunday strips from September through mid-October 1966), then by Al Plastino from March 1968 until the beginning of 1972 (with some aid by Nick Cardy in late 1971). In January 1972, the Ledger Syndicate abruptly dismissed the DC Comics staff and began producing its own stories, which ran into 1974.

Batman's most recent newspaper appearance was due to his third mass-media resurrection in 1989, via the Robinless hit motion picture created by director Tim Burton and starring Michael Keaton as Batman and Jack Nicholson as the Joker. This *Batman* strip, with an integrated daily and Sunday story line, ran from November 6, 1989, through August 3, 1991, through the Creators Syndicate.

This latest *Batman* strip carried the byline of Marshall Rogers for its first story (artist Rogers was assisted by John Nyberg, and Max Allan Collins was the writer) and "Loebs-Cinfa-Nyberg" (writer William Messner-Loebs and artists Carmine Infantino and John Nyberg) for the seven following adventures. These stories emphasized Batman's famous villains (Catwoman, the Penguin, the Joker, etc.) in a continuing story line with a major subplot showing Bruce Wayne's personal relationship with Harvey Dent, Gotham City's district attorney who, when his face was scarred, went mad and became the criminal Two-Face.

F.P.

BEETLE BAILEY
1950–present

The usual way it was done was that a young man served his time in the military and then attended college (most often on the G.I. Bill) to prepare for a career. Beetle Bailey turned it around. He left college to join up and has gone on to serve the equivalent of more than two retirement-eligible careers—all as a private.

Beetle Bailey was the first of nine strips the one-man cartoon factory Mort Walker was to create. Walker, whose success as a cartoonist started in his early teens, was the top-selling magazine gag cartoonist of the late 1940s. After his military hitch in World War II, which he described as his "four years of free research," Walker enrolled at the University of Missouri, where he created cartoon characters for the school's humor magazine. One of them, a goof-off named Spiders, caught the eye of *Saturday Evening Post* cartoon editor John Bailey, who suggested that Walker feature him in more of his cartoons for the *Post.* Spider's name was changed, initially to Beetle Botts, and then Beetle Bailey, using the last name of the *Post* editor. The one-panel gags featuring Beetle grew into a strip on September 11, 1950, a day after Walker's twenty-seventh birthday.

The strip, contracted by King Features, started out as a continuity about Beetle's first week at Rockview U, but changed into a gag-a-day comic almost immediately. The inaugural strip gave the flavor of the ne'er-do-well character. Beetle is getting off the bus at the university when he is asked, "Aren't you going to get your luggage?" Beetle holds up his toothbrush. "How can you get along eight months with just that?" asks his fellow traveler. "Haven't you ever heard of roommates?" Beetle rejoins.

As a college strip, *Beetle Bailey* apparently did not bring the "rollicking" fun King announced it would, for after six months, only twenty-five clients signed on. Unknown to Walker, King planned to dump the strip at the end of the year's contract, but the Korean War proved to be the strip's savior. As the war heated up, Walker decided, against King's advice, to substitute Beetle's pork-pie hat for a soldier's overseas cap. On March 13, 1951, Beetle's two roommates drag the "enlistee" into the induction center, restrain him while he signs the papers, and help hold up his right hand so the recruiting officer can administer the oath. Because military experience was a common bond in the country at the time, a hundred newspapers rather quickly picked up the strip. *Beetle Bailey* eventually went on to become the third most widely distributed strip in comics history.

Walker made adjustments to his drawing style once Beetle was at Camp Swampy. In the college strips, he drew arches, ivy, or shadows across the campus, but no matter how hard he tried, he could not dress up an army barracks. Nevertheless, in its first years, the strip was embellished with much detail, shading, dialogue, and many elaborate scenes full of panoramas and large casts of supporting characters. These techniques were possible in the 1950s when people spent more time with the strips and editors were more generous with space.

Later, when he quit spotting uniforms with Benday grays, Walker gained his variety by adding blacks, usually in the

backgrounds and out of the center of focus. He accommodated to the smaller panel sizes by shrinking his characters' bodies without changing their head proportions and by cutting much dialogue, the results being rounder and cuter characters and an overall more precise, crisp, and direct strip.

Walker's simple but well-composed drawings have been a model for the profession. He (and Charles Schulz) tell jokes, not stories, thus making the humorous function paramount. Very often the humor is visual, associated with what R. C. Harvey, in *The Art of the Funnies,* calls the "charming comic abstractions of the human form." Characters in *Beetle Bailey* have elastic anatomies—Miss Buxley bending into an upside down *U* as she files, prompting General Halftrack to extend his entire body into a perfect horizontal plane as he sneaks a peek at her from behind his desk and doorway, or Beetle flattened into an accordion shape or a mass of separated body parts by Sarge.

Walker experiments with layout occasionally, using elongated panels to provide panoramic sweeps, strips full of handwritten dialogue or commentary, or simply twenty pictures of Sarge's head, all identical save one that, through his expression, gives the punchline.

But, more than anything else, *Beetle Bailey* derives its humor from the personalities of its characters, many based on Walker's friends from college or military days. Plato is patterned after his cartoonist buddy, Dik Browne, and Otto, Sarge's dog, is the spitting image of its owner. Walker used to try out a new character at least once a year, until it became confusing to deal with such a large cast. As a result, some characters were written out of the strip, such as Canteen, Snake Eyes, Big Blush, Fireball, Bammy, Dawg, Moocher, Pop, Cosmo, Ozone, and others.

Of his continuing stars, Walker favors drawing Sergeant Orville P. Snorkel, because he looks funny in all positions and because he takes up a lot of space that normally required filling in with backgrounds or other characters. In Walker's 1984 book, *The Best of Beetle Bailey,* Beetle's philosophy is summarized as "Whenever the urge to work comes over me, I lie down until it goes away," and Sergeant Snorkel is characterized as a career army type who is so immersed in military life that he thinks a "civilian is a soldier in drag," while Zero is an "innocent young farm boy as sweet, honest, and unsophisticated as an ear of corn," and General Amos T. Halftrack is a leader who "couldn't lead a cub scout to a candy store."

The introduction of two characters, Lieutenant Flap and Miss Buxley, caused Walker some headaches. Lieutenant Flap, with his afro and goatee, was one of the first blacks in modern strips portrayed in a positive way. In his first appearance on October 5, 1970, he barks to Sarge, "How come there's no blacks in this honkey outfit?" Initially, some readers protested that Walker was either propagandizing for or

Beetle Bailey (M. Walker), © 1970 King Features Syndicate

ridiculing blacks. Three Southern newspapers refused to carry any Lieutenant Flap episodes, and *Stars and Stripes* temporarily banned the strip. In 1971, the voluptuous, miniskirted Miss Buxley appeared, much to the delight of most readers, and by 1982, to the chagrin of feminists who said she was a sexual stereotype and that Walker promoted sexual harassment. Some editors censored the strip, but Walker kept her in, even writing a book, *Miss Buxley: Sexism in Beetle Bailey?*, about the brouhaha.

At other times, the military did not look kindly at *Beetle Bailey*. In 1954, *Stars and Stripes* banned the strip, claiming it was bad for morale (whose, the officers'?) and gave a negative view of the military. King Features capitalized on the ban, which lasted a decade, by advertising "Send your soldier in the Far East something he wants—his hometown paper with *Beetle Bailey*."

Walker contends that the strip is neither sexist nor antiarmy, that it is about "these dumb people that act" sexist and that it plays on our common resentment of any authority, not just the military. He admits that *Beetle Bailey* is "full of constant comment," that it is "ambivalent and bilateral," and that it usually pokes fun at bureaucracy and the system. Other messages find their way into the strip, including private jokes, potshots at other cartoons and their characters, and hype for the profession, the international cartoon museum Walker has created, and the funnies' centennial.

Beetle Bailey is a tribute to Walker's complete mastery of the comic strip, blending visual and verbal gags, slapstick, social commentary, and very funny and memorable characters.

J.A.L.

BELVEDERE
1974–present

While ostensibly a dog strip named for the brown pooch with black spots that is its main protagonist, *Belvedere* actually depends more for its appeal on screwball humor, even surreal fantasy, than on predictable canine shenanigans. It started as a daily panel, drawn and written by George Crenshaw, and distributed by Field Enterprises, in March 1974, but soon evolved into a full-fledged newspaper feature.

By all outward appearances, Orville and Myrtle Dibble are a typical suburban couple living in a typical frame house in typical Floogle County. Their nuclear family is made up of Jezebel the cat and Chi-Chi the parrot in addition to Belvedere, the family mutt, rebel, and ringleader. A stickler for rights (his), Belvedere insists on his master wearing a coat and tie while watching the *Lassie* show, as well as on getting his meals on time (he uses a starter pistol to signal he is ready for chow); and he once went to Washington, D.C., to lobby for a bone-stamp program. A playful pup, he likes to engage in friendly boxing matches (Marquess of Queensbury rules) with surprised visitors, and the Dibbles were astounded once to see him pop up in the middle of a televised football game running for a touchdown.

Belvedere (G. Crenshaw), © George Crenshaw

While his nemesis remains the neighborhood dog-catcher (to whom he once sent a cruise ticket through the Bermuda Triangle as a birthday gift), Belvedere spreads his special brand of cheer to all and sundry. Indeed, so dreaded has his name become that people have been known to barricade their doors, disconnect their phone, or move in with their in-laws upon hearing the Dibbles were coming to visit with their dog.

On those occasions when he has to stay home, Belvedere can count on every possible comfort, human as well as canine. His doghouse has air-conditioning, a gourmet kitchen, and cable TV, as well as an L-shaped sofa and an elevator, among other amenities, and its owner keeps constantly adding to it. A nosy neighbor casually inquiring about the dog shoveling dirt in the backyard would get the answer: "Digging the basement under his doghouse to make room for a pool table." Belvedere and his cohorts would oftentimes turn the house upside down—literally—and the pet-sitter hired for the evening would get the number for "dial-a-prayer" just in case.

Yet the strip's zaniest moments are only tangentially connected to the main situation. "There's another skyscraper going up," Orville nonchalantly observes as a city building lifts off skyward. A bluejay dressed up in coat-and-tails, high hat, and spats gets ticketed for jaywalking. The Dibbles' camper gets snatched up by a giant condor during a trip to the mountains. A lake cruise unaccountably ends up with Orville and Belvedere stranded on a desert island. On a thematic level *Belvedere* relates less to such traditional dog strips as *Napoleon* or *Marmaduke* than to Bill Holman's anarchic *Smokey Stover*. In this respect it may be suggestive to note that Crenshaw started his strip only one year after Holman had retired his.

M.H.

BEN CASEY
1962–1966

When NEA decided to adapt the popular *Ben Casey* television show into newspaper-strip form, it called upon Neal Adams, already a seasoned veteran at age 21. The strip premiered on November 26, 1962, with a Sunday page added September 20, 1964.

As in the TV series, Ben Casey was resident surgeon at

County General Hospital, a metropolitan institution with a surfeit of extreme medical and psychological cases. On the screen Casey was played by Vince Edwards in a perpetually surly mode, but his dour persona was somewhat toned down in the strip. He kept, however, his integrity and the sense of moral duty that made him battle disease and the medical establishment with equal vigor. A no-nonsense practitioner, he didn't believe in coddling his patients, and chronic whiners and sob sisters got short shrift with him. He was tacitly supported in his one-man crusade by the elderly chief of surgery, crusty Dr. Zorbe; and in his rare leisure hours he entertained a discreet romance with his anesthesiologist, the alluring Dr. Maggie Graham.

Casey never performed such mundane tasks as an appendectomy or the removal of a cyst; he always got patients with severe cranial traumas, multiple bullet wounds, or aggravated spinal-chord injuries. The story lines did not shrink from tackling controversial problems, such as heroin addiction, illegitimate pregnancy, and attempted suicide. These were usually treated in soap-opera fashion, with light shining bright at the end of the proverbial tunnel, but there was also a touch of toughness to the proceedings, well rendered by Adams in a forceful, direct style that exuded realism and tension and accorded well with the overall tone of the strip.

The *Ben Casey* show ended its run at the close of its fifth season, on March 21, 1966, and the newspaper page version followed suit later that year: the last release appeared on Sunday, July 31.

M.H.

BEN FRIDAY
See BODYGUARD

BEN WEBSTER
See PHIL HARDY

BETTY
1920–1943

The first of the glamor-girl strips, *Betty* was the creation of Charles Voight, a noted magazine and fashion illustrator, specializing in the drawing of beautiful women in elegant surroundings. The feature made its debut on April 4, 1920, in the Sunday color pages of the *New York Tribune*, and was later distributed nationally by the Herald-Tribune Syndicate.

Voight had previously done *Petey Dink* (later known simply as *Petey*), a daily strip about a comical little man always sur-

rounded by bevies of beautiful young women. This short exercise proved to be of invaluable assistance to the artist in his drawing of *Betty*, where beautiful young women were very much in evidence. Betty Thompson (her full name) was a dark-haired, patrician lovely who led an existence of comfort, elegance, and ease. Her mind unfortunately did not match her looks, and she was to remain a rather vacuous character throughout the life of the strip. Her time was spent in visits to her dressmaker, attendance at fashionable dance parties, dates with eligible young men of the upper crust, and in the summertime trips to the seashore, which allowed the artist to display her figure and those of her female companions in skimpy bathing suits and advantageous poses.

The strip's humor (what there was of it) was provided by Lester De Pester, the heroine's hapless, frustrated suitor whose parakeet nose, bulging eyes, and shrimpish appearance were in comical contrast with Betty's svelte silhouette and delicate features. *Betty* was a typical product of the Roaring Twenties and looked more and more out of place in the grim environment of the Great Depression; yet it survived the decade of the 1930s, adding a touch of style and glamor to the comic pages. The war years, however, proved lethal to a heroine whose indolence now seemed downright unpatriotic (although Betty did war work on occasion). In desperation Voight turned to week-to-week continuity in tales of varying interest, but he could never quite make up his mind as to what he wanted his creation to be. The strip, Coulton Waugh wrote, was "a strange mixture of straight humor, plausible situations, and now and then a dash of pure fantasy." The last page appeared on June 13, 1943.

Betty remains much admired, even today, for its style and draftsmanship. Voight was first and foremost an illustrator, and the atmosphere of his strip was bathed in the creamy elegance of the slick magazines of the period. There was an air of opulence, sophistication, and class about *Betty* that later newspaper strips tried to emulate: these include Frank Godwin's *Connie* (in its early incarnation), Jefferson Machamer's *Petting Patty*, and Russell Patterson's *Almost a Bride*. Voight's creation now comes across as an oddity that, like the characters it depicted, is agreeable to look at but uninteresting to listen to.

M.H.

Betty **(C. Voight), © 1921 New York Tribune**

BETTY BOOP
1934–1937, 1984–1988

Max Fleischer's *Betty Boop* cartoon shorts were all the rage in the early 1930s, spawning dolls, toys, and assorted other products in their wake. It is therefore not surprising that King Features, ever on the lookout for new properties to develop, acquired the comic-strip rights to the character in 1934, with a daily version coming out in July 23 of that year. Credited to Fleischer and drawn by long-time cartoonist Bud Counihan, it met with enough popular success to warrant the addition of a Sunday page on November 24, 1934.

Many of the anecdotes in the strip revolved around movie actress Betty starring in every conceivable kind of film, from weepy to jungle adventure, with mildly amusing results. She also had a number of run-ins with her domineering director, Von, and with the never-seen but omnipresent head of the studio, the Chief. Despite all these commotions she found time for romance too, on and off the set, being wooed in turns by European prince Okey Dokey and matinee idol Van Twinkle.

In her domestic life Betty had to cope with her pugnacious Aunt Tillie, who had appointed herself guardian of her niece's morals, and with her kid brother Bubby, who at one point abandoned a promising career as a film star for the company of his rowdy pals. Her small bulldog Hugo rounded out the family circle, though at one time Betty was made to adopt quintuplets in order to change her image as a vamp. The blandness of most of the gags, coupled with the *Betty Boop* cartoons' decline at the box office, led to the strip's demise. The last daily appeared on March 23, 1935, while the Sunday page lasted until November 27, 1937.

For reasons best known to themselves, the editors at King decided to resurrect the character half a century after its first appearance in the newspapers. It took the efforts of no fewer than four of Mort Walker's sons, Morgan, Neal, Brian, and Greg, to bring it off. Betty, now flanked by Felix the Cat, in the appropriately titled *Betty Boop and Felix*, made her comeback, daily and Sunday, in November 1984. She lost Felix along the way in 1987, and the strip, rechristened *Betty Boop and Friends*, managed to stay afloat until January 31, 1988.

M.H.

BEYOND MARS
1952–1955

At the height of their newspaper's circulation, the editors at the *New York News* decided to sport their own exclusive comic feature as a sign of success and status. They contacted noted science-fiction author Jack Williamson who came up with the idea of *Beyond Mars*. Drawn by veteran comic-book artist Lee Elias, the strip, occupying the entire last page of the *News* Sunday comic supplement, debuted on February 17, 1952.

Williamson developed continuities based on his novel *Seetee Ship*, in which an astroship built on the principle of C.T. or Seetee (short for contraterrene, another name for antimatter) was used to explore the farthest reaches of the universe, the C.T. effect counteracting the pull of gravity. The strip starred a two-fisted adventurer named Mike Flint, who was billed as "a licensed spatial engineer" but acted more like an agent of law and order from his base in the asteroid belt. Actually, many of the plot lines were derived from similar *Dick Tracy* episodes, and Chester Gould was reportedly called in at one point to advise Williamson on the finer points of comic-strip suspense. As it turned out, *Beyond Mars* was a fast-paced space-opera, beautifully rendered by Elias with a stunning use of color.

After a couple of years the executives at the *News* started losing interest in their experiment, which did not meet the high expectations they had pinned on it. In September 1954 *Beyond Mars* was cut to half-page size, as a prelude to its eventual demise. The final Sunday (there never was a daily version), dated March 13, 1955, tried to tie up some of the strip's loose ends in a halfhearted effort at wrapping up.

M.H.

BIFF BAKER
1941–1945

One of the many comic strips that, along with Hollywood movies, helped homefront America fight World War II vicariously, *Biff Baker* actually started life as a sports feature on Sunday, September 7, 1941, exactly two months before the Pearl Harbor attack. Under the collective pseudonym Henry Lee, it was originally drawn by Henry (Schlensker) and written by Lee (Ernest Lynn) for NEA Service.

Biff was a clean-cut, eager college senior who excelled in academics as well as athletics, with a patriotic streak that made him enlist in the Air Corps right upon graduation from Midwestern University. He saw action in both Europe and the Pacific, and he and his buddies seemed at times to turn the tide of war in both theaters of operations almost single-handedly. While Biff did not altogether rival on paper the dash and splash Errol Flynn was at that same time displaying on film, Schlensker and Lynn had him go through his paces with all the reckless abandon typical of newsprint and celluloid warriors alike.

Reality in this period had a way of catching up with cartoonists of draft age. In early 1943, just as he was hitting his stride, "Ka-boom! War!," as Schlensker himself later colorfully put it. He was replaced on the page by Walt Scott, a former Walt Disney alumnus, whose cutesy style didn't quite fit the he-man, no-holds-barred wartime tone of the feature. Biff Baker continued his military career somewhat unsteadily until he finally bowed out of the conflict in the summer of 1945, a few months short of V-J Day.

M.H.

BIG BEN BOLT
1950–1978

Elliot Caplin, kid brother to Al Capp and demon comics writer, came to King Features with the concept for a newspaper strip about the tribulations of a prizefighter on

Big Ben Bolt (**J. Cullen Murphy**), © 1961 King Features Syndicate

and off the ring. The syndicate bought the idea, John Cullen Murphy, a noted illustrator of boxing scenes, was brought in as the artist, and the resulting feature, titled *Big Ben Bolt,* made its debut as a daily strip on February 20, 1950, with a Sunday added on May 25, 1952.

While Caplin always steadfastly denied that *Big Ben Bolt* was a copy of *Joe Palooka,* the strip's formula, a mix of pugilistic machismo and soap-opera sentimentality, held more than a passing resemblance to Ham Fisher's successful concoction, from which it diverged only at the margins. Unlike Palooka, who was of working-class and ethnic European extraction, Ben Bolt came from old New England stock and held a degree from Harvard University; again unlike Palooka, who was prone to bloopers and malapropisms, Bolt expressed himself in educated English. In essentials, however—as kind and generous individuals who both retained their integrity in a brutalizing and corrupt world—they were brothers under the skin.

In the very first episode, Ben Bolt, on his way back to the United States, met aboard ship Spider Haines, who would later become his fight manager. For the next five years most of the strip would be devoted to Bolt's pugilistic exploits. The prototypical overachiever, Bolt found time to complete his college education while on his way to winning the world's heavyweight crown, a crown he would lose and regain with monotonous regularity.

The boxing theme faded out of the picture somewhat in 1955, when Bolt suffered an eye injury that kept him out of the ring for a time (he was eventually to come back). Becoming a journalist and sportscaster for a while, he would get involved in tales of mystery, adventure, and danger; he would also meet an endless string of beautiful women, all panting after him, in the course of his pursuits, professional, and otherwise. Still later he revealed that under his tough veneer he had been hiding all along the soul of a crusader for good causes, as he slipped easily into the part of conservationist, social reformer, and role model for troubled youth.

Murphy's graphic renditions greatly enhanced Caplin's sometimes stilted writing. He moved with ease in the different milieus the script led the artist to depict; but Murphy was best in boxing sequences where, like his two-fisted hero, he packed a mighty punch. Otherwise his graphic style was not much different from that of the other slick comic-strip artists who came to the fore in the 1950s (Stan Drake, Ken Bald, John Spranger, to name a few). Murphy had the help of assistants almost from the outset, but the trend accelerated after his accession to the *Prince Valiant* page in 1971. Among others there were Al Williamson, Angelo Torres, and principally Carlos Garzon. This incessant turnover resulted in the cancellation of the Sundays in April 1975. After a brief stint by Joe Kubert, the dailies devolved to Gray Morrow who started signing them in August 1977. Early in 1978 Neal Adams took over and guided the strip through to its shocking twist ending.

In April 1978 Ben Bolt received the Nobel Peace Prize for his work in the fields of philanthropy, ecology, and education. Due to the well-known squeamishness of comics editors, most U.S. newspapers ended *Ben Bolt*'s run on an upbeat note with the strip dated April 10 (a Monday), showing the hero getting ready to address the Award Committee; the remaining handful of American papers (and most of the foreign ones that carried the strip) followed the action through to its unexpected conclusion at week's end. The Nobel laureate, aware that a contract was out on his life, nevertheless took the podium: an assassin's bullet through the heart cut him down in the middle of his acceptance speech. Thus, on April 15, 1978, Ben Bolt's brilliant career as heavyweight champion of the world, benefactor of mankind, and Nobel Peace Prize winner, came to a violent end.

M.H.

BIG CHIEF WAHOO
See STEVE ROPER

BIG GEORGE!
1960–1990

After unsuccessfully trying to sell a daily panel series that would have used the preposterously outlandish situations for which his cartoons had become famous, Virgil Partch (known professionally as Vip) finally settled on a domestic comedy feature that was less likely to baffle simple-minded comics editors. Titled *Big George!,* his newfangled creation came out in 1960, distributed by Publishers Syndicate.

On the strength of Vip's name alone the panel soon was carried in more than three hundred newspapers, and the syndicate asked the artist for the addition of a Sunday page. Appearing early in 1961 and bylined with the cartoonist's full name, it marked Partch's debut as a bona fide comic-strip artist. George was a pointy-nosed, pot-bellied office worker who lived in a suburban house in the company of his pert wife Helen (named for the artist's own spouse) and his small, shaggy dog Ajax. While many of the jokes revolved around familiar situations, such as fighting crabgrass, getting to the rail station on time, keeping up with the neighbors, and other suburban concerns, there were occasional flashes of the outrageous humor Vip was renowned for. The city-bred George's clumsy attempts at mastering ordinary garden paraphernalia, from lawn mowers to folding chairs, often evidenced a slightly surreal tinge.

At any rate, Partch's distinctive manner, which Stephen Becker characterized as "a highly individual style, with sharp, heavy lines," is really what carried the feature through the years. *Big George!* always had a respectable, if not spectacular, list of client papers; and after Partch's death in a car crash in August 1984, the strip was continued in close imitation of the creator's style by other, anonymous hands. It reportedly ended in December 1990.

M.H.

BIZARRO
1985–present

Of all the many clones spawned by the success of Gary Larson's *The Far Side, Bizarro* is the most worthy of note. Created by Dan Piraro for Chronicle Features Syndicate, it first appeared in 1985 as a daily panel, to which a Sunday version was added some years later.

Unlike Larson, Piraro makes ample use of speech balloons, and there is plenty of dialogue in *Bizarro*. The panel's graphic mode can best be called "generic cartoony," with no stylistic flourishes or decorative touches. The feature consists of a series of jokes, some of them gems, some of them duds, that could be told without the help of pictures. A radio announcer repeats endlessly, "You've tuned in to 91.6, K-VOID. The one spot on your dial with no programming whatsoever.... You've tuned in to 91.6 K-VOID..." While operating on a patient, a surgeon suddenly stops in his tracks, declaring, "Nobody move! I've lost a contact lens." A fortune-cookie in a Chinese restaurant reads, "In less than one hour you will begin to regret the minuscule tip you left the last time you were here."

Like Larson again, Piraro is very good at animal jokes. A mare comes shopping for shoes at a blacksmith's, asking, "Could I see something in a black, spike-heeled pump?" A bald eagle puts on a hairpiece to impress his date, who declares, "You're not fooling me." Dinosaurs greet startled motorists with the announcement, "Hi there, folks! Welcome to the gas station that time forgot!" A pooch enters a couple's living room all dolled up in hat, dress, and high heels, with the wife observing to her husband, "I think the dog wants to go out."

Bizarro has steadily grown in circulation since its inception, and it greatly benefited from the retirement of *The Far Side* early in 1995. While not as startlingly original or screamingly funny as Larson's creation, *Bizarro* is often the most interesting of the "weird comics" currently appearing on the newspaper pages.

M.H.

BLACK FURY
See MISS FURY

BLONDIE
1930–present

Blondie was the creation of cartoonist Murat "Chic" Young, who was born in Chicago in 1901, grew up in St. Louis, and at age 22 moved to Cleveland to draw a comic strip for the NEA, the Newspaper Enterprise Association. While there, he created *The Affairs of Jane,* what was then known as a "pretty-girl" strip because it capitalized on the new woman of the 1920s: pert, pretty, savvy. He followed this with *Beautiful Bab,* a short-lived strip that just happened to attract the attention of William Randolph Hearst.

Hearst offered Young a job, he moved to New York, and in 1924 he created *Dumb Dora,* whose subtitle, "She's Not So Dumb As She Looks," set the tone for what was to be his crowning achievement: the creation of *Blondie,* which made its first appearance on September 15, 1930. It was originally conceived as a "girlie strip," with Blondie Boopadoop portrayed as an irrepressible gold digger in pursuit of an irresponsible playboy named Dagwood Bumstead. For a while the strip focused on the comic friction between Blondie and the Bumstead family. In the meantime, other suitors were beginning to compete for Blondie's affection. Soon, however, the grim reality of the depression made flappers and playboys irrelevant, and *Blondie* began to wane in popularity.

To breathe new life into the strip, Chic Young made some daring innovations in the format. Going against convention, he decided to bring Dagwood back and have him and Blondie get married, which they did on February 17, 1933. This immediately moved them from the frivolous 1920s into the serious 1930s. Then, he had Mr. Bumstead disinherit his son so that Dagwood became as poor as his readers. Perhaps the biggest change he made in the strip was to turn Blondie from a scatterbrained bimbo into a charming but dutiful wife and mother. Blondie became the sustaining force in the family, leaving Dagwood to be the bumbler who could always depend on Blondie for support. The recipe worked then, and it continues to work today. The Bumsteads, along with their two children, remain the symbol of the nuclear family.

Young concentrated on the comedy of newlyweds for as long as he could, but it soon became clear that he needed to introduce a new element. In 1934, in an inspired stroke,

Blondie (C. Young), © 1930 King Features Syndicate

Blondie (C. Young), © 1945 King Features Syndicate

he gave the Bumsteads a son, called Baby Dumpling, and from then on the strip became a family strip.

For a long time after that, Baby Dumpling was the center of attention as Young showed Dagwood trying to cope with such things as feeding the baby and changing its diapers. Then in 1941 the Bumsteads had their second child, Cookie (a name selected from among the 431,275 entries in a name-the-baby contest). Along with their dog Daisy and her five pups, the Bumstead family was now complete.

The more domestic the material, the higher circulation climbed. By the 1940s, Young had developed a style of household comedy that would make *Blondie* a worldwide favorite. His topics were simple, realistic, and universal, drawn from the daily routine of work and family that readers could readily identify with.

Dagwood works for Julius C. Dithers and Company and is constantly at loggerheads with Mr. Dithers himself. Dithers is the boss from hell who browbeats poor Dagwood mercilessly, yet Dagwood always comes back for more. When he attempts even the feeblest revenge, such as mocking Mr. Dithers when he thinks Dithers isn't watching, he lives to regret it. Because he hates the thought of getting up in the morning and facing Mr. Dithers, he often oversleeps, only to have to rush around in a frenzy to avoid being late for work. Invariably, as he dashes out the front door to catch his bus, he collides with poor Mr. Beasly, the postman, whose mail gets scattered all over the neighborhood.

At home, Dagwood squabbles with his neighbor, Herb Woodley, whose wife, Tootsie, is Blondie's best friend. When Dagwood takes a nap or a bath, his peace and privacy are predictably disturbed by an impertinent neighbor boy named Elmo. Dagwood also carries on running battles with door-to-door salesmen—and usually loses. Chic Young admitted once that he didn't mind salesmen coming to his door because they always gave him ideas for another strip. Dagwood also has frequent confrontations with household repairmen, meddling in their work and often driving them to retaliate.

Over the years Dagwood evolved into the stereotype of the bumbling husband. He always means well, he even tries his best, but he is basically lazy and inept—and forever

hungry (hence, the Dagwood sandwich!). While Dagwood became the central comic figure of the strip, Blondie became a model of stability and order, frequently helping Dagwood out of a jam. She does, however, have her own charming personality and her own wit, as revealed in her frustrating but hilarious brand of logic.

There were never any radical changes in the *Blondie* format, but subtle adaptations to accommodate changing times have kept it fresh. When Chic Young's son Dean took over, his concern that *Blondie* might become an anachronism led him to introduce modest changes and even at times break some of his father's rules: Blondie's kitchen gets periodically updated, Dagwood's garters have disappeared (in spite of protest from readers), and Elmo, the kid from down the block, has replaced Baby Dumpling and Cookie as the subject of little-kid gags. Otherwise, Dean Young has never strayed from the four basic elements of his father's original formula: eating, sleeping, raising a family, and making money.

Blondie is the most widely circulated comic strip in the world. It has been translated into most languages and has an international audience reaching into the hundreds of millions. Between 1938 and 1951, twenty-eight movies were made based on the *Blondie* comic strip, all of them starring Penny Singleton as Blondie and Arthur Lake as Dagwood. A TV series followed, and even a novel. There was also a *Blondie* comic book drawn by Paul Fung, Jr.

Young employed several assistants on the strip, including Alex Raymond and Ray McGill. Starting in 1935, Young's chief helper was Jim Raymond, Alex's brother, who took over all the drawing in 1950 when Young's eyesight began to fail. Jim Raymond continued in the Young tradition, drawing in a sharp, clean, often highly animated style that could create the illusion of agitated motion. After Young died in 1973, Raymond shared a byline on the strip with Young's son Dean who had helped his father with the writing since 1963. After Raymond's death in 1981, Michael Gersher, his longtime assistant, took over the drawing. But Gersher was soon replaced by Stan Drake, who was able to imitate the Young-Raymond style. By the late 1980s, *Blondie* had attained an international circulation of nearly two thousand newspapers, the result of never tampering with Chic Young's proven formula.

In the mid-1990s, *Blondie* continues to be drawn by Dean Young and Stan Drake, and the strip shows every sign of surviving into the twenty-first century.

T.W.

BLOOM COUNTY
1980–1989

*O*ne of a number of contemporary newspaper strips to come out of college-magazine pages, Berke Breathed's *Bloom County* had as its forerunner *Academia Waltz*, which appeared in the University of Texas's *Daily Texan* and ran the distance of 658 strips (by the author's own count) in 1978 and 1979. Two collections of Breathed's strips had come out in the meantime, attracting the attention of the *Washington Post* editors; and on December 8, 1980, *Bloom County* made its debut on the newspaper page, distributed by the Washington Post Writers Group.

Breathed was not long in introducing a variegated gallery of outlandish characters (some of them carryovers from his college strip) into his creation, whose setting was a fictional Midwestern county. There were Cutter John, a paraplegic but very active veteran from the Vietnam war, who loved to race downhill in his wheelchair; the crooked lawyer and ineffectual lover Steve Dallas; and the goofy blonde Lola Granola, a former flower child. The adults were upstaged at every turn by the children, who included Milo Bloom, leader of the band and copyboy emeritus on the *Bloom Beacon*, the local paper; the anxiety-ridden Mike Binkley, who had a closetful of insecurities hiding in his bedroom closet; and the black whiz-kid Oliver Wendell Jones, certified scientific genius and convicted computer hacker.

The human characters found themselves gradually displaced by a gaggle of animals who, for one reason or another, came to settle in Bloom County. Opus the penguin arrived first: a refugee from the Falklands war, he was adopted as a pet by Milo. Soon the bow-tied waterfowl started evincing human traits, such as gluttony, avarice, and lust; he eventually became gossip columnist and film critic for the *Beacon*. A little later, Bill the Cat blew in from Dubuque, Iowa, in search of fame and fortune as a comic-strip cat; a drug-crazed, bibulous feline, his most consistent comment on the vagaries of life was "Ack." Other animal characters joined in at one or another point in time, including Hodge-Podge the acerbic rabbit and the foul-mouthed groundhog Portnoy.

While most often devoted to daily or weekly gags, *Bloom County* has sometimes engaged in wild continuities. At one time Bill, Opus, and Hodge-Podge formed a rock band known as Billy and the Boingers, and left on a nationwide tour managed by Steve Dallas and sponsored by Dr. Schol's Odor-Eaters. At another time the animals organized the National Radical Meadow Party, which ran in the presidential elections with Bill and Opus at the head of the ticket.

Bloom County has often been compared to *Doonesbury*, but its humor was brighter and more whimsical, and the politics less egregious. Breathed did satirize politicians in his strip, including Ronald Reagan and Jeane Kirkpatrick (Bill the Cat's sometime date), along with journalists, television celebrities, pop-culture icons, and businessmen (Donald Trump was a favorite target), and this earned him a Pulitzer Prize in 1987, as well as a host of other awards. Amid all this acclaim the author, to everyone's surprise, decided to terminate the strip, explaining his move in the following terms: "I have grown stubbornly affectionate toward my characters, and I have little desire to see Opus, Bill the Cat, and others disappear from my life. But after ten years of squeezing Bloom Countians into smudgy, postage-stamp-sized stories, I thought it might be more comfortable for all concerned if we took a powder from the daily pages." The last daily strip appeared on August 5, 1989, and on Sunday, August 6, *Bloom County* and its denizens literally faded off the page, to make way for the author's new creation, Outland.

M.H.

BOBBY SOX
1944–1979

During World War II a new breed of young girls invaded the teenage scene; they were known as bobby soxers, after their penchant for wearing ankle socks with tennis shoes. The comics were not long in recognizing the phenomenon, and a spate of teenage girl strips came to the fore, among them *Bobby Sox* by woman cartoonist Martha (signing "Marty") Links. Originally produced for the *San Francisco Chronicle*, *Bobby Sox* was syndicated nationwide by Consolidated News Features as a daily panel from November 20, 1944. A Sunday page (with *Betty 'n' Ho-Hum*, about a little girl and her dog, as a companion piece) was added the following year. The feature was rechristened *Emmy Lou* for its heroine when Links switched to United Feature Syndicate in 1958.

Emmy Lou was an awkward, gangling, freckle-faced brunette whose days were mostly spent waiting for the phone to ring or in helpless dependence on her mooching, no-good boyfriend Alvin. Emmy Lou and Alvin were always breaking up (to the unconcealed glee of the girl's parents), only to make up again afterward with monotonous regularity. When she was not busy daydreaming about her love life, Emmy Lou was wont to talk about it in endless (and boring) detail to her infinitely patient school friend Taffy. After the change of syndicate, and perhaps in response to the youth rebellion of the 1960s, the strip, while still humorous, took on an increasingly pessimistic tone.

A pleasant, rather innocuous feature, *Bobby Sox/Emmy Lou* was drawn in a cartoony, wispy style, without great originality, but with a welcome emphasis on visual humor. In the second half of the 1970s the strip was mostly done by Links's assistant Ted Martine, while many of the gags were supplied by Jerry Bundsen. In 1979 Links decided to retire from the comics, because, she felt, her strip no longer represented the teens of the day. Accordingly, the feature was retired by the syndicate later that same year.

M.H.

Bobby Sox (M. Links), © 1941 Consolidated News Features

Bobby Thatcher (R. Storm), © 1932 Bell Syndicate

BOBBY THATCHER
1927–1937

A pioneering strip of intrigue and melodrama, *Bobby Thatcher*, drawn and written by Robert Storm, premiered on March 21, 1927, in a daily format. Its first distributor was the McClure Syndicate, for which Storm had earlier contributed a number of newspaper features.

Like every other young adventurer of the funny papers at the time, Bobby Thatcher was a spunky orphan who had run away from his heartless and avaricious stepfather, one Jed Flint. The continuities hovered between nineteenth-century sentimentality and hard-bitten realism. In one early episode, for example, the teenage hero, hitchhiking along a lonely road, was picked up by a kind stranger who turned out to be a wanted criminal. In another misadventure the farm on which Bobby had spent the night caught fire; the orphan was charged with arson and brutally manhandled by the police, but he managed to make it out of town with the help of a friendly hobo. This alternation between good fortune and hard knocks seems to have wearied the author after a while, and before the year was out *Bobby Thatcher* veered decisively, albeit not exclusively, toward straight adventure. For the next several years Bobby was involved in tales of hijacking, kidnapping, air and sea piracy, smuggling, rumrunning, and other assorted skullduggery, in which the honesty and integrity of the young hero shone bright against the array of sundry brutes and riffraff he encountered (and bested).

On June 6, 1930, Storm, who owned the rights to his creation, transferred *Bobby Thatcher* to the Bell Syndicate. Around the same time Bobby was finally reunited with his long-lost sister Hattie (he had kept her picture with him for all those years). He decided to settle down with his sibling and his aunt Ida Baxter amid the bucolic surroundings of Jonesboro, the small town where his extended family was living. There followed a number of rural escapades in the company of other teenagers like Tubby Butler and Pee-Wee Nimmo.

But Bobby couldn't be kept on the farm after he'd seen Panama (as he had), and after a couple of years he resumed his wandering life, flanked this time by an adult companion, a two-fisted sailor going by the name of Hurricane Bill. The time was now the mid-1930s and adventure strips had sprung up all around *Bobby Thatcher*, many of them better drawn and more cleverly plotted than Storm's feature. Faced with a diminished readership and a dwindling income, the author abruptly decided to close down the strip around the summer of 1937.

That *Bobby Thatcher* had managed to last for so long was due to the creator's energy and enthusiasm. While it lacked sophistication of drawing and strength of characterization, the strip displayed an exuberance and zest that carried everything before it for a time.

M.H.

BODYGUARD
1948–1953

I n the late 1940s the staid Herald-Tribune Syndicate decided to enter the field of adventure strips twelve or fifteen years after most of the newspaper syndicates had done so. Their first foray into this territory was *Bodyguard*. Written by Lawrence Lariar and illustrated by John Spranger, the feature made its debut on Sunday, May 2, 1948.

Long before Kevin Costner, there was Ben Friday. A returning serviceman and former intelligence officer, Friday took a job guarding cantankerous millionaire Hyram Tucker and his valuable stamp collection. The action, which extended almost over the entire year, took the hero in search of an elusive Nazi war criminal known as the Baron, from Mexico to Brazil, and to the Baron's mysterious island stronghold in the middle of the Atlantic Ocean, before getting back to New York where it had started. In the next adventure Tucker sent Friday, who meanwhile had found time to strike up a romance with the millionaire's bodacious niece Linda, to diverse locations in India, where for the first time the bodyguard-hero met the dumpy young native prince who would later evict him from his own strip.

In the summer of 1949 there came the addition of a daily strip and a change of name to *Ben Friday*. The hero, now shed of his bodyguard designation, was free to take on all kinds of assignments, on land, at sea, and in the air, involving him in tales of murder, smuggling, piracy, and high finance, all told in breathless fashion by Lariar. Friday enjoyed ownership of the strip for little more than a year. In some of his adventures he kept bumping into the swarthy little prince, and this should have aroused his suspicions (and those of the readers) that something was afoot. In 1950 the Bantam Prince, as he was known, attended Friday's wedding in Manila to a gorgeous blonde he had met in the course of his peregrinations, and later bade farewell to the former bodyguard and his bride.

The strip, titled *The Bantam Prince* from then on, took on a decidedly comedic turn. The prince, it turned out, was a baseball fan, and the locale was transferred from Asia to Texas, where the young prince had gone to study. In June 1951 Spranger left the strip to devote himself to *The Saint*, a newspaper feature similarly distributed by the Herald-Tribune Syndicate. Carl Pfeufer took over the artwork in creditable fashion until *The Bantam Prince*'s discontinuance in 1953.

The three-headed feature owed much to Spranger's nervous, dramatic style, full of restless action and forward momentum. In the dross generated by the rash of adventure strips coming to light after World War II, *Bodyguard*— a.k.a. *Ben Friday* a.k.a. *The Bantam Prince*—is a minor gem worthy of closer scrutiny.

M.H.

BONER'S ARK
1968–present

Mort Walker was already the successful author of a strip about military life *(Beetle Bailey)* and of another one about family life *(Hi and Lois)* when he conceived the idea of a feature about animal life as a change of pace. Signed with Walker's first name, Addison, and distributed by King Features Syndicate, *Boner's Ark* accordingly saw light as a daily on March 11, 1968, and as a Sunday the following March 17.

Asked to define the strip's genre, Walker once averred that it was "pure satire-fantasy," but it actually is more parody than satire and more allegory than fantasy. The animals all exhibit recognizable human traits, from Priscilla the female pig who fancies herself a heartbreaker to the five-hundred-pound ape Dum-Dum, whose slow-wittedness makes him the butt of dumb gorilla jokes. The ark on which they drift aimlessly is the same allegorical ship of fools than can be spotted in art and literature through the ages. At first there were hosts of animals on the ark, but Walker later wisely reduced cast and crew to more manageable numbers. Chief among the passengers are Cubcake, the cuddly koala bear; Duke the penguin, always dressed to the nines; a trio of would-be mutineers made

up of hyena, bear, and mouse; as well as a goose named Mom. The crew, as motley as they come, is comprised of Arnie Aardvark, the first mate much given to crying out "Land Ho!" as a joke; Giraffe, the ship's lookout; and Homing Pigeon, the navigator who gets lost in a walk-in closet.

The only humans on the ark are Captain Boner, whose amiably inept stewardship has so far kept the craft from coming anywhere close to shore, and his empty-headed wife Bubbles, whom he picked off of a drifting raft. Their antics rival those of the animals, and they have been keeping the ship's marriage counselor (the hyena) busy for years. The feature is drawn in a more stylized, less literal mode than Walker's other strips. From 1971 on, Walker's assistant, Frank Johnson, has been drawing *Boner's Ark*, finally getting to sign it in 1982. The gags, however, continue to be written by Walker, aided and abetted by his usual accomplices, Bud Jones and Jerry Dumas.

M.H.

BOOB McNUTT
1915–1934

Rube Goldberg came up with his most fondly remembered character, Boob McNutt, in the eponymous Sunday page he created in May 1915 for the *New York Mail;* it was later picked up for syndication by the Star Company.

In its first years the feature was done strictly in a gag-a-week format. Boob was a well-meaning simpleton, attired in ill-fitting clothes, with an innocent-looking face and flaming-red hair crowned with a tiny green hat. His efforts at doing good always ended in disaster, with the objects of his clumsy solicitude usually turning on him. Week after harrowing week he was set upon by enraged husbands thinking he was moving in on their wives, pursued by homicidal homeowners whose houses he had set ablaze in order to rid them of termites, and bloodied by frustrated second-story men whose routine he had innocently disrupted. The feature was drawn in a broad, slapdash, and slapstick style, with a zest and spirit that redeemed its formlessness and clutter.

Early in 1922 Boob fell head over heels in love with an attractive, if equally empty-headed, brunette named Pearl, and the strip took an abrupt turn. While unlucky at almost

Boner's Ark ("Addison"), © 1970 King Features Syndicate

Boob McNutt (R. Goldberg), © 1931 Star Company

everything else, Boob proved lucky in love: his sentiments did not go unrequited. There was a large hitch, however, in the person of Pearl's malevolent father Toby, who actively aided and abetted the murderous attempts made on the hapless Boob's life by his jealousy-crazed rivals. Week after week the imminent union between Pearl and Boob was again postponed, until pleadings from sympathetic readers persuaded Goldberg to relent and allow the couple to marry on September 24, 1924.

Instead of an end, however, the wedding proved only a new beginning, as Goldberg concocted wilder and wilder predicaments for his protagonists. Reminiscing about this aspect of the strip in 1968, more than a half-century after its inception, and only two years before the creator's death, Goldberg had this to say: "The modus operandi of an artist with a continued story on his hands may be described in a few words. His three essential characters—hero, heroine, and villain—are scrambled in a series of episodes involving hairbreadth escapes, heartburnings, and grotesque situations, all these adventures worked out in a serio-comic vein." Applying this formula to the letter, the author involved the newlyweds with bloodthirsty pirates, foreign agents, and homicidal maniacs. Weird creatures kept popping up at odd moments, starting with Bertha, the Siberian cheesehound that became Boob's pet. To round off his gallery of characters, Goldberg in 1927 brought back Ike

and Mike, the two bowler-hatted, half-pint twins he had created earlier, as the long-lost brothers of Boob's equally height-challenged adoptive father, Shrimp McNutt.

The climax to these adventures came in the 1930s, when Boob fell prey to the machinations of his viperine attorney, John J. Blackheart, and his demented accomplice, Dr. Zano. Declared legally incompetent, Boob had to turn all his assets over to his lawyer, but Ike and Mike hid away the loot in the nick of time. Zano and Blackheart then tried every conceivable means of persuasion, from water torture to hypnotism, to wring the location of the secret hideaway from the unwitting Boob. A couple of adventures in the same vein followed until Goldberg's inventiveness began to flag, and after a few more desultory episodes *Boob McNutt* came to an end on September 30, 1934.

No study of *Boob McNutt* would be complete without mention of the companion strips that complemented the main feature from the mid-1920s on. First came *Bertha*, starring Boob's cheesehound, whose weekly tribulations lasted from January 9 to July 11, 1926, followed the next Sunday by *Bill*. Despite the deprecating comments of some historians, *Bill* proved of more than passing interest. The hero of the piece was the opposite of Boob: an enterprising youngster of more than usual nerve, he displayed an ingenuity in his get-rich schemes that verged on the larcenous. In January 1934 Goldberg's demon inventor, Professor Gorgonzola Butts, dropped in to stay, and the strip became *Bill and Prof. Butts* until its demise on the same day *Boob McNutt* was discontinued. For most of its run, Bill had to give up a third of its space to *Boob McNutt's Ark,* in which Goldberg exercised his zoological fantasy, dreaming up such creatures (always in pairs) as the Weeping Wuks, the Brush-Faced Sklups, the Prowling Soot-Soots, and the Bag-pipe Toots-Toots.

M.H.

Boots and Her Buddies (E. Martin), © 1930 NEA Service

BOOTS AND HER BUDDIES
1924–1969

With the proliferation of girl strips going on all around them, the editors at Newspaper Enterprise Association (NEA) decided to start one of their own. Edgar Everett ("Abe") Martin, who was already working in the service's art department, was handed the job, and in the alliterative fashion of the times he came up with *Boots and Her Buddies,* which made its bow on February 18, 1924, as a daily strip.

Boots, an attractive blonde with a shapely figure, was initially a college girl who sported the latest collegiate fashions and affected the trendiest campus speech. Martin, a dyed-in-the-wool conservative, did not permit her, however, the freedom of behavior that was supposedly the norm among coeds of the Roaring Twenties. She sagely lived off campus, boarding with the gruff but kindly Professor Stephen Tutt and his thoughtful wife, Cora, who kept an eye on their protege. While the spotlight was pretty much on Boots's extracurricular activities (always innocent in spite of hordes of suitors whom she tactfully kept at bay), some glimpses of real college life were allowed into the strip, such as Boots cramming for an exam or tutoring a high-school senior to pay for a new dress. So popular did the character become in a few short years that she was known as "the sweetheart of the comics" throughout the decade. Among Boots's buddies, on and off campus, were her brother Bill, always ready with a hand or a buck, and the collegiate couple formed by the chubby, wisecracking Babe and her bumbling boyfriend, Horace, who acted as comic relief.

The success of the dailies spawned a Sunday version that underwent two distinct phases. Starting in 1926 *Boots* appeared as the topper to Gene Ahern's *Our Boarding House* Sunday page. Laid out in a single row of three panels, its format and gags were but an extension of the daily strip. In October 1931 it was dislodged from its position by Ahern's newly created *The Nut Bros.* Martin, given a full-size Sunday page of his own, brought out another chronicle of campus life, *Girls,* which made its bow at about the same time *The Nut Bros.* did. At first the new feature had a rotating cast of college coeds, but in July 1933 Boots started to drop in on the proceedings, and she soon asserted herself as the star of the page, which, on September 9, 1934, was retitled simply *Boots* in her honor. As an adjunct to his main feature, Martin produced *Babe 'n' Horace,* which focused on the comic misadventures of Boots's boisterous buddies.

In the 1930s Boots got herself a job as a fashion model, and her mildly romantic adventures only added to her popularity with the readers. On September 2, 1945, the heroine finally married her college sweetheart, Rod Ruggles; right on time, on July 4 of the next year, she presented her husband with a son and heir named Davey. Babe and Horace had also tied the knot in the meantime, and *Boots* changed from a girl strip to a family strip. The perennially attractive Boots, whose figure had fluctuated from thin to plump over the years according to fashion, settled down to the role of mother without skipping a beat, with the help of her incurably romantic maid Dory.

Martin in his later years had adopted some idiosyncrasies of style, such as square speech balloons and writing slanted backwards, that proved irksome to some readers. Upon his death in 1960 the daily strip was discontinued, while the Sunday page was taken over by his former assistant, Les Carroll. Drawing in a close approximation of Martin's style, Carroll managed to keep *Boots* alive for almost an additional decade, until March 30, 1969.

M.H.

THE BORN LOSER
1965–present

From 1945 to 1965 Art Sansom had virtually been the workhorse of NEA's art department, turning out the illustrations for such straight strips as *Chris Welkin, Martha Wayne,* and *Vic Flint.* In 1965 he decided to create a humor strip for a change of pace and style. He came up with the idea for a comic strip to be called "The Loser," but the syndicate head thought that would give the competition too much of an opportunity for cheap jokes, so he rebaptized it *The Born Loser.* Thus was the Loser born again, midwifed by NEA on May 10, 1965, in a daily format and on the following June 27 as a Sunday page.

Brutus P. Thornapple is a middle-aged, pot-bellied, balding suburbanite who lives in Catfish Hill, where he is much put upon by wife, family, neighbors, and strangers. He utterly and irrevocably gets no respect. His goldfish make snide remarks about him from their tank, and when his basement gets flooded he is told that his plumber doesn't make house calls. His five-year-old son Wilberforce regularly beats him at checkers, and his six-year-old neighbor, Hurricane Hattie O'Hara, uses him as a guinea pig for her science experiments. His smirking wife, Gladys, is a special trial to him: on his fiftieth birthday, for instance, she plays a recording of Frank Sinatra singing, "As the days dwindle down to a precious few..." from *September Song.* Yet the couple nicely complement each other in the cultivation of the social graces and the appreciation of high culture: at a party Brutus declares Tchaikovsky to be a quarterback, while Gladys maintains that "Paddy Tchaikovsky is the famous playwright."

Brutus fares no better at work in the neighboring town of Little Liversville whither he commutes every day. His boss, Rancid T. Veeblefester, head of the Veeblefester Corporation, keeps him toiling under a 40-watt lamp in a dingy office where he must wear a green eyeshade and arm garters. Sansom draws his antihero's predicaments with a relaxed line but considerable expressiveness, although he admits his cartoony style did not always come easily to him, and that he has to take pains not to get "a bit too arty in drawing women." Called by the syndicate "the winningest loser in the comics," Brutus Thornapple now allegedly appears in over twelve hundred newspapers (by somebody's count). For the past ten years Sansom's son Chip (as in "chip off the old block") has shared the byline with his father.

M.H.

BOUND TO WIN
See PHIL HARDY

BRENDA STARR
1940–present

In the spring of 1940 the *Chicago Tribune* editors, impressed by the spectacular rise of the comic book, decided to introduce a sixteen-page "comic book magazine" insert with their Sunday supplement. Some of the

Brenda Starr (D. Messick), © 1960 Chicago Tribune–New York News Syndicate

material was recycled from old Sunday pages, but after distribution was taken over by the Tribune-News Syndicate, original titles found their way into the magazine, notably *Brenda Starr, Reporter*. Drawn by woman artist Dalia (Dale) Messick, and under the supervision of syndicate editor Molly Slott, it premiered on June 30, 1940.

A tempestuous and flamboyant creature (whom Messick had originally wanted to portray as a woman bandit but was persuaded to make into a reporter instead), the red-headed Brenda has exhibited more than her share of neuroses, in contrast to such straight heroines of an earlier era as Connie. Always elegantly dressed and impeccably coifed, she has shuttled to the far corners of the earth on one glamorous assignment after another for her paper, *The Flash*.

Perpetually torn between the demands of her career and her romantic proclivities, her life has proved a long litany of frustrations. Romance, usually doomed, has dogged Brenda's footsteps throughout her long career. Along the way the sexual overtones of her private life have become more and more explicit. She has been abducted and sequestered a number of times by spurned lovers bent on taking their revenge and subjecting her to their libidinous fantasies, she has fallen with monotonous regularity for smooth-talking con men and mobsters only interested in using her as a front for their nefarious activities, and jealous rivals have on occasion sent her letter bombs and poisoned gifts.

While firmly rooted in soap-opera conventions, *Brenda Starr* has also touched upon many adventure genres, including mystery, fantasy, and even science fiction. On September 16, 1945, Brenda's life took a fateful turn when the red-haired reporter experienced a premonitory dream, that of a tall, dark, and handsome stranger attired in a black cape and wearing a black patch over one of his eyes. The stranger materialized the next week, and he was

to play a dominant role in the story line, amplified by the addition on October 22, 1945, of a daily strip (simply called *Brenda Starr*), with continuities tied in with those of the Sundays. The elusive figure, whom Brenda dubbed "the mystery man," turned out to be Basil St. John, a reclusive millionaire who cultivated a rare species of black orchids, the only known remedy for his "secret disease." The love affair between Brenda and her diffident admirer lasted for three decades of stormy reunions and heart-wrenching separations before Messick finally relented and allowed the couple to marry in January 1976. The union was soon interrupted again by one of St. John's mysterious disappearances, and the suspense was renewed as before.

Amid all this misery, Brenda's coworkers have provided her with some welcome solace. They are Mr. Livwright, the tough-talking, carpet-chewing editor of *The Flash;* Hank O'Hair, Brenda's plain-looking colleague, who is wont to exclaim after each of the heroine's many misfortunes, "Am I glad I am not beautiful!"; not to forget Brenda's goofy girl cousin from Pinhook, Indiana, Abretha Breeze. Their timely interventions add a humorous touch and an ironic counterpoint to the redhead's harrowing experiences.

Messick, almost from the beginning, had the help of a number of assistants, including John Oleson and Jim Mackey. After Messick's retirement in 1980, comic-book artist Ramona Fradon took over the drawing; the writing was entrusted to Linda Sutter, followed by Mary Theresa Schmich in 1985. Fradon handed over the artistic duties to June Brigman in 1995.

In its intensity of feeling, sense of angst, and overheated romantic atmosphere, *Brenda Starr* remains a rarity among the more aseptic soap-opera strips of the newspaper page.

M.H.

BRICK BRADFORD
1933–1987

Veteran newspaperman William Ritt was fascinated by the possibilities offered by the comic-strip medium, and he tried his hand at two short-lived newspaper strips, first *Chip Collins' Adventures* (with illustrations by Jack Wilhelm) and later *Gabby* (drawn by Joe King) before hitting paydirt with *Brick Bradford*. The new feature made its debut on August 21, 1933, as a daily strip illustrated by Clarence Gray and distributed by Central Press Association, the Cleveland-based subsidiary of King Features.

As originally conceived, Brick was a troubleshooter always ready to take part in any far-flung adventure, from exploring an underwater city deep in the Andes to thwarting a sect of assassins bent on the conquest of the world. Ritt's story lines were intricately plotted and suspense-filled, and Gray rendered them with an uncanny sense of mystery and an awesome power of evocation. Relying almost exclusively on black masses and white spaces, with very few halftones, he delighted in depicting the action in cinematic terms, with frequent panoramic and lengthy sequences unbroken by any dialogue: his battle scenes and nocturnals were particularly effective.

On November 24, 1934, a weekly page was added to the daily strip, and in this spacious format Gray could give free rein to his talent and flair for showmanship. Fired by Ritt's mythology-laden tales, he enfolded his hero in spectacular settings of futuristic cities and primeval jungles, peopled by lost races and legendary monsters, bathing the whole proceedings in an atmosphere of eerie poetry and festive pageantry, to which the use of color added immeasurably.

A companion strip, *The Time Top,* made a brief appearance for a few months in 1935, and its invention, "the chronosphere" (a device clearly derived from H. G. Wells's time machine) later found its way into the main feature, allowing Brick to span the eons, from earliest prehistory to the farthest reaches of the future. This plot development further enhanced the artist's opportunity for grandiose spectacle in his depictions of hypertechnological societies or in his renditions of primitive rituals and customs.

Brick Bradford was very much a star vehicle, with the titular hero sharing top billing with no one. He had no regular sidekick and no permanent love interest. His best friends were usually scientists, such as Kalla Kopak in the dailies and Horatio Southern in the weeklies, who sent Brick on the most outlandish missions. June Salisbury, daughter of Professor Salisbury, yet another scientist, was his most constant female companion, but he had innumerable other girlfriends of times past, present, and future, including English ladies, Mayan princesses, and queens from faraway galaxies.

Came the outbreak of World War II and Brick was one of the very few adventure-strip heroes to sit out the entire conflict. The Sundays were devoted to more time exploring, while in the dailies the blond hero was sent on an interminable journey, starting in 1940 in Antarctica and ending on the moon in 1946. With the return of peace, Ritt seemed to have regained his stride, but this did not last long. Growing gradually disenchanted with the strip, he left more and more of the writing to his collaborator until he was finally released from his duties by the syndicate.

In 1949 Gray became the sole author of the feature: he intended to concentrate on more concise, more focused stories, but these ambitions were cut short when he was diagnosed with throat cancer later in the year. Inevitably his work began to suffer, and in 1952 he had to relinquish both the writing and the drawing of the daily strip to Paul Norris (who had earlier ghosted some sequences Gray had been too ill to draw). Retaining only the Sunday page, he turned it into a series of science-fantasy tales; there were still traces of brilliance in some of the pages, but the old dash had gone. Nevertheless he doggedly kept grinding out the *Brick Bradford* Sundays, now only pale reflections of their earlier incarnation, almost up to the day when he finally succumbed to his illness in 1957.

Paul Norris then took over the entire strip. His graphic style had none of his predecessor's brio and tended to the heavy-handed; his writing, however, proved adequate and sometimes even excellent, and he piloted Brick into further space and time adventures for more than three decades, putting in almost twice as much time on the feature as Gray had done. Norris's last daily appeared on April 25, 1987, with the following valedictory:" So...fifty-three and a half years after *Brick Bradford* began his daily stints in the newspapers of America and throughout the world, his adventures wind down to the final curtain..." In the last strip there was also a strong hint that Brick was finally ready to settle down. Due to the vagaries of newspaper-strip production, the last Sunday page, while drawn earlier, appeared on May 10, 1987. And thus ended the saga of one of the most enduring of comic-strip adventurers.

M.H.

BRINGING UP FATHER
`1913–present`

*B*ringing Up Father is in very select company, surpassed in longevity only by *The Katzenjammer Kids* and *Mutt and Jeff.* It was launched January 2, 1913, by George McManus, who in the very first episode established the formula that was to serve him well for forty-one years. Immigrant worker Jiggs and his wife Mary have come into a lot of money (by what means, we are not told). Mary aggressively uses the wealth to unlock the doors of the upper crust of society, while Jiggs remains unchanged and unfazed, still yearning only for a night at Dinty Moore's tavern, playing cards and pool, and eating his favorite dish of corned beef and cabbage. In the inaugural strip, Mary insists that Jiggs dress up before the arrival of Miss Loose Change, a high-society lass coming to meet their son. After she gets there, Jiggs comes out holding his shoes and says, "Say, Mary, I cant [sic] wear these shoes. My corn hurts. Will you fix my tie?" In the next panels, Loose Change faints before departing in a huff, and Mary and the couple's daughter gasp and sob in disbelief.

There were some slight variations on this formula of a family trying to adjust to high-society life. By the 1920s, Maggie (Mary by then had acquired the more familiar name) was reacting furiously to Jiggs's interruptions of her attempts at social climbing, and from thence forward, in many strips the last panel showed Jiggs leaving the house in a hail of dishes, rolling pins, or bricks, or sporting a shiner. Maggie undoubtedly was a tough cookie who in modern society would be up on multiple counts of spousal abuse; Coulton Waugh observed that save for Popeye, very

Brick Bradford (Ritt and Gray), © 1937 King Features Syndicate

Bringing Up Father (G. McManus), 1919

few men in comicdom could stand up to her. In the beginning, Jiggs stood about as tall as his wife, although the proportion seemed to change from panel to panel. But like Barney Google, and for the same reason, Jiggs's size dwindled, McManus explaining, "It is simply ridiculous to believe that Maggie could do what she does to a husky, powerful roughneck such as Jiggs was originally. Pitted against such a tyrannical spouse, Jiggs's will to be himself (and to sneak off to Dinty Moore's) was indomitable. In many a strip, Jiggs is seen pulling the wool over Maggie's eyes and escaping from the house, immaculately dressed, complete with top hat and tails, along a route that necessitated walking on telephone lines, jumping from one building ledge to another, inching his way along steel girders, or using his cane to lower himself into a window at Dinty Moore's. Occasional stories were built around Maggie's never-do-well brother Bimmy, known for his mooching and for his sticky fingers, and Nora, their beautiful daughter who usually seemed to be a mannequinlike prop.

Pretty women adorned the panels from time to time, to accommodate Jiggs's ogling ways, and at other times, to show off the artist's masterly depiction of the female anatomy, hairstyles, and clothing. McManus women were shown as gorgeous and perfectly coifed in the Gibson style, and were attired in the latest fashions. Many strips had a sensuality about them, showing women in silhouette, the light shining through their dresses highlighting their shapely legs, or depicting them in provocative sitting positions. Even Maggie, ugly as she was, had an hourglass figure that could turn men's heads.

Bringing Up Father was a gallery of delicately executed patterns, designs, and decorations, shown in Maggie or Nora's latest dress or hat, or in the wallpaper, furniture, staircases, doors, vases, and rugs. McManus delighted in filling his strips with these ornate decorations replete with curlicues, and with prop pictures on the walls that had animated figures emerging from them and carrying on their own antics. The reader became used to focusing on these miniature characters throwing balls at each other or blowing smoke rings into the room. McManus was also known for shaping and sizing panels to suit the day's narrative, for drawing broad panoramas and detailed cityscapes that showed off his keen knowledge of architectural design, and for deviating from the standard of putting the one punchline per strip in the last panel; a Sunday *Bringing Up Father* might contain three or four punchlines scattered about. His assistant, Zeke Zekeley, felt McManus was heavily influenced by Japanese artists who also liked clean lines and solid blacks.

McManus's style was fully formed by 1905, and his main characters and themes evolved through the immense amount of work the prolific cartoonist did. Jiggs's facial features popped up in that early work, and he and Maggie can be found in another McManus strip dating from as early as November 1911. The domestic-life, relations-between-the-sexes topic dominated what historian R. C. Harvey, in his *Art of the Funnies,* termed the "McManus anthology"—"finite variations on aspects of a subject appearing in rotation as a series of individually titled comic strips." Among these strips that would have assured McManus a place in comics history had he not come up with *Bringing Up Father* were his first strip for the *St. Louis Republic, Alma and Oliver,* and the following for the *New York World* (1905–10): *Snoozer, The Merry Marceline, Nibsy the Newsboy in Funny Fairyland, Cheerful Charley, Panhandle Pete, Let George Do It, The Newlyweds,* and *Spareribs and Gravy.* In 1912, McManus was recruited by Hearst; he brought *The Newlyweds* with him and retitled it *Their Only Child.* His first creation for Hearst was *Outside the Asylum,* which lasted a month. *Bringing Up Father* came out immediately after, appearing only three or four days a week. On Sundays, McManus did a second page, *Love Affairs of a Muttonhead.* The Sunday version of *Bringing Up Father* came out on April 14, 1918.

After McManus's death in 1954, Vernon Greene drew the strip until his own death in 1965, after which Frank Fletcher and Hamlet Campana illustrated the Sunday and daily *Bringing Up Father,* respectively, and William Kavanagh wrote the script. At the time of McManus's death, *Bringing Up Father* appeared in five hundred newspapers in forty-six countries.

J.A.L.

Bronc Peeler (F. Harman), © 1936 Fred Harman Features

BRONC PEELER
1934–1938

Fred Harman had grown up on his father's ranch in Colorado, but he had always felt from earliest childhood the urge to become a cartoonist. After working briefly with his brother Hugh and the young Walt Disney in a Kansas City advertising agency, he moved to Hollywood, and while there decided to combine his knowledge of the West with his love of drawing at one blow in a cowboy strip, which he titled *Bronc Peeler*. Coming out early in 1934, Harman's creation, appearing both daily and Sundays, was self-syndicated by its author under the overblown corporate name of Fred Harman Features, and sold to a handful of western newspapers.

Bronc Peeler was a red-haired, callow ranch hand who chanced upon the most unlikely adventures in the early days of the strip. He later aged by a few years overnight and acquired additional wisdom. Like most newspaper-strip cowboys, he ranged far and wide from his New Mexico base of operations in the company of Coyote Pete, his grizzled, somewhat befuddled sidekick. The action was set in contemporary times, and Bronc more than once demonstrated that he was as expert at driving cars or flying planes as at riding horses.

While some of the plots were quite conventional—involving cattle rustlers, crooked lawyers, and bank robbers—others were quite original. At one point, for example, Bronc was recruited by the FBI and the Mexican secret police to uncover a sinister organization bent on causing trouble on both sides of the Rio Grande by means of a deadly virus ("the red plague"). On another occasion Bronc and Pete discovered the Lost Valley of the Aztecs, where the king's lovely daughter, Princess Moonbeam, inevitably fell in love with the carrot-topped hero and saved him and his companion from death at the hands of the wrathful Aztecs. At the conclusion of each of his exploits Bronc would always come back to his blonde, effervescent sweetheart, the long-suffering Babs.

After a few years, Bronc acquired a new companion, an Indian boy named Little Beaver, in hopes of attracting a juvenile readership, but to no avail. *Bronc Peeler* folded in 1938, despite Harman's appealing, if roughhewn, graphic style,

and his minute depiction of horses, cattle, and western scenery. Along with the *Bronc Peeler* Sunday page, Harman had also drawn a panel describing western life and lore. Called *On the Range*, the feature gave Harman the opportunity to indulge his penchant for didacticism, a trait he would never lose in the course of his long career.

M.H.

BRONCHO BILL
1928–1950

United Feature Syndicate came out with one of the earliest examples of a western comic strip in 1928. Drawn and written by Harry O'Neill, the strip started as *Young Buffalo Bill*, then was briefly changed to *Buckaroo Bill*, before acquiring its definitive title in 1932 (perhaps as a tribute to the first western movie star, Broncho Billy Anderson).

The action took place in a geographical area at the foot of the Rockies, perhaps Montana (some episodes have the mountains as background, others are set in the plains), at the time of the Civil War. In order to help the local sheriff cope with the influx of outlaws caused by the war and in the absence of most men of military age, Bill had organized a corps of youthful vigilantes known as the Rangers. Bill and his cohorts saw no paucity of action, what with cattle rustlers, claim jumpers, bank robbers, and other miscreants abounding.

Despite his young age Bill could outdraw any man west of the Missouri (he once shot the glasses out of the hands of a half-dozen outlaws with a single bullet); and, mounted

Broncho Bill (H. O'Neill), © 1945 United Feature Syndicate

on his faithful stallion Blackie, he was able to outrun any pursuing foe. Bill's enemies, fooled by his young age, often made the mistake of kidnapping him, but the teenage ranger would somehow manage to get loose and return with reinforcements to fall upon the unwitting bandits. His constant companion on many of his adventures was the dark-haired Nell, and between rides they found the time to strike up a stormy romance.

O'Neill's draftsmanship was not on a par with his ambitions, and neither was his writing. His graphic style was limp, and his action scenes lacked punch at the climax; the narrative and dialogue were written in an atrocious style. Yet there were some nice documentary touches in *Broncho Bill*, such as the correct depiction of weapons and riding equipment, and the timely allusions to real figures and incidents of the Old West.

Broncho Bill appeared only daily until September 24, 1933, when it also acquired a Sunday page, touted by the syndicate as an "exciting tale of action, suspense, and thrills." As a topper to the main feature, O'Neill, a former circus acrobat, created *Bumps,* a romance of the Big Top. The Sundays ended in the late 1940s, while the dailies lingered until January 8, 1950.

M.H.

BROOM-HILDA
1970–present

Russell Myers's hilarious *Broom-Hilda* first appeared on April 19, 1970, courtesy of the Chicago Tribune–New York News Syndicate. Myers was a designer at Hallmark Cards and a freelance artist, who after several unsuccessful comic-strip submissions used some creative magic to originate his famous feature. Frightfully funny, it follows the gag-a-day episodes of the eccentric denizens of the Haunted Forest: Broom-Hilda, a fifteen-hundred-year-old, cigar-chomping, beer-guzzling witch; Gaylord, the bespectacled, vegetarian buzzard whose quest for knowledge matches his unbounded cowardice; and Irwin the troll, a naively innocent hairball who spreads love and warmth wherever he goes, a benevolent beacon in an otherwise cynical world.

Hilda wields her wand usually with ineffectual results, and her hapless pursuit of practically any man is her unre-

Broom-Hilda (R. Myers), © Chicago Tribune–New York News Syndicate

quited lot. During the strip's early years, Hilda transported herself regularly back in time, popping in on such notables of history as the first caveman, King Henry VIII, Sir Walter Raleigh, and Benedict Arnold. Hilda's conquering of the fourth dimension opened up a floodgate of dating possibilities. Described by her creator as "a dirty old man in a dress," this silly sorceress was first married to Attila the Hun and still wears USMC undershorts from her previous Marine Corps training. One of the original supporting characters was Grelber, a mean and cynical—and unidentifiable—creature who lived in a cliffside log dispatching "free insults." An antagonist to all other cast members, its menacing demeanor and bizarre presence have no place in the current version. Rounding out the cast is Irwin's beanied nephew Nerwin, a diminutive yet more learned clone of his uncle who appears more adjusted than his adult counterparts. The Forest is a virtual circus of personalities, providing an odd supporting cast of additional foils for gags, such as talking animals, horrific monsters, and larcenous flowers that lift wallets from passersby. This manic menagerie is drawn in a solid, furiously loony style existing in a surreal landscape of ever-changing backgrounds, reminiscent of George Herriman's *Krazy Kat.* The effect is one of direct yet richly mannered brashness, which creates a perfect vehicle for the artist's depiction of absurd imagination and innocuously macabre fantasy. Striving for more sources of humor, the characters frequently have found themselves outside the sheltered environs of their forest; their exposure to everyday urban existence has provided Myers with an opportunity to more directly parody commonplace situations, subtly shifting his focus between philosophical reflection, slapstick, and commentary. The original feel of the strip was rooted in the psychedelic, and although expectedly less so now, it still remains one of the most unique-looking contemporary comics; a model of sophistication to a generation of humor features that have followed it.

Numerous paperback collections have been published of *Broom-Hilda;* and in 1971, shortly after the strip's debut, the characters starred in a Saturday-morning television series titled *Archie's TV Funnies,* along with Alley Oop, the Katzenjammer Kids, and others. Filmation studios captured none of the ingenuity of the various properties it animated, yet episodes were released again in 1978 as *The Fabulous Funnies.* Plush dolls and other merchandising followed, including signed lithographs by Stabur Corporation.

Despite Broom-Hilda's comically repulsive appearance, crass self-indulgence, and habitual irritability, she is an endearing character who clearly casts an enchanting spell on her millions of faithful readers.

B.J.

BRUCE GENTRY
1945–1951

Ray Bailey had assisted Milton Caniff on *Terry and the Pirates* and Frank Robbins on *Scorchy Smith;* it is therefore not surprising that he would want one day to have an aviation strip of his own. On March 25, 1945, he got his wish with *Bruce Gentry,* distributed daily and Sunday by the New York Post Corporation.

In the waning days of World War II Bruce Gentry indulged (in a series of flashbacks) in the standard heroics demanded by the times: as a flyer with the U.S. Air Force, the blond hero took part in the battles on the European continent, and he was later shot down while flying cover for a Marine Corps landing on a Japanese-held Pacific island. Returned to civilian life because of his wounds, he devoted himself to the more peaceful pursuit of carrying cargo and passengers over the rugged Andes from his base in the fictional South American country of Cordillera. His life did not remain untroubled for long: Southern Cross Airlines, the company that employed him, seemed perpetually beset by unscrupulous competitors, drug smugglers, and air pirates, and as its chief troubleshooter Gentry got involved in some hair-raising adventures.

True to the genre, Gentry had a sentimental life as agitated as his professional career. Latin American sirens with evocative names like Tango or Raven would throw themselves at the dashing flyer, while North American beauties would try to snare him into serious commitment, to the frustration of his loyal if neglected sweetheart Cleo Patric (whom he would marry in the closing days of the strip). The South American locale had played a large part in the initial appeal of *Bruce Gentry,* with the syndicate even expressing "hopes the comic will improve relations between North and South America," but it eventually proved too small to hold the hero, who went adventuring all over the globe.

Bailey drew the strip with a real feeling for space and atmosphere, especially in the daily black-and-white continuities, and his plotting and dialogue were workmanlike and agreeable, if hardly original. In an era when air transport had become commonplace, and in skies already crowded by the likes of Steve Canyon, Buz Sawyer, and Johnny Hazard, Bruce Gentry could no longer survive; and in January 1951 the strip came to an end. Its demise was evidence that the romance of aviation was now part of history.

M.H.

BRUTUS
1929–1938

While best known as the author of the Raggedy Ann and Andy books, Johnny Gruelle was also a well-established newspaper and magazine cartoonist, and the creator of at least two comic strips of merit. The first one, *Mr. Twee Deedle,* ran in the comic supplement of the *New York Herald* from 1910 to 1921; after an eight-year hiatus devoted almost exclusively to Raggedy Ann and Andy, Gruelle then came up with *Brutus,* which made its debut as a Sunday page distributed by the New York Herald-Tribune Syndicate from November 17, 1929.

Brutus Dudd was a portly little man much given to smoking big cigars and having mild arguments with his wife. His domestic life was further complicated by the shenanigans of his two pets, a cat named Mark Anthony

Brutus (J. Gruelle), © 1934 Johnny Gruelle

and a dog called Caesar (only Cleopatra was missing). The gags were only intermittently funny, but the page was redeemed by Gruelle's unconventional graphic style, a mixture of turn-of-the-century cartooning and fantasy illustration, with elements of cubism and surrealism thrown in.

In the 1930s *Brutus,* like so many other gag strips of the period, went for adventure—but it was adventure with a difference. The drawings became more ungeometrical and even weirder as time went on. His characters had tilted facial features and sported ill-fitting or wholly unaccountable pieces of clothing. Derby-hatted and cigar-chomping animals were running all across the page, involved in obscure pursuits whose relevance to the main narrative was never made clear. The plots were just as unpredictable as the drawings. The action ostensibly took place on a cattle spread called the Hot Dog Ranch. Brutus acquired preternatural strength, and his feats foreshadowed those of Popeye. He had as companions the slow-witted Sampson and Lilly Hoss, a strangely shaped, funny-acting creature presented by Gruelle as a mare. The action was full of non sequiturs and outlandish situations (at one point Lilly Hoss gulped down a bottle of hair lotion and ran around looking like a sheepdog).

Despite its creator's fame, *Brutus* never reached the popularity or acclaim as such other pioneering strips as *Krazy Kat* or *Thimble Theatre.* The last page appeared on February 27, 1938, a few weeks after Johnny Gruelle's death.

M.H.

BUCK NIX
See OLD DOC YAK

BUCK ROGERS
1929–1967, 1979–1983

Buck Rogers in the 25th Century was the immensely influential work that introduced futuristic, outer-space adventure to the comic strips, only a couple of years after the creation of this genre. It was not the first strip to present rockets-and-ray-guns melodrama, but its predecessors (such as C. W. Kahles's *Hairbreadth Harry*) did so only as individual and comedic sequences before returning to the contemporary real world. *Buck Rogers* came to typify interplanetary "space opera" so thoroughly that for the next five decades, science fiction of any sort was popularly known as "that crazy Buck Rogers stuff."

The daily strip began on January 7, 1929, by writer Phil Nowlan and artist Dick Calkins, as an adaptation of Nowlan's earlier pulp-magazine novelette, *Armageddon 2419 A.D.* Yet credit for the creation of Buck Rogers is claimed today for its distributor, John F. Dille. According to Ray Bradbury, in his preface to *The Collected Works of Buck Rogers in the 25th Century* (1969), Dille had been impressed by the rapid growth in popularity of the new "scientifiction" genre of pulp-adventure fiction, which had started with the April 1926 issue of *Amazing Stories.* He wanted a comic strip like this for his newspaper distribution syndicate, the John F. Dille Company. He already had a staff artist for it in Dick Calkins, a sports-page cartoonist who had served in the Army Air Corps during World War I (and who would sign his art as "Lt. Dick Calkins"). When Dille read Philip Francis Nowlan's futuristic thriller in the August 1928 issue of *Amazing Stories,* he had found his plot. Dille contacted Nowlan and hired him to turn his planned series of adventures of Anthony Rogers in the twenty-fifth century from magazine stories into a comic strip instead. (One more novelette, *The Airlords of Han,* appeared in the March 1929 *Amazing Stories.*) Dille is also credited with changing Nowlan's hero's name to the more dynamic "Buck."

In both versions, Rogers is investigating a strange gas in a deep mine shaft in present-day America when he is overcome and falls into suspended animation. He awakens five hundred years later, to an America that is fighting to regain its independence after four centuries of Mongol domination. Buck is recruited into the resistance by attractive Wilma Deering, who remained his main companion for the rest of the strip's existence. The Mongols are barely overthrown when Earth is attacked by tiger men from Mars, and the action moves into outer space.

Buck Rogers introduced most of the staples of science-fiction plotting to the newspaper-reading public during its first decade: rocket-powered space ships, antigravity belts, alien inhabitants of other worlds, space pirates, bubble-domed undersea cities, scientifically extended life spans, and much more. In addition to Buck and Wilma, the cast of continuing characters grew to include their main nemesis, "Killer" Kane (usually a space pirate but always involved in villainy); Kane's sultry aide, Ardala Valmar; Dr. Huer, an Einsteinlike brilliant scientist; and Black Barney, a reformed space pirate who became a loyal friend. Buck was often accompanied by hyperenthusiastic young teens—originally Wilma's kid brother Buddy Deering and his platonic pal, Princess Alura of Mars, and later such space-going hepcats as "Hot-Rocket" Horace and "Ram-Jet" Rosie.

A Sunday page began on March 30, 1930. Both strips were signed by Nowlan and Calkins until 1940, but the Sunday strip was actually drawn by Russell Keaton until 1933, then by Rick Yager. Nowlan was dropped from *Buck Rogers* in 1940, shortly before his unexpected death (which has led to an often-repeated claim that he wrote the strip until he died). Calkins and Yager each took over writing as well as drawing their strips until 1947, when Calkins resigned from the Dille syndicate. The daily strip was then written by Bob Barton from 1947 to 1951, and drawn by Murphy Anderson (1947–49) and Leon Dworkins (1949–51). Rick Yager took over writing and drawing both the daily and Sunday strips from 1951 until 1958, when he left the syndicate the year after Dille's death. Yager was replaced as the artist on both strips by Murphy Anderson again (1958–59) and George Tuska (April 1959 to 1965 for the Sunday strip and to 1967 for the daily strip, when each was canceled). There were several writers during the strip's last decade, including, briefly, the famous sci-fi author Fritz Leiber.

The greatest popularity of *Buck Rogers* was during the 1930s. A radio dramatization began in 1932 and lasted for years. King Features Syndicate assigned Alex Raymond to create a competing space-adventure strip, and his *Flash Gordon* began in January 1934. The two became legendary rivals, with the latter usually the more popular due to Raymond's superb artistry. But *Buck Rogers* retained its status as the stereotype for melodramatic science fiction—to the extent that when Warner Bros. staff animation director Chuck Jones and writer Michael Maltese parodied this genre in 1953, their cartoon was titled *Duck Dodgers in the 24½th Century. Flash Gordon* was the first to spin off two movie serials, featuring Larry "Buster" Crabbe in 1936 and 1938; these so solidly established Crabbe as moviedom's favorite space hero that he then starred as Buck in a similar *Buck Rogers* serial in 1939. The *Buck Rogers* newspaper

Buck Rogers (Nowlan and Calkins), © 1936 John F. Dille Co.

strips were reprinted in comic-book format almost continuously from 1940 through 1955, either as *Buck Rogers* or as *Famous Funnies.* Some new stories were produced for the comic book in the early 1950s, including some of the earliest comic-book art of Frank Frazetta.

Buck Rogers began to seem old-fashioned and overly juvenile during the U.S.-Soviet space rivalry of the late 1950s and early '60s. The Sunday strip was dropped in 1965 and the daily disappeared in 1967—ironically, just before a new wave of nostalgia for the "classic" newspaper strips and academic interest in their histories. A massive hardbound sampler, *The Collected Works of Buck Rogers in the 25th Century* (1969), presented lengthy selections from 1929 through Calkins's departure in 1947, soon followed by other reprint volumes.

This renewed interest culminated in a 1979 movie and a TV series, both titled *Buck Rogers in the 25th Century* and starring Gil Gerard, produced by Glen Larson and Leslie Stevens. The series ran from September 20, 1979, to April 16, 1981. *Buck Rogers* purists were nauseated by the *Star Wars* influences hammered into it, and by the portrayal of Buck as a fun-loving twentieth-century daredevil-astronaut who teaches the uptight twenty-fifth century "how to boogie." But it generated enough popularity that the comic strip was revived for four years, starting on September 9, 1979. Jim Lawrence and Gray Morrow were the first writer and artist. Cary Bates took over the writing in 1981, and Jack Sparling became the new artist in 1982. During these years, Gold Key produced comic books based on the TV series; but Buck Rogers was retired, from both print formats, for the last time by 1983.

F.P.

BUCKAROO BILL
See BRONCHO BILL

BUGS BUNNY
1942–1993

Bugs Bunny is undoubtedly the best-known rabbit in the world, eclipsing Peter Cottontail and even Peter Rabbit. He is also one of the few cartoon characters to make it big, not only in comic books and comic strips, but also in movies and television. He has even won an Oscar.

The *Bugs Bunny* comic books and strip were based on characters in animated cartoons produced by Leon Schlesinger with the help of many studio employees. Bugs first appeared in *Porky's Hare Hunt,* a Porky Pig cartoon directed by Ben ("Bugs") Hardaway and Cal Dalton and based on a story by Bob Clampett. The first rabbit, although quite unlike the final Bugs, was so popular that the same directors did *Hare-um Scare-um,* featuring a reworked version of the rabbit. Another version appeared in *Presto Change-o,* directed by Chuck Jones. In 1939, when it was apparent that the rabbit was becoming a star, two more films were made: *Elmer's Candid Camera,* directed by Jones; and *A Wild Hare,* directed by Fred ("Tex") Avery. It was in *A Wild Hare* that the character most closely resem-

Bugs Bunny (R. Heimdahl), © 1967 Warner Bros. Pictures

bling the wisecracking Bugs Bunny of international fame appeared, along with his sassy "What's up, Doc?" After this film was made the bunny was given the name Bugs, from director Hardaway's nickname.

Bugs Bunny's first appearance was in the movies, in 1938. A long series of Bugs Bunny cartoons and comic books followed. The cartoons were released (and later produced) by Warner Bros. until 1969. Most of them were directed by Tex Avery, Bob Clampett, Chuck Jones, Fritz Freleng, Robert McKimson, and Frank Tashlin, featuring voices by Mel Blanc. The cartoons continue to be television favorites, and Bugs Bunny tie-ins with all sorts of merchandise are commonplace.

His comic-book debut occurred in 1941 in the first issue of Dell's *Looney Tunes and Merrie Melodies.* Bugs appeared in this magazine along with several other popular members of the Warner Bros. animated menagerie, including Porky Pig, Elmer Fudd, and Sniffles. Win Smith, who had drawn the *Mickey Mouse* newspaper strip in its early days, drew the first solo story about the rabbit, but newspaper veteran George Storm took over in the second issue.

The *Bugs Bunny* comic book began as part of the Dell *Four Color* series and appeared in twenty-seven international issues, mainly by Chase Craig, before regular publication began in 1953 with issue number 28. Bugs also appeared in dozens of other comic books, such as *Golden Comics Digest, March of Comics,* and *Super Comics, Porky Pig,* and *Yosemite Sam.* Among the writers involved in Bugs Bunny stories were: Lloyd Turner, Don Christensen, Sid Marcus, Carl Fallberg, Tom Packer, Cecil Beard, and Mark Evanier. Artists have included Win Smith, Tom McKimson, Phil DeLara, Ralph Heimdahl, and John Carey.

Bugs began appearing in newspaper comic sections in 1942, at first only in Sunday editions. Although Bugs headlined the strip, the syndicate insisted that other familiar Warners cartoon characters appear with him.

The first six Sundays were written and drawn by Chase Craig. When Craig went into the navy, Roger Armstrong got the job. He was paid $25 a week for writing, penciling, lettering, inking, and mailing. He was replaced two years later by Carl Buettner. A great many writers and artists worked on the strip, including Fallberg, McKimson, Armstrong, and Heimdahl. In 1948 a daily *Bugs Bunny* strip was added. Heimdahl, who had experience drawing the Sunday, drew the daily as well, working over the next

The Bungle Family (H. Tuthill), © 1931 McNaught Syndicate

twenty-five years with various writers. Shawn Keller took over the artwork on the feature (now called *What's Up, Doc?*)in 1990, bringing it to its close in 1993.

T.W.

BUGVILLE LIFE
See THE LATEST NEWS FROM BUGVILLE

THE BUNGLE FAMILY
1918–1942, 1943–1945

Of the many comic strips centered on American family life that emerged in the teens and twenties of this century, perhaps none presented so bleak a view of domesticity as Harry J. Tuthill's acid-edged feature *The Bungle Family*. Originally a daily gag-strip appearing under the ironic title *Home, Sweet Home* in the *New York Evening Mail*, it presented the usual cliches of the bickering married couple, but it was to evolve into an imaginative continuity feature when it was taken over by the McNaught Syndicate in 1924. In the process, George and Jo acquired a last name and a full-grown daughter Peggy, and the strip added a Sunday page.

Relatively compatible themselves, the Bungles were remarkable among comic-strip families for their incompatibility with the rest of the world. Their lives were a perpetual conflict with relatives, employers, landlords, bill collectors, cops, and an endless stream of weird and hateful neighbors. (George summarizes his attitude with the words, "The way I look at neighbors, never hit them with your fist unless they grab the club out of your hand," and his rancor is fully reciprocated.) The opportunistic but perennially unemployed George bungles his way into and out of improbable scrapes in his pursuit of an easy buck; but as abrasive and spiteful as he and his wife are, those around them are usually even worse. Tuthill was an equal-opportunity misanthrope, and his satire was indiscriminately aimed at everyone in his cast. Even the bit players in the background contribute to the sour tone of the strip: "Your darling mother is so sweet," sneers a woman glimpsed for a moment, "—to my face!"

Richly peopled with inventive characters, the ingenious stories spun out in *The Bungle Family* were imaginative from its first days as a continuity strip, involving mistaken identity, romance, crime, and mysterious disappearances. In one 1928 episode, a fake swami, hired to cure George of what a doctor has diagnosed as malingeritis, hypnotizes him and deprives him of his memory, leading to an adventure with a new identity, an eccentric millionaire, a huge inheritance, and other elements of melodrama, all told

with wry humor. As Tuthill became more confident, and perhaps a little restless, in the 1930s, he drew his characters into increasingly fantastic situations, involving them in international politics, talking animals, alien creatures from the fifth dimension, and space- and time-travel.

The *Bungle Family* was retired on August 1, 1942, following some conflict between Tuthill and the syndicate, but the artist resumed publication nine and a half months later, on May 17, 1943, distributing the strip himself. It lasted for another couple of years and was finally put to sleep on June 2, 1945.

Original as its plotting, characterization, and dialogue are, *The Bungle Family* had little claim to graphic distinction. Graceless in composition and conventional in technique, its characters were typical stylized cartoon figures, with noses like cucumbers and bodies like either beanpoles or beanbags. The appeal of the strip, which remained popular throughout its long run, was not visual, but rather depended on Tuthill's mordant characterization and lively narrative, and a level of sardonic humor rarely equaled in the comics.

D.W.

BUNKY
1927–1948

On May 16, 1926, Billy DeBeck introduced *Parlor, Bedroom, and Sink* as the top piece to his Sunday *Barney Google* page. It concerned itself with the domestic and social predicaments of a couple of bickering lovebirds, Bunker Hill and his wife Bibsy. On November 13, 1927, Bibsy caught up with her runaway husband and presented him with a surprise package: a bundle containing his son, Bunker, Jr., a baby graced with a nose of Cyrano proportions. Nicknamed Bunky, the infant would soon take over the entire feature.

In a matter of months the baby blossomed into a pint-sized philosopher in control of a large and recondite vocabulary, who would spout words of wisdom and maxims of grave profundity from under his lace cap. From burlesque and low comedy the strip took a turn into picaresque adventure with the introduction in July 1930 of Fagan (later renamed Fagin in homage to the eponymous character in Dickens's *Oliver Twist*), an unredeemable villain whose depths of depravity were in abysmal contrast to Bunky's heights of innocence. From this point on Fagin time and again would cross paths with the pure-hearted infant vainly trying to thwart the black-souled adult's unspeakable schemes with the damning cry, "Fagin, youse is a viper!" In spite of their unrelenting antagonism Bunky and Fagin enjoyed a close, almost symbiotic relationship.

Even in Fagin's absence, Bunky experienced a host of harrowing adventures, which he was fond to relate in the high-fallutin' tones of Victorian fiction. One typically ironic example occurred in 1937, when the infant attempted to recount how he had rescued millionaire Gilhooley's pooch from a band of dognappers. "I was about to tell you the harrowing experience I had with the 'Black Widow' gang before I recovered the ransom money—on the dark and stormy night of August 16...," he started, but was unable to finish his tale.

In recognition of the infant's paramount role in the strip, the feature added a "starring Bunky" appendage to its title in 1932, before changing into simple *Bunky* in 1935. After DeBeck's death in 1942, his successors, Joe Musial and Fred Lasswell, were at a loss about what to do with a strip that belonged to no recognizable genre. *Bunky* was finally dropped on July 18, 1948.

M.H.

BUSTER BROWN
1902–1926

After leaving the Hearst organization in 1898, Richard Outcault tried his hand at a number of new comic series, notably *Pore Li'l Mose*, about a black little boy, for the *New York Herald*. None of these creations even remotely approached the success he had enjoyed with *The Yellow Kid*, until he came up with *Buster Brown*, which made its debut in the *Herald*'s Sunday comic supplement on May 4, 1902.

Buster Brown was a fresh-faced, nattily attired boy who hid the mind of a devil under his angelic appearance. His pranks extended to relatives and strangers alike, and no amount of spanking could cure him of his penchant for mischief. The world he lived in was a far cry from the Yellow Kid's slum: Mr. Brown was a prosperous and quietly distinguished businessman, Mrs. Brown an attractive and stylish woman of leisure (reportedly modeled on the artist's wife), and their only child was at once the pride and the bane of their lives. They loved to give dinners and receptions, occasions that all too often served as showcases for Buster's genius at mischief-making.

Buster had two constant companions who shared in the thrill of his nefarious enterprises but somehow always managed to escape their punishment. First there was his talking (and talkative) bulldog Tige whose asides provided an ironic commentary on the various goings-on. His powers of empathy were infinite: he would convulse in laughter at Buster's diabolical pranks, and hang down his head in sorrow at the spectacle of his master's inevitable comeuppance. Second came the affectionately named Mary Jane (as were both Outcault's wife and his daughter), a dark-tressed hellion and precocious vamp of the species the French call *ingenue perverse* (a type the great French writer Colette was delineating in her novels about the same time). Dressed in the latest fashions, with a large ribbon in her hair, she often egged her companion on to his wild schemes, such as giving a surprise party for himself or creating a panic in a department store. In those rare moments when he was not engaged in some prank, Buster loved nothing more than playing the role of young man-about-town. His blond looks and cherubic face made him quite a hit with girls his age, and he would take one for a spin around the dance floor while giving another the eye. There always was an underground current of childhood sexuality running through the strip, a current that would sometimes surface, as in the episode in which Buster, pinned down to the ground by two giggling schoolgirls, was made the unwilling object of a kissing contest.

Buster was always allowed a show of contrition in the form of a hand-lettered signed piously called "Resolution" at the end of each Sunday episode. Buster's facial expression (and his renewed pranks) left no doubt about the insincerity of his resolutions. Moving in middle-class surroundings, unlike the Yellow Kid, he had learned the virtue of hypocrisy. One of these "resolutions" runs so strikingly counter to the spirit of all resolutions, and so much in the spirit of the strip, that it deserves to be quoted: "Resolved! That I will quit making resolutions. If we don't make them, we can't break them. It's the fellow who does wrong who resolves to do right." The Voltairian tone of mockery is unmistakable. Buster plays a cat-and-mouse game with the grown-ups, just as Outcault played a cat-and-mouse game with the censors. At any rate, Buster's credo was summed up in another one of these resolutions: "There's too much seriousness loose on the market now.... I am going to laugh and work overtime at it."

Outcault drew the strip in a graphic style influenced more by the Charles Dana Gibson school of illustration than by the cartoon conventions of most other comic features, which may account for Buster's success among a more genteel class of readers. His drawings were always sharp and clearly delineated, with a minimum of exaggeration, and his compositions looked airy and attractive, even in crowd scenes. His graceful, easy line inspired a latter generation of cartoonists, from George McManus to Martin Branner.

Buster Brown (R. F. Outcault), 1903

Hearst couldn't help but notice Buster Brown's newly acquired star status, and in 1905 he hired his former employee for the second time. Outcault thus brought his characters over to the *New York American* the second Sunday of January 1906, while the *Herald* had the strip continued by William Lawler (who did a creditable job of imitating his predecessor's tone and style) and other hands, until its eventual demise early in 1911. Prohibited by court order from utilizing the strip's name, Outcault ran the feature under a variety of headings framed by the grinning likenesses of the boy prankster and his dog companion, which may have led to the strip being called "Buster and Tige" by some. At any rate, under whatever name, Outcault's creation soared to even greater heights of popularity. Buster and Tige appeared on a multitude of commercial products, from candy to whisky. In 1910 the founding of the Outcault Advertising Agency led to further promotion of the characters. Now a wealthy man, Outcault decided to leave the comic-strip field: his last page appeared in December 1921, although the strip continued in reprints until 1926.

Buster Brown's fame, while firmly rooted in the first two decades of this century, has lasted to this day in many forms. His name has given rise to a number of popular expressions still in currency today, as in "Wait a minute, Buster!" and "Who do you think you are, Buster?" There still exists a line of Buster Brown shoes, and all kinds of garments are still being manufactured by Buster Brown Apparel, Inc., of New York City, which also runs the Buster Brown Museum.

M.H.

BUZ SAWYER
1943–1989

In 1943, in the middle of a war, Roy Crane, the creator of *Wash Tubbs,* deserted NEA for King Features. There he created yet another punning title, *Buz Sawyer,* which debuted as a daily strip on November 1, 1943, followed by a Sunday page on November 28.

Crane had originally planned to make his hero, Lt. John Singer ("Buz") Sawyer a fighter pilot, "for the panache," he said, but was persuaded to have him fly a fighter-bomber for the U.S. Navy instead. This was a happy choice in that it gave the handsome, clean-cut Buz a ready-made foil in the person of his tailgunner, a tough-looking, pot-bellied enlisted man named Rosco Sweeney. In addition, to avoid the trap of too close an identification with current events, Crane set the action slightly back in time, which gave him the benefit of hindsight (the first daily episode, for instance, took place on Christmas Eve, 1942).

Buz's adventures during the war, while necessarily more melodramatic than they would have been in real life, stressed the collective contribution of all the sailors, marines, and flyers serving aboard the aircraft-carrier *Tippecanoe,* with fascinating depictions not only of combat scenes but of the daily routine undergone by fighting men at sea. Individual exploits were not slighted, however, with Buz and Rosco finding themselves stranded on a Pacific island, fending off the advances of sarong-clad native girls, taken prisoners by the Japanese and making a daring escape, mounting a perilous night operation to slow down an advancing enemy column, and much more.

All the strips born of the World War II boom faced the task of recycling themselves at the end of the conflict. Buz for his part went into private investigation and hush-hush government work (but not before he had cleared himself of the charge of murdering his fiancée Tot Winter). He also separated himself from his wartime buddy Rosco (who took over the Sunday page): from then on Buz would work mostly solo. His assignments involved him with gunrunners, diamond smugglers, Mexican bandidos, and African headhunters, not to mention the obligatory mad scientist, this time raising in his sinister garden a variety of man-eating plants. Buz also served the U.S. Navy in diverse capacities at the time of the Korean War, the Cuban Missile Crisis, and over North Vietnam.

Despite all this adventuring, Buz also found time to get married. His bride was Christy Jameson, the hero's wartime sweetheart who had been waiting patiently at home for her aviator boyfriend to return. This wasn't easy, as Buz was continually jetting from one end of the earth to another, occasionally jilting Christy for other love interests. She always kept the faith, however, and the home fires burning, and finally landed her restless fiancé in December 1948, even giving him a son, John Singer, Jr., better known as Pepper, in 1953. She also got involved in Buz's dangerous life and was in mortal peril herself more than once.

Crane soon repented for having made his hero so good-looking ("What a mistake!" he later said. "I had to spend hours on his face so he would always look the same.") and at the first opportunity had Buz's nose broken in a fight. He also endeavored to toughen up the former pilot's boy-scoutish image by getting him involved in brawls or having him use ethically debatable methods to achieve his admit-

Buz Sawyer (R. Crane), © 1964 King Features Syndicate

tedly laudable aims. The fact is Buz always remained a somewhat bland character, unlike Crane's earlier Captain Easy.

In contrast, Rosco turned out to be a highly colorful and interesting individual. Settling down in Indian Mound, Florida, in company of his equally homely sister Lucille, the former tailgunner devoted himself to cultivating his orange grove and trying (vainly) to find a bride. In one humor-and-pathos-filled episode, he passed himself off as a "Palm Beach swell" to impress a pretty blonde, taking her to fancy restaurants and nightclubs, only to be turned down by the simple farm girl terrified of high society. Around the brother and sister there ebbed and flowed an assortment of similarly picturesque characters, including their mooching relatives, the Squatleys, and the former circus performer Calliope Birdwell, whose nightly organ recitals kept her neighbors awake for miles around. In recognition of Rosco's newfound star status, the Sunday title was changed to *Buz Sawyer Featuring His Pal Rosco Sweeney*, and later to simply *Rosco Sweeney*.

Nowhere was Crane's use of doubletone as masterful as on *Buz Sawyer* in the 1950s. With approaching old age, however, he left more and more of the drawing to Henry Schlensker, while much of the scripting was done by Ed Granberry. Ill health and growing disinterest caused him to close down the Sunday page, now entirely done by other hands, on May 19, 1974. The daily strip survived the creator's death in 1977 and was carried by Schlensker and Granberry (now signing their names to the feature), and later by John Celardo, until its eventual demise on October 7, 1989.

Unlike Roy Crane's *Wash Tubbs* and *Captain Easy*, *Buz Sawyer* leaves a mixed record. While at its peak, from its inception to the late 1950s, it could be ranked among the classic adventure strips, it later went into a precipitous decline, with artwork often looking rushed and continuities turning muddled. The author also felt more restricted at King Features than at easygoing NEA. At any rate, *Buz Sawyer*'s all too evident deficiencies make it fall short of being a masterpiece, despite the claims of Crane's many fans.

M.H.

CALVIN AND HOBBES
1985–1995

Following a stint at political cartooning and advertising layout in the early 1980s, Bill Watterson was able, after several unsuccessful submissions, to sell *Calvin and Hobbes* to Universal Press Syndicate. The daily and Sunday feature appeared on November 18, 1985, much to the delight of readers, who found in this humor comic strip a highly original creation.

It was with some irony that Watterson named Calvin, a hyperactive six-year-old first-grader, and Hobbes, a stuffed toy tiger who came alive in Calvin's presence only, after the two humorless philosophers. These two best friends (they seemed to need no others) loved to play pranks on one another and fight as they called each other names for cheating or for simply reinventing the rules of familiar American childhood games to fit their purposes of the moment. Knowing no obstacle, no restraint, endowed with a limitless imagination and a sophisticated vocabulary, as well as with a vast knowledge of prehistory and science-fiction technology, Calvin could transform a wagon, a sled, or a box into all manner of airships that allowed both him and Hobbes to fly over wide precipices, down snow-covered slopes, or through time.

When Calvin was by himself—at school, for example, which he hated and where, like Einstein, he earned mostly C's, or at the dinner table, where food was rarely to his demanding standards—he alternated between assuming the guises of Spaceman Spiff and Safari Al, as he conquered enemy planets or tamed uncharted jungles. However, he was always rudely brought back to reality by teacher or parent, sometimes themselves metamorphosed into disgusting creatures. In the same way, as Stupendous Man, the caped superhero, Champion of Liberty and Defender of Free Will, he could be vanquished only by his "evil archenemy—Mom-Lady." Although "childhood is short and maturity is forever," a more thoughtful Calvin was also concerned over pollution and endangered species (especially tigers), the

Calvin and Hobbes (B. Watterson), © 1994 Watterson, distributed by Universal Press Syndicate

purpose of life, the incomprehensibility of death, the passing of time, and the meaning of friendship.

To counteract his young companion's pursuit of instant gratification, after he had indulged him for a while, a better educated and sometimes more mature Hobbes deflated the boy's imprudent or self-centered behavior by showing him the error of his thinking, much to Calvin's belated chagrin. When, for instance, the self-appointed dictator-for-life Calvin was singing their club anthem, Hobbes reminded him that he has the soprano voice of a sissy; or he would wish Calvin luck in getting the world handed to him on a platter. Besides having an exuberant nature of his own, Hobbes had a gentle, sentimental side, too, being very pleased not to be a human being, choosing starvation over spam, or simply enjoying nature. Above all, he had poetry and panache.

Calvin's parents, while loving, were not Dr. Spock disciples, as they tried to cope with their son's conduct. Dad, a lawyer, was an ineffectual man around the house whose enjoyment of camping and the great outdoors was unmatched by anybody else's. He often preferred working at the office to being in manic Calvin's company, and he wondered whether a DNA test might explain his negative popularity-poll results, as tabulated by Calvin. Mom, on the other hand, was a homemaker who was willing to tolerate or ignore Calvin's shenanigans up to a point, beyond which she would blow up in anger and frustration. This is why a precocious Calvin believed that "some women just weren't meant to be mothers."

Susie, Calvin's dark-haired classmate ("a babe!" in Hobbes's eyes) and a very good pupil, was often the butt of this juvenile male chauvinist's jokes. Yet she was more than able to give back in kind. Rosalyn, the strict and understandably well-paid babysitter; Miss Wormwood the old no-nonsense schoolteacher; and Moe, the nasty bully, completed the cast of recurring characters.

To balance slapstick, fantasy, and human emotions, Watterson, influenced to some extent by Charles Schulz's *Peanuts* and Walt Kelly's *Pogo*, drew the pictures and wrote the script with an aesthetic energy and a well-tuned ear that reinforced each other and brought the strip to life. It is no wonder then that, in addition to various deserved awards (including its creator's receipt of Outstanding Cartoonist of the Year [twice]), several of Watterson's paperback reprints have been long-term *New York Times* bestsellers, and that *Calvin and Hobbes* went from some 130 newspapers in 1986 to close to two thousand when Watterson decided to retire his strip; the last page appeared on December 31, 1995.

P.H.

CAP STUBBS AND TIPPIE
1918–1966

The joy of childhood during the early decades of this century were arguably no better portrayed in comic strip form than by Frances Edwina Dumm in *Cap Stubbs and Tippie*. Likely this country's first female political cartoonist, Edwina (as she signed her work) had created *The Meanderings of Minnie* for the *Columbus Daily Monitor,* which had caught the attention of the George Matthew Adams Service. Revamping the girl into a boy, *Cap Stubbs* was first released in 1918 with a then crewcut lad and his terrier launching their journey together. Resembling *Buster Brown*'s Tige, that first short-haired dog was transitory, for he was lost and adopted by a crippled boy, allowing Cap to foster the woolly-haired version that became famous.

Besides the two principals, the strip included Cap's nondescript parents Milt and Mary Stubbs, benevolent storekeepers Uncle Ben and Aunt Libbie, Cap's good friends Mary Margaret and Lonnie, as well as Ethel, prissy Sammy Sutton, surly Mr. Budge, and Jaspurr the cat. The anchor figure, though, was undoubtedly Gran'ma Sara Bailey, as this aproned behemoth was the fussy matriarch of the feature, solely raising the youth with her constant exasperated exclamation, "My Land!" Able to scold her mischievous grandson and amend him with cookies and ice cream, Gran'ma represented the responsible, motivated parenting that largely prevailed decades ago, personifying the guiding stability and lovable essence of the strip.

Having studied under the master anatomist George Bridgman, Edwina's drawing style was mature: a rich combination of airy spontaneity and solid illustrative realism. Added was an ample ability to create the convincing environments that were backdrops to her daily dramas. The artist's admiration for the dog illustrations of *Mr. and Mrs.*

Beans creator and *Life* cartoonist Robert L. Dickey helped fortify her aspirations to incorporate a love and respect for canines in her creations. All told, despite the rich characterizations instilled in Gran'ma and Cap, it wasn't long before Edwina's true specialty became recognized as the feature's highlight: portraying the adorable actions of the energetic Tippie the terrier. This authentically depicted dog staunchly accompanied his master, an inseparable sidekick and loyal friend to the end. The dog soon shared billing in the daily strip's title, and in 1934 Tippie took his own Sunday page, syndicated by King Features, as the Adams Service hadn't facilities for color distribution. Possibly in keeping up with Snoopy, Otto, and other comic peers, Tippie was endowed with thought balloons in the strip's final years, appropriate only then in the era of Pop Art after decades of decreed naturalism. Simultaneously, Edwina created two other dog features, *Sinbad* for the old *Life* magazine and illustrations for *Alec the Great,* a poetic column written by her brother Robert Dennis. Two ceramic figurines complemented the pair of Sinbad books published in 1930 and 1932, along with an equal number of Alec collections.

Not one for hilarious gags, the strip focused foremost on homespun, down-to-earth situations that readers could relate to from a child's viewpoint—attending school, playing games, going to the circus, building a clubhouse. Melodramatic yet unthreatening story lines crept in occasionally, but most of the scripts stemmed from Edwina's fond recall of her comfortable years as a youth in Upper Sandusky, Ohio. Virtually a solo act, the cartoonist briefly used a background assistant but preferred to do what came naturally, working alone. From 1937 until the strip's end in 1966, cartoonist Herbert "Peter" Wells rendered all the unique art deco lettering, which was yet another distinctive element in this authentic period piece.

In collaboration with songwriter Helen Thomas, a series of Tippie music folios were issued by the Boston Music Company, in addition to two Dell comic books in 1949. A long-overdue retrospective *Tippie and His Friends* paperback appeared in 1975. This author and Rick Marschall interviewed Edwina in an extensive article for the April 1987 issue of *Nemo* magazine.

The innocent era that Edwina fondly captured is sadly long past, but the genteel dignity she displayed in creating her quiet classic should be an inspiration to generations of discerning historians and creators in the future.

B.J.

Cap Stubbs and Tippie (Tippie; E. Dumm), © 1937 George Matthew Adams Service

THE CAPTAIN AND THE KIDS
1914–1979

The Captain and the Kids (R. Dirks), © 1934 United Feature Syndicate

After being granted the right to draw his characters by the Federal Court of Appeals, Rudolph Dirks lost no time turning out a revived *Katzenjammer Kids* page, minus the name. Starting publication in the *New York World* in June 1914, the new feature at first bore no running title, as the mention "by the originator of the Katzenjammer Kids" that graced each page seemed identification enough. It was eventually christened *Hans and Fritz* on May 23, 1915, but the anti-German feelings of World War I forced a new change of title in August 1918, to *The Captain and the Kids.*

Meanwhile, a new version of *The Katzenjammer Kids,* done by Harold Knerr, had been appearing in the Hearst papers, starting in November 1914. This novel arrangement was bound to result in fierce competition between the two artists, with each one trying to top the other in humor, originality, and characterization. They outrageously stole characters, ideas, and situations from each other, exuberantly escalating the antics of their unedifying heroes, letting the action run wild, pulling out all stops—both of them encapsulating the raucous spirit of the comics in the effrontery of it all.

For many years the two competing strips looked like mirror images of each other. In the period between 1915 and 1935, for instance, the two sets of *Katzenjammer* principals exhibited similar symptoms of wanderlust. At one point Dirks sent the Captain and the Inspector around the globe on a bet to see who would arrive first (the Inspector traveling alone, the Captain with Mama and her brood tagging along). They both completed their respective journeys at the exact same moment. (With Hans and Fritz perpetrating sabotage at every turn, it's a wonder the Captain arrived at all.) At another time the whole tribe went on a long sea voyage, got involved with Long John Silver and his merry crew of pirates (characters Dirks had earlier created in his *Katzenjammer* page, after Robert Louis Stevenson), and finally landed on a tropical island in the mid-1930s, settling there much as Knerr's Katzenjammers were doing on King Bongo's island about the same time.

Dirks experienced a series of ups and downs with *The Captain and the Kids,* as he had with the *Katzenjammer Kids* in earlier decades. He left the page entirely in the hands of his assistant Oscar Hitt (with the mention "directed by R. Dirks") in 1922. In 1932, following a contractual dispute with United Feature Syndicate (which had acquired the property in 1930 after the *World* folded), he walked out, leaving both the Sunday page and the daily strip (which he had started a few months earlier) in midstream: both versions were taken over by his former assistant Bernard Dibble. Only in 1937 did he finally come back to stay, closing down the dailies a few weeks after his return, to concentrate solely on the Sunday page.

Dirks's pages of the late 1930s were indeed inspired. Hans and Fritz rose to new heights of inventiveness in their guerrilla war against the Captain, the Inspector, the royal family ruling the island, and all comers, including visiting relatives and traveling salesmen. Dirks did not share Knerr's edenic vision of island life; his island was always raided by pirates, overrun by interlopers, and infested with hustlers. (In fact, even Hans and Fritz had to be called upon to help against some of the pests.) From Dibble he had inherited the character known as the Brain, a top-hatted, masked evildoer who came to plunder from his lair on a neighboring island in company of his animal accomplice, a stork (also masked) trained to carry the bundle of loot with its bill. Among Dirks's later creations mention should be made of a crabby hermit who more than once turned out to be a match for the Kids' deviltry.

In the 1940s Dirks's interest in the feature again flagged. Fortunately his son John, just returned from service in World War II, came to help him, beginning in 1946. As his father's failing health kept him more and more often away from the drawing table, John Dirks put more of his imprint on the strip, taking it into the field of humorous fantasy and science fiction. There were adventures involving the Isle of the Lost World, a rocketship from Venus, invading robots, and even the abominable Snowman. The artist alternated these often frenetic stories with situations and settings recreating his father's early pages. After his father's death in 1968, John Dirks got to sign the page until its demise in May 1979.

There has been much debate among historians of the medium as to the respective merits of the two competing strips, with a slight edge given to Knerr's *Katzenjammers.* There is no doubt that *The Captain and the Kids* was hurt by Dirks's many absences, while Knerr for the entire thirty-five years of his tenure concentrated all his energy and dedication on his feature. Yet, for all his lapses in draftsmanship and his sometimes slapdash execution, Dirks at his best remained a master storyteller and gag builder who could turn his version into an inspired creation when the spirit moved him.

M.H.

CAPTAIN EASY
See WASH TUBBS

CAPTAIN MIDNIGHT
1942–1945

Before television became a purveyor of presold titles to the comics, there was radio; and among the radio programs that later were turned into newspaper-strip series, *Captain Midnight* was a natural, since its formula had been copied almost wholesale on the *Don Winslow* radio serial, itself taken from the comics pages. Raymond William Stedman put it best in his perceptive study, *The Serials:* "As Winslow's Squadron of Peace had skirmished regularly with a foreign menace, the Scorpion, and his organization, Midnight's Secret Squadron jousted with the forces of the Barracuda and one Ivan Shark. Both heroes had to cope with the treacherous female offsprings of their adversaries.... And both heroes had less than adequate *aides de combat.*" Started on local station WGN in Chicago in 1939 and broadcast the next year over the Mutual Network, *Captain Midnight* finally reached the funny pages in 1942, courtesy of the Chicago Sun Syndicate.

Captain Midnight was in actuality Captain Albright (a nice contrast of names there), and he had earned his *nom de guerre* thanks to his nightly exploits during World War I. By the time the newspaper feature began, World War II was well underway, but the hero's rank surprisingly remained the same. Under the nominal command of Major Barry Steel, and with the encouragement of his comic but efficient mechanic Ichabod M. Mudd (better known as Ikky) and the active assistance of his juvenile sidekicks, Squadron members Joyce Ryan and Chuck Ramsey, the Captain, nattily attired in his own uniform with-clock-at-midnight insignia, took on the Nazis in heroic missions all over Europe. Not only did he destroy vital arms factories and strategic bridges, at the head of his squadron, he also frequently risked his life in secret assignments behind enemy lines, rushing in where commissioned Allied intelligence officers feared to tread. In these endeavors Captain Midnight and the Secret Squadron received help and succor from Allied headquarters. While this situation was anomalous it was not entirely unfounded: It perpetuated a form of irregular soldiering, embodied at that same time in Africa and the Middle East by Orde Wingate and his Gideon Force and in Burma by the Chindits.

In the course of his daredevil wartime career Midnight had repeated and emotional—though not romantic—encounters with the enticing Luna White, the "Moon Woman," a lady of twilight and mystery whom he suspected of being a German agent. The pair were in fact on the same side of the fence and in parting at story's end "proved friends at last."

Although cryptically credited to "Jonwan," *Captain Midnight,* which appeared in both Sunday and weekday formats, was actually penned by that stalwart comics scriptwriter, Russ Winterbotham, and drawn chiefly by Erwin Hess. With the war rapidly coming to its close in Europe, Captain Midnight concluded his newspaper-page exploits in the spring of 1945; his adventures continued for a while longer on the radio and in comic books. (There was also a *Captain Midnight* television show, which aired from 1954 to 1958.)

M.H.

CAPTAIN YANK
1940–1945

While public opinion may have wavered during the first years of World War II, before America entered the conflict, most newspaper heroes entertained no such doubts: they were firmly pro-Allies and anti-Axis, from Captain Easy to Terry and from Joe Palooka to Tim Tyler. The trend accelerated after the fall of France in June 1940, with many new, belligerent strips coming to the fore. One such was created by Frank Tinsley for the *New York Herald-Tribune* in October 1940, running daily and Sunday under the patriotic name of *Yankee Doodle.*

A test pilot and aeronautics engineer, Doodle, better known as Captain Yank, spent much of his time fighting spies, saboteurs, and traitors, with the help of Daniel Boone, a fellow pilot and linear descendant of the famous Indian fighter, and of Captain Algernon Jeeps, of the U.S. Air Force. His first adventure involved him with the Black Column (an obvious reference to Hitler's "fifth column"), which was out to steal the design of his secret aircraft, the *Bat.* There were more scuffles with an assorted lot of foreign agents (many spouting "Heil" and "Ach" with each sentence) and some seedy homegrown fifth-columnists.

On June 7, 1942, the McNaught Syndicate took over distribution, changing the name of the feature to *Captain Yank.* The titular hero was now a Marine Corps captain heading a crack outfit of specially trained commandos into dangerous missions behind Japanese lines and all over the Pacific theater of war. As a former pulp-magazine illustrator, Tinsley had a knack for drawing airplanes (his specialty) and other appurtenances of war, but his depiction of human characters was stiff and wooden. Coulton Waugh, perhaps uncharitably, summed up the feature thus: "This is straight adventure, having little to do with humor, sense of design, or beauty of appearance." Possibly aware of his shortcomings, Tinsley hired a number of ghosts to draw the strip in its later years, notably Lou Fine and John Lehti.

Captain Yank was one of the many war heroes of the funny pages who after the coming of peace couldn't make it in civilian life: in December 1945, like all good soldiers, he just faded away.

M.H.

CASEY RUGGLES
1949–1955

Warren Tufts abandoned a promising radio career to create *Casey Ruggles,* which he subtitled "A Saga of the West." The new strip was brought out by United Feature Syndicate in 1949, the Sunday page on May 22 and the dailies on September 19.

The action was set in the days of the California gold rush. Casey was initially an army sergeant serving in the U.S. Dragoons during John Frémont's 1848 expedition. After a brief interlude in the East, where he became involved with Lilli Lafitte, daughter of the fabled pirate Jean Lafitte, to the chagrin of his long-suffering fiancée Chris, Casey went back to California. There he met with violence and skullduggery among the conflicting claims of Yankee gold

Casey Ruggles (W. Tufts), © 1952 United Feature Syndicate

rape, torture, and murder were related matter-of-factly, and no hold was barred in this grim tale of human courage, resilience, and greed. Tufts topped himself in 1952, when Casey discovered that his new bride and longtime lover Chris was actually his sister.

The comics-reading public soon started to protest at these perceived outrages, and this outcry, coupled with a eighty-hour weekly working schedule, prompted Tufts to resign from the strip in 1954. He was followed in quick succession by Edmond Good, Ruben Moreira, and Al Carreño. *Casey Ruggles* did not long survive its creator's departure: it came to an end in October 1955.

M.H.

CATHY
1976–present

Cathy Andrews, the unwavering heroine of the comic strip that bears her first name, began her existence as a cartoon figure in letters home to illustrate various events in the life of her creator, Cathy Guisewite. Prodded by her mother, Guisewite sent some samples to Universal Press Syndicate in 1976. With Universal's immediate response of a contract offer, the *Cathy* comic strip was born, debuting on November 22, 1976.

Chronicling the trials and tribulations in the professional and personal life of a modern young woman, *Cathy* appeals to all, regardless of gender, whose relationships have ever involved grappling with an exploitative boss, struggling with a significant other, attempting to keep up with a "perfect" friend, or striving to coexist with loving but irksome parents.

Whether she realizes too late that her boss Mr. Pinkley's calculated flattery concerning her dependability has beguiled her into accepting an overload of work at the office ("I just traded two seconds of omnipotence for two weeks of grief") or openly confronts her mother concerning her ability as a grown woman to run her own house, only to backslide into rejecting a detergent in the supermarket because "it isn't the kind my mom always buys," Cathy has learned through such experiences to face the problems of living life single and to make her own way with unflinching honesty, admirable resilience, and a gentle self-mocking that endears her to her legions of fans.

Alternately pudgy or slim, but always with the wide-eyed innocence of a child and with her heart literally worn for all to see, Cathy perseveres regardless of the gravity of the situation and somehow manages to maintain an unshakable sense of hope and good cheer, as when she happily concludes, after a stern but accurate scolding from an on-again, off-again boyfriend on her inability to make up her mind, "At last! A man who really understands me!"

As if her troublesome human relationships are not enough, Cathy also must deal with a manipulative canine, the dizzying world of women's fashions, a relentless and unending weight problem, and the stress of complex modern life including, but not limited to, the countless products that never quite deliver according to their claims. If her dog Electra is not reducing Cathy to barking herself into a stupor in an effort to have Electra outperform a

prospectors, Spanish landowners, and dispossessed Indians. Tufts was especially sensitive to the plight of Native Americans, and one of the most attractive characters in the strip was Kit Fox, an Osage orphan boy Casey had adopted.

With his blond good looks, Casey Ruggles could pass for a younger brother to Flash Gordon. Tufts was much indebted to Alex Raymond and Harold Foster for his graphic style, but as time went by his artwork acquired its own stamp and personality. He favored long, cinematic sequences in which he alternated close-ups, medium and long shots, panoramics, and changes in angle, as in Casey's lyrical rides through the majestic landscapes of a still unspoiled California. To relieve his work schedule he had to rely on assistants for short periods, Alex Toth most notably among them.

Tufts's writing was on a par with his artistic skills. He was at his best in long-breathed narratives in which he could develop atmosphere and characterization. He cleverly mixed fictional characters with real-life figures like cavalry scout Kit Carson, outlaw Joaquin Murieta, even U.S. Presidents Zachary Taylor and Millard Fillmore, and he often recounted actual incidents from the Old West. None of those was as vividly recreated as the 1849 gold rush, and in his strip he directly dealt with the implications of the discovery of gold at Sutter's Mill, and he depicted with unadorned, sometimes even grim, authenticity the changes visited by greed and lust upon an idyllic countryside. In fact, *Casey Ruggles* flew in the face of all the pious conventions of comic-strip westerns. It was filled with sweat, blood, and tears, as Tufts graphically depicted the backbreaking labor, treacherous dealings, and dreary existence that went into the making of the western frontier. Occurrences of

Charlie Chan (A. Andriola), © 1938 McNaught Syndicate

friend's toddler, both of whom then congratulate one another on their game of "How goofy can I make my mother look," she is struggling with the latest fashion fad, unabashedly acknowledging that every time a new phase in women's awareness asserts itself via yet another fashion trend, "there's a whole new category of clothes I can't get into," or else apologizing for wearing an outfit suitable for an eight-year-old because "the sales clerk made me buy it."

In one of her frequent philosophical comments on the state of her life, after reducing all her wants and needs to a tidy group of items such as a bathroom cabinet with one product that works rather than forty-seven "hypothetical miracles"—or a refrigerator with one decent meal instead of a variety of expired dairy products and little fast-food condiment packets, or a closet with three outfits that fit rather than a hundred miscellaneous pieces that don't— she realizes in laconic self-recognition that what she really wants is "more out of life, but...less in it."

Last, but definitely not least, Cathy's complex relationship to food means she must constantly fight the battle of the bulge, a relationship intricately bound up with almost all her other relationships, whether they involve family, love life, or career. A classic *Cathy* finds her, on her way to lunch, musing in front of a candy store on Valentine's Day over how part of her "doesn't care" and part of her "wants an apartment full of flowers," part of her finds the holiday to be a "cheap, commercialized event" and part of her "is screaming" for poetry, and so on; alone at her restaurant table and with an almost serene look of surrender on her face, she then orders "nachos for six."

Although Guisewite—a three-time runner-up and then winner in 1993 of the National Cartoonists Society's Reuben Award—has said that if she had it to do over she wouldn't name her popular comic-strip character after herself, one cannot imagine this dauntless little heroine under any other name. *Cathy* has grown steadily in circulation since its inception and appears daily and Sundays in twelve hundred newspapers worldwide as well as in numerous book collections, television specials, and countless products from greeting cards to, not unsurprisingly, boxed chocolates.

M.B.C.

CHARLIE CHAN
1938–1942

Mystery novelist Earl Derr Biggers created the character of Charlie Chan, probably the best known Chinese detective of all time, in *The House without a Key*, which started serialization in the *Saturday Evening Post* in 1925. Five additional Charlie Chan novels appeared until the time of Biggers's death in 1933; in the meantime the epigram-spouting Chan had also become the protagonist of an extremely successful series of motion pictures starring the Swedish-born Warner Oland. This in turn spurred the interest of syndicate editors, with the McNaught Syndicate eventually obtaining the newspaper-strip rights to the character.

Alfred Andriola, who had worked as a factotum to Noel Sickles and Milton Caniff at the time when both men shared a common studio, was hired to helm the new feature, on the strength of the samples he had submitted (with more than a little help from his friends). The Sunday page first appeared on October 30, 1938, and the dailies followed the next day. *Charlie Chan* was bylined "Alfred Andriola," with the mention "character created by Earl Derr Biggers."

The Charlie Chan of the newspaper strip owed less to Biggers's characterization than to his portrayal by Oland, down to his physical appearance, mannerisms, and cryptic pronouncements. After only a few weeks Andriola left much of the drawing in the hands of assistants, Charles Raab foremost among them. It was Raab who was responsible for the feature's distinctive look, made of a sharp line that stood out against a background of black-and-white masses alternating in harmonious balance.

Andriola did not adapt any of the existing Chan novels, but wrote his own, often excellent, story lines. As a leftover from the movies he kept "number one" son Lee, but upstaged him by introducing the blond, two-fisted private eye Kirk Barrow, whose fighting abilities came in handy after Chan's logic had failed. Violence, almost nonexistent in the original novels, and of only secondary importance in the movies, was in full flight in the strip. In a 1939 episode, for example, there was a full-scale siege, complete with machine-gun fire, and the tossing of hand grenades and sticks of dynamite. But Andriola also proved capable of spinning some solid detection tales, and such episodes as the Hollywood murder of actress Norda Noll or the mystery of little Sally Minton remain models of the genre. He could also create worthy antagonists for the wily detective, and he brought out in *Charlie Chan* one of his most successful feminine creations, Gina Lane, an aspiring movie actress and Barrow's faithful girlfriend and helpmate.

As the 1940s rolled along, Charlie Chan put his detective skills at the service of his country. He helped crush a ring of German spies in an East Coast port city and routed a pack of Japanese saboteurs in his native island of Oahu. He also, somewhat incongruously, came up (in 1940) with the crackpot idea to dam up the Gulf Stream in order to freeze out the European belligerents, but that was a temporary lapse in his thinking powers.

The Sunday pages, which ran independently from the dailies, except for a brief period between November 1939 and March 1940, were in contrast most often given over to short tales of detection, lasting no more than a few weeks. In these stories Charlie solved the cases of, among others, the murder of an island heiress, the kidnapping of a Chinese statesman, and the disappearance of an entire baseball team. For some reason he showed himself more prone to sententiousness on Sunday, coming up with such aphorisms as "Fewer words spoken, fewer mistakes made" and "Through darkness light must shine."

Despite its many charms, *Charlie Chan* enjoyed only a short existence. The daily strip was discontinued in December 1941, while the Sundays came to an end on May 31, 1942.

M.H.

CHARLIE CHAPLIN'S COMIC CAPERS
1916–1917

In the second decade of the twentieth century Charlie Chaplin enjoyed unheard-of fame around the world. His image of the Little Tramp was on soda bottles, tobacco canisters, orange crates—and of course, in the comics. Charlie Chaplin comics popped up in England, France, and Spain, all of them unlicensed, as were two newspaper strips devoted to Charlie and done independently in the U.S., one by Ed Carey, the other by Pat Sullivan, who had just arrived from Australia. Sensing an opportunity, James Keeley, former editor of the *Chicago Tribune* and then the owner of the rival *Chicago Herald,* entered into an agreement with Essanay Studios, distributors of the Chaplin shorts, to produce an authorized version. *Charlie Chaplin's Comic Capers* made its bow, daily and Sunday, in March 1916, drawn by a fledgling cartoonist named E. C. Segar.

The drawings were admittedly crude and the jokes of the vaudeville circuit variety. Unlike the Carey and the Sullivan strips in which he spoke not a word, Charlie in Segar's version expressed himself in speech balloons, sometimes at great length. Other liberties were taken with Chaplin's screen image, with the cartoonist seeming to rely on the

older Keystone two-reelers, which he had ample opportunity to see during his days as a movie-house projectionist in his hometown of Chester, Illinois. While usually attired in his fabled tramp costume, Charlie worked at a number of different occupations: lifeguard, gamekeeper, even cop; and in the last days of the strip, after America had entered World War I, he appeared in uniform on several occasions. His habitual foil in the strip was an ape-faced little man named Luke with whom he kept up a friendly, if at times heated rivalry.

In 1917 Chaplin left Essanay for Mutual, and Keeley's agreement was terminated. *Charlie Chaplin's Comic Capers* appeared for the last time on Sunday, April 15, 1917. The strip is included here as an indication of Chaplin's extravagant popularity at the time and in recognition of a rare cartooning talent about to blossom.

M.H.

CHIEF WAHOO
See STEVE ROPER

CICERO'S CAT
1933–1982

Cicero's Cat appeared for the first time on December 3, 1933, as the top piece to *Mutt and Jeff.* While credited to Bud Fisher, the feature was in fact the creation of Al Smith, who had become Fisher's ghost on *Mutt and Jeff* the previous year.

The black-striped feline had been the office cat in *From 9 to 5,* a panel that Smith had been drawing from 1930 to 1932 for the *New York World,* and later for United Feature Syndicate; he simply transferred his creation to the *Mutt and Jeff* Sunday page after he had taken charge of it, making the cat into the pet of Mutt's small son Cicero (hence the title). A female, she may have been called Esmeralda in the first episodes, but became known as Desdemona ("Desi" for short) in 1934. On May 13 of that year, after reading that

Charlie Chaplin's Comic Capers (E. C. Segar), 1916

Desdemona was the heroine of Shakespeare's *Othello,* she had calling cards printed bearing her new name; and Desdemona she remained for the rest of the strip's existence.

Desi was not an anthropomorphic cat; although she could read (as we have seen), she couldn't talk, at least not to humans. She did, however, converse with other animals (and sometimes with the reader), and while she sported clothes on occasion, she preferred to run wild in Kat Alley, the only place she felt safe from dogs. She moved in a very catlike way but somehow never seemed at ease with domestic appliances: she would get herself rolled up in the window shade or spun around the record-player turntable. Her gluttony was only matched by her laziness, and while lying in wait for mice to come out of their hole she would often fall asleep (with the mice dancing a little jig in front of her eyes).

Smith drew the misadventures of Cicero's cat until his retirement in 1980: the feline was then turned over (along with Mutt and Jeff) to George Breisacher, before ending her long career in 1982.

M.H.

CIRCUS SOLLY
See SLIM JIM

THE CISCO KID
1951–1968

In the early 1950s King Features decided to add another old-fashioned western to their catalogue. They turned to a well-known property, in this case *The Cisco Kid,* based on O. Henry's short story "The Caballero's Way," which had already been the object of countless retellings on the screen. The writing was entrusted to staffer Rod Reed, while the syndicate reached all the way to Argentina to come up with a suitable artist, the talented José-Luis Salinas. *The*

Cisco Kid first appeared on January 15, 1951, in daily-strip format.

Like his *compadre* Zorro, the Cisco Kid was a Mexican righter of wrongs, fighting crime and corruption not in California but in the New Mexico territories at the turn of the century. Impeccably attired in a richly embroidered black outfit and wearing a huge sombrero, he had become one of the legendary figures of the American West. In the company of his comic sidekick, the pot-bellied and crafty Pancho, his rides often took him far from his usual field of operation. The first story involved the Cisco Kid in an entertaining story of graft, land speculation, and underhanded dealings, with a clever twist at the end. It also introduced the character of Lucy Baker, a blonde suffragette that no man, not even the sinister Judge Hook, the villain of the piece, could silence.

Other adventures found the Kid and Pancho pitted against a hooded extortionist calling himself the Black Ghost, fighting the redoubtable outlaw Big Bull, and bringing to heel a gang of train robbers led by the notorious Red Lariat. One of the most entertaining narratives came in 1959, when the hero confronted the gun-toting, tough-talking Babe Puma, a kind of Annie Oakley as adept at karate as at broncho-riding or at markswomanship. At first rivals, Babe and Cisco would join forces later to outwit a trio of swindlers trying to put the Babe Puma Wild West Carnival out of business.

The Cisco Kid enjoyed interesting story lines, good characterization, and superlative artwork from Salinas's pen. The magnificent scenery and open spaces of the West were lyrically evoked in the artist's black-and-white compositions (there never was a Sunday version). In spite of all its qualities the strip failed to hold its public, and it was discontinued on August 5, 1968, bringing to an end one of the most artistically crafted and thematically interesting adventure strips to come out of the 1950s .

M.H.

NOW TELL ME, SEÑORITA LUCY—WHAT IS WORRYING YOUR PRETTY HEAD?

The Cisco Kid (Reed and Salinas), © 1951 King Features Syndicate

CLAIRE VOYANT
1943–1948

Fresh from drawing *Hap Hopper,* Jack Sparling decided to create his own newspaper feature. The result was *Claire Voyant,* which first appeared in the pages of New York's pioneering tabloid *P.M.* on May 10, 1943, as a daily strip.

Claire Voyant made one of the most dramatic entrances of any comic-page heroine, being plucked from the sea in the opening strip. Having drifted for days in a lifeboat, she had lost her memory, but in compensation she had picked up extrasensory powers, a fact reflected in the name she chose for herself. Her abilities to detect bad vibrations were put to good use in the very first episode, when she exposed a saboteur among the crew of the freighter that had rescued her. There followed some more adventures at sea and on land, with the heroine putting her powers at the service of the Allied cause, helping to send marauding German submarines to the bottom of the Atlantic and foiling the intrigues of Japanese spies in the Pacific. The first years of the strip were marked by interesting plot developments writ-

Clarence (Holbrook and Fogarty), © 1948 New York Herald-Tribune

ten with verve by Sparling, who confided to an interviewer, "I talk about Claire Voyant running in and out of situations in my sleep." The artist devoted equal if not greater attention to the drawings, which were executed with unusual flair and vigor and a strong emphasis on composition and design.

Claire Voyant, who could foretell future events from the pattern in a dress or a fork in the road, could not divine ahead of time the end of the war, and peace found her still embroiled in wartime adventure. She did get back to the States in record time, however, and took up a civilian job. As a private investigator, she used her abilities to uncover financial skullduggery on Wall Street and expose mob activities in Little Italy. Claire, an attractive brunette, also rediscovered her past as a stage actress, and this allowed the author to introduce the worlds of the theater, fashion, and advertising into the story lines. Sparling, who had been at his best when depicting Claire as the only woman in a mostly male world, did not feel at ease in these posh surroundings, and the strip in the mid-1940s entered into a period of marked narrative and artistic decline.

By that time Field Enterprises had taken over distribution of the feature (having added a Sunday page in the process). The circulation did not increase appreciably, however, and Sparling grew more and more disenchanted with his creation. The loss of his home paper finally precipitated his decision: in winter 1948 *P.M.* sank without a trace, and Claire Voyant went down with the ship, this time for good

M.H.

CLARENCE
1924–1949

Clarence was one of the multifarious family strips to see light in the 1920s. It was created on April 6, 1924, by Crawford Young as a Sunday page distributed by the New York Herald-Tribune Syndicate.

The childless couple formed by the dumpy, bemustached, balding Clarence and his much younger wife, the blonde and perky Mary, were designed as a welcome relief

from the bickering, snarling marriage partners that were such a staple of the comics at the time. Clarence and Mary seemed on a prolonged honeymoon, as they faced the myriad frustrations of daily life in their suburban home with a spirit of give-and-take exemplified in such cheerful self-deprecations as, "It was very inconsiderate of me, honey," and "No, no, it was I who was in the wrong, dear." On the eve of a two-week separation Clarence would declare, "Gosh, I'm certainly going to miss you, Mary," to which his wife would respond, "Why, Clarence, you sentimental old darling—I had no idea." Such protestations of affection met with the gushing approval of Coulton Waugh. "A married pair that never seems to bicker. A married couple who never disagree," he enthused in *The Comics*.

In 1930 Young left to create another comic strip, *Mortimer,* and *Clarence* passed into the hands of Frank Fogarty for the drawing and Weare Holbrook for the writing. Perhaps it was all the years Fogarty had passed ghosting *Mr. and Mrs.,* *Clarence*'s neighbor in the *Herald*'s comic pages, but in a manner reminiscent of Jekyll and Hyde, Young's former loving couple was transformed into yet another antagonistic pair in a matter of a few months. Matters were not helped by Mary's spinster aunt, an old battle-ax named Hester, who had come to live with the couple in the mid-1930s. Clarence and Mary's marital woes finally ended in March 1949, when the strip came to a close.

M.H.

CLARENCE THE COP
1900–1904, 1907–1909

Like many of C. W. Kahles's early productions, *Clarence the Cop* was created for Joseph Pulitzer's Press Publishing Company. Coming out toward the end of the year 1900, it proved an immediate hit with the readers, and it was Kahles's longest running comic feature next to *Hairbreadth Harry.*

Clarence was one in a long line of comical cops whose misadventures so entertained audiences in the early years of the century. A rotund, moon-faced Irish street cop in the ranks of the New York City Police Department, he spent his

Clarence the Cop (C. W. Kahles), 1903

time mistaking store thieves for delivery men, helping second-story men up ladders, and collaring robbery victims while letting the perpetrators go free. As a reward for his well-meaning but ill-timed exertions, the befuddled Clarence found himself "transferr'd agin!" to some forsaken place like the upper reaches of the Bronx or the Gowanus Canal, mumbling all the while in a thick Irish brogue, "Now, Oi wonder what they sint me way out here fer?"

While the public took the fumbling flatfoot to its collective bosom (resulting in three silent *Clarence the Cop* movie comedies made between 1903 and 1905), police departments across the country did not cotton up to the depiction of uniformed officers as bungling nincompoops and, according to Kahles's daughter Jessie Kahles Straut, they succeeded in having the feature suspended a number of times, once for almost three years from mid-1904 to early 1907, finally stopping it altogether in the spring of 1909.

M.H.

COLONEL POTTERBY AND THE DUCHESS
1934–1963

Colonel Potterby and the Duchess appeared as the companion strip to Chic Young's *Blondie* toward the end of 1934, displacing *The Family Foursome*, which had occupied the space since April 1931.

In his new venture Young tried to get as far away as possible from the middle-class domesticity that had become the theme of his main feature. The Colonel was an elderly, portly, bald, and bemustached gent always attired in coat and tails and opera hat, even when playing golf or puttering in his garden. The Duchess was a middle-aged spinster, angular and much taller than her companion. The two entertained a romantic relationship of sorts and moved in high-class circles, going to posh parties, eating at swank restaurants, and attending fancy wedding receptions. Once in a while the Colonel would venture some amorous advance, only to be met with rebuffs, scoldings, or worse, blows over the head with broom, umbrella, or rolling pin, wielded with unforgiving fury by the not-so-shy maiden determined to defend her virtue at any cost. The next week, however, would find the pair reconciled and walking arm in arm down some country lane or city boulevard.

The gags in *Colonel Potterby* were told largely in pantomime, and the drawings were rendered in a more angular, nervous style than those in *Blondie*. Ray McGill, Young's

Colonel Potterby and the Duchess (C. Young), © 1942 King Features Syndicate

assistant at the time, helped with the artwork from the beginning. When the creator's eyesight began to fail him in the late 1940s, he left the entire strip in other hands, and consequently *Colonel Potterby*, then distributed as an independent half page by King Features, increasingly lost readership. Young's death allowed the syndicate to let the strip lapse gracefully into oblivion: the last page appeared on November 3, 1963.

M.H.

COMICS FOR KIDS
1986–present

In the mid-1980s King Features revived the Sunday miscellany children's page, a genre that had fallen into disuse in recent times. *Comics for Kids,* as the feature was straightforwardly called, had been concocted by Bob Weber Jr., the elder son of *Moose* creator Bob Weber, and it came out in 1986. The syndicate had so little confidence in the venture at the outset that it only marketed it to foreign publications. Only after the page had garnered over thirty client newspapers and magazines in Europe and elsewhere did King undertake to distribute it in the U.S., starting in 1987. Later a daily version, of somewhat smaller size, was also syndicated.

In addition to the usual regimen of puzzles, conundrums, and connect-the-dots diagrams, there is a continuing panel featuring the Pigglys, a porcine family of four, comprising Papa and Mama and their two offspring Petey and Pudgy. Aside from attending mud-wrestling matches and playing video games, the Pigglys also propose simple arithmetic problems to the juvenile readers. In recent years, however, they have been upstaged by Slylock Fox, a Sherlockian figure in vulpine guise, complete with Inverness cape, deerstalker cap, and magnifying lens, who solves minimysteries from clues given throughout the feature. Slylock, his assistant Max Mouse, Police Chief Mutt, and the other animal regulars are reportedly enjoying as much popularity as the denizens of Sesame Street with the kiddie audience.

Like Barney the Dinosaur on public TV, *Comics for Kids* is hated by adult readers (who regularly vote it last in preference polls) but adored by the small fry, to such an extent that the syndicate is now touting the piece as "the most popular kids' activity feature in the world."

M.H.

CONNIE
1927-1944

Upon leaving *Vignettes of Life,* the Sunday human-interest page of drawings he had created for the *Philadelphia Public Ledger,* Frank Godwin lost no time in turning out a new comic page centering around the doings of a young and pretty girl, along the lines of Charles Voight's contemporary *Betty.* Titled *Connie,* and distributed by the Ledger Syndicate, it made its appearance on November 13, 1927, only one week after Godwin had signed his last *Vignettes of Life* page.

In contrast to the scatterbrains who populated other girl

strips of the period, Constance Kurridge (known as Connie to her friends, of whom she had many), far from being the stereotypical dumb blonde, had a keen mind, an independent spirit, and a quick, ready wit. She lived with her parents in a comfortable suburban home, and her interests were those of the carefree, well-to-do young woman she was. She dated many eligible men, including crooners, pilots, and movie stars, but showed no inclination to settle down. Her weekly adventures were mildly humorous, often involving the discomfiture of her most persistent and bothersome suitor, the insufferable De Witt Van Dinglehoff.

Connie soon garnered enough success to warrant the addition of a daily strip on May 13, 1929. In the dailies Connie took her first (but firm steps) into adventure. She learned to fly a plane and promptly embarked on a wild series of suspenseful escapades. Among other early exploits, she foiled her dastardly cousin's scheme to cheat her out of her inheritance; went searching for buried treasure in Mexico; was made a field-marshal in the banana republic of Anchovy; and became a reporter for the *Daily Buzz,* for which she solved a string of baffling cases of kidnapping, skullduggery, and other assorted forms of mischief.

Taking a cue from the dailies, the Sunday page also veered gradually toward action and mystery. In 1934, with her family ruined by the stock-market crash, Connie went to work—not as a dilettante as she had done earlier, but to earn her living, first as a reporter, then as the operator of a one-woman detective agency. The Sunday and daily continuities, while still kept separate, took on the same coloring, that of high adventure, with a strong admixture of fantasy and science fiction. In a 1938 Sunday episode, for instance, Connie and her pilot friend Jack Bird discovered a lost city of advanced civilization in the Andes; while a 1940 adventure involved yet another lost city, that of Lahkpor, whose leaders were plotting the takeover of the entire world but only brought about their own self-destruction from the atom bombs they had developed. As a humorous counterpoint to the high-minded *Connie* Sunday page, Godwin in the mid-1930s created a bottom strip, *The Wet Blanket,* about the misadventures that befell a long gallery of boors and bores.

It was in the dailies, however, that Connie lived her highest moments of heroism. She excelled as a private eye, as an investigative reporter, even as a military strategist, and above all, as an interplanetary explorer who could disarm alien creatures with the same cool aplomb that she displayed with men of this earth. Her exploits, which showed her doing anything a man could do, and doing it better, mark her as the ultimate pioneer of woman's liberation in the funny papers. Two of her more revealing adventures were in this vein: in a 1936 story, she traveled a thousand years into the future to discover a civilization run by women, with men relegated to ancillary roles; in a tale spanning 1938–40, she explored the farthest reaches of our solar system in the company of Dr. Alden, not coincidentally another woman. Some have ascribed these science-fiction plot lines to Ray Thompson, but their strong profeminine stance unmistakably shows the hand of Godwin's first wife, Grace Congleton, who was an ardent feminist.

Godwin was a top-notch illustrator as well as a cartoonist, and he brought to *Connie* the gloss of the slick magazines for

Connie (F. Godwin), ca. 1937, © Ledger Syndicate

which he also worked. His graphic style, composed of a network of fine cross-hatchings and of a cursive line, is recognizable at a glance. Without hardly ever resorting to cinematic techniques, Godwin succeeded in endowing his drawings with a sense of movement thanks to his masterly depiction of the human figure in motion and his dynamic rendering of airplanes, astroships, and other machines.

Godwin's talents were displayed at their best in the Sunday illustrations. With the space of an entire newspaper page available to him, he could utilize his artistic skills to the fullest, while color further enhanced the visual appeal of his drawings. He also varied the design of each page to avoid monotony. Breaking with the geometric pattern so prevalent in most Sunday strips, each of his Sundays was punctuated in contrast with arrangements of diagonal panels, hexagonal panels, overlapping panels, sunbursts and compositions in spiral, all in a dazzling show of virtuosity that has made *Connie* unique among newspaper comics.

Despite its graphic excellence, *Connie* was only carried by a pitifully low number of newspapers. During the war years its elegance came to be seen as frivolous and its themes were judged irrelevant: it finally disappeared in 1944, its last years spent in utmost obscurity.

M.H.

COUNT SCREWLOOSE
1929–1945

Milt Gross's most celebrated creation saw print for the first time on February 17, 1929, as a Sunday page titled *Count Screwloose of Tooloose* and syndicated by Pulitzer's Press Publishing Company. In the fall of 1930 the zany strip was transferred to King Features, with its title shortened to *Count Screwloose.*

As his name indicated, Screwloose was a lunatic afflicted with delusions of grandeur signaled by his phony title to nobility ("Tooloose" may have been a left-handed homage to the painter Henri de Toulouse-Lautrec, a linear descendant of the genuine Counts of Toulouse). The diminutive count's weekly attempts at escape from Nuttycrest, the

Count Screwloose (M. Gross), © 1930 Press Publishing Co.

insane asylum where he was confined, provided the source for most of the gags. After each of his exposures to outside society, the would-be escapee was only too glad to go back to the saner environment of the mental institution. The feature's last panel depicted the chastened antihero's return under the gleeful eye of his fellow inmate, a cross-eyed dog in a Napoleonic hat named Iggy, with Screwloose exclaiming in heartfelt repentance, "Iggy, keep an eye on me!"

This gentle satire poked fun at every facet of modern life and its frenzied pace, from harried politicians to jittery gangsters to overreaching society wives. The strip was drawn in a loose, disjointed style as zany as its theme. All the characters had grotesque heads, bulging eyes, and perpetually manic expressions. The activity displayed in the strip was nothing short of alarming, with people, animals, even inanimate objects agitated by constant, frenzied motion.

As a feature, *Count Screwloose* experienced a career as chaotic as the life of its eponymous hero. In June 1931 it became the top strip to Gross's newly created *Dave's Delicatessen,* and Screwloose in December 1933 found himself a part of the main feature. The *Count Screwloose* topper disappeared completely in June 1934, only to resurface in January 1935 as the main feature, displacing *Dave's Delicatessen.* No longer set in an asylum, the action concentrated on the count's failed attempts at promoting his new canine companion, J.R. the Wonder Dog, to Hollywood stardom. In the 1940s Gross turned most of the drawing over to his assistant Bob Dunn, before ill-health and declining readership forced him to close down the feature in 1945.

M.H.

CRANKSHAFT
1987– present

*I*n a medium that has always focused on youth, it was a refreshing change to see the emergence of a strip celebrating crabbed age. Ed Crankshaft is not the first geriatric protagonist of a comic strip, but he may be the first curmudgeon to star in his own. He is a grandparent, but not a sly one like Charles Edward Schultze's *Foxy Grandpa;* nor is he a subversive partisan of youth like the heroine of Charles Harris Kuhn's *Grandma.* If Crankshaft has a prototype in the comics, it is *Dennis the Menace*'s Mr. Wilson; but where the Menace's grumpy neighbor is a helpless victim, Crankshaft is a dynamic force, actively doing his part for human inconvenience with engaging enthusiasm.

The saga of a school-bus driver with very much his own curriculum, *Crankshaft* confirms what every kid who has ever chased an accelerating school bus has always suspected—that the driver gets a kick out of making his passengers late. It's a part of the natural enmity between youth and the grown-up world. But it is not necessarily age or traumatic experiences with children that have generated the misanthropy of Ed Crankshaft; there is evidence that the roots of his grumpiness go very deep. His scrapbook shows him slapping General Patton during World War II. His beleaguered daughter Pam discovers that she has to go through not only the "terrible twos" with her children but the "insufferable sixties" with her father.

Despite his constant friction with the outside world, the old man is not without his pleasures. Among them are seeing how many cars he can back up behind him on the highway with his school bus (an event for which the School Bus Drivers Association gives an annual Pied Piper Award), exercising his skill in knocking over mailboxes, and centering his bus door in the middle of puddles. But there is also a secret side to Ed Crankshaft, reflected in the furtive joy he takes in jumping in leaf piles. And although he never has a kind word for animals, he is a complete pushover to his own cat Pickles. In fact, the old crank has considerable hidden resources of warmth and childlike vulnerability lurking within his withered frame, try as he will to keep them hidden.

Attractively drawn in a loose, sketchy style by Chuck Ayers and written by Tom Batiuk, creator of the popular high-school humor strip *Funky Winkerbean, Crankshaft* has been distributed by Creators Syndicate since 1987.

D.W.

CROCK
1975– present

*A*n untapped source of humor in the comics, the French Foreign Legion has proved a surprisingly fertile field of drollery in *Crock* since 1975, when Brant Parker created the unlikely strip for the North American Syndicate. A longtime collaborator with Johnny Hart, for whom he had drawn *The Wizard of Id* since 1963, Parker approached magazine cartoonist (and later writer of the strip *Goosemyer*) Don Wilder with the idea. Parker was too busy with *Wizard* to take on the drawing and offered the task to his friend Bill Rechin, whose career had included the post of art director of the Federal Systems Group at IBM and doing the short-lived strip *Pluribus* as well as a two-year army stint in Korea, which familiarized him with the discomforts and indignities of military life. The trio produced the strip together until 1977 (its first collection, published by Fawcett that year, was credited, "Drawn by Bill Rechin, Written by Don Wilder, Rewritten and Redrawn by Brant Parker"). Since 1977 Rechin and Wider have done it on their own.

Perhaps the last and certainly the broadest spoof of *Beau Geste,* the strip has none of the heroism of Wren's novel. Its generally unlovely cast of misfits includes a misbegotten troop of legionnaires stationed in an isolated desert post. The setting is as grim as the life they lead; the troop knows it's spring when they see the first vulture. Their malevolent commandant Vermin P. Crock, a man who, according to his creators, "could have taught Attila how to Hun," reflects when he hears the improbable report that his men love him, "Back to the drawing board," and reassures them when they ask for more green in their diet, "Wait'll you see tomorrow's meatloaf."

Rechin and Wilder's characters are a representative crew of comic types, clearly distinguishable in appearance and personality. Captain Poulet (French for "chicken") is a sensitive type; when invaders threaten the fort with "murderous cannon fire and savage hand to hand fighting," he sends back the reply, "Was it something we said?" The grotesque "Pretty Boy" Froyd wipes out a peace-keeping mission and expresses the hope that it will help to "make this world a safe place for aggression." Captain Preppie is mainly concerned with his appearance and Figowitz lives for the letters he receives from his girlfriend Probity. The low man on the troop's totem pole is the dimwitted Maggot, who got one answer right on his IQ test—his name—and smugly observes, "Who says it doesn't pay to cram the night before?" The supporting cast includes Grossie, the obese, understandably love-starved camp follower (who, when asked what she wants on her small dieter's salad, replies, "a stack of three cheeseburgers") and Quench, an articulate camel.

The French government downsized its Foreign Legion years ago, but Wilder's inventive scripting and Rechin's expressive, broadly caricatural art have kept its spirit alive in *Crock*.

D.W.

CURLEY HARPER
1935–1944

Curley Harper was created by Lyman Young on March 31, 1935, as a top strip to the *Tim Tyler's Luck* Sunday page, replacing *The Kid Sister*. It was at first distributed as a package in combination with *Tim Tyler* by King Features, but later graduated to a half page with syndication of its own.

Initially titled *Curley Harper at Lakespur*, it involved a clean-cut, all-American young man who excelled in every imaginable athletic activity, from basketball to water polo,

and thus garnered acclaim and honor for his alma mater, the fictional Lakespur College. There was also an undertone of class rivalry running through the early episodes (these occurred during the depths of the Great Depression, after all), with Curley, who had to work his way through college, being the object of harassment from snotty frat brothers.

Curley left the campus in search of gainful employment in 1937, and on November 7 of that year the strip's title was shortened accordingly to simply *Curley Harper*. The young man soon found himself reporting for his hometown paper, on investigative assignments that included municipal corruption, political skullduggery, even the kidnapping of the town's mayor. In his endeavors he was often aided and abetted by his unofficial sweetheart, the perky Brynn Brighton.

With the coming of the war, Curley put his investigative talents at the service of American counterintelligence. Nat Edson, who had been ghosting the strip from the beginning, proved at his best in these tales of intrigue and espionage, with virtuosic displays of draftsmanship and a subtle flair for shading and suspense. In spite of its formal qualities, *Curley Harper* seems to have disappeared sometime in 1944, although King Features has no record of its exact discontinuance date.

M.H.

CURLY KAYOE
See JOE JINKS

CURTIS
1988–present

The gritty and precarious environs of the city are the backdrop for *Curtis*, introduced on October 3, 1988, by King Features Syndicate. Cartoonist Ray Billingsley had previously drawn *Lookin' Fine* for United Feature Syndicate, and his experience proved him more than capable of creating one of today's most important and poignant features.

Essentially depicting the urban existence of African Americans, the strip's focus is on the family of Greg and Diane Wilkins, who live in a weathered brownstone, a quar-

Curley Harper (L. Young), © 1937 King Features Syndicate

relsome but tight-knit household. Eleven-year-old Curtis and his younger brother Barry are wholesome youths who do their best to live honorably within their ignoble neighborhood, avoiding the temptations of gangs, drugs, and other unlawful activities. Curtis is an emblematic preteen who shares a bed with his brother, does his homework when forced, and is raised by a pair of "tough-loving," hard-working parents. The boy's passion is for modern rap music, spending his allowance on the latest releases, which he dances to and blasts at full volume, much to the aversion of his father and neighbors. Defiance is reciprocated by Dad's refusal to cease smoking, and the inescapable arguments on these two subject are running themes. An undercurrent of conflict and animosity pervades much of the family's interaction, attributed to growing pains, close proximity, economic concerns, and the looming unpleasantry of their metropolis. An unrequited love triangle exists, as plaited tomboy Chutney is enamored with Curtis, whose gaze is on the sour and unreceptive Michelle. Classmates Sheila and Verbena compound the frustration with their cattiness, while flat-topped Derrick plays the heavy, an inexorable rogue in this morality play. Kinship is provided by Gunk, Curtis's Caucasian pal and the strip's obtuse, mystical figure. Capable of enigmatic feats of benevolence and discovery, he is a simplistic yet empowered omen in Gotham.

Faith and religion are regular subjects in *Curtis,* as prayers at bedtime and church sequences with Reverend Woodard are common and redeeming. Tales of African folklore and theology are often the subject of Billingsley's richly narrative Sunday episodes, and the generous dialogue enhances the strip's compelling story structure.

Additional players include schoolteacher Mrs. Nelson and the braggart Gunther, the resident barber whose tall tales prompt many an eye roll from his customers and resigned, caustic coworkers. *Curtis* is a socially conscious effort, wherein Billingsley delves into controversial subjects and societal ills such as substance abuse, abortion, crime, and racism. Avoiding the gag-a-day format, situational humor is the norm, mixed with melodrama and pathos. Always in a four-panel daily format, Billingsley's solid and detailed drawing style creates a fitting atmosphere for his forceful tragicomedy, reminiscent of the detail and craft displayed by his predecessors decades earlier.

To date *Curtis* has experienced virtually no merchandising, except for two paperbacks in 1993. It is hoped that the underrated qualities of this creator and his comic will gain the critical recognition they deserve, for the strip is an exceptional work of modern fiction and covers important subjects with great integrity.

B.J.

DAN DUNN
1933–1943

*I*n the early 1930s the success of *Dick Tracy* gave rise to a number of imitations, none as blatant as *Dan Dunn*. It was concocted by Norman Marsh, an artist of modest achievement and a writer of limited imagination, for Publishers Syndicate, and began circulation, both daily and Sunday, in September 1933.

As Secret Operative 48, Dan Dunn worked for the U.S. Secret Service, but his square-chinned profile, beat-up trenchcoat, and snap-brimmed fedora gave him away as a poor man's version of Dick Tracy. His casebook included affairs of counterespionage, along with more mundane investigations of counterfeiting and racketeering. Some of his choicest adversaries were Spider Slick, a mob chieftain of unusual cunning; Big Jim, the corrupt mayor of a big city; and Scarface Bruno, their murderous henchman. No self-respecting crime strip of the 1930s was complete without at least one sinister Asian: *Dan Dunn* had two. First there was Wu Fang, an ersatz Fu Manchu who dreamed of taking over the city; when he was put away by the dauntless Dunn, he was replaced by Fat Sing, who from his opium den in the Chinatown of the mythical city of San Fragel (a composite of San Francisco and Los Angeles) spun a dark web of intrigue and murder across the country.

Marsh found many of the situations in the pulps, but most characters derived from other newspaper strips. Thus in 1934 the secret operative befriended Babs, an orphan girl who allied Annie Rooney's cuteness with Orphan Annie's spunk. Along with Dan's sheepdog Wolf, they formed a fearsome threesome, with Dan detecting, Babs snooping around, and Wolf playing straight dog to both (to

their rhetorical questions his answer was invariably "Wuf"). In 1938 Dan also acquired a comic sidekick, the bumbling Irwin Higgs, whose antics gained him a certain amount of popularity among the younger readers. Accordingly, the Sunday page, which had hitherto run in continuity with the dailies, was spun off the main narrative in order to showcase a series of gags built around the newcomer.

Despite the help of several able assistants, Ed Moore and Jack Ryan chief among them, Marsh never succeeded in giving his strip a distinctive look; while in the 1940s, his plots became more and more muddled. So when Marsh, a former leatherneck, announced in the aftermath of the bombing of Pearl Harbor that he was reenlisting in the Marine Corps, the news came as something of a relief to his syndicate, which immediately began planning the termination of the strip to coincide with the end of Marsh's second five-year contract. Allen Saunders was called in to write the remaining continuities, while the artwork was supplied by Paul Pinson. In January 1943 Alfred Andriola was enticed to succeed Pinson with the promise of a strip of his own (it turned out to be *Kerry Drake*), and he brought *Dan Dunn* to its close right on time, with the Sunday page of October 3, 1943.

M.H.

DATELINE: DANGER!
1968–1974

*T*he 1960s were the decade during which the comics syndicates were most blatantly aping successful television shows in a desperate (and vain) attempt at regaining their fast-disappearing readership. One of the most noteworthy

Dan Dunn (N. Marsh), © 1935 Publishers Syndicate

entries in that crowded field was *Dateline: Danger!,* a strip based on the popular *I Spy* program starring Robert Culp and Bill Cosby. Written by John Saunders, drawn by Al McWilliams, and distributed by Publishers-Hall Syndicate in both daily and Sunday formats, it premiered in November 1968.

As in *I Spy,* the main protagonists of *Dateline: Danger!* were a racially integrated two-man team working for U.S. Intelligence. Danny Raven, a former gridiron star and an African American, and his white partner Troy (an acronym for Theodore Randolph Oscar Young) were both employed by an American news organization, and their cover allowed them to travel to any trouble spot where their investigative talents were needed. They would thwart revolutionary plots in South America, defuse explosive situations on Western Europe's borders, and expose the machinations of enemy agents planning to topple friendly regimes in Africa. On the home front Danny, helped by his sister, Wendy, and his kid brother, Lee Roy, confronted a ruthless black agitator named Robin Jackson, who used his newspaper, The Revolt, to inflame racial tensions.

There was much banter and wisecracking going on between the partners as they raced cars, engaged in fisticuffs, and dodged bullets in the course of their everyday activities. Although suspenseful and entertaining, *Dateline: Danger!* suffered from the same readers' disaffection that afflicted most adventure strips in the 1970s, and it disappeared in 1974.

M.H.

DAUNTLESS DURHAM OF THE U.S.A.
1913–1914

Shortly after he had folded his *Desperate Desmond* strip, Harry Hershfield revised his formula of American heroism confronting foreign villainy with innocent womanhood as the stakes, in a new daily strip called *Dauntless Durham of the U.S.A.,* which started publication in the Hearst newspapers on January 22, 1913.

The classic strip of stage melodrama was reconstituted in a new guise. The protagonists were Dauntless Durham, "the ideal of the young American of the same spirit that brought his ancestors to America on the Mayflower"; Katrina, a despoiled European princess who "left her home with her little savings to come to America...still unaware of her royal birth"; and the indispensable antagonist, Lord Havaglass of Sussex-by-the-Thames, whose "years of family name and wealth have brought out his dictatorial nature." Havaglass wasn't much of a match for Durham (in the first week of continuity he got knocked out in a boxing bout, involving the fair Katrina, in no time flat by the handsome hero), and he lasted only a few months as the villain of the piece, being succeeded in the role by none other than that old rascal, Desperate Desmond himself. From that moment on the trio went through their familiar paces at an even more furious speed, Hershfield having replaced the captions that used to run under the *Desmond* panels with sprightlier speech balloons.

Durham, Desmond, and Katrina pursued one another all over the planet, from Mexico to Russia to Japan to New York City (where Durham was elected mayor), before Hershfield tired of the situation. On the last day of the year 1914, he brought his creation to a close by having Durham and Katrina marry, while a repentant Desmond returned to his children and his forgiving wife (who exclaimed, "Despy, I knew you loved me all the time."). While brief in duration, *Dauntless Durham* bears witness to the vitality and vibrancy of newspaper comics in the first decades of this century in a format almost totally nonexistent today—that of humorous day-to-day continuity.

M.H.

DAVE'S DELICATESSEN
1931–1935

Another one among Milt Gross's nutty confections, *Dave's Delicatessen* was sprung on an unsuspecting public on June 7, 1931, as a Sunday page (with *Count Screwloose* as its top strip) distributed by King Features Syndicate. A daily strip was added a few weeks later.

The titular hero, variously referred to as "Honest Dave," "Davey," and "Mr. Dave," was the proprietor of a greasy-spoon eatery where a motley assortment of zany characters liked to congregate. A tall, chinless man with a sausage nose and a small mustache, Dave was a soft touch for every bum, con artist, and hard-luck guy who dropped by his store, despite the strenuous efforts of his gigantic, practical wife. In December 1933 the lunatic tenant of the strip upstairs came to visit and never left. In subsequent episodes Dave and Count Screwloose embarked on sundry adventures, including a sea voyage and a stint in the French Foreign

Dave's Delicatessen (M. Gross), © 1932 King Features Syndicate

David Crane (C. Flessel), © 1969 Publishers-Hall Syndicate

Legion. The count soon took over total control of the Sunday page, and in January 1935 *Dave's Delicatessen* came to an end.

The dailies meanwhile had enjoyed continuities of their own, but those didn't last. Instead they were replaced by gags focusing on Dave and his small hero-worshipping son (whose name was never revealed). In his daily incarnation Dave was a much more nefarious character, and his underhanded dealings, such as selling a sawdust-filled sausage to a gullible customer or paying his delivery boy in stale bagels, invariably elicited from his gleeful youngster the admiring cry, "That's my pop!" in the last panel. The daily *Dave's Delicatessen* folded in late 1934, but Gross kept the scheming Dave and his filial booster in his *Grossly Xaggerated* miscellany page, where the pair became such a hit that the feature (which ran until the late 1940s) is often incorrectly referred to as "That's My Pop!"

M.H.

DAVID CRANE
1956–1971

Possibly the only straight story strip with a clergyman as its hero, *David Crane* (sometimes referred to as *Reverend David Crane*) was reportedly suggested by a deacon of the Presbyterian church to the editors of the Hall Syndicate. Drawn by Winslow Mortimer and written at first by editors at the syndicate, *David Crane* debuted, daily and Sunday, on February 27, 1956.

Reverend David Crane was the pastor of a midwestern church (no denomination given). The feature unfolded against a rural setting and the issues were kept comparatively simple. The dailies evolved continuities covering social work, marital breakup, and sibling rivalry, with strong overtones of soap-opera; while the Sundays often propounded straight moral lessons and plain homiletics. At the end of the 1950s Mortimer, who by that time was writing the strip as well as drawing it, got tired of the meager returns the feature generated and decided to leave *David Crane* (then distributed by Publishers Syndicate).

Craig Flessel, who took over the strip in 1960, tried to bring a different tone to the feature. As he told an interviewer, "Since the strip is about a minister and Christianity, I often have a feeling that our stories ought to get down to the 'nitty-gritty' of today's life and problems a little more than they do." Accordingly he tackled some thorny social problems, including the plight of the hungry and the sting of racial discrimination. In one sequence the reverend tried to convince the hog farmers who had planned to slaughter their animals and bury their carcasses in protest against falling prices to give the meat to the needy instead. In the Sundays, by contrast, Flessel, who termed himself "a meat-and-potatoes, big-foot comic artist at heart," indulged in humorous anecdotes centered around some of the pillars of the church, a treatment often frowned upon by the syndicate.

Having carried out his mission for over a decade and a half in the face of declining readership, David Crane finally ended his evangelical career in 1971.

M.H.

DAVY JONES
See JOE JINKS

DEBBIE
1946–1961

Cecil Jensen is better noted as the longtime editorial cartoonist of the *Chicago Daily News*, but his secret aspiration was to become a successful comic-strip artist. His first effort in the field was *Syncopating Sue*, a flapper-era strip that enjoyed a very short career. Some twenty years later he tried again, and this time his new feature hung on for a lot longer, through a decade and a half and several changes of name.

It started as *Elmo* on October 28, 1946, and was distributed, daily and Sunday, by the Register and Tribune Syndicate. Elmo was a Candide-like character who always came by his good fortune through dumb luck (decades ahead of Forrest Gump). Jensen satirized big-city politics, movie-star pretensions, and financial skullduggery in his strip, but this initial phase didn't last long. In May 1947 a hometown acquaintance, a pigtailed little girl named Debbie, came to visit and elected to stay. Her mild antics soon eclipsed the hapless Elmo's misadventures, and in 1949 she received leading-girl status when the name of the feature was changed to *Debbie.*

Debbie turned out to be just another run-of-the-nursery girl strip, and its anecdotes never rose above the level of childhood pranks and girlish misunderstandings. It was drawn in a loose, casual style that got more casual with the passing years. Despite its lack of originality and uninspired writing, the strip breezed through the baby-boom decade of the 1950s, but found it rough going with the coming of the more demanding 1960s. The feature underwent one last title change (to *Little Debbie*) before finally expiring on September 30, 1961.

M.H.

DEBBIE DEAN
1944–1949

Another in a long line of working-woman comics, *Debbie Dean* came out on January 11, 1944, in the form of a daily strip drawn and written by Bert Whitman and distributed by the New York Post Syndicate.

While not otherwise startlingly original, *Debbie Dean* innovated in at least one small way. Its "Career Girl" subtitle was quite a step up from the "breadwinner" and "toiler" labels that had been affixed to girl strips of an earlier era, and was evidence of the increasing respect being shown by newspaper-strip artists and editors to an expanding female workforce during World War II. Debbie was a dark-haired and winsome heiress who, tiring of "the debutante life," turned to a career in journalism. Her adventures as an investigative reporter were standard comic-strip fare: she exposed graft at city hall, uncovered corruption in sporting halls, and even tangled with German spies. Leaving the newspaper game in 1946, she then tried her hand at local politics, succeeding her walrus-mustached uncle, the facetiously named Gunga Dean, as mayor of her hometown of Deansburg. As soon as she was elected she proceeded to achieve a balanced budget (already a concern at the time) and make the town into a tourist destination.

In her private life Debbie carried on a less than torrid romance (she was a bit on the priggish side) with her boyfriend, an adman named Cozy (the name said it all). More and more the story lines tended toward straight operatic continuities of the sudsy variety, and *Debbie Dean* finally drowned in a sea of soap bubbles in 1949. Whitman later told a credulous interviewer that the strip's demise was due to his using the word "dope" in reference to narcotics in one of his narratives. It is much more likely that *Debbie Dean* folded because it couldn't compete in a crowded field against more breathlessly plotted and more slickly drawn strips such as *Brenda Starr* and *Mary Worth.*

M.H.

DENNIS THE MENACE
1951–present

The postwar baby boom produced not only a bumper crop of new infants, it also created a new crop of often bewildered parents; and to those the cartoonists, always on the lookout for a trend, responded with a crop of comic-strip kids of their own. Among these one of the most memorable and certainly one of the most durable proved to be Dennis the Menace, who first appeared in a daily panel initiated by Hank Ketcham and distributed by the Post-Hall Syndicate on March 12, 1951. A year later a Sunday page completed the picture.

As a five-year-old, Dennis Mitchell cannot display the same deviltry as that shown by older boys like the Katzenjammers, but he makes up for this shortcoming in other ways. His counterfeit innocence, blunt candor, and joyous vandalism often cause discomfort and embarrassment to the adults whose small hypocrisies are unable to withstand the light of truth, and whose property is sometimes put at risk by the irrepressible tot's high spirits. While he is only a nuisance (and on rare occasions a comfort) to his harried parents, Henry and Alice, he is most definitely a pest to his neighbors, the elderly George and Martha Wilson. Poor Mr. Wilson is inevitably the foil of Dennis's initiatives, always undertaken with the best of intentions.

The tousle-haired tot's best pal is the close-cropped and admiring Joey, and his main nemesis the freckle-faced, eyeglass-wearing Margaret, who has a crush on Dennis. The object of her unwanted affections only meets her advances with rebuffs and, in the winter, adroitly aimed snowballs. So great is Dennis's annoyance at his juvenile admirer that he once told his mother at bedtime, "You're lucky, Mom. If you were Margaret's mother, you'd hafta kiss *her* goodnight!" While all this is going on, Dennis' shaggy and moronic dog Ruff keeps surveying the scene in gaping incomprehension.

A religious man, Ketcham has his little devil with a heart of gold always say grace before dinner and recite his prayers at bedtime (although he may mangle them a bit). The cartoonist has also interspersed a number of biblical sayings and parables amid Dennis's shenanigans, albeit not on the scale practiced by his colleague Charles Schulz. These have been numerous enough over the years, however, to give birth to a booklet dedicated by the author to his "Sunday School teachers at First Methodist Episcopal Church in Seattle," published in 1993 under the title *Dennis the Menace: Prayers and Graces,"* with a foreword by Ruth and Billy Graham.

Dennis the Menace, whose name has now passed into the language, has had his adventures drawn by Ketcham in an apparently slapdash but actually highly organized style. The kids in particular have always been captured with telling brio and an appropriately dynamic line. Ketcham, who for a long time resided in Switzerland, has often had recourse to assistants and ghosts in his long career. In the 1980s most of the drawing was done by Karen Donovan and Ron Ferdinand; today Ferdinand is in charge of the Sundays only. Ketcham still draws some of the daily panels, with in recent times an increasingly frequent assist by Marcus Hamilton (the panels left unsigned are Hamilton's work).

M.H.

DESPERATE DESMOND
1910–1912

It is a truism to say that popular culture eternally recycles its own themes (along with the themes of highbrow culture). The silent movies took up with relish the conventions of the romantic novel long after they had been discarded by the practitioners of serious fiction; and the early comics revived the situations of stage melodrama well after the legitimate theater had abandoned them. C. W. Kahles was first to mine this mother lode with *Hairbreadth Harry,* but Harry Hershfield was not far behind him when he created *Desperate Desmond* as a daily strip for the Hearst newspapers on March 11, 1910.

Emphatically recreating the classic trio of nineteenth-century stage blood-curdlers, Hershfield had his heroine, Fair Rosamond, involved in a tug-of-war between her two rival suitors, her fiancé Claude Eclaire and the dastardly villain Desperate Desmond—who tried by means fair and foul (but mostly foul) to win the maiden's heart and, failing that, to see to it that she didn't belong to his hated enemy. Rosamond underwent all the hair-raising ordeals that are the hallmarks of the genre: she was in turns tied to railroad tracks, left dangling from the Brooklyn Bridge, and locked up in a burning cabin, all predicaments from which she was rescued (in the nick of time, of course) by her boyfriend. The switch was that she managed to save her somewhat dull-witted lover as often as he rescued her.

The strip was named for the villain, and there were good reasons for it. The snarling, cursing, mustachioed Desmond, always attired in the costume of black-hearted malevolence (top hat, coat-and-tails, bespatted black shoes), was the real as well as the titular hero of the piece. The endless feats of cunning and imagination he displayed in his attempts to outwit his opponent and to win the object of his lust were what kept the strip suspenseful and the readers amused at the broad-handed satire. Hershfield ran a lengthy narrative under the pictures, but he used balloons for the tongue-in-cheek dialogue. "Desmond you cur, I hate you," Rosamond would exclaim at the villain who

had just abducted her. "I love only Claude Eclaire!"; while at another time Desmond would yell in the direction of the triumphant hero, "Claude Eclaire, you dime-store hero, I'll have my revenge yet!"

After a brief interlude during the presidential campaign of 1912, when Hershfield, on instructions from Hearst, launched his comic strip into an ill-conceived political satire, Desmond ended late in 1912. *Desmond* himself was too colorful a character to be kept away for long, however, and Hershfield accordingly was to bring him back a few months later in his next daily-strip venture, *Dauntless Durham of the U.S.A.*

M.H.

DICK TRACY
1931–present

Chester Gould was in 1931 a moderately successful cartoonist with such mildly inventive creations as *Fillum Fables* (a spoof of silent movies) and a sports miscellany to his credit as well as a ten-year record of unsuccessful submissions to the *Chicago Tribune.* Then, as Gould himself has recounted in *Comics and Their Creators,* "in the spring of 1931 came the inspiration for *Dick Tracy,* symbol of law and order, who could dish it out to the underworld exactly as they dished it out—only better." This time Gould's brainchild, which he had tentatively called "Plainclothes Tracy," was accepted by the head of the Chicago Tribune Syndicate, Captain Joseph Medill Patterson, who changed the name to *Dick Tracy,* and in October 1931 the new feature was finally launched in both daily and Sunday format.

In the very first daily episode (the continuities for dailies and Sundays were kept separate until May 1932), Tracy was the powerless witness of a holdup during which his girl-friend, Tess Trueheart, was kidnapped and her father murdered. In sheer revulsion Tracy joined the police force and tracked down the criminals. His career was launched. In all the ensuing years Tracy would never look back: a cop he was, and a cop he would remain, first, foremost, and always. It is this grim determination and unshakable integrity that have made the character so fascinating to the critics and the public alike.

Gould's inspiration had not come from the comic pages but from the news pages. The headlines and stories about the gang wars and the pervasive corruption Prohibition had engendered proved the immediate cause of Gould's slowly crystalizing theme—that of ruthless crime and inescapable punishment. Moral outrage had long been a source of artistic expression, but expression has to match conviction in clarity and forcefulness to become persuasive. Here lies Gould's greatest accomplishment: he made *Dick Tracy* into the vehicle for a unified thought and a single vision.

Gould found his theme first and evolved a style to fit this theme only second, but what a style it was. His renderings were black and ominous, his line sharp and nervous, the perspective compact and oppressive. His imagery Gould took directly from news photos, complete with sharp-edged contours and flattened backgrounds, photoprints of the city's soul, with its skyscrapers, its back alleys, its gaudy neon

Desperate Desmond (H. Hershfield), 1912

Dick Tracy (C. Gould), © 1944 Chicago Tribune–New York News Syndicate

signs, its grandeur and squalor; for just as Troy had been the real subject of the *Iliad,* Chicago was the real subject of *Tracy.*

The mastery of Gould's tales resided most of all in their telling. The action pulsed relentlessly ahead; it evoked the brutal unspooling of a newsreel rather than the smooth flow of a Hollywood picture. Duplicating the abstract space of the movie screen, each panel alternated close-ups, long shots, angle views, and more in quick succession, forcing a feeling of irresistible forward motion upon the reader.

Inevitably Tracy's first opponents were the conventional villains of pulp and movie fiction: racketeers, kidnappers, bank robbers, mob lawyers, with colorful names such as Larceny Lou, Ribs Mocco, Stooge Viller, Boris Arson, or Big Boy. These were gradually replaced with a grotesque rogues' gallery of criminals whose faces and names were a clue to their nefarious activities: Trigger Doom (a hired killer), the Mole (an underground racketeer), or even more directly, Mr. Bribery and Mr. Crime. Many of these felons met ends as terrible as their deeds, being variously shot through the head, impaled on flagpoles, or scalded to death.

Tracy's life has been one of unremitting danger and terror. He has been wounded many times, blinded with acid, tortured, and stabbed, and has seen his loved ones, including his sweetheart and later wife, Tess Trueheart, and his daughter, Bonnie Braids, threatened and sometimes abducted, as was his adopted son, Junior. He has also found solace in his work and in the company of his fellow cops, Pat Patton, Sam Catchem, Chief Brandon, and Lizz the policewoman. His homilies on law and order and on police techniques have long been an integral part of the strip.

For the almost fifty years Gould worked on *Dick Tracy* his

influence grew steadily stronger. He introduced the themes of violence, suspense, tension, and terror into the comics. Soon after *Tracy* had established itself, rival syndicates brought out police strips with the avowed aim of beating Gould at his own game. While the best of features soon went their own creative way, they all owe a debt of gratitude to *Tracy* for the trails Gould had blazed during the first years of Tracy's existence.

In his introduction to *The Celebrated Cases of Dick Tracy,* Ellery Queen details all the contributions made by *Tracy* to the field of crime fiction. While one may quibble with some of his assumptions, he makes a strong case for Gould as a pioneer in the area of procedural fiction as well as a major figure in the history of detective fiction. *Tracy* was in fact an aggregate—or better a synthesis—of many strands in crime fiction. Integrating the puzzle elements of the traditional mystery tale, the violent action of the thriller, the atmospheric overtones of the suspense story, and the shock treatment of the pulps (with a dash of science fiction thrown in), Gould's stories ultimately followed no tradition but imposed their own.

A number of milestones have marked Gould's half-century tenure on the strip, such as the introduction of the wrist radio (and later the wrist TV), the birth of a daughter named Sparkle to the smelly B. O. Plenty and his grotesque wife Gravel Gertie, the invention of the Space Coupe, Tracy's wedding to Tess, and Junior's marriage to Moon Maid, daughter of the governor of the Moon. All these events were celebrated by the syndicate in shrewd advertising and merchandising campaigns that resulted in loads of toys, clothing, and knickknacks being offered for sale to an appreciative public.

Gould signed his last daily strip and Sunday page on Christmas Eve and Christmas Day 1977, respectively. The following week Rick Fletcher, who had been assisting Gould on the feature since 1961, took over the drawing, while the writing was entrusted to mystery author Max Allan Collins (with Gould retaining a byline). At first Collins tried to stay close to the original flavor and tenor of the strip, even bringing back some of Gould's old characters, notably Big Boy, the gang boss responsible for the death of Emil Trueheart, the father of Tracy's wife. Despite such outward fidelity to the sources, friction soon developed between Collins and the strip's creator, who expressed dissatisfaction with what he perceived as a softening of the tough "an eye for an eye" ideology that had for so long permeated the feature. In 1981 the break became official when Gould withdrew his name from the strip; two years later Fletcher's death severed the last remaining link between the modern-day *Tracy* and its origins.

As a replacement for Fletcher the syndicate picked Pulitzer Prize–winning political cartoonist Dick Locher, which caused quite a stir in some circles. Locher, however, has shown himself quite capable of adapting to the strip's gritty, hard-edged style, and his tenure on *Tracy*, which started in May 1983, has so far proved craftsmanlike if not quite stellar. In 1992 Collins, who had tried to attune the tenor of the strip even closer to the sensibilities of the times, was unceremoniously bumped off the feature, which is now being scripted by Michael Kilian.

M.H.

DICK'S ADVENTURES
IN DREAMLAND
1947–1956

With its recollections of *Dickie Dare* and his echoes *of Little Nemo in Slumberland*, *Dick's Adventures in Dreamland* was a comic strip put together by a committee and looked it. It was conjured up by fiat from the Chief, the mercurial W. R. Hearst, who had proposed "incorporating American history in the adventure strips of the comic section" and who had driven his point forcefully to his underlings at King Features. It was ultimately decided to star a young lad of about 12 named Dick who would act as a lead-in to each historical happening. Max Trell was chosen as the writer, and the artwork was entrusted to Neil O'Keeffe. Dick finally embarked on his adventures on Sunday, January 12, 1947.

The opening sequence found Dick, a youth of our time, in Genoa, Italy, where he advised Christopher Columbus on how best to obtain financing for his voyage of discovery. Later Dick dreamed himself into Coronado's California expedition, rode with Paul Revere through Lexington and Concord, was with George Washington during the crossing of the Delaware, and assisted Andrew Jackson in the Battle of New Orleans, to cite only a few examples. Enjoying the luxury of an entire newspaper page, O'Keeffe laid out his compositions tastefully, with a judicious use of color, and each panel was rendered with great attention of detail as to time, place, and social conditions. There were no speech balloons, but a somewhat ponderous text running within the frame at the bottom or top of each picture.

Dick's Adventures (Trell and O'Keeffe), © 1948 King Features Syndicate

The feature was a laudable initiative, and it might have succeeded on spectacle alone. While *Dick's Adventures* was not a bestseller, it did have a respectable list of client newspapers in the early years. Unfortunately, following Hearst's death in 1951, the syndicate cut *Dick's Adventures* from fullpage size down to half-page, and later to third-page. Thus deprived of its main asset—space—the strip went into a downward spiral, and it was finally discontinued on October 7, 1956

M.H.

DICKIE DARE
1933–1957

Dickie Dare first saw the light of day in the form of sample strips submitted by the young Milton Caniff to the Associated Press to fill an upcoming opening in their full page of daily strips, a feature service. When the AP accepted his proposed strip, thus began on July 31, 1933, the long-running adventures of young Dickie and his dog Wags, later joined by Dan Flynn, a writer friend of Dickie's father. Flynn was a harbinger of the adult mentor–youthful hero relationship to come in the persons of Pat Ryan and, later, Colonel Flip Corkin, and of Terry Lee, in Caniff's subsequent and highly successful *Terry and the Pirates*.

Initially conceived by Caniff as a boy with a vivid imagination who daydreamed himself into the midst of adventure stories—for example, with Robin Hood, Robinson Crusoe, even General Custer at the Battle of Little Big Horn (whose terrible fate he escaped only by a propitious awakening from his dream state)—Dickie, now accompanied by the strapping, blond, and handsome Dynamite Dan, moved into reality, so to speak, with original story lines set on the high seas, in the desert, and in other exciting locales. Blue-black hair glistening in the sun's reflected rays, Dickie thereafter traveled with Dan around the world, sailing the seven seas and becoming involved with all manner of ne'er-do-wells, from smugglers to spies to tyrants.

Caniff's much admired cinematic style of drawing not yet developed, his rendering of this strip was attractive, and his story lines were quite entertaining. When Caniff left in October 1934 to draw *Terry and the Pirates* for Captain Joseph Patterson of the Chicago Tribune–New York News, Coulton Waugh took over the reins in midstory. With no notion as to what direction the departed cartoonist had intended to go, Waugh nonetheless picked up the adventure—this time involving an updated pirate band, whose ship was a submarine and whose leader, Von Slugg, was as mean as his name sounded—without any noticeable difficulty.

As Waugh's stewardship of the strip grew longer, and he became more comfortable in his role as the author of Dickie's adventures, he began to change the tone and style of the original, to which he had been fairly faithful from the point of his takeover. He favored brush lines for the figures in place of Caniff's then cartoonlike style and also experimented with various pen patterns, such as crosshatching, until he was satisfied that he had reached his own individual style.

Dickie Dare (M. Caniff), © 1934 The AP

For Waugh the seafaring theme, which with Caniff had been seen as only one of a variety of settings for high-spirited adventure and excitement, became the dominant one. He drew on his own love of sailing and of nature, as evidenced by the excellence of his drawing of sailing vessels and landscapes, and blended it with such nautical occupations as deep-sea diving for buried treasure, to keep Dickie's exploits centered on the sea. In further illustration of the natural world, birds and animals, whether friendly or not, were found in abundance. Another decision, to allow Dickie to remain around age 12, preserved the character's wide-eyed, youthful exuberance and avoided the stress of adolescence with all its accompanying complications.

When Waugh left *Dickie Dare* in mid-1944 to write a comic-strip history and to try his hand at a new strip for another paper, his former assistant and future wife, Mabel Odin Burvik, succeeded him and carried on ably enough, briefly followed by Fran Matera. Upon completion of his book, entitled *The Comics,* and with the failure of his new strip, he returned to the Associated Press and took up Dickie's adventures where he had left off. However, as time passed, he grew weary of Dickie's boyish reactions and, receiving permission from the syndicate, aged the twelve-year-old enough for him to enter the Naval Academy. With an increasingly dwindling base, though, Dickie's last voyage finally took place in October of 1957, as his remaining readers watched him sail off into history.

M.B.C.

DIE FINEHEIMER TWINS
1903–1914

It is a tribute to the popularity of Rudolph Dirks's *The Katzenjammer Kids* that a few short years after the feature's inception imitations were sprouting all over the land, and even across the ocean. Among others there were Kahles's *Tim and Tom, the Terrible Twins, Dem Boys* by a cartoonist who signed "Karls," not to mention *The Terrible Twins* and *The Twinkerton Twins* in Britain. None of them, however, approached in quality of style and wit *Die Fineheimer Twins,* which Harold Knerr started in the comics supplement of the *Philadelphia Inquirer* on February 15, 1903, the first Sunday page to be syndicated nationally by this publication.

In a close imitation of Dirks's page, Knerr had two boys, one blond, one brunette, engaged in a protracted duel of wits with their loving but naive Mama and a peg-legged, portly retired sea-captain whom they never tired of harass-

ing. All the principals sported mock-German accents and looked like they had just wandered in from the rival strip; and like Dirks, Knerr was fond of sending his two hellions and their victims on foreign trips, whether to the Caribbean or the South Seas. Drawn clumsily at first, *Die Fineheimer Twins* soon gained in self-assurance, as Knerr tried out a diversity of layouts and used the device of the speech-balloon as part of the page's design, in contrast to Dirks, whose placement of balloons was often slapdash.

It is indicative of Knerr's blossoming talent that of all the *Katzenjammer* imitations his proved the most enduring as well as the most popular. Indeed, he might have continued it indefinitely, thus sparking a Dirks-Knerr rivalry no matter what, had he not been tapped by W. R. Hearst to take over the real article at the conclusion of the celebrated Hearst vs. Dirks court trial. In 1914, therefore, he left *Die Fineheimer Twins* in the hands of cartoonist Jack Gallagher, who only managed to carry it to October 4. Years afterward Knerr modestly stated, "Perhaps I am better able to draw childhood effectively because my own...persisted long into manhood." *Die Fineheimer Twins* was thus not merely a dry-run for *The Katzenjammer Kids* (as most commentators have claimed), but rather an original set of variations on a theme that Dirks had himself borrowed from Wilhelm Busch.

M.H.

DILBERT
1989–present

A strip addressing both the preoccupations and the sensibility of the 1990s, *Dilbert* concerns a moderately alienated engineer and his sarcastic animal companion Dogbert, a bespectacled oval creature, presumably canine, who is never at a loss for a snide remark. When Dilbert decides to pattern himself on Dr. Frankenstein and tells Dogbert to fetch him a brain, the dog replies, "Like your present model, or one that works?"

Created by Scott Adams, a project manager for a telecommunications company and an engineer with an MBA from the University of California, *Dilbert* has been distributed by United Feature Syndicate since 1989. It reveals a wicked insight into the cruelty, duplicity, and sycophancy of office politics and a keen ear for the inanities of both technical jargon and office double-talk. One of the recurrent themes of the strip is the explication of the language of business and of science: "It is technically impossible," for example, is translated as meaning "I don't feel like doing it," and "The data bits are flexed through a collectimizer which strips the flow-gate arrays into virtual message elements" as "I don't know." If a company's product is killing customers, Dilbert suggests that the fact be presented positively, as "a decline in unsatisfied customers."

As soul-destroying as his office job is, however, Dilbert has a richly imaginative personal life at home. His hopes for a social life are unflagging, despite the discouragement of a pet who asks, when Dilbert reports that he is writing a completely honest "personals" ad, "What species are you targeting?" Dogbert is apparently not alone in his low estimate of his master's romantic potential: the hapless hero's suspicions that there is a conspiracy against him are confirmed when he finds a book entitled *Attractive Women's Secret Guide to Avoiding Dilbert*.

Although the strip is mainly devoted to their caustic badinage, at times the two receive some odd visitors. Their furniture is possessed by mischievous spirits who identify themselves as upholsterygeists but Dilbert is equal to the occasions; he threatens to play Jane Fonda tapes on the VCR, and the haunted easy chair flees in terror. Other supernatural guests include a minor devil, the ruler of Heck, who punishes only misdemeanors; instead of a pitchfork, he carries a large spoon, and as he doesn't have the authority to damn people, he darns them.

Dilbert is minimally drawn, with no aspirations to visual sophistication, but it is a literate piece of whimsy with occasional shrewd flashes of insight. A combination of satire on techies and businessmen, portrait of the contemporary isolated man, and madcap fantasy, it contains some of the wittiest wordplay on the comics page.

D.W.

THE DINGBAT FAMILY
1910–1916

On June 20, 1910, a few days after George Herriman's arrival in New York City, *The Dingbat Family* started running in the *New York Evening Journal*. A daily strip about the doings of an average big-city family, it was the first of the many creations the artist was to contribute to the Hearst papers.

The family portrayed by Herriman was not much different from the many other comic-strip families then proliferating in the newspaper pages. It was comprised of E. Pluribus Dingbat, a shrimpish and stuffy office clerk; his large and homely wife Minnie, better known as Ma; and their obnoxious offspring, Imogene, Cicero, and Baby. They all lived in a city apartment, the Sooptareen Arms, where most of the shenanigans took place, in the company of a cat and a dog, both of them unnamed. Herriman was getting nowhere with the strip, and he had started to concentrate on the putative head of the family, even renaming the feature *Mr. Dingbat*, when at the end of July a mysterious family took up residence in Apartment 33 directly above the Dingbats', and there began a tug of war that was to last for more than a year.

The anonymous family in "33" seemed to have a single goal in life, namely to annoy, pester, bedevil, and otherwise harass the Dingbats. They would tap-dance in their living room, thereby sending the chandelier crashing on Dingbat's head; they would bean poor Dingbat with a well-aimed flower pot when he leaned out of the window; and the boy upstairs would hit Cicero in the eye every time the two met in the stairway. Herriman knew he had a good thing going, and on August 1 the strip was renamed *The Family Upstairs*. The enraged Dingbat tried by every possible means to ambush or at least to identify his noxious neighbors, but they remain unseen to the end. The internecine warfare between the families came to an abrupt conclusion on November 15, 1911, when the apartment building was demolished to make way for a department store, and the Dingbats moved to California.

The strip, again titled *The Dingbat Family*, reverted to its original format of domestic maladjustment, and in its second incarnation it proved successful enough to last until January 4, 1916. The feature would have remained just another title, amusing but certainly not outstanding, in the Herriman canon, had it not been for the curious byplay between the family cat and an impudent mouse intent on stoning the hapless feline. In time this sideshow would turn into the artist's undisputed masterpiece, *Krazy Kat*, eclipsing the support that had given birth to it.

M.H.

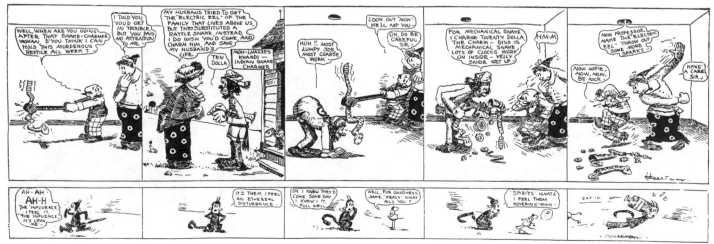

The Dingbat Family (G. Herriman), 1911

Dinglehoofer und His Dog (H. Knerr), © 1941 King Features Syndicate

DINGLEHOOFER UND HIS DOG
1926–1952

Harold Knerr created his last comic strip of any consequence, *Dinglehoofer und His Dog Adolph,* on May 16, 1926, as a topper to *The Katzenjammer Kids;* it was syndicated along with its companion strip by King Features.

Dinglehoofer featured a German-American bachelor of advancing age (whose benign face and rotund silhouette were modeled on the author's own father, Dr. Calvin Knerr), his small bullpup Adolph, and his black housekeeper Lillian. The humor was of a gentle variety, with Adolph causing all sorts of commotion through his friskiness and his eagerness to please. The action most often took place outdoors, and Knerr's winsome graphic style was displayed to the full in airy compositions and serene backgrounds. The artist must have regarded the strip as a welcome departure from the raucous and frenzied atmosphere of *The Katzenjammers.*

The feature thus coasted along at a bucolic pace that was somewhat shaken in 1934 by the introduction into Dinglehoofer's life of a little orphan boy, "Tadpole" (or "Tad") Doogan, whom the kindhearted bachelor soon adopted. The young boy brought some needed agitation to the strip, with the principals embarking on all sorts of adventure, from going on a butterfly chase to collaring a gang of burglars. While Dinglehoofer (whom Tad called "Mr. Dingy") spoke in a Germanized English similar to that of the Katzenjammers, Tad at first used a pseudo-Irish lingo that was almost indecipherable ("Uh big goose took his tail fer uh worm an' tried tu eat it!").

Unfortunately, the long reach of history in the person of a German dictator also named Adolph caught up with the gentle mood of the strip. Hitler's rise on the international scene made it no longer appropriate to give the name Adolph even to a dog. Knerr solved this knotty problem in his own understated way: on May 22, 1936, he had Mr. Dingy making a gift of Adolph to the daughter of a farmer friend, and the next Sunday another dog, a dachshund named Schnappsy, came to replace Adolph, with the strip acquiring its definitive title of *Dinglehoofer und His Dog.* Schnappsy proved to be as frisky a mutt as Adolph had

been, and the engaging trio of adult, boy, and dog carried on much as before, with episodes of mild adventure alternating with interludes of sweetness and humor. Knerr's death in 1949 did not interrupt the activities of the Dinglehoofer clan, which were continued by Doc Winner for a few more years, the final page appearing on February 3, 1952.

M.H.

DIXIE DUGAN
1929–1966

J. P. (Joseph Patrick) McEvoy and John Striebel, the creators of *Dixie Dugan,* had been friends since childhood; McEvoy later became a newspaperman and screenwriter, while Striebel turned to advertising and fashion illustration. In 1928 McEvoy sold a serial titled *Show Girl* to *Liberty* magazine, and Striebel was asked to illustrate it. *Show Girl* was later turned into a musical, and McNaught Syndicate, ever alert to new possibilities, approached the author with an offer to write a comic strip based on his creation. The new feature, also called *Show Girl,* premiered as a daily strip drawn by Striebel on texts by McEvoy, on October 21, 1929.

Legend has it that the new venture owed its early success to Ham Fisher's salesmanship. Fisher himself was not loath in taking credit. "I took the strip out during the worst period syndicates have ever known," he told an interviewer in 1942, "paid my own expenses and sold *Dixie Dugan* to some thirty-odd newspapers in forty days, a syndicate sales record." *Dixie Dugan* was consciously modeled on actress Louise Brooks, a woman of rare beauty and a personal friend of Striebel's, as Miss Brooks recounted in the film magazine *Image* in 1975. (Incidentally Louise Brooks may be the only woman to have inspired two comic-strip heroines, the other being Valentina by the Italian Guido Crepax.) Striebel caught her likeness when she was at her most pristine (she was 19 when the artist made his first sketches of the budding actress in 1926).

Dixie was such a radiant personality that she eclipsed with her presence the other characters in the strip, a serious flaw in such a popular medium as the comics were in the 1920s and 1930s. In order to recast her image as the girl next door, the author first took Dixie out of her theatrical

Dixie Dugan (McEvoy and Striebel), © 1945 McNaught Syndicate

surroundings, and the strip was renamed *Dixie Dugan*. Next the famous Louise Brooks hairbob disappeared in favor of shoulder-length hair, while Dixie, now a humble working girl, was thrown into an unending string of romantic and professional adventures. She was often seen in the company of her best friend, Mickey, a blonde debutante type whose conventional good looks helped set up, by contrast with the dark-haired heroine, the piquancy of Dixie's delicate face. In 1935 McEvoy's son Rennie took over the writing chores, increased by the addition of a Sunday page shortly thereafter.

In the 1940s, like so many other heroines of the funny pages, Dixie did her part for the war effort, helping trap foreign agents and black marketeers. After the war Striebel seems to have tired of Dixie, and he left more and more of the actual drawing to assistants. The heroine herself looked increasingly worn, and since she was the feature's main asset, the strip's readership began to drop. Bedeviled by trite situations and humdrum continuities, *Dixie Dugan* finally gave up the ghost in 1966.

M.H.

DON DIXON AND THE HIDDEN EMPIRE
1935–1941

Tired of paying top money for the syndicated strips they carried, the management at the *Brooklyn Eagle* decided to create their own newspaper service, the Watkins Syndicate. One of the first features to come out of the new organization was *Don Dixon and the Hidden Empire;* drawn by Carl Pfeufer on texts by Bob Moore, it saw light as a Sunday only in October 1935, along with a companion strip called *Tad of the Tanbark*.

The hidden empire of the title was Pharia, an unknown world reached by a scientist, Dr. Lugoff, and his two boy companions, Matt Haynes and Don Dixon. Once there they helped the legitimate king of the place regain his throne, and as a consequence Matt was rewarded with the hand of Princess Marcia, one of the king's daughters, and as a further consequence disappeared from the strip. Lugoff, Don, and Don's newfound girlfriend, Princess Wanda, another of the king's daughters, then joined forces against all the menaces threatening Pharia. In the swamps, through the forests, across the deserts, and over the mountains of this misbegotten world they trekked, in search of an egress to the outside world. In the course of his wanderings Don had to fend off scores of rivals lusting after the fair Wanda, fight against tigers and giant mice, escape the clutches of a lascivious sorceress, all in a passable facsimile of Flash Gordon's adventures.

With the years Pfeufer's style, at first slavishly imitative of Alex Raymond's, took on a rugged quality of its own, while Moore's writing acquired a dose of needed polish. These newly honed skills were much in evidence after Don and Wanda finally emerged to the surface in 1938. Their subsequent adventures on earth pitted them against the Destroyer, head of a secret organization headquartered in the Himalayas; they later fought Dr. Strunski, who schemed

Don Dixon (C. Pfeufer), © 1939 Watkins Syndicate

to subjugate the world with his army of robots, and Wulf, the captain of a pirate submarine. These sequences no longer owed a debt to *Flash Gordon* and were quite entertaining (unlike those of *Tad of the Tanbark*, a circus story turned jungle adventure that came to an unlamented end about this time).

The year was now 1940, and Germany was on the ascendancy. There followed *Don Dixon*'s next phase, marked by an almost unbridled Teutonic frenzy. In an episode lifted nearly whole from Richard Wagner's *Ring of the Nibelung*, Don, Wanda, and their companions arrived in the underground "kingdom of the caves," ruled by the dwarfish tyrant Mime. Armed with Balmung, Siegfried's magic sword, which he had unsheathed from its rock, and with the help of Alberic, Mime's brother, Don brought Mime's reign of terror to an end. There ensued a Celtic postlude, as Don and Wanda fell under the spell of the enchantress Morgan le Fay. They snapped out of it, and in the last *Don Dixon* page, which appeared on July 6, 1941, they were seen trying "to get back where everything is normal." (In the summer of 1941 this notion must have sounded to many as quaint as the strip's earlier conceits.)

M.H.

Don Winslow of the Navy (Martinek and Beroth), © 1937 Bell Syndicate

DON WINSLOW OF THE NAVY
1934–1955

Because the navy couldn't get enough recruits in the landlocked Midwest, former Lieutenant Commander Frank V. Martinek came up with the idea of a novel and, later, a newspaper strip showcasing the exciting adventures of a young naval officer, in order to spur enlistment. With some assistance from Colonel Frank Knox, secretary of the navy, he then sold the concept to the Bell Syndicate. Titled *Don Winslow of the Navy,* the new feature debuted in its daily format on March 5, 1934.

The first ten dailies did not show the titular hero, but provided the readers with a glimpse into the extensive headquarters of Scorpia, a dreaded secret organization bent on taking over the world (a favorite occupation of secret organizations at the time), which was headed by the baldheaded, cigar-smoking Scorpion, who in the course of the next twenty or so years would prove Don Winslow's most treacherous foe. Lieutenant (later Lieutenant Commander) Winslow worked in navy intelligence (as had Martinek), and it was his thankless task to track down the elusive Scorpion all over the world. In his efforts he was often helped by his short, fat associate, Lieutenant (never promoted) Red Pennington, and frequently comforted by the enticing Mercedes Colby, daughter of his commanding officer, Admiral Colby (later retired).

The Sunday page, which premiered in January 1935, had separate continuities that pitted Don and Red against a vast array of new adversaries. There was the Hawk, a magician-warlord, in 1935; the Crocodile, who planned the destruction of the American naval base at Cavite in the Philippines from his stratospheric island, in 1936; Dr. Centaur, the inventor of a paralyzing ray, in 1937; the Dwarf and his agents, the Duchess and Dr. Thor, in the following years; Don took care of them all. *Don Winslow* shared the Sunday page for a time with *Bos'n Hale, Sea Scout,* another strip of maritime adventure that lasted into the 1940s.

Don Winslow was the result of close teamwork. Martinek wrote the scripts and supervised the production. Lieutenant Leon A. Beroth, USN, drew the feature, with assistance from Carl Hammond (a mere civilian, which is perhaps why he remained uncredited). And the Department of the Navy was called upon to put its stamp of approval on the whole thing. While the plot lines remained the stuff of conventional pulp stories, there was also a great concern for authenticity. The naval bases were depicted under their real names, Cavite, San Diego, Guantanamo, etc., and the sites of such places as Manila Bay or Gibraltar were clearly recognizable in the drawings. The different battleships, cruisers, and hydroplanes appearing in the strip were also drawn from authentic models. This documentary preoccupation was further amplified in the "Winslowgrams," a series of vignettes about the navy and navy life that accompanied each weekly installment.

A number of changes took place over the years. In 1938 Ed Moore briefly joined the *Winslow* team, to be replaced in 1940 by Ken Ernst, who gave the feature a leaner, more realistic look. The war provided a boost to the strip's circulation, as did a number of comic-book and movie adaptations. Since Winslow was already in the armed services, he had a head start on all the other comic-strip heroes who had to scramble to get into uniform. The postwar years, however, proved not so propitious, as people became tired of military exploits. *Don Winslow* steadily lost readership. In 1952 it was picked up by the minor General Feature Syndicate, which brought about a number of story modifications. Winslow was now working directly for the Pentagon, with assistance from representatives of the other branches of the service. His adventures were now depicted by John Jordan, who had previously worked on the *Winslow* comic books. Martinek, after having suffered a heart attack, decided to scuttle the strip: it went down on July 30, 1955.

M.H.

DONALD DUCK
1936–present

Donald Duck made his bow in a 1934 *Silly Symphony* animated short, *The Wise Little Hen,* and the first line he uttered was: "Who, me? Oh, no! I got a bellyache." His character—cantankerous, ornery, and irascible—was established at the outset, and later developed even further in a series of *Mickey Mouse* shorts. The duck's violent and intemperate displays of emotion contrasted comically with Mickey's game determination and Goofy's phlegmatic unconcern. By the mid-1930s Donald had become Walt Disney's most popular character and was branching out in other media, including newspaper strips.

While Donald had made his appearance as early as September 1934 in the comic-strip adaptation of *The Wise Little Hen,* he only came into his own as a star character on August 30, 1936, in a weekly page titled *A Silly Symphony Featuring Donald Duck* that lasted until December 1937. It was during that period that Donald's nephews, Huey, Louie, and Dewey, made their first explosive appearance. Finally, on February 7, 1938, a *Donald Duck* daily strip saw the light of print, followed by a *Donald* Sunday page on December 10, 1939. The duck's adventures in all of their incarnations were distributed by King Features, with Disney retaining copyright.

Both dailies and Sundays were drawn from the start by Al Taliaferro (who had previously been the artist on the *Silly*

Symphony feature) and written by Bob Karp. They followed a strict gag format, with Donald often at odds with his sweetheart Daisy, a creation of the animated shorts transplanted with good effect to the newspaper page. The best and funniest of the gags, however, were those depicting Donald's invariably losing encounters with his nephews. The running confrontation between Donald and the devilish trio became in fact the central crux and the overriding theme of the newspaper feature.

Donald was in large part a one-joke strip, but it would not have lasted to this day if the jokes hadn't oftentimes been so excruciatingly funny and finely delivered. In one story Donald ordered his nephews to lower for their own safety the tightrope they were walking on, only to trip over it when they brought it down a mere four inches above the floor; in another episode the nephews had their uncle demonstrate his athletic prowess, and while he was busy running and jumping, they sneaked away to the neighborhood movie house. Donald didn't have better luck with Daisy; at one time he sent her a singing telegram to soothe her feelings after a spat and got a black eye by return delivery; another time, taking her on a hayride, the donkey suddenly refused to go further, and Donald had to pull both Daisy and the animal the rest of the way. Donald's angry reaction to all these indignities has been as funny as the gags themselves (in all fairness to Donald he did manage a few triumphs, but these were always short-lived.)

On the strength of his drawings, Taliaferro must be regarded as "the supreme duck artist," on a par with Carl Barks. That his name is far less known than that of his comic-book counterpart may be partly due to the fact that the newspaper *Donald* was never a continuity strip, and partly because Taliaferro died in 1969, before the time comic fandom had become fully established.

Taliaferro was succeeded after his death by Frank Grundeen, and in 1974 Karp turned over the writing to Greg Crosby. From that time on *Donald Duck* has been drawn by a variety of artists, including Frank Smith and Peter Alvarado, and scripted by several writers, Bob Foster and Larry Mayer chief among them. The obstreperous duck still carries on in today's newspapers, but without the verve and dash that Taliaferro had been able to impart to the character in his halcyon days.

M.H.

DONDI
1955–1986

The joint effort of Gus Edson (writer) and Irwin Hasen (artist), *Dondi* debuted on September 25, 1955, as a Sunday page, followed the next day by its daily version. The Chicago Tribune–New York News Syndicate took charge of the distribution.

Dondi (Edson and Hasen), © 1960 Chicago Tribune

Edson, whose version of *The Gumps* was on the skids, badly needed a comic-strip success to recoup his coming loss. Stories about children of dead American soldiers wandering across Europe were then in the news, and he chose just such a tale as the springboard for his new creation. He wisely refrained from drawing the feature himself and instead chose comic-book illustrator Hasen as the artist. In the strip version the basic situation was sanitized in that the orphan, named Dondi, was not the natural but the adopted son of an American G.I.

The first episode was a real tearjerker involving a bitter legal battle for guardianship over the orphaned Dondi between his adoptive father, Ted Wills, and Mrs. McGowan, the wealthy mother of his dead G.I. father. There followed more lachrymose continuities, as the spunky little boy fought to get into the United States, finally making it toward the end of the decade, and settling with Ted and his wife Katje in the small town of Midville. The story lines then becoming a lot tamer than they were at the beginning, there was not as much excitement as readers had come to expect from *Dondi*, and the strip began to sag in popularity. It received a boost, however, in 1961 when Columbia released a *Dondi* picture starring David Janssen and Patti Page, with David Cory playing the orphan boy.

In the 1960s *Dondi* became another family strip with soap-opera undertones on weekdays, while the Sundays were turned into a conventional kid-gang series of gags. Dondi and his fellow members of the Explorers Club, the bumbling Web and the disheveled Baldy, along with Dondi's inseparable dog Queenie, at times collided with the adult world in somewhat longer continuities involving star-crossed lovers, neglected housewives, and the suave con artists preying on them.

Edson died in 1966, and Hasen assumed sole authorship of the feature. With help from Bob Oksner and others he managed to keep *Dondi* afloat for two more decades. The strip finally expired from compassion fatigue (and increasing reader disaffection) in June 1986.

M.H.

DONNIE
1934–1937

Having been dispossessed of the Sunday *Little Annie Rooney* in favor of Nicholas Afonsky, Darrell McClure was offered a Sunday page of his own by King Features Syndicate. The resulting feature, *Donnie*, made its appearance in 1934. It was drawn in a crisp, pleasant style, but unfortunately the writing never rose above a juvenile level.

Donnie was an enterprising youngster of about 10 or 12 whose love of adventure led him to the farthest corners of the world. While the strip is best known as a seafaring series, Donnie's first exploits took place on terra firma, in the kind of mythical European kingdom that had been a mainstay of popular fiction since *The Prisoner of Zenda*. There were the usual palace intrigues, conspiracies, and plots, and Donnie found himself in the midst of all the action, just in time to save the legitimate heir to the throne. The young hero would have lingered a while longer (there was the beginning of a romance with a little princess), had not his parents asked him urgently to come home, with the further enticement of a yacht to bring him thither.

No sooner had Donnie set sail for America than there was a shipwreck on inhospitable shores. There were further complications, during which Donnie acquired a boy companion his own age, and together they pursued their adventures. They again tried to make it to the States aboard a yacht given them by yet another grateful monarch, but this time they were captured by Arab slave-traders. Liberated by a British patrol, they finally made their way home after numerous other vicissitudes early in 1937, thereby bringing the strip to an end.

M.H.

THE DOODLE FAMILY
See FRANKIE DOODLE

DOONESBURY
1970–present

Like many other newspaper strips of the 1970s, Garry Trudeau's *Doonesbury* had as its forerunner a feature the cartoonist did for his college paper (in this case Yale University's *Record*), which was called *Bull Tales*. The strip was then picked up by the slightly better circulated Yale *Daily News*, and it then attracted the attention of Jim Andrews, head of the fledgling Universal Press Syndicate. Renamed *Doonesbury* (for Michael J. Doonesbury, the putative hero of the piece), it made its national debut on October 26, 1970.

The motley crew congregating in the strip were all recognizable student types of the time, except for Doonesbury himself, who was a recognizable student type of any time—that of the eager, slightly befuddled undergrad who barely made it to college, seldom made good grades, and never made out with the girls. Around him were Mark Slackmeyer, the campus radical known as "Megaphone Mark," always ready to agitate in favor of every antiestablishment cause; B.D., the typical campus jock, so called for Brian Dowling, Yale's star quarterback; and B.D.'s girlfriend, Boopsy, the typical coed airhead. They drank beer, smoked pot, and held interminable midnight bull sessions on the meaning of it all.

In the early strips Trudeau spared nobody, figuratively shooting right and left at anything that moved. The students were seen as a likable but on the whole rather hopeless lot of misfits and dreamers, the campus cops as a sadistic mob of skull-crushers, and the administration as

Doonesbury (G. B. Trudeau), © 1984 G. B. Trudeau

made up of brown-nosers, incompetents, and nincompoops. The president of the university, "King" Brewster (a take-off on Yale president Kingman Brewster) appeared as a well-meaning goof. ("It's more kudos for Yale's youthful president as he starts out on his morning walk through the colleges to reduce tension.")

Later the protagonists went into the broader world, with mixed results. They founded Walden Puddle Commune, as more characters came into the strip. Later arrivals included the frizzy-haired Zonker Harris, a leftover from the drug culture and perpetual flower child; and his dope-guzzling, gin-swilling Uncle Duke, former newspaperman, stock manipulator, and corporate swindler, and future governor of American Samoa and U.S. ambassador to China.

Trudeau, a staunch supporter of the woman's liberation movement, also added strong female figures to the cast. One was Virginia ("Ginny"), a liberated black law student, who once ran for Congress; another is the fortyish Joanie Caucus, who dropped out of her marriage, and later became a congressional assistant to Lacey Davenport, a representative from the WASP establishment left.

"But," as critic Gary Wills has perceptively observed, "Trudeau's world opened up when he got into the realm of politics." At the height of the Watergate affair he had Megaphone Mark, now a disc jockey on a local radio station, declare on the air that everyone knew that Attorney General John Mitchell (who hadn't even been indicted yet) was "guilty! guilty! guilty!" On another occasion, macho B D., who had volunteered for Vietnam duty, had an eye-opening encounter with a Vietcong guerrilla named Phred who expressed astonishment that B.D. had never heard of him: "Who hasn't heard of Phred the Terrorist?" Or Henry Kissinger would plug on TV his latest book of memoirs, fittingly titled *The Whitewash Years*.

Trudeau's draftsmanship (or lack of it) has been duly noted in many quarters. "Anybody who can draw bad pictures of the White House four times in a row and succeed," Al Capp is reported to have grumbled, "knows something I don't." It should be mentioned, however that Trudeau's drawing style, consisting of a line reduced to its simplest expression, perfectly suited the purpose of the strip as it was then, literary rather than visual.

Trudeau's reputation soared with the passing years: his work was often quoted in the news media, his strips were collected in several bestselling books, and in 1975 he received the Pulitzer Prize for cartooning. At the height of all this acclaim, Trudeau (whose marriage to TV host Jane Pauley had in the meantime resulted in the production of an heir) chose to leave the rigors of turning out a daily and Sunday strip for the joys of househusbanding. The last Doonesbury installment appeared on New Year's Day 1983, with a promise from the author to be back in the fall of 1984.

True to his word, Trudeau restored Doonesbury to the newspaper page in September 1984, with the strip picking up even more papers than it had before its hiatus. More distinctions and rewards came Trudeau's way. There was a Doonesbury animated special on NBC-TV, and a musical comedy. More than fifty Doonesbury books have been published to date, and the author got people like Gloria Steinem, Studs Terkel, and William Buckley to write introductions (some of which are even readable). Unfortunately, a funny thing happened to Trudeau on his way back to the drawing board: he stopped being funny. The fact is that from the moment of his return Trudeau treated the nation's issues seriously (he once reprinted the seven original articles of the U.S. Constitution in their entirety in his Sunday page). High-mindedness is a trait laudable in a family man, perhaps, but a serious flaw in a funnyman. On the other hand, the drawing has became more artful and the design more inventive (due to improvement from his longtime ghost), but that has been poor compensation.

During the past five years Trudeau has increasingly traded liberal piousness for soap-opera titillation. Yet, to the author's everlasting annoyance, many newspaper editors keep grafting the strip onto the editorial page. The change in tone can be seen in some recent developments (courtesy of fellow contributor Bill Janocha): Boopsie serves on the O.J. jury, but is booted for sneaking out to go shopping.... Duke decides to personally capitalize on Newt Gingrich's suggestion that most homeless and/or troubled male youths would be better off in orphanages like Boy's Town. Duke sets up a scam operation posing as a priest, founding an orphanage, yet supplying little and pocketing the rest of the money intended for the children's care....

Drunk (or high), Duke caused a four-by-four vehicle driven by Zeke and his girlfriend, Mike Doonesbury's estranged wife J.J., off a mountain pass. J.J. had run away from Mike and their child, as in the film Thelma and Louise, to discover "her real self." Prone to lapse into acts of "performance art," she tried to fake a coma in order to get Mike to rush to her bedside.... Mike lost his lucrative advertising job back in 1991; out of work until 1995, he then moved from New York to the hot "new" epicenter for "Generation X," Seattle.

Despite its trying too hard to turn into a funny-looking version of Mary Worth with a political tinge, Doonesbury remains an interesting feature, keeping abreast of current events and providing a different, if now dated, view of American life.

M.H.

DOWN HOGAN'S ALLEY
See THE YELLOW KID

DR. KILDARE
1962–1984

Although writer Max Brand is better noted for his western novels, he also contributed a number of scripts to Hollywood movies, and one of these was for the 1938 medical drama *Interns Can't Take Money*. The two principal characters in the film, Doctors James Kildare and Leonard Gillespie, proved so popular that they were featured in ten more entries in the series (with Lew Ayres and Lionel Barrymore, respectively, in the lead roles). In 1961 NBC brought the characters to television, and the success of the program spawned a newspaper-strip version distributed by King Features, daily from October 15, 1962, and Sundays, starting on April 19, 1964. The writer was old hand Elliot Caplin, and the artist Ken Bald who had been drawing *Judd Saxon,* about an up-and-coming young executive, and who moved from the boardroom to the operating room without missing a beat.

Young, idealistic Dr. Kildare was an intern at the fictional Blair General Hospital, and his unorthodox ways clashed with the views of his superior, crotchety old Dr. Gillespie, who, as a representative of the Old Guard, tried to temper his subordinate's outbursts of indignation or enthusiasm. Dr. Stephen Kildare, the hero's father, tried to instill some sense into his hot-headed son. The medical emergencies included everything from gun wounds to cases of amnesia, and Kildare dealt with all of them with professional aplomb and a good deal of extramedical intensity. Some of the cases took decidedly romantic turns, but Kildare was married to his job, and none of the beautiful women who always crossed his path, whether they were nurses or patients, was ever able to get the handsome medic into more than fleeting involvement.

Caplin wrote the continuities in his usual soap-opera manner. Bald, who modeled the two principals on the actors who played them on television (Richard Chamberlain and Raymond Massey), drew the strip with breezy, self-assured elegance. The TV show ended in 1965, but the newspaper page *Kildare* managed to hang on for a considerably longer time, only coming to a close in 1984.

M.H.

DRAGO
1945–1946

Upon leaving *Tarzan,* Burne Hogarth lost no time coming out with a new adventure strip. Called *Drago,* it premiered on November 4, 1945, as a Sunday only, distributed by the New York Post Corporation.

Drago was a younger version of Tarzan, with bulging muscles under his shirt and dark good looks beneath his wide-brimmed hat. The hero was purportedly a gaucho, but the action was set in what looked like the tropical northern provinces of Argentina rather than the pampas. The first

Drago (B. Hogarth), © 1946 Burne Hogarth

and longest episode was actually a fable of good and evil. The good was represented by the handsome hero and his devoted sweetheart Darby O'Day, supported by Darby's engineer father and Drago's portly sidekick Tabasco. Evil was everywhere: they were confronted by Baron Zodiac, a sinister figure whose face was always obscured by shadow and cigarette smoke, and his minions, the knife-wielding Stiletto and the aptly named Hass-assein; most lethal of all was the beautiful and two-faced Tosca. Zodiac was a Nazi war criminal on the lam in Argentina, whose dream it was to rebuild the Third Reich in the wilds of South America. "But we shall rise from the ashes of defeat. Our new atom bomb is ready—discovered too late to save our armed might. With it we shall tear asunder the structure of civilization of the entire earth," he ranted in a taped communiqué, adding: "Already our new allies—war, famine, pestilence, death—march forward. In chaos and ruin we shall rise to victory. This is Operation Apocalypse...the master plan!" Drago put a stop to those iron dreams.

Hogarth's graphic style on *Drago* was even more restless than it had been on *Tarzan*. The action jumped from one panel to the next, often unencumbered by any separating frame, in a paroxysm of expressionistic fury and dramatic gesture. Color reinforced the sense of motion, of action and of suspense, as did the frequent elimination of all background, the silhouettelike characters moving in choreographed rhythm on a white ground.

Drago may have been too disconcerting in its symbolism, too rich in its dramatic effects for many of the readers. After the Zodiac story there was only one additional episode—a conventional tale of land grabbing—before the strip ended its run on November 10, 1946.

M.H.

DREAM OF THE RAREBIT FIEND
1904–1914

Winsor McCay contributed his first acknowledged masterpiece to the pages of the *New York Evening Telegram* in 1904. Titled *Dream of the Rarebit Fiend*, it was signed with the pseudonym "Silas," as were all of McCay's *Telegram* creations.

Some years later the author explained to an interviewer that the basic concept came about when he showed a gag cartoon about a cigarette addict to his publisher. "My employer suggested that I make him a series of pictures," he added, "and make them as rarebit dreams, and you know the result." The result, as McCay modestly called it, was a little masterpiece of whimsy, humor, imagination, and wit, full of observation, insight, and relevance. Unlike the later *Little Nemo*, each episode was self-contained and could be read and enjoyed independently of the others. There was no fixed protagonist, but a different dreamer was featured in almost every episode. During the fiends' nightmares caused by their inordinate ingestion of Welsh rarebits, one encounters themes and situations that probe the roots of human fears. Topics included nudity and the taboo attached to it, masks, transvestitism, the fear of castration, the fear of going insane, and the obsession of impotence.

Sexual overtones abounded. In one episode a man dreamt that he had moved to the state of Utah and married a dozen maidens; his bliss was short-lived, however, as his wives all ganged up on him to relieve him of his paycheck. In another sequence a rich old man, married to a much younger woman, longed to go back to his salad days; in his dream he witnessed his wish fulfillment turn into a nightmare as he slipped back into infancy and was only able to greet his startled wife with baby mumblings and whimperings. Other segments had spinsters dreaming that they were pursued by hordes of panting males fighting over their favors. Some dreams were explicitly sexual, with male and female protagonists performing strange rituals in bed or carrying on ambiguous conversations in a state of total nudity.

In his descriptions of the dream state McCay kept astonishingly close to the observations made by Sigmund Freud in his *Interpretation of Dreams* (1900): we must note that the dreams related in the strip were caused by the fiends' obsessive, manic cravings for Welsh rarebit—the resemblance to Freud's "libido" is too striking to be coincidental. McCay very consciously went back to the wellsprings of the unconscious, and the dream episodes, when considered in their staggering totality, virtually constitute a clinical catalogue of psychopathological symptoms.

Rarebit Fiend ran several times weekly in black and white in the pages of the *Telegram;* after 1907 the appearances became more or less weekly until 1911, when McCay left

Dream of the Rarebit Fiend (W. McCay), 1906

the Herald Company (parent of the *Telegram*) for the Hearst organization. For Hearst, McCay pursued his oneiric theme with such titles as *It Was Only a Dream, A January Day Dream, Midsummer Day Dreams, Dreams of a Lobster Fiend,* and others, while the *Herald* riposted by reprinting in full color some of McCay's old *Rarebit Fiend* strips. By 1914 the two competing series were both gone.

M.H.

DUMB DORA
1924–1935

Yet another flapper strip out of the 1920s, *Dumb Dora* began life obscurely as a Sunday page distributed by the misnamed Premier Syndicate (a Hearst outfit that functioned as a minor-league farm team to King Features). After a year of existence the feature proved promising enough to be picked up by the major-league syndicate, which added a daily strip to its new acquisition.

Dumb Dora was originated by Chic Young, who brought to the strip a great elegance of line as well as a flair for being cartoony without being overly caricatural. Dora Bell was a piquant brunette and coquettish college girl who kept a long roster of suitors on a string. For insurance, and in order to keep the fickle-female jokes flowing, Young also gave her in succession a pair of steady boyfriends, both of them equally love-smitten and judgment-impaired. First came Ernie, an owlish and prematurely aged grad student, whose clumsy attentions proved too much of a strain for the flirty brunette; he quickly went, and was immediately replaced by the dumpy, straw-hatted, and much put-upon

Rodney Ruckett. Despite the appellation "Dumb Dora" (which for a time became a byword for a scatterbrain) that had been pinned on her, the heroine was quite smart and quick-witted, running circles around the benighted males who were prone to underrate her and who frequently exclaimed in their discomfiture, "She ain't so dumb!" By the end of the 1920s the author lost interest in his creation and left the rest of the drawing to his assistant, Bud Counihan.

With the dawn of a new decade, Young finally jettisoned *Dora* to create *Blondie*. "Dora was a typical flapper strip," he confided to Martin Sheridan in 1942, "and in 1930 when flappers were on the way out I tried to picture the average girl of that age,

Dumb Dora (P. Fung), © 1930 Newspaper Feature Services

the kind who led in a complete return to femininity." The strip then devolved to Paul Fung, who had just had *Gus and Gussie* pulled from under him, the first Asian American to be in charge of a feature from a major syndicate. Fung drew the adventures of the spunky coed with his usual verve and perked up the gags with longer continuities, but he failed to take his heroine from flapperness to domesticity, as Young was doing on *Blondie*. After only a couple of years he left the feature in the inept hands of Bill Dwyer who, despite a great deal of help from Milton Caniff, could not maintain the strip on a proficient, or even adequate, level, and it ended in the early months of 1935.

M.H.

EEK AND MEEK
1965–present

A human fable in animal guise, *Eek and Meek* made its appearance in the first week of September 1965, in both daily and Sunday formats, drawn and written by Howie Schneider. It was, and still is, syndicated nationally by NEA Service.

The two title characters were initially a pair of field mice that poked gentle and sometimes pointed fun at human prejudices, foibles, and conceits. Eek was the loudmouth of the twosome: sporting a three-day stubble and a derby hat, he would hold forth on about any topic, from politics to welfare and civil rights, usually in acid-tongued terms. His most barbed sarcasm was directed at his companion, whose name said it all: the eternally bewildered Meek went through life in a daze, and he stood in awe of his buddy's breezy self-assurance. When the two weren't engaged in one-sided arguments they loved to make music: Meek strummed on the cello; Eek's instrument was the bugle, which he played so atrociously that he was once admonished by Leonard Bernstein to play "Taps" as his opening piece, so as to "set the tone for the evening."

Eek and Meek were both in love with the snotty Monique, a frizzy-haired mouse who had no use for either of them. Other characters of note included Luvable (who was anything but), a student rodent who preferred rioting and marching to the "mickey mouse" courses offered by the college; Fieldstone, the disreputable insurance sales-man; and slumlord J. Paul Ghetto, whose properties, his tenants claimed, were "nothing more than ratholes."

Sometime in 1977 Schneider realized that his strip was going nowhere and decided, with the approval of his editors, to bring his rodent characters up to full human status. The metamorphosis was gradual and only became fully realized in 1982. The pair have now more or less recognizable human features, but they still look like stick figures, and they behave pretty much as before. Eek still goes on drinking binges, and Meek has not yet worked up the nerve to propose to Monique. The circulation of the strip, however, has noticeably gone up since the switch, which goes to prove that the best laid plans of mice and men sometimes come aright.

M.H.

ELLA CINDERS
1925–1961

A n obvious twist on the old Cinderella fairy tale, *Ella Cinders* was the brainchild of two southern California newsmen, *Los Angeles Sunday Times* editor Bill Conselman (who wrote the script) and editorial cartoonist Charlie Plumb (who provided the artwork). It made its debut as a daily strip on June 1, 1925, syndicated nationally by the Metropolitan Newspaper Service (later absorbed into United Feature Syndicate).

The original premise was simple: the strip did not try to recount the Cinderella story in modern dress, but paralleled the well-known tale in broad outline, adding a number of parodic elements, somewhat along the lines of Rossini's opera on the same theme, *La Cenerentola. Ella Cinders* developed an amusing and tongue-in-cheek continuity, in which Ella toiled for her selfish stepmother, the domineering Mytie Cinders, and her two crabby daughters, Prissie and Lotta Pill, until one day she won a Hollywood contract and achieved a brilliant career in the movies, despite a freckled face and an ungainly figure. This was a common dream among millions of American girls, and the comics simply embroidered upon the theme. (In the case of *Ella Cinders,* the dream was to come true in the space of one short year, when the strip was made into a film starring Coleen Moore in the title role—another of the many instances of life imitating art.)

Yet the apparently unassuming story line always held more than met the eye (this was lucky for the reader, since Ella was such a plain-looking creature). The heroine, for

Eek and Meek (H. Schneider), © 1970 NEA Service

Ella Cinders (**Conselman and Plumb**), © **1934 United Feature Syndicate**

instance, was no sweet young thing waiting for Prince Charming: in point of fact she was married to a man named Patches, who for plot purposes was seldom around. Her pugnacity was such that the syndicate was at pains to explain it away. "It is this courage of Ella's," one press release read, "that has won her, as a star of comics, such a countless following of fans." She did have an ally in her kid brother Blackie, but otherwise had to face the cold world alone. The fairy-tale elements were all the result of happenstance: she won a movie-magazine beauty contest when her photo was picked at random by the editor; and she finally got a Hollywood contract from her wayward father, Sam Cinders, who had become a film studio head under an assumed name.

Plumb was as footloose as his characters (at one time he sent his drawings from a Pacific island), and his signature hid a string of ghosts, including Fred Fox, Henry Formhals, and Jack McGuire. His assistant at the outset had been Hardie Gramatky, who later went on to become a noted children's-book author and illustrator. It was Gramatky who was chiefly responsible (though uncredited) for the Sunday version (added on January 1, 1927), to which he gave a decidedly jazzed-up look. The weekly page is mainly remembered today as a series of gags, but in the 1930s it enjoyed a number of long-running episodes, often of an adventurous nature. In 1930, for example, Ella, along with the entire cast and crew of the movie they were filming, got marooned on a desert island; and she was later involved in a good many car accidents, plane crashes, and other disasters.

After Conselman's death in 1940, Plumb took sole credit for the feature, with Fred Fox supplying the drawings anonymously. Fox finally got to sign *Ella Cinders* when Plumb left in the mid-1950s. The first thing he did after taking charge was to get himself a ghost, Roger Armstrong, who drew the strip until its demise late in 1961.

M.H.

ELMER
1916–1956

A.C. Fera's genial chronicle of boyhood, *Just Boy,* started on May 6, 1916, distributed as a weekly color page by the Hearst Syndicate (and later by King Features).

Except for a few years in the late 1910s and early 1920s, the feature never boasted a daily version.

As the only child of the middle-class couple of Ella and Clem Tuggle, Elmer, who was, as the title indicated, "just boy," enjoyed a typical boyhood in a typical small American town. The ten-year-old was a mischievous kid in the tradition of all comic-strip boys, and his pranks often earned him a trip to the woodshed. Dressed in short pants, with tie and straw hat, he was the terror of the neighborhood and the bane of the household's black maid, Lotta. He also was a special target for the local cop on the beat, Officer Nolan, who often had to bring him home by the ear. Fera drew the strip in a straightforward, cartoony way, with some nice stylistic touches such as detailed goings-on in the background of the main action, until the time of his death in 1925. The feature was then turned over to King's most reliable bullpen resident, Charles ("Doc") Winner, who promptly retitled it *Elmer,* the name by which the page is best known.

Doc Winner has been charitably called "a journeyman cartoonist," but actually he was an execrable draftsman; his own syndicate thought so little of him that in their 1946 *Famous Artists and Writers* catalogue he only rated a single line, while most of his colleagues got two full pages. At first he tried to remain faithful to the style of his predecessor, but soon his mannerisms got the better of him, and his drawings became stiff and lifeless. Under his pen Elmer acquired the lunar face and bland expression that were his trademarks in later life. Winner was also a rather unimaginative gag writer, and the strip turned into a conventional feature about a boy and a dog, that is only remembered today for the exclamation that Elmer uttered in frustration or despair: "Crim-a-nentlies!"

It is a tribute to Winner's workhorse qualities that when

Elmer (*Just Boy;* **A. C. Fera**), © **1922 Newspaper Feature Services**

he died on August 12, 1956, he left enough finished pages to carry *Elmer* through to December 30, whereupon it was terminated.

M.H.

EMMY LOU
See BOBBY SOX

ETTA KETT
1925–1974

Paul Robinson started *Etta Kett* for King Features Syndicate in December 1925. Running both daily and Sunday, the feature was originally intended as a guide to good manners, with the young female lead, punningly named Etta Kett, dispensing daily advice on matters of taste, grooming, and clothing. It turned into a typical teenage-girl strip in the space of a few months.

A vivacious brunette, Etta lived with her parents: Pop, a portly, balding, pipe-smoking paterfamilias, and Moms, a chubby, gray-haired but stylish housewife. The heroine's life was a model of rectitude, and she never went beyond a chaste goodnight kiss when on a date. Even after the feature had outlived its pedagogic status, she remained true to her name by giving out tips on dress and manners, thereby keeping the teenage readers posted on the latest fads and fashions. Along with her best friend, the blonde Debby Davis, she was always ready to embark on a whirlwind of dates and parties, without nary a hint of hanky-panky as much as suggested. Later Etta acquired a steady boyfriend, the hollow-brained Wingey, whose only passion was for food, thus putting the reader's mind at rest concerning the nature of their relationship, which always remained proper.

For a number of years, from the late 1920s through the 1940s, *Etta Kett* sported a topper, *The Love-Byrds,* that often proved more entertaining than the main feature. It dealt with a newly married couple, Peggy and Horace Byrd, whose love life, made of bickerings and quarrels, contrasted sharply with the rosy promise of the title. A former animator, Robinson drew in an uncluttered, sinuous style that grew more desiccated as the years progressed. *Etta Kett* was discontinued following the creator's death, in November 1974, just short of its half-century mark.

M.H.

EVERETT TRUE
1905–1927

San Francisco–based cartoonist A. D. Condo (that was his real name) had already several comic strips to his credit when he created *Everett True* in 1905, under the initial title *A Chapter in the Life of Everett True.* The feature,

Etta Kett (P. Robinson), © 1934 King Features Syndicate

which appeared several times weekly and later daily in a vertical format, was syndicated by National Enterprise Association (now NEA).

Everett True was a middle-aged curmudgeon of the righter-of-wrongs variety. Fat, double-chinned, and sour-faced, he tried to hide his bald pate under a homburg and to contain his ample figure in an ill-fitting suit. Incapable of countenancing hypocrisy, cant, bullishness, or cruelty, he enforced his version of the golden rule with single-minded directness, with the help of his rolled-up umbrella, his cane, his fists, or his tugboat-sized boots. His targets were varied and many: brutal horse drivers, dishonest storekeepers, conniving politicos, bullying cops — they all experienced the fury of his blows or the lash of his tongue. In true comic-strip fashion, however, this paragon of straight-shooting manliness cowered in front of his formidable wife, whom he always called Mrs. True in cringing deference.

Everett True was drawn in a simple, unobtrusive line, somewhat reminiscent of C. W. Kahles's early style, and it always remained subordinate to the linear unfolding of each daily anecdote. (Apparently unable to contain his caustic verve within the confines of a single feature, Condo in 1907 created *Mr. Skygack, of Mars,* in which a visitor from the red planet was perpetually nonplussed by the seemingly absurd customs and rituals of people on Earth.)

The strip, long called *The Outbursts of Everett True* and later simply *Everett True,* was among the more popular features distributed by NEA, and it might have lasted forever had the cartoonist not been stricken with illness and forced to abandon his creation in January 1927. Everett True experienced a brief revival of notoriety when some of his exploits were reprinted in book form in the 1980s. The character was then appropriated by unscrupulous (and untalented) copycats who milked the concept for all it was worth in the pages of several comics publications.

M.H.

EXTRA, EXTRA
See SILLY MILLY

THE FAMILY CIRCUS
1960–present

Bil Keane (with one *l* in his first name) is a veteran cartoonist best known for his creation of the daily and Sunday newspaper feature, *The Family Circus,* which, according to his syndicate, "has become the most popular newspaper panel in the world," running in more than thirteen hundred newspapers. Twenty years of cartooning experience lay behind this overnight success. As a serviceman during and right after World War II, Keane had honed his cartooning skills in such military publications as *Yank* and *Stars and Stripes.* It was in fact, in the pages of the latter that he had created his first panel series, *At Ease with the Japanese,* an illustrated guide for the use of the victorious G.I.'s in Japan. Back to civilian life, as a staff artist on the *Philadelphia Bulletin,* he added two more features to his credit: *Silly Philly,* a Sunday comic that paid amused attention to the more egregious goings-on in the City of Brotherly Love, and *Channel Chuckles,* a running commentary on the foibles and follies of television and its audience. This latter series was picked up for distribution by the Register and Tribune Syndicate, which eventually led to Keane's creation of *The Family Circus* for the same organization.

The official birth date of *The Family Circus* is February 19, 1960, but Keane feels that the idea for a newspaper panel about family life came to him as early as 1952. The panel's situations revolve around an average American family originally made up of Mommy, Daddy, and three children—the elder son, Billy; his ponytailed sister, Dolly; and Jeffy, the tot of the family. In 1962 a third baby boy, P. J., was added to the household. Barfy, the family dog, rounds out the cast of principals.

Keane draws his daily panel within a circle to accentuate the feeling of closeness and also to symbolize the title by suggesting a circus ring. The Sunday feature is rectangular, but the ring motif is retained around the logo. Keane's own wife and family are the models for the panel's family, which may account for the close identification many readers feel with the feature. The happenings are ordinary, everyday events, only slightly exaggerated for humorous effect. "There's a general tendency among people who want to be funny to exaggerate," Keane stated in a 1966 interview. "I do just the opposite. I tone down every idea I get. I also keep my drawing style simple, only the lines necessary."

Success has amply rewarded Keane's simple cartooning

"I get the most 'portant job—
Cartoonist. You can be Editor."

The Family Circus (B. Keane), © 1989 Bil Keane

creed, with more than forty *Family Circus* books in print, several animated cartoon specials, as well as the Reuben Award for Best Cartoonist, among other distinctions. *The Family Circus* is a happy combination of Keane's skill as a cartoonist (with assistance on the inking by Bud Warner) and his experiences as a family man. "The feature," the artist wrote, "is based on the real-life Keane family as they were growing." The panels have described the myriad incidents and funny happenings involved in bringing up a large family. Now that many of the Keane children have become adults, "four grandchildren provide the inspiration," as the creator put it. This continual return to the source helps explain the vernal freshness of a feature that is now over thirty-five years old.

M.H.

THE FAMILY UPSTAIRS

See THE DINGBAT FAMILY

THE FAR SIDE
1979–1995

The progenitor of *The Far Side* was *Nature's Way,* a daily panel that Gary Larson created for the *Seattle Times* in 1978. Judged too weird by the paper's readers, that strip did not survive the year. Undaunted, the cartoonist tried again, and soon his new panel, *Gary Land,* started appearing in the *San Francisco Chronicle* and in syndication by Chronicle Features, which changed the title to *The Far Side* in 1979.

Larson's was the universe of the bizarre, the incongruous, and the absurd. A Cro-Magnon man had to write five hundred times on the blackboard, "I will not act primitive in class." A banner outside a dungeon proclaimed, "Welcome Bob, torturer of the month." A man was spotted buying happiness at an out-of-the-way "happiness store." Under the caption "What really happened to Elvis," the legendary rock 'n' roller could be seen checking in at the Bates Motel. A sinner in Hell confided to his neighbor, "I hate this place." An aborigine cried out in alarm, "Anthropologists! Anthropologists!"—prompting the rest of the natives to hurriedly place their television sets, telephones, and VCRs out of sight.

Larson once declared to an interviewer, "I've honestly never set out to offend anyone." Yet *The Far Side* has elicited howls of protest from readers, educators, politicians of the left and the right, clergymen, cigarette companies, lawyers, biologists, and even from Amnesty International. Pet owners and animal-rights advocates have been particularly vociferous, since the cartoonist had been prone to depict cats swung by their tails, dogs set upon by wildcats, and coyotes shorn of their coats. Animals have just as often turned the tables on the humans. A parrot dreamt of becoming the "parakeet of the Baskervilles," while a panel of fish gravely discussed whether spawning should be taught in school. Cows have been a favorite for Larson, who "found them to be the quintessentially absurd animal." He pictured the herbivores posing in front of the Grand Canyon, boarding a spaceship to the moon, or arguing the finer points of integral calculus. In one panel he managed to combine his two favorite subjects by showing a group of cavemen tossing a helpless cow into the air in an attempt to make a milkshake. To clarify the meaning of his more obscure panels Larson resorted to all kinds of explanatory devices: speech-balloons, hand-lettered captions within the frame, typeset captions outside the frame, and more.

The Far Side in the early 1980s enjoyed growing popularity, and in 1984 Larson switched from Chronicle Features to the more powerful Universal Press Syndicate, which added a Sunday page to the daily panel. The weekly feature was basically an extension of the weekday cartoon, with color added. Under UPS guidance *The Far Side* soared to even greater heights, giving rise to several paperback and hardcover anthologies, a number of exhibitions at art galleries across the country, and a torrent of merchandising, In an unexpected move Larson decided to terminate the feature with the release of Sunday, January 1, 1995. The cartoonist is only in his forties, and this may not be the last word on *The Far Side.*

M.H.

FARLEY
See TRAVELS WITH FARLEY

FEARLESS FOSDICK
1942–1977

Al Capp created *Fearless Fosdick,* Li'l Abner's favorite comic strip, as a gentle-humored spoof of Chester Gould's *Dick Tracy,* in August 1942. The eponymous hero of that strip-within-a-strip (credited tongue in cheek to a slightly moth-eaten cartoonist named Lester Gooch) was the most stupid police detective in the entire world, and as such enjoyed the unalloyed admiration of Li'l Abner, who tried to emulate his "ideal" in every respect (he already had the brains for such an enterprise).

Initially Fosdick was only used as a ploy to set up Abner's more outlandish experiments. Slavishly copying each of his idol's predicaments, the nit-witted hillbilly had himself in turns tied to a ticking bomb, dropped fifteen stories on his head, and thrown out of an airplane in flight without a parachute. The real crunch came in 1952 with Fosdick's wedding to his long-suffering sweetheart Prudence Pimpleton: a brokenhearted Abner likewise married his girlfriend, the faithful Daisy Mae. Fosdick's wedding turned out to have been a dream, but Abner's matrimony was for real (or as real as it gets in a comic strip).

Fearless Fosdick had meanwhile evolved into a full-fledged feature within the confines of the *Li'l Abner* continuity. The fearless cop acquired his definitive persona, that of implacable nemesis of crime at whatever cost. In one Sunday episode he gunned down forty-two innocent bystanders in his pursuit of an unlicensed balloon vendor (who got away). In his preface to a 1956 collection of Fosdick stories, Capp summed it up this way: "Fearless Fosdick is the ideal of all red-blooded American boys for the same reason that Buffalo Bill was and all the characters played by John Wayne are. He does his duty, no matter how imbecile it is and how harmful to the general public."

Fearless Fosdick (A. Capp), © United Feature Syndicate/Capp Enterprises

Capp in the course of the years created a hilarious gallery of villains for Fosdick to combat. In parody of *Dick Tracy*, there was the rodent-faced Rattop, along with the appropriately named Bomb-Face and Stone-Face. New heights of outlandishness were reached with such perpetrators as Sidney the parrot, who looked and acted like Edward G. Robinson in his movies, not to mention a homicidal Chippendale chair, the mastermind behind every criminal activity in Fosdick's jurisdiction. (As fitting retribution for its crimes, the Chippendale chair got the chair, clamoring "I'm innocent, I tell you, innocent!" all the way to the execution chamber.)

The Fosdick sequences continued with diminishing frequency through the 1960s but gained a new lease on life in the 1970s, when they appeared regularly up to the last year of the *Li'l Abner* strip, in 1977.

M.H.

FEIFFER
1956–present

Jules Feiffer's weekly feature of political and social commentary in comic-strip form started appearing (as a freebie) in the pages of the New York City radical publication the *Village Voice* in 1956 under the title *Sick, Sick, Sick* (it was later renamed simply *Feiffer* in recognition of the cartoonist's growing notoriety). A number of Feiffer's weekly strips were anthologized in a paperback also called *Sick, Sick, Sick;* the anthology then came to the attention of Robert Hall, whose syndicate started national distribution of *Feiffer* in 1960.

The pointed but on the whole amused criticism of accepted values in such strips as *Li'l Abner* and *Pogo* was transformed by Feiffer into a savage attack on the very fabric of American culture. In *A History of the Comic Strip* (published in 1968) I had this to say about the feature: "Feiffer's universe is the blackest and most depressing ever depicted by the comic strip. Drifting young men, neurotic young women, lovers who are strangers to each other, introduce us to a dehumanized world in which all communication and exchange of ideas is impossible, in which nothing happens and nothing is done. Like robots, the protagonists come and pour out, in plaintive, toneless voices, the account of their disappointments, the sum of their misfortunes." The intervening quarter of a century has not appreciably changed this assessment.

The arch-representative of this universe is Bernard Mergendeiler, whom I described as "a pathetic wreck devoured by tics and complexes." In the preface to his 1982 anthology, *Jules Feiffer's America*, the author elucidated this aspect of the strip. "Bernard Mergendeiler was my victim-hero and not hard to come by," he wrote. "I composed him out of my own life and the lives of friends." This asseveration helps explain the particular resonance that Bernard, above all other characters in the strip, arouse in the reader: in his voice one can recognize the undertones of self-hatred and self-pity.

Whatever his gifts for social observation and self-examination, it is as a political cartoonist that Feiffer is best noted. His targets have included not only the high and mighty but the self-aggrandizing and the prepossessing as well. His pounding of President Johnson's Vietnam policies was relentless. One strip showed Johnson impassively looking from his Oval Office window at placard-carrying peace demonstrators clashing with the White House police, then being brutally dragged away. "Freedom of speech is one of our most precious liberties," the president thoughtfully observed—to which a supine Dean Rusk dutifully replied, "Yes, Mr. President."

Richard Nixon provided Feiffer with his most constant target—and the cartoonist never tired of sniping at him, even before he became president. He especially delighted in showing up what was widely perceived as Nixon's lack of candor. During the 1960 presidential campaign, for instance, he had Nixon declare in his most unctuous tones, "I believe Senator Kennedy believes what he believes sincerely as I believe what I believe sincerely," while his eyes were constantly shifting from one side to the other.

Feiffer's attacks reached a crescendo during the Watergate crisis. Faced with tough questioning from journalists, Nixon typically went to the counteroffensive. "The question isn't over a free press," he sternly lectured, "it's over a *fair* press." Later, confronted with hard evidence of his wrongdoings, he unrepentantly declared that he would accept nothing short of "impeachment with honor." After Nixon's resignation Feiffer seemed to have lost some of his taste for the political jugular, and his subsequent lampoonings of Presidents Ford, Carter, and even Bush and Reagan became half-hearted. He now appears to kick only out of habit (as does the *Village Voice*, his initial outlet and one of the few papers that still carry the strip).

Nothing seems to come easy to Feiffer. An assessment of his play- and screenwriting career is not within the purview of this entry, but it should be noted that at best he has only obtained *success d'estime* in these fields. His newspaper-strip career has certainly not been a smooth one: he got a Pulitzer Prize in editorial cartooning only in 1986, years after his closest comic-strip disciple, Garry Trudeau, was awarded his. And in all American histories of the comics he appears only as a footnote, a sad commentary after more than four decades of labor in the field.

M.H.

THE FEITLEBAUM FAMILY
See NIZE BABY

FELIX THE CAT
1923–1967, 1984–1987

Felix's complicated genesis resulted from the collaboration of Pat Sullivan and his talented animator Otto Messmer, whom Sullivan had hired in 1916. The same year they developed a black feline character for use as the animal hero of a new series of cartoons that Sullivan was contracted to produce. The dry run for the series was released in 1917 after Messmer had left to fight with the American Expeditionary Force in Europe. Titled *Tail of Thomas Kat*, it can be considered the first Felix cartoon in all but name

Felix the Cat (O. Messmer), © 1934 King Features Syndicate

(already the cat was using his tail as a removable object to get him out of all kinds of predicaments).

With Messmer back from the war in 1919, the series was launched in earnest. The first entry was the 1920 *Feline Follies,* in which the cat was still called Tom. More titles followed, to the tune of two a month; in these cartoons the cat finally acquired his definitive name. Messmer directed most of the Felix cartoons, assisted by a team of animators that included at one time or another Al Hurter, Hal Walker and Raoul Barré. Felix was by then an established figure, enhanced by a catchy song played in movie houses showing the shorts: "Felix kept on walking / Kept on walking still."

On August 14, 1923, Felix starred in his own newspaper-comic page, drawn by Messmer and distributed through King Features Syndicate. The game little feline remained close to his cartoon film persona: he was depicted as quick-tempered, taciturn, and irascible, and he was drawn with angular, nervous lines. He was basically a vagabond, moving in rural surroundings peopled with animal characters. The backgrounds were stylized and often reduced to an outline suggesting a farm, a fence, or a clump of trees. As time passed, Felix became more humanized—rounder, warmer, and cuddlier, without ever getting cute or cloying—and the company he kept became increasingly composed of humans: dour-faced farmers and their surly wives, shifty tramps, unruly kids.

Felix's growing success led to the introduction of a daily strip on May 9, 1927. Unlike the Sundays, which were humorous in nature, intermixing one-page gags and short slapstick continuities, the dailies soon took an adventurous turn, albeit a comical one. The spunky black cat went exploring the wilds of Africa, was crowned king of a mythical country, traveled through time to a civilization of the future, and exposed a gang of sinister Asians in Chinatown. In all his exploits he displayed qualities of resourcefulness, courage, and ingenuity that clearly prefigured Mickey Mouse.

The Sundays through the 1930s also evolved toward longer continuities. At the beginning of the decade Felix was still a loner, kicked out of farmers' homes, spurned by Phyllis, his white kitten inamorata, and thwarted at every turn by a malevolent fate. Later his numerous adventures (in the land of Mother Goose, through the planets of the Zodiac, and back in America) allowed him to acquire kindred friends and companions, such as a tribe of elves in

Fantasy Land and a feisty six-year-old in a Boy Scout uniform named Bobby Dazzler (who would eventually star in a strip of his own). Color added immeasurably to the fantasy-fraught pages, as did the surrealistic use of signs and symbols (an interrogation mark turned into a crowbar, for instance, or an exclamation point used as a javelin) and of the conventions of the comic-strip itself (transforming a speech-balloon into a parachute, breaking through a panel border to escape a pursuing tiger, etc.). Bill Holman reportedly assisted Messmer on some of the Sundays from 1932 to 1935.

Messmer's imagination flagged notably in the 1940s, when he virtually went back to a simple gag format for both his dailies and his Sundays. The weekly page ended on September 19, 1943, and the artist finally retired from the strip in 1955; *Felix* will forever be remembered for his extraordinary contribution to the art of the comics all through the 1920s and 1930s. Mention should also be made of the three toppers that accompanied the *Felix* Sunday during his tenure: *Laura,* about a cantankerous parrot, which ran from 1927 to 1935; *Bobby Dazzler* (1935–1940); and finally *Gus the Ghost,* featuring a funny phantom, which ran from 1940 to 1943.

After Messmer's departure it was all downhill for the unlucky black feline. Joe Oriolo bought the rights to the character in 1954 and had the strip continued by a variety of ghosts with diminishing returns, until the feature's demise on January 9, 1967. Again proving that cats have indeed nine lives, the feline returned on November 19, 1984, as the lower half of the bill in *Betty Boop and Felix.* Again syndicated by King Features and now done by four of Mort Walker's sons, it was a noble effort at reviving the sagging career of two old cartoon movie stars. In 1987 *Felix* left the strip, now retitled *Betty Boop and Friends,* and he hasn't been seen in the funnies since that time.

M.H.

FERD'NAND
1947–present

A Scandinavian import that later became an American fixture, *Ferd'nand* was created by Danish animator Henning Dahl Mikkelsen in 1937. Signed simply "Mik," it was a pantomime strip that could easily be understood by readers of all nationalities A popular feature of many European newspapers, it was finally brought to the United States by United Feature Syndicate in 1947.

A strip of almost unendurable niceness, *Ferd'nand* appeals primarily to an older readership that finds the absence of conflict reassuring and the bland humor of the strip comforting. Another in a long line of comic-strip little men, Ferd'nand leads a quiet suburban life in the middle of a typical nuclear family made up of his wife, his small son and the family dog, all of them unnamed. The problems this model family encounters are slight. At one point the wife plans a candlelight dinner for the couple's anniversary: coming back from work and seeing the home darkened, Ferd'nand puts the electricity back on. At another time, while reading a volume of sea stories, Ferd'nand develops seasickness and falls out of his rocking chair. Mik's simple, clean, almost childlike style, allied to the almost complete absence of wording, helps elicit an indulgent smile at these innocuous anecdotes.

Following the acceptance of his strip in American newspapers, Mik moved to California where he developed a taste for real-estate speculation, leaving the strip increasingly in the hands of others. Since 1970 Al Plastino, signing "Al Mik," has carried on the strip, beyond its creator's death in 1982. In the mid-1990s, Henrik Rehr took over the feature, which is now creeping up to its half-century mark in American newspapers, a record equaled by no other transplanted comic strip.

M.H.

THE FIVE FIFTEEN
See SAPPO

FLAMINGO
1952–1953

A short-lived but extremely interesting newspaper strip, *Flamingo* was distributed by Jerry Iger's independent Phoenix Features and started in February 1952.

Flamingo was a dark-haired, full-bodied Gypsy dancer whose adventures took her all over Europe. In her righteous endeavors she was assisted by the entire tribe of fellow Gypsies and by her grandfather, Old Pepo, the mask-maker. She saved the victim of a kidnapping, proved the innocence of a wrongly accused man, and exposed a gang of house burglars, among other good deeds. Her dark beauty, shapely figure, and sultry dancing drove all males around her crazy with desire, but she remained steadfastly loyal to her one love, an American named Joe.

Ruth Roche, the scriptwriter, spun out suspenseful narratives and often dealt with such burning social issues as exclusion and intolerance (which the Gypsies, as a despised ethnic group, often encountered in their wanderings). It was the art of Matt Baker, the first illustrator on the strip, that provided *Flamingo* with its eye-popping appeal: as a veteran of so-called comic-book "good girl art," he endowed his heroine not only with a luscious figure, but also with fresh, innocent looks that added pathos to her tribulations.

Ferd'nand (H. Dahl Mikkelsen), © 1965 United Feature Syndicate

Unfortunately, Baker abruptly left the strip shortly after its inception (some sources say he died, others that he became incapacitated), and on July 3, 1952, John Thornton succeeded him.

Thornton, solid craftsman as he was, did not possess his predecessor's panache, and despite the addition of a Sunday page in August and continued excellent scripting by Roche, *Flamingo* lost much of its luster. The strip was guided to its conclusion on March 21, 1953, with the fiery Gypsy girl and her American lover getting married.

In addition to its purely formal qualities, *Flamingo* had the distinction, in those pre–civil rights, pre-feminist days, to have been guided at its outset by a team comprised of an African-American artist (Baker) and a woman writer (Roche).

M.H.

FLAPPER FANNY
1924–1939

D estined to become a synonym for a certain type of American womanhood, *Flapper Fanny* started life in 1924 as a daily newspaper panel created by Ethel Hays and distributed by NEA Service. Before the end of the decade the panel's success had spawned a color Sunday page (first appeared in 1928).

Fanny was a delicate, small, dark-haired cutie who affected sophisticated manners and languorous poses. Although one commentator characterized her as "chicly dressed," she was most often seen as chicly undressed, always wearing the latest style in negligees, petticoats, slips, and swimwear. She was fond of uttering flippant remarks, such as "In general, clothes that have the least cost the most" and "Kiss stealing is 'petty' larceny" (many of these sayings were credited to a mysterious E.F.). Fanny represented the emancipated girl of the Prohibition era, but her morals did not differ markedly from those of earlier generations of American women. Despite the general air of permissiveness about it, there was never any hint of sexual shenanigans in *Flapper Fanny;* emancipation was apparent only in clothes and speech. The Sunday page was even tamer, since it was supposedly read by children, and it oftentimes showed Fanny engaged in innocent escapades in the company of her kid sister Betty.

In 1932 Hays passed the torch to another woman, Gladys Parker, who proceeded to jazz up the feature and attune it closer to the times, without substantially altering its style or changing the heroine's personality. Fanny went to work while still keeping her interest in dances, cars, and rich boyfriends. She appeared as scatterbrained as before, but the artist endowed her with an acidulous charm and an often disarming ingenuity that were her redeeming graces. In 1938 Parker left *Fanny,* and the feature was drawn for the last months of its run by an artist who signed simply "Sylvia." Having outlived the era she symbolized, *Flapper Fanny* came to a close in 1939.

M.H.

FLASH GORDON
1934–present

Flash Gordon was created by cartoonist Alex Raymond and ghostwriter Don Moore as King Features' challenge to the popular science-fiction syndicated comic strip *Buck Rogers in the 25th Century.* The daily *Buck Rogers* debuted in 1929 and the Sunday in 1930.

Although *Brick Bradford* joined the intersyndicated sci-fi comic-strip wars in 1933, it wasn't until the arrival of *Flash Gordon* on January 7, 1934, that Buck's position as America's favorite sci-fi hero went down in flames to the artistic lash and spectacle of Alex Raymond's virtuoso artwork.

Flash Gordon (A. Raymond), © 1935 King Features Syndicate

Alex Raymond and *Prince Valiant* creator Hal Foster have been credited with bringing a new level of realistic, heroic, romantic realism to syndicated comics. A frequent debate among adventure-strip aficionados is who is the greatest cartoonist of this genre, Raymond or Foster. Because Hal Foster both wrote and drew *Prince Valiant,* I think he wins the category as the more complete cartoonist. His saga of medieval Europe was as superlative as his artwork.

For decades the myth was perpetuated that Alex Raymond did not have a ghostwriter on *Flash Gordon.* That is not true; Don Moore, borrowing heavily from Philip Wylie's and Edwin Balmer's novel *When Worlds Collide,* created the opening doomsday story of Flash and his companions—the beautiful Dale Arden and scientist Dr. Hans Zarkov—saving Earth from planet Mongo dictator Ming the Merciless.

The appeal of Raymond's *Flash Gordon* always had less to do with a rather silly plot filled with adolescent male fantasies than it did with the superlative artistry. Flash, Yale graduate and renowned polo player, originally had a physique that would make Superman cringe. He was the blond Nordic ideal hero. He was a natural leader of men, not a man of the people.

Spacecraft hurtling toward unknown civilizations in deep space, futuristic cities, exotic landscapes and seascapes, frozen worlds, flying Hawkmen, and especially beautiful, sparingly clothed queens, princesses, and maidens gave Raymond a full canvas to create memorable Sunday pages. Ming the Merciless and his lusty daughter Aura, who was redeemed by her love for Prince Barin of Arboria, became villains readers loved to hate.

Alex Raymond was working as a King Features staff artist ghosting *Tim Tyler's Luck* when he was tapped in 1933 to do the art for an action-based police strip, *Secret Agent X-9.* His work on this strip made him a star. *Flash Gordon* debuted with *Jungle Jim,* King Features' challenge to *Tarzan* but more importantly a marketing strategy by which *Flash* and *Jim* would capture an entire full Sunday comics page. Raymond's artwork for *Jungle Jim* was more purely illustration and lacked the grand design and scope of his work on *Flash Gordon.*

Formal composition combined with beautiful wet and dry brushwork and a dynamic sense of color set Raymond's *Flash Gordon* way above the competition. Exciting artwork was never a hallmark of *Buck Rogers.* Raymond's artwork did not illustrate the silly script; it transcended it and took *Flash* to a higher level.

The ongoing fight to defeat Ming the Merciless lasted from 1934 until the liberation of planet Mongo in 1941. Throughout the battle, Flash was accompanied by Dale Arden, whose purpose in the strip was to be captured by a variety of lechers, most notably Emperor Ming, and then saved from a fate worse than death by Flash.

In 1936 the success of *Flash Gordon* resulted in the first of three movie serials from Universal; Buster Crabbe and

Flash Gordon (A. Briggs), © 1940 King Features Syndicate

Jean Rogers starred as the perfect Flash and Dale in the film *Flash Gordon;* they reprised their roles in *Flash Gordon's Trip to Mars* (1938); the final classic serial was *Flash Gordon Conquers the Universe* (1940). In the series Charles Middleton's interpretation of Ming the Merciless became the most famous portrayal of an arch-villain in the genre.

There were *Flash Gordon* radio shows in the 1930s and 1940s and a television series in 1953–54. The last *Flash Gordon* film was produced by Dino de Laurentis and released in late 1980. While that movie bombed, the corresponding *Flash Gordon* comic books (Whitman's *Flash Gordon the Movie,* #'s 31, 32, and 33, 1980) adapted by Bruce Jones and drawn by Al Williamson are the best *Flash* work of recent years. Ironically, the *New York Times* gave a better review to the nudie parody film *Flesh Gordon,* which was released in December 1974.

Alex Raymond drew the Sunday *Flash Gordon* from January 7, 1934, until April 1944 when he entered the Marine Corps. Austin Briggs, a very talented artist and Raymond's assistant, took over the Sunday from May 1944 through June 1948. Briggs was also the artist of the daily *Flash Gordon* from its inception on May 27, 1940, until June 1944, when Mac Raboy took the daily over. Raboy continued to draw it until December 1967.

John Lehti, Paul Norris, Reed Crandall, and Al Williamson all worked on *Flash Gordon* before cartoonist Dan Barry became King Features' main artist on the strip in 1968. Much of Barry's *Flash Gordon* was written by Fred Dickenson, who offered better than average stories. He also wrote *Rip Kirby* during the same period. Barry's tenure on the strip ended in 1990.

Bruce Jones took over the writing in 1990–91, with artwork first by Ralph Reese and then Gray Morrow. Since 1991 the script has been written by Tom Warkentin. This includes the final, as of now, *Flash Gordon* daily, July 3, 1993, in which Flash exits the last panel saying, "I think I'll go fishing." That's hardly heroic.

But then Flash isn't the hot popular culture icon he once was. The mosaic strip is now available only as a Sunday, written by artist Jim Keefe. In the U.S. it reportedly is only published in the *Boston Herald;* overseas it probably does better. But there are rumors of a new Hollywood movie, and if that happens, and Flash is reinvented, he will surely be the heroic, larger-than-life Alex Raymond-inspired figure of yore. It is not impossible that Flash will be back more popular than ever.

B.C., Jr.

THE FLINTSTONES
1961–present

The Hanna-Barbera studios produced the first animation series ever to be seen on prime-time television. It was called *The Flintstones* and debuted on CBS in the fall of 1960. For this series Hanna and Barbera simply adapted the clichés of 1960s situation comedy to a Stone Age setting, the mythical town of Bedrock.

Reportedly modeled on the tremendously popular series *The Honeymooners, The Flintstones* featured the loud-mouthed, know-it-all Fred Flintstone (in a variation on the Jackie Gleason character) lording it over meek, gullible Barney Rubble (a takeoff on the Art Carney role). The "boys" were often in competition with their domineering spouses, the acidulous Wilma Flintstone and the sarcastic Betty Rubble, and they had to concoct all sorts of excuses in order to get out for an evening of bowling or a meeting of the Waterbuffaloes Lodge. The stories were carried in an adequate but pedestrian style of limited animation, a far cry from Hanna and Barbera's glory days at MGM.

The Flintstones nonetheless was Hanna and Barbera's most popular and successful creation. It was transposed to the movie screen, and adapted into comic books. It has also enjoyed a long career in newspapers, with a comic strip first distributed by McNaught Syndicate, starting in 1961.

The gags often dealt with the incongruity of modern appliances in prehistoric times: foot-propelled automobiles, pterodactyl-borne planes, dinosaur-powered cranes, and so on. After a while, however, these inventions began to wear thin. The marital fight that fueled the plots of many of the Sunday episodes also became hackneyed and increasingly repetitive. As on the small screen, two infants were introduced into the strip in an effort to bring new life to it: the mischievous Pebbles (daughter of the Flintstones) and the muscular Bamm-Bamm (son of the Rubbles). Later Dino, Fred's pet dinosaur, a pinkish, friendly beast of the species "runtasaurus," came more and more to dominate the jokes. Obviously the people involved believed that it would do for *The Flintstones* what Snoopy had done for *Peanuts,* but to date this has not happened. Dino dropping a stone newspaper on Fred's foot or dragging his master behind him in hot pursuit of the cave mouse are not gags aimed at eliciting approval from a discerning audience.

The first artist on the feature was Gene Hazelton, a veteran animator and funny-animal specialist. When

McNaught went out of business in the mid-1980s, *The Flint-stones* was picked up by Editors Press Service, with Don Sherwood put in charge of the drawings. The artwork is now being supplied by staffers at Hanna-Barbera.

M.H.

THE FLOP FAMILY
1943–1982

Created by the irrepressible George Swanson (better known as "Swan"), *The Flop Family* was initially called *Dad's Family* and enjoyed a career as durable as it was obscure. A Sunday page at its outset, on August 29, 1943, it was distributed, with the addition of a daily strip on May 1, 1944, by King Features Syndicate.

Swan once described his creation as "a strip of laughs that happen in the average family with three kids," but it turned into a little more than that. A cartoonist of the zany school, who had previously been responsible for such outrages as *Salesman Sam, High-Pressure Pete,* and *Elza Poppin* (this last one derived from Olsen and Johnson's fabled vaudeville show), he never kept his strip on a familiar domestic track. Philander Flop, the husband, was a small man, with a tiny sausage as a nose and a toothbrush for a mustache, who harbored a perpetually puzzled expression; his wife, Helen, contrary to comic-strip convention, was no taller than he was and only slightly more enlightened. The children (a college-age daughter, a teenage son, and their eight-year-old brother) were only peripheral to the gags, which centered on the married couple and their screwball encounters with the outside world. They had harrowing experiences with traffic cops, delivery men, streetcar conductors, and grocery-store clerks, from which they emerged sadder but no wiser. Helen proved a tad luckier than her husband in that she was able in these situations to wrangle from Philander the promise of a new dress or the consolation of a night on the town.

The drawings were rendered in a cartoony, slapdash graphic shorthand that harked back to the 1920s, and the jokes, while fresh in the vernal years of the feature, later became stale and repetitive. It is a wonder the strip lasted as long as it did, since it never seemed to glean either popular or critical success (the early historians of the medium all ignore it). The Sunday page was canceled on May 29, 1966, but Swan continued to turn out the dailies up to the time of his death at the end of 1981: the last *Flop Family* strip appeared on January 2, 1982.

M.H.

FLYIN' JENNY
1939–1952

Named for the JN-40 training plane of World War I, *Flyin' Jenny* was created by Russell Keaton and distributed, daily and Sunday, by the Bell Syndicate from October 1939.

Keaton brought to *Flyin' Jenny* skills he had honed to a fine point on *Skyroads,* a pioneer aviation feature he had been drawing for the previous six years. That ensured that

Flyin' Jenny (R. Keaton), © 1940 Bell Syndicate

the aircraft would be rendered just right down to the slightest detail, from the sleek Curtis P-51 Mustang pursuit plane to the stolid Ford A.T. transport. The heroine, Jenny Dare, whom an admiring female flyer characterized as "blonde, beautiful, cute, and cool," moved unintimidated amid all the equipment and machines. An old hand at the flying game, although she looked no older than 25, she could stand up to any male pilot in pylon contests or air races. In true comic-strip fashion she had a sidekick, another woman flyer named Wanda, as dark as Jenny was fair, and an unofficial boyfriend, Rick Davis, a handsome plane designer. The cast was rounded out by the obligatory comic relief in the person of the chubby and brash Spinner Martin.

As with many other strips born around that time, *Flyin' Jenny*'s heyday came during World War II. With dailies and Sundays running different continuities, Keaton decided upon an original division of labor: in the dailies Jenny would go through a series of spine-tingling exploits overseas, while the color pages would detail her adventures on the home front, each with their own supporting cast. Thus the blonde aviatrix flew dangerous missions over Europe in the company of news photographer Babe Woods on weekdays, while on Sunday she retained the strip's original cast. Together they fought fifth columnists and German infiltrators who had been dropped to sabotage the heroine's home field of Hillandia. All the villains were straight out of central casting: their chief, an egg-bald, monocled Nazi, when he saw himself cornered, threw his arms up in the air, shouting "Kamerad! I giff up!"

Keaton wrote the first stories himself. In 1940 the scripts were turned over to Hollywood screenwriter and former navy pilot Frank Wead (later the subject of the 1957 John Ford biopic *The Wings of Eagles*). Glenn Chaffin took charge of the writing in 1943 when Wead was recalled to service and was soon followed by Keaton, who was drafted as a flight instructor. The Sundays were ghosted for a time by Gladys Parker, before being entrusted to Marc Swayze, who also took over the drawing of the dailies after Keaton's sudden illness (and subsequent death in February 1945).

The Swayze-Chaffin team was confronted with the delicate task of reconverting the heroine to peacetime pursuits once again. This they did with a marked lack of cheer, and the strip at the end of the war started losing newspapers to such an extent that it was long believed that *Flyin' Jenny* had come to an end in 1946. Actually the feature had continued to cruise under the radar for six more years, concentrating on intrigue and romance, with generous displays of the heroine's charms, until its final landing in the spring of 1952.

M.H.

FOR BETTER OR FOR WORSE
1979–present

Based on the wit and sincerity of her three Meadowbrook Press books on carrying and raising children, Universal Press Syndicate approached Canadian illustrator Lynn Johnston to create a contemporary family strip from a woman's viewpoint. *For Better or For Worse* first appeared September 9, 1979, and was aptly named for its depiction of the triumphs, heartbreak, and simple pleasures of its participants. Drawn in a vivid, flowing anatomical style, the feature paints a vital portrait of family life that relies not on age-old comic clichés but on Johnston's original viewpoint.

Dentist John Patterson is the mild-mannered, loving husband who calmly comanages the household with his sometimes harried wife, Elly, who is clearly the strip's most developed consequential figure. She is full of all the hopes, fears, and tribulations that confront every conscientious, reflective woman and mother. As the feature is semiautobiographical, the characters often closely resemble their real-life counterparts, members and friends of the Johnson family, while often mirroring the thoughts and experiences of the cartoonist. Like those in the cast of *Gasoline Alley*, Johnston's subjects have aged slowly as time passes, helping reinforce the true-to-life aura that has been carefully developed.

Son Michael, currently in college, is a wholesome young man whose growth was recorded since boyhood within the course of the feature along with his sister Elizabeth. Typical sibling rivalry, household episodes, events at school, and dating rituals have been played out with gentle accuracy. Childhood was reintroduced in 1991 with the birth of April, who now experiences the fascinations of the young spirit once demonstrated by her brother and sister.

A situation drama such as this requires an expansive cast of supporting players to be catalysts to the strip's rich situational framework. Extended family such as grandparents, John's sister, and Elly's brother Phil appear occasionally. Elizabeth's friend Dawn and her obtrusive schoolmate Candice provide much material, as does Michael's mechanic chum, Gordo. Handicapped schoolteacher Sharon Edwards is an additional poignant character. The death of the beloved family dog Farley during a rescue sequence in 1995 evoked an emotional public response; a likable canine replacement, Edgar, is a recent adoption and evidence of life's continuing cycle.

Over fifteen comprehensive collections of the strip have been published in book form since 1981, most notably two anniversary chronicles, 1989's *A Look Inside* and *It's the Thought That Counts* from 1994. To date, seven animated television specials have been produced, initially by Atkinson Film Arts, followed by Lacewood Productions. The National Cartoonists Society bestowed the coveted Reuben Award to the cartoonist for the year 1985, making her the first woman to receive such distinction. Johnston's courage to periodically incorporate important social issues into the feature without exhortation is an admirable and unique feat in the profession today. *For Better or For Worse* has proven its prominence not only as one of today's best efforts, but also as one of the finest graphic narratives ever produced.

B.J.

THE FOUR ACES
1934–1935, 1936–1942

The Four Aces was created by Hal Forrest on January 7, 1934, in replacement of *Progress of Flight*, as a companion strip to *Tailspin Tommy*, and it is generally treated as a mere adjunct to the better known feature. It, however, deserves a study of its own.

Distributed along with *Tommy* by the Bell Syndicate, *The Four Aces* went through two distinct periods of unequal length. In its first incarnation, which came to an end on June 16, 1935, the Four Aces were Larry Gale, an American pilot with the Lafayette Escadrille during the Great War, and three of his wartime allies, one English, one French, and one Italian. Leisurely told in a single row of four panels, the first adventures involved the quartet in sporting (and sometimes unsporting) contests with a German stunt flyer known as the Red Baron. Later on, Audrey Ward, a lovely blonde American girl, entered the strip, which ended its initial run in a long flashback to World War I recounting the first meeting of Larry and Audrey. It was a tortuous tale of double- and triple-crosses in which Audrey, as an agent of French counterespionage, trying to smash an enemy espionage ring operating in France, masqueraded as a female German spy posing as a French spy.

After a stint trying his hand at a didactic feature, *How to Fly*, Forrest on March 22, 1936, returned to *The Four Aces*, but with a twist. In a bit of truly disastrous timing he replaced the Italian ace (the Italians were then unpopular because of the war in Abyssinia) with a German one. The scene now mainly took place in America, with the team competing in air races and aerial stunt contests, and occasionally tangling with gangsters. In 1939 Forrest switched from Bell to United Feature, revamping the series in the process and getting his heroes (there were now two American flyers) into the European conflict. This last-ditch effort proved of no avail, and the Four Aces, along with Tailspin Tommy, made their final landing in the spring of 1942.

M.H.

FOX TROT
1988–present

A recent addition to the literature of the family strip, Bill Amend's *Fox Trot* depicts the classic nuclear family of harried father, ironic mother, three manipulative youngsters, and a pet, but has an acerbic edge that saves it from the sentimental clichés of the genre. Distributed by Universal Press Syndicate since 1988, it was running in over 150 newspapers before the end of its first year.

Amend (whose name rhymes with Raymond) has created a thoroughly believable household for the 1990s. Roger Fox, a loving father, is defeated by life; his children routinely outsmart him, and he loses consistently to an electronic chess game programmed to deliver responses like "Nice move, moron. Checkmate. Ha ha ha ha." His wife Andy struggles unsuccessfully to get her children to eat properly, do their homework, and stop fighting, but embarrasses everyone in the family feature she writes for the local newspaper (her first column includes the passage "...and then there's my husband, Roger. A little chubby, a lot bald, and as nerdy as they come, but I love the goober anyway.")

Sixteen-year-old Peter agonizes over his inchoate love life but sometimes blunders into saying the right thing anyway. His sister Paige, 14, survives by means of romantic dreams, blackmail, invective, and occasional violence. Bespectacled Jason, 10, is the family genius; he has a rich inner life, part of it spent as a member of the cast of *Star Trek*, but he knows just what buttons to push in the Fox-family domestic warfare. Jason's pet, Quincy, a single-minded iguana, serves mainly as a weapon against women but has its own inner life, focused mainly on mealworms.

If the dramatis personae and the interpersonal dynamics of *Fox Trot* reflect long-established traditions of comic-strip families, the situations that illustrate them are unmistakably contemporary. Comics kids have always maintained the edge over their bumbling parents, but one of *Fox Trot*'s demonstrations of that fact is the ease with which Peter, Paige, and Jason master the computer while Roger is still trying to figure out how to turn it on. The evidence that the Foxes have struck a responsive chord in the American public is the successful publication of annual collections of the strip since 1989.

D.W.

FOXY GRANDPA
1900–1929[?]

Charles Schultze's engagingly drawn, unaffectedly funny *Foxy Grandpa* ushered in a new century of newspaper comics in the color section of the *New York Herald* on the first Sunday (January 7) of the year 1900.

Foxy Grandpa provided a twist on *The Katzenjammer Kids* in that the titular lead character always managed to turn the tables on the two prank-playing boys (never named and sometimes referred to as his nephews) who were constantly up to some deviltry with the oldster as their target. The mischief-makers, one fair-haired, one dark, like the Katzenjammers, time and again were outfoxed by the old gent, who lived up to his nickname. In one episode the two boys planted tacks on their parent's easy chair, but when they looked through the window to see how their trick had succeeded, the grinning Grandpa closed the pane on them, before administering a good spanking to the two culprits. In another instance the foxy old gent outwitted his

Foxy Grandpa (C. Schultze), 1905

nephews, who had loosened the bolt on the front wheel of his bicycle, by simply riding on the rear wheel.

These simple anecdotes were told in typeset texts under the pictures, with somewhat redundant subtitles such as "The Boys Were in a Very Mischievous Mood, but Grandpa Soon Cured Them," or "Foxy Grandpa Shows the Boys a Trick or Two." The pages, rendered always in a simple, rounded style, bore the signature "Bunny" accompanied by the drawing of a little white rabbit whose expressions or activities (laughing, weeping, covering his face, dancing a little gig, etc.) varied according to the mood of the piece.

Foxy Grandpa proved popular enough in the early years of the century to give rise to a musical show and a series of live-action shorts, all in the period 1902–03. This success attracted Hearst's notice, and on February 16, 1902, *Foxy Grandpa* transferred to the pages of the *New York Journal*. This proved a mistake on Schultze's part, as he had now to compete not only with *The Katzenjammers*, but with the creations of Swinnerton and Opper as well, and Schultze's strip steadily declined in popularity. Reacting to this downward trend, the artist toward the end of the decade involved his characters in lengthy narratives in faraway lands. In "Foxy Grandpa in Africa," for instance, Grandpa and his charges followed in the footsteps of Theodore Roosevelt on a hunting trip to the dark continent. The two boys on that occasion proved as much a help as a nuisance, saving he white-whiskered adventurer from the coils of a giant python and, in those politically incorrect times, rescuing him from the cooking pot of ravenous cannibals.

Despite the cartoonist's valiant efforts, *Foxy Grand-pa* was dropped from the pages of the *Journal* in 1910. It was then picked up by the *New York Press,* but did not outlast the decade. In the 1920s, Schultze revived his character as the emcee of *Foxy Grandpa's Stories,* where he narrated animal tales to children in a series syndicated by Newspaper Feature Service. This new venture seems to have disappeared at decade's end.

A number of commentators have argued that the strip then simply faded into oblivion, but this assumption is not entirely correct. The feature lingered in the fond memories of latter-day historians, such as Coulton Waugh, who called it "a gentle, plush-lined old epic," and it has survived in the popular expression "foxy grandpa" that serves to designate a sly, savvy senior citizen.

M.H.

FRANK AND ERNEST
1972–present

Bob Thaves, an industrial psychologist by profession and a cartoonist by avocation, started *Frank and Ernest,* a daily panel that occupies the entire space of a comic strip, for NEA in November 1972. The horizontal format—unusual for a panel feature—allowed Thaves to depict the action in the left side of the picture while the right side was taken up by text or dialogue lettered in large, bold print. The experiment proved successful, and a Sunday *Frank and Ernest* was added in April 1973.

Frank and Ernest are two zany characters hovering on the fringe of normal society. At first there were numerous protagonists in the strip, but the duo stood out to such an extent that the feature was almost entirely given over to them after only a few weeks. The shaggy, tall Frank, who does most of the talking, and the short, awestruck Ernest, who does most of the reacting, are placed by Thaves in the most unusual situations and in settings that vary from day to day. In the tradition of early cartoons, the two are bank tellers one day, door-to-door salesmen the next, and so forth, but they remain basically the same in character, and are most often pictured as two tramps sitting on a park bench or shuffling through desolate city streets.

The illogical and the outlandish are the main sources of the gags. In one instance, Frank looks bemusedly at the drooping beam issuing from his flashlight and mutters somewhat self-consciously, "Maybe the battery is getting weak." In another case, informed by his short friend that aliens have just taken over control of the world, Frank grinningly observes, "Boy, that's a load off my mind." As the pair goes through garbage cans, Frank again comments, "Boy, if money is the root of all evil, we gotta be two of the most right-minded guys in the whole world." On Sundays Thaves is wont to portray his two bums tramping through the crossword-puzzle page, making up their own definitions as they go along.

The runaway success of his feature (there have been a number of *Frank and Ernest* reprints and the strip consistently ranks among the top ten in readership and circulation) has allowed Thaves to devote his full time and attention to his creation.

M.H.

FRANKIE DOODLE
1934–1939

Starting out in 1934 as *The Doodle Family,* about an upper-middle-class household, this strip soon veered toward melodramatics, when young Frankie Doodle was orphaned and had to make it alone in an uncaring world. It was done from the outset by Ben Batsford for United Feature Syndicate.

Batsford, who had been one of the early artists on *Little Annie Rooney,* at first concocted narratives focusing on his ten-year-old hero, a spunky, curly-haired lad in knickers, trying to escape from the clutches of Mrs. Krule, the ruthless head of the orphanage from which he had, in true orphan-strip fashion, run away. Another relentless pursuer on Frankie's well-worn heels was Mr. Shady, a crooked lawyer intent on putting his hands on the Doodle inheritance. After a while the feature turned into a mystery tale, with Frankie helping Captain Ku, a Chinese secret agent, with his cases. Sporting a short goatee and a spaghettilike mustache, Ku was a cross between Charlie Chan and Ming Foo, and he was much given to mouthing cryptic aphorisms.

As *Frankie Doodle* approached the end of the 1930s, it was still not taking off. In desperation Batsford turned it into a humorous kid strip, but that didn't work either. The syndicate ultimately closed down the feature in 1939, at the end of its five-year run.

M.H.

FRECKLES AND HIS FRIENDS
1915–1973

Veteran cartoonist Merrill Blosser made his contribution to the already seried ranks of comic-strip kids with a winsome entry titled *Freckles and His Friends.* Distributed by NEA, it started life on September 20, 1915, as a daily strip, followed a short time later by a Sunday version.

Set in the placid midwestern town of Shadyside, the feature lived up to its title's promise by focusing on the youthful Freckles McGoosey and his friends, of whom he had many. Over the years Freckles grew from buck-toothed ten-year-old to gawky teenager to fresh-faced juvenile. There was, accordingly, a rapid turnover among his friends. Those had initially consisted of his kid brother, Tagalong (or Tag), his sister, Elsie, and pals Aleck, Slim, and the twin brothers Ray and Jay. Later there came the foppish Oscar, the voracious Lard Smith, the boy inventor Nutty Cook, not to forget Freckles's girlfriend, blonde and svelte June Wayman,

Freckles and His Friends (M. Blosser), © 1938 NEA Service

and Lard's sweetheart, Hilda Grubble. These different sets of friends kept crossing over from one period to another, thus keeping the continuity going, albeit in a somewhat confusing way.

Blosser's scripting tried similarly to keep pace with the protagonist going through all these age changes. A simple series of kid jokes at the outset, it later dealt with the concerns of teenagers, such as high school and the opposite sex; and at one time the plot had Freckles assembling a local band, with Lard as the lead singer. Toward the end of the 1920s and well into the 1930s Freckles went adventuring to exotic locales, from Labrador to Borneo. In many of these long, thrill-packed narratives he could often be found in the company of a grizzled old sea captain named Billy Bowlegs, who was fond of such presumably nautical oaths as "By the bones of the ten tinkers!"

Contrary to what some have averred, Freckles and his friends in the 1940s did their collective bit for the war effort. Queried on just that score by his father, the young hero proudly answered, "June and Hilda are rolling bandages for the Red Cross, Nutty is an assistant block warden, Tag is buying defense stamps, I've sold $1,200 worth of defense bonds, and Sue is assisting at a canteen for soldiers." Not content with those mundane activities, the gang also exposed an infiltrator spying on a nearby army base and even helped the police dismantle a black-market ring. The Sundays, meanwhile, were devoted to more peaceful pursuits, with the protagonists leading an existence far removed from the contingencies of war (though gas rationing was sometimes mentioned). In the 1930s and 1940s there also was a companion strip to the Sunday *Freckles;* called *Hector,* it concerned itself with the doings of Hilda Grubble's obnoxious kid brother.

After the heyday of the preceding two decades (at one point *Freckles* was syndicated to more than seven hundred newspapers across the country), the strip in the 1950s experienced a slow erosion in readership. Blosser decided to retire on the occasion of the feature's half-century anniversary, and his longtime assistant Henry Formhals than took over the strip, which he was allowed to sign in 1966. Fred Fox assumed the writing chores, and *Freckles* coasted along for several more years: the dailies ended on August 28, 1971, and the Sunday page was discontinued in January 1973.

M.H.

FRED BASSET
1965–present

*F*red Basset first appeared on July 9, 1963, in the *Daily Mail* of London, but only came to American newspapers two years later. It was created by Alex Graham, who had been drawing gag cartoons for years before he was enticed to try his hand at a comic strip by Julian Phipps, the *Mail*'s editor. The strip was an instant success in Britain, and in 1965 it was picked up for distribution in North America by Field Newspaper Syndicate, which added a Sunday page a few years later.

As his name makes clear, Fred is a basset hound. He wears a white-and-brown coat and possesses a very expres-sive face; he doesn't talk but muses aloud (in thought balloons, like Snoopy), and his comments add color to what would otherwise be a garden-variety family strip. "The basis of the humor is that he's a dog who thinks like a person," Graham once told an interviewer. "The unusual thing is that he's the character in the strip who's commenting on the behavior of the other characters in the strip." There are only two other characters of any permanence in the feature, and they are the suburban couple who are Fred's putative owners. It is indicative that they have remained nameless all through the years, while their pet is graced with a full name.

Despite his elongated shape, Fred is a well-rounded dog, a little inquisitive, a little cowardly, a little cunning, and more than a little hedonistic. His gourmet tastes allow him to eat only the best cuts of meat, and in addition he is a great bone connoisseur. "Ripe...crumbly...mature," he observes appreciatively after he had dug up a bone he had put down in 1972, adding, "It was a great year!" Most of his comments are directed at his masters, whom he chooses to acknowledge or to snub, at his convenience. Hearing his master's ultrasonic whistle from a distance, he disdainfully remarks to himself, "I intend to ignore it, of course, but it's a very clever gadget..." And when his mistress accuses him of having stolen the bone he is holding between his teeth, he simply walks away, sardonically musing, "It fell off a lorry..."

The strip is drawn in a deceptively sparse style, with only a few well-placed lines, skillful positioning of the characters, and only the slightest suggestion of background. An important element in the design of the daily strip is the lower-case hand-lettering (most strips use block letters for the texts) supplied by Leslie Hulme. As to the Sunday page (which is not published in Britain), Graham only drew and lettered it in pencil, leaving it to the syndicate to ink and color.

At age 80, Graham, of whom it was said that "he thinks like a dog but works like a horse," was still totally involved with *Fred Basset;* Graham died in 1992, and the strip (which is presently syndicated by Tribune Media Services) is now being done by other hands.

M.H.

FRIDAY FOSTER
1970–1974

*A*s the first comic strip starring and named for an African American ever released by a major newspaper syndicate, *Friday Foster* has a secure place in comic-strip history.

In 1968, Jim Lawrence, a middle-aged white writer, was reading the comics in the *Newark Evening News* and realized he was only seeing white faces. Having written *James Bond, Joe Palooka,* and *Captain Easy* for the comics, Lawrence developed the character of an ambitious, talented, beautiful black career woman, Friday Foster. He was also influenced by seeing the black model Donyale Luna on a television interview show.

Simultaneously the Chicago Tribune–New York News Syndicate was distributing a gag-a-day strip based on the hit television show *Laugh-In*. In it the syndicate had introduced black characters. Now it wanted a black continuity strip.

Lawrence found Jorge Longaron of Barcelona, Spain, to draw the strip. This gave the art for *Friday Foster* a realistic but decorative European style that offered a new look compared with other syndicate offerings of the time. It took two years before Lawrence's idea of a black comic-strip heroine was published.

Friday Foster debuted January 18, 1970, with a fourteen-week-long story that propelled her from "camera bunny" in a Playboyesque costume at Club Senegal in Harlem to assistant to high-fashion photographer Shawn North.

Friday was from Harlem in New York City and her family, especially her younger brother, gave her a reality check of the mean streets in contrast with the magazine-publishing-world intrigue she soon found herself in.

While some stories had a hard edge, ultimately *Friday Foster* became a romantic soap-opera strip about a gorgeous African-American woman making a success in the white world. The plots made Friday a globetrotter with trips to Europe, Hong Kong, and even Africa, where she became involved with a black American athlete who had dropped out to become a modern-day Tarzan-like character. She proved as pretty in front of as behind the camera, and Friday developed into a supermodel.

The strain of the lengthy lead time between Lawrence in New Jersey and Longaron in Spain and a decline in the popularity of the strip led to the art being turned over to Gray Morrow in early 1974. However, by May 1974, *Friday Foster* ended syndication.

In December 1975, American International released its film *Friday Foster*, starring Pam Grier. On assignment from *Glance* magazine, Friday helps unravel a plot to kill America's black leadership. The action-adventure film costarred Eartha Kitt, Yaphet Kato, and Godfrey Cambridge.

B.C., Jr.

FRITZI RITZ
1922–1968

Better noted as the feature that gave birth to the frizzy-haired Nancy, *Fritzi Ritz* is nonetheless worthy of a study of its own. It began on October 9, 1922, as a daily strip done by Larry Whittington and syndicated by Pulitzer's Press Publishing Company.

Like so many of her sisters on the comics page, Fritzi was a flapper, with a pleasant face, curly dark hair, and a curvaceous figure. She was apparently a woman of means, riding horses, driving expensive cars, residing in a fine mansion. After a few innocuous adventures, with clumsy American beaus and slick European fortune-hunters, she moved to Hollywood, where she started a modest screen career. At that point in her adventures, Whittington made the decision to leave Pulitzer (and the strip) for what he thought were greener pastures at Hearst's King Features Syndicate, for which he created another flapper strip, *Maisie the Model*, which promptly sank from view (as did Whittington).

Upon its creator's departure, *Fritzi Ritz* was continued by Ernie Bushmiller, who involved the spunky heroine in crosscountry adventures filled with thrills as well as gags. So

Fritzi Ritz (E. Bushmiller), © 1939 United Feature Service

successful was the new cartoonist with the strip that in 1929 a Sunday page was added to the dailies. The very next year Press Publishing went out of business, with a niggling number of its features being picked up by United Feature Syndicate, including *Fritzi*. At the request of the new distributing agency, Bushmiller added a companion strip, *Phil Fumble*, about a bumbling college type, to the Sunday *Fritzi*.

In 1933 Fritzi's young niece, Nancy, came to visit, and her antics soon upstaged the doings of the titular heroine. As a result the daily strip's title was enlarged to *Fritzi Ritz and Nancy* in 1938, becoming simply *Nancy* in the early 1940s. The weekly page also gave way to a Sunday *Nancy* with *Fritzi Ritz* turning into its two-tiered topper (expanding to a full page in the tabloid-sized newspapers that carried the strip). In it Fritzi continued her romantic adventures, with Phil Fumble now her perennially frustrated suitor. The *Fritzi Ritz* page also came to an end some time in 1968; the character still lives on, however, in *Nancy*.

M.H.

FU MANCHU
1931–1933

The 1931 publication of *Daughter of Fu Manchu* marked the return of Sax Rohmer's quintessential master of villainy after an absence of fourteen years. This fact, coupled with the concurrent appearance in American theaters of the Fu Manchu movies starring Warner Oland, may have prompted the ever-enterprising Bell Syndicate to come out that same year with a daily newspaper-strip adaptation of Rohmer's lurid tales of Far Eastern menace.

Following the example of the daily *Tarzan* strip, *Fu Manchu* did not make use of speech balloons; instead, the story was told in the first person by Dr. Petrie, one of the sinister Asian's stalwart adversaries, in a lengthy narrative running either alongside or beneath the pictures. In these tales of undiluted horror, torture, and death, Nayland Smith, British defender of Western civilization, foiled again and again the unspeakable designs of the diabolical Fu, more through luck than intellect. He was aided in his laudable endeavors by the aforementioned Petrie, and secretly protected by Karamaneh, Fu's sultry concubine who had fallen for Petrie's stiff-upper-lip masculinity.

"The door fits well," came Fu Manchu's mocking voice. "It is fortunate for us that is so. This is my observation window, Dr. Petrie. You are about to enjoy a unique opportunity of studying fungology. You know the poisonous properties of the puff-ball. I have increased its value . . ."

Fu Manchu (Rohmer and O'Mealia), © 1931 Bell Syndicate

The drawings were done by Leo O'Mealia in a grim, painstaking illustrative style, with a predominance of grays and blacks. Both in tone and in mood they were faithful to the spirit of the original stories, creating in the reader a vague feeling of unease and queasiness. The series concluded in April 1933 on the apparent triumph of the forces of good, with Fu Manchu meeting what looked like certain death in the path of an incoming train.

M.H.

FUNKY WINKERBEAN
1972–present

Funky Winkerbean was foreshadowed by a weekly cartoon series Tom Batiuk did for his hometown paper in Elyria, Ohio, in the late 1960s. Batiuk's years as a high-school teacher crystalized his interest in drawing a comic strip about teenage students (rather than teaching them), and he eventually sold his idea as a daily and Sunday feature to Publishers-Hall Syndicate in 1972.

Being only twenty-five years old at the inception of the strip, Batiuk held a vantage point close to his subjects, chronologically as well as pedagogically. On the whole the students at Westview High (as the fictional institution is called) are not a bad lot, a little goofy, perhaps, a little hare-brained, and a lot oversexed, but closer in their suburban setting to Dobie Gillis and his buddies than to the gang in *The Blackboard Jungle*. Funky Winkerbean stands as the representative of the student population, "someone that everybody identifies with," according to the author; as such, he is average in everything, especially in his scores, either in class or with girls, and his enthusiasm far surpasses his abilities. He is flanked by the usual suspects, offbeat characters like Bull Bushka, the jock with a negative I.Q. number; and Crazy Harry, the existential nut case. As for the girls, they are either giggling birdbrains or homely know-it-alls. The adults hardly rise a notch higher than the kids, except in hypocrisy. The principal only dreams about reaching retirement age without any trouble along the way; the teachers are either inept or unconcerned; and the band director is more interested in fund drives than in music. For a while the school shenanigans were often intermingled with the dubious scoops of the local TV anchorman, John Darling, who unfortunately left to star in his own, short-lived strip. Amid all this tomfoolery *Funky Winkerbean* has found time to deal—albeit gingerly—with such topical subjects as guns in the classroom, drugs, and teenage pregnancy. Batiuk periodically returns to his high school in Elyria for refresher courses in student fads and behavior, and he has in recent times introduced a new crop of students to Westview High in order to give some variety to the proceedings, which are still drawn in a basic Cartooning 101 style that neither adds to nor detracts from the anecdotes.

M.H.

THE FUSCO BROTHERS
1989–present

A flippant attitude, an offbeat angle of vision, and some wild wordplay combine to make J. C. Duffy's daily and Sunday strip *The Fusco Brothers* an appropriate feature

Funky Winkerbean (T. Batiuk), ca. 1979, © Field Newspaper Syndicate

for the 1990s. Produced for Lew Little Enterprises and distributed by Universal Press Syndicate since August 1989, the strip quickly acquired a following among sophisticated readers.

Described by their publishers as "nerds of the nineties," the four Fuscos all suffer from the same problems—existential malaise in the face of an essentially absurd universe and an inability to pick up girls—and they talk about them in much the same slightly skewed terms. Although Duffy has provided them with different hair color and styling and different nose shapes, they are more or less interchangeable in appearance as well, and they invariably address each other by name in an effort at providing them with recognizable identities; but the humor of the strip relies more on the cynical banter it contains than on character.

Lance, Lars, Rolf, and Al live together in Newark, New Jersey, with their dog Axel (a bizarre beast with a personality that shifts from that of Garfield to that of Snoopy, and who insists he is a wolverine but actually looks more like an anteater). Apparently none of them has a job (Lance can't get one because he suffers from PWS—prework syndrome—and the others never seem to think of it). Gloria, Lance's perpetually scowling girlfriend, apparently lives with them, though details about life at Fusco Manor are never precisely clear. Nothing seems to happen there except an endless round of caustic dialogue. They have little that is positive to say about or to each other: Lance advises Al to give someone who has angered him a piece of pie. "Don't you mean a piece of my mind?" ask Al. "It's like charity," Lance reminds him. "Only give what you can afford." Essentially a bunch of losers with delusions of life in the fast lane, they get high on Slurpees and celebrate Thanksgiving by sending out for a pizza with giblets.

The badinage in *The Fusco Brothers* has enough of the spirit of old-time vaudeville to reach a general audience, and enough madcap eccentricity and trendy references to appeal to the hip. Shifting from sarcasm to nonsense, and sometimes fusing the two, gives it a contemporary spirit that seems to speak for the last decade of the century.

D.W.

G.I. JOE
See MR. BREGER

GARFIELD
1978–present

Of all the great cats of cartooning, Garfield has to be the fattest, employing that word in its capitalistic as well as anatomical sense. By the 1990s, Garfield as a cottage industry had reached the scale of Peanuts, its Indiana plant, Paws, Inc., spewing out thousands (more than three thousand by 1988) of merchandising objects and producing the strip for more than twenty-five hundred newspapers. About forty people work at Paws, Inc., but only after attending drawing classes where they learn to draw Garfield in the same fashion. "Maintaining" (his word for what he does) the strip is its creator, Jim Davis, who still comes up with the gags and dialogue; penciling and final artwork are done by Gary Barker and inking by Valette Grene.

Before *Garfield,* Davis had tinkered with an insect strip, *Gnorm Gnat,* for about five years, never able to attract a syndicate's interest. Thinking that the public could not identify with a bug, he abandoned *Gnorm Gnat* and chose a cat to figure in his strip. He first did *Garfield* in 1976, but syndication did not come until June 19, 1978. Initially, the strip was called *Jon* after Garfield's owner, Jon Arbuckle, but when Davis realized that every time he wrote a gag, Garfield came up with the punchline, he turned the strip over to him and changed the title.

Although *Garfield* today is acclaimed worldwide, this was not always the case; the strip had a sluggish beginning. King Features rejected Davis's idea almost immediately, and the Chicago Tribune–New York News Syndicate after five months. United Feature eventually signed Davis to a contract. First reactions to *Garfield* also did not indicate a winner: one national magazine predicted a short life for the strip; Hallmark declined to merchandise the character, and newspaper-client growth was slow. After nearly two years, in March 1980, only 180 newspapers ran *Garfield.*

Garfield (J. Davis), © 1978 United Feature Syndicate

Then something unexpected happened. The first paperback collection, *Garfield at Large,* climbed to the top of the *New York Times* bestseller list, where it remained for one hundred weeks (four years on the list itself). Dailies clamored for the strip as the client list grew at the rate of one newspaper every day for the next three years. Meanwhile, more compilations appeared, and by November 1982, seven Garfield books were on the *Times* bestseller list simultaneously. The growth of new products grew apace.

Bill Blackbeard and Malcolm Whyte have written that the public took to Garfield so overwhelmingly because "he's everything we would be if only we could let ourselves go"—fat, lazy, grumpy, cynical, egotistical, and selfish, yet endearing. The character has been easy to identify with, simple in concept, and universal in appeal. Garfield cherishes eating (particularly lasagna) and sleeping and detests Mondays, diets, alarm clocks, and dogs; the latter he considers a form of life lower in the order of species than rocks. He spends a great amount of time verbally and physically beating up on Odie (whom he calls Bonebreath), the mindless mutt that shares his owner's house.

Everything in *Garfield* is distilled to the lowest common denominator. The art is very simple, drawn with bold, sure lines and with very little to clutter or distract either in dialogue balloons or backgrounds. Each strip has three equal squares, the center one left open. The characters stand out in *Garfield,* as do some of the star's quotable utterances, likely to find their way onto merchandisable objects. Among some of Garfield's more memorable sayings are: "Cute rots the intellect," "A stomach is a terrible thing to waste," "Show me a good mouser and I'll show you a cat with bad breath," or "Life's like a good bath; feels good while you're in it but the longer you stay the more wrinkled you get." Davis concentrates on his characters' expressions, especially through their eyes, which he believes tell it all. In a 1978 *Cartoonist PROfiles* interview, he said, "I start drawing with the eyeballs of all the characters. Then I fill the head in around the eyes and the body comes last."

Because *Garfield* is an international character, Davis stays away from topical themes and political comment, going so far as to avoid the use of seasons, holidays, rhyming gags, plays on words, or colloquialisms. His choice of an animal, rather than a human, for the main character has given him much more latitude with humor. As a cat, Gar-field is not black, white, male, female, young, or old, and thus can say and do much more than a race/gender/age-specific character.

Davis, who grew up on a farm surrounded by many cats, avoided copying real-life cats. Instead, he says (as related in a September 1986 *Cartoonist PROfiles* interview), "I took the characteristics of a cat and incorporated them into a form, rather than take the physical attributes of a real cat and try to resolve them into a cartoon character. Over the years he's become more the cartoon version of a cat than a real cat, in that there's been a Darwinian evolution of his features to better facilitate the gags." Thus, he has become a real cat that lies in the sunbeam, knocks things over, and hates dogs, but a caricature of a cat with human desires and, by the way, an opposable thumb that allows him to drink coffee in the morning.

The tremendous success of *Garfield* is attributable to its ability to tap into those things that perturb us, to its simplicity in style and universality in appeal, and to its distinctive, almost formulaic, approach. Davis has said that in a given week, he is likely to go for: one or two big laughs, sight gags usually depending entirely on the visual; one strip designed to provoke thinking; and a couple with "nice thoughts" that make some broad statement on life or perhaps a quotable quote suitable to be displayed on the wall.

These characteristics have made Garfield one of the most financially lucrative and multimedia-visible characters of all time—the winner of Emmys, the star of at least a half-dozen TV primetime specials and Saturday morning series, and the subject of many bestselling books.

J.A.L.

GASOLINE ALLEY
1918–present

Of all the veteran story strips distributed by Tribune Media Services (*Dick Tracy, Winnie Winkle, Annie,* and *Brenda Starr*), the most popular today is *Gasoline Alley*, written and drawn by Jim Scancarelli. That *Gasoline Alley* celebrated its seventy-fifth anniversary on November 23, 1993, makes this accomplishment all the more impressive. Jim Scancarelli has the unique distinction of being the only cartoonist to have worked on two major syndicated comic strips while they celebrated their seventy-fifth birthdays. Several years ago he was assistant to George Breisacher on the now defunct *Mutt and Jeff* during its three-quarter-century year, 1982.

The late Dik Browne, creator of *Hagar the Horrible,* believed all the truly great comic strips were family strips. If this is so, *Gasoline Alley* is the quintessential family strip, multigenerational and the embodiment of basic American values.

Back in 1918, cartoonist Frank O. King drew a Sunday feature for the *Chicago Tribune* called *Rectangle*. The human condition was cartooned in sections labeled "Pet Peeves," "AWOL, Absent without Leave," or "It Isn't the Cost, It's the Upkeep."

Gasoline Alley (F. King), © 1926 Chicago Tribune

On Sunday, November 24, 1918, the bottom quadrant of *Rectangle* featured Walt Wallet and his neighbors Bill, Doc, and Avery repairing their jalopies in the alley behind where they lived. The quadrant was titled "Sunday Morning in Gasoline Alley." King in this series successfully blended the humor of small-town America using his own hometown, Tomah, Wisconsin, and the country's love of the automobile. On August 24, 1919, *Gasoline Alley* became a full fledged seven-day-a-week syndicated comic strip.

In 1921, legendary *New York Daily News* publisher Captain Joseph Medill Patterson decided *Gasoline Alley* could gain readership if it had something to appeal to women. Patterson was the cousin and partner of Robert McCormick, publisher of the *Chicago Tribune*. His suggestion was that a baby be added to the strip.

Frank King decided the only logical way to do this was to have a foundling left on the doorstep of chubby bachelor Walt Wallet. This happened on Valentine's Day 1921. The baby was named Skeezix, slang for a mischievous child and a cowboy term for a motherless calf. *Gasoline Alley* now had its permanent direction and Skeezix proved an immediate merchandising marvel as the public took him into their hearts.

Unlike other cartoonists, King decided to let his characters age, albeit in comic-strip time. The strip functioned around the everyday trials and tribulations of small-town U.S.A. In time *Gasoline Alley* became the name of the fictional town the Wallet family lived in, not just the family's auto-garage business.

Millions of readers watched Walt Wallet's romance and marriage to Phyliss Blossom on June 24, 1926. Their son Corky was born in 1928 and they adopted Judy, a foundling, in 1935. This gave cartoonist King a family with three kids to work with in his stories. Under King's tenure on *Gasoline*

Alley the strip focused on Skeezix's coming-of-age saga. He had trouble with math and had fights in school. Puppy love and Latin gave him fits in high school, where he fell in love with his future wife, Nina Clock. (Having fun with names is a hallmark of *Gasoline Alley*; Nina Clock, as in nine o'clock, is the daughter of Seth Thomas Clock and has an aunt named Ada Clock.)

Skeezix and Nina married on June 28, 1944, while he was in the army. Having graduated high school just before World War II, Skeezix's wartime experiences filled the continuity from 1942 to 1945. However, unlike the guns-ablazing heroics of many comic strips of that period, true to its formula of success, *Gasoline Alley* focused on the everyday human and humorous side of being a G.I. in World War II. As would be expected, Skeezix's first son, Chipper Wallet, born in 1945, served in the Vietnam War.

The Wallet family is a large, extended one. Possibly that's a reason for the strip's continued success. For each age group of readers, there is someone in the strip to identify with.

While King's artwork on the daily strip was competent but bland, he could explode into amazing creativity on his Sunday page: Skeezix might have a dream sequence worthy of *Little Nemo*, or an aerial view of Gasoline Alley might be depicted. An annual event, continued by Jim Scancarelli, has been the fall walk though the woods by Walt and Skeezix, accompanied by swirling falling leaves and bright autumnal colors.

Bill Perry assisted Carl Ed on *Harold Teen* and began assisting Frank King on *Gasoline Alley* about 1925. In 1951, Perry took over the title's Sunday page as a stand-alone gag page. He retired from *Gasoline Alley* in 1976 but during his tenure the Sunday page never reached the heights it did with King or with those who followed him, Dick Moores and Jim Scancarelli.

Dick Moores joined the *Gasoline Alley* team in 1956. He had been an early assistant of Chester Gould on *Dick Tracy*, created his own strip, *Jim Hardy*, and from 1942 until he went to work for Frank King, worked for Walt Disney Studios. By 1960, Moores had almost completely taken over the writing and drawing chores of the daily *Gasoline Alley*. King went into semiretirement until his death in 1969. Moores's formula was to move the story along at a specific rhythm, develop the characters, and then add humor at the end.

When Bill Perry retired in 1976, Moores hired Bob Zschiesche to do the *Gasoline Alley* Sunday page, which he did until 1979. Zschiesche had previously assisted on *Gasoline Alley* between 1950 and 1963. In 1977, Moores added Jim Scancarelli to the creative team.

Under Dick Moores's leadership, *Gasoline Alley* flourished. Not only was his artwork exceptionally well designed, but he was extremely creative in his crosshatching and use of perspective. He also brought new characters to the forefront of the strip, such as the junkmen Rufus and Joel, and the lovely mayor of Gasoline Alley, Miss Melba, who forever has trouble keeping her dress from falling off her shoulders. While Moores's style was reminiscent of King's, it gave the strip a much more modern look. It was graphically exciting.

At Moores's death in 1986, *Gasoline Alley* was inherited by the very capable and creative Jim Scancarelli. In 1988, Scancarelli reached out to his readers with a story in which Walt Wallet had copies printed of the Wallet Family Tree. In the comic strip, Walt offered to send one to anybody who mailed in a self-addressed stamped envelope. A stunned Scancarelli sent out almost a hundred thousand family trees, all printed at his own expense.

Scancarelli has continued to keep *Gasoline Alley* contemporary. In 1991, the Gasoline Alley Garage was turned over by owner Skeezix to his daughter Clovia to manage when it became obvious she'd do a better job than the men available. Chipper Wallet found his wife through a computer-dating service. One of the characters is married to an Asian woman. Every effort is made to include minorities in the mosaic of everyday American life that *Gasoline Alley* portrays.

However, the Wallets are a large, loving, church-going family, definitely not dysfunctional, and Sunday pages coinciding with national holidays are often built around patriotic themes. Because of this, despite some of the prettiest artwork in semistraight humorous cartooning, *Gasoline Alley* seems to have rubbed some Generation X editors the wrong way. The classic example was in 1993, when the *Chicago Tribune*'s editors totally ignored a huge fan outcry when it dropped *Gasoline Alley*, which had been part of the fabric of that newspaper for generations.

For cartoonist Scancarelli, *Gasoline Alley* is a labor of love. His Sunday pages, which stand alone from the daily continuity, continue to experiment and push the limits of what one can do in syndicated cartooning. His artwork continues the improvements begun by Dick Moores.

Gasoline Alley is a part of American pop culture, overdue for a television sitcom and serious merchandising. It is the best that family values stands for. When Beavis and Butthead are deservedly in the trash heap of failed faddish comic-strip characters, the Wallet family will be just rolling along as usual.

B.C., Jr.

GEECH
1982–present

After a successful career as an editorial cartoonist for the *Wichita* [Kansas] *Eagle*, Jerry Bittle created *Geech* on July 19, 1982. The comic strip takes place in rural Grimace, Texas, and is peopled with a modest cast of typical small-town folks, each with his or her own set of recognized idiosyncrasies, qualities, and defects, who have known each other forever. Their world is bounded by a few select locales: bar, garage, women's store, barbershop, beauty parlor, movie theater, church, and even a gym-equipment store.

There is Fester (nicknamed Rabbit), the self-acknowledged antisocial—and divorced, of course—bar owner, so nasty that his mother will not give him her unlisted phone number. His black bartender is constantly trying to spruce up the place, or at least rid it of rats and roaches, over Fester's strenuous objections. Only the mild-mannered minister still insists on finding some semblance of decency in his heart, but even he has often had trouble. Another pair of dissatisfied people are Nadine, the blonde, overweight hairdresser, and her friend, Ruby, the red-haired waitress. Both in their fifties, with hairdos from the fifties to match, they are looking for an elusive Mr. Right at the bar, as they go through life eating too much junk food (with a giant tub of oversalted and underbuttered popcorn, "you get a free refill") and watching too many bad movies.

Fortunately, Vera and Artie Beemer, who have just celebrated their tenth anniversary, seem to be quite content, although he is at times too hyper for his all-too-perspicacious wife. This nervousness may be due in part to his diet and exercise, his increasing baldness, or his complete inability to put toys together for their two-year-old son, Jake (himself a precocious observer of his dad's shortcomings).

The two stars of the strip are definitely Merle and Geech, the unlikely hero. Merle is a garage proprietor of questionable competence and honesty: "Well, it took awhile, but we finally found what was wrong with your car. It was out of gas," he says, then adding the bad news: "We overhauled the engine first." His helper, a short, cowboy-hat-wearing fellow, is completely incompetent and, furthermore, does not run on all six cylinders—as when he questions the premise of a joke about two frogs walking into a bar and suggests instead that "they might *hop* into a bar..." Every so often, however, he has flashes of insight, preemptively telling his boss: "While you were gone...I didn't do anything and I didn't touch anything! I just sat right there on that stool and minded my own business!—It's my alibi."

Bittle's humor derives from well-observed everyday situations and true-to-life characters as well as an unencumbered caricatural graphic style. The strip is distributed by Universal Press Syndicate to over 150 daily newspapers and has been reprinted in paperback collections.

P.H.

GENE AUTRY
1940–1942, 1952–1955

Gene Autry, the first singing cowboy of the movie screen, had owed his success to an incredible western-cum-science-fiction movie serial entitled *Phantom Empire*, the first (and only) singing western set twenty-five-thousand feet underground. A shrewd businessman, Autry started merchandising himself, and one of his lesser efforts in the field was *Gene Autry Rides!*, which came out as a Sunday comics feature in the spring of 1940, distributed by Autry's own organization.

Written by Hollywood screenwriter Gerald Geraghty and drawn by Till Goodan, a cowboy turned cartoonist, *Gene Autry Rides!* was a laughable enterprise that seemed doomed from the start. Goodan's graphic style was stiff and mannered, and Geraghty's prose was at times unintelligible. The first story was a loose adaptation of *Phantom Empire* and had Autry shuttling maniacally back and forth between his ranch and the underground kingdom of Murania. More alarms and excursions followed as Autry, his elderly sidekick, Frosty, and his horse, Champion, rode the range. The hero rescued ranchers threatened with foreclosure, mine owners stalked by foreign agents, not to mention an assorted bevy of damsels in distress. Autry's screen popular-

ity did not rub off on the strip (of course, his main asset—his singing—was sorely missing), and Gene Autry stopped riding in the comic pages at the end of 1942, after Autry had gone to war.

Autry's renewed popularity on television in the early 1950s led to the release of a second newspaper feature about the singing cowboy, titled simply *Gene Autry*. This time the actor left the distribution in the hands of a professional, if second-string, syndicate, General Features, and only conserved copyright for himself. A daily strip started appearing on September 8, 1952, with a Sunday page following on April 26, 1953. The feature was purportedly written by Autry himself, and drawn by Bert Laws, assisted by Tom Cooke. The result was a tighter, pleasantly illustrated, and thoroughly conventional horse opera aimed at a juvenile public. After a promising start, the strip began to falter due to the mounting attacks against violent comics, including westerns. In 1954 Mel Keefer was brought in, but he could not stem the tide, and Gene Autry's second coming ended in 1955.

M.H.

GIRLS
See BOOTS AND HER BUDDIES

THE GIRLS IN APARTMENT 3-G
See APARTMENT 3-G

GORDO
1941–1985

Gus Arriola started *Gordo* for United Feature Syndicate on November 24, 1941, as a daily strip, but had to interrupt it less than a year later, on October 28, 1942, after being drafted into the air force. He later managed to send in, from the animation unit in which he was serving, a weekly *Gordo* page that United Feature started running on May 2, 1943. Finally, upon his discharge from the service, he resumed the daily as well, on June 24, 1946.

After this bumpy beginning, *Gordo* established itself as one of the more original features of the immediate postwar era. Gordo ("Fatso" in English) Lopez was a Mexican hombre with a large stomach, a big mustache, and a huge sombrero, who bore a marked resemblance to movie actor Leo Carrillo. Initially a dirt farmer in the small locality of Del Monte, he turned to the more lucrative profession of tourist-bus operator at the wheel of his rickety wagon, *El Cometa Halley*. A confirmed bachelor, living alone with his pets, Gordo was for decades the object of the wealthy Widow Gonzales's amorous pursuit. In order to get him to the altar the widow resorted to the services of a witch doctor, a hypnotist, and two local strongmen, even using a carnivorous plant (called Widow's Weed), all to no avail. At the same time the widow was relentlessly stalking him, Gordo's housekeeper, the matronly Tehuana Mama, was secretly pining for the portly bachelor. The fact is, Gordo was quite a ladies' man to the end, with an eye out for every local

Gordo (G. Arriola), © 1958 United Feature Syndicate

beauty and any cute American girl who happened to visit Del Monte.

With all the temptations before him, the paunchy Mexican preferred the pleasures of bachelorhood to the bliss of matrimony. He would frequently drop in on Pelon's tequila parlor, where he would hold forth with his cronies, chief among them the inebriated Poet Garcia and Juan Pablo Jones, the local windbag and raconteur. The dailies enjoyed long continuities, such as Gordo being enmeshed in the nefarious doings of a trio of scheming gringos, his pal Poet Garcia finally getting hitched to a visiting American tourist, and his twelve-year-old nephew, Pepito, discovering a putative Toltec stone head in the garden. And when things got too quiet around town, Little Coronado could always be counted on to enliven the somnolent scene with his infamous "bog of treeks."

The Sundays, especially in later years, were most often given over to simple, weekly gags, in pages attractively designed and embellished with decorative motifs. These Arriola frequently signed with punning pseudonyms such as "E. Z. Mark," "Fuller Dickens," or "T. Doff," to fit the mood of the piece. The animals, who formed part of the background in the dailies, came to the fore in the Sundays. Gordo's cat, the all-white Poosy Gato, indulged his antics there, from sleeping atop a telephone pole to banging on garbage cans in accompaniment to the local band. The cat could also be found engaged in deep conversations with the other animals in the strip, Popo the rooster, Señor Dog, Señor Pig, not to mention the artistically gifted spider Bug Rogers, weaver of the most intricate webs in all of the animal kingdom.

In later years *Gordo* declined in both originality and circulation. The Sunday page came to an end on February 24, 1985, while the dailies concluded on March 2, with Gordo finally wedding the long-waiting Tehuana Mama and bidding a fond *hasta la vista* to his readers.

M.H.

GORDON FIFE
1935–1941

Gordon Fife and the Boy King* was created for the *Brooklyn Eagle*'s Watkins Syndicate on October 7, 1935; also known as *Gordon Soldier of Fortune*, it was later commonly referred to by the simple title *Gordon Fife*. The writer was Bob Moore and the artist Jim Hales, who was replaced on December 28, 1936, by Carl Pfeufer, the titular artist on the syndicate's *Don Dixon*.

The action most often took place in the mythical central European kingdom of Kovnia, whose sovereign was the underage Nicholas (known as Nicki, the boy king of the early title). Because of his status as a minor, the actual ruler was the regent, his sister, the lovely Princess Caroline. After Gordon Fife, a dashing American adventurer, helped smash a plot against the throne, the princess, in best comic-strip tradition, fell in love with him.

Many of the adventures revolved around the schemes being endlessly hatched by Prince Karl, the devious monarch of neighboring Livonia, often in collusion with the Markala, a dreaded secret organization. Gordon, with the help of his Hindu manservant Ali and with the succor of Colonel Lorenz, head of Kovnia's intelligence service, would no less endlessly thwart the designs of his enemies and of the enemies of the throne.

The American adventurer often ventured far away from his usual base of operations, searching for a pharaoh's treasure in Egyptian sands, pursuing a high-living spy through Parisian nightspots, or exposing international conspirators in the shadow of Manhattan's skyscrapers. From 1940 on, Gordon would more and more frequently become embroiled in secret missions against the Axis powers, on assignment from the British Intelligence Service.

Hales drew Gordon in a relaxed, pleasant style, while Pfeufer's line was stronger, more incisive. His vigorous brushwork was perhaps displayed to even better advantage in the Sunday page, which came to supplement the daily strip (with separate continuities) on August 11, 1940. Both Sundays and dailies came to a premature end in July 1941.

M.H.

GRANDMA
1947–1969

Remarkable as a kid strip that essentially focused on an elderly heroine, *Grandma* had a somewhat old-fashioned look from its first appearance. Created by veteran *Chicago Tribune* editorial cartoonist Charles Harris Kuhn for the Richard Feature Service of Indianapolis, Indiana, it made its first appearance in 1947 but did not enjoy wide national circulation until Kuhn transferred the strip to King Features Syndicate a year and a half later. King distributed the daily strip from June 28, 1948, and a Sunday feature added on November 20, 1949, until both were regretfully retired on June 23, 1969.

An aged tomboy, Grandma was an anomalous figure to lead a boys' gang, but she filled that slightly subversive role with extraordinary gusto. Unfailingly wearing a long black dress with lace at the collar, a white apron, a cameo brooch, high-button shoes, and wire-rimmed spectacles, she was an archetypal sweet little old lady, endlessly cleaning her spotless house and baking cookies for the local kids. Nevertheless, she was never preachy and seldom even set a good example. The ideal indulgent grandparent, she supported her young friends when they got into mischief and was often involved in it herself. A typical story showed her hitting the baseball that breaks a neighbor's window and then hiding the team in her own home. Yet hoydenish as her behavior was, she was at heart the prim lady she appeared; when she had a chance, in a 1947 Sunday strip, she secretly swept out the gang's clubhouse, hung curtains on its windows, put up pictures, and set out vases of flowers, and was then dismayed to learn that the kids thought someone had made the place look like "a sissies' club room," and so they had "rearranged th' pictures, curtains, flowers an' vases out on th' trash pile!"

Grandma was drawn in an attractive, simple style, its uncluttered composition maintaining a pleasant distribution of clean line and solid planes of black with no shading or unnecessary detail. Much like its central figure, it had the look and the spirit of the idealized grandparent of the last century, and for over two decades it held its own in the marketplace against the growing tide of grimmer and more realistic depictions of youthful behavior and generational differences.

D.W.

Grandma (C. Kuhn), © 1965 King Features Syndicate

GRIN AND BEAR IT
1932–present

After a short stint as a sports cartoonist for the old *Chicago Daily Times* in the early 1930s, George Lichtenstein, better known as Lichty, created *Grin and Bear It* in March 1932. When Lichty retired at the end of 1974 (he died on July 18, 1983), it was taken over by Fred Wagner and drawn very much in the same loose, sketchy style. The gag series satirizes not only American mores and foibles but also greedy captains of industry, hopeful warmongering generals constantly in touch with the alert rooms at NORAD, and especially self-important politicians. Lichty's favorite was one Senator Snort, a "jewel in the national diadem" (according to a campaign poster) and an honorary member of the Guild of Guff Shooters; he once declared at a press conference: "I don't mind being quoted out of context, boys, since the context is usually the worst part of my speeches!"

The average man, too, has been a fit subject for ridicule, as have been love, death, and taxes. The institution of marriage has fared no better, always seeming to oppose a domineering, shrewish wife to a meek, emasculated husband.

Whether he commented on politics or the status of the modern family—from overeducated, intellectual sons, more interested in reading Kafka and the existentialists than in looking for a job, to parents worried over their liberated teenage daughters—Lichty was at heart a moralist concerned with outrageous behavior; and with this viewpoint Fred Wagner completely agrees. Successfully continuing his predecessor's series, Wagner attacks the same stupidities and types, since nothing has changed in the last twenty-odd years: "Part of Colin Powell's journey through America was in a pair of boots just like this!" asserts a salesman in an army-surplus store. Another example shows a TV repairman declaring to his customer, "Sometimes it doesn't pay to fix 'em," while an ad for some windbag politician blares out of the set.

Lichty's *Grin and Bear It* was a four-time winner of the National Cartoonists Society award for Best Newspaper Panel. It is now distributed by North America Syndicate.

M.B.C.

THE GUMPS
1917–1959

Although Martin Sheridan in *Comics and Their Creators* classified *The Gumps* as a married strip, it was always much more than that. *Chicago Tribune* editor Joseph Medill Patterson did conceive of it as a domestic strip about a lower-middle-class family with whom his newspaper readers (many of them working-class themselves) could identify. Accordingly, he called in cartoonist Sidney Smith, who was then doing *Old Doc Yak* for the *Tribune,* and handed him the assignment. On February 12, 1917, *The Gumps* made its appearance in daily-strip form in the pages of the *Tribune;* it was soon picked up for national distribution by the newly created Tribune-News Syndicate.

Under close supervision by Patterson, who always regarded *The Gumps* as his own brainchild, the dailies,

The Gumps (S. Smith), 1917

which starred the self-important Andy Gump, his long-suffering wife Minerva (Min), and their bright young son Chester, were drawn by Smith in a black, ungainly style. They often revolved around money concerns and financial dealings: thus Andy would lose his life savings in a stock swindle (but would catch up with the crooks eventually), or his billionaire Uncle Bim would be sued for breach of promise by a scheming widow. There was a lot of talk in these early dailies (perhaps due to Patterson's soapbox proclivities), and the action proceeded only in spurts.

In addition to the bald, toothless, and chinless Andy, "who invented the flower pot," and "introduced the polka-dot tie in this country," his no-nonsense spouse, Min, "the brain of the family," and little Chester, a precocious mischief-maker "whose pet stunt is turning in false alarms in zero nights to see the fire engines go by," there was Tilda, the family maid whose cooking was as awful as her looks. A little later, arriving from Australia, where he had made his fortune, there descended Uncle Benjamin ("Bim") Gump, who had trouble keeping his money, since his gullibility led him to invest in every worthless enterprise that came along. The secondary characters were all stock figures, from the callous Henry Ausstinn, whose heart was so black he rejoiced at his wife's suicide, to Mary Gold, the young, innocent maiden whom Ausstinn planned to marry.

The Gumps was among the first strips to introduce long-running continuities. In 1922 Andy ran for Congress on the promise of "100 percent for the people," and under the slogan, "He wears no man's collar." This allowed Patterson to mouth some of his pet peeves, such as the tariff, the worthlessness of both political parties, and the perverseness of the Red Menace. In 1934 Uncle Bim married a young and dizzy blonde who took him for all he had, giving Patterson an occasion to rail against marriage between members of different social classes.

On June 29, 1919, a weekly feature was introduced, and the Sunday pages, in contrast to the dailies, were bright and airy. They were often given over to young Chester, who went adventuring to faraway Pacific isles, the western desert, and other such exotic places. The best of the *Gumps*

weekly adventures occurred in the mid-1920s, when Chester and his aphoristic Chinese companion Ching Chow went in search of the fabled City of Gold. An old sailor, predictably named Sam Salt, occasionally dropped in on the proceedings, and Uncle Bim made cameo appearances as a kind of *deus ex machina*. Self-contained gag pages, in which Chester reverted to the role of high-spirited schoolboy, alternated with these more robust narratives.

In addition to Patterson, many ghosts took turns in writing story lines for *The Gumps*. Blair Walliser, a radio-station executive, helped with the daily continuities, as did Sol Hess, a Chicago jeweler who went on to create his own comic strip, *The Nebbs*, in 1923. Working on the Sundays was Brandon Walsh, who would eventually take the trio made up of boy adventurer, Chinese companion, and veteran sea-dog he had created from Smith and recycle them in his later Ming Foo page. Chester Gould and Harold Gray turned out some of the daily artwork before getting features of their own, while most of the Sundays were drawn by Stanley Link, who gave the page its distinctive flavor and outlook.

The popularity *The Gumps* enjoyed during Smith's tenure is hard to fathom today. What was impressive about it was not the debauch of merchandising the strip unleashed (a fact not uncommon even nowadays) but the genuine public involvement in the characters. The Minneapolis Board of Trade, for example, suspended its operations for several minutes in 1923 to allow the brokers to find out whether Uncle Bim had been conned into marriage with the widow Zander; and the death of Mary Gold in May 1929 caused thousands to mourn her passing like that of a real person. After Smith was killed in a car accident in October 1935, his obit in the *New York Times* (which then as now ran no comics in its pages) grew positively rhapsodic. "The death of Sidney Smith, creator of Andy Gump, and Min, and Uncle Bim, will be felt by literally millions of Americans," it ran. "Andy...was better known and more beloved to millions than the real characters that came and went on the front page."

Gus Edson, a cartoonist of dubious abilities, was picked

to succeed Smith. His style was even cruder than his predecessor's, but he had a certain knack for tear-jerking narratives. At any rate, the success of *The Gumps* continued almost unabated through the 1930s and during the war years. At war's end the strip started to decline precipitously in readership and circulation; through sheer determination Edson managed to carry the feature for a further decade and a half, only ending it on October 17, 1959.

M.H.

GUS AND GUSSIE
1925–1930

Show-business strips were flourishing in the 1920s, so it is no surprise that the powers-that-be at King Features would want one of their own. They asked Jack Lait, who for years had been writing a showbiz column about the doings of a small-time thespian named Gus, to come up with a strip based on his original character. The resulting daily feature, called *Gus and Gussie,* appeared in March 1925, with the drawing by Paul Fung.

The pint-sized, tow-headed Gus Donnerwetter was an aspiring Broadway comedian, while the dark-haired, leggy Gussie Abadab dreamed of becoming a Hollywood actress. The two maintained a platonic relationship that was fueled by their mutually sustaining ambitions. Together they went through all the familiar smiling-through-tears routines in the course of their up-and-down experiences in vaudeville and in cabaret, on stage and on screen, never making it to the big time, and never losing their faith. There was a bittersweet tinge to their tribulations, made of slight disappointments and small triumphs, a kind of gray overtone that didn't go down well with a public used to issues etched in black and white. A strip of unassuming qualities—charm, light-heartedness, jollity—*Gus and Gussie* didn't make it much past the decade: by 1930 it was gone. Lait went back to newspapering, and Fung went on to draw *Dumb Dora,* which Chic Young had just abandoned to create *Blondie.*

M.H.

HAGAR THE HORRIBLE
1973–present

One day in the early 1970s, Dik Browne announced to his family that he was retiring to his basement drawing board, not to emerge until he had a new comic strip. It did not take long for him to surface with what became one of the fastest growing and most popular strips of all time, *Hagar the Horrible.*

In his first appearance on February 5, 1973, Hagar, backed up by a gang of his Viking marauders, is dumbfounded as he is informed by the guard of the castle they are about to sack that it is the wrong address. It is the first of many disappointments Hagar must adjust to as the world around him changes. When other Vikings are blessed with terrors for sons, Hagar gets Hamlet, a Danish pastry, neat and studious, who has the "disgusting habit" of reading and an unheard of desire to be the first Viking dentist. As he badmouths and threatens menacing hordes armed to the teeth with axes, catapults, and battering rams, unbeknownst to him his own men have beaten a path back to the ship. Upon his return home from a year of looting and pillaging, his wife Helga never looks up from her cooking as she welcomes him with a loud, "Wipe your feet!"

Browne fashioned Hagar as a dichotomized individual, a henpecked, arrow-riddled warrior who refuses to go fighting without his teddy bear; a normally hapless fellow who occasionally gets in his own licks or comes up with a clever line. He is both capable of replying to a clerk that his middle name is "The" and remarking to his dog that he wishes people had tails so "we could tell when they're really happy." Browne called his star character "an underachieving vandal with a pacifist streak."

The secrets to the success of *Hagar the Horrible* lay in Browne's abilities to edit out nonessential elements, to create instantly and universally recognizable characters, to personalize the strip with family members and friends as models, and to vary the number, size, and aesthetics of panels. Some of Browne's reasoning for simplifying *Hagar* had to do with his own eyesight problems (he wanted a strip that was easily seen and read) and his family's background in show business (he learned early on to play to the balcony and not the boxes). His choice of a Viking as the lead character related to his belief that readers liked these terrors of the North who got away with the most atrocious behavior, and to the fact that Hagar matched Browne's own personality. In fact, the strip's title derives from the affectionate name Browne's children had given him years before its birth.

Although he had said the ideal number of characters for a strip is two, Browne had a whole cast of regulars and walkons, each exemplifying his keen sense of the comic. Besides Helga and Hamlet, other regulars were Honi, Hagar's daughter, still unmarried at sixteen; Snerd, his untrainable dog, who is about as disheveled as its master; Lucky Eddie, his dimwitted assistant, who is so unlucky that he once was knocked unconscious by a rainbow; Kvack, Helga's neat and clean duck companion; Lute, the aimlessly wandering troubadour who courts Honi; Hernia, the tough tomboy who laid claim to Hamlet, even sewing her name in all of his clothes; Dr. Zook, the quack medicine man who diagnoses Hagar as having the weekend plague; and Koyer, the

Hagar the Horrible (D. Browne), © 1977 King Features Syndicate

eloquent talking lawyer who "malaprops" legalese with whatever comes to mind (such as battery au gratin).

A *Hagar* strip under Dik Browne could consist of anywhere from one to four panels, be full or sparing of details, and differ widely in style. One day, the strip might be almost all white with perhaps one small figure and no backgrounds; on other days, the panels would be dominated by solid blacks, or a mixture of shading and solids. Browne's clever ways to "sell giggles"' (his term) were also applied to the few props he used, such as the animated Viking ship or a square (as opposed to globe) of the world mounted on a pedestal, and to the lettering. He used appropriate type fonts to express feelings such as pomposity or loyalty, a la Walt Kelly. In one strip, an evil-looking goon warns Lucky Eddie that he had better watch what he says if he wants to stay in one piece. In the next panel, Browne has dotted lines connecting Eddie's eyes to the speech balloon as he says, "I sure will."

A cartoon character in real life, Browne was known for the funny stories told about him and for his intellect. He was a favorite among his colleagues, who recognized his genius by voting him many awards, including an unprecedented two Reubens for two different strips *(Hagar* and *Hi and Lois)*. Calling his family a cottage industry, Browne involved his wife and two sons in the handling of the strips, and when he died in 1989, his son Chris inherited *Hagar.* By that time, more than eighteen hundred newspapers in fifty-eight countries carried the strip.

Chris has stayed true to the basic formula, at the same time exercising his own creativity. He has changed the strip in subtle ways, making Hagar spongier, softer, and less harsh and abrupt, and supplementing the gag-a-day format with week or longer continuity story lines. He has adjusted to the times in other ways. In his father's day, Hagar would be shown climbing a mountain in Tibet to see a wise man, or carrying off a maiden during one of his many raids, or being driven home in a wheelbarrow after a night of falling-

Hairbreadth Harry (C. W. Kahles), 1907

down drunkenness. Chris substituted a Nordic hill of wisdom for the Tibetan mountain, thus saving Hagar the numerous long trips; moderated the drinking scenes because he could not warm up to gags about drunks; and in deference to the women's movement, allowed Hagar to cart off a giant pizza or a French chef, instead of a maiden.

Under Chris Browne, *Hagar the Horrible* has continued to thrive, for he captures well his father's panache for sight gags, simplicity, and character development, while adding his own touches of continuity story lines, new characters (such as Tyrone Troll), and sensitivity.

J.A.L.

HAIRBREADTH HARRY
1906–1940

C. W. Kahles's *Hairbreadth Harry* is not, as some have claimed, the first adventure strip (an adjudication that rests on too many subjective definitions to be conclusive), but it certainly started the trend toward burlesque heroics in the comics. It premiered on October 21, 1906, as a Sunday page in the *Philadelphia Press.*

Initially called *Our Hero's Hairbreadth Escapes,* the series opened on a western scene in which our boy-hero, as he was described, was able through fast thinking and even faster riding to save the life of an innocent prospector wrongly sentenced to death by bringing in the governor's pardon in the nick of time. The first episodes were all self-contained, but after only a few months Kahles developed week-to-week continuities, along with a change of title (to *Hairbreadth Harry, the Boy Hero).*

In March 1907 Hairbreadth Harry (or *Harold Hollingsworth,* to give him his rightful name) met the man who would become his relentless nemesis, the top-hatted, black-coated Rudolph Rassendale. The classic trio of stage melodrama was completed six months later with the entrance of the heroine, Belinda Blinks, bound to a buzz-saw. Termed "the beautiful boilermaker," Belinda was actually a sorry-looking model of womanhood, about a head taller and ten years older than her rescuer. Harry, however, kept growing in both age and size with each passing year, and before long he was the same age as Belinda, who on her part had undergone a thorough beauty treatment to make her at least close to the "creature of dazzling loveliness" she was supposed to be. In the course of the years Harry encountered countless perils (such as marauding Indians, forest fires, and packs of wild animals), saved Belinda from the clutches of the fiendish Rudolph (who coveted the heroine for his bride) numberless times, and crisscrossed the globe in all directions, but with a marked predilection for the wide western spaces. One such 1907 adventure involved a gold mine, claim jumping, an ambush, and chicanery, as well as several gunfights and a landslide that put the hero and his sweetheart out of the reach of their pursuers. While there were suspense and action in the narratives, there was also a great deal of facetiousness and punning. In another 1907 episode, for instance, dealing with a race to the pole, Harry, pursued by a polar bear, climbed up a pole marked "'the one and only real North Pole," thereby winning the contest.

The Hall Room Boys (H. A. McGill), 1911

The adventures of Harry and Belinda (and Rudolph) briefly ended in 1915, but *Hairbreadth Harry* was revived the next year by the McClure Syndicate; and the trio again resumed their endless chase. In 1923 distribution of the feature was picked up by the Philadelphia Ledger Syndicate, which added a daily strip to the Sunday pages; Kahles drew both until his death in 1931. F. O. Alexander then took over the title, later getting Harry married to Belinda, who in the fullness of time presented him with a son, Harry, Jr. All these changes could not keep the strip from going down in circulation in the 1930s, under the weight of increased competition from more sophisticated adventure features. Alexander quit early in 1939, and *Hairbeadth Harry* limped along for a while longer under Jimmy Thompson's pen. The Sundays came to a close in August 1939, while the dailies ended in January of the following year.

On the strength of *Hairbreadth Harry* alone, Kahles should be given the recognition he deserves as the artist who established suspense in the comic strip as a sustained narrative device.

M.H.

THE HALL ROOM BOYS
1906–1923

H. A. (Harold Arthur) McGill is among the many unsung cartoonists who in the early decades of the twentieth century helped establish the comics form. The creator of such early girl strips as *Cinderella Peggy* and *Hazel the Heart-Breaker*, he is only remembered today for *The Hall Room Boys*, a strip of unwonted cynicism for its time. Appearing at first twice or thrice weekly in the pages of the *New York American*, starting in 1906, it later moved to the *Evening Journal*, before turning into a full-fledged Sunday feature in the *New York Herald* (as *Percy and Ferdie*).

Percy and Ferdie, "the Hall Room Boys," so named because they liked to hold forth in the hall room of Mrs. Pruyn's boarding-house, in which they were residents, were social climbers of a familiar type. They were pretenders whose performance did not live up to their pretense: when they tried to crash society parties they were thrown out by butlers, when they attempted to pass themselves off as visiting nobility they were put down by debutantes, and when they played the role of stage-door Johnnies they were waved away by doormen.

The two titular antiheroes had one eye solidly fixed on the fast buck and the other just as determinedly riveted on any skirt in sight. Whether they dated the fairest flower in the boarding-house, or cottoned up to a superior's homely daughter in order to win the father's favor, it was never a labor of love for the pair. No sentiment there, only a yearning for the elementals of social life: cold cash and warm flesh. It is therefore no wonder that the double-entendres in this strip were more blatant than in any other of the early comic features.

Later commentators have been hard on *The Hall Room Boys.* "McGill's picture of our social structure is unique," wrote Coulton Waugh, for one, "in that all the actors in his drama are driven by the same fierce motives, scrambling over each other like soulless puppets, unrelieved by any touch of friendliness, humanity, or even humor." Be that as it may, Percy and Ferdie pursued their nefarious schemes for many years in the papers, despite disappointments and letdowns; their optimism always belied their cynicism, and in this as in so many other traits they were quintessentially American. It is ironic that their joint career came to an end in January 1923, at a time when their type was in its fullest flower.

M.H.

HANS AND FRITZ
See THE CAPTAIN AND THE KIDS

HAP HOPPER
1940–1949

In 1939 newsmen Drew Pearson and Robert Allen, writers of the nationally syndicated "Washington Merry-Go-Round" column, conceived the idea of a newspaper strip dealing with the adventures of a rookie reporter on the capital beat. They enlisted the help of cartoonist Jack Sparling, then living in Washington, and presented their proposal to United Feature, which bought it. *Hap Hopper, Washington Correspondent* accordingly made its appearance in both daily and Sunday formats on January 29, 1940.

As originally conceived, Harold "Hap" Hopper was a bumbling stringer from the sticks, whose naiveness was only matched by his gullibility æ a kind of pencil-pushing Candide. Newspaper editors, however, did not like to see the noble calling of journalism being lampooned, and the authors soon changed Hopper into a whiz of a reporter, savvy and hard-hitting, picking up newspapers left and right in the process. As Sparling later recalled, "After suffering from having a dumb reporter, the strip got off to a flying start."

After a stint in the army at the end of 1940 and into 1941, Hopper reverted to his persona as a news reporter, while working for American counterintelligence on the side. Although credited to Pearson and Allen (and later to Pearson alone), *Hap Hopper* (as it was by then simply called) was actually written by William Laas, an editor at United Fea-

Hap Hopper (J. Sparling), © 1940 United Feature Syndicate

ture, who turned in an adequate job, though he was overly fond of punning names. Hopper's editor, for instance, was named Rushmore News, and the hero's girlfriend went by the moniker Holly Woode, and so forth. In 1942 Laas left the writing chores in the hands of Charles Verral, who involved his reporter hero in wartime intrigue, with continuities often featuring real-life personalities, from President Franklin Roosevelt to FBI director J. Edgar Hoover.

In 1943 Sparling left to create his own strip, *Claire Voyant,* and after a period of trial and error, Al Plastino was ultimately given the job of illustrating the strip (his signature first appeared on January 1, 1945). With the return of peace later that year, Hopper went back to the humdrum occupation of reporting on the national scene. In order to revive interest in the strip, Verral and Plastino came up with some suspenseful continuities, such as the 1946 episode in which a gang of racketeers threatened to kill Hopper's mother if the reporter came out in print with an exposé of their nefarious activities. The postwar readership decline continued unabated, and in a last-ditch effort to save the feature, a new character was introduced in 1947, a two-fisted private eye in the mold of Mike Hammer, who soon pushed Hopper out of the story line. *Barry Noble,* as the strip was now called in honor of the newcomer, lasted exactly two years, from May 1947 to May 1949.

M.H.

HAPPY HOOLIGAN
1900–1932

Frederick Burr Opper was already a political and magazine cartoonist of high repute when he entered the fledgling field of newspaper comics in the early months of 1900. His first effort for the new medium proved a masterstroke: it was *Happy Hooligan,* which first appeared as *The*

Doings of Happy Hooligan in the pages of W. R. Hearst's Sunday supplement *The American Humorist* on March 26, 1900.

A bedraggled little Irish tramp with a lunar face and a tin can for a hat, Happy was a hapless innocent who fell victim to his generous impulses; his various doings, as his adventures were initially called, were always half-baked attempts at winning sympathy from ungrateful strangers or correcting wrongs that invariably landed him in jail. Despite all these mishaps, Happy remained true to his name and smiled through every misfortune that fate and Opper's imagination could devise. In Happy we can already see the figure of the beaten-down but indomitable "little man" later epitomized in Charlie Chaplin's films; and like Chaplin's tramp, Happy in the end wins the girl, the pert Suzanne whom he courts under the very nose of her disapproving father.

Other characters came to populate the strip: Gloomy Gus, Happy's long-lost brother, whose good luck and lugubrious mien were in sharp contrast to his sibling's unbounded optimism and fathomless misfortune; another brother posing as an English lord, the bespatted and waistcoated Montmorency; his pet dog, Flip; his three young nephews, who could always be counted on to get into every conceivable scrap; and other Happy relatives.

Happy Hooligan soon developed from a collection of weekly gags into a continuing comic saga of epic proportions. As early as 1903 Opper introduced weekly cliff-hanging suspense to his stories, showing his characters dangling from aerostats or captives of Arab slave-traders at the end of an episode, only to be rescued from their predicament the following Sunday. By the end of its first decade Happy's adventures had become more and more extended, often taking the form of genuine picaresque narratives. Happy's luck, however, hardly changed over the years, and disaster always followed on the heels of each successive episode. On one of his round-the-world odysseys, for example, he would inevitably be captured by ravenous cannibals, set upon by ferocious head-hunters, or dragged away by assorted bands of pirates.

Happy's courtship of Suzanne brought new angles to his misfortunes, with his prospective father-in-law seizing upon every conceivable scheme to try and break up the pair. Even after the couple had married in 1916, their honeymoon was often thrown into turmoil by the machinations of jealous rivals, or simply the complications of domestic life. Through it all Happy maintained a cherubic countenance that proved as infuriating to his loved ones as it was disconcerting to his persecutors.

Opper was also in the habit of using some of his other creations from the comic pages to spice things up when the narrative sagged. Thus Happy was paired for a time with Mr. Dubb, a doughty little fellow in a plaid hat in whose competence Happy placed a blind if misguided faith; he later landed on the farm where Maud, the mule with the terrifying kick, held sway, and even met the two punctilious Frenchmen whose names have by now entered the language, Alphonse and Gaston. By the 1920s the narrative had become more and more involved, as the hero and his cohorts limped along helplessly from one ludicrous adventure to the next.

Happy Hooligan proved to be Opper's most enduring creation: his weekly adventures were reprinted in a number of illustrated books, and he was the subject of a series of early animated cartoons in 1917–19. Stylistically, Opper elevated the cartoon "doodle" into a fine art, giving his characters a wealth of facial expressions, with a simple circle and a few chosen lines used to depict emotions ranging from anger to ecstasy and from dejection to triumph. As Coulton Waugh noted in his study *The Comics,* "With this convention Opper carved a career." This career, however, came to an end in August 1932, when age and failing eyesight forced the artist into retirement.

M.H.

Happy Hooligan (F. B. Opper), 1905

HAROLD TEEN
1919-1959

The genesis of *Harold Teen,* one of the earliest comic features dealing with the life and customs of teenagers, was chronicled by its author, Carl Ed, in these terms: "A few months after the Armistice was signed I created a new strip portraying the activities of high-school youngsters, and called it *Seventeen.* I submitted the drawings to Captain Patterson, then coowner of the *Tribune.* "In accordance with syndicate practice (and because the name was identical to that of the famous Booth Tarkington novel), Patterson rechristened it *The Love Life of Harold Teen.* Distributed by the Chicago Tribune–New York News Syndicate, the feature started appearing as a Sunday page on May 4, 1919, and in a daily format in September of that year.

Harold, who as Ed's proposed title indicated, was 17, lived with his parents, the prematurely-aged Thomas ("Pops") and the rotund "Moms," and his kid sister, Josie, in a small midwestern town (modeled on Evanston, Illinois). The early episodes related Harold's hot and fruitless pursuit of Mae Preston, the town's belle (or "queen"). As the 1920s dawned, the strip's title was cut to *Harold Teen,* and the feature acquired the cast of characters that was to endure for the next four decades. The fickle Harold found himself a new, more pliant love interest in the person of a winsome brunette named Lillums Lovewell but this affair was often frustrated by his girlfriend's stern father, Lemuel. Like most teenagers of the time, Harold hung out at the local soda parlor, Pop Jenks's Sugar Bowl, in the company of his buddies, Horace the egghead, the shrimp-sized and contrarily named "Shadow" Smart, and Beezie the punster. *Harold Teen* thrived on the latest college slang, interminably spouted by the juvenile characters, and footnoted for the benefit of the "square" readers at the bottom of each panel (a 1922 strip, for instance, explained that "blaah" meant no good, and "noodle juice" was a synonym for tea). As Thomas Craven observed, "It is a fluid jargon, here today, gone tomorrow, and a little trying on the entrails," but the teenagers of America apparently lapped it all up.

The Roaring Twenties witnessed *Harold Teen*'s heyday. The strip ran in hundreds of newspapers across the country, was adapted to radio, and was made into a 1928 movie by Warner Bros. When the more somber 1930s rolled in, Ed kept current with teenage language and clothes, and brought in new characters, such as the elderly but swinging Aunt Pruny. During World War II the hero found himself working for American intelligence, but the author's talent did not lie with straight adventure, and the idea of Harold Teen as an undercover operative was simply ridiculous. In the late 1940s Harold and his cronies returned to the Sugar Bowl, but the postwar teenage scene had radically changed, and the characters' antics seemed totally out of place. More and more clients dropped the strip in the 1950s, and by the end of the decade it was only running in a handful of newspapers. Ed died in October 1959, and Harold Teen died with him.

Ed's graphic style had, with the help of several assistants, evolved over the decades from aggressively crude to barely adequate to pleasantly cartoony. His strip survives in memory as a nostalgic testament to a more innocent era and an untroubled adolescent world, both long gone.

M.H.

Harold Teen (C. Ed), © 1933 Chicago Tribune

HAWKSHAW THE DETECTIVE
1913-1922, 1931-1952

Having defected from Hearst's *Journal* to Pulitzer's *World* in 1913, Gus Mager created there another delightful Holmesian pastiche in the form of a Sunday page titled *Hawkshaw the Detective,* which started appearing on February 23, 1913.

Mager may have borrowed his detective's name from Tom Taylor's play *The Ticket-of-Leave Man,* but the new feature was otherwise modeled in close imitation of the cartoonist's earlier strip, *Sherlocko the Monk.* Mager kept the same team of clever sleuth and dumb assistant, casting them in human guise as Hawkshaw and the Colonel, and launching them into week-to-week continuing adventures. Their archenemy was the cunning master criminal known as the Professor (an obvious reference to Doyle's Professor Moriarty), whom they relentlessly pursued all over England and across Europe. This first phase came to an abrupt end in August 1922.

In December 1931 Mager was called in to revive *Hawkshaw* as a companion strip to his friend Rudolph Dirks's *The Captain and the Kids,* now distributed by United Feature Syndicate. Because he was doing another strip, *Oliver's Adventures,* at the time for another syndicate, Mager did not sign his name to this new version, which as a nod to the cartoonist's earlier creation, was bylined "Watso." This is the version that is best remembered today,

Hawkshaw the Detective (**G. Mager**), 1918

with its broad burlesquing of dime novels and detective stories and its outrageously far-fetched plots. Alternating with the Professor, a new nemesis was introduced, Galufo "the Demon," characterized by Hawkshaw as "the most dangerous criminal and international spy alive."

Aside from a period extending from May 1932 to December 1933, when he was replaced by Bernard Dibble, Mager drew the adventures of his comic detective until his retirement in 1952. *Hawkshaw,* like its predecessor *Sherlocko,* was more than mere parody: it was a cogent and endlessly imaginative variation upon the Sherlockian theme, and it deserves better than the cursory treatment it has been given in most comic-strip histories.

M.H.

HAZEL
`1969–present`

Like so many other newspaper-comic features, *Hazel* had its origins in the *Saturday Evening Post.* Actually, Ted Key's cartoons about a feisty and sarcastic maid had appeared in the early 1940s in such publications as *This Week* and *Collier's,* but the *Post* signed him to an exclusive contract in 1943, with *Hazel* putting in a weekly appearance that not even Key's induction into the army late in 1943 could interrupt. The panel's popularity was helped in no small measure by a highly successful television series, also called *Hazel,* with Shirley Booth in the title role; written by Key, it ran on NBC in 1961–65 and on CBS in 1965–66.

In 1969 the *Post* folded, but *Hazel* was quickly picked up by King Features for daily syndication.

Hazel still runs the household, comprised of George and Dorothy Baxter and their son, Harold, and adopted daughter, Katie. She keeps them all in check, along with the family dog, Smilie, and cat, Mostly, with an iron fist in a velvet glove, a withering look, and when everything else fails, a finely delivered putdown. The Baxters' guests often come in for their share of barbs, especially when they insist on treating her as mere house help. In her fight for dignity Hazel's most constant allies have proved to be the children and their little friends. Key has kept his one-joke panel fresh by introducing a host of secondary characters and by weaving imaginative twists on the basic situation, six times a week, for more than thirty-five years now.

"Ted Key took another working girl, slightly more mature and infinitely more domineering," Stephen Becker wrote in *Comic Art in America,* "named her Hazel and raised

her to the level of a national symbol." And there she has remained for all these years.

M.H.

THE HEART OF JULIET JONES
`1953–present`

Because King Features wanted to compete with the very successful *Mary Worth,* the syndicate readily agreed to purchase this soap-opera strip. Drawn by Stan Drake, like many other cartoonists an alumnus of the Johnstone & Cushing ad agency, and scripted by Elliot Caplin, Al Capp's younger brother, *The Heart of Juliet Jones* had its auspicious beginning as a daily on March 9, 1953, and as a Sunday feature on May 2 of the following year.

Set in the small town of Devon, of which Juliet Jones had once been mayor, the strip mostly relates the sentimental upsets, pleasures, and joys of the two female leads, although it also sends them on regular adventures. Juliet is a thirty-something, dark-haired classic beauty, always elegantly dressed. An intelligent and sensible career woman, she not only runs her widowed father's house but also tries to be a stabilizing influence on Eve, her younger sister.

The well-named Eve, on the other hand, is a pretty, vivacious blonde in her early twenties whose behavior at times is quite impulsive, in contrast to Juliet's proper demeanor. Of course, the most striking difference between the two sisters focuses on the way in which each thinks of romantic love. Whereas the mature Juliet falls in love from a mutual respect based on character, and the lovers in her life have been mainly professional men, secure and established, the flighty Eve is likely to become too easily entangled. Furthermore, since she believes in love at first sight ("It can happen as easily after one date as it can after seven years of courtship"), she often gets involved with the wrong man, much to the dismay of sister and father alike.

The head of the family is Howard Jones ("Pop" or "Pops"), a retired lumber executive who views the behavior of his two daughters with tolerance and understanding. Sometimes willing to accept Juliet's superintendence with amusement, sometimes checking Eve's too daring nature, he exudes affection and tenderness toward his dissimilar but equally lovable children, dispensing fatherly advice to both.

While Juliet has had many romances with eligible bachelors and has even been engaged a few times, she finally married the man of her dreams in a big church wedding on the

October 18, 1970, Sunday page. Then, with her husband, Owen Cantrell, a criminal lawyer, she moved to a city resembling New York, thus leaving the still unattached Eve to handle the love angle and center stage by herself. Unable to sustain Eve as the sole support of the strip, however, the authors eventually had Cantrell murdered, which allowed Juliet to go home to her father. Together the two women could then continue to solve as many thorny problems for others as for themselves.

The Heart of Juliet Jones presents sophisticated and realistic story lines, with continuity and innovative artwork that includes excellent adaptation of cinematic techniques. Drake was the first, for instance, to replace drawn cityscapes with xeroxed copies of photographs, which he would then go over with ink, thereby giving his cities an unsettling, ominous quality.

Other cartoonists, including Tex Blaisdell, Alex Kotzky, and Neal Adams, have over the years assisted with the illustrations. In 1984 Drake added *Blondie* to his drawing chores, but the burden of producing two newspaper strips simultaneously proved too great after a while: in May 1989 the artwork on *Juliet Jones* passed into the capable hands of Frank Bolle.

P.H.

HEATHCLIFF
1973–present

Cartoonist George Gately Gallagher, better known as simple George Gately to avoid confusion with his cartooning brother John Gallagher, came up with the idea of a comic cat for the McNaught Syndicate. Called *Heathcliff*, the feature first appeared on September 3, 1973, as a daily panel, to which a Sunday page was added a few years later.

Heathcliff was Gately's second attempt at a newspaper strip (the first one had been the short-lived *Hapless Harry*, about a roly-poly young man constantly thwarted by fate), and this time it proved a success. Far from possessing the tormented personality of his *Wuthering Heights* namesake, Heathcliff is the quintessential fat cat: smug, self-assertive, and underhanded, he stops at nothing to get what he regards as his due—a better than square meal, the easiest chair in the house, and complete sway over the neighborhood animal population. Nominally owned by the Nutmeg family, made up of Grandpa and Grandma and the two young'uns Iggy and Marcy, Heathcliff is pretty much his own cat, and he disdains the old couple's inducement to keep him home at night, preferring to roam the streets in search of garbage cans to overturn and stray dogs to harass.

Heathcliff does have his soft side, and he has been known to send sardines as a valentine to his pussycat love, a Persian named Sonja. The cocky, striped feline otherwise behaves more like a terror than a kitty cat. He is prone to scaring little kids on their way from school, chasing French poodles down blind alleys, beaning pigeons with a slingshot, and stealing fish from the local seafood store. Even the neighborhood bully, a huge bulldog named (what else?) Spike, cannot easily intimidate the pugnacious feline, who gives back as much as he gets.

With his sly mien and roguish demeanor, Heathcliff is a highly individualized, original character. A conscientious craftsman, Gately displays a fine sense of humor in his gags, and his graphic style is deceptively easy and agreeably cartoony, although of late he has been leaving more and more of the drawing to his brother. While not as wildly successful as *Garfield*, to which it is often compared and which it preceded by several years, *Heathcliff*, now under syndication by Tribune Media Services, has been able to hold its own in a crowded field.

M.H.

HENRY
1932–1995

Henry was a deceiving strip. Its economy of line, spare backgrounds, few characters, and lack of speech gave the impression that it was simple to draw. But this was not the case, as artists who succeeded *Henry*'s creator Carl Anderson found out. First of all, the character had no mouth, thus writing off considerable gag potential that involved smiling and happiness; and because Henry appeared in virtually all panels without variations in pose, dress, or activity, his features had to be consistently duplicated. The focus of attention was on him; there were no distracting elements in most panels. Finally, being a pantomime strip, *Henry* was as demanding of the cartoonist as that ancient performance tradition has been of actors and actresses.

Henry lasted the longest of the great pantomime strips that included Otto Soglow's *The Little King*, Oscar Jacobson's *Silent Sam*, and Irving Phillips's *The Strange World of Mr. Mum*. It carried on through the efforts of a number of cartoonists who succeeded Anderson—John Liney, Don Trachte, Jack Tippit, and Dick Hodgins, Jr.

The strip started almost as an afterthought to Anderson's long career, which dated from the first half-decade of the comic strip. Born in 1865, Anderson was already freelancing cartoons to *Judge, Life, Collier's,* and *Saturday Evening Post,* and drawing regular strips such as *Raffles and Bunny* and *The Filipino and the Chick* for New York dailies before the twentieth century began. Caught up in the staff raids endemic to yellow journalism at the time, Anderson switched jobs so often that even he had difficulty recalling where he had been at specific dates. His early strips were short-lived, mainly because the papers in which they appeared folded under him.

Anderson's big break in cartooning came late in his career when he was 67, and purely by accident. In 1932, hurt by the depression, he moved back to Milwaukee, thinking he might become a cabinet maker, which he had been in his teens. He took a job teaching cartooning at a vocational school, where one night, as part of his lecture, he drew a bald kid and nonchalantly called him Henry. The students liked the character and Anderson sent it off to the *Saturday Evening Post,* where it was accepted and became a regular feature. In 1934 William Randolph Hearst saw a German version of *Henry* and, in short order, signed Anderson with King Features. Within a year, *Henry* was made into a Sunday page, a Fleischer animated film, and a book. Eventually, 360 newspapers worldwide used the strip.

Henry (C. Anderson), © 1947 King Features Syndicate

Anderson, by then 70, recognized that he needed help to do this prodigious amount of work and hired Don Trachte, who drew the Sundays, and John Liney, who initially provided gags. After 1942, when Anderson's arthritis prevented him from drawing, Liney added the art for the dailies and comic books to his duties, which he continued after Anderson's death on November 4, 1948.

The strip had very few characters—Henry's girlfriend Henrietta, a little fat guy, the bully Butch, and a dog, plus occasional walk-ons, there for one gag only. Henry's main interests were Henrietta, ice cream, candy, and occasionally, running a sidewalk stand. He was mute in the strip, although minor characters sometimes talked, and convenient signs and labels were provided. But Henry was not expressionless, as some historians have written, for his eyebrows and body gestures cued the reader to his emotions.

To Jack Tippit, who drew the strip later on, Henry was essentially a "poor soul" who was lovable, good, and honest, but down deep, a sad person since he was "not allowed to smile." Historian Stephen Becker in his *Comic Art in America* characterized him as a winner, "his integrity, rarely corrupted by greedy motives, triumph[ing] over the forces of darkness and illogic." Whatever else he may have been, the pot-bellied, peanut-headed character was able to stroll down the street with his hands in his pockets for six decades, imperturbable and tenacious.

J.A.L.

HERMAN
1974–present

Like so many other gag features these days, Fred Unger's *Herman* (which started in 1974 and is distributed by Universal Press Syndicate) leads a double life: a single-panel cartoon on weekdays, it turns into a full-fledged newspaper strip on Sundays. In either version it is hilarious, in keeping with the artist's credo: "I feel my mandate is to make people laugh."

Herman is a misshapen man of advanced middle age, balding, with a bulbous nose and thick glasses—Unger's view of Everyman (or Everyherman). His kid sasses him, his dog bites him, and he tends to get scorned by waitresses, shoe salesmen, and receptionists. When he goes fishing he only catches mismatched boots, and comes back covered with graffiti from head to toe after a subway ride; to get company in his hospital room he has to call upon a rent-a-visitor service. His jobs (he keeps losing them) are as nondescript as his clothes: washroom attendant, department store Santa, even substitute Playboy bunny, all of them ending in disaster.

Herman's most constant aggravations, however, come from his run-ins with his acid-tongued, shrewish wife; the battle of the sexes rages with unparalleled ferocity in the Herman household. At their anniversary Herman wonders: "We been married fifty years, sixty years, or seventy years?" To his wife's complaint, "I've got to avoid stress," he replies without batting an eyelash, "Don't look in the mirror!" And when he gets lost on a farm, the first place his spouse goes looking for him is the pigsty.

Unger draws his comic in a loose yet very effective style, paying more attention to the gags than to the characters. Actually, his characters all look like Herman: his wife is Herman in drag, his son a diminutive version of Herman, and his dog a four-legged lump with a Herman mug. Once queried on precisely this point, the author replied: "His wife's named Herman. The dog's Herman. The kid is Herman, too. Herman is not anybody's name. Herman is a state of mind." Which goes to prove that his self-assumed mandate is to make people think as well as make them laugh.

M.H.

HI AND LOIS
1954–present

The successful suburban family strip *Hi and Lois* debuted daily on October 18, 1954, and October 14, 1956, Sunday, syndicated by King Features. A pure reflection of postwar domestic life, Hiram and Lois Flagston initially mirrored *Beetle Bailey* creator Mort Walker's growing family and was an offshoot of his military feature. Beetle visited his sister Lois on furlough in April of 1954, inspiring Walker to devise a contemporary version of a household strip for the Nuclear Age. Walker and artist Dik Browne created America's funniest young family and a model example of the modern humor epic.

Hi is a district sales manager and provincial Everyman whose attractive housewife shares equally in the comic's merriment, while helping to raise their four fair-haired children. Practically a youthful version of his Uncle Beetle, Chip is the teenaged son, having aged slightly during the feature's run to 15. Mildly rebellious, he is a typically wholesome young man who is anxious to obtain his driver's license, can talk for hours by phone to his current sweetheart, and maintains the messiest bedroom in the comics. The eight-year-old twins manage to dominate much of the spotlight; Ditto's naive innocence, naughtiness, and sense of discovery often clashes with his sister, Dot, whose bossy instincts and youthful aggressiveness complement her natural compassion and intelligence.

Hi and Lois (Walker and Browne), © 1972 King Features Syndicate

The strip's most endearing and popular character is Trixie, a precocious infant who was the genre's first thinking baby. Allowing the reader an opportunity to understand her humorously intuitive perceptions significantly broadened the possibilities for material; it's an idea since imitated by others. One particular theme is Trixie's amity with sunbeams, providing the baby with moments of wonderment and solace, often spent cuddled aside the family's sheepdog. Slovenly neighbor Thirsty and his frustrated wife, Irma, provide a burlesque contrast to the euphonic Flagstons, typically with the former's unkept yard and hedonistic habits a source for conflict and humor. Additional cast members include Hi's obdurate boss, Mr. Foofram, and the comedic team of garbagemen, Abercrombie and Fitch.

Browne's initial artistic influence was Harry Haenigsen's *Penny,* but soon imitation of the mentor's angular, controlled approach evolved into the warmer, colorful style Browne had mastered earlier during his tenure as an advertising artist and on *The Tracy Twins* for *Boy's Life.* During the strip's first decade, a number of the Sunday episodes focused on beautifully crafted nostalgic recollections of blissful days gone by, imaginary stories or other themes that honed the artist's ability to handle graphic challenges and highlighted his mature command of detail and design. Unlike the farcial slapstick found in *Beetle Bailey, Hi and Lois* maintains a more realistic and affectionate depiction of its environs, preserving a credibility in caricature. Its soft, genial view provides an honest and humble look at this average family's small tribulations and avoids most of the world's more menacing perplexities.

Hi and Lois has been a group effort from its inception. Writing assistance has come from a core of top-notch cartoonists, beginning with Jerry Dumas, Bud Jones, and Bob Gustafson, who instilled particular charm into the innocent doings of Trixie and the twins. Frank Johnson has deftly handled most of the inking since the early 1970s, and Fred Schwartz has provided lettering since the beginning. There was a gradual transition of the artistic reins from Dik Browne to his son Bob, and since his father's passing in 1989 Bob has maintained the strip's high quality and visual appeal. Brian Walker has assumed the considerable role of editor and chief writer, sharing the responsibility with his older brother, Greg. This meritorious team has updated the strip in several aspects: revamping Thirsty into a less chauvinstic, sober Thurston; introducing personal computers; and assigning more household duties to Hi, as a complement to Lois's part-time real-estate position.

Nearly forty paperback collections have appeared domestically over the years, including notably *The Best of Hi and Lois* from 1986 and 1990's *Here Comes the Sun.* Dell issued three comic books in the late 1950s, Charlton followed with a series from 1969 to 1971, and a set of cloth dolls was produced in 1985.

The classic strip created by the masterful pair of Walker and Browne over four decades ago continues just as strongly today, overseen by the next generation of talented cartoonists, amply fulfilling their comics legacies while keeping the exploits of the Flagstons enjoyable to readers well into the next century.

B.J.

HIGH-PRESSURE PETE
See SALESMAN SAM

HOGAN'S ALLEY
See THE YELLOW KID

HOPALONG CASSIDY
1949–1955

In the late 1940s William Boyd, who had played the lead in all of the almost seventy Hopalong Cassidy movies, bought the rights to the character and immediately set out on a merchandising campaign to sell the silver-haired Hoppy as a star of television, comic books, and every other conceivable medium. Consequently, a *Hopalong Cassidy* newspaper feature, licensed by Boyd's Hopalong Cassidy, Inc., organization, saw the light of print, daily and Sunday, in 1949. The strip was first distributed through the Los Angeles Mirror Syndicate and, starting in 1951, it was taken up by King Features. The artwork was assured by Dan Spiegle, who had been hand-picked for the job by Boyd himself.

The character as depicted by Spiegle was very close in his understated appearance and gentlemanly behavior to

Hopalong Cassidy (D. Spiegle), © **King Features Syndicate**

Boyd's screen persona. The first story was written by Dan Grayson, one of Boyd's finance managers (in its beginnings this was pretty much a mom-and-pop operation), but later a professional writer named Royal King Cole was brought in. Cole contributed many interesting narratives, often taking Hoppy out of his usual locale and putting him into strange surroundings, such as the San Francisco waterfront, and even Australia (where Hoppy was taken after being shanghaied aboard a smuggling ship).

Spiegle's draftsmanship kept improving with each passing episode. He gradually abandoned the rough-hewn linework of his early drawings in favor of a more subtle rendering based on a mix of Craftint and dry-brush techniques. His artwork became especially striking after King Features had taken over syndication of the strip. Around that time Spiegle also deepened his utilization of color in the Sunday pages, thus adding a further dimension of drama to the happenings. In the early 1950s *Hopalong Cassidy* was undoubtedly one of the best-looking of western strips. The stories, however, did not keep pace with the improvements in draftsmanship and were being diluted more and more under pressure from the syndicate. As the hue-and-cry against violence in the comics steadily increased during the decade, King Features quietly decided to drop the strip, which at its peak in the early 1950s had a list of over two hundred newspapers. By the summer of 1955 the silver-haired, black-suited cowboy was gone from the newspaper pages.

M.H.

HUBERT
1945–1994

Like many other aspiring cartoonists drafted into the U.S. Army, Dick Wingert found an outlet for his talents in a service publication, in his case the European edition of *Stars and Stripes*. His first efforts in 1942 resulted in a series of joke cartoons without any thematic or character-

istic unity, but little by little there evolved the small, ridiculous figure of Hubert, Private First Class, the victim of snarling noncoms and bullying fellow draftees alike. So popular did the little soldier with the big nose and the bewildered expression become that he edged out even Bill Mauldin's *Willie and Joe* in some readership polls.

On December 3, 1945, Hubert made his first appearance in civilian garb in a daily panel distributed by King Features Syndicate, followed on February 3, 1946, by a full-fledged Sunday page. Writing in 1947, a few short years after *Hubert*'s debut in the newspaper pages, Coulton Waugh sounded skeptical about the new feature's chances of survival amid the glut of former military cartoons turned civilian strips. "It is sharply drawn," he wrote, "but one wonders whether tubby Hubert's personality will click in the long run." He shouldn't have worried: Hubert was to flourish for over forty-five years more, outlasting such army rivals as *Sad Sack* and *Private Breger* by decades.

Now transplanted to the suburbs like so many other ex-G.I.'s, Hubert, as portly, clumsy, and unprepossessing as before, got himself married to an attractive blonde housewife named Trudi, and later fathered a daughter, Elli. His warlike encounters were now for the most part reduced to run-ins with his boss, the supercilious Dexter L. Baxter, and mix-ups with his unruly sheepdog, Freddy. His constant nemesis was his mother-in-law, who on occasion proved as formidable as his top sergeant in the army. Once, as Trudi was reminiscing back to her days as a schoolgirl, when she dreamed of marrying a handsome prince, her mother interjected, eyeing her son-in-law, "How come you couldn't even get a good-looking peasant?" The difference was that now poor Hubert could fight back, which he sometimes did in his sly, meek way. Waiting in a woman's store for the old battle-ax to pick a dress that would fit her ample silhouette, he suggested in a seemingly innocent tone, "Try the fat rack, mother-in-law."

The reasons for *Hubert*'s longevity are difficult to pin down. The gags were amusing but conventional, and the drawings pleasantly cartoony without great originality. In the late 1980s illness caused Wingert's line to grow shaky and almost indecipherable. The feature was finally discontinued on January 16, 1994, just shy of the half-century mark.

M.H.

HUCKLEBERRY FINN
See SCHOOL DAYS

HUNTER KEENE
1946–1947

In an attempt to duplicate the success he had achieved a decade earlier with *Dan Dunn*, Norman Marsh, freshly back from service in World War II, came up with a virtual clone of his previous creation, which King Features started distributing daily under the title *Hunter Keene* on April 15, 1946.

Hailed by the syndicate (perhaps tongue-in-cheek) as "a

man of sixteen cylinders—an adventurous, steely-eyed, God-fearing detective who tracks down dirty rats to the corners of the earth, in the interests of justice and right," the pipe-smoking, fedora-hatted Keene used his fists and his gun in his relentless pursuit of malefactors, much as Dan Dunn had been doing. He had a loyal female assistant named Peggy, and to complete the resemblance with his earlier feature, Marsh brought over Dan Dunn's old sidekick, Irwin Higgs, as the comic relief for Keene.

With the passing years Marsh's artistic skills had markedly improved to the point where his drawings looked almost professional. His scripts, however, were still lifted bodily from the pulp magazines of the 1930s, and with the changed public tastes of the immediate postwar years they didn't pass muster. There never was a Sunday page, and the dailies terminated after only one short year, on April 12, 1947.

Hunter Keene is noted less for any artistic or literary distinction than for Marsh's sheer doggedness and persistence. After the failure of *Keene* he went on to draw *Danny Hale,* a history-themed strip that only lasted for a couple years, thereby ending Marsh's somewhat anomalous newspaper-strip career.

M.H.

IN THE LAND OF WONDERFUL DREAMS
See LITTLE NEMO IN SLUMBERLAND

INSPECTOR WADE
1935–1941

*O*n account of a legal and business fluke, King Features' *Inspector Wade,* based on British best-selling author Edgar Wallace's novels, appeared first in Italy, serialized as an appendix to "I Romanzi del Cerchio Verde," a mystery-novel collection, on May 1, 1935. Only after some thorny copyright problems had been solved did it make its American debut on May 20 of that year, as a daily strip.

The first Wallace novel to be adapted was *The India-Rubber Men,* whose protagonist, Detective Inspector Wade of Scotland Yard, became the titular hero of the whole series (in the strip his first name was variously given as John and Jim). Other novels were similarly adapted (on the average a full-length novel yielded ten weeks' worth of comic-strip continuity) by Sheldon Stark, with drawings supplied by veteran pulp illustrator Lyman Anderson. The suave, pipe-smoking Wade and his bowler-hatted, mustachioed assistant, Donavan, not content on fighting crime on their home turf, often journeyed to foreign lands, such as Switzerland or even Arabia, in pursuit of their quarry. The stories had a leisurely air about them, especially as depicted in Anderson's cursive, laid-back style.

On July 4, 1938, Anderson was replaced by Neil O'Keeffe, who brought a darker, more nervous look to the drawings. The continuities were accordingly shifted away from Wallace's mystery and detection stories to his more violent thrillers, as well as to his exotic tales. The last *Inspector Wade*

Inspector Wade (L. Anderson), © 1935 King Features Syndicate

adventure, loosely adapted from Wallace's *Sanders of the River* stories, took place in western Africa and concluded, along with the strip, on May 17, 1941.

M.H.

THE INVENTIONS OF PROFESSOR LUCIFER G. BUTTS
1907–1948

*C*rackpot inventors have existed long before the industrial age began, but their numbers increased exponentially during the nineteenth century and in the first years of the twentieth. For every advance in technology there were hundreds of patents given out to people who were forever reinventing the wheel. Cartoonists were quick to recognize this trend, and some came up with preposterous devices of their own; but no cartoonist was as persistent (and as successful) in this line of endeavor as Rube Goldberg, who foisted the first of his "Inventions" on a bemused public as early as May 1907, in the pages of the *New York Evening Mail.* Soon this developed into a regular feature whose complete title, *The Inventions of Professor Lucifer G. Butts,* was as ludicrous as the goofy inventions devised by Goldberg's alter ego, Professor Lucifer Gorgonzola Butts, A.K.

Butts perfected such ingenious gadgets as a "safety device for walking on icy pavements," a "special foot warmer for tall people with short blankets," and a "machine for washing dishes while you are at the movies," all with a generous helping of pulleys, electric fans, bellows, and sundry household items arrayed in the most bewildering system imaginable. Every little mishap, accident or contretemps ever encountered by the professor was put to good use by the worthy scientist and resulted in one or another clever invention. For instance, Goldberg would write tongue-in-cheek: "Professor Butts chokes on a prune pit and coughs up an idea for an automatic typewriter eraser"; or, "Professor Butts gets his whiskers caught in a laundry wringer and as he comes out the other end he thinks of an idea for a simple parachute."

Along with his more mundane devices the professor also produced a host of life-enhancing and/or socially useful ideas, such as "how to keep from forgetting your rubbers," "how to protect yourself against a holdup man," and "how to get rid of a weekend guest." *The Inventions* (which was later syndicated through King Features) ran for decades, until Goldberg finally tired of the feature in the mid-1930s. He revived it, however, for the Register and Tribune Syndicate, which distributed it until 1948.

Of all Goldberg's creations, it is *The Inventions* that most contributed to his fame. Even after he had abandoned drawing them on a regular basis, he continued to throw in an "invention" or two, usually on some burning issue of the time, for a magazine or on a TV program. The "inventions" also earned him an entry in the dictionary as an adjective (a "Rube Goldberg" contraption is synonymous with an implausibly complicated device).

The reason for this enduring fame resides not only in the sheer outlandishness of the "inventions" but also in the underlying concept of the feature. As a civil engineer (he had graduated from the University of California School of Mining in 1904), Goldberg knew that some modern-day inventions, such as the internal-combustion engine, were no less complicated (only less fanciful) than most of Professor Butts's contraptions. He mocked the machine age, but also in a more subtle way extolled those that had made it possible. As Philip Garner put it in his study *Rube Goldberg: A Retrospective,* Goldberg "paid homage to the guy with the idea." Viewed in this light, Lucifer G. Butts was no crazier than Thomas A. Edison, just not as successful.

M.H.

INVISIBLE SCARLET O'NEIL
1940–1956

*T*he brainchild of Russell Stamm, a former assistant to Chester Gould, *Invisible Scarlet O'Neil* was to experience a newspaper-strip career as sinuous as the eponymous heroine's comely figure. Launched in a daily format on June 3, 1940, by the Chicago Times Syndicate, it followed every fad of the moment and finally died of indecision.

At the time of the feature's creation, super-powered characters had become the rage in the wake of the phenomenal popularity enjoyed by such superheroes as Superman. Accordingly, Scarlet O'Neil, the daughter of a scientist, acquired the power of invisibility by walking unwittingly in front of a ray-device invented by Dr. O'Neil. Finding out that she could make herself invisible or visible at will by simply pressing a nerve on her left wrist, she vowed to use her newly discovered gift in the service of good, thereby allowing the delighted syndicate to tout her as "America's new superheroine." And a superheroine she was to remain all through the war years and for some time afterwards. Red-haired, full-breasted, and long-legged, Scarlet was better outfitted for romance than for adventure, but she resolutely turned aside would-be boyfriends in favor of lachrymose orphans, hard-luck entrepreneurs, and frustrated inventors.

She later placed her abilities in the service of her country, as she infiltrated with equal ease Japanese spy rings and Nazi front organizations. (Not willing to waste his heroine's eye-pleasing assets, Stamm drew her in silhouette when she was supposed to be unseen.) Himself called to the colors in 1944, the author left *Scarlet* in the hands of ghosts before returning to his creation in 1946. Little by little, humor and satire seeped into the feature, and *Invisible Scarlet O'Neil* became as much a spoof of the genre as a straight superheroine strip.

By the end of the 1940s superheroics had started to wane and cowboy action was on the ascendancy. Dutifully, Scarlet lost her powers of invisibility, relocated to the fictional western place known as Deathless Valley, and acquired a cowboy sidekick named Chips; the strip was rechristened *Scarlet and Chips* in the fall of 1949. It pledged, in the syndicate's copy, "superb character drawing, fast-paced continuity, humorous dialogue," but failed to deliver on its promise. In 1950 the title reverted to simply *Scarlet O'Neil.*

Stamm and his syndicate (which in the meantime had changed names as often as its ill-starred feature and was now called Field Enterprises) kept plugging at it. In 1952 a new character, a two-fisted Texan with a drawling sense of humor, made his appearance in the story, and his growing popularity with the readers caused one last title change, to *Stainless Steel* (that happened to be the newcomer's improbable name) on October 24, 1954. With the help of a new assistant, Emery Clarke (who later cosigned the strip), Stamm managed to keep the feature going until 1956.

M.H.

The Inventions of Professor Lucifer G. Butts (R. Goldberg), 1919

THE JACKSON TWINS
1950–1979

Perhaps to make up for his late entry into the field, Dick Brooks came up with not one but two protagonists for his teenage-girl strip, *The Jackson Twins*. Distributed by the McNaught Syndicate, the feature started running daily and Sunday in November 1950.

The twins were two attractive, dark-haired and exceedingly cute girls named Jan and Jill who lived in the idyllically neat and manicured suburban setting of Gardentown with their parents and an obnoxious kid brother named Junior. Their identical looks at first provided a source of gags for the Sundays, but after a while Brooks equipped Jill with eyeglasses to distinguish her from her sibling. While the Sundays concentrated on weekly anecdotes of a mildly humorous nature, mostly about the twins' adventures at home and at school, the dailies often spun off into lengthy continuities. The twins in one episode tried to find out the identity of a mysterious newcomer to the neighborhood they both had a crush on (he turned out to be married and writing a book à la *Peyton Place*); in another story they engaged in a battle of wits with the modish and snotty Imogene, daughter of the wealthiest man in town.

During the almost three decades of the strip's run the twins managed not only to keep their teenage looks but also to go through one of the most eventful periods in the history of American youth without losing their manners or their virtue. While student protests, teenage sexuality, and teenage drug addiction were being reported in the news pages, Jan and Jill blissfully pursued their sheltered existence in the comics pages. Brooks drew the adventures of his two young heroines in a pleasant, somewhat old-fashioned style reflective of the strip's somewhat old-fashioned values. While he had assistants to help him, notably Ed Moore and Warren Sattler, he always wrote the scripts himself. For his "idea farm," as he put it, he often relied on his own two daughters, Ginnie and Laura. The strip's nostalgic appeal did not prove strong enough for it to survive the turbulent 1970s, and it was discontinued on March 24, 1979.

M.H.

JANE ARDEN
1928–1968

One of the best-known features ever distributed by the Register and Tribune Syndicate, *Jane Arden* experienced a career as checkered as it was long. It started on

The Jackson Twins (D. Brooks), © 1968 McNaught Syndicate

November 26, 1928, during the heyday of the girl strip, when veteran newspaperman Monte Barrett came up with the idea of yet another career girl. The first artist was Frank Ellis and he drew the daily strip in a conventional line: Jane was then a flirty young thing, much in the same tradition as Charles Voight's Betty and of Frank Godwin's Connie in her first impersonation. The strip did so well that a Sunday page was added in 1933 (Jack McGuire was assigned to draw it). In 1935 Russell Ross succeeded both McGuire and Ellis, and he gave Jane her most remembered look.

Ross, who lived in Hollywood, modeled his heroine on actress Irene Dunne (Mrs. Barrett had allegedly served as the model for the earlier Jane). A painstaking stickler for realism, Ross particularly excelled in the rendering of human anatomy and the drawing of strongly individualized faces; he once explained his working method to an interviewer thus: "I spent most of my Saturday afternoons at the public library.... Rather than attracting attention by sketching the people, I attempted to memorize each individual's characteristics, carrying the mental images home to put down on paper." By then Jane had undergone much the same metamorphosis as Connie had around that time, and was now a woman reporter who hopped all around the globe, shunning romance for adventure. Her new, go-getting persona was popular enough to warrant a Warner Bros. movie in 1939, *The Adventures of Jane Arden*, with Rosella Towne in the title role.

Throughout the 1930s and into the 1940s the *Jane Arden* Sunday, like so many other features of the period, sported a line of cutout dolls titled *Jane Arden's Wardrobe*, as well as a companion strip, *Lena Pry*, about a prying (what else?) spinster. Ross introduced suspense and mystery into the strip, with Jane engaging in dangerous investigations with the help of Tubby the office boy (whom Ross had plucked bodily out of his earlier feature, *Slim and Tubby*). The mood of intrigue was further heightened in the 1940s, when Jane took it upon herself to combat foreign spies and homegrown fifth-columnists wherever she could ferret them out.

In the late 1940s, however, *Jane Arden* started on its slow downward slide. Barrett died in 1949, and he was replaced by Walt Graham. In the mid-1950s Ross quit the strip; his successor was Jim Speed (whose signature started appearing in 1956); and at the end of the decade William Hargis was entrusted with the artwork.

In 1964 there was a radical departure from the strip's entire premise when Bob Schoenke took over total control of the feature. He had previously done a western called *Laredo Crockett*, and his cowboy hero was simply transplanted to *Jane Arden*, with the locale changed to a small western town, the time to the 1880s, and Jane into her own mother, also named Jane, and also a newspaper reporter. This reincarnation, baptized *Laredo and Jane*, was not without merit, but the breezy gusto of the earlier version was gone from the strip; and in 1968 it was finally canceled.

M.H.

JEFF COBB
1954–1975

Tired of ghosting for other people, Pete Hoffman decided to create a story strip of his own. As a result, *Jeff Cobb* made its debut on June 28, 1954, syndicated in a daily format by General Features Corporation.

Jeff Cobb was a newspaper reporter, and in the tradition of comic-strip newsmen, this meant his getting involved in every conceivable situation, from cracking a case of bribery at city hall to rescuing a kidnap victim. A blond, handsome, clean-cut chap, the hero, while investigating a case of arson lost the vision in one eye, which allowed him to wear a sexy black patch over his right eye and get twice as many chicks as before.

Hoffman drew the strip in a neat, crisp, efficient, if rather bland, style. *Jeff Cobb* initially met with fair success, and a Sunday page was added in 1955, but it lasted only a couple of years, as the writing deteriorated into a collection of pulp-story clichés. Hoffman had previously ghosted Allen Saunders's *Steve Roper*, and to repay a debt Saunders in the 1960s contributed anonymously a number of continuities to *Jeff Cobb*, anchoring it firmly to the soap-opera mode.

By his own admission, Hoffman always had trouble "seriously battling cartoon deadlines," and in 1972 he relinquished the artwork to Winslow Mortimer. Now distributed by the Los Angeles Times Syndicate (which had absorbed General Fea-

Jeff Cobb (P. Hoffman), ca. 1960, © General Features Corp.

tures), *Jeff Cobb* continued on a downward path. The last daily appeared on October 11, 1975.

M.H.

JERRY ON THE JOB
1913–1932, 1947–1954

Walter C. Hoban started *Jerry on the Job* in the *New York Journal* on December 29, 1913, as a daily strip. After a shaky start it was picked up for national syndication by Hearst's International News Service; there again it was slow to catch on, adding a Sunday page only in the summer of 1921.

Jerry Flannigan (to give him his full name) started on the job as a normal-sized seventeen-year-old, but he kept getting younger and shorter with each passing month, until he finally assumed his definitive appearance, that of a towheaded kid of about 12, afflicted with a big head and a diminutive stature. He first found employment as an office-boy in the corporation run by one Frederick Fipp (what the corporation actually did was never made quite clear), and he promptly singled himself out for his alacrity and application, though not for his custodial skills. As a matter of fact, Jerry did not long linger in his office job, quitting early in 1915 to seek his fortune variously as a grocery clerk, a pet-shop employee, a messenger boy, and even as a flyweight boxer known as the Cyclone Kid (his bout against the equally shrimp-sized "Locomotive" Ginsberg marked one of the high points of the strip's early years).

In December 1915 Jerry finally settled into a more or less permanent job with a suburban railroad company, where he remained for the rest of the strip's existence, except for a bout of wanderlust on the protagonist's part in 1916, and a stint in the U.S. Army on the creator's part in 1917–18. His new boss was Mr. Givney, a bewhiskered, befuddled old gent, whose absent-mindedness was such that he had been known to put his umbrella to bed while he himself spent the night sitting on the umbrella stand; his entire staff was comprised of Jerry who acted in turns as ticket seller, train conductor, troubleshooter, and all-round boy Friday. The station apparently served only one destination, a mysterious locality referred to as New Monia that seemed to attract only the weirdest sort of passengers. In the course of his duties Jerry had to deal with deadbeats, card sharks, snake-oil salesmen, and insane asylum escapees, not to mention bomb-throwing Bolsheviks, and he acquitted himself with uncommon aplomb and unmitigated nerve.

Hoban drew the strip with a verve that bordered on the manic. His characters never stood still for an instant, they were always seen running around, jumping up, often zipping in and out, and sometimes plopping down. Jerry in particular was a cyclone of activity, sweeping used tickets under the rug, mishan-

Jerry on the Job (W. Hoban), © 1921 King Features Syndicate

dling packages, sassing passengers, and causing general pandemonium. The backgrounds—especially in the Sundays—also seemed in constant flux. The one-room railway station had more nooks and crannies, cavernous closets and hidden passageways than a Scottish castle; while the immediate surroundings looked like an immense empty lot planted with oddly-shaped trees and crisscrossed by boardwalks leading nowhere.

Jerry did not long survive the mad decade of the 1920s. In 1931 the daily strip was discontinued, while the Sunday feature only appeared as the top strip to Hoban's latest creation, *Rainbow Duffy*. Even in this attenuated format it only lasted for one more year. The character wouldn't stay dead, however, and late in the decade he was revived in an ad strip for Grape-Nuts drawn and written by Hoban and after his death in 1939, by Bob Naylor. In 1947 King Features was persuaded by Naylor to resurrect *Jerry on the Job* as a daily strip once more. While Naylor caught the caricatural aspect of the strip with dead-on accuracy, his writing lacked the raucous humor and the punch of the earlier incarnation. The feature came to an unlamented end in 1954.

An underrated artist who has been ignored by the early historians of the comics, Hoban left a far from negligible body of comic-strip work. In addition to *Jerry on the Job,* which remains the showpiece of his professional career, he turned out *Rainbow Duffy*, concentrating on a teenage bank clerk who was as lazy as Jerry was hyperactive, and *Needlenose Noonan*, about an amiably incompetent cop on the beat. It should be noted that all these creations played sympathetic variations on well-known Irish stereotypes, much as that other great Irish-American cartoonist, George McManus, had done with *Bringing Up Father*.

M.H.

JET SCOTT
1953–1955

In 1953 the editors of the New York Herald-Tribune Syndicate decided to round out their already impressive roster of adventure comics with a science-fiction feature designed to attract the public of young adults then enamored of science and technology. As the author on the project they called upon Sheldon Stark, who had written such strips as *Inspector Wade* and turned out scripts for Hollywood movies; the artist they picked was Jerry Robinson, who had made his career up to then in comic books.

Starting on September 28, 1953, *Jet Scott* pursued its course fitfully weekdays and Sundays, for a period of some two years. The title hero was a darkly handsome agent for a hush-hush organization connected with the Pentagon. The action was set in the near-future and the plots were recycled from current news headlines (theft of plutonium, rogue scientists on the loose, etc.), resulting in what Joe Brancatelli in *The World Encyclopedia of Comics* called "a mediocre science-fiction feature." Robinson's style, while adequate, was too academic and lacking in the fantasy that might suggest the unlimited promise (and danger) of the future.

Jet Scott ended in September 1955. Robinson went on turning out comic strips like *Still Life* and *Flubs and Fluffs* with little success. Always better as a promoter than as a cartoonist, he has found his niche as the head of his own organization, the Cartoonists and Writers Syndicate.

M.H.

JIM HARDY
1936–1942

After years of anonymous toil on Chester Gould's *Dick Tracy*, Dick Moores decided to branch out on his own with a newspaper strip about a tough operator whom he named Jim Conley. Mailing out his samples to a number of syndicates, he finally got a positive response from United Feature, which after many changes and alterations, took on distribution of the strip (now rechristened *Jim Hardy*), touting it as "a new daily strip that is as true to life as it is dramatic!" The first release came out on June 8, 1936.

A six-footer with dark, curly hair and an honest, somewhat tormented face, Jim had been initially conceived by Moores as an ex-convict, but the character was much toned down by the time he reached the newspaper page. In the first episode the armored car he was guarding got hijacked, and Jim immediately fell under suspicion. With the help of his policeman friend, Pinky, he succeeded in clearing his name and putting the collar on the real perpetrators, Rocks Roskal and his gang. Despite the entreaties of the town mayor's daughter, the pert Betty Lee, who was secretly in love with him, the hero then left the city and went West to work as a reporter on his Uncle Joe's newspaper, later coming back East to fight racketeers, corrupt politicians, and bank robbers in the fictional Hub City.

Moores could never quite make up his mind as to which way he wanted his strip to go. Drawn in a style more than a little reminiscent of *Dick Tracy*, it never managed to exude the same atmosphere of suspense and fear. The stories were quite good, but didn't have *Tracy*'s nasty, self-righteous tinge, though not for want of trying on Moores's part. He even gave his hero a ridiculously small hooked nose to make him look closer to Gould's detective, and had him use expletives like "You gutless yellow skunk!" It was all for naught. The strip was never popular enough to warrant the addition of a Sunday page, and from the late 1930s on, its pitifully small circulation shrank even further. In a last-ditch effort to salvage the feature, *Jim Hardy* was phased out of the picture in favor of a western character named Windy and his horse Paddles. *Windy and Paddles*, as it came to be known, only lasted for a short while, breathing its last in October 1942.

M.H.

JINGLET
See SWEENEY AND SON

JOE AND ASBESTOS
1925–1926, 1928–1966

There have been many horse-racing strips in the history of the funnies (*A. Piker Clerk* and *Mutt and Jeff* were two early examples), but none as durable (or as lucrative) as *Joe and Asbestos*. Ken Kling, a former assistant to Bud Fisher on *Mutt and Jeff*, decided to branch out with a newspaper strip of his own, starring a horse-race bettor who would consistently lose his stake day after day. Named after its protagonist, *Joe Quince* debuted in the fall of 1925 in one newspaper, the *Baltimore Sun*, on a one-year trial basis.

Kling had Joe Quince pick real horses in actual races, and according to his own accounts, he built his gags around Joe's hunches. Amazingly, the horses Joe played all won, and the *Sun* soared correspondingly in circulation. Other newspapers across the country, upon hearing the news, rushed to pick up the strip. After a few months, Kling tired of having his lone protagonist talk to himself, and he brought in a black stable boy as Joe's comic relief; the newcomer soon upstaged his mentor and became the costar of the feature, now renamed *Joe and Asbestos*.

Upon the termination of his contract, Kling dropped the strip and went on a vacation. Coming back to the comics after a year, he created *Windy Riley*, about a blowhard not unlike Major Hoople of *Our Boarding House*. Readers wanted *Joe and Asbestos* back, however, and in the spring of 1928 the cartoonist obliged. The two horse players turned up at Belmont, at Saratoga, at Santa Ana, and in other venues around the country, dispensing tips as they went. While the strip ran in only a score of metropolitan newspapers, these were the most lucrative markets in the U.S. Kling, who owned the strip, became a millionaire many times over (in 1942 alone he reportedly earned more than $100,000); he started playing the ponies himself and even acquired a stable of trotters he occasionally drove himself; and as he once jokingly declared, he wrote it all off as "research expenses" on his tax return.

Joe and Asbestos ended its long career in 1966. It never was a terribly well-drawn strip, and most of its gags were old and tired. Since the feature generally ran on the racing page, these esthetic considerations probably never bothered any of Kling's readers.

M.H.

JOE JINKS
1918–1971

When Vic Forsythe started his humorous daily strip *Joe's Car* for the Press Publishing Company in the spring of 1918, little did he foresee that his modest little feature would not only outlive him, but that it would last for over half a century, through two world wars, four title changes, and the hands of a dozen different cartoonists.

Joe was a balding, agitated little man, afflicted like most comic-strip husbands with a nagging wife, named Blanche in this case. He found an outlet for his many domestic frustrations in his passion for automobiles, and later for airplanes. From there he branched out into the fight game and became the manager of a heavyweight boxer named Dynamite Dunn, whom he guided to a world championship. Cars had long ceased to be of any import to the action, and in recognition of the fact the strip was rechristened *Joe Jinks*, for its shrimpy protagonist, in August 1928; and in December of the same year a gag page, focusing on the domestic tribulations of the Jinkses, was added.

Forsythe drew Joe's adventures in a peculiar style better suited for slapstick than for pugilistic action. He managed to foreshorten all his characters, with the result that his heavyweights looked more like puffed-up flyweights. After he left in 1933 to create *Way Out West*, he was replaced by sports cartoonist Pete Llanuza, who bowed in his turn to Moe Leff in 1936. During his short tenure (little more than one year) Leff succeeded in giving the strip a more realistic as well as a more visually appealing look. He was followed in quick succession by the returning Forsythe, then by editorial cartoonist Bill Homan on the dailies, while the Sunday page was taken over by Henry Formhals. From the time of Homan's death in 1939 up to 1944, no fewer than five different artists tried their hand at the strip (now carried by United Feature Syndicate). Finally Sam Leff came in, bringing his brother Moe (whose work went unaccredited) back with him. A new, blond boxer of manly good looks soon took over the daily strip, which was renamed *Curly Kayoe* in his honor on December 31, 1945.

In 1947 Joe quit the fight game, ostensibly to care for his ailing wife, and Curly was free to pursue a number of extracurricular activities, such as solving a murder mystery, going to hunt for sunken treasure, and getting involved with a great many sultry and often dangerous beauties. For a while in the 1950s the dailies and the Sundays proceeded along the same narrative track; but in December 1958 the weekly page returned to its original gag format, and it ceased publication a couple of years later. Early in 1961 a strapping young sailor named Davy Jones started to loom large in the dailies, and astute readers could scent that another title switch was in the cards.

Having been born on land, the strip was now to undergo

a burial at sea. Changed into a maritime adventure series in June 1961, *Davy Jones* was written by Sam Leff, and drawn in succession by Al McWilliams, John Celardo, and Wayne Boring. It chugged along fitfully until the spring of 1971, when it was unceremoniously double-sixed by its syndicate.

M.H.

JOE PALOOKA
1930–1984

In a sport not noted for its civility, prize fighter Joe Palooka stood out like a sore thumb, or more appropriately, a black eye. Joe personified the ideals of the American majority of old—the simple life, the virtues of the Boy Scout code, and goodness for its own sake. He also exemplified toughness and power and could be moved to intense anger when his or someone else's toes were stepped on.

Joe Palooka graced the funnies for almost fifty-five years, during which time he found himself, willingly and otherwise, in a number of adventures in and out of the ring. Usually, he shared these experiences with a cast of equally homely and likable characters. Most memorable of them were his bald and seemingly toothless (a trait shared by all male characters in the strip) manager, Knobby Walsh; friend Jerry Leemy; longtime sweetheart (and wife after 1949), the cheese heiress, Ann Howe; the mute kid, Max; Ma Palooka; the butterball Humphrey Pennyworth and his homemade shack on wheels; Big Leviticus, the hillbilly Al Capp contributed before the creation of his own *Li'l Abner*, and Joe's children, Joannie and Buddy (Joe, Jr.).

Although it attained a long and successful run (being one of the top five most popular strips in 1950), *Joe Palooka* almost did not get off the drawing board. Ham Fisher got the inspiration for his character in 1926, after he had interviewed a gentle, childlike boxer ("unsophisticated but good-natured," was how Fisher described him) for the *Wilkes-Barre* [Pennsylvania] *Herald*, where he worked as staff cartoonist. The following year, Fisher went to New York to continue plugging for the strip. Over and over, all the syndicates turned it down. To make a living when he first went to New York, Fisher worked in a nondescript job at the *New York Daily News,* and shortly after he moved to the McNaught Syndicate. One of his assignments there was to take the *Dixie Dugan* strip on the road to seek new clients. Successful in this salesmanship task, Fisher decided to do the same with *Joe Palooka*. When the McNaught general manager went on vacation, the young cartoonist also took off, and in three weeks he sold the strip to twenty newspapers. Thus, the first sports-adventure strip was launched on April 19, 1930.

Fisher developed a formula that mixed suspense, romance, and humor with occasional bits of liberal polemics and unabashed patriotism. The result was, as Coulton Waugh wrote, that *Joe Palooka* was neither eye-catching, smart, nor "smart-alecky; it was simply an easy-going story packed with heart, human love, and long, drawn-out fights. The character that Fisher fashioned was a simple man—shy, easily embarrassed, and laid-back. His

Joe Palooka (H. Fisher), © 1944 McNaught Syndicate

mangling of the language ("Kin ya 'magine?") and naive notions about high society (a New York penthouse to him was "where they keep people that's got measles and things, ain't it?") endeared Joe Palooka to the working class. He was liked because he was humble and dedicated and because he knew his limits. For example, rather than accept a military commission, Joe enlisted as a buck private, feeling he did not know enough to be an officer. He fought throughout the entire war at that rank.

At times, Fisher chopped off stories and transported Joe into completely different places and roles. That's how Joe ended up in the military. Upon being offered a lucrative fight in Cuba, Joe abruptly declared that he had other plans and joined the armed forces. This was considerably before the U.S. entry into the war, at a time when many newspapers carrying *Joe Palooka* still were isolationist. Joe's action has been credited with persuading many Americans to enlist, for which the government was grateful, singling out *Joe Palooka* as the one strip that truly reflected the military and the U.S. cause. Fisher himself was caught up in the wartime fervor, touring army camps to capture their flavor and to contribute to soldier morale. For the war years, the strip was dominated by a theme of usefulness: Knobby worked in a defense plant, tackling absenteeism and tardiness; Ann Howe was a Red Cross nurse; and Joe and his army buddy, George, fought bravely in every corner of the globe, interrupting their skirmishes to give spiels that promoted cooperation and warned about fifth-columnists and fascists.

Joe Palooka showed off the excellent storytelling techniques of Ham Fisher and his ghostwriters, Al Capp and Moe Leff. Fisher crafted his strip much as a playwright creates a script, shifting scenes, molding delightful characters, polishing dialogue, and setting interest traps to string the reader on. To provide play by play of the long fight scenes, Fisher occasionally tucked one or two commentary panels in between the visual ones, also relieving himself of drawing every left cross, uppercut, or right hook. Other times, especially while Joe was in the army, word panels would be used in the form of written letters between Joe and Knobby.

After Fisher's suicide in 1955, Moe Leff took over *Joe Palooka;* he was succeeded by Tony Di Preta in October 1959. The strip ended on November 4, 1984.

J.A.L.

JOE'S CAR
See JOE JINKS

JOHNNY COMET
1952–1953

Frank Frazetta's only credited foray into the newspaper-strip medium, *Johnny Comet* was sprung on an unsuspecting public by the McNaught Syndicate on January 28, 1952, as a daily strip, followed the next February 3 by a Sunday version.

Centering in and around the world of automobile races, the strip was credited to Peter de Paolo, a champion racing-car driver, but the famous ace did not actually write the continuities, which he left in the hands of a Hollywood script-writer named Earl Baldwin. De Paolo contented himself with dispensing the car-racing tips that accompanied the Sundays, and acted in the general role of technical adviser. Under his tutelage the strip exuded an authentic pit-stop aroma (you could almost smell the spilled oil and

burning tires). The locale was California, and the competitions ran the gamut from midget-car races to fifty-lap classics.

The titular hero was a dark, handsome hunk of impressive build and attenuated brains, whose passion for fast cars excluded any other diversion. His steady girlfriend, a curvy blonde bombshell named Jean Fargo, a racing-car designer in her own right, tried to get Johnny's puny mind off the next race once in a while, but her efforts were always in vain. Once when Jean told him meaningfully, "Johnny, I feel a little chilly," the big flummox only responded, "I'll go get you a sweater." Around them there swirled a little world of car mechanics, garage proprietors, pit-stop operators, small-time chiselers, and big-time crooks.

What made the strip stand out was the forcefulness of Frazetta's drawings. His racing machines pulsated with awesome power, and the action scenes displayed an almost epic quality. His dynamics extended even to his characters, who were seldom seen at rest and always seemed to exude a restless energy. The stories, however, did not match the quality of the illustrations, concerning themselves with tales of jealousy between drivers and racetrack manipulations. In August 1952 the Sundays eschewed continuity and turned into a series of self-contained gags; and in November the protagonist, for some unaccountable reason, underwent a name change to Ace McCoy (with the feature retitled accordingly). *Ace McCoy* lasted for only a few more months, the dailies to January 31, 1953, and the weeklies to the next Sunday. *Johnny Comet,* a.k.a. *Ace McCoy,* is chiefly remembered today for the twenty-four-year-old Frazetta's contribution, which represents an important milestone in the artist's career.

M.H.

Johnny Comet (F. Frazetta), © 1952 McNaught Syndicate

JOHNNY HAZARD
1944–1977

Johnny Hazard began his long career in the middle of World War II, a fact made plain by the very first adventure, during which the pilot hero made his daring escape from a German POW camp. Created by Frank Robbins for King Features Syndicate after the artist's departure from *Scorchy Smith,* Hazard saw the light of newspaper print in the daily of June 5, 1944, the eve of D-Day, and in a Sunday page that appeared not long afterward, on July 2.

Having wreaked havoc behind enemy lines, Johnny Hazard now surfaced on the Italian front, where he was to meet his main squeeze (albeit not his exclusive one by a long shot), the tempestuous Brandy, a war photographer accredited to the U.S. forces. This proved only an interlude, and soon thereafter the hero was found leading a hardy band of guerrilla fighters harassing the Japanese in China, where not surprisingly Brandy caught up with him in short order. Before the war was over, the American flyer and his troops had blown up innumerable enemy installations, liberated large tracts of territory, and even captured a Japanese general.

Like so many real-life airmen, Hazard couldn't get flying out of his system after the return of peace. He became a kind of world-class troubleshooter whose plane allowed

Johnny Hazard (F. Robbins), ca. 1944, © King Features Syndicate

him to take cases in any place under the sun. In October 1946 Robbins started running subtitles to Hazard's adventures, serving as clues to the hero's global reach and his universal expertise in problem solving. There were, for instance "Death Wears an Orchid" (involving a homicidal orchid collector in South America), "The Mountain of the Dancing Devils" (kidnapping and murder in the Gobi desert), "When Time Stood Still" (searching for Rommel's buried treasure in Libya), and "London Bridge Is Falling Down" (saving the crown jewels). So great had his reputation become that no sooner had Hazard arrived, assassins were trying to do him in with gun, blade, bomb, or lariat, any place he happened to be, from a ski chalet in the French Alps to an opium den in Singapore, and even at the opera (there, the hit was cunningly devised to coincide with the execution scene in *Tosca*).

In the mid-1950s real-life events caught up with Hazard, and he found himself working for the U.S. State Department on a secret mission in Nepal, and later on other delicate assignments fighting the Communist menace all over Asia. Being a civilian at heart, he never displayed in these official tasks the same gusto as Milton Caniff's Lieutenant Colonel Steve Canyon, to whom he was often compared in this period. He felt more at ease in later years being an agent of the World International Network Guardian (WING), an international counterespionage organization.

During the entire life of the strip, Sunday and daily narratives unfolded on independent tracks. Not only did this device allow Robbins to vary his locales during the same week, it also allowed Hazard to meet twice as many beautiful women. Many fell for him, and some tried to kill him, but he handled every one of them with equal aplomb, whether they were airline executive, animal tamer, or gangster moll. Like Caniff, Robbins had a knack for conjuring evocative feminine names: among many others there were Paradise, Velvet, Fern, Cha-Cha, not to mention Lady Jaguar, Lady Mist, and Baroness Flame. As for the males, they sported handles like Snap Hunter, Blitz Martin, and Wild Bill Hiccup.

Robbins brought all his superlative skill and awesome technique as an artist to these adventures. The strip seemed possessed with perpetual motion, as the backgrounds, the action, and the characters flew by at dizzying speed. Even at a time when newspaper strips were being shrunk to the size of postage stamps, Robbins could cram in an incredible

amount of detail in each of his panels, varying the angle of vision or the perspective in such a way that his drawings never seemed cramped. It was as a storyteller that his enthusiasm started to flag as he saw the strip's circulation dwindle down in the 1970s. His narratives, which had exhibited great originality up to then, became pale James Bond imitations, and the strip declined further. In its last years *Johnny Hazard* had become a ghost of its former self, and the syndicate finally brought it down, with the Sunday ending on August 14, 1977, and the dailies following suit at the end of the same week, on August 20.

M.H.

JOHNNY REB
1956–1959

An interesting but ultimately ill-conceived attempt to explore the intricacies of the American Civil War through comic-strip narration, *Johnny Reb and Billy Yank* (as it was originally called) was hatched in the editorial offices of the New York Herald-Tribune Syndicate. The first page of this Sunday feature appeared on November 18, 1956.

This chronicle focused on two protagonists, a Southerner and a Northerner with symbolically charged names: a Virginian, Johnny Reb, and a New Englander, Billy Yank. At first these tales were told evenhandedly, as Johnny and Billy took turns starring in the feature. Perhaps because the Civil War—and the stories related to it—have always exercised greater fascination in the South than in the North, the strip soon began tilting in favor of the Confederate hero, starting with the shortening of the title to *Johnny Reb*.

The artwork looked eerily in step with this changed point of view. Frank Giacoia, the tale's illustrator, had at the outset exhibited a very welcome flair for spectacle, drama, and the pathos of war. His documentation seemed accurate, and he brought off the cameralike sequences of battle and action with gusto. As time passed, however, he seemed to lose interest in the stories he was telling, and his drawings became hurried and lackluster, his backgrounds sketchy, his action scenes lifeless. Circulation steadily declined along with the declining quality of the strip, and by the summer of 1959 *Johnny Reb* simply petered out— another noble effort gone awry.

M.H.

JOHNNY-ROUND-THE-WORLD
1935–1938[?]

*T*he Amazing Adventures of Johnny-Round-the-World, to give this Sunday page its full title, was one of King Features Syndicate's periodic attempts at cultural uplift. Written by William LaVarre, F.R.G.S. (Fellow of the Royal Geographic Society), it debuted in February 1935.

The title was something of a misnomer, since Johnny didn't get 'round the world, but confined his wanderings to a tiny part of it, what were then the colonies of British Guiana (now Guyana) and Dutch Guiana (now Suriname), where he had accompanied his father, Major Jupiter, on a scientific expedition. The major and his son traveled in true Rudyard Kipling fashion, with an imposing retinue of native porters and the requisite accouterments of knee-boots, sidearms, and pith helmets. The only modern touch was the zoom camera—then a novelty—that young Johnny had brought with him. The titular hero was an earnest, eager teenage boy who bravely went rafting down the rapids of the Suriname River, faced leopards and wild boars with suitable aplomb, and kept a very British stiff upper lip when the expedition's provisions were stolen or some of the porters deserted. But though there were river floods, jungle stampedes, and forest fires a-plenty, the action itself never caught fire.

The comic relief (what there was of it) was provided by Johnny's small fox terrier, Peppy, who often got into scrapes with wild animals or prank-playing native children. Johnny filmed all the incidents with his camera, which resulted in a different black-and-white photo every week, looking incongruous smack in the middle of the full-color page. The reader was thus regaled with a parade of native warriors in full battle dress, native women grinding sorghum, and native monkeys making faces, in a funny-page version of the *National Geographic*.

Although Coulton Waugh called it "pioneering and interesting," the feature never lived up to its billing. The texts and dialogues were trite and patronizing (with a heavy dose of racism and colonialism thrown in), and the drawings, executed by anonymous hands from the syndicate's bullpen, never proved better than adequate. *Johnny-Round-the-World* was carried by a handful of newspapers, and it finally disappeared toward the end of 1937 or early in 1938 (King Features didn't even bother to list it in its catalogue).

M.H.

JOSÉ CARIOCA
See WALT DISNEY'S SUNDAY PAGES

THE JOURNAL TIGERS
1898–1903

*A*t the turn of the century James Swinnerton created for the Sunday comic supplement of Hearst's *New York Journal* a number of color pages that ran alternately with one another. Among those there were a Noah's Ark–type strip (most often referred to as *Mount Ararat*) and, more importantly, beginning in 1898, a series dealing with the comic adventures of little tiger cubs who became so identified with the newspaper that they became known as the "Journal Tigers."

The "Tigers" page was not really a comic strip: it used speech-balloons only sparingly and developed no sequential narratives, but displayed instead a series of vignettes amusingly arranged around a common theme. "The Journal Tigers Give a Wild West Show," for instance, showed the winsome little felines riding bucking broncos, showing off their marksmanship, or driving a stagecoach (pulled by a goat) and fighting off some of their compatriots dressed like Indians. In another page, titled "Our Tigers Go Abroad," the merry little band carried on aboard an ocean liner, some dancing the gig, others getting seasick, two young ones having a tryst behind their sleeping parents' backs; and all finally leaving the sinking ship in lifeboats and rafts. In 1902 Swinnerton plucked a cocky, roguish little tiger out of the lineup and starred him in his own strip called *Mr. Jack*. After that the Tigers only made sporadic appearances in the *Journal*, finally fading out the next year.

Swinnerton's Tigers were great favorites of Hearst's: they were often prominently featured on the front page of the *Journal*'s Sunday supplement and received ample promotion in other Hearst publications. Engaging and lovingly delineated, *Tigers* deserves to be remembered as little masterpieces of fantasy and humor.

M.H.

JUDGE PARKER
1952–present

*B*uoyed by the success of his medical soap-opera comic strip, *Rex Morgan, M.D.*, Dr. Nicholas Dallis decided to strike again into the field of newspaper strip melodramatics. Choosing this time the noble profession of the law as his new area of concern, and using the pen-name Paul Nichols, he came up with *Judge Parker* in November 1952.

Judge Allan Parker, a tall, handsome, distinguished man in his fifties, was reportedly modeled on Dr. Paul Alexander, a Toledo juvenile-court judge Dallis had known in his earlier days as a psychiatrist.

Parker is a pillar of the community and a knowledgeable as well as understanding magistrate on the bench; but in true soap-opera fashion, he also meddles (albeit discreetly) in other peoples' lives, mending broken marriages or reconciling estranged father and son on occasion.

"The fact is, an individual cannot be entertained unless he feels he is learning something, whether it be factual or something pertaining to emotion," Dallis wrote in 1962. "This is the reason for our fidelity to authenticity and realism in *Rex Morgan, M.D.* and *Judge Parker.*" True to his credo the author had his jurist tackle not only problems of corruption, graft, embezzlement, and other felonies, but also more personal concerns, such as unwanted pregnancy, adoption, and divorce, never failing to expound some object lesson in jurisprudence or psychology along the way. The readers usually skipped reading the dailies in which these little homilies were spun out and stuck instead to the sure-fire soap-opera developments.

The judge, a pipe-smoking widower in the early days of

the strip, remarried in the 1960s, and he also gave up smoking (perhaps on the advice of Dr. Rex Morgan). At the same time a new protagonist came onto the scene: Sam Driver, a crusading young attorney who gradually took center stage in the feature, over which Judge Parker is now presiding only nominally. Unlike the judge, the handsome, muscular newcomer could (and did) engage in fisticuffs when needed, and he also leads an active social life, with many attractive young women vying for his attentions. He remains, however, steadfastly loyal to his blonde and wealthy girlfriend, Abbey Spence.

Dan Heilman, a former assistant to Ken Ernst on *Mary Worth*, drew the strip from its inception to the time of his death in July 1965. Heilman closely hewed to the illustrative style that is the norm in soap-opera comics, but he also occasionally indulged in some humorous asides, especially in the drawing of minor characters. His assistant, Harold LeDoux, took over the artwork assignment in the time-honored tradition of newspaper comics, and he is still the artist of record today. Dallis died in 1991, and Woody Wilson now does the scripting, without any appreciable change of tone or substance. Distributed at the outset, daily and Sunday, by Publishers Syndicate, *Judge Parker* is now being carried by North America Syndicate, an affiliate of King Features.

M.H.

JUDGE RUMMY
See SILK HAT HARRY'S DIVORCE SUIT

JUDGE WRIGHT
1945–1948

Credited to Bob Brent, as the writer, and Bob Wells, as the artist, *Judge Wright* was actually the work of Robert Bernstein, who scripted the piece, and Bob Fujitani, who drew it. It first appeared on October 9, 1945, as a daily strip distributed by United Feature Syndicate.

Both creators were comic-book alumni (Bernstein having been a writer on the notorious *Crime Does Not Pay* comic book and Fujitani having long worked on such titles as *The Hangman* and *Black Angel*) and they lost no time getting the strip in high gear. The very first week Judge Jon Wright had to sentence to the electric chair a man declared guilty of murdering his wife, but secretly convinced that the convicted man was innocent, he set out to find the real killer (which of course he did in due time). The judge was a darkly handsome man of middle years, married to a beautiful and younger woman, the former Ann Sage, who happened to be a newspaper reporter and enthusiastically supported her husband in his unrelenting quest for justice. Together they brought to heel ruthless mobsters, corrupt politicians, and stealthy conspirators who thought they had escaped the clutches of the law. Amid all this, the loving couple found time to argue and fight, only to later make up in an orgy of hugs and kisses.

Fujitani drew the strip in a dark, brooding cinematic style, with a predominance of ominous angles and long shadows, reflecting the film-noir cinema style of the same period. Despite its undeniable narrative and graphic qualities, the feature did not take hold, and Fujitani left in December 1946 in search of greener pastures. He was succeeded for a few months by Fred Kida, followed by George Roussos, who took over in June 1947 but only lasted until February of the next year. Both men acquitted themselves creditably, but for the last few weeks of its run *Judge Wright* was plunged into the lower depths of draftsmanship by an untutored hack who didn't dare sign his name. His tenure was mercifully brief, ending along with the strip on April 3, 1948.

M.H.

JULIET JONES
See THE HEART OF JULIET JONES

JULIUS KNIPL, REAL ESTATE PHOTOGRAPHER
1988–present

One of the most distinctive voices in the alternative press, Ben Katchor suffuses his offbeat strip *Julius Knipl* with a poignant combination of nostalgia and defeat. The atmospheric eight- or nine-panel vignettes contain neither action nor commentary; rather, they are devoted to pensive examinations of the deteriorating underside of the city, focusing on odd little details of its marginal lives and trashy artifacts. Knipl, a middle-aged real-estate photographer, remains uninvolved in the decaying world he records, ruminating on the significance of its curious detritus. His name is a Yiddish word for nest-egg, "the little treasure you store away for a rainy day," Katchor explains. "And the strip's all about the little treasures of the city."

Described by one reader as "a two-bit Leopold Bloom," Knipl is a short, stocky gent with a thin moustache and no apparent personal life, sadly reflecting on others who make meager livings as rubber-band salesmen, shoe-tree manufacturers, rebuilders of malted-milk machines, and necktie appraisers. He speculates on the symbolic meaning of the eternal flame keeping sauerkraut warm at an all-night hot-dog stand, and wistfully recalls such drinks, now impossible to find, as Grape Bosphorus, Normona, Hoyvel's Coconut Champagne, and Hubert Water (soda water topped with a dash of syrup and half-sour milk). His bailiwick is the Cheap Merchandise District, with its second-floor restaurants and its signs for used hats, day-old bread, and patent mustard fountains.

An elegy for a passing scene, the strip is drawn with an unerring sense of the gritty streets of its unnamed locale. Its dark, soft-toned settings and sudden shifts, from long angle shots to minute close-ups, recall film noir, but Katchor denies the source. "On the contrary," he insists, "film-noir directors...were influenced by the same comics that influenced me." Deceptively simple in appearance, his captions, dialogue, and drawings interact to evoke a sense of the city and the observer's complex emotional response to it.

Julius Knipl was created in March 1988, for *the New York Press,* where it ran weekly until the *Village Voice* picked it up in 1994. Katchor has also syndicated the strip to alternative

Jump Start (R. Armstrong), © 1994 United Feature Syndicate

newspapers in Miami, San Diego, Seattle, Providence, Washington, D.C., and half a dozen other cities in the U.S., and it has a loyal following in Italy. Its first book-length collection, *Cheap Novelties: The Pleasures of Urban Decay,* was published in 1991 by Viking; edited by *Maus* creator Art Spiegelman, it was well received and earned the artist a profile in the *New Yorker* in 1993.

Despite the subtitle of his book, neither Katchor nor his equally detached hero takes any particular pleasure in the squalor they so perceptively observe, and much of the strip's appeal lies in its deadpan, dispassionate tone. Julius Knipl Real Estate Photographer focuses his lens on a world suffused in a light at once startlingly clear and movingly poetic.

D.W.

JUMP START
1990–present

In its advertising, United Feature Syndicate accurately portrays *Jump Start* by Robb Armstrong with the following: "A reflection of today's middle-class America, *Jump Start* follows a young African-American family as they chase their dreams and care for each other."

The strip revolves around the humorous happenings in the lives of recently married Joe, a police officer in an urban setting, and Marcy, a nurse. (When the strip began in 1990, Robb Armstrong himself was recently married.) Now, as the marriage has matured, the couple have a baby daughter, Sunny, and are looking to buy a house.

Cartoonist Robb Armstrong is successful in bringing an upwardly mobile African-American family to the comics because of his background. Just as his characters Joe and Marcy work on getting a "jump start" on life, so did the cartoonist under the guidance of his late mother.

Born and raised in West Philadelphia, Robb Armstrong left the public-school system after the sixth grade to attend the Shipley School, an exclusive private school on Philadelphia's Main Line, a reference to the commuter-rail line that serves suburban areas outside the city. His serious art education began at Shipley; from there he attended Syracuse University and earned a bachelor's degree in fine arts.

Robb Armstrong's mother died during his freshman year at Syracuse, and it was a major trauma for him. He took the negative energy from this event and put it into *Hector,* a comic strip he created for the Syracuse student newspaper. Hector, an African-American college student with attitude,

was cool, wore fogged-up goggles, and was a big hit on campus. By Armstrong's senior year, *Hector* was given a serious look by Tribune Media Services, which ultimately rejected the strip as being too collegiate and isolated.

Graduating from college, Robb Armstrong went to work in the advertising industry. His attempts at a syndicated feature focused on *Cherry Top,* a strip about cops. He researched the strip by talking with a retired police officer who was the father of a good friend. *Cherry Top* at first went nowhere; but eventually Armstrong's friend Mark Cohen showed it to United Feature. That syndicate was interested in an African-American strip, and *Cherry Top* evolved into *Jump Start.*

Armstrong has a distinctive style that features rounded rather than square corners to his panels and a delightful attention to detail that goes beyond what might be called big-foot cartoon style. His police car bounces along with all four wheels off the ground as Joe and his partner, Crunchy, talk about life; Crunchy is white and a generation older than Joe. Cartoonist Armstrong realized that as a police officer, Joe would not only be involved in the African-American community but would be a role model as well.

The same holds true for Marcy being a nurse. Like Joe, she meets all types of people in her job and this broadens the appeal of the strip. *Jump Start* is as successful in part because it isn't only a genre strip about African Americans, it is a strip about life in America in the 1990s. Just as Joe's fellow cops offer subjects for gags, the nurses and doctors at the hospital Macy works in offer a widely varied cast of characters for Robb Armstrong to work with.

As an African American who knows middle-class hopes and dreams in the broadest sense, Robb Armstrong is successful and funny in *Jump Start* because he is comfortable with the material and because the strip is all-inclusive in presenting the mosaic that is America.

B.C., Jr.

JUNGLE JIM
1934–1954

By the end of 1933 King Features, then as now the largest purveyor of comics in the U.S., had a worthy arsenal of adventure strips, such as *Brick Bradford* and *Tim Tyler's Luck,* but none that could compete with the likes of *Tarzan* or *Buck Rogers.* This gap was filled at one blow by the Sunday page Alex Raymond contributed to the King roster, starting in January 7, 1934: its main feature was *Flash Gordon,* and occupying the top third of the page there was its companion strip, *Jungle Jim.*

In the opening sequences Jim Bradley, better known as Jungle Jim, was an animal trapper and tamer working for American and European zoos, very much in the mold of Frank Buck. Later on his professional reputation would lead him to more esoteric activities, recasting him as a kind of exalted privateer, midway between an international troubleshooter and a secret agent, who would be called upon by government agencies and commercial interests alike as an instrument of last resort from the Indian frontier to the China seas. Jungle Jim certainly looked tailor-made for the role: with his tall and elegant silhouette he recalled Gary Cooper, and like Cooper he appeared equally at home in the jungle and in the drawing-room. In jodhpurs and pith helmet he was the very image of heroic determination, and he cut a stylish, dashing figure in a white dinner jacket with a red carnation adorning its lapel.

Jungle Jim was too handsome a man not to attract the attention of the women he encountered, but early on he fixed his choice, albeit not an exclusive one, on Lilli de Vrille, an adventuress also known as Shanghai Lil (in direct reference to the role played by Marlene Dietrich in the movie *Shanghai Express*). A dark-haired, sultry temptress, Lil was reformed by the hero's love, and together they embarked on many a swashbuckling enterprise, with Lil's wiles nicely complementing Jim's brawn in their common fight against crazed warlords, shady traffickers, and international conspirators. Jim's most constant companion remained, however, his loyal Hindu assistant, the turbaned and knife-wielding Kolu. A man of few words and swift action, Kolu was a master guide and tracker, and his jungle skills often proved invaluable to his companion in danger.

After a desultory string of adventures involving mad hunters, wild animals, and bloodthirsty savages, *Jungle Jim* settled on a more disciplined mode of storytelling. In tales cleverly mixing elements of espionage, suspense, intrigue, and mystery, Jim successively put down a rebellion in Mongolia, tussled with a renegade prince in Burma, searched for Genghis Khan's treasure in Afghanistan, and fought pirates on the Malay seas. There were also adventures taking place in Borneo, in the Celebes, in Shanghai—in an unending travelogue of steamy jungles and teeming Asian cities.

With war coming closer and closer to American shores, Jim was called back to the States and given various coun-terespionage missions, in the Panama Canal zone, in South America, even in Washington, D.C. The coming of hostilities after the bombing of Pearl Harbor allowed Jim to return to his old stomping-grounds of Asia, where he could best display his prowess. After getting reunited with Kolu, he joined now the guerrilla-fighters in Yunnan, now the Chindwin commandos in Burma, blowing up munitions dumps, setting oil installations ablaze, and ambushing Japanese columns all over the China-Burma-India theater of war. Lil on her part enlisted in the Marine Corps, soon to be followed in real life by Alex Raymond.

After Raymond's departure a number of different artists worked on the strip, although King Features' catalogue lists only Austin Briggs from May 1944. It is clear that the artwork was initially done by Raymond's brother Jim until 1945, when Briggs actually took over; in later years Briggs would be assisted by ghosts, including Jim Raymond again and John Mayo. Briggs's elegant brushwork and fine eye for colorful detail can clearly be seen in the episodes of the uranium mine mystery (1945–46) and the kidnapping of Lita Carson (1946–47). In addition, scantily clad ingenues and lascivious femmes fatales, two of Briggs's specialties, were pretty much in evidence in this period, and their loving depiction leaves no doubt as to the identity of the artist.

In July 1948 Paul Norris, who had been drawing the *Jungle Jim* comic books, was entrusted with the drawing of the newspaper strip as well. With Norris's advent, Don Moore, who had been writing the strip's continuity from the beginning, was finally allowed to get his name under the title. Norris, an adequate draftsman, did not possess the talents of Raymond or even Briggs, and his plodding style robbed the strip of much of its romantic appeal and all of its poetry. After a long, painful decline, *Jungle Jim* finally expired on August 8, 1954.

Jungle Jim is mostly remembered today for Alex Raymond's vibrant, exhilarating artwork. Raymond often lavished more care on his secondary feature than on *Flash Gordon,* and he delighted in dramatic effects and subtle color harmonies. His evocation of mood and depiction of action was masterly. Even more than *Tarzan, Jungle Jim* epitomized the dream of exotic adventure; and the place names nonchalantly strewn all along the narratives—names like Borneo, Tibet, Mandalay, Gobi Desert, Khyber Pass, Java Sea—remain forever linked in memory with the name of Jungle Jim.

M.H.

Jungle Jim (A. Raymond), © 1937 **King Features Syndicate**

JUST BOY
`See ELMER`

JUST KIDS
`1923–1957`

The lively tradition of the kid strip is one of the earliest to appear in comics, and no major syndicate was without at least one. When Gene Byrnes's *Reg'lar Fellers* proved a success in the *New York Herald,* Hearst was eager to compete and contracted Augustus Daniel ("Ad") Carter to revive an old kid strip of his called *Our Friend Mush* for King Features Syndicate. Retitled *Just Kids* but featuring some of the same characters, the new strip began as a daily on July 23, 1923, and added a Sunday page on August 20 of the same year.

Just Kids was considered by many to be an imitation of Byrnes's popular strip in both visual style and content; its setting, the little town of Barnsville, had the same quaintly stylized architecture as the unnamed setting of *Reg'lar Fellers,* and even the name of Carter's character Fatso Dolan seemed to echo that of Byrnes's Jimmie Dugan. But the kids in *Just Kids* had a character of their own, just as reg'lar but a shade more aggressive. Mush Stebbins, the leader of the band, was a wholesome lad who never passed up the chance for a fight; indeed, the standard formula among his friends when a confrontation approaches was "I'll hold your coat." His buddies were clearly distinguishable from each other in appearance—Fatso Dolan was chubby, Pat Chan was Chinese, and every boy in town had his own unique headgear—but they all spoke and acted pretty much the same.

A more distinctive characteristic of the strip was the sometimes bizarre characters in the background: a strange old man always seen roller-skating down the street talking to his infant grandchild, a musical street cleaner, and other eccentrics made Barnsville one of the more colorful communities in the comics.

After about a decade, *Just Kids* shifted gears and became a continuity strip. Although the Sunday page continued to offer self-contained weekly gags, the daily strip carried its cast to distant places and involved them in suspenseful stories of mystery and crime as well as pure adventure. Essentially good children, for all their pugnacity, Mush, Fatso, and Pat always supported the forces of law and social order in their escapades.

Although the minimal backgrounds in *Just Kids* had little claim to graphic distinction, the kids themselves and the goofy characters around them were drawn with a certain primitive charm. Although faithful to the conventions of 1920s cartoons, the stylized faces of the characters were capable of considerable expressiveness. As the style became increasingly dated, the strip began to lose its audience. The daily feature was discontinued on August 18, 1947, although the gag-based Sunday page lasted until December 20, 1957, six months after Ad Carter's death. (For a time in the 1930s and 1940s the Sunday page sported an interesting companion strip, *Nicodemus O'Malley and His Whale*—years before *Free Willy.*)

D.W.

Just Kids (A. Carter), © 1932 King Features Syndicate

THE KATZENJAMMER KIDS
1897–present

The oldest strip in existence and the only one to have spanned the entire history of the comics, *The Katzenjammer Kids* saw light on December 12, 1897, in the pages of "The American Humorist," the comic supplement of W. R. Hearst's *New York Journal*. It was the *Journal's* editor, Rudolph Block, who suggested to German-born cartoonist Rudolph Dirks that he try his hand at adapting Wilhelm Busch's highly successful picture story *Max und Moritz* for the fledgling medium. On the strength of the sketches he then submitted, Dirks got the assignment: Busch's urchins were rechristened Hans and Fritz, with the surname Katzenjammer (literally "howling of cats," but meaning a hangover in German slang) bestowed upon them, allegedly by Block himself.

In the first comic pages Dirks established his two juvenile antiheroes, the blond Fritz and the dark-haired Hans, known jointly as the Katzies, as incorrigible pranksters who would play tricks on the maid, the butcher, the neighbors, even the family cat, simply for the fun of it. With their foppish attire and innocent-looking faces, they were both the pride and the bane of their German-American family. Their dumpy mother ("Die Mama"), a busy and happy housewife, was always baking pies for "her liddle anchels" and turning a blind eye to their shenanigans; their ineffectual father could merely sigh after each of the twins' depredations, "Sich a family!" Only the grandfather would try to whip some discipline into the boys (vainly as it turned out) by way of repeated spankings—thus starting the familiar pattern of mischief and retribution that was to become one of the hallmarks of the strip.

This domestic setting changed with the gradual disap-

pearance of the two male adult members of the family. They were replaced by Der Captain, an old seadog taken in by Die Mama as a boarder in August 1902, and Der Inspector, a bewhiskered truant officer who had come to look for the terrible twins in January 1905 and stayed on as Der Captain's pinochle-playing crony. The arrival of these two irresistible targets, nicknamed respectively "the walrus" and "the goat" by Hans and Fritz, caused the twins to raise their mischief to the level of inspired deviltry. Not confining their pranks to these more immediate targets, the Katzies literally waged war on the entire adult world, causing Der Inspector to exclaim in despair: "Mit dose kids, society iss nix!"

Dirks also turned *The Katzenjammers,* which at first had only made use of silent pantomime, into the first genuine comic strip, complete with panel sequences and speech balloons. He also built suspense and excitement into the series with lengthy adventures lasting months and even years, sending his characters on a cataclysmic cruise around the world, or having them prospecting for gold out West.

At the height of the strip's popularity, Dirks and Hearst engaged in a bitter legal battle over the strip's ownership. In a judgment worthy of Solomon, the federal courts ruled in appeal that Hearst had title to the name but that Dirks could go on drawing the characters for the competition. Hearst then turned to Harold Knerr, who for years had drawn *Die Fineheimer Twins,* the most successful of the many *Katzenjammer* imitations, as a replacement for Dirks. His signature started appearing in November 1914 on what was now billed as *"The Original" Katzenjammer Kids* (to differentiate this version from the one Dirks was concurrently doing for the *New York World*).

Having inherited a cast of already legendary characters from Dirks, Knerr then set out to elevate the basic situation

The Katzenjammer Kids (R. Dirks), 1905

The Katzenjammer Kids (H. Knerr), ca. 1915

to quasi-mythological proportions. During the first twenty years of his stewardship, he dispatched the Katzenjammer tribe on a worldwide path of destruction extending from the Arctic to the Sahara desert, and from Hollywood to the Congo forest. They even briefly claimed to be Dutch citizens during the anti-German hysteria of World War I, with the strip's title switched to *The Shenanigan Kids* (it reverted to its original name in 1920).

The Katzenjammers' wanderings ended in 1935 when they all landed on an island off the coast of Africa ruled by the benevolent King Bongo. After they had settled there, they were joined subsequently by Miss Twiddle, an English governess who was brought in for the thankless task of teaching the Kids civilized manners, and her niece Lena. Knerr rounded out his cast of characters with the introduction of the foppish Rollo Rhubarb, Miss Twiddle's star pupil, whose underhanded schemes often proved more than a match for the Kids' devilish tricks. In addition, there were literally thousands of extras: palace guards, tax collectors, traveling salesmen, not to mention visiting royalty, lost explorers, and hosts of wild animals, each last one of them delineated and individualized with a sure hand and a fine comic touch.

On this broad canvas Knerr painted countless variations of his basic theme of all against all with unbounded verve and gusto and an unerring eye for composition and motion. His single-minded devotion to his characters shone through in his minute attention to detail, his accomplished draftsmanship, his flair for comic effect. Much admired by Picasso and the Surrealist painters, his is the version most often associated with *The Katzenjammer Kids*. His death in 1949 brought to an end the most brilliant phase of the strip.

A long succession of cartoonists, some reasonably talented, some barely adequate, have tried since then to take on the mantle once worn by Dirks and

Knerr. First there was Doc Winner, followed in 1956 by Joe Musial who drew the feature until his death in 1977. After a brief interim period (1977–81) when it was done by Joe Senich, the Katzenjammers passed into the hands of Angelo De Cesare, with Hy Eisman taking over in 1986. *The Katzenjammer Kids* is now fast approaching the century mark, and indications are that the only strip still surviving from the last century will make it into the next millennium.

M.H.

KEEPING UP WITH THE JONESES
1913–1945

Arthur "Pop" Momand started his strip *Keeping Up with the Joneses* about an aspiring middle-class family in the summer of 1913, the same year that George McManus created *Bringing Up Father* on a similar theme. The feature, which initially appeared in Joseph Pulitzer's *New York World*, may have been meant as a swipe at McManus, who had deserted Pulitzer for Hearst the year before.

The phrase "keeping up with the Joneses" was not invented by Momand, but dates back to the last century and refers to an actual New York family, that of George Frederic Jones and his wife Lucretia Rhinelander, possessors of large tracts of Manhattan real estate (and parents to the novelist Edith Wharton), whose lavish lifestyle bedazzled the local citizenry. Momand, who was born in 1886 and educated in Manhattan, was certainly familiar with the coinage, and he dreamed up a fictitious Jones family for snobbery-minded middle-class folks to look up to. The strip (which was simply signed "Pop") dealt with just such social climbers, the middle-aged, bewhiskered Aloysius McGinis, and his ample spouse Clarice. Anything the Joneses did, the McGinises would endeavor to emulate. Aloysius would try to get into the same club as Mr. Jones, Clarice would buy her furniture from the same store the Joneses patronized, and on weekends the couple would go to the same spa the Joneses had journeyed to the week before.

Keeping Up with the Joneses ("Pop"), 1913

The McGinises had a pretty and nubile daughter (in further imitation of Maggie and Jiggs) whose name was Julie, and a black maid called Belladonna. Momand drew the strip in a well-rounded, winsome cartoon style that stood out of the newspaper page. *Keeping Up with the Joneses* enjoyed considerable success from the start, and it was adapted to the musical stage and made into a series of animated cartoons in 1915–16. In the meantime, the feature had inspired a daily spin-off, *Cats,* derived from the byplay between the Jones cat and other animal creatures that had gone on for months in the *Keeping Up* strip, in the manner of George Herriman (another Pulitzer defector).

After the *World* folded in 1930, syndication was taken up by Associated Newspapers, which added a Sunday page to the daily strip. In the grim climate of the Great Depression, conspicuous consumption was no longer a theme in keeping with the times, and accordingly Momand turned his creation into a conventional strip of domestic life. It proved more and more difficult for the feature to compete successfully in this crowded field, and it steadily lost circulation, finally disappearing in 1945. That it managed to thrive for over three decades, however, is proof of the cartoonist's underrated talent.

M.H.

KERRY DRAKE
1943–1983

Kerry Drake was launched, daily and Sunday, in October 1943, in replacement of *Dan Dunn,* which had just come to an end. It was distributed by Publishers Syndicate, and the credited author was Alfred Andriola.

Like *Dan Dunn* before it, but in more subtle ways, *Kerry Drake* was an imitation of *Dick Tracy.* While Andriola handled the overall concept, he very soon turned to others to do the drawing for him. As for the actual scripting, it was carried out almost from the start by Allen Saunders, who was Publishers' unofficial writer-in-residence. The first stories were genuinely suspenseful. They involved cases of kidnapping, extortion, serial murder, and gang violence. Kerry was a tow-headed, handsome-looking private eye working for the local district attorney; he didn't hesitate to use his fists or his gun in the course of investigations. Like every other self-respecting PI, he had a pretty and adoring secretary, named Sandy Burns, and a comic sidekick, a red-haired office boy called Firetop. In the Tracy tradition, the villains he encountered and subjugated had colorful names like Dr. Zero, Stitches, No Face, Kid Gloves, DDT, and Mr. Goliath. There was a great deal of violence and sadism going on in the early years, prompting Coulton Waugh in 1947 to ask rhetorically (and disapprovingly), "Is this what the public wants?" "Many of us doubt it," was his own answer.

After his former secretary and current fiancée Sandy had been murdered, Kerry quit DA work and became a detective on the police force. Saunders then gave vent to his proclivities, and the strip soon veered toward soap-opera continuities, a step Andriola explained thus: "I try to incorporate the human issue—how crime affects the peo-

Kerry Drake (A. Andriola), ca. 1964, © Field Enterprises

ple involved—rather than spelling out crime for crime's sake." The trend solidified in 1958 with the hero's wedding to Mindy, the widow of a slain policeman (with Mary Worth in attendance!), and culminated in 1967 with the birth to the happy couple of quadruplets.

The strip had gotten so far away from its initial premise that a kid brother named Lefty was discovered to take his older sibling's place in the fisticuffs division: as chance would have it, he also happened to be a detective. From the 1970s on, Lefty took care of the rough stuff, while Kerry played house husband. William Overgard, who had taken over the writing chores in 1971, authored some interesting and suspenseful continuities in the rediscovered tradition of the early *Kerry Drake.* Meantime the parade of ghost artists had come to an end in 1955, when Sururi Gumen became the official assistant on the strip, which he was finally allowed to cosign in 1976. All these changes did not help circulation, and throughout its final decade *Kerry Drake* steadily lost client papers. Andriola died in March 1983, and the feature he had steadfastly claimed as his own despite all evidence to the contrary died with him.

M.H.

KEVIN THE BOLD
1948–1972

One of the most tortuously plotted of all comic strips, *Kevin the Bold* began life as a Sunday feature called *Mitzi McCoy* on November 7, 1948, and was the creation of Kreigh Collins for NEA Service.

Mitzi McCoy was a blonde heiress with a passion for adventure and a knack for getting herself into hot water, in her sentimental as well as in her adventurous life. With her exuberance untempered by any shred of wisdom, she seemed a cross between Frank Godwin's Connie and Al Capp's Daisy Mae. In the first episode, fleeing, in her private plane, from a disastrous union on the eve of her marriage, she crashed in the north Canadian woods. After

Kevin the Bold (K. Collins), © 1955 NEA Service

being rescued by Tim Graham, a handsome reporter on her hometown paper, the *Clarion,* she got herself mixed up with an assortment of unsavory characters attracted by her money and her looks.

Seeing that he was getting nowhere with his heroine, Collins tried a new tack. In September 1950, Mitzi was told of a distant Irish ancestor named Kevin and nicknamed "the bold" for his prowess in war and in love. The following October 1, Kevin materialized in the flesh, Mitzi disappeared from view, and the entire page got itself rechristened *Kevin the Bold.* Under the new title it was to last for another two decades.

Collins drew the adventures of his Irish rogue with gusto and a flair for dramatic effect. The very first page dropped Kevin in the midst of the fray, fending off with fists and sword Barbary pirates who had come to raid the Irish coast in search of slaves and booty. The hero was only a lowly shepherd but he proved, in the author's own words, "arrogant as a baron." This all took place in the year 1497, and soon Kevin found himself in the employ of King Henry VIII of England, for whom he carried out secret and highly dangerous missions that took him all over Europe and into America. He also found time for rest and relaxation in the midst of his adventures, courting French princesses and Indian maidens during his time off, though most of the lighter moments in the strip were provided by Kevin's oversize Spanish lieutenant Pedro, and by his youthful squire Brett.

Collins gave himself considerable leeway in the telling of his hero's adventures, and the narrative meandered quite a bit. There were even flashbacks within flashbacks, as in 1965 when the author stopped the action to retell the legend of Robin Hood and his Merry Men. Russ Winterbotham, who had come on board as scriptwriter in 1964, was responsible for this one, as he was for winding down the historic setting with a flash forward that brought the strip back to the present.

The ground was laid for another change of title, and *Kevin the Bold* on November 11, 1968, turned into *Up Anchor,* about a couple of enterprising seafarers in far-flung adventures around the globe. The feature, which was never popular enough to warrant a daily strip, did not last long in its new guise; on February 27, 1972 it ended its eventful run.

M.H.

THE KEWPIES
1905–1918, 1935–1937

Contrary to widely held belief, there were quite a number of women cartoonists in the newspaper field at the turn of the century. One stellar example was Rose O'Neill, who in the course of her long career had contributed countless creations to magazines, periodicals, and newspapers, beginning in 1896. In 1905 she hit it big with the Kewpies, cupidlike creatures that she claimed came to her in a dream. Before long, the Kewpies were a national craze, carried first in the pages of the *Ladies' Home Journal,* transferring in 1910 to the *Woman's Home Companion,* and finally to *Good Housekeeping* in 1913. The Kewpies' fame was spread further by the celebrated Kewpie doll, the ultimate in cuteness, and by a flood of assorted merchandise.

The Kewpies entered the newspaper field in 1917 with a daily Kewpies panel along with a Sunday page. O'Neill, the owner of the copyright, syndicated the feature herself. In the Sundays, the Kewpies were seen cavorting, dancing, and making merry in a series of vignettes linked thematically, while the panel had some cute saying mouthed by one or the other of the Kewpie characters. O'Neill closed down both newspaper versions in 1919, as a gesture of mourning for the Allied losses in World War I.

On February 5, 1935, O'Neill came back to the newspaper pages with a Sunday feature again called *The Kewpies,* which was distributed by King Features Syndicate. In true comic-strip fashion, this revived version told a weekly story in a succession of panels. With the use of dialogue balloons, the Kewpies were now further individualized: there were Uncle Hob, a curmudgeonly kind of hobgoblin, and

The Kewpies (R. O'Neill), 1918

his infant nephew Gobby; the twins Katie and Johnny Kewp; Bobby, the information Kewp; along with animal characters such as Frisky Freddie the jumping frog and Squabby the duck. Scootles, an inquisitive four-year-old, also wandered into the place and stayed on as "Kewpieville's favorite tourist."

In the gloomy depression years, O'Neill's cheerful, rosy, and overly cute creatures could not long survive, and by the end of 1937 the Sunday page was gone from the newspapers. The artist, however, continued to draw the Kewpies for various publications until the time of her death in 1944.

M.H.

THE KID SISTER
1927–1935

Under prodding from his younger brother Chic, Lyman Young, an advertising artist, decided to try his hand at cartooning. In 1924 he took over *The Kelly Kids,* a brother-and-sister strip that had been created by C. W. Kahles in 1919. In 1927 he followed his brother to King Features, for which he created *The Kid Sister* as a daily strip. When his better-known creation, *Tim Tyler's Luck,* acquired a Sunday version on July 19, 1931, *The Kid Sister* became its companion strip on the page.

Anticipating Ruth McKinney's "My Sister Eileen" stories by a full ten years, *The Kid Sister* starred two sisters from the sticks living at a boarding-house in the big city: blonde, flirtatious Jane Dale, the title character, and her older, more sedate sibling, Trixie. Jane had dreams of the stage, while her sister only wished to marry some nice young man from a respectable background. The dailies were mildly humorous, centering on the many contretemps encountered by the sisters in the pursuit of their respective goals. With the advent of the Sundays, the soap-opera elements, already in evidence in the daily version, came to dominate the story lines. There were tales involving a lost inheritance, mysterious doings in a dark house, and the like. At one point the sisters even became rivals in love, but it all ended happily with a double wedding on March 24, 1935. Whether Jane and Trixie lived in matrimonial bliss ever after was left to the readers' imaginations.

Lyman Young at first drew the strip in a broad, cartoony style, but it soon acquired a more glittering look thanks to assistance from brother Chic, who had a knack for drawing pretty girls. In 1931, Alex Raymond, who had in the meantime been hired as Lyman Young's assistant, glamorized the feature even further, lavishing special care on the two lovely protagonists. This was particularly apparent in *Sister's Cutout,* a series of weekly pinups that functioned as an adjunct to the main feature and showed Jane and Trixie in various states of undress. After Raymond's departure late in 1933, Charles Flanders was given the task of supplying the artwork in close imitation of his predecessor's style.

While hardly a masterpiece, *The Kid Sister* deserves recognition if only for the exquisite artwork Alex Raymond produced during his two-year tenure on the strip.

M.H.

THE KIN-DER-KIDS
1906

To compete with W. R. Hearst's rival *Chicago American,* the *Chicago Tribune* sent its representative, James Keeley, to Germany in 1905 with a view to recruiting local cartooning talent for the paper's color comic section. Chicago was then home to a sizable German population and the *Tribune* was eager to attract their readership. Keeley's mission proved highly successful: in a matter of a few months he signed up such notable German illustrators as Lothar Meggendorfer, Karl Pomerhanz, and most important of all, Lyonel Feininger. Born in America to German immigrant parents in 1871, Feininger had later moved to Germany, where he had become a cartoonist of repute, working regularly for French and German magazines. *The Kin-der-Kids,* his first contribution to the art of the comics, premiered on April 29, 1906.

The new strip was ushered in with great hoopla. A double-page spread displayed on one side a gigantic self-portrait of the artist (dubbed "Your Uncle Feininger") as a puppet-master with his various characters dangling from his fingers, and on the other side "the Kin-der-Kids portrait gallery." There was Daniel Webster, the intellectual of the group, who couldn't take his eyes off any book he happened to be reading at the time, and whose reply to any query invariably was, "Don't disturb me!" Strenuous Teddy (an obvious reference to President Theodore Roosevelt) was an all-around athlete always engaged in lifting weights, kicking footballs, or jumping rope. Rounding up the little band, the voracious Pie-mouth could always be counted on to scrounge up needed provisions, even in the Siberian wilds or in the middle of the ocean. The Kin-der-Kids had

The Kid Sister (L. Young), © 1932 King Features Syndicate

King Aroo (J. Kent), © 1965 Jack Kent

two pets to accompany them on their adventures: one animal, the gloomy-looking dachshund Sherlock Bones, the other mechanical, a life-size robot called Little Japansky that exhibited extraordinary strength when wound up.

The title had been dreamed up by Keeley (with a side glance no doubt toward *The Katzenjammer Kids*), but otherwise Feininger's kid strip had little to do with Rudolph Dirks's creation. On a tenuous narrative thread, proceeding by non sequiturs, Feininger detailed the round-the-world odyssey of the Kids in the family bathtub. By land and by sea (the tub was amphibious), they successively encountered a whale, won a motorboat race, and were taken prisoners by Cossacks, among other adventures. In hot pursuit after them was the dreaded Aunty Jim-Jam, who was hellbent on administering a double dose of castor oil to the Kids.

An accomplished painter, Feininger suffused his pages with expressionistic colors, shades of green, brown, and purple, sharpening and underlining the ludicrous goings-on. His graphic style, very angular and only slightly caricatural, served less the purpose of the story than the logic of the composition. The placement of the speech-balloons proved a special headache for Feininger (as they did for Winsor McCay), who subordinated them to his overall layout scheme; this often resulted in long stretches of dialogue being squeezed into too tight a space, rendering them virtually illegible. With all its faults, *The Kin-der-Kids* displays such visual splendor and nonstop motion that to a modern eye they sweep aside any literal objection.

Following a dispute between the artist and his employers, *The Kin-der-Kids* came to an abrupt end in misadventure, the last, extraneous page appearing on November 18, 1906, after a run of exactly seven months. Never has such a short-lived comic strip elicited so much long-winded oratory from art-journal types, who finally discovered Feininger's cartooning artistry after everyone else had. "Feininger drew...in a studio on the Boulevard Raspail," Adam Gopnik, as one example, wrote in the catalogue of the 1990 "High and Low" show at the New York Museum of Modern Art, "all the while simultaneously absorbing, and sending back in simplified and slightly deflected form, the burgeoning manners of Cezannist faceting and Fauvist simplification..." Let it be simply said that *The Kin-der-Kids* was an artistic masterwork as well as a pioneering comic strip.

M.H.

KING AROO
1950–1965

*O*ne of the few newspaper strips worthy of comparison with *Krazy Kat* and *Barnaby*, Jack Kent's *King Aroo* made its debut, daily and Sunday, in a modest number of newspapers in November 1950, under the distributorship of the McClure Syndicate.

An engaging blend of twisted fairy-tale nonsense story, fantasy yarn, and mock epic, the strip had as its locale the kingdom of Myopia, a country so small that the princess from the kingdom next door could drop in to borrow a cup of sugar. Despite its tiny size, Myopia boasted a number of topographical features, from the Spindly Thicket, home to an incredible variety of flora and fauna, to the Eerie Woods, rumored to be full of spooks and hobgoblins—except at vacation time. The moat circling the royal castle was a world unto itself, containing desert islands and carrying on its placid waters bottled messages from seafarers shipwrecked on distant shores.

This peaceable land was ruled with a benign hand and a light touch by King Aroo. A short monarch with a short beard and mustache, Aroo cut a somewhat less than regal figure, even when attired in full royal apparel: his ermine was molting, his velvet robe was covered with patches, and the gold plate had rubbed off his crown. The modesty of his position in the world was equally matched by the modesty of his ambitions in life. Apprised at one point of all the requirements needed to successfully win a princess's hand, he opted to go to bed instead, sagely concluding, "It's a wonder all princesses aren't spinsters."

King Aroo's entire retinue consisted of Yupyop, a bald, bespectacled little man who acted in turn or simultaneously as royal adviser, master of protocol, keeper of the seal, and occasional nursemaid to his dumpy sovereign. Yupyop frequently engaged in friendly, if heated, arguments with the top-hatted Prof. Yorgle, a scholar versed in all things (and then some), who resided appropriately enough on Highbrow Hill. Other royal subjects of note included Dipody Distich, a poet for all occasions; Mr. Elephant, who often thought himself a mouse or a lamppost; the letter-carrying kangaroo Mr. Pennipost, whose supervisor hid in his pouch to remind him of the service's proud motto, "The postman always rings twice"; and Drexel Dragon, who had learned to play dead in order for King Aroo to impress visiting princesses. On the fringes of the kingdom, at the edge of the Eerie Woods, there lived Wanda Witch, who came to town to ply her trade with a sign on the side of her handcart reading: "Spells cast and hemstitching done while you wait."

The characters' sundry adventures were all of a gentle, whimsical quality: King Aroo buying a magic three-and-a-half-leagues boot (he didn't have the dime needed to buy the whole pair); Mr. Pennipost flying to the moon and back on Wanda Witch's broomstick; or Yupyop learning to crow to rouse the sun in replacement for the laryngitis-stricken rooster on duty that day. Those stories sometimes spun out for weeks, and Kent's imagination never flagged, as he piled incident upon improbable incident.

The drawings, rendered in a curving, graceful line, had a rounded airiness in keeping with the open-endedness of the story lines. Together they encompassed a definite vision of the world. As Gilbert Seldes rightly observed, "Jack Kent brings to the small company of fantasists the primary faculty of being able to create a compact universe that adheres strictly to a logic of its own." Never carried by a great many newspapers, *King Aroo* was dropped following the merger of McClure with the Bell Syndicate. Revived for a time by Golden Gate Features, an outfit expressly created for the purpose, it finally came to an end on June 14, 1965.

M.H.

KING OF THE ROYAL MOUNTED
1935–1954

In the mid-1930s publishing entrepreneur Stephen Slesinger somehow persuaded the popular western novelist Zane Grey to create an adventure strip for him; on the strength of Grey's reputation, he then sold the distribution rights to King Features Syndicate. In due time the new feature made its appearance in the comic pages on February 17, 1935, under the title *King of the Royal Mounted*.

Sergeant King (only his last name was known) was one Canadian mountie who always got his man. In his relentless pursuit of fur thieves, cattle rustlers, and train robbers, his demeanor invariably remained one of dogged earnestness, and he never cracked a joke or a smile. His first adventure involved him in the search for stolen treasure under the Arctic Circle, where he first met Betty Blake, his love interest, and her brother Kid, who became his inseparable boy-companion. The artist on the weekly page was Allen Dean,

King of the Royal Mounted (A. Dean), © 1937 **King Features Syndicate**

who excelled in the depiction of the Canadian Northwest, its snowcapped peaks, vast pine forests, icy-blue waters, and boundless snowfields against which King's uniform burned bright.

King met with enough popular success to warrant the addition on March 2, 1936, of a daily strip: Dean took charge of it, relinquishing the Sunday page to Charles Flanders. The dailies would alternate mystery plots, spy tales, and rescue missions, along with the more traditional western themes of land grabbing, claim jumping, and bank robbing. Rounding out the cast of characters was the French Canadian Jerry Laroux, a pilot for the Royal Mounted who spoke in heavily accented English.

In April 1938 Dean left the strip, which was also taken over by Flanders: his tenure on both the Sunday and daily versions was creditable rather than spectacular. If he proved stiff in the drawing of characters, his deft handling of western scenes got him promoted to the newly minted *Lone Ranger* strip; Jim Gary succeeded him in the drawing of *King*. Gary at first brought a more relaxed, less brooding feel to the strip, as well as a welcome humanity to the characters, and some of his early stories were genuinely thrilling. As time went by, however, he seemed to tire of his assignment, and left more and more of the drawing to "ghosts"; when *King* was finally discontinued in February 1954, few mourned its passing.

King was never an adventure strip of the first rank, but it did enjoy a fair amount of success in the 1930s and 1940s; it was even made into a movie serial in 1942.

M.H.

KRAZY KAT
1910–1944

Inarguably the most celebrated comic strip of all time, George Herriman's *Krazy Kat* experienced an exceedingly complicated period of gestation before finally coming to light and fruition. As the creator once declared, "*Krazy Kat* was not conceived, not born, it jes' grew." The first stirrings made themselves felt on July 26, 1910, when Herriman, "to fill up the waste space" at the bottom of *The Dingbat Family*, the daily strip he was then doing for Hearst's *Evening Journal*, had the family cat beaned with a stone thrown by an impudent mouse. This simple byplay continued for weeks as a sideshow (or rather a bottom show) to the action in the main feature (retitled *The Family Upstairs* for a while before going back to its original appellation). Slowly the protagonists grew into their definitive selves: the mouse became Ignatz, and the nameless cat turned into Krazy Kat. A thin line separated the main action from the cat-and-mouse game going on below: this subsidiary strip ran variously as *Krazy Kat and Ignatz* and *Krazy Kat and I. Mouse*. Finally, on October 28, 1913, the feature that "jes'grew" appeared for the first time as an independent strip under its definitive name, thus marking *Krazy Kat*'s coming of age.

The initial premise was very simple. Krazy Kat, a creature of indeterminate gender (Krazy once described him/herself as both a bachelor and a spinster, wryly adding that this situation would last "until I get wedded"), loves Ignatz

Krazy Kat (G. Herriman), 1918

Mouse. Ignatz in turn despises Krazy for that unwanted love and in exasperation devotes all his time and energy to finding innumerable ways to hit Krazy with a brick, which has the opposite effect of reinforcing Krazy's unrequited passion. It seems that Krazy was the linear, though infinitely distant, descendant of Kleopatra Kat's daughter, whose love for a lowly mouse had been kindled by a *billet doux* chiseled on a brick tablet; and in his atavistic memory Krazy mistook the brick hurled by Ignatz as a message of love. This bipolar situation was further complicated some time later when Offissa Pupp, bulldogged representative of law and order, deemed it his duty to toss Ignatz in jail after the mouse had thrown his brick. In this way there developed a complex triangle presenting limitless plot possibilities that Herriman was prompt to exploit.

The apex of the triangle was constituted by Offissa Pupp, the one solitary figure among the principals. One side was made up of the "Kat Klan," namely Krazy himself, Aunt Tabby, Uncle Tom, Krazy Katbird, Osker Wildcat, Alec Kat, and Krazy Katfish. The other side was comprised of the House of Mouse, including Ignatz, his wife Matilda, their offspring Irving, Milton, and Marshall, along with countless "marauding mice" and "robber rodents." Around the three principals there was a wide circle of acolytes (the triangle in a circle was a constant in Herriman's iconography), among whom Joe Stork, "purveyor of progeny to prince and proletariat" took pride of place. Others in the cast were Gooseberry Sprigg, "the Duck Duke," a holdover from an earlier Herriman strip; the ineffectual knight Don Kiyoti and his lethargic assistant Sancho Pansy; Joe Bark, the moon hater; Mock Duck, "launderer de luxe and sage of the Orient"; and Kolin Kelly, dealer in bricks, to name but a few.

Initially *Krazy Kat* had no backgrounds and was set in no specific geographical location. Little by little, however, Herriman established the setting of the action as Coconino County, Arizona, and the adjacent Navajo country, especially Monument Valley, whose landmarks and features became an integral part of the strip. The addition of a full weekly page (in black and white, tucked away in the arts and drama section of the newspaper) on April 23, 1916, allowed the artist full scope in his lyrical depictions of Southwestern landscapes and vistas. The Enchanted Mesa, Rainbow Bridge, the Thunder Needle, the Painted Desert (or "Desierto Pintado"), and especially the Mittens—two rock formations in the shape of fingerless hands pointing heavenward that Herriman like to join together in what he

termed "a lithic applause"—all became silent (and sometimes not so silent) witnesses to the action, itself rich in allusions and symbols and bathed in an atmosphere of inconclusion and flux. Backgrounds and objects were constantly changing and being transformed: a rock became a battleship, a mountain took on the appearance of a cathedral, space lost its continuity, and strange shapes arose out of the void, all in a pantheistic display of elemental forces. In this respect Herriman participated in the great artistic movement that ranges from the Dadaists to the Surrealists and whose aim it was to redefine reality in new esthetic terms.

This constant landscape-shifting went on equally in the daily strip, but the crosspage, linear format did not allow for the same feeling of spectacle. In compensation, Herriman went in for long narratives that extended for days and even weeks. None of these tales is as famous as the "Tiger Tea" sequence, which ran from June 1936 to the end of the year. In the course of the narrative, Krazy left Coconino, to come back from his mysterious errand, bringing with him a catnip brew guaranteed to turn the meekest cat into a tiger. With his nerve fortified by the concoction, Krazy stood up to Ignatz and the other denizens of Coconino eager for a sip of the potent brew, finally deciding to secrete the potion away in a safe place where no one could get at it. In this episode Herriman harked back to the innocent, cartoony style of the strip's beginnings, delightfully matching the spareness of the drawing to the simplicity of the plot.

If theme, setting, and style were the three planes delimiting *Krazy Kat*'s space, language provided the fourth dimension. It transcended space and time not only in its use of African-American dialects, Spanish locutions, Navajo word-sounds, and Yiddish colloquialisms, but also in its recourse to Old English, Latin, and even Greek, in an amalgam at once poetic and vernacular, a kind of Esperanto of the funnies. The language sometimes took the form of clever pastiche, as in Offissa Pupp's high-flown "Rhodes, Babylon, Memnon, Rome, and Chichenitza have given the world colossi at which to wonder" (an obvious swipe at Alfred, Lord Tennyson's bombast) or in Krazy's whimsical "And the foolish kittens which get lost in high trees, don't they make nice pussy-willows" (an affectionate spoof of Edward Lear's nonsense verse). There were also more personal and lyrical accents to Herriman's poetry, as in these lines from his oft-quoted elegy to Krazy Kat, "At some time will he ride away / To you, people of the twilight, / His password will be the echoes of / A vesper bell, his coach / A zephyr from the west."

In addition to an unerring sense of design, Herriman brought an undeniable theatrical flair to his Sunday pages. He would often bathe his panels in limelight or frame them with curtains. He also loved to set up a scene by presenting the actors in the mock-grandiloquent tones of commedia dell' arte: "Ignatz Mouse, possessor of obscure wealth...Don Kiyoti, Castilian nobleman of a most soapy nature...Sancho

Pansy, his amanuensis..." While he was an astute student of past dramatic practice, he was also a pioneer in other ways, anticipating the Theater of the Absurd by several decades. Lines like "The ocean is so innikwilly distribitted. Take Denva, Kollorado, and Tulsa, Okrahoma, they ain't got no ocean a tall while Sem Francisco, Kellafornia, and Bostin, Messachoosit, has got more ocean they can possibly use" and "I'd give my right and my wrong eye for it, Offissa Pupp" are worthy of Eugene Ionesco; while a lament such as "You can't make this day too dark for me, for the nonce I have no need of light, for the moment give me night" with its echoes of Shakespeare foreshadows similar perorations by Samuel Beckett.

In 1935 color became a permanent feature of the *Krazy Kat* page (there had been some antecedents in the 1920s). With color added, the mythical elements of the landscape became more apparent, even as blinding as the desert sun. Reds, oranges, greens, and blacks dominated, substituting form for line, and moving closer to the aesthetics of Surrealism, from which Herriman borrowed freely, just as the Surrealist painters, Joan Miró above all, had previously borrowed from him. The pantheism implicit in his universe also became evident, since with color the artist could now fully replicate Indian motifs and designs not only in the margins but within the page, making the mountains, the rocks, the sun, and the stars participate in the mysterious rites of Coconino County.

Herriman died in 1944, and *Krazy Kat* ended with him. *Krazy Kat* had endured not because of its artistic and literary excellence but despite it: only W. R. Hearst's will had kept it alive against the wishes of the bean-counters at King Features. *Krazy Kat* has now become emblematic of the best there is in comic art, just as Herriman has now attained the status of quasi-literary saint. There is irony in this, but it is irony Herriman would have comprehended; as early as 1937 he had written of Krazy Kat, "Forgive him, for you will understand him no better than we who linger on this side of the pale."

M.H.

KUDZU
1981–present

Doug Marlette, the award-winning political cartoonist for *New York Newsday,* began publishing his daily comic strip on June 15, 1981, and the Sunday entry on the following June 21. Named after a fast-growing vine that covers much of the southern United States, Kudzu is in his late teens, a tall, skinny young man who dreams of becoming a writer. To reach this goal he feels he must leave his hometown of Bypass, North Carolina, for the stimulating environment of New York City, so he can finally experience "life." Each time the subject comes up (or is even hinted at), however, his possessive mother fakes paralysis or a deadly illness, and good son that he is, he stays home, working in his Uncle Dub's garage.

Kudzu intellectualizes over philosophical questions and metaphysical doubts, sometimes regarding the most trivial concerns, such as whether he should have looked in the directory rather than asked the phone operator for a number. This and his ignorance of tools, hunting, fishing (the fish make fun of him), his "sissy" journal-keeping, his lack of chest hair, all contribute to an uneasiness over his manhood by his virile and powerful uncle, the epitome of the good ol' boy. No more successful at overcoming the resistance of the blank page, when he finally sends a story off to the *New Yorker,* he receives a rejection letter addressed "Dear Twit," accompanied by a handwritten note asking him, "Is this some sort of sick joke?" To add insult to injury, the magazine cancels his subscription.

Love, of course, is not an easier pursuit for Kudzu, despite his having much to offer in affection and tenderness. Veranda, the object of his undying adoration, is a lovely blonde flower of the South who hardly knows he exists (he usually has to spell out his last name) and has so many beaus that they each take a number to line up outside her door. Described by her own mirror as "a bit of a bimbo, but actually quite fetching," she is vain, self-absorbed, and capricious, yet not heartless.

To help him cope with the world and the human condition in general, Kudzu often engages the Reverend Will B. Dunn in discussion. The black-clad, tobacco-chewing preacher is barely interested in his parishioners and pays more attention to his soap operas than to their troubles—until he gets presidential ambitions, at which point he becomes more accommodating and remembers his motto: "Human relations is my field." Yet such questionable conduct does not deter the young man from unburdening himself to the Reverend. For more useful advice, Kudzu relies on Maurice, a sophisticated black contemporary, who has both feet solidly planted on the ground. His main role is not to deflate his best friend's unrealistic desires but to make him realize the difficulty of fulfilling them. Finally, there is Doris, Kudzu's very human silent parakeet. Although she refuses to utter a word, her thoughts speak volumes, mostly about her owner, whom she considers to be nice and considerate, but totally ineffectual.

Still, Kudzu is far from being a loser. This is due in large part to the sympathetic and understanding way Marlette portrays him as he depicts the problems and painfulness of growing up. Furthermore, by re-creating life in a small Southern town, a milieu he knows very well, he gently satirizes social mores and human foibles applicable to all.

The strip, which is alternatively a self-contained unit or a continuity series, is distributed by Creators Syndicate and appears in more than 150 newspapers worldwide. It has been collected in numerous paperback books as well.

P.H.

LADY LUCK
1940–1946

In true comic-book fashion, Will Eisner's *Spirit* newspaper insert had a number of back-up features through the years, none as interesting as *Lady Luck*. Eisner himself wrote the first two stories under the pseudonym Ford Davis, Chuck Mazoujian was the illustrator, and *Lady Luck,* along with *The Spirit,* first made its appearance on June 2, 1940, under distribution by the Register and Tribune Syndicate.

Lady Luck was in reality Brenda Banks, a beautiful blonde "debutante crime buster bored with social life" who, as the introductory text explained, decided to become "a modern lady Robin Hood." Unlike other crime fighters, Lady Luck did not don some exotic, skintight outfit in her secret activities, but dressed in matching green gown, high-heel pumps, and Cordoba hat; for disguise she would draw a green silken veil over her face. She had no superpowers but used her wits and wiles to achieve her righteous ends. She acted more like a private investigator, in cases involving kidnapping, blackmail, political intrigue, and occasionally espionage, in the four color pages she was allowed each week. An ironic twist was that Police Chief Hardy Moore, whose duty it was to bring Lady Luck to justice, was in love with her alter ego, Brenda Banks.

Following Eisner, Dick French and later Toni Blum (a woman) took care of the story lines, and Nick Cardy succeeded Mazoujian on the drawings. In 1942 Klaus Nordling took over the entire feature, and he stamped it with his own brand of storytelling that mixed satire and slapstick with mystery and suspense. For the next four years the strip enjoyed its most entertaining period under Nordling's half-illustrative, half-cartoony brush. Lady Luck's run in the newspapers came to a close in 1946, although her adventures continued for a while longer in comic books.

M.H.

LALA PALOOZA
1936–1939

In every creator's career there is at least one work they look back on with much despondency. In Rube Goldberg's case it was *Lala Palooza:* he never once mentioned it in his memoirs, and a pained look would come to his face any time he was queried about it. He turned out the feature for the obscure Frank Jay Markey Syndicate, starting on September 20, 1936.

Lala was an overweight heiress whose consuming passions were chocolates and social climbing. Having acquired the title of countess through marriage, she then tried to

Lady Luck (K. Nordling), © 1946 Will Eisner

parlay her newfound status into acceptance by high society, all in vain (which caused her to hit the candy box again). She was abetted in her upstart dreams by her equally fat stumblebum of a brother, whose harebrained schemes to push his sister up the social ladder always backfired on both of them. After a while Lala lost most of her excess poundage, but got no luckier in her ambitions. There was a great deal of joking about money, position, and compulsive eating in the strip, but it all came out as bad taste rather than satire.

Discouraged by the public response to his strip (there hardly was any), Goldberg late in 1938 decided to leave Lala Palooza to her fate. Her cause was then taken up by Bernard Dibble, with no changes in her fortunes: it all finally ended in the summer of 1939.

Lala Palooza is mentioned here because it was Goldberg's last major effort at crafting an original comic strip. From then on he would largely confine himself to gag and editorial cartooning, along with book and magazine writing.

M.H.

LANCE
1955–1960

After his departure from *Casey Ruggles* in 1954, Warren Tufts proposed to United Feature (which had right of first refusal) a science-fantasy strip called *The Lone Spaceman* in the expectation that the syndicate would reject it. He was not disappointed and, thus free to indulge his own taste, he created *Lance*, a western he syndicated himself with the help of his immediate family. The feature debuted in a full-Sunday-page format on June 5, 1955.

Lance St. Lorne, the titular hero, was a second lieutenant with the U.S. First Draggons, headquartered at Fort Leavenworth, Kansas, in the early 1840s. Lance's outfit was assigned the policing of the territories west of the Missouri, and the task led them into a bloody confrontation with the Sioux. Like *Casey Ruggles*, *Lance* was a history-oriented feature, and Tufts described the Indian campaigns with documentary accuracy, even introducing historical figures such as the fabled Indian scout Kit Carson into the narrative. The storytelling was highly realistic: blood flowed copiously, and sexual relationships were detailed with unusual candor.

Even more than *Ruggles*, *Lance* was a morality tale of good versus evil, but with good and evil distributed in unequal parts between the white men and the Indians, and even within each individual. In the second episode, for instance, a white woman was seen abandoning her priggish husband to share the life of a Sioux chieftain. In 1957 another episode showed the army in cahoots with the fur-trade monopoly in their efforts to despoil the Indians. In 1958 and again in 1959 the depredations committed by the army (massacres, rapes, plunder) were depicted with matter-of-fact realism. Yet Tufts did not harbor any vision of the Indian as a "noble savage." In one story an Indian chief deserted his own braves in the middle of a charge he knew to be hopeless, and surrendered to the U.S. Cavalry rather than face certain death; and scenes of white settlers being tortured to death by their Indian captors were rife.

Each page of the *Lance* saga presented itself as one pictorial composition, with no use of dialogue balloons, the narrative being relegated to blocks of text within the panels (like *Prince Valiant,* on which stylistically *Lance* was modeled). At first these texts were typeset; later hand-lettering was used, but in 1957, for commercial reasons, Tufts had to resort to balloons for the dialogue. The images themselves were grandiose in their meticulousness and dramatic in their effect; scenes of bloody battles and senseless violence alternated with peaceful interludes such as formal dances in the pioneer towns or St. Lorne's wedding in 1957. Color was used to enhance the action in blotches of shocking reds or icy blues.

Between January 1957 and May 1958 Tufts added dailies in narratives tying in with those of the Sunday page. Lance, after a fast start (picking up about a hundred newspapers, many of them in the larger cities) began to falter a few years later. Tufts cut back the feature to half-page, then third-page size. In spite of his last-ditch efforts, Lance went steadily down, until its creator ultimately abandoned it on May 29, 1960, bringing down with it the best hope for a renewal of the American adventure strip.

M.H.

THE LATEST NEWS FROM BUGVILLE
1901–1912

Gus Dirks, Rudolph Dirks's younger brother, was also a cartoonist of some note, and in the course of his tragically short life he was a prolific contributor to all the major humor magazines of his day. His specialty was drawing the very humanlike carryings-on of bugs and other small creatures, a genre in which he excelled. The cartoons on this theme that he did for *Judge* magazine in the late 1890s were later collected (with added verses by humorist R. K. Munkittrick) in a book called *Bugville Life.* This anthology drew the attention of the ever-vigilant W. R. Hearst, and in 1901 Gus Dirks joined his older brother in the ranks of the Hearst organization.

There the younger Dirks drew a weekly color half-page (and sometimes a full page) devoted to his beloved varmints. Called *Bugville Life* (and later retitled, for copyright reasons, *The Latest News from Bugville*), it featured ladybugs, June bugs, and other insects living in small houses amid the underbrush and the wild mushrooms, in drawings executed with broad pen strokes and subtle cross-hatching, and enhanced with a fine sense of color. The gags were often provided by a newsboy hawking the *Snail News,* who might arrive out of breath in a three-cornered hat, shouting, "Extra! Extra! All about Washington crossing the Delaware!" This recurrent joke eventually earned the feature its definitive title.

Shortly before Christmas Day 1903, Dirks committed suicide at the lamentably young age of 24, and his page passed into the hands of another animal depicter, Paul Bransom. Bransom continued the feature in the Dirks tradition and in a pleasant approximation of his predecessor's style. He also experimented with a multipanel format and with speech-balloons, thus bringing the feature closer to being an authentic comics page. *Bugville* ended in 1912, when Bransom left for greener pastures as a magazine and book illustrator. His departure coincided with the waning of public interest in talking-bug and -bird cartoons, a tradition revived only decades later in *Right Around Home* by Dudley Fisher, who might have remembered Dirks's and Bransom's cartoons from childhood.

The Latest News from Bugville was representative of the wide variety of the features offered by the color newspaper supplements at the beginning of this century, a sharp contrast to today's situation. It also stands as testament to Gus Dirks's promising talent, which might have resulted in the most exciting brother act in the history of the comics had the young cartoonist allowed his life to run its natural course.

M.H.

LATIGO
1979–1983

Latigo was the western strip created by Stan Lynde after he gave up his popular *Rick O'Shay* due to a dispute with the Chicago Tribune Syndicate. *Latigo* began in June 1979, with the Field Syndicate.

Latigo was modeled upon the successful elements of *Rick O'Shay:* a deep love for the historic American West that was communicated to the readers; a Montana Territory locale set exactly a hundred years in the past; and realistic adventures moderated by a dash of humor, indicated most heavily by punny names such as Jordan Rivers (a preacher) and Oliver Sudden. But there was no joke in the hero's name. Cole "Latigo" Cantrell was the child of a white frontier father and an Indian mother. He left home to fight in the Civil War, and returned to find that his parents had just been killed by agents of the Python Corporation, a fictitious composite of all the robber-baron-owned trusts that sought to control the wealth of the West. After spending several years more as a bitter fast gun avenging his parents, then as a civilian scout for the U.S. Cavalry at Fort Savage under arrogant Major Fairweather, Latigo settled down to became a deputy U.S. marshal, headquartered in Rimfire, Montana Territory.

The episodes ranged from Latigo's keeping the peace in Rimfire to being sent on missions elsewhere around the West by his boss, crusty old Marshal Hoodoo Hawks. Serious adventures usually alternated with humorous interludes. Every so often Latigo had a run-in with the Python Corporation, stopping some illegal scheme and making himself an increasing annoyance to Python's master, the megalomanically dissolute Claudius Max. Lynde had always enjoyed presenting the western landscape as God's Country, but in 1980 he became a born-again Christian and modeled a couple of story sequences upon well-known biblical parables. Lynde later acknowledged that there were complaints, but in general readers continued to appreciate the high quality of the plotting and drama.

After four years, faced with the continuing decline in the popularity of the continuity strip, Lynde brought *Latigo* to an end. He wrapped up the ongoing Python Corporation plot thread in the final story, which ended in May (daily) and June (Sunday) 1983. *Latigo* was collected a few years later in *Comics Revue*, the strip-reprint magazine. In the 1990s Lynde reprinted *Latigo* in three attractive albums from his own Cottonwood Graphics press.

F.P.

LIFE IN HELL
1980–present

Asked why he had given his weekly comic page such a provocative title, Matt Groening had a typical tongue-in-cheek answer ready. "My strip started running when Reagan was running for president in 1980," he declared to a *Washington Post* interviewer in 1988, "so *Life in Hell* was an appropriate title." *Life in Hell* grew out of a series of cartoons Groening drew in his college newspaper; after his cartoons started appearing in the *Los Angeles Reader* they soon acquired a cult following, and in a matter of a year or so they were carried by a score of newspapers nationwide.

Groening did not originate the free-form comic page, an innovation some commentators have given him credit for. (Tad Dorgan and Rube Goldberg, among other cartoonists of the first decade of this century, had both experimented with the format of the miscellany page.) He did, however, revive it long after it had fallen into disuse and refine it for modern tastes. In keeping with its title, the weekly page (each with its own subtitle) is often broken down into subheadings ("Love Is Hell," "School Is Hell," "Work Is Hell," etc.), but many pages belong to none of these subdivisions and simply reflect the cartoonist's concerns or pet peeves of the moment.

The variations on the "love is hell" theme provide some of the funniest as well as the more poignant moments of the strip. The pages' various titles give a clue to their contents; there are "The Crimes of Love," "Why You Are So Screwed Up," "Questionable Opening Lines," and "Homo vs. Hetero: Which Is Better?" Groening's prototypical anti-hero, a floppy-eared, crazy-eyed rabbit named Binky, expounds endlessly on the theme in "Binky's Guide to Love," which opens with the line, "Je t'aime, I think," while the gay couple of Jeff and Akbar eternally ask each other, "Do you love me?" In one especially revealing episode Binky, after a spat with his girlfriend, decides to bring her a bottle of wine as a peace offering, but on his way to her home he gets thirsty and ends up totally smashed on her doormat.

Binky's son Bongo, a one-eared bunny of rebellious bent, is usually the protagonist of the "School Is Hell" segments. He refuses to learn anything, and his recitations of the Pledge of Allegiance never fail to drive his teachers up the wall. "I pledge allegiance to Frank Zappa / Of the United Mutations of America / And to the Duke of Prunes and Grand Wazoo / For which he stands / One size fits all, centrifugal / With yellow sharks and hot rats for all," one version runs. To supplement his limited cast of characters Groening often draws himself (unkempt and unshaven, looking somewhat like a befuddled porcupine) and his sons Abe and Will into the strip. As a cartoonist he credits himself with "malicious frivolity" (or alternatively with "frivolous maliciousness"). The graphic style is as chaotic as the writing, with Groening's drawings sometimes resembling the doodles in schoolboys' notebooks, at other times looking like the hieroglyphs on Egyptian mastaba walls, and at yet other moments approximating the scrawlings on lavatory partitions.

The runaway success of Groening's animated television series *The Simpsons* in the 1990s has spurred a renewal of interest in *Life in Hell,* which is now being syndicated under the corporate banner of Acme Features in the artist's home state of Oregon.

M.H.

LI'L ABNER
1934–1977

Some of the harshest commentary on American society and the human condition appeared in a comic strip that featured a hillbilly whose distinguishing trait was his abject stupidity. In fact, almost all the hundreds of characters Al Capp showcased in *Li'l Abner* were "dumb," as well as lazy and extremely gullible. Capp was fair in that he was no kinder to his characters than he was to those he lampooned.

During its forty-three years, starting on August 13, 1934, the strip entertained millions of readers hooked on the bizarre adventures of an equally odd cast of characters. Many, John Steinbeck prominent among them, saw *Li'l Abner* as social satire at its best.

An excellent writer, who for years did continuity for the strips *Abbie an' Slats* and *Long Sam,* Capp had a knack for plotting, characterization, storytelling, and parodying. He entangled the Yokum family and their Dogpatch, U.S.A., neighbors in all types of intrigue, some fashioned by conniving outsiders who recognized an easy mark when they saw one. One favorite theme revolved around the dogged

Li'l Abner (A. Capp), © 1934 United Feature Syndicate/Capp Enterprises

determination of the typical Dogpatch woman to snatch a man. In 1937, Capp gave the women a day set aside for them to chase and hunt down their prey. Sadie Hawkins Day became an unofficial national holiday in real life, as hundreds of college campuses celebrated it. Li'l Abner himself escaped the "hoomiliation" of marriage half a dozen times before Daisy Mae Scragg finally nabbed him in March 1952. Preacher Marryin' Sam gave the occasion his $1.35 special ceremony and *Life* magazine its cover story.

Capp would no sooner end one story before starting another, usually in the middle of the week so as not to have readers wander off on the weekends. Stories ended rather quickly, as he had difficulties with endings. Although he set most episodes in Dogpatch and the hills around it, Capp varied the scenery, as *Li'l Abner* was temporarily shifted to the streets of New York, or the craters of the moon, or the wastelands of Lower Slobbovia. Wherever the strip meandered off to, a good story full of parody, puns, and appropriate dialect was guaranteed.

In one 1941 sequence, Abner returned from the moon with a slew of pictures scientists drooled to see. However, all were mug shots of Abner, who had taught the moon varmints photography. In the Lower Slobbovia story, the people lived miserably in the twin cities of Tsk-Tsk and Tck-Tck, while King Nogoodnik took up residence in the capital of Caesar Siddy. One of the leading citizens of Lower Slobbovia was Harry S. Rasputintruman. Another episode was built around the emblem of Lowest Slobbovia (apparently the other side of the tracks from Lower Slobbovia), a cuddly creature called Bald Iggle, whose redeeming quality was that when humans looked into its brown eyes, they were compelled to tell the whole truth. In introducing the character, Capp told his readers, "This, of course, makes it impossible to carry on any courtship, many businesses, and most political speeches." As would be expected, Bald Iggle was not long for this world; it was slaughtered by government agents at the demands of the military, businessmen, spouses, salesmen, and others.

There were other stories that gripped the country, making Capp the most famous and visible cartoonist from the 1940s to the 1970s. One story featured a zoot suit, set off by huge shoulder pads and long lapels that protruded like angel wings, that Abner won the honor of endorsing by having the lowest IQ in America. The Root Toot Zoot Suit Manufacturing Company had held a competition to find someone stupid enough to risk his life to advertise the merchandise. Two of the most popular and satiric sequences starred the Shmoo and the Kigmy, both very amiable creatures that were menaces to the establishment. Shmoos provided all human needs: they produced eggs, grade A milk, creamery butter, and even cheesecake; when they were broiled, they tasted like fine steak, and boiled, they became boneless chicken. They reproduced prodigiously, required no upkeep, and loved to be sacrificed for humans. The Shmoos kept the people of the United States engrossed for a couple of months with their anticapital, antilabor, and economy-of-plenty implications, while congressmen and other benefactors of capitalism thought Capp had hit too close to home.

After he dropped the Shmoo, Capp came right back with the Kigmy, a character that represented all scapegoats

Li'l Abner (A. Capp), © 1936 United Feature Syndicate/Capp
Enterprises

rolled into one. With targets painted on their posteriors,
Kigmies loved to be kicked, thus allowing humans to
release aggression. Eventually, the Kigmies learned how
nice it was to kick people around, and as the kickees
became indistinguishable from the kickers, they were sent
back to Australia.

Capp attacked prejudice in other stories. In one
sequence, a square-eyed family that moved to Dogpatch was
shunned by all until Mammy Yokum figured out they were
basically the same as normal round-eyed folks.

Except for Chester Gould's *Dick Tracy*, no strip had such
a collection of grotesques as *Li'l Abner*. Each character was
very well defined and memorable, from Abner and Daisy
Mae to Marryin' Sam, Adorable Jones, and Silem. Other
characters around which stories often were built were Evil-
Eye Fleegle from Brooklyn, who possessed one mean
whammy; bullet-riddled Fearless Fosdick, the hapless
detective who was a parody of Dick Tracy; Joe Btfsplk, the
jinx with the ever-present rain cloud over his head; Sir Cecil
Cesspool, the snobbish Englishman; Moonbeam McSwine,
a pipe-smoking woman with a fantastic figure and pungent
smell; Henry Cabbage Cod, the Boston socialite; Lonesome
Polecat and Hairless Joe, cave-dwelling roommates who
concocted Kickapoo Joy Juice, which in reality became a
licensed soft drink; and Appasionata von Climax, one of
many erotic manifestations in the strip.

Capp labored hard to make *Li'l Abner* stand out among
other strips. His goal was impact, which he achieved
through heavy black borders, silhouettes, electriclike balloons to portray excitement and anger, heavy lettering with
some words boldfaced, and various methods of shading—
not to mention colorful characters and dialect. The artwork was meticulously done and appropriate for the
settings: statues, paintings on office walls, and tall buildings
for the city; characters framed in a bright moon or back-
grounded with shacks, pines, or beautiful hills for Dog-

patch. Beautiful women in provocative dress and poses,
with deep cleavage and full thighs showing, further called
attention to the strip.

Capp made *Li'l Abner* intensely personal, reflecting his
political views and professional feuds. For example, after
giving play to a belief contrary to his own, he would sarcasti-
cally add the word "Right!!!" in boldface over his signature.
Most opinions were subtly presented as parts of entertaining stories, but in the 1960s, Capp's style became much
more strident and his views very conservative. Previously
the darling of the liberals, Capp now attacked college students and demonstrators (labeled S.W.I.N.E.—Students
Wildly Indignant About Nearly Everything), bureaucrats,
and the welfare state. Likenesses of Joan Baez (Joanie
Phoanie) and Jane Fonda (Nancy Nuisance, with her
vicious dogs, Mao Tse Tung and Karl Marx) replaced beautifully curvaceous women, and the day's headlines took
over from commentary on the human condition. Capp
made campaigning against the left a major part of his life,
going on the college lecture tour and writing a newspaper
column to that end. Called a fascist by those who paid
homage to him before, Capp argued that he had not
changed over the years, that he simply defended the "poor
son-of-a-bitch who *worked*, who was being denounced by liberals."

The professional feud portrayed in *Li'l Abner* concerned
Ham Fisher, creator of *Joe Palooka*. Capp assisted Fisher for a
brief time in the early 1930s, during which he introduced a
hillbilly character, Big Leviticus, to the boxing strip. When
Capp left to start *Li'l Abner*, Fisher was furious and yearly
thereafter, he reprinted pages of the Big Leviticus sequence
to remind readers that a hillbilly was in *Joe Palooka* first.
Capp countered by regularly caricaturing Fisher in *Li'l
Abner* as a cartoonist who had others do his work for him,
usually artists shown hidden in closets slaving for a dollar a
day. The feud was devastatingly brutal, resulting in lawsuits
and professional censure before Fisher's suicide in 1955.

Capp retired his strip on November 13, 1977, two years
before his own death. However, *Li'l Abner* has endured
through book-length analyses of the character and its creator, reprintings of the series year by year, and remembrances of those who recognized Capp for the creative
genius that he was.

J.A.L.

LITTLE ANNIE ROONEY
1929–1966

King Features Syndicate had for some years nursed the
idea of a newspaper strip based on Mary Pickford's
1925 movie *Little Annie Rooney*, but it took considerable
time for the project to come finally to fruition. The writing
was entrusted to Brandon Walsh, who had previously been
a ghostwriter on *The Gumps*, with the first daily seeing the
light of print on January 10, 1929. While it had a writer,
Little Annie Rooney was clearly a strip in search of an artist:
in the short span of only twenty months, to the despair of
the editors, it had known no fewer than three different
draftsmen. The first one was Ed (or Ernie; accounts differ)
Verdier, who signed simply "Verd"; he was officially suc-

Little Annie Rooney (D. McClure), © 1933 King Features Syndicate

ceeded on July 22, 1929, by Ben Batsford, before Darrell McClure took over on October 6, 1930. McClure, who had earlier drawn Harry Hershfield's *Vanilla and the Villains* and *Hard-Hearted Hicky* for King, turned out to be the perfect man for the job. So pleased was the syndicate with *Annie Rooney*'s vastly improved look that a Sunday page was added on November 30, 1930.

Annie Rooney had at first been conceived as a riposte to Little Orphan Annie, and in the beginning she was a feisty, belligerent moppet, but the syndicate soon found out that newspaper editors were not interested in a watered-down version of Harold Gray's creation. Taking advantage of McClure's advent, they charted a change of course. Annie now became much more passive and accepting, closer to the tear-jerking tradition of Little Nell and countless other orphan girls of fiction, stage, and screen. The little heroine was a fresh-faced, dark-haired girl of about 12, whose precocious coquettishness and girlish mannerisms anticipated Shirley Temple's movies by several years. Her nemesis was the ugly, cruel Mrs. Meany, head of the orphan asylum Annie had escaped from in the company of her faithful white fox terrier Zero. No matter how far the little fugitive got, or how long she remained hidden, Mrs. Meany's hired detectives would always track her down, and the orphan was once again forced to flee into the cold and into the night. In the course of her peregrinations Annie often relied on the kindness of strangers (usually men) who would offer her temporary refuge. It is this dual, ambiguous outlook that caused French critic Jean-Claude Romer to call *Little Annie Rooney* a cross between the Countess de Segur and the Marquis de Sade. (The countess is known as the author of cloyingly sweet novels and the marquis of course gave his name to the sexual perversion now called sadism.)

Walsh knew how to play variations on this basic theme, and gritty continuities depicting Annie and Zero wandering deserted roads or shivering under rainy skies alternated with rosier adventures, often verging on fairy tales. In one such episode of the mid-1930s Annie was adopted by a kind and elderly millionaire aptly named M. Bullion, and she was given her heart's desire for herself and her little friends. Her bliss was short-lived when Mr. Bullion disappeared after a financial crash, and the hapless orphan had to hit the road again, with Mrs. Meany and her henchmen in hot pursuit.

McClure drew the daily strip without interruption until its demise on April 16, 1966. On instructions from the syn-

dicate he had to relinquish the Sunday page in February 1934 to Nicholas Afonsky, who turned the little heroine into an even more pathetic-looking creature. After Afonsky's death in 1943, McClure regained possession of the Sunday feature, which he illustrated until its discontinuance on May 30, 1965. McClure also proved surprisingly adept at storytelling when he also took over the writing of the strip following Walsh's death in 1954.

Annie Rooney owed its longevity to Walsh's imaginative and often suspenseful plots and McClure's sinuous line and effortless evocation of mood. When both men were at their best, in the depression years of the 1930s, they often transcended the shopworn conventions of the genre.

M.H.

THE LITTLE BEARS
1895–1901

Animals in the comics are as old as the comics form itself. As early as 1895, in what some regard as the first American comic strip, *The Little Bears*, James Swinnerton had chronicled in more or less weekly fashion the frolics of a merry crew of cute little bear cubs in the pages of the *San Francisco Examiner*. Actually Swinnerton's creation goes back to 1893, when he used the bears, adapted from the emblem on the California flag, as spot illustrations (which he signed "Swin") for diverse items and announcements; so when he was asked to contribute a weekly feature to the *Examiner*'s children's page he naturally turned to the cuddly little animals as protagonists of what was intended to be a simple page of illustrations for the kiddies.

The little bears were shown cavorting, skipping rope, and indulging in other such children's activities. They were occasionally joined in their games by small human urchins, which led the feature to be informally called "The Little Bears and Tykes." (Early histories of the comics, making an unwarranted amalgam between Swinnerton's bears and his later Journal Tigers, came up with "Little Bears and Tigers," a feature that never existed.) After a while the cartoonist dropped the tykes, probably feeling that the presence of the kids was superfluous in a feature where the cubs all acted and behaved like small children of an unusually furry kind. When Swinnerton left for New York at the end of the nineteenth century, he took his bears with him, and they ran sporadically in the pages of Hearst's *Journal* until 1901.

While *The Little Bears* was in no sense a comic strip (the pictures did not unfold in sequence and they make no use of speech-balloons, for instance), it certainly represents one of the earliest examples of funny animals in the comics pages. Swinnerton was to bring the talking-animal strip one step further with a contemporary series (most often referred to as *Mount Ararat*) in which an ark full of animals of all species would engage in human activities ranging from planting crops to building houses. In this Sunday page feature the artist developed some of his more sophisticated compositions, often humorously commenting on his own craft, the work of his cartooning colleagues, and even the medium of the comics, in which he perceived with remarkable insight the dawning promise of a new art form.

M.H.

LITTLE DEBBIE
See DEBBIE

LITTLE IODINE
1943–1986

Iodine Tremblechin made her appearance in the 1930s in Jimmy Hatlo's panel feature, *They'll Do It Every Time.* The shenanigans of the little brat became an increasingly frequent fixture of the series until she was finally given a Sunday half-page of her own. Called *Little Iodine*, it started syndication on July 4, 1943, under the aegis of King Features.

Initially the seven-year-old, pony-tailed Iodine was not so much malicious as she was boorish, self-centered, and inconsiderate of others. She would play havoc with the mannequins in a store window, for instance, or throw dozens of volumes onto the floor of the library in search of a book "with pitchers," causing one librarian to muse aloud that "a book could fall on her accidentally." She gradually grew in deviltry (though not in years) as time went by. Her favorite targets were her own parents, the meek and over-burdened Henry, her father, whom she never tired of bedeviling and hoodwinking, and her prepossessing mother, Effie, whose social pretensions she delighted in deflating. And every time the Tremblechins would invite Henry's pompous boss, Mr. Bigdome, in hopes of a raise or promotion, one could be sure their obstreperous daughter would in the course of dinner sabotage any chance her father had with her obnoxious behavior and her cynical, if seemingly innocent, questions about the boss's waistline or his wife's hat. In addition to being the despair of her parents, Iodine was also the bane of the neighborhood, playing all kinds of pranks on her suburban neighbors with the help of her admiring boyfriend, Sharkey.

Little Iodine never approached its parent feature in popularity. Although drawn in the same broad, disjointed style, it lacked *They'll Do It*'s genial sense of the absurdities of social life. Bob Dunn, who had ghosted *Little Iodine* almost from its inception, took over the strip at Hatlo's death in 1963. Al Scaduto drew the feature while Dunn mainly con-

tributed the gags and the dialogue. In 1967 Hy Eisman succeeded Scaduto on the artwork, and together with Dunn managed to carry it along for another two decades until its close in 1986.

M.H.

LITTLE JIMMY
1904–1941, 1945–1958

James Swinnerton's most enduring (and endearing) creation as well as his own favorite, *Little Jimmy* began life as simply *Jimmy* on February 14, 1904. Carried in the Sunday color section of the Hearst papers, it only appeared sporadically at first, but soon, as it gained wider and wider reader acceptance, it became a weekly fixture on the comics page.

Jimmy Thompson (to give him his rightful name) was a young boy of 5 or 6, round-headed and small-sized, with a diffident demeanor and an ardent curiosity about everything. Not malicious or even mischievous, he found himself embroiled in various misadventures through innocence or indolence. *Little Jimmy* was a strip of distractions and contretemps, and the slight anecdotes it related (Jimmy getting lost in the streets while following a parade, or getting side-tracked while on an errand by an organ-grinder and his pet monkey) were in odd contrast to the incident-filled gags of *The Katzenjammer Kids,* the other great child strip of the Hearst supplement. The wide-eyed little boy was as much an observer as he was a player, as he meandered endlessly through the town where he lived, fascinated as he was by the world surrounding him. The tempo of the strip was slow, sunny, and relaxed, like a Sunday afternoon stroll in the park.

Swinnerton's rocketing career was almost cut short in 1906, when he was definitely diagnosed with tuberculosis. He then decided to move back to his native West in pursuit of a cure, first to Colton, a then-famed resort for tubercular patients in the California desert, then to Arizona in 1914; his health fully restored, he again returned to California, but every year he took lengthy trips back to the Arizona desert, with which he had fallen in love.

This love reflected itself first of all in *Little Jimmy.* Using the ploy of the Thompson family going to the desert for

Little Jimmy (J. Swinnerton), 1905

vacation, Swinnerton shifted the strip's locale to the Southwest with greater and greater frequency, finally having the family settle there. Jimmy gained new companions in this unfamiliar setting: his bulldog Beans, a pet bear cub he called Lil' Ole Bear, a Mexican fighting rooster by the name of Poncho, and numerous other animals. Jimmy and his equally diminutive pal, Pinkie, were later joined in their adventures by several Navaho Indians who had crossed over from *Canyon Kiddies,* a weekly series of picture-stories Swinnerton was doing at the same time for Hearst's *Good Housekeeping* magazine. In the 1930s a wise Indian brave named Somoli, who was able to talk to animals and served as guide and mentor to the plucky little band, joined the cast.

In July 1920 a daily strip was added to the Sunday page, and up to its demise in October 1937, it too revolved mainly around wondrous experiences in the Great American Southwest. This is the period that has most fascinated later commentators. "Though recent," Coulton Waugh wrote in 1947, "this phase is really from the old days; quiet, dreamy, and without bitterness." (It should be noted, however, that throughout the 1920s and 1930s a number of releases, left unsigned by Swinnerton, were in fact the work of Doc Winner.)

In 1941 Swinnerton was enticed into doing a straight western page, the ill-fated *Rocky Mason, Government Marshal,* and the *Little Jimmy* Sunday went into a four-year hiatus. It resurfaced in November 1945 and wound its leisurely, bucolic way through the comic pages until April 27, 1958, when age and ill-health forced the artist to regretfully abandon his long-running feature.

Little Jimmy is a work of understated lyricism, warm and reserved at the same time. At first glance Swinnerton's style may seem quaint and old-fashioned, but the reader is soon won over by the simple humor, quiet poetry, and subtle charm of this, his most renowned creation. Unlike most other contemporary cartoonists, Swinnerton cultivated unobtrusiveness: his characters were likable and contemplative, his landscapes sunny and serene, and his anecdotes engaging rather than rambunctious. *Little Jimmy* was a meditative, almost ruminative strip, and in this regard it has few peers in the history of the comics and should be recognized as one of the true originals of the medium.

M.H.

LITTLE JOE
1933–1969

*O*n October 1, 1933, the Chicago Tribune–New York News Syndicate came up with a western feature called *Little Joe.* The credited author, Ed Leffingwell, was Harold Gray's assistant (as well as his cousin), and the resemblance between *Little Joe* and *Little Orphan Annie* was not coincidental. There is no doubt that the syndicate banked heavily on the graphic and philosophical similarities between the two strips to bring in at least some of the many newspapers then subscribing to *Annie.*

Little Joe Oak lived on his widowed mother's ranch, which was managed by a gruff character (and former gunfighter) named Utah. Soon Joe and Utah found themselves

involved in innumerable adventures, some of them humorous and other ones melodramatic, like the one in which Utah and Joe outsmarted a pair of shyster lawyers from the East who were trying to defraud Mrs. Oak of her title to the ranch with the help of forged documents.

Harold Gray, who actually wrote most of the continuities and a great deal of the dialogue, never lost an opportunity to poke political fun at the various dude types who came to visit Joe's ranch. Trade unions were Gray's special *bêtes noires,* and he would often compare union officials to rattlesnakes and buzzards intent on seeing the cattle dispatched in order to pick the carrion. In the late 1930s he added to the strip's cast the comic figure of a Mexican general (simply known as Ze Gen'ral), the better to pick on politicians of the New Deal by using the situation in Mexico as a thinly disguised parable of events then taking place in Washington, as Gray saw them.

During World War II Joe, Utah, and Ze Gen'ral joined with gusto the fight against the Axis powers. Characteristically theirs was a private war in the course of which our heroes rounded up assorted gangs of alien spies or homegrown fifth-columnists. They even captured a landing party of Japanese saboteurs, whom Utah, with his usual business acumen, put to work on the ranch (at no pay, of course).

Since 1936 Joe's adventures had been drawn by Robert Leffingwell, following his brother Ed's death from a botched surgical operation, without any perceptible change in style of draftsmanship. (The page was simply signed "Leffingwell," so few readers were aware of the switch.) After the war Gray seems to have lost interest in the feature, and *Little Joe* from 1946 on was entirely done by Leffingwell (who added a top strip called *Ze Gen'ral*). Reduced to a mere series of weekly gags, Leffingwell's page lost most of its appeal, and by the 1960s it was appearing in only a handful of newspapers. As a result of Gray's death in 1968, the syndicate decided to kill the money-losing strip, which came to an end in the early months of 1969.

Little Joe should be remembered chiefly for its always intelligent, often arresting narratives of the 1930s and early 1940s, as well as for the Leffingwell brothers' subtle but masterly depiction of western scenes, from breathless rides through craggy and awe-inspiring canyons to wild stampedes across the limitless expanses of prairie country. It is certainly a minor classic worthy of greater appreciation than it has hitherto received.

M.H.

THE LITTLE KING
1934–1975

*O*tto Soglow's king was the antithesis of most real-life monarchs in that he was extremely kind and gentle, jovially playful, and very democratic. He was an uncomplicated man who, take away the royal robe and crown, could have passed for the fellow down the street.

Without being abrasive, or even conscious of it, he tweaked the noses of the pompous uppity-ups around him, doing the simplest, most unexpected, and most nonsensical thing, rather than the most ceremonial. In one story,

The Little King (O. Soglow), © 1934 King Features Syndicate

the king gets up from his luxurious bed, traverses the length of his magnificent palace, has the drawbridge opened, and takes in the morning quart of milk. On another occasion, when he learns on his way to the pool that the royal dishwasher has been fired, he simply picks up the tub of dirty dishes and takes them swimming with him. Or, when a dolphin in the royal aquarium refuses to eat alone, the king doffs his robe, but not his crown, and joins the mammal in the water.

The Little King was one of the pre–World War II pantomime strips and, as with *Henry* of that time, the main figure preferred to be mute, although minor characters sometimes spoke to set the scene or advance it. The nonverbal nature of the strip sometimes required more than the usual number of panels. The episode about the fussy dolphin, for example, took fourteen panels, including six just to introduce the royal aquarium keeper to the king. But, because the panels were clean and neat and flowed rhythmically, the reader was not aware of this long trek in telling a simple story. The strip was also unique in that everyone was nameless, as was the kingdom.

Soglow's drawing style was characterized by economy of line, precise spotting of black, and exaggeration. The royal attendants didn't just stand at attention, but were so erect that their chests protruded like surrealistic caricatures of baseball umpires. The king was so dumpy that his dinner-bell-like body was not only legless, but footless as well. But his crown was always there, even when he was in bed or swimming. Except for Ookle the Dictator, introduced for six months in 1940, and the king's wife and daughter, who were shown occasionally, there were no other featured characters; they would have been superfluous.

The Little King was Soglow's major work among a number of *New Yorker* and other magazine gag cartoons and a few other strips—the companion feature, *Sentinel Louie*, also pantomime; *The Ambassador*, the 1933 predecessor to *The Little King*; and *Travelin' Gus*, a kind of Toonerville trolley, which appeared in the *New York Journal-American*.

The Little King showed off Soglow's mastery of the gag. It had an appeal that was difficult to explain: although the punchline was expected to be nonsensical, perhaps even embarrassingly silly, nevertheless it was clever enough to entice the reader to seek it out. The strip is a classic because it gets its gags across despite the absence of usually essential elements such as speech, names, multiple characters, and artistic detail. *The Little King* was discontinued on July 20, 1975, following Soglow's death earlier that year.

J.A.L.

LITTLE LULU
1950–1969

Little Lulu Moppet starred in a *Saturday Evening Post* gag panel, many comic books, including her own title, an advertising campaign for a facial tissue, a Broadway show, many songs, and at least twenty-six Paramount cartoon films before the Chicago Tribune–New York Times Syndicate put her on the funny pages in June 1950. By that time, *Little Lulu*, always identified as the creation of Marge (Marjorie Henderson Buell), was written and drawn by others.

The resourceful and mischievous Lulu first appeared as a flower girl in a February 23, 1935, *Saturday Evening Post* panel; she was shown tossing banana peels behind her to trip up the bride and groom. Marge, who already had been doing *Post* gags for nine years, was asked to do the panel as a replacement for *Henry*. In 1945, Lulu started a ten-issue run in Dell's *Four-Color Comics* before appearing in her own book, *Marge's Little Lulu*, in 1948.

Marge did not draw the comic book—that chore was given to John Stanley—nor the strip, for in 1945 she sold the rights to the character to Western Publishing Company. The West Coast office of Western, responsible for overseeing the production and sale of some strips to syndicates, decided to package *Little Lulu* for the newspapers. The strip never really took off, remaining marginally viable because of a small client list of sixty-five and because of a six-way split of revenues among Western, the syndicate, artists, writers, Marge, and her agent. Nevertheless, Western retained the strip for nineteen years, primarily to help promote the many Little Lulu products on the market.

First to write and draw the strip was Woody Kimbrell, who had the longest tenure (1950–64). During the next two years, Roger Armstrong was the artist, while Al Stoffel was chief writer, assisted by Del Connell and Armstrong. Stoffel and Connell also wrote the strip during its waning years (1966–69), when Ed Nofziger was the artist.

Lulu was a strong character—ingenious, intelligent, confident, and tough as nails, sometimes bordering on nastiness and maliciousness. She believed she was sexually equal and demonstrated it, as she regularly outwitted her pal (and sometimes boyfriend) Tubby and his gang. In the strip, as well as in the comic books, Lulu showed that intelli-

Little Lulu (M. Henderson Buell), © 1952 Chicago Tribune–New York News Syndicate

gence and wit did triumph over violence, that beauty and wealth did not necessarily represent quality, and that subservience to all authority did more harm than good. She conveyed these notions in unobtrusive and fun-filled ways, avoiding sermonizing at all costs.

The little girl in corkscrew curls and unchanging red dress certainly made a lasting impression. Sixty years after her debut, fan clubs, the fanzine *Hollywood Eclectern,* and an organization called Friends of Lulu, dedicated to encouraging more women creators and readers of comics, serve as testimonies to her popularity and spirit of independence.

J.A.L.

THE LITTLE MAN
1979–present

A former trumpet player, art instructor, and college dean, Ray Salmon drew the self-caricatural "Little Man" as a signature on his personal stationery. Prompted by the response the small figure enjoyed with friends and business associates, he decided to self-syndicate *The Little Man* as a daily panel, which has been appearing since l979.

Described by the author as "a special commentary humor panel," *The Little Man* stars a short, balding, middle-aged man with a walrus mustache (not unlike Salmon himself), and it pokes gentle fun at the social and political scene. As can be expected, he often comments on his favorite subject, art, with references to abstract expressionism (he is against it), television cartoons (he likes them), and the art market (he wishes it could be healthier). All this is mixed in with jokes about overpriced lawyers, crash diets, dissembling politicians, and Everyman's civic responsibilities. It is an engaging and funny feature, infused with a discreet and subtle charm.

Distributed only to about forty newspapers, *The Little Man* is typical of the dozens of self-syndicated features judged too individual or too controversial by the major syndicates. As in every other field of endeavor, there are the gems and there are the dogs; but at their best these self-starters may represent the future of newspaper comics at a time when big-city (and not so big) dailies increasingly fold,

merge, or shrink. By necessity cartoonists in the next century will have to cater to smaller markets, whether print or electronic, where large syndicates fear to tread.

M.H.

LITTLE MARY MIXUP
1917–1957

R. M. (Robert Moore) Brinkerhoff, a cartoonist and illustrator on the *Evening World,* was enticed by his colleague Will B. Johnston to try his hand at a comic strip. Almost casually, Brinkerhoff turned out a feature about a trouble-prone little girl, which the *World* to his amazement started running in 1917 and later syndicated through its own Press Publishing Company.

At the inception of the strip Little Mary was a blond-tressed, primly-dressed five-year-old with an angelic expression and a propension for saucy remarks and tart rejoinders. Although never nasty or malicious, she proved a trial not only to her family but also to strangers fooled by her cute looks and innocent mien, in the tradition pioneered more than a decade earlier by Penny Ross's *Mamma's Angel Child.* In the 1920s the author began to experiment with daily continuities, often on fantasy themes, involving his spunky little heroine in encounters with elves, flying dragons, and enchanted princesses. The Sundays, on the other hand, remained wedded to humorous anecdote.

This adventurous trend accelerated in the 1930s, after United Feature had taken over distribution, following the *World*'s demise. Mary, now a venturesome teenager, tangled with gangsters, kidnappers, and animals of the wild in a series of entertaining episodes. As the years went by, Mary managed to grow into young womanhood, and by the end of the decade she was in love with a handsome lout named Elmer. She recovered from that and when World War II started she put her talents at the service of her country, helping the relatives of young men at the front, and even exposing a Nazi spy ring. She resumed her freewheeling ways after the war, adventuring West and going on a treasure hunt. Like the Hollywood heroines whose exploits she was trying to emulate, she always emerged from these ordeals with her poise unruffled and her appearance undisturbed.

Brinkerhoff in the course of his long career never found it expedient to change his style, and the strip at the end of its forty-year run was still "drawn in the sketchy pen manner of an earlier period," as Coulton Waugh described it in 1947. In the feature's last years the artist's line grew even sketchier until ill health finally forced him to retire *Little Mary Mixup* in 1957, some months before his death in February of the next year.

Little Mary Mixup (R. M. Brinkerhoff), 1918

M.H.

Little Miss Muffet (F. Cory), © 1937 Fanny Y. Cory

LITTLE MISS MUFFET
1935–1956

In 1935 Fanny Cory was drawing *Babe Bunting*, a strip about a little orphan girl, which proved successful enough to draw the notice of King Features' editors. Asked to create yet another feature about a waif for King, Cory came up with *Little Miss Muffet,* which debuted as a daily strip (there never was a Sunday) on September 2, 1935.

Milly Muffet (her surname was inspired by a well-known nursery rhyme) was an orphan girl of about 5, clearly modeled on Shirley Temple (as Babe Bunting had also been), with blonde curls and bright eyes. Like any other self-respecting orphan, Milly (or Millie as the name was sometimes spelled) had the requisite cruel stepmother as well as a dog companion called Hash, to whom she confided at length. She also found a fairy godmother in the person of a middle-aged, unmarried woman named Mrs. Grayson, who often took the orphan under her wing, much to the frustration of the second Mrs. Muffet. There were stories of kidnapping, embezzlement, and financial skullduggery, but no violence in a feature the syndicate had touted as "a girl adventure strip filled with thrills and heartbreak."

Cory's style was delicate and soft-edged, with an elaborate use of halftones, grays, and some well-positioned blacks. She had a flair for delineating faces, and her adult characters were neatly categorized as to class and type in just a few lines. The artist often complained about not being able to write her own stories, the continuities being handed to her by King Features' writers for her to illustrate. At any rate, she drew the adventures of the little moppet until old age (she was going on 80) forced her to retire in the mid-1950s. Her last strip appeared on June 30, 1956.

M.H.

LITTLE NEMO IN SLUMBERLAND
1905–1914, 1924–1926

On October 15, 1905, *Little Nemo in Slumberland*, Winsor McCay's best known and most beloved creation, made a spectacular entrance in the pages of the *New York Herald*. It showed a very young boy of about 5 cavalcading through the stars amid a wild bestiary of fantastic animals, the whole sequence of pictures bathed in dazzling color and light.

The plot of the series was simple: each night Little Nemo, the young boy hero, was carried in a dream to Slumberland, and each morning he was brought back down to earth by the rude shock of awakening. This abrupt conclusion, however, in no way impeded what might be called the ineluctable development of the plot: on each of his nocturnal rambles Nemo penetrated a little deeper into the kingdom of dreams. A well-read man, McCay may have heeded the warning expressed by Homer at the very beginning of the *Iliad:* "A dream can also be a message from Zeus." The message here issued from a lesser Olympian deity, King Morpheus, who peremptorily summoned Nemo to his kingdom. From this simple premise there would ensue as many tribulations as in any Homeric legend.

It took no fewer than twenty weeks for Nemo to reach Slumberland, only to find the entrance gate closed; once inside, however, the cast of characters that were to dominate the strip all came into place. The first of them to greet Nemo was Flip, a green-faced, grimacing dwarf perpetually wearing a big hat and chewing on a fat cigar, who was described as "a bad and brazen brat...an outcast relative of the Dawn family." Initially Nemo's arch-rival and implacable enemy, he later turned into a somewhat unsettling companion who involved the little hero in increasingly dangerous escapades. In one of these, a visit to the uncharted Candy Islands, they brought back a grass-skirted cannibal named Impy (or Impie), a holdover from McCay's *Jungle Imps* days. The trio of Nemo, Flip, and Impy would have turned McCay's creation into yet another boys' adventure strip had it not been for the presence of the Princess of Slumberland, who presented an image of feminine poise, grace, and charm in the weird surroundings of the her kingdom. It was her longing for companionship that had prompted King Morpheus, her father, to summon Little Nemo to Slumberland as a playmate for the little princess, whose name was never disclosed in the entire course of the strip.

Finally, there was Little Nemo himself, who would change and grow as the stories progressed. The timid, wonder-struck mama's boy of the early episodes became more assured and rose in his own esteem as he entered into

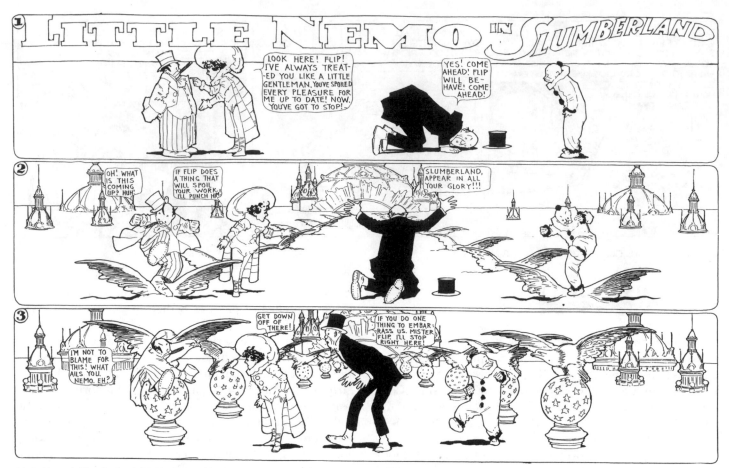

Little Nemo in Slumberland (W. McCay), 1909

closer intimacy with his weird milieu; the shadowy little figure, who wore the Latin name for "nobody," was gradually transformed from dreamer to doer: where he had once fled from giants and been thrown from horses he would later fight pirates and polar bears. His heroic attributes would even grow to messianic proportions, as he walked on water at least twice, and even healed the lame and the sick. Ultimately Nemo would become the ruler of his dream after he had learned to master its powers, interpret its laws, and conquer its universe.

And what a universe it was to conquer! If it did have a center in the form of the rococo palace over which King Morpheus held sway with the assistance of his officious majordomo, the black-coated Dr. Pill, Slumberland's circumference, like that of the kingdom of Heaven, extended toward the infinite. Its approaches were as vast as St. Peter's Square in Rome, while its architecture was a curious amalgam of Italian baroque, world's-fair eclecticism, and art nouveau decoration.

Unfortunately King Morpheus, who despite his looking like God the Father in the Michelangelo frescoes, was a rather benign despot (except when suffering from the gout), had let the immense domains beyond the palace walls go to seed. At the behest of the imperious princess or perhaps prompted by his own sense of curiosity and adventure, Nemo therefore went on to explore the icebound land of Jack Frost, restore some civilization to the rundown tenements of Shanty Town, and confront the perils of Befuddle Hall; he even journeyed as far afield as the moon and the planet Mars. All these adventures were punctuated

by a vast diorama of coruscating images—such as the dramatic dismantling of Jack Frost's palace; the multiple duplications, dislocations, and transmogrifications suffered by the hero and his companions in Befuddle Hall's chamber of illusions; or the visit to the weird zoo of Mars—images that stayed in the mind with the vividness of remembered dreams.

McCay's imagery was greatly enhanced by the use of color. Color brought sharper focus to forms and objects, pointedly distancing Nemo's universe from the mundane reality of the waking state. Color made it easier for the artist to manipulate the laws of perspective as when, for instance, Nemo grew magically taller or smaller, as the situation required, in relation to an environment that acquired the transience of insubstantial things. Doggedly McCay proceeded with his methodological exploration of the dream. Lovingly he detailed its transpositions, its fulgurations, its transformations. Graphically and pictorially he recreated its sensations, the sense of free fall, of flight, of dizziness, of estrangement. Yet he also knew how to put slapstick and buffoonery to good use, his cartooning abilities being all the more effective for being displayed with such wit and elegance.

In 1911, in a move all too familiar to American cartoonists of the time, McCay left the Herald Company, enticed by the siren song (and a higher salary) from W. R. Hearst's *New York American.* Before leaving the *Herald,* he indulged in one last fling, a grand tour of all the North American cities where *Little Nemo* was published. To the *American* McCay contributed a number of short-lived strips, such as

The Man from Montclair, Dear Dad and His Daughter, Mr. Bosh, and Nobody Cares for Father (the last named may have been autobiographical); more importantly, he continued to write and draw Nemo's adventures there under the title In the Land of Wonderful Dreams. McCay's awesome mastery of line and color was still very much in evidence in his retitled Nemo page, but his inventiveness seemed to have gone, leading to a disconnected gallery of beautiful pictures with no narrative peg on which to hang them. This second series of Nemo adventures came to an end in 1914, the same year that McCay also abandoned his other comic-strip stories.

Nemo was one dream that would not die, however; after a ten-year hiatus, at the end of his contract with Hearst in 1924, McCay returned to the *Herald* and one last crack at *Little Nemo in Slumberland,* down to the restoration of the feature's full and hallowed title. The born-again Sunday page, while visually dazzling, had lost much of the poetry and pathos that had characterized the original version, and it soon faltered before ending on the last Sunday of 1926, thereby providing a sad epilogue to McCay's career in the comics. In 1947 Winsor McCay's son Robert tried to revive his father's strip for syndication, but this last effort met with almost no success.

M.H.

LITTLE NO-NO
See NORBERT

LITTLE ORPHAN ANNIE
1924–1979; as ANNIE, 1979–present

A continuity strip containing adventure, pathos, humor, and a social message as elemental as its drawing, Harold Gray's *Little Orphan Annie* began on August 5, 1924, in the New York *Daily News* and made its first appearance in color in the Sunday *News* on November 2 of the same year. Employing some of the conventions of popular sentimental fiction and rendered in a bold, simple graphic style, it quickly became a national favorite.

Gray had apprenticed as an assistant to Sidney Smith, working on *The Gumps* at the *Chicago Tribune* for five years before approaching Chicago Tribune–New York News Syndicate president Joseph Medill Patterson with the idea of a strip about an orphan. Legend (which Gray always denied) has it that his original proposal was for a strip to be called *Little Orphan Otto* and that Patterson convinced him to turn Otto into a girl. Gray's version of the character's origin was that Annie was his own idea, chosen because there were forty comic strips featuring boys and only three starring girls running at the time.

In its first month, *Little Orphan Annie* focused on the pathetic waif's indomitable spirit. From the beginning, Annie epitomized Gray's ideal of spunky, resourceful childhood, and for the forty-four years he drew the strip, the unaging eleven-year-old went through an endless succession of misfortunes and adventures with courage, ingenuity, humor, and a clear moral vision. As her creator

described her in 1964, "Annie is tougher than hell, with a heart of gold and a fast left, who can take care of herself because she has to." Despite the trademark empty ovals Gray drew for her eyes, she was more perceptive than most of the adults in the strip, unfailingly recognizing villainy and seeing through social pretension.

Annie was almost always accompanied by her loyal dog, Sandy, whose sole vocal response was "Arf!" but who made up in facial expressiveness for what it lacked in vocabulary. After two months, she was joined by "Daddy" Warbucks, a zillionaire who took her under his protection but frequently relied on her help.

Unpretentious despite his usual costume of dress suit and huge diamond stickpin, Warbucks is a self-made man and a strident champion of conservative values, clearly those of his creator. The story line of *Little Orphan Annie* repeatedly reflected Gray's support of big business and his dislike of government interference. Among his targets over the years were income taxes, the New Deal, and what he characterized as "Commies."

Warbucks's far-flung enterprises have brought him many mysterious friends, among the most useful of whom are Punjab, a turbaned giant of unlimited physical strength and a knowledge of magical spells, and Asp, a sinister Asian of unstated but manifold powers who, like Warbucks, always wears a tuxedo. Variously serving as bodyguards and hit men, they are unfailingly loyal to both the industrialist and his ward.

Like many classic strips, *Little Orphan Annie* has had enough vitality to overflow into other media. From 1930 to 1943, it gave its name and characters to a popular radio program, beginning on station WGN in Chicago, and later, sponsored by Ovaltine, in network syndication on ABC. Its theme song—beginning "Who's that little chatterbox? / The one with pretty auburn locks? / Cute little she / It's Little Orphan Annie"—became one of the most familiar tunes on radio. Less of a hit in Hollywood, Gray's heroine figured in two unsuccessful films called *Little Orphan Annie,* one from RKO in 1932 and another from Paramount in 1938; it was not until the successful Broadway musical, called simply *Annie,* in 1977, and the even more successful Columbia Pictures film version of it in 1982, that the moppet was to achieve national celebrity in the theater.

Gray has often been compared with Charles Dickens for his exaggerated characterization, his blend of pathos and humor, and his simplistic social philosophy. Another Dickensian trait was his ingenious coinage of names that fit the personalities or situations of his characters. Miss Asthma, the director of the orphanage in which Annie began her epic, and Oliver Warbucks, the munitions magnate who became her patron, were the first of a cavalcade of memorably named characters, which also includes the brat Selby Adelelbert Piffle (every bit the sap his acronym suggests), the devious Frenchman Count de Tour, the ballet teacher Anya Toze, and the charlatan Dr. LeQuaque.

One measure of the universal familiarity of the strip is the frequency with which it has been parodied. Its well-known cast of characters, graphic style, and political stance have proved irresistible to many other cartoonists as subjects for good-natured lampoons. Al Capp, in his *Li'l Abner,* did a strip-within-a-strip called *Sweet Fannie Gooney* spoofing

Little Orphan Annie (H. Gray), © 1925 Chicago Tribune

Gray's characters; Sandy and Annie appeared as guests in Walt Kelly's *Pogo,* renamed "Li'l Arf an' Nonnie," in 1952; and in 1961 Harvey Kurtzman turned Annie into an adult sexpot in his irreverent *Playboy* strip *Little Annie Fanny.*

The frequent violence of Annie's adventures and the right-wing politics of its message brought complaints and occasional cancellations, but the strip was appearing in four hundred newspapers when Gray died in 1968. It was carried on by its creator's cousin and longtime assistant, Robert Leffingwell, but the public was so dissatisfied with his work that he was quickly replaced. After a series of other artists and writers failed, the syndicate gave up trying to find a successor for Gray; by the mid-1970s classic *Little Orphan Annie* strips from the 1930s were being reprinted—a moderate success as nostalgia, but sadly fallen off from its days as one of the top strips in the national polls.

With the renewal of interest in *Little Orphan Annie* sparked by the successful Broadway musical, and in breathless anticipation of a blockbuster film, the syndicate made another stab at resuscitating Gray's characters in 1977. Leonard Starr, creator of the realistically drawn and scripted *On Stage,* was chosen for the job. In a deliberate effort at differentiating the new avatar from Gray's by-now somewhat dated opus, the strip was renamed *Annie* when it made its reappearance on December 9, 1979, and it was drawn in a sleeker, less primitive style. But Starr has not departed significantly from the essential simplicity of the original. His stories, too, have retained Gray's blend of physical excitement and homespun humor, although they have abandoned his conservative preaching. Starr has also updated the strip in several ways to give it a contemporary look. He has varied Annie's wardrobe, allowing her to change out of the nondescript red dress that was almost her only garment for the first four decades of the strip's. He has also permitted her a chaste little romance with a boyfriend named Huckie Flynn, and her vocabulary, for many years a stylized version of what Gray considered working-class vernacular, now includes some living slang.

But while Annie may experience other superficial alterations with the passing years, she is too much of a national icon to undergo any really fundamental change. However she dresses or speaks, she is a symbol of much that is central to America's self-image: independence, self-reliance, diligence, and wholesome moral values.

D.W.

THE LITTLE PEOPLE
1952–1970

In 1952 Walt Scott wisely gave up drawing *Captain Easy,* for whose illustrative style his talents were unsuited, and started concentrating on funny animals and cute elves, for which, as a former Disney animator, he was eminently qualified. His first foray into the field of comic-page whimsy was *Huckleberry Hollow,* a talking-animal strip that he started on Sunday, February 24, followed by the more durable *The Little People* a little later, on June 1.

Actually the Little People, a tribe of cute, small-sized, forest-dwelling creatures, had undergone a dry run during Christmas week 1951, as a special holiday feature, and they were judged popular enough to be later given their own Sunday page (with *Huckleberry Hollow* as a companion piece). The Little People, with their enormous heads, floppy ears, and tiny bodies, had the appearance—and appeal—of big babies. They sported names like Chub, Woosh, Loop, and Jink, and lived in the Valley of the Small People, where they consorted with friendly animals and managed to keep out of the clutches of the nasty ones. Their adventures, jolly rather than frightening, were clearly aimed at young children, as was Scott's rounded, cozy drawing style, a style most adults found a little too cute.

Scott died in 1970, and NEA, which distributed the feature, allowed *The Little People* to lapse; the last page appeared on September 6, 1970.

M.H.

LITTLE SAMMY SNEEZE
1904–1906

At the invitation of James Gordon Bennett, head of the New York Herald Company, Winsor McCay came to New York at the end of 1903 to work for Bennett's two dailies, the *Herald* and the *Evening Telegram.* It was in the pages of the *Telegram* the following year that McCay's first veritable comic creations made their appearance: the artist was well past 30 when he entered the medium. *Mr. Goodenough, Sister's Little Sister's Beau,* and *Phoolish Philip* were early examples of McCay's comic series: they don't yet reveal the artist's full-blown talent, but in their detailed renditions, their skillful depiction of minute events they stylistically stand head and shoulders above most of the comic features of the period.

The *Herald* was the *Telegram*'s sister publication, and in its Sunday color section McCay's most striking efforts were published (his work for the *Telegram* had all been in black and white). On July 24, 1904, he created there *Little Sammy Sneeze*, a weekly series involving the cataclysmic sternutations of a foppishly dressed little boy and the disasters that ensued: in six panels disposed in two tiers, the artist developed his theme in almost invariable fashion. The first four panels depicted the mounting symptoms of Little Sammy's bout of sneezing, leading up to its eruption in the penultimate frame, and ending with the hapless boy being booted out in the last picture. Sammy's sneezes could be ranked in the same category as natural catastrophes in their magnitude and their destructive power: they shattered windows, leveled houses, blasted workshops, and even at one point blew out the strip's panel borders.

Despite the disclaimers McCay placed on either side of the strip's logo, "He just simply couldn't stop it" and "He never knew when it was coming," the unfoldings of the gags were easily predictable. "The pleasures of the strip," wrote McCay biographer John Canemaker in his outstanding study *Winsor McCay: His Life and Art,* "include seeing how McCay varied the climactic moment in the explosion panel and the subtle differences he put into details in the panels leading up to Sammy's sneeze."

The artist's conscious strivings toward an original form of graphic expression that would amalgamate striking imagery and dynamic motion can best be seen in *Little Sammy* and the contemporaneous *The Story of Hungry Henrietta* (the catastrophe-prone little boy and the ravenous little girl actually met in a 1905 episode). In these early pages McCay displayed, along with a masterly sense of color and composition, a fine visual wit and the larger-than-life vision that remained his trademarks all through his career.

M.H.

THE LOCKHORNS
1968–present

In addition to drawing gag cartoons for a number of magazines, Bill Hoest began writing *The Lockhorns* on September 9, 1968 (daily), followed on April 9, 1972, for the Sunday page. Since his death in 1988, his widow, Bunny, and his very able assistant, John Reiner, have successfully continued to amuse readers with the marital bickerings of the very well-named Lockhorns.

This childless couple has been married for many years, but it seems longer to both as they constantly quarrel about everything. Leroy complains about Loretta's cooking, which "speaks for itself...it says, 'Yecch'," her failed attempts at self-beautification (especially of her hair), her accident-prone driving, her incessant gossiping, her spendthrift ways, and her unbearable singing ("Either Loretta's tone deaf...or we are"). However, he is far from blameless himself, as she points out to her sympathetic girlfriends, the minister, and her mother. She does not like his drinking whether at home, parties, or at Arthur's, his favorite water-

ing hole, and resents his roving eye and flirtatious behavior toward young, beautiful women. Nor does she appreciate his lying on the couch all day, watching sports on TV, or—more likely—sleeping: "There he is...not doing all the things he wanted to do all winter."

That each should at times contemplate murder is not too surprising; that they do not follow through is. This is because, deep down, they in fact love each other, as is evidenced by their visits to the marriage counselor, an occasional gift of flowers and candy on his part, and a rare purchase of "a dozen red roses and a white flag," again on his part, while she does her best to keep house or introduce him to culture and the finer things in life. Ultimately, they find that tolerance of each other's foibles and shortcomings is the key to surviving marriage: why else would she have kept his IOU from their first date?

Bill Hoest's panel cartoon series, so successfully carried on by his successors, is based on, and uses the humor of, the traditional husband-and-wife conflicts, both in the pithiness of its one-liners and in the caricatural portrayal of the two protagonists, with their bulbous noses and foreshortened bodies. For his work, which is distributed by King Features Syndicate to more than five hundred newspapers worldwide, Hoest received awards from the National Cartoonists Society for Best Syndicated Panel in 1975 and 1980.

P.H.

THE LONE RANGER
1938–1971, 1981–1984

One dark day in the 1880s, a group of six Texas Rangers led by Captain Dan Reed was ambushed by the murderous Butch Cavendish Gang. All the Rangers were killed, with the exception of the captain's younger brother, John, who was rescued by Tonto, an Indian. To deceive Cavendish, Tonto dug six graves, one for each of the Rangers. John Reed, once he had been nursed back to health, donned a mask so he wouldn't be recognized, and solemnly vowed vengeance on the Cavendish gang and on all evildoers. Thus was the legend of the Lone Ranger born.

Conceived by Fran Striker as a radio play, *The Lone Ranger* had begun on January 30, 1933, on Detroit's radio station WXYZ, carried on the strains of the *William Tell* overture. Its success had been phenomenal, spawning movie serials and a barrage of merchandising. In 1938 King Features bought the rights to the character, and the new feature made its debut, in both daily and Sunday formats, in September 1938.

The first artist on the strip was the much-maligned Ed Kressy. While he can hardly be regarded as a great (or even good) cartoonist, his awkward drawings displayed a quality of spontaneity that well fitted the loose script (at first written by Striker himself). After a brief interim with Jon L. Blummer, Charles Flanders, who had cut his teeth on *King of the Mounties,* took charge of the drawing in January 1939. Flanders did a creditable job on the strip, and his characterization of the masked rider must be accounted the definitive one. His long tenure on the feature caused him to grow disenchanted and careless, and toward the end of its run *The Lone Ranger* often lapsed into unintended self-parody (when it was not ghosted outright by other hands).

The "Lone Ranger" appellation was always something of a misnomer since the hero actually had at least two constant companions. The first one was the faithful Tonto (to whom the Lone Ranger was "Kemo Sabay," the Trusty Scout), who would accept torture rather than put the Lone Ranger's life or identity in jeopardy; the other one was the Ranger's white stallion, Silver, toward whom he dis-

The Lone Ranger (C. Flanders), © 1946 Lone Ranger, Inc.

played an affection he never showed any woman. The battle-cry "Hi-Yo, Silver!" became the Lone Ranger's familiar trademark. (Tonto also had a recognizable mount, the paint Scout, who was to Silver what he himself was to the Lone Ranger.) In the mid-1940s, following the fashion of the radio plays, there was introduced into the strip a teenage companion to the Ranger: his nephew, Dan Reid, Jr., son of slain Captain Dan Reid, and future father of Britt Reid, the Green Hornet.

While he excelled at the depiction of the masked hero and his companions, as well as in the drawing of horses, cattle, wagons, and other paraphernalia of the West, Flanders somehow never seemed to get the backgrounds right. The scenery in *The Lone Ranger* was one of the barest ever to appear in any newspaper-strip western: often a cluster of trees, a few mesquites, or a faraway mountain range were all there was to mark the location. A sense of place was consequently never achieved. The familiar landmarks of the western locus were sketched in rather than delineated in detail; they looked more like sets than locations. *The Lone Ranger* had the strange look of a storyboard for a grade-B western movie; the real thing somehow always eluded the artist. The secondary characters were also pictured hastily, and they all looked interchangeable and more often than not could only be told apart by the shape of their Stetsons or the color of their shirts.

Plot and situations were the conventional staples of western adventure. Usually there would be a stagecoach robbery, a bank holdup, or a string of cattle rustlings that the Lone Ranger would be called in to solve. There were also a number of stories dealing with defrauded widows, victimized orphans (often young and pretty girls), and wronged ranch owners. One familiar plot twist was to have the Lone Ranger wrongly accused of some crime, with the masked avenger then setting out to find the real culprit. In the course of his adventures the Lone Ranger often came close to getting himself killed or to having his identity revealed.

No outlaw, however, succeeded in lifting the mask off the face of the western nemesis of crime. At the end of each episode the triumphant Ranger would ride off on his horse, leaving behind him one of his silver bullets, as the existential trace of his passage.

The greatest popularity of the strip came in the 1940s, when Flanders reached his peak. Then erosion set in, as Flanders did less and less of the work and Tom Gill, who was drawing the comic-book version at the time, often came over to ghost the newspaper strip as well. Despite some imaginative scripting by Paul Newman (who had succeeded Bob Green, who himself had replaced Striker), *The Lone Ranger* eventually lost its following, and it was finally dropped by the syndicate in late 1971.

At the time of its demise, *The Lone Ranger* had been appearing in newspapers for over thirty-three years, the longest run of any western strip. A good deal of its appeal, of course, lay with the title character's ambiguous role, a characterization so artfully contrived by Striker that it has resisted countless debunkings, spoofs, and satires. Its popularity also resided in the resiliency of the western myth itself. Hemming close to the timeless themes of western legend, *The Lone Ranger,* as it was done from its inception through the 1950s, was probably the most representative of all western strips.

Following on the heels of the *Legend of the Lone Ranger* movie, a revival was attempted by the New York Times Special Features Syndicate. The new *Lone Ranger* strip was handsomely drawn by comic-book veteran Russ Heath, on texts by Cary Bates. It never achieved the success of the earlier version and only ran from September 13, 1981, to April 1, 1984.

M.H.

LONG SAM
1954–1962

*I*n *Li'l Abner* Al Capp had stood sex on its head, picturing most of his female characters as oversexed and eagerly in pursuit of the unwilling, harassed men—a common male fantasy. All this tomfoolery reached its zenith every year on Sadie Hawkins Day. That fateful day any girl able to catch one of the fast-fleeing males got to marry him. And in Al's madCapp world, that was as fiendish a fate as could be devised.

Later Capp simply reversed this premise in *Long Sam,* a

daily and Sunday comic feature he created, and which made its debut on May 31, 1954, under distribution by United Feature Syndicate. Sam was a nubile girl who lived in seclusion in a little cabin in the hills in the sole company of her mother, who had sheltered her from the ways of the world (and especially of men). She later made up for her ignorance in a variety of ways, as she finally ventured into the outside world and immediately became the object of desire of every leering, panting man around. Her adventures, Stephen Becker wrote in *Comic Art in America,* "ranged from the simple contretemps of refusing ardent suitors to the more complex task of escaping a band of Brooklyn science-fiction addicts disguised as Martians." Among other escapades, she was lured into a mail-order marriage with a disfigured man wearing a face mask and entertained a platonic relationship with an older, shorter, overweight millionaire she called Uncle Al.

As the artist on the strip Capp picked Bob Lubbers, and he couldn't have made a better choice: Lubbers's professional motto has always been "cherchez la femme," and his talents in this field were never displayed to better advantage than in *Long Sam.* He pictured the naive heroine as an impossibly leggy and bosomed creature, with luscious, dark hair and a fresh, rosy face, according to the canons of beauty prevalent in her days. Unfortunately he was instructed by Capp to draw every other character in a caricatural way that was not the artist's forte: Sam's Maw in particular looked like Mammy Yokum brought over from *Li'l Abner.* The juxtaposition of straight illustration with grotesquerie did not blend easily and eventually detracted from the excellence of the artwork.

Long Sam did not live up to Capp's monetary expectations, and after a couple of years he turned the feature over to his younger brother, Elliot Caplin, who became disenchanted in his turn by the meager financial returns from the strip. Stu Hampel then took over for a brief period; in its final years the feature was scripted by Lubbers. The syndicate ultimately decided to pull the plug on Long Sam's sexually simmering but commercially tepid career: the last release appeared on December 29, 1962.

M.H.

THE LOOK-ALIKE BOYS
See MIKE AND IKE

LOOY DOT DOPE
See NIZE BABY

THE LOVE BYRDS
See ETTA KETT

LUANN
1985–present

Greg Evans had taught junior and senior high school art in his native California, worked as promotion manager and graphic artist for a TV station in Colorado, and entertained with a robot at trade shows and fairs before he sold *Luann* to News America Syndicate in 1984. On March 17 of the next year, NAS launched the strip with little fanfare. Since then the thirteen-year-old titular heroine and her seventeen-year-old brother, Brad, have not grown any older, but the strip has kept up with the times in the subjects it has addressed. *Luann* neither sentimentalizes nor demonizes the period of life it features: rather, its sometimes poignant humor derives from its honest portrayal of the sibling hostility, academic tedium, and adolescent angst of its characters.

Luann DeGroot agonizes about all the usual things that beset her age: the injustice of school ("I don't know much about prepositions, the Civil War, or photosynthesis," she admits, "but I know a lot about clothes, video games.... How come I never get asked about the stuff I *know?!*"); her senior prom is only three years away and she still doesn't have a date; no one understands her; and her gorgeous clasmate Aaron Hill doesn't know she's alive. She plays out the modest drama of her life against a no less typical social background: her awkward, sullen brother, with whom she lives in a state of hostile symbiosis; her realistic best friend, Bernice, who acts as sounding board and advisor; and the African-American swinger Delta, who uses eyeliner, mascara, shadow, lipstick, and blush to attain an effect called "natural innocence."

Although it is Luann's strip, her brother Brad is a well-defined character with his own problems, not the least of them the fact of having a little sister (whose face he threatens to remove if she continues waving to him when he's with his buddies). A lazy, slovenly lout, he yearns for social grace, his confidence not supported much by his sister's advice as he heads for

Long Sam (Capp and Lubbers), © 1962 United Feature Syndicate

his first date: "Say 'excuse me' when you belch," she suggests. Then she holds her nose and asks, "Got on enough cologne?"

Luann has remained a genial, good-natured strip, but it has reflected the advances the comics industry has made in candor by presenting the coming-of-age rites of its characters frankly. Luann has suffered the indignity of wearing braces, she has defied parental opposition to get her ears pierced, and in 1991 she underwent that most significant transitional experience of her age, unprecedented in mainstream comics, her first menstruation. Evans admitted that he expected some negative reaction to introducing such a delicate topic, but said that he hoped the strip would open communications and ease discussion on the subject. Handled delicately, the event was announced on May 7 by Luann screaming from the bathroom, *"Aaaaaa!! It's happened!! I'm.... It's.... Go get Mom!"* There were a few complaints, Evans reported, but the reaction from mothers, teenage girls, and school counselors was overwhelmingly positive.

Simplistically drawn with all heads either egg- or pear-shaped, *Luann* remains a sympathetic record of the changing lifestyles of contemporary youth. Teenagers of both sexes find in the strip much that is familiar and the reassurance that they are not alone.

D.W.

LULU AND LEANDER
1903–1907

Many, if not most of the creators in the early years of the comic-strip medium were graduates from the nineteenth-century humor magazines, notably *Judge, Life,* and *Puck.* Many of these practitioners had pioneered the sequential form of narratives-in-pictures that foreshadowed the newspaper comic strips. Among the latter, F. M. Howarth got his chance in 1903 at turning out a genuine comic page for the Hearst newspapers, and while he didn't succeed, the feature he created there, called *Lulu and Leander,* provides an interesting sidebar to the early history of the medium.

Lulu was a much-courted young woman, dark-tressed and dark-eyed, with an hourglass figure stylishly draped in the fashions of the Gay Nineties. On his part Leander was "an oily social climber," according to Coulton Waugh, who added, "His only charm is that he usually gets thrown out on his ear, which relieves the customers." He often involved Lulu and her gullible "Mommer" and "Popper" in nefarious schemes from which he alone managed to extricate himself. Lulu was steadfastly loyal to her slick-haired, fast-talking Romeo, despite all his shortcomings, even in the face of hot competition from such worthies as Charley Onthespot and Lieutenant Sharpnell.

Howarth drew the feature in his fastidious, minutely detailed style. All his characters had enormous heads, and they seemed to move like mannequins. Instead of dialogue balloons he used text under the pictures and at a time when the comics were going into freer, less formal directions, along with competition in the same comics section from

strips like *The Katzenjammer Kids* and *Happy Hooligan,* this may have proved to be the page's biggest drawback with the readers. In an effort to redress the situation, the author got Lulu and Leander married in August 1906. This ploy, which would work wonders with later comic-strip characters from Blondie to Dick Tracy, failed to achieve the desired result in this case, and *Lulu and Leander* ended its run in the course of the following year.

M.H.

LUTHER
1969–1986

Luther is one of the trio of comic strips by African-Americans, along with *Wee Pals* and *Quincy,* that blazed a path into national syndication with major newspaper syndicates in the late 1960s and early 1970s.

Of the three, *Luther,* by Brumsic Brandon, Jr., had the hardest edge to its humor. The strip began with Reporters' News Syndicate and then shifted to the powerful Los Angeles Times Syndicate.

The strip's namesake is a grade-school child. School's tough, even in the second or third grade, when your teacher's named Miss Backlash. When his little white pal asked Luther how he had done on a test, his response was that although all the questions had been answered correctly, "Miss Backlash said I must have cheated."

Luther's classmate Hardcore wore a baseball cap with the sun visor over his eyes; Pee Wee was younger, only in prekindergarten. The kids in *Luther* wondered aloud how the teacher already knew that Pee Wee wasn't college material. The black girls in the strip, Mary Frances and Oreo, had different personalities and sometimes played off of blonde Lily.

Brumsic Brandon, Jr., also drew editorial cartoons and received his art education at New York University. His first published cartoon was in 1945. Although his gags were often about racism, Brandon was successful in using his nicely designed urban inner-city kids to get his message of racial equality across. Luther, in one instance, told Pee Wee that the first slave ship landed in Virginia in 1619. Pee Wee's response was to ask, "When were the good old days, Luther?" The artwork focused on the kids talking, with only minimal backgrounds.

As a young girl, Barbara Brandon, the daughter of *Luther*'s creator, had colored in silhouettes and drawn the border-lines for her father's strip. As a woman, she brought to real life the comment by Luther to Pee Wee, "I'll bet when you grow up...you'll still be able to be the first black something." Barbara Brandon became the first African-American woman to have a nationally syndicated comic strip when Universal Press Syndicate debuted her *Where I'm Coming From* in September 1991.

Like her father's cartoons, her work doesn't go for the belly laugh. *Where I'm Coming From,* a Sunday feature, portrays a revolving cast of seven black women whose heads and hands, often holding telephones, are only shown; Barbara Brandon wants the reader to notice the eyes of her characters and not the more obvious parts of their bodies. Her technique combines that of her father and the talking-to-the-audience style developed by cartoonist Jules Feiffer.

Barbara Brandon deals with the same themes of racism that her father emphasized. However, she's added single parenthood, sexism, and women's rights to the mix. Working to debunk stereotypes, her women characters range from self-absorbed and man-obsessed to socially conscious.

Although not nationally syndicated now, *Luther* continues to make published appearances. At least six *Luther* books have appeared, including *Luther from Inner City* and *Luther Tells It as It Is,* and *Where I'm Coming From* reprints have also been published in book form.

B.C., Jr.

MADGE, THE MAGICIAN'S DAUGHTER
1905–1910

W. O. Wilson was the creator of *Madge, the Magician's Daughter,* a weekly color page that came out in the summer of 1905. It was syndicated nationally by the North American Company (not to be confused with the later North America Syndicate).

Madge was an early fantasy strip that was based on the same premise as the celebrated folk tale of the Sorcerer's Apprentice. The titular heroine was a young girl with blonde curls who would often perform tricks with her father's wand. Her efforts at magic inevitably backfired on her. She would, for instance, try to conjure up a goat to surprise the guests at a party, and a hippopotamus would appear instead and wreak havoc on the proceedings. This recurrent gag line constituted the core of each Sunday episode, and Wilson milked it for all it was worth. He was unfortunately not adept at building suspense, and the subtitles running under the main title would always give the joke away. "Just a slight mix-up—camels came instead of pheasants," one caption read, while another proclaimed, "Oops, wrong again! That Easter egg was a turkey."

Madge was a precocious vamp who also delighted in playing pranks on her unsuspecting playmates. Like a latter-day Circe, she once transformed her boy companions into pigs, making them perform all kinds of tricks. The feature was drawn in a pleasant, innocuous style closely patterned on Outcault's *Buster Brown,* down to the foppish clothes and upper-class trappings. It lasted for five years, disappearing at the end of 1910.

M.H.

MAGGIE AND JIGGS
See BRINGING UP FATHER

MALE CALL
1943–1946

Although drafted twice, Milton Caniff was declared 4F because of phlebitis. Still, no cartoonist with the possible exception of Bill Mauldin contributed as much during World War II to improving the general morale of Allied troops.

Caniff's *Terry and the Pirates* was already a superstar of syndicated comics when the Second World War began. It seemed natural for Caniff to write and draw a special weekly *Terry and the Pirates* pinup/gag strip featuring sultry blonde Burma for the Camp Newspaper Service clip-art sheet. This he began October 11, 1942.

However, in south Florida the special army version of *Terry* with bodacious Burma and racy double-entendre gags was also used by the regular press, causing complaints to the Chicago Tribune–New York News Syndicate from subscribers of the regular *Terry and the Pirates* adventure strip. The syndicate ordered Caniff to cease using any *Terry* characters and the *Terry* name. However, Caniff could continue doing his part for the war effort with a new strip and a new female character.

Caniff's new character was the opposite of worldly, seemingly available Burma. He designed Miss Lace to be "innocent but sexy as hell." She was brunette to Burma's blonde, and she pushed the boundaries of what was acceptable to publish in a military newspaper. The Camp Newspaper Service staff named the strip *Male Call,* a play on words, and Caniff approved the title. The last special *Terry* was published January 10, 1943. *Male Call* began January 24, 1943, and continued through March 3, 1946.

After the Dragon Lady, Miss Lace was the most famous

Male Call (M. Caniff), © 1945 Milton Caniff

female character created by Caniff. Appearing in three thousand military newspapers on land and sea, Miss Lace thrilled and tantalized a minimum audience of fifteen million readers, not counting civilians. Her innocent but suggestive adventures were each a self-contained gag strip.

Caniff basically did two versions of each week's strip. The first, with outlines inked and benday patterns noted, was converted into a stencil for mimeograph reproduction. The original art was then returned to Caniff, who inked it in his classic style for use in *Stars and Stripes, Yank,* and military newspapers printed at regular commercial printers. During the World War II prephotocopy era, the mimeograph machine was everywhere and spread the fame of *Male Call* close to the front lines.

Miss Lace was femininity itself. She was the stuff of dreams, available but not available, a sexy lady in a low-cut evening dress who called enlisted men "general" or "admiral" depending on their branch of service. Her popularity with G.I.'s ranked with Rita Hayworth's and Betty Grable's as the leading pinup of the war.

In 1945, Simon & Schuster published a reprint of 112 *Male Call* strips. A 152-strip reprint was published in 1959. The complete *Male Call,* including the *Terry and the Pirates* strips featuring Burma and eight censored versions of Miss Lace, was published by Kitchen Sink Press in 1987 and is still available.

The sexy and titillating Miss Lace continued to be drawn by Caniff for military reunion groups, special drawings at their request. However, he saw her as being locked in the time frame of World War II and did only one upgraded version of her, for *Airman* magazine in 1970.

B.C., Jr.

MAMA'S BOYZ
1990–present

The main characters of *Mama's Boyz* are the Porter family, African Americans in a urban setting who live over their bookstore. Pauline Porter, a widow, inherited the bookstore from her late husband, Virgil. Sons Tyrell, age 18, and Yusuf, age 16, help out reluctantly when they aren't in school.

The extended Porter family includes Mama's parents, Gran'pa, a retired chef, and the rarely seen Gran'ma. Mama's thirty-six-year-old bachelor brother, Greg—Uncle Greggo to the kids—is often shown, as is Keisha, the love of Tyrell's life, who is a student and part-time bookstore employee.

Cartoonist Jerry Craft, a graduate of the School of Visual Arts in New York, began self-syndicating *Mama's Boyz* in 1990. He'd freelanced work for both Harvey and Marvel Comics and had cartoons published in *Ebony* magazine. As with other African-American cartoonists before him such as Ted Shearer of *Quincy,* black newspapers were first to publish his work. In New York City, Craft's work is a regular feature in the *City Sun.*

Currently a staff artist at King Features Syndicate, Craft and *Mama's Boyz* joined King's Weekly Service package for distribution to fifteen hundred small- to midsized newspapers in February 1995. Other comic strips in the package include *Popeye, Flash Gordon, Henry, Bringing Up Father,* and *Krazy Kat and Ignatz,* older King properties, as well as up-and-coming comic strips. *Mama's Boyz* is the only African-American strip in the package.

Yusuf, the "Imelda Marcos" of the sneaker world, has never seen a hip haircut he doesn't want to try. He's a good athlete and a "babe" magnet. A senior in high school, Tyrell is too old to be a "hip-hopper" but too young to be taken totally seriously by adults.

Jerry Craft's goal is to bring mainstream black family humor to the comics. Mama (Pauline Porter) is the cornerstone of strength holding the family together and keeping *Mama's Boyz,* with all its trials and tribulations of an inner-city urban environment, on the road for success.

Although given general distribution by King Features Syndicate, a different version of *Mama's Boyz* is still distributed to black newspapers. These, usually in Sunday-page format, have a harder edge. In a parody of *Where's Waldo?,* for example, Craft drew "Where's Security?" and asked the reader to count how many people are watching Tyrell and Yusuf shop in a department store. The answer is twenty. Black male teenagers are often not made to feel welcome in stores.

With a believable cast of characters, the cartoonist's own urban background to draw on, humor, and the ability to keep up with latest trends among African-American teenagers, Jerry Craft's *Mama's Boyz* is the rare strip distributed nationally that features black male teens.

B.C., Jr.

MAMIE
1951–1956

Canadian-educated Russell Patterson is best known as a magazine illustrator with a special flair for drawing pretty women (at one time the Patterson girl was as celebrated as the Gibson Girl), but he did turn out a comic strip, *Pierre et Pierrette,* for the French language *La Patrie* in the second decade of this century. Only forty years later did he recidivate with *Mamie,* a Sunday page he created for United Feature Syndicate in 1951.

Mamie was a long-limbed, lovely-shaped blonde, always dressed in up-to-date fashions, and with her equally beauteous and stylish girlfriend, the dark-haired Daisy, she had mild adventures, mainly involving suitors and admirers. The latter included passersby and cops on the beat, and in those prefeminist days the ladies didn't seem to mind being ogled or whistled at. While they supposedly held positions in an office, they were seldom seen at work (which, after all, was legitimate, since the strip appeared only on weekends). They were usually shown shopping, dancing, and especially going to the beach, which allowed the artist to display their charms to the fullest.

The setting was undeniably (and unabashedly) New York, with Patterson lingering lovingly over its buildings, nightspots, and street signs. To counterbalance their more frivolous activities, the girls sometimes took the subway or ate at the Automat; despite these concessions to the times, *Mamie* was basically a flapper strip that had somehow wandered into the wrong decade.

As could be expected, *Mamie* was an elegantly drawn, exquisitely composed page, as easy on the eye as its glamorous heroine. The anecdotes, however, were thin and rarely elicited as much as a grin. This shortcoming eventually doomed the feature, and by the spring of 1956 it was gone.

M.H.

MANDRAKE THE MAGICIAN
1934–present

Ever since its inception, Lee Falk's *Mandrake the Magician* has provided its readers with a daily dose of the occult and the fantastic. Falk sold his project to King Features on the strength of the samples he had submitted. *Mandrake* started appearing on June 11, 1934, as a daily strip, with the artwork taken over two weeks later by Phil Davis, a much better draftsman than Falk had been. A Sunday version, written by Falk and drawn by Davis, followed on February 3, 1935.

At the outset, Mandrake, always impeccably attired in coat and tails, top hat, and opera cape, was a real magician who could change his size at will, conjure a sandwich or an umbrella out of thin air, or materialize himself over great distances. In his first adventure his white magic was pitted against the black magic of the Cobra, a sinister, hooded figure whose aim was nothing less than total domination of the earth. Later on, following protest from Christian readers who objected to magic on religious grounds, Mandrake became a simple master of hypnotism, who could cloud people's minds into believing that he was actually performing bona fide feats of witchcraft.

The very first daily strip introduced Mandrake's Herculean sidekick Lothar. The dethroned king of an African tribe whose life Mandrake had saved, he put himself at the magician's service out of gratitude. His fists would often succeed where his companion's powers had failed, and on more than one occasion he got to repay his debt of honor by rescuing Mandrake from mortal danger. In later years the relationship between Mandrake and Lothar became more equal, turning into a solid, mutually beneficial partnership.

While he had only one friend (in addition to his magic), Mandrake had innumerable enemies. His archnemesis was the aforementioned Cobra, an erstwhile Tibetan sage named Luciphor, whose disfigurement consequent to a laboratory accident had turned him into an embittered instrument of evil.

Mandrake the Magician (Falk and Davis), © 1936 King Features Syndicate

There have also been Saki, "the Clay Camel," a master of crime and of disguise; the Great Grando, a creature of smoke and illusion; Paulo, the mad tyrant of Dementor; and a gallery of sundry other antagonists, human, animal, or artificial. Finally, there were all those eccentric scientists who kept sending the magician on dangerous errands: journeying to the moon, for instance, or traveling into the "X" dimension.

As for the ladies, they were forever throwing themselves at the handsome magician. Princess Narda, of the mythical kingdom of Cockaigne, made her appearance the very first year of the strip, trying to murder Mandrake in order to protect her no-good brother Segrid. She became his constant companion in the dailies, but in the Sundays the suave magician was at liberty (at least for a time) to play the field. The beautiful females Mandrake has met and left behind have included lady explorers, women astronauts, harem slaves, society women, and a passel of reformed bad girls. His predilection, however, has always gone to damsels in and out of distress.

In the 1930s Mandrake and Lothar kept hopping around the world, and often beyond it, variously turning up in Transylvania, in the Amazon, at the South Pole, on Mars, and even on Broadway, as whim or happenstance dictated. Falk was then at the peak of his imaginative and narrative powers, and he wove tales of unequaled inventiveness, suspense, and wit. His writing was matched by Davis's evocative artwork and mastery of line.

During World War II, Mandrake, like so many of his fellow adventurers, felt duty-bound to put his awesome powers at the service of his country. Not content to fight enemy saboteurs and master spies, such as the Octopus, on the home front, he also saw action in the Pacific. Once the hostilities ended he seemed to have suffered the same letdown (known as the "peace trauma") that afflicted many other returning veterans, losing some of his former *élan* and even some of his erstwhile powers. While he continued on his explorations of fantastic (and uncharted) lands in the Sundays, the dailies often found him close to home, in mundane investigations of burglaries or blackmail, a situation symbolized by his now quasi-official union with Narda. Perhaps in compensation, the readers were treated to tantalizing glimpses of the magician's past, including his apprenticeship in Tibet. Mandrake's personal life stood further revealed with the introduction of his evil twin, Derek, and the irruption of his younger sister, Lenore.

In 1964 Davis died, and after a short interim period filled by his widow Martha, his succession passed into the hands of veteran comic-book artist Harold ("Fred") Fredericks, who brought a more down-to-earth sensibility to the strip. Falk took this opportunity to bring about some changes in an effort to revitalize the feature. Mandrake, now firmly anchored in his fortress-residence of Xanadu, acts less and less as a lone operator. He often collaborates with likeminded international organizations, such as Inter-Intel, a crime-fighting outfit headed by a cigar-chomping, foultempered robot.

After more than sixty years of existence, *Mandrake* still remains a fascinating creation, at least intermittently. Fredericks's tenure on the strip has now exceeded in length of years that of Phil Davis, while Lee Falk's octogenarian status doesn't seem to have slowed him down.

M.H.

MARK TRAIL
1946–present

What Jay "Ding" Darling had done for conservation through editorial cartoons, Ed Dodd and Jack Elrod have accomplished on the funnies page. Their strip, *Mark Trail,* one of the few nature stories in the history of American comics, exposed the devastation possible from oil slicks in the early 1970s, long before Exxon spoiled the Alaskan seascape. All along, Dodd and Elrod have pushed for the need to preserve the country's dwindling wetlands and wildernesses, remove ugly billboards from scenic areas, and protect wildlife from grubby poachers. The message of the strip has always been a simple one—preserve the woods, waters, and wildlife for future generations.

The characters and plots also have been out of the ordinary. The star of the strip is Mark Trail, a handsome, rather rugged individual who has never aged beyond 30. In his capacity as outdoor writer and photographer for *Woods and Wildlife Magazine,* as well as private citizen, he roams the wildernesses of the world, exposing corruption and catching poachers. On other occasions, he has been busy protecting his girlfriend, Cherry, from hoodlums. At the end of the work day (or week or months), Mark would return to his rustic house out West on the Lost Forest game preserve, owned by Cherry's father, Doc Davis. Constantly at his side while at home has been his dog, Andy.

Other characters were added by Elrod when he took over the strip upon Dodd's retirement in 1978. These are the boy Rusty, his dog Sassy, and Kelly, a good-looking woman used by the cartoonist as a foil to make Cherry jealous. Mark's lifestyle has been the envy of many men, according to Elrod in a *Cartoonist PROfiles* story, because "he makes his living at hunting, fishing, and camping and he is constantly being harassed by beautiful women."

Dodd and Elrod met while they were in the Boy Scouts, Dodd as a scout leader, Elrod as a young scout. Dodd was an advertising agent at the time. In 1946, Dodd sold *Mark Trail* to a syndicate, and four years later he hired Elrod as a lettering and background artist.

Mark Trail has not been memorable for zany personalities or snappy dialogue, yet it has been moderately successful, carried by more than two hundred newspapers at one time. Its appeals lay in a clean artistic style, smoothflowing and authentic plots, excellent panel composition, and stories involving animals. The stories seem continuous: Mark would still be in Cherry's welcoming embrace upon his return from an adventure, when, spotted in the background of the panel would be the person who would lead him to his next mission. Authenticity has been achieved by keeping characters, plots, and scenes realistic. Some stories actually have been based on true accounts Elrod found in newspapers, and regularly the Fish and Wildlife Service and Forest and Park services have been consulted to document aspects of outdoor life. Panels are often executed with the eye of a photographer much like Mark Trail himself, with animals eating, playing, or posing featured big in the foreground and word balloons seen coming from a cabin or from one of the characters in the very distant background.

Mark Trail is one of those "sleeper" strips whose characters and creators have not dominated the limelight, such as did Al Capp and *Li'l Abner,* but nevertheless have caught the fancy of many readers through the strip's simplicity and socially conscious messages.

J.A.L.

MARMADUKE
1954–present

The already long list of newspaper dogs increased by one in June 1954, with the irruption of Brad Anderson's Great Dane, whose name—Marmaduke—is as impressive as the gigantic meat-hound who bears that moniker. Based on the antics of Anderson's parents' dog, *Marmaduke* was first distributed as a daily panel by National Newpaper Syndicate, and was later picked up by United Feature, acquiring a Sunday version in the process.

While technically owned by the suburban couple of Phil and Dottie Winslow, Marmaduke acts more like the house master than the house pet. He naps on the living room sofa, runs on roller blades around the house, and helps himself to a midnight snack of peanut-butter sandwiches (his favorite food), pepperoni pizza, and apple-cherry pie from the refrigerator whenever he feels like it. Even his luxuriously appointed doghouse (complete with leatherlined walls, air conditioning, color TV set, water cooler, and other amenities) fails to hold him for long; he often elects residence in the main house while now and then subletting his own quarters to other animals.

Unlike many of his comic-strip kin, Marmaduke is not an anthropomorphized canine, but he exhibits many human traits nonetheless. He is lazy (rolling on the rug in laughter when asked to fetch Phil's slippers), avaricious (hoarding pilfered hamburger patties in his cooler), lecherous (picking up every female dog in sight), and mendacious (fingering one of the kids when asked who stole the tarts he'd just gulped down). He does have a few good points, however; he is always ready to lend a paw helping the kids play pranks on the neighbors or barking off pesky relatives who have come to visit the family. Even his most commendable efforts often end in disaster, and one can be sure that the errant baseball or stray newspaper that he catches between his teeth will arrive back to their owners mangled beyond recognition.

Anderson draws *Marmaduke* in a relaxed, unassuming style that sticks to essentials; and while the jokes may at times sound tired, even corny, their appeal to pet fanciers should not be underestimated: Anderson has over the years received thousands of fan letters from dog owners, and their support and loyalty have kept the feature going strong for more than four decades.

M.H.

MARVIN
1982–present

om Armstrong's *Marvin,* which made its debut in August 1982, is a very amusing strip revolving around the activities and thoughts of a one-year-old toddler named Marvin. A typical child, he spends most of his days dreaming of his future as a star football player or a fearless private eye, chewing on his ABC books, playing with his zillions of toys, and using his crayons on books and walls. Naturally, he enjoys running around the house in a baby walker and terrorizing every man, woman, and beast in sight with his "four on the floor," or spilling his food, rolling out the toilet paper, emptying cabinets out, and safely tucked in bed, declaring: "I love days when I can't seem to do anything right." But above all, he finds special pleasure in running his parents ragged, particularly in the middle of the night, for, despite child-expert books, "babies set the agenda."

The other members of his immediate family include Jeff, his dad, and Jenny, his mom. Both are doting parents whose world seems to have shrunk since Marvin's birth. Before, they used to ski, attend sports events, go on romantic getaways. Now, "parenthood is the art of converting disposable income into disposable diapers." Only Bitsy the mutt is unwilling to tolerate Marvin's shenanigans. That is because, first, Bitsy understands his thoughts and responds in kind; second, dignity and self-confidence serve as shields against the boy's demands and tantrums; and third, the dog is aware of its legal rights as an animal.

Megan, the daughter of Jenny's sister Janet, and therefore Marvin's cousin, lives with her mother at her aunt and uncle's house since her parents are separated. Being of Marvin's age and a feminist from way back, she is a perfect match for his untempered machismo as she points out the inequities of a male-dominated culture, sometimes with the help of a sexual discrimination attorney. Finally, Grampa passes on tidbits of grandfatherly wisdom and knowledge, along with a semblance of tradition, when he is not hidden by his ever-present camera.

Distributed to some two hundred newspapers by North America Syndicate and reprinted in paperback editions, Armstrong's strip portrays families coping with modern problems by using humor and common sense and presents lovable children with minds of their own, all in strong and uncloying fashion.

M.B.C.

MARY PERKINS
See ON STAGE

MARY WORTH
1934–present

merica's favorite grandmother, Mary Worth was born Apple Mary on October 29, 1934, in a daily strip distributed by Publishers Syndicate. Her character was derived from Damon Runyon's Apple Annie, later made famous in Frank Capra's comedy *Lady for a Day.* Like her inspiration, Apple Mary was a fruit peddler who tried to eke out a meager living in depression-era America. The strip was drawn and written by Martha Orr, the niece of *Chicago Tribune* editorial cartoonist Carey Orr, and it enjoyed enough success from the start to warrant the addition of a Sunday page in July 1935.

Orr drew *Apple Mary* in a competent, pleasant style midway between cartooning and illustration. As initially conceived, Mary was a dowdy old lady in ill-fitting clothes, whose main problems were paying the rent and keeping her relatives out of trouble. In-between-whiles she also found the time to do some matchmaking, notably in a 1936 episode when she succeeded in getting together two antagonistic radio personalities, Sally Blue, better known on the airwaves as "Sally the Sob," and Mike Wires, an investigative reporter. Later she concentrated on helping her grandson (not her nephew, as has been said) Dennie get back on his feet (he was lame), to such a degree that in 1938 the strip was rechristened *Apple Mary and Dennie.* Shortly afterward Orr resigned, ostensibly to get married, but actually because the feature's readership was declining and her editors thought that her naturalistic, lower-class continuities were no longer in sync with the times.

In 1939, therefore, another woman, Dale Conner Ulrey, who for some time had been assisting Orr on the strip, was substituted as the titular artist, while Allen Saunders, former drama critic and the scriptwriter of *Big Chief Wahoo,* was called in to revamp the story lines. Working in tandem under the joint name "Dale Allen," they gave the feature (now called *Mary Worth's Family*) a considerably modernized outlook. The process was speeded up in 1942, when Ken Ernst, a talented illustrator, took over the artwork from the departing Ulrey, and completed in 1944, when the strip acquired its definitive *Mary Worth* logo, putting an end to a decade of title-switching.

Mary Worth (Saunders and Ernst), © 1959 Publishers Syndicate

In 1963 Saunders described his new, improved heroine in these terms: "Mrs. Worth, a refined, well-educated widow with a generous endowment of plain common sense, has seen her late husband's once worthless securities regain sufficient value to afford her a modest income. This she augments occasionally by taking a job." While he also averred that he "tried avoiding making her a meddlesome busybody," she actually turned into just that, spending the majority of her time dispensing advice to the (fashionably) distressed and the obviously lovelorn. Now conservatively dressed and leading an existence of comfort and ease, the aging heroine moved amid a throng of mostly middle-class characters, many of them young and glamorous, to whom she would offer her own brand of conventional, grandmotherly wisdom.

In the wartime years Mary put her snooping skills to a higher purpose, contriving to expose the furtive Save America Society, actually a front for pro-Nazi activities, and later, as a volunteer hospital worker, helping wounded war veterans with their emotional problems. But the halcyon days of the strip were the 1950s, when Saunders's continuities, boosted in no small measure by Ernst's crisp drawings, rivaled in popularity any soap opera the small screen had to offer. Among other accomplishments, Mary has helped a television comic regain his self-esteem and his wit after his wife had left him; has gotten a returning Korean War vet to reconcile with his estranged sweetheart; has straightened out the messed-up life of an aging Hollywood actress; and has turned down a marriage offer from an elderly, blind business tycoon. In 1955 she was reunited with her grandson, Dennis Worth, now hale and hearty and a business executive, who would later marry "and start

a new generation in the life of the feature," as Saunders put it.

Saunders always kept close to the concerns of the times. Throughout the 1960s and into the 1970s the strip tackled such topical problems as alcoholism, drug addiction, student unrest, and the plight of unwed mothers. Saunders retired in 1979 and passed the torch to his son John, thus preserving *Mary Worth* as a family strip in more ways than one. In 1985 Ernst died, and his longtime assistant Bill Ziegler took responsibility for the artwork, helped by Bill Armstrong and Gene Colan. Due to illness, Ziegler was replaced in the early 1990s by comic-book veteran Joe Giella, who is currently drawing both daily and Sunday versions of the feature in a somewhat simplified, austere style.

Mary Worth is best noted as the mother (or grandmother) of all soap-opera strips, and its popularity in the 1950s was responsible for unleashing a torrent of "suds" onto the newspaper pages. It is also a feature worthy of study for its fascinating psychological and sociological subtext.

M.H.

MAUD THE MULE
See AND HER NAME WAS MAUD!

THE MEDIEVAL CASTLE
1944–1945

During World War II the government ordered newspaper syndicates to reduce the size of the comics so that more could fit on less newsprint and thus save paper for the war effort. However, if your syndicate controlled a whole page of space, you didn't want a competitor to get any of it. That was the dilemma King Features faced in early 1944.

Its solution was to ask *Prince Valiant*'s creator, Hal Foster, to produce a new strip to fill the one-third of a page that *Valiant* would lose when the comics had to shrink. *The Medieval Castle* was born. The three-panel companion feature to *Prince Valiant* began on April 30,1944, and ended November 24, 1945. The week after it ended newspapers were again publishing *Valiant* as a full page.

While Foster acknowledged in interviews why he created *The Medieval Castle*, he lavished as much attention on it as he did on *Valiant*. However, during this period of time the plot in *Valiant*, with Val kidnapping and then falling in love with Aleta, Queen of the Misty Isles, was so strong that *The Medieval Castle* was completely overshadowed. The stories of two young lads, Arn and Guy, in England during the time of the First Crusade included the stock feuding-families plot along with much detail on the life of a squire.

The Young Knight, A Tale of Medieval Times, a book published in 1945, reprinted part of *The Medieval Castle* but the time frame was switched to that of King Arthur. In 1957, Hasting House's *The Medieval Castle* retold the whole story of Arn and Guy with numerous panels from the strip.

B.C., Jr.

"OOO!" SQUEALS HIS PERMANENT AUDIENCE, "YOU MUST BE THE BEST ARCHER IN THE WHOLE WORLD!" ARN ACCEPTS THIS SWEET FLATTERY WITH BECOMING MODESTY.

COPR. 1945, KING FEATURES SYNDICATE, Inc WORLD RIGHTS RESERVED 8-26-45

The Medieval Castle (H. Foster), © 1945 King Features Syndicate

Merely Margy (J. Held, Jr.), © 1930 John Held, Jr.

MERELY MARGY
1927–1935[?]

All through the 1920s John Held's depictions of pleasure-mad flappers, gin-guzzling college boys, and top-hatted partygoers seemed to be everywhere, in the pages of *Vanity Fair* and *Collier's*, on the covers of the *New Yorker*, and in ads for cigarettes. Held was the illustrator of the Jazz Age in print just as F. Scott Fitzgerald was its chronicler in prose. His elegant drawings came to the newspaper pages in 1927 in the form of a daily panel titled *Oh! Margy!* and distributed by the Press Publishing Company. In 1929 the artist transferred his creation to King Features, which syndicated it as a daily strip and a Sunday page renamed *Merely Margy*.

Margy was a typical Held flapper, angular and flat-chested, with a penchant for expensive clothes, fast cars, and rich suitors. She liked to strike languorous poses, a long cigarette-holder between her fingers. Her main flirt was the equally empty-headed Arab, whom she would have loved more were he not chronically broke. Margy, who lived with her mother and father, was a lot tamer than the female characters on Held's covers for *Vanity Fair* or *College Humor*. Should any of her dates forget his manners, even innocently, there was always a parent close at hand to put him in his place. The Sunday *Margy* also sported a companion strip, *Joe Prep*, about a raccoon-coated prep-school twerp whose pranks always backfired on him. The antics of these holdovers from the Roaring Twenties were no longer in step with the gloomy reality of the depression. By 1935 Margy, Arab, Joe Prep, and their consorts were all gone.

Held drew *Margy* with his usual acuity of line, but his gags were flat (no pun intended) and his situations trite. The strip is mentioned here mainly because of its creator's fame.

M.H.

MICKEY FINN
1936–1976

Mickey Finn was created by sports cartoonist Lank Leonard for the McNaught Syndicate. It began as a daily strip on April 6, 1936, with a Sunday version starting on the following May 17. It was a good-natured, fairly humorous strip about patrolman Michael Aloysius Finn, a big-city-beat cop who was thoroughly Irish and totally honest. As such, it was one of the few comic strips ever to portray a city policeman in a manner that avoided either sentimentality or sensationalism.

When the strip first started, Mickey was living at home with his widowed mother and her brother, his Uncle Phil, and working at the Schultz Soap Company. Mickey lost his job through a comic accident, but on his way home he managed to rescue a runaway steer with his bare hands. On the strength of this feat, Mickey was offered a chance to take a police physical, which he passed. From that point (May 26, 1936), Mickey was a beat patrolman.

For more than three decades Leonard presented the upbeat but slow-paced story of Mickey, his sweet mother, and his witless Uncle Phil. Even though Phil was to become a sheriff and an alderman, he remained the butt of other people's jokes.

Mickey Finn was early teamed with another patrolman, named Tom Collins, and somehow or other their names became associated with two totally different drinks. "To slip someone a mickey," a phrase now somewhat dated, means to slip knockout drops into someone's drink. By contrast, a Tom Collins is a rather tame blend of gin, lemon or lime juice, carbonated water, and sugar.

Mickey was also frequently involved with the off-the-wall activities of a reporter named Gabby, and he conducted a rollercoaster romance with a girl named Kitty Kelly. Other regulars were Clancy, the bartender; Sergeant Halligan, Mickey's immediate superior; Mr. Houlihan, Uncle Phil's nemesis; Flossie Finn, Mickey's niece; and Red Fedder, a baseball player. *Mickey Finn* was never a violent strip. It usually included nothing worse than a black eye after one of Uncle Phil's brawls or the peaceful arrest of a petty crook. It was the winsome side of the Irish character that was stressed, not the hot-tempered.

Sports were at the center of Lank Leonard's life. He had done the sports-page cartoon for more than a decade in the *New York Sun* before launching *Mickey Finn*, and he occasionally introduced actual sports personalities into the strip, particularly the Sunday page. Lou Gehrig, Joe Louis, Jack Dempsey, and others appeared over the years. This was also a feature of Ham Fisher's *Joe Palooka* strip (although the noted figures were more likely to be politicians and show people), and for that reason, plus the fact that the two strips appeared together in many papers, readers tended to associate the two in their minds. The fact that both Mickey Finn and Joe Palooka had more brawn than brain, not to mention comic sidekicks, made this association inevitable.

The artwork in the *Mickey Finn* comic strip was fairly simple and straightforward, in keeping with its superficial characters and thin plots. In its best years, it appeared in nearly three hundred papers. Morris Weiss worked as

Mickey Finn (L. Leonard), © 1947 McNaught Syndicate

Leonard's assistant and sometimes-ghost during the feature's first year, after which Mart Bailey took over. Bailey was a comic-book veteran who had drawn the Finn characters on the covers of several comic-book reprints of the strip.

When Lank Leonard retired in 1968, Weiss succeeded him, but the strip was never quite the same. Leonard died in 1970, but Weiss kept the strip going for a few more years. Finally, on December 21, 1975, the Sunday *Mickey Finn* ended; the daily ended on July 31, 1976, three months after its fortieth birthday.

T.W.

MICKEY MOUSE
1930–present

According to legend, Walt Disney conceived his most celebrated character in the course of a 1927 train ride back to Hollywood from New York, where he had just lost the rights to his *Oswald the Rabbit* series to Charles Mintz. He wanted to name the little rodent creature he had in mind Mortimer but was talked out of it either by his wife or by one of his distributors (according to which source one is willing to listen to). Thus was Mickey Mouse born.

Once the concept had crystalized, Disney sketched out the broad outlines of "the Mouse." "He had to be simple," he later reminisced, adding, "His head was a circle with an oblong circle for a snout. The ears were also circles so they could be drawn the same, no matter how he turned his head. His body was like a pear and he had a long tail. His legs were pipestems and we stuck them in big shoes to give him the look of a kid wearing his father's shoes."

Retaining overall direction, Disney turned over the actual drawing to his talented assistant, Ub Iwerks. On September 19, 1928, the first Mickey Mouse animated short, *Steamboat Willie,* the first cartoon to use sound and music, opened at the Colony Theater in New York, and proved an instant hit. Other shorts starring the Mouse followed, along with a torrent of merchandising and licensing, including a *Mickey Mouse* daily newspaper strip that premiered on January 13, 1930, distributed by King Features Syndicate (with Disney retaining copyright).

Mickey Mouse was drawn in the early months by Ub Iwerks, assisted by Win Smith, and it was scripted by Disney himself. After a few months the feature found its ideal *auteur* in a former gag cartoonist named Floyd Gottfredson, who variously penciled, inked, and wrote the strip (with the assistance of a number of Disney staffers, who have included over the years Al Taliaferro, Ted Osborne, Merrill de Maris, Bill Walsh, Dick Shaw, and Roy Williams) from May 1930 until his retirement in 1975. When King Features felt that a Sunday page was in order, the studio again turned to Gottfredson (after a sample page done by Earl Duvall), and his version began appearing in January 1932, lasting well into 1938, when Manuel Gonzales took over.

The 1930s were Mickey's golden years, the time when Gottfredson was in closest control of his material. He made full use of the cartoon cast, the irascible Horace Horsecollar, the hapless Clarabelle Cow, Uncle Mortimer, Mickey's dog Pluto, and his comic sidekick Goofy. Present also from the first was Mickey's inamorata, the incomparable Minnie, for whose love Mickey would summon incredible amounts of energy, stamina, and sheer resilience.

Adventure was the keynote in the daily strips. There Mickey could fully reveal the extent of his prowess, whether fighting a ruthless gang of cattle rustlers out West, outwitting a phantom assassin, or vying for Minnie's favors against an oily city slicker. Mickey's adventurings took him to the remotest corners of the earth, the lowest depths of the ocean, and the furthest reaches of space. His two most implacable enemies, the brutish Peg Leg Pete and the cunning Sylvester Shyster, lay trap upon fiendish trap for him, but Mickey always emerged triumphant from these encounters, in succession beating out the unholy duo for the ownership of Uncle Mortimer's gold mine, leaving them stranded on a cannibal island, thwarting them in their attempts to steal the Sacred Jewel of Zwoosh, and even foiling their mad plot to take over the world with their pirate dirigible. In addition to fending off Pete and Sylvester, Mickey did find time at odd moments for running a newspaper, entering a prize-fighting contest, making a movie, hunting for whales, even playing monarch to the cuckoo kingdom of Medioka.

The English writer E. M. Forster summed it all up quite nicely: "Mickey's great moments are moments of heroism, and when he carries Minnie out of the harem as a potplant or rescues her as she falls in foam, herself its fairest flower, he reaches heights impossible for the entrepreneur."

The Sunday pages were more anecdotal and often given over to sundry gags involving Mickey with his favorite foil, the slow-witted Goofy, or having him play host to his two mischief-making nephews, when he was not busy courting Minnie with clumsy attentions. There too Gottfredson managed to spin a few rip-roaring adventure yarns, such as Mickey and Goofy being mistaken for two ruthless killers while prospecting for gold, or Mickey meeting up with

Robin Hood and later having to rescue Princess Minerva. Color greatly enhanced Gottfredson's exquisite artwork in these stories, and their irrepressible high spirits and inexhaustible gag building rank them high as classics of their kind.

In the 1940s adventure ceased to animate the Sunday pages, which were given over entirely to self-contained gags, while action continued unabated in the dailies. There were some breathless stories taking place in this period, the most notable of which occurred in 1940–41, when Mickey found himself back in the Stone Age. There were also episodes involving, respectively, Aladdin's lamp, a homicidal hypnotist, and a gang of bumbling hotel burglars. Mickey's perennial nemesis, Peg Leg Pete (now minus his wooden leg and renamed Black Pete), also returned to plague the feisty little hero in a number of entertaining adventures. During the war Mickey and his companions did their obligatory bit for the Allied cause, helping combat enemy spies and saboteurs. Science fiction became the hallmark of the postwar *Mickey Mouse* daily, with Mickey and Goofy venturing to alien planets and traveling back in time.

The 1950s signaled the end of *Mickey Mouse* as an adventure. From then on, the feature followed a strictly gag format, with the familiar characters experiencing mild tribulations in a suburban setting. In the meantime Gottfredson had stepped down as art director and had been succeeded by Frank Reilly. Until his retirement in 1975 he devoted himself to drawing the dailies exclusively, while the writing chores devolved mainly to Bill Walsh. In addition to the regular *Mickey Mouse* daily strip there also was, from September 1958 to March 1962, a daily feature called *Mickey Mouse and His Friends* that was drawn in pantomime by Julius Svendsen.

Following Gottfredson's departure, the dailies were taken over by Roman Arámbula, with scripts provided by Del Connell. Gonzales meanwhile had retained the Sundays, which he continued to draw until 1981. After a series of short stints put in by Tony Strobl, Daan Jippes, and Bill Wright, Arámbula toward the end of 1983 became the titular artist on both dailies and Sundays, a position he retained until 1989. Rick Hoover then stepped in to take charge of the artwork until 1993, at which time *Mickey Mouse* went into reprints.

M.H.

Mickey Mouse, © 1932 Walt Disney Company

MIDGET MOVIES
See MINUTE MOVIES

MIKE AND IKE, THEY LOOK ALIKE
1917–1928

Rube Goldberg's celebrated duo of twins had their forerunners in a weekly comic page the cartoonist syndicated through the World Color Company of Saint Louis. They were then called Tom and Jerry, but they already had their definitive personas: two shrimp-sized, stubble-bearded, and bald-pated bums who had zany encounters with a netherworld of hustlers, contortionists, and geeks, and who performed sleight-of-hand tricks with their derby hats. Called *The Look-Alike Boys,* the feature first appeared in September 1907 and lasted only some six months.

The loony pair were to enjoy a much longer existence a decade later, when Goldberg decided to resurrect the twins in 1917 inside the miscellany strip he was then turning out for the *New York Mail.* Giving them a separate panel of their own, and renaming them Mike and Ike, he had them perform a series of vaudeville turns, generally based on knockabout questions and word games. Some examples will suffice: "What two things cause most of the unhappiness in married life?" one of the identical twins would ask, and the other would reply, "The husband and the wife"; or, "Name a single word with double meaning," the response being "Trousers."

Most often seen in the form of a single-cartoon panel, *Mike and Ike, They Look Alike* was sometimes laid out in comic-strip sequence by the simple expedient of dividing the panel's space into a four tiny boxes. When that was the case, the resulting ministrips frequently sprouted self-explanatory subtitles, such as "Mike and Ike Classical Dancers" or "Mike and Ike Tame a Tiger." Alternating with such other recurring features as *I'm the Guy* and *Foolish Questions, Mike and Ike* appeared sporadically until 1928, when Goldberg abandoned his strip of miscellany to initiate *Bobo Baxter.*

Mike and Ike had become too popular with the general public by that time for Goldberg to drop them altogether. In August 1927 already he had introduced them into the continuity of *Boob McNutt,* where they often saved the hapless Boob's bacon. They remained in the strip until its discontinuance in September 1934, after which the twins were seen no more. They lived on, however, in their repeated refrain, "I'm Mike," "I'm Ike," which became a popular catchphrase for a time.

M.H.

MIKE HAMMER
1953–1954

It is a little-known fact that Mickey Spillane, before he started on his wildly successful series of Mike Hammer novels, was a comic-book writer, working notably on such titles as *Captain America, Captain Marvel,* and *Target.* So when Jerry Iger's tiny Phoenix Features Syndicate approached him with an offer to transplant his tough-guy private detective to the comics pages, he readily accepted; to him it was less a business proposition than a homecoming. Accordingly, *Mike Hammer* started appearing daily on April 20, 1953, and weekly the following Sunday.

In addition to Mike, who narrated the action in the first person, the dailies introduced Velda, the detective's faithful secretary and paramour, and Mike's police pal, homicide captain Pat Chambers. Ed Robbins drew the strip in a scratchy, clumsy style that blurred much detail. The continuities were written by Joe Gill at first, and later taken over by Robbins.

The Sunday came out with separate continuities under the high-sounding title *From the Files of...Mike Hammer,* and ran a chapter heading alongside the main title to showcase each story. ("Comes Murder!", "The Sudden Trap," and "Dark City" were the three episodes that were to make up the entire run of the Sundays.) The story lines were allegedly penned by Spillane himself, and the writing did indeed sound like it was his. ("Trouble comes anytime and when it starts and when it ends there's always that nasty taste left in your mouth.") Perhaps due to that fact, Robbins's work on the Sunday page was a little more artful than usual.

Daily or Sundays, the continuity did bear all the hallmarks of a Mike Hammer novel: fast-paced action, tough-talking and tough-acting characters, sultry dames, and of course sadism. There was a mounting outcry in the right-thinking press, and when a particular Sunday panel appeared showing a half-naked woman tied to a bed and about to be tortured by a grinning thug, that proved too much for many newspapers, including the *New York Post,* which dropped the feature. Iger asked Spillane to tone down the stories but met with a firm refusal. Reluctantly, he then decided to bring down the curtain on Mike Hammer, whose comic-strip career came to an end in March 1954.

M.H.

MING FOO
1935–1943

*T*he genesis of *Ming Foo* is complicated and took place over a full decade. In the mid-1920s Brandon Walsh was writing (uncredited) the continuities for the Sunday version of *The Gumps,* wherein he sent young Chester Gump adventuring around the globe in the company of an old sea captain and a sententious Chinese. Having switched to King Features and *Little Annie Rooney* at the end of the decade, he introduced in 1933 the character of Joey Robbins, an enterprising lad who became Annie's closest friend. Joey was later joined by an old salt named Tom Trout and an aphoristic Chinese known as Ming Foo, thereby reconstituting a trio similar to the one Walsh had created in *The Gumps.* Soon the *Annie Rooney* Sunday was turned over to the maritime adventures of Joey and his companions, pushing Annie out of her own strip for long stretches at a time. Finally, on March 17, 1935, the seafaring adventurers were given their own berth in the form of a Sunday page titled *Ming Foo* and distributed by King Features Syndicate.

Drawn by Nicholas Afonsky on Walsh's scripts, *Ming Foo* was a handsome-looking feature, painstakingly illustrated with a slightly cartoony tinge that admirably suited the strip's slightly cartoony characters. Joey was the prototypical American youth, perpetually curious and active, Tom Trout the quintessential sea-dog, resourceful and hard-bitten. Then there was Ming Foo, the titular hero of the piece and the very image of a stereotypical Chinese: pigtailed, wearing a traditional Chinese robe, his head always crowned with a mandarin hat, he was much given to the recitation of sonorous maxims and epigrams. In the course of one Sunday page alone he spouted no fewer than four aphorisms: "Who can deny: The careless shepherd is the friend of the wolf?", "It has been truly said: He who could see two days ahead would rule the world!", "Who can deny: There is a time to fish, and a time to dry nets?", and "It is written: Even the gods will not help a man who loses opportunity!" It is a wonder his companions didn't strangle the moralizing Asian, no matter how sagacious his advice.

Aboard their yacht, the *Sea Swallow,* the three went roaming the seven seas, and met with no paucity of action along the way. Their most implacable enemy was Chang Ho, a bloodthirsty pirate chieftain plying his trade along the China coast; they also had to confront the Steel Brethren, a secret organization of men in armor bent on taking power in their corner of the world, not to mention a tribe of Melanesian headhunters and a cohort of South American revolutionaries. They were shipwrecked countless times, but always managed to salvage their vessel; in compensation they also laid hands on vast troves of rubies, emeralds, pearls, and gold, with which to finance their further explorations.

The momentous odyssey of the *Sea Swallow* came to an unfortunate end in 1943. After Afonsky had become too ill to draw Ming Foo, the syndicate decided to discontinue the feature. The last page appeared on March 28, leaving behind the memory of an offbeat and enjoyable tale of high adventure.

M.H.

MINUTE MOVIES
1917–1936

*T*o say that the comics and the movies share a great number of conventions, themes, and characteristics has by now become a truism: they were born around the same time, in the last decade of the nineteenth century, from the same motivations—a mix of artistic striving and crass commercialism—and evolved along more or less parallel tracks. From the beginning, there had been a continuous crosspollination between the two forms, and the fact was nowhere better epitomized than in a series of daily strips that Ed Wheelan started turning out for the Hearst papers as early as 1917.

At first they appeared without a running title at the top of the sports section, and they spoofed all kinds of moviemaking, from feature films to short subjects to travelogues. Soon Wheelan filled his strip—which had taken on the permanent title *Midget Movies* in 1918—with paro-

Minute Movies (E. Wheelan), © 1933 George Matthew Adams Service

dies of movie columns, movie magazines, and even movie-studio releases. He even organized his own awards, giving them out to various mock movie people, years before the Oscar ceremonies were established. At the beginning of the 1920s the strip had reached a high level of popularity, at which time Wheelan decided to quit the Hearst organization after a dispute with the autocratic head of the newspaper chain.

Moving over to the George Matthew Adams Service in 1921, he simply continued his creation under the new title *Minute Movies,* under which it is best known. True to its name, the feature now ran daily in a two-tier row of minute panels, in which the artist was able to cram an enormous deal of graphic detail and an extraordinary amount of narrative and dialogue. Styling himself the head of this improvised film studio, appropriately named Ed Wheelan Ink, he endeavored to become the greatest purveyor of picture-stories ever to come out of that city of glitz and glamour, which he called Follywood, USA.

As with any other studio head, Wheelan's first task was to assemble a stable of reliable contract players. First came Dick Dare, a young actor of good looks and impressive chin who specialized in heroic roles and soon became the studio's male star. Hazel Dearie was his female counterpart: she usually played the ingenue, a role for which her blonde, innocent good looks made her well suited, in a variety of productions, from *Hamlet* (she played Ophelia, of course) to blood-curdling melodramas. Blanche Rouge was the vamp, a position she filled with gusto; and there were such other wonderfully named characters as the villainous Ralph McSneer, the bumbling Fuller Phun, the wisecracking Lotta Talent, and the foppish Paul Vogue. They were all briskly put through their paces by Art Hokum, the busiest director on the lot.

Ed Wheelan Ink produced all genres of pictures, but action films were its specialty. There were melodramas like "Serpents of the City" and "Fingers of Fear," westerns such as "The Mysterious Bandit," sea epics called "Blood and Booty" or "Piracy," not to forget Saturday-matinee serials, of which "The Perils of Hazel" was but one. In these and other productions Wheelan used all types of cinematic techniques, the close-up, the diaphragm shot, the fade-out, and more, which would later allow him to claim the title of pioneer of the continuity strip, a dubious distinction at best since there were other cartoonists who had used at least some of these devices before he did. He did, however,

popularize and generalize these techniques, a fact that paradoxically proved his undoing.

In the late 1920s and early 1930s new story strips came to the fore that were better drawn and more grippingly told than *Minute Movies,* Hal Foster's *Tarzan* and Roy Crane's *Captain Easy,* to name just two. Wheelan, beaten at his own game, then took to adapting literary classics a full decade before Classics Illustrated comic books were to do the same. *Don Quixote, Ivanhoe, Treasure Island, The Count of Monte Cristo,* even Blasco Ibañez's *Blood and Sand* were thus translated into comic-strip continuities: these were often ghosted by Nicholas Afonsky and later by Jess Fremon. Although these adaptations were praised by educators, they steadily lost favor with the general public, until *Minute Movies* finally faded out of the newspaper pages sometime in 1936. (It did resurface at the end of the decade in *Flash Comics,* a comic book in which it ran intermittently for a couple of years.) As a final note we should mention that at the height of its popularity *Minute Movies* gave rise to a number of imitations, the best known of which is *Fillum Fables* that a young Chester Gould did between 1924 and 1929, prior to creating *Dick Tracy.*

M.H.

MISS FURY
1941–1952

*M*iss Fury (originally titled *Black Fury*) was created by Tarpe Mills as a Sunday feature distributed by the Bell Syndicate. The first installment appeared on April 6, 1941.

Born June Mills, the artist had been one of the few women working on horror comic books, with such hair-

Miss Fury (T. Mills), © 1943 Bell Syndicate

raising titles to her credit as *The Purple Zombie, Daredevil Barry Finn,* and *Devil's Dust.* Mills brought two clichés from the comic books to her Sunday page: the costumed justice-fighter and the protagonist's dual identity. A luscious socialite named Marla Drake by day, the heroine would don a tight-fitting black leopard outfit to go on her errands at night under the guise of the Black Fury. Her dates included racketeers, blackmailers, and gangsters' molls, to whom she would indistinctly administer her own brand of justice. Unlike many other heroines of the funny pages, the Black Fury did not shrink from violent physical action, but displayed her ferocious powers with fist, tooth, and claw.

After America had entered World War II, she turned her attentions (as Miss Fury) to fifth columnists, Axis agents, and Nazi infiltrators. The action, which had started hard-boiled, heated up to hellish temperatures in scenes involving not only grue and gore but torture, whipping, branding, and bondage as well. One of the standouts of this period was an episode taking place in Brazil, where the monocled, bald-headed, and one-armed German general Bruno Beitz tried to take over the country in cahoots with a local politician named Pepe Manero. Miss Fury put an end to his ambitions with the help of Era, a fierce woman guerrilla-fighter. Other adventures took place in Manhattan, in Panama, and in the South Seas, with Miss Fury meeting such colorful characters as the fanatical Baroness Erica von Kampf, a Nazi sexpot who under her platinum-blonde hairdo sported a swastika branded on her forehead; an American-Indian graduate of Harvard named Albino Joe; and the mysterious U.S. intelligence agent Dan Carey.

Miss Fury reached the peak of its popularity during the war years, with laudatory articles appearing in such publications as *Time* and the *Miami Daily News.* After the war Mills, on instructions from the syndicate, started toning down the more sadistic elements in the strip. The continuities also became tamer, with Miss Fury now fighting the likes of voodoo witch doctors and crazed inventors. The feature went into a steady decline and ultimately vanished from the comic pages in the summer of 1952.

M.H.

MISS PEACH
1957–present

On February 4, 1957, Mell Lazarus opened the doors of the Kelly School, a fictional school named after Walt Kelly, the creator of *Pogo,* in a comic strip entitled *Miss Peach.* First published in the *New York Herald-Tribune,* it is distributed through Creators Syndicate and has also been reprinted in several paperback collections.

At the head of this elementary school is Mr. Grimmis, the principal, fiftyish, grumpy, and increasingly disgusted with the exploits of his disobedient charges. He is joined in his frustration by Miss Crystal, an old-maid schoolmarm. On the other hand, Miss Peach is young, pretty, and pleasant; she is the only one to feel affection for her ill-mannered pupils, who, in turn, like her a lot. However, she is not the focus of the strip bearing her name, although she

does bring some semblance of order to the permissive and chaotic world of the Kelly School. That role is taken with panache and dazzle by the gang of little rascals of both sexes. Disguised as schoolchildren, these form an efficient fifth column, undermining the authority of the principal, the faculty, the parents, and the entire adult world.

The last word always belongs to the children, whose superiority over their elders is evident in all areas psychological, pedagogical, and especially sophistic. First, there is Freddy, who from the first day of school took his seat in the last row to hide the brilliant qualities that would make him an A+ student (a horrible fate!). Thanks to his territorial immunity and his insolence—which he carefully cultivates along with a solid cynicism—he is in a good position to attack middle-class virtues such as friendship, discipline, and respect for others.

If Freddy is the small group's inspirer, Marcia is its leader, for she knows her rights both as pupil and female and uses them impudently. A pretentious quibbler and schemer, she monopolizes the presidency of every club and even creates new ones just to satisfy her hunger for power. A cheat and a nasty girl with a big mouth, she is disliked by all her classmates; she nevertheless can get them to admit—usually through physical or verbal abuse—that she is the prettiest, most charming and generous person at Kelly.

Ira, who has been persuaded by Marcia's "striking" arguments to accept his role as her fiancé, is her complete antithesis: he is afraid of everything and everyone, particularly of his bullying girlfriend. Young Arthur is the perfect example of the gullible kid, unassuming and gentle, full of quiet dignity. Of a melancholy bent, he continually drags around his sorrow over the flight of Tweetie, his pet parrot and a well of learning, who got tired of his master's limited intellect. While waiting for his bird to return, Arthur spends his free time in the school hothouse cultivating various species of weeds with all the passionate care of an orchid grower.

Lester is the sickly child of the class. In fact, the older he gets the more he shrinks; the more he eats the more he loses weight. Weak and puny, he is saved from total nothingness by his clever comebacks. Yet he has the secret hope of having his revenge and becoming a great athlete—but only after he beats every classmate, of course. Where Marcia uses force, Francine succeeds through feminine wiles in leading the boys by the nose. She wears makeup and lipstick and generally does her best to act the part of the vamp. Attributes such as gossipy, jealous, and chatterbox round out her description. The other children behave in similar fashion. Lazy, lying, inconsiderate, stubborn, stupid, and narrow-minded, they will become perfect adults when their turn comes.

Not surprisingly, very little teaching takes place in this school. Miss Peach or Miss Crystal try from time to time, but without conviction, to explain insect behavior or talk about George Washington, only to be interrupted by the ludicrous observations of one student, the silly questions of another, or the humorous comments of a third. At the Kelly School, the pupils either know a lot more than their teachers or are completely incapable of learning anything.

Since they are already set in their knowledge, their igno-

Miss Peach (M. Lazarus), © 1958 New York Herald-Tribune–Publishers-Hall Syndicate

rance, and their prejudices, the children spend most of their time playing—playing at being adults and copying their activities. Thus, they imitate museum guards, journalists, police officers, judges; sometimes they are perverse enough to become the principal and teachers of the Kelly School. Their greatest pleasure, however, is to create, like their elders, endless and pointless committees and clubs, whose bylaws are vague but strict. If the band is always ready to assume adult privileges, it is less inclined to take on responsibilities. To her classmates who would like to be already grown up, Marcia shows the drawbacks of adulthood by portraying in turn a local officer, an IRS auditor, a boss, etc., until they all run away in terror before the vision of this nightmarish world.

Miss Peach is drawn in the simple style typical of modern humor strips. The protagonists are generally seen full-length and in profile. The children carry large heads on tiny bodies, and the characters all show the peculiarity of having their eyes set on the same side of their faces. For *Miss Peach* and *Momma,* Lazarus was named Best Humor Strip Cartoonist by the National Cartoonists Society (1973 and 1979) and received its Reuben Award for Best Cartoonist in All Categories in 1982.

P.H.

MITZI McCOY
See KEVIN THE BOLD

MODESTY BLAISE
1963–present

Modesty Blaise first appeared in the British *Evening Standard* in May 1963, just in time for the fad for sophisticated secret-agent spy thrillers that was started by the first James Bond film that year. Modesty has the allure of a redeemed fallen angel, a femme fatale who uses her deadly talents against evil.

Modesty is a retired crime lord of about 26, though her real age is unknown. She lost her parents in World War II and suffered as an orphan through the worst refugee camps from Greece to Persia. An old professor in the camps educated her and named her Modesty; she chose her surname from the legends of King Arthur. Around age

16 she became a croupier for a small-time Tangier gang. Her skills soon made her its leader, and she built it into a major international organization. "The Network dealt in many crimes, but never drugs or vice. Modesty Blaise loathed human degradation and those who dealt in it. For this she would kill..." While she had many lieutenants, it was Willie Garvin, a Cockney whose gutter accent belied his own intelligence and extensive education, who became her inseparable partner, as their relationship grew into a platonic friendship of mutual trust as equals. By the time Modesty was 25, the Network had become so successful that she and Willie were able to retire in England with large personal fortunes. But both soon realized that they were bored. They had become addicted to the excitement of their old lives, if not its cruelty. At this point Sir Gerald Tarrent of the Foreign Office's Intelligence Division entered their lives. He had been keeping a discreet eye on such notorious characters, and realized that their reformation coupled with their expertise in extralegal affairs could be invaluable if applied in a socially useful direction.

From 1963 through the present, Modesty and Willie have experienced a series of more than eighty adventures, usually running daily for up to three months, in which they alone or with two or three allies act as a commando team to overthrow some utterly ruthless and sadistic criminal genius or foreign espionage organization, usually operating from an impregnable fortress. The strip is known for its clever dialogue, and the plausibility of its well-planned crime and spy-type action, presenting deadly battles of both cunning and martial arts.

Modesty and Willie are up-to-date in current technology in weaponry, electronic spying aids, and so forth, but not beyond the limits of plausibility to exaggerated superscientific devices. The strip does acknowledge some metaphysics and psychic talents, notably Willie's "prickling of his ears" when some unexpected disaster is about to befall, cueing them to prepare for action. Creator Peter O'Donnell has elaborated upon this to rationalize why his protagonists have far more adventures than normal people (a common condition of comic-strip adventure heroes, which is not usually deliberately addressed). Some people have good or bad luck; Modesty and Willie are "magnets for trouble."

O'Donnell has been writing British strips since the early 1950s. In 1956 his humor strip *Romeo Brown,* for the *Daily Mirror,* was passed to a new artist, Jim Holdaway. Their collaboration worked so well that *Modesty Blaise* was developed as a team effort. Holdaway's sophisticated "good girl" art set its permanent look; when he unexpectedly died in 1970, he was replaced by Spanish artist Enrique Romero, who has done an excellent job of continuing Holdaway's style.

Modesty Blaise is carried in newspapers around the world, though it has been in only a few in America, such as the *New York Post* during the 1960s and 1970s. Fortunately, O'Donnell has been extremely accommodating in making the strip available through high-quality reprint collections available in America, often with informative personal notes, and in adventure-strip reprint magazines. In 1994 O'Donnell wrote an original story for DC Comics as a 144-page graphic novel, illustrated by Dick Giordano. O'Donnell also wrote twelve *Modesty Blaise* mystery books, eleven novels, and a short-story collection between 1965 and 1985. There was a major motion picture in 1966 and a TV movie (an unsold TV series pilot) in 1982, about which O'Donnell has publicly expressed his dissatisfaction.

F.P.

depicts his aunt, my sister Helen, who, as everyone knows, is the person 'Momma' is modeled after." Mrs. Lazarus's disclaimer to the contrary, there is a strong autobiographical element in *Momma,* which serves to further enhance the flavor of the strip.

Lazarus's drawing style is suited to the unconventionality of his texts. His characters are drawn in a broadly caricatural manner, with the eyes pictured on the same side of the head (not unlike Picasso and the Cubist painters). His somewhat awry method of drawing reflects his somewhat wry vision of the world—a bit offside but nonetheless recognizable. Asked to comment on his working philosophy, the artist once wrote: "I like to compare doing each daily strip to producing a play.... First I write the gag, or script, in finished form, even as a play would be written before the production process could begin. And it is, I hope, a playlet which will note something about the human condition of which the audience may have been aware but had never themselves articulated."

A favorite with readers for over twenty years, *Momma* has often been reprinted in paperback form.

M.H.

MOMMA
1970–present

Mell Lazarus, the creator of *Miss Peach,* came up with another winner, *Momma,* which he started on October 26, 1970, for Field Newspaper Syndicate. Mrs. Hobbs ("Momma") is the embodiment of the mother-hen syndrome. When she is not bragging about her children's achievements (real or fancied) to friends and neighbors, she is berating these selfsame children for their shortcomings (usually their lack of concern for her feelings). Her eye is especially stern on her two unmarried offspring, the ne'er-do-well Francis and the flighty Marylou, whom she ordinarily pelts with a barrage of motherly advice and unsolicited prescriptions (not to mention home cooking). Her married son, Thomas, also comes in for his share of barbs, but Momma's most pointed remarks are, of course, directed at her daughter-in-law, Tina.

In her tongue-in-cheek foreword to *The Momma Treasury* (1978), the author's mother, Frances Lazarus, wrote: "I approve of the way [Mell] sees fit to make a living.... What I don't approve of about Melvin's work is the way he

THE MONK FAMILY
1904–1913

One of the pioneers of the comics, Gus Mager had been drawing funny animals since the beginning of the century. His depictions for the Hearst papers in 1903 and 1904 of jungle animals cavorting under the trees, holding town meetings, and exchanging society gossip had been particularly popular under the general title of *Jungle Land.* From these Sunday episodes there evolved a series of more or less daily strips involving apes or "monks" (short for monkeys) in human dress engaged in human pursuits (fishing, carousing, playing golf, etc.). The first such strip, titled *Knocko the Monk,* appeared in the *New York Journal* in April 1904. Due to popular demand, Mager introduced more "monk" strips in alternation, each with its own descriptive title (*Rhymo the Monk, Groucho the Monk, Nervo the Monk,* and so forth); as the years went by his "monks" became more and more anthropomorphized, and by 1910 they were hardly recognizable from caricatural humans. These series of interconnected strips have been sometimes called

Momma (M. Lazarus), © 1979 Field Enterprises

"Mager's Monks," although Mager himself occasionally referred to them as "the Monk Family," which is the name adopted here. Among this simian society the author introduced on December 9, 1910, a newcomer who proceeded to take over the entire feature: this was Sherlocko, who played a private detective in the grand tradition, complete with Holmesian violin, pipe, and deerstalker cap, not to mention a gullible and admiring sidekick transparently called Watso.

There was no continuity from strip to strip, as Sherlocko solved a different minimystery in each installment. The other "monks" turned up as the detective's clients, and most often than not as the perpetrators. Each episode was highlighted with its own colorful subtitle, often in the Conan Doyle manner, such as "The Curious Case of the Hat That Didn't Fit," "The Mysterious Incident of the Faithful Watchdog," or "The Adventure of the Disappearing Passenger." In a series of six panels disposed in three vertical rows, Sherlocko solved these and other baffling mysteries in a logical chain of deductions, commented upon in awestruck tones every step of the way by his dumbfounded assistant. "Marvelous," "wonderful," "most extraordinary," and "too deep for me" were some of Watso's exclamations as the investigation unfolded.

In February 1912, Mager adopted for his strip the cross-page, horizontal format that had become the standard for daily newspaper strips. The reshaped strips did not allow for as much narrative development, and this fact, coupled with Mager's growing dissatisfaction with his employer, led to his abandoning *Sherlocko* and the Hearst organization for Pulitzer's *New York World* in February 1913. This was not the end of the character, however; Mager briefly revived him in a *Sherlocko* strip that he syndicated himself between October 1924 and March 1925.

M.H.

The Monk Family (Mager's Monks/Sherlocko the Monk; G. Mager), 1910

MOON MULLINS
1923–1993

In 1922, Frank Willard, a former assistant to Billy DeBeck and the veteran cartoonist of a number of short-lived newspaper strips, including *Tom, Dick, and Harry, Mrs. Pippin's Husband,* and *The Outta Luck Club,* heard that the Chicago Tribune–New York News Syndicate was looking for new properties. Having successfully offered his services, he was told by Captain Joseph Patterson, head of the syndicate, that he "should do a strip about a roughneck" named Moonshine (for the homemade bootleg liquor, a sure sign of low life). Subsequently, *Moon Mullins* made its appearance as a daily strip on June 19, 1923, followed by a Sunday page on September 9 the same year.

The strip's initial setting was a boxers' training camp (Moon tried to fob off his sidekick Mushmouth as a sparring partner for Jack Dempsey), and then shifted to the circus, before settling in 1924 into its definitive locale, the suburban boarding house run by the scraggly spinsterish Emmy Schmaltz, whose newest tenant Moon became. The seedy Schmaltz establishment was inhabited by enough of life's failures to stock several road companies of *Death of a Salesman,* a grim, if hilarious, cross-section of losers as long on color as they were short on funds and morals. They included Moon himself, whose reputation as a shady, fast-talking hustler had been established early on; his kid brother, Kayo, a miniature version of Moon complete with derby hat and foul mouth, who slept in a desk drawer; run-down Lord Plushbottom ("Plushie"), whom Emmy finally

Moon Mullins (F. Willard), © 1931 Chicago Tribune

dragged to the altar in 1934; and Mamie, the elephantine cook and washerwoman, wife to Moon's ne'er-do-well Uncle Willie. Emmy vainly tried to put on airs, but she was always put down by one or another of her boarders, whose affronts she invariably greeted with the seldom-carried-out threat "I'll smack your sassy face!"

Because it dealt with low-life characters, the strip more than any other could indulge in sexual overtones. Riches and sex were the twin—and never fulfilled—ideals of the small band of outsiders and misfits. Plushbottom, when not looking down his nose at the other boarders, was on the prowl for every shapely young woman in sight, in the great comic-strip tradition of henpecked husbands. Amid the less than shining lights in the strip, Little Egypt, Emmy's carnival dancer of a niece, twinkled bright, a creature of beauty and glamour; indeed, every male in the boarding house lusted after her. Their efforts were of course doomed: success unachieved and sex unobtained were the two sides of the same debased coin. Only Moon, whose pursuit of Little Egypt was as unashamed as it was unsubtle, made any headway with her.

This points out the originality of the strip: loser as he might be, rogue as he certainly was, Moon was very much the hero (or antihero) of the feature, and he somehow always managed to come out on top in his various adventures, whether getting himself out of trouble with the law, foiling a kidnap plot, or helping Plushie open a nightclub in Florida. His triumphs were always short-lived, and he never succeeded in keeping more than a half-step ahead of whoever was after him, but he displayed an indomitability of spirit that was as admirable as his aims were reprehensible.

The daily *Moon* episodes were intricately plotted and kept the readers in suspense for weeks. The twists and turns of the narratives sometimes stretched to the fanciful, but they were always kept within the bounds of verisimilitude, whether involving Uncle Willie saving (in spite of himself) a rich clubman from drowning or Moon using Little Egypt as bait for one of his get-rich schemes. The Sunday page, on the other hand, usually featured a series of weekly gags (and hilarious they were). From 1930 on the

ple matter for the syndicate to turn over the entire strip to Johnson. In his hands *Moon Mullins* became, if not quite civilized, at least less raucous than it was in its early years. From the genuine saga of low life and low morals that it was in its heyday, it turned into another chronicle of middle-class life, which abruptly ended in 1993.

M.H.

MOOSE
1965–present

Moon Mullins Sunday was given a companion strip, *Kitty Hawkins*, starring Kayo's young female playmate. Both Sundays and dailies were drawn with superlative flair, a fine sense of composition, and a masterly economy of line by Willard, ably assisted by Ferd Johnson, who had come on board during the first year of the strip.

So good indeed was Johnson that, beginning in the 1940s, Willard turned over more and more of the drawing to him. When Willard died suddenly in 1958 it was therefore a sim-

Bob Weber was a successful magazine cartoonist as well as a former assistant on a number of comic strips when he was asked by King Features Syndicate to come up with a character that would be an American answer to England's Andy Capp, then hitting it big in U.S. newspapers. The resulting feature turned out to be *Moose*, which made its debut, daily and Sunday, on September 20, 1965.

Termed "the all-American loafer," Moose Miller lives in what appears to be a more than slightly dilapidated suburban home with his patient wife, Molly, his two sons, the teenaged Bunky and the five-year-old Blip, his small daughter, and a multitude of pets, including Grits the family dog, a thieving parrot, a goat, and a garter snake. Predictably, many of the gags revolve around Moose's aversion to work. When Molly tells him she dreamed he found a job and asks him, "What's that a sign of?" he imperturbably answers, "That's a sign you *were* dreaming." On those rare occasions when he does get gainful employment, he is usually booted out his first day on the job. To avoid doing housework he is capable of any manner of subterfuge, from pleading a backache to waxing falsely romantic. To his wife accusing him of having forgotten what day it is comes the florid oration "Does the brook forget to babble? Do flowers forget to blossom? Do the stars forget to twinkle? Happy anniversary, Molly." (Whereupon he is reminded to his chagrin that it is garbage day.)

Along with sloth, Moose's other cardinal sin is gluttony. During a short hospital stay he wolfs down all the other patients' dinners; for his wife's birthday he buys her a cold pizza; and the only thing that can get him out of his easy chair is the announcement of an invitation to dinner over at the neighbors' house. His neighbors are the much-put-upon Chester and Clara Crabtree (Weber has a fondness for alliterative names), and they regularly get their barbecue steaks swiped right off the grill, their swimming pool used as a pet's drinking station, and their lawnmower borrowed without permission by the ever ingenious Moose. Theirs is friendly antagonism, however, with Moose and Chester often going to bowling tournaments or on camping trips together.

Drawn in a broad, exaggerated, bigfoot style, *Moose* (now called *Moose Miller*) is one of the few remaining American strips still devoted to the tradition of old-time slapstick and buffoonery.

M.H.

MOPSY
1939–1965

Fresh from drawing the *Flapper Fanny* feature, Gladys Parker decided to do her own girl strip. Called *Mopsy* and distributed by Associated Newspapers, John Wheeler's syndicate, it started slowly in 1939 as a daily panel, but it soon gathered speed, and by 1945 a Sunday page had been added.

Mopsy, a pert, tousle-haired brunette patterned after Parker herself, liked to play dumb to the hordes of solici-

tous males who were always around her, but she displayed a fine sense of realism and practicality when the occasion required. ("People like dumb characters best," the artist is reported to have said; "it flatters their intelligence.") In her efforts to cope with suitors, female rivals, and the myriad aggravations of daily life, she was sometimes exasperated, sometimes dejected, but always smiling through at the end. Though perpetuating many stereotypes of women (the ritual visits to the beauty salon, the backbiting, the fussing with physical appearance, all things that were a large part of Mopsy's life), Parker also used her strip to deflate male pretensions.

Mopsy prospered mightily throughout the 1940s, especially during the war years, when she did her bit for the country, appearing variously as a WAC, a WAVE, an army nurse, and a munitions-plant worker. After the war she went back to civilian life with her popularity undiminished, so much so that *Newsweek* ran a piece on the strip and its creator in March 1949. The feature declined in circulation at the end of the 1950s, however, and it ended in 1965, shortly before its creator's death the next year.

A fresh, funny, ingratiating feature, *Mopsy* is recalled with affection by its many former readers.

M.H.

Mopsy (G. Parker), © 1946 Associated Newspapers

MOTHER GOOSE AND GRIMM
1984–present

Like some of his predecessors, Mike Peters started his strip in one direction but shifted gears when he realized that one of his characters was getting most of the gags.

Originally, *Mother Goose and Grimm* dealt with funny twists on fairy tales; however, for most of its life, the strip has been built around the antics of Mother Goose's dog. Characterized as "everyman's dog," Grimmy obviously passed up obedience school (and all schools, for that matter) and etiquette instruction. He gets great pleasure out of chasing cars, terrorizing the cat, raiding the garbage can, and trying to figure out the world around him. With the latter, he usually stumbles pitifully. In one sequence, he is standing in the middle of the street, puzzling over a foreign-language word that is approaching: "Ecna?" "Ecnalub?" "Ecnalubma?" In the last panel, he is seen embedded in the grill of an ambulance.

Peters makes his characters very expressive, using a few lines to exaggerate distinctive features—droopy eyes or the esophagus-visible throat of a screaming cat. Grimmy is almost as funny to look at as to listen to, as Peters balances the visual and verbal elements. Drawings are bold, with minimal details, and gags are clever, zany, and irreverent.

Launched October 1, 1984, by Tribune Media Services, the strip has appeared in more than 550 newspapers worldwide, has been the subject of at least a dozen books and a Saturday morning CBS cartoon show, and has adorned more than a hundred licensed products.

Peters is also a Pulitzer Prize–winning editorial cartoonist for the *Dayton* [Ohio] *Daily News*. For some time, he did animated editorial cartoons, called *Peters Postscripts,* which appeared regularly on *NBC Nightly News*. It was the first

Mother Goose and Grimm (M. Peters), © 1991 Grimmy, Inc.

time animated editorial cartoons were used regularly on a prime-time network-news program. In 1992, Peters was named Cartoonist of the Year by the National Cartoonists Society, adding to the many awards he has received.

J.A.L.

MOTLEY'S CREW
1976–present

In 1975 Tom Forman, a television comedy writer, tired of the scant assignments he was getting from TV studios, decided to try his hand at writing a comic strip with a sporting slant. He contacted cartoonist Ben Templeton and the two put together a feature they called "Super Fan." The comics editor at the Chicago Tribune–New York News Syndicate accepted the strip but suggested the authors satirize current social and political events along with sports. Renamed *Motley's Crew,* the new venture started on September 6, 1976, daily and Sunday, and it was soon carried by an impressive number of newspapers.

The beer-drinking Mike Motley and his cigar-chomping bosom buddy Earl are both blue-collar workers at Drudge Industries, but the products they turn out remain something of a mystery (it may be widgets one week, flanges the next). Actually, they seem to spend more time at the local tavern than at the plant, and this gives them the opportunity of meeting some outlandish characters. There is Tacoma, the town belle, who claims to have dated extraterrestrials and astounds the two pals by announcing not all of them are green. There is Yuri Greygorovitch Litvin, a big, jovial, hairy Russian the pair met in Moscow in 1987 (they get around). Later escaping from Russia as a ballet dancer, Litvin turns up now and then in Motley's hometown. Cameo appearances have also been put in by, among others, a Tibetan monk, a Martian, and the Devil himself.

A number of gags were, as promised, devoted to sports and sports fans, but they soon diminished and even disappeared, as Forman and Templeton created a daily panel (and later a Sunday page) to that purpose, the ephemeral *The Sporting Life.* Instead Forman, a government-affairs graduate and a former history teacher, went in for political satire with a vengeance. In 1977 he had President Jimmy Carter come to Motley's house and his neighborhood to find out what typical middle-class Americans were thinking. So impressed was he by his sojourn that the very next year Carter invited Mike and Earl to a dinner honoring American blue-collar workers. Since that time Forman and Templeton have featured in their strip every American president in office, along with a number of senators and governors, not to mention foreign bigwigs such as the former head of the Soviet Union, Mikhail Gorbachev. They have also commented on topics ranging from farm subsidies to California's now infamous Proposition 13. Now entering their twentieth year, Motley and his crew give no signs of slowing down.

M.H.

MOUNT ARARAT
See THE LITTLE BEARS

MR. A. MUTT
See MUTT AND JEFF

MR. ABERNATHY
1957–present

Former *Beetle Bailey* assistant Ralston ("Bud") Jones conceived in tandem with Frank Ridgeway the amusing saga of an elderly Romeo. Drawn by Jones, scripted by Ridgeway, and distributed by King Features, *Mr. Abernathy* came out as a daily strip on October 14, 1957, followed by a Sunday page on November 8, 1959.

Mr. Abernathy (no first name given), a diminutive, white-haired, moustachioed, and top-hatted millionaire, is an art collector, a wine connoisseur, a food lover, and above all an unrepentant, if hardly successful, Casanova. Aided and abetted by his faithful retainer Dudley, he wines and dines bevies of beauties in his penthouse, plying them with liquor and covering them in furs, all in vain; at best he gets rewarded with a buss on the forehead, at worst he is gratified with blows of purse or umbrella on the skull. Mr. Abernathy's amorous approach is as unsubtle as it is unconvincing: to his intended conquests he boasts of his wealth and possessions—a Maurice Chevalier he is not. To diversify the jokes, the old gentleman is sometimes shown in feckless disputations with fellow club members or in luckless tries at bridge, golf, and piano playing. Drawn in an enjoyable version of Mort Walker's bigfoot style, and scripted with some amount of wit and humor, *Mr. Abernathy* remains an ingratiating comic of the old school.

In the late 1970s Jones sold his interest in the strip to his partner, who then received sole credit for the feature. Done in the same graphic style as before, Mr. Abernathy blissfully went on strutting his stuff, though now only on weekdays. With Ridgeway's death in 1994, the strip has now passed into the hands of syndicate staffers, and it is rumored to be on the verge of termination.

M.H.

MR. AND MRS.
1919–1963

Having drawn for years such celebrated daily panels as *When a Feller Needs a Friend* and *Ain't It a Grand and Glorious Feelin'?* for the *New York Tribune*, Clare Briggs decided it was time for him to add a color Sunday page to his black-and-white exertions. The result was *Mr. and Mrs.*, which made its debut on April 20, 1919, in the *Tribune* comic supplement.

The Mr. and Mrs. of the title were respectively Joseph (Joe) and Violet (Vi) Green, he an office worker of advancing age, bald, bemoustached, and bespectacled, she a lanky and ordinary-looking housewife some years his junior. While the page is mostly remembered for the couple's endless bickerings, there was more subtlety to it, at least in the early years, than the basic situation would suggest. In one 1921 episode, for example, while Vi was trying to cajole her husband into buying her an expensive birthday gift, Joe was seen reading his newspaper and mumbling to himself, "Well, I see that Mrs. Titcomb got her divorce"; continuing to read as his wife carried on, he came to the end of the article, "She gets the custody of the kids and ten thousand a year," whereupon he got up from the breakfast table, leaving a hundred-dollar bill for his wife to buy whatever she pleased with it.

The relationship between the couple was less one of antagonism than of mutual disenchantment. In the rare moments when Joe would assert himself, Vi would stop her nagging and meekly back down. She would also melt when her husband showed some sign of affection, such as buying her a Valentine's Day gift. Only in later years did the situation degenerate into a climate of acerbic and ceaseless recrimination, punctuated in bitter irony by the refrain "Papa love Mama?" (or "Mama love Papa?") invariably uttered at the end of each episode by the couple's young son Bertram (who may have been renamed Roscoe at a later date).

This bleak depiction of middle-class married life proved paradoxically so popular with the *Tribune*'s middle-class readers that not only did the *Mr. and Mrs.* Sunday page survive the death of its creator in 1930, it added a daily strip the next year. The texts for both were written by Arthur Folwell, the *Tribune*'s former drama critic, with the dailies being drawn by Ellison Hoover, and the Sunday page mostly done by Frank Fogarty. Whatever charm there was to the feature had resided mainly in Briggs's drawings, executed in a scratchy, slightly caricatural style. His successors did not display the same winsomeness, prompting Thomas Craven in his 1943 anthology *Cartoon Cavalcade* to scowl, "I don't think that anyone draws *Mr. and Mrs.* now: it is self-spawning," adding, "Every day, at the crack of dawn, I look at it, always praying that the Greens will have taken their unending quarrels into the divorce court, and that I may never behold their snarling faces again."

Craven had to wait twenty years to see his prayer answered. *Mr. and Mrs.* ultimately died, along with its parent newspaper, in 1963. By that time it was being done by Kin Platt, who had taken over the drawing of both daily and Sunday in 1947.

M.H.

MR. BREGER
1942–1970

One of the more tantalizing bits of trivia in the history of World War II is the fact that G.I. Joe, probably the most famous American cartoon character to come out of this conflict, was born because Dave Breger's *Private Breger* was under copyright to a civilian publication, the *Saturday Evening Post,* where it had been running as an interrelated series of joke cartoons since 1941. Having to come up with an alternative name for his civilian-in-uniform hero, Breger reportedly coined the term "G.I. Joe" (G.I. standing for "Government Issue") while on leave in New York City from military maneuvers in Louisiana. At any rate, *G.I. Joe* started running in the army's weekly *Yank* magazine and daily *Stars and Stripes,* while simultaneously appearing as Private Breger stateside. Under either name he kept the same appearance and identity. "Breger's hero, a reduced and sharpened version of Breger himself," Stephen Becker wrote in *Comic Art in America,* "was neither warrior nor stumblebum, but somewhere in between, like most American soldiers."

Private Breger started its newspaper career—as distinct from its magazine run—on October 19, 1942, in a daily panel distributed by King Features Syndicate. The diminutive, freckle-faced, bespectacled hero got himself in all kinds of scrapes in every theater of war, trying to swat mosquitoes in the North African desert while his buddies were busy fighting off a German assault, or taking snapshots of locals in quaint costumes while his unit was inching its way through Italy. Both Bregers (the real and the fictional versions) got their discharge papers in the latter half of 1945; the daily panel was accordingly renamed *Mr. Breger* on October 22, 1945. (*G.I. Joe* was terminated around that same time.) On February 3, 1946, a Sunday *Mr. Breger* page saw light of print, with the title character now tackling all the perils of civilian life.

Mr. Breger tried his hand at diverse occupations, while

Mr. and Mrs. (C. Briggs), © 1922 New York Tribune

not succeeding at any. He was the same lovable, plodding, somewhat befuddled little man he had been in military life, but now his troubles seemed to multiply, and his enemies no longer wore recognizable uniforms: those might be nasty bosses, querulous neighbors, or backbiting colleagues. For all his woes, he managed to marry an attractive redhead named Dorothy and father a son named Harry. The cartoonist's acidulous view of American life and society was not to every reader's taste, and the strip plodded along, in the manner of its eponymous hero. Following Breger's death in January 1970, his feature was discontinued by the syndicate later that same year, the daily panel on March 16, and the Sunday version on March 22.

It is a sad irony that *Mr. Breger* is hardly acknowledged today, despite a respectable run of some twenty-five years, while *Private Breger* is still fondly remembered by anyone who lived through World War II.

M.H.

MR. GEORGE
1904–1914

Harold Knerr in his early comic-strip career would, like any other fledgling cartoonists in their twenties, painstakingly copy the style of artists he particularly admired. If in *Die Fineheimer Kids* he imitated in theme and style (at least in the beginning) the work of Rudolph Dirks, it is to George McManus he turned for the drawing of *Mr. George*. It should be noted, however, that in both the aforementioned features Knerr's line, while imitative, was already confident and craftsmanlike. As with most of Knerr's pre-1914 creations, *Mr. George* (also called *Mr. George and Wifey* and *Mr. George and Dear Wifey*), which started as a Sunday page in January 1904, was carried by the *Philadelphia Inquirer*, which syndicated it to other publications.

While the drawings were modeled on McManus's artwork, *Mr. George*'s theme was clearly derived from James Swinnerton's *Mr. Jack*. George (or Georgie, no surname given) was a married man with a roving eye and an unbridled lust for any cutie that was around; he also had a bossy wife (always referred to as Wifey) who didn't take kindly to his philanderings. Sneaking out for some furtive embrace, he would always be found out by his irate spouse, who would then vent her anger by bopping poor Hubby on the head with umbrella, purse, or parasol, as the case may be, while exclaiming in disgust, "Reprobate!" or "Perfidious villain!" The lengthy subtitles Knerr stuck over each episode told it all: "George Steals a Kiss Under the Goo-Goo Tree—He Also Gets Beat Up Under the Goo-Goo Tree" and "Did Wifey Catch the Fish? No but She Caught Hubby!" are two examples. Even as early as 1907 Knerr managed to slip some humorous asides into the dialogue, like Wifey trying to bolster her claim of botanical knowledge by asserting: "Didn't my grandfather study farming by correspondence?" These ironic quips were of course to become one of the artist's hallmarks on *The Katzenjammer Kids*.

Like his other series, *Mr. George* was abandoned by Knerr

upon his taking charge of the Katzies in 1914; the page was continued until October 25 of that year by Jack Gallagher and then disappeared.

MR. JACK
1902–1904, 1912–1919, 1926–1935

Mr. Jack grew out of *The Journal Tigers*, the Sunday page James Swinnerton had been drawing at the turn of the century for the Hearst papers, all about the frolicsome escapades of a merry crew of feline characters. Among the band there was a cocky cat-about-town that stood out, and in 1902 he was given his own Sunday feature to cavort in. A small, impeccably attired cat with a roguish streak, he was fond of ogling every female in sight, to the chagrin of his long-suffering wife. In 1903 the philandering feline was given a name, Mr. Jack, but his amorous escapades lasted only for another year before the feature was pulled out of the sanitized environment of the Sunday comic supplement, where children could see it, because of its racy overtones.

In 1912 *Mr. Jack* came back in the form of a daily strip, with the title character disporting himself pretty much as before. Mr. Jack was the prototypical cool cat, and his many discomfitures, such as his being put down by kittenish vamps, set upon by enraged husbands, or hit on the head by his exasperated wife, hardly seemed to affect his outward composure. No trick was too low, no lie too shabby for the crafty feline in his unrelenting pursuit of the opposite sex. With the passing years his shenanigans became so outrageous that Swinnerton had to close down the strip, purportedly on orders from W. R. Hearst himself, in the summer of 1919. Stubbornly, Swinnerton tried once again: his rakish hero, now no longer married, resurfaced on February 7, 1926, as frisky as he ever was, in *Mr. Jack*, the top piece to *Little Jimmy*. Again he got into trouble with the syndicate editors, and in June 1935 he was gone for good.

As a much-married man (no fewer than four times) with a perpetually roving eye, Swinnerton seems to have had a special fondness for Mr. Jack. Certainly there is more than

Mr. Jack (J. Swinnerton), ca. 1904

a touch of self-revelation in some of the more poignant turndowns and indignities suffered by the feline hero. In Swinnerton's world, much given to idyllic depictions of childhood and outdoor life, *Mr. Jack* stands out much as a naturalistic novel would next to *Little Lord Fauntleroy*.

M.H.

MR. MUM
See THE STRANGE WORLD OF MR. MUM

MR. MYSTIC
1940–1944

Faced with the task of producing a sixteen-page weekly comic-book insert for newspapers, Will Eisner, in addition to reserving *The Spirit* for himself, created two back-up features, one of which was *Mr. Mystic,* which appeared on June 2, 1940.

Credited to "W. Morgan Thomas," *Mr. Mystic* was modeled on one of Eisner's earlier creations, *Yarko the Great, Master Magician*. The first story related how Ken, a young American, got lost over the Himalayas, where he received magical powers—and a new name—from a mysterious Council of Seven Lamas who would guide his actions through telepathy. "Endowed with vast supernatural powers, Mr. Mystic steadily carries on his war against Evil," an inset tersely proclaimed at the opening of each weekly episode. Thus, on instructions from the secret council, Mr. Mystic continually traveled the earth, one week in Dakar, Africa, the next one in the wilds of Amazonia, always nattily dressed in a blue costume, red cape, and yellow turban. All this flying around played havoc with the magician's love life (he was quite a ladies' man) as his protectors would send him on some assignment to battle evil right after he had sat down at some exotic cafe with a date. He later found a permanent mate in the former agent of darkness Elena, whom he converted to his side. Together, and for the rest of the feature's run, they would fight the Nazis all over the globe.

Bob Powell was the first artist on the title, and each five-page episode crackled with action and suspense. After Powell was drafted in 1943, Fred Guardineer, who had previously drawn *Zatara the Master Magician*, one of the better Mandrake imitations, replaced him, but not for long. The next year he was called into service in his turn, and *Mr. Mystic* ended on May 14, 1944, in the newspapers (in comic books the character continued his existence through the 1940s).

M.H.

MR. TWEE DEEDLE
1910–1921

In 1910 the editors of the *New York Herald,* alarmed at the prospect of losing the soon-to-depart Winsor McCay, organized a contest with a $2,000 prize to find a replacement for McCay's *Little Nemo*. Johnny Gruelle, a cartoonist

of already recognized talent, sent in the winning comic page, *Mr. Twee Deedle,* which started appearing later that year, and its innocent contents and moral tenor proved so popular with the *Herald* readers that in 1911 it relegated *Nemo* to the interior (black-and-white) pages of the paper for the brief remainder of its run.

Mr. Twee Deedle was more of a fairy tale than a fantasy. A typeset text of paragraph length ran beneath and sometimes above each picture, and the dialogue was conveyed indirectly in quotes, instead of being enclosed in speech-balloons in imitation of direct conversation. Yet there was an undercurrent of wonder and dazzlement as well as a splendid dreamlike imagery in these adventures of a trio (sometimes enlarged to a quartet) of mismatched characters on a quest of undetermined origins amid alien worlds. Mr. Twee Deedle was a male fairy of attenuated size and less than impressive powers (in some ways he anticipated *Barnaby's* Mr. O'Malley) who guided a plucky blond boy named Dickie to "lands beyond the imagination." Dickie himself, clearly modeled on Little Nemo in age, size, and pleasant appearance, was always ready to follow his mentor into whatever mischievous escapade he devised. In the course of their wanderings the two companions acquired a third associate in the person of the bumbling Moon Man, a white-bearded, beanpole-shaped deposed monarch who always wore a crown on his head as a sign of his former exalted rank. At some point the Rubber Man, whose elasticity and shape-changing abilities saved the friends from many a thorny thicket, joined the little band, but he dropped out just as mysteriously as he had come.

Drawn with exquisite line and written in passable prose, *Mr. Twee Deedle* was a work of great imagination. Its monsters, weird creatures, and strange landscapes were depicted with a stirring use of color and in a friendly style guaranteed not to frighten children, unlike similar scenes in *Little Nemo*. Gruelle's Sunday page lasted until 1921, when the artist left to devote himself to his immensely successful series of Raggedy Ann and Andy books. While not quite on a par with McCay's masterpiece, which it was meant to replace, *Mr. Twee Deedle* remains a fascinating oddity and perhaps the best example of a hybrid between the classic picture-story and the modern comic strip.

M.H.

MRS. FITZ
1957–1972

Among the many comic-strip ideas thought up by Mort Walker, there was one "about a perky old lady who owned an apartment building occupied by an outlandish assortment of tenants," in Walker's own words. Drawn by Frank Roberge and distributed by King Features, *Mrs. Fitz's Flats* (as it was originally titled) started syndication as a daily (there never was a Sunday) on January 7, 1957. At first Walker wrote the jokes, then only contributed gag ideas, finally relinquishing full authorship to Roberge.

A spunky, white-haired oldster always attired in a black dress and a white apron even when going out, Mrs. Fitz served most often as the anchor around which the antics of

Mrs. Fitz (F. Roberge), © 1967 King Features Syndicate

the various building occupants revolved. Her tenants were a motley group, as diverse as any city building ever sheltered, including Umber, the artist whose main stock in trade was painted turtles; Ludvig, the lazy slob, and his nagging mountain of a wife, Danube; the bibulous Turf, who ran a bookmaking operation from his apartment; and Linseed, the accident-prone janitor. There also were a fashion model, a couple of phony aristocrats, and other eccentric characters. While Roberge's style was eye-pleasing and uncluttered, and many of his gags amusing (those involving Professor Neutron's periodic encounters with space aliens proved quite imaginative), the great number of different characters kept the readers from identifying with any of them.

Sensing this disaffection, Roberge in the mid-1960s got Mrs. Fitz married (she had been a widow), had the newlyweds move into a retirement home in Florida, and renamed the strip simply *Mrs. Fitz.* He soon tired of old-age jokes, however, and a couple of years later brought Mrs. Fitz (minus her husband) back to her flats.

The move back didn't help either, and the strip, which never had list a large list of client newspapers to begin with, sank even further. Roberge bravely carried on, spicing up his gags with topical allusions and sexual undertones, to no avail. *Mrs. Fitz* finally fizzled out on October 22, 1972.

M.H.

MUGGS AND SKEETER
1927–1974

One of the many kid strips to come out of the 1920s, the undistinguished but likable *Muggs and Skeeter* (originally known as *Muggs McGinnis*) managed to outlive the competition through luck and resilience. Created in 1927 by Wally Bishop for Central Press Association as a small-town answer to King Features' *Skippy*, it found itself the next year in the Hearst camp, after the Hearst interests had acquired Central Press. On December 31, 1934, *Muggs* was picked up for direct syndication by King, thus coming full circle.

As befits a man born in Normal, Illinois (as Bishop was), the cartoonist had his ten-year-old hero as a regular representative of American boyhood, neither tough nor sentimental, but given to good-natured pranks and other

healthy signs of a normal childhood. He lived with Grandpa and Grandma McGinnis, who were both very understanding of the boy's small problems and heartaches. Other principals in the gang included the scrappy Beauregard, the precocious tot Knothaid, Effie Mae, the feisty female member of the band, and the overaffectionate Junior, a dachshund. Shortly after King Features took over distribution, Skeeter, an orphan boy, joined the activities and became Muggs's bosom pal in the strip, which acquired its definitive title in July 1936.

The anecdotes told in the strip (usually as daily gags, but sometimes extending over a couple of weeks) were slight, and generally revolved around some of the kids' shenanigans, or dealt with typical childhood games like softball, marbles, or cops-and-robbers. On the other hand, the little band was seldom seen taking part in classroom activities, though most of its members were certainly of school age. This was a rosy, nostalgic view of childhood, reflected in the quaint quality of the drawings, somewhat stiff but always engaging. *Muggs and Skeeter* achieved only modest critical and commercial success (it is not mentioned in any of the early histories of the comics, and it never got a Sunday page) during a long career that ended on February 25, 1974, a forty-seven-year run matched by few other kid strips of the period.

M.H.

MUTT AND JEFF
1907–1983

Mutt and Jeff has been the anomaly of comic strips. In artwork, it left much to be desired, its creator, Bud Fisher, preferring crude, rushed, and amateurlike drawings to the above-average cross-hatching and shading he was capable of doing. The verbal part also lacked verve and often imagination, depending very regularly upon vaudevillian pie-in-the-face punchlines and gags recycled threadbare.

Yet, the strip proved itself a survivor and innovator, lasting longer than all others except *The Katzenjammer Kids,* and adding many important dimensions to the medium. *Mutt and Jeff,* from its beginning in 1907 in the *San Francisco Chronicle,* helped mold the funnies. Preceded by Clare Briggs's daily *A. Piker Clerk* three years earlier, Fisher's creation found its niche in history as the first successful six-days-a-week, multiple-panel strip that used a regular cast, and technically as one of the first comic books. The latter occurred in 1911, when *Mutt and Jeff* strips were collected into an eighteen-inch-wide, six-inch-high book used as a circulation stunt for subscribing dailies. (By the way, when *Famous Funnies* ushered in the modern comic book in 1934, *Mutt and Jeff* was one of the strips included.)

The very ineptness with which Fisher drew the strip also left an impact, telling other cartoonists by its example that this was the way to do comics. Fisher's characters often had mismatched body and head proportions and unrealistic anatomical features. Mutt sometimes had six or seven fingers on a hand, for which Fisher made no apology. In an early interview, he said, "All I have is an idea and I want to express it. It matters little to me whether a man's arm is drawn longer than his body or whether he wears a straw hat in winter time."

Further, the strip was partly responsible for making comics topical. In its earliest days, before syndication, when it was drawn for the next day's newspapers, *Mutt and Jeff* dealt with many current affairs. In February 1908, during A. Mutt's six-week court ordeal brought about by his stealing from a pay phone to feed his gambling habit, Fisher plopped into the strip a number of sledgehammer-like references to San Francisco politicians involved in high-level corruption. He daily fashioned the strip as the top of a newspaper, with a banner and a succession of "newspaper photos" he drew, complete with captions of principals in the corruption cases. That same year, on March 27, Mutt met Jeff, an insane-asylum patient who thought he was the prizefighter Jim Jeffries, thus his name. Jeff became a regular in the strip about a year later.

When elections came around in 1908, Mutt was the first strip character to announce his candidacy for president of the United States, running as a Bughouse Party nominee with Jeff as his vice-presidential mate. In 1916, Mutt was the Bull Mole party candidate, and this time, Jeff was his campaign manager. Mutt must have tossed in the towel rather early, as he was seen in bed snoring as the narrator explained that Mutt's doctor advised the avoidance of all excitement and complete rest and quiet. Mutt's natural reaction was to run for vice president and go to sleep. In 1932, the Lion Tamers' convention made its one attendee, A. Mutt, the nominee, while another one-member party gave its nod to Jeff.

Fisher introduced newsworthy figures to the strip from time to time, showing Mutt training for a 1929 fight with Max Schmeling on a regimen of running (which came in handy when he got in the ring with the champ), and working as Herbert Hoover's butler on Inauguration Day. In the latter episode, Mutt hoped to get an important government post by making a good impression on the president. However, when he answered Hoover's early-morning coffee call, he found Jeff already there, stretched out on the bed next to the president, his new pal.

Fisher's exploitation of current topics in the strip made him very popular with racing fans. When he was still with the San Francisco dailies, Fisher introduced into the strip the names of real horses running at Emeryville Track across the bay. He chose horses' names in a whimsical fashion—those that inspired a gag in that day's strip—but readers thought of them as hot tips. Horse betting was the basis for most early gags, with Mutt shown exhausting every legal and illegal means of getting a stake and then dashing to the window to place his bet. A low-brow life was depicted, mainly based on gambling, playing pool and cards, searching for shortcuts to wealth, avoiding work, and keeping ahead of Mrs. Mutt's flung rolling pin. Both Mrs. Mutt and son Cicero date from the fourth episode in 1907.

The strip occasionally showed flashes of genius, such as when Mutt and Jeff reminisced with readers about the first forty-five years of the strip's history in a sequence lasting from December 31, 1951, through February 2, 1952, or on the numerous occasions when the characters carried on conversations with their "boss" (Fisher, or his successor, Al Smith), who would appear in the strip with them, or at times when characters interacted with the readers. In one sequence Jeff would not disrobe to bathe until Mutt held up a towel to block the readers' view.

The chief characters—one tall and smart, the other short and feeble-minded—brought to the comics page stereotyped vaudeville, and later film, funny combinations. Jeff, the short fellow in the top hat, was usually the butt of the jokes in early strips, but eventually his unanswerable illogic and successes with beautiful women wore Mutt down. In exasperation, he would flatten Jeff, often seen on the floor sporting a shiner as stars and globes danced about his head, or he would stick a gun in one of his own ears and a finger in the other to drown out the sound, feigning suicide.

Not only did the roles of the strip's characters and the topics change, but also the artwork. By 1915, Fisher began adding splotches of blacks that made parts of the panels

Mutt and Jeff (H. C. "Bud" Fisher), 1916

stand out. The artwork changed at other times over the years—to even simpler, less cluttered panels—but it is unlikely that Fisher had much to do with these alterations. Already in the 1920s, he had delegated most responsibilities of the strip to Ed Mack, who drew *Mutt and Jeff* until his death in 1932. He was succeeded by Al Smith, who not only did the ideas and drawings for the rest of his life (1982) but also created a Sunday tag to *Mutt and Jeff,* called *Cicero's Cat,* which he fully credited to Fisher. In 1982, George Breisacher of the *Charlotte Observer* inherited the strip, which was still distributed by Field Newspaper Service and owned by Fisher's second wife of four months, Countess Aedita de Beaumont. Field ended *Mutt and Jeff* just before selling out to Rupert Murdoch, the idea being to dump borderline strips to make the syndicate appear healthy and worth purchasing.

By that time, the strip did not hold much of an audience or command much respect, a shell of its former self seven decades before, when it made Fisher the wealthiest and most popular cartoonist. In those days, the cartoonist boasted earnings of $150,000 a year from the strip alone, and at least another $100,000 from animation, books, merchandise, and his vaudeville act, all connected to *Mutt and Jeff.* Fisher hobnobbed with the likes of Ring Lardner and Jack Dempsey and regularly showed up at nightspots with beautiful showgirls on both arms, all the time snubbing cartoonist colleagues. He died a lonely and sad man in 1954.

J.A.L.

MYRA NORTH, SPECIAL NURSE
1936–1941

Drawn by Charles Coll on texts by Ray Thompson, *Myra North, Special Nurse* made its daily appearance on February 10, 1936, followed by a Sunday page on June 12 of the same year; the strip in both versions was nationally syndicated by NEA Service.

While she conspicuously wore the regulation nurse uniform and cap, Myra North's activities were more often than not very special indeed and routinely involved matters of murder, conspiracy, and espionage. Among other cases she handled were blackmail and piracy affairs. Year in, year out, she solved a baffling series of murders in Hollywood, put out of business a sinister spy network masquerading as a peace organization, and even uncovered the secret of the Great Pyramid at Gizeh.

In addition to her multifaceted talents, Myra also possessed good looks and an attractive figure, and that made her prey to a number of lecherous males, such as escaped racketeers, mad scientists, and even some of her employers. When she was not getting in harm's way on her own, she was thrust into peril through her relationship with her boyfriend, Jack Lane, an insurance investigator (Lane, a handsome if rather dense fellow, would probably have ended up on the breadlines like so many others during the depression had it not been for his girlfriend's acumen and resourcefulness).

To be fair, Myra did carry out her professional duties on occasion, and even acted as an angel of mercy in an unnamed European country ravaged by civil war, but her assignments often led her to the discovery of some unsavory activity. It would always happen that the director of the clinic where she was nursing turned out to be experimenting on human guinea pigs, or that the English dowager whose nurse and companion she had become would get bumped off by an heir. She sometimes also used her nursing credentials as a cover, getting into a prison for the criminally insane, for instance, in order to expose an inmate who was masterminding his gang's activities from his cell, or posing as a navy nurse as a means to ferret out a spy ring that had infiltrated a naval base.

Myra's adventures were well plotted and adequately drawn, but in the end proved too tame for a public used to sturdier comic-strip fare. Her career as a special nurse ended on March 25, 1939, in the dailies, and on August 31, 1941, her Sunday adventures also came to a close.

M.H.

Myra North (Thompson and Coll), © 1936 NEA Service

MYRTLE
1941–1965

In 1935 *Columbus Dispatch* cartoonist Dudley Fisher was working on a weekly feature called *Jolly Jingles* when he decided one fine day to draw one huge panel taking up the whole page and depicting what happens to a farm family when city relatives come to visit them for Christmas. His innovation was so well received that Fisher dropped *Jolly Jingles* to devote himself entirely to his new creation, which got its definitive title, *Right Around Home,* not long afterward. In January 1938 King Features Syndicate picked up the panel for national distribution.

The most striking characteristic of Fisher's page was its bird's-eye view (looking downward at about a forty-five-degree angle), which the cartoonist recreated based on his experiences flying over enemy-held territory as a lieutenant in the 45th Photo Section of the U.S. Army Air Corps during World War I. His other distinguishing artistic trait was the incredible crowding of his compositions. Working the whole scene into single giant panel filling an entire newspaper page, Fisher crammed his characters into small, tight groups engaged in some activity or other in every corner of his panel.

Gradually the action in the feature shifted from a rural to a suburban setting, centering more and more on such activities as barbecues, bridge games, car washing, etc. Revolving around an extended American family, *Right Around Home* had a cozy, homey, carefree flavor, and it enjoyed wide enough popularity to give rise to a spin-off, a daily strip that started syndication on May 26, 1941, marking the date of the feature's entrance into bona fide newspaper comicdom.

Called *Myrtle* in honor of the daughter of the family who had in the meantime stolen the show from the other protagonists, the dailies took on the appearance (and the substance) of a traditional kid strip. The title character was a mischievous ten-year-old who always wore a hat and indulged in mildly amusing pranks. The catastrophes she brought about were the result of high spirits rather than malice, and she was ever ready to profess contriteness—more in the mold of Dennis the Menace than of the Katzenjammers. Her best friend was the freckle-faced and two-toothed Sampson, who was in constant awe of his female companion. Her pop, Freddie, and her mom, Susie, were a well-adjusted and loving twosome, in contrast to most married couples of the comics. Myrtle's young Aunt Minnie and her boyfriend Slug provided the juvenile angle; while her grandma represented the older set; and the family's neighbors, the Smaltzes, were played off as foils to Myrtle's pranks. There were also the black cat Hyacinth, the dogs Bingo and Sunshine, plus two cynical birds, Alice and Archie, who commented on the action.

Fisher died of a heart attack in July 1951. The daily strip and the Sunday panel (with its title now expanded to *Right Around Home with Myrtle,* in recognition of the star status enjoyed by the daughter of the house) were picked up by Stan Randall, followed by a succession of syndicate staffers. The durable feature managed to last into 1965, with the dailies closing on April 26 and the Sunday coming to an end on May 2.

M.H.

NANCY
1938–present

Nancy, the slot-nosed, bristle-headed kid created by Ernie Bushmiller and introduced in the early 1930s in *Fritzi Ritz* (a stereotypical flapper strip originated by Larry Whittington, then carried on by Bushmiller) as Fritzi's niece, slowly but surely eclipsed her aunt in the public eye. The year 1938 marked both the appearance of Nancy's rough-around-the-edges pal, Sluggo Smith, and also the daily strip's name change from *Fritzi Ritz* to *Fritzi Ritz and Nancy* and later to simply *Nancy*—reflecting the initially peripheral child character's move to center stage. Bushmiller's Sunday strip also gave way to a Sunday *Nancy*, with *Fritzi Ritz* as its top, and by the late 1940s the mischievous little girl found herself in one of the most popular comic strips in the country, growing to a peak circulation of nearly one thousand papers by the 1970s. *Nancy* has also been translated into many foreign languages, being especially popular in South America and Japan.

Continuing story lines were succeeded by a daily gag format that often relied as much on visual as verbal punchlines. Bushmiller's mastery of gag building was not matched by his artwork, however, which early on was more interesting and drawn with a certain attention to detail, but which in the cartoonist's quest for simplicity eventually became tired and repetitive. This led to efforts by newspapers in the 1950s and 1960s to drop the daily and Sunday strips—to no avail, for Nancy's fans were legion and their devotion to her unabashedly simple-minded action and unrelenting plainness prevented any such attempts.

The years between 1944 and 1959 are commonly viewed as *Nancy*'s classic period, when Bushmiller perfected his craft, distilling his gags and his graphic style to their barest minimum. In spite of the strip's unsophisticated nature, it must be said that Bushmiller's Nancy was not a one-dimensional character. She displayed an offbeat cleverness when solving problems,

Nancy (E. Bushmiller), © 1946 United Feature Syndicate

such as improving the appearance of Sluggo's cracked and torn plaster wall by incorporating the odd-shaped holes into a mural she drew on the wall. Her relationship with Sluggo also developed into a lifelong association, whether they were fighting or making up. As for her all-too-human characteristics, Nancy could fly into jealous rages when Sluggo looked at a pretty girl, she constantly fretted about her appearance, and her rich dream life bordered on the surreal, with animated school houses gleefully awaiting hapless kids at summer's end.

Afflicted with Parkinson's disease, the cartoonist was unable to draw for the last few years of his life, so his assistants, Will Johnson and Al Plastino, who did the daily and Sunday strips respectively, handled the workload while he supervised his creation. He suffered a heart attack and died at home on August 15, 1982.

Nancy, however, has lived on through the efforts of other artists: Mark Lasky, until his own death in 1983, followed by Jerry Scott, who has drawn the strip since that time. Scott has given *Nancy* a more modern look and has brought a fresh feeling to the strip by gradually updating it without altering its basically simple nature and gentle humor. As for Nancy herself, still self-centered, she can make a ruckus to focus attention on her high dive or fancy hoop shot, only to lose her temper and berate the very onlookers she has courted for witnessing her consequent bellyflop or her beaning by the basketball. She remains as concerned with her appearance as ever, dressing up in high heels or applying gobs of makeup—without permission, of course. And although Nancy may look at others, Sluggo is still her best pal and true love. She also retains her fierce competitive edge: Sluggo, after beating her at a board game, declares that winning when playing with Nancy "can be more painful than losing," as tokens bounce off the helmet he's just donned in preparation for the aftermath of his victory.

Thanks to Scott's superb efforts, *Nancy* has rebounded in popularity and has begun to build the kind of recognition it once enjoyed. Unfortunately, with Scott's recent departure to concentrate on his other strip, *Baby Blues*, United Feature, *Nancy*'s syndicate, has decided to return to the original style and story lines, a change to which its readers have not enthusiastically taken. While the current artists, Guy and Brad Gilchrist, have certainly captured the Bushmiller look and gag style, today's readers, especially kids, are much more aware and demanding than were their counterparts in 1940. Thus, it is possible that this new/old look may doom *Nancy* to once again suffer the fading popularity of strips too closely linked to a bygone era.

M.B.C.

NAPOLEON
1932–1961

While there were many cats in the vying for the position of most successful comic-strip feline in the 1930s, the most beloved and most popular dog strip of the decade was undeniably *Napoleon and Uncle Elby* (later simply *Napoleon*). Clifford McBride created the feature as a daily strip for the obscure Lafave Syndicate on June 6, 1932, with a Sunday page following on March 12 of the next year. (It should be noted, however, that the two title characters had earlier appeared in a weekly gag page McBride had been doing for the McNaught Syndicate.)

Napoleon was an enormous mutt of indeterminate origin, ungainly and uncouth, the very epitome of shaggy dogs. His well-meaning intentions always ended in catastrophe, and for just such occasions, Napoleon could harbor a wonderful range of expressions, from utter disgust to doleful contrition. He found his perfect foil in Uncle Elby, a portly, bespectacled, finicky old bachelor, whose neatness and primness were on a permanent collision course with Napoleon's sloppy habits.

As befitted his jumbo size, Napoleon was endowed with an enormous appetite. Ordinary dog food never satisfied his fastidious tastes, and in contrast to his usual clumsiness

Napoleon (C. McBride), © 1935 Arthur J. Lafave

he could show remarkable dexterity when it came to pilfering food, squeezing into butcher's carts, meat showcases, even shoppers' baskets in order to gulp down sausages or chops. "No, I don't know his breed," Uncle Elby once declared to an inquiring friend, "but I've always thought he was some sort of hunting dog. He points beautifully and has a superb nose for game"; whereupon Napoleon proceeded to prove his master right by pointing to the stuffed animals in a taxidermist's window.

The interactions between dog and master were the crux of the strip, as the original title implied. McBride soon decided, however, to vary the gags by introducing Uncle Elby's ten-year-old nephew, Willie, and his pals. In the tradition of comic-strip kids, they played all kinds of tricks on poor Napoleon, but the mutt often had the last laugh, lapping up the lemonade they were selling or upsetting their games of hide-and-seek by barking vigorously in the direction of whoever was "it." While the gags were rather bland, it was the artist's outstanding pen-and-ink mastery that carried *Napoleon* to the heights of popularity the strip enjoyed all through the 1930s and 1940s.

After the creator's death in 1951, his widow, Margot McBride, assumed the writing of the strip, while Roger Armstrong, McBride's longtime assistant, took over the drawing in a style almost indistinguishable from that of his predecessor. Armstrong, who was also drawing *Ella Cinders* at the time, resorted more and more to ghosts, including Ed Nofziger and Foster Moore, with the result that *Napoleon* eventually declined in quality and subsequently in readership. It finally disappeared in 1961.

M.H.

THE NAPS OF POLLY SLEEPYHEAD
1905–1906

Famed magazine cartoonist and children's-book author Peter Newell made his only recorded contribution to the comics with *The Naps of Polly Sleepyhead*, which he syndicated himself to a number of big-city newspapers (and particularly to the *New York Herald*, where it appeared in the Sunday supplement). The first of these weekly tableaux came out in June 1905.

Polly was a young girl with a wild imagination and an inclination to sleepiness, and her nightmares sprang from the last object upon which she had laid eyes before dozing off. Thus, a cat in front of the fireplace would be transformed into a huge spider ready to ensnarl her in its web; a stork on a Japanese screen would peck at her; a placid cow browsing in a meadow would be turned into a menacing monster; or the bunnies in their cage would multiply so fast they would stifle her under their numbers.

These pages were drawn in an attractive, graceful, and quite sophisticated illustrative style. Polly herself was depicted as a blonde, rather pleasant if indolent young girl whose resemblance to John Tenniel's Alice was probably not coincidental. The drawback was the lengthy narrative inserted between the pictures, which made *Polly Sleepyhead* look more like a heavily illustrated girls' book than a genuine comic strip. These conventions, carried over from

Navy Bob Steele (Starbuck and Greenwood), © 1941 McClure Syndicate

nineteenth-century picture books, were already becoming outdated by early 1900s. Furthermore, the one-note premise, despite the imaginative variations Newell played upon it, proved tiresome after a while. Its artistic excellence was not enough to save the feature, and by December 1906 it was gone.

M.H.

NAVY BOB STEELE
1939–1945

Before America's entrance into World War II on December 8, 1941, and even before the conflict had officially broken out in Europe, many newspaper strips had already taken a definite stand on the issue. As a case in point, Wilson Starbuck, a former lieutenant in the U.S. Navy during the First World War and a current novelist and playwright, in the early months of 1939 conceived the idea of a strip about authentic naval life at sea, with a view toward supporting President Franklin Roosevelt's policy of war preparedness. In the psychological wake caused by Germany's invasion of Poland later that year, the author finally sold his concept to the McClure Syndicate. Drawn by Erwin Greenwood, *Navy Bob Steele* made its bow as a Sunday half-page on November 5, 1939.

Lieutenant Robert ("Navy Bob") Steele, was a clean-cut hero with a square chin and a fleeting resemblance to movie actor Robert Young. Unlike Don Winslow, who worked mainly on matters of counterespionage, Navy Bob was a fleet officer, serving on a variety of craft in the Pacific.

His usual sidekick was fellow lieutenant Bill Sheridan; Tommy Andrews, gunner's mate first class, and Red Malone, seaman first class, rounded out the cast of regulars. During the first two years of the strip Navy Bob and his cohorts took part in such operations as dismantling a secret radio station sited on a remote Pacific island by a foreign power, and joining in naval maneuvers aimed at foiling a possible invasion of the Hawaiian islands. The foreign power was not named, but the uniforms of its officers and the markings on its planes looked suspiciously close to those of the Japanese.

On the exact day of the Pearl Harbor bombing, December 7, 1941, Navy Bob happened to be aboard a destroyer engaged in a daring rescue at sea. He was not long in joining the general fray, however, and from early 1942 on he seemed to take on the Japanese almost single-handed. His earlier adventures had displayed at least a veneer of verisimilitude, but now his exploits acquired a decidedly Hollywoodian cast, as he bagged a Japanese submarine or set up an observation post on an enemy-held island. Meanwhile, Starbuck had reenlisted in the navy with the rank of commander, and his work on *Navy Bob Steele* became more and more hurried. Late in 1944 Greenwood, who possessed a pleasant if conventional illustrative style, was replaced by William King, who had no recognizable style at all. The strip began to falter. Its main attraction—the war setting—likewise waned as the conflict in Europe came to an end and the defeat of Japan appeared certain. By the summer of 1945 *Navy Bob Steele* was gone from the newspaper page.

Among newspaper strips advocating (however covertly) American intervention in the war, *Navy Bob Steele* was partic-

The Nebbs (Hess and Carlson), © 1926 Bell Syndicate

ularly emblematic on at least two counts. In a literal sense, its timespan coincided almost exactly with the conflict's duration; while on a more contextual level the real feeling of urgency generated by the strip at the time of American neutrality seemed to evaporate as soon as the United States had entered the war, when, like so many other wartime features, it degenerated into sheer melodrama.

M.H.

THE NEBBS
1923–1946

Among the more amiable families in the early days of American comics, the Nebbs had little of the acerbic tone of such predecessors as the misanthropic Bungles in Harry Tuthill's *The Bungle Family* or the eternally bickering Joe and Vi Green in Clare Briggs's *Mr. and Mrs.* Their creator, Sol Hess, set out deliberately to avoid the caricature of the contentious American couple then common in the funnies. "In presenting the Nebb family," he wrote for their first appearance on May 22, 1923, "I will try to portray from day to day, in a humorous way, the things that happen in everyday life. The Nebbs are just a little family like thousands of other families...good, wholesome people."

According to Hess, Rudy Nebb got his name from *nebich* (now more commonly spelled *nebbish*), a Yiddish term combining pity and contempt for an ineffectual nobody. But Rudy was not the henpecked husband his name suggests; in fact, he ruled the Nebb roost—or at least his patient wife, Fanny, and two slyly perceptive children allowed him to think he did. The proprietor of a hotel–health resort, he meddled with and attempted to manipulate the manifold goings-on among his guests, usually as unsuccessfully as he dominated his family. If the humor of *The Nebbs* was often at Rudy's expense, the would-be bully never realized it . The only character who stood up to him openly—and the only one drawn from real life, according to Hess—was his good-hearted and level-headed neighbor, Max Guggenheim, an emphatic little man who was unafraid to set him straight when he needs it. Rudy never admitted being wrong, but he usually saved himself by taking Max's advice.

The family members surrounding the pompous Rudolph Nebb were believable, each with a fully developed personality. His realistic and infinitely tolerant wife Fanny accepted her husband's bluster and listened to his get-rich-

quick schemes with a good-natured smile. Betsy Nebb was a modern, knowing teenager and clearly her mother's daughter. And ten-year-old Junior was a lively, imaginative kid with an active life of his own. In the Sunday feature, which maintained separate stories, Junior often starred in his own adventures, including traveling with a circus and outwitting a gang of western desperadoes.

According to legend, Sol Hess was a successful businessman who liked to hang around cartoonists and used to provide Sidney Smith, creator of *The Gumps*, with ideas. As that earlier family strip became a national sensation and Smith offered Hess a regular job writing dialogue, Hess decided to go into business for himself, hired the artist Wallace A. Carlson (who had drawn an animated-film version of *The Gumps*), and developed *The Nebbs*. It was quickly accepted by the Bell Syndicate and became a great national favorite, appearing, according to syndicate claims, in over five hundred papers. When Hess died in 1941, his daughter Betsy and her husband Stanley Baer carried on with the scripting and Carlson continued the art, although the credit line remained "by Hess" until the strip came to an end in 1946.

The Nebbs was drawn in the somewhat primitive cartoon style of the time, the characters looking very much like those of *The Gumps;* but the layout of the panels was always handsomely composed, and the strip had a generally attractive look. The warm humor, the more or less plausible story lines, and the likable characters earned the feature a large and loyal audience.

D.W.

NED BRANT
1929–1948

One of the longest-running sports newspaper strips ever published, *Ned Brant* started existence in 1929 as a daily feature distributed by the Register and Tribune Syndicate. The writing was credited to famous University of Illinois football coach Bob Zupke, and the artwork was supplied by Bill W. Depew.

Ned Brant was a college jock and the star athlete of his alma mater, good old Carter U. (in fact the strip was initially called *Ned Brant at Carter*). A tall, blond, wholesome young man, whose only woman interest was his widowed mother, Ned triumphed in any sport he tried his hand (or his foot) at, whether it was swimming, high jumping, or the two-hundred-meter dash; he often led his teammates to victory in football, basketball, volleyball, or hockey. He was a straight arrow on the field and off, and upheld a high code of integrity, even when it meant personal sacrifice (he once lost a race to a cheating competitor rather than snitch on his dishonest rival). In other words, he was in the honored tradition of such dime-novel heroes as Burt L. Standish's Frank Merriwell. (Ironically, a comic strip based on the real thing, William Ritt and Jack Wilhelm's *Frank Merriwell's Schooldays,* lasted only three years, from 1931 to 1934.) In the early 1930s *Ned Brant* (which in the meantime had picked up a Sunday version) enjoyed enough popularity to give rise to imitations. It is probable that the radio program *Jack Armstrong the All-American Boy* (started in 1933) was inspired by *Ned Brant;* and it is more than probable that Lyman Young's *Curley Harper* (begun in 1935) was directly based on it. Ned got his own back, however, in 1939, when he started work as a reporter on his hometown paper, two years after Curley had done the same. Like most heroes of the funny pages, Ned enlisted at the time of World War II, serving in the navy during the Pacific campaign. The postwar period saw him back at school (on the GI Bill) and back into sports. In 1940 Zupke was replaced in the writing chair by George Marcoux, later succeeded by Ted Ashby. Through all these changes Depew gamely carried on in his limp, plodding style, until the strip's end in 1948.

M.H.

THE NEWLYWEDS
1904–1918, 1944–1956

George McManus's first acknowledged masterpiece, *The Newlyweds* initially appeared as a full Sunday page in Pulitzer's *New York World* on April 10, 1904.

Writing in *Cartoon Cavalcade,* Thomas Craven averred that while the battle of the sexes had been depicted with unbridled ferocity in the comic pages, "the charms of sex

The Newlyweds (G. McManus), 1907

have never found their way into American cartooning." His statement, accurate as far as it goes, could never have applied to *The Newlyweds,* where the charms of sex were indeed pretty much in evidence, albeit under the respectable cloak of connubial bliss. The interminable cooing between Mr. and Mrs. Newlywed (who called themselves by such names as "lovely" and "dearie") drove most of their friends and relatives to distraction. Hubby was fond of writing love poems to his wife (one such ended with the lines, "Oh let me press thee to my heart / And we will never part"), while Wifey would buy small gifts for her husband (like a recording of Caruso singing Puccini's aria "Addio, mio dolce amor," which she presented to Hubby before leaving on a seaside trip with her mother).

After a suitable waiting period, starting in January 1906, when *The Newlyweds* disappeared from the comic pages, the inevitable result of such passion showed up on May 19, 1907, heralded by a change of title, to *The Newlyweds—Their Baby* (and later to *The Newlyweds and Their Baby*). The infant (known as Snookums), with his one tooth, bulb nose, and moronic expression, had a face only a mother could love. His parents indulged his every whim, and for the remainder of McManus's tenure the baby's tantrums constituted the mainspring for the gags.

In 1912 McManus left Pulitzer for Hearst, and *The Newlyweds* was continued in close approximation of McManus's style by Albert Carmichael until the latter's death in 1917. Meanwhile McManus had revived his characters on September 1, 1912, in a Sunday page titled *Their Only Child.* Again the obnoxious baby was at the center of the action (such as it was), and his idiotic pranks would elicit cries of delight from his deluded parents and dark mutterings from his helpless victims (some of whom would try to do the nefarious infant in). The Newlywed family's tribulations ended in 1918, when *Bringing Up Father* was permanently established on the Sunday page. That the American public preferred the jaundiced view of married life expressed in *Bringing Up Father* to the rosy picture presented by *The Newlyweds* is in itself a social comment of no small importance.

The family made one last appearance, on November 19, 1944, under the title *Snookums,* as the companion piece to *Bringing Up Father.* The former baby was allowed to grow up without his parents (now middle-aged and renamed Wedlock!) stopping to dote upon him. The strip survived its creator's death in 1954, and only ended its long career on December 30, 1956. (In its last years it had been drawn by Frank Fletcher.)

M.H.

NIBSY THE NEWSBOY
1905–1906

Among George McManus's early gems, *Nibsy the Newsboy* must take pride of place, short-lived as it was. Started in April 1905 in the pages of Joseph Pulitzer's *New York World,* it only lasted to late July 1906, but in the course of its brief existence it displayed the cartoonist's talent at its most extravagant.

The strip dealt with the outlandish adventures of a young

newspaper vendor who found himself transported each Sunday from the streets of New York to the strange byways of the kingdom of Fairyland. All it took was a complacent fairy, and these apparently could be found at every corner and in many guises: it could be a cop, a fruit peddler, a street cleaner. Once in the place, the skinny boy in a brown derby would check out the situation, and whatever it was—a mob riot, a prolonged drought, an epidemic of sneezing sickness—he somehow managed to make it worse before beating it back to his station in downtown Manhattan.

After *Little Nemo in Slumberland* began its run in the *Herald* in October 1905, McManus turned his strip into an affectionate spoof of Winsor McCay's masterpiece, even amplifying its name to *Nibsy the Newsboy in Funny Fairyland*. The king of Fairyland was meek and slow-witted, his wife a surly battle-ax, and his daughter, the princess, an ugly harridan. McManus's drawings were as elaborate and detailed as McCay's, but the backgrounds were slightly askew, the colors subtly off-key, and the characters caricatural to the point of grotesquery. All in all, this was a very funny strip, beautiful to boot, whose run was regrettably all too short.

M.H.

NIPPER
See SCHOOL DAYS

NIZE BABY
1927–1930

In addition to being a prolific cartoonist, Milt Gross was also a screenwriter (he worked on Charlie Chaplin's *The Circus*, most notably), a raconteur, a book writer, and a newspaper columnist. It was in his columns for the *New York World* that he first recounted the adventures of the Jewish Feitelbaum family in their new home in America. In 1926 some of his columns were reprinted in book form with the title *Nize Baby*, which later also became the name of Gross's newspaper page that started appearing on Sunday, January 2, 1927, under syndication by the *World*'s Press Publishing Company.

The family—composed of Mama or Mom Feitelbaum, a middle-aged woman of ample size; her short, bald-headed husband, Morris; their grown son, Looy (better known as "Looy Dot Dope"); their six-year-old, Isidore; and Nize Baby—all lived in a big-city tenement. The Feitelbaums were a dysfunctional family even before the term was invented. Isidore, instead of minding the baby as he had been instructed, would always get distracted by something or other and leave his infant brother to his own devices, with catastrophic results. On these occasions he would receive a severe tanning by his incensed father, while Mama admonished from the sidelines, "Morris, not on de head!" As for Looy Dot Dope, he would always involve the family in his harebrained get-rich schemes and be rewarded with kicks in the pants or flower vases thrown at his head.

Gross sprinkled the dialogue with liberal doses of Yiddish dialect. "Morris I got to put to sleep de baby," was Mama's plaintive refrain, while her husband would smack Isidore around for chewing tobacco, all the time exclaiming, "A cooke-snuffer you'll grow opp maybe, ha?" *Nize Baby* was drawn in a style as idiosyncratic as the language, with perspective all askew and odd-shaped houses, sidewalks, and trees. The page prematurely ended in February 1929.

A daily strip called *The Feitelbaum Family* had meanwhile come into being shortly after the start of the Sunday page. Focusing on the nefarious doings of the elder scion of the family, it had its title changed to *Looy Dot Dope* in 1930, after Gross had left in the wake of the *World*'s collapse. Distributed by United Feature Syndicate, it was drawn first by Johnny Devlin, a former Gross assistant, and later by Bernard Dibble. In its latter incarnation the strip had no longer any connection to Gross's inspired creation, and it is here mentioned for the sake of completeness.

M.H.

NORBERT
1964–1983

This unique and funny comic by former engineer and sportsman George Fett began syndication as *Sniffy* on June 29, 1964. Based on the city-wise pets he owned, the all-animal cast initially consisted of a motley gang of neighborhood dogs: Sniffy (named for Fett's pet beagle), Sniffy's mischievous nephew Caesar, his lanky pal Charley, and the curly-topped love interest, Queenie. Also along were Clyde the cat, Big John, a mouse who had a penchant for homemade wine, and a large-billed "Ooh" bird, aptly named for his painful exclaims during bumpy landings.

The strip was very crudely drawn at first, but Fett quickly honed his concise and unique cartoony style, which perfectly suited the zany, farcical nature of his humor. His direct delivery mirrored the successful format comanded previously by Johnny Hart in *B.C.* Fett's strip lacked Hart's philosophical or theological context, relying more on situational humor than distinctive characterization.

As the sixties progressed, so did the increasing number of cast members. Added was Hervy the horse, who became the bird's comedic partner, menacing Albert the bulldog, who added opposition and competition to Charley's futile courtship of fickle Queenie. There were also Sam the near-sighted, unkempt sheepdog, and a menagerie of talking fish, frogs, rabbits, insects, and even flowers that appeared regularly.

Norbert (G. Fett), © George Fett

On January 3, 1966, an orphan pup was left on Sniffy's doorstep, who exclaimed, "I think I've been had." That sentiment was prophetic, as Little No-No replaced Caesar and soon became the focus of attention, sharing the strip's title in *Little No-No and Sniffy* by 1970. Simultaneously, Sniffy ceased appearing, allowing the more defined characters Uncle Charley and No-No to gradually develop a father-and-son-like relationship. In 1973 No-No was being called Norbert, and again the strip was retitled accordingly. Finally, the human element was introduced, as a boy named Sydney and his playmate Cynthia added a more conventional context. Now the final cast was intact, and more traditional situations of a milder sort complemented the increasing domestication that dominated this later period.

Only a daily release and never widely syndicated by Bell-McClure or later by United Feature Syndicate in 1972, the strip met with more success abroad than domestically. Three Australian paperbacks were published in the early 1970s, and much character-related merchandise appeared in Japan later that decade.

Tired and shaky, Fett's final strip appeared on January 2, 1982, when *Winthrop* cartoonist Dick Cavalli took over. Although an accomplished artist and gag writer, Cavalli's treatment was rather static and lacked the raucous spontaneity that earmarked the old strip in its prime. This canine comic appeared for the last time on September 26, 1983. George Fett was a solid humorist whose hilarious comic quietly helped cement the conventions of the contemporary humor strip. His best work deserves rediscovery.

B.J.

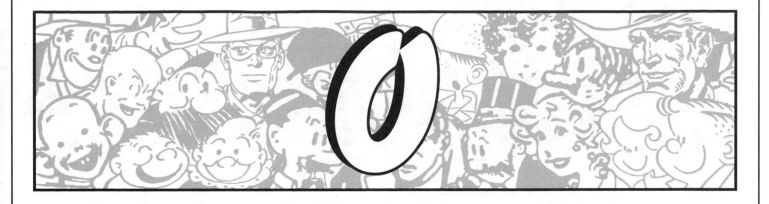

OAKY DOAKS
1935–1961

In the mid-1930s the AP Feature Service was enjoying a modest success with its stable of newspaper strips (of which *Scorchy Smith* was the star). To spruce up the line-up a little, William T. McCleery, the AP's comics editor, thought of a humorous continuity strip set in medieval times that would ally good-natured parody with tongue-in-cheek adventure, somewhat along the lines of Mark Twain's *A Connecticut Yankee in King Arthur's Court.* Ralph Briggs Fuller, an already established magazine illustrator and cartoonist, was chosen as the artist on the new feature; titled *Oaky Doaks,* it made its bow as a daily strip on June 17, 1935.

Oaky Doaks himself was the antithesis of Prince Valiant, whom he preceded by some two years. A lowly ploughboy, he had decided to take up the lance as a knight errant, somewhat in the manner of Don Quixote, mounted on his faithful mare Nellie, as the Don was on Rosinante. He found his Sancho Panza in King Cedric, a dumpy monarch more interested in food and women than in ruling his kingdom, and later in King Cornelius (Corny for short) of Uncertainia. Many episodic characters, all delineated with a sure hand, appeared in turn in this leisurely paced saga, from bumbling sheriffs to goofy highwaymen and ineffectual wizards. Best of all were the many women strewn across Oaky's path, most of them fast and breezy damsels whom Fuller loved to depict as long-legged and full-breasted lovelies.

The zany character of the strip was established early on, with the titular hero masquerading as a shepherd; asked how many sheep he was tending, Oaky earnestly answered he didn't know, because he would fall asleep every time he started counting them. The continuities for the first two years were written by McCleery, and then by M. J. Wing, before devolving to Fuller in 1938. Hal Foster's *Prince Valiant* had made a spectacular newspaper entrance the previous year, and Fuller, now in full control of his strip, launched into a full-blown parody of tales of chivalry in general and *Valiant* in particular. There were jousting tournaments, fights against dragons, and encounters with brigands a-plenty, without anybody getting killed or even seriously hurt.

Oaky's adventures sometimes paralleled Prince Val's. In 1939, for instance, while Valiant was fighting the invading Saxons, Oaky was engaged in repulsing the dreaded invaders known as the Zoobies, whose king, to avert possible conspiracies, had a corner on every conceivable position in Zoobia. "Here iss da chudge!," he would declare to Oaky on trial for high treason. "I also iss da chury.... Da verdict iss guilty!" The spoofing became even more evident when Oaky in the 1940s traveled to Camelot, and experienced a string of daffy adventures in the company of King Arthur, Merlin, Launcelot, and other Round Table stalwarts.

In 1941 a Sunday page was added, with continuities kept separate from those of the dailies. Fuller wrote the scripts, but the artwork was provided by Bill Dyer until 1944. From that time on, Fuller kept supplying a double dose of mock-medieval shenanigans for the duration of the feature, art and story, weekdays and Sundays. Like Prince Valiant again, Oaky finally settled down, marrying King Corny's daughter, Pomona, who gave him a son. *Oaky Doaks* proved one of the most popular of AP's strips, ending only when the press association closed down its syndicate operation in 1961.

M.H.

Oaky Doaks (R. B. Fuller), © 1939 AP Feature Service

OH, DIANA
1940–1957

While Harry Haenigsen's *Penny* is usually credited as the first of the bobby-soxer comics that sprouted up throughout the 1940s, it was preceded by quite a few years

Oh, Diana (V. Clark), © 1944 AP Feature Service

script outfits. The approach had been devised to attract older women readers, and it apparently worked, since *Oh, Diana* gained additional circulation along with a Sunday page in the latter half of the 1940s. Clark's work on the feature drew praise from Coulton Waugh, who commented somewhat patronizingly that she "has proved that a woman cartoonist can turn in an excellent job."

In the 1950s Clark left *Oh, Diana,* and the strip coasted along for a few more years under the helmsmanship of Phil Berube before coming to an end in 1957.

M.H.

by *Oh, Diana,* an obscure strip (but not without merit) started in 1940 by Don Flowers. Syndicated initially by AP Newsfeatures as a daily, it added a Sunday page later in the decade.

Diana was an auburn-haired, long-legged teenage girl of about 17 who lived at home with Mom and Pop, and whose (usually) mild antics always elicited from her rotund, pipe-smoking father the resigned reproof "Oh, Diana," which became the strip's mantra. While all his older characters were caricatures, Flowers, who had been drawing the daily pin-up panel *Modest Maidens* for the previous ten years, generally graced his young women with a healthy dose of sex appeal. Even Diana's homely girlfriend Kitty, who by her own admission had a face "that curdles cold cream," possessed a shapely figure she wasn't loath to display on occasion.

At the end of 1941 Flowers got the opportunity to do a full-color *Modest Maidens* Sunday page and, deciding his workload had become too heavy, left *Oh, Diana* in the hands of his former assistant, Bill Champs, who tried as best he could to maintain the Flowers look for the two years of his tenure. Early in 1944 the feature passed into the hands of Virginia Clark, who under the nom-de-plume Virginia Huget had drawn a number of flapper strips through the 1920s and 1930s (*Campus Capers, Babs in Society,* etc.). Clark proceeded to take the strip away from its exclusively teenage trappings. For starters she made her characters somewhat older (Diana was now a "junior college gal") and put them in "smartly styled clothes," in contrast to their younger bobby-sox sisters who were usually seen in nonde-

OLD DOC YAK
1912–1919, 1930–1935

Sidney Smith's *Old Doc Yak* had its origins in an earlier newspaper strip the artist had turned out for the *Chicago Examiner.* Started in 1908, it featured an anthropomorphized and penurious goat appropriately named Buck Nix, who was perpetually in search of the bucks he didn't have. An early example of Smith's obsession with money, *Buck Nix* was terminated when its author moved to the *Chicago Tribune.* At the *Tribune* Smith basically recycled the themes and conceits of his earlier strip, changing his goat character into a yak and renaming the feature—which started its run as a Sunday page on March 10, 1912—*Old Doc Yak.*

As in *Buck Nix,* many of the plots in *Old Doc Yak* revolved around the financial problems of the bearded Doc, whose get-rich-quick schemes always backfired on him, and who had a hard time providing shelter and subsistence for himself and his small son, Yutch. Doc's only consolation was his dilapidated speedster that proudly displayed the plate number "348" on its front bumper. (Once, to raise money for the rent, Yak tried to auction off his beloved car, but the highest he was bid was one dime.) For a couple of years there also was an *Old Doc Yak* daily strip, which often went in for lengthy continuities. In February 1917, Yak, unable to pay the rent, skipped out of town and out of the strip, with a new family moving into the vacated space the next Monday—the Gumps. The process was repeated a few years later, when Smith in June 1919 closed down the *Doc Yak*

Old Doc Yak (S. Smith), 1917

Sunday to make room for the newly minted weekly color version of *The Gumps*.

After an absence of more than ten years, *Old Doc Yak* made its comeback on December 7, 1930, as an adjunct to the *Gumps* Sunday page. This revived version consisted of a four-panel strip, generally running at the bottom of the page, whose gags mainly involved Yak in a repeated duel of wits with his constant nemesis, a crotchety black bear variously named Metzler and Greisheim. By hook and by crook the bear would always win the contest, whereupon he would hit Yak on the behind with any instrument at hand (baseball bat, two-by-four, pick handle, etc.) and then skedaddle, laughingly exclaiming, "That's fun!" In October 1935 Smith was killed in a car accident, and *Old Doc Yak* did not long survive him, coming to an end on December 8, 1935.

M.H.

THE OLD GLORY STORY
1953–1965

At the height of the anticomics crusade of the 1950s, the Chicago Tribune–New York News Syndicate launched a Sunday half-page devoted to American history in order to try to prove that comic strips could be educational. Written by historian Athena Robbins and illustrated by *Tribune* stalwart Rick Fletcher, *The Old Glory Story* made its debut in May 1953.

True to its title, *Old Glory* focused principally on U.S. military history. The events of the Revolutionary War and of the War of 1812 were briefly recounted, but the feature soon placed greatest emphasis on the opening and conquest of the West, and the role played by the U.S. Army in this context. The scripts were fairly accurate as far as they went, but since this was before the days of political correctness, there was more attention paid to military exploits than to the plight of the Indians. The strip garnered a number of awards and medals from such organizations as the American Veterans Association, the American Legion, and the Freedom Foundation, but despite all these kudos circulation remained weak outside the feature's home papers.

What gave the series a boost were the Civil War centennial celebrations, starting in 1961. Robbins and Fletcher were not long in cashing in on the festivities, coming up with the more relevant title *Old Glory at the Crossroads* and giving a week-by-week, blow-by-blow description of the events, beginning with the cannonade at Fort Sumter, long before PBS had thought of latching onto the same concept. Fletcher had become quite adept at battle scenes by that time, and he displayed special illustrative flair in the depiction of such military highlights as Pickett's charge at Gettysburg, the duel between the *Monitor* and the *Merrimac*, and, inevitably, the burning of Atlanta. The timing proved excellent, and *Old Glory* picked up a goodly number of additional newspapers, especially in the South. The Civil War eventually came to an end, as did the centennial, and the papers that had come on board at the beginning of the conflict started to peel off after the close; in the summer of 1965 *Old Glory* was finally struck down.

M.H.

OLIVER'S ADVENTURES
1927–1934

Oliver's Adventures constituted a first for both Gus Mager, who created it, and the McNaught Syndicate, which distributed it: it was the first straight adventure strip ever attempted by either of them. Running daily only, it debuted in February 1927.

Mager, better noted for his depictions of humanized monkeys and other animals, found himself at pains to come up with a suitable illustrative style for *Oliver,* and his work on the strip looked labored and unconvincing. Like his namesake in Dickens's novel, Oliver was an orphan, and after undergoing the obligatory indignities at the hands of black-hearted guardians and cruel landlords, in true comic-strip fashion he went roaming the world. His adventures took place on land, at sea, and principally in the air, in the company of a daredevil pilot named Captain Breeze. In the 1930s, at a time when other cartoonists were rushing their characters into heroic action, Mager reverted his strip, now renamed *Oliver and His Dog,* to the setting of a conventional kid comic feature.

Oliver came to a close at the end of 1934 and is hardly remembered today. As one of the early attempts at defining the parameters of the modern adventure strip, it deserves mention, however misguided it turned out to be in execution.

M.H.

ON STAGE
1957–1979

After submitting several comic-strip ideas to various syndicates, Leonard Starr succeeded in 1956 in placing *On Stage* with the Chicago Tribune–New York Daily News, and the strip made its debut on February 10,1957. The title was later changed to *Mary Perkins on Stage* with the December 17, 1961, Sunday page. However, at the end of 1979, the syndicate decided to end Mary Perkins's career, since Leonard Starr was to revive the *Little Orphan Annie* strip, following the musical's smash hit on Broadway two years earlier and the forthcoming John Huston film.

Mary Perkins, a cheerleader and beauty queen from a small town, was typical of so many star-struck young women who moved to New York City to find fame in the theater. What distinguished her from her fellow actresses was the genuine wonderment with which she looked at life around her and accepted her good fortune. That, despite disappointments and reverses, she was easily and quickly able to land parts on Broadway, in summer stock, and in Hollywood only reinforced her idea of how welcoming the theater is at bottom. Her initial naiveté was just as evident when she met unsavory characters whose intentions toward her were far from pure. Whether these people were insensitive directors, unscrupulous producers, ambitious understudies, or mad Phantoms of the Opera, they were portrayed with flair and intelligence, for Starr never turned them into clichés or caricatures. And solid protagonists, like her talented black music coach and other dedicated

On Stage (L. Starr), © 1957 Chicago Tribune

performers, further contributed to the reader's interest in this most fascinating world.

In addition to her work on stage and in movies, Mary enjoyed a full sentimental life, mostly with Pete Fletcher, a very successful photojournalist whom she met a few months after her arrival in New York, and Johnny Q., a handsome gangster who rescued her from a movie producer's dishonest designs. She finally married Pete in Switzerland on December 13, 1959, in a German-language civil ceremony. Together or separately, a distinctly more mature Mary and her husband participated in exciting, even thrilling adventures as they shuttled between the worlds of show business and of magazines, whose glitter and glamour and romance Starr faithfully recreated.

The plots were entertaining and skillfully developed, the backstage atmosphere realistic, the dialogue sophisticated, and the characters, especially the women, well drawn, and none more so, of course, than dark-haired Mary Perkins. From the bubbly, good-looking ingenue with the turned-up nose and doelike eyes, who upon seeing Times Square and its traffic, stores, crowds, and neon lights for the first time exclaimed, "Glory! The Great White Way!" under a policeman's amused look, she became a beautiful and elegant woman, full of poise and self-assurance, and with a new hairdo to frame the classic shape of her face. If at first Mary's physical charms were often emphasized (smoothing her stockings while dressed in a black slip or seductively soaking in a tub and washing her leg), she soon was given a more demure conduct, especially after her marriage, although roles might still require her to show her thighs and cleavage. She in fact exemplified a certain type of modern woman: plucky yet vulnerable, idealistic yet open-eyed, considerate of others' feelings yet unwilling to be taken advantage of.

Because love and its vicissitudes were not its main concerns, *Mary Perkins* can almost be considered an adventure strip rather than a soap opera through its use of suspense, humor, irony, and even poetic language. As for its art, Starr's photographic realism, evolved from Hal Foster's

romanticism and Milton Caniff's impressionist realism, was highly polished, with startling wide-angled black-and-white renderings of cityscapes and backgrounds. Understandably, therefore, the National Cartoonists Society presented him with the Best Story Strip award in 1960 and the Reuben Award in 1965.

P.H.

OUR BOARDING HOUSE
1921–1984

The pretender and mountebank has been a popular target for writers of comedy from Aristophanes to Neil Simon. In the comics the type had been used in several Herriman and Segar creations, but never was it delineated with more finality than in *Our Boarding House,* created by Gene Ahern as a daily panel for NEA Service in September 1921.

Just as in a Neil Simon play, Ahern initially based his vignettes of life in *Our Boarding House* on his recollections as a boarder in exactly that kind of an establishment during his hungry years as an art student in Chicago. The action—what there was of it—revolved round the schemings and bickerings of the various boarders, who ranged from shoe salesmen to bank clerks, and their encounters with the implacable Martha, owner of the place and a woman of formidable size and forbidding mien. The series changed character early the next year with the irruption of Major Amos B. Hoople, the landlady's errant husband, whose personality soon came to dominate the proceedings. Hoople has been compared to the type created on-screen by W. C. Fields, but he was probably closer to Falstaff. A retired military man of dubious achievement like Shakespeare's Sir John, he boasted of soldierly exploits that were perhaps not all invented, and his buffoonery sometimes concealed real pathos. Like Falstaff again "in the waist two yards about," with his florid manner of speech and his extravagant claims, Hoople cut an imposing, if bogus, figure, and his larger-than-life persona proved to be an instant hit with the readers.

Our Boarding House (W. Freyse), ca. 1940, © NEA Service

The first signs of success appeared in 1924 when a Sunday page was added to the daily panel. In a series of weekly gags, with Hoople often the butt of children's jokes, Ahern tried to get out of the confines of the boarding house and spice up the proceedings with zany scenes and multipanel action. The result was only a mitigated success. From October 1931 on, *The Nut Bros.* ran as an adjunct to the main feature. It was truly an inspired creation in the tradition of old vaudeville turns, wherein the two nutty siblings (named Ches and Wal for emphasis) engaged in loony bits of business and in no less outrageous puns.

Meanwhile the daily panel forged claustrophobically on. Under the pressure of popular success the author reduced Hoople from the complex character he originally was to the one-dimensional figure of fun most people remember today. In the process he placed the Major squarely in a long line of American schemers who, as Stephen Becker perceptively observed, "have an eye for the main chance; and...stubbornly refuse to believe that hard work is better than quick wits." A high-flown windbag as well as a hollow dreamer, Hoople would often hold forth in the parlor of the boarding house on any subject under the sun, harumphing his way around any logical objection that might be put to him. His disquisitions were always met with a chorus of jeers from a trio of cynical boarders named Clyde, Buster, and Mack, whose clear-sightedness did not extend to their own self-delusions. In the course of the years Ahern also expanded his small cast of characters, adding the Major's irksome nephew Alvin and scapegrace brother Jake to the Hoople family tree.

In 1936 Ahern left NEA for King Features, and *Our Boarding House* passed into the hands of a bewildering array of artists and writers whose enumeration would be too fastidious. Succeeding Wood Cowan and Bela "Bill" Zaboly, Bill Freyse was the artist most closely associated with the feature, which he drew from 1939 until the time of his death in 1969. After a brief stint by Jim Branagan, Les Carroll took over in 1971 as the next and, as it turned out, the last cartoonist to draw *Our Boarding House*. The Sundays were discontinued on March 29, 1981, and the daily panel came to an end on December 22, 1984.

M.H.

OUR NEIGHBORS
See THE RIPPLES

OUT OUR WAY
1921–1977

James Robert Williams was one of the shrewdest and most versatile cartoonists of the first half of this century, and his "way" was the multifaceted American way of life. In daily panels produced for NEA Service from November 22, 1921, until his death in 1957, he created a warm and perceptive panorama of many aspects of everyday existence. The recurring tag lines under which *Out Our Way* appeared included "Curly and the Cowboys," featuring vignettes of western ranch life; "The Bull of the Woods," a

Out Our Way (J. R. Williams), © 1930 NEA Service

much-loved feature set in a machine shop; "Heroes Are Made—Not Born," a sympathetic series on the vicissitudes of growing up; "Born Thirty Years Too Soon," an often poignant evocation of home life in the early 1900s; "The Worry Wart," featuring the mishaps of an irresistibly slovenly youngest child; and "Why Mothers Get Gray," the definitive picture of a warm nuclear family and the harassed mother who holds it all together. Together these engaging little sagas were among the most popular newspaper features in America; in 1940 *Out Our Way* was carried in 725 daily and 230 Sunday papers, reportedly more than any other comic in the world.

Williams's many popular family-centered panels had such wide appeal that NEA persuaded him to create—or, at least, to authorize—a Sunday strip during the first year of their association. In 1921 he expanded the little domestic comedies and near tragedies of the Willit family, featured in "Why Mothers Get Gray," into a full half-page. Williams signed the strip, but he is generally credited only with supervising its weekly production, and indeed it lacked the trenchancy of his daily panels. The Sunday strip was initially done by Neg Cochran, who took over the daily "Why Mothers Get Gray" panels after Williams died; subsequent artists who worked on the strip include Paul Gringle, Ed Sullivan, and Walt Wetterberg. From the beginning, the ghosted strips were gracefully drawn, with a tidy, cleaned-up look, and lacked the endearingly blowzy charm that characterized Williams's visual style.

Running under the title *Out Our Way, with the Willits,* the Sunday feature related the cozy domestic dramas of a middle-class suburban family whose squabbles generally centered on the efforts of its children to escape their household chores. Willis and Lillian, the Willit teenagers, were in constant conflict, with their parents and with each other, but it never went very deep, and the blustering complaints of their long-suffering parents had no real acrimony.

The bland *Out Our Way, with the Willits* outlived by some twenty years the many panel series that earned Williams his reputation, but those features have contributed an enduring gallery of homespun characters to our literature. As *Time* magazine wrote of Williams in 1940, *Out Our Way's* "homely humanity, black realism, and salty, Mark Twainish humor have attracted the attention of Americana-collecting high-brows [and] have earned for is author the title 'Will Rogers of the Comic Strip.'"

D.W.

OUTLAND
1989–1995

On Sunday, September 3, 1989, Berke Breathed's much-awaited sequel to *Bloom County* appeared. Called *Outland*, it was distributed only as a weekly page by the Washington Post Writers Group.

The author himself described *Outland* as a country for "those who don't fit in," half nightmarish dystopia, half escapist fantasy. The main protagonist was a little black girl named Ronald-Ann Smith, who had sought refuge there from all the calamities of urban ghetto life; she was soon joined by Mortimer Mouse, Mickey's brother and stunt double, who after forty-five years of knocking around Europe had returned to the Walt Disney studio (asking for his old job back, he got his ear chewed up—literally—by Michael Eisner). A few weeks into the strip, the first of the old Bloom County denizens dropped in unannounced in the form of Opus the penguin looking for his mother. (Upon learning she was detained in Sea Jamboree Marine Park, California, he mounted a hilarious rescue operation to get her out on Christmas Day.)

The trouble with the strip was that it tried to go in several directions at once. On a purely artistic level, it was a sometimes stunning, sometimes incomprehensible fantasy, harking back to the innovative, unfettered tradition of the early funnies, with shifting landscapes evocative of Herriman's *Krazy Kat*, and odd perspectives reminiscent of McCay's *Little Nemo*. On another, more topical, level, it was a cartoon of social commentary, with sarcastic references to George Bush, Dan Quayle, Leona Helmsley, and Bill Gates. It was a humor strip last of all, only occasionally rising to moments of inspired zaniness, such as Opus filling out his census form and putting down "Antarctic-American" as his ethnic origin.

Such a departure from Breathed's earlier gag-filled feature soon alienated a large part of the cartoonist's public, and the number of subscribing newspapers began to drop alarmingly when compared to the circulation of *Bloom County*. As a way to alleviate the situation, more characters were brought back from the old strip: Bill the Cat after a few months, followed by Steve Dallas, now married and turned househusband; Binkley and Cutter John also made cameo appearances in what was turning into a demented version of *Bloom County*. Nothing helped; *Outland*, like so many other noble experiments, went unappreciated. In January 1995, the author announced the strip's demise in these terms: "There are more stories to discover and, if permitted, I shall spend much of my life telling them in places other than the newspaper funny page—a great American story in itself, shrunken in size and buffeted by new technology, still bravely resisting its own ending." The last page appeared on March 26, 1995.

M.H.

OVERBOARD
1990–present

Neither the nautical setting nor the character types of *Overboard* were particularly new when Universal Press Syndicate began distribution of Chip Dunham's strip in July 1990, but the ingenious fusion of contemporary concerns and vocabulary with the life of a band of eighteenth-century pirates was an inspired idea. *Overboard* does for pirates exactly what Dik Browne's *Hagar the Horrible* and Brant Parker's *Crock* do for Vikings and Foreign Legionnaires. A wryly witty strip, it examines the latest preoccupations with a modern sensibility, and with all the latest buzzwords, but in the voices of a band of cutthroats.

The cast of *Overboard* is the crew of the good ship *Revenge*, a gang that would have made Blackbeard go into some other line of work. Their captain, Henry Crow, is not exactly the scourge of the Seven Seas; he ties himself up trying to untangle a piece of rope, sails into the polar seas looking for Jamaica, and immerses himself in the owner's manual as his ship sinks. But if the captain seems ill-suited to his profession, his men are even more unlikely as pirates. Seahawk and Charley, the Duffy brothers, refuse to take their swords ashore on a raid because "when you take swords along, people wanna fight you—plus, there's always a chance of an accident cuz the dumb things are so sharp." Another crew member, Boof, notes with alarm that "this big metal anchor thing in the water is getting totally *wet*" (prompting Captain Crow to ask his mate, "You ever get the feeling that some of these guys lied on their resumés?"). The huge, bearded Nate, who conducts seminars in knife fighting, holds sharks' heads underwater till they get mad and then wrestles them, prompting Seahawk to observe, "And the guy wonders why he's uninsurable." Two unnamed figures in the crow's nest, known to captain and crew as "the two crow's nest guys" and distinguished visually by their polka-dot pirate hats, conduct their own private war with reality.

A blend of slapstick action, absurd anachronism, and witty banter, all rendered in a loose, sketchy style appropriate to its broad humor, *Overboard* was nominated for the Best Newspaper Comic Strip award by the National Cartoonists Society in 1991.

D.W.

OZARK IKE
1945–1958

Well before the likes of Beau Jackson, Ozark Ike McBatt of Wildweed Run, nestled in the Ozark mountains, not only excelled at baseball and football but also played some basketball on the side. A highly successful continuity sports strip created and drawn by sports car-

Ozark Ike (R. Gotto), © 1947 King Features Syndicate

toonist Ray Gotto, *Ozark Ike* was sold to King Features Syndicate and began on November 12, 1945, running until September 1958, although Gotto himself left the strip in 1954. The cartoonist subsequently started a new baseball strip, *Cotton Woods*, which did not enjoy the same success; he then went on to a celebrated career with *Sporting News*.

Notwithstanding some similarities to *Li'l Abner* (the heroes of both strips were simple country boys with gor-

geous girlfriends who sported long blonde hair and nearly identical form-fitting outfits), *Ozark Ike* eventually focused more on sports than on the hillbilly world of Ozark's origin. Thus the Hatfields-and-McCoys-style backwoods feud between the Fatfields and McBatts—the families of Dinah, Ozark's girl, and Ozark, respectively—settled annually by a football match billed as the "Football Brawl," faded from view, with the Fatfields making only occasional appearances thereafter.

Further in contrast to Abner, who successfully escaped marriage with Daisy Mae for years, Ozark, who played Romeo to Dinah's Juliet, actually wanted to marry the voluptuous Dinah rather than avoid matrimonial bonds. It was only the obstacles of their warring families' running feud, and later, when the rural setting was phased out, Ozark's lack of money (often as a result of underhanded behavior toward this naive, kindhearted rube) that kept the couple from wedded bliss.

Gotto drew in a bold cartoon style, and it has been said that some of his best artwork was done in his Wildweed Run sequences, with great attention paid to complex and intricate crisp detail. The sports sequences, on the other hand, were cleaner, so as not to obstruct the action and excitement of a ball speeding from the pitcher's mound or on the way literally out of its panel off the bat of the lanky left-fielder or that of one of his Bugs teammates.

The suspense of not knowing whether a runner was safe or out, a long fly was caught, or a ball was fair or foul till the next day pointed up Gotto's yarn-spinning talent and ability to hold the reader's interest. When Gotto moved on, the strip was taken over by Bill Lignante, but it ended, after a few more years, in 1958.

M.B.C.

PA'S SON-IN-LAW
1914–1942

Charles H. Wellington was drawing political cartoons and doing general illustrations for the *New York Evening Mail* in 1914 when he saw an opportunity to do a regular daily feature for the McClure Syndicate. The social-climbing, nouveau-riche family was already providing a rich vein of humor in those days of a burgeoning economy, and Wellington chose to mine it with a strip called *Pa's Imported Son-in-Law*. Taking many hints from George McManus's popular *Bringing Up Father*, begun the year before, Wellington created the Splutterfuss family, including the huge, masterful Ma, her dwarfish husband, the Pa of the title, and their foppish, upper-class son-in-law, Cedric, a monocled, elegantly clad Englishman who catered to Ma's fantasy of acceptance by the British upper crust. Hopelessly obtuse, Cedric spoke in what Americans believed to be an aristocratic dialect and, apparently like all members of his island race, was always pictured wearing spats.

As *Pa's Son-in-Law* had taken its masterful, status-seeking matriarch from *Bringing Up Father*, it was in debt to Cliff Sterrett's strip *Polly and Her Pals* for its character Woe-Sin, Pa's droll Chinese servant. Like Neewah, the servant of Polly's Pa, Woe-Sin was sympathetic to his diminutive employer's problems, and although his command of the English language was tenuous, he was wise to the ways of the world. Addressing all non-Asians with the title "Missy," and always speaking of himself in the third person, he repeatedly introduced schemes to Missy Pa with the words "Woe-Sin ketchee idee." That his ideas usually backfired was no reflection on his cunning, but rather on the hopelessness of trying to escape Missy Ma's powerful authority.

The graphic style of *Pa's Son-in-Law* was no less derivative than its characters. Wellington's figures were broadly drawn and conventional cartoon stereotypes, and they were usually posed in stiff tableaux. But the compositions of the panels were usually clean, well balanced, and simple, and the general look of the strip was reasonably attractive.

When Wellington left the *Evening Mail* during Pa's first year, the strip was maintained by Ed Carey under the name *Pa's Family and Their Friends,* but Wellington resumed it for the *New York Tribune,* restoring the focus on the contrast between Pa and Cedric by calling it *That Son-in-Law of Pa's!* The strip's nomenclatural variability finally came to an end when the title was fixed as *Pa's Son-in-Law* shortly afterward. In 1920, Wellington took the strip to the New York Herald-Tribune Syndicate, where it remained a moderately popular feature for the rest of a career spanning more than a quarter of a century.

D.W.

PANCHITO
See WALT DISNEY'S SUNDAY PAGES

Pa's Son-in-Law (Pa's Family and Their Friends; E. Carey), 1916

PANHANDLE PETE
1904–1907

The first decade of this century was one of feverish comic-strip creation, and no cartoonist was more feverishly at work than young George McManus. Among the many features he contributed to the *New York World*, *Panhandle Pete* is one that shines bright. It started publication on Sunday, February 28, 1904, one short month after McManus's twentieth birthday.

As his name suggested, Pete was a tramp, and he proved as wise at his avocation as Happy Hooligan was innocent. He knew how to put the touch on credulous hayseeds, dim-witted farm wives, and suspicious burghers alike with his hard-luck stories. Pot-bellied, unshaven, and in tatters, he cut the sorriest figure of any comic-strip bum, past, present, and to come. His small-time connivings made way in late 1905 to bigger game. In raucous adventures extending from Sunday to Sunday, Pete and his two fellow vagabonds, a wiry, tall hobo named Cecil and a short, fat one who remained nameless, swindled their way around the globe, pocketing prize money for races they won by hook and crook, and even taking over whole native kingdoms.

Each Sunday page was replete with incident and detail, and peopled with a weird assortment of vaguely recognizable human characters, and hardly recognizable animals. Ending on October 13, 1907, in the pages of the *World* (it may have continued for a while longer in lesser outlets), *Panhandle Pete* constituted for the three years of its run one of the more fascinatingly bizarre creations to come out of the comics pages.

M.H.

PATORUZU
1941–1949

The first comic strip ever carried by the liberal New York newspaper *P.M.* (starting in August 1941), *Patoruzu* was not a U.S. feature but an Argentinean product, born in the pages of the Buenos Aires daily *La Razón* in 1931. Created by the prolific pen of Dante Quinterno, *Patoruzu* soon met with dazzling success, being exported to other South American countries and to Europe, and finally cracking the North American market through the efforts of the George Matthew Adams Service.

For the benefit of U.S. readers a short introduction explained the origins of the character in these terms: "The adventures of Patoruzu begin in far-off Argentina, where elders of the Tehuelche tribe witness the coming of age of their new chief, Patoruzu. But his fabulous inheritance of gold, land, and cattle carries the obligation to win the three tribal feathers; the first by his defense of the oppressed, the second by his power to right wrongs, and the third by his humility."

A kind of Patagonian Don Quixote, Patoruzu went to Buenos Aires in search of his Sancho Panza. He found him in the person of Renaldo, a ne'er-do-well looking for the main chance, hooked up with the naive Indian in hopes of having some of his companion's wealth rub off on him. Other characters in the strip included the arrogant Isidoro Cañones, godfather to Patoruzu, and the hero's Herculean brother, Upa.

In the course of his adventures in the United States, Patoruzu received, as reward for his services to a Native-American tribe, a magic flute with the power of attracting any listener to the path of reform and goodness. After using it first on Renaldo with complete success, the hero then went in search of the Devil himself to make him mend his ways. The protagonist, in his naive quest, may have seemed to many a simplistic, even simple-minded, do-gooder, but he was not without his defenders. Coulton Waugh called him "a symbol of democracy, of the power of the people."

In 1948 *P.M.* ceased publication, and the following year the Adams Service discontinued syndication of the strip in North America, though it may have appeared in a few smaller markets for a while longer. (In Argentina, *Patoruzu* continued publication until 1977.)

M.H.

PATSY
1935–1956[?]

While they had a boy's adventure strip in the form of *Dickie Dare*, the editors of AP Newsfeatures in 1934 felt the urge to add a story strip starring a girl for balance. They tapped Mel Graff, who was working in the association's art department at the time, to come up with a suitable theme and an appropriate cast of characters. Thus was *The Adventures of Patsy* born, making its daily strip appearance on March 11, 1935.

Graff had initially decided on a fairy-tale setting, complete with goblins, midgets, giants, and witches. The five-year-old Patsy and her diminutive companion Thimble experienced a wild succession of adventures (as the title promised) in the land of Odds Bodkins ruled by King Silhouette. They often had to be extricated from their many predicaments by the Phantom Magician, a *deus ex machina* in cape and mask in whom some see the first costumed superhero of the comics.

The fantasy theme did not gel, and Graff decided to bring his moppet back to reality—if Hollywood, where the action next took place, can be considered reality. Therefore in December 1936, Patsy, flanked by her uncle, Phil Cardigan, who had shed in the meantime his Phantom Magician persona, arrived in Tinsel Town to embark on a child-star movie career. Again there were adventures aplenty, on and off screen, as Patsy and her guardian contended with would-be kidnappers, disgruntled film technicians, and homicidal cameramen, not to mention J. P. Panberg, the mercurial head of Paragon Pictures. These later episodes were drawn in an atmospheric, stormy style that lent credence to the proceedings.

In May 1940 Graff heard the siren call of King Features and went over to take charge of *Secret Agent X-9*. He was replaced by Charles Raab, who with more than a little help from his friend Noel Sickles, did an impressive job on the dailies. After Raab was called to military duty, there came in quick succession George Storm, who imparted to *Patsy* a nervous, high-strung look from 1942 to 1944, followed by Al McClean and Richard Hall, each lasting less than one

Patsy (M. Graff), © 1935 The AP

used in greeting cards, advertising campaigns, and merchandising for some three hundred companies.

Peanuts is credited with reviving the child strip, which had fallen into disuse during the 1940s, but it was a child strip unlike any that had come before. From the start it has not featured mischievous or cute children, or contrasted a child's view of life with that of adults, but has rather presented a self-contained world of young people with clearly defined and complex personalities. Suffering all the anxieties, frustrations, and conflicts normal to childhood, these articulate moppets are precocious only in their use of a sophisticated adult vocabulary, rich in the jargon of psychology and theology, to express their attitudes and reactions.

The origin of *Peanuts* is as modest as its characters. Schulz was holding down a part-time job correcting lessons for the correspondence school Art Instruction, Inc., in his native St. Paul, Minnesota, in the late 1940s when he sold a weekly panel feature called *Li'l Folks* to the St. Paul *Pioneer-Press.* Simply drawn and engagingly gentle in tone, it featured the prototypes of the *Peanuts* gang, three-, four-, and five-year-olds examining and responding to their world with a naive insight that found an audience among both children and adults. After *Li'l Folks* had run for some two years and Schulz had freelanced a few gag cartoons featuring the same ambiguously youthful characters to the prestigious *Saturday Evening Post,* he felt emboldened to ask the *Pioneer-Press* to increase the publication of *Li'l Folks* to daily. The paper's response—one of the greatest blunders in the history of journalism—was to fire him.

Schulz determined to persevere and offered a strip developed from his panel feature to several syndicates. The response was not very encouraging. The strip was rejected half a dozen times before United Feature Syndicate agreed to take it on. Because there had been an earlier strip named *Little Folks,* United decided to change the name to *Peanuts,* and although Schulz has never been happy with the name, he consented. With no fanfare, the new strip was launched on October 2, 1950, in seven newspapers.

The early strips featured Charlie Brown (always identified and addressed by his full name) and three of his friends, with little to distinguish them. Charlie Brown, as Schulz has written, was at first "a flippant little guy, who soon turned into the loser he is known as today." The others faded into the background. The sensitive, trusting Charlie Brown, failing at everything and accepting the blame for all his failures but undeterred in his pursuit of his modest goals, quickly became the central figure in a growing cast of characters. Before the end of 1950 he acquired the pup Snoopy, who seemed to have an intellectual edge even before he was endowed with the power to think in human language, and who found the children's follies hilariously funny. Within a few years, the personality of Snoopy was to be elaborated, and the pooch was to become a rival of his master for star billing in the strip. Snoopy never speaks—at least, not to humans—but his imagination is clearly articulated in thought balloons in which his fantasies have become increasingly complex: he has seen himself as a fearsome dinosaur, a sinister vulture, an ice-hockey star, a figure skater, a Foreign Legionnaire, a bestselling author, a world-famous lawyer, and most famously, a World War I flying ace; his doghouse has been fitted out with a billiard table, tapes-

year. In the meantime a Sunday page had been added to the feature under the denomination *Patsy in Hollywood* and then simple *Patsy,* which also became the definitive title of the daily strip.

In 1946 Bill Dyer was entrusted with both the daily and Sunday versions, and he took *Patsy* back to its origins as a child strip. His tenure, the longest of any artist on the feature, was marked by an unfortunate penchant for cartooniness and slapstick, which resulted in a long artistic and narrative decline that only ended some ten years later with the strip's demise. Because the Associated Press scuttled its syndicate operation in the early 1960s and subsequently destroyed all the archives, it is difficult to pinpoint with precision the exact date of *Patsy's* discontinuance. From all indications it seems, however, that it happened at the end of 1955 or early in 1956.

M.H.

PEANUTS
1950–present

Charles Schulz's *Peanuts* has surely achieved the largest and most devoted following of any strip in comics, and earned its creator richer rewards than any other in the history of the medium. Carried by more than two thousand newspapers in sixty-eight countries and twenty-six languages, it has been reprinted in countless books around the world, dramatized in a hit Broadway musical, four motion pictures, and numerous television specials, and

Peanuts (C. Schulz), © 1953 United Feature Syndicate

tries, and a van Gogh (destroyed in a fire in 1966 and replaced by an Andrew Wyeth), and although none of this is seen or verbalized, he has somehow communicated it clearly to his human companions.

Schroeder, an infant musical prodigy who began to play virtuoso pieces on his toy piano the moment he received it, was added to the band in 1951, and his devotion to Beethoven has remained constant through the years. Some conflict was introduced into the strip with the arrival of Lucy Van Pelt, who joined the group in the first Sunday page on January 6, 1952. The crabby little girl who rejects the idea that life has its ups and downs by demanding that hers have only "ups and ups and ups" was quickly to develop into Charlie Brown's main antagonist. Hearing herself called a natural-born fussbudget, she protests, "Natural-born nothing!... I've worked hard to be what I am!!" But Lucy is more than a fussbudget; she is an aggressive bully who dramatizes her belief in her natural superiority by violence if necessary. Year after year she pulls away the football as Charlie Brown runs up to kick it, and year after year her hapless victim gives her another chance to trick him, patiently accepting his destiny with a resignation born of experience. Lucy's little brother, Linus, is as powerless as Charlie Brown, despite his subtle intellect and his fantastic skills—she demolishes the elaborate crenelated castles he constructs in the sand with the same ferocity she directs at all the boys in the strip—but he has a flannel blanket to which he can cling for comfort. Linus's dependence on this piece of fabric was to put the term *security blanket* in the American vocabulary.

New characters have been added to *Peanuts* over the years: Charlie Brown's little sister Sally appeared in 1959 and quickly evidenced a determination that her wishy-washy brother lacked: she consents at last to the prospect of going to kindergarten but resolves that she will not learn Latin. In 1972 the Brown family was increased further by the addition of a baby brother, Rerun, for Charlie. In 1966 the rugged little tomboy "Peppermint" Patty arrived and was joined in 1971 by her respectful little friend Marcie, who has ever since persisted in calling her "Sir" and trying unsuccessfully to reconcile her to the Tiny Tots concerts they are forced to attend. Pig-pen, always pictured in a cloud of dust, is described as the only person who can get dirty in a snowstorm. In 1968 Schulz added a token African American, Franklin, but has never assigned any particular identity to him.

Even Snoopy has acquired a circle of friends. In 1970 he

became acquainted with a flock of birds, whom he guides on nature walks and who occasionally take over his doghouse for bridge games. His particular chum among them is the fledgling, Woodstock, who, since he cannot learn to fly, has his own modest avian fantasies. Another late arrival is Snoopy's long-lost brother Spike, who has been living in the desert with coyotes and who, even lonelier than Charlie Brown, talks to cactuses.

Although the original theme of *Peanuts* was, in the artist's words, "the cruelty that exists among children," the essential appeal of the strip has always depended on the tragic sense of life that informs it. Linus annually renews his unsupported faith in the Great Pumpkin, a Halloween equivalent of Santa Claus, whom he expects to rise every year from the most sincere pumpkin patch to reward good children with gifts. Another recurring theme has been unrequited love: Lucy pursues Schroeder despite his obvious preference for Beethoven; Sally insists that Linus is her Sweet Babboo; Linus suffers the pangs of a crush on his teacher, Miss Othmar; and Peppermint Patty has set her cap for Charlie Brown, who yearns hopelessly for a never-shown little red-haired girl he dreams will one day share his solitary lunch at school. Such bittersweet echoes give *Peanuts* a dimension that is unprecedented in the literature of the comics.

The depth of psychological and philosophical insight that has endeared *Peanuts* to an audience spanning generations and cultures has earned it many honors: Schulz received Yale University's Humorist of the Year Award in 1958, the National Education Society's School Bell Award in 1960, honorary degrees in 1963 and 1966, and a Big Brother of the Year Award in 1973. The National Cartoonists Society voted him its highest honor, the Reuben, in 1955 and 1964, and a place in the Cartoonists Hall of Fame in 1987. But perhaps a more important testimony to the breadth of his vision than these professional accolades is the praise his work has received outside the cartoon field. Theologian Robert L. Short, in his 1964 book *The Gospel According to Peanuts,* describes the strips as "wonderfully imaginative parables of our times" and counts the devoutly religious Schulz, along with Søren Kierkegaard, Blaise Pascal, Paul Tillich, and Karl Barth, among the significant voices in modern thought.

D.W.

PENNY
1943–1970

Wishing to introduce a new comic strip starring a girl, the New York Herald-Tribune syndicate looked no further than the creator of its *Our Bill* feature, Harry Haenigsen, in 1943. On June 20 of that year *Penny* first appeared, featuring the cheery exploits of bobby-socked teenager Penelope and her prominently correct, traditional parents Roger and Mae Pringle. A conservative middle-class family, they represented a well-characterized caricature of an able American household who quietly aspire to a more refined existence in their own serene, cultured way. Penny was pert and popular with her schoolmates of both genders; often she found herself mired in the adolescent dilemma of deciding which handsome boy to accompany to the school dance, while pondering new ways to ask father for permission or the funds to purchase the latest style skirt or a ticket to a current movie.

Haenigsen's unique combination of fluid design and mature scripting gave the feature an aura that was both droll and fey, recounted by the pedantic dialogue, elaborate graphic framing, and Penny's own blithe spirit and balletic posturing. Despite these peculiarities the humor was direct and solid, occasionally underscored by some form of moral resolve. During the strip's peak in the 1950s, Penny bore more than a passing resemblance to actress Katharine Hepburn, both in appearance and attitude, and as his "princess," was lovingly doted upon by her pipe-smoking, well-read father. The strip's earlier years displayed the artist's penchant for jive and teenage slang, quoted either directly from actual contemporary phrases or ofttimes made up by Haenigsen himself.

Situational humor required the occasional appearances of regular cast members Judy, Elsa, Doodie, Aunt Ellen, and any one of the myriad of Penny's boyfriends, but their fungible nature and nondescript personalities reinforced their sole purpose as story vehicles to showcase the daily activities of the Pringle family.

For years Howard Boughner lettered and assisted in the writing, along with Stan Kay. From 1947 until 1949, Avon published six *Penny* comic books, and a paperback collection appeared in 1953. Now syndicated by Publishers-Hall, during its last decade the strip's artwork was simplified down to its bare essentials, yet Haenigsen still managed to use unorthodox design elements such as off-camera action, extreme close-ups, and mannered spatial placement to preserve its uniqueness. The straight-haired coed now befriended an unkempt hippie named Delbert and appeared a bit impertinent; a reflection on the changing times and then-topical Generation Gap.

In the late 1960s Haenigsen was seriously injured in an automobile accident, prematurely ending his involvement with the strip. Bill Hoest, who was then introducing his famous panel *The Lockhorns*, stepped in to write and ghost

Penny, revitalizing it with the introduction of some new characters and his trademark craftsmanship. An artist named Flannery finished out the strip in its last days, which ended in 1970.

B.J.

PETE THE TRAMP
1932–1963

Cartoonist Clarence D. Russell had always professed a kinship with "bums"; it is therefore not surprising that he created that paragon of bumhood, Pete the Tramp. "I started drawing tramps for *Judge*, the old humorous magazine," he once declared, "and pretty soon Pete began to evolve. He was my escape valve. Pete did the things I always wanted to do." The redoubtable W. R. Hearst was not long in spotting these cartoons as fodder for his syndicate, and on January 10, 1932, a *Pete the Tramp* Sunday page, signed "C. D. Russell," started appearing, distributed by King Features.

Pete was a sad-faced little tramp with a stubble beard and a shuffling gait who roamed alone the streets, parks, and back alleys of the city in search of food and shelter and an occasional handout. Later he acquired a yellow mongrel dog called Boy, and a toddler whose forlorn expression reflected his own. The little tramp found himself the butt of rough handling from O'Leary, the cop on the beat, but he found consolation in the kindness of Linda the cook, who would put away a piece of meat and a slice of pie for her hobo friend. Some companionship also came to him in the person of Doc, the older, pipe-smoking hobo with whom he often engaged in existential disputations on how best to mooch a meal, steal a chicken, or swipe a cigar.

Pete was the polar opposite of Chaplin's Little Tramp: he didn't ask for sympathy, didn't claim to be a victim, didn't blame his plight on society, didn't pine after beautiful girls (there were no beautiful girls in Pete's world, only ugly harridans); above all, he didn't aspire to a higher, or a better, or a safer life. He loved being a tramp; he asked, nay demanded, only to exercise his calling in peace and with a measure of dignity. In his own self-deprecating, humble way he cut a grand figure—the bum as existential hero. And on occasion Pete could indeed display incredible feats of heroism in pursuit of a meal. Once he got himself hired as a restaurant waiter in order to help his accomplice Doc

Penny (H. Haenigsen), © 1952 New York Herald-Tribune

pilfer a pharaonic meal that the two later shared in the privacy of their vacant lot. At another time, lured by the irresistible offer of a free dinner given to any veteran in uniform, he presented himself in a suit of armor lifted from a nearby museum.

When everything else failed, he would even accept work. He was thus employed at various times as a golf caddie, a street cleaner, a store clerk, and as a magician's assistant (he stole the rabbit for stew). But the job he favored above all others was that of sandwich-man: it allowed him to stroll leisurely through city streets looking for cigar butts. (When it rained he would use the two sign-boards as a tent.) Even without a union he knew his rights as a working man; in one instance when he had been cheated out of his compensation by a stingy farmer's wife, he spent an entire night nailing back the logs he had split in the daytime.

As was usual for Sunday features of that time, *Pete the Tramp* had to share the page with several toppers during the 1930s. *The Tucker Twins,* about a rascally pair of identical six-year-olds, came first. It was followed in 1933 by *Pete's Pup,* which detailed the romps enjoyed by the tramp's dog away from his master. Finally *Shorty,* dealing with a diminutive, derby-hatted bum of Herculean strength, arrived in 1935 and lasted the longest, into the early 1940s. Between February 1934 and June 1937 there also was *a Pete the Tramp* daily strip.

Pete the Tramp is one of the minor glories of the comics. It lasted for more than three decades, coming to an end only on December 22, 1963, on the heels of the artist's death. Its longevity was due in great part to C. D. Russell's extraordinary devotion to his theme. He was the poet of hobo camps, of shantytowns, and of freight yards. His image of a multitude of hobos disgorging from a freight car in the weirdest array of torn-up garments, mismatched shoes, and beat-up headdresses imaginable may have inspired director Preston Sturges's similar shot in his 1941 film masterpiece *Sullivan's Travels.* Russell felt a genuine affection for his downtrodden characters, whom he portrayed in an understanding yet unsentimental light, without derision or condescension.

M.H.

Pete the Tramp (C. D. Russell), © **King Features Syndicate**

PETER PAT
1934–1935

Mo Leff was one of the countless cartoonists who for years toiled anonymously on other people's strips, in his case Al Capp's *Li'l Abner* and Ham Fisher's *Joe Palooka.* In the mid-1930s he got his one opportunity to shine, if only for a brief moment, with a creation of his own, a Sunday page called *Peter Pat* that United Feature started syndicating on June 3, 1934, to a scant number of American newspapers (and a few foreign ones).

"Dreaming to know what was beyond the clouds," Peter Pat, a venturesome young lad of about 12, climbed the highest mountaintop, from which he was plucked by a giant winged warrior who looked like the Norse god Thor, to be plunked down in the midst of a strange other-world inhabited by dwarfs, giants, wizards, and monsters. Befriended by the Pagos, a race of mighty midgets, he helped them defeat their enemies the Kilgos, and later liberated the little princess Judy, ruler of the Golden Castle, from the clutches of conspirators intent on usurping the throne. All these adventures were told in a straight narrative mode without the use of speech balloons.

Peter Pat was, as Pierre Couperie commented on the French version of the strip, "a weird story...whose style creates a vague sense of unease: the children, in particular, with their heavy, short-legged bodies and their oversized heads, are disquieting..." Leff largely drew for his inspiration on Victorian fairy tales and their disturbing illustrations. He also borrowed imagery from sources as diverse as *Little Nemo* (the eagle carrying Peter on its back), *Flash Gordon* (Peter's fight with the two-headed hydra), and even Hal Foster's *Tarzan* (the struggle with a giant alligator), but somehow succeeded in blending all these disparate elements into a coherent whole.

With story lines deliberately aimed at children and artwork better suited for adult tastes, *Peter Pat* was too much of an oddball strip to please either audience. The last page appeared on July 28, 1935, after a run of little over one year.

M.H.

PETER RABBIT
1920–1956

The prolific book and magazine writer Thornton W. Burgess conceived the character of Peter Rabbit (not to be confused with Beatrix Potter's creation of the same name) in his daily-newspaper *Bedtime Stories.* First published in the pages of the *New York Globe* in February 1912, they were later transferred to the *New York Tribune* in February 1920, appearing there six days a week for over three decades.

Each of these *Bedtime Stories* was illustrated with a drawing by Harrison Cady, who had illustrated some of Burgess's magazine stories as far back as 1911. Cady had started his art career in the last years of the nineteenth century, and while he was better noted at the time for his work in books and magazines and for his gag cartoons, he was also a comic-strip artist, having toiled in this field for the *Philadel-*

phia Press from 1905 on. It was perhaps inevitable, therefore, that he would try his hand at a *Peter Rabbit* newspaper comic feature; the first page appeared on Sunday, August 15, 1920, in the *Tribune,* and it was later distributed nationally by the New York Herald-Tribune Syndicate. Despite repeated demands from readers, there never was a *Peter Rabbit* daily strip.

In addition to drawing the feature, Cady also wrote the story lines. At first he stuck close to Burgess's rustic locales of Green Meadows and Smiling Pool, but he later transferred his bunny hero to the suburban setting of Carrotville, and also devised stories of his own. A portly, middle-aged white rabbit of dignified mien, Peter lived in the company of his chubby wife Hepsy and his two mischievous sons (one or both of whom were indifferently called Peter Jr. or Petey). He was apparently a rabbit of means: he drove a car, had a large wardrobe, belonged to a country club, and engaged the services of a maid named Bridget Possum.

Peter and his offspring always pursued some innocent activity that quickly turned into full-scale disaster. Peter would knock down an entire row of houses with his car, or bean a number of players with one golf ball, or his sons would blow up their classroom in one of their science experiments. These accidents would inevitably end up with a lynch mob hot on the culprit's heels, brandishing canes, cudgels, baseball bats, and hockey sticks, and screaming imprecations like "After 'im, boys," "We'll fix 'im," and "Get th' villain." Peter and his kids would then make mile-a-minute tracks back to their house, which they would barricade against the enraged citizenry.

With the exception of World War II, which was hard to ignore, Cady seldom let events from the outside world intrude on the goings-on around Carrotville and its surroundings. A staunch conservative, he would, however, take oblique swipes at the Roosevelt administration in the 1930s. This aspect of the strip did not go unnoticed by Coulton Waugh, who wrote in 1947, "Peter himself may be a rabbit, but more precisely he is one of the earliest comic business fathers...an exceedingly Republican rabbit forced out to make needless reports on his business."

Cady drew *Peter Rabbit* in a more concise version of his minutely detailed style. The drawings were eye-pleasing, and the frenzied action was rendered with tongue-in-cheek naturalness. The anecdotes, however, were repetitious and got cloying after a while. Cady retired at age 70 in 1948 (his last page appeared on July 25), and he was succeeded by Vincent Fago, a former Max Fleischer animator, with disastrous results. Fago tried to remake Peter into a Bugs Bunny clone, with limp drawings and stale jokes. The feature, now carried almost exclusively by the lonely *Herald-Tribune,* managed to last until March 11, 1956.

M.H.

THE PHANTOM
1936–present

Buoyed by the growing success of *Mandrake the Magician,* Lee Falk came up less than two years later with the idea for another adventure strip centering around

The Phantom (Falk and Moore), © 1939 King Features Syndicate

a masked justice-fighter. Accordingly, *The Phantom,* drawn by a St. Louis artist friend of Falk's, Ray Moore, and distributed by King Features Syndicate, made its daily debut on February 17, 1936.

The first week of continuity concentrated on Diana Palmer, a young and lovely woman explorer just back from the East Indian seas on her yacht anchored in New York Harbor. When a band of gangsters tried to hijack the cargo of ambergris aboard the ship, the mysterious Phantom saved the day; thus started a sultry romance that was to last for decades. All the elements that made up the long saga of the Phantom were already there, with the action soon moving away from America to the Far East: there were the exotic locales, the fast-paced action, the sinister antagonists ranging from Singh pirates to big-city mobsters, all against a background of mystery and romance. At the end of this first adventure the Phantom revealed to Diana the secret behind the myth: he was the last in a long line of fighters for right and justice, waging a private and unrelenting war against crime, a tradition passed on from father to son since the sixteenth century. Thus the Phantom was not just a man but a legend, "the ghost-who-walks," thought by friend and foe alike to be immortal and endowed of supernatural powers. Like all legendary figures, he would leave the existential trace of his passage, "the sign of the skull," after each of his interventions, and the dreaded symbol was often enough to strike fear and confusion in the minds of his enemies.

From his base of operation deep in the Indian jungle, the Phantom ranged far and wide in his pursuit of evildoers. He was assisted in his task by his faithful gray wolf, Devil, and by Guran, leader of the feared Bandar pygmies, who was the only one to know the secret of the ghost-who-walks. The first years of the strip alternated between Indian locations and more urban settings: New York, London, Paris. In the jungle the Phantom would don a tight-fitting costume, over which he would throw a double-breasted overcoat during his travels, completing his disguise with a hat and a pair of dark sunglasses. (A few people did get suspicious, but the Phantom had a way of discouraging their curiosity.)

Moore drew the Phantom's adventures with a supple line and subtle shading that created just the right aura of suspense and anticipation. Whether in repose or in movement, the Phantom always appeared as a superhuman figure whose long shadow pervaded the action. On May 28, 1939, a Sunday page was added (with continuities kept separate from those of the dailies); saddled with this additional burden, Moore developed a less evocative, heavier line, and he came to rely more and more on his assistant, Wilson McCoy, who took over the feature in 1942–45, while Moore was serving with the U.S. Air Force. After the war Moore came back to reclaim *The Phantom,* but a nervous disorder related to wounds he had suffered in the war forced him to relinquish the strip to McCoy again, this time for good, in 1949.

Under McCoy, a mediocre draftsman at best, the Phantom lost much of his mystery and gained a lot of weight. At the same time Falk changed his name from Christopher Standish to Kit Walker, and his nationality was now that of an American citizen (he had previously been a British subject). India was then in full political turmoil, and Falk found it expedient also to change the venue to the African wilds, with the Phantom electing residence in the Deep Woods. He was still surrounded by his loyal tribe of pygmies, but had now an entire organization of peacekeepers, the Jungle Patrol, to work for him. When McCoy died in 1961, he was briefly succeeded by Bill Lignante; in 1962 Seymour (Sy) Barry took over the feature and, with the help of several assistants, notably George Roussos and Joe Giella, he has restored *The Phantom* to the top rank of illustrated strips.

Since the 1960s Falk has hewed closer to modern-day concerns and preoccupations, such as preservation of the environment and control of nuclear weapons. While still fighting pirates, gangsters, and other miscreants, the Phantom has also tried to prevent the encroachments of unscrupulous businessmen upon the wilderness, and he has thwarted time and again the schemes of foreign agents to set up missile bases or nuclear facilities in the Deep Woods. Falk has also increasingly shown his hero at rest and at play, and even in domestic surroundings. This trend culminated in his wedding to his long-waiting sweetheart Diana in December 1977; and in the spring of 1979 he became the caring father of twins, Kit and Heloise. Kit Jr. is now being groomed to take over the family business, thus living up to the proud motto of his line: "There will always be a Phantom!"

Because of its longevity, its international popularity, and its resonance among younger readers, the Phantom can be considered the "granddaddy" of all costumed superheroes. This seems ironic since, as Coulton Waugh pointed out, he "is not a superman in the wild, modern meaning of the word; he happens to be able to outfight, outrun, outswim, outjump, outclimb, outshoot, and outride everyone else in the world. But the Phantom, if shot neatly and completely between the eyes, would, presumably, drop dead." For all his lack of supernatural powers, the Phantom may yet survive the hordes of comic-book superpowered beings who have risen in his wake.

M.H.

PHIL HARDY
1925–1941

Phil Hardy resulted from the chance encounter between cartoonist and illustrator George Storm and writer and journalist Jay Jerome Williams. Both men wished to branch out into the lucrative newspaper-strip market, and their joint effort saw light of print on November 2, 1925, as a daily strip distributed by the Bell Syndicate.

Williams, a great admirer of the Horatio Alger stories, signed with the transparent pseudonym "Edwin Alger, Jr.," and the strip's premise was that of countless nineteenth-century rags-to-riches boys' novels. "This is the story of Phil Hardy's climb to fame and fortune," the opening sentence in the very first panel straightforwardly announced. Williams's illustrator had, however, other ambitions, and under his increasing involvement with the scripts, the feature soon veered toward violent adventure. The fifteen-year-old boy hero went to work for a shipping company, only to find himself shanghaied aboard the steamer *Black Castle* on a seven-week voyage that included tempests, fire, and a mutiny at sea. It was during the last incident that several sailors were killed, prompting some to assert this as the first instance of violent death graphically depicted in the comics (a claim nearly impossible to substantiate).

Other adventures, some at sea, some on land, followed, enlivened by a highly colorful cast of characters that included hard-bitten sea captain Eli Bent; Jason Royle, ship's cook and resident sage; and Phil's close friend, the equally teenaged Ben Kittredge. Williams peppered the narrative with stern Puritan admonitions, such as "Work hard—that's the foundation of all success," but it was Storm's nervous, evocative drawings that carried the action forward. Abruptly the *Phil Hardy* strip came to an end, but the title neatly segued in September 1926 into *Bound to Win,* also written by Williams, with Storm working on the first sequence to insure a smooth transition.

The narrative concerned another plucky lad of fifteen who embarked on sundry adventures in the company of his dog, Briar. After a while the strip took on the name of its young protagonist, starting with the Sunday version (added in 1934) called *Ben Webster's Page.* Still written in earnest boys'-book style by Williams and illustrated with varying degrees of proficiency by diverse anonymous hands, *Ben Webster,* despite its faults, exuded enough period charm to last until 1941.

M.H.

A PILGRIM'S PROGRESS BY MISTER BUNION
1905–1910

While Winsor McCay is most acclaimed for his mastery of line and color, and the splendor and inventiveness of his imagery, his catholicity of interests led him to create in the pages of the *Evening Telegram* the most literary of his masterpieces, a modern-day allegory whose title, clearly inspired by the eponymous work of the seventeenth-century religious writer John Bunyan, read *A*

Pilgrim's Progress by Mister Bunion. (Mister Bunion was the pilgrim whose progress it was, not the purported author of the piece as some unenlightened commentators have claimed; the strip was clearly signed "Silas," the pen-name McCay used for all his *Telegram* work.)

The premise of the strip was clearly laid out by McCay in a note penned to his editor. Mister Bunion, whom the artist sketched as a tall, gaunt man in a black suit and stovepipe hat, carrying with him a suitcase labeled "Dull Care," desperately "tries all manners of schemes to get rid of his burden 'Dull Care,' but like the cat it comes back.... He will always be looking for 'Glad Avenue' and will have an occasional visit to Easy Street but his burden will stick with him. I will have him try to burn it, bury it, throw it in the sea, blow it up, advertise it for sale or give [it] away, get it run over by trains, hit by autos and hundred[s] of things he will try to do to get rid of it but can't—I hope you will see my scheme it's a good one." The editor, Mr. Harris, must have indeed seen the point, for on June 26, 1905, *A Pilgrim's Progress* made its appearance in the daily *Telegram*, where it alternated with *Dream of the Rarebit Fiend.*

True to his word, McCay exposed the fatal suitcase to all the mishaps he had detailed in his note, and then some. Subjected to flood, fire, conflagration, or target practice, the unwanted baggage always turned up again with nary a scratch. The allegorical image of the suitcase as the existential burden man eternally carries with him is of course a recurrent symbol of the human condition in twentieth-century literature, from Franz Kafka to Eugene Ionesco. It is to the work of Samuel Beckett, however, that *A Pilgrim's Progress* is most thematically linked. In one episode, for instance, the downcast Bunion is comforted by a kind passerby who assures him soothingly "to wait right here and I'll send relief right up"; the pilgrim waits and waits and waits until he grows a long white beard, and in the last panel he leaves in despair. In its striking sparseness this parable could serve as a synopsis of *Waiting for Godot.* It is unlikely that the Irish playwright knew of the American artist's work, but is indicative of the theme's pervasiveness in modern times that a similar development could have been arrived at independently by creators from two different eras and two different continents.

A Pilgrim's Progress (W. McCay), 1908

It was somehow foreordained that, unlike Bunyan's protagonist, who found enlightenment at the end of his quest, this pilgrim wouldn't be anymore unburdened at the close of his progress than he had been at the beginning of it. For all the commotions it had caused, his itinerary had brought him back to the starting point, in what French writer Alfred Jarry called *un voyage immobile* ("a motionless journey"). On this sobering note the strip came not to a conclusion but to a stop, in December 1910.

Because of its black-and-white austerity and somber overtones, which are a far cry from the dazzling pyrotechnics and chromatic opulence of *Little Nemo, A Pilgrim's Progress* has been unjustly neglected. It is time to have it restored to the top rank of Winsor McCay's canon.

M.H.

PINKERTON, JR.
See RADIO PATROL

Pogo (W. Kelly), © 1963 Walt Kelly/OGPI, Inc.

POGO
1948–1975, 1989–1993

For more than twenty years, first in comic books and then newspapers, *Pogo* was comics as high art, the one strip that utilized all aspects of the medium in almost perfect harmony. While other strips have been known for their excellence in one category or the other, *Pogo* was top-rated in all of them—characterization, language, dialect, use of satire and parody, story, art, and lettering. Even more impressive was the fact that this was a one-man performance, that of Walt Kelly.

Pogo could not have succeeded in any other way, certainly not as the product of a comics assembly line, for the intricacies of the strip depended solely on the fertile mind of its creator. Kelly had a knack for uniting the verbal and visual elements into an interdependent whole, while complicating the Okefenokee setting with an ever-increasing lineup of real characters dressed in allegorical costume and going in all directions through free association, double entendres, and figures of speech.

To keep track of the characters required a directory. Some main inhabitants of the swamp were Pogo (possum), Albert (alligator), Howland (owl), Churchy (turtle), Rackety Coon Chile, Beauregard Bugleboy (dog), and Porkypine, while others made appearances depending on the story—Sis Boombah (chicken), Miss M'amzelle Hepzibah (skunk), Deacon Mushrat, Moonshine Sonata (frog), Seminole Sam (fox), Wiley Catt, or Choo Choo Curtis. Still others were strictly political, sociological representations. Kelly put more than six hundred named and otherwise identifiable creatures in the swamp, each with a distinct personality, language, and set of mannerisms. Most were difficult to describe because they were many-sided characters who reacted differently as situations changed.

Kelly had an ear for language and dialect and a love of words, strengthened by his civilian work with the U.S. Army Foreign Language Unit during World War II. He mixed Elizabethan English, French, and black dialects to create a poetic language that set the swamp apart; historian R. C. Harvey called it "Southern fried" dialect. His characters talked and argued constantly, parodying what passes as communication among humans. Many strips contained Kelly's unique version of poetry and song, made up of "gobbledygook verses," the most lasting of which was "Deck Us All with Boston Charlie." First sung in a 1961 strip, "Deck Us All" sounded the way a three-year-old (or an Okefenokee Swamp creature) might hear the words of the famous Christmas carol.

Kelly instinctively came up with double entendres, puns, quotable one-liners, and plays on words, especially in names. Thus, when Albert, in the role of an editor, called for legmen to get the news for him, a stork and a caterpillar appeared, and when Pogo and Churchy discussed the idea of edible money printed on food, they innocently made the wry comment, "Just think! Folks with money would never have to starve." Some one-liners that were memorable were Pogo's comments about boating, applicable more generally to life: "If you ask me the hardest work a body can do...is to sit still, keep quiet...and don't splash"; Congressman Frog's "I'll tell you, son, the minority got us out-numbered!"; Porkypine's appraisal of death as something he "could live without"; and the most quoted of all, Pogo's sad observation upon seeing the garbage-cluttered swamp, "Yep, son, we have met the enemy and he is us." The very names of characters were funny twists of words: Horrors (Horace) Greeley, P. T. Bridgeport (P. T. Barnum, from Bridgeport, Connecticut), Simple J. Malarkey (Senator Joseph McCarthy), Tammany Tiger (New York's corrupt Tammany Hall political machine), or Sarcophagus MacAbre, the vulture.

On at least one occasion, Kelly had said that the comic-strip industry was a safe haven where one had to lean over backward to get into trouble. As he acknowledged, he leaned over backward "fairly well." His daily strip represented some of the century's most caustic and ingenious satire in any form. In fact, it was so pointed politically that Kelly prepared alternative "bunny-rabbit strips" on innocuous themes that were distributed to timid newspapers. The Sunday *Pogo* also avoided topicality in order to entice new subscribers and to appeal to children. But, in his regular daily strips Kelly was merciless as he took the unprecedented risk of naming names in his mockery of the high and mighty—forces such as J. Edgar Hoover, the D.A.R., the John Birch Society, George Wallace, Richard Nixon, Spiro Agnew, Nikita Khrushchev, Fidel Castro, and Joe McCarthy. He did his number on the Wisconsin demagogue a full year before Edward R. Murrow's devastating broadcast. In one series, he used questioning similar to what the main witch-hunt body, the House Un-American Activities Committee, employed: Turtle was asked by Mole, "What kind of an owl are you?" "I ain't no owl; I ain't even a bird," Turtle replied. "Were you ever a bird or are you thinking of becoming one?" Mole persisted.

Richard Nixon was Kelly's most represented figure, portrayed as Malarkey's sidekick, Indian Charlie, and later as a teapot-shaped spider named Sam. Much meaning could be derived from the way other political personalities were drawn: Agnew as a uniformed hyena, Khrushchev as a pig, Castro as a goat, and Hoover as a bulldog.

Early on, Kelly decided the day's news offered the best material for stories. He took particular delight in parodying national elections and made strong comments on five campaigns between 1952 and 1968. Starting in 1952, he also ran Pogo for the president of the United States, with his own campaign song, "Go Go Pogo." Kelly's importance as an election critic was recognized in 1956 when NBC hired him to do radio and television commentary during the Democratic National Convention.

Throughout the 1960s, he drew increasing numbers of caricatures of real people into the strip, sparking some newspapers to oppose this practice editorially. By 1968, the humor in *Pogo* had become more strident and much less subtle, and Kelly refused to provide alternative strips to newspapers afraid to carry the regular ones. As a result, some newspapers transferred *Pogo* to the editorial page, while others canceled it altogether.

The artwork of Pogo was no less outstanding. It was meticulous and well worked out with full backgrounds, including detailed panoramas of the swamp, and wide use of deep space, many patterns, and dense, dark drawings. Kelly drew his characters with flesh so that the animals seemed to have a certain amount of human anatomy in them. The art was also irreverent, articulate, and varied. In a 1990 talk, Bill Watterson of *Calvin and Hobbes* said that the drawings in *Pogo* represented comic art at its peak, and that Kelly used his art to enhance, not just prop up, his strip. Kelly made all parts of a panel serve his artistic purposes, including borders and dialogue balloons.

Albert struck matches against panel borders to light his cigar, and dialogue balloons carried varied typefaces, allowing characters to be defined not only by what they said but by how their words looked. The grim vulture, Sarcophagus MacAbre, spoke within balloons that resembled black-bordered death announcements; the promoter, P. T. Bridgeport, in circus posters and newspaper headlines complete with photographs of himself; and Deacon Mushrat, in a Gothic typeface.

Kelly picked up some of his artistic skills while working at Disney from 1935 to 1941. After that, he returned to New York, where he did comic books for Dell, in one of which, *Animal Comics* #1 (December 1941–January 1942), he introduced Albert, Pogo, and a black kid named Bumbazine. These characters were dropped after the twelfth number of *Animal Comics,* but they reappeared in *Four Color, Our Gang,* and *Santa Claus Funnies,* and eventually were featured in their own *Pogo Possum,* which had sixteen issues between 1949 and 1954. In 1948, Kelly joined the *New York Star,* where he was in charge of editorial cartoons and other art. That October, he started a daily strip version of *Pogo* in the *Star,* which lasted until the paper's folding three months later. Hall Syndicate picked up the strip on May 16, 1949, and for the next six years *Pogo* was available simultaneously in comic books and newspapers. By 1954, Kelly's rela-

tionship with Western, the parent company of Dell, had soured, prompting him to quit doing the books and concentrate on strips.

Pogo started out slowly in syndication, but after a year, 126 U.S. newspapers subscribed. The number went up to 225 newspapers with thirty-seven million readers in 1952, and peaked at almost 600 in the late 1950s. Kelly regularly reprinted *Pogo,* resulting in more than three dozen paperbacks during his lifetime. Only one animated cartoon based on the strip, *Pogo's Special Birthday Special* in 1969, was produced before his death in 1973.

The strip continued until 1975 through the scissors-and-pastepot efforts of Kelly's widow, Selby, and son Stephen. On January 8, 1989, *Walt Kelly's Pogo* appeared in about three hundred newspapers, the work of writer Larry Doyle and artist Neal Sternecky. When Doyle left the strip in February 1991, Sternecky went solo with it until Kelly's children Pete and Carolyn took it over on March 23, 1992; it ended the next year.

As hard as these individuals have tried to revive *Pogo,* none has been able to come remotely near the masterly work done by Kelly.

J.A.L.

POLLY AND HER PALS
1912–1958

Cliff Sterrett has been described as the "most gifted" and "least celebrated" graphic artist; his *Polly and Her Pals,* as one of the great sleepers of comic strips. Although he was a professional cartoonist for fifty-five years, during which he innovated many aspects of the funnies, Sterrett was never given the acclaim of most of his contemporaries. He was seldom interviewed or honored, and his long-lived strip was not spun off into serialized movies, radio shows, or even much merchandising.

The genesis of *Polly and Her Pals* was an evolutionary one. Sterrett had been doing four strips for the *New York Telegram,* one of which was *For This We Have Daughters,* built around a father, a mother, a comely daughter (Molly), and

Polly and Her Pals (C. Sterrett), © 1935 King Features Syndicate

a cat. It and his other *Telegram* strips were rather tame, for, as Sterrett was to complain later, the censorship was rigid: "We couldn't show a girl's leg above the top of her shoe." In 1912, he left the *Telegram* to work for William Randolph Hearst's *Journal,* where he drew a variation of *For This We Have Daughters* called *Positive Polly.* The first Sundays were called *Polly!* with the daily and color versions becoming *Polly and Her Pals.* Either the censorship standards changed or Sterrett ignored them during the intervening years, as Polly was a leggy beauty who wore fashionable clothing cut low at the neckline and high at the hemline. Initially, the strip revolved around this independent young lady who dared to use lipstick, bob her hair, wear flapper dresses, and even play some golf occasionally. She had an address book full of boyfriends, from whom her father was constantly trying to protect her through his various schemes.

Polly and Her Pals pioneered the pretty-girl strip, featuring a female type that historian Coulton Waugh said was "based on the French doll: bulging brow, tiny nose and mouth, deep-set eyes." Sterrett showed Polly in profile, a trait picked up by other pretty-girl cartoonists who made this category of strip prominent in the 1920s and 1930s.

Rather quickly, Polly receded to supporting-character status as Paw (Samuel Perkins) became the strip's star. Paw, usually decked out in loud, checkered, and unmatched clothing, served as an easy target, his tradition-bound sentiments coming under attack from both Polly and Maw (Susie), and at times others in the crammed household. Among the hangers-on at the Perkins abode, who were usually thorns in Paw's side, were Delicia Hicks, a not-very-much-of-anything (not smart, not attractive) niece; Ashur Url Perkins, a scheming, stupid nephew; Carrie Meek, a sharp-tongued sister-in-law; Gertrude, Carrie's daughter; Aunt Maggie Hicks; three maids, Cocoa, Liza, and Manda; Neewah, the valet who was an Asian version of Paw, and Kitty the cat (a.k.a. Dot and Em). The last two often took sides with Paw.

Sterrett's work was unique, and that has made it difficult to describe. Stephen Becker tried to pinpoint it in his *Comic Art in America,* saying, "In the art professor's terms, Sterrett composed beautifully; each of his daily panels is a delicate balance of black and white, and often one panel leads into another through the simple rhythm of the lines. Sterrett usually dresses his characters in striped or checked garments, and the play of line against shape is masterly. If heads, hands, and feet were removed, what remained would be pen-and-ink abstraction of a high order." Historian-critic Rick Marschall credited Sterrett with doing things artistically that no other strip cartoonist had ever done, singling out his panel arrangements, color, "striking lines,...playful treatment of reality,...teasing of readers' perception." Another historian, R. C. Harvey, cautious not to pigeonhole Sterrett's work, labeled it futuristic and surrealistic, with "high comedy in the visuals."

The comedy is often overlooked by those enamored of Sterrett's high art, but the visual comedy is very significant for its fresh gags, its highlighting of characters' personality quirks, and its parodying of fads and national institutions. The humor is sometimes filtered through unusual perspectives, such as the abstract world Paw and Maw see when they get their glasses switched, or the completely underwater peek at Paw's flirtatious shenanigans with an attractive young lady and Maw's subsequent thrashing of him.

Beginning in the 1920s, Sterrett added a second, smaller strip over the top of the Sunday version of *Polly and Her Pals.* Syndicates at the time required "top strips," giving the illusion of double the number of strips, at the same time getting full services out of their cartoonists. The first to appear over *Polly* were *Damon and Pythias* and *Dot and Dash,* both pantomimes about animals. Later, Sterrett pulled ideas from his first strips at the *Telegram* for his top strips, *Sweethearts and Wives* and *Belles and Wedding Belles* and *Then They Were Married.*

Sterrett had to give up drawing the daily strip because of his rheumatism; Paul Fung drew it from March 9, 1935, on. The dailies appeared without signature after that because Sterrett refused to sign work that he did not draw. He stayed with the Sunday strip until it ended on June 15, 1958.

J.A.L.

POP
1929–1950

An outstanding British import, *Pop* was not the first foreign newspaper strip to be syndicated in the United States (this distinction belongs to Australian James Bancks's *Ginger,* which was briefly distributed in North America by the Arthur J. Lafave Syndicate during the 1920s). Created by J. Millar Watt for the *Daily Sketch* of London in 1921, the strip was picked up for daily syndication by the Bell Syndicate in 1929.

Pop was a rotund, bald-headed, cheerful little man who tried (not always successfully) to maintain a very British unflappability in the face of outrage or adversity. Always attired in waistcoat and striped pants, the pint-size hero was afflicted with a very un-British wife, Mag, a woman twice his size and his better half five times over, and burdened with an unruly family of two teenage daughters named Phoebe and Moreen, a son called Johnny, and a baby girl christened Babs. To console himself about his domestic woes Pop often repaired to his club, where he exchanged barbs with his nemesis, an exceedingly tall and stuffy gentleman known as the Colonel. During World War II the diminutive protagonist seemingly enlisted in every branch of the British armed forces, in all of which he displayed the same guilelessness and ineptness.

Pop was drawn in a very simple but highly effective style, with the action and the spare backgrounds crossing over from panel to panel, and the last one registering the reaction to the gag in the previous panel. As Coulton Waugh noted, the strip was "outstanding in pure, expressive drawing ability." For a while the American syndicate used to redraw the uniforms on the soldiers and policemen in order to make them appear American, but the practice was discontinued following protests by the copyright holders.

The *New York Sun,* which had published *Pop* from the start of its syndication in the U.S., folded in 1950, and with the loss of its flagship newspaper, Bell halted distribution of the strip. (*Pop* continued to appear in British and other foreign papers until 1960.)

M.H.

Pottsy (J. Irving), © 1960 Chicago Tribune–New York News Syndicate

POPEYE
See THIMBLE THEATRE

POSITIVE POLLY
See POLLY AND HER PALS

POTTSY
1955–1970

*T*he son, grandson, and nephew of New York City cops, Jay Irving, on admonition from his father, turned to journalism and cartooning rather than police work. Uniformed policemen were never far from his mind, however, and between 1932 and 1945 he contributed a weekly series of police-gag cartoons to *Collier's* magazine, appropriately called *Collier's Cops*. In 1946 he unsuccessfully tried his hand at a comic strip about a lovable city cop, *Willie Doodle*, which in a roundabout way was to lead to *Pottsy*, his most enduring creation. Started as a Sunday only in the summer of 1955, the feature was distributed by the Tribune-News Syndicate.

Pottsy was a pudgy street cop with an innocent face and a mild countenance. His beat looked more like a pleasant suburban neighborhood than the asphalt jungle of inner-city precincts, with its clumps of trees, neat metal fences, and orderly rows of houses. The gags were equally pleasant and unassuming. Hiding a childlike heart under his blue uniform, Pottsy would often gambol along with the neighborhood kids in the wintry and deserted streets of the city; or he would go about his rounds jumping over manholes or playing hopscotch with fire hydrants. His unconventional behavior would often come in for scolding from his superior officer, but as soon as the snarling sergeant had his back turned, the rotund little cop would comfort himself with the snack and the soda bottle he had hidden in his call box. The problems on Pottsy's beat were few and slight, such as a stolen street sign or a cat stranded up a tree.

There were no drugs, no riots, no political protests to disturb the protagonist's placid disposition.

Irving drew *Pottsy* in an uncluttered, unhurried, doodling style that harked back to the cartooning simplicity of an earlier, sunnier era. The artist was so proud of his police connections that under his byline he drew the honorary police badge he had been awarded by the New York City Police Department. Termed "the mildest policeman in the business" by Stephen Becker, Pottsy did not long survive the death of his creator in June 1970; with the page of July 26 he was gone.

M.H.

PRINCE VALIANT
1937–present

*F*rom the moment it debuted Sundays, on February 13, 1937, *Prince Valiant* has been one of the premier adventure strips in newspaper comics. Even today, when adventure strips are considered passé by some younger newspaper feature editors, *Prince Valiant* remains an entrenched favorite with readers of top-circulation newspapers because of its tradition of good stories and good drawing. This a full sixteen years after Valiant's creator, Harold R. Foster (1892–1982), gave up artistic control.

Prince Valiant is the saga of a Norse prince who's a knight of King Arthur's Round Table at Camelot. Val, as he's often referred to, and his family struggle in the rough and tumble world of the late fifth century. At the strip's beginnings, in 1937, Val was an adolescent full of the bravado of youth. Today he's a powerful knight and adviser to King Arthur. He and his wife, the beautiful Aleta, Queen of the Misty Isles, have five children and one grandchild.

Their oldest son, Prince Arn, has married Maeve, daughter of King Arthur's evil half-brother, Modred. Arn and Maeve's child is their granddaughter, Ingrid. Next are twins Karen and Valeta. Karen, always the tomboy, "became" an Amazon in her late teens. She has subsequently married an Italian named Vanni, the son of the legendary Prester John.

VAL ASKS THE KING FOR A MISSION, ANY MISSION, NO MATTER HOW DANGEROUS. THE KING, KNOWING HIS TROUBLES AND NOTING THE DESPERATE, RECKLESS LOOK IN HIS EYES, REFUSES.

Prince Valiant (H. Foster), © 1939 King Features Syndicate

Valeta, the quiet one, recently gained new confidence ruling the Misty Isles in her mother's absence. She has an on-again-off-again courtship with Cormac, a Druid priest. He's a pagan element in an otherwise Christian story.

Of all Val's children, second son Galan seems most similar in temperament. As he enters adolescence, he may develop into the hot-blooded firebrand his father was. Youngest son Nathan, now about 10, is the scholar of the family.

There's been some criticism among fans that *Prince Valiant* is becoming more a family strip than an adventure strip, that Valiant's sword is rusting in its jeweled scabbard. But as a young man, Val had the fastest and deadliest sword in the Middle Ages.

In an interview late in life, Hal Foster stated that he thought his work would not endure for the ages. That opinion underestimates the power of King Arthur, Camelot, and the fact that *Prince Valiant* is now part of that centuries-old legend.

In 1929, Foster was doing advertising illustrations in Chicago. Business was slow, so he drew three hundred illustrations for a newspaper adaptation of Edgar Rice Burrough's *Tarzan of the Apes*. Foster hated the story. He felt it silly and unrealistic. However, in 1931, during the Great Depression, when Burroughs himself chose Foster to draw a syndicated *Tarzan* Sunday page, he was happy for the

work. Times were hard. He moved his family to Topeka, Kansas, his wife's home area, because it was cheaper than Chicago. During the depression, according to Foster, "we ate ape."

The fact that William Randolph Hearst, newspaper tycoon, comics fan, and owner of King Features Syndicate, was impressed by Foster's *Tarzan* changed everything. Hearst wanted Foster to do a strip for King Features. When Hearst put forth a decree, King Features moved heaven and earth to make it happen. Foster had already been developing ideas for a new strip. He created a character in the King Arthur period, Derek, Son of Thane. It was creative types at King Features who gave Foster's creation the symbolic name Prince Valiant. How badly Hearst wanted Foster to work for King Features is shown by the fact that Foster was given ownership of the strip. That was something granted few cartoonists.

The saga began with a swirl of fantasy that befits the legend of King Arthur. However, soon Foster discovered his characters were too real for him to indulge much in fantasy. His own preference was heroic realism. The early stories featured Val as squire to Sir Gawain, in the time of the Saxon invasions of Britain (450–510). Val lost his first love, the slim blonde Ilene, to the war, but gained his knighthood by helping King Arthur's forces defeat the Saxons.

Val's father, King Aguar of Thule (think Norway), first fled to the swampy fens of Britain after a coup by Sligon the Traitor. Sir Valiant's first quest was to regain his father's throne. During the story of the doomed Maid Ilene, Val had been given the Singing Sword (June 12, 1938) by his rival for Ilene's hand, Prince Arn of Ord. When used for justice this charmed sword, forged by the same sorcerer who made King Arthur's Excalibur, made its owner nearly invincible as its blade whistled many a death knell in battle. Sligon wisely accepted a forced retirement in the British fens.

A hot-blooded young man, Val set out from Thule with his Singing Sword for many an adventure. Some were with Sir Gawain and Sir Tristram, some with Viking raider Boltar. Val was the sole survivor of the fall of Castle Andelkrag in Europe to Attila the Hun. He lived to organize an army that stopped the Huns in their tracks. This adventure, published in 1939 and 1940, so enraged Hitler that wherever the Nazis took over in Europe, *Prince Valiant* was immediately banished.

Hal Foster is credited with bringing classic illustration technique to the comics. Certainly Alex Raymond did somewhat the same thing, but Foster's work, more solid, less flashy than Raymond's *Flash Gordon* and light years more realistic in story, characterization, and anatomy, took Raymond's achievements one step further.

Prior to his marriage (October 2, 1946) to gray-eyed Aleta, the story of star-crossed romance and of Val under Aleta's spell proved Val's greatest quest. Foster was basically a Victorian gentleman with a strong sense of honor, of right and wrong. He personally was put off by the pliable, single, often near-ravaged Dale Arden trailing after Flash Gordon all over the universe. Foster's hero would find his true love after great trials and tribulations, be married, and have a family. Skeptics at King Features thought it would be the end of the strip.

On the contrary, the marriage of Val and Aleta gave Foster a whole range of new material. Foster was himself blessed with a long happy marriage. His wife, Helen, as his portraits of her as a young woman show, was idealized as the model for Aleta. The Queen of the Misty Isles has never been a woman to take lightly. Resourceful, strong-willed, sexy, knowledgeable of how to use both diplomacy and the business end of a dagger, she is, although Foster most likely never thought of her as such, a medieval feminist.

Prince Valiant over the years has included as many vignettes of family humor as jousts. Foster would usually follow a violent story with a light one. Ultimately, the success of the strip is that it is about life, about happiness and tragedy. Being set in the Middle Ages, when medicine was minimal, several main characters in *Prince Valiant* have been maimed and have lost limbs; such realism transcends most comic strips.

Often praised for his authentic research, Hal Foster knew he was playing fast and loose with several centuries in presenting King Arthur's fifth-century world with mostly Norman castles and eleventh-century armor. Still, Foster was a perfectionist in showing architecture, costume, and plant life that was correct for wherever the *Prince Valiant* saga was geographically. He created the right medieval mood for the strip.

Of all the emotions Foster successfully showed in *Prince Valiant,* the strong love between Val and Aleta is the most memorable. While critics and politicians complain of moral decay in the media, the fact is that syndicated comics were sexier years ago. While a matron and grandmother now, the young Aleta and all the women in Foster's first two decades of *Prince Valiant* favored a very sexy no-bra look. Today's political correctness keeps the young women in *Prince Valiant* from showing off their figures in a similar manner.

Hal Foster was age 45 when he created *Prince Valiant.* In 1970, at 78, he decided to find an artist as his replacement. Three tried out, and John Cullen Murphy was selected. Foster knew Jack Murphy's work on the story strip *Big Ben Bolt,* syndicated by King Features. He also was comfortable with Murphy's formal training in art and experience as an illustrator.

From fall 1971 until Foster ceased to draw his creation in early 1980, he gave Murphy a nicely penciled layout to complete. (*Prince Valiant* has always been published only on Sunday.) Foster numbered each page. His last published page was #1788. It was also the last full-broadsheet *Prince Valiant* offered by King Features. The pre–World War II full-size newspaper page (broadsheet) measured 14 by 20 inches. It gave Foster a wonderful size to work with. During World War II, the secondary Foster strip, *Medieval Castle,* took a third of the page, from April 1944 until November 1945. In 1971 the largest format *Prince Valiant* pages available became full tabloid or half-page broadsheet.

Word balloons are never used in *Prince Valiant.* More than any other syndicated comic, the Valiant saga is an illustrated epic novel. Foster's writing was that of an instinctive storyteller. This format helped keep the strip distinct and added to its formal grandeur. In 1975 Foster finally sought outside sources for *Prince Valiant* stories. Cullen Murphy, who now writes the strip and is John Cullen Murphy's son,

began submitting scripts. Cullen Murphy, whose college degree is in medieval history, is currently managing editor of the *Atlantic Monthly.* A year later, Foster asked Bill Crouch to submit stories also. He wrote six published stories over the next four years.

After forty-three years of guiding *Prince Valiant,* Hal Foster submitted his last pencil layout to Murphy, whose finished artwork appeared on February 10, 1980. Foster realistically never tried to have Murphy copy his style. Murphy's style is more angular than Foster's; he prefers pen work to Foster's rounded brushstrokes. But John Cullen Murphy is a pro, and *Prince Valiant* remains among the most handsome comic strips published. The lettering and coloring on *Prince Valiant* is now done by Murphy's daughter, Meg Nash.

Reduced size and modern plastic-plate printing have ended forever the beauty that was possible in the old large hand-engraved comics. Still, there is always room for a quality adventure strip such as *Prince Valiant.* As long as the legend of King Arthur lives, *Prince Valiant* will live on.

B.C., Jr.

PRISCILLA'S POP
1947–1983

While adventure strips enjoy on average the lifespan of mayflies and humor comics turn over faster than television sitcoms, family strips seemingly go on forever. A case in point is *Priscilla's Pop,* which Al Vermeer started for NEA in 1947 and which was interrupted only by its creator's death.

Vermeer began his professional career in California as a sports reporter and later illustrated his own stories; these landed him the job of sports cartoonist for NEA in 1945. In his autobiography for the *National Cartoonists Society Album,* he stated that he did "a bit of cartooning for fun but never thought of it as a profession," a shortcoming that's painfully evident in *Priscilla's Pop.*

Priscilla was a five-year-old whose pranks were more irritating than amusing. Her pop was a youngish sort and formed with his pretty wife, Hazel, a typical suburban couple. A six-year-old son, Junior, with whom Priscilla always feuded, and the family dog rounded off the cast. By Vermeer's admission the strip was "based on life with wife, Jo, and our two children"; but its inspiration came as much from *Blondie* as from life. Unfortunately, Vermeer possessed neither Young's ease of drawing nor his talent at gag-building. His characters were stiff and their faces looked like blobs; as to his jokes, they were impossibly sophomoric. Yet the family setting was enough to carry it through several generations of American parents. Priscilla and her pop came to the end of their trite adventures, looking not one day older than they did at their beginning, early in 1983, thereby surviving their creator by a few months.

M.H.

PRIVATE BREGER
See MR. BREGER

Professor Phumble (B. Yates), © 1972 King Features Syndicate

PROFESSOR PHUMBLE
1960–1980

Noted more for its longevity than for its artistry and for its grit rather than its wit, *Professor Phumble* was the brainchild of Bill Yates, a former gag cartoonist and ghost on other people's comic strips. King Features Syndicate began distributing the daily strip nationally on May 9, 1960.

The title character was yet another variation on the absent-minded professor stereotype. A white-haired, portly, pipe-smoking, tweedy sort of a fellow, Phumble liked to tinker in his basement laboratory in the hope of devising the perfect instrument for cutting one's own hair or of coming up with the converter that would allow motorcars to run on water. He was not, however, just a loony inventor in the mold of Rube Goldberg's Lucifer G. Butts; he was just as inept in his academic and domestic life as he was in his creative endeavors, and he was often shown in run-ins with his wife, his in-laws, his colleagues, and his neighbors. An avid golfer, Yates managed to work into the strip a number of golf gags that had nothing whatsoever to do with Phumble's vocational or avocational activities.

Phumble later became a lecturer on physics at Hoohaw U., and this allowed the cartoonist to paint an acidulous—though not jaundiced—picture of academic life. Drawn in a loose style with a certain flair for telling detail, *Professor Phumble* (or *Prof. Phumble,* as it was often spelled) was an amiable and pleasant strip rather than an inspired or a riproaring one. Its twenty-year run, ending on June 17, 1980, brought many smiles to its readers, and perhaps even an occasional guffaw. What better epitaph for a comic strip?

M.H.

THE PUSSYCAT PRINCESS
1935–1947

Grace Drayton was one in a number of select women cartoonists who made it big in the comics in the early decades of the century. She had known fame (under her own name and as Grace Wiederseim, the name of her first husband) as the illustrator of *Toodles* and *Dimples,* among other comic pages, and especially as the graphic creator of the Campbell Kids, the two urchins that were for a long time the standard-bearers of the Campbell Soup Company. Nicknamed the Queen of Cute for her depiction of chubby, seraphic, cuddly little children, she had seen her income dwindle to nothing as the depression years deepened, her last comic creation, *Dolly Dimples and Baby Bounce* having been terminated in 1932. So, when she was contacted some years later by King Features Syndicate to illustrate a fairy-tale strip written by Ed Anthony, she eagerly accepted. The feature, titled *The Pussycat Princess,* was launched, as a Sunday page only, on March 10, 1935.

The scene was set in the storybook kingdom of Tabbyland, exclusively peopled with cuddly, round-faced kittens, all of them graced with big eyes and the heart-shaped mouths that were Drayton's trademark. The king was a democratic kind of monarch, ready to mingle with the populace at the drop of a crown, and always riding with the train engineer when taking a trip on the Royal Express. His daughter, the Princess of the title, was also a generous soul who liked to take orphan kittens on day trips and distribute fish to the felines in the poorer neighborhoods. The court was a brilliant affair, with its retinue of knights in armor, ladies-in-waiting, and sumptuously attired palace guards. They were all a bunch of happy, pleasure-loving cats, except for the aptly named Earl of Sourface, the court chamberlain, whose dictatorial manner always ran afoul of the Princess's forbearance. There was also a local police force, headed by the no-nonsense Sgt. Snoop of Scatland Yard in full Sherlockian paraphernalia, but they never had anything more serious to investigate than the theft of the royal goldfish or the mysterious appearance of drill-holes throughout the palace.

Drayton died early in 1936, and the feature passed into the hands of children's-book illustrator Ruth Carroll, who worked in close imitation of her predecessor's style. Under her tutelage some contemporary concerns started to creep into the strip, such as unemployment and the threat of war, but overall *The Pussycat Princess* remained squarely aimed at younger children all through World War II and beyond.

The Pussycat Princess (Anthony and Carroll), © 1939 King Features Syndicate

The text abounded in jokes, riddles, and little rhymes, but was mostly noted for its puns on the word "cat" (the local currency was the ducat, the social registry was known as the Royal Catalogue, etc.).

The Pussycat Princess was widely praised by educators and social workers for its wholesomeness. No less an authority than Dr. William Moulton Marston, a noted psychiatrist as well as the creator of *Wonder Woman,* extolled its "constructive influence" on children, an aspect of the strip Carroll never tired of pointing out. "I think the *Princess* is the kind of funny that mothers can read to their small children," she once stated. "We make a slight concession to the teenage fans by introducing such modern developments as a flying elephant and a flying carpet, but on the whole the accent is on gentle, humorous adventures among the kittens." The adventures did not prove to have enduring appeal, however, and the feature was dropped on July 13, 1947.

M.H.

QUINCY
`1970–1986`

King Features Syndicate debuted *Quincy* on June 17, 1970, as its offering in the area of African-American comic strips, a genre pioneered by Morrie Turner's *Wee Pals* in 1965. Whereas *Wee Pals* was influenced by *Peanuts* and has a suburban feel. *Quincy* was urban and set in Harlem, New York City, the boyhood home of its creator, Ted Shearer.

When he began *Quincy,* Shearer resigned his position as a television art director at Batten, Barton, Durstine & Osborn (BBDO), one of the major advertising agencies in the United States; he'd been with it for fifteen years. A painter and illustrator as well as cartoonist, Shearer created an extremely stylish strip.

Quincy was a ten-year-old inner-city kid being raised by his grandmother, Granny Dixon. He had a younger brother, Li'l Bo. They lived just above the poverty line. Other characters included his sassy girlfriend, Viola, and his best friend, Nickles, who was white.

Commuting into New York City by train from Westchester County, where he lived, Shearer had some of his drawings praised by King Features artist Bill Gilmartin. Shearer had previously sold King panel cartoons for its *Laff-A-Day* feature. His meeting with Gilmartin was just a chance encounter on the train. Shearer also told him about his cartoons that had been published in *Saturday Evening Post, Collier's,* and other major magazines.

Gilmartin brought Ted's work to the attention of King Features. The result was a request to develop an African-American strip. Shearer was already a "name" within the black community. At age 15, while a student at DeWitt Clinton High in New York City, he had sold a cartoon to the city's major African-American newspaper, the *Amsterdam News.* The paper, for which he developed the weekly panel *Next Door*, had continued to publish him ever since.

A veteran of the U.S. Army's 92nd Division in the segregated military of World War II, Ted Shearer knew from personal experience the pain of racism. However, he didn't feel *Quincy,* featuring a poor black child, was the right character to vent too much about social injustice. Rather, he used *Quincy* to be ever optimistic and upbeat, with a sunny outlook and a white best friend that was a parody of the cliché, "Some of my best friends are black."

Shearer's mentor in cartooning was E. Simms Campbell, creator of the *Esquire* magazine logo, the full-page sultan-and-his-harem cartoons, and a sexy, stylish *Cuties* panel for King Features. Few of his thousands of readers in mainstream America knew E. Simms Campbell was African American. He was an inspiration to Shearer who met him while still a high school student. He taught the young Shearer the ins and outs of the cartoon business.

Quincy was blessed with artwork of strong design and a creative use of ziptone. Visually, it jumped off the page at the reader. During its sixteen years in syndication, *Quincy,* along with Morrie Turner's *Wee Pals* and Brumsic Brandon, Jr.'s *Luther,* paved the way for the current generation of successfully syndicated African-American cartoonists.

B.C., Jr.

Quincy (T. Shearer), © 1972 King Features Syndicate

100 Years of Color Comics

THE AMATEUR DIME MUSEUM IN HOGAN'S ALLEY.

R. F. Outcault, *Hogan's Alley (The Yellow Kid),* 1896. Outcault's *Yellow Kid* was the object of fierce competition between Joseph Pulitzer's *New York World* and W. R. Hearst's *New York Journal.* This rivalry gave birth to the term *yellow journalism,* used to characterize the practices of the sensationalist press.

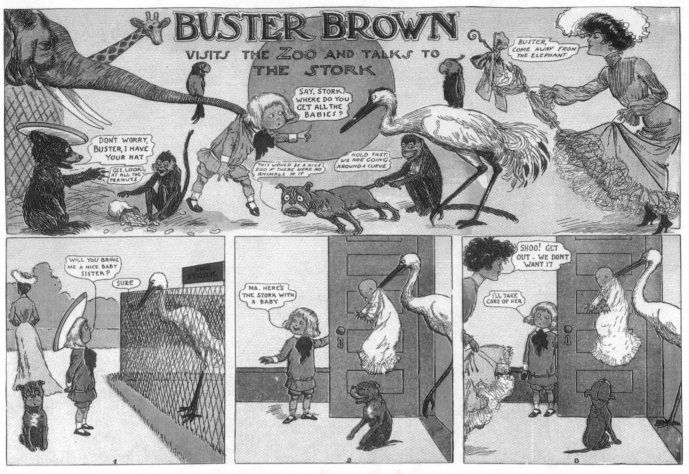

R. F. Outcault, *Buster Brown*, 1903. Shortly after abandoning *The Yellow Kid*, Outcault created his even more famous character, Buster Brown, in 1902.

R. F. Outcault, *Buster Brown*, 1903

R. F. Outcault, *Buster Brown,* © 1922 Newspaper Feature Service. A late example of the strip.

James Swinnerton, *M'Manus's Fence*, 1898. One of many series that Swinnerton contributed to the *New York Journal* at the turn of the century.

James Swinnerton, *Mount Ararat*, 1902. As early as the first years of this century, cartoonists such as Swinnerton had already become aware of the comics' potential as an art form, hence the self-referential character of this page.

James Swinnerton, *Little Jimmy*, 1915

F. M. Howarth, *Uncle Henpeck*, 1901. An example of the already outmoded picture story with typeset text instead of speech-balloons, by the creator of *Lulu and Leander*.

Rudolph Dirks, *The Katzenjammer Kids*, 1898. Born in 1897, *The Katzenjammer Kids* is the oldest newspaper strip still published.

Rudolph Dirks, *The Katzenjammer Kids*, ca. 1907

Harold Knerr, *The Original Katzenjammer Kids*, 1916. Knerr took over the Katzies after the celebrated court battle that pitted Hearst against Dirks for possession of the strip.

Rudolph Dirks, *The Captain and the Kids*, © 1931 United Feature Syndicate. After he left Hearst, Dirks drew his Katzenjammer characters under a new title.

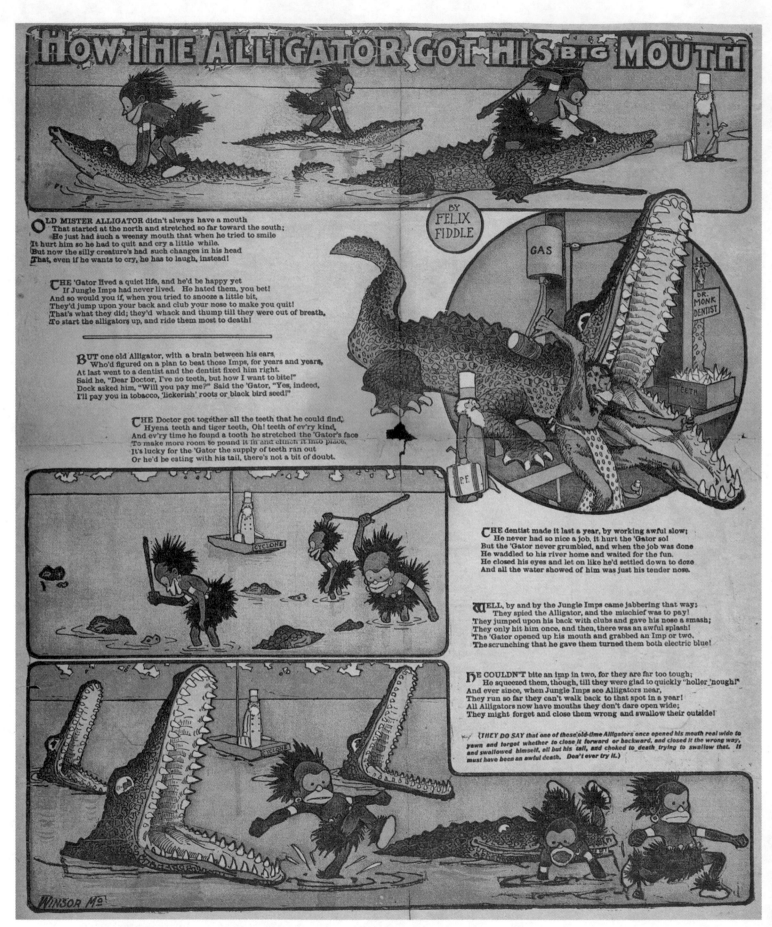

Winsor McCay, *Tales of the Jungle Imps,* 1903. *Jungle Imps* was McCay's earliest comic-page series.

Winsor McCay, *Tales of the Jungle Imps*, 1903

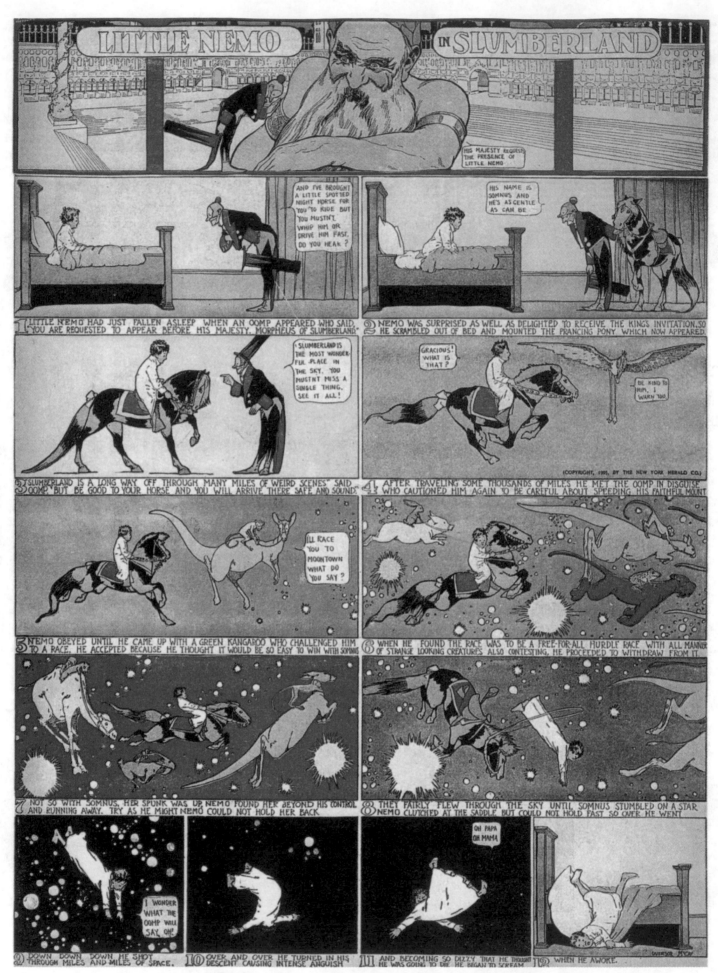

Winsor McCay, *Little Nemo in Slumberland*, 1905. This very first *Little Nemo* page appeared in the *New York Herald* on October 15, 1905.

Winsor McCay, *Little Nemo in Slumberland*, 1907. *Little Nemo* was McCay's greatest creation, and for artistic mastery of perspective, architectural details, and decorative design it has never been surpassed.

Winsor McCay, *Little Nemo in Slumberland*, 1907

Winsor McCay, *In the Land of Wonderful Dreams*, 1914. McCay's version of *Little Nemo* retitled for the Hearst newspapers.

Lyonel Feininger, *The Kin-der-Kids*, 1906. Before gaining fame as a fine artist associated with the Bauhaus school in Germany, Feininger enjoyed a cartooning career of outstanding achievement. *The Kin-der-Kids* is his most celebrated comics creation.

Lyonel Feininger, *The Kin-der-Kids*, 1906

Lyonel Feininger, *Wee Willie Winkie's World*, 1906. In Feininger's amazing surrealistic creation, Wee Willie Winkie, a naive little boy, finds himself in the midst of an enchanted universe where inanimate objects spring to life and familiar landscapes take on fantastic shapes.

This is the way the thunderstorm came the other day: At first a couple of clouds crept up, like scouts, over the hill, back of the little fern-house there, and peered over into the fields below.

They must have decided that there was a good wide space for an invasion, for soon a gigantic trumpeter-cloud mounted the hill-top, leading on a disorderly array of cloud-soldiery, with eager, threatening faces, and a great gray cat flew sprawling along overhead, so that things took on a very weird and uncomfortable appearance.

Lyonel Feininger, *Wee Willie Winkie's World*, 1906

F. B. Opper, *And Her Name Was Maud!*, 1906. Opper was an early practitioner of the comics medium. Among his creations were Happy Hooligan, Alphonse and Gaston, and (shown here) Maud the Mule.

F. B. Opper, *Happy Hooligan*, 1912. Opper's Alphonse and Gaston characters make a guest appearance.

Ed Carey, *Simon Simple*, 1906. Carey was a prolific cartoonist, and Simon Simple turned out to be his most popular creation.

George McManus, *The Newlyweds*, 1910. McManus's most famous comics feature prior to *Bringing Up Father*.

George McManus, *Nibsy the Newsboy*, 1906. So great was *Little Nemo*'s renown that shortly after its inception it gave rise to this delightful parody by the up-and-coming George McManus.

George McManus, *Their Only Child*, 1912. When McManus left Pulitzer for Hearst, he took his *Newlyweds* characters with him but changed the title of his strip.

George McManus, *Their Only Child*, 1912

George McManus, *Bringing Up Father,* 1918

Jim Nasium [?], *M. D'Auber*, 1908. An example of the wide variety of features offered by the newspapers' comic supplements in the first decade of the twentieth century; in this case, a satirical strip by the pseudonymous Jim Nasium.

C. W. Kahles, *Hairbreadth Harry*, 1909

C. W. Kahles, *Hairbreadth Harry*, 1923

Johnny Gruelle, *Mr. Twee Deedle*, 1912. A fine example of this fantasy strip by the author of the Raggedy Ann and Andy books.

Rube Goldberg, *Boob McNutt*, 1918. Goldberg's zaniest comic strip.

Rube Goldberg, *Boob McNutt,* © 1934 King Features Syndicate. An example from the last year of the strip.

Sidney Smith, *The Gumps*, 1919. *The Gumps* was the first comic strip to win a million-dollar contract for its author.

Sidney Smith, *The Gumps*, © 1928 Chicago Tribune–New York News Syndicate

Billy DeBeck, *Barney Google,* © 1922 King Features Syndicate

Billy DeBeck, *Barney Google,* © 1932 King Features Syndicate

Fontaine Fox, *Toonerville Folks,* © **1924 Bell Syndicate**

Frank King, *Gasoline Alley,* © 1924 Chicago Tribune

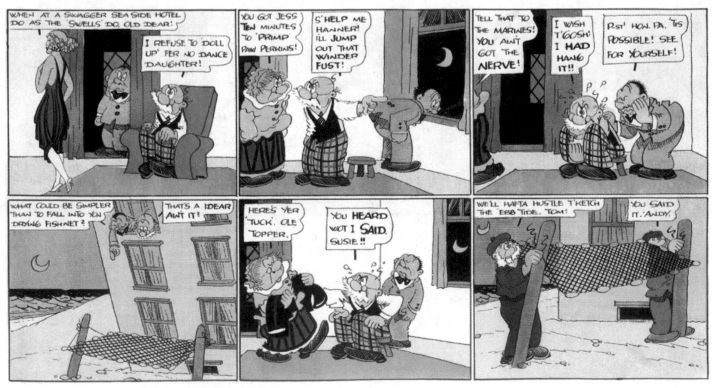

Cliff Sterrett, *Polly and Her Pals,* © 1922 King Features Syndicate

Cliff Sterrett, *Polly and Her Pals,* © 1926 King Features Syndicate. Sterrett's *Polly* is revered for its sophisticated, almost cubistic sense of design.

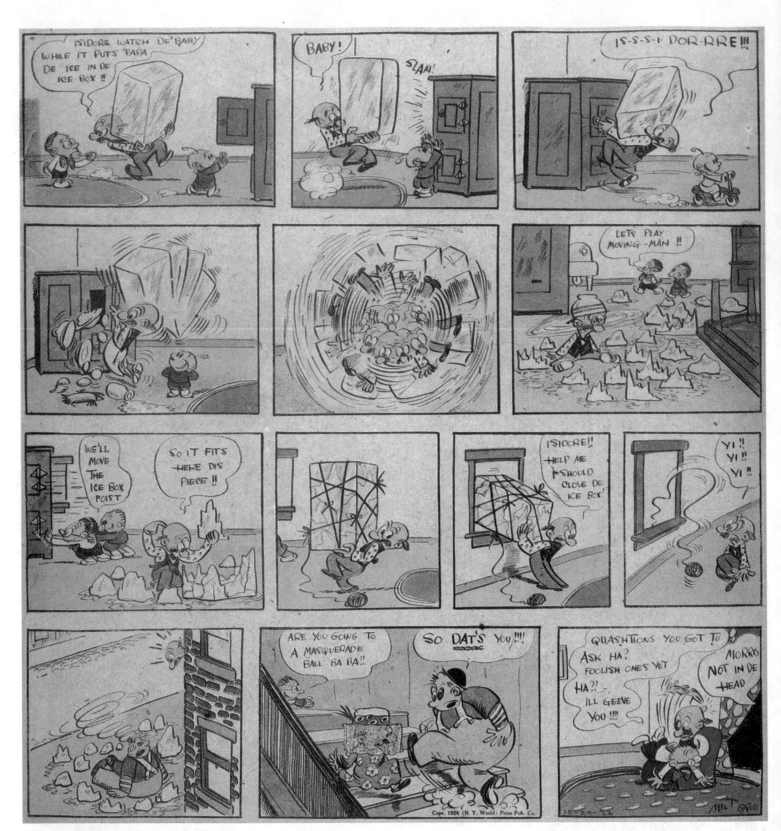

Milt Gross, *Nize Baby*, © 1926 Press Publishing Co.

Frank Willard, *Moon Mullins*, © 1928 Chicago Tribune–New York News Syndicate

Garrett Price, *White Boy*, © 1933 Chicago Tribune–New York News Syndicate. One of the most artistically literate of the comic strips of the 1930s, *White Boy* unfortunately did not last long.

Phil Nowlan and Dick Calkins, *Buck Rogers*, © 1933 National Newspaper Syndicate. Started in 1929, Buck Rogers is the granddaddy of science-fiction comics.

Roy Crane, *Captain Easy*, © 1934 NEA Service

Fred Harman, *Bronc Peeler,* © 1934 Fred Harman Features. At the bottom is a beautiful example of Harman's "original cowboy drawings," offered as prints to contest winners.

V. T. Hamlin, *Alley Oop*, © 1935 NEA Service

Rose O'Neill, *The Kewpies,* © 1935 King Features Syndicate

E. C. Segar, *Thimble Theatre*, © 1935 King Features Syndicate. This strip was the theater of Popeye's exploits.

Percy Crosby, *Skippy*, © 1935 King Features Syndicate

Alex Raymond, *Flash Gordon,* © 1935 King Features Syndicate. A fine example of Raymond's dynamic and expressive illustration.

Alex Raymond, *Jungle Jim,* © 1935 King Features Syndicate

Allan Dean and Zane Grey, *King of the Royal Mounted*, © 1935 King Features Syndicate

Harold Gray, *Little Orphan Annie*, © 1937 Chicago Tribune–New York News Syndicate

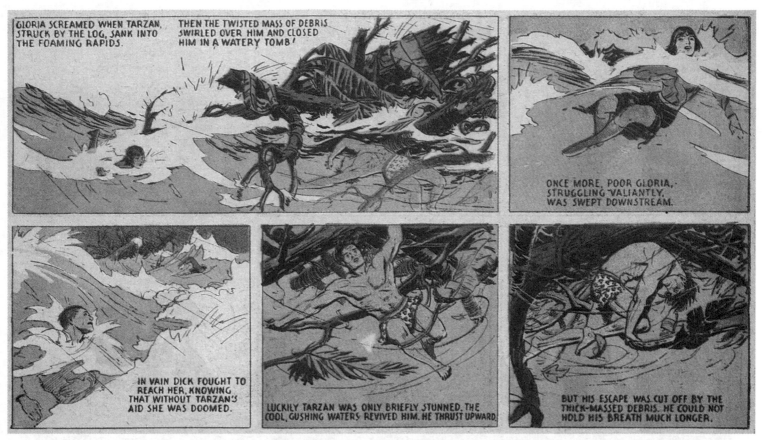

Harold Foster, *Tarzan*, © 1936 ERB, Inc.

Harold Foster, *Prince Valiant*, © 1951 King Features Syndicate. Foster's masterpiece is considered one of the finest examples of the illustrator's art in the comics medium.

Burne Hogarth, *Tarzan*, © 1943 ERB, Inc.

Frank Godwin, *Connie*, © 1936 Ledger Syndicate. One of the best-looking strips of the 1930s.

Frank Godwin, *Connie,* © 1937 Ledger Syndicate

William Ritt and Clarence Gray, *Brick Bradford*, © 1937 King Features Syndicate

Bill Holman, *Smokey Stover*, © 1938 Chicago Tribune–New York News Syndicate

Hal Forrest, *Tailspin Tommy*, © 1939 United Feature Syndicate

George Herriman, *Krazy Kat*, © 1940 King Features Syndicate

Edwina Dumm, *Tippie*, © 1940 George Matthew Adams Service

Lee Falk and Phil Davis, *Mandrake the Magician,* © 1940 King Features Syndicate

Ray Thompson and Charles Coll, *Myra North,* © 1941 NEA Service

Bob Moore and Carl Pfeufer, *Don Dixon,* © 1941 Watkins Syndicate

Milton Caniff, *Terry and the Pirates*, © 1941 Chicago Tribune–New York News Syndicate

Milton Caniff, *Terry and the Pirates*, © 1944 Chicago Tribune–New York News Syndicate. **Caniff used cinematic storytelling to make *Terry* and *Steve Canyon* landmarks of American comics.**

Milton Caniff, *Steve Canyon*, © 1968 Field Enterprises. Caniff drew the editor of this encyclopedia into the last panel.

John Lehti, *Tales from the Great Book*, ca. 1955, © Publishers Syndicate

Chester Gould, *Dick Tracy,* © 1942 Chicago Tribune–New York News Syndicate

Will Eisner, *The Spirit*, © 1948 Will Eisner. A fine example of Eisner's inventive page layouts and use of film-noir pictorial composition and moods.

Walt Kelly, *Pogo*, © 1953 Walt Kelly/OGPI, Inc. Kelly's philosophical, political, and insightful strip is one of the highlights of comics history.

Winter sets upon the plains. Lance, Blaze, and Fitzpatrick race it through the Nebraska badlands, then fight their way west through ice and snow. At last—800 miles out of St. Louis—Fort Laramie looms like an oasis on the broad plain stretching to the mountains . . .

The double gates swing open and a rousing welcome greets the travelers. But suddenly there is a hush—

. . . One of the travelers is a white orphan child! She speaks a language the mountain men have all but forgotten—English—and crusty old hearts melt with nostalgia.
And so the Princess of the Plains is enthroned!

Lucien Fontenelle, post trader, gushes with joy. "I am host! I 'ave guests! Once more, for a fleeting moment, ze blood on my knife weel dry as I become a gentleman! Come, m'sieurs—a small feast!"

Fontenelle serves crocks of milk, a luxury. When this is gone he brings on French wine. Then—
"Sacre! Wat ees zat commotion in ze quadrangle?!"

31 1-1-56   ©1956, WARREN TUFTS ENTERPRISES All rights reserved

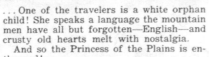

More travelers!
"If you, Sir, are the commander of this post I demand you order your savages to unhand me and my wife! We are citizens of the United States, Sir, and I bear authority of the government on my person! Do you hear me, Sir?"
"But . . . ze milk ees all gone!" Fontenelle says.

Warren Tufts, *Lance*, © 1956 Warren Tufts Enterprises

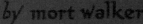

Mort Walker, *Beetle Bailey,* © 1963 King Features Syndicate

Mort Walker and Dik Browne, *Hi and Lois,* © 1963 King Features Syndicate

Stan Lynde, *Rick O'Shay*, © 1969 Chicago Tribune–New York News Syndicate

Stan Lynde, *Rick O'Shay*, © 1970 Chicago Tribune–New York News Syndicate

Dale Messick, *Brenda Starr*, © 1970 Chicago Tribune–New York News Syndicate

Jim Lawrence and Jorge Longaron, *Friday Foster*, © 1970 Chicago Tribune–New York News Syndicate

Leonard Starr, *On Stage*, © 1970 Chicago Tribune–New York News Syndicate

Jim Scancarelli, *Gasoline Alley,* © 1989 Chicago Tribune–New York News Syndicate. A recent version of a venerable strip, notable for its inventive use of color and its array of comic characters.

On this last, nostalgic note this hundred-year odyssey comes to its conclusion: around the world (of comics) in more than ninety pictures. This eventful journey has taken us from crude humor to fantasy, from satire to adventure, from politics to social commentary. Traveling through the comics is traveling through time: in these images we can recognize the hopes, longings, fears, fads, and fancies of the century better and more immediately than in the headlines of the very newspapers that had given the comics shelter. These images, some seemingly so quaint and passé, reveal the temper, the tenor, and the flavor of their times more graphically than any newsreel, because they have been filtered through the talent, style, and sensibility of each individual artist and writer.

The comics—the funnies—had been originally conceived for Sundays and for color (black-and-white daily strips came later), and the colorful panorama that has unfolded on these pages has hopefully captured the fun, joy, and excitement of lazy Sundays spent at home or far away. So, happy birthday to the comics—and to all our childhoods.

RACE RILEY AND THE COMMANDOS
1941–1945

Arguably the most obscure of all the gung-ho strips to come out of World War II, *Race Riley and the Commandos* was United Feature Syndicate's belated entry into the field. While rival organizations had been fighting the enemy for years, with the help of such worthies as Terry, Captain Easy, and Don Winslow, UFS only joined the fray late in 1941 with this daily strip drawn by Milburn Rosser.

Riley was a blond, clean-cut, all-American hero who itched to take part in the good fight and enlisted in a British commando unit for the purpose. Soon he was leading his group in raids into enemy-occupied Europe and had many a close shave, with the Gestapo breathing hard down his neck, before making it back to England, in the hallowed traditions of the genre. Finding even this kind of action too tepid for his taste, he later joined the French underground, battling the German occupiers in the company of a female resistance fighter, an authentic princess of royal blood who wore mask and cowl to disguise her identity in order to spare her relatives from Nazi reprisals.

The scripts were predictable and hackneyed, and Rosser's drawings, while adequate, did not convey the kind of patriotic spirit necessary to sustain a strip of this kind. Race Riley and his commandos ended their wartime service with the cessation of hostilities, in the summer of 1945.

M.H.

RADIO PATROL
1933–1950

In August 1933 Eddie Sullivan, the night city editor of the Hearst-owned *Boston Daily Record*, and Charlie Schmidt, the art editor of the paper, got together to pro-

duce a police strip called *Pinkerton, Jr.*, about the exploits of a young crime-solver. The feature attracted the notice of King Features editor Joseph Connolly, and on April 16, 1934, it started national syndication as a daily strip renamed *Radio Patrol*.

As the new title implied, the action centered on a radio police car (a novelty then) occupied by red-headed, handsome Sergeant Pat and his fat, speech-impaired partner, Stutterin' Sam. The two men were often helped in their investigations by their young protégé, Pinky Pinkerton (the Pinkerton, Jr., of the earlier version) and his Irish setter called, with a remarkable lack of invention, Irish. The romantic interest was provided by blonde Molly Day, a woman detective with whom Pat enjoyed a platonic relationship. The pair of uniformed cops acted more like police investigators than patrolmen on the beat, nabbing bank robbers, bringing protection racketeers to heel, and practically constituting a two-men SWAT team (before the concept even existed) that swept every perpetrator in range of their police radio out of commission.

Radio Patrol enjoyed enough popularity to warrant a weekly color page in November 1934. The first episode was packed with thrills, and involved a gang of smugglers, the abduction of Molly, and a breathless speedboat chase across Boston Harbor. There were scenes of violence and even sadism, with Molly on the verge of getting raped. Sullivan was told by the syndicate to tone down the story lines, however, for fear of offending the parents of comics-reading kiddies, and the page settled into a humdrum chronicle of petty street crimes solved (usually with muscle) by two-fisted Pat.

By the end of the 1930s the emphasis was placed on the main protagonist, and the feature rechristened *Sergeant Pat of Radio Patrol*. The hero acquired a more or less permanent nemesis in the person of crafty gang leader Big Dan, and a rival on the force represented by the loutish and invidious

Radio Patrol (Sullivan and Schmidt), © 1934 King Features Syndicate

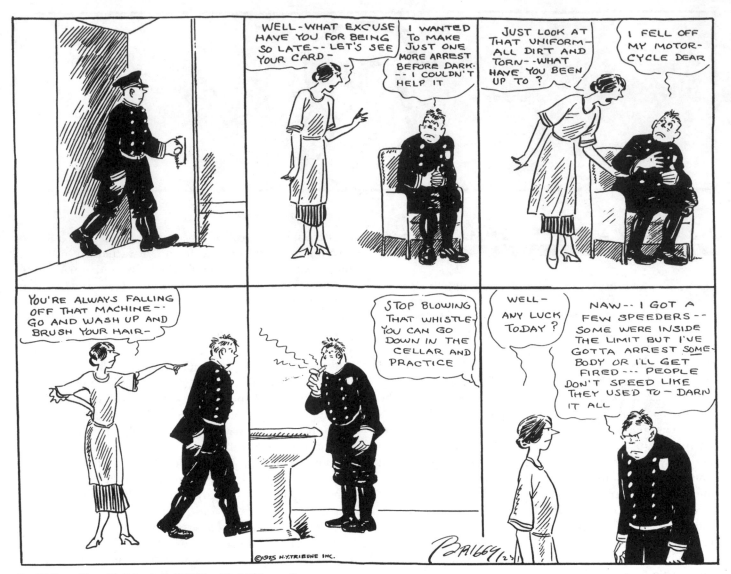

Real Folks at Home (C. Briggs), © 1925 New York Tribune, Inc.

Inspector Maggin, who tried at every turn to get Pat demoted. He also found an ally in "the Buster," a short, feisty district attorney clearly modeled on Tom Dewey. Despite Sullivan's interesting continuities, and incisive, atmospheric drawings by Schmidt, *Radio Patrol* could not compete with *Dick Tracy* or the syndicate's own *Secret Agent X-9*. Termed "a fast, clean, very modern and very illustrative detective strip" by Coulton Waugh, it was always regarded as something of a second-string feature by King. In the mid-1940s its readership steadily declined, and the Sunday was discontinued on October 20, 1946, with the dailies hanging on a little while longer, to December 11, 1950.

M.H.

REAL FOLKS AT HOME
1924–1929

Among the many alternating series that Clare Briggs contributed to the *New York Tribune*, none came as close to being a genuine comic strip as *Real Folks at Home*. While these vignettes did not have recurring characters, they had a recurrent theme, and they were usually laid out, comic-strip fashion, in two rows of three panels each. *Real*

Folks at Home started running, several times weekly, in 1924 and came to an end only with Briggs's death in 1929.

The series focused on men from different walks of life coming home from work and imagined how their respective occupations might affect their homecoming. The songwriter, for instance, would announce his arrival with the lilting refrain, "Mammy, Maam-m-mee, is dinner ready for your baby?" adding, "I've been earning for you a lot of money"—to which his wife would reply, "And I've been yearning for you a lot, my honey." An orchestra leader would barge in imperiously, waving his baton and asking, "Is my supper ready? Answer pianissimo!"—to which his spouse would reply in operatic tones, "Yes-s, supper is ready, oh it is read-ee!" and so on *ad jocularum*. One of the funniest variations on this theme consisted in having the husband come in late and trying to explain himself. Thus an aviator would say, "I couldn't get here sooner. My inductor went on the blink and I had to come down in Ireland to fix it," while an astronomer sheepishly asseverated, "Well, I was kinda waiting for the moon to come up..."

These short sketches of imagined domestic life were sometimes excruciatingly funny, and never less than inventive and witty. Briggs drew the series in his usual scratchy style, with a minimum of background detail and a strong attention to faces and gestures. His characters always looked right on target—his song plugger, in straw hat and checked pants, appeared suitably upbeat and emphatic, his traffic cop consonantly dumb and flustered, his radio announcer fittingly brash and sonorous. While other Briggs series may be better remembered, *Real Folks at Home* deserves recognition as an imaginative study in typology and characterization.

M.H.

RED BARRY
1934–1938

As an answer to the tremendous success enjoyed by *Dick Tracy*, King Features in 1934 fielded no fewer than three different police strips. Among them was *Red Barry* by Will Gould (no relation to Chester Gould), which first appeared as a daily on March 19, 1934; when a Sunday version was added on February 3, 1935, it received the full-blown title *Red Barry, Undercover Man*. The daily and Sunday versions ran separate continuities, except for a period between June 1936 and August 1937.

Detective Red Barry looked, behaved, and sounded like Jimmy Cagney. A man of few words and brutal action, he showed scant regard for the legal niceties of police procedure, and in his rough-and-tumble ways he anticipated Mike Hammer more than he emulated Dick Tracy. His superior, Inspector Scott, often winked at his subordinate's sometimes questionable practices, as long as he got results (and get results he certainly did). Like most tough guys of the time, Red had no use for dames, and time and again he spurned the advances of the lovely Mississippi, a blonde, Jean Arthur type, who was sick with yearning for the red-haired detective. As compensation he played big brother to the street urchin Ouchy Mugouchy and his two youthful pals, collectively known as the Terrific Three, who often served as Red's ubiquitous eyes and ears.

The action took place in a big city, unnamed but easily recognizable as New York (Gould didn't bother to disguise some of its landmarks or street names), and was most often set in Chinatown, whose dives and alleyways the author had gotten to know well in his former capacity as reporter on the real-life *New York Daily Graphic*. (His experience served him equally well in his frequent depictions of newsroom scenes.) As the Sunday title indicated, Red often worked undercover, passing himself off variously as a boxer, a cab driver, a journalist, and a hoodlum. In his investigations he came up hard against a rogues' gallery of evildoers, from the oily "Count" Rinaldi to the crazed ventriloquist Sarno and his homicidal puppet. One of his more unusual antagonists was the Flame, a slinky Eurasian gang leader who used her feminine wiles along with more direct means of persuasion to hold Chinatown in thrall. The red-haired cop more often than not cracked his cases (and a few

skulls) the hard-boiled way, with his fists, but he sometimes also used his powers of deduction, as when he was able to indentify the culprit in the murder of a Tin Pan Alley composer upon hearing the suspect humming the song the tunesmith had been working on when he was killed at his piano (where Red had learned to read music was never explained).

Because of the strip's high violence content and its explicit sexual overtones, Gould soon found himself in hot water, and he was told by the syndicate to tone down the proceedings. This led him to leave more and more of the artwork in the hands of his assistant, Walter Frehm, and the feature suffered a precipitous decline. The dailies were discontinued on August 14, 1937, while the Sunday version, soon minus Red Barry, who was sent away to recover from wounds received in the line of duty, continued with only the Terrific Three to sustain reader interest. This proved insufficient, and the weekly continuity also came to an end, on July 17, 1938.

A footnote: King Features in 1940 turned again to Will Gould and Red Barry for a comic-book insert they were planning as an answer to Will Eisner's highly successful *Spirit* supplement (this was confirmed by Eisner). Gould turned out several weeks' worth of continuity, but to all appearances the project never saw print.

Red Barry would deserve to be remembered only as a solid, second-tier crime strip, were it not for one paradigmatic story that ran daily for almost a full year, from July 1935 to June 1936. The real star of the piece was the Monk, a hooded master criminal who from a lair in Chinatown spun a web of corruption, blackmail, and murder all over the city. The action reeked of violence, agony, and torture. In a series of low, claustrophobic panels Gould created an atmosphere of unrelieved blackness, with a predominance of night scenes, dark skies, and sinister shadows. It was in this story that Mississippi made a dramatic entrance, saved from drowning by Red Barry after her attempted suicide. Soon the detective started to suspect that his protégé was somehow involved in the goings-on. Pursuing a series of seemingly unrelated leads, Red finally broke through all the way to the Monk, who was revealed to be a woman, Mississippi's sister Lola.

Red Barry (W. Gould), © 1935 King Features Syndicate

Had Gould been allowed to develop more tales of the same artistic quality and breathless suspense, *Red Barry* might indeed have become a worthy rival to *Dick Tracy*, as it had been intended at the outset.

M.H.

THE RED KNIGHT
1940–1943

In the late 1930s the newspaper syndicates became alarmed at losing more and more of their juvenile audience to the upstart medium of comic books with their colorful array of costumed superheroes. Some, in an "if you can't beat 'em, join 'em" move, turned out syndicated-strip versions of comic-book titles; others decided to create their own superpowered champions. This was the case with the Register and Tribune Syndicate, which in the month of June 1940 not only managed to release the *Spirit* comic-book section for newspapers but also came up with a superhero to call its own in John Welch and Jack McGuire's *The Red Knight*.

Writer Welch cut right to the chase in the very first panel of the new feature. "In his secret laboratory, secluded deep in a wood," it read, "Dr. Van Lear is completing an incredible experiment that is destined to astound the whole world." The experiment turned out to be the Red Knight, an ordinary mortal endowed with supernatural powers, thanks to the scientist's "plus power" that gave the Knight superstrength, superspeed, even invisibility, though, unlike Superman, he couldn't fly.

It was to *Superman* indeed that *The Red Knight* was most closely related, but in order to appeal to the adults as well as to the kiddies, the fantastic elements were toned down and never reached the heights of absurdity that were the hallmarks of comic-book superheroes. As a result *The Red Knight* ended pleasing nobody, despite some amusing scripting by Welch and agreeably campy drawings by McGuire (the Red Knight himself ran around in a colorful Roman centurion costume that made him look like an extra in a Hollywood epic). After a couple of years the authors gave up on the superhero concept and turned the protagonist into simple Alan Knight, secret agent for the

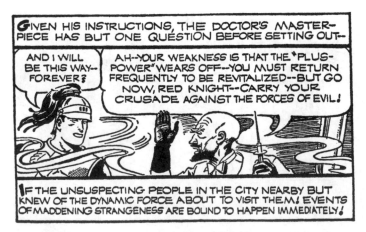

The Red Knight (Welch and McGuire), © 1940 Register and Tribune Syndicate

U.S. government. Like its hero, the strip unfortunately couldn't fly, and in September 1943 it finally ground to a halt, another casualty of the "me too" syndrome.

M.H.

RED RYDER
1938–1964

After the failure of *Bronc Peeler* in 1938, Fred Har-man went east in the hope of securing a permanent syndicate position. He un-successfully tried out for *King of the Royal Mounted* but attracted the attention of Stephen Slesinger, who had developed *King* for syndication, and was asked to try his hand at another western strip, along the lines of his earlier creation. Thus was *Red Ryder* born on November 6, 1938, as a Sunday feature, to be followed by a daily strip on March 27, 1939. Both versions were distributed by NEA Service.

In the very first installment, the strip's red-haired hero, looking very much like an older brother to Bronc Peeler, acquired his famous Navaho sidekick, the ten-year-old Little Beaver, himself a holdover from the earlier feature. *Red Ryder,* however, was more realistic, less juvenile than *Bronc Peeler* had been. Harman skillfully mixed elements of derring-do, suspense, and humor and came up with a winning combination that was to make his new creation into the champion of western strips in the space of little more than a year.

Of particular importance to the popularity of the strip was the authentic flavor of time and place that Harman was able to convey. The period—the 1890s, after the last of the Indian wars but before the advent of the automobile—and the setting—the little town of Rimrock, in southwestern Colorado, at the foot of the San Juan Mountains, in the Blanco Basin—looked just right. Harman knew the region well. He had been raised there, and later bought a ranch in Pagosa Springs, which we can imagine as being not too far removed from Rimrock.

The locale was depicted with almost archeological authenticity. The mining towns were pictured in all their rough-and-tumble rambunctiousness; the Mexican settlements looked like not much more than adobe shantytowns; the ranch houses were rendered with gruff simplicity and no Hollywood glamour; while the Indian pueblos were drawn with almost photographic precision and without glossing over the squalor. Most impressive of all was the formidable presence of the Rocky Mountains, whose peaks and gorges towered over the pathetic goings-on among the men below.

In these surroundings Red emerged as one of the most unconventional of western heroes. While his innate sense of justice drove him into some of his adventures, he could also be guided by more pragmatic motives, like tracking down a clever con-man in order to get back the thousand dollars he had been swindled out of, or joining a traveling circus to pay off some unexpected expenses. He had also been known to hire out his gun on occasion. "There are people who need me," he once declared on just such an assignment, judiciously adding, "and I'm bound to make a heap of money." Throughout the years he remained an impenitent bachelor, while at the same time keeping an appreciative eye out for the ladies, be they blonde-tressed demure schoolmarms, fiery Mexican senoritas, or wayward Indian princesses. At any rate, why should he have married? As Red himself once stated, he already had a family: his aunt, "the Duchess," a strong-willed, no-nonsense matriarch who helped him manage his ranch, and his adopted son, Little Beaver.

Red Ryder (F. Harman), © 1949 McNaught Syndicate

Little Beaver, next to Red the most important character in the strip, was a Navaho Indian dressed in the correct attire of his tribe: hair hanging loose, with a simple strip of cloth around his forehead, loin-cloth and hip-high chaps. His language, however, was the sort of pidgin English favored by Hollywood hacks, such as "Him gettum plenty bad, Red Ryder!" A boy of unusual resourcefulness and pluck, Beaver would often get Red out of some tight spot, as in the episode in which he triggered a horse stampede to divert the attention of the outlaws who held Red captive, and liberated the carrot-topped cowboy in the ensuing confusion.

If characterization, attention to detail, the slightest touch of pathos, and a penchant for wry humor were the hallmarks of *Red Ryder,* action remained the keynote of the strip, as befitted a good western of the old school, as *Ryder* was. With its muddy, unpaved streets, shaky houses, and rundown general stores, Rimrock, for some reason, proved an irresistible magnet for outlaws of every stripe and description. Those desperadoes would have before long taken over the town (whose lone defender was the cantankerous, ineffectual Sheriff Newt) had it not been for Red. Armed with his trusted .45 Colt revolver and his Winchester rifle, he could face any number of opponents. In the course of his adventures Red knew many scary experiences. He was hung by the neck, his feet precariously resting on a shaky board; was left to drown in a caved-in mine tunnel; was closeted in a dark room with a rattlesnake. He was shot through various parts of his body, had his leg broken, was blinded with acid, and was left spread-eagled under the scorching desert sun.

Red's enemies included a whole slew of offbeat villains, such as the sinister gambler and hired assassin Ace Hanlon; Banjo Bill, the music-loving killer who kept a gun concealed in his instrument; Donna Ringo, the seductive leader of a gang of train robbers; and a roving band of circus freaks working their depredations out of a traveling tent show. There was smaller fry, too, like the thieving twins, Oliver and Bolivar, and the incorrigible con-man Buckskin. Around those characters and hundreds more, Fred Harman and his scriptwriters, chief among them the talented Russ Winterbotham, wove tales filled with excitement and humor.

In the 1940s *Red Ryder* had become the most popular of western strips by far. It was adapted into comic books and brought to the screen; it was also voted "favorite comic strip" by the Boys' Clubs of America. Harman drew the feature in his forceful style, but with greater technical proficiency than he had shown in his earlier *Bronc Peeler.* He displayed a virile line made of an odd mixture of awkwardness and concision. The Sunday page was often accompanied by an educational panel called *Red Ryder's Corral of Western Lingo,* in which Harman indulged his weakness for grammar-school pedagogics.

In the 1950s *Red Ryder,* which in the meantime had been picked up by the McNaught Syndicate, gave increasing signs of deterioration, as Harman more and more came to rely on ghosts. These included, at one time or another, Edmond Good, Jim Gary, and John Wade Hampton. In the early 1960s Harman made his retirement from the strip official, and Bob McLeod carried on as best he could for a while longer. King Features, which had meanwhile taken over the syndication, decided to discontinue carrying the property late in 1964.

M.H.

REDEYE
1967–present

Born in Utah and living in Idaho, Gordon Bess was ideally suited as a cartoonist to try his hand at a comic-strip western; this he did with *Redeye,* which started syndication by King Features as a daily on September 11, 1967, with the Sunday version coming out at the end of the same week.

What *Tumbleweeds* had been doing to the myth of the rugged cowboy, *Redeye* was to do to the legend of the noble Indian. The Chickiepan tribe without a doubt comprise some of the most fainthearted, soft-headed braves ever assembled around a wigwam—always ready to follow the warpath in the wrong direction or to barter their tomahawks for smuggled firewater. Their sachem, the pudgy, slightly befuddled Redeye, tries to keep his warriors in line, to little effect. His dreams of military glory are always thwarted not only by the marked lack of mettlesomeness shown by his unruly troops but, closer to him, by the contrariness of his mustang, Loco. As his master orders a

Redeye (G. Bess), © 1971 King Features Syndicate

charge, Loco would be sure to run the other way; when he is instructed to keep quiet in order to surprise an enemy war party, the cowardly mount would go "clippety-clippety-clop" with a vengeance.

Nor is the sachem better served at home. His wife's cooking gives him heartburn, his small son, Pokey, drives him bananas with his practical jokes, and his lovely and nubile daughter, Tawny, is in love with the tribe's most hapless warrior, the accident-prone Tanglefoot. Their smooching and cooing drive Redeye to homicidal fury but, as with most of his other efforts, to no effect. Try as he might with bow and arrow, lance or tomahawk, the incensed sachem has not been able to dispatch this Indian Romeo to his ancestors.

Until the time of his death in 1990, Bess strove, in his own words, to "draw and ink the six dailies and Sunday page by myself." This dedication was apparent in the expressiveness and polish of the drawings: the action proceeded in seamless sequence, and the actors moved with the elasticity of animated-cartoon characters. In addition the screwball situations blended effortlessly with the author's firsthand knowledge of the West, and scenery, animals, and customs were depicted with a deft, if satirical, hand.

Following Bess's death, the team of Bill Yates (scripting) and Mel Casson (drawing) has taken over the feature. While they have not exhibited the same flair for absurd situations and unexpected twists the creator often brought to *Redeye*, they have at least managed to keep the strip on an even keel for the past few years.

M.H.

REG'LAR FELLERS
1917–1949

Begun inconspicuously as a single-panel daily feature in 1917, Gene Byrnes's ingratiating *Reg'lar Fellers* blossomed into a full-fledged comic strip in the early 1920s. Like many other titles of that era, its history proved tortuous and unlinear. *Reg'lar Fellers* was originally conceived by Byrnes as a throwaway segment of his highly popular *New York Telegram* series *It's a Great Life If You Don't Weaken* (which became the unofficial motto of the American Expeditionary Forces in Europe during World War I), but the Reg'lar Fellers (they were children) soon caught the fancy of the public, and in 1920 became the protagonists of their own reg'lar daily strip. In the meantime the cartoonist had started a Sunday page for the *Telegram*'s parent newspaper, the *New York Herald,* under the title *Wide Awake Willie,* whose kid characters resembled the *Reg'lar Fellers* cast in all but name. In November 1920 the Sunday feature changed its name to *Reg'lar Fellers,* and from then on dailies and Sundays functioned as one.

The Reg'lar Fellers consisted of Jimmie Dugan, the ringleader, always neatly dressed in dark suit with cap and bowtie; his best pal, the voracious Puddinhead Duffy; Puddinhead's little brother, Pinhead; the nondescript Baggy Scanlon; and Bump Mahoney, a precocious curbstone philosopher in overalls. Later Aggie Riley, Jimmie's sweetheart, and a mutt of undetermined pedigree, Bullseye, also joined the little band. They all resided in a working-class Irish neighborhood of a big city (possibly Brooklyn, which was pretty rural in spots at the time), along with their extended families. The kids' parents, grandparents, and other relatives often figured in some of the jokes, and on Sundays the readers were frequently given glimpses into their homes. Other walk-on roles were taken by Mister Duffy the "pleecemin'," Mister Oomlauf the deli owner, Mister Case the street cleaner, and assorted neighborhood stalwarts.

The Fellers were an active and ebullient lot, jumping over fences, playing pranks on the neighbors, cutting classes, and generally indulging in all the activities their age entitled them to. In the street they engaged in games of one-upmanship (or one-upkidship), boasting about their respective fathers' sporting exploits, or their uncles' exalted positions in life, and trying to mooch candy or ice cream from one another. They were also uncannily aware of the less savory facts of life: Bullseye was told as he watched the pork-butcher's shop window, "There's your papa 'n Aunt Lena 'n Uncle Willie 'n Li'l Walter 'n Cousin Jim 'n everybody!" When it came to formal learning, however, they didn't fare as well. Asked by his teacher to locate San Diego, Jimmie declared that it was between Boston and Montreal because "that's where it is on our radio!" Another time, queried as to his excuse for coming in late, he breathlessly answered, "I hurried so fast I forgot to make one up!"

Byrnes, who owned the copyright on the strip, grew dissatisfied with the Herald-Tribune distribution, and he jumped ship for the Bell Syndicate in the 1930s, before deciding to go the self-syndicating route. Despite an auspicious start at the beginning of the 1940s (in 1941 there was

Reg'lar Fellers (G. Byrnes), © 1926 New York Tribune, Inc.

a *Reg'lar Fellers* motion picture, with child actor Billy Lee in the lead, as well as a radio show), the move proved ultimately detrimental to the strip, which in the post–World War II era went into a downward slide. In 1949 Byrnes, seeing the writing on the wall, terminated the strip on a high note.

A minutious, painstaking cartoonist with a great flair for drawing kids and nonstop action, Byrnes imposed his style on the various assistants he employed over the years (Tack Knight, Burr Inwood, George Carlson), and he proved a great influence on many of his colleagues, especially in the 1920s and 1930s. Long after his newspaper strip had become a fond memory, he kept his position as a guiding light in his profession by publishing an important number of how-to books, using the *Reg'lar Fellers* cast as examples.

M.H.

REX MORGAN, M.D.
1948–present

When *Rex Morgan, M.D.*, first appeared on May 10, 1948, the strip signaled an advance in the naturalism vein in the comics, at the same time that it helped spark an American obsession with the stories of the sick and dying. Rex and his admiring nurse, June Gale, minded their patients' medical and personal lives in a soap-operalike fashion similar to that which would dominate a chunk of television from the 1950s until the present.

Created by Dr. Nicholas Dallis, a medical-school graduate who later specialized in psychiatry, the strip is a fast-moving continuity that deals with real-life people and their encounters with medical problems. Rex is a straightforward physician who does not lecture or talk down to his patients. He occasionally philosophizes about trends and dilemmas in the profession and crusades for change. In one 1950 episode, he criticized the system of elective coroners, pointing out that individuals without medical credentials could end up in that important position. In other sequences, Rex helped destroy stereotyped myths surrounding different diseases—for instance, that leprosy is highly contagious and totally disfiguring. He hinted at euthanasia in at least one story and was the first comic-strip character to talk about cancer quackery, epilepsy, blindness, and cerebral palsy. By the 1970s, Rex (and by extension, Dallis) let his disenchantment with medicine be known as he told June: "A doctor can no longer practice medicine to the best of his ability and moral judgment! He must practice as though preparing a brief for the day he's taken into court!"

Rex Morgan, M.D., reflected a trend at the time of its launch that packaged teams of specialists to produce comic strips. Dallis, under various pseudonyms and anonymously, provided imaginative stories with roughed-out sketches of characters, while Marvin Bradley drew the major characters and Frank Edgington, minor characters and backgrounds. Later, Tony DiPreta worked on *Rex Morgan, M.D.* The artwork of Bradley and Edgington was realistic, with ample depth of field rather full backgrounds, and vivid contrasts of blacks and whites.

The strip was also one of the early results of marketing

Rex Morgan (Bradley and Edgington), © 1965 Publishers Newspaper Syndicate

research and analysis entering the comics. Publishers Syndicate, which took a chance with Dallis's idea, had used public opinion sampling to determine the extent of an audience and to shape *Rex Morgan, M.D.* Originally, seventy newspapers carried the strip, and rather quickly, the list of clients grew to three hundred, including some abroad.

For the last twenty-nine years of his life, Dallis wrote three daily comic strips, the other two being *Judge Parker* (1952) and *Apartment 3-G* (1962). He died in 1991 at age 79, leaving to the comics a legacy of accurate and socially relevant portrayals of the medical and legal fields that were both instructive and entertaining. Woody Wilson is now writing the strip, with Tony DiPreta doing the artwork.

J.A.L.

RICK O'SHAY
1958–1981

Rick O'Shay was one of America's last notable western strips. It was created in April 1958 for the Chicago Tribune–New York News Syndicate by Stan Lynde, a young Montanan who had been raised on his father's ranch and knew the West from personal experience. Lynde had wanted to draw a serious adventure strip, but the heyday of such strips was over and the syndicates were interested only in gag humor strips, so Lynde took what he could get.

The original setting was Conniption, a barely populated stereotypical western semi–ghost town in contemporary America. Its inhabitants were all western stereotypes with punny names: Rick O'Shay, the amiable young sheriff; Manuel Labor, his well-meaning but lazy deputy; Deuces Wilde, the flamboyant gambler; Hipshot Percussion, the deadly gunfighter who really had a heart of gold; Gaye Abandon, owner of the town saloon; the neighboring Kyute Indian tribe, and so on. These characters, mostly good

Rick O'Shay (S. Lynde), © 1965 Chicago Tribune

friends, were satisfied to lead a laid-back rural life. The humorous plots during the strip's early years generally involved culture conflicts between their old-fashioned lifestyle and stereotypes of modern America: a visit by Rick's big-city private-investigator cousin, Shamus (a parody of the then-current TV mania for private-eye series like *77 Sunset Strip*); Hollywood's hiring of a couple of Kyute braves as experts on Indian authenticity, which dazzles them into "going Hollywood"; and so forth.

As the strip evolved, Lynde developed and enriched the personalities of his main cast, and made his art style more seriously realistic. By 1964 he had established its popularity solidly enough that the syndicate allowed him to transform it into the genuine historical adventure strip that he had always wanted. The time was changed to the 1880s, and Conniption became a live frontier town in Montana Territory. The cast kept their punny names but took on a continuing soap-opera relationship. In the daily strip, Rick's job as sheriff became serious, and his life was often in danger. The Sunday pages were more relaxed, and became famous for Lynde's panoramas of the western countryside and his graphic essays on the pleasures of camping out and staying in touch with nature.

In 1977, after a dispute with his syndicate over his rights to *Rick O'Shay*, Lynde abandoned it to create a new strip that he could control. *Rick O'Shay* was continued for a short time longer by writer Marian Dern and artist Alfredo Alcala, but it lacked Lynde's personal familiarity with the West. It was discontinued in 1981. In the late 1980s, Lynde started his own publishing company, Cottonwood Graphics, Inc., and bought the rights to Rick O'Shay. He has since been reissuing the strips in a series of high-quality trade paperback editions, such as *Rick O'Shay, The Dailies, 1959–1960*. In 1992 he wrote his first new Rick story in fifteen years for publication in comic-book format, *Rick O'Shay and Hipshot: The Price of Fear* (two issues of thirty-two pages each).

F.P.

RIGHT AROUND HOME
See MYRTLE

RIP KIRBY
1946–present

Rip Kirby celebrates his fiftieth anniversary as a syndicated comic strip in 1996, due in no small part to the excellent work done by John Prentice, who has drawn the strip for forty years. However, Prentice's work is usually overshadowed in discussions of *Rip Kirby* by that of Alex Raymond, who created the strip in 1946 and drew it until his death in an automobile accident in September 1956.

Given the excellence of *Rip Kirby,* the strip's lack of popularity with American newspaper editors is a mystery to cartoon fans and historians; it has been much better received in Europe. With the decline in popularity of *Dick Tracy*, it is highly possible for *Rip Kirby* to become the premier syndicated detective comic strip.

Alex Raymond was a genuine Cartoon Hall of Fame legend. Prior to World War II he'd received the adulation of fans and inspired his peers with work on three successful comic strips for King Features: the daily *Secret Agent X-9*, a police strip written by Dashiell Hammett that debuted January 22, 1934; *Flash Gordon,* hero of the fight against the evil Ming the Merciless of planet Mongo, created by Raymond and scripted by ghost writer Don Moore, which debuted January 7, 1934; and *Jungle Jim,* created as a companion piece to *Flash Gordon,* and which began the same day. These three strips were King Features' challenge to *Dick Tracy, Buck Rogers,* and *Tarzan.*

When he left the U.S. Marine Corps as a major in 1946, Alex Raymond had the syndicated cartoon world in the palm of his hand. King Features even gave him ownership of *Rip Kirby,* the detective strip he'd been given carte blanche to create. Raymond's heirs still own it. Raymond created a bachelor private detective who preferred to be called a criminologist on March 4, 1946. Rip's stock-in-trade is using his brains to solve cases, but when needed the necessary brawn is also applied.

Rip Kirby (A. Raymond), © 1953 King Features Syndicate

Rip Kirby was written by Raymond until 1952 and he gave the detective many of his own attributes, including being a former Marine major. Rip is moneyed, suave, and urban. He doesn't suffer fools lightly. For years he smoked a pipe until changing public perception of smoking nixed it. Intellect, good instincts, and strong detective work are how Rip solves most of his cases. More often than not the criminals are operating at the high end of the social ladder. With New York City as home base, Rip's the type of fellow who knows not only the desk sergeant at the local police precinct but the police commissioner as well. His adventures take him all over the world.

Beautiful women, many with larcenous hearts, fill Rip's address book. Originally his steady was blonde high-fashion model Honey Dorian, but she can disappear from the story line for years at a time. Marriage is not part of Rip's agenda as much as his love of beautiful women and fast cars.

In 1952, Raymond turned the writing over to the able Fred Dickenson, who wrote *Rip Kirby* until his death in the late 1980s. Briefly, John Prentice wrote the strip, until former newspaperman Bruce Smith came on board as writer. In winter 1966, Maxwell MacRae was added to the writing staff. His first story featured gold-digging starlet Heidi Highprow.

For humor, and a sense that his detective lives the good life, Raymond gave Rip a majordomo named Desmond, a reformed safecracker from London who's still very British.

Rip Kirby has always been only a daily strip. Although famous for his brushwork pre–World War II, Raymond chose pen over brush as his main technique in *Rip Kirby*.

The black-and-white style used to draw the strip has been flawless, and even today, although not as intricate as the style of the 1960s and 1970s, John Prentice's work remains on a level above many other story strips. The point-of-view angles move constantly; characters make eye contact with the reader; the Raymond technique of the establishing landscape shot with dialogue continues; and creative and unique crosshatching is used.

Rip Kirby is a mature story strip with a bright future. Many hope that King Features will realize this and give *Rip Kirby* the promotion and sales push it seems to have lacked from the syndicate for many years.

B. C., Jr.

Rip Kirby (J. Prentice), © 1964 King Features Syndicate

round-faced and bespectacled, was an office worker always wearing suit and tie; his wife, Alice, was an attractive, red-headed hausfrau. They had a five-year-old son, the wide-awake Butch, who unlike most comic-strip kids was very respectful to his parents. Most of the incidents were provoked by his overeagerness to help, like his falling through the roof while trying to put back some tiles blown off by the wind. Referring to Clark, Stephen Becker noted, "He has never attempted to induce the belly laugh; he feels that a gently humorous reminder of something that has probably happened to his reader will suffice." Unfortunately, the cartoonist's love of understatement was sometimes carried to soporific extremes. *The Ripples* was most of the time a genuinely unfunny feature; it somehow managed to last into the early 1960s.

The Ripples had as a bottom piece throughout the 1940s *Aunt Peachy's Pet Shop*, about an old maid and her menagerie of talking animals. This secondary offering was oftentimes more amusing than the main attraction.

M.H.

THE RIPPLES
1939–1961[?]

George Clark, who had created the long-lasting panel *Side Glances* for NEA in 1929, decided ten years later to jump ship and join the higher-octane Chicago Tribune–New York News Syndicate. There he came up with another daily panel, *The Neighbors,* in 1939, which proved popular enough to give rise the following year to a Sunday page called *Our Neighbors.* Unlike the daily panel, which presented a wide variety of different characters, the Sundays soon focused on a single family. Accordingly, the feature became known as *Our Neighbors the Ripples,* and then simply as *The Ripples.*

The Ripples lived in a neat house in the suburbs: Harvey,

RIVETS
1953–1986

One of the longest-lived dogs in the comics, Rivets wagged his tail for the first time in the pages of the *Saturday Evening Post.* George Sixta, a veteran cartoonist of some fifteen years, had sent the cartoon in from the public-relations office of the Department of the Navy, where he was currently serving. The frisky, friendly mutt won the affection of the readers and became a regular fixture of the *Post* from 1944 until March 2, 1953, when he was picked up for national distribution by Publishers Syndicate. *Rivets* appeared at first as a daily panel, with a Sunday page added a few years later.

A cross between a fox terrier and a cocker spaniel, the small white dog was modeled after the Sixtas' own dog, Terry, and the appeal of the strip precisely lay in the verisimilitude of Rivets's alarums and misadventures, and

Rivets (G. Sixta), © Field Enterprises

of his interaction with the various members of the family that owned him. His crashing through a window running after a ball, messing up the house in the family's absence, or breaking up a game of checkers by upsetting the board must have rung a bell with most dog owners. As could be expected, his most constant playmates were the children of the house, named in descending order, like the artist's own children, Steve, Jamie, and Virginia. The little dog would retrieve their stray balls, sit with them at the barber's, and occasionally swipe their ice-cream cones. Rivets did not talk (except to himself) but he was extraordinarily perceptive, always choosing Be Kind to Animals Week for his more reprehensible pranks.

A steady, reliable journeyman, Sixta produced over the years a feature that was, like his drawing style, a little corny, a little dull, but easily recognizable and reassuringly predictable. These low-key qualities kept *Rivets* going until the cartoonist's death, in January 1986.

M.H.

ROCKY MASON, GOVERNMENT MARSHAL
1941–1945

On August 24, 1941, veteran cartoonist Jimmy Swinnerton (who had temporarily suspended his *Little Jimmy*) tried his hand at a straight western. A weekly tabloid page titled *Rocky Mason, Government Marshal*, it was distributed by King Features Syndicate, which pinned high hopes on the new strip.

The first episode introduced Rocky Mason riding into town and taking on the local Mr. Big. The story involved a series of highway holdups masterminded by a mysterious boss-man (no mystery as to who the mastermind was, however). As could be expected from Swinnerton, who had been living in the West since early in the century and who had become by then a renowned desert painter, the locales and backgrounds were quite authentic, revisiting the same southwestern scenes and vistas he had depicted for years in *Little Jimmy* and *Canyon Kiddies*. The continuities unhappily were a different thing altogether: obviously the author felt ill at ease within the conventions of the action genre, and all his stories had a borrowed air about them. They dealt with claim jumping, range feuds, bank robberies, and the like, with a marked lack of zest (and an unfortunate absence of suspense) that went against the rules of the

game. In addition, the drawing was too cartoony for a straight shoot-'em-up, and the artist's old-fashioned page layouts did not allow for visual excitement. *Rocky Mason* ended its run on October 28, 1945, and Swinnerton went back to the gentler pace and more familiar plotting of *Little Jimmy*.

As much as one wishes to say only kind words about the work of one of the great comic-strip pioneers, it must be conceded that *Rocky Mason* was not one of Swinnerton's better efforts. As it is, the strip remains an oddity in the artist's canon.

M.H.

ROOM AND BOARD
1928–1930, 1936–1958

Impressed by the success of Gene Ahern's *Our Boarding House*, the editors at King Features decided to launch their own rooming-house daily panel in the fall of 1928; Sals Bostwick, a former assistant to Frank King on *Gasoline Alley*, was picked as the artist on the feature, which under the title *Room and Board*, took place at a residence hotel called the Fizzbeak Inn. There was a large cast of boarders and transients but no central character to hold the piece together, and it never even approached the popularity of *Our Boarding House*. Consequently, after Bostwick's death in 1930, the syndicate allowed the panel to lapse.

When Ahern himself was lured away to King a few years later, he picked up the *Room and Board* title and turned it into a clone of his own *Our Boarding House*, with a daily panel and a Sunday page simultaneously started in June 1936. The central character in the strip was Judge Homer Augustus Puffle, like Hoople a self-aggrandizing and paunchy windbag kept on a short leash by his harridan of a wife, Nora, with the help of her maid Delia's vigilant eye. Living with the Judge were his brother Robin, as lazy and

Room and Board (G. Ahern), ca. 1941, © King Features Syndicate

Rosie's Beau (G. McManus), ca. 1940, © King Features Syndicate

mendacious as his sibling, his nephew, the good-for-nothing Conrad, and his uncle Bert, a geriatric overachiever. There was the obligatory chorus of wisecracking boarders, who exercised their wit at the expense of the harrumphing Puffle brothers but reserved most of their barbs for one another. There was some semblance of daily and weekly continuity, especially during the war years, when Puffle and his brother were civilian defense workers under the command of archdisciplinarian Uncle Bert, the senior neighborhood warden. Otherwise most of the gags seemed to revolve around Puffle trying to sneak out of the house for a game of billiards at the Bat Roost Club, in the manner of Jiggs in *Bringing Up Father*.

Ahern did not enjoy at King the same freedom he had had at NEA, even if the pay was better. The syndicate executives laid down a set of rules and strictures under which the artist had to labor. "I have a rigid code for my characters," he told an interviewer in 1942. "They are never allowed to cash in on a laugh at the cost of human suffering. They never jest about things which some persons may revere." In other words satire, mockery, derision, and cheerful cynicism, all of which had been hallmarks of *Our Boarding House*, were out. Under these conditions it is no wonder that *Room and Board* steadily lost its pungency and bite. In the 1950s, with fewer and fewer newspapers carrying the feature, the lights finally went out; the Sunday page was dropped on May 31, 1953, while the daily panel hung on a while longer, coming to an end on November 24, 1958.

M.H.

ROSCO SWEENY
See BUZ SAWYER

ROSE IS ROSE
1984–present

The popularity of Pat Brady's *Rose Is Rose* is evidence that there remains a taste for simple, wholesome domestic comedy in America. Almost completely devoid of conflict, this engaging daily and Sunday strip is a celebration of the normal, happy, loving family. Brady reports that the strip was inspired by a television talk show featuring "women who were defiantly proud of being housewives." Unfashionable as its stance is, the strip has been popular from its inception; according to its publisher, *Rose Is Rose* has ranked among the top three favorite strips in newspa-

per polls since it was first syndicated by United Feature in 1984.

The strip centers on Rose Gumbo, an independent, intelligent housewife whose handyman husband Jimbo and two-year-old son Pasquale keep her busy and fully satisfied. Like Bil Keane's *The Family Circus,* it depicts its tight little nuclear family with warmth but without sentimentality. Rose guides her menage with a sure and loving hand, Jimbo is attentive but neither henpecked nor uxorious, and their son is an endless source of affectionate amusement as he interprets the world, expressing his discoveries in a phonetically transcribed language that sometimes requires his loving parents to translate. Pasquale patiently waters a phone pole, trusting it to grow telephones; he wonders that airplanes stay in hangars instead of their nests when they're not flying; and he proposes, when the month seems to be passing slowly, that the calendar needs winding. But the toddler's observations are not always naive; when Rose tells him he may not have another ice pop now, he notes, "Now it'z now...*Now* it'z now...*NOW* it'z now...It'z *always* now!" The reasoning is too much for her. "Your philosophy better not be rusty when you're in charge of ice pops," she reflects as she turns one over to the winner of the argument.

Gracefully drawn and consistently upbeat, *Rose Is Rose* is a pleasant, uncritical strip, and one that confirms some universal truths of the human heart. If it doesn't reflect typical American family life at the end of the century, only the most cynical reader would question that it represents an attractive ideal.

D.W.

ROSIE'S BEAU
1916–1918, 1926–1944

After joining the Hearst organization, George McManus pursued his craft with wild abandon, coming up with one comic-strip idea after another, and discarding them almost as fast as he had conceived them. Standing out from these ephemeral creations, *Rosie's Beau,* which made its bow in the comic sections of the Hearst papers on Sunday, October 15, 1916, was there to stay.

With the Newlyweds impeded in their public displays of affection by the presence of their insufferable baby, McManus in short order had come up with another loving couple—unmarried this time. Rosie was a typical McManus cutie courted by a fat, double-chinned office worker named Archie (or Archibald). Her beau's amorous ardors never grew tiresome to the love-smitten Rosie, who was as short on brains as she was long on looks. The couple carried on the most outrageous cooing and petting at every opportunity, oblivious of fire, flood, burglary, or whatever catastrophe was currently taking place around them.

In April 1918 *Rosie's Beau* vanished to make room for the *Bringing Up Father* Sunday page but resurfaced on June 13, 1926, as the top strip to McManus's better-known feature. The couple picked up exactly where they had left off eight years before, but with a twist—Rosie's father was now Archie's boss. No matter; nothing could stop the couple's renewed transports of ecstasy, not the roar of incoming traffic, not the news that Archie had gotten fired, not even the unexpected irruption of characters from the strip downstairs who had gotten off on the wrong floor (or rather the wrong story). The onset of World War II, which caused Archie to be drafted, did not disrupt the couple's romantic activities in the slightest: Rosie's lovesick beau would get back to his sweetheart's waiting arms every Sunday, despite forced marches, KP duty, stockade, and threats of court-martial.

Rosie and her beau didn't know much, but they knew they had a good thing going, and wisely kept their relationship from the risk of ever getting stale. When the strip ended on November 12, 1944, they were still unmarried.

M.H.

ROY POWERS, EAGLE SCOUT
1937–1942

*I*n the mid-1930s the minor Ledger Syndicate had embarked on an ambitious expansion program. Having experienced its first taste of success with the FBI-authorized strip *War on Crime*, it decided to develop a new property dealing with the exploits not of G-men but of Boy Scouts, perhaps reasoning that the Boy Scouts had even more members than the FBI. Dubbed "the official strip of the Boy Scouts of America" and credited to Paul Powell, the new feature made its bow as a daily only in March 1937. Titled *Roy Powers, Eagle Scout*, it purported to chronicle the adventures of a scout troop called the Beaver Patrol, led by the seventeen-year-old Roy, with some comic assistance from his fat friend Chunky. The boys' first adventures, drawn by Kemp Starrett in an imitation of Ledger's star comics artist Frank Godwin's style, were pretty sedate. They would straighten out a neighborhood bully, for instance, or track down a gang of burglars.

Roy Powers, Eagle Scout (F. Godwin), © 1938 Ledger Syndicate

In its advance publicity, the syndicate had billed *Roy Powers* as a "thrilling, clean-cut story," but it might have proved a bit too clean-cut for American boys used to sturdier comic-book fare. At any rate it didn't click, and the master himself, Frank Godwin, was brought in later in 1937 to try to perk up the strip. In short order he had the boys shipped out to exotic locales, where his draftsmanship could be displayed to best advantage. In an extended travelogue the entire Beaver Patrol journeyed to Africa on a photo safari, went treasure hunting in the Caribbean, and even found time to solve a five-thousand-year-old mystery in Egypt.

After a couple of years Godwin went off the strip, replaced in quick succession by Ledger stalwarts Jimmy Thompson and Charles Coll. Gamely, Roy, Chunky, and the rest of the Beaver Patrol carried on scouting in pretty much the same manner as before, and their further adventures carried them into 1942, when the strip finally ended its run.

M.H.

ROY ROGERS
1949–1961

*T*he 1940s saw the heyday of the western newspaper comics, and the last cowboy strip to come out of the decade was *Roy Rogers*. Under copyright of the famed western star, it was distributed by King Features Syndicate, beginning on December 2, 1949.

The continuities clearly followed the plots and the themes of the Roy Rogers movies, minus of course the musical interludes. The hero would usually ride into town only to be confronted by trouble of some sort (a rancher unjustly accused of murder, a holdup in progess) and, with the help of his faithful stallion, Trigger, he would bring the culprits to justice. There always were some good action scenes, with long panoramic panels and good page layout on Sundays. Dale Evans did not figure as prominently in the strip as she did in the movies; on the other hand, Roy's sundry sidekicks often got featured parts. The dialogue and characterization, unfortunately, never rose above those found in grade-B movie westerns ("The ol' coot ain't packin' hardware, Slim!" was typical of the writing that went on in the strip).

Roy Rogers was initially drawn by the brothers Chuck and Tom (signing Al) McKimson, and they did a proficient and sometimes excellent job. In May 1953 the initials M.A. started appearing on the panels; they turned out to belong to Mike Arens, who later signed the artwork, done in a crisp, cool style, with his full name. By the end of the decade, however, cowboy comics went out of favor; Roy Rogers and Trigger enjoyed their last ride in the funny papers in 1961.

M.H.

RUDY
1983–1984

After leaving *Steve Roper,* which he had written and drawn for almost three decades, in 1982, William Overgard set out to create a humor strip that would utilize to the full his knowledge of the television and movie scene. The resulting feature, *Rudy,* which the author described as "a gag strip about a talking monkey in Hollywood, drawn in a realistic continuity style," made its debut, daily and Sunday, in the first week of 1983, distributed by United Feature Syndicate.

After a hiatus of some thirty years following a dispute over billing (the producers of *Bedtime for Bonzo,* in which he was to costar, insisted on having Ronald Reagan's name before his in the credits), Rudy, "the thinking man's chimpanzee," felt the urge to return to his show-business roots. Taking up residence in the Garden of Allah II (a modern-day replica of the fabled Hollywood apartment hotel of the 1930s), he planned his showbiz comeback with extreme method and utmost care. Alas, his strenuous efforts availed him little; he was offered such jobs as singing waiter in a monkey suit, spokesman for a pet deodorant, and host of a "dial-a-chimp" call-in show.

Rudy was a simian takeoff on comedian George Burns, complete with upraised cigar, slow-burn delivery, and spiffy clothes. He was abetted in his endeavors by a broad assortment of oddball characters, including Sol Sizzle, the 106-year-old theatrical manager; Arnold, who doubled as a garbageman between engagements; Stay-awake Wasserman, the foul-mouthed host of a nighttime radio talk show; and Spangle, the eternally aspiring movie starlet. Of particular note were Bonita, the singing and piano-playing parrot that had been the talking chimp's partner in bygone vaudeville days; and Rudy's monumental landlady, Mrs. de Mayo, who when she was not hosing down her garden, kept a shrine to her departed husband, "Lightning" Rod de Mayo, a streetcar conductor inducted into the Motorman Hall of Fame after his death (from drinking too much of his own bathtub gin). Despite his dry wit and deadpan humor(or perhaps because of them), Rudy didn't make it in comicdom anymore than he did in show business: his farewell performance took place in December 1984.

M.H.

RUSTY RILEY
1948–1959

In the mid-1940s acclaimed illustrator Frank Godwin suffered the indignity of having to work for low-paid, little-regarded comic books. Fortunately, big-hearted King Features came to the rescue and offered the artist a contract to create an original newspaper strip. Called *Rusty*

Rusty Riley (F. Godwin), © 1950 King Features Syndicate

Riley, the new feature debuted, as a daily strip scripted by Rod Reed, on January 26, 1948; a Sunday version came out on June 27 of the same year, on texts by Harold Godwin, Frank's brother.

A sandy-haired, bright lad of about 14, Rusty was, inevitably, an orphan, no less inevitably accompanied by his faithful dog, a fox terrier named Flip. In his dream of becoming a jockey, Rusty wandered the Kentucky horse country, finally finding work as a stable boy for the wealthy Mr. Miles. Encouraged by the gruff but big-hearted Tex Purdy, manager of the Miles estate, he gradually worked his way to trainer and then to jockey, riding his horse, Bright Blaze, to victory in the Derby.

While his life centered on horses and racetracks, Rusty also ventured far afield, often in the company of his boss's daughter, Patti Miles, an attractive teenager with whom the boy hero shared a discreet and youthful romance. Together they discovered a race of midget horses in the recesses of the Grand Canyon, took part in a rodeo in Wyoming, and even foiled the schemes of a trio of riverboat gamblers on the Mississippi. Although the story lines in *Rusty Riley* were sometimes trite and often pedestrian, Godwin's superb draftsmanship always carried the day. His delineation of faces was exquisite, his depiction of horses and other animals masterful, and his compositions were laid out with finesse and taste. Godwin put a great deal of love and dedication into his work on the strip up to the time of his death in August 1959; fittingly, *Rusty Riley* died with him. The last daily appeared on September 14, and the Sunday page ended on November 1.

M.H.

RUSTY ROLLINS, COWBOY
1935–1938

After leaving *Tailspin Tommy* at the end of 1933, Glenn Chaffin returned to Hollywood and screenwriting for a while. Early in 1935 he was persuaded to take a stab at writing another comic strip; drawing on his experiences as a cattle rancher and gold prospector, Chaffin came up with *Rusty Rollins, Cowboy,* which was illustrated by Irwin Shope and distributed by McClure Syndicate.

Rusty was a young cowhand who underwent all the rigors of frontier life on his way to becoming an ace roper, cattle driver, and rodeo rider. In addition to the minutious depiction of western customs and traditions, there were the inevitable episodes of melodrama, involving highway robberies, cattle rustling, and claim jumping. One of the more intriguing continuities took place in 1936–37 and had Rusty living for a time among the Indians and adopting their outlook and way of life, half a century before Kevin Costner's *Dances with Wolves.* Chaffin was well served by Shope, who drew Rusty's adventures in a loose, laid-back version of the Caniff style.

Late in 1937 Shope was replaced by Bob Naylor, who had charge of *Rusty Rollins* until the end of the feature's run sometime in the summer of 1938.

M.H.

THE RYATTS
1954–present

*T*he Ryatts was created in October 1954 by Calvin (Cal) Alley, the son of famed cartoonist James Pinckney Alley, as a daily strip based on his own family, for the Hall Syndicate (which became af-ter many a name change the North America Syndicate).

The composition of the Ryatt family exactly duplicated that of the Alleys. In addition to mother and father, there were three daughters, Pam, Kitty, and Missy, and two boys, Tad and Winky, along with Junior, the family dog. Alley drew the strip in an unpretentious, cartoony style, which accorded well with the general blandness of the situations and the slight humor of the punchlines. The feature enjoyed moderate success and it coasted along on its diffi-

dent charm until ill-health forced its creator to retire in 1965.

As a replacement the syndicate called on Jack Elrod, who had been assisting Ed Dodd on *Mark Trail.* Without abandoning his assistant job, Elrod took over *The Ryatts,* keeping its premise and approach unchanged, but giving it a more incisive visual look. "My first consideration is to get a good gag," the artist told an interviewer. "I also try to keep a good, warm relationship between mem-bers of the...family, hoping in many cases it will help the reader to recall with delight his own family background." This formula seemed to work and *The Ryatts* soon picked up circulation. By the late 1960s it also picked up a Sunday version called *Winky Ryatt* (for the younger son of the family), and centering on the boys' (usually mild) antics.

In the last quarter-century, as the problems bedeviling the American family have increased exponentially both in number and in intensity, *The Ryatts*'s sunny view of domestic life has correspondingly waned in the eyes of the public. The Sunday page was discontinued in the 1980s, and the daily strip is now carried by a dwindling list of newspapers.

M.H.

The Ryatts (C. Alley), © Hall Syndicate

S'MATTER POP?
1910–1940

One of the earliest examples of what was to become a sturdy convention in American comics, Charles M. Payne's *S'Matter Pop?* was a domestic strip featuring a cast of characters in roles that had already become American stereotypes: the masterful wife, the weak, helpless father, and the manipulative child. If Payne contributed anything original (besides his always innovative and imaginative graphic style), it was the freshness of his language and the occasional flashes of grotesque humor that emerged among the clichés. Undergoing a variety of name-changes (it was known as *Nippy's Pop* and *Say Pop!* before it assumed the title by which it is now remembered), *S'Matter Pop?* was carried daily by the *New York World* from its inception in 1910 and also ran for many years as a Sunday feature in the *New York Sun*. In 1917, distribution of *S'Matter Pop?* was taken over by the Bell Syndicate.

The strip's final title, which was to enter the American vernacular during the 1920s as something of a stock formula, was a phonetic reduction of "What's the matter, Pop?"—the recurrent question asked (usually after some defeat or humiliation of Pop's) by his naive older child, Willyum. The question was rhetorical; the matter with Pop laid deep within the nature of things.

Pop was not the victim of mischievous or even particularly clever children, a convention exploited by other comics of the period. He was, rather, the victim of his own limitations of character. A type well known in popular fiction and vaudeville, and one going back to Rip van Winkle, he was a simpleminded, indolent, self-indulgent dreamer who submitted willingly to the domination of his shrewish wife. His neighbor's child, who identified himself as "Desper't Ambrose," was the closest thing to a villain, and the closest thing to an original character, in the strip: a willful moppet who spoke in a curious, stilted dialect derived from historical novels and a vivid imagination, he sometimes introduced himself to the scene with the theatrical announcement "'Tis I, Desper't Ambrose" and never failed to impose his will; but an occasional visit from his even more desper't little brother made him seem relatively amiable.

The relationship between Pop and his world was not really one of conflict. The subordinate role he played to his formidable wife was clearly defined and apparently unresented. His baby (whose communications were limited to unintelligible noises, often without vowels) was undemanding, and the trouble Willyum made was usually innocent. The existential question posed in the title, and reiterated daily as a sort of choral device, remained unanswered.

Drawn with a loose, fluid line and pleasing composition, *S'Matter Pop?* remained fresh and popular until the late 1930s. Payne discontinued it in 1940, as its characters and situations were beginning to pass out of fashion.

D.W.

THE SAD SACK
1945–1958

Sergeant George Baker had already been in the army for some months when he conceived the idea of a comic strip about a lowly buck private, partly out of his own experiences, partly out of stories told to him by fellow draftees. Called *The Sad Sack,* the feature made its first appearance in the pages of the weekly army magazine *Yank* in May 1942. Its popularity with the G.I.'s grew steadily, and in 1943 the publication even issued an advertising poster in order to gain new subscribers with the enticement, "Subscribe to *Yank* and get the Sad Sack every week."

S'Matter Pop? (C. M. Payne), 1916

The Sad Sack (G. Baker), © 1945 George Baker

Baker, a former Disney animator, drew his hapless soldier victim in a winsome, loose style that tended to tone down the Sack's dreary experiences, usually in two rows of four borderless panels each. The first episodes showed the Sack going through "The Physical," "The Uniform," "Drill," and "Orders" in a state of listlessness bordering on stupor. There was no dialogue, and not even any sound effects in the strip, which was strictly done in pantomime. The sorry-looking little private was sent to every army post under the sun but was never promoted for his efforts. "The underlying story of the Sad Sack," Baker later wrote, "was his struggle with the army in which I tried to symbolize the sum total of the difficulties and frustrations of all enlisted men."

The last *Sad Sack* page appeared in *Yank* in October 1945. Titled "Happy Day," it showed the Sack bouncing with joy upon receiving his discharge, only to end up dejected again after reading the headlines blaring nuclear threats and international crises out of the newspapers. In the meantime Baker's creation had been picked up for national distribution by the Bell Syndicate, which first ran only reprints of the *Yank* strips, with the first civilian *Sad Sack* page appearing on May 5, 1946. Even out of uniform, the Sack was a figure of helplessness and ridicule, kicked around by his boss, browbeaten by bureaucrats, snubbed by salesclerks, and spurned by women. The whole of society seemed to have turned into one giant barracks for the Sack. Despite its gloomy, even fatalistic outlook, *The Sad Sack* managed to last until 1958 in the newspapers (and even longer in comic books).

M.H.

THE SAINT
1948–1962

Leslie Charteris created the character of Simon Templar (nicknamed the Saint for his initials) in his 1928 novel *Meet the Tiger*. At first a gentleman-burglar like Raffles, Templar later turned into a justice-fighter and righter of wrongs. The popularity of the novels starring the Saint grew by leaps and bounds in the 1930s, especially after Charteris had moved to the United States and become an American citizen. *The Saint* was successfully brought to radio and film (and later to television), so a newspaper strip seemed a logical extension. On September 20, 1948, *The Saint* made its appearance in the dailies, followed by a Sunday version in the spring of 1949; the feature was distributed by the Herald-Tribune Syndicate, which in the late 1940s went in big for adventure.

Apparently Charteris wrote his own continuities (he was a prodigiously fast wordsmith) and from the first forcefully introduced his permanent cast of characters. The Saint, termed "the modern Robin Hood" by his creator, was a handsome and suave hero, a man of impeccable taste and manners who always left his calling card—the drawing of a stick figure surmounted by a halo—on the scene of his exploits. He was flanked by a comic sidekick, a reformed mob strongman named Hoppy Uniatz, whose malapropisms were in humorous contrast to his boss's literate epigrams; and his most constant adversary (and sometimes partner) was Inspector John Fernack of the New York City police. Patricia Holm, his woman companion in the novels, also made sporadic appearances, but in the strip at least the Saint mostly played the field.

Charteris was known for his skill at recycling old material, and one could spot here and there plot elements from *The Saint in New York*, *The Last Hero*, and *Thieves' Picnic*, among others. Much of the action took place in the States: in addition to New York, favorite places were southern California, Las Vegas, and Miami. In the course of his forays abroad the Saint traveled to the Bahamas, London, several European countries, and Rio de Janeiro. There were tales of mystery, suspense, and intrigue, as the "happy highwayman" tangled with the mastermind behind a rash of kidnappings, tackled a murder-for-hire syndicate, mounted a sting operation (to benefit himself) aimed at a ring of thieves, and rid the world of a sinister conspiratorial circle plotting to trigger a third world war.

The first man to illustrate *The Saint* was Mike Roy, and he acquitted himself creditably if unspectacularly. He was replaced in 1951 by John Spranger, who left a distinctive imprint on the feature. An underrated artist whose work deserves to be better noted, Spranger gave the dailies a suitably sophisticated look, but he lavished his greatest care on the Sundays, where his understated use of color and his harmonious sense of composition were displayed to best advantage. The overall design of the page was helped by its simple but attractive logo setting off a drawing of the famous Saint emblem. After an auspicious start, *The Saint* began to falter as a result of the antiviolence and anti-comics crusades of the 1950s. Spranger abruptly quit early in 1959, and after a brief interim period filled by Bob Lubbers, Doug Wildey took over the artwork at the end of the year. He had planned to revamp the feature, but shortly afterward the Herald-Tribune Syndicate was absorbed into Field Enterprises, which closed down the strip in 1962.

M.H.

SALESMAN SAM
1921–1936

One of the wackiest comic strips ever concocted first came out on September 6, 1921. The perpetrator was George O. Swanson (or "Swan," as he signed his work), a

Salesman Sam (C. D. Small), © 1936 NEA Service

former film animator on such cartoon series as *Mutt and Jeff* and *The Gumps,* and his creation was called *Salesman Sam* (or *$alesman $am,* as the author preferred to spell it). A daily strip distributed by NEA Service from its inception, it received the added benefit of a Sunday page in December 1922.

Sam Howdy was an ebullient, eager, bumbling go-getter of a young man, and he encapsulated in his grinning, wide-eyed, open-mouthed expression all the energy and brainlessness of the Jazz Age. He worked, as the qualifier denoted, as a sales clerk in a general store under the close supervision of his sarcastic and sometimes abrasive boss, J. Guzzlem (whom he always addressed as "Chief"). The early strips were gag-a-day anecdotes detailing Sam's encounters with larcenous customers, pesky solicitors, and sassy delivery boys. Within a few years (perhaps under the artistic prodding of another one of NEA's strips, which had started with a similar store setting, *Wash Tubbs*) Swan got his hero involved in extended hair-raising escapades bordering on the surreal. In 1925, for example, a burglary at Guzzlem's store led to a car chase on busy highways, a pursuit through the woods, an airplane hijacking, and finally a parachute drop from five thousand feet in the air.

Swan's training as an animator showed in the nonstop depiction of movement. The characters were forever popping their hats in the air, falling backward, jumping out of their shoes, or flying over their desks. In addition to all the store merchandise that could be crammed into the panels, the cartoonist also hung signs everywhere, with punning

inscriptions like "Yes, we have ana cigars," and (over a showcase displaying spectacles) "For your eyes only."

In 1927 Swan was hired by King Features to create a strip in the same vein, *High-Pressure Pete,* and C. D. Small succeeded him on the NEA feature. While he didn't indulge in Swan's flights of narrative fancy, Small proved in his gags even loonier than his predecessor.

The strip became a hurricane of separate and sometimes contradictory actions going on all at once, while the puns grew more and more outrageous. Sam would refuse to drop the store's invoices into a mailbox, for instance, because a nearby sign proclaimed, "Post no bills." Small's feverish brain worked overtime for almost a decade until, as so many other funnymen did, he took his own life, and *Salesman Sam* died with him. The last release was dated September 26, 1936. (*High-Pressure Pete,* on the other hand, was to continue until February 7, 1938.)

M.H.

SAM AND SILO
See SAM'S STRIP

SAM'S STRIP
1961–1963, 1977–present

In the early 1960s Jerry Dumas and Mort Walker dreamed up the idea of a place where newspaper-comic characters, past and present, would meet and mingle (a scheme later used for animated cartoon characters in *Who Framed Roger Rabbit?*). This enclave was presided over by a pudgy little man in a porkpie hat named Sam and his nameless assistant. The whole concept was sprung on an unsuspecting public on October 24, 1961, in the form of a daily strip distributed by King Features Syndicate.

In this strip, far from their own strips, the characters went on acting as was expected of them: Buster Brown and the Katzenjammers would play pranks on Sam and his hapless helper, and Maggie would still keep Jiggs away from his pinochle game with Moon Mullins and the Little King. In other ways, however, they behaved pretty much like free agents, holding forth on the finer points of comic art, and reminiscing about the pioneer days of the form. The high point of the strip occurred in 1962, in what was termed

Sam's Strip (Walker and Dumas), © 1961 King Features Syndicate

"International Comics Week," when a multitude of comic figures (sixty-three by someone's count) took the floor to air their grievances (such as not getting a five-day work week "like any other working stiff") or to engage in some outrageous activities involving rolling pins or custard pies. It is indicative that this particular strip came out in the early 1960s, at a time when the study of the comics as a serious art form was gathering momentum on both sides of the Atlantic. While it pleased the aficionados, *Sam's Strip* failed to attract the general public, who couldn't understand the many inside jokes or indeed recognize many of the characters cavorting throughout the strip. With circulation (which had never been high to begin with) steadily falling off, Dumas and Walker decided in June 1963 to close down the strip.

The authors resurrected Sam and his assistant (now named Silo) in a daily and Sunday feature appropriately called *Sam and Silo* on April 18, 1977. The two are now the entire police force of a small burg, where they face mildly humorous situations involving run-ins with the town mayor and wild-goose chases after imaginary malefactors. Shorn of the nostalgia and whimsy of its earlier incarnation, the feature is just another well-crafted but bland confection routinely turned out by the Walker comics factory. (The Sunday version was dropped in 1995.)

M.H.

SANDY HIGHFLIER
See THE AIRSHIP MAN

SAPPO
1920–1925, 1926–1947

In 1920 E. C. Segar, who was already doing *Thimble Theatre* for King Features, was asked to create another daily strip for the syndicate. The result, called *The Five-Fifteen*, about a suburban commuter named John Sappo, came out in the last week of the year.

In the already hallowed tradition of comic-strip husbands, Sappo was a small man afflicted with a large and bossy spouse (ungentlemanly named Myrtle after Segar's own wife). The couple lived in a suburb called Despaire, and the strip's title referred to the commuter train Sappo had to take every morning to his work in Murkville-City. In February 1923 the feature was renamed *Sappo the Commuter,* and a little later simply *Sappo,* in recognition of the fact that the shrimp-sized, mild-mannered suburbanite had now become a hero of sorts in a series of slightly humorous adventures. This phase of Sappo's life came to an end on February 17, 1925. When Segar felt the need to provide his newly created (in 1925) *Thimble Theatre* Sunday page with a top strip, he turned once again to *Sappo,* which he revived on February 28, 1926. Sappo, now no longer a commuter, engaged with his wife in weekly arguments that he would always lose. Loose gag continuities were sometimes established, as in 1927 when Sappo joined the Hardboiled Husbands' Club and got rewarded week after week with rolling-pin blows on the head by his incensed wife.

Sappo was running the risk of degenerating into a second-rate *Bringing Up Father* when Segar, sensing the danger, changed direction and in the 1930s launched the strip on two separate occasions into the field of humorous science-fantasy. In May 1932 the white-bearded Professor O. G. Wottasnozzle, called by Sappo "the greatest scientific mind of the age," came to live with the couple as a boarder, and his zany inventions provided the springboard for a series of imaginative adventures. In one sequence, lasting for three months in 1933, Wottasnozzle and Sappo left in a spaceship of the professor's invention for a gag-filled tour of the moon, Mars, and Venus. Other continuities involved a shrinking machine, an invisibility process, and an all-out war pitting Wottasnozzle against his scientific rival, Professor Finklesnop. After an eighteen-month hiatus in 1935–36 when *Sappo* was used for cartoon lessons, Segar came back to the science-fiction theme. In a lengthy sequence extending from April to November 1937, Sappo and Wottasnozzle, accompanied this time by Finklesnop and Myrtle, who had stowed away, embarked on another space trip in search of a perfect world. Of course, they met only with a series of nightmarish experiences and in the end were glad to get back to Earth.

After its creator's death in 1938, *Sappo,* along with *Thimble Theatre,* passed briefly into the hands of Doc Winner before being entrusted the following year to the team of Bela Zaboly and Tom Sims. The feature soon degenerated into a string of mindless gags, and it was dropped by the syndicate on May 18, 1947.

M.H.

Sappo (E. C. Segar), © 1934 King Features Syndicate

SCAMP
1955–1988

Scamp was born (literally) in the 1955 Disney animation feature *Lady and the Tramp,* when Lady presented the Tramp at the conclusion of the film with four puppies, one of whom was the frisky Scamp. The mischievous, winsome pup was brought to the comics pages, first in a daily strip started on October 31, 1955, followed by a Sunday page on January 15, 1956. Like all Disney comic-strip properties, *Scamp* was distributed by King Features.

Lady and the Tramp had been based on an idea by King Features editor Ward Greene, and it was Greene who suggested a comic-strip sequel to the film; he also wrote the first stories, on illustrations by Dick Moores. Scamp was a gray-coated, spunky pup who could converse with the other animals in the strip but acted dumb in the presence of humans. Despite his good intentions, he was often rebuffed by adults, who spurned his importune displays of affection, while the kids liked to play pranks on him. He fared little better with his animal brothers: a huge neighborhood bulldog was his nemesis, always pursuing him back to his doghouse every time he ventured out; and when he seemed to hit it off with a cute female dog, he found out she was interested only in the bone he had just dug up. Aimed at a very young audience, *Scamp* developed simple gags and situations, and its humor always remained at a juvenile level.

Greene and Moores left the series in May 1956, and were replaced by Bill Berg for the scripts and Bob Grant on the drawings. From the 1960s on, a number of artists in addition to Grant worked on *Scamp*, including Chuck Fuson (1962–65), Glenn Schmitz (1968–69), and Richard Moore (1976–78). In 1978 Roger Armstrong became the titular artist on the strip, and he brought it to its conclusion in June 1988.

M.H.

SCARLET O'NEIL
See INVISIBLE SCARLET O'NEIL

SCHOOL DAYS
1904–1942

Clare Victor Dwiggins, who signed all his work "Dwig," created a number of comic strips during his long and fruitful career; they sometimes had different titles, but they all shared an overarching theme, that of remembered boyhood, and in that sense they can be said to constitute a single body of work, with several branches conjoining to form one meandering river of thoughts, musings, and drawings. Since *School Days* is the appellation most often associated with Dwig and in its shorthand encapsulates his whole motif, it will be used here as an overall title.

These interrelated (and often overlapping) series featured basically the same cast of characters. There were Ophelia, the cross-eyed girl who was wont to chalk up wise sayings on her slate; Pip Gint, the school bully; Frog Tadhopper, the local fat boy and champion girl-baiter; Patches, the artful bulldog; and assorted urchins, tomboys, and schoolmarms. Produced by Dwig for the McClure Syndicate, these series ran under a variety of titles as early as 1904, but finally the cartoonist settled on *School Days* around 1910. Most of the shenanigans took place in a rural schoolhouse where the pupils played with all sorts of fantastic contraptions made up of wires, pulleys, and buckets, not to mention sundry animals used in the propulsion of these ingenious devices.

This first series of half-page panels ended in 1914, but that was not the end of the story. Dwig kept turning pages after hilarious weekly pages, still using his old cast of characters. In 1917 he revived the *School Days* title for a daily

School Days (C. V. Dwiggins), © 1924 McClure Syndicate

panel series again extolling the joys of boyhood in his native Ohio; and in 1918, by permission of the Mark Twain estate, he started a Sunday page called *Tom Sawyer and Huck Finn*. While Tom and Huck, as well as Becky, did appear in this new feature, and some of the anecdotes were based on incidents related in Twain's novels, this was basically the same old setting with Tom and Huck thrown in for good measure. As a matter of fact the title was amplified in 1924 to *The School Days of Tom Sawyer and Huck Finn*, and in 1928 it reverted to simply *School Days*—which in theme and treatment it had been all along. Dwig closed down his daily *School Days* panel in 1932, and by the end of the decade the Sunday page was also gone, thus ending Dwig's long association with McClure.

In the meantime the indefatigable cartoonist had hooked up with the Ledger Syndicate, for which he created in 1931 *Nipper*, a daily and Sunday feature. *"Tom Sawyer and Huck Finn...was modernized somewhat and merged into Nipper,"* Cal Dobbins wrote in his introduction to a 1977 reprint anthology of *School Days* "all with a similar cast of characters and all dealing with boyhood adventures in rural America."

Nipper came to an end in 1937, but Dwig, nothing daunted, then revived the Twain characters in *Huckleberry Finn*, a daily strip he turned out for Ledger again. It starred Huck and Tom in wild adventures in the Far West and among the "cannibals" of Africa. The strip lasted from 1940 to 1942; thus ended the longest and most intricate newspaper cycle ever attempted by a single cartoonist. (In the mid-1940s Dwig drew further boys' adventures for comic books, but these go beyond the purview of this essay.)

M.H.

SCORCHY SMITH
1930–1961

Toward the end of the 1920s the Associated Press decided to go into the newspaper-strip syndicating business under the corporate name of AP Newsfeatures. Adventure strips, and more particularly aviation strips, were the rage

Scorchy Smith (N. Sickles), © 1935 The AP

at the time, so it is not surprising that among the first handful of features AP proposed to client papers there inevitably was a strip about an airplane pilot: that was *Scorchy Smith,* which made its debut on March 17, 1930.

Scorchy Smith was modeled on Charles Lindbergh, whose solo transatlantic flight in 1927 was still fresh in everybody's mind. Everything was there: the lanky silhouette, the tousled hair, the freckled face (hence the "Scorchy" nickname). John Terry, a former newspaper cartoonist and the brother of *Terry-Toons* creator Paul Terry, was given the task of drawing the new feature. His line was shaky, his compositions ill-defined, yet the strip became a mild success on the strength of its story line.

Stricken with tuberculosis, Terry in 1933 gave up the feature to a talented newcomer, Noel Sickles, who proceeded to transform *Scorchy Smith* into one of the best-drawn newspaper strips of the decade. In April 1934, following Terry's death, Sickles's signature finally appeared on the drawings. Thus given free rein, Sickles endeavored to fashion out of the feature "a romantic adventure strip, filled with thrills and spectacle, and innovative on an artistic level," to quote the artist. In order not to disorient the readers by effecting too brutal a change, this metamorphosis took place over a period of months. Terry's muddy network of cross-hatchings made way little by little to a sharper line, while the compositions were opened up by way of airy perspectives against which the characters took on added relief. By the end of 1934 the drawings in *Scorchy Smith* were displaying a mastery that few other strips of the period could equal.

At that time Sickles and Milton Caniff were sharing a studio, and they started sharing their work as well. A veritable artistic osmosis developed between the two men, with Sickles sometimes penciling whole sequences of *Terry and the Pirates,* while Caniff was scripting entire continuities for *Scorchy Smith.* Under this partnership the stories drawn by Sickles took on a more humane, more credible look. Scorchy remained an airman for hire, ready to take part in a gun-running operation or a search for a kidnapped

heiress, but his actions now sprang from subtler motives than simple need for money or love of adventure. Sickles also gave his hero a companion in the person of Heinie Himmelstoss, a former German ace of the Great War; at first a relentless foe, Himmelstoss turned into the most loyal ally of the man he kept calling in heavily accented English "Scorcher Schmidt." Toward the end of 1935 Scorchy met, in the middle of the Canadian wilds, Mickey Lafarge, a pretty blonde with a sharp tongue and a golden heart, and for a while the duo merged into a trio; but in the summer of 1936 Mickey and Heinie went off to get married, and Scorchy regained his status as a lone eagle.

In the course of his short comic-strip career Sickles's manner constantly evolved, but it was always grounded in the desire to give the strip a greater appearance of life and movement. He was ultimately to adopt a style that was more pictorial than graphic, with greater attention given to light than to line, a style related less to illustration than to film-making. Pioneered by Sickles and Caniff, this new technique would soon spread like wildfire throughout the cartooning fraternity.

In October 1936, due to contractual disagreements with his syndicate, Sickles abandoned his hero in the Amazon forest, smack in the middle of an adventure. He was then replaced by another one of AP's youthful (and underpaid) wonders, Bert Christman, who tried as best he could to follow in his predecessor's footsteps during his short tenure, which extended to April 1938. Christman's line soon lost its initial awkwardness, and while his characters remained rather undefined, he excelled on the other hand in the drawing of airplanes and other machines. Christman has become known less for his work on *Scorchy Smith* than for his heroic death in combat: as a pilot with the Flying Tigers, he was shot down and killed during aerial fighting against Japanese planes that had come to bomb Rangoon.

After Christman came Howell Dodd. A solid craftsman, he supplied competent if unspectacular artwork on scripts by Frank Reilly, before handing the strip over to Frank Robbins in May 1939. At first the continuities were written by Bob Farrell, but early in 1940 Robbins took over entire responsibility for *Scorchy Smith* and turned it anew into an adventure strip of uncommon brilliance. His drawings, accented by heavy lines and solid black masses, had a vigor, a virility that were quite striking. So successful had the feature become that a Sunday page was added late in 1942.

Robbins left in 1944 to create *Johnny Hazard* for King Features. His successor, Edmond Good, turned out to be an able replacement, hardly inspired but reasonably gifted, and under his stewardship Scorchy's wartime and postwar adventures were not without attractiveness. He was unfortunately succeeded in 1946 by Rodlow Willard, who botched the job so hopelessly that circulation went into freefall.

From 1954 to 1959 George Tuska tried to straighten out this wretched situation with eye-catching drawings and interesting plots, but it was too late: readership kept declining inexorably. In a final touch of irony the task of bringing down the curtain on the feature that had once been AP's pride fell upon John Milt Morris, one of the most inept men ever to wield a brush. The firstborn among AP strips, *Scorchy Smith* was the last one to die, early in 1961.

M.H.

SECRET AGENT CORRIGAN
See SECRET AGENT X-9

SECRET AGENT X-9
1934–present

Novelist Dashiell Hammett was at the height of his fame in 1933, having garnered critical acclaim as well as popular success with such hard-boiled stories of mystery and suspense as *The Maltese Falcon* and *Red Harvest;* so it was no surprise when King Features turned to him for a police strip that would rival *Dick Tracy.* Hammett hastily put together a script, and to illustrate it the syndicate called upon a talented young artist, Alexander Gillespie (Alex) Raymond. Heavily promoted in the Hearst papers and on the radio, the new feature premiered on January 22, 1934, under the title *Secret Agent X-9* .

Of all the great comic-strip creators, Alex Raymond unquestionably possessed the most versatile talent. Some artists may have surpassed him in creative power or in boldness of execution, others in evocation of mood or in accuracy of detail, but none displayed such an awesome variety of talents—talents that enabled him to master with ease all the different types of strips at which he tried his hand. Light years distant from the futuristic settings of *Flash Gordon* and the exotic locales of *Jungle Jim* (the two strips Raymond was also turning out at the time), Hammett's was a netherworld teeming with crooks, shysters, racketeers, chiselers, gunsels, and treacherous females of all classes. Working exclusively in black and white (there never has been an *X-9* Sunday), Raymond devised a style at once gritty and graceful, sinewy and elegant, that matched Hammett's wary and cynical worldview with dead-on accuracy.

As imagined by Raymond and Hammett, X-9 was a handsomely virile hero, tall and agile, who moved with equal ease among murderers and thieves and in the company of high-society swells. He was a secret operative for an unspecified government agency, and his beat was the jungle of cities—all cities. Men, be they cheap hoods or wealthy tycoons, he dealt with summarily ("You can call me Dexter. It's not my name, but it'll do," he announced himself to the multimillionaire Tarleton Powers); women, whether gangster molls or society dames, he treated with icy contempt ("I don't like you. I really don't," he tersely told one of them). The Hammett-scripted episodes dealt with criminal conspiracies in high circles, air piracy, kidnapping, counterfeiting, and of course murder. After a while the writer and the syndicate grew mutually disenchanted, and in February 1935, Hammett left. Leslie Charteris, the creator of *The Saint,* succeeded him, but his stories had neither the dash of his Saint novels nor the pace of the Hammett continuities; pleading overwork, Raymond, on November 16, 1935, quit in his turn.

The feature was then turned over to Charles Flanders, who was to draw the adventures of the famous G-man (as X-9 was now known to be) until April 9, 1938. Being in charge of *Secret Agent X-9* was no easy task. Hammett and Raymond had imparted to the strip an atmosphere and a look that were difficult to change and hard to emulate. Laboring under these handicaps, Flanders did a creditable job. He was able to tell the story visually with a maximum of clarity and a minimum of irrelevant detail. There was a literalness in Flanders's drawings that was at once endearing and infuriating, hovering as they did between integrity and mindlessness. It was a far cry from Raymond's artistry, but if Flanders's performance was markedly inferior to that of his predecessor, it was nonetheless competent and workmanlike.

Because of his limitations, Flanders had to rely on the strength of the stories he was given to illustrate, and on this score he was fortunate, getting the help of good writers. After Charteris, whose work had improved during the last months of his tenure, there came Max Trell (using the alias Robert Storm). Surprisingly, Trell proved at least as adept as his predecessor, and went on getting better all the time. His narratives had a flavor of their own. While retaining the loose frame of the classic gangster story, he leaned more toward the technical and scientific aspects of crime-fighting, dwelling at length on the methods of fingerprint analysis, laboratory work, and code-breaking. In his themes he slowly veered away from the stereotyped tales of gang-busting and racket-cleaning to more relevant stories of detection and counterespionage.

After a brief interlude by Nicholas Afonsky, Austin Briggs took charge of the artwork on November 7, 1938, and his first story was a doozie. Three years before America's entry into World War II and even before the conflict had officially broken out in Europe, X-9 was hunting down a spy ring headed by one Captain Ludwig, whose name, monocle, shaved neck, and arrogant bearing left no doubt about his nationality. Briggs displayed an elegance of line and a stylistic brilliance that often recalled Alex Raymond. Trell on his part proved just as inspired in narratives bearing such subtitles as "Terror in Cafe Society" (murder and blackmail on Broadway), "Helium Thieves" (German-looking and -sounding spies out to get the precious gas for their dirigibles), and "The Big Ditch" (sabotage on the Panama Canal).

Secret Agent X-9 (A. Raymond), © 1934 **King Features Syndicate**

In yet another instance of the Peter Principle at work, in April 1940 Briggs was plucked off the modern-day trappings of *X-9* (he had to leave in such haste that he didn't have time to finish the story he had already begun), which he was ideally suited to depict, and plunked down on the science-fictional settings of *Flash Gordon,* to which he never warmed up. On May 13, 1940, after several other candidates had auditioned for the job, the task of drawing *X-9* fell to Mel Graff: his turned out to be the longest tenure of any artist on the strip, and after the first few years it proved a disaster. His style was different from that of his predecessor, closer to Caniff than to Raymond, but it adapted well to the stories of espionage and detection he was given to illustrate.

In 1943 Graff persuaded the editors at King Features to dump Trell, who had anchored the strip through three changes of artists, and turn the scripting over to him. He then proceeded to give X-9 a name—Phil Corrigan—a busy romantic life, and even a likable personality, transforming him from a lone wolf into an avuncular figure, not unlike the almost eponymous Phil Cardigan in the *Patsy* strip Graff had earlier produced for the Associated Press. To top it all off, he got the G-man to marry (in June 1950) and a few years later to father a child. X-9's family life turned into a soap opera of such cloying sentimentality that it would have made Hammett cringe, had he bothered to read the strip (he didn't). In addition, Graff had developed a drinking habit that put him out of commission for weeks, and he had to resort to ghosts who filled in for him, a practice that resulted in a hodgepodge of styles and in plots desultory to the point of incoherence. In March 1960 he was finally asked to leave.

X-9 was then entrusted to Bob Lubbers, who had been drawing it for long stretches at a time anyway, and who signed "Bob Lewis" because of a conflict of interest (he was also drawing *Long Sam* for another syndicate at the same time). Lubbers gave greater prominence to the G-man's professional life (it was a police strip, after all) and turned in a generally agreeable, if hardly memorable, performance. Lubbers left in January 1967, and he was succeeded by Al Williamson, who had been drawing the *Flash Gordon* comic book in close mimicry of Alex Raymond's style. Williamson brought on Archie Goodwin as scriptwriter on the strip, which was now retitled *Secret Agent Corrigan.* Both men were strong admirers of the James Bond movies, and Corrigan accordingly undertook many missions in foreign lands and amid exotic locales peopled with bevies of enticing beauties. In the early years of his tenure Williamson drew the G-man's adventures in a visually exciting and dynamic style, with long shots and elaborate action scenes alternating with expressive close-ups. As the 1970s passed the midpoint, however, his work became more hurried and sloppier. Furthermore, he got into the annoying habit of drawing himself as Corrigan, making the hero look more like the sensitive artist Williamson is than the tough operative X-9 was supposed to be.

In February 1980 the Williamson-Goodwin team, discouraged by the modest returns generated by their endeavors, finally called it quits, and George Evans, another comic-book alumnus, took over *Corrigan,* which he guided with skill, vigor, and integrity. It is unfortunate that, because of the feature's limited circulation, few people are able to read and appreciate one of the genuinely interesting action strips still extant, a strip still carried on in dashing style by Evans.

M.H.

SECRET OPERATIVE DAN DUNN
See DAN DUNN

SERGEANT PAT OF THE RADIO PATROL
See RADIO PATROL

SERGEANT STONY CRAIG
See STONY CRAIG OF THE MARINES

THE SHADOW
1939–1942

As befits the elusive character of the protagonist, there is a mystery about the *Shadow* newspaper strip. Vernon Greene, who illustrated the feature for its entire duration, claimed that he had drawn it from 1938 to 1942. Other sources give the starting year as 1940. Since the strips were not dated, different newspapers published it at different times, which makes the matter no easier. From close examination of the evidence, it seems that Greene did indeed start drawing the strip in 1938, but that it made its published appearance in 1939 (one strip whose original is in the author's collection is clearly marked July 22, 1939). Written by Walter Gibson (a.k.a. Maxwell Grant) in partnership with Greene, *The Shadow* was distributed in daily format only by the Ledger Syndicate.

The newspaper strip was of course based on the famous radio program that made its debut on the Mutual network in March 1931, with Frank Readick as the voice of the protagonist (Orson Welles, the most famous Shadow of all, came later, in 1937), and Harry Charlot as the first scriptwriter. The radio series became an overnight success and, sensing a hit, Street and Smith issued *The Shadow* pulp magazine beginning in April 1931. Walter Gibson wrote most of the pulp stories under his alias of Maxwell Grant. The Shadow had a split personality from the start. On the air he was Lamont Cranston, "a wealthy young man about town," who had learned in the Orient "a strange and mysterious secret, the hypnotic power to cloud men's minds so they cannot see him." On the printed page, by contrast, he was a cloaked figure of justice using disguise, night, and the shadows as a means of concealment, along with many aliases.

The strip used both personas alternatively, but only one alias for its hero, that of Lamont Cranston, and only one girlfriend, the lovely and spunky brunette Margo Lane. In the early continuities the Shadow had no powers of invisibility but relied on fist and gun and wits to achieve his righteous ends. There were murders, kidnappings, and

The Shadow (V. Greene), ca. 1940, © Ledger Syndicate

gunfights a-plenty in these adventures, patterned on the pulp stories. In 1940 the hero learned to turn invisible, and his exploits followed at least in spirit some of the radio scripts. The narratives now involved tales of espionage, as the Shadow placed his abilities at the service of the U.S. government and its armed forces. One of the later episodes, for instance, had the invisible protagonist foil a German plot to sabotage the American fleet at anchor in Norfolk, Virginia.

Greene at first drew *The Shadow* in an adequate if unimaginative approximation of Alex Raymond (with *Secret Agent X-9* as his model). He later turned in an appropriately dark version of the stories, and his sense of atmosphere and mood was often remarkable, perfectly matching the sardonic quality of the scripts. In 1942 the artist was called to military duty, and the strip was dropped by the syndicate that same year.

M.H.

SHERLOCK HOLMES
1930–1932, 1954–1956

While newspaper strips starring detectives have traditionally done well, the greatest detective of them all, Sherlock Holmes, never proved successful in a comic-strip format. The first Sherlock Holmes version to run in the comics pages appeared in 1930, the year of Arthur Conan Doyle's death (it is possible that Doyle, a very conservative man, frowned upon the funnies as a proper vehicle for his detective). It was an extremely respectful adaptation based on the stories that make up *The Memoirs of Sherlock Holmes*.

The lengthy, typeset text, tastefully abridged from the Doyle narratives, took up almost half of each of the panels drawn by Leo O'Mealia in a dark, brooding style better suited to the nefarious doings of Fu Manchu (which O'Mealia was to undertake later) than to the ratiocinations of the Baker Street detective. Nationally distributed by the Bell Syndicate, *Sherlock Holmes* lasted less than two years, disappearing early in 1932.

The sleuth in the Inverness cape and the deerstalker cap had been absent from the comic pages for more than two decades when the Herald-Tribune Syndicate decided to bring him back, starting in March 1954. The new *Sherlock Holmes* was drawn by Frank Giacoia, with a strong assist by Mike Sekowsky, on texts by Edith Meiser. Unlike O'Mealia's version, which had appeared only in a daily format, this second rendition came out in both daily and Sunday settings. The look of the strip was undeniably influenced by the movies, with the detective hero and his memorialist, Dr. Watson, resembling Basil Rathbone and Nigel Bruce respectively. The continuities were only loosely based on Doyle's stories and contained more action than detection. The Victorian atmosphere, backgrounds, and costumes were recreated with some faithfulness but couldn't quite duplicate the charm and appeal of the original tales. Neither fish nor fowl, this second Sherlock Holmes avatar also lasted two years, ending in the spring of 1956.

M.H.

SHERLOCKO THE MONK
See THE MONK FAMILY

SHOE
1977–present

The brainchild of political cartoonist Jeff MacNelly, *Shoe* began publication in September 1977. It is a humor strip in which the characters come from various species of birds. Nevertheless, they act and speak very much like regular people and in fact display all-too-human frailties and neuroses.

As befits its creator, the strip takes place at a newspaper entitled *Treetops Tattler Tribune*, with offices aptly located in a gigantic tree. P. Martin Shoemaker (Shoe, for short, and PMS for initials), a tough editor-in-chief and a hard-drinking, cigar-chomping (good for crowd control and to kill the awful toothpaste taste) racetrack aficionado, is the titular protagonist. Just like other newspapermen of the old school, he is sarcastic, insensitive, sharp-tongued ("This stinks" is his usual critique), and more often than not refuses to answer letters from readers because "it only encourages them." One redeeming side of his otherwise mean nature is the fact that he turned down a job at the *New York Times* because it does not print comics.

Shoe is aided in his journalistic pursuits by "Perfesser" Cosmo Fishhawk, an irascible reporter and analyst, whose range of expertise is as wide as it is superficial. He is the messiest accumulator of memos, letters, notes, bills, and receipts, making his desk a disaster area, which he cleans every so often at his boss's urging, only to start all over again. A big drinker and eater, he is always trying to lose weight and exercises with *The Orson Welles Workout Book,* his favorite fitness manual, while he drinks diet sodas—with beer chasers. His precocious nephew and ward, Skyler, is the typical nerdy teenager and terrible student. Unprepared, he usually answers in such convoluted circumlocutions that he sometimes receives a C in essay questions, although he has a tougher time in mathematics.

Roz is the owner of a greasy-spoon cafe, where "only major gas credit cards" are accepted and *haute cuisine* is indeed a foreign concept. Like so many fellow birds, she is not shy about saying what she thinks, whether about the Perfesser's unwritten Great American Novel or the litigious lawyer knocked out by her skillet ("If I'm getting sued, I want it to be for something worthwhile"). Indeed, only preppie Muffy Hollandaise, the newly hired general reporter, and the not-too-bright Loon, the messenger and deliveryman, never utter a nasty word. She actually calls her boss Mr. Shoemaker and draws happy faces inside her O's, while Loon believes he is playing fish with poker sharks from the paper. Finally, Battson D. Belfry, the mildly corrupt senator from East Virginia, who bears a passing resemblance to Tip O'Neill, has a politician's natural gift of gab and desire to live on the dole. He finds it hard, therefore, to decide between a press conference, where he can truly shine, and a fact-finding mission to the Bahamas, where he can do so much good.

The strip satirizes the military-industrial complex, consumer fads, the post office (now able to deliver mail overnight by using Federal Express), off-the-wall teaching innovations, government grants and matching funds, and sensational murder trials: "He must be superhuman to sit through this day after day.... There must be a limit to what one man is forced to take. Hasn't he suffered enough?" "Well, Roz, he has been charged with two counts of murder..." "I'm talking about Judge Ito," she replies. At times, if the humor can be biting, it is because it is on target. As in his editorial cartoons, MacNelly is not afraid to attack sacred cows and debunk accepted ideas about human relationships, management styles, or even child-rearing techniques: "Three D's, a C, and an F?" asks Uncle Cosmo of his nephew, adding, "Maybe you're just dumb as a post."

Shoe is distributed to more than a thousand newspapers by Tribune Media Services and has been reissued in numerous book collections. In 1979, it was honored with the National Cartoonists Society's Reuben Award.

P.H.

SHORT RIBS
1958–1982

Frank O'Neal was already a successful magazine cartoonist at the time he sold NEA Service his slightly off-the-wall comic strip, *Short Ribs.* Debuting as a daily on November 17, 1958, the feature added a Sunday version on June 14 of the following year.

Traveling back and forth in time and space, *Short Ribs* had several sets of fixed but unrelated characters, from a court jester in medieval England to a pair of Soviet apparatchiks during the cold war period. Among these inspired creations there were an inept but incorrigibly hopeful western sheriff, whose exclamation after each shootout, "Still the slowest gun in the West," found its ironic correlative in the boast of a feisty old witch who could change a prince into a frog and back again in the twinkling of an eye, "Fastest wand in the kingdom!" A permanent feature of the strip was a delightful sense of offbeat humor that carried into the dialogue, sprinkled with puns and non sequiturs reminiscent on one level of old vaudeville turns and on a higher plane of the contemporary absurdist playwrights. This wordplay was nicely complemented by the visuals, with their incongruous backgrounds and slightly awry perspective, all rendered with an extreme economy of line and a fine sense of design by the artist.

In his autobiographical contribution to the *National Cartoonists Society Album* (1972 edition), O'Neal wrote, "My principal ambition is to make *Short Ribs* an outstanding strip." This ambition was not fulfilled—at least not financially—to the cartoonist's satisfaction, and O'Neal left the strip in the hands of his assistant, Frank Hill, in 1973. Hill worked in close approximation of his predecessor's graphic style, and he tried to maintain the strip's caustic bite. His wanderings into some of the topical concerns and issues of the day dated the feature more than they updated it. Never a great commercial standout to begin with, it steadily lost the coterie of fans that had at least assured it of critical suc-

Short Ribs (F. O'Neal), © 1960 NEA Service

cess, and it was permanently retired with the Sunday release of May 2, 1982.

Under the aegis of its creator, *Short Ribs* was a strip ahead of its time, and it proved the forerunner of such later hits as *The Wizard of Id*, *Broom-Hilda*, and *Shoe*.

M.H.

SILENT SAM
1922–1955

Among the dozen or so foreign comic strips that have made it into American newspapers, *Silent Sam* occupies a special niche. Born *Adamson* in the Swedish humor weekly *Søndags-Nisse* ("Sunday Troll") in 1920 from the talented pen of Oscar Jacobsson, it was imported to the United States as early as 1922, and later syndicated as a daily by Consolidated News Features (with its creator's name simplified to Jacobson).

Silent Sam (to give him his American name) was small, almost bald (except for three hairs on his pate), and always chomping on a cigar. He was not only mute but also impassive, and his stone-faced expression was not unlike Buster Keaton's when confronted with contretemps big and small, as he often was. Jacobson drew his strip entirely in pantomime: no dialogue was ever exchanged and there was no wording of any kind, except for an occasional sign or a few sound effects. The graphic style was simplicity itself, with almost no props and no backgrounds; the characters were delineated with a bold, uncluttered line. "Jacobson, Sam's creator, succeeded because the idea that was outlined was almost always good," Coulton Waugh wrote in *The Comics*. "His was a reverse sense, a distortion of the ordinary."

In 1936 Henry Thol took over the drawing of the strip, and he was succeeded in 1944 by Jeff Hayes, who made it into a more conventional feature, using backgrounds and speech balloons, while in Sweden Jacobsson imperturbably carried on with the original version of the strip until his death in 1945. The American version proved successful enough to survive until 1955. Jacobson, or Jacobsson, paved the way for other Scandinavian strips to follow his into the American market, notably Henning Dahl Mikkelsen's *Ferd'nand* and *Alfredo* by Jorgen Morgensen and Cospar Cornelius.

M.H.

SILK HAT HARRY'S DIVORCE SUIT
1910–1929

Thomas Aloysius Dorgan (known professionally as Tad) was reportedly the highest-paid sports cartoonist in the country, but in the early years of this century, try as he might, he never managed to come up with a successful newspaper strip. *Johnny Wise,* for instance, starring a grizzled, grinning, gin-guzzling Irish reprobate, lasted for only one year, in 1902–03. Finally in 1910, inspired by the legal shenanigans in the two consecutive trials (in 1907 and 1908) of Arthur K. Thaw, accused of the murder of famed architect Stanford White, he created a series of interlock-

ing panels on a judicial theme, often running in sequences, which were called *Judge Rummy's Court* and *Old Judge Rumhauser* before settling on *Silk Hat Harry's Divorce Suit* later in the 1910s. In the middle of the decade a Sunday page, syndicated by King Features, was added, further solidifying the feature as an authentic comic strip.

All the protagonists in Dorgan's feature were canine characters with very human traits and foibles (especially foibles). Silk Hat Harry was a bon vivant, wine connoisseur, and admirer of female pulchritude, a fancy that, not illegitimately, put his wife's nose out of joint. The enraged Harry (who owed his nickname to his classy attire when visiting Broadway actresses on opening nights), as a result, sought a divorce on a variety of flimsy grounds that Judge Rummy, ruling from the bench, airily dismissed out of hand. When the aggrieved Harry averred that his spouse hadn't spoken to him in a month, the judge smilingly admonished him in soothing Irish tones, "Don't tell everybody about her; you'll never get a wiff [sic] like that again."

While Harry was the official center of the strip, Judge Rummy was its most colorful and popular character. Apparently versed in all facets of the law, he made rulings in cases ranging from unruly behavior to aggravated felony. Rummy's escapades away from the chamber were as picturesque as his court appearances. An inveterate lover of the opposite sex, he pursued the objects of his desire with unalloyed ardor, in restaurants, in theaters, on the street, pressing third parties—maitre d's, ushers, cops on the beat—into love's service with the unvarying instruction "Tell her it's the Judge." As his advances met only with rebuffs, the judge naturally turned to the solace that had earned him his nickname. So great was his reputation on that score that when he failed to reappear after court recess, the police report stated: "A full quart of hooch found yesterday in the Judge's chambers proves conclusively that the jurist did not leave of his own accord."

Regulars on the strip included McIntyre Bunk, a sleazy con-man; Paul Fedinck, a French pretender; not to forget Matt Soupbone, bailiff in the judge's court, and a bulldog detective that went by the name of Curlock Holmes. The judge's long-suffering wife and his small-town brother, Ima Rummy, also put in occasional appearances. They were drawn in a scratchy, hasty style, with little adornment but great vigor, by the cartoonist.

One didn't go to Tad for his graphic abilities but for his raucous narratives and slangy expressions. He joyously deflated the pretensions of small-town hucksters, would-be financiers, and self-appointed experts. He had as fine an ear for language as he had an eye for observation, and the dialogue he put in the mouths of his bums, mountebanks, and social climbers was accurate and more often than not excruciatingly funny.

In 1920 Tad was diagnosed with a serious heart ailment, and he had to cut down on his output, concentrating on his humor cartoons and his *Indoor/Outdoor Sports* panels, to the detriment of his strip work. In 1922 Silk Hat Harry argued his last in front of Judge Rummy's court. The cockeyed magistrate, however, sporadically continued his checkered career in-between Tad's regular daily panels until the cartoonist's death in 1929.

M.H.

SILLY MILLY
1938–1952

A daily strip of inspired zaniness, *Silly Milly* began life as *Extra, Extra* in the pages of the *New York Post* on January 8, 1938. It was written and drawn by Stan McGovern, a cartoonist of the old school much given to puns and vaudeville turns, whose grotesque yet somehow winsome graphic style exactly complemented his loony brand of humor.

In its initial incarnation the strip would pick up on a minor news item and milk out a series of verbal and visual gags from it, much in the manner of today's stand-up comics. Thus the announcement that the police in many metropolitan cities were using all kinds of vehicles to trap criminals would be followed by images of policemen riding in milk trucks, Mardi Gras floats, even commandeering ice-cream carts, with the instruction to "follow that bandit!" In the early 1940s, when swing was the thing, the strip changed its title to *Swing on the News*, while conserving the same format.

The feature had no recurring character save for one: a dark-haired, moon-faced girl in a polka-dot dress who looked like a rag doll and acted like a souped-up comedian, punctuating each sentence with "har, har" and "yuk, yuk." She was there to comment on the screwy goings-on. She eventually became known as Silly Milly and her popularity with the readers grew to such an extent as to warrant a new title change for the strip, which took on the name of its main character.

Silly Milly had a coterie of loyal fans, including Coulton Waugh, who in his study *The Comics* declared that McGovern belonged "to the classic tradition of the true funnymen." Yet despite the valiant efforts of the Post Syndicate, the strip was never carried by more than a handful of big-city newspapers; and in 1952 Silly Milly uttered her last "yuk, yuk."

M.H.

SILLY SYMPHONIES
1932–1942

I n the early 1930s most Sunday comic pages featured a companion strip (usually occupying one-third of the page) in addition to the main attraction. The *Mickey Mouse* Sunday, debuting on January 10, 1932, was no exception, and as its topper Walt Disney chose *Silly Symphonies,* the name of the series of musical animated shorts he had started in 1929. Like the Sunday *Mickey,* the first *Silly Symphonies* page was written and drawn by Earl Duvall; and the entire page was distributed by King Features Syndicate.

Oddly enough, the first (and longest) of the series, which ran from January 1932 to March 1934, was not based on any of the short cartoon films. Rather, it featured the epic adventures of a smart ladybug named Bucky fighting for the salvation of his hometown, Junkville, and the light of his love, June, against invading hordes of flies. It was an engaging and funny tale, and it marked the birth of a major comic-strip talent, that of Al Taliaferro, who had taken over the strip soon after its inception, in April 1932. Taliaferro had for writers on the story Ted Osborne and

Merrill de Maris, and the text made a number of topical references. As early as December 1932, for instance, the king of the flies justified his planned invasion of Junkville in this way: "Flyburg is crowded.... We've got to expand! We've got to have money! We've got to have land! So let's declare war upon Junkville Town!"—an eerie echo of *Mein Kampf,* whose author, Adolf Hitler, was to take over as chancellor of Germany the very next month.

Following the Junkville saga, most of the later stories (now titled *Silly Symphony* in the singular) were derived from a number of their screen namesakes, such as *Birds of a Feather, Peculiar Penguins, The Little Red Hen* (in which Donald Duck made his first appearance), and *The Robber Kitten.* In all of these fables the text was written in rhyme, as in the opening of "The Little Red Hen" strip: "In Barnyard Village, on the farm / there lives a hen and ten small chicks / They have their joys and sorrows, but / no income tax nor politics!"

It would be a mistake to think that these Sunday-page tales were only a reduction of the animated cartoons; it was rather an adaptation in the best sense of the word, and Taliaferro displayed great ingenuity in translating the screen stories into graphic terms. The two tales featuring the Three Little Pigs were long developments on the initial theme and were constructed along sound narrative lines and around firmly delineated characters. This development was perceptively noted by Allen Dean Foster, who wrote: "A mere villainous presence in the *Three Little Pigs* film, the Big Bad Wolf emerges as a real character in the strip offshoots, with a full range of emotions in which he is permitted to converse instead of simply huff and puff."

Stylistically innovative but commercially expendable, the stories derived from *Silly Symphonies* cartoons were often interrupted by the introduction of more enticing Disney fare: thus Donald Duck was starred in a series of weekly gags running from August 30, 1936, to December 5, 1937, while between December 12, 1937, and April 24, 1938, there appeared an adaptation of *Snow White and the Seven Dwarfs* drawn by Hank Porter on texts by de Maris. Taliaferro came back to draw a further number of *Silly Symphonies* pages, such as "Timid Elmer" and "The Ugly Duckling." In April 1939 he definitively left the feature. "Pluto the Pup" (April–December 1939) was drawn by Bob Grant, who assisted Hank Porter on the adaptation of *Pinocchio* (December 1939–April 1940). "Little Hiawatha" was the last title in the *Silly Symphonies* series. Starring a little Indian boy and his irascible chief of a father, it unfolded its simple gags (superbly drawn by Bob Grant) from November 10, 1940, to July 12, 1942, marking the official end of the *Silly Symphonies* title.

M.H.

SIMON SIMPLE
1904–1914[?]

T he comics pages of the American Sunday supplements in the first decade of this century were literally hothouses of new cartooning talent. Among the most prolific comics creators of this era special mention should be made of the unjustly forgotten Ed Carey, whose *Simon Simple,*

Simon Simple (E. Carey), 1904

of mild social satire and pun-heavy wordplay. Comparisons have been made with Jack Kent's *King Aroo*, but its closest counterpart was probably Jay Ward's television-cartoon series, *Fractured Fairy Tales*.

Sir Bagby was set in a stereotypically mythical Middle Ages that was rife with anachronisms, such as the sleazy used-horse salesmen billed "Oaf & Churl—Used Horses Since 1044." Its hero was Sir Bagby, a young knight who (like Walt Kelly's Pogo Possum) never let his cynicism wear down his innocence, or at least his good manners. He was a soft touch for every noble cause that came along, or every half-baked government mission that his monarch, King Filbert, sent him on; and even though his attitude and commentary usually implied that he was fully aware of their impossibility, he was simply too polite to refuse undertaking them.

The main trio consisted of Bagby himself; Solly, the court jester, his regular traveling companion and sarcastic Greek chorus; and henpecked King Filbert, whose royal court was a setup for sardonic jabs at the contemporary national political scene. In a 1962 sequence, shortly after President Kennedy announced that America would put an astronaut on the moon by the end of the decade, King Filbert decided to send a man to the moon, with Sir Bagby delegated to finding a witch who could build a broomstick powerful enough to fly there. "Where are you going?" Solly asked Bagby. "On a witchhunt." "I thought that was a function of the legislature." "Not these days." However, the next day's four-panel strip opened with Bagby recapping, "The king needs a witch to advise him about riding broomsticks, so I have to find one. Let's go." The two middle panels were blank. Solly, startled, said in the last panel, "Hey...we just skipped two panels." "I know," replied Bagby. "A good witchhunt always starts on the far left or the far right." Similar examples of this humor: an Asian crockery salesman, Moe T. Soong, who was unable to find any customers for his Red China; B. O. Wolf, a Viking raider (he didn't wear a horned helmet; the horns grew through holes in his headgear), who was fast-talked into becoming the royal tax collector; James Patriot, an ultraconservative who teamed up with Sir Dudley Dull of the Royal Unpatriotic Activities Committee to accuse everyone in the kingdom of disloyalty; and Phineas Figg, an adman (from Neatsfoot, Flummery, and Figg) who brought high-pressure Madison Avenue tactics to knight-versus-dragon bouts.

The humor was not all topical or cynical, however. Snerk the Magician became the royal weatherman to try to improve the quality of medieval weather, but kept having "raining cats and dogs" accidents. A dragon turned out to be more interested in culture than combat; she became King Filbert's Social Dragon, haughtily enforcing etiquette at royal soirees and advising Bagby on the proper manner

which began as a weekly color page in 1904 for the T. C. McClure Syndicate, for a time rivaled in popularity *Buster Brown* and *Happy Hooligan*.

Simon Simple was a clownish figure accoutered in baggy pants, a huge bowtie covering half his lunar face, and a waistcoat three sizes too short for his elongated body. He was a character whose innocence and incomprehension in some ways prefigured Bill Griffith's Zippy the Pinhead. A victim of society, human malice, and unkind fate, Simon tried to put up a brave front, but it was a losing battle. He always found himself set upon by dogs, harassed by kids, hassled by cops, put down by girls, and affronted by total strangers. His bad luck was contrasted by the good fortune of his constant companion, a little black boy named Mose. In 1908 he acquired a pet tiger, and the animal allowed him occasionally to turn the tables on his tormentors but didn't change his misfortune: Simon walked into banks just as a holdup was in progress, got run over by ice wagons while waiting for a streetcar, and couldn't go hiking without triggering a fire, a flood, or a rockslide. The page, now retitled *Simon Simple and Ben-Gal* (adding his tiger), lasted for a few years longer, but seems to have disappeared in 1914, when Carey took over *Pa's Family* from C. H. Wellington.

Simon Simple was a hit for most of its run, and earned its creator acclaim and fortune (Carey was reportedly paid as much as five hundred dollars for a single page, a considerable sum at the time). The feature is now totally forgotten, and while it is no masterpiece, it exudes a welcome period charm and a humorous touch that make it worth revisiting.

M.H.

SIR BAGBY
1959–1967

Krazy *Kat* is probably the best-known example of a comic strip that had a fame and prestige among the literati that far outpaced its mass popularity. There have been many strips that never gained large followings but did win a small but devoted readership. One of the more charming of these was *Sir Bagby*, a gently humorous fantasy

Sir Bagby (R. Hackney), © 1960 Adcox-Lenahan, Inc.

in which to rescue fair maidens. Mrs. Harpy was a soft-hearted witch who could always be sweet-talked into using her spells to help rather than to harm. A gryphon turned up in a variety of situations.

Sir Bagby was the creation of Rick (art) and Bill (writing) Hackney. The two Minnesota-raised humorists opened a studio in San Francisco in the mid-1950s for freelance advertising art and producing comic-book features for the Catholic *Our Sunday Visitor.* When they decided to create *Sir Bagby* they offered it to a conveniently local but small syndicator, Jim Lenahan, in mid-1958. He was only able to place *Sir Bagby* in about a half-dozen papers, until he teamed up with Glenn Adcox to create Adcox-Lenahan, Inc., a year later. *Sir Bagby* leaped into several major newspapers in May 1959, and stayed there when Adcox-Lenahan dissolved a year later due to Lenahan's declining health; the *Sir Bagby* distribution contract was sold to the McClure Syndicate. But the number of papers never increased. The Hackneys felt that McClure (which became the Bell-McClure Syndicate in April 1963) was not promoting their strip, and they reclaimed it when their contract expired at the end of June 1964. *Sir Bagby* carried the credit "R. & B. Hackney Feature" from July 1964, but the brothers were working full-time to support their families as it was, and they discovered that they did not have time for new promotion as well as for production and distribution of the strip to their existing clients.

After about two and a half years, a week's continuity was published in which Bagby, Solly, and King Filbert said good-bye to their readers. This was intended to be a hiatus, not a final conclusion, while Rick Hackney took an extensive promotional tour, including a trip to Europe to drum up foreign sales. But interest was scant, and by the time that he returned to America, Bill was suffering from stomach cancer (which killed him in 1970). *Sir Bagby* was never resumed, despite requests from most of the newspapers that were carrying it when it was discontinued.

F.P.

SKIPPY
1925–1945

The first half-century of the comics spawned many kid strips, but only one could be elevated to the status of classic. Percy Crosby's *Skippy*, which innovated a number of sophisticated and refined touches used later by Charles

Schulz and Bill Watterson, filled a void in kid comics with its use of realistic characters engaged in the trifling daily happenings of a boy's world.

Skippy, perpetually decked out in checked hat, bow tie, shorts, and drooping socks, was alternately charming, philosophical, cunning, and mischievous, but most of all, he was real. Crosby knew boys well and had a good ear for their idiom. He portrayed Skippy and friends as puritanical, considerate, and happy, but also as quarrelsome, lonesome, troublesome, and sad. At times, Skippy was shown hurdling a series of death-defying obstacles to pick a bouquet of flowers for his mother or praying that her day-long headache be given to him for a while; occasionally, he was downright romantic, but only on his own terms and unbeknownst to Sooky and his other buddies. Usually rebuffed by the pretty little girl with black hair, Skippy always bounced back quickly and went on his merry way. In one episode, after the hoped-for love of his life slammed the door in his face, Skippy fed the flowers he had bought for her to a cow, and then chopped down the tree on which he had carved their names and made kindling of it.

To Skippy, school was a last resort, somewhere to go when there was nothing else to do, and sequences often revolved around his efforts to skip school by presenting forged excuses or to avoid punishment for a bad report card. Most of Skippy's world was full of activities unrelated to school—plummeting down a hill in his flying boxcart, squabbling over who was to be first at bat, looking in on the branches of his lemonade-stand empire, or just hanging out on the curb, daydreaming and philosophizing with Sooky.

Much of the philosophy was whimsical and clever. When Skippy's father reminded him that "we were put here to do good for others," Skippy asked, "What were the others put here for?" When Sooky announced that "Republicans is the only real people," Skippy agreed, adding, "Only I was goin' to say Democrats." In one episode, when Skippy and Sooky were adrift in a rowboat without oars, Skippy nonchalantly summed up their choices: "Well, if the tide's with us we'll get home; if it ain't we'll go to Europe for nothin'." Some rather adultlike sayings rolled out of the kids' mouths as well, as when Skippy said, "Chop people up in little pieces an' I'll bust out laughin', but show me a stained glass winder in a church an' I'll cry like a little child," or as he prayed, "Oh Lord, please give me the strength to brush my teeth every night and if Thou cannot give me the strength, give me the strength not to worry about it."

By the 1930s, political polemics replaced the cute sayings as Crosby became the first cartoonist to break the unwritten rule that specific political issues should not be injected into strips. A very intense man who earlier had drawn political cartoons for the *New York Daily Call, Brooklyn Eagle,* and *Life,* Crosby began to use *Skippy* for his very strong denouncements of Roosevelt, Al Capone, J. Edgar Hoover, censorship, and tyranny of any type, and his equally powerful defenses of press freedom, the rights of individuals, and high morality. Some days, the strip was almost solid dialogue, as evidenced in one Memorial Day discourse on patriotism and disarmament that went on for four hundred words. In the strip and the many books and articles he wrote, Crosby let it be known that he could not be bought, and when publishers refused to use his work, he self-published (books such as *A Cartoonist's Philosophy* in 1931) or paid to have his articles and cartoons used as advertisements. In a two-year period, he spent more than $30,000 on the advertising of his viewpoints.

Such prodigious outputs of work and money were possible through the incredible speed with which he produced and the huge sums of money he made. From 1928 to 1937, Crosby did 3,650 episodes of *Skippy,* ten books of fiction, philosophy, politics, drawings, and cartoons, and numerous pamphlets and essays, while also mounting a dozen exhibitions of his oils, watercolors, lithography, drypoints, and drawings in New York, Paris, Rome, Washington, and London. He normally worked nine hours at a stretch, during which he would produce six daily strips, plus the Sunday *Skippy* and its two toppers, *Bug Lugs* and *Always Belittlin'.*

When King Features syndicated the strip in 1926, after it had appeared in *Life* for two years and with other syndicates for still another year, Crosby was given a contract calling for a salary of $1,150 weekly against 50 percent of gross receipts. Adaptations of the strip to other media, such as a film (in 1931), songs, novels, a radio show (in 1934), and one of the very first comic books (also in 1934), brought in additional money that enabled him and his family to live royally at Ridgelawn in Virginia.

But the tremendous success was short-lived, as alcoholism, melancholia, loneliness, and deep depression took their toll on Crosby's life after the mid-1930s. A devastating divorce and the loss of most of his belongings, both attributable to his bizarre drinking behavior, came first, followed by the demise of *Skippy* on December 8, 1945, Crosby's fifty-fourth birthday. After unsuccessful attempts to revive the strip and a series of other setbacks, Crosby attempted sui-

Skippy (P. Crosby), © 1936 Skippy, Inc.

cide in 1948. That incident and his increasing paranoia about perceived (and real) adversaries landed him in an insane asylum, where he spent the remaining sixteen years of his life. Even then, he refused to give up and spent much of his time writing novels and his opus, a series of books on the arts (done mainly from memory), as well as drawing and painting. He died in 1964 on his seventy-third birthday.

Crosby's hallmark in cartoons and paintings was motion—swift, clean, and simple. In *Skippy,* he exhibited a type of impressionism that favored blurred and hazy details, disconnected lines, and spontaneity, all designed to call more attention to the characters noted for their realism. Crosby was both an expert draftsman and wordsmith, and *Skippy* excelled because the humor worked equally well in pantomime and in words.

J.A.L.

SKULL VALLEY
See WHITE BOY

SKYROADS
1929–1942

Soon after the inception of *Buck Rogers,* the small but enterprising John F. Dille Company launched another soaring adventure strip, *Skyroads.* An aviation feature purportedly written by Lieutenant Lester J. Maitland, a crack

Skyroads (R. Keaton), 1933, John F. Dille Co.

Slim Jim (S. Armstrong), 1916

pilot and air pioneer, and drawn, like *Buck Rogers,* by Dick Calkins (who liked to sign himself "Lt. Dick Calkins"), it left ground on Monday, May 27, 1929.

The first daily opened on a rousing oration to the glory and romance of flight, then settled down to introduce the protagonists of the piece, Ace Ames and Buster Evans, founders of Skyroads Unlimited, a fledgling air service. After only a few months of flying, they were joined by a third partner, the dark-haired and headstrong Peggy Mills, who, challenged derisively on her gender, indignantly replied, "Girl! I'm no girl—I'm an aviatrix!" As it happened, Peggy's father was a wealthy tycoon who, in the interest of science, offered to finance the trio's "flight to the headwaters of the Amazon." From then on there was no turning back.

Calkins was only a mediocre illustrator and, burdened by two strips to draw, he hired early in 1930 a pair of young draftsmen barely out of art school to take care of the artwork. One was Zack Mosley, who soon left to create *Smilin' Jack;* the other one, Russell Keaton, stayed on, however, and with him at the controls *Skyroads* turned into an artistic tour de force, though it remained only a modest commercial success (there never was a Sunday, for instance). Keaton had an uncanny feeling for space, action, and speed, and a fine sense of drama and style. He brought excitement and suspense to the feature, and endowed it with an airy and elegant look. *Skyroads* was incontestably the best-designed aviation strip of the period until Noel Sickles took command of *Scorchy Smith.*

In 1933 Maitland's name was dropped from the credits, just as Keaton's signature started appearing on the strip. A restless experimenter, Keaton scrapped the original *Skyroads* team and replaced them with an array of manly heroes, decked out with colorful nicknames. There were in quick succession Hurricane Hawk, Speed McCloud, and Clipper Williams. In an ironic touch the latter physically resembled Keaton and, like him, was a native of Corinth, Mississippi. They were all daredevil adventurers who rid the skies of air pirates, international terrorists, and self-proclaimed masters of the world.

In 1939 Keaton moved on to create in October of that year *Flyin' Jenny* for another syndicate. Before he left, however, he indulged in a nostalgic homeward journey: fresh from a harrowing adventure in the Himalayas, Clipper came back to Corinth for rest and recuperation. While there he foiled a bank robbery; with the reward money he

bought two old biplanes and turned a hangarful of eager town boys into junior pilots, organizing them into the Flyin' Legion to combat a foreign saboteur known as the Flying Ghost. As a loving tribute to his birthplace, Keaton drew many of Corinth's schoolchildren into what he knew to be his valedictory tale. All in all it had been an exciting ten-year itinerary, and it somehow seemed fitting for Keaton to conclude his commitment to the strip just as the high-flying decade of the 1930s similarly drew to its close.

It fell to Leonard Dworkins (signing Leo Gordon) to pilot the strip in its final years. Coming in as he did in the initial stages of World War II, Dworkins concerned himself with continuities involving spies and agitators, and mysterious menaces from the skies. On this warlike note *Skyroads* ended in the spring of 1942.

M.H.

SLIM JIM
1910–1937

In the fall of 1910 the World Color Printing Company of St. Louis, which specialized in supplying smaller rural papers with inexpensive Sunday comic pages, brought out George Frink's very funny *Slim Jim* for national syndication. The feature proved a hit with its small-town readers and soon added a number of metropolitan papers, such as the *Oakland Tribune,* to its roster.

Slim Jim had been foreshadowed years before by another Frink creation, *Circus Solly,* which had started life on February 21, 1903, in the *Chicago Daily News.* A stringy and elastic circus acrobat turned hobo, Solly was continually hounded by a corps of bumbling Keystone Cops trying vainly to nab him. For World Color, Frink rechristened his beanpole Slim Jim and had him escape the clutches of the entire Grassville constabulary, a trio of comical and extremely tenacious gendarmes known collectively as the Force. Frink prematurely died in 1911, and the feature passed into the hands of James Crawford Ewer, who for little over three years displayed an inexhaustible inventiveness along with a baroque sense of design in his depictions of the slippery antihero's escapades.

In 1914 Ewer died and, after a period during which several cartoonists, including C. W. Kahles and Clarence Rigby, had a stab at the feature, *Slim Jim* (its title now amplified to that of *Slim Jim and the Force*) finally devolved to Stanley Armstrong in 1915. An unjustly maligned cartoonist, Armstrong, while he did not possess the stylistic excellence of his predecessors, exhibited a robust sense of humor and a raucous narrative flair that were ideally suited to the hyperkinetic, almost demented shenanigans of Slim Jim and the Force. He developed the characters of Bill Barnacle, Jim's old salt of an uncle, and of Shark-Eye and his murderous crew of pirates. The strip's relentless pursuit now turned into a no-holds-barred steeplechase in which the multiple protagonists ran across, under, and over one another, on land, in the air, at sea, and even under the seas in a submarine demolition derby that was as hair-raising as it was hilarious.

Like so many other strips of burlesque adventure, *Slim Jim* could not resist the 1930s competition of the straight action features that had come to the fore during the decade. In 1937 Slim Jim and his pursuers ran their last chase.

M.H.

SMILIN' JACK
1933–1973

*S*milin' Jack was one of the earliest and most enduring aviation-based adventure strips. Created for the Chicago Tribune–New York News Syndicate by Zack Mosley, an amateur pilot and aviation enthusiast, it began as a Sunday feature called *On the Wing* on October 1, 1933. That December Mosley changed it to *Smilin' Jack* and added a daily strip on June 15, 1936.

On the Wing began as a comic series about jittery flying students and was based on Mosley's own flying experiences. It was not too successful during its fourteen-week trial run, but that all changed when its name was changed to *Smilin' Jack*. From then on, it took on a momentum that continued for the next forty years. Mack Martin, the edgy student-pilot, became Jack, a dashing figure who sported a trim mustache above a winning smile that not even four decades of perilous adventures could wipe off his handsome face.

"Smilin' Jack" Martin was a pilot by profession, which meant, especially during the period the comic strip took place, that Smilin' Jack had to be a jack-of-all-trades, involving himself in everything from tracking down lost explorers to solving bank robberies. In his exploits he was assisted by his boy companion, Pinfeathers; his faithful cook and handyman, Fat Stuff; and an obese ex-head-hunter he had picked up in the South Seas who kept popping his shirt buttons into the open mouths of hungry chickens. He also had two eccentric sidekicks, the boisterous Velvet Harry and the sinister but sensual Downwind Jaxon, whose face was so handsome, he was never seen in more than quarter profile.

Jack became a commercial pilot whose consignments of freight and passengers took him to remote places and required a remarkable variety of talents. Although he was always embroiled in conflicts with crooks and spies, Jack never lost his cool. He was endlessly resourceful, devilishly clever, and extremely lucky. His most heinous foes included the Head, whose drooping eyelids and sinister face bespoke evil; the Claw, who used his prosthetic hook to deadly pur-

pose; and Toemain the Terrible, whose pet piranhas thrived on human flesh.

Jack never lacked for female companionship, including Cindy, the Incendiary Blonde, and the tempestuous Gale—not to mention an endless string of anonymous sexpots, his famous "li'l de-icers," who were so hot they could de-ice an airplane's wings. In spite of an abundance of amorous opportunities, Jack did get married—to his boss, Joy, no less—and they had a son with the improbable nickname of Jungle Jolly. Soon thereafter, Joy disappeared mysteriously, only to pop up during the war suffering from amnesia and then to vanish again, this time for good.

Always suspenseful, even when they stretched the limits of credibility, Jack's escapades were fast paced, and the occasional romantic interlude (women could no more resist his smilin' face than they could Downwind's averted one) was never long enough to interrupt the nonstop action.

Unlike most continuity strips, *Smilin' Jack* had genuine development. Characters grew up, grew old, even died. Jack married twice, and his son, Jungle Jolly, matured from a babe-in-arms to a young man as good-looking as his father but with a captivating smile all his own.

Zack Mosley remained active in aviation, and that helped him keep *Smilin' Jack* accurate and up-to-date. Even though his plots were outlandish, his aircraft drawings were flawless. Readers who grew up with *Smilin' Jack* received a solid education in basic aeronautics. Mosley's drawings of wind tunnels, for example, and his careful accompanying explanations could have served as textbook illustrations and instructions. Among Mosley's capable assistants in the rendering of his entertaining but informative strip were Gordon "Boody" Rogers and Ward Albertson.

Smilin' Jack was widely reprinted in comic books by Dell. In addition, the strip was the basis of a thirteen-episode movie serial produced by Universal in 1943.

Gradually the novelty of aviation wore off, and the readership for adventure comics in general declined. Even so, *Smilin' Jack* lasted well beyond its time, coming to end on April 1, 1973, after a forty-year run, the longest of any aviation strip.

T.W.

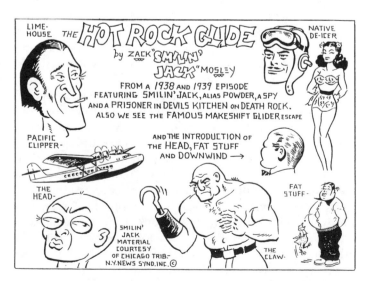

Smilin' Jack (Z. Mosley), © **Chicago Tribune–New York News Syndicate**

Smitty (W. Berndt) © 1928 Chicago Tribune–New York News Syndicate

SMITTY
1922–1974

A number of the strips of the 1920s and 1930s were set in the office, as was Walter Berndt's *Smitty*, originally titled *Bill the Office Boy* when it first appeared in the *New York World* in 1922. Berndt knew his subject matter well, having been an office boy himself for the *New York Journal*. It was on the *Journal* that he broke into cartooning, first substituting for "Tad" Dorgan and eventually taking over the panel *Then the Fun Began* when its creator, Milt Gross, left the paper.

Bill the Office Boy resided in the *World* for two weeks before Berndt was fired. The same day of his dismissal, he showed the strip to Joseph Patterson, who added it to his stable of Chicago Tribune–New York News Syndicate comics. One condition was that the name be changed. Berndt obliged, picking at random the name Smith from the telephone book.

Many of the strip's episodes revolved around the twelve-year-old Smitty and his maneuvering to impress, and at the same time to outwit, his boss, Mr. Bailey. As Stephen Becker wrote in *Comic Art in America*, "Underlying the whole relationship is the certainty, known all along to Smitty and gradually communicated to the readers, that the indispensable man in this office is not the boss but the boy." Also central to the cast was Smitty's four-year-old brother, Herby, who spoke with a lisp ("Thay, Thmitty") and wore a smock that always seemed to be catching a gust of wind that blew it forward. Herby's antics were often more adventuresome and cuter than those of Smitty. Mr. and Mrs. Smith made occasional appearances (more frequently later on), as did others of the neighborhood.

Berndt's drawing style was rather simplistic, with characters and backgrounds not very detailed, but full enough to give a sense of reality. Each four-panel strip carried its own gag and was part of a five- or six-week continuity.

One such story in 1932 featured Smitty's brief sojourn at military school. Smitty got to the prestigious academy in a roundabout way that was shared with the readers over weeks. Mr. Allen, a business friend of Mr. Bailey, was impressed with Smitty and asked him to live at his mansion and be his son's playmate. Smitty took to the socially and athletically inept rich kid and helped make him a bit tougher and streetwise. Mr. Allen rewarded Smitty for his devoted friendship by sending him and his new playmate to

military school. There, Smitty used his smarts to sabotage the academy's regimen and to ward off one cadet officer in particular whose preoccupation was to humiliate and denigrate the two boys. Eventually, the officer got the upper hand, as he framed the Allen boy. Smitty retaliated by planting evidence that put the blame on him, thus saving Cadet Allen and getting Smitty tossed out of the academy. Smitty's family learned of his unselfish act and welcomed him home as a hero.

In another 1932 series, Smitty playfully manipulated famous people (Babe Ruth, Calvin Coolidge, Douglas Fairbanks, etc.) to give him their autographs. Each daily strip featured a celebrity in caricature and concluded with a gag, the person's signature, and the suggestion that readers add the autographs to their scrapbooks.

Berndt maintained a mutually beneficial relationship with Joseph Patterson, even acting as his unofficial talent scout, and continued to draw *Smitty* for fifty-two years, until his retirement in 1974.

J.A.L.

SMOKEY STOVER
1935–1973

A long-running nonsense and screwball feature, *Smokey Stover* started spinning out its weekly string of outrageous gags and puns on March 10, 1935, under distribution by the Chicago Tribune–New York News Syndicate. The perpetrator was Bill Holman, who had honed his wacky skills on such self-revealing strips as *Billville Birds, G. Whizz Jr.,* and *Wise Quacks*.

Though never syndicated in a daily format (with the exception of a short period in the mid-1930s), *Smokey Stover* enjoyed great popularity for decades. Smokey was a fireman, and under his leather helmet he hid the mind of a Surrealist poet. He could use metaphors as outlandish as "You look as broken up as a gravel driveway" and "Any guy with my crust would know how to bake a pie," or concoct a scheme to conduct skywriting without an airplane. The firehouse was a hotbed (naturally) of zany characters, from Chief Cash U. Nutt, whose desk chair was in the shape of a bare foot, to the firehouse cat, a scrawny black feline with a red ribbon on its tail, named Spooky (who for a long time

Smokey Stover (B. Holman), © 1948 New York News Syndicate

had a Sunday strip of his own). The Stover household, comprising wife Cookie and son Earl, was just as colorful, with odd-shaped furniture and bizarrely tilted pictures on the walls.

The feature's main attractions were the puns, of which there was a gaggle included with each Sunday installment. Most of them were affixed to the screwy pictures they were supposed to enlighten. Thus an aspirin bottle atop a mound would be labeled, "The bottle of Bunker Hill"; a picture of a lamp bulb singing "O Sole Mio" would carry the caption, "Light Opera"; and so forth. Sometimes the puns were all related to that week's installment: thus, in a gag involving the annual firemen's ball there could be found "1-2-3-4 fife," "down beets," and "Little Organ Annie" (showing a little old lady with a hearing horn).

Borrowing a routine from vaudeville, the recurring catchphrase, Holman gave immortality of sorts to expressions entirely of his own devising: "Foo," "1506 nix-nix," and "Notary Sojac," for which he gave explanations as ingenious as they were contradictory. (He once maintained that "Notary Sojac" was Gaelic for "horsecrap," while at another time he averred that it meant "Merry Christmas" in the same language.) *Smokey Stover*'s drawings were as outrageous as the puns, portraying (in another nod to Surrealism) characters literally falling apart, heads flying off shirt collars, and incongruous objects popping into the most unexpected places. As Stephen Becker commented, Holman "created so many departures from reality that his work must be ranked with that of uninhibited geniuses like Rube Goldberg and Milt Gross."

Holman frequently added recurring side panels to the main feature, such as "Foomous People," which paid homage to the likes of "I. Otto Nekkum, tip-top tycoon who manufactures all the collars people get hot under" and "Buckboard K. Whipsocket, the barnstormer who raises all the gift horses that people never look in the mouth."

Holman retired in 1973 at age 70, and his Sunday page was retired along with him.

M.H.

SNAKE TALES
1982–1991

Allan Salisbury (signing "Sols") was the first Australian cartoonist to make it for any length of time in U.S. newspapers, and he did it by using what is usually regarded as the lowest form of humor—the pun. *Snake Tales* came out in Melbourne's *Daily Telegraph* in 1974, and it met with almost immediate success, being reprinted in several anthologies and adapted to animated cartoons in Sols's native Australia; in 1982 it was picked up by NEA Service for syndication in North America.

The action took place in the Australian outback, which accounted for the exotic fauna that populated the strip along with a few eccentric humans. S. Snake, the reptilian protagonist, liked to hang around a pile of rocks, throwing puns at his only friend, the kangaroo (otherwise nameless), who invariably displayed outrage at his companion's wordplay. Some examples will suffice: "Why did the drunk kamikaze pilot survive the war?" "He got smashed before he

took off"; "Why did so many turn up at the optician's party?" "He promised them all a spectacle"; "How do you stop your telly running all night?" "Make sure it has commercial brakes." And when he decided to break up with his female friend, he sent her a toy drum with a note reading, "Beat it!" For his pains Snake got tied up in knots, strung up trees, thrown off cliffs, bashed with sticks, and smashed under rocks, but he always came back for more.

In the strip everybody punned. An ice-cream-sundae vendor got asked what he sold on weekdays (his answer: "fish"). To a door-to-door salesman trying to sell her a vacuum cleaner a housewife replied: "Thanks. I don't have a vacuum." A native game hunter tried to locate a floating poker game with a spy glass. A customer looking for a loudspeaker ended up with the sales clerk's wife. Asked if he could write shorthand, an applicant wrote down *shorthand* on his form. And a toddler crawled up to the mining office to apply for a "minor's license." These and similar affronts seemingly kept readers amused—or perhaps bemused—for the almost ten years the strip ran in American newspapers.

Snake's reputed lack of friends provided the other main source of humor. Yelling, "Hi, I'm your friend" at Echo point he got "Hi, I'm your echo" in reply. In order to get into a private party he was forced to mutter the password: "The snake is a little creep and we all hate him." And when he despairingly asked what was wrong with his life, his interlocutor imperturbably ticked off, "No mum, no dad, no friends, no mates, no acquaintances," and on and on, for days. Readers must have finally agreed with this assessment, and *Snake Tales* ended its North American run in 1991.

M.H.

SNIFFY
See NORBERT

SNOOKUMS
See THE NEWLYWEDS

SNUFFY SMITH
See BARNEY GOOGLE

SOMEBODY'S STENOG
1916–1941

When stenographers became commonplace across the country in the first decade of this century, cartoonist Dink Shannon came up with *Sallie Snooks, Stenographer,* probably the earliest example of a career girl in the comics. The strip started in 1907 but proved an isolated phenomenon that lasted only a few years and spawned no immediate imitator. The picture changed a decade later, when A. E. (Alfred Earle) Hayward picked up the theme again, first in a daily panel that ran for only a month in 1916 in the *Philadelphia Evening Public Ledger* under the title *Somebody's Stenographer.* Hayward revisited

Somebody's Stenog (A. E. Hayward), © 1931 Public Ledger Syndicate

an independent person, tied to neither parents nor husband, and making her way in the world through work, charm, ingenuity, and more than a little nerve.

M.H.

SPACE CADET
See TOM CORBET, SPACE CADET

SPEED SPAULDING
1939–1940

the theme in a daily strip shortened to *Somebody's Stenog* and distributed by the Ledger Syndicate from December 16, 1918, with a Sunday page added on April 30, 1922.

Born of the manpower shortage of World War I, this epitome of office girls was named Cam O'Flage (a bit of wartime humor there) and she worked as a girl Friday in a nut-and-bolt factory run by the much put-upon Sam Smithers. Blonde, attractive, and unmarried, she seemed to spend as much time on romantic pursuits as on office work, a tradition that would be perpetuated in the hordes of girl strips to follow in her footsteps. She repeatedly fended off the clumsy advances of Reggie, the boss's son, and on a bet entered the Miss America contest, which she won. She also displayed brains in addition to looks, a startling departure from comic-strip tradition. Among her coworkers were the pudgy Mary Doodle, Cam's best friend; the rival stenographer, a backbiting brunette named Kitty Scratch; and Venus, the spinster business secretary.

Hayward drew *Somebody's Stenog* in an uncluttered, bold style, with a few judicious penstrokes and an acute sense of shortening and caricature. In 1933, due to illness, he had to relinquish the drawing of the dailies to Ray Thompson and others. Following the creator's death in July 1939, the feature passed into the hands of Sam Nichols, and faded out on May 10, 1941, thereby neatly spanning the entire era between the two world wars.

Somebody's Stenog inarguably helped break new ground in the comics; for the first time in a long-running and reasonably successful strip there was a woman who was seen as

A short-lived but extremely interesting science-fiction strip, *Speed Spaulding* was based on *When Worlds Collide,* a novel written by Philip Wylie on a schema by Edwin Balmer. Both men shared credit for the script, with Marvin Bradley taking care of the drawing.

Running daily and Sundays, *Speed Spaulding* unfolded along a single narrative track, seven days a week. It is difficult to pinpoint the exact start day of the feature since the John F. Dille Company, which had charge of the syndication, did not date the strips (or copyright them either, except for the first week of dailies, which gives us at least the start year—1939). From external evidence, however, it is probable that *Speed Spaulding* began publication in September, around the time the world conflict erupted in Europe. As in the original novel, the Earth found itself threatened with extinction by a cosmic disaster from beyond the stars, of which the populace was only dimly aware. "Extry! Extry! World menaced by mysterious discovery," clamored newshawks at every city corner in the strip's opening panel, "Scientists form secret league!" Exclaiming, "I'm going to find out what it is," Speed Spaulding, a square-jawed, handsome, all-American football quarterback (who in the novel was nowhere to be found) went to investigate.

The menace in question turned out to be two planets discovered from his observatory in South Africa by Professor Bronton (who modestly named them Bronton-Alpha and Bronton-Beta). The two celestial bodies having been reckoned to move on a collision course with Earth, a secret league of seven scientists from different countries had been formed under the leadership of the American professor Gale Pendon, to cope with the impending catastrophe. The

Speed Spaulding (M. Bradley), 1939, John F. Dille Co.

only solution, grim as it was, consisted in having a representative portion of mankind transferred to another planet aboard a spaceship of Pendon's invention. This was the cheerless background. In the foreground, however, there were romance, involving Speed and Pendon's daughter, a lovely brunette named Ann, and skullduggery in the shape of gangsters plotting to steal the plans to the spaceship in cahoots with a rogue scientist from an unspecified country (the felon's name happened to be Mitusiki, letting the readers draw their own conclusions).

Speed Spaulding didn't live up to the expectations of the syndicate, and never even approached the success of *Buck Rogers*, a feature Dille also distributed. It seemed that the American public was less interested in the danger posed by alien planets than by the dual, and far less distant, menaces looming right over the eastern and western horizons. Furthermore, the writing (probably the work of syndicate hacks) was less than peerless, and the drawing, while adequate, was heavily borrowed from the much-underrated, much-imitated Austin Briggs, who was doing *Secret Agent X-9* at the time. Barely a year after it had all begun, the world ended with a bang, and the strip ended with a whimper, a sad case of good intentions and bad timing.

M.H.

The Spirit (W. Eisner), © 1949 Will Eisner

THE SPIRIT

1940–1952

While he may be known in more conservative circles as a pioneer in the use of comics in administrative and classroom instruction, Will Eisner is generally regarded by comics fans and the general public as the creator of the mystery-and-humor feature *The Spirit*. This was a weekly seven-page series, part of a comic-book-sized Sunday supplement (which also included two back-up stories not by Eisner, *Lady Luck* and *Mr. Mystic*) carried in the comics section of a number of newspapers. It premiered on June 2, 1940, with distribution assumed by the Register and Tribune Syndicate.

A year after its first appearance, Eisner recalled the creation of his already famous series for the *Philadelphia Record:* "When I decided upon the Spirit," he declared, "I worked from the inside out, you might say. That is, I thought first of his personality—the kind of a man he was to be, how he would feel about life, the sort of mind he would have. When that was worked out, I didn't have to imagine him as a person. I began to see him. Handsome obviously, powerfully built, but not one of those impossibly big, thick-legged brutes. He was to be the kind of man a child could conceive of seeing on the street."

The masked justice-fighter known as the Spirit was in reality Denny Colt, a criminologist believed dead by almost everybody and who fought crime from his secret headquarters in Wildwood Cemetery. His identity was known only to gruff Police Commissioner Dolan, the head of the regular law-enforcement agency in Central City (a stand-in for New York City), where the action took place, and his blonde ingenue of a daughter, Ellen. In her double capacity as bearer of the flame and keeper of the secret, Ellen was oftentimes involved in lurking peril, from which she was always rescued—in the nick of time, of course—by her boyfriend hero.

The greatest danger to Ellen, however, came from the many vamps the Spirit encountered on his path; worst of all, most of them took an immediate fancy to the hero, who was not always insensible to their charms. They were women with seductive wiles, shapely figures, and evocative names. In addition to the prototypical Lorelei Rox—a modern siren luring unsuspecting mariners to their death—there were Autumn Mews, Sparrow Fallon, Wisp O'Smoke, Plaster of Paris, Silk Satin, P'Gell, and countless others.

The Spirit also had to contend with less accommodating male enemies. These included the malevolent mastermind, the Octopus, leader of a gang of cutthroats; the oily Belabaruk, "jewel dealer"; and during the war an assortment of arrogant and monocled Nazi *Schweinhunden*. In order to track his quarry the Spirit had to wander far afield from Central City, to the sands of Araby, the snows of the Himalayas, and the nightspots of Paris. In his endeavors he was often ably served by Ebony White, a black shoeshine boy who became his constant companion and sidekick.

From October 13, 1941, to March 11, 1944, there was also a daily-strip version of *The Spirit,* but the Sunday section remained its mainstay. In 1942 Eisner was drafted into the army, and the feature was temporarily taken over by Lou Fine, with the assistance of artist Jack Cole and scriptwriters Manly Wade Wellman and Bill Woolfolk. Eisner was demobilized in the fall of 1945, and he lost no time in reclaiming *The Spirit* (his first postwar story appeared in December and was called, appropriately enough, "The Christmas Spirit").

Eisner had come back from the war in a more detached, more reflective mood, and this found its counterpart in the stories he now wrote and drew. As I stated in *The World Ency-*

clopedia of Comics: "In its seven-page narrative each *Spirit* episode constituted a self-contained short story, but the weekly unfolding of the tales revealed a peculiar rhythm, a cadence evoking not so much the prose narrative as the prose poem (even down to the suggestion of blank verse in the text). In this aspect *The Spirit* probably has few counterparts in comics history."

In 1950 Eisner left more and more of the drawing and writing to others, including Wally Wood, Klaus Nordling, Al Wenzel, and Jules Feiffer. This period saw the publication of the famous "Outer Space" story, in which the Spirit journeyed to the moon. It was drawn by Wally Wood in a stunning display of draftsmanship, on text by Eisner and Feiffer.

As a newspaper feature *The Spirit* ended on October 5, 1952, at a time when adventure and action were beginning to wane from the comic pages. Gone, but not forgotten, its spirit was kept alive by a small but appreciative public in the form of comic books and other reprints. After *The Spirit* was revived for a unique piece in the *New York Herald-Tribune* in 1966, the floodgates really opened for a full-fledged reappraisal of the feature and its creator. Since that time Spirit stories have again become widely available, as a number of publishers have rushed into print with the old episodes and an occasional new tale.

M.H.

SPOOKY
1935–1954

Spooky first appeared as the firehouse cat in Bill Holman's *Smokey Stover* Sunday page in March 1935. A month later, on April 7, the scrawny black feline with the

Spooky (B. Holman), © 1948 New York News Syndicate

red ribbon on its tail became the star of *Smokey's* newly minted companion strip: simply called *Spooky,* it was distributed, like *Smokey,* by the News-Tribune Syndicate.

Spooky, a female, averred herself as the proverbially unlucky black cat. She couldn't run into the street without being splashed by a water truck, or walk in front of a store in renovation without having a bucket of paint dropped on her (in remorse the painter hung a "Wet Paint" sign on her). Her master was a flaky character named Fenwick Flooky, whose vocation was lying in bed and whose hobby was embroidery. His house was filled with such knickknacks as scatter rugs on ball bearings, hanging fishbowls, and pictures tilted at odd angles, among which Spooky moved gingerly. Because of her master's penchant for somnolence, the goofy cat often found herself locked out at the end of her nightly rambles, and she had to display all her animal cunning to get back in. Once she serenaded the neighborhood from the windowsill, and after the resulting bombardment of brickbats, rolling pins, and mismatched boots, she coolly jumped in through the broken window. At another time she scattered a bagful of tacks in front of the house, waiting for the ensuing pandemonium of screeching tires and blasting horns to wake up the fast-asleep Fenwick.

Dogs were the constant bane of Spooky's life, and she was never able to shake off her tormentors. To escape a snarling canine, the luckless cat would sneak into a theater, only to zip out frantically a few moments later with an entire pack of performing dogs in hot pursuit. She wasn't even safe at home; when she came down with a case of anemia, the vet would prescribe a sure-fire cure in the form of a ferocious mutt to chase the fear-crazed feline all around the house. These and similar outrages kept the strip lively for a goodly number of years.

Spooky ran, in an increasingly attenuated format, for almost two decades, coming to an end in 1954. Afterward the black feline appeared, until the cartoonist's retirement in 1973, not only in *Smokey Stover* but in Holman's daily *Nuts and Jolts* panel as well, often as a dismayed observer muttering such phrases as "Oh no!" and "Here they go again."

M.H.

THE SQUIRREL CAGE
1936–1960

***T**he Squirrel Cage* was created to serve as the topper to *Room and Board,* the Sunday page Gene Ahern had started for King Features Syndicate on June 21, 1936. A fantasy strip imbued with nonsense and absurd humor, it soon garnered more acclaim than the main feature.

Starring an irascible little man in a long white beard, dressed in a black coat and wearing what looked like an oversized tam o'shanter, it took place in the cuckoo country of Foozland. Posted at a busy crossroads and muttering his persistent and incomprehensible refrain "Nov shmoz ka pop?" the diminutive oldster week after week tried to thumb a ride to the city of Swolz, but in spite of his best efforts, whether traveling by car, oxcart, wheelbarrow, or on the shoulders of a tramp, he always ended up at the place he had started from. Once he became so disgusted with the situation that he crossed (on foot) to the neighboring country of Skoobozia, only to find white-bearded hitchhikers at every crossroads, and he returned in resignation to his habitual station. The nameless old geezer in time became known as the Little Hitchhiker. While the other characters in the strip all spoke English, the Little Hitchhiker for some reason persisted in expressing himself in a mysterious tongue, which Ahern sometimes interpreted, and sometimes not. (For instance, we learned that "Osh golop vsk" translated as "This settles it," but we never got to know what "Nov shmoz ka pop?" meant.)

Due to its popularity with the readers, *The Squirrel Cage* outlived the *Room and Board* Sunday by a number of years, ending only with Ahern's death in 1960. It left in its wake a cult following as well as fond remembrances of its star performer. Robert Crumb, for instance, has acknowledged that the Little Hitchhiker was the inspiration for his Mr. Natural character.

M.H.

STEVE CANYON

1947–1988

After World War II Milton Caniff, then at the height of his popularity, tried to negotiate a better contract for himself on *Terry and the Pirates,* but the negotiations broke down and the artist signed to create a new strip for Field Enterprises. Even before Caniff drew the first line, and without knowing the new feature's name or theme, more than two hundred newspapers (according to Reinhold Reitberger and Wolfgang Fuchs) contracted for the series. The new strip turned out to be *Steve Canyon,* and it first appeared on January 19, 1947 (Caniff had drawn his last *Terry* page a few weeks earlier). "Here was Caniff approaching his full power," Stephen Becker in *Comic Art in America* observed of *Steve Canyon.* "His use of 'camera angles,' his alternation of close-ups, long shots, middle distance, his creation of suspense in two or three panels—all were superb."

A former air force captain, Stevenson Burton Canyon (to give him his full name) came upon the stage as the head of Horizons Unlimited, a shaky air-transport company. His first assignments took the reader back to the freewheeling days of the 1930s, as Canyon flew from South America to the Middle East to the Himalayas in search of lucre and adventure. Two years after the strip's inception, Caniff sent his hero to the familiar grounds of the Far East, where Canyon, at the head of an escadrille of foreign volunteers, tried to stem the red tide of Mao's armies. Under China skies Canyon would meet Leighton Olson, another American flyer, whose wife, Summer, would play an increasingly large role in the hero's life.

The outbreak of the Korean War caused Canyon to get back into air force uniform, and he would eventually rise to the rank of full colonel. His missions, mostly undercover, were many and included rescuing American captives in China, detecting an enemy mole in Thailand, and flying all kinds of hush-hush new aircraft. Caniff's attention to characterization extended even to secondary players, whose

Steve Canyon (M. Caniff), © 1946 Field Enterprises

very human traits, weaknesses, and strengths were delineated with a sure touch. There were Happy Easter, the gruff old mechanic type; Pipper the Piper, a happy-go-lucky pilot; and the other military men, from enlisted Joes like Sweet Joseph and Chigger to the wise-cracking Lieutenant Upton Bucket to the vinegary General P. G. "Shanty" Town.

Constantly strewn into Canyon's path were bevies of female beauties, some of them his antagonists, some of them his helpmates, and all of them in hot pursuit of the blond and ruggedly handsome hero. Cooper Calhoon, for one, a female tycoon whose ruthless ways had earned her the title "She-Wolf of Wall Street," went after Steve with a forceful single-mindedness. There also were Miss Mizzou, a Marilyn Monroe look-alike; the two-faced Madame Lynx; the poisonous Duchess of Denver; the soft-hearted Dr. Deen Wilderness; and many others too numerous to mention. Through it all Summer Olson would remain Steve's one true love. The pair for many years remained locked in noble frustration, as Summer's husband was a war invalid whom her sense of honor prohibited from leaving. In 1970 Leighton Olson had the good grace finally to keel over, and the two star-crossed lovers were allowed to marry.

The field was now open for Poteet Canyon, Steve's pert and spirited ward and "kissin' cousin" from Texas, who sometimes managed to steal the show from her suave guardian. A latter-day entry in the *ingénue perverse* category, she never made a secret of the crush she had on her handsome relative, and much hanky-panky was always suspected by the readers (a fancy tantalizingly fed by Caniff himself in his story lines). A graduate of Maumee University, Poteet later became a working reporter and a flyer in her own right who would at one time compete in the famed Powder Puff Derby air race.

The last twenty years were difficult ones for Canyon and for Caniff. The protagonist had reenlisted into the air force for the second time at the height of the Vietnam War; this stung many of Caniff's readers, who organized protests and boycotts. The strip started bleeding to death, as more and more newspapers canceled the feature. In a desperate bid to regain popularity, Caniff showed Canyon more and more frequently out of uniform, and the strip veered closer to soap opera, focusing on Steve and Summer's marital woes, eventually culminating in separation.

As circulation kept dwindling, Caniff slowly lost heart. He delegated an increasing share of the work to his assistants, Ray Bailey, Bill Overgard, Fred Kida, Alex Kotzky, Don Heck, and Doug Wildey among them. In latter years, while still writing the continuities, he left the penciling in the hands of Dick Rockwell (nephew to Norman Rockwell) and only inked the finished artwork. In 1986, however, Caniff entirely wrote and drew a nostalgic episode that took Steve on a sentimental journey to China, where he met the heroes of a long-gone but never-forgotten era, Terry and Pat and Connie.

Caniff died in his sleep on April 3, 1988, and his strip was likewise allowed to lapse peacefully. The last daily appeared on June 4, drawn by Rockwell with the single caption, "All honor to his art and name"; while the final Sunday, on the following day, carried a drawing by Caniff's long-time friend and colleague, Bill Mauldin, along with the signatures of eighty-seven comic-strip artists and writers. This genuine sense of loss was less for the demise of *Steve Canyon* than for the passing of one of the great masters of the comics and for the end of an era.

M.H.

STEVE ROPER
1936–present

Like most of the strips distributed by Publishers Syndicate, *Steve Roper* has had a tortuous history. First called *The Great Gusto* for its main protagonist, it had been renamed *Big Chief Wahoo* when it finally came out in November 1936. Elmer Woggon, who had drawn the short-lived aviation strip *Skylark* for the syndicate, was the artist, and Allen Saunders, former drama critic for the *Toledo News-Bee* and a cartoonist in his own right, wrote the scripts.

Wahoo was initially conceived as a parodic western, a genre that was particularly flourishing in the mid-1930s. The title character was a cigar-stand Indian used as a stooge by a medicine-show operator named J. Mortimer Gusto (the great Gusto of the original title and a dead ringer for the comedian W. C. Fields). Gusto was selling a universal panacea known as Ka-Zowie Kureall and, like all traveling show con-men, felt he needed an Indian as a foil; Wahoo, newly rich from oil discovered on his lands, fell for it. En route to New York City they picked up a little Indian girl named Pigtails, and later had a number of gag encounters in the Big Apple. Eventually Gusto faded out of the strip, and Wahoo, along with his sweetheart, Minnie-Ha-Cha, a former nightclub singer, pursued his humorous exploits in Tepee Town, his native reservation.

As Martin Sheridan noted, Saunders and Woggon (who signed "Wog") had a peculiar way of working together. The two collaborators, he wrote, "discuss the story and agree upon the main outlines. Saunders...draws rough sketches and fills in the balloons. These are submitted to Publishers Syndicate.... When the roughs are returned with approval, or with change suggested, Woggon redraws them completely and inks them in." Woggon worked in an old-time, big-foot style, and toward the late 1930s Saunders, who was writing longer and more straightforward continuities, became disenchanted with the strip's cartoony look. As a result ghosts were brought in to draw the feature in a more illustrative style: Bill Woggon (Elmer's brother) first, then Don Dean, and starting in 1944, Peter Hoffman, while Woggon retained overall artistic direction and continued to sign the strip.

In 1940, meanwhile, *Big Chief Wahoo* had taken a new turn with the arrival in Teepee Town of Steve Roper, a big-city news photographer. A ruggedly handsome hero, Roper soon stole Minnie-Ha-Cha's affections from Wahoo; more gallingly, he also stole the spotlight from the hapless Indian chief. As the strip delved deeper and deeper into wartime adventure, it was retitled *Chief Wahoo and Steve Roper,* then *Steve Roper and Wahoo,* and finally in 1947 simply *Steve Roper,* while Wahoo rode out into the sunset.

With Roper now on his own, the feature took on a more serious cast, hovering midway between straight adventure and soap opera. In 1953 Woggon and Hoffman were displaced by Bill Overgard, who started signing the strip the following year as well as contributing significantly to the scripting. Overgard's slick, dynamic, and eye-catching style gave a considerable boost to *Steve Roper,* whose popularity had been sagging in the postwar years. One of the attractions of this polished version of the strip was its loving depiction of beautiful women, including the irresistibly piquant Bobbie Burnem and Roper's secretary, a blonde bombshell named Honeydew Mellon. In addition to beauty, Overgard also brought brawn to the strip in the person of tough, two-fisted Mike Nomad, who soon shared the scene with Roper. The feature in the late 1970s switched titles once again, to *Steve Roper and Mike Nomad,* a denomination it has managed to conserve to this day.

With Woggon's death in 1978 and Saunders's retirement the next year, Overgard was hoping to get sole authorship of the feature, but Saunders imposed his son John as the scriptwriter. Disappointed, the artist left to create his own strip, *Rudy,* in 1983. Since that time John Saunders and illustrator Fran Matera have guided the destinies of *Steve Roper and Mike Nomad,* which is now being distributed by King Features under the banner of the North America Syndicate.

M.H.

STONY CRAIG OF THE MARINES
1937–1946

After a dry run in the *Boston Traveler, Stony Craig of the Marines* started national distribution as a daily strip on September 20, 1937, under the aegis of the Bell Syndicate. The strip's creators, themselves like their hero members of the Marine Corps, were Sergeant Frank Rentfrow (script) and Lieutenant Don Dickson (art), both then on the staff of the Corps's magazine *The Leatherneck.*

The action focused on a group of marines led by Sergeant Stony Craig, a hard-bitten, no-nonsense veteran of World War I. Under him were "Slugger" Wise, a tough-talking, belligerent street pug; the seemingly naive but ultimately resourceful Jed Fink; and the blond, handsome Jimmy Hazard, who played the romantic lead, most often in his encounters with his sweetheart, a pretty army nurse named Helen, in the quieter interludes between fights. And fights there were a-plenty. In the early episodes the quartet formed part of a company of leathernecks dispatched to guard the American settlement in Shanghai, and they took it upon themselves to fight their own guerrilla war against the Japanese army that surrounded the city on all sides. They even hooked up with a band of Chinese freedom-fighters led by Tania, a Eurasian beauty in the mold of the Dragon Lady, assisted by her half-brother Ivan, a former White Russian army colonel of gigantic size. The marines were often aided and abetted in their freelance activities by a suave British Intelligence officer named Jeremy Blade, who looked like Clark Gable, talked like Cary Grant, and behaved like John Wayne.

In June 1940, with war looming large over the horizon, a Sunday page titled *Sergeant Stony Craig* was added. Having two separate continuities to cope with, the authors sent their heroes all over the globe, from Alaska to the Canal Zone to the Pacific. Dickson continued drawing their adventures (along with a Sunday topper called *Daredevils of Destiny*) in a rugged, somewhat primitive style that accorded well with the rugged, primitive action. At the end of 1940, he was called back to service, and Gerard Boucher, an artist of uncertain skill, replaced him till the end of 1944. Then came Bill Draut, for eighteen months in 1944–45, followed by Lin Streeter, who guided the strip for the remainder of its existence. In December 1946 Sergeant Stony Craig retired from the Corps, and Sergeant Rentfrow, who had steadfastly scripted the hero's adventures in war and peace, likewise retired from the comics.

M.H.

THE STRANGE WORLD OF MR. MUM
1958–1974

Irving Phillips's *The Strange World of Mr. Mum* began as a daily panel on May 5, 1958, under distribution by the Hall Syndicate (and later by Field Newspaper Syndicate). It enjoyed moderate success from the start, and a Sunday page was added in 1961.

Mr. Mum was a small, middle-aged, bespectacled man, always wearing a hat to conceal his bald pate. He seemed to have no occupation other than that of a bystander on life's outer limits. His world was strange indeed. A single mother with a brood of children would shoot the stork at the local zoo. A sailor would be shown a fish tank containing the merbaby born to him at the maternity ward. A coven of witches would take off from an airport gate on a jet-powered broom. Under the familiar sign "The Marine Corps Builds Men," a noncom leatherneck could be seen assembling a robot in a marine uniform. On the Texas Central a conductor punched out train tickets with a six-shooter.

Animals and primitive men were favorites of Phillips's, as they later proved to be of Gary Larson's. A swan followed by its cygnets entered the New York City Ballet theater through the stage door for a performance of *Swan Lake*.

Microbes observed through a microscope would carry signs reading, "Help Stamp Out Penicillin" and "Stop Medicare." A caveman would return several overdue stone tablets to a bemused librarian.

As the sole witness to all these weird happenings, Mr. Mum sometimes raised an eyebrow but, true to his name, he never spoke a word (and neither did any of the participants). To relieve the stress caused by his experiences, the protagonist would often repair to Joe's Health Bar for a pick-me-up of mango juice with sassafras or a triple turnip juice tweerple. Mr. Mum shed his observer status only in his dreams, when he pictured himself as a fearless explorer trekking through the desert or an Eastern pasha surrounded by bevies of nubile harem girls.

As could be expected of a feature published seven times a week, there were a number of duds, but the strokes of inspiration outnumbered them by far. Its anything-can-happen brand of humor was ahead of its time and provided the impulsion—acknowledged or unacknowledged—for such contemporary strips as Jim Unger's *Herman,* Gary Larson's *The Far Side,* and Dan Piraro's *Bizarro.* Mr. Mum had enough of a following to appear in a number of paperback collections but never appealed to a broad section of newspaper readers. The syndicate finally decided to drop the strip in 1974, despite the protestations of many fans.

M.H.

STUMBLE INN
1922–1926

George Herriman's last comic strip of any significance, *Stumble Inn* came out while the author was concurrently working on *Krazy Kat*. Under syndication by King Features, the first daily appeared on October 30, 1922, and a Sunday color page followed in December.

Herriman's was a world of moochers and dreamers, and the ramshackle, rundown Stumble Inn had plenty of both. Uriah Stumble was the disorganized hotel keeper, and Ida, his soft-hearted wife, tried hard to be practical. The place was a magnet for a wide assortment of oddball patrons who

Stumble Inn (G. Herriman), © 1922 King Features Syndicate

stumbled upon the inn for the weirdest of reasons, from a crackpot inventor who wished to test his diving suit in the inn's deep bathtub to the army major who dropped in because the hotel's spartan amenities reminded him so much of his old quarters in Flanders during the First World War. The inn's most permanent fixture was Joe Beamish, a holdover from Herriman's earlier creations—moocher, loafer, and chair-warmer extraordinaire. The establishment's most constant visitor was a safecracker known as Dynamite Dan who raided the place with maddening regularity. Trying to keep a handle on the goings-on was the ineffectual house detective Owleye, who under his rough exterior was as big a dreamer as Krazy Kat. His dream was to catch Dynamite Dan, and every time he came close to his quarry, like Krazy he got beaned with a brick.

The *Stumble Inn* daily folded in May 1923, and Herriman carried on with the Sunday page in the grand manner, lavishing great care on its composition, color scheme, and design. Visually it was a delight, with unexpected little details cropping up in the margins and good, original pieces of business going on in the background. The gags however kept getting feebler, a sure sign the author was wearying of the feature's basic situation. Early in 1926 the Stumble Inn closed its doors for good.

M.H.

SUPERMAN
1939–1966, 1977–1993

The story of how Superman came into being has been told so often that it has become a staple of pop mythology: how in 1933 two teenagers from Cleveland, Jerry Siegel and Joe Shuster, had conceived *Superman* as a comic strip extolling the exploits of a superhuman justice-fighter from another planet; how they tried to sell their brainchild for years, only to be turned down by every newspaper-comics syndicate in the land; how it finally came to the attention of M. C. Gaines, who sold the idea in 1938 to Harry Donnenfeld, owner of the nearly bankrupt Detective Comics (DC) company; and how Superman, reunited with its creators, who happened to have been even then working for DC, burst forth to universal (kiddie) acclaim, thus saving the financial fortunes of DC and setting the tone and substance of the comic-book form in one swift stroke. This is the stuff of legend, and it is therefore fitting that a copy of the first issue of *Action Comics,* in which Superman first appeared, should now rest in the Smithsonian Institution.

The phenomenal sales recorded by the comic books featuring Superman (two million copies were being sold monthly a few months after Superman's initial appearance) finally prompted the McClure Syndicate to assume the title's newspaper distribution in 1939 (the dailies on January 16, the Sundays on November 5).

There have been many retellings of Superman's origins, but only the version imagined by Siegel and Shuster in the first week of dailies needs to detain us here. Superman was initially the lone survivor of the doomed planet Krypton, a baby rocketed to Earth by his scientist-parents. Landing in America, the infant was found and adopted by a human couple, Jonathan and Martha Kent, and later discovered that he had superhuman abilities, which he decided to dedicate to serving truth, justice, and his adopted country as the Man of Steel or the Man of Tomorrow; all the while, he hid his true self under the assumed identity of "meek" Clark Kent, who became a reporter for a big-city newspaper.

Superman's syndicated adventures were of the predictable comic-book variety: the Man of Tomorrow used his superpowers to fight and bring to heel mobsters, kidnappers, conspirators, foreign agents, and other miscreants. His finest hour came in 1942 when he destroyed the Atlantic Wall in preparation for the Allied landing, causing a fuming Josef Goebbels to rant in the pages of the Nazi sheet *Der Stürmer,* "Superman is a Jew!"

Siegel wrote and Shuster drew the newspaper exploits of Superman for the first couple of years, whereupon they turned the chores over to Wayne Boring, who got to sign his name to the feature in 1945. He had the help of a number of assistants, including Jack Burnley, Paul H. Cassidy, and Whitney Ellsworth, under the editorship of Mort Weisinger. Boring, who had a thicker, more muscular line than Shuster, managed to guide the fortunes of the Man of Steel for more than two decades, until May 1966, when the strip was canceled by the syndicate due to poor sales.

In 1977 Superman resurfaced in the newspaper pages within the framework of *The World's Greatest Superheroes,* a feature concocted by DC to showcase its most famous characters. The next year the clamoring success enjoyed by the first *Superman* movie starring Christopher Reeve caused the Chicago Tribune–New York News Syndicate, which distributed the newspaper version, to expand the title to an impossible *The World's Greatest Superheroes Present Superman,* thankfully shortened a little later to simply *Superman.* The new adventures of the Man of Steel were written in a more nervous style by Martin Pasko and Paul Kupperberg, while George Tuska and the Argentine artist José Delbo supplied the illustrations. This second coming of the savior from Krypton lasted until 1993.

M.H.

Superman (Siegel and Shuster), 1944, TM & © DC Comics

Sylvia (N. Hollander), © 1987 Nicole Hollander

SWEENEY AND SON
1933–1960

Al Posen was already a veteran gag and comic-strip cartoonist by the time he created *Sweeney and Son* for the Chicago Tribune–New York News Syndicate. The new feature premiered on Sunday, October 1, 1933.

"Pop" Sweeney (no first name given) was the proprietor of a toy and novelty shop that he ran with a light hand and a whimsical touch. His ten-year-old son (called Sonny or Junior) often accompanied him on his frequent holidays from work. Later another, adopted, son, a three-year-old nicknamed Me-Too for his habit of amplifying every last sentence pronounced by his father or his sibling, joined the family. Ma (or Mom) tried to keep a grip on her husband's and her children's vagaries, but she never nagged or even remonstrated very much. In fact the Sweeneys must have been the most harmonious family in the comics. The cast of regulars was rounded off by Pushface, Sweeney's worshipful assistant, and his scatterbrained girlfriend, Beverly.

As a companion strip to the main feature, Posen used *Jinglet,* a four-panel strip narrated in rhyme that he had created back in 1927. In the 1940s and afterward he alternated *Jinglet* with two similarly constructed strips, *Them Days Are Gone Forever* (based on his earlier and most famous panel, dating from 1922) and *Rhymin' Time,* in which he encompassed a greater variety of themes.

An affable man, Posen made *Sweeney and Son* into an affable, likable feature. The happenings were kept simple and displayed a gentle, understated humor, and Posen's graphic style perfectly matched the unhurried pace of the anecdotes. "*Sweeney* is drawn simply and effectively," Stephen Becker wrote. "The style might be called 'basic,' and is reminiscent of the unadorned style of a few very early strips." Posen died in October 1960, and his Sunday feature survived him by only a few weeks.

M.H.

SYLVIA
1978–present

Nicole Hollander, a former art teacher and book illustrator, created *Sylvia* in 1978 for a suburban Chicago newspaper. It was picked up for national syndication by Universal Press Syndicate in 1979. Field Enterprises took over the syndication of *Sylvia* in 1981 and added a Sunday page. The strip is now being distributed as a daily only by the author herself under the corporate name of the Sylvia Syndicate.

Sylvia is a fiftyish, dark-haired, somewhat plump woman who lives (like Hollander) in Chicago in the company of a finicky cat upset at her sloppy eating habits (a food junkie, she has a sign on her refrigerator reading, "Remember: You can't take it with you, so eat it now"). A woman given to caustic remarks, she loves to trade barbs with Harry, the proprietor of the neighborhood bar, and Gernif, an alien from Venus whose language only she can understand. Her obnoxious personality is such that she has only one woman friend, Beth-Ann, whose companionship she retains by agreeing with anything she says. Her most constant target, however, is her trendy daughter, Rita, whom she deluges with motherly advice during daily telephone calls and frequent home visits.

For a living Sylvia writes an advice column ("Dear disgusting wimp," is how she began her answer to one of her correspondents). In her spare time she keeps sending CBS proposals for new game shows (one would have featured recently divorced couples trying to guess each other's most annoying habits) or for a comedy miniseries about a woman with a three-way split personality (brain surgeon, housewife, and hair stylist; housewife, snake handler, and educator; and so on).

Sylvia also likes to dream up "menacing supercops of the future," like the "love cop" (trying to break up incompatible couples), the "credit card cop" (seeing to it that people don't overspend), the "nutrition cop" (watching over children's diets), and the "exercise cop" (looking to uncover couch potatoes).

Sylvia is drawn in a simple, even crude, graphic style, with balloons haphazardly hand-lettered; yet the unconventional artwork is well suited to the strip's iconoclastic humor. Carried only by a small number of newspapers, the feature has acquired a loyal readership, and many *Sylvia* collections have appeared over the years, most of them sporting characteristic titles such as *I'm in Training to Be Tall and Blonde, That Woman Must Be on Drugs,* and *Ma, Can I Be a Feminist and Still Like Men?* (Sylvia's answer: "Sure...just like you can be a vegetarian and like fried chicken.")

M.H.

TAILSPIN TOMMY
1928–1942

The first newspaper strip exclusively devoted to aviation, *Tailspin Tommy* (originally called *Tail-Spin Tommy*) was the collaborative creation of veteran scriptwriter Glen Chaffin and sometime cartoonist (and airplane enthusiast) Hal Forrest. Distributed by the Bell Syndicate, the pioneering feature made its debut as a daily on May 14, 1928.

The very first panel laid out the strip's premise in a nutshell. Next to a full-length drawing of the blond hero in a dark suit it read, "Tommy Tomkins, a modern American youth, who lives in Littleville. He has talked 'airplane' so much that the village 'wit' has nicknamed him 'Tail-Spin Tommy'." A car mechanic who resided with his mother in a "little cottage," Tommy realized his dream of flight when he got his pilot's license and started work for the small, Texas-based Three-Point Airlines. He shared his adventures there with Skeets Milligan, a freckle-faced, wisecracking plane mechanic, and with Betty Lou Barnes, a spunky brunette and a pilot in her own right. Betty had the added advantage of a rich uncle named Abner, a fact that later allowed the trio to take over ownership of the company.

The early dailies kept pretty close to the realities of commercial flying. Tommy was seen transporting cargo, carrying the mails, or delivering needed medical supplies to isolated towns in his airplane. Later on he participated along with his companions in the rescue operation mounted during the catastrophic Mississippi floods and fought forest fires.

Chaffin's writing was often stilted and always wordy, while Forrest's drawings were sometimes awful and never more than adequate. *Tailspin Tommy* soared to clamoring success in the early 1930s on the strength of its exuberant fascination with the romance of flight, the sheer sense of freedom it projected. This success was jeopardized by a bitter dispute that opposed the two creators, with Chaffin ultimately selling his share to his partner and leaving the strip. His last byline appeared on the Sunday for December 31, 1933.

A *Tailspin Tommy* Sunday had started on October 20, 1929. In contrast to the earnest tone of the dailies, adventure, suspense, and exoticism were the keynotes of the weekly page. In lengthy episodes that unfolded over months the fearless trio went exploring a lost civilization in the Andes, rescued ships lost in the Sargasso Sea, or led an expedition to the South Pole in a dirigible chartered by Uncle Abner. Forrest reserved his best (such as it was) for these Sunday escapades, and his drawings, while still clumsy, exuded a certain boyish charm. He also indulged in a bit of eroticism, with near full-page depictions of half-naked dancing girls, and lingering shots of squirming maidens about to be sacrificed to the volcano god. The Sunday also carried a secondary feature, *Progress of Flight,* about "the pioneers who have made aviation what it is today."

Following Chaffin's departure, Forrest took over the writing chores as well, with the result that all the continuities, daily and Sunday, took on an unalloyed heroic glow. No longer having to share his cut of the considerable revenue generated by the strip, he now could afford to hire talented assistants, and from the middle to late 1930s *Tailspin Tommy* enjoyed an attractive visual look that added a measure of handsomeness to the often far-fetched narratives.

Tailspin Tommy (H. Forrest), © 1933 Hal Forrest

There were tales of air piracy (with phantom planes piloted by skeletons), stories of foreign intrigue (involving the plans for a secret stratospheric aircraft), and episodes of pure fantasy (about a mad scientist bringing down airplanes with his death ray).

By 1939 the competition among aviation strips was fierce (with *Scorchy Smith* and *Smilin' Jack* leading the pack), and *Tailspin Tommy*'s popularity began to falter. Seeing his income steadily shrink, Forrest, who held the copyright to his strip, switched from Bell to United Feature and sent his hero into the European war cauldron. Nothing seemed to help. In the spring of 1942 Tommy flew his last flight, got married to Betty Lou, and settled down for good.

M.H.

TALES FROM THE GREAT BOOK
1954–1972

Given the religiousness of the American people, it is surprising that there was no nationally syndicated strip on Biblical themes before the 1950s. Perhaps influenced by the short-lived *Bible Tales for Young Folk* series of comic books Atlas put out in 1953, John Lehti, always on the lookout for neglected and potentially profitable genres, came up with a Bible-inspired idea for a newspaper strip, which he sold to Publishers Syndicate. Titled *Tales from the Great Book*, it made its bow, as a Sunday only, sometime in 1954.

The familiar stories (of Jacob and his brothers, of David and Goliath, of Daniel in the lion's den, and many others) were given to the reader in bite-size nuggets, the continuities lasting usually a few weeks, and rarely more than a couple of months. The general tone was respectful but not sanctimonious. These were "tales" indeed, more in the spirit of Hollywood Bible epics than of Sunday homiletics. The overwhelming majority of the tales were derived from the Old Testament, probably because those provided for greater spectacle and more drama, and they used both text narratives and speech-balloons. For dramatic contrast they did not follow the canonical order of the books but alternated violent episodes with more serene interludes. Thus a tale from Judges might follow a story from the Book of Esther, for instance.

On the other hand, the narrative pattern hardly ever varied. Each tale bearing its own subtitle ("The Sword of Gideon" or "Jacob's Toil," for example) would be framed by a short introduction and, in the last panel, an appropriate summation. "And all Israel hears the wise judgment of their king and marvels at his wisdom which he has received from the Lord, all of which is recorded in I Kings chap. 3: 16–28," one such summation read. The dialogue was an admixture of King Charles English and American vernacular. "Oh Samson! Will thou truly tell me thy secret?" Delilah would coo, adding, "and not trick me with lies as thou hast three times already?"

Lehti's drawing style was pleasant, if hardly groundbreaking. He had a flair for spectacle, as shown in the battle scenes between the Hebrews and the Amalekites, or in the depiction of Samson bringing down the temple upon the Philistines, but he could also compose serene tableaux of shepherds tending their flocks in the shadow of purple hills. At any rate, *Tales from the Great Book* displayed enough visual appeal to last for almost two decades, only ending in the summer of 1972. This, however, did not curtail Lehti's involvement with the Book: in the 1980s he drew and self-syndicated a panel dealing with biblical themes.

M.H.

TALES OF THE GREEN BERET
1966–1969

Robin Moore's novel *Tales of the Green Beret*, about a member of the U.S. special forces in Vietnam, became a bestseller in the mid-1960s, and this prompted the Chicago Tribune–New York News Syndicate to attempt a comic-strip adaptation. For the task they turned to veteran comic-book artist Joe Kubert, who had won much acclaim for his work on war stories with titles like *Our Army at War, Enemy Ace,* and *Sgt. Rock.* The joint effort of Moore and Kubert, the newspaper feature made its appearance in the early months of 1966.

The strip followed the fortunes of the tough-talking, hard-bitten, cigar-chomping Lieutenant Ross, and his hardened company of Vietnam veterans on special commando missions for the army. The texts were written with a breathless urgency, and the horrors depicted with full force. Burning villages, fleeing civilians, and snarling Vietcong guerrillas greeted the small troop at every halt; and there was more firepower exchanged between the American soldiers and the enemy in the course of the strip's run than was expanded in the whole of World War II. Kubert drew the action with his usual vigor and purpose, sparing no sensibilities. "His highly stylized, gritty, piercing illustrations," Michael Uslan wrote of the artist in *America at War,* "embody all the horrors of war and the intricacies of detailed war machines. When Kubert's soldiers crawl...on their bellies, you see the pain, the weariness, the insanity of war..."

At the same time as the strip extolled the heroism of the soldiers in Vietnam, the war itself was becoming more and more unpopular with the American public. In response to the national mood, Kubert quit late in 1967, and the feature was taken over by John Celardo, who carried it over into 1969.

M.H.

TALES OF THE JUNGLE IMPS
1903

On January 11, 1903, Winsor McCay created for the *Cincinnati Enquirer* a weekly page filled with jungle drawings of wild animals and half-naked natives cavorting amid luxuriant scenery and with an overblown text set in mackerel verse. These pages, later to become known as *Tales of the Jungle Imps,* lasted only until November 9, 1903, but, short-lived as they were, they constitute an important milestone in the development of the comics.

The full-page feature was credited to one "Felix Fiddle," in actuality George Randolph Chester, an editor at the paper. Felix Fiddle himself appeared in each installment in the series as a little man sporting a long white beard and wearing a top hat, who observed all the outlandish activities with the same impassive expression. Each page carried a descriptive title, such as "How the Alligator Got His Big Mouth" or "How the Rhinoceros Lost All His Beauty"—reminiscent of some of Rudyard Kipling's *Just So Stories for Children*—and it was signed variously "Winsor" or "Winsor Mc."

As McCay's biographer John Canemaker observed, "*Tales of the Jungle Imps* was Winsor McCay's first attempt in an extended series format to bring together all of his eclectic talents in a cohesive graphic style." The series, extending over only forty-three weekly installments was not yet a genuine comic strip, but it was more than mere illustration; in this pioneering work McCay proved himself a magician of image and color a few short years before he was to become a master of the comics idiom. Some of the characters, such as one of the Imps, would later reappear in his comic series; while he would time and again come back to the experiments into perspective and design that he had pioneered in his *Tales*. This series must therefore be considered a seminal work in McCay's canon.

M.H.

TANK McNAMARA
1974–present

Sports, even more than politics, is probably America's number-one obsession; it is therefore not surprising that this national institution has also come in for its share of knocks at the hands of fast-shooting cartoonists. In 1974 *Houston Chronicle* film critic and humor columnist Jeff Millar came up with the idea for a humorous sports strip. Drawn by Bill Hinds, *Tank McNamara* made its bow in August of that same year, distributed by Universal Press Syndicate.

Tank is a former pro-football player turned TV sports announcer. A lovable hulk of a man who fumbles his words ("Here's norts spews...I mean sports news"), likes to reminisce about his days in the pro leagues, and never quite makes it with the ladies, he goes through life as if it were a permanent football huddle. In the course of the strip Millar and Hinds have poked gentle fun at temperamental tennis stars, moronic sports fans (they once depicted one such who dropped dead after watching eight days straight of football games on television), overpaid sports superstars, and the corrupting influence of big business, big money, and television on all games.

Among the long-running, slightly skewed characters gravitating around the hapless jock, special mention should be given to Sweatsox, Tank's sports-crazed buddy and manager of the junior league; Murray, his money-mad promoter; and his personal therapist, the demented Dr. Tszap. Their antics, and those of the real-life sports personalities who, under their own or assumed names, keep turning up at strategic moments of the story line, have helped maintain the strip's popularity through the years.

M.H.

Tarzan (H. Foster), © 1936 ERB, Inc.

TARZAN
1929–present

Edgar Rice Burroughs created the Lord of the Jungle in 1912: the novel in which he first appeared, *Tarzan of the Apes*, started publication in *All-Story Magazine* in October of that year, and it made publishing history.

The saga of the infant son of Lord and Lady Greystoke, born in a log cabin on the African shore where his parents had been left stranded by a mutinous crew, must be known to millions of readers throughout the world. Raised among the apes after the death of both his parents, he later became a leader of their tribe, as well as a recognized figure of justice holding sway over the African jungle. The success of the tale was immense and immediate, and led to many more narratives to follow. At the time of his death in 1950, Burroughs had penned no fewer than forty-five original Tarzan novels and stories (some of them were published posthumously).

Tarzan's fame spread to the movies (the first Tarzan picture dates back to 1918), to radio, to television, and to the stage. Yet, of all the media in which the Lord of the Jungle has appeared, the comics have inarguably been the most truthful to Tarzan's image and to his legend. Tarzan came late to the comics (or more accurately, the comics came late to Tarzan). The newspaper-strip rights had been acquired by an advertising executive named Joseph H. Neebe, who in 1928 asked Allen St. John, Tarzan's book illustrator, to adapt *Tarzan of the Apes* into a series of daily strips. St. John turned down the offer, and it fell upon Harold Foster, then an advertising artist, to provide the illustrations over a lengthy text running underneath each picture. This adaptation was syndicated by the Metropolitan Newspaper Service and ran from January 7 to March 16, 1929, in a handful of newspapers, but its success with the readers was such that a sequel soon followed. Based on Burroughs's second Tarzan novel, *The Return of Tarzan*, it was drawn by Rex Maxon, again with great success.

United Feature Syndicate absorbed Metropolitan in 1930, and the new editors decided to capitalize on the pop-

Tarzan (B. Hogarth), ca. 1948, © ERB, Inc.

ularity of the dailies by following up with a Sunday page, which made its debut on March 15, 1931. It was drawn by Maxon with such appalling results that Foster was called back a few months later, on September 27, 1931. With the space of an entire newspaper page at his disposal, Foster could give free rein to his artistic flair and to his awesome technical skills. He revolutionized the newspaper-strip field by incorporating cinematic techniques, such as angle shots, panoramics, and depth of field, into the syntax of the comics. The adventures of the apeman, now no longer based on adaptations from novels but underpinned by original stories created for the purpose, took on a striking sense of immediacy, with the feel of the steaming jungles and the splendor of the African scenery practically leaping off the page. Whether exploring the mysteries of a lost civilization (half Egyptian, half Phoenician), foiling the schemes of a power-mad white hunter, or searching for the fabled elephant graveyard, Tarzan, in Foster's hands, took on the mythopoeic dimension with which Burroughs had originally endowed him.

In 1937 Foster went on to create *Prince Valiant,* and *Tarzan* passed into the hands of Burne Hogarth (his first signed page appeared on May 9). At first imitative of his predecessor, Hogarth later developed his own style, which made him into one of the most celebrated artists of the comics. During a first phase, Hogarth drew the Sunday exploits of Tarzan until December 1945. Written by Don Garden, the stories evidenced a solid knowledge of Burroughs's thematology. In the course of this first cycle of adventures, Tarzan took up the challenge hurled at him by a fierce tribe of Amazon warriors, rescued a worthy family of Boer pioneers from the machinations of black-hearted villains and the fury of spear-throwing savages, and discovered the twin civilizations of the Peoples of the Sea and of

the Fire. As a nod to the temper of the times, he also thwarted a Nazi attempt to set up a secret base in Africa in 1943. Hogarth translated these episodes into pages in which images were in constant flux, moving inexorably from one climax to the next. Tarzan appeared literally to fly across the page or to bound out of the frame.

After a two-year absence from *Tarzan,* during which time the Sunday page was drawn with clumsy brushstrokes by "Rubimor" (Ruben Moreira), Hogarth went back to the Lord of the Jungle, following the promise that he would write the texts as well as draw the pictures. Accordingly, he turned out some of his most awe-inspiring work in the three short years from his return to the *Tarzan* page in August 1947 to the time of his final withdrawal in August 1950.

In Tarzan's adventures of the period—fighting the monstrous Ononoes, exploring the sinister island of Mua-Ao, or foiling the intrigues of ruthless treasure-hunters—Hogarth aimed at a visual treatment that achieved the grandeur of myth. More than any other artist, he established his vision of Tarzan as the embodiment of the Lord of the Jungle. In this respect he ranks even above Harold Foster.

Throughout the 1930s Maxon meanwhile plodded along on the dailies, with a break between June 1936 and January 1938 when, following a contractual dispute, they were drawn with a certain panache by William Juhré. Under Juhré's tenure the daily strip finally shed its antiquated narrative mode in favor of a text enclosed within each panel. Upon his return Maxon was allowed to write his own scripts, and he kept turning out the feature with modest skills until his final exit from *Tarzan* in August 1947.

From that point there followed a bewildering succession of artists. Hogarth took charge of the dailies for a few months in late 1947, and after him there came at a quick pace Dan Barry (1947–49), John Lehti (1949), Paul Reinman (1949–50), and "Cardy" (Nicolas Viskardy) till July 1950. Finally, Bob Lubbers took over the artwork of the dailies as well as that of the Sundays, thereby unifying for the first time both versions of *Tarzan* under a single artist.

Lubbers's tenure lasted only until January 1954, when he relinquished the feature to John Celardo. Over an arc of some fourteen years, Celardo restored some stability—though very little luster—to *Tarzan;* while hardly inspired, his illustrations displayed enough workmanlike qualities to carry the strip over a difficult period. Early in 1968 Russ Manning, who had been drawing the comic-book adventures of the Lord of the Jungle, took over the newspaper feature, which under his able stewardship regained some of its former visual splendor. He managed to blend the elegance of Foster's version with the power of Hogarth's rendition in a series of eye-catching episodes that for a time seemed destined to revive the comic-strip fortunes of the apeman.

Tarzan continued to decline in spite of Manning's best efforts, and in 1972 the syndicate closed down the dailies (which went into reprints). The Sunday version, however, continued with Manning at the helm. In 1979 the team of Gil Kane (artist) and Archie Goodwin (writer) took it over until 1981, when it passed into the hands of Mike Grell. Two years later Gray Morrow became the titular artist, with Don Kraar as his scriptwriter; and there the matter rests for now.

M.H.

TED STRONG
1935–1938

One of the more intriguing western strips to come out of the 1930s, *Ted Strong* started life in the summer of 1935 as part of an eight-page Sunday color comic section distributed nationally by the George Matthew Adams Service. The artist was Al Carreño, a Mexican national who had come to the United States in the late 1920s and was an expert on ranch life and lore.

Drawn by Carreño in a loose, forceful style, *Ted Strong* was a taciturn, fast-acting hero, not unlike some of the screen characters played by Gary Cooper. His adventures, which took place in modern times, involved fast-riding horse chases, hair-raising escapes, and some of the most entertaining gun battles ever depicted on a newspaper page.

Unhappily, Adams's comic section (which contained such obscure strips as Paul H. Jepsen's *Rod Rian of the Sky Police*) did not fare well and only picked up a meager list of client newspapers. To shore up its fortunes, *Ted Strong* was changed into a mystery strip, with the hero carrying diverse counterespionage missions as an undercover agent. This metamorphosis, started early in 1938, did not save the feature, which went down along with Adams's entire comic package at the end of the year. Ted Strong, however, still drawn by Carreño, was to continue his career for a while in comic books.

M.H

TED TOWERS, ANIMAL MASTER
1934–1939

In the 1930s King Features, having come late to the adventure-strip sweepstakes, decided to make up for time lost by having at least two different features in each and every action genre. Hot on the heels of Alex Raymond's *Jungle Jim* the syndicate launched yet another jungle-adventure weekly page; covering every commercial angle, it was called *"Bring'em Back Alive" Frank Buck Presents Ted Towers, Animal Master* and came out on November 24, 1934, in the Saturday tabloid-size color supplement King had started earlier that year.

Frank Buck enjoyed then a great reputation as an animal trapper and explorer (though many of his exploits may have been bogus), as well as a lecturer and author, so much so that even when the title was shortened to a more manageable *Ted Towers, Animal Master*, he still received credit for the feature. It is doubtful, however, that he wrote any of the scripts; more probably they were the work of Ed Anthony, a King Features stalwart (he was writing the texts for *The Pussycat Princess* at the time) and an occasional collaborator on some of Buck's literary enterprises. While *Ted Towers* had only one putative author, many were the artists who drew the feature. Glen Cravath was the first and by far most interesting one; a former film animator, he endowed his compositions with a graceful sense of motion, especially in the hunting scenes. He was also the illustrator of *Animal Land*, the wildlife-strip topper that ran conjointly with *Ted Towers*

for some months in 1935. After his departure in February 1935, then came an anonymous hand, then Joe King, followed by Paul Frehm, all this in a matter of a few months. On June 7, 1936, the strip finally stabilized with Ed Stevenson illustrating it with heavy-handed industriousness until its conclusion on May 21, 1939.

Ted Towers was a clean-cut, strong-jawed young man who trapped animals for a living, at least in the beginning. His base of operation was India, and in his activities he was most often flanked by his faithful retainer Ali, a trained tracker and guide, and by his no less adventurous girl-friend, a perky blonde named Catherine Custer. The first episodes were faithful to the spirit of Buck's *Bring'em Back Alive* anecdotes: in particular there was the lengthy narrative detailing the suspense-filled stalking and eventual capture of a Bengal tiger, depicted with credible graphic skill by Cravath. Later on the continuities degenerated into hair-raising tales of adventure, featuring such villains as the leader of a native rebellion, a rival animal trapper, and a lust- and power-crazed maharajah. A pleasant enough adventure strip, *Ted Towers* never could compete with the likes of *Tarzan* or *Jungle Jim*, and its demise went more or less unnoticed.

M.H.

TEENA
1941–1964

One fine day in the summer of 1941 the editors at King Features received a peremptory cable signed W. R. Hearst: "Get Hilda Terry." One of the leading women cartoonists of the time, Terry was just then enjoying great popular success with her series of cartoons about teenage girls that were appearing in the *Saturday Evening Post*. In due time she was signed to a King Features contract, and the resulting feature started appearing as a daily panel called *It's a Girl's Life* on December 8, 1941, the day after Pearl Harbor was bombed. The panel and the Sunday page that soon followed were both retitled *Teena*, for the main character, in 1945.

Teena (H. Terry), © 1954 King Features Syndicate

Terry later averred that her character was inspired by a visiting fourteen-year-old cousin of hers. Over the years Teena changed from perky brunette to bubbly blonde, but her bobbysoxer persona and her teenage status altered hardly at all. She remained thin, gangly, and angular for the duration of the strip, but the artist endowed her with an acidulous and unforced charm that won over a large public. Her doings, in the company of girls named Penny or Marcelle, were mild and typical of a girl her age at that time: waiting for the phone to ring, buying clothes, and talking about boys while dreaming of Frankie (Sinatra). These slight anecdotes were rendered in Terry's winsome graphic style, an eye-pleasing amalgam of old-line illustration and wispy cartooniness. The strip's greatest popularity occurred in the late 1940s when it was, as Coulton Waugh wrote in 1947, "a star of the Saturday color section of the *New York Journal American.*"

The bobbysoxer type gradually faded in the 1950s, and by the next decade it was gone—as was *Teena,* which came to an end in 1964.

M.H.

THE TEENIE WEENIES
1914–1970

Although not a comic feature in the strict sense, *The Teenie Weenies* occupied such an important place in many metropolitan newspapers that it cannot be ignored in any encyclopedic survey of the American newspaper strip. It was the work of William Donahey, who with his older brother James Harrison ("Hal") had made the *Cleveland Plain Dealer* into a cartooning powerhouse among American dailies. The younger Donahey was doing a Mother Goose page for the *Plain Dealer* when he was asked by Joseph Patterson to create a children's activity page for the *Chicago Tribune.* The first release appeared on June 14, 1914.

The page generally consisted of one huge panel depicting some activity engaged in by the Teenie Weenies, a clan of tiny people about two to three inches in height living in an universe of normal-sized people (never seen). Most of the little creatures looked like human children (but were in fact adults) and wore colorful medieval garb, but some sported more contemporary attire, such as cowboy dress or soldiers' uniforms. They had domesticated mice to serve as mounts or beasts of burden, and made houses out of hatboxes, biscuit canisters, and other discarded items of general use. A typeset text would accompany the pictures and often propound an object lesson or offer riddles and simple math problems. One of the more popular aspects of the feature were the cutouts that children could assemble to form a whole village of Tennie Weenies.

In 1923 *The Teenie Weenies* went into national syndication and soon acquired a number of big-city papers such as the *New York News,* making it one of the most widely read pages of its kind in the country. Donahey continued to draw his diminutive protagonists until the time of his death in January 1970. His colorful and endearing creation was allowed to die with him after a remarkable run of well over a half-century.

M.H.

THE TERRORS OF THE TINY TADS
1905–1911

Gustave Verbeck (or Verbeek), who had earlier perpetrated *The Upside Downs of Little Lady Lovekins and Old Man Muffaroo,* came up with yet another weird confection for the Sunday supplement of the *New York Herald.* Titled *The Terrors of the Tiny Tads,* it made its bow on May 28, 1905, preceding the more celebrated *Little Nemo in Slumberland* by several months.

The feature presented itself in the almost immutable format of a newspaper half-page consisting of two tiers of three panels each, with two lines of doggerel verse running beneath each panel. There were occasional speech-balloons, but these were used mainly for elaboration or amplification. The opening quatrain of the very first page established from the outset the tone and premise of the strip: "The wonderful Hippopautomobile / Has licked the last drops of his gasolene meal. / Then away for some far off, magical land / He carries the Tiny Tad band." The Tiny Tads were four venturesome young boys (not otherwise named) gone to explore a weird and wondrous world where all varieties of fantastic creatures abounded. In a symbiosis and mating of the animal, the vegetal, the mineral, and the artificial, there could be encountered such freakish (and punning) combinations as the Kangarooster ("who jumps from peak to peak and every morning just at dawn lets out an awful shriek"), the Cariboogaboo ("a spooky kind of beast"), and the Vermicelligator ("a fish that's often found just west of the equator").

The strip was drawn in a delightfully matter-of-fact, uncluttered style by Verbeck, who excelled in depicting the fantastic as commonplace. His composite monsters displayed a deadpan literalness that seemed at odds with their nightmarish evocation. While Verbeck was obviously intending his creation for the children, he also winked in the direction of the adults who couldn't but chuckle at his tongue-in-cheek contrivances.

The Terrors of the Tiny Tads appeared with decreasing frequency through 1910, and disappeared the following year.

The Terrors of the Tiny Tads (G. Verbeck), 1905

It is a wonder that Verbeck could have sustained this weekly level of maniacal inventiveness for close to six years.

M.H.

TERRY AND THE PIRATES
1934–1973, 1995–present

Raiding other press organizations for new talent had been a hallowed practice of newspaper syndicates ever since the days of W. R. Hearst and Joseph Pulitzer. So when Joseph M. Patterson, head of the Tribune-News Syndicate, decided to add an exotic action title to his lineup of syndicated comics, he turned to Milton Caniff, then drawing the *Dickie Dare* strip for AP Feature Service. Responding to the challenge with his usual alacrity, Caniff produced what was to become one of the most admired comic features of all time, *Terry and the Pirates,* which made its debut as a daily on October 22, 1934, followed by a Sunday page on December 9 of the same year.

When Caniff started on his assignment, the newspaper strip of exotic adventure was already a well-established genre. With Harold Foster calling Africa his own in *Tarzan,* and Alex Raymond having annexed Southeast Asia in the wake of *Jungle Jim,* Caniff decided on China as the setting of his new feature. Years later he was to describe his research methodology in these terms: "I have never been to China, so I go to the next best place, the public library. From its picture file and with careful clipping of every scrap of data on things oriental, combined with a dash of *Encyclopedia Britannica,* I am able to piece together a pretty fair background of Far Eastern lore. For authentic speech mannerisms I plow through a pile of books by traveled people from Pearl Buck to Noel Coward."

As his lead characters Caniff chose the same combination of manly hero and boy companion that had assured the success of his earlier *Dickie Dare,* of which *Terry and the Pirates* (the "Pirates" had been added by Patterson) seemed not so much an offshoot as a duplication. The youthful Terry was a slightly more with-it version of Dickie, and his adult companion and mentor, Pat Ryan, was there for guidance and protection. At the outset the continuities between dailies and Sundays were kept separate, with Pat, Terry, and their Chinese sidekick Connie venturing far into the interior of China on weekdays, while experiencing a number of sea adventures along the Chinese coast on Sundays.

Terry's graphic style was at first stiff and mannered, but it soon underwent a radical transformation under the influence of the pioneering work done at the time by Noel Sickles. Caniff and Sickles had known each other from childhood; by the end of 1934, while Caniff was working on *Terry,* Sickles had taken over *Scorchy Smith* and evolved a comic-strip style of his own, based on the use of brush-drawing in order to achieve quasi-impressionistic atmospheric effects and a startlingly visual delineation of action. In view of the two men's long-standing friendship and close working relationship (they shared the same studio), constant interchange between Sickles's brilliant draftsmanship and Caniff's dramatic talent became inevitable. When dailies and Sundays merged into a single story line in August 1936, the famous Caniff style, a synthesis of cinematic narration,

Terry and the Pirates (M. Caniff), © 1944 Chicago Tribune–New York News Syndicate

careful framing, elaborate lighting effects, and skillful manipulation of space, was already in full bloom.

This sophistication was duplicated in the plotting, which acquired added authenticity, humor, and suspense. Most important, Terry was now growing up, from boyhood into adolescence, and often striking out on his own. There were still tales of smuggling, piracy, and banditry, which had been the staples of popular fiction since time immemorial, but they now blended into the tapestry of a China ravaged by war. Terry and Pat found themselves confronted by a colorful roster of villains, from the sinister Captain Judas to the epicene Papa Pyzon, and from the ruthless Klang to the slimy Tony Sandhurst; but always lurking in the background were the heroes' real enemies, the occupying Japanese army, simply referred to as "the invaders."

Caniff's *Terry* is perhaps best remembered for his gallery of beautiful women. The Dragon-Lady came first: she was conceived at the outset as an Eurasian villainess, the leader of a band of cutthroats and murderers, whose real name was Lai Choi San (allegedly meaning "mountain of wealth" in Chinese). Enigmatic yet devastating, with high cheekbones and jet-black hair, the Dragon-Lady was also intelligent and highly sophisticated, well versed in the ways of the world (and of men), conversant in Shakespeare and Confucius, and without illusion. Next came Normandie, spoiled, capricious, and headstrong, who would marry the despicable Sandhurst out of spite, and remain faithful to him out of duty and a sense of *noblesse oblige.* The golden-haired, golden-hearted Burma, a fugitive from justice, completed this triptych: brash, obvious, and almost outrageously endowed with lascivious charms, she went after Pat with single-minded determination.

The entry of the United States into World War II propelled *Terry* to the front rank of newspaper strips, as the wild adventures of Pat and Terry gradually gave way to the realities of the war. Terry, having finally passed the adolescent stage, became a lieutenant and pilot in the U.S. Air Force, and his commanding officer, Colonel Flip Corkin, moved into the role heretofore occupied by Pat Ryan, but with greater equality between the two men. *Terry* became a different kind of strip, in which individual deeds were muted before collective heroism. This culminated in the famous Sunday page of October 17, 1943—the first comic strip ever included in the *Congressional Record*.

After the war Terry and Pat stayed in China, and lived through a series of missions and complications, with a new foe hovering in the background: the Chinese Red Army. Caniff had intended to marry Pat, who had risen to the rank of lieutenant commander during the war, and Burma, who had finally obtained a pardon as a consequence of her war services, and to bring Terry back to the States; but this was not to pass. As the negotiations for his new contract broke down, he abandoned *Terry* on December 29, 1949, in an atmosphere of inconclusion.

As a replacement the syndicate settled on George Wunder, an event heralded thus in *Newsweek:* "Wunder never has drawn comic strips. But the Tribune-News Syndicate picked him out of a flock of candidates largely on the basis of his weekly, comic-strip-like backgrounds to the news in the AP's weekly-feature sheet." Wunder never lived up to his billing. His drawings were stiff and graceless, his depiction of characters heavy-handed, and his compositions static; despite the help of talented assistants such as Wallace Wood, Frank Springer, Don Sherwood, and George Evans, *Terry* became almost a parody of its former self. After the outbreak of hostilities in Korea, Terry reenlisted in the air force as a captain, later rising to the rank of major. This allowed Wunder, who had greater affinity for the drawing of machines than the depiction of characters, to picture airplanes, tanks, and other paraphernalia of war in accurate and loving detail. Carried by the winds of the cold war, the strip cruised along for more than a quarter-century, until the antiwar climate of the Vietnam era finally brought it down on February 25, 1973. The characters wouldn't remain dead, however, and in March 1995 Terry and Pat were brought back to the newspaper pages in a version written by Michael Uslan and drawn by the brothers Hildebrandt.

M.H.

TEX THORNE
1936–1937

A rugged and sometimes brutal western, *Tex Thorne* was credited to Zane Grey (who may have actually written the text—its story lines were very close to the themes Grey made familiar) and drawn by Allen Dean, who had been the original artist on *King of the Royal Mounted*. Put together by comic-strip packager Stephen Slesinger, it was distributed as a Sunday half-page by King Features Syndicate, starting on September 13, 1936.

Tex was a gunfighter who hired out his gun for justice, not money. His first task was to clean out West Texas from the dreaded menace of the outlaw Jed Blackstone. Spurning the love of his boss's daughter, Anita Wayne, he then followed a mysterious woman, who had saved his life on two previous occasions, in order to track down his old enemy (and the woman's former lover) Colt Ashton. Again victorious, Tex would once more leave the town he had just pacified, impervious to the entreaties of his friends and disdainful of the imploring glances of the woman, Susan Locke, and continue on his self-appointed rounds.

Tex Thorne was not the garden-variety type of western hero. He had qualms of conscience, and he actually foreshadowed a familiar figure of latter-day movie westerns such as *Shane,* that of the morally troubled gunfighter. After the gunning down of one of his foes he once confided to his only trusted friend (characteristically it was his horse): "Another notch in my gun handle to haunt me nights, Topaz." He would sometimes hunger for a more sedate life, and he was almost tempted when Anita pleaded with him. Yet in the end he could only answer a higher calling. "Sorry, ma'am," he would simply reply, "but the grass won't just grow under my feet."

Allen Dean depicted the adventures of this latter-day knight errant with his usual economy of line and his flair for authentic detail. The feature, however, did not click with the public; perhaps the action was too straightforward, too sparse. At any rate *Tex Thorne* lasted less than one year, coming to an end on June 30, 1937. It is worthy of mention here because of its originality and its contribution, however brief, to the western canon.

M.H.

TEXAS SLIM AND DIRTY DALTON
1925–1928, 1932–1933, 1940–1958

Probably one of the most aleatory of all newspaper strips, Ferd Johnson's *Texas Slim* started in the *Chicago Tribune* on August 30, 1925, as a Sunday page nationally distributed a short time later by the Chicago Tribune–New York News Syndicate. A parodic western (one of the first such in the comics), it starred an exuberant, outgoing cow-

Texas Slim (F. Johnson), © 1946 Chicago Tribune

hand with a knack for landing in trouble. Along with his cowboy buddy, a rather untidy, bemoustached saddle-tramp known (with good reason) as Dirty Dalton, he managed to wreak havoc on his boss's cattle spread in Texas. Then the scene shifted to an unnamed city (clearly Chicago), which provided Johnson with a good opportunity at low humor, with Slim and Dalton playing their tricks on the unsuspecting city slickers. Particularly funny were Slim's ham-handed efforts at courting boss Akers's daughter, Jessie. Despite its title, the strip's star attraction turned out to be the uncouth Dalton, who had an unreconstructed but ingratiating way of dealing with every emergency with a closed mind and an open mouth.

Texas Slim was dropped in 1928, then briefly resurfaced as a gag strip used as the topper to another of Johnson's Sunday page confections for the *Tribune, Lovey Dovey,* which only lasted for under one year (1932–33).

Starting its third life on March 31, 1940, in the comic-book supplement of the *Tribune,* the lanky antihero soon had to share equal billing with his costar in the renamed *Texas Slim and Dirty Dalton.* In this latter (and final) reincarnation, the feature for the first time displayed some real fireworks, as Johnson unfolded a number of suspenseful and action-packed narratives interspersed among the more familiar comic routines.

All the while Johnson had kept assisting Frank Willard on *Moon Mullins,* which he took over at Willard's death in January 1958. Judging that this added responsibility did not justify his continuing a strip that, in his own words, "didn't amount to a hill of beans," he closed down *Texas Slim* for good later in 1958.

M.H.

THEIR ONLY CHILD
See THE NEWLYWEDS

THEY'LL DO IT EVERY TIME
1929–present

Jimmy Hatlo was sports cartoonist on the *San Francisco Call-Bulletin* when, according to syndicate copy, he was asked to do a funny drawing in replacement of a syndicated cartoon that got lost in the mail, "and out of a clear sky, unpremeditated, unsung, dropped *They'll Do It Every Time.*" The date was February 5, 1929, and little did the artist know then that his unpretentious cartoon would mushroom into a nationally syndicated feature and give rise to a catchphrase that has now entered the American lexicon.

The cartoon series soon attracted the attention of readers who started sending in suggestions for the artist to use in his daily depictions of people's inconsistencies, hypocrisies, and downright stupidities. When these suggestions were used in his panel, the authors would receive acknowledgment in print, along with a note of thanks (later expanded to the famous "tip of the Hatlo hat"). In recognition of the growing local popularity enjoyed by *They'll Do It Every Time,* King Features Syndicate started national distribution of the panel series on May 4, 1936,

adding a Sunday half-page consisting of a group of interrelated cartoons (and sometimes of one huge panel) on May 8, 1949.

The daily feature most usually juxtaposed two contrasting panels showing, for example, a man polite to a fault at work turning into a raging insult artist once he got into his car, or an office tyrant reduced to putty at home by his domineering wife. At first Hatlo used no recurring characters, but he later introduced into the feature a meek little Everyman called Henry Tremblechin who cowered before his boss, his formidable spouse, and even his daughter, Little Iodine, who would later star in a feature of her own.

After Hatlo's death in 1963, the feature passed into the hands of his longtime assistant, Bob Dunn, who shared credit with his own assistants, Tommy Thompson first, and Al Scaduto later. In 1989 Dunn died, and Scaduto took over sole authorship of *They'll Do It Every Time,* which he is still doing to this day.

M.H.

THIMBLE THEATRE
1919–present

E. C. (Elzie Crisler) Segar initially conceived his *Thimble Theatre* (so called because of the tiny size of its panels arranged in a vertical row) as a filler on the comics page of daily newspapers. It thus appeared in its diminutive form on December 19, 1919, in a number of Hearst papers, with distribution taken over the following year by King Features Syndicate.

After a brief period during which he spoofed current movies, Segar decided to focus the limelights of his "thimble theatre" on its main protagonists, the slightly seedy Oyl family. The parents, Nana and Cole Oyl, were a couple of bumbling nonentities and they played only subsidiary roles in the strip, which concentrated instead on the younger generation, made up of brother and sister. Castor Oyl was a pint-sized, ill-tempered blowhard, short in talents but long in expectations, and his laughably inept enterprises contributed the source of most of the plots. His sister was Olive Oyl, the surly rosebud of the Oyl clan, and the comic love affair between Olive and her banana-nosed boyfriend Harold Ham Gravy provided the crux of the action for a while; but soon Olive took off after bigger game. Along with her nincompoop of a brother she would embark on a multitude of harebrained undertakings. With her nondescript face perched atop her scrawny figure, she presented a sorry example of womanhood. In 1925 Castor met his future wife, the fickle Cylinda, and the sextet was complete.

Up to then *Thimble Theatre* had consisted of a series of gags and short continuities. A radical change occurred on January 25, 1925, with the advent of a color Sunday page. With ample space now at his disposal, Segar could indulge his secret penchant for spectacle. He soon developed lengthy narratives, the most famous and complex of which involved Castor and Ham Gravy in a wild goose chase after lucre in the Great American Desert, and lasted for two years, between March 1928 and March 1930.

By the end of the 1920s the *Thimble Theatre* cast was clearly six characters in search of not an author but a star performer. As if on cue he unexpectedly turned up on January 17, 1929, in the unlikely guise of a one-eyed, craggy-faced seadog named Popeye. His first spoken words (in answer to Castor's query whether he was a sailor) were the immortal "'Ja think I'm a cowboy?" At the outset Segar had intended Popeye to be just another episodic character walking through his part, but like the man who came to dinner, the sailor stayed on and on and on, until he had taken over the entire stage. Only on March 2, 1930, the same day Castor and Ham Gravy came back from their western odyssey, did he make his appearance in the Sundays, but there again he stole the spotlight from the other players in short order. (Years later the page would carry a trailer proclaiming "Starring Popeye" after the title in recognition of the fact.)

Thimble Theatre (E. C. Segar), © 1935 King Features Syndicate

Even in these early years, Popeye may have become a star, but he certainly was no matinee idol. In addition to his missing eye, he had an unprepossessing appearance, with his bulging forearms attached to toothpicks, his feet the size of tugboats, and his roughhewn mug from which his corncob pipe seemed to sprout. He was also uncouth, unmannered, and uneducated, and his speech was peppered with curses, swearwords, and malapropisms. His pugnaciousness led him to pick fights with almost anybody, and he assiduously nurtured his strength, residing in his enormous forearms, with the help of barbells and the frequent ingestion of spinach.

In the course of the years Segar assembled a stellar cast around the one-eyed sailor. First came J. Wellington Wimpy, who initially popped up as the referee of one of Popeye's boxing matches. He would later become the sailor-man's best friend, although he was nowhere to be found in a pinch. Lazy, cowardly, selfish, conniving, larcenous, penurious, and above all voracious, he exhibited a love of hamburgers as great as Popeye's fondness for spinach. To satisfy his craving Wimpy could rise to heights of mooching, cajoling, and dissembling unmatched even by W. C. Fields in his screen persona. Even his frequent flights of poetry or wisdom concealed an ulterior motive, and his self-serving and self-protecting phrases, "I'll gladly pay you Tuesday for a hamburger today," "Let's him and you fight," and "I'm one of the Jones boys," have passed into the language. His surfeit of sins made him the perfect foil for Popeye's straight-arrow personality, and Wimpy soon became *Thimble Theatre*'s costar (especially in the Sundays).

Swee'pea, Popeye's "adoptid infink," arrived in a box left on the sailor's doorstep in July 1933; baptized with a pot of spinach, he would display boxing abilities belying his tiny size. Another surprise package, sent from "darkest Africa" by Olive's explorer uncle and opened in March 1936, contained Eugene the Jeep, a fantastic, marsupial-like animal who always knew (and told) the truth. Eugene, whose only cry was "jeep," and Swee'pea, whose only utterance was "glop," became fast friends in league against the world of human adults. In response to the syndicate's demands that Popeye clean up his language and cut down on the fisticuffs, Segar brought up next (at the end of a grueling and hilarious search) Poop-deck Pappy, Popeye's father, who turned out to be a ninety-nine-year-old cuss, querulous, cantankerous, and obnoxious, who swore a blue streak and beat up on everybody in sight (particularly if the body in question happened to be Olive's). Even secondary roles were filled with such colorful characters as the Sea-Hag, "the last true witch on earth"; George W. Geezil, Wimpy's homicidal nemesis who, try as he might with gun, blade, or poison, never managed to dispatch the indestructible moocher; and Rough-House, the unflappable owner of the cafe where Popeye took Olive on their first date and where Wimpy would hang out in hopes of a free hamburger.

Of the old, pre-Popeye cast only Olive remained as a regular. In that fateful month of March 1930 the gawky spinster finally found her mate in the person of the invincible sailor, who won her in a fair fight at the end of which he had decisively knocked his luckless rival, Ham Gravy, out of the running (and out of the strip). Popeye and his "sweet patootie" (as he fondly called his ungracious girlfriend) were to know together many an adventure, where the sailor's integrity of character and physical strength would be further heightened for the presence of his heart's delight. In the name of love, fair play, and the nutritive superiority of spinach, the fearless Popeye fought the Sea-Hag on Plunder Island, cleared a murderous gang of cutthroats out of Black Valley, made himself "dictipator" of Spinachova, and restored King Swee'pea to the throne of Demonia. (Segar's skill at conjuring mythical lands was as great as his talent for creating unforgettable characters.)

A number of commentators uncognizant of dramaturgical theory have categorized *Thimble Theatre* as "low comedy," citing as evidence the number of low characters, the use of vernacular and/or ungrammatical language, and the prevalence of farcical elements in the strip. This is to ignore the fact that all these ploys were a staple of Attic and Roman comedy and are pervasive in the plays of Shakespeare and Molière, as well as in the stage works of Eugene Ionesco and Samuel Beckett. Indeed, it is to the Absurdist playwrights that Segar should be compared. Like them he depicts a black and unredeemable universe, and he uses impossible situations to break through the comforting illusions and agreed-upon hypocrisies of civilized society. His characters (with the exception of Popeye) are innocent of any moral compulsion and (with the possible exception of Wimpy) are ignorant of all intellectual surrogations. It is a universe of louts, boors, knaves, loons, shams, and barbarians. All the adult characters are ugly, and their unlovable mugs, misshaped figures, and physical deformities are rendered in drawings of unflinching if hilarious cruelty. This ugliness would be unbearable were it not tempered by Segar's feelings of sympathy and understanding bordering on an amused complicity between the author and his creation. (Robert Altman elected to emphasize the ugliness and ignore the complicity in his thoroughly despicable *Popeye* movie, scripted with a total absence of wit by Jules Feiffer.)

Segar died on October 13, 1938, and his vision died with him. As a valuable commodity, *Thimble Theatre* continued in other hands. Doc Winner, who had previously ghosted a number of sequences in 1938 that Segar had been too ill to draw, was called in to take over the strip as a temporary replacement. In 1939 the feature was turned over to the team of Bela "Bill" Zaboly (artist) and Tom Sims (writer), who carried on as best they could until 1959. Bud Sagendorf, Segar's son-in-law and sometime assistant, then took over control, but he had to relinquish the dailies in 1986 to Bob London. Having received instructions to bring the strip, which in the meantime had been officially renamed *Popeye,* in closer harmony with the times, London, a former underground-comix practitioner, introduced in 1992 the issue of abortion and was promptly fired by the syndicate brass (whose mindset was still mired in the 1950s). In 1994 Sagendorf died; the *Popeye* Sundays are now being done by Hy Eisman, while the dailies are reprinting earlier Sagendorf continuities.

M.H.

TIGER
1965–present

One of King Features' perennial efforts to revive the traditional kid strip, Bud Blake's *Tiger* has fared better than most other shots in that direction in recent years. Started in both daily and Sunday formats in May 1965, it is still going strong today, more than thirty years after its inception.

The children in the strip are neither the hellions of *The Katzenjammer Kids* nor the precocious intellectuals of *Peanuts* but are more closely related to the *Reg'lar Fellers* gang in their normal childhood pursuits and their youthful

dreams. Tiger, with his cap hiding half his face, is indeed a reg'lar boy, always flanked by his flaccid dog, Stripe, and in annoyed charge of his kid brother, Punkinhead, who despite his nickname turns out to be a lot shrewder than he lets on. The ravenous Hugo, with his short-cropped hair, his animal strength, and his huge appetite, is the obligatory dimwit, counterbalanced by the bespectacled Julian, the only one in the little band to indulge in philosophical excursions as a regular exercise.

There are also the two girls, the blonde Suzy and the dark-haired Bonnie, who often serve as the targets for the boys' aggressions, being pelted with snowballs in the wintertime and shoved into thornbushes in the summer. And when Suzy asks one of the boys to escort her to a party, Tiger and Hugo fight over who will do the honors—with the prize going to the losing side. School seldom intrudes on the goings-on, which are rendered with a sure hand and a painstakingly neat line by Blake, who was already a seasoned cartoonist at the time he started the merry little band on their frolicsome way.

The assessment I gave of the feature twenty years ago still stands. "Relaxed, agreeable, and unassuming, *Tiger*...is proof that even the most worn-out comic-strip formula can still work if it is done with integrity and skill."

M.H.

TILLIE THE TOILER
1921–1959

The post-Victorian era brought with it an opportunity of independence for many American women, and this prospect was reflected in several burgeoning strips of the period, including *Tillie the Toiler.* Created by Russ Westover, it first appeared daily on January 3, 1921, and on October 10 of the next year as a Sunday syndicated by King Features and rapidly became one of its most popular titles. Young brunette Tillie Jones was a secretary, stenographer, and part-time model at the fashion salon of J. P. Simpkins, the representative authority foil for her and her most ardent admirer, diminutive coworker Clarence "Mac" MacDougall. Acutely aware of her attractiveness and the attention she created, Tillie often had the last word and

Tillie the Toiler (R. Westover), © 1929 King Features Syndicate

inadvertently contrived more of the office affairs than general manager Wally Whipple, Mac's Jazz Age nemesis.

Most situations centered around office banter, yet mild adventures occurred during the 1930s. During World War II Tillie joined the WACs and stepped out of character, losing all frivolity in exchange for conscientious military duty. Mac joined the army in 1943 in order to be closer to her and maintain the unrequited-love theme that was the strip's main premise. Keeping the fickle heroine in the latest fashions was a unique topical element and mainstay, as readers contributed patterns that appeared in the Sunday topper alongside the family strip *The Van Swaggers*.

Westover's drawing style displayed a great virtuosity of the pen with his deft handling of Tillie, yet it turned hasty and rather elemental. Her appealing yet expressionless, lithe figure and wooden, conventional suitors were juxtaposed against a sketchy, roughed-in backdrop peopled mostly by bulbous, clownish figures. Rudimentary rendering and spontaneous inking gave an uninhibited appearance to the usually static compositions. Over the years, several artists and writers assisted the cartoonist, beginning with a young Alex Raymond in 1930, Charles "Doc" Winner, and Westover's son Alden among others.

Tired of Westover's tardy delivery of new strips, the syndicate eventually assigned the writing to Bill Kavanagh and the art to Bob Gustafson, who initially ghosted by combining new drawing with paste-ups of older material. Now drawing all new episodes, Gustafson's signature first appeared January 1, 1952, when immediately, except for a few lapses, *Tillie* dropped its story format in exchange for gag-a-day. New characters were added to help revitalize the feature, including Oafley, Mac's rotund rooming-house friend and Tillie's boarding Uncle Dudley. Despite the improved version, now drawn in a cleaner comic style similarly adopted by Connecticut contemporaries such as Mort Walker and Bill Yates, King Features canceled the strip in March of 1959, just as Tillie and Mac were finally preparing to marry. Their destiny now set, this thirty-eight-year saga had decisively reached its conclusion.

Generous book collections of *Tillie* reprints were issued throughout Westover's tenure, with eight Cupples and Leon collections from 1925 to 1933 and fourteen Dell comic-book titles during the 1940s. In addition, jigsaw puzzles, coloring and paper-doll books, a novel, and a 1927 feature film were produced.

Tillie had a harder edge than her peer strips of similar genre, yet it still depicted flirtatious adventures that were good clean fun. The roles and essence of these simple characters encapsulated the naive yet respectful nature of a time that in some ways is regrettably long gone.

B.J.

TIM TYLER'S LUCK
1928–present

Lyman Young was never a great talent at cartooning, but he was infallible when it came to spotting a trend. At the time when orphan strips were in fashion in the newspaper comic pages, he promptly produced one; when airplanes became the rage, he transformed his creation into an aviation strip; then changed it to a jungle strip, then to a war strip, as times dictated. This chameleon-hued feature was called *Tim Tyler's Luck*, and it came out on August 13, 1928, as a daily strip, followed by a Sunday page on July 19, 1931.

The hero of the piece, young Tim Tyler, was put out of the orphanage that had hitherto sheltered him, upon reaching his fourteenth birthday (those were tough times for welfare recipients). Later on he met up with another, slightly older, waif named Spud Slavins, who became his constant companion. In October 1929 they both went to work for Sky Lane Airways, an aviation company, and under the tutelage of pilot Roy Fleet, the first in a long line of father-figures, they learned to fly. Soon the trio went adventuring to all the exotic spots on the map in their airplane, from Alaska to India, and from China to Arabia. In the course of their wanderings they eventually landed in the heart of Africa, where Roy met his future bride, a white princess of the jungle, and where the boys met Fang, the black panther that became their pet and protector. It was on the dark continent in April 1934 that Tim and Spud (now bereft of Roy, who had gone back to America) were to know their most memorable adventures when they joined the Ivory Patrol. In many ways the Patrol represented the colonial ethos, as it was understood at the time. Initially made up of white settlers eager to regulate the traffic in elephant tusks (hence the name), it soon took upon itself to keep peace and order in its part of the African continent (which part was never made too clear).

Under the leadership of Sergeant (later Captain) Paul Clark, Tim and Spud, looking spiffy in their new uniforms, set about their task of rounding up wild-game poachers, fighting river pirates, and rescuing explorers in peril. Their most implacable foe was "Spider" Webb, a bandit chief who was in the nasty habit of stringing up his victims in a web of jungle vines and leaving them there to die. But the boys also found time to discover lost jungle civilizations, quell a number of native uprisings, and even help a European princess regain her throne. Their adventures ranged over vast expanses, from torrid desert zones to steamy jungles to snow-capped mountain peaks to palm-fringed sea coves.

Meanwhile the war clouds that had gathered over Europe were coming ever closer to American shores, and the two young heroes in the spring of 1940 went back to the States, after an absence of almost ten years. Having by then reached young adulthood, they decided to enlist in the Coast Patrol, an outfit that seemed to fulfill many of the same functions as the real-life Coast Guard. There they had the surprise of coming under the command of their old friend Roy Fleet, who in the meantime had himself become a lieutenant with the Patrol. Prior to America's official entrance into World War II, they spent their time in the service thwarting the nefarious schemes of Nazi spies and Japanese saboteurs, alarmingly active under the cover of such names as Captain Phantom, the Octopus, or the White Dragon. They were often helped—and sometimes hindered—in their investigations by the dark-haired Trixie Keene, a female agent of American counterespionage. In 1944 they found themselves transferred to the Navy Commandos, with whom they performed a series of dangerous

Tim Tyler's Luck (L. Young), © 1932 King Features Syndicate

missions, all in the Pacific theater of war, such as landing behind enemy lines for reconnaissance purposes, getting in contact with Chinese guerrilla-fighters, or blowing up Japanese outposts. The end of the war found them in a military hospital recovering from wounds sustained in the course of their latest exploit.

Honorably discharged after the war, Tim and Spud became for a while investigators for the World-Wide Insurance Company, headed by the former Lieutenant Fleet. In that capacity they solved a number of cases involving, among others, a disappearing corpse in the bayous of Louisiana, stolen museum pieces whose trail took them all the way to Alaska, and a mysterious cascade of stage accidents in a Broadway theater. The strip, however, seemed to have lost much of its exotic appeal and, in the hope of recapturing some of the magic, Young in 1947 sent his two heroes back to Africa.

After numerous vicissitudes, they joined yet another paramilitary organization in the 1950s, the Jungle Patrol (Young seems to have had a fondness for the word *patrol*). Their adventures there echoed more or less those they had experienced with the Ivory Patrol of prewar days; even Fang made a return in 1952. While the dailies were depicting an Africa not too dissimilar from that shown in many Hollywood movies of that time, the Sunday page, more often than not, conjured up the continent of myth and legend, with wild tales of black magic, phantom safaris, cities of gold, even talking jungle animals.

Lyman Young, a cartoonist of limited artistic abilities, had early on hired ghost artists to assist him with the drawing of the strip. The first one was Alex Raymond, who honed his skills on the feature from late 1931 to 1933, and in the process made *Tim Tyler's Luck* into one of the most eye-catching strips of the time. Charles Flanders and Burne Hogarth also put in some time on the strip, but it was Nat Edson (Gus Edson's brother) who gave *Tim Tyler* its best-remembered look, during his tenure which extended from 1935 to 1946. Upon his departure the artistic qualities of the feature, daily and Sunday, went steadily down, first under the pen of Clark Haas, a mediocre craftsman at best, and later under that of Tom Massey, who proved no better but got to sign the Sunday page, starting in 1952, while the daily was cocredited to Lyman's son, Bob Young. The Sunday version limped along until July 1972, when it came to an end.

Tim and Spud, however, bravely soldier on in the daily

strip, which has survived the death of its creator, in 1984. That makes *Tim Tyler's Luck* one of the most durable of all adventure strips, as well as one of the very few still in existence.

M.H.

THE TIMID SOUL
1924–1953

The image of the defeated male, browbeaten by his boss, henpecked by his wife, and manipulated by his kids, has a long lineage in the comics, but in none has the character been more thoroughly cowed than in Harold Tucker Webster's feature *The Timid Soul*. The hapless hero of the series appeared first in May 1924, in one of the many panel series Webster offered through the *New York World*, but he traces his origins to yet earlier features. A series called *Are You One of Those Spineless Creatures?*, which ran briefly in 1919, foreshadowed the weak-kneed hero of *The Timid Soul*, and H. T. Webster's first comic strip, *The Man in the Brown Derby*, featured the valiant but futile attempts at glory of the hopelessly commonplace Egbert Smear in 1923. The eternally defeated Mr. Smear gave up the struggle in 1924, to be reborn as the gentler and more modest Caspar Milquetoast, the Timid Soul, described by comics critic Coulton Waugh as "the reduction ad absurdum of the whole generation of feeble, wife-bitten, flaccid American strip-husbands."

Chinless and bespectacled, Caspar picked his way cautiously through the perils he saw everywhere about him. Sure that every youth was carrying a knife and every policeman waiting to arrest him for some unnamed crime, he followed all instructions to the letter: he sacrificed his hat rather than disobey a "Keep Off the Grass" sign, stood obediently before a billboard commanding, "Watch This Space!", rushed past a "No Loitering" sign, and postponed reading the news because an advertisement ordered him to "Read Every Word of This!" In 1941 he patriotically remained standing for hours while the little boy next door practiced the *Star Spangled Banner*, and in 1948, during the cold war, he refused Russian dressing on his salad. His wife did not bully him, but she treated him like the child he was, his thin white hair notwithstanding, and he dutifully returned home on a sunny day to take umbrella, muffler, and galoshes because, as she pointed out, "It *might* rain." Of

MR. MILQUETOAST!
MR. CASPAR MILQUETOAST!

HA! HA! HA!

CAN YOU IMAGINE ANYONE ANSWERING TO TH' NAME OF MILQUETOAST? I'D SURE LIKE TO SEE TH' BIRD WHO OWNS THAT MONICKER! HAW! HAW! HAW! HE MUST BE A HOT SKETCH

HE MISSES AN IMPORTANT PHONE MESSAGE—

The Timid Soul (H. T. Webster), © 1931 New York Tribune

course, he conceded every point at golf to his boss, Mr. Grouchmore.

The Timid Soul put *milquetoast* in the dictionary with a small *m* as a common noun for a pusillanimous, apologetic person, and the use of the word has long outlived the cartoon feature that generated it. Gracefully drawn in a barely exaggerated illustrative style, the panels appeared weekly and were perhaps the most popular of the many Webster did over the years, appearing in a book-length collection in 1931. On May 3 of that year Webster joined the *New York Herald-Tribune* and added a *Timid Soul* Sunday page, developing at greater length, if no greater depth, his endless variations on the theme of his hero's timidity. Both the comic-strip and the daily black-and-white panels continued till Webster's death in 1952 and, written and drawn by his longtime assistant Herb Roth, for a year longer. Their unflagging popularity over a period of nearly three decades and their frequent republication since are perhaps a testimony to the candor of an American public that recognizes the universal relevance of Caspar's timidity.

D.W.

TINY TIM
1931–1958

Stanley Link had been laboring anonymously on the Sunday page of *The Gumps* for some ten years when he finally was given the chance at his own feature by the Chicago Tribune–New York News Syndicate. Aiming his new venture at children, he confected a fantasy strip whose

hero was a young boy of Lilliputian size confronted to a real-sized world. Unfolding only on Sundays, Tiny Tim's adventures began in the summer of 1931 (and not in 1933, as has often been asserted).

Right from the outset Tim had a series of close escapes from the clutches of ravenous field mice and malevolent dragonflies, but he soon learned to fend for himself in this hostile environment. In the early months Tim was often accompanied by his equally minuscule sister, Dotty, but this inconvenient sibling simply disappeared from the action a while later. By the fall of the following year the tiny tyke had managed to lay his hands on a toy aircraft carrier, and he later found a model airplane that he parked on the carrier's deck; both were means of transport that he used in a string of gripping adventures. (As the opening panel in a November 1932 page stated, "The little fellow, his plane, and the carrier have become an inseparable trio.")

Thanks to a Gypsy woman's magic, Tim grew back to normal size in the mid-1930s. As a regular boy, Tim underwent all the trials and tribulations that were the usual lot of orphan boys in the comic strips of the thirties. He was ruthlessly exploited by greedy landlords, hounded from place to place by suspicious gendarmes, and got himself entangled with mad scientists and bank robbers on the lam. His fate took another twist in April 1943, when the same obliging Gypsy woman gave the young hero an amulet through which he could change at will from his normal size to his erstwhile two-inch height and back again. Thus endowed with the power of transformation, Tim would foil the designs of real-life villains by changing into a tiny tad and hiding in a tin can or behind a clump of daisies. The author would vary the tenor of his strip from time to time, getting his hero variously involved in tales of suspense, science-fantasy yarns, and soap-opera continuities. Link drew the boy's adventures Sunday after harrowing Sunday in a flat, scratchy style, sometimes embellished by a few color-splashed panels, until his death in 1957. The last *Tiny Tim* page appeared on March 2, 1958.

Over two decades, the 1930s and 1940s, *Tiny Tim* enjoyed wide popularity, especially among the younger set, before fading into undeserved obscurity. It should be remembered as a charming, often winning feature, and its author as one of the journeymen cartoonists who contributed mightily to the vitality and appeal of the newspaper-strip medium at the time of its greatest expansion.

M.H.

TIPPIE
See CAP STUBBS AND TIPPIE

TOM CORBETT, SPACE CADET
1951–1953

Tom Corbett, Space Cadet was CBS's answer to the Dumont network's highly popular *Captain Video* science-fiction program. Based on Robert Heinlein's novel *Space Cadet*, it debuted on October 2, 1950, spawning in its wake toys, costumes, games, and, in due time, a newspaper strip as well as a series of comic books.

The newspaper feature made its first appearance on September 9, 1951, in the form of a Sunday color page, followed the next day by the first daily strip, under syndication by Field Enterprises. It was drawn by veteran comic-strip artist Ray Bailey and scripted by Paul S. Newman, who hewed closely to the TV series. Set in the year 2351, the first weekly lost no time in planting the backdrop, the U.S.-headquartered Space Academy where young men from the Solar Alliance (formed by Mars, Venus, and Earth) were trained to become Space Guards, the organization charged with maintaining peace and order on the planets. It also introduced the three principals: two cadets from Earth and one from Venus. The Earthlings were the earnest Tom Corbett and the wisecracking Roger Manning, while the man from Venus was appropriately called Astro. On the TV program Astro was a sober-sided sort, but in the strip he served as comic relief for the two Earth cadets, a blatant case of anthropocentric discrimination. On following Sundays the readers were treated to slices of life at the Space Academy, where the cadets trained under the tutelage of father figure Captain Strong, and to glimpses of such futuristic wonders as the Luna space station and the Venusport.

The dailies on the other hand plunged headlong into space adventure aboard the rocket cruiser *Polaris*. The missions included repulsing alien invaders who had attacked Venus, collaring smugglers who had set up shop on the dark side of the moon, and putting down an attempted rebellion on Mars led by the treacherous Count Venger, whose rocketships fought a spectacular battle with the *Polaris*—one of the high points of the strip. After a while the Sundays caught up with the dailies, thus allowing the *Polaris* and its occupants to travel a single interplanetary and narrative path.

While the continuities were standard space-opera fare, the artwork was excellent, and sometimes outstanding. Bailey was proficient at depicting the spaceships, moving sidewalks, air-conditioned cities, and other marvels of twenty-fourth-century science and technology. His forte, however, was the portrayal of women, a skill he had learned from his mentor, Milton Caniff. Among his more remarkable feminine creations were Sultra, Venger's slinky accomplice, and the alluring Lorelei, a dancing girl Manning fell head over heels for. Meanwhile, the *Tom Corbett* TV series had migrated to ABC, and from there to NBC, where it finally ended its career on September 26, 1952. The newspaper strip lasted one year longer, until September 1953.

M.H.

TOM SAWYER AND HUCK FINN
See SCHOOL DAYS

TOMMY OF THE BIG TOP
1946–1950

For some as yet unexplained reason, circus stories have never been popular in the comics. In the 1930s there had been *Bumps*, the topper to Harry O'Neill's *Broncho Bill* Sunday and, briefly, Ed Wheelan's *Big Top*, but neither of them had clicked with the public. Shortly after the war, John Lehti decided to try his hand at this neglected genre. The resulting *Tommy of the Big Top* saw the light of print on October 26, 1946, as a daily strip distributed by King Features Syndicate.

The sixteen-year-old Tom Tilton got to achieve what other small-town boys his age could only dream of, becoming part of "the greatest show on earth." Thanks to the friendship of the equally teenaged Lisetta Graham, the daughter of a couple of equestrians, he joined a traveling circus troupe that was visiting his hometown. Tommy was hired at first as a lowly roustabout but, as he aged both in years and in wisdom, he became a sort of troubleshooter for the organization, helping some performers down on their luck, solving a string of robberies, or foiling the schemes of unscrupulous speculators trying to get control of the circus. In the course of his career he also had the opportunity of becoming in turns a lion tamer, a clown, and a ringmaster. He had the further task of coping with Lisetta, who had also grown up in the meantime, and whose jealous temperament provided fodder for some of the plots.

As can be inferred from the foregoing, the story lines weren't particularly exciting, but they were redeemed by many nice documentary touches dealing with circus life and circus lore, and by Lehti's attractive graphic style. *Tommy* never really caught on with the readers, there never was a Sunday version, and the daily finally ended its run in 1950.

M.H.

THE TOODLES
1941–1966[?]

An uninteresting strip with an interesting history, *The Toodles* began life as *The Toodle Family* in the first week of December 1941, as a daily and weekly feature distributed by the Chicago Sun Syndicate and released on Sunday, December 7, the date of the Pearl Harbor bombing. The strip's creators were Betsy Hess Baer, daughter of Sol Hess, the originator of *The Nebbs*, and her husband, Stanley Baer. On the last day of 1941 the elder Hess died after a long illness, and the Baers found themselves having to cope with two different newspaper strips for two rival syndicates (*The Nebbs* was distributed by Bell).

Unsurprisingly the Baers' new venture followed the same formula that had assured the success of the earlier series. It was a mixture of soap opera, humor, and sentimentality (with a dash of patriotism, added in those war years) that went over well in the 1940s. The Toodles were a well-to-do family (father was an industrialist) with two college-age children and two very young nonidentical (boy and girl) twins. The feature was drawn in a semi-illustrative, lively style by Rod Ruth, a former pulp-magazine illustrator. After a few years of carrying two strips on almost identical themes, the Baers decided to merge *The Nebbs* (which they never signed) into *The Toodles*, which they considered their own. They did it by simple osmosis, sending the Toodle twins (who by coincidence turned out to be relatives) to live with the Nebbs, and later having the Nebbs move next door to the Toodles. In August 1946 the merger was completed, and *The Toodles* remained as the sole successor to *The Nebbs*

Toonerville Folks (F. Fox), © 1934 Fontaine Fox

(although some papers may have carried the combined strip under its old name as late as the early 1950s). Wallace Carlson, who had been drawing *The Nebbs* since its inception, was let go (he went on to create an office-comedy strip, *Mostly Malarkey*).

The Toodles continued on a steady, if unspectacular, path until the mid-1950s. Then it started on a downward spiral, as the Baers, who owned other business concerns, lost interest in the strip. Ruth quit in 1958, and he was succeeded by Peter Winter. The feature coasted along for some more years, with circulation decreasing to the point of invisibility; it was finally discontinued either in late 1965 or early in 1966.

M.H.

TOONERVILLE FOLKS
1915–1955

In 1908 cartoonist Fontaine Fox started drawing a series of weekly cartoons for the *Chicago Post* featuring the escapades of a high-spirited bunch of suburban kids. These attracted the attention of Bob Wheeler, head of the Wheeler Syndicate, who in 1913 signed Fox to a contract to draw his kid cartoons for national distribution by the syndicate. Only in 1915 did Fox's cartoons start daily syndication, acquiring their definitive title *Toonerville Folks* the following year, a title consolidated with the creation of a Sunday page in 1918.

What was most striking about the feature was the proliferation of characters, all highly individualized, all finely delineated, not only visually but psychologically as well, thanks to a dead-on tagline bestowed on each character. There were the Terrible-Tempered Mr. Bang (reportedly modeled on Fox's father), whose tantrums escalated with each of his appearances; Mickey (Himself) McGuire, the schoolyard bully who would beat up his classmates regularly, then charge them for boxing lessons; the Powerful Katrinka, who could lift a car (and its occupants) with one arm; Aunt Eppie Hogg, "fattest woman in three counties"; "Skyscraper" Smith, who left a trail of busted street lights every time he crossed the road; not to mention Grandma, the Demon Chaperone, the terror of romancing couples all through town. The Wortles formed a clan apart, so numerous were they; their ranks included John Greenleaf Wortle, the poet-laureate of Toonerville; Pop Wortle, the old string

saver; Pinkney Wortle, the world's laziest man; Lem Wortle, the practical joker; Grandma Wortle, "who controls all the money in the family"; and little Woo Woo Wortle, "who has never been spanked." Among the innumerable kids who populated Toonerville (many of whom belonged to the Little Scorpions Club), Little Stanley, a spunky and imaginative six-year-old, was singled out for special treatment when in the 1920s he became the titular hero of the Sunday *Toonerville Folks* companion strip, named *Little Stanley*.

But the real hero of the piece was the Toonerville Trolley That Meets All the Trains, a ramshackle contraption that wound its way throughout the suburban county, making stops at such points as Melton's Corners, East Scurvee, Knob Hill (which commanded a view of the entire length of the trolley line), Goat Hill, and Dead Center. Looking as ancient as his vehicle, the trolley's motorman, a bewhiskered, wizened little man known only as the Skipper, smoked a corncob pipe and took gaff from nobody, least of all the Transit Commission. The machine would often leave the tracks, smashing into outhouses, snapping clotheslines, and sometimes falling into a pond, from which it had to be extricated by its passengers. In the early 1940s, when trolley lines were falling into disuse, and again in the 1950s, the Skipper became the driver of the Bus That Connects with the Toonerville Trolley; but the fabled Trolley is what remains in memory.

Fox drew *Toonerville Folks* in a scratchy, doodling style that was as effective as it was unsophisticated. Many commentators have noted that the artist favored compositions drawn from a vantage point slightly above the goings-on; it was indeed one of Fox's stylistic idiosyncrasies, but he used the device only in the drawing of his daily panels (and not in all of them, at that). In his Sunday page, where narrative flow from panel to panel was paramount, he used conventional perspective. From 1927 on, Fox employed an assistant, Arthur Clark, who propounded gag ideas and inked the drawings. When there were six parallel lines over Fox's signature, it meant that the drawing was all his; fewer lines indicated the extent to which Clark had assisted him.

Toonerville Folks enjoyed its greatest popularity between the two world wars, when it was distributed by the Bell Syndicate, and later by the McNaught Syndicate. The postwar era witnessed radical changes in suburban life, which were not reflected in Fox's nostalgic feature. Having reached the age of 70, the artist decided it was time to retire the feature, which came to an end early in 1955. Now almost completely forgotten, except by the medium's historians, *Toonerville Folks* remains as a lyrical paean to a vanished America.

M.H.

TOOTS AND CASPER
1918–1956

There is little domestic conflict between the partners in Jimmy Murphy's cheerful family strip *Toots and Casper.* This attractive young couple meet their minor problems together in a spirit of solidarity and affection, and with a shared dimness of perception that the public was to find engaging for many years. One of an emerging class of comics that marked a transition from daily gags to family continuity, *Toots and Casper* was to present the circumstances of the young married couple with warmth and humor for a third of a century.

Murphy had been an editorial cartoonist for several years and had already been widely syndicated before he created the strip for which he is now best known. He had worked as a freelancer and served as staff cartoonist with the *Portland* [Oregon] *Journal* for five years and the *San Francisco Call-Post* for three when William Randolph Hearst invited him to New York to join his *New York Journal* in 1918. *Toots and Casper* began in Hearst's *American* in December of that year and was accepted for national distribution by King Features Syndicate in 1920. A Sunday feature was added on January 22, 1922.

One feature *Toots and Casper* shared with other family strips of its time was a leading man half the size of his wife, but the devoted Casper was not the victim of a dominatrix. Indeed, one of the most distinctive things about the new strip was the charm and physical beauty of its heroine. Toots was neither an amazon nor a vamp but a new type just coming into being, the modern, liberated girl with a mind and a will of her own, somewhat scatterbrained but fully the equal of her not very challenging husband; and her adoring Casper was a model of wedded bliss.

After a few years of conventional daily gag strips, frequently centering on such innocuous subjects as the changing sartorial styles of the time, the plot, such as it was, thickened somewhat. In November 1920, Toots and Casper's union was blessed with issue, and from then on the

couple's attention focused largely on their improbably named son, Buttercup, destined, his doting parents were sure, to be president. As the decade progressed, the content and cast of the strip became increasingly complex. Although Buttercup never grew beyond the age of a toddler, new characters entered the scene, including Buttercup's goofy-looking dog, Spare-Ribs, and such broadly conceived caricatures as Colonel and Mrs. Hoofer and their son and various rich uncles of Casper's. The strip was to shift during the 1920s from daily gags to somewhat bland domestic continuities, with the occasional seasoning of a touch of drama and romance. Never a full-fledged soap opera, it achieved a pleasant balance of character-based humor and narrative suspense.

Clearly the progenitor of such comic-strip star turns as Chic Young's 1930 *Blondie,* Murphy's strip was one of the first to depict a happy young couple and a normal, nonmischievous child. *Toots and Casper* was to wear somewhat thin by the end of its long run—the daily strip lasted until November 12, 1951, and the Sunday feature until December 30, 1956—but in its day this engaging picture of domestic felicity was an innovative addition to the field.

D.W.

TORCHY BROWN
1937–1940, 1950–1955

The first ever nationally distributed newspaper strip created and drawn by an African-American woman, Jackie Ormes's *Torchy Brown, From Dixie to Harlem,* started appearing in the summer of 1937 in the black-owned *Pittsburgh Courier,* which subsequently syndicated it as a daily to nearly a score of black newspapers.

True to the promise of its title, the first continuity involved the title heroine, a jet-haired brown beauty, in a trek north from the impoverished rural community in the Deep South where she was born. In New York City she found heartbreak and disappointment but also hope and support from other people, men and women in the black community, on her way to becoming a performing artist at the famed Apollo Theater in Harlem. In filigree to Torchy's artistic and personal ups and downs there were woven vignettes of black life in the 1930s that gave the strip its special poignancy. Because of its limited circulation (no white paper would touch it), *Torchy Brown* produced only meager returns to its author, and Jackie Ormes in 1940 reluctantly decided to go back to magazine and advertising illustration at a time when new markets were opening up in these fields.

Ten years later Ormes brought back her attractive heroine in a weekly color half-page titled *Torchy in Heartbeats.* While the greater part of the story lines were given over to the heroine's sentimental affairs with a doctor, a jazz musician, and other black professionals, there was also heightened concern about the racial and economic problems gripping America in the 1950s, topics that were largely ignored by mainstream newspaper strips. "What kept *Torchy Brown* from being a black soap opera," Trina Robbins wrote in *A Century of Women Cartoonists,* "was Ormes's treatment of segregation, bigotry, and, in an age when ecology was a vir-

Toots and Casper (J. E. Murphy), © 1934 J. E. Murphy

tually unknown word, environmental pollution." Financial considerations again forced the artist to end the feature in 1955, this time for good. *Torchy Brown* can be read on two levels: as an interesting newspaper strip in its own dramatic and artistic right, and as a social document dealing with black conditions and concerns in the years prior to the civil-rights movement.

M.H.

TRAVELS WITH FARLEY
1975–present

A charming and good-natured strip with an ecological bent, *Travels with Farley* (the title was inspired by John Steinbeck's *Travels with Charley*) has never enjoyed the success it deserves. Conceived by cartoonist (and former Hallmark greeting cards alumnus) Phil Frank, it debuted on June 16, 1975, in only one newspaper, the *Portland Oregonian;* but slowly it garnered enough support to incite Chronicle Features of San Francisco in 1978 to undertake daily syndication of the strip (there never was a Sunday version).

Farley was created at the outset, in the author's own words, as "a character roaming the country in search of America.... Traveling on foot, rather than in a car, he'd meet many more people face to face." In the course of his wanderings this typical flower-child of the times has indeed met a host of uncommon (to say the least) characters. There have been Sergeant Major J. D. Campbell, a veteran of World War II and escapee from the Golden Years Retirement Home; Major Mishap, the fumbling officer in charge of the nuclear-safety program, who was forever tripping on atomic warheads; Baba Re Bop, a car mechanic turned guru, who could explain many of life's mysteries, starting with those by Agatha Christie; not to mention Bob the Wonder Dog, whose favorite travel destination was Bone, Idaho. Most memorable of all have been the Asphalt State Park Bears, Alphonse, Tyrone, Floyd, and Bruin Hilda (who had a crush on Farley and sent him mash notes on Valentine's Day).

Frank has used the strip to touch upon a number of ecological and social topics, such as the paving over of America, shoddy construction practices, the danger posed by pesticides, or the controversy over wearing fur. As he moved from coast to coast, and from one state to the next, Farley has played the role of observer and catalyst, leaving active participation to more vocal (or more self-righteous) characters. His travels have left him time at several points to fall in and out of love with his spunky girlfriend, Jan the mail clerk.

In 1980 Frank temporarily abandoned Farley to create *Miles to Go* for Field Newspaper Syndicate, about another little man (named Miles, naturally) traveling America's back roads. After this new strip folded in the mid-1980s, Frank came full circle, resurrecting his old character in just one newspaper. Now simply called *Farley*, it runs as a daily exclusive in the *San Francisco Chronicle:* in this new, attenuated version, the title character no longer wanders the land but stays close to his home base in the Bay area.

M.H.

TREASURY OF CLASSIC TALES
1952–1987

S ometime at the beginning of the 1950s, Walt Disney Productions made the decision to unify all the various newspaper comic pages it had been turning out under different titles into one portmanteau series. Thus, on July 13, 1952, *Treasury of Classic Tales* made its official entrance under distribution by King Features Syndicate.

The first entry in the series was "Robin Hood." This was not an adaptation of the animated feature, which would come later (in 1973–74), but a transposition of the 1952 live-action movie *The Story of Robin Hood*, which starred Richard Todd and Joan Rice. Frank Reilly was the writer and Jesse Marsh the artist. This dynamic duo stayed with *Treasury* for ten years, with Marsh specializing in illustrated adaptations of live-action films, such as *The Sword and the Rose, Rob Roy, 20,000 Leagues under the Sea*, and *Swiss Family Robinson*. When it came to transposing animated cartoons to paper, the task in the same period fell to various Disney cartoonists (Floyd Gottfredson, Manuel Gonzales, Ken Hultgren, etc.). Comic-strip versions of *Peter Pan, Lady and the Tramp, Sleeping Beauty,* and *101 Dalmatians* all saw light of print at that time.

From 1962 to 1972 the artwork on all stories was entrusted to John Ushler, who in the unanimous judgment of critics proved the worst draftsman in the entire run of the series. Among the adaptations he bungled were the animated features *Mary Poppins, The Jungle Book,* and *The Aristocats,* along with the live-action films *The Moon-Spinners, The Happiest Millionaire,* and *The Love Bug.* Mike Arens succeeded him, with somewhat happier results, on *Cinderella, Robin Hood* (the animated version), and *Alice in Wonderland.*

In 1976 Richard Moore took over the drawing chores, and under his facile pen the series got a new lease on life. Among his most skillful adaptations were those of such animation classics as *Pinocchio, Snow White and the Seven Dwarfs,* and *The Adventures of Mr. Toad,* along with the more contemporary *The Rescuers, The Fox and the Hound,* and *Mickey's Christmas Carol.* He was no less proficient in straight illustration, and did his best work adapting *The Watcher in the Woods* and *The Cat from Outer Space.* Several diverse hands later worked on the series, which experienced a serious decline in the 1980s. The last tale, titled "Tramp's Cat-astrophe" and starring the canine hero of *Lady and the Tramp,* concluded on February 15, 1987.

M.H.

TRUDY
1963–present

J erry Marcus created *Trudy* as a daily panel on March 18, 1963; a Sunday page was added on June 5, 1966. Both have been distributed from their inception by King Features Syndicate.

Described by the syndicate as "a humorous sendup of marriage, parenthood, and nosy next-door neighbors," *Trudy* revolves around the joys, sorrows, and tribulations of a winsome suburban couple. In true comic-strip fashion, Trudy is the head (in more ways than one) of the family,

Tumbleweeds (T. Ryan), ca. 1980, © North America Syndicate

calm, collected, and down-to-earth, trying to keep in check both her slightly bewildered husband, Ted, and her less-than-upstanding son, Crawford. The hen-pecking order is preserved. with Ted more often than not outwitted and upstaged by his wife, while both are hoodwinked in turn by their obnoxious offspring.

While Ted is the typically harrowed husband and father, Trudy finds time for reflection, self-improvement, and even philosophical meditation. She can be in turns romantic ("I'm going to the beauty parlor—now, remember, Ted, the girl that walks in here in a couple of hours from now will be me, your wife"), thoughtful ("What wine goes best with a husband who hates fish?"), or wryly perceptive ("I know you're not listening when you get that idiotic attentive look on your face!"). In a reversal of situation Ted sometimes stands up to her: "Here we are," he declares at one point, putting a record on the turntable, *"Music to Nag By."* And Trudy herself does not shrink from using forceful arguments on her son when he gets way out of line; lifting him by his tee-shirt and shaking him violently on just such an occasion, she soothingly declares: "Of course Mother still loves you, Mother may be a little annoyed at her little boy, but Mother still loves him."

A warm, unpretentious feature, *Trudy* is drawn in a simple, ingratiating style. An inveterate practical joker, Marcus loves to surprise his cartoonist friends by sneaking some of their characters into his own strip.

M.H.

TUMBLEWEEDS
1965–present

The history of the Wild West got rewritten starting on September 6, 1965, when the Lew Little Syndicate first printed *Tumbleweeds* by former commercial artist Tom K. Ryan. The setting is the dilapidated town of Grimy Gulch, where sarcasm and dry wit reign. The concept and clean design made it an original, unique offering, and it has remained so. A Sunday page was added in 1967, by then distributed by the Register and Tribune and, later, United Feature and North America syndicates.

Tumbleweeds is a laconic cowpoke who travels the prairie on his indolent, disheveled horse Epic, who sports a moptop. A nuisance to "Weeds" is the town's sole spinster, Hildegard Hamhocker. Her endless pursuit to drag him to Judge Horatio Frump for nuptials is the classic drama of unrequited love, and one of the standard story lines. The only other female in town is Hildegard's niece, Echo, who dotes on the "world's laziest dog," Pajamas.

The Nugget Saloon is the only social outlet, the constant hangout of local drunk Soppy Sopwell, arguably the strip's most colorful clown. In sharp contrast is the town gambler and smooth-talker, Ace, a straightman among straightmen. Not exactly *High Noon*, the struggle between law and order pits grimacing criminal Snake-Eye McFoul against a dour sheriff and his no-witted deputy, Knuckles. For the unfortunate souls who fail to dodge Snake-Eye's gunsights, undertakers Claude Clay and Wart Wimble eagerly offer their services ("You plug 'em, we plant 'em").

The neighboring tribe of Poohawk Indians fares no better. The depressed Chief laments over his sect's collective incompetence, exemplified by village idiot Limpid Lizard. This buck-toothed wacko haplessly courts the elder's daughter, Little Pidgeon, hilariously paralleling the Weeds-Hamhocker endeavor. The only mild success the ill-starred tribe enjoys is annoying the cavalry of Fort Ridiculous, led by Colonel G. Fluster. The most cultured and insubordinate "warriors" are the diminutive Lotsa Luck and Screaming Flea, whose introduction marked real innovations in Ryan's analysis of the fractured science of communication. Originally mute, snobbish Lotsa Luck stole punchlines by scribbling sardonic retorts tossed callously at their recipients, while Screaming Flea's beautifully calligraphic, ornate speech balloons were as striking and surreal in appearance as he was. Unfortunately, these eccentricities have been dropped; the mute now speaks and all speech is typeset, obviously allowing the cartoonist to maintain his ample quantity of dialogue despite the continued shrinkage of newspaper space allotted comic strips.

Twenty *Tumbleweeds* books have been published since 1968. The strip was animated for Saturday-morning television in the late 1970s, but because of the cartoonist's exclusion from the project the results were lackluster. In 1983 a *Tumbleweeds* musical production debuted, supplemented in Las Vegas in a live stage attraction at the MGM Grand theme park; started in 1993, it is titled *Tumbleweeds Gulch*. One other noteworthy point is that cartoonist Jim Davis was Ryan's studio assistant from 1969 until 1978, when he departed to launch *Garfield*.

Ryan's mastery of verse, prose, and sardonic banter has made *Tumbleweeds* into a highly literate feature and an exemplary model: much of today's style of comics humor follows the manner of this feature, and its contributions to the field of newspaper strips has yet to be fully appreciated.

B.J.

TWIN EARTHS
1952–1963

Former comic-book editor Oskar Lebeck teamed up with veteran comic-book artist Alden (Al) McWilliams to produce an original science-fiction newspaper series titled *Twin Earths*. With distribution by United Feature Syndicate, it debuted on June 16, 1952, as a daily strip; a Sunday page was added on March 1 of the next year.

Posited on the familiar science-fiction premise of a planet (called Terra in this case) identical to Earth in every respect and symmetrically located on the opposite side of the sun, *Twin Earths* presented to the readers the image of a Terran civilization one full century ahead of our own. Having mastered space travel, the Terrans (the majority of whom were women) had been observing the doings on Earth for some time in their astro-vehicles in the shape of flying saucers (a neat touch). There were some amusing sendups of earthbound customs as contrasted to the coldly rational behavior of the alien observers, but soon the strip veered toward the more traditional themes of melodrama and soap opera. The story line developed into a romance

between the FBI agent charged with the investigation into the UFOs, the handsome and dapper Garry Verth, and one of the Terran visitors, a bodacious lass named Vana, who fell head over heels in love with the Earthman, proving thereby that rationality has its limits. Later the Terrans would even help the forces of law and order on this planet to eradicate crime, thanks to their superior weapons and methods.

The narratives unfolded at a rather slow pace, and the long pauses were filled with depictions of futuristic gadgets and weaponry, along with the portrayal of numberless Terran women, all of them easy on the eyes. McWilliams's polished drawings kept *Twin Earths* interesting and attractive for a long period of time, but at length the lack of coherent plots did the feature in: it was finally discontinued in 1963.

M.H.

Twin Earths (A. McWilliams), © 1955 United Feature Syndicate

UNCLE REMUS AND HIS TALES OF BRER RABBIT
`1945-1972`

Anticipating Disney's 1946 live-action and animation medley *Song of the South* by almost a year, *Uncle Remus and His Tales of Brer Rabbit* started appearing as a Sunday page distributed by King Features Syndicate on October 14, 1945. The following year Disney, bowing to protests from literary historians and others, added the tag line "Based on the stories by Joel Chandler Harris."

In contrast to Harris's tales and to *Song of the South*, where he was impersonated by James Baskett in a memorable performance, Uncle Remus never appeared in *Uncle Remus* (it is possible that either Disney or King were loath to show a black character in a favorable light for fear of losing newspapers in the South). At any rate, the series opened immediately on the conflict opposing the carefree Brer Rabbit to the crafty Brer Fox and the slow-witted Brer B'ar intent on gobbling him up. In a string of fast-paced incidents, Brer Rabbit would always extricate himself from various predicaments thanks to his quick thinking and his ready wits. The episodes centering on the "Tar Baby" and the "Briar Patch" tales were especially diverting and nicely drawn.

These longer continuities soon gave way to self-contained gag pages with an extensive use of Southern dialect.

Uncle Wiggily (Garis and Campbell), 1919

Brer Rabbit was no longer depicted as the immaculate hero, and he as often as not ended up the victim of his own underhanded schemes The cast of characters was gradually expanded to include Brer Tarripin, Brer Possum, Brer Gopher, Brer 'Gator, and Sis Goose, along with the protagonist's Mammy Rabbit and his sweetheart Molly. Each page ended on a little homily like "Jumpin' into trubble is a heap easier than jumpin' out" and "Twixt right an' wrong thar ain't no middle path!"

Writer Bill Walsh and penciler Paul Murry had charge of the first year's worth of stories. George Stallings, who had a hand in the writing of *Song of the South,* then took over the scripting, and he was succeeded in 1963 by Jack Boyd. Dick Moores was the principal artist on the page from 1946 to 1951, followed by Riley Thompson and Bill Wright. In 1962 John Ushler brought in the rear (in a stylistic as well as a chronological sense) in a succession of limp *Uncle Remus* pages until the series' end on December 31, 1972.

M.H.

UNCLE WIGGILY
`1919-1929, 1947-1953`

Howard R. Garis, a newspaperman turned fiction writer, came up with the idea of a series of tales about a wise old rabbit character after a walk in the woods in the fall of 1909. He brought the concept to his former employers at the *Newark Evening News,* and on January 30, 1910, the first story about Uncle Wiggily (as the rabbit was called) appeared in print. Picked up for syndication by the McClure organization, these bedtime stories were published, at the rhythm of six a week, in newspapers around the country. The success of the tales prompted the syndicate to ask the author to create a comic page that would star the rabbit, and early in 1919 *Uncle Wiggily* made its debut as a Sunday color feature.

Uncle Wiggily Longears (to give him his full name) was a neatly dressed old bachelor who lived in a bungalow nestled in the hollow of a tree stump, where Nurse Jane Fuzzy Wuzzy, an elderly muskrat character, served as his housekeeper. Despite his age and his rheumatism, which forced him to use a crutch, Wiggily was sprightly and cunning. In Animal Land, he always managed to outrun and outsmart the baddies, such as Skillery Skallery Alligator, Woozie Wolf, the mean-minded Pipsisewah, and the slippery Skeezicks, who all were after the souse that grew in the rabbit's ears. These attempts at mayhem never amounted to much, however. As Martin McCaw observed, "Nothing very bad happened to anyone in Animal Land, although the bad chaps got banged up a little."

In the first years of *Uncle Wiggily*'s Sunday run, the texts appeared in typeset form neatly arranged in boxes under each picture. In September 1925 this outdated narrative device was discarded in favor of regular speech balloons. *Uncle Wiggily* was now a bona fide comic feature in all respects. A few months previously Uncle Wiggily had finally married: not Nurse Jane, who in proverbial fashion had cried at his wedding, but a Mrs. Jump, a widow rabbit with six bunny children; this circumstance allowed the author to turn *Uncle Wiggily* into a kid strip as well as an animal feature.

From the outset the stories had been illustrated by Lansing ("Lang") Campbell, a veteran from such publications as *Judge, Puck,* and *Life,* whose charming and whimsical line perfectly suited the simplicity of the tales. In the mid-1920s there was also a daily strip, *Uncle Wiggily's Tricks,* drawn in its early months by Campbell, who relinquished it to Hubert Main, followed by an artist who signed simply "Rich." The definitive version, however, belongs to Campbell, who was emphatically not "a gifted lady," as some have claimed, but a certified male, a married man and a father. He was also a prolific cartoonist. According to his biographer, Suzanne Shaub, "Mr. Campbell wrote and illustrated several comic strips of his own in the early 1930s —*Paddy Pigtail, Paddy the Pup, Dippy Doodlebug, Bizzy Izzy Humbug, The Dinky Ducklings, Duck and Applesauce,* and *Dicky Bird's Diary.* (At least one, *Piggy Pigtail,* was published by McClure Syndicate.)"

The *Uncle Wiggily* Sunday page was discontinued at the end of 1929. In March 1947 *Uncle Wiggily* was brought back to the Sunday newspaper pages by the Bell Syndicate. Illustrated now by Francis Kirn in an imitation of the Disney cartoon style, with none of the charm and winsomeness of Campbell's drawings, it only lasted until 1953.

M.H.

UP ANCHOR
See KEVIN THE BOLD

THE UPSIDE DOWNS OF LITTLE LADY LOVEKINS AND OLD MAN MUFFAROO
1903–1905

*I*n the first decade of this century, the *New York Herald* editors for some as yet unexplained reasons decided to go all out for whimsy and fantasy in the pages of their Sunday comic supplement, and none of their features was as whimsical or fanciful (starting with the title) as Gustave Verbeck's *The Upside Downs of Little Lady Lovekins and Old Man Muffaroo,* which started publication on October 11, 1903.

Next to Winsor McCay, Verbeck (who signed "Verbeek") was the most prolific contributor to the *Herald* comic pages; *The Upside Downs* was his first effort there, so he must have been at pains to make a splashy entrance —and he did. The premise was very simple: each week Lady Lovekins, a rather

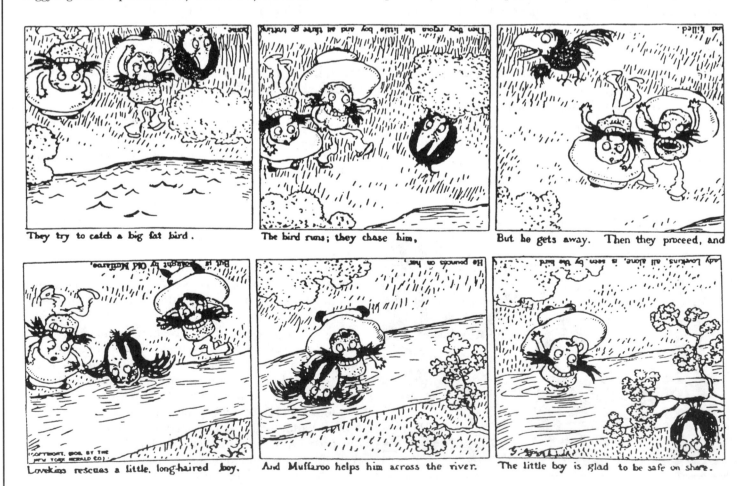

They try to catch a big fat bird.

The bird runs; they chase him,

But he gets away. Then they proceed, and

Lovekins rescues a little, long-haired boy.

And Muffaroo helps him across the river.

The little boy is glad to be safe on shore.

The Upside Downs (G. Verbeck), 1904

shapeless maiden, and her mentor, the potato-headed Old Man Muffaroo, found themselves confronted with perils and predicaments steadily increasing in intensity as the strip progressed. In one episode Lady Lovekins was snatched up by a flying dragon; in another, she got engulfed by a giant tidal wave; in yet another, hordes of hobgoblins attacked her. On each and every occasion she was rescued by the fearless Muffaroo in great displays of ingenuity and daring.

This was clearly a narrative of epic proportions, and since he disposed of only a half-page in the interior (monochrome) spread of the *Herald* supplement, Verbeck hit upon an ingenious way by which to expand the feature into a full page in half the space. After reading each six-panel episode of *The Upside Downs* in the normal way, one would turn it upside down (hence the clever title) to find out how it ended. The acrobatics required to get the composition of each panel to match its upside-down image and still make sense were enormous: Thus Lady Lovekins would metamorphose into Muffaroo, a clump of trees would change into the head of a giant, and the moon at twilight would become the sun at dawn, in an endless cavalcade of weird transpositions.

The Upside Downs carried on in this way for sixty-four weeks, winding down on January 15, 1905. While Peter Newell had used the same technique in his *Topsys and Turveys* in the last decade of the nineteenth century, no one since Verbeck has ever tried to duplicate this original method of storytelling, and in all probability no one will.

M.H.

VANILLA AND THE VILLAINS
`1928–1929`

In the late 1920s Harry Hershfield, whose *Abie the Agent* was then flourishing in the comic pages, perhaps in a bout of nostalgia decided to go back to the kind of burlesque melodrama that had been his hallmark during his salad days. With the help of cartoonist Darrell McClure, then in his twenties, he confected (anonymously) *Vanilla and the Villains,* which on September 10, 1928, started its daily appearance in the Hearst chain of newspapers.

Set in the nineteenth century, the strip was a compendium of all the clichés of Victorian fiction Hershfield had read as a boy. Vanilla Graingerfield was a heroine of truly epic proportions who made her entrance riding a white horse amid a throng of singing, clapping, black slave cotton-pickers. The first continuity was a parody of *Uncle Tom's Cabin,* wherein Vanilla, with the help of her boyfriend Stonewall and the intervention of the U.S. Marines, thwarted the schemes of her dastardly stepfather Bourbon Mash (who was trying to cheat her of her inheritance), and at the end of which she freed the grateful slaves. Hershfield next introduced Lambert Leer, a top-hatted, black-suited, bemustached, snarling villain in the tradition of his earlier Desperate Desmond, for Vanilla and Stonewall to combat. Leer and his secret organization, the Sinister Six, pursued their adversaries all over the globe, from the wilds of the Rockies to the snowbound steppes of czarist Russia, in a series of hilarious adventures spoofing a variety of adventure-fiction classics.

The strip owed much to the graphic artistry of its cartoonist, who in a wink to his uncredited scriptwriter's famous creation, often signed "Desperate Darrell McClure." Obviously inspired by all the foolery he was given to illustrate, McClure drew with equal abandon tableaux of ridiculous pageantry, scenes of comic mayhem, and vignettes of tender reunion in a loose, devil-may-care style, half cartoony and half illustrative, that served to highlight the absurdities of the plot. Hershfield, however, soon tired of this one-note situation, and at the end of 1929 he brought the feature to an abrupt close. Brief as its existence was, *Vanilla* left the memory of a tiny epic that foreshadowed the straight adventure strips to come out of the 1930s.

Hershfield was to take one last stab at humorous melodrama on the heels of *Vanilla and the Villains.* Again in tandem with McClure and again uncredited, he came out with *Hard-Hearted Hicky,* about yet another villain plotting against the world. *Hicky* too lasted only one year, being abandoned in 1930 when McClure took over the drawing of *Little Annie Rooney.* On this note Hershfield's career as an irrepressible purveyor of comic adventure came to an end.

M.H.

VIC FLINT
`1946–1967`

Vic Flint was conceived in the immediate postwar era as a continuity strip built on the personality of a tough private-eye hero, to take advantage of the public's infatuation with hard-boiled novels and movies. It started on Sunday, January 6, 1946, with the story line being picked up without a break the following Monday in daily form; it was drawn by Ralph Lane and written, under the pseudo-

Vic Flint (R. Lane), © 1946 NEA Service

nym Michael O'Malley, by Ernest "East" Lynne, an editor at NEA, the syndicate that distributed the feature.

The narrative was told in the first person by the titular hero, a handsome blond private investigator, always spiffily attired in a sports jacket adorned with a white carnation. He was often helped in his assignments by his dark-haired, loving secretary Libby Lang, and sometimes stymied by the appropriately named Inspector Growl of the city police. His casebook included such delicate missions as exposing a blackmailer without damage to his victim, recovering a stolen necklace from a foreign diplomat for an insurance company, and snatching an amorous heiress from the clutches of a fortune-hunting Romeo.

A former marine, Flint was never loath to use his fists or his gun to close his cases. His lighthearted manner and mercenary instincts ranked him closer to Michael Shayne than to Philip Marlow, to whom he has been compared. Once asked what he intended to do with the fat check he had just received for his services, he airily answered, "Give it to my favorite charity—myself."

On October 8, 1950, Lane, who had been drawing the feature in an easy, pleasant illustrative style, was replaced by Dean Miller, whose line was clearly heavier and clumsier. The strip went on a marked decline, and in January 1956 the dailies were dropped, leaving only the Sundays. In 1961 Art Sansom, a versatile artist who could work in a realistic manner as well as in a bigfoot vein, took over the artwork. The writing continued to be credited to O'Malley but actually was the work of a number of anonymous house scribes. In August 1965 the title was changed to *The Good Guys*, with Flint teaming up with another investigator, the millionaire Joe Thunder. The continuity was taken up by the talented Russ Winterbotham (who signed "J. Harvey Bond"), while the drawing was entrusted, interestingly enough, to John Lane, the son of the original artist. The feature acquired some welcome humor, and even a satirical outlook spoofing the entire private-eye genre, but it only lasted for a few more years, to March 12, 1967.

M.H.

VIC JORDAN
1941–1945

The editors of the liberal-progressive New York daily *PM* were among the earliest and most vocal supporters of the Allied cause in World War II, and their advocacy extended even to the comics page. On December 1, 1941, there appeared *Vic Jordan,* a daily strip credited to "Paine" (a pseudonym that covered staff writers Kermit Jaediker and Charles Zerner) and drawn by Elmer Wexler, a former comic-book artist. A Sunday version later followed.

Vic Jordan was a press agent for an American musical show, and he found himself stranded in Paris at the time of the German invasion. Having thumbed his nose at the Nazi occupiers, he barely escaped the clutches of the Gestapo, and later joined up with the forces of the French resistance movement. There he eventually helped harass the enemy at every turn, blowing up bridges, attacking lonely outposts, and getting Allied airmen back to Britain. Vic was often aided in these commendable endeavors by Marty O'Brien,

a former prizefighter who added brawn to the proceedings, and was assisted by a blonde British agent named Sue, who contributed her charm as well as her feminine wiles to the fight.

While the action often paralleled that of contemporary Hollywood war movies, there was also an emphasis on the grim, no-holds-barred contest between the French resisters and their ruthless occupiers. Just as Vic and his partners were fighting their private war in the comic pages, the actual war continued unabated in the real world. Wexler enlisted in the Marine Corps in 1942, and was succeeded by Paul Norris, who entered service in his turn in 1943, in a repeated instance of life imitating art. David Moneypenny, a staff artist, and ultimately Bernard Baily assumed the artwork on *Vic Jordan* for the remainder of its run.

With Paris and most of France liberated in the summer of 1944, Vic took the fight to enemy soil, spearheading the Allied advance into Germany; by the spring of 1945, however, it had become clear that the strip had lost its raison d'etre. On April 30, 1945, John P. Lewis, the editor of *P.M.*, announced the end of the feature in these terms: "The victory in Europe has been reflected on our comic page. *Vic Jordan,* our first comic strip, which was devoted to dramatizing the fight against Fascism in the underground of Europe, has bowed to the fact that military victory is at hand. In the Sunday paper Vic made his exit. He was wounded, you remember, and has come back home for a rest."

Despite the constant change in artists, the look of the feature remained surprisingly steady and of good, if not outstanding, quality. The first comic strip to reflect sympathy with the plight of the occupied peoples of Europe, preceding by several months *The Adventures of Pinky Rankin* in the communist *Daily Worker, Vic Jordan* deserves to be remembered as more than just another wartime comic routinely turned out by the syndicates in those parlous times.

M.H.

Vic Jordan (P. Norris), ca. 1943, © **Field Newspaper Syndicate**

WAGS, THE DOG THAT ADOPTED A MAN
`1905–1908`

In the dawning years of the century William Marriner was the mainstay of T. C. McClure's syndicate. Among the many comic pages he created there, *Wags, the Dog That Adopted a Man,* which started running in March 1905, is perhaps the best remembered.

Wags was a white mongrel dog with black spots, whose mistake it was to attach himself to a man who hated animals. With typical canine loyalty he followed the surly old geezer in whiskers and top hat—he called him "my nice man"—home every day, despite rebuffs, kicks, and blows to the head. In desperation the reluctant pet-owner tried to shake Wags by getting out of town, barricading himself in his house, and even paying kids to drown the accursed mutt, but nothing availed: Wags would turn up in his suitcase, come down the chimney, or get ashore by holding a rope tied to a rowboat. Often the presence of the unwanted Wags would trigger all kinds of mishaps for the putative owner, who would exclaim at the end of every painful episode, "But it ain't my dog!" Each Sunday page was drawn in an attractive, expressive style that blended cartooniness with observation.

"In his time William F. Marriner was known to as wide an audience as Opper, Dirks, Outcault, and McCay were," Stephen Becker wrote in *Comic Art in America,* adding with a note of regret, "Today he is forgotten and neglected even by historians." For history's sake, therefore, let it be mentioned here that, in addition to *Wags,* Marriner drew many other noteworthy comic strips, most of them about animals or children, such as *The Fortunes of Foolish Ferdinand, Mary and Her Little Lamb,* and most especially *Sambo and His Funny Noises,* dealing with a little black boy who always got the better of his white tormentors.

M.H.

WALT DISNEY'S SUNDAY PAGES
`1942–1945`

After the discontinuation in 1942 of *Silly Symphonies* as an overall title for Walt Disney's Sunday comic pages, these sundry features kept coming out for a period of some three years under titles that changed with every new story. For convenience's sake these are usually regrouped under the appellation "Walt Disney's Sunday Pages" adopted here. The first story, in direct succession to the lapsed *Silly Symphonies,* was an adaptation of *Bambi,* written by Merrill de Maris and drawn by Bob Grant, that ran from July 19 to October 4, 1942. A lyrical tale skillfully scripted by de Maris and lovingly detailed by Grant, it was followed without a break by the longest entry in the group, the raucous "José Carioca."

The first Sunday page opened with a panoramic tour of Rio de Janeiro before closing up on the shack that was "the home of a young man-about-town, a gay carefree Brazilian *papagaio* named José Carioca." This marked the first U.S. appearance of the nattily dressed, pleasure-seeking parrot, some four months ahead of his starring role in the 1943 *Saludos Amigos* cartoon film. The gags were quite unsophisticated and revolved around three main themes: the anti-hero's scheming to get a free meal, his pursuit of the opposite sex, and his imaginative avoidance of work. These proved sufficient to sustain the title for a full two years, to October 1, 1944.

The following Sunday José made way for another Latin-American knockabout, the fiery rooster Panchito, thus anticipating the character's appearance in 1945's *The Three Caballeros.* As energetic as José was lazy, the sombrero-hatted, gun-toting Mexican fowl was always shown riding horses, fighting bulls, and lassoing cattle, when he was not busy wooing his chick, the fickle Chiquita. His adventures came to an end October 7, 1945. The team formed by writer Bill Walsh, penciler Bill Murry, and inker Dick Moores had kept "Panchito" going, and the very next week they plunged without a pause into *Uncle Remus* (discussed elsewhere in this book).

As a postscript to the cycle, two later adaptations of Disney animated films should be mentioned: the 1950 *Cinderella* and the 1951 *Alice in Wonderland.* In 1952 *Treasury of Classic Tales* would again provide a catchall denomination for all the weekly color pages turned out by the Disney studio and distributed by King Features Syndicate.

M.H.

WAR ON CRIME
`1936–1938`

Following a thorough shakeup in 1936, the small Ledger Syndicate embarked on an ambitious course of expansion. It scored a major coup when it got the rights to adapt into newspaper-strip form some of the best-known cases ever cracked by the Federal Bureau of Investigation.

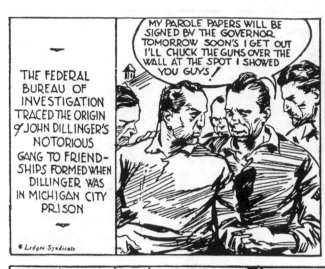

War on Crime (K. Starrett), © 1936 Ledger Syndicate

felons natural-born killers, and that was that. Compared to the fictional *Dick Tracy* or *Secret Agent X-9*, the fact-based *War on Crime* looked and sounded dry and dreary. It ended its run with the conclusion of the Tri-State Gang case, on January 22, 1938.

M.H.

WASH TUBBS
1924–1988

One of the great adventure strips of all time started life inauspiciously on April 14, 1924, as *Washington Tubbs II*. Its author, Roy Crane, had wanted to turn out a sophisticated slice of big-city life, but he was persuaded to produce a daily feature about a store clerk in a small midwestern town instead.

Better known as Wash Tubbs, the titular hero was a diminutive, bespectacled, but spunky adolescent who in the early months of the strip was clerking for a grocery store in the Midwest. Soon the wandering bug bit him and he went in search of sunken treasure in the South Seas. In the process he also grew in years and in resourcefulness (though not in height) and developed a taste for pretty girls that even topped his love of adventure. In 1926 he hooked up with another young wayfarer, the gawky, cocky Gozy Gallup, and the pair met with a great many dangers in situations that were half-realistic and half-humorous, in locales ranging from Mexico to North Africa.

What distinguished *Wash Tubbs* (as the feature was now called) from contemporary action strips like *Oliver's Adventures* or *Bobby Thatcher* were its openly erotic overtones. In the course of his numerous wanderings Wash met countless beauties (usually double his size) with whom he would invariably fall in love. There were Dottie, his hometown crush who later turned into a movie star; Hula of the South Seas, who almost got him to the altar; Jada in the Sahara Desert, who saved him from the clutches of Hudson Bey, the slave trader; not to mention the Countess, a clever con-woman who had him convicted of her partner's murder, dispossessed of all his money, and ruined in the eyes of his friends before meeting her comeuppance at the end. None of them, however, matched the fiery Tango, the tiger tamer, who would not hesitate to take the whip to her bemused boyfriend.

Up to that time humor had dominated over adventure in the unfolding of the tales. The situation was to change radically in May 1929 when Wash met, in the jails of the middle-European kingdom of Candelabra where he had been traveling, the man who was destined to steal the show

Written by Rex Collier, a *Washington Star* newsman who had reported on many of these cases, and closely monitored by the FBI, the new feature, which the editors claimed to be "true stories...modified in the public interest," made its appearance as a daily titled *War on Crime* on May 18, 1936.

Based on official FBI files, the strip related in somewhat breathless fashion the criminal activities of such notorious mob figures as John Dillinger, "Pretty Boy" Floyd, and "Machine-Gun" Kelly, and the dogged police work of the fearless G-men who brought them to heel. The artist who gave the strip its dark-accented, gloom-laden stamp was Kemp Starrett, with an assist from such ghosts as the apocryphal "Hammon" and the uncredited Frank Godwin. He was replaced in July 1937 by Jimmy Thompson, who supplied the artwork for the remaining few months of the strip in his usual, plodding manner.

Jay Maeder, the enterprising journalist of Miami and New York who, through the Freedom of Information Act was first to bring out the facts of the FBI's involvement with the strip, claims that the feature's demise was due to the Bureau running out of interesting cases to illustrate. This is partly true; but the main responsibility lay within the strip itself. Perhaps due to excessive official tampering and to overcautiousness on the part of Collier, the continuities never built upon picturesque anecdotes or stylistic embellishments to relieve the monotonous recitation of dates, places, and facts. In addition, character motivation was never explored: all the agents were noble heroes, all the away from him. Calling himself Captain Easy, gentleman adventurer, he soon escaped from prison along with his pint-sized companion, and together they embarked on a new series of adventures, more suspenseful, more thrill-packed, and less humorous than before. The longest and most fateful of these adventures occurred during their perilous voyage from Holland to Alaska aboard the whaling ship *Jonah,* on which they had been shanghaied. There Wash finally settled accounts with his old nemesis, the brutish Bull Dawson, thanks to his tough companion's mastery of fisticuffs and the martial arts.

More adventures followed, on the seven seas and across the five continents, in Cuba, in China, and in the fictional banana republic of Costa Grande. Little by little the readers learned of the taciturn Easy's turbulent past: expelled from West Point for eloping with a superior officer's daughter, later divorced, he had served as a mercenary in the armies of several Latin American, European, and Asian countries. Tall, muscular, and tough-featured, he soon edged out the shrimpish Wash from his own strip, starting with the Sunday page, which from February 1927 had unfolded its weekly (and weak) gags atop the *Out Our Way* feature, and which on July 10, 1933, was rebaptized *Captain Easy* in his honor.

Purporting to recount Easy's exploits before his meeting with Wash, the Sunday episodes (now unfolding over the space of a full newspaper page) were filled not only with sound and fury but with pathos and humor as well. With Easy as his proxy, Crane could now vicariously indulge his wanderlust (which in his youth had caused him to roam the roads and byways of the United States and even to hire out as a seaman aboard ship). He sent his hero not only to lands he had always dreamed of visiting, such as China and India, but also to unknown countries of the mind, like the mysterious Himalayan region that "no white man has seen since the days of Marco Polo."

It is for the operetta kingdoms of Europe that Crane showed the greatest affection. Thus Easy found himself successively imprisoned by the dictator of Hitaxia; decorated for valor by the monarch of Kleptomania, Prince Hugo Maximilian von Hooten Tooten, whom he had restored to the throne; and taking part in the war between Nikkateena and Woopsydasia. In the course of this latter episode (in 1935) Crane, in counterpoint to the underlying heroic ethos of the strip, interpolated a bitter elegy to the futility of war: "Generals decorate each other with medals; profiteers grow rich; and the flower of Nikkateena's manhood falls like autumn leaves in a gust of wind."

In January 1938 the weekly page reunited Easy and Wash in circumstances similar to those that had thrown them together nine years before, thereby conjoining Sundays and dailies on the same temporal plane. The two companions' reunion proved brief, however, as Wash got himself married soon afterward and settled into domestic life. This left Easy free to resume his swashbuckling exploits solo, which he

did with his usual gusto. Following the outbreak of war in Europe he put his talents at the service of the FBI in the fight against spies and saboteurs, and after Pearl Harbor he had his rightful rank of captain in the U.S. Army restored to him. On this redemptive note Crane left his hero and his syndicate to create *Buz Sawyer* for King Features.

As an artist of the comics, Crane occupies a place apart, and it is in *Wash Tubbs* that his artistry can best be appreciated. He allied a forceful pen-line that sometimes resembled brushwork to a complex of atmospheric effects achieved with the judicious application of Doubletone. These devices never detracted from the clarity of his compositions that at once stood out on their own and served the narrative line. Black masses were applied as a counterpoise to the impressionistic, often detailed outlines of the backgrounds. These processes were subtly transposed to the Sunday feature, in which the shimmer of color and the freedom of layout allowed by the spaciousness of the newspaper page were firmly anchored by the solidity of the underpinning line. If we consider that it only came to full fruition with the arrival of Captain Easy, *Wash Tubbs* then should take its place as one of the heralds of the modern adventure strip, alongside the two other outstanding features that came out of that fateful year 1929, *Tarzan* and *Buck Rogers.*

In June 1943 Leslie Turner, who had been assisting Crane for the past six years, found himself in charge of the daily strip. While Walt Scott was at the same time turning out the Sunday *Captain Easy* with dubious results, Turner on his part proved himself an able and sometimes inspired exponent of the Crane style. In 1949 dailies and Sundays became unified under the *Captain Easy* banner, and in 1952 Turner became solely responsible for both aspects of the feature. Paradoxically, just as it was being consolidated formally and artistically, *Captain Easy* bifurcated thematically. While the dailies continued on an adventurous path, with Easy resuming his thrill-packed wanderings from Arabia to South America, the Sundays were given over to weekly gags often involving Wash's superrich father-in-law, J. P. McKee, and the swindling Kallikak clan, who tried to divest him of some of his wealth.

In 1960 Mell Graff took control of the Sunday page, which he skippered until 1969 (with the exception of a brief return by Turner in 1961). Graff on the whole acquit-

Wash Tubbs (Captain Easy; R. Crane), © 1931 NEA Service

ted himself better than he had done during the final years of his tenure on *Secret Agent X-9*, although he made no effort at maintaining the graphic look his predecessors had imparted to the feature. At the end of 1969 dailies and Sundays devolved to Bill Crooks, who had assisted Turner from 1945 on. With scripts supplied by Jim Lawrence, and later by Mick Casale, Crooks restored *Captain Easy* to some of its erstwhile glitter, in both style and tone. Easy again went adventuring to the far corners of the earth as, successively, an agent for the federal government, a troubleshooter for the McKee Foundation, and a private investigator. On this downbeat note the daily strip came to an end in 1988, a few years after the Sundays had been discontinued.

M.H.

Wee Pals (M. Turner), © 1971 Register and Tribune Syndicate

WEE PALS
1965–present

Morrie Turner, who is in his early seventies and the senior African-American cartoonist published today, has met success by being always true to his ideals with his comic strip *Wee Pals*.

Following encouragement from Charles Schulz at a San Francisco meeting of the Northern California Cartoon and Humor Association in 1964, Turner developed his truly integrated strip in 1965 for the Lew Little Syndicate. Lew Little later merged with the Register and Tribune Syndicate, and now *Wee Pals* is distributed by Creators Syndicate.

Peanuts is Turner's favorite strip and it occurred to him that he could do his own version geared for the African-American market. He soon expanded the idea into an integrated strip for the general marketplace.

Wee Pals is populated with schoolchildren of all races and religions. The humor of their interaction is the central theme of the strip. Nipper, the black kid whose eyes are hidden by a Confederate kepi hat, was named for Nipsey Russell, the comedian. His "pals" include: Sybil the no-nonsense peacemaker; Diz, who sports a dashiki shirt, sunglasses, and beret; George, who's Chinese and quotes Confucius; the white girl Connie, who's a feminist; Jerry, the strip's resident Jewish intellectual; Rocky, a full-blooded Native American; and the cast goes on and on.

Morrie Turner was not a novice cartoonist when he began *Wee Pals*. He started drawing cartoons while serving with the famed all-black 477th Bomber Group during World War II. Later he freelanced cartoons for publications such as the *Saturday Evening Post* and *Argosy*. In the early 1960s he drew the panel *Humor in Hue* for *Black World,* the former *Negro Digest* magazine. His cartoon *Dinky Fellows* appeared in the *Chicago Defender,* a leading black newspaper.

Prior to the success of *Wee Pals,* Morrie Turner worked for over a decade as clerk and unofficial artist for the Oakland, California, Police Department. In 1966, after winning the Brotherhood Award of the National Conference of Christians and Jews for his work on *Wee Pals,* Turner was quoted in a National Cartoonists Society publication on some of the rationale behind *Wee Pals*. "I decided that just by exposing readers to the sight of Negroes and whites playing together in harmony, rather than pointing up aggrava-

tions, a useful, if subliminal, purpose would be served, and ultimately would have as great effect for good as all the freedom marchers in Mississippi."

Turner devotes part of each Sunday page to "Soul Corner," where he explores minority historical personages and current leaders who have often been overlooked in the mainstream media.

A number of *Wee Pals* reprints have been issued in paperback. For many years *Wee Pals on the Go* was aired as a kids' show on local San Francisco television. A piece of *Wee Pals* merchandising sums up the theme of the strip: two characters are shown with the statement underneath, "Freedom is holding hands with whoever you wish."

The growing ranks of successful African-American syndicated cartoonists owe a debt of gratitude to Morrie Turner, whose *Wee Pals* did some serious pioneering work for them.

B.C., Jr.

WEE WILLIE WINKIE'S WORLD
1906–1907

Shortly after the appearance of his pioneering feature *The Kin-der-Kids*, Lyonel Feininger made a second contribution to the comic pages of the *Chicago Tribune* with *Wee Willie Winkie's World*, which started publication on August 19, 1906.

Wee Willie Winkie's title was inspired by an English nursery rhyme (which had also been used by Rudyard Kipling), but in mood and content the strip was much closer to such German fairy tales as Hansel and Gretel. The titular hero was a little boy lost amidst the wonders and perils of the natural world. Feininger fashioned an allegorical universe of marvel and terror that Willie had to face alone, his small, pathetic silhouette standing in incongruous contrast to the stately presence of the trees, the hills and the clouds surrounding him on all sides. This world was not malevolent but simply impersonal; to the lonely little boy, however, it sometimes appeared as threatening as if it were peopled with ogres and monsters. "A solitary traveler, Wee Willie has neither friend nor enemy. He is the sole actor in the strip's drama," Judith O'Sullivan wrote in *The Great American Newspaper Strip*. "Conflict is achieved by Willie's interaction with an anthropomorphized natural environment, its roots deep in Teutonic pantheism."

Wee Willie Winkie was in one respect a throwback to the earlier narrative form of the picture story. There were no speech-balloons, Feininger employing instead printed legends between the pictures, themselves framed with exquisite animal, floral, or mythological decorations. The imagery was spectacular, involving intricate transmogrifications of forms and objects and terrifying depictions of natural forces, creating an aura of unease and disquiet that even the reassuring text at the end of each Sunday episode failed to dispel.

Feininger's esthetic preoccupations are evident throughout the strip. In the geometrical precision of the landscapes and the deliberate exaggeration of movement there can already be detected elements of the burgeoning Expressionist school as well as intimations of the nascent Cubist discipline. These heady experiments came to a premature close on January 20, 1907, marking the end of Feininger's promising comic-art career. Had he been able to continue, his innovations, operating together with those of Winsor McCay in the same period, might have changed the artistic course of the American newspaper strip.

M.H.

WHAT'S UP, DOC?
See BUGS BUNNY

WHEN A FELLER NEEDS A FRIEND
1912–1929

The first and longest-running of Clare Briggs's motto series, *When a Feller Needs a Friend* debuted as a single-panel daily feature in the *Chicago Tribune* in 1912, transferring in 1914 to the more upscale *New York Tribune* (which later became the *Herald-Tribune*).

When a Feller was only one in a glorious parade of Briggs daily panels, some boasting phrases that still resonate today: *Ain't It a Grand and Glorious Feelin'?*, *Somebody Is Always Taking the Joy Out of Life,* and *It Happens in the Best Regulated Families;* others were tagged with simple descriptive titles like *The Days of Real Sport, Golf,* and *That Guiltiest Feeling,* which alternated with one another, according to the artist's whim and inspiration. As Thomas Craven observed, "Briggs delineated the humors of golfers and poker players, the irritations of domestic life, and the memories of boyhood, investing his drawings with the muscular enthusiasm and kindliness of his personality." *Feller,* however, partly because of its longevity, partly because of the extra note of poignancy the artist brought to it, has become for posterity the epitome of the entire Briggs catalogue.

These vignettes of life described the pangs of growing up from boyhood to young manhood under the gaze of others. There were the frustrations of not being able to play with other kids on account of new clothes, the embarrassment of having a first mash note discovered by mocking parents, the pain of being turned down by a girl in favor of the school's jock. There was a tinge of sadness to these remembrances of things past, and a pathos that was uncontrived. These all came to an end in 1929, when Briggs died at age 55.

M.H.

WHITE BOY
1933–1936

On October 8, 1933, only a short week after the inception of Ed Leffingwell's *Little Joe,* the Chicago Tribune–New York News Syndicate released another offbeat western series, Garrett Price's *White Boy,* a Sunday half-page as stunning as it is obscure. Price, who was then working in the *Tribune* art department, was asked to turn out a feature that would appeal primarily to a juvenile audience. "I was hampered by authentic knowledge of the West," the artist later confided. "My folks...left Kansas when I was a year old. Until I was nineteen we lived in Wyoming, Oklahoma, South Dakota—mostly in Wyoming." Price, however, set to work with a sense of purpose and an undeniable vision of what the strip should be.

Set in the late nineteenth century, the strip has its adolescent hero (simply known as White Boy) captured by the Sioux, then rescued by a rival tribe, nursed to health and loved by an Indian girl named Starlight. Even after a scout, Dan Brown, entered the story, White Boy decided to stay with his Indian friends, much as the Kevin Costner character would do over a half-century later in *Dances with Wolves.*

The story line was an amalgam of Indian lore and legend (how the snowshoe rabbit got his fur, for instance), gag situations often involving White Boy's pet bear Whimper, and some genuinely gripping narratives, such as the famous tale of the white Moon Queen lording it over an utterly cowed Indian tribe.

When a Feller Needs a Friend (C. Briggs), 1920

The main appeal of the strip, however, resided in Price's incredibly evocative artwork. The artist would often draw in a flat, patterned line, dominated by earth colors, reminiscent of Indian sand paintings. His horses, cattle, and buffaloes were frozen in the hieratic pose of animals in cave drawings. His light was sometimes subdued, sometimes dazzling, in harmony with the days and the seasons.

Then, in April 1935, on instructions from the syndicate, Price switched the time and place to those of a modern dude ranch. White Boy's love interest, Starlight, his blood brothers, Woodchuck and Chickadee, and all his Indian friends were dropped. White Boy turned into Bob White, and a new heroine by the name of Doris Hale was introduced. The strip, rechristened *Whiteboy in Skull Valley,* and later simply *Skull Valley* (there is an actual place called Skull Valley in Arizona) was changed to a routine western, with the usual stories about cattle rustlers, bank robbers, and masked bandits. Price did his best to sustain the interest of his readers, but when *Skull Valley* degenerated into a tired gag feature, he decided to call it quits, later concentrating on a successful career as a *New Yorker* cartoonist and a magazine illustrator. The last *Skull Valley* page appeared on August 16, 1936.

M.H.

WILL-YUM
1953–1967

Dave Gerard's *Will-Yum* originated in 1949 in the *Woman's Home Companion* magazine as a monthly feature about a boy from a middle-class family. When the artist was asked to create a comic strip by John Dille, head of National Newspaper Syndicate, he simply took *Will-Yum* to the syndicate, which started distributing it, daily and Sunday, in June 1953.

Will-Yum would have been just another innocuous kid strip if Gerard hadn't endowed the feature with his own personality and gentle brand of humor. The children were a mischievous but on the whole ingratiating bunch led by the cocky Will-Yum, a know-it-all whose self-assurance matched that of Lucy Van Pelt in *Peanuts.* Will-Yum, however, had neither her drive nor her nastiness; his idea of a prank was to show his girlfriend Madeline his bleeding finger to hear her shriek.

The kids held long disputations about which illness was deadlier, the mumps or the measles, and engaged in dares

as to which one of them could skip the longest on one foot. In all these innocent diversions Will-Yum was shown to be not only a born leader, but a pioneer in sartorial fashion as well—he always wore his farmer's cap backwards, thereby proving himself decades ahead of his time.

A native and resident of Crawfordsville, Indiana (whose mayor he was for a number of years), Gerard depicted an idyllic view of small-town childhood rarely seen since the days of Tom Sawyer and Huckleberry Finn. *Will-Yum* could not outlast the rebellious 1960s, and this charming, understated strip, so much at odds with the times, was finally canceled in 1967.

M.H.

WINDY AND PADDLES
See JIM HARDY

WINKY RYATT
See THE RYATTS

WINNIE WINKLE
1920–present

Martin Michael Branner was already doing two Sunday comic strips when he sold *Winnie Winkle the Breadwinner* to the Chicago Tribune–New York News Syndicate in 1920. In 1919 he had sold the Bell Syndicate a gag strip called *Looie the Lawyer,* and the next year the *New York Sun* and the *New York Herald* bought *Pete and Pinto.* But both of these primitive gag strips, in the broad old vaudeville tradition of set-up and punchline, were quickly handed over to others when Branner undertook the full-time job of a daily and Sunday strip.

Winnie was a humor strip, featuring daily gags in the same style as *Looie* and *Pete and Pinto,* when it began on September 20, 1920, but its original and credible characters soon led Branner to turn it into a continuity strip. There had been working girls in the comics before—A. E. Hayward had started *Somebody's Stenog* in 1916—but Winnie was the first real career girl in the medium. She too started as a stenog, working for the Bibbs Pin Company and living up to the strip's subtitle by supporting her warmhearted but helpless ma and her improvident father, appropriately named Rip.

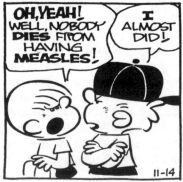

Will-Yum (D. Gerard), © 1963 National Newspaper Syndicate

Winnie Winkle (M. Branner), © 1928 Chicago Tribune

In April 1922, the family increased with the addition of an adoptive brother, Perry, whose punning name identifies the child with the humble flower and the mollusk, reflecting both Branner's still jocular approach to the strip and the modest pretensions of the character. Perry and his street gang, the Rinkydinks, gradually took over the Sunday feature, providing an independent series of self-contained gag strips, while the dailies developed long, continuous stories. The Rinkydinks were a rowdy bunch, in the time-honored comic-strip tradition of mischievous kids, their most notable member being the appealing simpleton Denny Dimwit. Poorer even than his ragged companions, Denny was more often a victim than a participant in the gang's pranks, but his innately sweet disposition and innocent heart made him impervious to the cruelty of his friends. Perry's adventures began to fuse with the daily continuities during the 1950s, and by 1954 Denny and the rest of the Rinkydinks had become minor background characters.

Winnie's function as a breadwinner began to fade during the early days of the strip, and the subtitle was dropped. In 1937 she married an engineer, Will Wright, and for a time the strip dealt with the problems of a conventional young married couple, but Will joined the army in 1941 and disappeared, leaving his wife pregnant. Winnie, the first war widow in the comics, coped as resourcefully with the problems of single motherhood as she had with those of supporting her parents. Over the years, the character has increased in both complexity and social stature: she has evolved from a stenog to a successful fashion designer— even before she had her own business, Branner had dressed her with notable taste and style—and her daughter Wendy and kid brother Perry have grown up to be a credit to her.

With Branner's retirement in 1962, the strip was taken over by his long-time assistant Max van Bibber, who recast the appearance of the characters from comic-strip stereotypes to attractive, fairly realistic figures, in keeping with the strip's contemporary stories. Frank Bolle maintained the illustrative style and updated the stories still further

when van Bibber turned *Winnie Winkle* over to him in 1980. In Bolle's skillful hands, the strip has dealt with such social problems as crime and narcotics as well as the characters' perennial romantic complications.

Something of an anachronism by the 1990s, *Winnie Winkle* has nevertheless held its own as other continuity strips have disappeared. By adapting in both look and narrative content to the changing tastes of the times, it has shown the same resourcefulness as its engaging heroine.

D.W.

WINTHROP
1966–1993

Neither a mischievous scamp like Buster Brown or a Katzenjammer Kid nor a simple, natural child like Tiger, Winthrop belonged rather to that more recent category of cartoon character, the ironic child. The creation of gag-cartoonist Dick Cavalli, he delivered tart observations on life and the state of the world, which, like those of the figures in *Peanuts* and *Miss Peach*, derived much of their humor from the contrast between the youth of their speakers and the worldly wisdom that informed them.

Winthrop began his long career as a bit player in the cast of Cavalli's strip *Morty Meekle*, a rather conventional feature detailing the dismal career of a beleaguered office worker. Morty and his girlfriend Jill made their first appearance in 1955, syndicated by NEA. In the time-honored tradition of Dagwood Bumstead and his belligerent boss Mr. Dithers, the meek Mr. Meekle endured the tyranny of his thunderous employer E. G. Boomer; but if, like Dagwood, he never rebelled in word or deed, the strip carried a background chorus of snide youngsters with a perceptive take on the human condition. Increasingly through the early 1960s, the articulate kids provided the sharpest humor in the daily strip, and on February 27, 1966, Morty, Jill, and Boomer were retired and the juvenile cast took over.

Renamed *Winthrop* for the most frequent spokesman of

the little band, the spinoff strip took on a new lease on life and has prospered in the company of a growing number of *Peanuts* clones. Cavalli's cartoons in such national magazines as the *Saturday Evening Post* and *Collier's* had earned him such success that *Writer's Digest* wrote of him in 1956 that he had "risen to the top faster than any other cartoonist in the business." Working in much the same style, he brought to *Winthrop* an attractively clean look and a mildly sardonic wit that struck a nice balance between the sentimental and the acerbic.

Winthrop and his pals were not sharply characterized—except for the compulsively tidy Spotless McPartland, none had a very distinctive identity—and the strip contained little reference to anything outside their timeless world. But Cavalli's contemporary language and the wry outlook of his precociously cynical kids kept the spirit of the feature timely up to 1993, when it ended.

D.W.

THE WISH TWINS AND ALADDIN'S LAMP
1904–1907

Born in the United States in the 1890s, the comics soon sprouted in all directions. Two major themes emerged: children, who were everywhere in sight, and fantasy, whose presence was more subtle but in some ways just as significant. No newspaper in the early years of the medium was as skillful in merging these two strands as the *New York Herald*. *Little Nemo* remains, of course, the exemplar of this creative coupling, but there were many others, including *The Wish Twins and Aladdin's Lamp,* which ran in the interior (monochrome) pages of the *Herald* between 1904 and 1907.

Drawn by W. O. Wilson (who was turning out *Madge, the Magician's Daughter* for the McClure Syndicate about that same time), *The Wish Twins,* unlike *Nemo,* was more humorous than oneiric. After getting hold of the fabled magic lamp, the twins (two young boys of about 10) used it to satisfy childhood wishes (to soar into the air, to have the run of a candy store) or to play pranks on unsuspecting adults. They also sometimes used their magic to right some wrong, forcing a brutal wagon driver to take the place of his horse in the shafts, for instance, or getting an insensitive mother to wear the same tight-fitting corset she'd inflicted on her teenage daughter.

The Wish Twins was no masterpiece in either the kid-strip or the fantasy-page departments: its drawings were pleasant if conventional, and its jokes only mildly amusing. It is included here as representative of the wide range of offbeat features the newspapers of the time were offering.

M.H.

THE WIZARD OF ID
1964–present

In 1963, Johnny Hart, the creator of *B.C.*, wanted to move out of the environment of his prehistoric world and approached Brant Parker with the idea of a medieval comic strip. Aided by his *B.C.* team, Dick Boland and Jack Caprio, Hart would write the script, and Parker would handle the art. Thus, *The Wizard of Id* appeared as a daily on November 9, 1964, and a weekly soon after.

Set in and around a castle circled by a moat filled with hungry crocodiles, dragons, and monsters to be fed by simply removing the "No Swimming" sign, the strip relates the activities of the King of Id, his vassals, and subjects. Although the era presented is the Middle Ages, the modern world sometimes invades the story, from the Berlin Wall and feminism to crabgrass and pizza delivery.

The King, a self-described "tyrant's tyrant," dominates the script. He is a cruel, petty ruler with a cynical sense of humor and an innate pessimism about human nature. To his chamberlain, who reads him the day's schedule ("9:15: The hanging of Intrepid Irving...11:30: The decapitation of Mad Marlowe...2:00: The drawing and quartering of Dirty Dirk"), he replies, "Cancel everything...I'm in no mood for merriment today." Furthermore, he gleefully enjoys his nastiness, including that directed at his generous and benign father ("Ten years in solitary might bring him to his senses") and his mother-turned-charwoman, who rightly accuses him of being a cheapskate.

However, being the smallest man in Id (or maybe anywhere), he is extremely sensitive about any reference to size, even if made in the most innocent manner. Indeed, such an insult will send the culprit to the rack or the dungeon, where he will hang upside down in chains with a skull for sole company. The fact that the King wears a crown made up of suits of cards (clubs, diamonds, etc.) and that he drags his royal train behind him and sits on the throne with his feet thrust into the air hardly diminishes the impact of his overall conduct, notwithstanding the Lone Haranguer's oft-repeated cry, "The King is a fink."

Unlike the legendary Merlin, the Wizard of the title is never sure of the results of his concoctions and spells. Whether he tries to light his fire logs by magic and burns his armchair instead, or changes a suitor into a disgusting frog, or actually succeeds in his attempts, he reacts with an equanimity born of years of searching and experimenting. The only person who can usually best him is his wife, Blanch, an ugly and obese nag—which explains why the Wizard is so glad to make her vanish—albeit by sending her to visit her mother. A cloudlike genie assists him, with an insolent reluctance, although unable to transform Blanch into a beautiful woman. For reasons grounded in folklore and chivalric literature, the Wizard, along with Bung, the drunken court jester, can say and do anything to the King and get away with it. This is done not out of righteous correcting of fault (which is the monk's vocation) but rather as a reminder to the King of unknown powers and truths.

The King's squire, the stupid Rodney, is the very antithesis of the medieval knight. Not only is he a coward who finds lame excuses to avoid fighting enemy warriors (for example, he needs to repair the drawbridge, or his suit of armor has been recalled by the manufacturer), but he does not even like to court ladies fair. His personality and behavior, however, do not deter blonde Gwen from being madly in love with him and shamelessly pursuing him, to no avail. Another recurrent figure is a prison lifer, whose long, dirty hair and beard earned him the nickname of The Spook.

The Wizard of Id (Hart and Parker), © 1968 Publishers-Hall Syndicate

Having once beaten the King at croquet, he now rots in a dank cell under the watchful eye of his jailer, as both spend their time talking about food: slop for one, swill for the other.

Rounding out the cast of characters are an obfuscating lawyer who looks like W. C. Fields; the Duke of Marinello, the perfect snob; Troob, the pretentious troubadour; the loud night timekeeper; and the Idian subjects, who always ask for better conditions and are always shamelessly exploited and overtaxed by the King. Ultimately, all the inhabitants of the aptly named Kingdom of Id show instinctual impulses and demands for immediate satisfaction of primitive needs. Sigmund Freud would have been flattered.

Parker's graphic style is simple, almost caricatural, especially in the drawing of the protagonists' bulbous noses, while Hart's humor is sarcastic and biting in its satire of the less attractive side of human nature. The strip, distributed to over a thousand newspapers and anthologized in more than thirty paperback collections, has won several accolades, including the National Cartoonists Society's Reuben Award in 1984.

P.H.

WONDER WOMAN
1944–1945

William Moulton Marston, a noted psychologist and the inventor of the polygraph, created Wonder Woman to counteract what he saw as a predominance of male superheroes in the comic books sold to American youth. His superpowered heroine made her entrance in the December 1941 issue of *All-Star Comics,* published by National Periodical Publications, which also owned the

Superman character. Drawn by Harry G. Peter and written by Marston himself (under the pen-name Charles Moulton), the newcomer rapidly graduated to her own *Wonder Woman* comic book in 1942. Two years later National struck a deal with King Features to syndicate a *Wonder Woman* newspaper strip. Also drawn by Peter and scripted by Marston, the feature made its first appearance on May 8, 1944.

While its existence was brief (a little over one year), the *Wonder Woman* newspaper strip is notable because it allowed its author to develop in this supposedly more mature medium his themes and his personal obsessions in more explicit ways than he had been allowed to do within the confines of comic books aimed primarily at children. The newspaper continuities closely adhered to the premise and the setting of the comic books, albeit with greater emphasis on the ambiguous sexual relationship between the two main protagonists. The daughter of Hippolyte, queen of the Amazons, Wonder Woman had come especially from her home on Paradise Island to help defeat the Axis menace. In the olive-drab environment of World War II America she cut a dazzling (and fulsome) figure in her star-spangled hot pants and golden breastplate; she also proved the bane of Nazi spies and foreign infiltrators, whom she easily overcame thanks to her superhuman strength, her golden lasso, and her bullet-deflecting bracelets. In her guise as frumpy army nurse Diana Prince, however, she was hopelessly in love with the dull-witted Major Steve Trevor, whom as Wonder Woman she had rescued countless times from enemy traps and the intrigues of sultry women spies.

Yet with all the occasions that arose out of these encounters, the superheroine apparently never got even close to romantic fulfillment with Trevor in either of her personalities. To the defense of Wonder Woman, whose cause was eventually taken up by the women's movement, sprang none other than Gloria Steinem, who declared, "Wonder Woman hinted at an answer [to her sexual dilemma] when she alternately admired strength in Steve and said she could not love a man who dominated her. Apparently she could only love an equal." Unlike comic-book audiences who lapped it all up, newspaper readers never found these psychological intricacies particularly compelling. In August 1945 the *Wonder Woman* strip was unceremoniously dumped by the syndicate.

M.H.

YANKEE DOODLE
See CAPTAIN YANK

THE YELLOW KID
1895–1898

Now universally regarded as an icon of popular culture, R. F. Outcault's *The Yellow Kid* can only with reservations lay claim to being the first comic strip, but it had the good luck of being at the right place at the right time in the history of American newspapers.

Born into a well-to-do family of German descent, Richard Felton Outcault started his cartooning career in the early 1890s with contributions to many humor magazines, including *Judge, Truth,* and *Life.* In 1894 he began his fruitful collaboration with Joseph Pulitzer's *New York World,* and it was in the pages of the *World* that for the first time appeared an ugly-looking little slum kid with a bald head and big ears, who increasingly drew the interest of both the newspaper's editors and its readers.

The urchin began appearing weekly in his own feature in the Sunday supplement of the *World* on February 17, 1895. From then on its progress toward genuine comic-strip status proceeded by increments. On May 5, the first color cartoon in the series (now officially known as *Hogan's Alley*) was published, and a little later the Kid acquired a name—Mickey Dugan. The year 1896 proved crucial in setting the true origin of the newspaper comic: in January the Kid's only garment, his nightshirt, was definitively colored yellow (it had previously been of several different hues), thus earning him his popular nickname; and in March the Kid's yellow garment sported its first word, later expanded to longer and longer sayings. A forerunner of today's "talking tee-shirts," the nightshirt not only spouted sarcastic inscriptions but also "commented on the most important political issues of the day," as comics historian Bill Blackbeard observed, "from Free Silver and William Jennings Bryan's campaign for

the presidency to the Spanish-American War." Around that time Outcault also began using text and dialogue enclosed within one huge panel that took up half, and sometimes the whole, of a page. In Outcault's chaotic and teeming drawings could already be discerned all the harbingers of a new and exciting artistic form.

The feature became a prize in the struggle between Joseph Pulitzer and William Randolph Hearst for mastery over the New York newspaper market, with Hearst winning the contest and bringing Outcault over to his *New York Journal* in October 1896. Promptly, the now-famous Kid became the main attraction of the *Journal*'s Sunday supplement, while the *World* hired painter George Luks to continue *Hogan's Alley* for a time. Under Hearst's prodding, Outcault made increasing use of sequential narratives and of speech-balloons in a series of comical misadventures named, in honor of the hero, *The Yellow Kid;* thus were the terms "comics" (applied to the Sunday feature for obvious reasons) and "yellow journalism" (used to describe the practices of the sensational press) born at the same time.

The Yellow Kid proved the first merchandising phenomenon of the comics. The character was portrayed on key chains and collector cards, appeared on stage and in book form, and even had a short-lived magazine named after him. Because of its avowed vulgarity *The Yellow Kid* soon aroused the ire of the censors, and despite the windfall his creation was earning for him, Outcault walked away from the feature in January 1898. He did not abandon his character altogether, however, and the Yellow Kid kept putting in cameo appearances in the artist's later creation, *Buster Brown,* in the first decade of this century.

The Yellow Kid (R. F. Outcault), 1897

Following Outcault's death in 1928, the Yellow Kid, unlike Buster Brown, virtually faded from memory, and he was only rescued from oblivion by the early historians of the comics. Coulton Waugh in his pioneering study *The Comics* (1947) set up an imaginary scene whereby the foreman of the *World* decided on his own accord to try out the color yellow from his new presses on the nightshirt of Outcault's Kid. Twelve years later Stephen Becker in *Comic Art in America* picked up on the legend, with each successive generation of historians embroidering further on the theme. Thus, the Yellow Kid's posthumous fortune owes less to Outcault's talents (though they were many) than to the happiest of happy accidents.

M.H.

YOU KNOW ME AL
1922–1925

Baseball strips have never fared well with comics readers, and *You Know Me Al* was no exception. Yet when the Bell Syndicate bought the rights to adapt Ring Lardner's "Busher's Letters" stories, it must have seemed like a good idea: Lardner was the most popular sports columnist of the era between the two world wars, and his stories had enjoyed great success from the time they had first appeared in the *Saturday Evening Post* in March 1914. So when *You Know Me Al* started publication as a daily strip in September 1922, great hopes were pinned on it.

Subtitled "The Adventures of Jack Keefe," the strip adapted the original stories from the point they had started. They followed the "busher" Jack Keefe's career, from the day he was picked from the bush leagues (in his case Terre Haute, Indiana) by the Chicago White Sox, through his checkered record as a pitcher for the big leagues, and chronicled his clumsy courtship of and later marriage to Edna Cannon, an empty-headed chorus girl. The letters the busher sent to his friend Al Blanchard back in Indiana provided an ironic commentary on the various goings-on, showing the protagonist's naiveté as well as a certain native savviness. "Women don't never give you nothing Al and it's a wonder they ain't all umpires," ran one, while another averred, "That's the hell of it in baseball Al it costs too much to take your wife on a trip and it ain't safe to leave them home."

Keefe's domestic problems, however, were not terribly amusing, nor were his attempts at crashing high society. The strip only came alive when baseball was in season: Lardner peppered his narratives with baseball lingo and statistics, and many of the game's players and officials made cameo appearances under their real names. Yet the strip failed to catch fire, partly because the cartoonists hired to provide the artwork proved inadequate for the job. Will B. Johnstone, who was first to illustrate *Al*, was competent, but his drawings were stiff. Dick Dorgan, who succeeded him, in March 1923, owed his job to his brother Tad's fame and made a terrible mess of the strip. In January 1925 Lardner quit, and Dorgan tried to keep *Al* afloat as best he could on his own, until the end of 1925.

M.H.

You Know Me Al (D. Dorgan), © 1924 Bell Syndicate

ZIGGY
1971–present

Tom Wilson, an alumnus, like so many of his cartooning colleagues, of the greeting-card school of humor, tried his hand in 1966 at a newspaper-panel series about the sundry mishaps and contretemps encountered by a rotund little man named Ziggy, only to be repeatedly turned down. In 1968 he compiled a number of his rejected cartoons along with some new ones into a small volume, *When You're Not Around,* which was published by his then employer, the American Greetings Corporation, and promptly became the company's best seller. This in turn attracted the attention of Jim Andrews, the editor of Universal Press Syndicate, and *Ziggy* finally made it to the newspaper page, as a daily panel on June 1971, to be followed by a Sunday series two years later.

Ziggy, originally an elevator operator, is now an individual of no particular profession and no discernible talent. He is well-meaning, endearingly inept, and preternaturally unlucky, not unlike Happy Hooligan in an earlier era. He mistakenly sprays his armpits with shoe polish, squeezes toothpaste out of the wrong end of the tube, and rolls himself up in the window shade. Even his canary calls him a twerp.

The Sunday format allows Wilson to go beyond the boundaries imposed by the single-gag concept of the daily panel. He frequently sends his diminutive antihero for long walks, sometimes along with his pet companion, a pudgy little bulldog called Fuzz; an unwelcome surprise usually awaits at the end of these leisurely outings. Thus, on one occasion when he takes a stroll through festive city streets during the Christmas season, Ziggy is held up by a Santa. Another time, at the end of the proverbial rainbow he only finds a pot filled with IOU's. He is no luckier at home: he finds spiderwebs in his mailbox, ants in his sugar bowl, a

Ziggy (T. Wilson), © 1994 Ziggy and Friends, Inc.

seagull nesting in his fireplace, and moths flying out of his closet, upon which he only sighs: "Oh well...we all have to live!"

All is not unremittingly bleak in his universe, however, and even a Ziggy can manage a few moments of epiphany. In one 1977 episode, while reaching for a star he is gently touched on the shoulder by the finger of God. His very Ziggy-like comment on this wondrous encounter is simply: "I don't think I'll tell anybody about this." So, gamely Ziggy endures, while waiting for the meek to inherit the earth.

It is this simplicity of tone, allied to genuine pathos, and carried by a drawing line reduced to its essentials, that have made a commercial winner out of this existential loser. *Ziggy* appears in hundreds of newspapers in the U.S. and abroad, is reprinted in countless books, and has been adapted into two animated television specials.

M.H.

ZIPPY THE PINHEAD
1974–present

Cartoonist Bill Griffith first conceived the character of the Pinhead (he was called Danny at the time) in 1970, and he premiered him the next year in the underground comic book *Real Pulp.* It was in the pages of Griffith's own *Tales of Toad* that the character fully blossomed into his Zippy the Pinhead persona, complete with polka-dot clown suit, non sequiturs, and good-natured shenanigans. Concurrently with his work for the undergrounds, Griffith had started syndicating a *Zippy* comic strip intended for college newspapers in 1974. Later the character came to the attention of King Features Syndicate, which picked up national distribution of the feature in 1980.

While touching only gingerly upon the sexual and scatological themes that had been the twin concerns of his underground days, Zippy still indulges his bouts of raucous zaniness, and it is this aspect of the strip that makes the character such a unique phenomenon among the tame denizens of the comic pages. Fueled by a diet of Ding Dongs and tacos, Zippy roams the world through space and time, turning up in the most unexpected places under the most outlandish guises, variously materializing as a beat poet in a San Francisco coffeehouse of the 1950s, as a Greek soldier tucked inside the wooden horse during the Trojan War, and as an art critic in modern-day Paris. While he meets people from all walks of life and all levels of sanity during his peregrinations, the Pinhead's most telling encounters involve media-created celebrities, and on that score David Letterman and Princess Diana appear just as fictional as Sergeant Bilko or Barney the Dinosaur.

To make a point Griffith resorts to the old-fashioned device of running subtitles over each of his daily strips. These subtitles might be descriptive ("Zippy's Mystical Experience," "John and Jane Q. Public Seek Asylum"), evocative ("Studebaker Lust," "Daydreaming, Media-Soaked Pinhead"), allusive ("Bedtime for Ronald," "Zippy, Drugs & Rock 'n' Roll"), and most often pun-accented ("Sports Simulated," "Docu-Dramamine," "Dismemberment of Things Past"). Recurring subtitles are used by Griffith to introduce series within the strip, such as his "Helpful Hints," which are anything but; on putting out garbage, for example, the advice given is: "Wait until a big flood...then put the garbage can in the street and pray that it lands in Hewlett, Long Island!"

Griffith draws *Zippy* with scratchy, sharp lines, in contrast to the greeting-card cuteness of so many other comic strips. And on Sundays his colors blind the eye. The artist's crude style and love of primary colors, allied to his penchant for nonsense and pop culture, have oddly enough not proved detrimental to the strip, which enjoys a respectable if smallish circulation, along with a loyal following among highbrows and lowbrows alike. As Bernard Kliban once observed, "Another thing I like about *Zippy* is that although it is definitely not done for idiots, I have actually seen many idiots enjoying him on some level." On a more rarefied plane, Judith O'Sullivan in *The Great American Comic Strip* found *Zippy* to be "the anthem of our national absurdities," perhaps too weighty an assessment for the creation of an artist who claims as his major contribution to Western civilization the phrase "Are we having fun yet?"

M.H.

Bibliography

Contributors

Biographical Index

THE AMERICAN
NEWSPAPER STRIP:
A BIBLIOGRAPHY

Only books dealing wholly or substantially with some important aspect of the American newspaper strip are listed. Monographs, how-to books, book reprints, and anthologies of individual strips have been omitted. For a more comprehensive bibliography refer to John A. Lent's *International Bibliography* mentioned below.

Becker, Stephen. *Comic Art in America.* Simon and Schuster, 1959.

Berger, Arthur Asa. *The Comic-Stripped American.* Walker and Company, 1974.

Blackbeard, Bill. *A Century of Comics* (two volumes). Kitchen Sink Press, 1995.

———— and Martin Williams, eds. *The Smithsonian Collection of Newspaper Comics.* Abrams, 1978.

Couperie, Pierre, and Maurice Horn. *A History of the Comic Strip.* Crown Publishers, 1968.

Craven, Thomas. *Cartoon Cavalcade.* Simon and Schuster, 1943.

Davidson, Sol. *Culture and the Comic Strip.* New York University Press, 1959.

Fern, A. *Comics as Serial Fiction.* University of Chicago Press, 1968.

Galewitz, Herb. *Great Comics Syndicated by the Daily News–Chicago Tribune Syndicate.* Crown Publishers, 1972.

Gifford, Denis. *The International Book of Comics.* Deans International Publishing, 1984.

————. *American Comic Strip Collections.* G .K. Hall, 1990.

Glubok, Shirley. *The Art of the Comic Strip.* Macmillan, 1979.

Goulart, Ron. *The Adventurous Decade: Comic Strips in the Thirties.* Arlington House, 1975.

————. *The Encyclopedia of American Comics.* Facts on File, 1990.

————. *The Funnies: 100 Years of American Comic Strips.* Adams, 1995.

Harvey, R. C. *The Art of the Funnies: An Aesthetic History of the Comic Strip.* University Press of Mississippi, 1995.

Herdeg, Walter, ed. *The Art of the Comic Strip.* Graphis Press, 1972.

Hogben, Lancelot. *From Cave Painting to Comic Strip.* Chanticleer Press, 1949.

Horn, Maurice. *Comics of the American West.* Winchester Press, 1977.

————. *75 Years of the Comics.* Boston Book & Art, 1971.

————. *Sex in the Comics.* Chelsea House Publishers, 1985.

————. *Women in the Comics.* Chelsea House Publishers, 1977.

————. *The World Encyclopedia of Comics.* Chelsea House Publishers, 1976.

Inge, M. Thomas. *Comics as Culture.* University Press of Mississippi, 1990.

Kempkes, Wolfgang. *International Bibliography of Comics Literature.* R. R. Bowker, 1974.

Kurtzman, Harvey. *History of Comic Art from Argh to Zap.* Nostalgia Press, 1973.

Kutlowski, Edward. *Cavalcade of Old Time Comic Strips.* Tower Press, 1967.

Lent, John A. *Comic Books and Comic Strips in the United States: An International Bibliography.* Greenwood Press, 1994.

Marschall, Richard. *America's Great Comic-Strip Artists*. Abbeville Press, 1989.

Murrell, William A. *A History of American Graphic Humor*. Macmillan (two volumes), 1933 and 1938.

O'Sullivan, Judith. *The Great American Comic Strip*. Little, Brown, and Company, 1990.

Perry, George, and Alan Aldridge. *The Penguin Book of Comics*. Penguin Books, 1967; revised edition, 1971.

Reitburger, Reinhold, and Wolfgang Fuchs. *Comics: Anatomy of a Mass Medium*. Little, Brown, and Company, 1972.

Robbins, Trina. *A Century of Women Cartoonists*. Kitchen Sink Press, 1994.

————— and Catherine Yronwode. *Women and the Comics*. Eclipse Books, 1985.

Robinson, Jerry. *The Comics: An Illustrated History of Comic Strip Art*. Putnam, 1974.

Scott, Randall W. *Comic Books and Strips*. Oryx Press, 1988.

Sheridan, Martin. *Comics and Their Creators*. Hale, Cushman, and Flint, 1942.

Siegfried, Joan C. *The Spirit of the Comics*. University of Pennsylvania Press, 1969.

Stanley, John, and Mal Whyte. *The Great Comics Game*. Price Stern Sloan, 1966.

Walker, Mort. *Backstage at the Strips*. A & W Visual Library, 1975.

Waugh, Coulton. *The Comics*. Macmillan, 1947.

White, David Manning, and Robert H. Abel. *The Funnies: An American Idiom*. The Free Press of Glencoe, 1963.

Winterbotham, Russell Robert. *How Comic Strips Are Made*. Haldemann-Julius, 1946.

Wood, Art. *Great Cartoonists and Their Art*. Pelican Publishing, 1987.

NOTES ON THE CONTRIBUTORS

MARY BETH CALHOUN is a research associate for an Ohio research and consulting firm and is also a freelance writer and editor. Previously, she worked as an editorial assistant at a scientific journal. While growing up, she enjoyed reading all the comics in the *Pittsburgh Press*, and she has kept up her interest in the field ever since.

BILL CROUCH, JR., a Connecticut Yankee, has written about cartooning since he was first published in *Cartoonist PROfiles* in 1974. For that magazine he interviewed Hal Foster, Noel Sickles, and Norman Mingo (the first artist to paint Alfred E. Neuman in full color for the cover of *Mad*. With Mrs. Walt Kelly he edited five *Pogo* trade paperbacks for Simon and Schuster. He wrote *Dick Tracy: America's Most Famous Detective* for Citadel Press and coauthored a Dick Tracy collectibles book. In addition, he was a contributor to *The World Encyclopedia of Cartoons*. He has also written scripts for syndicated comics and humorous comic books, specifically *Yogi Bear, Top Cat, Hong Kong Phooey*, and *The Flintstones*. His book *The ABCs of Cartooning* will be published in 1997.

MAURICE HORN, the editor of *100 Years of American Newspaper Comics*, has also edited *The World Encyclopedia of Comics, The World Encyclopedia of Cartoons*, and the multivolume "Contemporary Graphic Artists" series. Among the books on the subject of comics he has authored are *Women in the Comics, Comics of the American West*, and *Sex in the Comics*. He is also the coauthor of *A History of the Comic Strip*. He was coorganizer of the exhibition "Bande Dessinée et Figuration Narrative" at the Louvre in Paris, and organized the "75 Years of the Comics" exhibition at the New York Cultural Center in 1971. He has written scores of articles on comics and cartoons, has lectured extensively on these subjects, and has been the recipient of many awards and distinctions in the field. He is currently at work on an update of both *The World Encyclopedia of Comics* and *The World Encyclopedia of Cartoons*.

PIERRE HORN is professor of French at Wright State University in Dayton, Ohio, where he also holds the Brage Golding Distinguished Professorship of Research. He has written extensively on French literature and civilization, including biographies of Louis XIV and Lafayette. In addition, he has lectured on popular culture and contributed numerous entries to *The World Encyclopedia of Cartoons* and the multivolume series "Contemporary Graphic Artists." He is also the editor of the *Handbook of French Popular Culture*.

BILL JANOCHA is a freelance artist who has been studio assistant to Mort Walker on *Beetle Bailey* since 1987. He has contributed articles to *Nemo, Inks*, Comicana Books and Kitchen Sink Press. Editor of the 1988 and 1996 editions of *The National Cartoonists Society Album*, Janocha helped with the development of the 1995 "Comic Strip Classics" U.S. postage stamps and with exhibitions for the Newspaper Features Council and for the International Museum of Cartoon Art.

JOHN A. LENT has had a longtime academic interest in comic art, dating from 1963. Since then, he has written scores of books and articles on the subject; overall, he is the editor or author of forty-seven books and monographs. Dr. Lent started, and has chaired since

1984, the Comic Art Working Group of the International Association for Mass Communications Research. He is also managing editor of *Witty World International Cartoon Magazine,* an international editor of *Comics Journal,* editor of *Asian Cinema,* editor of *Berita,* and chair of the Asian Cinema Studies Society. He founded the Malaysia/Singapore/Brunei Studies Group, which he chaired for seven years. He has been a professor in universities throughout the United States, the Philippines, and Malaysia, where he established the first mass-communications program in that country.

FRED PATTEN became active in comics fandom in the early 1960s, serving for four annual terms as central mailer of *Capa-alpha,* comics fandom's first amateur press association. He has written lengthy articles on international comic art and edited the book review section of *Graphic Story Magazine* (later *Wonderworld*). This led to a specialization in Japanese *manga* and *anime.* Patten was a cofounder of the Cartoon/Fantasy Organization, America's first Japanese-cartoon-art fan club. He coauthored the series "The Great European Comic Heroes" for *Nemo* magazine, and has written many articles on comics and cartoons for various publications. He has also written several comic-book short stories since the late 1980s.

DENNIS WEPMAN has taught English at the City University of New York and held the post of cultural affairs editor of the *New York Daily News.* The holder of a graduate degree in linguistics from Columbia University, he is the author of twelve volumes of biography and history and has contributed to numerous publications in linguistics, literature, art, and popular culture, as well as to several standard reference books on cartooning. He has been a contributor to "Contemporary Graphic Artists" and to *The Encyclopedia of American Comics,* and is the chief review editor of *Witty World,* the international cartoon magazine.

TOM WHISSEN is professor of English, emeritus, at Wright State University, in Dayton, Ohio. His works include *A Way with Words, The Devil's Advocate: Decadence in Modern Literature,* and *Classic Cult Fiction: A Guide to Popular Cult Literature.* He has written numerous articles on such diverse popular figures as Daphne du Maurier, Joseph Heller, Tom Wolfe, S. I. Hinton, Truman Capote, and Mary Higgins Clark. His forthcoming books include *A Guide to American Cinema: 1930–1965* and *Return to Danger,* a suspense novel. Whissen is also a composer/lyricist, with three musicals to his credit.

100 Years, 100 Cartoonists: A Biographical Index

The following group of listings serves not only as an index of comic artists/writers for easy reference to the title entries in the alphabetical section of this book, but also provides brief biographies of a hundred of the most important newspaper-strip artists. Special emphasis has been given to the "old-timers," since biographical information on contemporary cartoonists is now—happily—readily available.

A

AHERN, Gene. Born 1895, Chicago, Ill.; died November 17, 1960, Hollywood, Cal. See: *Our Boarding House, Room and Board, The Squirrel Cage.*

ANDRIOLA, Al. Born 1912, New York, N.Y.; died March 29, 1983, New York, N.Y. See: *Charlie Chan, Kerry Drake.*

B

BAILEY, Ray. Born 1913, New York, N.Y.; died 1975, San Francisco, Cal. See: *Bruce Gentry, Tom Corbett.*

BERNDT, Walter. Born November 22, 1899; died 1979. See: *Smitty.*

BRANNER, Martin. Born December 28, 1888, New York, N.Y.; died May 19, 1970, New London, Conn. See: *Winnie Winkle.*

BREATHED, Berke. Born June 21, 1957, Encino, Cal. See: *Bloom County, Outland.*

BREGER, Dave. Born April 15, 1908, Chicago, Ill.; died January 16, 1970, South Nyack, N.Y. See: *Mr. Breger.*

BRIGGS, Austin. Born September 8, 1908, Humboldt, Minn.; died October 10, 1973, Paris, France. See: *Flash Gordon, Jungle Jim, Secret Agent X-9.*

BRIGGS, Clare. Born August 5, 1875, Reedsburg, Wisc.; died January 3, 1930, New York, N.Y. See: *A. Piker Clerk, Mr. and Mrs., Real Folks at Home, When a Feller Needs a Friend.*

BROWNE, Dik. Born August 11, 1917, New York, N.Y.; died June 4, 1989, Sarasota, Fla. See: *Hagar the Horrible, Hi and Lois.*

BUSHMILLER, Ernie. Born August 23, 1905, New York, N.Y.; died August 15, 1982, Stamford, Conn. See: *Fritzi Ritz, Nancy.*

BYRNES, Gene. Born 1889, New York, N.Y.; died July 26, 1974, New York, N.Y. See: *Reg'lar Fellers.*

C

CADY, Harrison. Born June 17, 1877, Gardner, Mass.; died December 9, 1970, New York, N.Y. See: *Peter Rabbit.*

CALKINS, Dick. Born 1895, Grand Rapids, Mich.; died May 13, 1962, Tucson, Ariz. See: *Buck Rogers, Skyroads.*

CANIFF, Milton. Born February 28, 1907, Hillsboro, Oh.; died April 3, 1988, New York, N.Y. See: *Dickie Dare, Male Call, Steve Canyon, Terry and the Pirates.*

CAPP, Al. Born September 28, 1909, New Haven, Conn.; died November 5, 1979, Cambridge, Mass. See: *Abbie an' Slats, Fearless Fosdick, Li'l Abner, Long Sam.*

CORY, Fanny. Born 1877, Waukegan, Ill.; died 1972, on her ranch near Helena, Mont. See: *Little Miss Muffet.*

CRANE, Roy. Born November 22, 1901, Abilene, Tex.; died July 8, 1977, Orlando, Fla. See: *Buz Sawyer, Wash Tubbs.*

CROSBY, Percy. Born December 8, 1891, Brooklyn, N.Y.; died December 8, 1964, New York, N.Y. See: *Skippy.*

D

DAVIS, Jim. Born July 28, 1945, Fairmount, Ind. See: *Garfield.*

DAVIS, Phil. Born March 4, 1906, St. Louis, Mo.; died December 16, 1964, New York, N.Y. See: *Mandrake the Magician.*

DeBECK, Billy. Born April 15, 1890, Chicago, Ill.; died November 11, 1942, New York, N.Y. See: *Barney Google, Bunky.*

DIRKS, Rudolph. Born February 26, 1877, Heinde, Germany; died April 20, 1968, New York, N.Y. See: *The Captain and the Kids, The Katzenjammer Kids.*

DRAKE, Stan. Born November 9, 1921, Brooklyn, N.Y. See: *Blondie, The Heart of Juliet Jones.*

DUMM, Edwina. Born 1893, Upper Sandusky, Ohio; died 1990. See: *Cap Stubbs and Tippie.*

DWIGGINS, C. V. Born June 16, 1874, Ohio; died 1959. See: *School Days.*

E

ED, Carl. Born July 16, 1890, Moline, Ill.; died October 10, 1959, Evanston, Ill. See: *Harold Teen.*

EDSON, Gus. Born September 20, 1901, Cincinatti, Ohio; died September 26, 1966, Stamford, Conn. See: *Dondi, The Gumps.*

EISNER, Will. Born March 6, 1917, Brooklyn, N.Y. See: *Lady Luck, Mr. Mystic, The Spirit.*

ERNST, Ken. Born 1918, Stanton, Ill.; died August 6, 1985, Salem, Ore. See: *Don Winslow, Mary Worth.*

F

FEININGER, Lyonel. Born July 17, 1871, New York, N.Y.; died January 13, 1956, New York, N.Y. See: *The Kin-der-Kids, Wee Willie Winkie's World.*

FISHER, Bud. Born April 3, 1885, Chicago, Ill.; died September 7, 1954, New York, N.Y. See: *Cicero's Cat, Mutt and Jeff.*

FISHER, Ham. Born 1900, Wilkes-Barre, Penn.; died December 27, 1955, New York, N.Y. See: *Joe Palooka.*

FLANDERS, Charles. Born 1907, Mayville, N.Y.; died January 10, 1973, Palma de Mallorca, Spain. See: *King of the Royal Mounted, The Lone Ranger, Secret Agent X-9.*

FOSTER, Hal. Born August 16, 1892, Halifax, Canada; died July 25, 1982, Winter Park, Fla. See: *The Medieval Castle, Prince Valiant, Tarzan.*

FOX, Fontaine. Born March 3, 1884, Louisville, Ky.; died August 9, 1964, Greenwich, Conn. See: *Toonerville Folks.*

FULLER, R. F. Born March 9, 1890, Capac, Mich.; died August 16, 1963, Boothbay Harbor, Maine. See: *Oaky Doaks.*

G

GODWIN, Frank. Born October 20, 1889, Washington, D.C.; died August 5, 1959, New Hope, Penn. See: *Connie, Roy Powers, Rusty Riley.*

GOLDBERG, Rube. Born July 4, 1883, San Francisco, Cal.; died December 7, 1970, New York, N.Y. See: *Boob McNutt, The Inventions of Professor Lucifer G. Butts, Lala Palooza, Mike and Ike.*

GOTTFREDSON, Floyd. Born May 5, 1905, Kaysville, Utah; died July 22, 1986, Orange County, Cal. See: *Mickey Mouse.*

GOULD, Chester. Born November 20, 1900, Pawnee, Okla.; died May 11, 1985, Woodstock, Ill. See: *Dick Tracy.*

GRAFF, Mel. Born 1907, Cleveland, Ohio; died November 1, 1975, Orlando, Fla. See: *Patsy, Secret Agent X-9, Wash Tubbs.*

GRAY, Clarence. Born November 14, 1901, Toledo, Ohio; died January 5, 1957, Cleveland, Ohio. See: *Brick Bradford.*

GRAY, Harold. Born January 20, 1894, Kankakee, Ill.; died May 9, 1968, La Jolla, Cal. See: *Little Joe, Little Orphan Annie.*

GROSS, Milt. Born March 4, 1895, Bronx, N.Y.; died November 28, 1953, aboard S.S. *Lurline* between Hawaii and the U.S. mainland. See: *Banana Oil, Count Screwloose, Dave's Delicatessen, Nize Baby.*

GRUELLE, Johnny. Born 1880, Arcola, Ill.; died January 8, 1938, Miami Springs, Fla. See: *Brutus, Mr. Twee Deedle.*

H

HARMAN, Fred. Born February 9, St. Joseph, Mo.; died January 2, 1982, Phoenix, Ariz. See: *Bronc Peeler, Red Ryder.*

HART, Johnny. Born February 18, 1931, Endicott, N.Y. See: *B.C., The Wizard of Id.*

HATLO, Jimmy. Born 1893, Providence, R.I.; died November 30, 1963, New York, N.Y. See: *Little Iodine, They'll Do It Every Time.*

HERRIMAN, George. Born August 22, 1880, New Orleans, La.; died April 25, 1944, Los Angeles, Cal. See: *Baron Bean, The Dingbat Family, Krazy Kat, Stumble Inn.*

HERSHFIELD, Harry. Born October 13, 1885, Cedar Rapids, Iowa; died December 15, 1974, New York, N.Y. See: *Abie the Agent, Dauntless Durham, Desperate Desmond, Vanilla and the Villains.*

HOEST, Bill. Born February 7, 1926, Newark, N.J.; died November 7, 1988, Lloyd Neck, N.Y. See: *Agatha Crumm, The Lockhorns.*

HOGARTH, Burne. Born December 25, 1911, Chicago, Ill.; died January 28, 1996, Paris, France. See: *Drago, Tarzan.*

HOLMAN, Bill. Born 1903, Crawfordsville, Ind.; died February 27, 1987, New York, N.Y. See: *Smokey Stover, Spooky.*

J

JOHNSON, Crockett. Born October 20, 1906, New York, N.Y.; died July 11, 1975, Norwalk, Conn. See: *Barnaby.*

K

KAHLES, C. W. Born January 17, 1878, Lengfurt, Germany; died January 21, 1931, Great Neck, N.Y. See: *The Airship Man, Clarence the Cop, Hairbreadth Harry.*

KEATON, Russ. Born 1910, Corinth, Miss.; died February 13, 1945, Corinth, Miss. See: *Buck Rogers, Flyin' Jenny, Skyroads.*

KELLY, Walt. Born August 25, 1913, Philadelphia, Penn.; died October 18, 1973, Hollywood, Cal. See: *Pogo.*

KETCHAM, Hank. Born March 14, 1920, Seattle, Wash. See: *Dennis the Menace.*

KING, Frank. Born April 9, 1883, Cashton, Ill.; died June 24, 1969, Winter Park, Fla. See: *Gasoline Alley.*

KNERR, H. H. Born September 4, 1882, Bryn Mawr, Penn.; died July 8, 1949, New York, N.Y. See: *Die Fineheimer Twins, Dinglehoofer und His Dog, The Katzenjammer Kids, Mr. George.*

L

LAZARUS, Mell. Born May 3, 1927, Brooklyn, N.Y. See: *Miss Peach, Momma.*

M

MAGER, Gus. Born October 21, 1878, Newark, N.J.; died July 17, 1956, Murrysville, Penn. See: *Hawkshaw the Detective, The Monk Family* .

MARTIN, Edgar. Born July 6, 1898, Indianapolis, Ind.; died August 30, 1960, Clearwater, Fla. See: *Boots and Her Buddies.*

McBRIDE, Clifford. Born January 26, 1901, Minneapolis, Minn.; died May 22, 1951, Pasadena, Cal. See: *Napoleon.*

McCAY, Winsor. Born September 26, 1869 (?), Spring Lake, Mich.; died July 26, 1934, Brooklyn, N.Y. See: *Dream of the Rarebit Fiend, Little Nemo in Slumberland, Little Sammy Sneeze, A Pilgrim's Progress, Tales of the Jungle Imps.*

McCLURE, Darrell. Born February 25, 1903, Ukiah, Cal; died February 27, 1987, Ukiah, Cal. See: *Donnie, Little Annie Rooney, Vanilla and the Villains.*

McMANUS, George. Born January 23, 1884, St. Louis, Mo.; died October 22, 1954, Santa Monica, Cal. See: *Bringing Up Father, The Newlyweds, Nibsy the Newsboy, Panhandle Pete, Rosie's Beau.*

MESSICK, Dale. Born April 11, 1906, South Bend, Ind. See: *Brenda Starr.*

MESSMER, Otto. Born August 16, 1892, Union City, N.J.; died October 28, 1983, Teaneck, N.J. See: *Felix the Cat.*

MONTANA, Bob. Born October 23, 1920, Stockton, Cal.; died January 4, 1975, Meredith, N.H. See: *Archie.*

MOORES, Dick. Born December 12, 1909, Lincoln, Neb.; died April 22, 1986, Asheville, N.C. See: *Dick Tracy, Gasoline Alley, Jim Hardy, Scamp, Uncle Remus.*

MOSLEY, Zack. Born December 12, 1906, Hickory, Okla.; died September 2, 1993, Stuart, Fla. *See Buck Rogers, Skyroads, Smilin' Jack.*

O

O'NEAL, Frank. Born May 9, 1921, Springfield, Mo.; died October 10, 1987, Pacific Grove, Cal. See: *Short Ribs.*

O'NEILL, Rose. Born June 24, 1874, Wilkes-Barre, Penn.; died April 6, 1944, Springfield, Mo. See: *The Kewpies.*

OPPER, F. B. Born January 2, 1857, Madison, Ohio; died August 28, 1937, New Rochelle, N.Y. See: *Alphonse and Gaston, And Her Name Was Maud!, Happy Hooligan.*

OUTCAULT, R. F. Born January 14, 1863, Lancaster, Ohio; died September 5, 1928, Queens, N.Y. See: *Buster Brown, The Yellow Kid.*

P

PARKER, Gladys. Born about 1905, Tonawanda, N.Y.; died April 28, 1966, Glendale, Cal. See: *Flapper Fanny, Mopsy.*

R

RAYMOND, Alex. Born October 2, 1909, New Rochelle, N.Y.; died September 6, 1956, Westport, Conn. See: *Flash Gordon, Jungle Jim, Rip Kirby, Secret Agent X-9.*

ROBBINS, Frank. Born September 9, 1917, Boston, Mass.; died December, 1994, San Miguel de Allende, Mexico. See: *Johnny Hazard, Scorchy Smith.*

RUSSELL, C. D. Born 1895, Buffalo, N.Y.; died October 22, 1963, the Bronx, N.Y. See: *Pete the Tramp.*

S

SANSOM, Art. Born 1920, East Cleveland, Ohio; died July 4, 1991, Cleveland, Ohio. See: *The Born Loser, Vic Flint.*

SCHULTZE, Charles. Born May 25, 1866, Lexington, Ky.; died January 18, 1939, New York, N.Y. See: *Foxy Grandpa.*

SCHULZ, Charles. Born November 26, 1922, Minneapolis, Minn. See: *Peanuts.*

SEGAR, E. C. Born December 8, 1894, Chester, Ill.; died October 13, 1938, Santa Monica, Cal. See: *Charlie Chaplin's Comic Capers, Sappo, Thimble Theatre.*

SMITH, Sidney. Born February 13, 1877, Bloomington, Ill.; died October 20, 1935, near Trudehurst, Wisc. See: *The Gumps, Old Doc Yak.*

SOGLOW, Otto. Born December 23, 1900, New York, N.Y.; died April 3, 1975, New York, N.Y. See: *The Little King.*

STARR, Leonard. Born October 28, 1925, New York, N.Y. See: *Little Orphan Annie, On Stage.*

STERRETT, Cliff. Born December 12, 1883, Fergus Falls, Minn.; died December 28, 1964, New York, N.Y. See: *Polly and Her Pals.*

STORM, George. Born 1893, Arkansas; died 1976, Enid, Okla. See: *Bobby Thatcher, Joe Jinks, Patsy, Phil Hardy.*

SWANSON, George. Born 1897, Chicago, Ill.; died December 1, 1981, New York, N.Y. See: *The Flop Family, Salesman Sam.*

SWINNERTON, James. Born November 13, 1875, Eureka, Cal.; died September 5, 1974, Palm Springs, Cal. See: *The Journal Tigers, The Little Bears, Little Jimmy, Mr. Jack, Rocky Mason.*

T

TALIAFERRO, Al. Born August 29, 1905, Montrose, Colo.; died February 3, 1969, Glendale, Cal. See: *Donald Duck, Silly Symphonies.*

TUFTS, Warren. Born December 12, 1925, Fresno, Cal. Died July 6, 1982 (in plane crash). See: *Casey Ruggles, Lance.*

V

VERBECK, Gustave. Born 1867, Nagasaki, Japan; died 1937, New York, N.Y. See: *Terrors of the Tiny Tads, The Upside Downs.*

W

WALKER, Mort. Born September 3, 1923, El Dorado, Kan. See: *Beetle Bailey, Boner's Ark, Hi and Lois, Sam's Strip.*

WATTERSON, Bill. Born 1958, Chagrin Falls, Ohio. See: *Calvin and Hobbes.*

WESTOVER, Russ. Born August 3, 1886, Los Angeles, Cal.; died March 6, 1966, San Rafael, Cal. See: *Tillie the Toiler.*

Y

YOUNG, Chic. Born January 9, 1901, Chicago, Ill.; died March 14, 1973, St. Petersburg, Fla. See: *Blondie, Colonel Potterby and the Duchess, Dumb Dora.*

YOUNG, Lyman. Born October 20, 1893, Chicago, Ill.; died February 12, 1984, Port Angeles, Wash. See: *Curley Harper, The Kid Sister, Tim Tyler's Luck.*